*Praise for*

# LES MISÉRABLES

"There are plenty of translations of this extensive, exuberant novel that cut out anything that feels superfluous. But God is in the detail, and Julie Rose has returned all the detail, making a language that is rich and gorgeous."—JEANETTE WINTERSON, *The Times* (London)

"[A] bold new translation."—GRAHAM ROBB, *The Times Literary Supplement*

"One of civilization's great books in a new translation that couldn't be more welcome."—*The Buffalo News* (editor's choice)

"I am absolutely loving these Modern Library re-issues and re-ups of the classics. The latest out ... is *Les Misérables*. ... Talk about value for your entertainment dollar; for a mere 28 bucks, you'll bring home a riveting classic ... with notes, introductions and more than a few useful what-nots. ... What really distinguishes this edition [is] the introduction and the translation. ... Some of us may have read *Les Misérables* back in the day, but ... between Gopnik and Rose, you'll get two introductions that will offer you all the pleasures of your college instruction with none of the pain."—The Agony Column (bookotron.com)

"Julie Rose's new translation of *Les Misérables* is very well done. Vibrant and readable, idiomatic and well suited to a long narrative, it is closer to the captivating tone Hugo would have struck for his own contemporaries."—DIANE JOHNSON

# LES MISÉRABLES

# Victor Hugo

# Les Misérables

*A new translation by Julie Rose*

*Introduction by Adam Gopnik*

*Notes by James Madden*

THE MODERN LIBRARY

NEW YORK

2009 Modern Library Paperback Edition

Published in the United States by Modern Library, an imprint of
The Random House Publishing Group, a division of Random House, Inc., New York.

MODERN LIBRARY and the TORCHBEARER Design
are registered trademarks of Random House, Inc.

Originally published in hardcover in the United States by Modern Library, an imprint of
The Random House Publishing Group, a division of Random House, Inc., in 2008.

LIBRARY OF CONGRESS CATALOGING-IN-PUBLICATION DATA
Hugo, Victor, 1802–1885.
[Misérables. English]
Les misérables/Victor Hugo; a new translation by Julie Rose;
notes by James Madden; introduction by Adam Gopnik.
p.   cm.
ISBN 978-0-8129-7426-3
1. Paris (France)—Fiction.   2. Ex-convicts—Fiction.   3. Orphans—Fiction.
I. Rose, Julie   II. Madden, James.   III. Title.
PQ2286.A36 2008
843'.7—dc22     2008009711

Printed in the United States of America

www.modernlibrary.com

2   4   6   8   9   7   5   3   1

# VICTOR HUGO

Victor-Marie Hugo was born in Besançon in 1802, the third and youngest son of Léopold Hugo, an officer in the Revolutionary and Napoleonic armies, and his wife, Sophie. The family followed Major Hugo to Italy, Elba, Corsica, and finally Spain, where Léopold rose to the rank of general thanks to the protection of Joseph Bonaparte, whom Napoléon had installed on the throne in Madrid. The Hugos' marriage, however, was an unhappy one, and Madame Hugo left her husband for good in 1812, returning to Paris with their three sons. Madame Hugo blamed the collapse of the marriage on her royalist principles, a polite half-truth that her poet son echoed—famously describing himself as the son of "my father the old soldier, and my mother the *Vendéenne*"—but in fact their separation was due to far more banal causes. Sophie Hugo saw to it that her sons received an excellent education, which included the great works of French and classical literature, as well as political writings in sympathy with their mother's beliefs. Victor and his two elder brothers were largely estranged from their father until their mother's death in 1821.

Young Victor displayed a precocious literary talent while still in his teens, winning prizes for his poems and even founding, with his brothers, a literary magazine entitled *Le Conservateur littéraire*. He was barely twenty when he published his first collection of verse, *Odes et poésies diverses,* which earned him a national reputation and a royal pension that allowed him to marry Adèle Foucher, who had been his playmate as a child. In 1825, Hugo was named to the Legion of Honor, and invited to be the official poet of the coronation of Charles X, youngest brother of Louis XVI and the last Bourbon king of France.

But Hugo's youthful royalism quickly gave way to a growing liberalism. The famous preface to his play *Cromwell* became a manifesto for a generation of French Romantics. In 1829 he published a remarkable novel, *Le Dernier Jour d'un condamné* (The Last Day of a Condemned Man), which was an eloquent denunciation of the death penalty (a lifelong cause of Hugo's), and his poetry began to show more political ambiguity than had been evident in his earlier work. In the history of French literature, the legendary "*bataille d'*Hernani"— when the Parisian literary and political worlds were divided between pro- and anti-Hugo camps—marks the triumph of Romanticism in nineteenth-century France. Hugo's play broke with all the rules of the neoclassical tradition that had dominated French theater. There were literally fistfights in the audience between Romantics and conservatives. In retrospect, the "*bataille d'*Hernani" came to be viewed as a cultural precursor of the Revolution of 1830.

Under the July Monarchy of 1830–48, Hugo's status as the leading figure in French literature increased steadily as he successfully published the novel *Notre-Dame de Paris* (1831) as well as several collections of poetry, including *Les Feuilles d'automne* (1831), *Les Chants du crépuscule* (1835), *Les Voix intérieures* (1837), and *Les Rayons et les ombres* (1840); he also enjoyed considerable success as a playwright. Even after he became a member of the literary establishment, Hugo's work continued to reveal a growing concern for social justice. In 1834, he published *Claude Gueux,* a brief account of a murderer who went to the guillotine; Hugo used his book to dare his bourgeois readers to consider their responsibility for a society that drove men to crime, and women to prostitution. In his poetry too, amid Romantic contemplations of nature and celebrations of his love for his children or his mistress, Hugo's social and political conscience is clearly present. Publicly, the 1840s brought Hugo to new professional and political heights, as he was elected to the Académie Française and named by the king to the Chambre des Pairs. Personally, Hugo was devastated in 1843 by the sudden death by drowning of his eldest and favorite child, Léopoldine, a loss that would inspire some of his best-known poems.

It was in 1845 that he began work on a novel, first called *Jean Tréjean* renamed *Les Misères,* the story of a convict, a poor man persecuted by a system in which justice has been overshadowed by the law. Hugo had completed most of the book when the Revolution of 1848 drew him back into politics. Elected to the new National Assembly of the nascent Second Republic as a member of the center-right, Hugo was soon calling for such progressive measures as free public education, penal reform, including the abolition of the death penalty, and international cooperation. In June of 1848, Hugo played a leading role in the suppression of a popular insurrection that saw barricades raised up in the streets of Paris. It was a searing moment for Hugo, who was appalled by the misery that provoked the uprising, but felt compelled to side with civic order. Hugo also supported the return from exile of Napoléon's nephew Louis-Napoléon Bonaparte, as well as his subsequent candidacy for the presidency. By the time the so-called "prince-président" seized power as Emperor Napoléon III, Hugo had become one of his most vocal and courageous opponents. Hugo soon judged it prudent to leave France, eventually taking up residence in the

English Channel Islands, where he would await the fall of the Second Empire for almost twenty years.

It was in exile that Hugo's political transformation became complete. The poetry he wrote in exile—*Les Châtiments, La Légende des siècles, La Fin de Satan*—was politically and artistically daring, and revealed a greater commitment to changing the social order of France and Europe than his previous writings. Hugo also publicly lent his support to such movements as abolitionism in the United States and Italian unification under Garibaldi. This was the Hugo who in 1860 returned to *Les Misères,* which he had given up for politics in 1848. In 1861, sixteen years after he began, and with significant revisions to his original, unfinished novel, Hugo traveled to Belgium, where the book now called *Les Misérables* was to be published, and visited the battlefield of Waterloo, in order to verify certain details for a brief digression he intended to include in his novel. A massive publicity campaign in every capital of Europe preceded the publication of the first volume, *Fantine,* in April 1862. The Parisian literary establishment did not quite know what to make of the novel, which defied every expectation of the genre. Critical reaction was typified by the Goncourt brothers' pronouncement that a man of genius had written a novel intended for the *cabinets de lecture* (i.e., the uneducated people who visited the reading rooms). Such cautious snobbery was not reflected in the book's sales. In Paris, bookstores sold every copy within three days. Factory workers were reported to have pooled their money to buy shared copies. Conservatives denounced a book that presented a criminal as a hero. Pope Pius IX placed *Les Misérables* on the Church's Index of proscribed books, and copies were publicly burned in Spain. In Paris and all around the world, *Les Misérables* solidified Hugo's reputation as the champion of the poor and the enemy of tyranny. The novel was devoured by everyone from Tolstoy and Dostoyevsky to soldiers on both sides of the American Civil War.

When the Franco-Prussian War brought down the government of the Second Empire, Hugo returned to France, his status as a national icon unquestioned. He served again in government, the last time as a senator of the Third Republic. He also continued to write, including a sentimental verse collection entitled *L'Art d'être grand-père.* In 1874, his last novel, *Quatre-vingt-treize* (Ninety-three), reached back to the previous century to examine the lost opportunity that was the French Revolution.

Victor Hugo died on May 23, 1885. He had outlived his wife, his principal mistress, and three of his four children. More than two million people—a number greater than the official population of Paris—turned out to witness the funeral procession as, according to Hugo's instructions, a pauper's hearse bore his casket from the Arc de Triomphe, where Hugo had lain in state for twenty-four hours, to the Panthéon, which had been reestablished as a national mausoleum just in time to receive his mortal remains.

# CONTENTS

## LES MISÉRABLES

### PART ONE: FANTINE

### PART TWO: COSETTE

# Introduction

*Adam Gopnik*

One of the permanent and popular works of Western literature, Victor Hugo's *Les Misérables* is a rare book that is both a major literary novel and a miracle of popular entertainment. I write these words having just returned from a packed Boxing Day performance of the operetta version of the book by Schönberg and Boublil, whose emblematic image of an embattled, wide-eyed nymphet, taken directly from the illustration of Cosette in the first French edition, has by now become familiar to the world. A thousand Christmas-sated New Yorkers sat, silent and rapt with emotion, at the nearly three-hour-long rendition of Hugo's seemingly remote story of a failed revolt in 1832 Paris. Only the Dickens of *Oliver Twist* and *A Tale of Two Cities* rivals Hugo as a popular poet who is also a great writer—and Dickens, for all his radicalism, worked more comfortably within the essentially progressive and ameliorative society he was settled within than Hugo, who wrote in exile at a time of autocracy in France, ever could. Dickens was responsible to reform, and Hugo to revolution. Dickens was the storyteller to a nation; Hugo was the conscience of a people. A possibly apocryphal story relates that shortly after *Les Misérables'* heavily hyped publication, Victor Hugo sent to his publisher a telegram with the single character "?" The response came back in perfect symmetry: "!" That exclamation point was meant to suggest the commercial success of the book, but it remains intact as a reader's response too.

But readers expecting simply the operatic version of the novel, the tale of Jean Valjean and his implacable pursuit by Inspector Javert, counterpoised with the love story of his adopted daughter, Cosette, with the romantic revolutionary Marius, may be struck, or puzzled, by the novel as it really is. *Les Misérables* is (to use an image Hugo would have liked) a huge Gothic cathedral of a book, ornamented with gargoyles of malice and flying buttresses of digressions and some suspiciously restored-looking statues of saints. It includes a famous, long descriptive analysis of the Battle of Waterloo, which plays very lightly on the action, essaylike paragraphs and pages on the meaning of names, the nature of genius, the importance of slang, and the social origins of prostitution, not to mention aphorisms of general applicability, only gently tied to the material, present on every page. It seemed a little old-fashioned to critics when it was first published in 1862, a time when Manet and Baudelaire were already working, and the stenographic irony and elegance of French modernism was already alive. It can still seem a little old-fashioned today.

There is, as a consequence, a natural urge on the part of the reader to skip the gassy bits and go directly to the dramatic bits. This would be a mistake, and one that this new translation by Julie Rose, which marvelously removes the yellowed varnish from Hugo's prose and gives us the racy, breathless, and passionate intelligence of the original, makes easy to avoid. The gassy bits in *Les Misérables* aren't really gassy. They're as good as the good bits. They're what give the good bits the gas that gets them aloft.

Hugo wrote *Les Misérables* on the Channel island of Guernsey in the late 1850s while in exile from the Second Empire of Louis-Napoléon, Napoléon's nephew and the autocratic mountebank who began to build modern Paris. It was in some ways a self-chosen exile—an amnesty had been issued in 1859 which Hugo might have taken advantage of, though at the cost of self-censorship on his return. But it was serious exile, not at all the self-saving, semi-theatrical exile that Voltaire had known a century before in Switzerland. It was modern political exile, of the kind that countless Russian and German and South American writers would undergo in the next century, an uprooting with only a remote chance of ever getting home.

And it was an exile earned as the accumulated result of almost sixty years of national history, years about as "tumultuous" as any sixty years of history have ever been. In France, since Hugo's birth in 1803, nearly every option of human governance, short of matriarchal Amazonianism, had been tried out—one regime after another, in rapid and disjointed succession and often with the same people playing similar roles in different hats. The French Revolution in 1789, the great unlooked-for revolt against a thousand years of hereditary absolutism, had been deformed into the Terror only a few years later, and then suddenly metamorphosed into Napoléon's Empire—a thing not seen since the days of Alexander the Great, an imperial cult of charismatic conquest. That had ended, dramatically and abruptly, at Waterloo—the place where the French Revolution stops and modern French politics begins, which explains why Hugo spent so much time thinking about the mechanisms of the battle—only to be followed by a restoration as inept as had been envisioned but considerably less cruel than had been feared. This failed restoration led to the second revolution, of 1830, which brought a "bourgeois King" to the throne of France and created a crucial breathing space in which the civil society of France grew and became recharged. This was followed by the central event of Hugo's maturity—the great, specifically liberal uprising of 1848, which was in turn shut down a mere two years later in a coup d'état organized by Louis-Napoléon, returning an autocratic, but far from charismatic, empire to the French: a corrupt, business-friendly regime, something like the Peronist regime in modern Argentina.

No nation in modern history has seen so many political options played out over the space of one lifetime. In *Les Misérables* Hugo is writing a kind of account book of all those possibilities, and the credits and debits they had incurred. Was Waterloo a triumph of reaction or a preamble to reform? Did the restoration of 1830 betray the Republic or provide it with a crucial breathing space? Had the revolution of 1848 been betrayed or fulfilled, ironically, in the only way it could be? Hugo's own life had been formed, in the spirit of the melodramatic vertigo he admired, by all of these experiences. His father, an atheist Bonapartist, had been a high-ranking officer in la Grande Armée; his mother, on the other hand, with whom he lived for most of his boyhood, was a fanatic Roman Catholic reactionary; and his first poems and political writings were all for King and Faith. His movement toward Republicanism, so decisive in his later years, was in some sense a move away from his mother and poetry and toward egalitarianism and his father, with the proviso that he could only find Republicanism convincing if it wore a romantic, semimystical garb. There was always tension between his feeling for glory and dash and glow—the Napoleonic virtues—and his sympathy with reason and piety and fairness— the Republican principles. *Les Misérables* is a kind of long argument Hugo is having with himself about whether the Republic will ever be sufficiently romantic. His early hero, Chateaubriand, gloomy poet-prophet of French romanticism, always haunted him, but he was trying to turn Chateaubriand's aristocratic pessimism into a form of liberal optimism while keeping the same poetic intensity—trying to turn aristocratic pessimism into liberal optimism without making it fatuous.

Though it was agonizing to live through these crazy oscillations—which didn't really end until the Fifth Republic in 1958—Hugo's particular, and particularly French, kind of humanism is rooted in them, too. Shifting from pole to pole is a good way to learn that the world is round. Though unequivocal in his own politics, Hugo, as a novelist, accepts the contradictions of social life rather than trying to wrest them round to a simple idea of good and evil. For Hugo civilization is dialectic without a synthesis. Pointless riot and necessary revolution, romantic love and self-infatuated flirtation, poetry and slang, all mix together in a messy human whole. He loves the coexistence of extremes and hates the golden mean: "For everything there is a theory that proclaims itself 'common sense,' Philinte versus Alceste, the offer of a compromise between the true and the false; explanation, admonition, a somewhat arrogant mitigation that, because it is mixed with blame and excuse, believes itself to be wisdom yet is often only pedantry."

Yet *Les Misérables,* though touched by a young man's passions, is very much a mature writer's book—Hugo had been a figure in French letters for almost forty years when he wrote it—whose interpolations and asides are part of a deliberate, "achieved" aesthetic. His first, instantly famous acts as a young writer involved taking sides against French classicism—against the neoclassical unities and the chilly, elegant formalism that have always been far more alluring in France than in England, something imbibed rather than inculcated. The first scandal connected with his name involved his now-unreadable plays of the 1820s *Cromwell* and *Hernani,* which made the case, forcibly, against neat plays with neat points, in favor of a "Shakespearean" drama of messy scenes and high emotion. Neatly woven stories were inadequate to modern times, Hugo always believed, while Gothic forms, with their shadows and side chapels and façade ornaments, spoke more directly to our experience. This paradox, central to all romantic art and fiction, where the Middle Ages are not the nostalgic past but the transposed theater of the present, informs his first great novel *Notre Dame de Paris,* which we know as *The Hunchback of Notre-Dame.* It luxuriated in its medieval setting while scoring its increasingly liberal points.

His choice, yet again, of an implicitly Gothic form for *Les Misérables*— a form that is as potent in its ornaments as in its architecture and defies every notion of "unity"—is neither accidental nor without a kind of politics of its own. Hugo *does* write in a way that will seem odd to the modern reader, who is accustomed to the smooth psychological flow of the Gustave Flaubert or Henry James novel. Hugo doesn't just describe. He describes, then dramatizes, and then editorializes on the drama, in a way that violates the decorum of the psychological novel as we have inherited it. He imagines his characters, sees what they do, and then charts his course on that basis.

This "all-over," freewheeling structure gives Hugo the opportunity to *talk.* What the reader is likely to remember longest and be stirred by most in *Les Misérables* is Hugo's own voice as the narrator, and his wry, amused, impassioned, pluralistic, inclusive running commentary on the action. At a "micro" level, Hugo's active delight at contradiction is expressed in the constant flow of antitheses that fill every page of the book and crowd its corners. The love of contradiction, expressed in sonorous antithesis, is there when he hymns the abandoned Napoleonic "Elephant" monument in Paris that has become a squatter's delight: "O, the unforeseen usefulness of the useless! The charity of big things! The goodness of giants! The outsize monument that had once held an idea of the emperor's had become a poky home for a little street kid." It's evident in Hugo's wonderful descriptions of Paris in a time of revolution: "Only such vast enclosures can contain civil war and an indescribably odd tranquillity at the same time. . . . People shoot at each other at street corners. . . . A few streets away, you can hear the clinking of billiard balls in the cafés. The curious laugh and chatter two feet away from these streets full of war; the theaters open their doors and perform vaudeville. The fiacres roll along; people go off to dine *en ville*." (The whole tone of the French upper punditry still derives from Hugo's prose—the praise of the "voluptuous cruelty of life" or the "horrible lucidity of journalism," and so on, which one can still bump one's shin against in any high-minded magazine.)

Though some of Hugo's antitheses are *merely* sonorous, and a few baffling, their constant drumming presence do suggest a view of life more accepting, more deeply tolerant of moral frailty, than our own Anglo-American liberalism, which still tends to put characters into neat boxes marked *nasty* and *nice*. This is what Hugo's humanism consists of, and what makes the long editorial digressions so passionate but still so convincing. It is in the opposites of his prose that what is romantic and "old-fashioned" and what is modern and ever-contemporary in Hugo meet. The "doubleness" in Hugo's voice, his fascination with what Browning called "the dangerous edge of things" ("the honest thief, the tender murderer, the superstitious atheist") means also that certain crucial scenes and actions in the book are a lot more complicated than we have chosen to recall them in popular memory.

Hugo is a champion of the people, but he is far from a sentimental populist; his portrait of the Thénardiers, the innkeepers who mistreat Cosette and then play a role on the barricades, is withering, and might have been written by that arch-reactionary Balzac. More important, the moral dilemmas that Jean Valjean faces throughout the book are rarely simple choices between Republican virtue and reactionary vice. Although Hugo is generally "anti-clerical," he makes sure to have Valjean, at a crucial moment, rescued by a priest, who, out of Christian compassion, pretends to have made him a "gift" of silver candlesticks that Valjean has in fact stolen from him. At another early turning point in the narrative, Valjean, in his disguise as Madeline, a factory owner, has essentially escaped Javert's pursuit; another man has been mistaken for him. Valjean's decision to go to the wrongly accused man's rescue and identify him, also involves the loss of his own small factory and the destitution of his workers. It's not an obvious choice.

Even the novel's climactic scenes on the barricades are not, as most people think or recall, images of the 1830 revolution or the glorious (if soon betrayed) ones of 1848, but of a smaller, largely forgotten Parisian *fronde* in 1832, which Hugo recognizes from the beginning as doomed and probably pointless, and certainly from a narrow strategic point of view counterproductive. It keys his great meditation on the difference between a riot and a revolution, a difference which Hugo, a passionate revolutionary, is willing to concede is much smaller and more contingent than one might like. In every case, where we recall a simple morality play, Hugo gives us a complicated essay on chance, contingency, and the cruel workings of moral necessity.

Above all, while the popular imagination remembers Inspector Javert as an implacable and relentless pursuer, it is not, for Hugo, Javert's malice and mercilessness that drive him to hunt down Jean Valjean. It is Javert's absolute, and on its own terms admirable, commitment to justice, which Javert interprets as a commitment to the rules and their administration, to the parallel paper universe of abstract principles and absolute laws. At what is perhaps the real climax of the book, Javert's death, the drama is driven from inside by the poetry and is preceded and climaxed by a flurry of Hugo's antithesis. The crisis for Javert is that he is not able to accept the multiplicity of motive in human life. After Valjean's own mercy to Javert has persuaded the inspector to allow Valjean to carry Marius to safety, Javert "saw two roads before him, both equally straight, but he saw two of them, and this terrified him, for he had never in his life known more than one straight line." As Hugo tells us in one of his most memorable aphorisms, thinking always involves a certain amount of inner revolt: I think, therefore I doubt. To be alive is to be skeptical about one's own certainties. The complexity of Valjean's behavior is so frightening to Javert that it drives him to his own death, ornamented by a sudden shower of those antitheses:

> Jean Valjean threw him. All the axioms that had propped up his whole life collapsed before that man. Jean Valjean's generosity toward him, Javert, devastated him. . . . A benevolent malefactor, a compassionate convict . . . offering forgiveness in return for hate, favoring pity over revenge, preferring to be destroyed himself to destroying his enemy, saving the one who had brought him down . . . this loathsome angel, this vile hero, who outraged him almost as much as he amazed him.

Devastating generosity, loathsome angels—what destroys Javert is not his implacable lack of compassion but his absolute certitude, which is inadequate not merely to the complexity of life but to Hugo's conviction that life is necessarily double, inexorably two-pathed even when we struggle to stay on one.

Yet, though Hugo has a complex view of the world, the popular memory isn't wrong to remember *Les Misérables* best as exhortation and example. In the end, Hugo kept Republican liberalism from seeming fatuous by insisting that its acceptance of pluralism was not timid compromise but a sign of wisdom. For Hugo, it is the rational, "procedural" liberal Republican who alone has mystic romantic insight into the intrinsic doubleness of life. Hugo is a romantic, and a Republican: he believes in individual acts, even heroic individual acts, and he believes that liberty is the precondition of that kind of heroism.

At the height of the twentieth century's calamities, Hugo's romantic republicanism could seem fragile and unconvincing. Beginning with Karl Marx himself, Marxists always condescended to Hugo. Marx wrote that Hugo had failed to see the inevitable workings of the bourgeois scheme in the making of the Second Empire and wrongly thought that the problem was Louis-Napoléon when the problem was the Republic, which was bound to be a fraud. Hugo, though, believed that liberty was not a bourgeois ruse but a gift, like fire, that ought to be available to everyone. Hugo thought the problem was not with the Republic but with Louis-Napoléon, who had betrayed it. The horror of capitalism lay in its cruelty to the poor—reform the cruelty and one could reconcile with capitalism. Any absolutist scheme that enslaved men was wrong; the Republican scheme, at least, pointed the way to their liberation. Though Hugo would have been, like Dickens, an exasperating man to talk practical politics with (and was a failure in them), he had a vision of political life that remains remarkably sane and prescient. True Republicanism meant increasing the sphere of liberty in every arena of life—more freedom to rise, to sing, to act without fear, to accept contradictions without panic—and it meant breaking down the false fears among people. That's the "romantic" in Hugo, and that's the vision of *Les Misérables:* all men are creatures of lust and will and cruelty, who can be broken not by slow education but by sudden passionate bursts of empathy and conscience, and indignation at the treatment of other human beings.

Almost exactly halfway through *Les Misérables* Hugo introduces an amazing extended metaphor of intellectual work as mining. Against the Enlightenment metaphor of intellectual work as tower-making or bridge-building, reaching upward toward heaven or the far shore, Hugo proposes that thinking is a kind of delving in the dark, a Dante-like descent toward something mysterious and unknown. At each level the miners find new jewels, but farther down is a deeper inferno of pure will. You dig deep to reach wisdom, but if you dig deeper you find raw hate and animal passion. It is a Freudian, self-canceling metaphor of the kind that modern literary critics love—the deeper into the darkness you go, the more light you shed (presumably the light from the sky that comes down into the shafts, but that isn't clear or poetically convincing). But Hugo's real point is apparent: sane minds are always forged over an inferno of passion and hatred; the job of the poet or philosopher is to open a vein into the mind that delves into the possibilities of the soul without getting us too deep into the rule of the will. It's dark down there, but the darkness is the only place where we can work, and in the darkness something can be found. Accepting will, passion, lust, cruelty, rage, and violence—all the things *Les Misérables* describes—as inevitabilities of life, we can still believe in compassion, liberty, and light as the possibilities of civilization. The light of the mind is visible in human eyes, he tells us, and he means it.

It is a little startling to think that Hugo's dream for France and Europe, albeit after a century of unprecedented cruelty and suffering, has actually been brought to pass: a democratic France in a united Europe, allergic to warfare, with poverty reduced to pockets. Republican revolution, completed, does not look at all Romantic. (It is hard for Francophiles today to realize that all the petty bureaucratic schemes of Brussels and the depressing sonorities of compromised politics are the dreams that men died on barricades for, but they are.) One need only look at life in South America or Asia, though, to see the same enduring conflicts between mass poverty and "mere" freedom, and, more deeply, between the frightened insistence on authority and the love of liberty. As Mario Vargas Llosa's tribute to Hugo, *The Temptation of the Impossible,* has shown, Hugo's vision is still contemporary in a "globalized" world, reminding us that a courageous championing of the poor and a love of liberty aren't in tension but the same impulse expressed at different moments. Hugo's romantic republicanism, of which this book is the permanent manifesto, looks a lot saner than all the alternatives that have risen to replace it. The question marks remain; *Les Misérables* continues to provide the exclamations.

---

ADAM GOPNIK is the author of *Paris to the Moon* and *Through the Children's Gate,* and editor of the Library of America anthology *Americans in Paris.* He writes essays on various subjects for *The New Yorker,* and has recently written introductions to works by Maupassant, Balzac, Proust, and Alain-Fournier.

# TRANSLATOR'S PREFACE

*Les Misérables* is not just a novel; it is a monument. As a piece of French *patrimoine*, it is as sacred in France as the "Marseillaise" and the notion of the Republic. It is a piece of world treasure, too, a projectile of the imagination, sacred to its readers everywhere as it soars over the rocky landscape of the modern world. Translating it has not been remotely like any other experience I've ever had, for if it's true, as the saying goes, that you do not emerge from reading *Les Misérables* the same person, this is even truer of translating it. You are, for one thing, less inclined to take life lightly—or lying down.

Since I first sat down to work on this translation seasons have come and gone, some days bitterly cold, some days too hot to sit there, in my study, tapping away, without a fan. At one stage I had to wheel in an occupational therapist to reorganize the desk and lighting and come up with a more ergonomic chair; my hair didn't quite go white with the struggle, like Jean Valjean's does when he gives himself up to save another man's skin, but gray hairs appeared and accumulated with building speed and toward the end I needed stronger reading glasses—for you don't tackle a monument with impunity.

Hugo, it seems, wrote standing up, not something my occupational therapist thought of. He wrote *Les Misérables* standing in the room he'd nicknamed "the lookout" at the top of Hauteville House, on the isle of Guernsey, looking out over the water beyond St. Peter Port. When he wasn't upstairs writing, or producing spectacular artworks way ahead of their time, he was downstairs entertaining visitors, enjoying family, or somewhere else in the house doing things with the maid. And when he wasn't in the house, he was either down the road at his intimate friend Juliette Drouet's, or out walking for mile after mile with one of his beloved dogs—Chougna, Ponto, or Sénat (Senate). Hugo, too, was a monument, a man of huge appetite and lust for life.

Keeping pace with this monumental man is a very physical challenge. For though some parts of *Les Misérables* are more compelling than others, Hugo's energy never seems to flag. His interest in, his passion for, the real world, and the world beyond, beneath, and behind it, are indefatigable. I often thought of him, Victor Hugo, already a monument in his own lifetime, as I set out with my beloved dog, Poppy, heading for her favorite haunts along the Parramatta River. If all translators should have dogs, this is axiomatic when it comes to translators of Hugo.

Hugo once claimed that he'd had two great affairs in his life: Paris and the ocean. As I walked, I thought of that generous, gregarious yet wild man in self-imposed exile on a tiny island in the English Channel, cut off from his beloved Paris but in full possession of his other great love, the sea. And the connection with the oceanic quality of the novel, which is a book about everything, not merely a narrative, seemed obvious. So, too, did the connection with the level of detail and the loving specificity throughout the book.

There is Hugo, tramping over grass and rocks and along the shore, in the bracing salt sea air, taking in the briny tang in great gulps, *remembering* Paris. In as much detail as his phenomenal memory—or powers of invention—would allow, as though he was trying to bring back a face he loved (his mother's face, he says) from out of the mists of time.

God is in the details, as we know. Hugo wrote from an omniscient narrator's point of view with an eagle eye for detail—at a time when details of every stripe were being swept away. That turbulent century saw the sudden speeding up of History, the installment of change as a new mode of being—political, social, physical change.

Hugo bears witness to that process of change, to all the changes he had lived through. He describes everything he remembers—fixes forever—times, events, things, people, "facts," standing on the seashore, facing the tidal wave of History, as though standing on shifting sands. He *was* standing on shifting sands.

That is the whole point of detail. And if I seem to be hammering the point, it's because I have taken great care to give you, the reader, all of the detail that Hugo wanted you to read. I am, to my knowledge, one of the few translators to have rendered all of Hugo's magnificent novel without censorship.

For there is a whole censorious tradition of translating *Les Misérables*. In this tradition, Hugo's great, original, exuberantly wordy book is "cleaned up." It's cleaned up of rude words and vulgar images, which the translator views as offensive and unnecessary, as though Hugo's use of such words and images was accidental or abhorrent. This is not merely losing bite and punch. Much more seriously, it's misreading the entire book. For if *Les Misérables* can be reduced to a meaning, it is surely the connection Hugo is forever making between the sewer and society, the gutter and the stars.

Offensive matter is not the only thing this tradition has cleaned out of existence. It has also gone after mixed metaphors, grammatical improprieties, and, above all, detail, even where that detail is inoffensive.

We lose the vibrant density of what Hugo was writing about as a result. When Hugo says Cosette was married in "Binche guipure lace," for example, that surely gives us something more than hearing she wore "a lace frock." It tells us where the lace was made, that there was a whole industry of making lace of a very specific kind there, and it tells us what that lace was: guipure. Such a beautiful word. If you don't know what it is, you can always look it up. Hugo's descriptive scope was encyclopedic, and encyclopedias, like dictionaries, still exist, online and off. Knowledge, like virtue, is its own reward.

For some previous translators, *Les Misérables* has been valued solely for its central story and anything that departs from that narrative or doesn't directly advance it is superfluous and *should* go—or be lopped, or banished to an appendix. When you see the book as a narrative—in fact, a detective story–cum-psychological thriller as well as a very moving moral tale—embedded in a much larger work, the impetus behind such a stance seems bizarre. Some of Hugo's finest writing is in the discursive bits and these are tethered to the narrative of moral struggle by many threads, each digression investigating another battlefield, from the military campaign of Waterloo that changed the course of the century, to religious fundamentalism, to the dark battlefield of poverty and crime, and on to the disposal of human effluent, actual and metaphorical.

The digressions don't detract from the narrative, they enhance it. Hugo the orator and polemicist clearly had a good time writing them, just as he had a wonderful time with certain of his characters, who instantly achieved what today we'd call iconic status, entering the language as so many proper nouns and staying there.

The relationship between translator and writer is very like a marriage. In this "marriage," I've wanted to be completely faithful. And I hope the translation is more readable, not less, as a result. I did it in my house in Sydney, Australia, a place put on the modern map by Captain James Cook, whose *Voyages* Jean Valjean lugs around with him in his little suitcase as one of the few precious things he owns. The house was built in 1869, seven years after *Les Misérables* came out—in ten volumes over nine months, complete with its own advertising merchandise—to become the biggest hit in the history of publishing. The first owner of the house was a woman named Marie Paull, and she hailed from St. Hélier, Jersey. When Hugo docked there in 1855, already a world-renowned celebrity-hero, he was greeted by a crowd of fans. Whether Marie Paull was in the crowd or not we'll never know, but I'd like to think she was. She would certainly have known of Hugo—and the Hugo of the Channel Islands, who conducted séances and talked to the spirits of the dead, would have liked the connection.

The whole effort of this translation has been to respect the work—all of it—and to let it speak, driven by the surprising freshness of Hugo's prose, the muscularity of his rhythms, the vitality of the book's cast and ideas, and the stunning prescience and relevance of a novel once called "the Magna Carta of the human race."

At times I really did feel like I was "channeling" Hugo, and it was every bit as euphoric and draining as such a theatrical experience ought to be. In a sense, all translation is a performance, a piece of theater. You try to "be" the role you're playing, to stay "in character." This is one way of expressing how I was taken over by this masterpiece in the process of translating it. Censorship is an old tradition in translating—and adaptation. Think of Alexander Pope reinterpreting Shakespeare so primly that it was like a bad translation, with Hamlet thinking of taking up arms against a "siege" of troubles instead of a "sea" of troubles, to avoid the horrors of mixing metaphor. Hugo knew about translating. His son, François-Victor, translated Shakespeare. Yet Hugo claimed translation was censorship. I've done my humble best to prove him wrong.

———

Heartfelt thanks to the team at Random House who've worked so hard on this edition: production editor Vincent La Scala; Holly Webber, a copy editor who misses nothing; and my editor, Judy Sternlight, for unerring judgment and support.

*This translation is dedicated to Allan.*

—Julie Rose, Sydney, February 2008

# CHRONOLOGY

1797        Marriage of Joseph-Léopold-Sigisbert Hugo, an officer of the Revo-
            lutionary armies, and Sophie Trébuchet, in Nantes.

            Birth of Abel Hugo.

1800        Birth of Eugène Hugo.

1802        Victor-Marie Hugo, the Hugos' third son, is born in Besançon on
            February 26.

            Publication of Chateaubriand's *René*.

1803–10     Léopold Hugo joins the staff of Joseph Bonaparte, eventually be-
            comes his aide-de-camp, serving in southern Italy when Joseph is
            named king of Naples by his brother, then follows him to Spain in
            1809 after Napoléon's conquest of that country and Joseph's transfer
            to the throne in Madrid. He is promoted to the rank of general and
            named a count by Joseph in 1809.

            As the Hugos' marriage deteriorates, Sophie intermittently follows
            her husband to his postings with the children and eventually moves
            to Paris, where her lover, General Lahorie, acts as tutor to their chil-
            dren. In 1810, Lahorie is implicated in a conspiracy against
            Napoléon; he is arrested in Madame Hugo's house and later exe-
            cuted by firing squad (1812).

            Goethe's *Faust* is published in 1808.

1811        Madame Hugo takes her sons to Madrid, where Joseph Bonaparte
            has encouraged the Hugos to resolve the conflicts in their marriage.

1812        Sophie Hugo returns to Paris with the children; she and General
            Hugo permanently separate.

            Byron's *Childe Harold* is published.

| | |
|---|---|
| 1814 | General Hugo, having returned to Spain with the retreating French armies the previous year, is assigned by Napoléon to command the fortified border city of Thionville, in Lorraine, on the Moselle River. General Hugo refuses to surrender even after Napoléon's abdication. |
| 1815 | During the Hundred Days, General Hugo rallies to Napoléon and is again given the command of Thionville; he again holds out long after Napoléon's surrender, giving up the city in November, some five months after Waterloo. General Hugo lives mostly in the city of Blois during the Restoration, largely estranged from his children and feuding with Madame Hugo about financial support of their children. |
| 1817 | Victor-Marie Hugo is awarded honorable mention in a poetry contest sponsored by the Académie Française. |
| 1818 | Hugo begins work on his first novel, *Bug Jargal* (The Slave King), the story of a slave uprising in Saint-Domingue (modern-day Haiti). |
| | Mary Shelley's *Frankenstein* is published. |
| 1819 | Hugo's poems, including an ode on the restoration of a statue of Henri IV on the Pont-Neuf in Paris, win first prize in the prestigious Jeux Floraux de l'Académie de Toulouse. With his brothers, he founds a literary periodical, *Le Conservateur littéraire*. |
| | Sir Walter Scott's *Ivanhoe* is published. |
| 1820 | Hugo's ode in honor of the recently assassinated Duc de Berry, nephew of Louis XVIII, is awarded 500 francs by the king. Hugo publishes *Bug Jargal* in serial form in *Le Conservateur littéraire*. |
| 1821 | Death of Sophie Hugo. Hugo and his brothers will reconcile with their father over the next several years. |
| 1822 | Publishes his first collection of poetry, *Odes et poésies diverses*. Hugo's poems display sufficient orthodoxy and royalism to earn him a pension that allows him to marry Adèle Foucher, whom he has known since childhood. Hugo's elder brother Eugène, who was also in love with Adèle, suffers a nervous breakdown the night after the wedding from which he will never recover, spending the rest of his life in institutions. |
| 1823 | Publishes his second novel, *Han d'Islande* (Hans of Iceland or The Demon Dwarf), a historical novel set in Scandinavia inspired by the work of Walter Scott. |
| | Birth of a son, Léopold-Victor, who will die in infancy. |
| 1824 | Publishes his second volume of poetry, *Nouvelles Odes*. |
| | Birth of a daughter, Léopoldine. |
| 1825 | Hugo is named chevalier of the Légion d'Honneur and official poet |

of the coronation of King Charles X, youngest brother of Louis XVI, who will be the last Bourbon king of France.

1826    Publishes a revised version of *Bug Jargal* and *Odes et poésies diverses.*

Birth of a son, Charles.

1827    Publishes a play, *Cromwell,* which is never produced; the *préface* is a manifesto of the growing movement of French Romanticism, famously containing Hugo's defense of the role of the *grotesque* in literature and art.

Publishes a long poem, *Ode à la Colonne de la Place Vendôme,* a celebration of the glory of the French military under the Empire, which is seen as a sign of his growing rift with royalism and conservatism.

1828    Hugo's play *Amy Robsart,* an adaptation of Walter Scott's *Kenilworth,* is produced but poorly received.

Birth of a third son, François-Victor.

Death of General Léopold Hugo. As the third son of an imperial count, Victor begins to use the title of baron, even though his father's title was never recognized by the restored Bourbon government.

1829    Publishes the novel *Le Dernier Jour d'un condamné* (The Last Day of a Condemned Man), a first-person interior monologue of a man facing his imminent execution, and a powerful statement of opposition to the death penalty, which will be a lifelong cause of Hugo's.

*Marion de Lorme,* the story of a courtesan who is reformed by love, is staged by the Comédie-Française before being banned by the government for its alleged moral and political subversiveness.

Publishes *Les Orientales,* a collection of poems heavily marked by the Romantic fascination with the exotic East.

1830    In February, the premiere of Hugo's much anticipated play *Hernani* becomes a cultural and political event, provoking near riots between liberal Romantics and neoclassical conservatives.

In July, the government's attempts to promulgate authoritarian laws provoke the July Revolution. The Bourbons go into exile, and their cousin Louis-Philippe d'Orléans accedes to the throne under a new constitutional monarchy.

Birth of another daughter, Adèle, named for her mother.

Stendhal publishes *Le Rouge et le noir* (The Red and the Black).

1831    Publishes *Notre-Dame de Paris* (The Hunchback of Notre-Dame).

Publishes *Les Feuilles d'automne* (Autumn Leaves), a collection of intimate verse inspired by paternity and family life.

Madame Hugo begins an affair with Charles-Augustin de Sainte-

Beuve, celebrated literary critic and one of Victor's closest friends. From this point on the Hugos' marriage is a platonic partnership.

1832      *Le Roi s'amuse* (The King Takes His Pleasure) premieres at the Comédie-Française. The play is soon banned for its alleged immorality as it depicts the French king François I as a dissolute tyrant, abusing his power in pursuit of a young woman. This is the first act of censorship of the July Monarchy, of which Hugo was and remained a supporter. Giuseppe Verdi's *Rigoletto* (1851) is based on *Le Roi s'amuse*.

The Hugos rent an apartment in the elegant place Royale (today's place des Vosges), where they live until 1848.

Widespread unemployment and economic distress lead to insurrections in Lyon and Paris, events that would play a key role in *Les Misérables*.

1833      Premiere of *Lucrèce Borgia*, Hugo's greatest popular and financial success in the theater. During rehearsals, Hugo falls in love with Juliette Drouet, an actress and celebrated courtesan who had a minor role in the play. She would be Hugo's *maîtresse en titre* for the rest of her life.

Another historical play, *Marie Tudor*, was far less successful.

1834      Publishes *Claude Gueux*, a fact-based account of a poor man in prison who was executed for assaulting a guard; as with *Le Dernier Jour*, Hugo used literature to campaign against the death penalty.

Publishes *Philosophie et littérature mêlées*, a collection of critical essays.

1835      Publishes *Chants du crépuscule* (Songs of Twilight), a collection of poems, many of which suggest Hugo's growing republican sympathies.

The historical play *Angelo, Tyran de Padoue* premieres at the Comédie-Française.

Balzac's *Le Père Goriot* is published.

1836      Hugo is twice nominated, but not elected, to the Académie Française.

1837      Publishes *Les Voix intérieures* (Interior Voices), a collection of poems inspired by both Hugo's personal life and political events.

His elder brother Eugène dies in Charenton asylum. Victor now uses the title of vicomte.

1838      Premiere of *Ruy Blas*, considered by many to be Hugo's finest play. Ruy Blas is a servant who, disguised as a nobleman, becomes the lover of the queen of Spain. Hugo's condemnation of a corrupt aristocracy scandalizes conservatives and enjoys great popular success.

Dickens publishes *Oliver Twist.*

1840     Publishes *Les Rayons et les ombres* (Rays and Shadows), a poetry collection that contains some of Hugo's most famous poems.

Hugo again fails to win election to the Académie Française.

1841     Hugo is at last elected to the Académie Française.

1842     Publishes *Le Rhin,* ostensibly a travel narrative that reflects Hugo's interests in history, legend, and politics, including an early call for international cooperation between the French and the Germans.

Publication of Eugène Sue's *Les Mystères de Paris,* a sprawling novel chronicling the Parisian underworld. Sue's novel is immensely popular, and heavily influences both Balzac's *Splendeurs et misères des courtisanes* (The Splendor and Misery of Courtesans) and Hugo's *Les Misérables.*

1843     *Les Burgraves* (The Robber Lords of the Rhine) is a critical and popular failure, marking the end of Hugo's career as a playwright and, it is generally agreed, of the Romantic theater in France.

On September 4, his daughter Léopoldine, who had married Charles Vacquerie on February 15 and was pregnant, was killed along with her husband in a boating accident on the Seine at Villequier. The death of Hugo's favorite child would cast a shadow over the rest of his life and inspire some of his best-known poetry.

1845     After being named a peer of France by King Louis-Philippe—Hugo is by now an intimate of the royal family, in particular of the crown prince and his wife—Hugo is arrested for adultery, caught in flagrante with Léonie d'Aunet (Madame Briard).

He begins work on a novel entitled *Jean Tréjean,* which will take on the working title of "Les Misères."

Poe publishes *The Raven.*

1848     In February, the July Monarchy falls before popular insurrection provoked by continued economic hardship among the working class. Hugo is elected to the Constituent Assembly as a conservative. Hugo's political activity will take precedence over his literary production for the next three years. He will not return to "Les Misères" until 1860.

In June, continued economic distress and unemployment lead to another violent popular insurrection; Hugo takes a major role in repressing the uprising, after which he begins a marked shift to the left in his politics.

With his son Charles as its public face and titular publisher, Hugo founds a political newspaper, *L'Événement* (The Event), which strongly advocates the election of Louis-Napoléon Bonaparte as president of the new Republic.

The *Communist Manifesto* of Marx and Engels is published.

1849     Hugo, still viewed as a conservative, is elected to the National Assembly, where he gives a noted speech calling for an end to poverty.

Hugo serves as president of an international peace conference in Paris, where his public address calls for the formation of a "United States of Europe" (*États Unis d'Europe*).

Dickens's *David Copperfield* is published.

1850     Hugo's speeches in the Assembly call for universal suffrage, freedom of the press, and free, compulsory education for all children.

1851     Hugo directly challenges the increasing authoritarianism of the "prince-président" Louis-Napoléon Bonaparte in the National Assembly.

Charles and François-Victor Hugo are arrested and imprisoned for publishing articles in *L'Événement* that are critical of the government.

In December, Louis-Napoléon and his supporters stage a successful coup d'état which establishes the Second Empire. Hugo attempts to rouse public resistance before fleeing to Brussels in disguise and in the company of Juliette Drouet, soon followed by Madame Hugo and his three children.

Melville publishes *Moby-Dick.*

1852     In Brussels, Hugo publishes *Napoléon le Petit,* a scathing indictment of Louis-Napoléon's rise to power, from the presidency of the Second Republic to the Second Empire.

The Hugos travel to London before taking up residence on the Channel Island of Jersey.

Harriet Beecher Stowe publishes *Uncle Tom's Cabin.*

1853     Publishes *Les Châtiments* (Chastisements), a collection of satirical poems aimed at Louis-Napoléon.

Hugo begins to participate in séances, seeking to contact the spirit of Léopoldine.

1854     Hugo begins work on *Dieu* (God) and *La Fin de Satan* (The End of Satan), visionary poems inspired by biblical and literary accounts of God and the devil that will not be published until after his death.

1856     Publishes *Les Contemplations;* subtitled *Memoires of the soul, Contemplations* is often considered Hugo's poetic masterpiece. The collection contains some of Hugo's greatest and best-remembered poems, many inspired by the loss of Léopoldine.

The success of *Les Contemplations* enables Hugo to purchase Hauteville House, on the island of Guernsey.

Hugo's daughter Adèle shows the first signs of mental illness.

1859  Publishes the first volume of *La Légende des siècles* (The Legend of the Centuries), a poetic retelling of human history, drawing heavily on the Bible as well as legend.

Hugo refuses an offer of amnesty from the government of Louis-Napoléon and issues a public call for the pardon of American abolitionist John Brown.

1860  Hugo returns to the unfinished manuscript of "Les Misères"; he will make significant revisions and additions to the manuscript of what will become *Les Misérables*.

1861  Hugo, accompanied by his wife, sons, and mistress, travels to Brussels, where his completed novel will be published. He makes a trip to the battlefield of Waterloo to verify his impressions of the terrain for the famous "digression" of *Les Misérables*.

1862  *Les Misérables* is published in Brussels, Paris, and throughout Europe. The novel is an instant popular success. Madame Hugo, who has been spending the winter season in Paris for some years, acts as Hugo's representative among the French literary community.

1863  A stage version of *Les Misérables*, written by Charles Hugo, debuts in Brussels.

The Hugos' daughter Adèle, in a state of delusion, runs away to Canada in pursuit of Charles Pinson, an English officer whom she discovers to be already married. She writes to her parents that she has married Pinson.

1864  Hugo writes the preface to a French edition of Shakespeare, translated by his son François-Victor. The preface is in fact a wide-ranging essay on the nature of genius.

1865  Publishes *Chansons des rues et des bois* (Songs of the Streets and the Woods), a collection of pastoral poems.

Tolstoy's *War and Peace* begins to appear in serial form.

1866  Publishes *Les Travailleurs de la mer* (The Toilers of the Sea), a novel depicting the lives of fishermen of the Channel Islands.

Dostoyevsky's *Crime and Punishment* is published.

1868  Birth of Georges Hugo, Charles's son and Hugo's first grandson. Hugo's wife, Adèle, dies in Brussels. Hugo accompanies her coffin to the Franco-Belgian border, en route to her burial in Paris.

1869  Publication of *L'Homme qui rit* (The Man Who Laughs or By the Order of the King), a historical novel set in seventeenth-century

England, deeply infused with Hugo's political, humanitarian, and literary preoccupations.

Hugo presides at an international peace conference in Lausanne, Switzerland.

Birth of Charles Hugo's daughter, Jeanne.

1870    The Prussian invasion of France brings about the collapse of the Second Empire. Hugo returns to Paris a national hero on the day after the Third Republic is declared.

1871    The Franco-Prussian War ends in French surrender, following a four-month siege of Paris by the Prussian army. Hugo is elected to the National Assembly but resigns in frustration in the face of a conservative, Bonapartist majority.

The Republican insurrection known as the Commune takes control of Paris for fifty-four days; some 25,000 supporters of the Communard government, mostly working-class, are killed before the national government regains control of the capital.

Death of Charles Hugo.

Émile Zola publishes *La Fortune des Rougon* (The Rougons' Fortune), the first volume of his great naturalist epic, the Rougon-Macquart series.

1872    Publishes *L'Année terrible* (The Terrible Year), a collection of poetry inspired by the political events of Paris since his return.

Hugo's advocacy of amnesty for the Communards leads to his electoral defeat.

Troubled by a reactionary turn of the government, Hugo returns to Guernsey.

Hugo's daughter Adèle returns to France from Barbados, where she had been living under the care of a housekeeper-cum-nurse for some time. She will be institutionalized until her death in 1915.

1873    Death of François-Victor Hugo.

1874    Publication of *Quatre-vingt-treize* (Ninety-three), Hugo's last novel, set in Brittany during the French Revolution, specifically under the Convention and the Terror. The novel's young hero, Gauvain, embodies the idealism and, implicitly, the lost opportunities of the Revolution.

1875    Publishes *Actes et paroles* (Actions and Words), a collection of his political speeches and essays.

1876    Hugo is elected to the Senate, where he advocates amnesty for the Communards of the 1871 insurrection.

| | |
|---|---|
| 1877 | Publishes second volume of *La Légende des siècles* (The Legend of the Centuries) and *L'Art d'être grand-père* (The Art of Being a Grandfather), a collection of intimate verse inspired by his grandchildren. |
| | Hugo plays a leading role in defending the Republic against an attempted reactionary coup d'état led by President MacMahon. |
| | Zola's *L'Assommoir,* the story of the miseries of the working class of Paris, is published. |
| 1878 | The stage adaptation of *Les Misérables* is presented at the Théâtre de la Porte-Saint-Martin. |
| | Hugo suffers a mild stroke that effectively puts an end to his writing career; further publications will be of revised manuscripts. |
| 1879 | Publishes *La Pitié suprême* (Supreme Pity), a poem advocating amnesty, a cause he also takes up in the Senate. |
| 1880 | Publishes *Religions et Religion* and *L'Âne* (The Ass), two long poems composed in exile. *Religions et Religion* draws a sharp distinction between belief in God and organized religion; *L'Âne* satirizes the pretentions of erudition, science, and philosophy. |
| | Hugo at last succeeds in obtaining amnesty for the Communards. |
| 1881 | Publishes *Le Quatre Vents de l'esprit* (The Four Winds of the Mind), a varied collection of poems. |
| | Hugo's seventy-ninth birthday—the beginning of his eightieth year—is declared a national holiday. Over the course of the day, an estimated six hundred thousand people file in tribute past his windows near the place de l'Étoile. His street, the avenue d'Eylau, is renamed the avenue Victor Hugo in his honor, a name it still bears today. |
| 1882 | Hugo's play *Torquemada,* written in 1869, is performed. |
| | Hugo is reelected to the Senate. |
| 1883 | Publishes the final volume of *La Légende des siècles.* |
| | Juliette Drouet dies on May 11. |
| 1885 | On May 22, Hugo dies of pneumonia. His last words are reported to be *"Je vois de la lumière neuve"* (I see a new light). |
| | Hugo lies in state under the Arc de Triomphe as a reported two million people come to pay tribute. The first of June is declared a national day of mourning. Legislation to reestablish the Panthéon as a national mausoleum is passed. According to Hugo's wishes, his coffin is borne on a pauper's cart, following eleven wagons overflowing with flowers, to his final resting place on top of Mount Sainte-Geneviève. |
| | Zola's *Germinal,* the epic story of a coal miners' strike, is published. |

1886      Publication of the unfinished *La Fin de Satan,* one of the visionary and metaphorical poems Hugo began in 1854. Its companion poem, *Dieu* (God), also unfinished, will be published in 1891.

1902      On the centenary of Hugo's birth, his former home in the place des Vosges is established as a museum, the Maison de Victor Hugo.

1905      The first full-length feature film produced in the United States is an adaptation of *Les Misérables.*

As long as social damnation exists, through laws and customs, artificially creating hell at the heart of civilization and muddying a destiny that is divine with human calamity; as long as the three problems of the century—man's debasement through the proletariat, woman's demoralization through hunger, the wasting of the child through darkness—are not resolved; as long as social suffocation is possible in certain areas; in other words, and to take an even broader view, as long as ignorance and misery exist in this world, books like the one you are about to read are, perhaps, not entirely useless.

—HAUTEVILLE HOUSE,[1] *January 1, 1862*

PART ONE

# Fantine

# BOOK ONE

# A JUST MAN

### I. MONSIEUR MYRIEL

In 1815, Monsieur Charles-François-Bienvenu Myriel was bishop of Digne. He was an elderly man of about seventy-five and he had occupied the seat of Digne since 1806.

There is something we might mention that has no bearing whatsoever on the tale we have to tell—not even on the background. Yet it may well serve some purpose, if only in the interests of precision, to jot down here the rumors and gossip that had circulated about him the moment he first popped up in the diocese. True or false, what is said about people often has as much bearing on their lives and especially on their destinies as what they do. Monsieur Myriel was the son of a councillor of the Aix parliament, a member of the *noblesse d'robe.*[2] They reckoned his father had put him down to inherit his position and so had married him off very early in the piece when he was only eighteen or twenty, as they used to do quite a lot in parliamentary families. Charles Myriel married or no, had, they said, set tongues wagging. He was a good-looking young man, if on the short side, elegant, charming, and witty; he had given the best years of his life thus far to worldly pursuits and love affairs. Then the Revolution came along, events spiraled, parliamentary families were wiped out, chased away, hunted, scattered. Monsieur Charles Myriel emigrated to Italy soon after the Revolution broke out. His wife died there of the chest infection she'd had for ages. They had no children. What happened next in the destiny of Monsieur Myriel? The collapse of the old society in France, the fall of his own family, the tragic scenes of '93,[3] which were, perhaps, even more frightening for émigrés[4] watching them from afar with the magnifying power of dread—did these things cause notions of renunciation and solitude to germinate in his mind? Was he, in the middle of the distractions and amorous diversions that filled his life, suddenly hit by one of those mysterious and terrible jolts that sometimes come and strike at the heart, bowling over the man public calamities couldn't shake, threatening as these did only his existence and his fortune? No one could say; all that was known was that, when he came back from Italy, he was a priest.

In 1804,[5] Monsieur Myriel was the curé of Brignolles.[6] He was already old and lived like a real recluse in profound seclusion.

Around the time of the coronation, a small parish matter—who can remember what now?—took him to Paris. Among other powerful persons, he called on Cardinal Fesch,[7] Napoléon's uncle, to petition him on his parishioners' behalf. One day when the emperor was visiting his uncle, the worthy curé, who was waiting in the anteroom, found himself in His Majesty's path. Napoléon, seeing the old boy give him the once-over with a certain curiosity, wheeled round and said brusquely: "Who is this little man staring at me?"

"Your Majesty," said Monsieur Myriel, "you see a little man, and I see a great man. Both of us may benefit."

That very night, the emperor asked the cardinal what the curé's name was and some time after that Monsieur Myriel was stunned to learn that he'd been named bishop of Digne.

But, when all's said and done, what was true in the tales told about the first phase of Monsieur Myriel's life? No one could tell. Few families had known the Myriel family before the Revolution.

Monsieur Myriel had to endure the fate of every newcomer in a small town, where there are always plenty of mouths blathering and not many brains working. He had to endure it even though he was the bishop, and because he was the bishop. But, after all, the talk in which his name cropped up was perhaps nothing more than talk; hot air, babble, words, less than words, pap, as the colorful language of the Midi[8] puts it.

Whatever the case, after nine years as the resident bishop of Digne, all the usual gossip that initially consumes small towns and small people had died and sunk without a trace. No one would have dared bring it up, no one would have dared remember what it was.

Monsieur Myriel arrived in Digne accompanied by an old spinster, Mademoiselle Baptistine, who was his sister and ten years his junior.

They had only one servant, a woman the same age as Mademoiselle Baptistine, called Madame Magloire. Having been the servant of Monsieur le curé, she now went by the double title of personal maid to Mademoiselle and housekeeper to Monseigneur.[9]

Mademoiselle Baptistine was a tall, pale, thin, sweet person, the personification of that ideal expressed by the word *respectable;* for it seems a woman must be a mother to be esteemed. She had never been pretty, but her entire life, which had been merely a succession of holy works, had ended up laying a sort of whiteness and brightness over her; as she aged, she had gained what you could describe as the beauty of goodness. What had been skinniness in her youth had become transparency with maturity; and this diaphanous quality revealed the angel within. She was more of a spirit than a virgin. She seemed a mere shadow with scarcely enough of a body to have a gender; just a bit of matter bearing a light, with great big eyes always lowered to the ground, an excuse for a spirit to remain on earth.

Madame Magloire was a little old lady, white skinned, plump, round, busy, always wheezing, first because of always bustling about and second because of her asthma.

When he first arrived, Monsieur Myriel was set up in his episcopal palace with all the honors required by imperial decree, which ranked bishops immediately after field marshals.[10] The mayor and the president of the local council were the first to visit him, and on his side, he made his first visits to the general and the chief of police.

Once he had moved in, the town waited to see their bishop on the job.

## II. MONSIEUR MYRIEL BECOMES MONSEIGNEUR BIENVENU

The episcopal palace of Digne was next door to the hospital. The episcopal palace was a vast and handsome town house built in stone at the beginning of the previous century by Monseigneur Henri Puget, doctor of theology of the faculty of Paris and abbé of Simore,[1] who had been bishop of Digne in 1712. The palace was truly a mansion fit for a lord. Everything about it was on the grand scale, the bishop's apartments, the drawing rooms, the bedrooms, the main courtyard, which was huge, with covered arcades in the old Florentine style, and the gardens planted with magnificent trees. It was in the dining room, which was a long and superb gallery on the ground floor opening onto the grounds, that Monseigneur Henri Puget had, on July 29, 1714, ceremoniously fed the ecclesiastical dignitaries, Charles Brûlart de Genlis, archbishop prince of Embrun, Antoine de Mesgrigny, Capuchin bishop of Grasse, Philippe de Vendôme, grand prior of France, abbé of Saint-Honoré de Lérins, François de Berton de Crillon, bishop baron of Vence, César de Sabran de Forcalquier, lord bishop and lord of Glandève, and Jean Soanen, priest of the oratory, preacher in ordinary to the king, lord bishop of Senez.[2] The portraits of these seven reverend fathers embellished the dining room and the memorable date of July 29, 1714, was engraved there in gold lettering on a white marble panel.

The hospital was a low, narrow, single-story house with a small garden.

Three days after his arrival, the bishop visited the hospital. When his visit was over, he politely begged the director to accompany him back to his place.

"Monsieur le directeur, how many sick people do you have in your hospital at the moment?"

"Twenty-six, Monseigneur."

"That's what I counted," said the bishop.

"The beds are all jammed together," the director went on.

"That's what I noticed."

"The living areas are just bedrooms, and they're difficult to air."

"That's what I thought."

"Then again, when there's a ray of sun, the garden's too small for the convalescents."

"That's what I said to myself."

"As for epidemics, we've had typhus this year, and two years ago we had miliary fever—up to a hundred were down with it at any one time. We don't know what to do."

"The thought did strike me."

"What can we do, Monseigneur?" said the director. "You have to resign yourself to it."

This conversation took place in the dining-room gallery on the ground floor. The bishop fell silent for a moment, then suddenly turned to the hospital director.

"Monsieur," he said, "how many beds do you think you could get in this room alone?"

"Monseigneur's dining room?" cried the astonished director.

The bishop sized up the room, giving the impression he was taking measurements and making calculations by eye alone.

"It could easily hold twenty beds!" he mumbled, as though talking to himself. Then he spoke more loudly. "Look, my dear director, I'll tell you what. There has obviously been a mistake. There are twenty-six of you in five or six small rooms. There are three of us here and we've got enough room for sixty. There's been a mistake, I'm telling you. You've got my place and I've got yours. Give me back my house. This is your rightful home, here."

The next day, the twenty-six poor were moved into the bishop's palace and the bishop was at the hospital.

Monsieur Myriel had no property, his family having lost everything in the Revolution. His sister got an annuity of five hundred francs, which was enough for her personal expenses, living at the presbytery. Monsieur Myriel received a salary of fifteen thousand francs from the government as bishop. The very day he moved into the hospital, Monsieur Myriel decided once and for all to put this sum to use as follows. We transcribe here the note written in his hand.

HOUSEHOLD EXPENDITURE

| | |
|---|---:|
| For the small seminary | 1500 livres |
| Mission congregation | 100 livres |
| For the Lazarists of Montdidier | 100 livres |
| Seminary of foreign missions in Paris | 200 livres |
| Congregation of the Saint-Esprit | 150 livres |
| Religious institutions in the Holy Land | 100 livres |
| Societies of maternal charity | 300 livres |
| For the one at Arles | 50 livres |
| For the betterment of prisons | 400 livres |
| For the relief and release of prisoners | 500 livres |
| For the release of fathers of families imprisoned for debt | 1000 livres |
| Salary supplement for poor schoolteachers in the diocese | 2000 livres |
| Upper Alps public granary | 100 livres |
| Ladies' Association of Digne, Manosque, and Sisteron,[3] for the free education of poor girls | 1500 livres |
| For the poor | 6000 livres |
| My personal expenses | 1000 livres |
| TOTAL | 15000 livres |

The whole time Monsieur Myriel held the see of Digne, he made almost no change in this arrangement—what he called, as we shall see, "taking care of his household expenses."

Mademoiselle Baptistine accepted the arrangement with absolute submission. For this devout spinster, Myriel was both her brother and her bishop, the friend she grew up with and her superior according to ecclesiastical authority. Quite simply, she loved him and revered him. When he spoke, she listened, and when he took action, she was right behind him. Only the servant, Madame Magloire, grumbled a bit. As you will have noticed, the bishop kept only a thousand livres for himself which, added to Mademoiselle Baptistine's pension, meant fifteen hundred francs a year. The two old women and the old man all lived on those fifteen hundred francs.

And when some village curé came to Digne, the bishop still managed to find a way of entertaining him, thanks to the assiduous scrimping and saving of Madame Magloire and Mademoiselle Baptistine's clever management.

One day, when the bishop had been in Digne for about three months, he said, "With all that, things are pretty tight!"

"They certainly are!" cried Madame Magloire. "Monseigneur hasn't even claimed the money the *département* owes him for the upkeep of his carriage in town and his rounds in the diocese. In the old days, that was standard for bishops."

"You're right, Madame Magloire!" the bishop agreed. And he put in his claim.

A short while later, after considering this application, the department council voted him an annual stipend of three thousand francs, under the heading, *Bishop's Allowance for Carriage Upkeep, Postal Costs, and Travel Expenses Incurred in Pastoral Rounds.*

The local bourgeoisie was up in arms over this and an imperial senator,[4] who had been a member of the Council of Five Hundred[5] promoting the Eighteenth Brumaire and was now provided with a magnificent senatorial seat near Digne township, wrote a cranky little private letter to the minister of public worship, Monsieur Bigot de Préameneu.[6] We produce here a genuine extract of a few lines:

"Carriage upkeep? Whatever for, in a town with less than four thousand people? Travel expenses incurred in pastoral rounds? To start with, what's the good of them anyway? And then, how the hell does he do the rounds by post chaise in such mountainous terrain? There are no roads. One has to proceed on horseback. Even the bridge over the Durance at Château-Arnoux[7] can barely take a bullock-drawn cart. All these priests are the same. Greedy and tight. This one played the good apostle when he first turned up. Now he acts like all the rest. He must have a carriage and a post chaise. He must have luxury, the same as the old bishops. Oh, these bloody clergy! Monsieur le comte, things will only come good when the emperor has delivered us from these pious swine. Down with the pope! [Things were not good with Rome at that point.][8] As for me, I'm for Caesar alone." And so on and so forth.

Madame Magloire, on the other hand, was delighted.

"Hooray!" she said to Mademoiselle Baptistine. "Monseigneur put the others first but he's wound up having to think of himself, finally. He's fixed up all his charities. Here's three thousand livres for us. At last!"

The same night, the bishop wrote a note, which he handed to his sister. It went like this:

### CARRIAGE UPKEEP AND TRAVEL EXPENSES

| | |
|---|---|
| Beef broth for the sick in the hospital | 1500 livres |
| For the society of maternal charity of Aix | 250 livres |
| For the society of maternal charity of Draguignan | 250 livres |
| For abandoned children | 500 livres |
| For orphans | 500 livres |
| TOTAL | 3000 livres |

And that was Monsieur Myriel's budget.

As for the cost of episcopal services, redemptions, dispensations, baptisms, sermons, consecrations of churches and chapels, marriages and so on, the bishop took from the rich all the more greedily for giving it all to the poor.

It wasn't long before offerings of money poured in. The haves and the have-nots all knocked on Monsieur Myriel's door, some coming in search of the alms that the others had just left. In less than a year, the bishop became treasurer of all works of charity and cashier to all those in distress. Large sums passed through his hands, but nothing could make him change his style of life in the slightest or get him to embellish his spartan existence by the faintest touch of the superfluous.

Far from it. As there is always more misery at the bottom of the ladder than there is fraternity at the top, everything was given away, so to speak, before it was received, like water on thirsty soil. A lot of good it did him to be given money, he never had any. And so, he robbed himself.

The custom being for bishops to put their full baptismal names at the head of their mandates and pastoral letters, the poor people of the area had chosen, out of a sort of affectionate instinct, the one among all the bishop's various names that made the most sense to them, and so they called him Monseigneur Bienvenu—Welcome. We'll do likewise whenever the occasion arises. Besides, the nickname tickled him.

"I like that name," he said. "Bienvenu pulls Monseigneur into line."

We are not saying that the portrait of the man we offer here is accurate; we will restrict ourselves to the claim that it is a passing likeness.

## III. A Good Bishop for a Hard Bishopric

Though he may have converted his carriage into alms, that didn't stop the bishop from doing his rounds. Digne was a particularly exhausting diocese to tour. There was precious little flat land and a great deal of mountain. And there were almost no roads, as we said earlier. Thirty-two parishes, forty-one vicarages, and two hundred and eighty branch parishes. To visit all of that is no mean feat. But the bishop somehow managed. He did it on foot locally, in a cart on the plains, and in a chair on a pack mule in the mountains. The two old women went with him. When the going was too tough for them, he went on his own.

One day he rode into Senez, a town that was once an episcopal city, mounted on a donkey. He had been bled dry at the time and couldn't afford any other mode of transport. The mayor of Senez, who had come to greet him at the gate of the bishop's palace, watched him get down from his donkey, completely scandalized. A few good burghers stood around snickering.

"Monsieur le maire," said the bishop, "and you dear gentlemen, I see I've shocked you. You think it's terribly arrogant of a poor priest to ride the same beast that Jesus Christ rode. I only did so out of necessity, let me assure you, and not out of vanity."

On his rounds, he was giving and gentle and he didn't preach so much as chat. He never represented a virtue as though it were beyond an ordinary person's reach. He never drummed up far-fetched arguments or examples. To the inhabitants of one area, he cited the example of the inhabitants of a neighboring area. In cantons where those in need were dealt with harshly, he would say, "Look at the good folk of Briançon. They have given their poor and widows and orphans the right to mow their meadows three days before everyone else.[2] When their houses are tumbling down, they rebuild them for free. And so it is a place blessed by God. For a whole hundred years, they have not had a single murderer."

At harvest time in villages where people were greedy for gain he would say, "Look at the good folk of Embrun. If a man with a family finds himself at harvest time with his sons in the army and his daughters working as domestics in town, and he's sick and can't work, the curé offers up prayers for him and on Sunday, after mass, all the people in the village, men, women, and children, go into the poor man's field and harvest his crop for him and they take the straw and grain and put it in his granary." To families torn by money worries and inheritance wrangles he would say, "Look at the Devolny mountains, a place so wild you'll only hear the nightingale there once every fifty years. Well, when the father in a family dies, the boys go off to seek their fortunes and leave the girls the property, so they have a better chance of finding a husband." In cantons where people had a taste for litigation and where farmers went broke over engraved stationery,[3] he would say, "Look at the fine peasants of the valley of Queyras. There are three thousand souls there. Lord! It's like a small republic. Judges and bailiffs are unheard-of. The mayor does everything. He divvies up taxes, assessing each person fairly, mediates quarrels for free, distributes personal assets without charging any fees, hands down sentences without cost. And he is obeyed because he is a just man among simple men." In villages that he found to be without a schoolteacher, he also cited the case of Queyras. "Do you know what they do?" he would ask. "Since a tiny place of some twelve to fifteen households can't always feed a teacher, they've got teachers who are paid by the whole valley, who whip around the villages, spending a week here, ten days there, teaching. These teachers do the fairs—I've seen them. You can recognize them by the quills they wear in their hatband. The ones who only teach how to read wear one feather, those who teach reading and sums have two feathers, and those who teach reading, sums, and Latin have three feathers. Those last I mentioned are real scholars. What a shameful thing it is to be ignorant! You should do what the folk of Queyras do."

That's how he talked, in a fatherly fashion, gravely. If he lacked examples, he made up parables that went straight to the point, with few pretty phrases and lots of images—and with the same eloquence as Jesus Christ himself, sincere and persuasive.

### IV. He Puts His Money Where His Mouth Is

In conversation, he was affable and cheery. He spoke at the same level as the two old ladies that spent their lives by his side; when he laughed, it was the laugh of a schoolboy.

Madame Magloire liked to call him *Your Highness.* One day, he got up out of his armchair and went to find a book. The book happened to be on one of the top shelves and, as the bishop was fairly short, he couldn't reach it. "Madame Magloire," he said, "bring me a chair, will you. My Highness doesn't extend to this shelf."

One of his distant relatives, Madame la comtesse de Lô, rarely let an opportunity slip to enumerate in his presence what she called "the hopes" of her three sons. She had several very elderly relatives at death's door of whom her sons were the natural heirs. The youngest of the three was to collect from a great-aunt a tidy sum of a hundred thousand livres in bonds; the middle son was to step into his uncle's title as duc; and the eldest was to succeed to a peerage held by his grandfather.[1] The bishop would listen in silence to this innocent and forgivable maternal showing off. Once, though, he seemed more dreamy than usual as Madame de Lô was going over all these successions and "hopes" in lavish detail. She stopped midsentence somewhat impatiently.

"Heavens, cousin! A penny for your thoughts!"

"I was thinking," said the bishop, "about something strange that is, I think, in Saint Augustine.[2] 'Put your hope in Him who has no successor.'"

Another time he received the death notice of a gentleman of the district, which laid out, in one long page, not only the honors of the deceased but all the feudal ranks and titles of nobility of every one of his relations.

"What a broad back has Death!" he cried. "You can cheerily pile up any number of titles on it. And how cunningly people manage to feed their vanity via the tomb!"

He occasionally went in for gentle raillery but there was almost always a serious message involved. One year, during Lent, a young vicar came to Digne and preached eloquently enough in the cathedral. The subject of his sermon was charity. He called upon the rich to give to the poor and thereby avoid hell, which he painted in the most alarming colors imaginable, and to get to heaven, which he made out to be desirable and extremely pleasant. In the audience there was a well-heeled retired merchant, a bit of a cheapskate, named Monsieur Géborand, who had made half a million manufacturing serge and other kinds of coarse woolen cloth, known as *cadis* and *gasquets*. Monsieur Géborand had never in his life given alms to those less fortunate than himself. But from the date of this sermon, everyone noticed that he gave a sou every Sunday to the old beggar women who hung around the door of the cathedral. There were six of them who had to share that sou. One day, the bishop saw him performing his act of charity and said to his sister with a smile, "I see Monsieur Géborand's busy buying a sou's worth of paradise."

When it came to charity, he did not allow himself to be put off, even by a knock-back; in such a case, he would find words that gave pause for thought. Once he was collecting money for the poor in a salon in town. The marquis de Champtercier happened to be there—a rich old tightwad who had found a way to be an ultra-royalist and an ultra-Voltairean at once,[3] though at the time he was not alone in such a feat. The bishop came to him and put a hand on his arm. "Monsieur le marquis, you must give me something." The marquis turned to him and said sharply, "Monseigneur, I have my own poor." "Give them to me," came the bishop's reply.

One day he gave the following sermon in the cathedral:

"Dearly beloved brethren, my good friends, there are in France thirteen hundred and twenty thousand peasant's homes that have only three openings; eighteen hundred and seventeen homes that have only two openings, the door and one window; and, lastly, three hundred and forty-six thousand cabins that have only one opening, the door. This, thanks to something called the tax on doors and windows.[4] You put poor families, old women, young children, in such abodes, and just watch the fevers and diseases! Alas! God gives men air, the law sells it to them. I do not blame the law, I praise God. In the Isère, in the Var, in the two alpine regions, the Upper Alps and the Lower Alps, the peasants don't even have wheelbarrows; the men carry cow dung on their backs. They don't have candles; they burn twigs and rope soaked in pine resin. It's the same throughout the highlands of the Dauphiné. They make bread to last six months, they bake it with dried cow dung. In winter they break the bread with the aid of an ax and soak it in water for twenty-four hours before they are able to eat it. My brothers, have pity! Look at all the suffering around you."

A native of Provence, he had easily picked up all the different dialects of the south. He could say, *"Eh bé! moussou, sès sage?"* (Hey there! Mister, you behavin'?), as they said in the Lower Languedoc, and *"Onté, anaris passa?"* ('Morning, what gives?), as they said in the Lower Alps, and *"Puerte un bouen moutou embe un bouen froumage grase"* (A good sheep gives a good fat cheese), as they said in the Upper Dauphiné. People appreciated this and it was no small factor in giving him access to everyone's innermost thoughts. He made himself at home everywhere, whether in a humble cottage or in the mountains. He had a knack for expressing great things in the most common idioms. Speaking all tongues, he entered all hearts and minds.

Besides, he was the same to everybody, the high and mighty and the humble alike.

He was never quick to condemn and he always took into account the surrounding circumstances. He would say, "Let's see how this sin came to pass."

Being, as he laughingly described himself, an ex-sinner, he had nothing of the purist about him and boldly professed, without the mad frowning of the ferociously virtuous, a doctrine that may be summed up as follows:

"Man is made of flesh and that flesh is both a burden and a temptation to him. He drags it around with him and he yields to it.

"He should keep a close eye on it, put the lid on it, repress it, and only give in to it at the last extremity. There may still be some sin in giving in to it even then; but such a sin is venial. It is a slip, but a slip onto one's knees, which may well end in prayer.

"To be a saint is the exception; to be a just person is the rule. Err, stumble, commit sin, but be one of the just.

"Sin as little as possible—that is the law of mankind. Not to sin at all is the dream of the angel. All earthly things are subject to sin. Sin is like gravity."

Whenever he saw people indignant over something, rushing to get on their high horse, he would say, with a smile, "Tut! Tut! This would seem to be a serious crime that everyone commits! The hypocrites are so shocked they can't point their fingers and duck for cover fast enough."

He went easy on women and the poor, feeling that the weight of human society fell on them. He would say, "The sins of women and children, domestic servants and the weak, the poor and the ignorant, are the sins of the husbands and fathers, the masters, the strong and the rich and the educated."

He would also say, "Those who are ignorant should be taught all you can teach them; society is to blame for not providing free public education; and society will answer for the obscurity it produces. If the soul is left in darkness, sin will be committed. The guilty party is not he who has sinned but he who created the darkness in the first place."

As you can see, he had a strange, idiosyncratic way of looking at things. I suspect he got it from the Gospel.

In someone's drawing room one day he heard a tale about a criminal case that was about to go to court. Some miserable wretch, for love of a woman and the child he'd had with her, found himself at the end of his rope and had gone in for a bit of counterfeiting. Counterfeiting was still punishable by death in those days. The woman had been arrested trying to pass the first false coin the man had made. She was held in custody, but they had no proof against the man. She was the only one who could point the finger at her lover and sink him by telling all. She denied his guilt. They put the pressure on, but still she denied his guilt. At that point the public prosecutor[5] had a bright idea. He told her that her lover had been unfaithful and he managed to cobble together fragments of letters and so persuade the poor woman that she had a rival and that the man was betraying her behind her back. She was immediately overcome by a fit of jealousy and swiftly denounced her lover, admitted everything, offered proof. The man was lost. He was shortly to be tried in Aix along with his accomplice. When the tale was told, everyone there was in raptures over the cunning of the prosecuting magistrate. By bringing jealousy into play, he had provoked the woman's rage and the truth had shot out of her; he had brought about justice by sparking revenge. The bishop listened to all this in silence. When they were finished marveling, he had a question.

"Where are the man and woman to be tried?"

"In the circuit court."

"And where is the public prosecutor to be tried?"

A tragic event occurred in Digne. A man had been condemned to death for murder. It was some poor unfortunate who was not quite literate, but not completely illiterate; he had been a tumbler working the fairs as well as a public letter-writer. The trial was the talk of the town. The day before the date set for the condemned man's execution, the prison chaplain got sick. A priest was needed to attend the prisoner in his last moments, so they went for the local curé. Apparently this curé refused, saying, "That's not my problem. Not my job. Besides, I don't want anything to do with that circus monkey. I'm sick, too. And anyway, it's not my place."

When the bishop was told of this response he said, "The reverend father is right. It's not his place, it's mine."

And with that, he sped off to the jail, rushed to the cell of the "circus monkey," called him by his name, took his hand and talked to him. He spent all day and all night with him, forgetting about food and sleep and praying to God for the soul of the condemned man, as well as praying to the condemned man for his own soul. He spoke to him of the highest truths, which are the simplest ones. He was a father, brother, friend; and only acted as a bishop to bless him. He taught him everything he could, reassuring him and consoling him as he did so. This man had been about to die in despair. Death for him had been an abyss. Standing, trembling, on the ghastly brink, he had shrunk back in horror. He was not ignorant enough to be completely unmoved. His sentence had come as a terrible shock and had somehow, here and there, broken through the wall that inures us to the mystery of things and that we call life. He couldn't take his eyes off the fatal chinks in the wall and what lay on the other side and he could see only darkness. The bishop made him see a light.

The next day, when they went to get the poor man, the bishop was there. He went with him and showed himself to the crowd decked out in his purple cape and with his episcopal cross around his neck, at the side of this poor wretch whose hands were tied with rope.

He climbed into the cart with him, he mounted the scaffold with him. The doomed man, so gloomy and horror-stricken the day before, was radiant. He felt his soul reconciled and he trusted himself to God. The bishop embraced him and, just as the blade was about to fall, he said to him, "Whomsoever man puts to death, God restores to life; whomsoever his brothers chase away, finds the Father. Pray, believe, enter into life! God the Father is there!" When he got down again from the scaffold, there was a look in his eye that made the crowd stand back. They would have been hard-pressed to say which was the most impressive, his pallor or his serenity. When he got back to his humble abode, which he fondly called his palace, he said to his sister, "I've just been officiating pontifically."

As the most sublime things are often also the most misunderstood, there were those in town who said, commenting on the bishop's conduct, "Talk about laying it on thick!" But that was parlor talk. Ordinary people do not view saintly acts with malice and they melted with admiration.

As for the bishop, seeing the guillotine up close had been a shock, one from which he was a long time recovering.

The scaffold, when it is standing there, tall and straight, can, indeed, make you think you're seeing things. You may think you are indifferent to the death penalty,[6] can't say whether you are in favor of it or not—as long as you haven't clapped eyes on a guillotine. When you come across one, the shock is brutal and forces you to take a stand, for or against. Some, like Maistre, admire it; others, like Beccaria,[7] abhor it. The guillotine is the ultimate embodiment of the Law; its name is Retribution. It is not neutral and doesn't allow you to remain neutral, either. Whoever sees it quakes in their boots with the most mysterious of terrors. Every social issue hooks its question mark around this chopper. The scaffold is not a framework, the scaffold is not a machine, the scaffold is not some inert mechanism made of wood, iron, and rope. It is more like some sort of living being that has taken who knows what somber initiative of its own. You'd think that the framework could see, that the machine could hear, that the mechanism could understand, that this wood, this iron, this rope, had a will of its own. In the frightened reverie into which your soul is thrown by its presence, the scaffold appears terrifying and somehow actively involved in what it does. The scaffold is the executioner's accomplice. It devours, it eats flesh, it drinks blood. The scaffold is a kind of monster manufactured by judge and carpenter together, a specter that seems to have a kind of ghastly life of its own arising out of all the death it has dealt.

And so the impression was horrible and cut deep. The day after the execution and for many days following, the bishop seemed devastated. The almost brutal serenity of the fatal moment had vanished; but the phantom of social justice haunted him and would not leave him alone. He, who usually came home beaming with satisfaction after performing his duties, now seemed to blame himself. At times, he talked to himself, muttering gloomy monologues under his breath. This is one that his sister overheard one night and wrote down: "I had no idea it was so monstrous. It is wrong to be so absorbed in divine law that you take no notice of human law. Death belongs only to God. By what right do men tamper with a thing so unknowable?"

With time, his impressions faded and probably were erased altogether. But it was remarked how the bishop from that point on avoided going near the square where executions took place.

Monsieur Myriel could be called to the bedside of the sick and dying at any time of the day or night. He was well aware that this was his greatest duty and his greatest work. Widowed or orphaned families didn't have to ask, he came of his own accord. He knew exactly how to sit and keep quiet for hours at a stretch by the side of a man who had lost the woman he loved, the mother who had lost her child. Just as he knew when to keep quiet, he also knew when to say something. Such a wonderful comforter! He did not seek to efface pain in forgetfulness, he sought to elevate it and to dignify it with hope. He would say, "Be careful how you turn to the dead. Don't think of the rotting. Hold your gaze and you will see the living light of your dearly loved departed up above in heaven." He knew how healthy believing is. He sought to counsel and to calm the desperate by pointing to those who were resigned, and to transform the grief that gazes on the freshly dug grave by showing it the grief that gazes up at a star.

## V. HOW MONSEIGNEUR BIENVENU MADE HIS CASSOCKS LAST TOO LONG

Monsieur Myriel's inner life was brimming with the same thoughts as his public life. If you could have seen it close up, the self-imposed poverty in which the bishop of Digne lived would have been a grave and moving spectacle.

Like all old men and like most thinkers, he slept little. But his short sleep was deep. In the morning, he reflected for an hour, then said mass, either in the cathedral or in his oratory. Once he'd said mass, he breakfasted on a bit of rye bread dunked in milk from his cows. Then he got down to work.

A bishop has a lot on his plate. Every day he must receive the secretary of the diocese, who is usually a canon, and almost every day his grand-vicars.[1] He has congregations to oversee, privileges to bestow, a whole ecclesiastical book trade to look into, with the publication of missals and diocesan catechisms, books of hours and so on, pastoral letters to write, sermons to endorse, priests and mayors to make peace between, stacks of clerical and administrative correspondence, with the government on the one hand and with the Holy See on the other. In short, a thousand matters to tackle.

The free time left to him by these thousand matters and by his church services and his breviary was given first to the needy, the sick, and the downtrodden; the time left to him by the downtrodden, the sick, and the needy was given to toil. Sometimes he took a shovel to the garden, sometimes he did a bit of reading and writing. He had one word only for these two different kinds of work: he called both gardening. "The mind is a garden," he would say.

At midday, he would stop to eat and the midday meal was virtually the same as his breakfast.

At around two in the afternoon, when the weather was fine, he would go for a walk in the countryside or around town, often poking into the poorest hovels. He could be seen ambling about, alone, his head in the clouds, his eye to the ground, leaning on his long cane, snug as a bug in his warm quilted purple overcoat, purple stockings,[2] and great clodhopper shoes, his head capped by his flat tricorn hat with three golden "spinach-seed" tassels dangling off the corners.

Wherever he appeared, there was a party. You would have said that he brought warmth and light wherever he went. Children and old folk rushed to their front doors to see the bishop as they would run to look at the sun. He blessed and was blessed in return. Anyone who needed anything was shown to his door.

Here and there, he would stop and talk to the boys and girls and have a laugh with their mothers. He visited the poor whenever he had money, and when he had none, he visited the rich.

As he made his cassocks last a very long time,[3] but didn't want anyone to know this, he never went to town without his padded purple overcoat. This was a bit uncomfortable for him in summertime.

At eight-thirty at night, he dined with his sister, Madame Magloire in position behind them waiting on the table. Nothing could be more frugal than their evening meal. Though, if the bishop had one of his priests to dinner, Madame Magloire took advantage of the occasion to serve Monseigneur some wonderful fish from the lake or some fine game from the mountains. Any curé was a good excuse for a good meal. The bishop went along with it. But apart from this, his usual diet consisted of little more than boiled vegetables and soup made with olive oil. And so, the saying went in town, "When the bishop isn't feeding a priest, he's feeding a Trappist."[4]

After dinner, he would chat for half an hour with Mademoiselle Baptistine and Madame Magloire before returning to his room and writing a bit more, sometimes on loose sheets of paper, sometimes in the margins of one of his folios. He was well read and rather erudite. He has left us five or six somewhat curious manuscripts, among others a dissertation on this passage in Genesis:[5] "And the spirit of God moved upon the face of the waters." He contrasts this with three other texts: the Arabic version, which goes, "the winds of God blew"; Flavius Josephus,[6] who says, "a wind from on high descended upon the earth"; and finally the Chaldean paraphrase of Rabbi Onkelos, which goes, "a wind from God blew upon the face of the waters." In another dissertation, he examines the theological works of Hugo, bishop of Ptolemaïs[7] and great-great-uncle of the Hugo writing this book, and he demonstrates that sundry little tracts published in the last century under the pseudonym of Barleycourt should be attributed to this bishop.

Sometimes, while he was in the middle of reading, and no matter what book he happened to have in his hands, he would fall into the most profound meditation and emerge only to scribble a few lines over the pages of this same volume. These lines often had no bearing on the book containing them. We have before us a note written by him in the margin of a quarto volume entitled, *Correspondance du lord Germain avec les généraux Clinton, Cornwallis et les amiraux de la station de l'Amérique. À Versailles, chez Poinçot, libraire, et à Paris, chez Pissot, libraire, quai des Augustins.*

Here is the note:

Oh, Thou who art!
Ecclesiastes names you the Almighty; the Maccabees name you the Creator; the Epistle to the Ephesians names you Liberty; Baruch names you Immensity; the Psalms name you Wisdom and Truth; John names you Light; the Book of Kings names you Lord; Exodus calls you Providence; Leviticus, Holiness; Esdras, Justice; Creation names you God, mankind names you Father; but Solomon names you Mercy and of all your names, that is the most beautiful.[8]

At around nine o'clock at night, the two women retired and went upstairs to their rooms on the first floor, leaving him on his own on the ground floor until morning.

Here we really need to give you a more precise idea of the bishop of Digne's abode.

## VI. HOW HE PROTECTED HIS HOUSE

The house he lived in, as we've said, consisted of a downstairs and an upstairs: three rooms at street level, three bedrooms on the upper floor, and an attic above. At the back of the house, a quarter-acre garden. The two women occupied the upper story. The bishop lived below. The first room, which opened onto the street, served him as a dining room, the second, as a bedroom, and the third as an oratory. There was no way out of this oratory except through the bedroom, and no way out of the bedroom except through the dining room. In the oratory, at the back, there was an alcove, closed off by a screen, with a bed for the odd guest. The bishop offered this bed to country curés brought to Digne on business or to attend to the needs of their parish.

The hospital pharmacy, a small building tacked onto the house and extending into the garden, had been turned into a kitchen and cellar.

There was also a stable in the garden, which had once been the hospital kitchen and where the bishop now kept a couple of cows. Whatever the quantity of milk they produced, he invariably sent half of it every morning to the sick in the hospital. "I'm just paying my dues," he would say.

His bedroom was fairly big and fairly hard to heat up in winter. As wood is very dear in Digne, he'd had the bright idea of dividing the cow stable with a partition made of wooden boards and that way creating a sealed compartment for himself. And that was where he spent his evenings when it got really cold. He called it his winter salon.

Like the dining room, the winter salon was very nearly bare, the only furniture being a square pine table and four straw-seated chairs. The dining room had the additional enhancement of an old sideboard mottled pink with distemper. The bishop had made the altar that decorated his oratory out of a similar sideboard, and suitably decked it out with white doilies and imitation lace.

His wealthy female penitents and the devout women of Digne had chipped in to provide a fine new altar for the monseigneur's oratory; he had taken the money every time and given it to the poor. "The finest altar," he said, "is the soul of some poor wretch who finds comfort and gives thanks to God."

There were two wicker prie-dieu chairs in the oratory, and an armchair also made of wicker in the bedroom. When he happened to have seven or eight visitors at the same time, the prefect of police, or the general, or officers of the regiment stationed in the garrison, or some students from the little seminary, someone had to go and get the chairs from the winter salon in the stables, the prie-dieux in the oratory, and the armchair in the bedroom; that way, he managed to collect up to eleven seats for his visitors. At each new visit, a room was laid bare.

Sometimes there were twelve, and the bishop would cover up the embarrassment of the situation by remaining standing in front of the fireplace if it was winter, or proposing a turn in the garden if it was summer.

There was an extra chair in the enclosed alcove, but half the straw seating was missing and it only had three legs to stand on, so that it could only be used propped up against a wall. Mademoiselle Baptistine also had a huge bergère[1] in her room made of wood that had once been gilt and covered in a soft floral

Pekin silk, but this bergère had had to be winched up to her room upstairs through the window, as the stairway was too narrow, and so it could not be counted among the movable furniture.

Mademoiselle Baptistine's ambition was to be able to buy a lounge made of carved mahogany in a swan's-neck design and with cushions covered in yellow rose-print Utrecht velvet. But this would have set her back at least five hundred francs and since she'd only managed to save forty-two francs and ten sous[2] for this object in five years, she'd finally given up the idea. Well, anyway, who ever manages to attain their ideal?

You couldn't imagine anything simpler than the bishop's bedroom. French doors opening onto the garden and facing them, an iron hospital bed with a green serge canopy; on the other side of the bed, behind a curtain, toiletries that still betrayed the old habits of an elegant man of the world; two doors, one close to the fireplace, opening into the oratory, the other, close to the bookcase, opening into the dining room; the bookcase, a big cabinet with glass doors full of books; the fireplace, its wooden surround painted to look like marble, usually without a fire; in the fireplace, a pair of wrought-iron firedogs decorated with two vases garlanded with flowers, the fluting once plated in silver, which was something of an episcopal luxury; above, where the mirror would normally go, a copper crucifix that had lost its silver paint was attached to a threadbare piece of black velvet in a wooden frame that had lost its gilt. Next to the French doors, a great big table with an inkstand, piled high with papers all in a heap and enormous tomes. In front of the table, the wicker armchair; in front of the bed, a prie-dieu borrowed from the oratory.

Two portraits in oval frames hung on the wall on either side of the bed. Small gilt inscriptions on the plain canvas mount around the faces indicated that the portraits represented the abbé of Chaliot, bishop of Saint-Claude, and the abbé de Tourteau, vicar-general of Agde, abbé of Grand-Champ, Order of Cîteaux,[3] diocese of Chartres. When he took the room over from the hospital patients, the bishop had found these portraits and he had left them where they were. They were priests, probably donors—two good reasons to respect them. All he knew about these two characters was that they had been appointed by the king,[4] one to his bishopric, the other to his living, on the same day, which happened to be April 27, 1785. When Madame Magloire took down the paintings to shake the dust off, the bishop had found this detail written in faded ink on a little square of paper yellow with age, stuck behind the portrait of the abbé of Grand-Champ with four sealing wafers.

At his window hung an ancient curtain made of coarse woolen material that got so old in the end that, to save buying a new one, Madame Magloire was forced to sew a great big patch smack in the middle. This patch was in the shape of a cross. The bishop often called attention to it. "Doesn't that do you the world of good!"

Every room in the house, upstairs and down, without exception, was white-washed with slaked lime, just like army barracks or hospitals.

And yet, in later years, as we shall see further on, Madame Magloire found decorative paintings on the walls of Mademoiselle Baptistine's chamber under-neath the distempered wallpaper. Before becoming a hospital, the house had been an assembly hall where well-heeled burghers gathered together, and it had been decorated accordingly. The bedrooms were tiled in red bricks, which were washed once a week, with woven straw mats at the foot of the beds. For the rest, the place, being kept by two women, was always in a state of exquisite cleanliness from top to bottom. This was the sole luxury the bishop allowed. He used to say, "The poor don't lose anything by it."

But we must confess that he still hung on to a few things left over from all he once possessed; these were a set of six silver knives and forks and a big soup ladle that Madame Magloire loved to see sparkling gorgeously every day against the coarse white linen tablecloth. And since we're painting the bishop of Digne here in his true colors, warts and all, we must add that he was heard to say more than once, "It would be very hard for me to give up eating with silver."

We should add to the list of silverware, two big solid silver candlesticks that had come down to him as part of his inheritance from a great-aunt. These two candlesticks held two wax candles[5] and they sat as a rule on the bishop's man-telpiece. Whenever he had anyone to dinner, Madame Magloire would light the two candles and put the two candlesticks on the table.

In the bishop's bedroom, of all places, at the head of his bed, there was a small cupboard in which Madame Magloire would lock up the silver cutlery and the soup ladle every night. Though we have to say that no one ever took the key out of the door.

The garden, which was somewhat spoiled by the rather ugly buildings we mentioned earlier, was laid out with four paths forming a cross centered around a drainage well. A separate path ran around the outer edge of the garden and along the white wall that enclosed it. Within the paths were four squares bor-dered with shrubs. In three of them, Madame Magloire grew vegetables; in the fourth, the bishop had planted flowers. There were a few fruit trees dotted around to boot.

Once Madame Magloire had said to him with a kind of gentle malice, "Monseigneur, you are always so keen to put everything to good use, yet there's a useless garden bed for you!" "Madame Magloire," the bishop replied, "you are mistaken. The beautiful is just as useful as the useful." After a pause, he added, "Perhaps more so."

This square with its three or four beds kept the bishop nearly as busy as his books did. He would happily while away an hour or two pottering around prun-ing, weeding, and digging holes here and there to sow seeds. He was not as hos-tile to insects as a regular gardener would have liked. Besides, he had no pretentions to botany; he knew nothing at all about genera or other theories of classification such as "solidism"; he didn't give the difference between Tournefort and the natural method a moment's thought; he didn't take sides either way in contests involving the utricles versus the cotyledons or Jussieu versus Linnaeus.[6] He did not study plants, he loved flowers. He had a lot of respect for the learned, but even more respect for the ignorant, and, without ever falling short in either respect, he watered his beds every evening in summer with a tin watering can painted green.

The house did not have one single door that locked. The door of the dining room, which, as we have seen, opened straight onto the square in front of the cathedral, was once as loaded with locks and bolts as the door of a prison. The bishop had had all the locks and bolts removed and now, night and day, this door was closed only by a latch. Anyone passing by, whatever the hour, had merely to push it open. In the early days, the two women had been particularly tormented by this door that was never really shut, but the monseigneur of Digne had said to them, "Get locks put on your bedroom doors if you like." They had wound up sharing his confidence or, at least, acting as though they did. Madame Magloire alone had the odd fright. But as far as the bishop himself went, you can find his thoughts explained, or at least noted, in these three lines written by him in the margin of a copy of the Bible: "Here's the difference: a doctor's door should never be closed, a priest's door should always be open."

In another book, entitled *Philosophie de la science médicale,* he'd written this other note: "Am I not a doctor just as they are? I, too, have my patients; to start with, I have theirs, whom they call the unwell; and then, I have my own, whom I call the unfortunate."

Elsewhere he had written: "Do not ask the name of the person who asks you for a bed for the night. He whose name is a burden to him needs shelter more than anyone."

It happened that a worthy curé, I don't remember if it was the curé from Couloubroux or the one from Pompierry, took it upon himself one day to ask him, probably at Madame Magloire's instigation, if Monseigneur was quite sure he wasn't being a little foolhardy in leaving his door open, day and night, at the disposal of whoever felt like coming in, and if he didn't, at the end of the day, worry that something bad would finally occur in a house so unguarded. The bishop put his hand on the man's shoulder with gentle gravity and said to him, "*Nisi Dominus custodierit domum, in vanum vigilant qui custodiunt eam,*"[7] from the Psalms: Except the Lord keep the house, the watchman waketh but in vain. Then he changed the subject.

He liked to say, "There is such a thing as priestly courage just as there is the courage of the colonel of the dragoons. Only," he would add, "ours should be quiet."

## VII. Cravatte

This is the place for a fact that we must not leave out, for it is one of those that bring out most clearly what kind of man Monseigneur, the bishop of Digne, really was.

After the disbanding of Gaspard Bès's gang of crooks,[1] which had overrun the gorges of Ollioules, one of its lieutenants, a man named Cravatte, decided to seek refuge in the mountains. He hid for a while with his fellow bandits, the remnants of Gaspard Bès's troop, in the county of Nice before cutting across to Piedmont.[2] Then he suddenly popped up again in France, down Barcelonnette way. He was spotted in Jauziers first, then in Tuiles. He holed up in the caves of Joug-de-l'Aigle[3] and from there he made raids on local hamlets and villages via the ravines of Ubaye and Ubayette. He even pushed as far as Embrun, broke into the cathedral there one night and emptied out the sacristy. His looting devastated the countryside. The police were set on him but in vain. He always got away, sometimes resisting with violence. He was a brazen bastard. The bishop turned up in the middle of this campaign of terror, doing his usual rounds. At Chastelar, the mayor came to fetch him and urged him to turn back. Cravatte held the mountains as far as Arche and beyond. It would be dangerous to venture farther even with an escort. It would mean risking the lives of three or four poor gendarmes for no purpose.

"And so," said the bishop, "I intend to proceed without an escort."

"You can't be serious!" cried the mayor.

"I am so serious that I absolutely will not accept your gendarmes and I will be off in an hour."

"Be off?"

"Be off."

"Alone?"

"Alone."

"Monseigneur! You can't do that."

"In the mountains," the bishop resumed, "there is a humble little community, tiny, minuscule, that I haven't seen for three years. They're good friends of mine, gentle, honest mountain people—shepherds. They own only one in thirty of the goats they look after. They make extremely pretty wool yarn in different colors and they play mountain ditties on little six-holed flutes. They need someone to talk to them about the good Lord from time to time. What would they think of a bishop who was frightened off? What would they think if I didn't go there?"

"But, Monseigneur, what about the bandits? What happens if you run into the bandits!"

"Don't worry," said the bishop, "I haven't forgotten about them. You're right. I could run into them. They, too, surely need someone to tell them about the good Lord."

"But, Monseigneur! It's a gang! They're a pack of wolves!"

"My dear mayor, perhaps it's precisely this flock that Jesus has made me pastor of. Who can tell the mysterious ways of Providence?"

"Monseigneur, they will take everything you've got."

"I have nothing."

"They'll kill you."

"A little old priest like me, getting along mumbling poppycock? Go on! Why would they bother?"

"God love us! Just imagine if you run into them!"

"I'll ask them for money for my poor."

"Monseigneur, don't go, for Christ's sake! You're taking your life in your hands."

"My dear mayor," said the bishop, "isn't that just the point? I'm not in this world to take care of my life. I'm here to take care of souls."

There was nothing anyone could do to stop him. He set off, accompanied only by a boy who offered to act as his guide. His pigheadedness created quite a stir throughout the district and terrified the locals.

He did not want to take either his sister or Madame Magloire along and so he left them behind. He crossed the mountains by mule, met no one, arrived safe and sound in the bosom of his "good friends" the shepherds. He stayed there a fortnight, delivering sermons, administering rites, teaching, preaching. When the time drew near for him to leave, he resolved to sing a Te Deum[4] with all the pomp of a pontificate and he spoke to the curé about it. But what were they to do? There were no episcopal props. All that could be placed at his disposal was a paltry village sacristy with a few old chasubles of worn-out damask dolled up with imitation braid.

"Bah!" said the bishop. "My dear father, we'll go ahead and announce our Te Deum during the sermon. Things will work out somehow."

All the neighboring churches were scoured. But the assembled glories of all these humble parishes put together were not enough to suitably deck out a single cathedral chorister.

While they were in this predicament, a great chest was brought in and deposited in the presbytery for Monseigneur the bishop by two unknown horsemen who promptly turned their mounts and charged off. When the chest was opened it was found to contain a cope of gold cloth, a miter studded with diamonds, an archbishop's cross, and a magnificent crosier, all the pontifical raiment stolen the previous month from the treasure of Our Lady of Embrun.[5] In the chest, there was also a scrap of paper on which were written these words: "Cravatte to Monseigneur Bienvenu."

"I told you things would work out!" said the bishop. And he added, with a smile, "To him who contents himself with a priest's surplice, God shall send an archbishop's cope."

"Monseigneur," muttered the curé, shaking his head with a smile, "God—or the devil!"

The bishop looked the curé in the eye and replied with authority, "God!"

When he set out again for Chastelar, the people came out and lined the roadside to gawk at him out of curiosity. At the presbytery in Chastelar, he found Mademoiselle Baptistine and Madame Magloire waiting for him and he said to his sister:

"Well, was I right or wasn't I? The poor priest goes to those poor mountain folk with his hands empty and he comes back with his hands full. I set out with only my trust in God, and I bring back the treasure of a cathedral."

That night, before going to bed, he went on to say, "Never be afraid of thieves and murderers. They represent the dangers without, which are not worth worrying about. Be afraid of ourselves. Prejudices are the real thieves, vices are the murderers. The greatest dangers are within us. Who cares who threatens our heads or our purses! Let's think only of what threatens our souls."

Then he turned to his sister and said, "My dear sister, a priest must never take precautions against his fellow man. What your fellow man does, God permits. Let's confine ourselves to praying to God when we feel danger approaching us. Pray to him, not for ourselves, but so our brother does not fall into sin on our account."

Other than this, nothing much ever happened to him. We can only relate what we've heard, but generally he spent his life doing the same thing at the same time every day. A month of his year was like an hour of his day.

As for what became of the treasure of Embrun Cathedral, it would embarrass us to be questioned on that score. There certainly were some lovely items, most tempting and well worth stealing on behalf of those less fortunate. And anyway, they were already stolen. Half the job had already been done; it only remained to steer the treasures in another direction and help them along their journey into the hands of the poor. We are not saying this is what happened, of course. Only that among the bishop's papers a rather obscure note was found which may have some bearing on this affair and which reads as follows: "The issue is whether it should be returned to the cathedral or go to the hospital."

## VIII. PHILOSOPHY AFTER A DRINK OR TWO

The senator mentioned earlier was a smart man who had made his way in life with a single-mindedness oblivious to any of those stumbling blocks known as conscience, sworn oaths, justice, duty; he had gone straight for his goal without ever deviating from the path of self-interest and his own advancement. He had once been a prosecutor, but had gone soft with success; there was not a nasty bone in his body, and he was happy to do whatever he could for his sons, his sons-in-law, his relatives, even his friends, having sensibly opted for the best that life had to offer, the best opportunities, the best deals.

To do anything else struck him as positively dimwitted. He was witty and just literate enough to consider himself a disciple of Epicurus[1] while being, perhaps, nothing more than a product of Pigault-Lebrun.[2] He laughed easily, and infectiously, at anything to do with infinity and eternal life and "the twaddle of the dear old bishop." He even laughed at times, with an amiable authority, in Monseigneur Myriel's face, though the latter, of course, never seemed to take offense.

At some semi-official ceremony or other—I can't remember what—the comte ―――― (this senator) and Monseigneur Myriel were lined up to dine with the prefect at home. During dessert, the senator, who was a bit tipsy by then, although still dignified, suddenly launched himself.

"I say, dear bishop, why don't we get right down to it. It's hard for a senator and a bishop to look each other in the eye without a wink and a nudge. We are both oracles. I have a confession to make to you. I have my own philosophy."

"And you're right to do so," replied the bishop. "As you make your philosophical bed, so shall you lie in it. You lie on a bed of purple, my dear senator."

The senator, encouraged, took up the challenge: "Come on, let's be good fellows."

"Good devils, if you like," the bishop cut in.

"I tell you," the senator began again, "that the marquis d'Argen, Pyrrhon, Hobbes, and Monsieur Naigeon[3] are no slouches. I have all my philosophers in my book collection—and gilt-edged, to boot."

"Like you yourself, my dear comte," the bishop cut in.

The senator plowed on regardless: "I detest Diderot.[4] He's an ideologue, a raving lunatic, and a revolutionary, and underneath it all he believes in God and is even more of a bigot than Voltaire.[5] Voltaire had the nerve to make fun of Needham,[6] but he was wrong, for Needham's eels prove that God is pointless. A drop of vinegar in a spoonful of dough replaces the *fiat lux*.[7] Suppose the drop is fatter and the spoonful bigger and what have you got? The world! Man is the eel. So what's the point of the Eternal Father? My dear bishop, the Jehovah hypothesis bores me rigid. All it's good for is producing featherbrained weaklings. Down with the great All, who gives me the willies! Long live Zero, which leaves me in peace! Just between you and me, while we're at it, I'll make my confession to my confessor as is only right and admit I have common sense. I'm not mad about your Jesus preaching renunciation and sacrifice at the drop of a hat. Advice of a miser to beggars. Renunciation! What for? Sacrifice! What to? I don't see a wolf setting itself on fire to make some other wolf happy. So let's stick to nature. We are at the pinnacle, so let's have a higher philosophy. What's the good of being on top if you can't see past the next man's nose? Let's live and be merry. Life is all there is. The notion that man has another life, elsewhere, up above, down below, somewhere—I don't believe a single blasted word of it. Ah, they tell me to go in for sacrifice and renunciation, that I should watch my every step carefully; I'm supposed to give myself migraines worrying about good and evil, the just and the unjust, the *fas* and the *nefas*.[8] Why? Because I'll have to account for my actions, apparently. When? When I'm dead. What idle fancy! When I'm dead, it'll take a smart man to collar me. You try and get a ghost's hand to grab a handful of ashes. Let's be honest, we who are in the know, who've looked up Isis's skirt: there is neither good nor evil, there is only growth. Let's go for what is real. Let's dig deep. Let's get to the bottom of things, for God's sake! You need to sniff out the truth, scratch around in the dirt and grab it. When you do, it gives you untold joy. And you become strong and you laugh. Me, I call a spade a spade. My dear bishop, the immortality of man is a fabulous fairy tale. Oh, what an unbeatable promise! You had better believe it! What a winner Adam's on! One is a spirit, one will be an angel, one will sprout blue wings from one's back. Help me out here, is it not Tertullian[9] who says that the blessed will go from star to star? So be it. We'll be grasshoppers to the stars. And we will then see God. Blah blah blah. What utter piffle, all this stuff about paradise! Talk about chasing rainbows. God is a monstrous bit of balderdash. I wouldn't say that in the *Moniteur*[10]—Christ, no! But I can whisper it among friends. *Inter pocula*.[11] To give up the world for heaven means chasing rainbows. Being hoodwinked by infinity! I'm not that big an idiot! I am nothing. I call myself Monsieur le comte Nothing, senator. No, really. What am I? A bit of dust embodied by an organism. What am I supposed to be doing on this earth? I have a choice. To suffer or to enjoy myself. Where will suffering get me? Nowhere. But I will have suffered. Where will enjoying myself get me? Nowhere. But I will have enjoyed myself. I've made my choice. It's eat or be eaten. I eat. Better to be the scythe than the blade of grass. That's my philosophy for you. In the end, come what may, the gravedigger is waiting, the Panthéon[12] for some of us, but we all end up in that big hole in the ground. The end. Finis. Total liquidation. That is the point of no return. Death is dead, believe me. The idea that there is someone there with something to tell me—I laugh just thinking about it. A nursemaid's tall tale. A bogeyman for little kiddies, Jehovah for grown-ups. No, our tomorrow is darkness. Beyond the grave all that's left is equal nothings. Whether you're Sardanapalus or Vincent de Paul,[13] it comes to the same old *niente*.[14] That's the real situation, if you want to know. So live it up. Make use of your self while you've got a self to use. Truly, my dear bishop, I tell you, I have my philosophy and I have my philosophers. I don't let myself be hoodwinked by make-believe. But having said that, it is of course essential that the little people, the barefoot tramps, the small-timers, all those poor bastards, be given a few fables to swallow, chimeras, the soul, immortality, heaven, the stars. They eat that up. They butter their lousy dry bread with it. Even if you have nothing else, you have the good Lord. Better than nothing. I don't have a problem with that but I keep Monsieur Naigeon for myself. The good Lord is good only for the people."

The bishop clapped his hands.

"Great speech!" he cried. "This materialism of yours is a splendid thing, really, marvelous! Pity those who can't bring it off. Ah, because when you can, you're nobody's fool anymore. You're not about to let yourself be stupidly exiled, like Cato, or stoned to death like Stephen, or burned alive like Joan of Arc.[15] Those who have managed to avail themselves of this admirable materialism have the joy of feeling totally irresponsible and of imagining they can devour everything without a worry—positions, sinecures, honors, power rightly or wrongly come by, lucrative recantations, handy betrayals, juicy little capitulations of conscience—and they'll go to their grave, having digested the lot. How sweet it is! I'm not attacking you, of course, my dear senator. But I just can't stop myself from congratulating you. You great lords have, as you say, a philosophy that is all your own and that is as exquisite and refined as you like, accessible only to the rich, fit for every occasion, wonderfully adding spice to the sensual pleasures of life. This philosophy has been dragged from the depths and unearthed by specialists in the field. But you are good princes and you don't mind if the masses have their belief in God as a philosophy—a bit the way you don't mind them eating goose with chestnuts: the poor man's turkey with truffles."

## IX. The Brother as the Sister Tells It

To give you an idea of the domestic life of Monseigneur, the bishop of Digne, and the way in which those two saintly women subordinated their actions, thoughts, and even their instincts as women easily frightened, to the habits and designs of the bishop, without his even needing to go to the trouble of putting anything into words, we cannot do better than to set down here a letter of Mademoiselle Baptistine to Madame la vicomtesse de Boischevron, her childhood friend. This letter is in our possession.

*Digne, December 16, 18—*

My dear Madame,

Not a day goes by without our talking about you. It is something of a habit we've gotten into. But there is another reason. Would you believe that when Madame Magloire was washing and dusting the walls and ceilings, she made a few discoveries? Now our two bedrooms, which used to be covered with old wallpaper whitewashed with lime, would not be out of place in a château as fine as your own. Madame Magloire ripped all the paper off. There were things underneath. My sitting room, which has no furniture in it and which we only use as a drying room on wash days, is fifteen feet high and eighteen feet wide, with a ceiling that was once gilded, and beams the same as at your place. It was covered in material from when it was a hospital. And on top of that, there was wainscoting from our grandmothers' day. But it is my bedoom you should see. Under at least ten layers of paper that were stuck all over it, Madame Magloire uncovered paintings, not good, but not bad, either. There is Telemachus received as a knight by Minerva[1] in one, another one of him in the gardens of . . . the name escapes me. Well, anyway, the place where Roman ladies used to go for just one night. What can I tell you? I have Romans, men and women [here the word is illegible]—the whole retinue. Madame Magloire has cleaned them all up and this summer she's going to fix up a bit of damage here and there, revarnish the lot and the room will be a real little museum. She also found in a corner of the attic two wooden console tables, antique style. They were asking two écus six livres to regild them, but it would be better to give the money to the poor. Anyway, they are as ugly as can be, and I'd prefer a round table in mahogany.

I'm as happy as ever. My brother is so good. He gives everything he has to the sick and needy. We are feeling the pinch. The winters here are bitterly cold and of course we have to try and do something for those in need. We manage to stay warm and have light, though. You see how well off we are.

My brother has his little ways. When he mentions them, he says that's just how a bishop should be. Just imagine—the front door of the house is never locked. Anyone can just walk in off the street and make themselves right at home in the middle of his room. He's not afraid of anything, even at night. That's his form of courage, as he says.

He doesn't want me to be frightened for him or for Madame Magloire to be frightened. He exposes himself to every danger and he doesn't want us to even look as though we notice. You've got to know him to know what he's about.

He goes out in the rain, he walks in the water, he travels in winter. He is not afraid of the dark or of dangerous roads or of running into someone.

Last year, he went all on his own into territory full of thieves. He wouldn't hear of taking us along. He stayed away for a fortnight. When he came back, nothing had happened to him, we thought he was dead and he was in great spirits, and he said: "You see how they robbed me!" And he opened up a chest full of all the jewels from Embrun Cathedral which the thieves had given him.

That last time I'd gone with some friends of his to meet him at a spot a couple of miles away, and as we were returning home, I couldn't help but scold him a little, being careful only to talk when the carriage was making a racket, so no one else could hear.

In the old days, I used to say to myself: "There is no danger that can stop him, he's terrible." Now I've ended up getting used to it. I motion to Madame Magloire not to go against him. Let him take whatever risks he will. I cart Madame Magloire away, go to my room and I pray for him and I fall asleep. I'm perfectly calm, because I know full well that if anything happened to him, it would be the end of me. I'd go to the good Lord with my brother and my bishop. It's been a lot harder for Madame Magloire to come to terms with what she calls his recklessness. But now we have our routine. We both pray, we are both frightened together, and we fall asleep. If the devil came into the house, we'd let him do his worst. After all, what can we be frightened of in this house? There is always someone with us who is the strongest. The devil might pass through, but the good Lord lives here.

That is it. My brother doesn't even have to say a word to me now. I understand him without his needing to speak and we put ourselves in the hands of Providence.

And that is how one should be with a man with his greatness of spirit.

I asked my brother for the information you requested concerning the Faux family. You know how he knows everything and how good his memory is, for he is still a good royalist. They are really and truly a very old Norman family from the Caen region. They go back five hundred years to a Raoul de Faux, a Jean de Faux, and a Thomas de Faux, who were all noblemen, one of them being a seigneur de Rochefort. The last was Guy-Étienne-Alexandre and he was a colonel and something or other in the light horse of Brittany. His daughter, Marie-Louise, married Adrien-Charles de Gramont, son of the duc Louis de Gramont, a peer of France, colonel in the Gardes Françaises and lieutenant general in the army. It is spelled Faux, Fauq, and Faoucq.

My dear Madame, commend us to the prayers of your holy relative, the cardinal, won't you? As for your dear Sylvie, she was right not to spend the brief moments she had at home with you in writing to me. She is well, works as you would like her to, and still loves me. That is all I could wish for. Her regards reached me through you and I am very happy to have them. My health is not too bad, though I get thinner by the day. Goodbye for now, I'm running out of paper so I must leave you here, very best wishes,

BAPTISTINE.

P.S. Your sister-in-law is still here with her young family. Your grand-nephew is a delight. Did you know he will be five soon? Yesterday he saw a horse going past; someone had put knee pads on it and he said: "What's he got on his knees?" He is so sweet, that boy! His little brother drags an old broom around the apartment like a carrriage and says: "Giddyup!"

As you can see from this letter, the two women managed to adapt them-selves to the bishop's way of life with that special genius of women who know a man better than he knows himself. The bishop of Digne, beneath that soft can-did air that never failed him, sometimes committed acts of greatness, daring, even magnificent acts, without appearing remotely conscious of it. They would tremble, but they let him get on with it. Sometimes Madame Magloire tried to remonstrate with him before; never during or after. They never disturbed him, not even by a sign, once he had begun any course of action. At certain times, without his needing to say a word, when he himself, perhaps, was not aware of it, so perfect was his artlessness, they felt vaguely that he was acting the bishop; then they were nothing more than two shadows moving about the house. They would serve him quietly, and if compliance meant making themselves scarce, they disappeared. They knew, by a wonderfully subtle instinct, that certain kinds of concern can get in the way. So even when they thought he was in dan-ger, they knew, I won't say what he was thinking, but what he was like, to the point where they no longer watched over him. They entrusted him to God.

Besides, Baptistine used to say, as you have just read, that her brother's death would be her own. Madame Magloire didn't say so, but she knew it.

## X. THE BISHOP BEFORE AN UNKNOWN LIGHT

Not long after the date of the letter quoted above, the bishop did something, if the entire village is to be believed, even more risky than the trip through the mountains held by the bandits.

In the countryside near Digne, there was a man who lived alone. This man had once been, not to mince words, a member of the National Convention.[1] His name was G——.

In the small world of Digne, G—— the Conventionist was spoken of in the hushed tones of horror. A Conventionist! Imagine! He went back to the days when people addressed each other familiarly as *tu* and used the word *citizen.* This man was more or less a monster. He had not exactly voted for the death of the king, but as good as. Which made him a semi-regicide.[2] He had been terri-ble. Why, when the legitimate princes returned to power, was this man not put on trial in a provost court without appeal? They might not have cut his head off if you like, since clemency is, of course, necessary; but a good banishment for life would have done the trick. Set an example, for heaven's sake! And so on and so forth. The man was an atheist, into the bargain, like all his kind. It was like geese cackling around a vulture.

But was this G—— really a vulture? Yes, if you were to judge him by the fierceness of his isolation. Not having voted for the king's death, he had not been included in the decrees of exile and so had been able to remain in France.

He lived three quarters of an hour outside town, far from any hamlet, far from any road, in a godforsaken hole of a place in an extremely wild valley. He had a sort of field there, they said, and a bolt-hole, a hideout. No neighbors, no one even passing through. Since he'd been living in the valley, the path to it had disappeared under grass. People spoke of the place as the house of the hangman.

Yet from time to time the bishop gazed at the horizon where a clump of trees marked the valley of the old Conventionist and he would say, "There is a soul there who is all alone."

And in the back of his mind, he would add, "I owe him a visit."

But, to be frank, this idea, at first so natural, seemed to him, after a moment's reflection, weird and impossible, almost repulsive. For at heart he shared the general view and the Conventionist inspired in him, without his being fully aware of it, that feeling which verges on hate and that is so aptly expressed by the word *aversion*.

Yet, should the sheep's mange cause the shepherd to recoil? No. But what a sheep!

The good bishop was torn. Sometimes he would head off that way, but then he would turn around and come back.

One day the word went out around town that a kind of shepherd boy who looked after G—— the Conventionist in his pigsty had come to find a doctor; that the old geezer was dying, that he was half-paralyzed, and that he wouldn't last the night. "Thank God!" some chimed in.

The bishop grabbed his stick, put his overcoat on to hide his cassock, which was getting too threadbare, as we've seen, and also because the evening breeze would not be long in rising, and left.

The sun was low in the sky, almost touching the horizon, when the bishop reached the unholy spot. He knew by the way his heart pounded that he was nearing the lair. He leaped over a ditch, jumped over a hedge, lifted a gate, stepped into a tiny overgrown yard, rather boldly struck out across it and there, suddenly, at the end of an empty plot, behind a tall clump of bushes, he saw the cavern.

It was a very low-roofed hut, dilapidated, small and neat, with a climbing vine tacked onto the outside.

By the door, in an old wheelchair, the armchair of a peasant, was a man with white hair smiling at the sun.

Next to the old man sitting in the wheelchair stood a young boy, the little shepherd. He was handing the old man a bowl of milk.

While the bishop looked on, the old man spoke up. "Thank you," he said, "I don't need anything more." And his smile switched from the sun to the boy.

The bishop came forward. At the sound of his footsteps, the old man turned his head and his face expressed all the surprise a person could muster at the end of a long life.

"In all the years I've lived here," he said, "this is the first time anyone has been to my home. Who are you, Monsieur?"

The bishop answered: "I call myself Bienvenu Myriel."

"Bienvenu Myriel! I've heard that name. Are you the one the people call Monseigneur Bienvenu?"

"That's me."

The old man continued with a tiny smile: "In that case, you are my bishop?"

"In a way."

"Come in, Monsieur."

The Conventionist held out his hand to the bishop but the bishop did not take it. The bishop did no more than comment:

"I'm happy to see that I've been misinformed. You certainly don't look sick to me."

"Monsieur," the old man replied, "I'll get over it." He paused and then added: "I'll be dead in three hours."

And then he went on: "I'm a bit of a doctor; I know what happens in the final hour. Yesterday, only my feet were cold. Today, the cold has reached my knees; right now I can feel it climbing up to my stomach. When it gets as far as the heart, I will cease to be. The sun is beautiful, isn't it? I had myself wheeled outside so I could cast my eyes over everything one last time. You can talk to me, it doesn't wear me out. You've done the right thing, coming to see a man who is about to die. It's good that such a moment has witnesses. We all have our quirks; I would have liked to have got as far as dawn. But I know I'm only good for another three hours, at most. It will be night. At the end of the day, it hardly matters. Giving up the ghost is a simple business. You don't need the morning for that. So be it. I'll die by starlight."

The old man turned to the boy.

"You, go to bed. You stayed up the other night. You're tired."

The boy went back inside the hut. The old man watched him go and then added, as though talking to himself: "I'll die while he's sleeping. We can keep each other company in sleep."

The bishop was not as moved as perhaps he might have been. He didn't feel he could sense God in this way of dying. To spell it out, for the little contradictions of great souls clamor for recognition like all the rest: The man who laughed so heartily at "Your Highness" was a bit shocked not to be addressed as Monseigneur and he was almost tempted to lob a "Citizen" in reply. He felt an impulse to use the gruff familiarity common enough with doctors and priests, which was not at all his usual bedside manner. This man, after all, this Conventionist, this representative of the people, had been one of the masters of the universe; for perhaps the first time in his life, the bishop felt an urge to be harsh.

The Conventionist, on the other hand, gazed at him with a humble congeniality in which one might have discerned, perhaps, the humility that is appropriate when a person is so close to returning to dust.

The bishop, for his part, though normally careful not to show curiosity, curiosity being as far as he was concerned very nearly a crime, could not prevent himself from scrutinizing the Conventionist with an attention that, not having its source in sympathy, would have gone completely against his conscience if the man in question had been any other man. This Conventionist affected the bishop as an outlaw might, beyond the reach even of the law of charity.

Calm, practically straight-backed, voice vibrant, G—— was one of those great octogenarians that dumbfound physiologists. The Revolution produced plenty of men like him, equal to the era. You could see just by looking that the old man had been through the mill and been strengthened by it. Even now, so close to his end, he had preserved all the energy of health. There was something in his bright eyes, in his firm tone, in the robustness of his shoulders, that was enough to throw death off the scent. Azrael, the Mohammedan angel of the sepulchre,[3] would have turned on his heels, feeling he'd come to the wrong door. G—— seemed to be dying only because that is what he wanted to do. His agony smacked of freedom. His legs alone were immobile. The dark had him by the lower limbs. His feet were already dead and cold but his head was alive with all life's potency and seemed powerfully illuminated. At this solemn moment, G—— was like the king in the oriental tale, flesh above, marble below.

There was a stone nearby. The bishop sat down on it. He delivered his exordium *ex abrupto.*

"I must congratulate you," he said in a tone of reprimand. "At least you didn't vote for the death of the king."

The Conventionist appeared not to hear the bitter innuendo implied in those words: At least, he had no trace of a smile on his face when he answered.

"Go easy with the congratulations, Monsieur, I voted for the end of the tyrant."

This was said in a tone of austerity to match the tone of severity.

"What do you mean?" asked the bishop.

"I mean that man has a tyrant, ignorance. I voted for the demise of that particular tyrant. That particular tyrant has engendered royalty, which is authority based on falsehood, whereas science is authority based on truth. Man should be governed by science alone."

"And conscience," added the bishop.

"It's the same thing. Conscience is the quota of innate science we each have inside us."

Monseigneur Bienvenu listened, a little amazed by this brand-new way of talking. The Conventionist went on: "As for Louis XVI, I said no. I don't believe I have the right to kill a man; but I feel I have a duty to exterminate evil. I voted for the end of the tyrant. That is to say, the end of prostitution for women, the end of slavery for men, the end of darkness for children. In voting for the Republic, that is what I voted for. I voted for fraternity, for harmony, for the dawn of a new age! I helped hasten the downfall of prejudices and bad habits. When bad habits and prejudices come crashing down they create light. We brought down the old world, some of us, and the old world, that chamber pot of miseries, tipped over and turned into an urn pouring joy over humankind."

"Not all joy," said the bishop.

"You could say clouded joy and now, after the fatal return of the past known as 1814,[4] evaporated joy. Alas, our work was incomplete, I admit; we demolished the structures of the ancien régime, but we didn't quite manage to obliterate its ideas. To wipe out abuse is not enough; you have to change people's whole outlook. The mill is no longer standing, but the wind's still there, blowing away."

"You demolished. Demolition may be useful; but I don't trust any demolition that's caught up in rage."

"The law has its rage, my dear bishop, and the wrath of the law is part of progress. Come what may and no matter what they say about it, the French Revolution was the greatest leap forward for mankind since the coming of Christ. Incomplete, yes; but sublime. It released all kinds of social unknowns. It sweetened people's minds; it soothed, relieved, enlightened; it caused waves of civilization to wash over the world. It was good. The French Revolution is mankind's crowning achievement."

The bishop could not prevent himself from muttering: "Oh, yes? What about '93!"[5]

The Conventionist sat bolt upright in his chair with an almost mournful solemnity and, as much as a dying man can, he shouted: "Ah! You got there at last! Seventeen ninety-three! I was wondering when you'd get to it. A cloud had been hanging over us for fifteen hundred years. At the end of fifteen centuries, it finally burst. You want to take the thunderclap to task."

The bishop felt, without perhaps admitting it to himself, that something in him had cooled down, gone out. But he put a brave face on it. He replied: "The judge speaks in the name of justice, the priest speaks in the name of pity, which is only a more exalted kind of justice. The thunderclap should not err."

And he added, fixing the Conventionist with his eye: "What about Louis XVII?"[6]

The Conventionist reached out and clutched the bishop's arm: "Louis XVII? Let's see. Who are you crying over? Over the innocent child? You're right, if so, and I cry with you. Over the royal child? Then I beg to reflect. For me, Cartouche's brother,[7] an innocent child, hung by the armpits in the place de

Grève[8] until death resulted, for the sole crime of having been Cartouche's brother, is no less lamentable than the grandson of Louis XV, an innocent child, martyred in the Temple tower for the sole crime of having been the grandson of Louis XV."

"Monsieur," said the bishop, "I don't like those names being connected."

"Cartouche? Louis XV? Which of them do you claim to represent?"

There was a moment of silence. The bishop almost regretted having come, and yet he felt obscurely and strangely shaken.

The Conventionist went on: "Ah! My dear priest, you don't like your truth so raw. Christ loved it. He took a scourge and scoured the temple. His flashing whip was a rude teller of home truths. When he cried: *Sinite parvulos*[9]—suffer them to come unto me—he didn't distinguish among the little children. He wouldn't have been too hard put to make a connection between the dauphin of Barabbas and the dauphin of Herod.[10] Monsieur, innocence is its own crown. Innocence has no truck with highness. It is as august in rags as it is draped in the fleur-de-lis."[11]

"That's true," said the bishop in a low voice.

"I say again," continued the Conventionist G——, "you brought up Louis XVII. Let's understand each other. Are we to cry over all the innocents, all the martyrs, all the children, those at the bottom as well as those at the top? I am with you. But then, as I've told you, we have to go back further than '93 and it's well before Louis XVII that we need to begin shedding tears. I will cry over the children of kings with you as long as you cry with me over the children of the people."

"I cry for them all," said the bishop.

"Equally!" cried G——. "And if we must tip the balance, let it be on the side of the people, for they have been suffering longer."

There was another silence. It was the Conventionist who broke it. He raised himself on one elbow, took a pinch of his cheek between his thumb and his crooked forefinger, as you do mechanically when you interrogate and judge, and he fired at the bishop a look that contained all the intense energy of approaching death. It was like an explosion.

"Yes, Monsieur, the people have been suffering for a long time. Then again, you realize, that is not all. What are you doing coming here and quizzing me and talking about Louis XVII? I don't know you. Since I've been in the region, I've lived in this paddock, on my own, never set foot outside it, or seen anyone apart from the boy who gives me a hand. Your name, it's true, has more or less reached me, and, I have to say, what I've heard of you is not all bad. But that doesn't mean a thing; clever folk come up with all kinds of ways of trying to put one over on the good people. Speaking of which, I didn't hear you roll up in a carriage—no doubt you left it behind the vine over there, at the fork in the road. I don't know you, I say. You tell me you're the bishop but that doesn't tell me anything about what sort of man you are. So, I repeat my question: Who are you? You are a bishop, that is to say, a prince of the Church, one of those gilded, emblazoned, salaried men who have big fat prebends—the see of Digne, fifteen thousand francs fixed salary, ten thousand francs in commissions, total, twenty-five thousand francs—who have kitchens, who have liveried retinues, who entertain lavishly, who eat guinea fowl on Fridays, who parade around, lackeys in front, lackeys behind, in a gala-standard berlin,[12] and who have palaces, and roll along in a carriage in the name of Jesus Christ who went barefoot! You are a prelate; meaning annuities, palaces, horses, valets, a fine table, all the sensual pleasures of life, you have all that, like the rest of them, and like the rest of them you enjoy it and that's fine, but it says too much or not enough. It doesn't enlighten me as to your intrinsic and essential worth, you who have come here most likely presuming to bring me enlightenment. Who am I talking to? Who are you?"

The bishop dipped his head and replied: *"Vermis sum."*[13]

"A worm in a carriage!" the Conventionist growled.

It was the Conventionist's turn to show human weakness and the bishop's turn to show humility.

Gently, the bishop replied: "So be it, Monsieur. But explain to me how my carriage, which is two paces away behind the trees, and my fine table and the guinea fowl I eat on Fridays and my twenty-five-thousand-francs income and my palaces and my lackeys prove that pity is not a virtue, that clemency is not a duty, and that '93 was not hideously ruthless."

The Conventionist passed his hand over his forehead as though to brush off a cloud.

"Before I answer you," he said, "I beg your pardon. I was wrong just now, Monsieur. You are in my home, you are my guest. I owe you courtesy. You are debating my ideas, so I should confine myself to combating your arguments. Your wealth and your pleasures are advantages I have over you in the debate, but it is not in good taste for me to make use of them. I promise not to use them again."

"Thank you," the bishop replied.

G—— went on: "Let's go back to the explanation you requested. Where were we? What were you saying? That '93 was hideously ruthless?"

"Ruthless, yes," said the bishop. "What do you make of Marat applauding the guillotine?"[14]

"What do you make of Bossuet singing the Te Deum as the dragoons savaged the Protestants?"[15]

The comeback was tough but it hit home with the sharpness of a rapier's blade. The bishop winced; he had no riposte, but he was taken aback to hear Bossuet's name used in this way. The best minds have their soft spots and sometimes feel somewhat bruised by the scant respect of logic.

The Conventionist began to gasp for breath; the asthma produced by approaching death, which makes the last intakes of air so labored, broke up his voice, and yet the perfect lucidity of his soul shone on in his eyes. He continued: "I'd like us to keep talking a bit. Beyond the Revolution, which, taken as a whole, is an immense affirmation of humanity, '93 alas! was a refutation. You find it hideously ruthless, but what about the whole of the monarchy, Monsieur? Carrier was a crook, but what do you call Montrevel? Fouquier-Tinville was a ghoul, but what is your opinion of Lamoignon-Bâville? Maillard was appalling, but what do you say of Saulx-Tavannes? 'Le père Duchêne' was ferocious, but how would you describe 'le père Le Tellier' for me? Jourdan-Coupe-Tête was a monster, but not as big a monster as the marquis de Louvois.[16] Monsieur, Monsieur, I feel sorry for Marie Antoinette, archduchess and queen.[17] But I also feel sorry for the poor Huguenot woman who, in 1685, under Louis le Grand,[18] Monsieur, was breast-feeding her baby when she was tied to a post, naked to the waist, the baby held at a distance. Her breast swelled with milk and her heart swelled with anguish. The little mite was pale and hungry and he could see her breast and he was dying for a feed and he bawled and sobbed and the executioner said to the woman: Recant! forcing her to choose between the death of her child and the death of her conscience. What do you say to that bit of torture, worthy of Tantalus,[19] applied to a mother? Monsieur, remember this: The French Revolution had its reasons. Its fury will be absolved by the future. Its outcome is a better world. Its most terrible actions led to tender loving care for the human race. I'll leave it at that. I must stop, it's too easy— I hold all the cards. Anyway, I'm dying."

And, ceasing to gaze at the bishop, the Conventionist polished off his argument with these few quiet words: "Yes, the brutalities of progress are called revolutions. When they are done, we recognize one thing: that the human race has been badly manhandled, but that it has moved forward."

Little did the Conventionist suspect that he had swept aside, one after the other, all the bishop's entrenched internal defenses. There was one left, however, and from this supreme entrenchment, the last fastness of Monseigneur Bienvenu's resistance, these words poured forth, almost as harshly as his opening gambit: "Progress should believe in God. Good can't be served by impiety. An atheist is a bad leader of the human race."

The old representative of the people did not answer. A shiver ran through his body. He looked up at the sky and a tear formed slowly in his eye. When his eyes were full to brimming, his tears ran down his livid cheeks and he said, almost stammering, in a low voice, to himself, his eyes lost in the depths: "O you! O ideal! You alone exist!"

The bishop experienced an inexpressible commotion.

After a moment's silence, the old man raised a finger to the sky and said: "Infinity is. It is there. If infinity had no self, the self would be its limit; it would not be infinite. In other words, it would not be. But it is. So it has a self. This self of infinity is God."

The dying man had uttered those words in a loud voice and with a shudder of ecstasy as though he could see someone. When he finished speaking, his eyes closed. The effort had exhausted him. It was clear that he had just lived the few hours remaining to him in one moment. What he had just said had brought him closer to the one who stands at death's door. The final moment was coming.

The bishop knew that time was running out. It was as a priest that he had come; his initial extreme coldness had gradually turned to extreme emotion. He looked at the closed eyes, he took the age-ravaged hand, wrinkled and icy, and he leaned toward the dying man: "This hour is the hour of God. Don't you think it would be a shame if we had met in vain?"

The Conventionist opened his eyes again. A gravity in which there was a shadow was stamped upon his face.

"My dear bishop," he said, with a slowness that came more, perhaps, from the dignity of the soul than from his waning strength, "I've spent my life in meditation, study, and contemplation. I was sixty years old when my country called me, and commanded me to take part in its affairs. I heeded the call. There were abuses, I fought them; there were rights and principles, I confessed them and professed them. The land was invaded and I defended it; France was threatened, I offered my breast. I was never rich; now I am poor. I was one of the masters of the state, the vaults of the Treasury were piled so high with coins that we were forced to prop up the walls which were ready to burst under the weight of all that gold and silver; I dined in the rue de l'Arbre-Sec at twenty-two sous a head. I succored the oppressed, I relieved the suffering. I tore up the altar cloth, it's true, but only to bandage the wounds of my homeland. I have always supported the forward march of the human race toward the light and I have sometimes resisted progress pitilessly. I have, on occasion, protected my own enemies—you lot. And at Peteghem in Flanders, on the very spot where the Merovingian kings had their summer palace, there is an Urbanist convent, the abbey of Sainte-Claire en Beaulieu, which I saved in 1793. I've done my duty as much as my strength would allow, and what good I could. After which I was hunted, hounded, pursued, persecuted, slandered, scoffed at, spat on, cursed, ostracized. For many years now, from the time my hair turned white, I've sensed that many people think they have the right to look on me with contempt; for the poor ignorant hordes, I wear the face of the damned and, hating no one, I accept the isolation hate brings. Now I am eighty-six years old; I am about to die. What have you come to ask of me?"

"Your blessing," said the bishop.[20] And he went down on his knees.

When the bishop raised his head again, the face of the Conventionist had become august. He had died.

The bishop returned home deeply absorbed in we know not what thoughts.

He spent the whole night in prayer. The next day, a few brave nosy parkers tried to talk to him about the Conventionist, G——. All he did was point to the sky. From that moment, he became more gentle and fraternal than ever toward the little children and the suffering.

Any allusion to "that old rotter G——" caused him to lapse into a strange meditative trance. No one could say that his spirit's passing encounter with that spirit and the reflection of that great conscience over his own did not have something to do with his approaching perfection.

That particular "pastoral visit" was naturally an occasion that set the little local coteries buzzing: "Was the place for a bishop by the bedside of a man like that, even if he was dying? Obviously he couldn't have been expecting a conversion from that quarter. All these revolutionaries are irreligious. So why go there? What did he think he'd find? He must have been really keen to see a soul carted off by the devil."

One day, a dowager of the breed that mistake impertinence for wit took a swipe at him: "Monseigneur, we are all wondering when Your Grace will get your red bonnet." "Oh, well, red's a pretty rich color," the bishop shot back. "Luckily those who despise it in a bonnet revere it in a hat."[21]

## XI. A QUALIFICATION

You would risk getting it badly wrong if you imagined from this that Monseigneur Bienvenu was "a philosopher bishop" or "a patriot priest."[1] His meeting, we might almost say, his communion, with G——, the Conventionist, left him in a state of amazement that made him sweeter than ever. That's all.

Although Monseigneur Bienvenu was anything but a political animal, this might well be the place to sum up, very briefly, his position in relation to the events of the day, assuming Monseigneur Bienvenu ever thought of having a position.

For this, we need to go back a few years.

Some time after the elevation of Monsieur Myriel to the episcopacy, the emperor had made him a baron of the empire, along with several other bishops. The arrest of the pope, as we know, took place during the night of July 5–6, 1809;[2] on that occasion, Monsieur Myriel was appointed by Napoléon to the synod of the bishops[3] of France and Italy, convened in Paris. This synod was held in Notre-Dame and assembled for the first time on June 15, 1811, under the presidency of Cardinal Fesch. Monsieur Myriel was one of the ninety-five bishops who made the journey. But he only attended one sitting and three or four special conferences. It seems that as the bishop of a mountainous diocese, living such a basic, rustic life so close to nature, he brought to this assembly of eminent personages ideas that dampened the whole atmosphere. He rushed back to Digne, and when queried about his prompt return, said: "I got on their nerves. I brought a draft from the great outdoors in with me. It was like I'd left the door open."

Another time, he said: "What do you expect? Those gents are princes. I'm just a poor country bumpkin of a bishop."

The fact is he put them off. Among other odd things, he let slip one evening when he found himself at the home of one of the most eminent of his colleagues: "What fine clocks! What fine rugs! What fine liveries! It must make you most uneasy! Heavens! I'm glad I don't have all these luxuries bellowing forever in my ears: 'There are people who are starving! There are people who are shivering with cold! There are people who have nothing! There are people who have nothing!' "

We should note in passing that hatred of luxury is not an especially bright form of hatred. Such hatred implies hatred of the arts. And yet, in a man of the Church, outside ritual and ceremony, luxury is a sin. It would seem to stimulate habits that have nothing much to do with charity. A wealthy priest is a contradiction in terms. A priest should stay close to the poor. Now, is it possible to be in constant contact, day and night, with every kind of distress, every kind of calamity, every kind of destitution, without some of this saintly misery rubbing off on oneself, like dirt from hard work? Can we imagine a man standing close to a fire and not feeling warm? Can we imagine a laborer toiling away incessantly at a furnace without either a hair on his head getting burned or a nail blackened or a drop of sweat or a speck of ash settling on his face? The first proof of charity in a priest, and especially in a bishop, is poverty.

That, no doubt, is what the bishop of Digne thought.

Besides, you must not think that he shared, on certain delicate points, what used to be called "the ideas of the century." He rarely got involved in the theological quarrels of the day and he kept his silence on matters where the Church and the State were compromised; but if you applied pressure, it appears you would have found him to be more of an Ultramontane than a Gallican.[4] Since we are painting a portrait of the warts-and-all kind, we are obliged to add that the decline of Napoléon left him unmoved. From 1813, he supported and applauded all demonstrations of hostility toward him. He refused to go and gawk[5] at the emperor as he passed through on his return from the island of Elba and declined to prescribe public prayers in his diocese for him during the Hundred Days.

Apart from his sister, Mademoiselle Baptistine, he had two brothers: One was a general, the other, a prefect of police. He wrote fairly often to both. He was pretty stiff with the first for a while because, having a command in Provence at the time of Napoléon's landing in Cannes, the general had placed himself at the head of twelve hundred men and pursued the emperor so half heartedly you'd have sworn he was determined to let him get away.[6] His corre spondence remained more affectionate with the other brother, the former police prefect, a brave and worthy gentleman who lived in retirement in Paris, in the rue Cassette.

And so Monseigneur Bienvenu, like anyone else, had his hour of partisanship, his hour of bitterness, his dark cloud. The shadow of the passions of the day passed over this sweet and exalted soul, busy as he was with eternal things. It goes without saying that such a man deserved not to have political opinions. Don't get me wrong; we are not confusing what are called political opinions with the great aspiration toward progress, with that sublime patriotic, democratic, human faith which, these days, should be the very foundation of all generous intelligence. Without going further into issues that only indirectly touch on the subject of this book, we will simply say this: It would have been a good thing if Monseigneur Bienvenu had not been a royalist and if his gaze had not been turned for a single moment from that serene contemplation where we see, shining clearly above the stormy hustle and bustle of human affairs, those three pure lights, Truth, Justice, and Charity.

While we agree that it was not for some political role that God had created Monseigneur Bienvenu, we would have understood and admired him if he had protested in the name of right and liberty, if he had put up fierce opposition, perilous and just resistance to Napoléon, when Napoléon was all-powerful. But what pleases us in those on the way up, does not please us as much when they are on the way down. We don't like fighting unless there is danger; and, in any case, only those who have fought from the very beginning have the right to annihilate at the very end. A man who has not been a relentless opponent in fair weather, when the enemy is at his peak, should keep quiet in foul, when the enemy collapses. Only the man who has denounced the enemy's success can legitimately proclaim the justice of his downfall. As for ourselves, when Providence intervenes, we let it do its worst. The year 1812 comes along and disarms us. In 1813, the cowardly breach of silence on the part of the taciturn legislative body, emboldened by disaster, was worthy only of outrage, and it was a crime to applaud; in 1814, faced with those treacherous marshals, faced with a senate that lurched from one dirty deed to another, insulting where once it had deified, faced with this idolatry collapsing and then spitting on the idol, it was a duty to turn away. In 1815, as the ultimate disasters were in the air,[7] as France shuddered at their sinister approach, as Waterloo could dimly be perceived opening up before Napoléon, the sorrowful acclaim of the army and of the people, cheering on a man who had been condemned by destiny, had nothing laughable about it, and with all our reservations about the despot, a heart like the bishop of Digne's should not, perhaps, have been so impervious to all that was noble and moving, at the edge of the abyss, in the tight embrace of a great nation and a great man.

With that one exception, he was and always would be, in everything, just, true, fair, intelligent, humble and dignified, beneficent and benevolent, which is another form of beneficence. He was a priest, a sage, and a man. Even in the political stance we have just chided him for and that we are inclined to judge almost severely, we have to say he was tolerant and even-keeled, which is, perhaps, more than can be said for the man addressing you now. The doorkeeper of the *mairie* had been put in place by the emperor. He was an old noncommissioned officer of the old guard, a legionnaire of Austerlitz,[8] as Bonapartist as the eagle.[9] From time to time thoughtless words would escape this poor devil's lips, which the law of the day defined as seditious. Since the imperial profile had vanished[10] from the insignia of the Legion of Honor, he never dressed in regulation dress, as he liked to say, so as not to be forced to wear his Legion of Honor cross. He had himself religiously removed the imperial effigy from the cross Napoléon had given him; this created a hole that he did not want to fill with anything else. "I'd rather die," he would say, "than wear those three toads[11] over my heart!" He laughed out loud at Louis XVIII. "That gouty old bastard[12] with his English gaiters!" he would say. "Let him take his pigtail and bugger off to Prussia!"—only too happy to be able to get the two things he hated most, Prussia and England,[13] into the same imprecation. He said more than he should have and finally lost his job. There he was on the street with his wife and kids without a scrap of bread. The bishop sent for him, gently chastised him, and appointed him verger of the cathedral.

Monsieur Myriel was the real pastor of the diocese, a friend to all.

In nine years, by dint of holy works and gentle manners, Monseigneur Bienvenu had filled the town of Digne with a sort of tender, filial veneration. Even his attitude toward Napoléon had been accepted and more or less tacitly forgiven by the people, a good but feeble flock who worshipped their emperor but loved their bishop.

## XII. MONSEIGNEUR BIENVENU'S SOLITUDE

There is almost always a squad of small-time abbés around a bishop, just as there is a covey of junior officers around a general. They are what the delightful Saint Francis de Sales[1] somewhere describes as "whippersnapper priests." Every profession has its cadets[2] who mill around those at the top. There is no figure of authority who doesn't have his entourage; no man of fortune without his court. Those in quest of a future flutter around the leading lights of the present. Every metropolis[3] has its general staff. Every bishop worth his salt has his squadron of cherubic seminarians on patrol maintaining order in the episcopal palace and mounting guard over monseigneur's smile. Pleasing a bishop is a foot in the door for a subdeacon.[4] After all, a person has to carve out a niche for himself and so clerics never disdain sinecures.

Just as there are bigwigs elsewhere, so there are big miters in the Church. These are the bishops in vogue, rich, well-heeled, smart men of the world, men who doubtless know how to pray but also know how to lobby, not too scrupulous about setting themselves up as conduits for a whole diocese, hyphens between the sacristy and the diplomatic world, more abbés than priests,[5] more prelates than bishops. You know you've got it made if you are one of the happy few who manage to get near them! With their stocks so high, they shower those around them—overzealous sycophants and favorites alike and all the young men who've learned how to flatter them—with fat parishes, livings, archdeaconates, chaplaincies, and cathedral posts, as a prelude to episcopal honors. By advancing themselves, they bring their satellites forward; a whole solar system swings into motion. Their radiance bathes their retinue in reflected rays of purple. Their prosperity scatters its crumbs over those waiting in the wings in the form of handy little promotions. The bigger the patron's diocese, the bigger the favorite's parish. And then there is always Rome. A bishop who gets himself made an archbishop, an archbishop who gets himself made a cardinal, takes you along for the ride as a conclavist;[6] you get onto the Rota,[7] you are handed a pallium[8] to wear, suddenly you are an auditor, suddenly you are a chamberlain, suddenly you are a monseigneur, and from His Grace to His Eminence there is just a step, and between His Eminence and His Holiness there is just the smoke of a burned ballot. Any clergyman in a skullcap can dream of the papal tiara. Nowadays the priest is the only man who can routinely become king—and what a king! The ultimate king. And so, what a hotbed of ambition is a seminary! How many blushing choirboys, how many fresh-faced abbés, run around like the dreamy milkmaid Perrette,[9] with a milk jug on their heads! How easily ambition calls itself vocation, maybe—who knows?—in all good faith, even hoodwinking itself, drooling with rapture as it is!

Monseigneur Bienvenu, humble, poor, peculiar, did not rate as one of the big miters. This could be seen by the complete lack of young priests flocking around him. We saw that he "didn't take" in Paris. No glorious future on the make sought to hitch his star to this lonely old man. No budding ambition was silly enough to attempt to blossom in his shadow. His canons and grand-vicars were good old codgers, a bit common like himself and immured like him in the diocese with no way of rising to the cardinalate, and they resembled their bishop, with this difference: They were finished and he was complete. The impossibility of getting anywhere under Monseigneur Bienvenu was so palpable that, scarcely out of the seminary, the young men ordained by him promptly got themselves recommendations to the archbishops of Aix or Auch and swiftly disappeared. For, after all, we all need a push. A saint who leads a life of excessive self-denial is dangerous to be around. He could well infect you by contagion with incurable poverty, numbing of the joints used for climbing the ladder, and, in short, a tad more renunciation than you'd like. People flee from such squalid virtue. Hence the isolation of Monseigneur Bienvenu. We live in a somber society. How to get ahead, succeed—that is the lesson that trickles down, drop by drop, from the overriding corruption on high.

We might say, by the way, that success is pretty awful. Its deceptive resemblance to merit has people fooled. For the hordes, success looks just like supremacy. Success, that dead ringer for talent, has a dupe: history. Only Juvenal and Tacitus[10] grumble about it. In our time, a more or less official philosophy has entered into service as Success's handmaiden, wears its livery and works its antechamber. Succeed: That's the whole idea. Prosperity presupposes Capability. Win the lottery and you are a clever man. The winner is revered. Be born with a silver spoon in your mouth, that's all that counts. Be lucky and the rest will fall into place. Be fortunate, and you'll be thought great. Apart from the five or six illustrious examples that are the glory of their age, contemporary admiration is as shortsighted as it is possible to be. All that glitters *is* gold. There's nothing wrong with being an arriviste as long as you've arrived. Vulgarity is an old Narcissus who adores himself and applauds the common vulgarity. That mighty genius by which one becomes a Moses, an Aeschylus, a Dante, a Michelangelo, or a Napoléon[11] is discerned by the multitude and wildly applauded in any man at all who achieves what he set out to achieve, no matter what that may be. Let a notary rise to become a deputy, let a sham Corneille write *Tiridate*,[12] let a eunuch come into possession of a harem, let some military Prudhomme[13] accidentally win the decisive battle of an era, let an apothecary invent cardboard soles for the Sambre-et-Meuse army[14] and let him, with this cardboard sold as leather, build himself four hundred thousand livres a year in income, let a hawker get into bed with usury and cause it to give birth to seven or eight million of which he is the father and she the mother, let a preacher become a bishop by talking through his hat, let an intendant of a great estate be so loaded on leaving the service that he is made minister of finance—people call that Genius, just as they call Mousqueton's face Beauty and Claude's[15] bearing Majesty. They mistake the constellations of the cosmic void for the stars made by ducks' feet in the soft mud of the bog.

## XIII. What He Believed

From the point of view of orthodoxy, it is not up to us to sound out the bishop of Digne. Before such a soul, we can feel nothing but respect. The conscience of a just man should be taken at face value. Besides, with certain kinds of people, we allow for the potential development of all the beauties of human virtue within a faith that is different from our own.

What did he think of this dogma or that mystery? These secrets of the profound inner life are known only to the grave, which all souls enter naked. What we are certain of is that for the bishop problems of faith were never resolved by hypocrisy. There can be no possible corruption in a diamond. He believed as much as he could. *Credo in Patrem*[1] was his cry. Besides, he drew from good works that degree of satisfaction that meets the demands of conscience and whispers softly to you, "You are with God."

What we feel we should point out is that, outside his faith, so to speak, and beyond it, the bishop had an oversupply of love. And it was due to this, *quia multum amavit*,[2] that he was judged vulnerable by the "serious," the "solemn," and the "sensible"; those favorite labels of our sad little world where egoism borrows its clichés from pedantry. What was this surplus of love? It was a serene benevolence, flowing over all people, as we have seen, and sometimes extending even to things. He lived without scorn. He was indulgent toward God's creation. Every man, even the best, has in him an unthinking harshness that he holds in reserve for animals. The bishop of Digne had none of that harshness, peculiar though it is to many priests. He did not go as far as the Brahmans,[3] but he seemed to have taken these words of Ecclesiastes to heart: "Who knoweth the spirit of man that goeth upward, and the spirit of the beast that goeth downward to the earth?"[4] External ugliness or the deformities of instinct did not worry him or make him angry. He was stirred by them, very nearly moved to tears. He seemed to be thoughtfully looking beyond the life of appearances to the underlying cause, explanation, or excuse. He seemed at times to be asking God to hand down lighter sentences. He examined, dispassionately and with the eye of a linguist deciphering a palimpsest, the level of chaos that exists even in nature. Such reveries occasionally caused strange words to pass his lips. One morning, he was in his garden; he thought he was alone, but his sister was strolling behind him without his being aware of it; all of a sudden he stopped and peered at something on the ground. It was a huge spider, black, hairy, horrible. His sister heard him say: "Poor creature! It's not her fault."

Why not record this almost divine infantilism, evidence as it is of goodness? Puerile trifles, if you like; childishness, but sublime childishness such as that of Saint Francis of Assisi and Marcus Aurelius.[5] One day he actually twisted his ankle trying to avoid treading on an ant.

And that is how this godly man lived. Sometimes he nodded off in the garden and when he did, there was nothing more venerable.

In the past, if we believe the tales told about him as a young man and even as a more mature man, Monseigneur Bienvenu had been a man of passion, perhaps even a violent man. His universal goodwill was not so much a natural instinct as a firm conviction that had trickled into his heart from life, slowly dripping into him, thought by thought; for a person's nature, like a rock, can be drilled into by drops of water. Such channels bored through are ineffaceable; such formations, indestructible.

In 1815, as I think we might have said, he had reached the age of seventy-five, but he did not look a day older than sixty. He was not tall; he was a bit over-weight, and to combat it, he cheerfully went on long walks; his step was firm and he was only very slightly stooped, a detail from which we do not claim to draw any conclusion. Pope Gregory XVI,[6] at eighty, held himself perfectly straight and smiling, but this did not stop him from being a lousy pope. Monseigneur Bienvenu had what is commonly known as "a handsome head," but he was so sweet that you forgot he was handsome.

Whenever he chatted away with the childlike gaiety that was one of his graces, and that we have already mentioned, you felt at ease in his company; joy seemed to stream from his whole being. His ruddy, fresh coloring, the full set of pearly white teeth that he'd held on to and that his laugh showed off, gave him that open, easygoing air that prompts people to describe a young man as "a good lad" and an old man as "a good old stick." This was, as you'll recall, the effect he produced on Napoléon. At first, and especially at first sight, he hardly seemed to be anything more, indeed, than a good old stick. But if you then spent a few hours with him, and saw him in a thoughtful mood, the good old stick was gradually transfigured and took on an ineffably imposing quality; his broad and serious forehead, made noble by a full head of white hair, was also ennobled by meditation; grandeur emanated from his goodness, but without that goodness ceasing to shine. You felt something of the emotion you would experience if you saw a smiling angel spread its wings without ceasing to smile. Respect, a respect beyond words, spread through you by degrees and made its way to your heart and you couldn't help but feel that you were in the presence of one of those great spirits, tried and tested and full of compassion, whose thinking is on such a large scale that it can't be anything but gentle.

As we have seen, prayer, celebration of religious offices, charity, consoling the afflicted, cultivating a little patch of ground, fraternity, frugality, hospitality, self-denial, trust, study, and work filled every day of his life. Filled is exactly the word, for the bishop's day was full to the brim of good thoughts, good words, and good deeds. And yet it was not complete if cold weather or rain stopped him from passing an hour or two every night, after the two women had retired, in his garden before he went to bed. It seemed as though this was a kind of rite with him, a way of preparing for sleep by meditating in full view of the great spectacle of the night sky. Sometimes, even well into the small hours, if the two old ladies could not sleep, they would hear him slowly circling the property. Then, he was alone with himself, rapt, peaceful, adoring, connecting the serenity of his heart with the serenity of the ether, overcome in the darkness by the visible splendors of the constellations and the invisible splendors of God, opening his soul to the thoughts that rain down from the Unknown. In moments like these, offering up his heart at the hour that night flowers offer up their perfume, lit up like a lamp in the middle of the starry night, full of ecstasy in the middle of the universal radiance of creation, he could not perhaps have said himself what was happening in his spirit; he felt something soar up out of him and something fly down into him. Mysterious exchanges between the bottomless well of the soul and the bottomless well of the universe!

He would muse about the greatness and the living presence of God; about the strange mystery of the eternal future; about the even stranger mystery of the eternal past; about all the infinities streaming in every direction before his very eyes; and, without trying to comprehend the incomprehensible, he saw it. He did not study God, he was dazzled by Him. He considered the magnificent collisions of the atoms that produce what we see of matter, showing the forces at work by observing them, creating individuality within unity, proportion within extension, the numberless within the infinite, and producing beauty through light. Such collisions are constantly taking shape, bringing things together and pulling them apart; it is a matter of life and death.

He would sit on a wooden bench with his back against a decrepit trellis and he would gaze at the stars through the scrawny stunted silhouettes of his fruit trees. This quarter-acre patch of ground, so sparsely planted, so crowded with sheds and shacks, was dear to him, was all he needed.

What more could an old man need when he divided whatever spare time his life allowed, he who had so little spare time, between gardening of a day and contemplation of a night? Surely this small enclosure, with the sky as a ceiling, was enough to enable him to worship God by regarding His loveliest works and His most sublime works, one by one? Isn't that all there is? Indeed, what more could you want? A little garden to amble about in, and infinite space to dream in. At his feet, whatever could be grown and gathered; over his head, whatever could be studied and meditated upon; a few flowers on the ground and all the stars in the sky.

## XIV. WHAT HE THOUGHT

One last word.

These sorts of details, particularly in this day and age, might give the bishop of Digne a certain "pantheist" profile, to use an expression currently in vogue, and promote the idea, either to his debit or his credit, that he had one of those personal philosophies peculiar to the age that sometimes take root in solitary souls and build and grow there until they replace religion. So we must insist on this: No one who knew Monseigneur Bienvenu would have allowed themselves to think anything of the sort. What showed this man's way with such clarity was his heart. His enlightenment came from the light the heart sheds.

No theories, just lots of good works. Abstruse speculations are dizzying, and nothing indicates that he polluted his mind with mystical claptrap. An apostle may be reckless, but a bishop has to tread carefully. He probably made a point of not going too far in certain issues and conundrums reserved to a certain extent for towering and terrifying minds. There is holy horror at the gates to enigma; the doors gape open wide but something tells you, you, life's passerby, not to go there. Woe betide the person who does! In the unfathomable depths of abstraction and pure speculation that, for all intents and purposes, lie beyond dogma, geniuses offer up their ideas to God. Their prayer boldly invites debate. Their worship is probing. This is direct religion, full of anxiety and liability for those who risk themselves on its dizzying cliffs.

Human thought knows no bounds. At its own peril, it analyzes and explores its own dazzlement. You could almost say that, through a kind of magnificent reaction, it dazzles nature; the mysterious world that surrounds us gives back what it takes, and it seems likely that the contemplators are contemplated. Whatever the case may be, there are in this world men—if that is what they are—who clearly perceive the pinnacles of the absolute at the far horizons of dream and who have a terrible vision of the infinite mountain. Monseigneur Bienvenu was not one of those men. Monseigneur Bienvenu was no genius. He would have dreaded those sublime peaks from which a few rare, not to say great, men, like Swedenborg or Pascal,[1] have slid down into madness. Of course such powerful daydreams have their moral usefulness and it is only by such arduous roads that we can approach ideal perfection. But our man took the shortcut: the Gospel.

He did not try to fold his chasuble in imitation of Elijah's mantle;[2] he did not throw any ray of light from the future onto the shadowy unfolding of events; he did not seek to condense the glimmer of things into a flame; there was nothing of the prophet or the seer about him. This humble soul was filled with love, that's all.

More than likely he inflated his praying into a superhuman longing; but you can't pray too much any more than you can love too much. And, if it was heresy to pray outside the sacred texts, then Saint Teresa and Saint Jerome[3] were heretics.

He gravitated toward those in pain and those who wished for atonement. The world seemed to him like one massive disease; he could feel fever everywhere; everywhere he heard the rattle and wheeze of suffering in people's chests with his special stethoscope and, without seeking to solve the enigma, he tried to stanch the wound. The awesome spectacle of things as they are produced in him compassion; his sole concern was to find for himself and to help others to find the best way to sympathize and bring relief. All that exists was for this good and rare priest constant grounds for the sadness that seeks to console.

There are men who work hard, digging for gold; he worked hard, digging for pity. The misery of the world was his mine. Pain everywhere was an occasion for goodness always. *Love one another.*[4] He declared this to be complete, desired nothing more; it was the sum total of his doctrine. One day, the above-mentioned senator, who styled himself a philosopher, said to the bishop: "But just take a good look at the world; it's the war of each against all; might is right. Your *love one another* is nonsense." "Ah, well," replied Monseigneur Bienvenu without arguing, "if it's nonsense, the soul should shut itself up in it like a pearl in an oyster." And so, he shut himself up in it, he lived in it, he was utterly happy there, leaving aside the prodigious questions that lure and terrify, the unfathomable perspectives of abstraction, the heady precipices of metaphysics, all these profundities that converge, for the apostle, on God, and, for the atheist, on nothingness: fate, good and evil, the war of being against being, man's conscience, the pensive sleepwalking of animals, transformation by death, the summing up of existences in the grave, the incomprehensible grafting of successive loves on the enduring self, essence, substance, being and nothingness, the soul, nature, freedom, necessity—thorny problems that are sheer drops, murky depths, over which the colossal archangels of the human mind hover; awesome abysses that the likes of Lucretius, Manu, Saint-Paul, and Dante[5] contemplate with blazing eyes that, by staring hard at infinity, seem to cause stars to hatch there.

Monseigneur Bienvenu was, quite simply, a man who observed mysterious matters from the outside without scrutinizing them too closely, without stirring them up, and without troubling his own mind with them, a man who had in his soul a serious respect for the unknown.

# BOOK TWO

# THE FALL

## I. THE NIGHT AFTER A DAY'S WALK

In the first days of the month of October 1815, about an hour before sunset, a man traveling on foot entered the small town of Digne. The few inhabitants who found themselves at their windows or front doors at that moment watched the traveler with a vague anxiety. You would have been hard-pressed to come across anyone on the road more derelict in appearance. He was a man of average height, stocky and strong and in the prime of his life. He might have been around forty-six or forty-eight. A cap with a turned-down leather peak partly hid his face, which was sunburned and windburned and streaming with sweat. His shirt of coarse yellow twill, fastened at the neck with a small silver anchor, gaped open, exposing his hairy chest; he had a cravat that looked like twisted rope, trousers of blue drill, worn out and threadbare, with one knee frayed white and one knee in holes, a tattered old gray peasant's smock, with one elbow patched with a bit of green sheeting sewn on with string; on his back, a brand-new soldier's knapsack crammed to bursting and tightly buckled up; in his hand, an enormous knotted stick; on his stockingless feet, hobnailed shoes. His head was shorn and his beard was long.

The sweat, the heat, the journey on foot, the dust, added a strange sordidness to his shabby appearance.

Though his hair had been shaved off it still managed to stick out all over his head, for it was beginning to grow back and looked as though it hadn't been cut in quite a while.

No one knew who he was. Obviously he was just passing through. Where did he come from? From down south. Maybe from the coast. For he made his entrance into Digne from the same street that, seven months before, had seen the emperor Napoléon go by on his way from Cannes to Paris. The man had to have been walking all day. He looked extremely tired. Women from the old quarter at the bottom of the town had seen him stop under the trees on the boulevard Gassendi and drink from the fountain that stands at one end of the esplanade. He must have been really thirsty because the children trailing after him saw him stop again for a drink two hundred feet farther along at the fountain in the marketplace.

When he got to the corner of the rue Poichevert, he turned left and headed for the *mairie*.[1] He went in, then came out a quarter of an hour later. A gendarme was sitting by the door on the stone bench General Drouot[2] had mounted on March 4 to read to the terrified assembled residents of Digne Napoléon's proclamation[3] on his landing in Juan Gulf.[4] The man lifted his cap and humbly saluted the gendarme.

Without returning his greeting, the gendarme stared intently at him, watched him closely for a while as he moved off, then went inside the *mairie*.

In Digne in those days there was a very good inn known as La Croix de Colbas. The innkeeper was a man named Jacquin Labarre and he was held in high esteem in the town because he was related to another Labarre, who kept another inn, the Trois Dauphins in Grenoble and who had served in the Guides. At the time of the emperor's landing, the Trois Dauphins had been the talk of the region. It was said that General Bertrand, disguised as a carter, had made frequent trips to it during the month of January and that he had handed out *croix d'honneur* there to the soldiers and fistfuls of napoléons to the good burghers.[5] The truth is that once he entered Grenoble, the emperor had refused to move into the prefecture building; he had thanked the mayor for his offer with these words: "I'm going to stay with a fine fellow I happen to know"—and with that, he promptly took himself off to the Trois Dauphins. The glory of this Trois Dauphins Labarre was reflected twenty-five miles away on the Labarre of the Croix de Colbas. They liked to say of him in town: "He's the cousin of the one in Grenoble."

The man headed for the inn, which was the best in the district. He went into the kitchen, which opened directly onto the street. All the stoves were burning; a great fire blazed merrily in the fireplace. The host, who was also the cook, was going from the hearth to the saucepans, totally engrossed in supervising an excellent dinner destined for some cart drivers who could be heard cackling and yapping away furiously in the next room. If you've ever been on the road you know that nobody eats better than cart drivers. A fat woodchuck, flanked by white partridges and grouse, was turning on a long spit in front of the fire; on the stoves were two huge carp from the lac de Lauzet and a trout from the lac d'Alloz.

The host, hearing the door open and a newcomer enter, said without taking his eyes off his stoves: "What are you after, Monsieur?"

"Bed and board," said the man.

"Nothing easier," replied the host. At that point he turned his head, gave the traveler a thorough once-over, and added: "—it'll cost you."

The man pulled a fat leather purse from the pocket of his smock and answered: "I have money."

"In that case, at your service," said the host.

The man put his purse back in his pocket, hoisted his pack off his back and dropped it on the floor by the door; then, still holding his stick, he went and sat on a low stepladder by the fire. Digne is in the mountains. Nights in October are cold there.

As the host came and went, he still kept a steady eye on the traveler.

"Will dinner be ready soon?" the man asked.

"Shortly," said the host.

While the newcomer warmed up with his back turned, the worthy innkeeper Jacquin Labarre took a pencil from his pocket and then tore off a corner from an old newspaper lying on a small table near the window. He scribbled a line or two in the empty margin, folded it without sealing it, and handed the scrap of paper to a boy who appeared to serve him as both kitchen hand and lackey at once. The innkeeper had a word in the boy's ear and the child skipped off in the direction of the *mairie*.

The traveler had not seen any of this.

He asked again: "Will dinner be ready soon?"

"Shortly," said the host.

The boy came back—with the note. The host hurriedly unfolded it as though anxious for an answer. He read it with apparent interest, then shook his head and thought for a moment. Finally he took a step toward the traveler, who looked to be lost in thoughts that were not particularly serene.

"Monsieur," he said, "I can't put you up."

The man half-rose in his seat.

"What! Are you frightened I won't pay? Do you want me to pay you in advance? I have money, I tell you."

"It's not that."

"What then?"

"You have money—"

"Yes," said the man.

"But I," said the host, "I don't have a room."

The man replied calmly: "Put me in the stable."

"I can't."

"Why not?"

"The horses take up all the room."

"Well then," the man shot back, "a corner of the hayloft. A bale of straw. We'll look into it after dinner."

"I can't give you any dinner."

This declaration, made in a measured but firm tone, struck the stranger as serious. He got up.

"What the—! But I'm dying of hunger. I've been walking since sunrise. I've covered twelve leagues.⁶ I'm paying. I want to eat."

"I haven't got anything," said the host.

The man burst out laughing and turned toward the chimney and the stoves.

"You haven't got anything, eh! What's all that?"

"All that is taken."

"Who by?"

"By those gentlemen, the cart drivers."

"How many of them are there?"

"Twelve."

"There's enough there to feed twenty."

"They reserved all of it and paid for all of it in advance."

The man sat back down and said, without raising his voice:

"I'm at the inn, I'm starving, and I'm staying put."

At that, the host bent down to his ear and said to him in a tone that made him jump: "Get out of here."

The traveler was bent over at that point, poking a few embers in the fire with the metal tip of his stick; he wheeled round and, as he was opening his mouth to reply, the host fixed him with his eye and added, again in a low voice: "Listen, enough talk. Do you want me to tell you who you are? You are Jean Valjean.⁷ Now would you like me to tell you what you are? When I saw you come in, I was suspicious, I sent word to the *mairie* and here's what they sent back. Can you read?"

So saying, he handed the stranger the note, now unfolded, that had just made the trip from the inn to the *mairie* and from the *mairie* back to the inn. The man glanced at it. The innkeeper continued after a moment's silence:

"I'm in the habit of being polite to everyone. Get out of here."

The man dipped his head, picked up his bag, and left.

He took the main street. He walked willy-nilly, putting one foot in front of the other, slinking alongside the houses with his tail between his legs, humiliated and sad. He did not look back once. If he had looked back, he would have seen the innkeeper of La Croix de Colbas on his doorstep, surrounded by all the travelers at the inn and all the pedestrians in the street, talking animatedly and pointing at him, and seeing the looks of suspicion and fear on their faces, he would have guessed that before too long his arrival would be the talk of the town.

He saw nothing of all this: People who are overwhelmed with troubles never do look back. They know only too well that misfortune follows in their wake.

He walked along for a while without stopping, aimlessly tramping down whatever unknown streets cropped up, forgetting his fatigue, as can happen in a bout of sadness. All of a sudden he felt a real pang of hunger. Night was falling. He looked around to see if he could see any kind of lodging.

The fine hotel trade was closed to him, so he looked for a humble tavern, any sleazy dive.

Just then a light came on at the end of the street; a pine branch, hanging from an iron stand, stood out against the white sky of twilight. He headed straight for it.

It was in fact a tavern, the one in the rue de Chauffaut.

The traveler stopped in his tracks for a moment and gazed through the windowpane into the low-ceilinged tavern, which was lit by a small lamp on a table and by a great fire in the fireplace. A few men were inside drinking. The host was warming himself by the fire. The flames were causing an iron pot hanging on a hook to hiss.

You can enter this tavern, which is also an inn of sorts, by one of two doors. One door opens onto the street, the other leads to a small courtyard full of dung. The traveler did not dare take the street entrance. He slipped into the courtyard, stopped again, and then gingerly lifted the latch and pushed the door.

"Who goes there?" asked the publican.

"Someone who'd like a meal and a bed."

"That's good, because in this house we eat and we sleep."

He went in. All the drinkers turned to look at him. The lamp shone on him from one side, the fire from the other. They examined him for a while as he was taking off his pack.

The host said to him: "There's the fire. Supper's in the pot. Come and warm yourself, friend."

He went and sat close to the fireplace and stretched his aching feet out in front of the fire. A delicious smell was wafting from the pot. All that could be seen of his face beneath the lowered cap took on a vague look of well-being mingled with that other, very poignant look that the habit of suffering produces.

His was, besides, a strong face, energetic and sad. He had the strangest physiognomy, which started off looking humble and ended up looking harsh. His eyes were shining under his eyebrows like fire under scrub.

But one of the men at the table was a fisherman who, before coming into the tavern in the rue de Chauffaut, had stopped to put his horse in the stable at Labarre's. Chance would have it that he had come across the stranger that very morning as he made his way between Bras d'Asse and—well, . . . I forget the name. I think it was Escoublon. Now, when he had come across him, the man, who already seemed beat, had asked him to give him a ride on the back; to which the fisherman had replied only by doubling his pace. This fisherman had been part of the group gathered around Jacquin Labarre only half an hour before and he had himself related his unpleasant encounter of the morning to his mates at La Croix de Colbas. He subtly motioned to the taverner from his seat. The taverner went over to him. They exchanged a few words softly. The man had sunk into his thoughts once more.

The taverner went back to the fireside, clapped his hand roughly on the man's shoulder, and said: "On your way!"

The stranger turned to face him and replied mildly: "Ah! So you know?"

"Too right I know."

"They turned me away from the other inn."

"And we're kicking you out of this one."

"Where am I supposed to go?"

"Somewhere else."

The man took his stick and his bag and left.

As he was leaving, some children who had followed him from La Croix de Colbas and who seemed to be waiting for him began throwing stones at him. He retraced his steps furiously and threatened them with his stick; the children scattered like a flock of birds.

He came to the prison. An iron chain attached to a bell hung from the prison door. He rang.

A grate slid open.

"Doorkeeper," he said, respectfully taking off his cap, "would you kindly open up for me and let me stay here for tonight?"

A voice replied: "This is a prison, not an inn. Get yourself arrested. Then we'll open up for you."

And the grate closed again.

He turned into a little street where there were a lot of gardens. Some were enclosed by hedges, which cheered up the street. Among these gardens and these hedges, he saw a little single-story house with a light in the window. He peered through the glass as he had done at the tavern. It was a large whitewashed room with a bed draped in Indian cotton and a cradle in a corner, a few wooden chairs, and a double-barreled musket hanging on the wall. A table was set in the middle of the room. A brass lamp lit a tablecloth of coarse white cotton, a pewter pitcher that gleamed like silver, and a smoking brown soup tureen. At this table was seated a man in his forties, with an exuberant, open face, bouncing a toddler on his knees. Next to him a very young woman was breast-feeding another baby. The father was laughing, the toddler was laughing, the mother was smiling.

The stranger was momentarily spellbound before this sweet and soothing scene. What was going through his mind? Only he could have said. Most likely he was thinking that such a joyful home would be hospitable and that there, where he saw so much happiness, he would perhaps find a bit of pity.

He knocked ever so faintly on the window.

No one heard.

He knocked again.

He heard the woman say to her husband: "I think I heard someone knock."

"No," said the husband.

He knocked for the third time.

The husband got up, took the lamp, and went and opened the door.

He was a tall man, half peasant, half artisan. He was wearing a vast leather apron that fastened over his left shoulder, with a pouch for a hammer, a red handkerchief, a powder horn, all kinds of objects held in place by his belt as though they were in a pocket. He threw his head back; his shirt, which was collarless and largely open, showed his bull neck, white and bare. He had thick bushy eyebrows, enormous black side-whiskers, bulging eyes, a muzzle of a chin, and over it all that indefinable air of being right at home.

"Forgive me, Monsieur," said the traveler. "If I pay you, could you give me a bowl of soup and a corner to sleep in in that shed down there in the garden? Tell me, could you? If I pay?"

"Who are you?" asked the man of the house.

The man replied: "I've come from Puy-Moisson. I've been walking all day. I've done twelve leagues. Could you? If I pay?"

"I wouldn't refuse to put up any decent man who could pay. But why don't you go to the inn?"

"There's no room."

"Gah! That's not possible. There's no fair on today and it isn't market day. Did you try Labarre's?"

"Yes."

"Well then?"

The traveler replied in some embarrassment: "I don't know, he wouldn't let me stay."

"Did you go to the other joint, rue de Chauffaut?"

The stranger's embarrassment increased. He stammered: "He wouldn't let me stay either."

The peasant's face took on a suspicious expression; he looked the newcomer over from head to toe and suddenly he bellowed with a sort of shudder: "Are you the man . . . ?"

Casting another glance at the stranger, he took three steps back, put the lamp down on the table and took the gun off the wall.

But the wife had leaped up at the peasant's words: "Are you the man . . . ?"; she had swept her two children into her arms and swiftly taken refuge behind her husband, gazing at the stranger in horror, her throat bare, her eyes wild with fright, murmuring almost inaudibly in French alpine patois: *"Tso-maraude"*— *chat de maraude*, or cat of a thief.

All this happened faster than you could have imagined. After studying "the man" for a moment, the way you would study a viper, the man of the house came back to the door and said: "On your way."

"For pity's sake," the man cried, "a glass of water."

"I'll give you a bullet!" said the peasant.

With that he banged the door shut violently and the man could hear two heavy bolts shooting home. A moment later, the shutter closed over the window, and the sound of an iron bar being put in place reverberated outside.

Night kept on falling. The cold wind from off the Alps came up. By the dying light of day, the stranger spotted in one of the gardens lining the street a sort of hut that looked as though it were built out of clumps of turf. He resolutely hurdled a wooden fence and found himself in the garden. He approached the hut; for a door it had a very low and narrow opening, and it looked like one of those buildings that road menders throw up by the side of the road. No doubt he thought that was what it was, a road mender's shed; he was suffering from cold and hunger—he had resigned himself to the hunger, but at least here was shelter from the cold. These sorts of sheds are usually empty at night. He lay down on his stomach and slid into the hut. It was warm inside and he found quite a decent bed of straw. He lay resting for a moment stretched on the bed, unable to move a muscle he was so tired. Then, as the bag on his back was uncomfortable and it would make a good pillow, he started to unbuckle one of the straps. At that moment a ferocious growl could be heard. He looked up. The head of an enormous mastiff was outlined against the hut's entrance.

It was a dog kennel.

He was himself vigorous and formidable; he grabbed his stick as a weapon, used his bag as a shield, and got out of the hut as best he could, not without making the rips in his tattered clothes much worse.

He also made his way out of the garden, walking backward, obliged, to keep the dog's respect, to resort to that maneuver with the stick that masters of this style of fencing call *la rose couverte*.

When he had scrambled back over the fence, not without difficulty, and he found himself once again on the street, alone, without a place to stay, without a roof over his head, without shelter, driven even from a straw bed in a miserable dog kennel, he sank down rather than sat on a rock, and it appears that someone going past heard him cry out: "I'm not even a dog!"

Soon he got back to his feet and began walking again. He left the town behind, hoping to find a tree or a haystack somewhere in a field where he could take shelter.

He ambled along for some time with his head hung low. When he felt he was far away from all human habitation, he raised his eyes and looked around him. He was in a field; in front of him was one of those low hills covered in very short stubble that, after the harvest, look like shaved heads.

The horizon was pitch black, due not only to the thickness of night but also to very low-lying clouds that seemed to press down on the hill itself and then to rise, filling the whole sky. But as the moon was about to come up and a last faint crepuscular light hovered at the zenith, the clouds formed a sort of vault of whitish light at the highest point of the sky, from which a shaft of light fell to earth.

This made the ground lighter than the sky, which is a particularly sinister effect, and the hill, with its meager and stunted contour, stood out pale and wan against the shadowy horizon. The whole scene was hideously bleak, mean, gloomy, hemmed in. Nothing in the field or on the hill, apart from a gnarled tree that seemed to twist and rustle just a few feet from the traveler.

This man was obviously far from possessing the ingrained subtlety of intelligence and sensitivity that makes you susceptible to the mysterious appearances of things; and yet there was in that sky, in that hill, in that plain, and in that tree something so profoundly desolate that after standing there motionless for a moment and musing, he swiftly turned back the way he came. There are times when nature itself strikes you as hostile.

He retraced his steps. The gates of Digne were closed. In 1815, Digne, which had sustained sieges in the wars of religion,[8] was still surrounded by ancient walls flanked by square towers that have since been demolished. He slipped through a breach and was back inside the town.

It might have been eight o'clock at night. Since he did not know the streets, he struck out again at random.

And so he came to the prefecture, followed by the seminary. As he passed by the cathedral square, he shook his fist at the church.

In a corner of the square there is a printing works. This is where the proclamations of the emperor and the Imperial Guard to the army, dictated by Napoléon himself and brought back from the island of Elba, were printed for the first time.

Exhausted and past caring, he lay down on the stone bench that sits at the door of the printing works.

An old woman emerged from the church at that moment. She saw the man lying there stretched out in the dark.

"What are you doing there, my friend?" she said.

His reply was sharp and angry: "As you can see, my good woman, I'm trying to sleep."

The good woman, most worthy of the name in fact, was Madame la marquise de R——.

"On that bench?" she continued.

"For nineteen years I've had wood for a mattress," said the man. "Today I have a mattress of stone."

"Were you a soldier?"

"Yes, my good woman. A soldier."

"Why don't you go to the inn?"

"Because I don't have any money."

"Alas," said Madame de R——, "I've only got four sous[9] in my purse."

"Give them to me anyway."

The man took the four sous. Madame de R—— went on: "You can't get yourself a room in an inn with that paltry sum. Have you tried, though? You can't possibly spend the night out here. I bet you're cold and hungry. Someone could have put you up out of charity."

"I knocked on every door."

"What happened?"

"Everyone drove me away."

The good woman put her hand on the man's arm and pointed out a small low house next to the bishop's palace on the opposite side of the square.

"You knocked," she asked, "on every door?"

"Yes."

"Did you knock on that one?"

"No."

"Knock there."

## II. PRUDENCE IS RECOMMENDED TO WISDOM

That evening, the bishop of Digne had stayed shut up in his room after his stroll around town. He was busy with his great work on Duty[1] which, unfortunately, has remained unfinished. He was carefully going through all that the Fathers and Doctors[2] have said on this grave subject. His book was divided into two parts. First, the duties of all; second, the duties of each one according to his station in life. The duties of all are the major duties. There are four categories of them. Saint Matthew has listed them as: duties to God (Matthew 6); duties to ourselves (Matthew 5:29–30); duties to our neighbor (Matthew 7:12); and duties to all God's creatures (Matthew 6:20, 25). As for other duties, the bishop found them listed and prescribed in other places; those of sovereigns and subjects in the Epistle to the Romans; those of magistrates, wives, mothers, and young men by Saint Peter; those of husbands, children, and servants in the Epistle to the Ephesians; those of the faithful in the Epistle to the Hebrews; and those of virgins in the Epistle to the Corinthians. He was committed to the laborious task of bringing all these prescriptions together into one harmonious whole that he hoped to offer up for the souls of mankind.

He was still toiling away at eight o'clock, writing inconveniently enough on little squares of paper with a great big book open on his knees, when Madame Magloire came in, as was her wont, to take the silverware out of the cupboard by the bed. A moment later, the bishop sensed that the table was set and that his sister was perhaps waiting for him, so he closed his book, got up from his table, and went into the dining room.

The dining room was a long room with a fireplace and with a door that opened on to the street, as we said, and a window that opened onto the garden.

Madame Magloire was indeed just finishing laying the table. While going about her business, she was chatting with Mademoiselle Baptistine.

A lamp was sitting on the table and the table was near the fireplace. A pretty good fire had been lit.

You can easily imagine these two women, who were both over sixty now: Madame Magloire, small, fat, lively; Mademoiselle Baptistine, sweet, thin, frail, a bit taller than her brother, dressed in a puce-colored frock, a color in vogue in 1806 when she had bought it in Paris, and which was holding up well. To borrow one of those vulgar phrases that have the merit of expressing in a single word ideas that can scarcely be expressed in a page, Madame Magloire had the look of a peasant and Mademoiselle Baptistine of a lady. Madame Magloire was wearing a banded white bonnet, a little gold chain with a cross known as a *jeannette* around her neck, the only article of women's jewelry in the house, a bright white shawl known as a fichu peeking out of a homespun black dress with short wide sleeves, a red and green checked cotton apron, tied at the waist with a green ribbon, with a similar bodice piece, a stomacher, pinned up at the top at both corners; on her feet she wore clunky shoes and yellow stockings like the women of Marseilles. Mademoiselle Baptistine's dress was cut along the lines of 1806 models, with a short waist, narrow skirt, sleeves with padded shoulders, and with plackets and buttons. She hid her gray hair under a curly wig in the style known as *à l'enfant*. Madame Magloire looked intelligent, sharp, and good; the corners of her mouth were crooked when she smiled and her top lip was fatter than her bottom lip, which made her look somewhat obdurate and imperious. While Monseigneur remained silent, she hammered at him relentlessly with a mixture of familiarity and respect; but as soon as he opened his mouth, as we've seen, she became as meekly docile as Mademoiselle. Mademoiselle Baptistine did not even speak. She simply knuckled under, quietly complying. Even when young she had not been pretty. She had big blue eyes bulging out of her head and a long hooked beak. But her whole face, her whole person, as we said at the beginning, exuded ineffable goodness. She had been predestined to generous indulgence; but faith, hope, and charity, those three virtues that gently warm the soul, had gradually elevated this indulgence to saintliness. Nature had made her a mere sheep; religion had made her an angel. Poor saintly spinster! Sweet memory now vanished!

Mademoiselle Baptistine told what happened at the bishop's place that night so many times afterward that there are still people living who remember it down to the last detail.

When the bishop came in, Madame Magloire was talking somewhat animatedly, discoursing with Mademoiselle on a familiar subject to which the bishop was long accustomed. This concerned the latch on the front door.

It seems that while Madame Magloire was out shopping for supper, she had picked up a few things in various places. There was talk of a bad-looking prowler; of how a dubious-looking tramp had popped up out of nowhere and was lurking in town somewhere and how you wouldn't want to run into him in a dark alley if you were foolish enough to come home late that night. How the police were totally useless, to boot, given that the prefect of police and the mayor hated each other and tried to do each other harm by staging incidents to show the other up. How it was accordingly up to sensible people to be their own police and to protect themselves and to make doubly sure that their houses were duly shuttered, bolted, and barricaded and to make doubly sure the doors were securely locked.

Madame Magloire stressed those last words; but the bishop had just come from his room where he had been rather cold, so he went and sat in front of the fire to warm up and then started thinking about something else. He didn't hear a word of what Madame Magloire had let slip. She repeated it. Then, Mademoiselle Baptistine, wanting to satisfy Madame Magloire without annoying her brother, timidly ventured to say:

"My dear brother, did you hear what Madame Magloire was saying?"

"I heard something vaguely," he replied.

Then he turned his chair half round and put his hands on his knees, and raising his friendly, good-humored face, lit from below by the fire, to his old servant, he said:

"Come on, what is it? What is it? Are we in mortal danger, then?"

So Madame Magloire told her story all over again, unwittingly exaggerating here and there. It appeared that some bohemian, some barefoot gypsy, a dangerous beggar of a man was in town at that actual moment. He had turned up for bed and board at Jacquin Labarre's but Labarre had refused to take him in. He'd been seen arriving by the boulevard Gassendi and prowling about the streets at dusk. A man with a pack and a rope and a terrible face.

"You don't say?" said the bishop.

This willingness to question her encouraged Madame Magloire; it seemed to her to indicate that the bishop was not far from being alarmed himself and so she went on, triumphantly:

"Yes, Monseigneur, that's the size of it. Something awful will happen in town tonight. Everybody says so. Add to that, the police are less than useless [a useful repetition]. Fancy living in the mountains and not even having street-lamps! You go out. It's black as the ace of spades, for heaven's sake! So I say, Monseigneur, and Mademoiselle also says—"

"Me?" the sister interrupted. "I say nothing. Whatever my brother does is the right thing to do."

Madame Magloire continued as though she had not heard this protest.

"We both say that this house is not a bit safe; that, if Monseigneur will let me, I'll go and tell Paulin Musebois, the locksmith, to come and put the old locks back on the door; they're just over there, it'll only take a minute. And I say we must have locks, Monseigneur, if only for tonight; you see, I say that a door that opens from outside with just a latch that anyone can open, well, nothing could be more dreadful. Add to that the fact that Monseigneur is in the habit of always telling people to come in—even in the middle of the night. Heaven help us! They don't even need to ask permission—"

At that very moment, a loud knock was heard at the door.

"Come in," said the bishop.

### III. The Heroism of Passive Obedience

The door opened.

It opened suddenly, wide, as though someone had given it a vigorous and determined shove.

A man entered.

We know this man already. It was the traveler we saw a moment ago wandering around in search of a place to stay.

He came in, took a step, then stopped, leaving the door open behind him. He had his bag over his shoulder, his stick in his hand, and a rugged, reckless, tired, and violent look in his eyes. The fire in the grate shone on him. He was awful. It was a sinister apparition.

Madame Magloire did not even have the strength to utter a cry. She stood trembling with her mouth hanging open.

Mademoiselle Baptistine turned round, saw the man come in, and half-rose with shock, then, slowly turning her head back to the fireplace, she took a good look at her brother and her face became once more profoundly calm and serene.

The bishop fixed a tranquil eye on the man.

He was about to open his mouth, no doubt to ask the newcomer what he wanted, when the man leaned on his stick with both hands and let his eyes wander over the old man and each of the two women in turn and, without waiting for the bishop to speak, said in a loud voice: "All right. My name is Jean Valjean. I'm a convict. I've spent nineteen years in the clink. I've been free for four days and I'm on my way to Pontarlier, which is where I'm aiming. Four days I've been walking since Toulon.[1] Today, I've done twelve leagues on foot. This evening when I got to this place, I went to an inn and I was sent packing because of my yellow passport,[2] which I showed them at the *mairie*. I had to do that. I went to another inn. They said to me: Get lost! At the first place, at the other place. No one would have me. I went to the jail, the doorkeeper wouldn't open. I was in a dog kennel. The dog bit me and chased me away like it was a man. You'd have thought it knew who I was. I went into the fields to sleep under the stars. There were no stars. I reckoned it was going to rain and that there was no good Lord to stop it from raining, so I came back to town to try and find a doorway. Here, in the square, I was about to lie down on a stone. A good old biddy showed me your house and told me: Knock there. I knocked. What is this place? Are you an inn? I've got money, my life savings. One hundred and nine francs fifteen sous that I earned in the clink working for nineteen years. I'll pay. What do I care? I've got money. I'm very tired, twelve leagues on foot, I'm very hungry. Is it all right with you if I stay?"

"Madame Magloire," said the bishop, "set one more place."

The man took three steps and went over to the lamp that was on the table.

"Listen," he continued, as if he had not quite understood, "it's not like that. Didn't you hear me? I'm a galley slave. A convict. I come from the galleys."

He pulled out of his pocket a large sheet of yellow paper, which he unfolded.

"Here's my passport. Yellow, as you can see for yourself. This serves to get me kicked out everywhere I go. Would you like to read it? I can read, you know. I learned in the clink. There's a school for anyone who wants to learn. Look, here's what they put on the passport: 'Jean Valjean, freed convict, a native of'—you don't need that bit—'has spent nineteen years in jail. Five years for breaking and entering. Fourteen years for trying to escape four times. This man is extremely dangerous.' There! Everybody's kicked me out. Would *you* put me up? Is this an inn? Would you give me something to eat and a place to sleep? Do you have a stable?"

"Madame Magloire," said the bishop, "put clean sheets on the bed in the alcove."

We have already explained the absolute nature of both women's obedience.

Madame Magloire went out to carry out her orders.

The bishop turned to the man.

"Monsieur," he said, "sit down and get warm. We'll have supper shortly and your bed will be made up while you're eating."

At that, the man finally understood. The expression on his face, till then glum and hard, shifted from stupefaction to doubt, then to joy, and finally became extraordinary. He started to stammer like a madman: "True? You mean it! You mean you'll keep me? You're not chasing me away? A convict! And you call me *monsieur*! You don't talk down to me! Get lost, you cur! everybody else always says. I really thought you'd send me packing. So I told you straight out who I was. Oh, that fine woman who sent me here! I'm going to have supper! And a bed! A bed with a mattress and sheets! Like everyone else! I haven't slept in a bed for nineteen years! You really don't want me to go! You are wonderful people! Anyhow, I've got the money. I'll pay well. Pardon me, Monsieur innkeeper, what's your name? I'll pay all you want. You're a good man. You are an innkeeper, aren't you?"

"I," said the bishop, "am a priest and I live here."

"A priest!" the man went on. "Oh! A priest and a good man! Does that mean you don't want money from me? You'd be the curé, isn't that right? The curé of that big church? Right, of course! I'm such an idiot! I didn't see your skullcap!"

While he was speaking, he had put his sack and his stick down in a corner, put his passport back in his pocket, and sat down. Mademoiselle Baptistine was studying him sweetly. He continued:

"You are humane, Monsieur curé. You don't have contempt. A good priest really is a good thing. So you don't need me to pay?"

"No," said the bishop. "Hold on to your money. How much do you have? Didn't you tell me a hundred and nine francs?"

"Fifteen sous," the man added.

"A hundred and nine francs fifteen sous. And how long did it take you to earn that?"

"Nineteen years."

"Nineteen years!"

The bishop let out a deep sigh.

The man went on: "I've still got all my money. In four days, I've only spent the twenty-five sous I earned helping unload carts in Grasse. Since you're an abbé, I'll tell you, we had a chaplain in jail. And then one day I saw a bishop. Monseigneur, he was called. It was the bishop of the Majore, in Marseilles.[3] He's the curé who's above the other curés. You know, sorry, I'm not saying that right, but you know, for me, it's all so far away!—you know what we're like, us lot! He said mass in the middle of the jail, at an altar; he had a pointed thing, gold, on his head.[4] In the heat of the day, it shone like blazes. We were in rows, on three sides, with the cannons, their wicks lit, facing us. We couldn't see too well. He said something but he was too far back, we couldn't hear. So that's a bishop for you."

While he was speaking, the bishop had gone to shut the door, which had remained wide open.

Madame Magloire returned. She was carrying a plate, which she placed on the table.

"Madame Magloire," said the bishop, "put that plate as close to the fire as possible." And then, turning to his guest: "The night wind is bitterly cold in the Alps. You must be cold, Monsieur?"

Every time he said that word *monsieur* in his gently grave yet so very companionable voice, the man's face lit up. *Monsieur* to a convict is a glass of water to a man shipwrecked on the *Medusa*.[5] Ignominy is thirsty for respect.

"Now here's a lamp," the bishop went on, "that does not give much light."

Madame Magloire understood and immediately went and fetched the two silver candlesticks from the mantelpiece in Monseigneur's bedroom and placed them on the table with the candles lit.

"Monsieur curé," said the man, "you are goodness itself. You don't despise me. You take me into your home. You light your candles for me. Even though I didn't hide from you where I've been or the fact that I'm a poor cursed man."

The bishop was sitting next to him and he gently touched his hand. "You didn't have to tell me who you were. This is not my house, it's the house of Jesus Christ. That door does not ask who enters whether he has a name, but whether he has any pain. You are suffering, you are hungry and thirsty; you are welcome. And don't thank me, don't tell me I'm taking you into my home. No one is at home here except the man who is in need of a refuge. I'm telling you, who are passing through, you are more at home here than I am myself. Everything here is at your disposal. What do I need to know your name for? Besides, before you told me your name, you had one I knew."

The man opened his eyes in amazement.

"True? You knew what I was called?"

"Yes," replied the bishop. "You are called my brother."

"Listen, father!" cried the man. "I was as hungry as a wolf before I came here; but you are so good, that, now, I don't know what's hit me; it's gone."

The bishop looked at him and said:

"You have suffered a lot?"

"Oh! The red *paletot*,[6] the ball-and-chain at your feet, a plank to sleep on, the heat, the cold, hard labor, the galleys, the stick! Double shackles for nothing. The dungeon for a word. Even sick in bed, the chain. Dogs, dogs are better off! Nineteen years! I'm forty-six. And now I've got a yellow passport! There."

"Yes," the bishop said, "you have come from a place of sadness. Listen. There will be more joy in heaven over the tearful face of a repentant sinner than over the white robes of a hundred righteous men. If you come out of such a painful place full of hate and rage against men, you are worthy of pity; if you come out full of goodwill, gentleness, and peace, you are worth more than any of us."

Meanwhile Madame Magloire had served supper. A supper composed of water, oil, bread and salt, a bit of bacon, a chunk of mutton, figs, a *fromage frais*, and a large loaf of rye bread. She had taken it upon herself to add to the bishop's normal meal a bottle of old wine from Mauves.

The bishop's face immediately took on that expression of gaiety peculiar to hospitable natures: "Let's eat!" he said brightly. As he was accustomed to doing whenever a stranger dined with him, he sat the man on his right. Mademoiselle Baptistine, perfectly peaceful and natural, took her place at his left.

The bishop said grace, then himself served the soup as was his wont. The man began to gulp it down.

Suddenly the bishop said: "But it seems to me there's something missing from the table."

Madame Magloire had, in fact, only laid out the three place settings strictly necessary. Well, it was the custom of the house that when the bishop had someone to supper, the complete set of six silver place settings were laid out on the tablecloth in an innocent display. This gracious semblance of luxury was a kind of childish game all the more lovable in this sweet austere household that turned poverty into an art of great dignity.

Madame Magloire knew exactly what he was getting at, turned on her heel without a word, and a moment later the three extra place settings required by the bishop were gleaming on the tablecloth, symmetrically arranged in front of each of the three guests.

## IV. The Cheesemakers of Pontarlier

Now, to give you an idea of what happened at the table, we can't think of anything better than transcribing a letter from Mademoiselle Baptistine to Madame de Boischevron in which the conversation of the convict and the bishop is narrated with guileless meticulousness.

> ... The man paid no attention to anyone. He ate voraciously, as if he were starving. But after the soup, he said: "Monsieur le curé of the good Lord, all this is still far too good for me, but I must tell you the cart drivers who didn't want me to eat with them live better than you do."
>
> Just between us, the remark shocked me a little. My brother replied: "They are a lot tireder than I am."
>
> "No," the man went on, "they have more money. You are poor. I can see that pretty clearly. Maybe you're not even a curé? Are you a curé, even? Ah, for crying out loud, if the good Lord was just, you'd be a curé for sure."
>
> "The good Lord is more than just," my brother said.
>
> A moment later he added: "Monsieur Jean Valjean, is it Pontarlier you are going to?"

"The itinerary is compulsory."

I'm fairly sure that's what the man said. Then he went on: "I have to be on the road tomorrow at the crack of dawn. Travel's hard. The nights may be cold but the days are hot."

"Where you are going," my brother said, "is fine country. In the Revolution, my family was ruined. I took refuge in Franche-Comté to start with and I lived there for a time by laboring with my bare hands. I was willing and able. I found plenty to occupy myself. There's plenty to choose from. There are paper mills, tanneries, distilleries, big clock factories, steel mills, copper foundries, at least twenty iron foundries—four of them at Lods, Châtillon, Audincourt, and Beure are very big concerns—"

I think I'm not mistaken and that those are the names my brother mentioned. He then stopped and turned to me: "My dear sister, don't we have relatives around there somewhere?"

I answered: "We did have; among others Monsieur de Lucenet, who was captain of the old city gates at Pontarlier under the ancien régime."

"Yes," my brother went on, "but in '93 no one had relatives anymore, we only had our bare hands. I labored. What they have in the countryside around Pontarlier, where you are going, Monsieur Valjean, is an industry that's completely family-run and absolutely delightful, my dear sister. I'm talking about their cheese dairies, which they call *fruitières*."

So then my brother, all the while getting the man to eat more, explained to him in great detail what these Pontarlier *fruitières* were, how they were divided into two types: the big barns, which are for the rich, and where there are forty or fifty cows that produce seven or eight thousand cheeses a summer; and the *fruitières d'association* or associated dairies, which are for the poor; these are the peasants of the mid-mountain area who pool their cows and share the produce. They hire a cheesemaker that they call a *grurin*. The *grurin* is brought the associates' milk three times a day and he notes the quantities in duplicate. Toward the end of April the work in the dairies begins and toward mid-June the cheesemakers take their cows up into the mountains.

The man picked up again as he ate. My brother gave him some of the good Mauves wine that he doesn't drink himself because he says it's too dear. My brother gave him all these details with that easygoing cheeriness you've seen in him, stopping now and then to graciously make a fuss of me. He kept coming back all the time to the job of being a *grurin*, as though he were hoping that the man realized, without giving him hard advice directly, that this would be a refuge for him. One thing struck me. The man was what I told you he was. Well! During the meal and throughout the evening, my brother did not once say anything, apart from a few words about Jesus when he first arrived, that would remind the man who he was or reveal to the man who my brother was. On the surface, it was a perfect occasion to get in a bit of a sermon and for the bishop to lean on the galley slave in order to give him something to think about. Anyone else, if he had had this poor unfortunate in his hands, might have seen it as an opportunity to feed the man's soul at the same time as his body and to deliver a reprimand seasoned with morality and advice, or else a touch of commiseration with the exhortation to behave himself better in future. My brother did not even ask him what part of the country he was from or about his history. For in his history lies his crime and my brother seemed to avoid anything that might remind him of that. It got to the point at a certain moment, while my brother was talking about the mountain folk of Pontarlier who have "sweet work close to the heavens" and who, he added, "are happy because they are innocent," where he stopped short, fearing that in that word that had escaped his lips there was something that could rub the man the wrong way. Having thought about it quite a bit, I think I know what was going through my brother's mind. He no doubt thought that this man, whose name is Jean Valjean, was only too well aware of his misery, that the best thing to do was to distract him from it and to make him believe, if only for a moment, that he was a man like any other, by being perfectly normal with him. Indeed, isn't that what charity is, properly called? Isn't there, my good madame, something truly evangelical in the sort of delicacy that abstains from sermons, moral lessons, allusions, and isn't the highest form of pity, when a man has a sore spot, not to touch it at all? It seemed to me that this might well have been what my brother was thinking in his heart of hearts. In any case, what I can say is that, if he did have all these ideas, he didn't let on for a moment, not even to me. From start to finish, he was the same as he always is, every night, and he dined with this Jean Valjean the same way and acted just the same as if he were dining with Monsieur Gédéon Le Prévost or with the parish priest.

Toward the end, as we were up to the figs, someone banged on the door. It was mother Gerbaud with her little one in her arms. My brother kissed the child on the forehead and borrowed fifteen sous I had on me to give to mother Gerbaud. While this was going on the man didn't pay much attention. He had stopped talking and looked extremely tired. Once poor old mother Gerbaud had gone, my brother gave thanks for the meal and then turned to the man and said to him: "You must be in great need of your bed." Madame Magloire swiftly removed his plate and I realized we were supposed to retire and let the traveler get some sleep, so we both went upstairs, but I sent Madame Magloire back down an instant later with a deerskin from the Black Forest that is in my room to put on the man's bed. The nights are icy cold and it keeps you warm. It's a pity the skin is old; it is losing all its hair. My brother bought it in the days when he was in Germany, at Tottlingen, near the source of the Danube, along with the little ivory-handled knife I use at table.

Madame Magloire came back up almost immediately, we set to praying to God in the room where we hang the washing, and then we each went to our rooms without a word.

## V. TRANQUILLITY

After saying good night to his sister, Monseigneur Bienvenu took one of the silver candlesticks from the table, handed the other to his guest, and said to him: "Monsieur, I'll show you to your room."

The man followed him.

As you may have gathered from what was said earlier, the abode was so laid out that, to get into the oratory where the alcove was and to go out of it, you had to go through the bishop's bedroom.

Just as they were crossing this room, Madame Magloire was locking the silver in the cupboard at the head of the bed. It was the last chore she completed each night before retiring.

The bishop set his guest up in the alcove. A bed with fresh white sheets had been made up. The man placed the candlestick on a small table.

"Well, then," said the bishop, "have a good night. Tomorrow morning before you leave you will have a cup of milk from our cows, nice and hot."

"Thank you, Monsieur abbé," said the man.

Scarcely had he said those words full of peace than suddenly and without any transition, he made a strange movement that would have chilled the two saintly women to the bone with horror if they had witnessed it. Even now it is hard for us to grasp what was driving him at that moment. Was he trying to issue a warning or to launch a threat? Was he simply obeying some sort of instinctive impulse obscure even to himself? He suddenly turned to the old man, folded his arms, and fixing his host with a savage glare, cried out in a hoarse voice: "Hah! I don't believe it! You're putting me up at your place, right next to you, just like that!"

He broke off and added with a laugh that held something monstrous: "Have you really thought about this? Who's to say I'm not a murderer?"

The bishop raised his eyes to the ceiling and answered: "That is the good Lord's concern."

Then, gravely, and moving his lips as though he were praying or talking to himself, he raised the two fingers of his right hand and blessed the man, who did not bow his head, and without turning his head and without looking back, he went back to his bedroom.

Whenever there was someone staying in the alcove, a big heavy serge curtain was drawn from one side of the oratory to the other, and it hid the altar. The bishop knelt before this curtain in passing and said a short prayer.

A moment later, he was in his garden, strolling, dreaming, contemplating, heart and soul wholly occupied with the great mysteries that God reveals at night to those whose eyes remain open.

As for the man, he really was so tired that he did not even enjoy the nice white sheets. He had blown out the candle by snorting through one nostril the way convicts do and dropped onto the bed fully clothed, and in an instant he was fast asleep.

Midnight rang out as the bishop left the garden and went back into his apartment.

A few minutes later everyone in the little house was sound asleep.

## VI. JEAN VALJEAN

In the middle of the night, Jean Valjean woke up.

Jean Valjean was from a poor peasant family from Brie.[1] As a child he had not learned to read. When he reached adulthood, he became a tree pruner in Faverolles. His mother's name was Jeanne Mathieu, his father's name was Jean Valjean or Vlajean, probably a nickname, a contraction of "voilà Jean."[2]

Jean Valjean was thoughtful without being glum, which is typical of affectionate natures. All in all, though, there was something rather sleepy and insignificant, in appearance at least, about Jean Valjean. He had lost his mother and his father when he was very young. His mother died after childbirth of a bout of milk fever that was not properly treated. His father, a pruner like him, died when he fell from a tree. All that remained to Jean Valjean was his sister, who was older than he was, a widow with seven children, girls and boys. This sister had brought Jean Valjean up and, while her husband was still alive, she had lodged and fed her younger brother. Then the husband died. The eldest of the seven children was eight years old, the youngest, one. Jean Valjean had just turned twenty-four. He took the father's place and in turn supported this sister who had brought him up. This was done automatically, as a duty, and even with a certain gruffness on Jean Valjean's part. His youth was thus spent in hard and badly paid labor. He had never been known to have a "sweetheart" in the region. He had never had the time to fall in love.

At night he came home tired out and ate his soup without a word. While he ate, his sister, mother Jeanne, would often take out the best bits of his meal from his bowl—the chunk of meat, the strip of bacon, the cabbage heart—to give to one of her children. He would go on eating, hunched over the table with his head practically in the soup, his long hair falling around the soup bowl, hiding his eyes. He behaved as though he didn't see a thing and did nothing to stop it. There was in Faverolles, not far from the Valjeans' cottage, on the other side of the lane, a farmer's wife named Marie-Claude. The Valjean children, who were always starving, sometimes went to "borrow" a pint of milk from Marie-Claude on their mother's behalf, which they then guzzled behind a hedge or in some corner of the alley, snatching the pot away from one another so greedily that the little girls would spill some on their smocks and down their gullets. If the

mother had known about this pilfering, she would have chastised the delinquents severely. Jean Valjean, brusque and gruff as he was, paid for Marie-
Claude's pint of milk behind their mother's back and the children went
unpunished.

In the pruning season, he made twenty-four sous a day;[3] after that he would
hire himself out as a harvester, as an unskilled worker, as a farmhand or
cowherd, as any kind of casual laborer. He did what he could. His sister worked,
too, but what can you do with seven children? They were a sad bunch, enveloped by a poverty that was slowly squeezing them dry. One winter was particularly rough. Jean had no work. The family had no bread. No bread. Literally.
Seven children!

One Sunday night, Maubert Isabeau, the baker on the church square in
Faverolles, was getting ready to go to bed when he heard a loud crash and the
sound of breaking glass at the barred window of his shop. He arrived just in
time to see an arm shooting through the hole punched into the wire-meshed
glass. The hand at the end of the arm grabbed a loaf of bread and the thief made
off with it. Isabeau rushed out; the thief was running away as fast as his legs
would carry him. Isabeau ran after him and stopped him. The thief had
chucked the loaf of bread but his arm was still bleeding. It was Jean Valjean.

This happened in 1795. Jean Valjean was brought before the court of the
day for "breaking and entering an inhabited house at night." He had a gun,
which he could use better than any marksman in the world, and he was something of a poacher and that went against him. There is a legitimate prejudice
against poachers. The poacher, like the smuggler, verges a little too closely on
the out-and-out crook. And yet, we might just say in passing, there is still a gulf
between this species of men and the murderous city-dwelling criminal. The
poacher lives in the forest; the smuggler lives in the mountains or by the sea.
Cities turn out ferocious men because they make men corrupt. The mountains,
the sea, the forest, make men wild. They bring out the fierce side of human nature but often without destroying the human side.

Jean Valjean was found guilty. The terms of the code were categorical.
There are some fearful moments in our civilization; these are the moments
when a sentence delivers a verdict of shipwreck. What a mournful instant it is
when society withdraws and consummates the irreparable abandonment of a
sentient being! Jean Valjean was condemned to five years in the galleys.

On April 22, 1796, Paris resounded with the hue and cry over the victory
of Montenotte,[4] carried by the commander in chief of the Army of Italy, whom
the message from the Directoire to the Five Hundred,[5] dated Floréal 2, Year IV,[6]
called Buona-Parte; that same day a great human chain was shackled together
at Bicêtre prison.[7] Jean Valjean was part of that chain. An old prison doorman,
who is close to ninety years old today, still remembers perfectly the poor

wretch who was put in irons at the end of the fourth row in the north corner of the courtyard. This man was sitting on the ground like the rest of them. He appeared not to comprehend anything about his situation, except that it was awful. Most likely he also made out, through all the hazy notions of a poor and completely ignorant man, something excessive in it. As they were riveting the bolt of his collar shackle with great whacks of the hammer at the back of his neck, he wept, he choked on tears that prevented him from speaking; the only thing he managed to get out from time to time was: "I was a pruner in Faverolles." Then, sobbing all the while, he raised his right hand and lowered it gradually seven times as though patting seven heads at different heights and through this gesture you could guess that whatever it was he had done, he had done it to feed and clothe seven small children.

He left for Toulon. He arrived there after a journey of twenty-seven days, on a cart, with the chain at his neck. In Toulon he was dressed in a red smock known as a *paletot*. Everything about his life was erased, right down to his name; he was no longer even Jean Valjean, he was number 24601. What became of his sister? What became of the seven children? Who was going to worry about that? What becomes of the handful of leaves from the yellow tree sawn off at its base?

It's the same old story. These poor living beings, God's creatures, now without support, without a guide, without shelter, drifted off aimlessly, scattered on the wind, who knows? each on their own, perhaps, plunging further and further into the cold mist that swallows up solitary destinies, an opaque gloom into which so many luckless people disappear, one after the other, in the solemn march of the human race. They left their home county. The bell tower of what was once their village forgot them; the boundary of what was once their field forgot them; after a few years' sojourn in jail, Jean Valjean himself forgot them. In that heart where there once was a wound, was now a scar. That is all. During the whole time he was in Toulon he had only once heard talk of his sister. It was, I think, toward the end of his fourth year of captivity. I no longer remember through what channel the news reached him. Someone, who had known them back home, had seen his sister. She was in Paris. She lived in a mean street near Saint-Sulpice,[8] the rue du Gindre. She had only one child with her by then, a little boy, the baby of the bunch. Where were the other six? She herself, perhaps, did not know. Every morning she went to a printer's in the rue du Sabot, no. 3, where she was a folder and stitcher. She had to be there at six in the morning, well before daybreak in winter. In the same building as the printing works there was a school and she took her little boy, who was seven there. Only, as she started work at six o'clock, and the school did not open till seven, the child had to wait for an hour, in the courtyard, for the school to open an hour in the dark in winter in the open air! They wouldn't let the boy come into the printer's because he got in the way, they said. As they passed by of morning, the workers would see the poor little mite sitting on the cobblestones, nodding off to sleep and sometimes sound asleep in the dark, crouched and curled up over his basket. When it rained, an old lady, the concierge, would take pity on him; she would take him into her shabby squat, where there was nothing but a pallet, a spinning wheel, and two wooden chairs, and the little boy would sleep there in a corner, cuddling up to the cat for warmth. At seven o'clock, the school would open and in he would go. That is what someone told Jean Valjean. They spoke to him about it, one day, and just for a moment, there was a flash of lightning, like a window suddenly opening on the destiny of these creatures he had loved, then everything shut again; he never heard another word about them again, not ever. Nothing further about them ever reached him; he never saw them again, never ran into them, and for the rest of this painful story, we will not stumble across them again.

Toward the end of this fourth year, Jean Valjean's turn to escape arrived. His inmate pals helped him as they do in such sad places. He escaped. He wandered about for two days, free, in the fields; if you can call it being free to be hunted down, to whip your head round at every instant, to start at the slightest noise, to be frightened of anything and everything, of smoke coming from a roof, of a man passing by, of a dog, of a galloping horse, of the sound of the hour striking, of daylight because you can see, of night because you can't see, of the road, the path, the bushes, of sleep. The night of the second day he was nabbed again. He had not eaten or slept for thirty-six hours. The maritime court sentenced him for this felony to a further three years, which gave him eight years. The sixth year, it was his turn to escape again; he took it, but he was not able to consummate his flight. He had missed roll call. A cannon was fired and that night the men on patrol found him hiding under the keel of a boat that was being built. He resisted the guards who seized him. Escape and resisting arrest—this infraction was dealt with by the provisions of the special code; the punishment was an increase of five years, two of them in double chains. Thirteen years. The tenth year, his turn came again, he took advantage of it again. But he did not make a better go of it this time, either. Three years for this latest attempt. Sixteen years. Finally, it was, I think, during the thirteenth year that he tried one last time, succeeding only in being caught again after a mere four hours on the outside. Three years he copped for those four hours. Nineteen years. In October 1815 he was released; he had gone in in 1796 for having broken a windowpane and taken a loaf of bread.

This is the place for a short parenthesis. This is the second time, in his study of the penal issue and of damnation by the law, that the author of this book has come across the theft of a loaf of bread as the point of departure for the destruction of someone's life. Claude Gueux[9] stole a loaf of bread; Jean Valjean stole a loaf of bread. British statistics show that in London four out of five thefts have hunger as their immediate cause.

Jean Valjean had gone to jail sobbing and shaking; he came out impassive. He had gone in desperate; he came out grim.

What had gone on in his soul?

## VII. Despair from the Inside

Let's try to put it into words.

Society must look these issues in the face since it is society that produces them.

The man was, as we have said, an ignoramus; but he was not an imbecile. That inborn light was on inside—and there was somebody home. Tragedy, which sheds its own light, intensified the thin light of day that was in his mind. Under the bludgeon, under the chains, in solitary confinement, in exhaustion, under the harsh sun of jail, on the plank bed of the convict, he withdrew into his conscience and reflected.

He turned himself into judge and jury.

He began by passing judgment on himself.

He acknowledged that he was not an innocent man unjustly punished. He admitted to himself that he had committed an extreme and blameworthy act; that he might not have been refused the loaf of bread if he had asked for it; that, in any case, he should have waited for it to come to him either through pity or through work; that it is not altogether an unchallengeable comeback to say: Who can wait when they're hungry?; that, to start with, it is extremely rare to literally die of hunger; second, that, happily or unhappily, man is so constituted that he can suffer for a long time and a great deal, morally and physically, without dying; that he should accordingly have had patience; that this would have been a lot better even for the seven poor children; that it was an act of madness, on his part, poor puny man, to grab society as a whole violently by the throat and to imagine that a person could get out of dire poverty by theft; that, in any case, it was the wrong door for getting out of dire poverty that admitted a man into infamy; in a word, that he had been in the wrong.

Then he asked himself:

If he were the only one who had been in the wrong in his fateful story? If it wasn't a serious matter to start with that he, who was a worker, lacked work; that he, who was industrious, lacked bread. If, subsequently, with the wrong committed and confessed, the punishment hadn't been ferocious and wildly excessive. If there hadn't been more abuse on the part of the law than on the part of the one guilty of the wrong. If there hadn't been too much weight in one of the pans of the scales, the one for expiation. If the excess weight of the penalty did not wipe out the crime and did not end in this result: reversing the situation, replacing the wrong of the delinquent with the wrong of the crackdown on him turning the guilty party into the victim and the debtor into the creditor, and putting right squarely on the side of the very person who had violated it. If the sentence, complicated by the successive extensions of time for the escape attempts, did not wind up being a sort of assault by the strongest on the weakest, a crime committed by society against the individual, a crime that was committed afresh each day, a crime that went on for nineteen years.

He asked himself whether human society could have the right also to subject its members, on the one hand, to its crazy lack of foresight and, on the other, to its pitiless foresight, and to hold a poor man forever between a lack and an excess—lack of work and excess of punishment. If it were not outrageous that society dealt in this way precisely with those of its members who were the worst off in the parceling out of goods, which is the work of chance, and so, the most worthy of being handled with care.

These questions being put and resolved, he passed judgment on society and he condemned it.

He condemned it to his hate.

He made it responsible for the fate he suffered and told himself that he would quite likely not hesistate to call it to account for this one day. He said to himself that there was no balance between the damage he had done and the damage done to him; he finally concluded that his punishment was not, in all honesty, an injustice, but that it was without the shadow of a doubt an iniquity.

Rage can be wild and unfounded; you can be wrongfully stirred up. But you only feel outraged when you are fundamentally right to do so somewhere along the line. Jean Valjean felt outraged.

And then, human society had only ever done him harm. Never had he seen anything of it but this wrathful face that it calls Justice and that it shows to those it strikes. People had only ever touched him to wound him. All contact with them had been, for him, a blow. Never, since his childhood, since his mother, since his sister, never had he met with a kind word or a kind look. He had lurched from one suffering to the next and had gradually arrived at the conviction that life was a war; and that in this war he was the vanquished. He had no other weapon but his hate, and he resolved to hone it in jail and to take it with him when he got out.

There was in Toulon a school for the convicts run by the Ignorantine friars,[1] where those of the wretched inmates who had the will to learn were taught the bare essentials. He was one of the ones who wanted to learn. At the age of forty, he started school and learned to read, write, and do sums. He felt that to strengthen his knowledge was to strengthen his hate. In certain cases, instruction and enlightenment can serve to shore up the harm done.

It is sad to have to say it, but after having judged the society that had brought him undone, he passed judgment on the Providence that had brought about that society.

He condemned it, too.

And so, during those nineteen years of torture and slavery, this poor soul both rose and fell at the same time. Light entered on one side and darkness on the other.

Jean Valjean was not, as we have seen, naturally bad. He was still good when he arrived in jail. Inside, he wrote society off and felt himself turn wicked; inside, he wrote Providence off and felt himself turn impious.

At this juncture it is hard not to ponder a little.

Can human nature turn itself inside out like that, so completely? Can man, created good by God, be made wicked by man? Can the soul be entirely remade by destiny and become bad if that destiny is bad? Can the heart become warped and catch incurable diseases and turn ugly under the pressure of some abnormally great woe, the way the vertebral column becomes warped under a too-low ceiling? Isn't there in every human soul, wasn't there in the soul of Jean Valjean, in particular, an initial spark, a divine element, incorruptible in this world, immortal in the next, that good can bring out, prime, ignite, set on fire and cause to blaze splendidly, and that evil can never entirely extinguish?

Grave and obscure questions, to the last of which any physiologist would probably have answered no, and without hestitating, if he had seen—in Toulon, in hours of rest, which were for Jean Valjean hours of reverie, as he sat, arms crossed, on the bar of some capstan, the end of his chain stuffed in his pocket to stop it from dragging—this forlorn galley slave,[2] grave, silent, and pensive, a pariah of laws that look on man with anger, one of civilization's damned, who looked so harshly on the heavens.

Certainly, and we do not wish to pretend otherwise, the observant physiologist would have seen irremediable misery there, would perhaps have felt sorry for this man made sick by the law, but he would not even have attempted a cure; he would have averted his gaze from the bottomless pit he had glimpsed in that soul and, like Dante at the gates of hell, he would have erased from that existence the word that the finger of God nonetheless writes on the forehead of every man: *Hope!*

Was the state of mind that we have been trying to analyze as perfectly clear for Jean Valjean as we have tried to make it for our readers? Did Jean Valjean distinctly see, once they were formed, and had he distinctly seen, as they were forming, all the ingredients that went into his moral destitution? Did this uncouth illiterate really grasp the succession of ideas by which he had, step by step, climbed and slid down until he reached that mournful outlook that had for so many years now been the inner horizon of his mind? Was he fully conscious of all that had happened within him and all that stirred there? We would not dare say such a thing; we do not even think it. There was too much ignorance in Jean Valjean for him not to remain fairly unclear, even after so much misery. At times, he did not really know for sure what he felt. Jean Valjean was in darkness;

he suffered in darkness; he hated in darkness; you could say he hated whatever was in front of him. He lived constantly in such shadow, groping like a blind man or a dreamer. Only, at intervals, there would suddenly come to him, from within or from without, a gust of rage, an added burst of suffering, a pale and rapid flash of lightning that would illuminate his entire soul and would suddenly reveal all around him, before and behind, in the glare of a ghastly light, the awful sheer drops and grim overhangs of his fate.

Once the lightning had passed, night would fall once more, and where was he? He could no longer tell.

The peculiar feature of sentences of this kind, in which what is pitiless, meaning brutalizing, dominates, is to gradually transform a man into a wild animal through a sort of stupid transfiguration. Sometimes into a ferocious animal, at that. Jean Valjean's repeated and dogged attempts to escape are enough to prove how strangely the law worked on the human soul. Jean Valjean would have tried to break out again and gone on trying, however utterly crazy and pointless such attempts might be, as many times as the occasion presented itself, without thinking for an instant about the consequences or about his previous experiences. He escaped impulsively, like a wolf that finds its cage open. Instinct told him: Run! Reason would have told him: Stay! But faced with such a violent temptation, reason vanished; only instinct remained. The animal alone acted. When he was nabbed again, the new severities inflicted on him only served to make him wilder.

There is one detail that we should not leave out and this is that not one of the galley inmates could hold a candle to him in physical strength. In hard labor, for twisting a cable or turning a windlass, Jean Valjean was equal to four men. He would sometimes lift and carry enormous weights on his back and would occasionally himself replace the tool known as a *cric*, or jack, which used to be called an *orgueil*, or pride, from which, by the way, the name of the rue Montorgueil near Les Halles[3] in Paris derived. His inmate pals had nicknamed him Jean-le-Cric. Once, when the balcony of the Toulon *mairie* was being repaired, one of Puget's wonderful caryatids,[4] which support the balcony, came loose and was about to fall off. Jean Valjean, who happened to be there, propped the caryatid up by his shoulder, giving the workers time to get there.

His suppleness actually surpassed his strength. Certain convicts, who are always hatching escape plans, end up turning combined strength and skill into a veritable science—the science of muscles. A whole mysterious regimen of statics is practiced on a daily basis by prisoners, those eternal enviers of flies and birds. To scale a sheer vertical wall and find toeholds and handholds in places where you could barely see a bump was child's play for Jean Valjean. Give him a chunk of wall, and with the tension of his back and his knees, with his elbows and heels jammed into the rough edges of the stone, he would hoist himself up three stories, as though by magic. Sometimes he would climb up to the rooftop of the jail like this.

He said little. He never laughed. Some extreme emotion was required to wring out of him, once or twice a year, that lugubrious cackle of the convict, which is like the echo of a demon's laugh. To look at him, you would think he was busy staring endlessly at something terrible.

He was, in effect, absorbed.

Through the unhealthy perception of a stunted nature and an intelligence that had been laid to waste, he felt vaguely that something monstrous was sitting on his back. In the dim bleak haze in which he crawled, every time he craned his neck and tried to look up, he saw, with a mixture of terror and rage, piling up and looming in tiers that soared out of sight above him, with horrible sheer walls, a sort of horrifying heap of things, laws, prejudices, men, and deeds, whose contours escaped him, whose bulk terrified him, and which was nothing more than that prodigious pyramid we call civilization. Here and there he could make out, in this teeming, amorphous mass, now close up, now far away on inaccessibly high plains, some group, some detail sharply illuminated; here the guard with his truncheon, here the gendarme with his sword, over there the mitered bishop, and at the very top, in a sort of blaze of sunlight, the emperor, crowned and dazzling. It seemed to him that these remote splendors, far from dispelling his own darkness, made it all the more funereal and black. All that— laws, prejudices, deeds, men, things—was coming and going above him, according to the complex and mysterious movement God imparts to civilization, walking on top of him and crushing him with an unspeakably calm cruelty and remorseless indifference. Souls who have hit rock bottom as far as possible calamity goes, unhappy men lost in the depths of that limbo where no one looks anymore, the law's rejects feel the full weight on their heads of this human society, so forbidding if you are outside it, so terrifying if you are underneath it.

In this situation, Jean Valjean mused, and what do you think was the nature of his musings?

If the millet seed under the millstone had thoughts, it would doubtless think exactly what Jean Valjean thought.

All these things, realities full of phantoms, phantasmagoria full of realities, had ended up providing him with a sort of inner state you would be hard pressed to put into words.

At times, in the middle of his prison labors, he would stop . . . and think. His reason, at once more mature and more disturbed than before, would revolt. All that had happened to him seemed absurd; all that surrounded him did not seem possible. He told himself it was a dream. He looked at the guard standing a few feet away; the screw seemed like a phantom, yet suddenly the phantom would give him a whack with his truncheon.

The natural world scarcely existed for him. It would almost be true to say that for Jean Valjean, there was no sun, there were no lovely summer days, no radiant skies, no fresh April dawns. Only an awful thin light managed to reach him through the basement window of his soul.

By way of conclusion, to sum up what can be summed up and translated into concrete terms in all that we have just outlined, we will just say that, in nineteen years, Jean Valjean, the harmless tree pruner of Faverolles, the fearsome galley slave of Toulon, had become capable, thanks to the way the galleys had molded him, of two kinds of bad deed: first, some swift, unpremeditated act full of frenzy, performed entirely instinctively as a sort of reprisal for the wrong endured; second, some seriously criminal act, consciously debated and mulled over with the false notions such misery can give rise to. His premeditated ideas went through the three successive phases available only to natures of a certain cast: reasoning, will, determination. What moved him was habitual indignation, the bitterness in his soul, a profound sense of the iniquities he had been subject to, a reaction against even the good, the innocent, and the just, if such there be. The beginning and end of all his thoughts was the same: hatred of human law, the hatred that, if it is not nipped in the bud by some miraculous event, turns, within a certain time frame, into hatred of society, then hatred of the human race, then hatred of creation, and is translated into a vague and constant and brutal desire to do harm, to anyone at all, to any living being, whoever they may be.

So, as you can see, it was not for no reason that the passport described Jean Valjean as a very dangerous man.

Year by year, slowly but surely, his soul had dried up. Dry heart, dry eye. When he got out of jail, he had not shed a tear in nineteen years.

## VIII. The Dark and the Deep

Man overboard!

Who cares! The ship does not stop. The wind is blowing and that particular doom-laden ship has a course to keep. On it sails.

The man disappears, then reappears, he dives down and comes back to the surface, he calls out, he waves his arms around; no one hears him. The ship shudders in the gale, fully focused on its maneuvering, and the sailors and the passengers can't even see the submerged man anymore; his miserable head is just a dot in the vastness of the waves.

He hurls desperate cries out into the depths. The sail looks so ghostly as it vanishes into the distance! He watches it, he watches it for all he's worth. It is moving away, it is becoming faint, it is getting smaller. He was on that ship just a moment ago, he was part of the crew, he came and went on deck with the rest of them, he had his share of air, of sunlight, he was alive. What the hell happened? He slipped, he fell, and now, the jig's up.

He is in the monstrous waters with only their roiling and heaving beneath him. The waves are torn and ripped to shreds by the wind and close in on him sickeningly; the rolling abyss sweeps him away, all the tattered water whips around his head, a mob of waves spits at him, vague tunnels of water half-devour him; every time he goes under, he glimpses sheer drops of unfathomable darkness; weird unfamiliar plants seize him, bind his feet, pull him under; he feels himself becoming one with the abyss, he is part of the foam, the waves toss him from one to the other, he gulps down bitterness, the spineless ocean is raring to drown him, the vastness toys with him, dragging out his last gasps. All that water feels like liquid hate.

Yet he struggles, he tries to defend himself, he tries to keep going, he makes an effort, he swims. His pitiful strength immediately exhausted, he struggles against the inexhaustible.

Where can the ship have got to? Over there. Barely visible in the pale blur of the horizon.

Gusts of wind come up; each head of foam batters him. He looks up and all he sees is the lividness of the clouds. In his death throes, he witnesses the immense madness of the sea. He is tortured to death by this insanity. He hears sounds unfamiliar to man that seem to come from beyond the earth—from some unimaginable and awful otherworld.

There are birds in the thick cloud cover, just as there are angels hovering over human hardships, but what can they do for him? They fly, sing, and soar while he, he moans in agony.

He feels buried at once by those two infinities, the ocean and the sky; the one a grave, the other a shroud.

Night comes bearing down and he has been swimming for hours, his strength is almost gone; the ship, that distant speck where once there were men, has faded from view; he is alone in the dreadful crepuscular gulf, he goes under, he is getting stiff, he thrashes around, he feels the monstrous waves of the invisible below him, he calls out.

There are no men anymore. Where is God?

He calls and calls. Anyone! Anyone! He goes on calling. Nothing on the horizon. Nothing in the sky.

He implores the expanse stretching away, the waves, the seaweed, the rocks; they are all deaf. He pleads with the storm; the imperturbable storm obeys only infinity.

Around him, darkness, mist, solitude, the oblivious thundering tumult, the endless chaotic puckering and churning of the wild waters. Inside him, horror and fatigue. Under him, the drop. Nothing to hang on to, no foothold. He thinks of the murky adventures of his corpse falling through the limitless gloom. The bottomless cold paralyzes him. His hands clench and curl up and grasp at nothingness. Winds, clouds, whirlpools, gusts, useless stars! What can he do? The despairing give up, the weary decide to die, they stop resisting, they go with the flow, let go, and off they go, the drowned, rolling away forever in the gloomy depths of engulfment.

O relentless march of human society! All the men and souls lost along the way, written off! Ocean into which all those that the law drops, fall! Vile withdrawal of all help! O moral death!

The sea is that inexorable social darkness into which the penal system casts those it has damned. The sea is measureless misery.

The soul, drifting with the current in the plumbless deep, can turn into a corpse. Who will resuscitate it?

## IX. FRESH GRIEVANCES

When the time came for him to get out of jail, when Jean Valjean heard in his ear those strange words: *You are free!* the moment was unreal, unbelievable; a ray of blinding light, a ray of the real light of the living suddenly shot through him. But this light swiftly faded. Jean Valjean had been dazzled by the idea of freedom. He had believed in a new life. He very soon saw what kind of freedom a yellow passport entails.

And this brought much more bitter disillusionment. He had calculated that what he had saved during his stay in jail amounted to one hundred and seventy-one francs. To be fair, we should add that he had forgotten to include in his calculations the fact that Sundays and public holidays were compulsory days off, which, over nineteen years, meant deducting around twenty-four francs. On top of that his savings had been reduced by various local charges to the sum of one hundred and nine francs and fifteen sous, which had been counted out and handed over to him as he was leaving.

He did not understand any of this and believed himself to have been short-changed—let's not mince words, robbed.

The day after he was released, in Grasse, he saw some men unloading bales of orange blossom outside a distillery.[1] He offered his services. The job was urgent so they took him on. He set to work. He was smart, robust, and adroit; he did his best, and the foreman seemed happy. But while he was working, a gendarme came past, spotted him, and demanded to see his papers. He had to show his yellow passport. That done, Jean Valjean went back to work. A bit before this, he had quizzed one of the workers about the daily rate they earned for the job; they told him that it was thirty sous. That evening, since he was forced to head out the following morning, he turned up at the distillery foreman's and asked for his pay. The foreman didn't say a word, just handed him twenty-five sous. He demanded the rest. The foreman replied: "That's good enough for the likes of you." He stood his ground. The foreman looked him in the eyes and said: "Watch out you don't end up back inside!"

Once more, he considered himself robbed.

Society, the state, in diminishing his savings, had robbed him in a big way. Now it was the turn of the individual to rob him in a small way.

Release is not the same as liberation. You get out of jail, all right, but you never stop being condemned.

So that is what happened to him in Grasse. We have seen the welcome he was given in Digne.

## X. The Man Wakes Up

And so, as the cathedral clock struck two in the morning, Jean Valjean woke up.

What woke him up was that the bed was just too good. He had not gone to sleep in a bed for going on twenty years and although he had not taken his clothes off, the sensation was too novel not to disturb his sleep.

He had slept for over four hours. His weariness had passed. He was used to not giving many hours over to rest.

He opened his eyes and peered into the darkness around him for a while, then he closed them again to go back to sleep.

When your day has been teeming with different sensations, when you have things on your mind, you can get to sleep to start with but you can't get back to sleep. Sleep comes a lot more easily than it comes back. This was the case with Jean Valjean. He could not get back to sleep and he began to think.

He was in one of those states where our ideas get blurred. There was a sort of cloudy swirling in his brain. His old memories and his most immediate memories floated around pell-mell and bumped into each other at random, losing their shapes, becoming crazily magnified, then evaporating suddenly, like mud stirred up in a pool of water. Many thoughts came to him, but there was one that would not go away and that sent all the others scurrying. This thought we will tell you without further ado: He had spotted the six silver knives and forks and the silver ladle that Madame Magloire had laid on the table.

These six silver sets of cutlery obsessed him. They were just sitting there. A few feet away. The very moment he crossed the room next door to come into the room he was now in, the old servant had put them away in a cupboard at the head of the bed. He had, naturally, noted this cupboard. On the right, as you enter by the dining room. They were solid silver. And old silver, at that. For the ladle, you'd get at least two hundred francs. Double what he'd earned in nineteen years. True, he would have earned more if the "administration" hadn't "robbed him."

His mind wavered for a good hour, and his hesitation certainly involved some struggle. The clock struck three. He opened his eyes again, promptly sat up, shot out his arm, and groped for his haversack, which he had thrown into the corner of the alcove, then swung his legs over the side of the bed and placed his feet on the floor and found himself sitting up straight on the bed, not knowing how he'd got into that position.

He remained sitting there in that position, thinking, for some time, and anyone who'd seen him sitting there in the dark, the only person awake in the sleeping household, would have found him a sinister sight. Suddenly he bent down, took off his shoes, and put them gently on the mat beside the bed, then he resumed his position, sitting still and thinking.

In the middle of this vile rumination, the ideas we just mentioned kept stirring around in his brain, coming and going and coming back again, seemingly bearing down on him like a ton of bricks; and then, without knowing why, and with that automatic persistence of reverie, he thought at the same time about a convict named Brevet whom he had known in jail, and whose trousers used to be held up by a single brace of knitted cotton. The checked pattern of that brace kept coming back to him without letup.

He remained sitting there and would perhaps have stayed there like that until daybreak if the clock had not struck a single note—to mark the quarter hour or half hour. The clock seemed to say to him: Let's go!

He rose to his feet, hesitated a moment longer and listened; all was quiet in the house, so he headed straight for the window, which he could make out, taking small careful steps. The night was not very dark; there was a full moon with big clouds racing across it, chased by the wind. This produced bursts of light and dark outside, eclipses and lightning flashes, and inside, a sort of twilight. This twilight, enough to guide his path, intermittent because of the clouds, was like the livid light that falls from a basement window when people are coming and going outside. When he reached the window, Jean Valjean looked closely at it. It had no bars, it opened on to the garden, and it was shut, in keeping with the custom of these parts, with only a tiny latch. He opened it, but as cold, sharp air rushed in, he closed it again instantly. He looked at the garden with that penetrating gaze that sizes up more than it sees. The garden was enclosed by a fairly low white wall, easily scaled. Behind it, on the other side, he could make out the tops of trees evenly spaced, which indicated that the wall divided the garden from an avenue or lane planted with trees.

Having given the scene the once-over, he acted like a man who knows what he's doing, walked over to his alcove, grabbed his haversack, opened it, fumbled around inside, took out something that he placed on the bed, stuck his shoes in one of his pockets, did the bag up again, hoisted it onto his shoulders, clapped his cap on his head, jamming the peak down over his eyes, felt for his stick, and went and put it in the corner of the window, then returned to the bed and resolutely seized the object he had laid on it. It was a short iron bar, sharpened at one end like a hunting spear.

In the dark it would have been hard to work out what this piece of iron was made for. Was it perhaps a lever? Was it perhaps a club?

In daylight, you would have recognized that it was just an ordinary miner's spike. In those days convicts were sometimes put to work quarrying stone from the high hills that surround Toulon, and it was not unusual for them to carry around miners' tools. Miner's spikes were made of solid iron, with a point at the bottom end for hoeing into the rock.

He took this spike in his right hand and, holding his breath and treading softly, he headed for the door of the room next door, the bishop's room, as you'll recall. When he reached the door, he found it ajar. The bishop had not closed it.

## XI. What He Does Next

Jean Valjean listened. Not a sound.

He pushed the door.

He pushed it with one finger, lightly, with that furtive anxious restraint of a cat that wants to come inside.

The door yielded to the pressure, silently and imperceptibly opening the gap a little wider.

He waited a moment, then pushed the door again, more forcefully.

It continued to yield in silence. The gap was wide enough now for him to slip through. But near the door a small table was in the way, forming as it did a sort of awkward angle with the door.

Jean Valjean saw the problem. But he had to open the door wider no matter what.

He steeled his resolve and pushed the door a third time, more energetically. This time a badly oiled hinge suddenly sent out a prolonged and raucous screech into the darkness.

Jean Valjean jumped. The noise of the hinge rang in his ears, as resounding and terrible as the trumpet of the Last Judgment.

In the eerie amplification of that initial moment, he almost imagined that the hinge had come alive, suddenly taking on a terrible life of its own and barking a warning to the world like a dog rousing the sleeping from their slumber.

He stopped in his tracks, shivering, distraught, and tipped back from the balls of his feet onto his heels. He could hear his pulse thumping in his temples like a pair of sledgehammers, and it seemed to him that his breath came from his chest with the sound the wind makes rushing out of a cave. It seemed to him impossible that the horrible clamor of the outraged hinge had not shaken the whole house like the shock of an earthquake; the door, pushed by him, had taken fright and screamed; the old man would soon be up, the two old women would cry out, someone would come running to their aid; before a quarter of an hour was up, the town would be buzzing and the gendarmerie on the move. For a moment, he thought the jig was up.

He stayed where he was, petrified like the proverbial pillar of salt, not daring to make a move. Some minutes passed. The door was wide open now. He risked a peek at the room. Nothing had moved. He cocked an ear. Nothing in the house was stirring. The noise of the rusty hinge had woken no one.

This initial danger was over, but he still felt a dreadful turmoil inside. Yet he did not back down. Even when he had thought the jig was up, he had not backed down. His only thought now was to get it over with as quickly as possible. He stepped into the room. The room was perfectly still. Here and there various blurred shapes could vaguely be made out, which, by day, were papers scattered over the table, open folios, books piled on a stool, an armchair heaped with clothes, and a prie-dieu, but at this hour, they were no more than dark shadows and whitish spots. Jean Valjean crept forward carefully to avoid bumping into the furniture. At the back of the room he could hear the quiet, even breathing of the bishop, fast asleep.

Suddenly he stopped. He was on top of the bed before he knew it; it had taken no time at all.

Nature sometimes makes connections between our actions and its own special effects and star turns with a sort of somber and intelligent aptness, as though it wanted to make us sit up and think. For nearly half an hour, a huge cloud had covered the sky. The very moment Jean Valjean stopped, facing the bed, this cloud broke up as though it had done so on purpose and a ray of moonlight shot through the long window and suddenly lit up the bishop's pale face. He was sleeping peacefully, untroubled. Though in bed, he was almost fully dressed because of the bitterly cold nights of the Lower Alps, decked out in a brown woolen garment that covered his arms to the wrists. His head was thrown back against the pillow in the abandoned attitude of sleep; over the side of the bed his hand dangled, adorned with his pastoral ring—the hand that had performed so many good works and saintly deeds. His whole face was luminous with a vague expression of contentment, hope, and bliss. It was more than a smile, almost a radiance. On his forehead lay the ineffable reflection of a light invisible to the naked eye. The souls of the just in sleep contemplate a mysterious heaven.

A reflection of this heaven lay over the bishop.

It was at the same time a luminous transparency, for this heaven was inside him. This heaven was the internal light of his conscience.

At the moment that the moonlight superimposed itself, so to speak, on this inner limpidity, the sleeping bishop appeared bathed in glory. And yet that glory remained soft and veiled in an ineffable half-light. The moon in the sky, dozing nature, the garden so still, the house so calm, the hour, the moment, the silence, added something oddly solemn and moving to the venerable rest of this good man, and wrapped in a sort of majestic and serene aureole his white hair and those closed eyes, this face where all was hope and where all was trust, the head of an old man sleeping like a baby.

There was something almost divine about the man, so unself-consciously august was he.

Jean Valjean, on the other hand, was in the shadow, his iron spike in hand, standing erect, rigid, terrified at this luminous old man. He had never seen anything like it. Such trust horrified him. The moral world offers no greater sight than this: a troubled and overwrought conscience, brought to the brink of some evil deed, gazing upon the sleep of a just man.

Such sleep, in such isolation, with only the likes of him for company, had something sublime about it that he was dimly but powerfully aware of.

No one could have said what was happening inside him, not even himself. To try to grasp it, we need to imagine the most violent of men in the presence of the most gentle. Even on his face, you could not have made out anything distinct with any certainty. His expression was one of a sort of crazed amazement. He saw what he saw, and that was that. But what was he thinking? It would have been impossible to guess. What was obvious was that he was moved and deeply distressed. But what kind of emotion was that, exactly?

He couldn't take his eyes off the old man. The only thing that could clearly be discerned in his demeanor and on his countenance was a strange indecisiveness. You would have said he was hesitating on the brink of two yawning chasms, the one where you are lost and the one where you are saved—doom or salvation. He looked as though he was ready either to smash the old man's skull in or to kiss his hand.

After a few moments, Jean Valjean raised his left hand slowly to his forehead and took off his cap, then let his arm fall back just as slowly, and with that he retreated into his thoughts, his cap in his left hand, his club in his right, his hair standing up on end over his savage head.

The bishop went on sleeping in profound peace beneath this frightening stare.

A reflection of moonlight made the crucifix above the mantelpiece dimly visible; it seemed to be opening its arms to both of them, in benediction for the one and forgiveness for the other.

All of a sudden Jean Valjean clapped his cap back on his head, then strode to the head of the bed without giving the bishop another glance and straight to the cupboard, which he could make out next to the head of the bed; he raised the miner's spike as though he was about to force the lock. But the key was in it. So he turned it. The first thing he saw was the basket of silverware. He grabbed it, bounded across the room without worrying about the noise, whipped through the door, ran back to the oratory, shoved the window open, grabbed his stick, climbed over the windowsill, threw the silver into his knapsack, flung the basket away, raced across the garden, leaped over the wall like a tiger and fled.

## XII. THE BISHOP AT WORK

The next day at sunrise, Monseigneur Bienvenu was circling his garden. Madame Magloire ran to him, quite beside herself.

"Monseigneur, Monseigneur," she cried, "does Your Grace know where the silverware basket is?"

"Yes," said the bishop.

"God be praised!" she replied. "I didn't know what had happened to it."

The bishop had just picked the basket from out of a garden bed. He handed it to Madame Magloire.

"Here it is."

"But!" she said, flustered. "There's nothing in it! What about the silver?"

"Ah!" said the bishop. "So it's the silver you're worried about? I don't know where that is."

"Good God in heaven! It's been stolen! That man from last night! He's stolen it!"

In the blink of an eye, with all the sprightliness of a frisky old watchdog, Madame Magloire tore off to the oratory, into the alcove, and back again to the bishop. The bishop had just bent down, heaving a sigh, and was examining a cochlearia *des Guillons* that the basket had broken when it landed in the garden bed. He straightened up again at Madame Magloire's shriek.

"Monseigneur, the man's gone! The silver's been stolen!"

While she was yelling the news, her eyes fell on a corner of the garden where you could see traces of a scramble. A brick in the wall had been ripped out.

"Look! That's where he got away. He jumped over into the ruelle Cochefilet! Ah! The swine! He stole our silver on us!"

The bishop remained silent for a moment, then he looked up with a grave expression on his face and spoke softly to Madame Magloire: "To start with, was the silver really ours?"

Madame Magloire was flabbergasted. There was another silence and then the bishop went on: "Madame Magloire, I was wrong to hang on to that silver—and for so long. It belonged to the poor. What was that man? He was poor, evidently."

"God help us!" Madame Magloire retorted. "It's not me or Mademoiselle I'm worried about. We couldn't care less. It's Monseigneur. What is Monseigneur going to eat with now?"

The bishop looked at her in amazement.

"Ah, is that all! Don't we have any pewter cutlery?"

Madame Magloire shrugged her shoulders.

"Pewter smells bad."

"Well, then, iron."

Madame Magloire pulled a face.

"Iron tastes bad."

"Well, then, wood."

A few moments later, he was eating at the same table that Jean Valjean had sat at the night before. While he ate, Monseigneur Bienvenu chirruped gaily to his sister, who said nothing, and to Madame Magloire, who muttered under her breath that there really was no need for spoons or forks, even of wood, to dunk a bit of bread in a glass of milk.

"Did you ever hear such a thing!" Madame Magloire said to herself as she came and went. "Fancy letting a man like that come into your home! And to put him up, right next to your own bed! And what a stroke of luck that all he did was steal! Mary, Mother of God! It makes your hair stand on end just thinking about it!"

Just as the brother and sister were getting up from the table, there was a knock at the door.

"Come in," said the bishop.

The door opened. A weird and wild-looking bunch stood on the doorstep. Three men were holding a fourth by the scruff of the neck. The three men were gendarmes; the other man was Jean Valjean.

A sergeant of the gendarmerie, who seemed to be the leader of the group, stood nearest the door. He came in and strode over to the bishop, giving him a military salute.

"Monseigneur—" he began.

At that, Jean Valjean, who looked glum and broken, lifted his eyes, startled.

"Monseigneur," he murmured. "So this isn't the local curé?"

"Quiet!" said one of the gendarmes. "This is Monseigneur, the bishop."

But Monseigneur Bienvenu had gone over to the men as fast as his old pins would carry him.

"Ah, there you are!" he cried, looking straight at Jean Valjean. "Am I glad to see you! But, heavens! I gave you the candlesticks, too, you know; they are made of silver like the rest and you can get two hundred francs for them, easily. Why didn't you take them with the cutlery?"

Jean Valjean's eyes nearly popped out of his head; he looked at the venerable bishop with an expression no human tongue could convey.

"Monseigneur," said the sergeant, "is what this man said true, then? We saw him hotfooting it out of town. He looked like he was on the run. So we arrested him to be on the safe side. He had all this silver—"

"And he told you," the bishop broke in with a smile, "that it had been given to him by some old codger of a priest whose place he'd spent the night in? I can see how it looks. So you've brought him back here? There has been a misunderstanding."

"If that's the case," the sergeant said, "can we let him go?"

"You must," said the bishop.

The gendarmes released Jean Valjean, who visibly shrank back.

"Are you really letting me go?" he said in a voice that was barely articulate, as muffled as if he were talking in his sleep.

"Yes, we're letting you go; something wrong with your ears!" said one of the gendarmes.

"My dear friend," said the bishop, "before you go, here are your candlesticks. Take them."

He went to the mantelpiece, swept up the two silver candlesticks, and handed them over to Jean Valjean. The two women watched the bishop without a word, without a movement, without a glance that might upset him.

Jean Valjean's whole body was shaking. He took the two candlesticks automatically and with a stricken look on his face.

"Now," said the bishop, "go in peace. Speaking of which, when you come back, my friend, there's no need to go through the garden. You can always come and go through the front door on the street. It is only ever on the latch, night and day."

He then turned to the policemen and said:

"Gentlemen, you may go."

The gendarmes headed off.

Jean Valjean looked as though he were about to pass out.

The bishop went over to him and said to him in a voice just above a whisper: "Don't forget, don't ever forget, that you promised me to use this silver to make an honest man of yourself."

Jean Valjean, who had no memory of ever having promised a thing, remained stunned. The bishop had emphasized every word as he spoke. He went on with a kind of solemnity: "Jean Valjean, my brother, you no longer belong to evil but to good. It is your soul that I am buying for you; I am taking it away from black thoughts and from the spirit of perdition, and I am giving it to God."

## XIII. PETIT-GERVAIS

Jean Valjean left town as though he were still on the run. He practically broke into a trot when he hit the open countryside in his anxiety to get away, blindly taking whatever paths and tracks he stumbled on without realizing that he was going round in circles. He snaked about like this all morning, without eating a thing and without feeling in the least hungry. He was in the grip of a whole host of new sensations. He felt a kind of rage, he knew not at whom. He couldn't tell whether he felt moved or humiliated. A strange sensation of tenderness came over him at times, but he fought it and threw the hardness of the last twenty years up against it like a screen, warding it off. This state wore him out. He watched in alarm as the kind of frightening calm that the injustice of his lousy fate had produced melted away inside him. He wondered what on earth could take its place. There were moments when he really would have preferred to be slammed behind bars with the gendarmes and for things not to have taken such an incredible turn; at least he wouldn't have been so churned up. Even though the season was fairly advanced, there were still a few late-blooming flowers here and there in the hedges, and as he walked along, clouds of perfume brought back childhood memories. These memories were almost unbearable, it was so long since they had last appeared.

A welter of whirring thoughts he could not have put into words banked up inside him like this the whole day.

As the sun set at the end of the day, dragging out the shadow on the ground of the tiniest pebble, Jean Valjean sat behind a bush in a great red plain that was absolutely deserted. The only thing on the horizon was the chain of the Alps. Otherwise, not even a church steeple in a distant village. Jean Valjean might have been about three miles from Digne. A path that cut through the plain ran past just a few feet from the bush.

While he was lost in thought, a meditative state that would have contributed not a little to the frightening effect of his rags on anyone unlucky enough to run into him, he heard a joyful sound.

He turned his head and saw a young Savoyard,[1] an itinerant chimney sweep, of about twelve skipping along the path singing, a hurdy-gurdy, or *vielle*, at his side and a cherrywood box on his back; he was one of those chirpy little strays that roam the countryside, with their knees peeping through the holes in their pants.

Still singing, the child paused now and then to play jacks with a few coins he was carrying—his entire fortune, probably. One of the coins was a forty-sou piece.

The boy stopped beside the bush without spotting Jean Valjean and tossed his handful of sous into the air. Up until that moment, he had caught them all pretty skillfully on the back of his hand.

This time the forty-sou piece eluded him and went rolling toward the bush over to Jean Valjean.

Jean Valjean instantly slammed his foot on top of it.

But the boy had followed it with his eyes, and saw what happened.

He was not put out at all and went straight over to the man.

The place was completely isolated. As far as the eye could see there was no one on the plain or walking along the track. The only sound was the feeble cries of a flock of migratory birds flying across the sky at immense height. The boy stood with his back to the sun, which shot through his hair, turning it to threads of spun gold and flushing the savage face of Jean Valjean with a blood-red glow.

"Monsieur," said the little Savoyard with that childish trust that is a blend of complete ignorance and complete innocence, "my coin?"

"What's your name?" asked Jean Valjean.

"Petit-Gervais, Monsieur."

"Get lost," said Jean Valjean.

"Monsieur," the child persisted, "give me back my coin."

Jean Valjean lowered his head and did not respond. The child repeated:

"My coin, Monsieur!"

Jean Valjean went on staring at the ground.

"My coin!" cried the child. "My silver coin! I want my money!"

Jean Valjean seemed not to have heard him, or to understand plain French. The boy grabbed him by the collar and shook him, at the same time trying hard to shift the great hobnailed boot from off his treasure.

"I want my piece! My forty-sou piece!"

The child began to cry. Jean Valjean's head shot up. He was still squatting on the ground. His eyes looked troubled. He examined the boy with a sort of wonder, then he reached for his stick and yelled in a terrible voice: "Who's there?"

"Me, Monsieur," the boy replied. "Petit-Gervais! Me! Me! Give me back my forty sous, please! Take your foot away, Monsieur, please!"

Then, tiny as he was, the boy lost his temper and managed to sound almost threatening: "For pity's sake! Will you take your foot away? Take your foot away, right now!"

"Ah, you're still here!" said Jean Valjean, and suddenly springing up, foot still on the coin, he added: "I'd get cracking if I was you!"

The terrified child looked at him and then began to quiver from head to toe and, after a few seconds of standing there stunned, he ran away as fast as his little legs would carry him, not daring to look back or to let out a whimper.

But after a certain distance, he was out of breath and forced to stop, and Jean Valjean, lost in a daze as he was, heard him sobbing.

A few seconds later, the boy had vanished.

The sun had gone down.

The shadows gathered around Jean Valjean. He hadn't eaten all day; it is likely that he had a fever.

He stayed on his feet, rooted to the spot, not having budged since the boy fled. His chest heaved as he breathed slowly and unevenly. His eyes were riveted to a spot ten or twelve feet ahead, as though he were completely fixated on a shard of old blue pottery lying in the grass. Suddenly he shuddered; he had begun to feel the cold night air.

He pulled his cap down over his forehead, fumbled mechanically to do up his smock, took a step forward and stooped to pick his stick up off the ground.

At that moment he spotted the forty-sou coin that he had half-ground into the dirt with his foot and that was glistening among the pebbles. The sight of it was a bolt from the blue.

"What the hell is that?" he hissed between clenched teeth.

He took a few steps back, without being able to take his eyes off the spot he had trampled underfoot only a moment before, as though the thing shining there in the darkness were an open eye staring up at him.

After a few moments he lunged convulsively at the coin, snatched it off the ground, and stood holding it, motionless, staring off into the farthest reaches of the plain, casting his eye at all points along the horizon, upright and shivering like a frightened wild animal looking for a place to hide.

He couldn't see a thing. Night was coming down, the plain was cold, and murky, great violet mists were swirling up in the glimmering twilight.

He let out an "Ah!" and set off at a fast pace in the direction the child had taken before he disappeared. After a hundred feet or so, he stopped and looked around but still saw nothing.

Then he called out at the top of his lungs: "Petit-Gervais! Petit-Gervais!"

He shut his mouth and waited.

No one answered.

The countryside was deserted and mournful. He was surrounded on all sides by empty space. There was nothing all around but semi-darkness, in which his gaze was lost, and silence, in which his voice was lost.

A freezing northerly wind was blowing, the icy blast of winter, lending the things around him a sort of woeful life. Stunted shrubs shook their skinny little limbs in unbelievable fury. You would have sworn they were threatening someone and chasing after him.

He started walking again and then he started running, from time to time stopping and calling out in the lonely wilderness in the most fearsome and the most desolate voice you could possibly imagine: "Petit-Gervais! Petit-Gervais!"

Naturally, if the boy had heard him, he'd have been frightened stiff and quickly ducked for cover. But the child was already, no doubt, far away.

He ran into a priest on horseback and went up to him and said: "Monsieur le curé, have you seen a boy go by?"

"No," said the priest.

"Kid by the name of Petit-Gervais?"

"I haven't seen a soul."

He took two five-franc pieces out of his bag and handed them to the priest

"Monsieur curé, for your poor . . . Monsieur curé, he's just a little kid of about ten with a wooden box on his back, I think, and a hurdy-gurdy. He was heading this way. One of the chimney-sweep kids. A Savoyard, you know?"

"I haven't seen him."

"Petit-Gervais? He's not from any of the villages around here, is he? Can't you tell me?"

"If it's as you say, my friend, the boy must be a foreigner. They come through here in droves. We haven't a clue who they are."

Jean Valjean swiftly produced two more five-franc pieces and handed them to the priest.

"For your poor," he said.

Then he added on a wild note: "Monsieur abbé, arrest me. I am a thief."

The priest dug his heels in and galloped away, frightened out of his wits.

Jean Valjean started to run again in the direction he had first taken.

He ran on for quite some distance, peering around, calling out, shouting, but he met no one. Two or three times he ran toward something off the beaten track that looked to him like someone lying down or crouching; it always turned out to be a clump of brushwood or a flat outcrop of rock. At last, where three paths intersected, he stopped. The moon had risen. He strained to see in the distance and called one last time: "Petit-Gervais! Petit-Gervais!" His cry died out in the mist without even raising an echo. He mumbled once more, "Petit-Gervais!" but his voice was weak now, barely a murmur. That was a last-ditch attempt; his legs suddenly gave way beneath him as if an invisible power had suddenly bowled him over with the weight of his guilty conscience; he dropped, exhausted, onto a big slab of rock, his hands balled into fists and buried in his hair, his head propped on his knees, and he cried: "I am a miserable bastard!"

His heart broke at that point and he burst into tears. It was the first time he had cried in nineteen years.

When Jean Valjean left the bishop's, as we saw, he was in a state far beyond anything he had experienced till that moment. He did not recognize himself. He could not make sense of what was happening to him. He steeled himself against the old man's angelic act and against his gentle words. "You promised me to make an honest man of yourself. It is your soul that I am buying for you; I am taking it away from the spirit of perversity, and I am giving it to the good Lord." Those words kept coming back to him. He defended himself against such heavenly forgiveness by means of pride, which is like a stronghold of evil inside us. He felt indistinctly that the old priest's forgiveness was the greatest assault and the most deadly attack he had ever been rocked by; that if he could resist such clemency his heart would be hardened once and for all; that if he gave in to it, he would have to give up the hate that the actions of other men had filled his heart with for so many years and which he relished; that this time, he had to conquer or be conquered and that the struggle, a colossal and decisive struggle, was now on between his own rottenness and the goodness of that man.

In the glimmering light of all these thoughts, he staggered like a drunk. While he was flailing about, did he have any real idea what his adventure in Digne might mean for him? Did he hear all those mysterious warning bells that alert us or jog our spirits at certain turning points in life? Was there a voice that whispered in his ear that he had just passed the most solemn moment of his destiny, that there was no longer a middle course for him; that from now on, he would either be the best of men or he would be the worst of men; that he now had to rise higher, so to speak, than the bishop or fall even lower than the galley slave; that if he wanted to be good, he had to be an angel; that if he wanted to stay bad, he had to be a monster from hell?

Here, once more, we need to ask those questions we have already asked elsewhere: Did some dim notion of all this take shape in his mind? Certainly, as we've said before, adversity sharpens the wits and calamity is the highest form of education; yet it is doubtful that Jean Valjean was in any state to unravel all the strands we have singled out here. If such notions occurred to him, he would have half-glimpsed them rather than clearly seen them and they would only have thrown him into a painful and very nearly agonizing crisis. When he had just gotten out of that ugly, dark, deforming place we call jail, the bishop had wounded his soul the way a sudden flash of blinding light would have hurt his eyes coming out of the dark. His future life, the life that opened up to him now, all pure and radiant, filled him with trembling and fear. He no longer really knew where he was. Like an owl suddenly confronted by sunrise, the convict had been dazzled and blinded by virtue.

One thing was certain, and he himself did not doubt it: that he was no longer the same man, that already everything about him had changed, and it was no longer in his power to act as though the bishop had not spoken to him, had not touched him to the quick.

In this frame of mind he had encountered Petit-Gervais and stolen his forty sous from him. Why? It was way beyond his powers to explain; was it the final effect, a last-ditch attempt, on the part of the bad thoughts that he had brought with him from jail, a lingering residue of evil impulse, a result of what is called in physics *cumulative energy*? It was that and it was also, perhaps, something less than that. To put it simply, it was not he who had stolen, it was not the man, it was the beast who, out of habit and instinct, had stupidly stuck its foot over the money while his mind tried to grapple with so many new and bewildering obsessions. When his mind snapped out of it and saw what the brute had done, Jean Valjean recoiled in anguish and let out a cry of horror.

The thing is—and it's a strange phenomenon, one that could not occur outside the situation he was now in—in stealing the money from that child, he had done something he was already no longer capable of.

Be that as it may, this final bad deed had a decisive effect on him; it suddenly pierced through the chaos in his mind and cleared it, rolling the blanket of darkness to one side and making way for the light on the other; and it acted on his soul, in the state in which it found itself, the way certain chemical reactants act on a cloudy solution by precipitating one element and clarifying another.

At first, before he had time to think, lost as he was, like a drowning man clutching at straws he had tried to find the child to give him back his money; then, when he realized that this was pointless and impossible, he gave way to despair. The very moment he shouted "I am a miserable bastard!" he saw himself for what he was, and he was already so dissociated from himself that he felt he was now no more than a ghost. What he saw, in front of him, in flesh and blood, with his stick in his hand and his smock on his back and his sack filled with stolen goods over his shoulder, with his grim and granitelike face and his mind full of abominable schemes, was the hideous galley slave Jean Valjean.

Too much misery, as we have noted, had turned him into something of a visionary. And this was like a vision. He truly saw this Jean Valjean, that sinister face, before him. He was on the point of asking himself who this man was, and he was horrified.

His brain was in one of those states that are both violent and yet frighteningly calm, in which thought runs so deep it blots out reality. You no longer see the objects around you, yet you can see the shapes in your mind as though they are outside your body.

And so he contemplated himself, so to speak, face-to-face, and at the same time, through this hallucination, he saw, at a mysterious distance, a sort of light which he took at first to be a torch. Looking more closely at this light that dawned in his conscience, he saw that it had a human shape, that the torch was the bishop.

His conscience considered each of the two men in turn as they stood before him, side by side: the bishop and Jean Valjean. Any lesser person than the first would have failed to soften the second. Through one of those strange effects that are peculiar to this kind of ecstasy, the longer the trance went on, the bigger and greater the bishop grew and the more he shone resplendent in his eyes, the more Jean Valjean shriveled and faded away. At a certain point he was no more than a shadow. Then, all of a sudden, he evaporated completely. The bishop alone remained. He flooded the entire soul of this miserable bastard with a glorious radiance.

Jean Valjean cried for a long time. He shed hot tears, he sobbed, more helpless and fragile than any woman, more terrified than any child.

While he was crying, day dawned brighter and brighter in his spirit, and it was an extraordinary light, a light at once ravishing and terrible. His past life, his initial downfall, his long atonement, his increasingly brutal outside appearance, his hardening interior, his release from custody jollied along by so many schemes of revenge, what had happened to him at the bishop's, the last thing he had done, stealing forty sous from a child, a crime even more cowardly and monstrous for coming after the bishop's pardon, all this came back to him clearly, but with a clarity he had never before that moment known. He looked at his life and it looked horrible to him; at his soul, and it looked revolting. And yet, a new day was dawning and its soft light was settling over his life and over his soul. He felt like he was seeing Satan in the light of paradise.

How many hours did he spend crying his heart out? What did he do when he stopped crying? Where did he go? No one ever knew. The only thing that is known, apparently, is that, that same night, the coach driver who made the Grenoble run got to Digne at around three in the morning and saw, as he drove along the street where the bishop's residence was, a man who looked like he was praying, on his knees on the cobblestones in the shadows outside Monseigneur Bienvenu's front door.

# BOOK THREE

# IN THE YEAR 1817

## I. THE YEAR 1817

Eighteen seventeen is the year that Louis XVIII, with a certain royal aplomb not devoid of arrogance, called the twenty-second year of his reign.[1] It is the year Monsieur Bruguière de Sorsum,[2] the translator of Shakespeare, became famous. All the wigmakers' shops, hoping for the return of powdered wigs along with the royal bird, were awash with azure and fleurs-de-lis.[3] It was the age of innocence when the comte Lynch[4] sat every Sunday as churchwarden in the official pew at Saint-Germain-des-Prés decked out as a peer of France, with his red sash and his long beak and that majestic profile peculiar to a man who has done a remarkable deed. The remarkable deed performed by Monsieur Lynch was that, as mayor of Bordeaux, he had handed the town over a little too soon to Monsieur le duc d'Angoulême,[5] on March 12, 1814. Hence his peerage. In 1817, it was all the rage to bury the heads of little boys from four to six years old under enormous tanned leather caps with earflaps, which looked rather like Eskimo cowls. The French army was dressed in white, Austrian style, the regiments were known as legions, and instead of numbers they wore the names of *départements*. Napoléon was on Saint Helena, and as England refused his request for green cloth, he was having his old riding habits turned.[6] In 1817, Pellegrini sang, Mademoiselle Bigottini danced, Potier reigned, Odry did not yet exist.[7] Madame Saqui took over from Forioso.[8] There were still Prussians in France.[9] Monsieur Delalot[10] was somebody. Legitimacy[11] reared its ugly head, first by cutting off the hand, then the head, of Pleignier, Carbonneau, and Tolleron.[12] The prince de Talleyrand, grand chamberlain, and the abbé Louis, finance minister designate, looked at each other and laughed the laugh of a pair of soothsayers, both having celebrated the mass of the Federation in the Champ de Mars, on July 14, 1790, Talleyrand saying the mass as bishop, Louis serving him as deacon.[13] In 1817, on the footpaths that laced the same Champ de Mars, big wooden cylinders were to be seen, lying on their sides on the grass, rotting in the rain, their blue paint still bearing traces of eagles and bees that were losing their gold leaf. These were the columns that, two years previously, had supported the emperor's podium in the Champ de Mai.[14] They were scorched and charred here and there by the bivouac fires of the Austrians camped in barracks close to Gros-Caillou.[15] Two or three of the columns had disappeared altogether in these fires, which warmed the great hands of the *kaiserlichen,* or imperialists. What was remarkable about the Champ de Mai celebration was that it was held on the Champ de Mars and in the month of June. In the year 1817, two things were popular: the Touquet edition of Voltaire[16] and the Touquet snuffbox *à la Charte.* The latest Paris sensation was the murder committed by Dautun,[17] who had hurled his brother's head into the Marché-aux-Fleurs fountain. The ministry of the navy was beginning to be questioned over the sinking of the doomed frigate the *Medusa,*[18] an event that was to cover the captain Chaumareix with shame and the painter Géricault with glory. Colonel Selves[19] went to Egypt to become Suleiman Pasha there. The Palais des Thermes, in the rue de la Harpe, served as a cooper's shopfront. You could still see on the roof of the Hôtel de Cluny's octagonal tower the little clapboard shed that had served as an observatory to Messier,[20] naval astronomer to Louis XVI. The duchesse de Duras[21] read the unpublished manuscript of *Ourika* to three or four friends in her boudoir, done out by X in sky blue satin. The *N*s were all scratched out at the Louvre.[22] The pont d'Austerlitz abdicated and called itself the pont du Jardin du Roi,[23] a double riddle that disguised both the pont d'Austerlitz and the Jardin des Plantes. Louis XVIII, who was busily annotating Horace with his thumbnail and worrying about heroes who get themselves made emperors and clogmakers who get themselves made dauphins, had two causes for concern: Napoléon and Mathurin Bruneau.[24] The Académie Française proposed an essay prize[25] on this theme: "the happiness that comes from study." Monsieur Bellart was officially eloquent. Broë's future attorney general could be seen germinating in his shadow, before becoming, when ripe, the butt of Paul-Louis Courier's sarcasm.[26] A Chateaubriand impersonator named Marchangy popped up, followed by a Marchangy impersonator named d'Arlincourt.[27] *Claire d'Albe* and *Malek-Adel* were masterpieces and Madame Cottin[28] was declared the premier writer of the age. The Institut de France let the academician Napoléon Bonaparte[29] be struck off its list of members. A royal ordinance established a naval school at Angoulême,[30] for the duc d'Angoulême being a grand admiral of the fleet, it was obvious that the town of Angoulême had to be found by rights to have all the qualities of a seaport, failing which the whole principle of monarchy would have been dented. Ministerial councils fretted over the issue of whether the vignettes of acrobatics that spiced up Franconi's posters[31] and lured the street rabble should be tolerated. Monsieur Paër, author of *L'Agnese,* a good old fellow with a square face and a wart on one cheek, directed the small private concerts offered by the marquise de Sassenaye, rue de la Ville-l'Évêque. All the young girls sang "L'Ermite de Saint-Avelle," with words by Edmond Géraud.[32] The *Nain jaune* turned into the *Miroir.*[33] The Café Lemblin was for the emperor, as opposed to the Café Valois,[34] which was for the Bourbons. Monsieur le duc de Berry had just been married off to a Sicilian princess, though the duc was already regarded most darkly by Louvel.[35] Madame de Staël[36] had been dead a year. The bodyguards hissed and booed Mademoiselle Mars.[37] The big newspapers were quite small. The format had shrunk but freedom of expression had mushroomed. The *Constitutionnel* was constitutional.[38] *The Minerve*[39] spelled Chateaubriand *Chateaubriant,* like the steak, and that final *t* gave the bourgeoisie a lot of laughs at the great writer's expense. In the turncoat press, old newspaper hacks prostituted themselves and insulted the outlaws of 1815:[40] David had lost his talent, Arnault had lost his wit, Carnot had lost his integrity, Soult had never won a battle, and certainly Napoléon had lost his genius.[41] Everyone knows that letters addressed to a man in exile rarely reach him,[42] the police making it a religious duty to intercept them. This is nothing new; Descartes complained about it when he was banished.[43] But when David moaned about not receiving the letters people wrote to him, in the columns of some Belgian newspaper, the royalists found this hilarious and jeered at the exile in their rags. Whether you said "regicides" or "voters," "enemies" or "allies," "Napoléon" or "Buonaparte"[44] divided you from the next man more decisively than any yawning chasm. All reasonable people agreed[45] that the age of revolutions had been closed forever by King Louis XVIII, fondly known as "the immortal author of the Charter." On the tip of the central island by the Pont-Neuf the word *Redivivus* was sculpted on the pedestal that awaited the statue of Henri IV.[46] In the rue Thérèse, no. 4, Monsieur Pieté[47] was hatching his plans for the consolidation of the monarchy. In critical situations, the leaders of the right invariably wheeled out the phrase: "We must write to Bacot."[48] The ultra-royalists Messieurs Canuel, O'Mahony, and de Chappedelaine were working, not entirely without the approbation of Monsieur, the king's brother, on what would later become known as "the Waterside Conspiracy."[49] The ex-army officers of L'Épingle Noir were also plotting away. Delaverderie teamed up with Trogoff.[50] Monsieur Decazes, showing somewhat liberal tendencies as police minister, prevailed.[51] Chateaubriand, on his feet every morning at the window at no. 27, rue Saint-Dominique, in stirrup pants and slippers, his gray hair tied up in a Madras scarf, his eyes glued to a mirror, a complete dental surgeon's kit open in front of him, was cleaning his teeth, which were perfect, while dictating variations on *La Monarchie selon la Charte*[52] to his secretary, Monsieur Pilorge. The most influential critics preferred Lafon to Talma.[53] Monsieur de Féletz signed himself "A"; Monsieur Hoffmann[54] signed "Z." Charles Nodier[55] wrote *Thérèse Aubert.* Divorce was abolished.[56] High schools were called colleges. The college students, sporting decorative gold fleurs-de-lis on their collars, thrashed each other over the king of Rome.[57] The palace secret police informed her royal highness, Madame,[58] about the portrait, everywhere on show, of, Monsieur le duc d'Orléans,[59] who looked better in the uniform of a colonel general of hussars than Monsieur le duc de Berry in the uniform of a colonel general of dragoons—which was a real worry. The city of Paris dipped into its own coffers to have the dome of the Invalides[60] regilded. Serious men wondered what Monsieur de Trinquelague would do on such and such an occasion; Monsieur Clausel de Montals differed, on this or that point, with Monsieur Clausel de Coussergues; Monsieur de Salaberry was not happy.[61] The actor Picard,[62] who belonged to the Académie, which Molière had never been able to get into, put on *Les deux Philibert* at the Odéon,[63] on the pediment of which, though the letters had been torn off, you could still clearly read: THÉÂTRE DE L'IMPÉRA-TRICE. You were either for Cugnet de Montarlot[64] or against him. Fabvier was seditious; Bavoux[65] was revolutionary. The bookseller Pélicier[66] brought out an edition of Voltaire under the title *The Works of Voltaire,* by the Académie Française. "That brings the customers in," the naïve publisher reckoned. Popular opinion had it that Monsieur Charles Loyson[67] would turn out to be the genius of the century; envy was beginning to nip at his heels, a sure sign of glory, and he was the butt of this line of verse:

Even when Loyson takes wing, you know his paws are firmly on the ground.

Cardinal Fesch refused to step down, so Monsieur de Pins, archbishop of Amasie, took over the administration of the diocese of Lyon.[68] The fight over the valley of Dappes[69] kicked off between France and Switzerland with a memo from Captain Dufour, who was later made a general. Saint-Simon,[70] then unknown, was busy constructing his sublime dream. At the Académie des Sciences, there was a celebrated Fourier whom posterity has forgotten, and in some godforsaken attic or other, there was a Fourier the future will remember.[71] Lord Byron was beginning to shine; a note in a poem of Millevoye's introduced him to France as "a certain Lord Baron." David d'Angers[72] tried to knead marble. The abbé Caron spoke with praise, in a small committee of seminarists, in the cul-de-sac of the Feuillantines, of an unknown priest named Félicité Robert, who was later known as Lamennais.[73] A thing that smoked and sloshed along the Seine with a noise like a dog swimming came and went beneath the windows of the Tuileries, from the pont Royal to the pont Louis XV; it was a crummy bit of machinery, a sort of toy, the invention of a daydreaming crackpot, a utopia: in a word, a steamboat. Parisians regarded the useless object with indifference. Monsieur de Vaublanc,[74] an Institut de France reformer whose preferred tools were the coup d'état, the royal decree, and the lot, proved to be the making of several academicians, but did not manage to become one himself.

The faubourg Saint-Germain and the pavillon Marsan[75] wanted Monsieur Delavau[76] as chief of police because of his devoutness. Dupuytren and Récamier[77] argued in the amphitheater of the École de Médecine and virtually came to blows over the divinity of Jesus Christ. Cuvier,[78] with one eye on Genesis and the other on Nature, tried to satisfy the bigots[79] by getting fossils to fit in with the scriptural record and having Moses backed up by the mastodons. Monsieur François de Neufchâteau, the praiseworthy keeper of the flame of Parmentier's memory,[80] did his level best to see that *pomme de terre*—potato—was pronounced *parmentière,* but he did not pull it off. The abbé Grégoire,[81] ex-bishop, ex-Conventionist, ex-senator, acquired the status of "the infamous Grégoire" in royalist polemics. The expression just used—"to acquire the status of"—was denounced as a neologism by Monsieur Royer-Collard.[82] You could still distinguish by its whiteness, under the third arch of the pont d'Iéna,[83] the new stone that plugged the hole made two years earlier by Blücher[84] when he tried to blow up the bridge. The Law called to its bar a man who, on seeing the comte d'Artois[85] enter Notre-Dame, was reckless enough to say out loud: "I'll be buggered! How I miss the days when I used to see Bonaparte and Talma going into the Bal-Sauvage arm in arm."[86] Seditious words—six months' jail. Traitors crawled out of the woodwork; men who had gone over to the enemy the day before a battle did not bother hiding a sou of what they'd earned in bribes and strutted about shamelessly in broad daylight full of the cynicism wealth and honors bring; the deserters of Ligny and Quatre-Bras,[87] in their unchecked and financially rewarded depravity, paraded their monarchical devotion brazenly, for all to see—forgetting what is written on lavatory walls in England: *Please adjust your dress before leaving.*

And that, willy-nilly, is what dimly survives of the year 1817, otherwise now largely forgotten. History neglects nearly every one of these little details and cannot do otherwise if it is not to be swamped by the infinite minutiae. And yet, the details, which are wrongly described as little—there are no little facts in the human realm, any more than there are little leaves in the realm of vegetation—are useful. The face of the century is made up of the lines of the years.

In the year 1817, four young Parisians played "a great practical joke."

## II. A Double Foursome

One of these Parisians was from Toulouse, one from Limoges, the third from Cahors, and the fourth from Montauban; but they were students, and once you're a student, you're a Parisian; to study in Paris is to be born in Paris.[1]

These young men were of no account, everyone has seen their type. Pull the first four passersby off the street and they would be perfect examples; neither good nor bad, neither knowledgeable nor ignorant, neither geniuses nor morons; good-looking in that charming fresh-faced way known as being twenty. They were four Oscar what's-his-names, for in those days Arthurs had not yet come into their own. "Burn the perfumes of Arabia for him," the romance cries, "Oscar[2] is coming, Oscar—soon, I'll see him!" Everything was straight out of *Ossian,*[3] elegance was either Scandinavian or Caledonian, and the first of the Arthurs, Wellington, had only just won the battle of Waterloo.

These Oscars were called Félix Tholomyès, of Toulouse, Listolier, of Cahors, Fameuil, of Limoges, and lastly, Blachevelle, of Montauban. Naturally, each one had his mistress. Blachevelle loved Favorite, so named because she had been to England;[4] Listolier adored Dahlia, who had adopted the name of a flower as her nom de guerre;[5] Fameuil idolized Zéphine, a diminutive of Joséphine; Tholomyès had Fantine, known as "the Blonde" because of her beautiful hair, the color of sunlight.

Favorite, Dahlia, Zéphine, and Fantine were four ravishing girls, perfumed and sparkling, still a bit on the working-class side, not having entirely abandoned their sewing needles, troubled by torrid romances of the railway novel kind, but with traces of the serenity of labor on their faces and in their hearts that bloom of purity that survives a woman's first fall from grace. One of the four was known as "the baby" because she was the youngest; and one was known as "the old girl." The old girl was twenty-three. To be frank, the first three were more experienced, more nonchalant, and more familiar with the ways of the world than Fantine, the Blonde, who still harbored a few illusions.

The same could not be said for Dahlia, Zéphine, and especially not Favorite. There had already been more than one chapter in their barely begun romantic novel, and the amorous young man who was called Adolphe in the first chapter turned into Alphonse in the second and Gustave in the third. Poverty and coquetry are two deadly counselors; one upbraids, the other flatters, and the beautiful daughters of the working class have both of them whispering in their ears, each with its own agenda. Such defenseless creatures listen. Hence their falls from grace and the stones thrown at them. The splendor of all that is immaculate and inaccessible is hurled at them, heaped upon them. Alas! What if the Jungfrau[6] had been starving?

Favorite, having been to England, was much admired by Zéphine and Dahlia. She'd had a home of her own at a very early age. Her father was an old brute of a mathematics teacher who swaggered like a Gascon[7] and was an out-and-out braggart; he had never married and he still chased skirt despite his age. When he was young, this teacher had one day seen a chambermaid's dress snag on a fender, and he had fallen in love with the accident. Favorite was the result. She ran into her father from time to time and he would say hello. One morning an old woman who looked a bit dotty turned up on her doorstep and said, "Don't you know me, Mademoiselle?" "No." "I'm your mother." Then the old woman opened the buffet cupboard, ate and drank her fill, sent for a mattress she had lying about somewhere, and settled in. This mother, a terrible nag and pious on top of it, never spoke to Favorite, could sit for hours on end without uttering a sound, ate enough breakfast, lunch, and dinner for four, and would go down to the porter's lodge to peer at visitors and stab her daughter in the back.

What had driven Dahlia into Listolier's arms and, perhaps, into the arms of others, into an idle life, was her pink fingernails, which were far too pretty. How could anyone expect those nails to do any work? If a girl wants to remain virtuous she can't be too soft on her hands. As for Zéphine, she had conquered Fameuil with her cute little mutinous way of simpering: "Oui, monsieur."

The young men were pals, the young women, friends. Such love affairs are always coupled with such friendships.

It's one thing to be good and quite another to be philosophical; the proof, if proof were needed, is that Favorite, Zéphine, and Dahlia were able to come to terms with these illicit little pairings off because they were philosophical, but Fantine was a good girl.

Good, I hear you say? What about Tholomyès? Solomon would reply that love is part of goodness. We'll say only that Fantine's was a first love, a unique love, a faithful love.

She was the only one of the four to whom one man alone had whispered sweet nothings.

Fantine was one of those beings who spring up, so to speak, in the very bosom of the people. Emerging from the absolute dregs of the social morass, she bore the mark of anonymity and disconnection on her forehead. She was born at Montreuil-sur-mer. Who were her parents? Who could say? No one had ever known her to have a father or a mother. She called herself Fantine. Why Fantine? No one had ever known her to go by any other name. At the time of her birth, the Directoire[8] still held sway. She had no family name, since she had no family; she had no Christian name, since the Church had become a spent force. She was called whatever the first person who had happened along felt like calling her when they ran across her as a tiny toddler padding around the streets barefoot. A name had fallen upon her the same way water from the clouds fell on her head when it rained. They called her *la petite Fantine.* That was all anyone knew about her. This human being had come into existence just like that. At the age of ten, Fantine left town and went into service with a farming family in the district. At fifteen, she came to Paris "to seek her fortune." Fantine was beautiful and remained pure for as long as she could. A pretty blonde with beautiful teeth, she had gold and pearls for a dowry, but her gold was on her head and her pearls were in her mouth.

She worked in order to live; then, also in order to live, she loved, for the heart has its own hunger.

She loved Tholomyès.

For him it was a simple love affair, for her, passion. The streets of the quartier Latin, which were crawling with students and working girls,[9] saw the beginning of this idyll. In the labyrinth of the Panthéon hill, where so many amorous adventures coalesce and dissolve, Fantine had run away from Tholomyès for a long time, but always in such a way that she would run into him again. There is a way of running away that looks a lot like chasing after. To cut a long story short, the pastoral idyll happened.

Blachevelle, Listolier, and Fameuil formed a sort of group with Tholomyès at the head. He was the wit.

Tholomyès was the original world-weary student. He was rich, with four thousand francs annual income[10]—four thousand francs, annual income— a splendid scandal on the montagne Sainte-Geneviève.[11] Tholomyès was a wasted high roller of thirty. He was wrinkled and gap-toothed, and he was starting to develop a bald patch, of which he himself said without a hint of regret: "the noggin at thirty, the knees at forty."[12] His digestion was pretty lousy and he had suddenly developed a weeping eye. But the more his youth faded, the gayer a blade he became; he replaced his teeth with gibes, his hair with hilarity, his health with irony, and his weeping eye laughed nonstop. He was falling apart yet blooming. His youth, packing it in long before its time, beat an orderly retreat in a fit of laughter, and all that could be seen of it was its fire. He'd had a play turned down at the Vaudeville. He would toss off mediocre verses whenever he had the urge. What's more, he maintained a superior skepticism about all things, a great strength in the eyes of the weak. And so, being ironic and bald, he was the chief. Iron is a strong metal. Could that be where the irony came in?

One day Tholomyès took the other three aside, made an oracular gesture, and said to them: "It's nearly a year since Fantine, Dahlia, Zéphine, and Favorite have been asking us for a surprise. We promised them solemnly to give them one. They keep harping on it, especially to me. Just as the old women of Naples cry to Saint Janvier, *Faccia gialluta, fa o miracolo*—'Yellow face, do your miracle!'— so our beauties are always saying to me, 'Tholomyès, when are you going to produce your surprise?' At the same time our parents are appealing to us. Let's kill two birds with the one stone. The time has come, it seems to me. Let's see what we can come up with."

On that note, Tholomyès lowered his voice and mysteriously intoned something so hysterically funny that a huge and wildly enthusiastic guffaw went up from all four in concert and Blachevelle cried: "Now, that's not a bad idea!"

A small smoke-filled bar cropped up, they went in, and the rest of their conference was lost in shadow.

The result of this secret conference was a wonderful pleasure trip that took place the following Sunday, the four young men inviting the four young women along.

## III. Four by Four

What a trip to the country meant for students and their girls forty-five years ago can hardly be imagined today. Paris no longer has the same outskirts; the face of what we might call circum-Parisian life has completely changed in half a century. Where there was once the battered old rattletrap there is now the railway car; where there was once the rickety old two-masted cutter, there is now the steamboat; today we say Fécamp the way we once said Saint-Cloud.[1] The Paris of 1862 is a city that has the whole of France as its suburbs.

The four couples conscientiously got through all the *folies champêtres*[2] then possible in the country. It was the start of the holidays and a bright hot summer's day. The night before, Favorite, the only one who could write, had written a note to Tholomyès on behalf of all four: "It is a good time to set out in good time." This is why they got up at five o'clock in the morning. They caught the coach to Saint-Cloud, looked at the dry waterfall, and cried, "Must be fabulous when there's water!" had breakfast at the Tête-Noire, to which Castaing[3] had not yet been, treated themselves to a game of quoits on the paths by the main pool, climbed up to Diogenes' Lantern, bet macaroons on the roulette wheel at the pont de Sèvres, picked bunches of flowers at Puteaux, bought toy reed pipes at Neuilly,[4] ate apple turnovers everywhere they went, and were perfectly happy.

The girls trilled and twittered away like warblers who'd escaped from their cages. They were delirious. Now and then they'd give the young men a few soft girlish pokes. Ah, the intoxication of life's clear morning! What wonderful years! The wings of dragonflies are quivering. Oh, whoever you are, don't you remember? Have you never walked in the undergrowth beneath the trees, holding branches out of the way because of the lovely head following behind you? Have you never slipped, laughing, on a slope wet with rain with a woman you love holding on to you by the hand and squealing: "Oh, my brand-new lace-up boots! Look at them now!"

We hasten to add that this good-humored crowd missed out on that thrilling setback, the squall, even though Favorite had said at the outset, in an authoritative and motherly tone, "The slugs are wandering all over the paths. Sign of rain, children."

All four girls were deliriously pretty. A good old classic poet well-known at the time, the knight of Labouïsse[5]—a nice man who had an Eléanore stashed away somewhere—was strolling under the chestnuts of Saint-Cloud that day and when he saw them go by at about ten in the morning, he shrieked, "There's one too many!"—thinking, of course, of the Graces. Favorite, Blachevelle's girlfriend, the one who was twenty-three, the old girl, was running ahead under the great green branches, jumping over ditches, madly leaping over bushes, and presiding over the general high spirits with the verve of a young female faun. As chance would have it, Zéphine and Dahlia were beautiful in a complementary way that was enhanced when they were seen together, so they never left each other's side, more out of some instinctive vanity than out of affection; leaning on each other's arm, they struck English poses. The first sentimental keepsakes had just started to appear at the time, melancholy was coming into vogue for women just as Byronism would later be all the rage for men, and the hair of the tender sex was beginning to stream down in a weeping habit. Zéphine and Dahlia wore their hair in rolls. Listolier and Fameuil were engaged in a discussion about their teachers and were explaining the difference between Monsieur Delvincourt and Monsieur Blondeau[6] to Fantine.

Blachevelle seemed to have been born to carry Favorite's limp dun-colored shawl on his arm on Sundays.

Tholomyès brought up the rear, dominating the group from behind. He was as gay as a lark, but you could sense that it was all very controlled; there was a whiff of the dictatorial about his joviality—he was pulling the strings. His principal adornment was a pair of "elephant-leg" pants—ballooning nankeen trousers, with stirrups of copper braid; he had a strong rattan cane in his hand that had cost two hundred francs, and, as his boldness knew no bounds, he had the strangest thing, a cigar, in his mouth. Since nothing was sacred to him, he'd taken up smoking.

"You've got to hand it to Tholomyès," said the others with reverence. "Those pantaloons! All that energy!"

As for Fantine, she was pure joy. Her magnificent teeth had clearly been given her by God with one purpose only, and that was to laugh. She had a little straw hat with long white ribbons, which she preferred to carry in her hand rather than to wear on her head. Her thick blond hair, which was inclined to come adrift and needed to be pinned back up constantly, seemed made for some enactment of Galatea's flight beneath the willows,[7] tresses floating free. Her rosy lips babbled with delight. The corners of her mouth, voluptuously turned up like those of the antique masks of Erigone,[8] seemed to encourage bold advances; but her long shadowy eyelashes were discreetly cast down over the suggestive animation of the lower part of her face, as though to rein it in. Her whole getup had something wildly poetic and flamboyant about it. She wore a frock of mauve barège, little bronze-colored ankle boots whose laces traced Xs on her fine white openwork stockings, and a sort of muslin spencer, originally invented in Marseilles and called a *canezou,* the name being a corruption of the words *quinze août*—15 August—as pronounced on the Canebière[9] in Marseilles, and connoting the warm sunny weather of the south. The other three were not so timid, as we said, and wore boldly low-cut dresses without further ado; in summer, under hats covered in flowers, they looked extremely graceful and alluring, but next to such daring attire, the *canezou* of the blond Fantine—transparent, indiscreet, yet understated, covering and revealing at the same time—seemed like one of decency's more provocative brainwaves, and the famous court of love presided over by the vicomtesse de Cette,[10] the woman with the sea green eyes, would perhaps have awarded the prize for seduction and sex appeal to this little *canezou* that had entered the modesty stakes. The most naïve is sometimes the most knowing. It can happen.

Stunning face-on, delicate in profile, with her deep blue eyes, lustrous eyelids, small, beautifully high-arched feet, wrists and ankles admirably turned, white skin that showed, here and there, a bluish arborescence of veins, fresh young cheeks, the robust neck of the Aegean Juno, the nape firm and supple, shoulders modeled as though by Coustou,[11] with a voluptuous hollow between them visible through the muslin; a gaiety cooled by dreaminess; sculptural and exquisite . . . That was Fantine. You could sense the statue beneath the ribbons and glad rags, and in this statue, a soul.

Fantine was beautiful, without being too conscious of the fact. Those rare dreamers, mysterious priests of the beautiful, who compare all things to perfection, would have glimpsed the sacred antique harmony in this little working-class miss through the transparency of Parisian grace. This daughter of darkness had class. She possessed both types of beauty—style and rhythm. Style is the shape the ideal takes, rhythm, its movement.

We said Fantine was joy itself. Fantine was also decency.

What any observer studying her closely would have picked up, emanating from her through all the intoxication of her age, the season, her little love affair, was invincible reserve and modesty. She was always a bit on the wide-eyed side. That peculiarly chaste bewilderment is the subtle difference between Psyche and Venus.[12] Fantine had the slender long white fingers of the vestal virgins who once stirred the ashes of the sacred fire with golden rods. Although she would never have refused Tholomyès anything, as was all too clear, her face at rest was utterly virginal; a sort of serious and almost austere dignity would suddenly come over it at certain moments, and nothing was as strange and disturbing as seeing the gaiety so swiftly eclipsed by withdrawal—without any transition. This sudden gravity, sometimes severely pronounced, was like the contempt of a goddess. Her forehead, nose, and chin offered that balance of line, as distinct from the balance of proportion, that constitutes the harmony of the whole face; in the expressive space that separates the base of the nose from the upper lip, she had that barely perceptible but enchanting line that is a mysterious sign of chastity and that made Barbarossa fall in love with a Diana dug up in the excavations in Iconium.

Illicit love is a sin; so be it. Fantine was the innocence that rises above this sin.

## IV. Tholomyès Is So Cheery He Sings a Spanish Ditty

That particular day was pure sunshine from dawn to dusk. All of nature seemed to be on holiday and to smile on them. The parterres of Saint-Cloud were fragrant with scent; the breeze from the Seine gently stirred the leaves; the branches waved in the wind; the bees were having their way with the jasmine; a whole bohemia of butterflies fluttered in the milfoil, clover, and wild oats; there was a swarm of those vagabonds, the birds, in the stately playground of the king of France.

The four frolicking couples, at one with the sun, the fields, the flowers, the trees, were radiant with happiness, too.

And in this shared magic, talking, singing, running, dancing, chasing butterflies, picking convolvulus, getting their stockings wet in the long grass, fresh, wild, but nice, all the girls earned kisses now and then from all the boys, except Fantine, remote in her vague resistance, dreamy and fierce, and full of love. "You know," Favorite said to her, "you always come across as a bit odd."

These are the joys of life. This casual coming together of happy couples is a profound rallying of life and nature and brings out the light and the love in everything. Once upon a time, there was a fairy who made meadows and trees just for people in love. Whence the eternal clandestine school of the open air, that school of love that just keeps starting over again and that will keep on as long as there are bushes and schoolboys. Whence the popularity of spring among thinkers. The patrician and the small-time operator, the duke and the peer and the gownsman, the people of the court and the people of the town, as they used to be called, are all in thrall to this good fairy. You laugh, you play hide-and-seek, the air has never been so bright and clear, love transfigures every little thing! Notary clerks are gods. And the little squeals, the games of chasing in the grass, waists encircled on the sly, all that mumbo jumbo that is music to the ear, the adoration that breaks out in the way a syllable is said, those cherries sucked from one mouth by another—all this blazes and burns into heavenly rapture. Beautiful girls throw themselves away so sweetly. You feel that it will never end. Philosophers, poets, painters look on these ecstasies and don't know what to do with them, so dazzled are they. "The embarkation for Cythera!" cries Watteau; Lancret, the commoner's painter, contemplates these bourgeois sailing off into the blue; Diderot opens his arms wide to all the fleeting romances, and d'Urfé sticks a few Druids in among them for good measure.[1]

After breakfast, the four couples went off to what was then called the king's patch to look at a plant that had just arrived from India, the name of which escapes us for the moment but which drew all Paris to Saint-Cloud at the time; it was a bizarre and lovely shrub with a long stem and numerous fine threadlike branches, all tangled and leafless and covered with thousands of tiny white stars, which made the bush look like a head of hair crawling with flowers like lice. There was always a crowd standing around admiring it.

The bush having been viewed, Tholomyès shouted: "Donkeys, everyone—my treat!" And once they agreed on a price with the donkey man, they rode back via Vanves and Issy. At Issy, there was a bit of an incident. The park, now part of the Bien National[2] but at the time owned by the army supply officer Bourguin,[3] was open, as luck would have it. They went in through the gates, visited the statue of the anchorite[4] in its grotto, gave themselves a few thrills in the famous hall of mirrors, a lascivious snare fit for a satyr-*cum*-millionaire or a Turcaret metamorphosed into Priapus.[5] They rattled the swing that hung from two chestnuts celebrated by the abbé de Bernis.[6] While he gave each gorgeous girl a turn on the swing, one after the other, amid general hilarity due to a flying up of skirts that would have been grist for the mill for Greuze,[7] the Toulousian Tholomyès, who was something of a Spaniard, Toulouse being a sister city of Tolosa, sang to the tune of a melancholy lament the old *gallega* song[8] probably inspired by some beautiful girl zooming high in the air on a rope between two trees:

> I am from Badajoz.
> Love calls me.
> My whole soul
> Is in my eyes
> Because you are showing
> Your legs.

Fantine alone refused to swing.

"Talk about laying it on thick," Favorite muttered sharply.

The donkeys finished with, a new pleasure: They took a boat down the Seine and then walked from Passy to the barrière de l'Étoile.[9] They had been on their feet since five o'clock in the morning, as you'll recall, but that meant nothing! "No petering out on Sunday," according to Favorite. "Tiredness doesn't work Sundays." Toward three o'clock the four couples, delirious with happiness, were racing down the roller coaster, a strange structure that sat on Beaujon heights[10] then, and whose snaking line could be seen over the tops of the trees in the Champs-Élysées.

From time to time, Favorite cried out:

"What about the surprise? I want the surprise!"

"Patience," Tholomyès retorted.

## V. AT BOMBARDA'S

The roller coaster exhausted, thoughts turned to dinner, and the radiant eight, finally a little weary, came to rest at the Cabaret Bombarda, a branch establishment opened on the Champs-Élysées by the famous restaurateur Bombarda,[1] whose sign could then be seen hanging on the rue de Rivoli next to the passage Delorme.

A big but ugly bedroom, with an alcove and a bed at the back (given how full the dive was on Sundays they had to put up with this as a place to rest); from two windows you could gaze through the elms at the quai and the river; a magnificent shaft of August sunlight grazed the windows; two tables, on one, a triumphant mountain of bouquets interspersed with men's and women's hats, on the other, at which our four couples had plonked themselves down, a cheery clutter of dishes, plates, glasses and bottles, jugs of beer jumbled up with flasks of wine—not much order on the table, quite a bit of disorder under it.

As Molière[2] says:

Their feet made under the table
The worst racket that they were able.[3]

So that was as far as they had got, at four-thirty in the afternoon, with the pastoral gambol that had started at five in the morning. The sun was going down and appetite was fading.

The Champs-Élysées, full of sunshine and people, was nothing more than glare and dust, the two components of a haze of glory. The Marly horses,[4] those whinnying chunks of marble, reared up in a golden cloud. Carriages drove up and down. A squadron of magnificent Gardes du Corps, bugler at the head, was passing down the avenue de Neuilly; the white flag, faintly pink in the setting sun, floated over the dome of the Tuileries.[5] The place de la Concorde, by that time once more the place Louis XV,[6] was crawling with happy strollers. Many of them were sporting the silver fleur-de-lis dangling from the moiré ribbon that, in 1817, had not yet disappeared[7] from all buttonholes. Here and there, in the middle of a circle of applauding spectators, clusters of little girls were tossing off a Bourbon round then famous, intended to crush the Hundred Days;[8] the chorus went like this:

Give us back our Père de Gand.[9]
Give us back our Father.[10]

A host of faubourg folk decked out in their Sunday best, sometimes even sporting a fleur-de-lis like good bourgeois,[11] were scattered over the great carré

Marigny,[12] playing skittles and zipping round on the merry-go-round on wooden horses; others were drinking; a few apprentice printers were wearing paper caps; you could hear them laughing. Everyone was radiant. It was a time of incontestable peace and of profound security of a royalist kind; it was the age when a private and special report on the Paris faubourgs, drawn up by the prefect of police, Anglès,[13] and handed to the king, ended with these lines: "All things carefully considered, Your Majesty, there is nothing to fear from these particular people. They are as carefree and indolent as cats. The lower echelons of the provinces are restless, those of Paris are not. They are all small men. Your Majesty, two of them would need to be placed end to end to make up one of your grenadiers. There is nothing to worry about on the part of the populace of the capital. It is remarkable that the average height has fallen further in this group in the last fifty years; and the populace of the Paris faubourgs are smaller than before the Revolution. They are not dangerous. To sum up, rabble they are, but good rabble."

Police chiefs don't think a cat can possibly turn into a lion; and yet, it happens. And that is the miracle of the people of Paris. Besides, the cat, so despised by the comte Anglès, enjoyed the esteem of the republics of antiquity; the cat was freedom incarnate in their eyes, and, as though to serve as a counterpart for the wingless Minerva[14] of Piraeus, there used to be a bronze colossus of a cat in the public square in Corinth. The simpleminded police of the Restoration tended to view the people of Paris through rose-colored glasses. They are not quite the "good rabble" some people think. The Parisian is to the French person in general what the Athenian was to the Greek; no one sleeps more soundly, no one is more openly frivolous and lazy, no one seems quite so oblivious. But don't be fooled; the Parisian is given to every species of nonchalance, but when there is glory to be had, he comes through in the end, proving capable of all kinds of rage. Give him a pike and he'll do you the tenth of August;[15] give him a gun and you'll get Austerlitz.[16] He is Napoléon's crutch and Danton's mainstay.[17] Is the homeland at stake? He signs up! Is it freedom that's at stake? He rips up the cobblestones. Watch out! That hair standing up on his head in fury is epic; his smock drapes itself into an antique chlamys, a purple cloak. Take care. He will turn the first rue Greneta that crops up into the Caudine Forks.[18] If the tocsin tolls, this *faubourien*, a product of the backblocks, this will grow, this little man will rise up and his eyes will be merciless and his breath will blast like a tempest, and from that narrow, weedy chest he'll produce enough wind to rearrange the folds of the Alps. It's thanks to the Paris *faubourien* that revolution conquers Europe, once the armies get involved. He sings, it's what he loves to do. Tailor the song to his nature and stand back! As long as he has only the "Carmagnole"[19] for a refrain, he will only overthrow Louis XVI; get him to sing the "Marseillaise," and he will free the world.

Having scribbled this note in the margins of the Anglès report, we can now get back to our four couples. The dinner, as we were saying, was winding down.

## VI. A Chapter Where Everyone Adores One Another

Table talk and amorous talk are equally impossible to grasp; amorous talk is all pretty bubbles, table talk, hot air.

Fameuil and Dahlia were humming; Tholomyès was drinking; Zéphine was giggling; Fantine smiled. Listolier blew into a wooden trumpet bought at Saint-Cloud. Favorite gazed at Blachevelle tenderly and said: "Blachevelle, I adore you."

This prompted a question from Blachevelle: "What would you do, Favorite, if I stopped loving you?"

"Me!" cried Favorite. "Ah, don't say that, not even for a laugh! If you stopped loving me, I'd race after you, I'd claw you to bits, I'd scratch your eyes out, I'd throw water over you, I'd have you arrested."

Blachevelle smiled with the self-satisfied smugness of a man whose vanity is tickled. Favorite went on: "Oh yes, and I'd set the guards on you! Hah! I wouldn't think twice, you mongrel!"

Blachevelle, in ecstasy, leaned back in his chair and proudly closed both eyes.

Dahlia, still eating, whispered to Favorite through all the din: "Do you really idolize him that much, then, your Blachevelle?"

"Me? I can't stand him," replied Favorite in the same tone, taking up her fork once more. "He's a tightwad. I'm in love with the character over the road from my place. He's very good-looking, is that young man, do you know the one I mean? You can tell he'd make a good actor. I love actors. As soon as he gets home, his mother says: 'Oh, Lord! There goes my peace and quiet. He'll be shouting his head off again any moment. Dear boy, you give me such a headache.' Because he goes up to the very top of the house, right up to the attic, with all the rats, up into some dark cubbyhole, up as high as he can go, and he sings and recites and carries on—you can hear him down in the street! He's already making twenty sous a day working for an attorney writing out crooked legal stuff. He's the son of an old chorister from Saint-Jacques-du-Haut-Pas.[1] Oh, he's gorgeous and he idolizes me! I mean, one day when he saw me making pancake batter, he said, 'Mamselle, make your gloves into fritters and I'll eat them.' Only an artist could come up with a line like that. Ah, he really is gorgeous. I'm nearly going crazy over him. But, so what? I still tell Blachevelle I adore him. What a whopper, eh? What a whopper!"

Favorite paused, then added: "Dahlia, you know, I feel quite sad. It's done nothing but rain all summer, the wind is driving me nuts, it never stops, Blachevelle's too mean to roll downhill, it's hard to find fresh peas at the markets, no one knows what to eat anymore—I've got the blues, as the English say—butter is so dear! And then, you know, to top it off, what could be worse than dining in a joint with a bed in it?! It makes me tired of living."

## VII. The Wisdom of Tholomyès

Meanwhile, while some were singing, others were talking away at the top of their lungs and all at the same time; the place was nothing but noise. Tholomyès decided to intervene: "Let's not just say whatever comes into our heads or talk too fast," he shouted. "Let's think about what we're saying if we want to sparkle. Too much improvisation drains the old brain. Flowing beer gathers no head. Messieurs, what's the hurry? Let's season this blowout with a bit of dignity; let's eat with a bit of restraint; let's savor the feast—slowly. Let's take our time. Take spring; if it comes too early, it's had it, meaning everything's frostbitten. Too much zeal is the death of peach trees and apricots. Too much zeal kills the grace and joy of a fine meal. No zeal, gentlemen! Grimod de la Reynière is of the same opinion as Talleyrand!"[1]

Mutiny rumbled through the group.

"Tholomyès, cut it out," said Blachevelle.

"Down with the tyrant!" said Fameuil.

"Bombarda, Bombance, and Bambouche!" cried Listolier.

"There's such a thing as Sunday, you know," Fameuil resumed.

"We are sober, what's more," added Listolier.

"Tholomyès," put in Blachevelle, "behold *mon calme*."

"You are the marquis of calm," replied Tholomyès.

This mediocre play on words—the marquis de Montcalm was a famous royalist of the day—had the effect of a stone tossed into a pond. All the frogs stopped croaking.

"Friends," cried Tholomyès in the tone of a man regaining control of his empire, "as you were. You mustn't let yourselves be so stunned by this rather stunning pun. Not everything that falls out of the sky is worthy of enthusiasm and respect. Puns are the droppings of the mind in flight. The joke falls where it will; and the mind, after releasing its inane remark, takes off into the blue. A whitish spot splattering a rock does not stop the condor from soaring. Far be it from me though to put down the pun! I give it its due, nothing more. All the most august, the most sublime, the most delightful minds of humanity, and perhaps beyond humanity, have gone in for the play on words. Jesus Christ made a pun about Saint Peter—Petrus, the Rock—Moses about Isaac, Aeschylus about Polynices, Cleopatra about Octavius. And note that Cleopatra's pun preceded the battle of Actium and that, without it, no one would have remembered the city of Toryna,[2] whose name derives from a Greek word for dipping spoon. Having conceded that, I return to my exhortation. Brethren, I repeat, no zeal, no din, no excess, even of witticisms, quips, jubilant bons mots, and plays on words. Hear me out, for I have the prudence of Amphiaraüs[3] and the baldness of Caesar. There must be a limit, even to conundrums. *Est modus in rebus.*[4] There must be a limit, even to dinners. You like apple turnovers, mesdames, but don't eat too many of them. Even with turnovers, art and good sense are required. Gluttony punishes the glutton. Gula punishes Gulax.[5] Indigestion was invented by God to force morality on stomachs. And remember this: Each of our passions, even love, has a stomach that must not be overloaded. In all things, we must write the word *finis* in time, we must contain ourselves, even when our urges are urgent, we must slam the door on our appetite and shoot the bolt, stick fantasy in the lockup, turn ourselves in. He is a wise man who knows when the moment has come to put himself under arrest. Have a little faith in me. Just because I've done my bit of law, or so my exam results tell me, just because I know the difference between a hypothetical matter and a matter pending, just because I've submitted a thesis in Latin on the ways torture was meted out in Rome in the days when Munatius Demens was quaestor of parricide,[6] and just because it seems I'm about to be made a doctor of law, it does not necessarily follow that I am a complete idiot. I recommend moderation in your desires. As sure as my name is Félix Tholomyès, what I say is well said. Happy is he who, when the time comes, makes a heroic stand and abdicates, like Sulla or Origen of Alexandria."[7]

Favorite listened as though she hung on every word.

"Félix!" she cried. "Such a pretty name! I love it. It's Latin. It means Prospero."[8]

Tholomyès went on: "*Quirites,* gentlemen, *caballeros, mes amis*! Do you hope to feel no sting of desire, to pass up the nuptial bed and thumb your nose at love? Nothing easier. Here's the formula: drink lemonade, get far too much exercise, do hard labor; wear yourselves out, drag around heavy logs, do not sleep, stay up all night, fill yourself till you're ready to burst with carbonated drinks and water-lily tisanes, sip emulsions of poppies and agnus-castus; season this for me with a strict diet, practically starve to death, and throw in cold baths, herbal belts, applications of lead poultices, lotions containing lead solution, and fomentations of vinegar and water."

"I'd prefer a woman," said Listolier.

"Woman!" Tholomyès shot back. "Never trust Woman. Woe to him who surrenders to her changing heart! Woman is perfidious and devious.[9] She hates the serpent out of professional rivalry. The serpent is the shop across the road."

"Tholomyès," cried Blachevelle, "you're drunk!"

"Like hell I am!" said Tholomyès.

"Well, lighten up a little, then," Blachevelle insisted.

"All right, then, I will," said Tholomyès.

And, filling his glass, he got to his feet.

"Glory be to wine! *Nunc te, Bacche, canam!*[10] Sorry, girls, that's Spanish. And the proof of that, señoras, is this: Give me the wine cask and I'll give you the people. The *arroba* of Castille contains sixteen liters, the *cantaro* of Alicante twelve, the *almuda* of the Canaries twenty-five, the *cuartin* of the Baleares twenty-six, Czar Peter's boot thirty. Long live the czar, who was big, and long live his boot, which was even bigger! Mesdames, a friendly word of advice: Go to bed with the wrong man, if you feel like it. The whole point of love is to stray. A love affair is not meant to grovel and slave like a frowsy British maid with calluses on her knees from scrubbing. It's not made for that; it's made to rove gaily, sweet fling! They say: To err is human. I say: To err is to be in love. Mesdames, I idolize you all. O Zéphine, O Joséphine, with your face like a slapped backside, you'd be lovely if you weren't so cross. You look like you had a pretty face until someone accidentally sat on it. As for Favorite, O nymphs and muses! One day Blachevelle was crossing the gutter at the rue Guérin-Boisseau when he spotted a beautiful girl with taut white stockings showing off her legs. The overture was to his liking, so Blachevelle fell in love. The one he loved was Favorite. O Favorite, you have Ionian lips. There was once a Greek painter named Euphorion who was known as the painter of lips. Only this Greek would have been worthy of painting your mouth. Listen! Before you came along, there was no creature worthy of the name Favorite. You are made to be handed the apple, like Venus,[11] or to eat it, like Eve. Beauty begins with you. I just mentioned Eve, it is you who created her. You deserve a patent for inventing the beautiful woman. O Favorite, I'll stop using the familiar form of address, since I'm now moving from poetry to prose. Just now, you spoke my name. I was deeply moved; but, whoever we are, let's not get stuck on names. Names can be deceptive. My name is Félix but I'm not happy. Words lie. Let's not blindly accept what they tell us. It would be a mistake to write to Liège for corks or to Pau for gloves.[12] Miss Dahlia, if I were you, I'd call myself Rose. Flowers should smell good and a woman should have wit. I'll say nothing of Fantine, she is a thinker, a dreamer, a ponderer, a sensitive soul; she is a phantom in the form of a nymph with the prudery of a nun who has strayed into the life of a grisette, but who takes refuge in her illusions, and who sings and prays and gazes up into the blue without a clue what she's seeing or what she's doing; with her eyes planted on the heavens, she wanders into a garden where there are more birds than exist in real life! O Fantine, know this: I, Tholomyès, I am an illusion. But she doesn't even hear me, this blond daughter of pipe dreams! Everything about her is fresh, smooth, young, sweet morning light. O Fantine, a girl worthy of calling yourself Marguerite[13] or Pearl, you are a woman of the most beautiful Orient. Mesdames, a second bit of advice: Don't get married. Marriage is like a grafted plant; it either takes well or not at all; shun the risk. But, heavens! What am I going on about? I'm wasting my breath. Girls are incurable when it comes to weddings; and no matter what the rest of us, we wise men, may say, nothing will prevent these vest makers and bootie knitters from dreaming of husbands loaded with diamonds. Well, so be it; but, sweethearts, remember this: You eat too much sugar. You have only one fault, O women, and that is nibbling sweets. O gnawing sex, your pretty little white teeth crave sugar. So, listen carefully, sugar is a salt. All salt is drying. Sugar is the most drying of all salts. It sucks the fluids out of the blood through the veins; coagulation follows, then the blood solidifies; then you get tuberculosis in the lungs, then death. This is why diabetes verges on consumption. So don't munch on sugar and you will live! I now turn to the menfolk. Messieurs, make your conquests. Steal your beloveds from each other remorselessly. Thrust and parry. In love, there are no friends. Wherever there is a pretty woman there is open hostility. No quarter, all-out war! A pretty woman is a *casus belli;* a pretty woman is a *flagrante delicto.* All the invasions in history have been caused by petticoats. Woman is Man's right. Romulus carried off the Sabine women, William the Conqueror carried off the Saxon women, Caesar carried off the women of Rome. The man who is not loved hovers like a vulture over other men's lovers; and, as for me, to all those unfortunate men without women, I throw down the sublime proclamation Bonaparte delivered to the Italian army: 'Soldiers, the enemy has everything you lack!' "

Tholomyès broke off.

"Take a breather, Tholomyès," said Blachevelle.

At the same time, Blachevelle, backed by Listolier and Fameuil, struck up to the tune of a lament one of those workingmen's songs composed of the first words that spring to mind, heavily rhymed or not at all, as meaningless as the movement of a tree or the noise of the wind, which emerge out of pipe smoke and lift and evaporate with it. This is the ditty they came up with in response to Tholomyès's harangue:

> The father turkeys gave
> Some money to an agent
> So 'is Grace Clermont-Tonnerre[14]
> Was made pope on Midsummer's Day;
> But Clermont could not be
> Made pope, not being a priest;
> So their raging agent
> Gave 'em their money back.[15]

This was not effective in dampening Tholomyès's improvisation; he tossed back his glass, refilled it, and started off again.

"Down with wisdom! Forget everything I said. Let's not be prudes or prudent or prudhommes. I drink to merriment; let's be merry! Let's polish off our little lesson in law with madness and food. Indigestion and the Digest. Let Justinian be male and revelry female! Joy to the very depths! Live, O creation! The world is a great fat diamond! I am happy. The birds are amazing. It's all one big party! The nightingale is as good as Elleviou[16]—and it's free. Summer, I salute you. O Luxembourg, O Georgics of the rue Madame and of the allée de l'Observatoire![17] O dreamy chickadiddies! O, all those lovely maids who keep themselves amused sketching their little charges while they mind them! The pampas of South America would appeal to me, if I didn't have the arcades of the Odéon. My soul soars over virgin forests and savannas. Everything is beautiful. The flies buzz in the sunbeams. The sun has sneezed hummingbirds. Kiss me, Fantine."

He kissed Favorite by mistake.

## VIII. Death of a Horse

"The food's better at Edon's[1] than at this Bombarda's!" cried Zéphine.

"I prefer Bombarda to Edon," declared Blachevelle. "It's more luxurious. It's more Asian. Look at the room downstairs. It has great looking-glasses on the walls."

"I prefer *glaces*[2] on my plate," said Favorite.

Blachevelle was not deterred.

"Look at the knives. The handles are silver at Bombarda's and bone at Edon's. Well, silver's worth more than bone."

"Unless you've got a silver chin," Tholomyès observed.

At that moment he was gazing out at the dome of the Invalides, visible from Bombarda's windows.

There was a lull.

"Tholomyès," cried Fameuil, "a moment ago, Listolier and I were having a discussion."

"A discussion is good," replied Tholomyès, "an argument is better."

"We were arguing about philosophy."

"So far so good."

"Who do you prefer—Descartes or Spinoza?"[3]

"Désaugiers,"[4] said Tholomyès.

This ruling handed down, he drank and resumed: "I agree to live. All is not over on this earth, since we can still go on ranting. For this, I give thanks to the immortal gods. We lie, but we laugh. We assert, but we doubt. The unexpected springs out of a syllogism. That is beautiful. There are still human beings here below who can merrily open and shut the surprise box of paradox. What you are quietly drinking, mesdames, is Madeira, don't you know, from the Coural das Freiras vineyard, which is three hundred and seventeen fathoms above sea level! Take note while you drink! Three hundred and seventeen fathoms! And Monsieur Bombarda, the magnificent restaurateur, gives you these three hundred and seventeen fathoms for four francs fifty centimes!"

Fameuil butted in once more: "Tholomyès, your opinion is law. Who's your favorite author?"

"Ber—"

"—Quin?"

"No. Choux."[5]

Tholomyès went on: "All honor to Bombarda! He would be on a par with Munophis of Elephanta if only he could pick me up an *almeh*—a dancing girl, to you—and with Thygelion of Cheroneus[6] if only he could bring me a hetaera! For, O mesdames, there were Bombardas in Greece and Egypt. So Apuleius[7] tells us. Alas, it's always the same old story, there is nothing original anymore in the creator's creation! *Nil sub sole novum,*[8] as Solomon says—nothing new under the sun; *amor omnibus idem,*[9] says Virgil—love is the same for all of us. Julie hops in a boat at Saint-Cloud with her Jules, just as Aspasia embarked with Pericles in the fleet of Samos.[10] One last word. Do you know who this Aspasia was, ladies? Though she lived at a time when women did not yet have souls, she had a soul; a soul tinged pink and purple, hotter than fire, fresher than the dawn. Aspasia was a creature in whom Woman's two extremes met; she was the prostitute goddess. Socrates, plus Manon Lescaut.[11] Aspasia was created in case Prometheus[12] needed a trollop."

Tholomyès was off and racing and would have been hard to stop if a horse had not fallen down in front of them on the quai at that precise moment. The shock stopped both the cart and the orator in their tracks. It was a mare from Beauce,[13] old and skinny and ready for the knacker's, and it had been pulling a very heavy cart. Having got as far as Bombarda's, the exhausted animal was overcome and refused to budge another inch. The incident had drawn a crowd. The outraged cart driver, cursing furiously, had barely had time to pronounce with suitable energy the sacramental word *mongrel!* backed by an implacable lash of the whip, when the nag fell, never to get up again. At the clamor of the bystanders, Tholomyès's merry little audience whipped round and Tholomyès took the opportunity to close his address with this melancholy verse:

> She was of this world where cuckoos and carriages
>     Have the same fate,
> And, rotten as she was, she lived the way the rotten live,
>     For the space of a morning—the mongrel![14]

"Poor horse," sighed Fantine.

And Dahlia cried: "There goes Fantine, pitying horses now. Have you ever seen anyone so soft in the head!"

At that point, Favorite, crossing her arms and throwing her head back, looked Tholomyès firmly in the eye and said: "Right! So, what about the surprise?"

"Quite right. The moment has come," replied Tholomyès. "Gentlemen, the hour has struck when we surprise the ladies. Ladies, wait for us a moment."

"It begins with a kiss," said Blachevelle.

"On the forehead," added Tholomyès.

Each man gravely planted a kiss on his mistress's forehead; then all four men headed for the door in single file, placing a finger over their lips.

Favorite clapped her hands as they filed out.

"It's already fun," she said.

"Don't be too long," murmured Fantine. "We're waiting."

## IX. Happy Ending to Happiness

Left to their own devices, the girls propped their elbows on the windowsills in pairs, chatting and leaning their heads out the window and talking over one another.

They saw the young men leave the Cabaret Bombarda arm in arm; the men looked back and waved, laughing, then vanished in the dusty Sunday throng that invades the Champs-Élysées once a week.

"Don't be long!" Fantine shouted.

"Wonder what they'll bring us back?" said Zéphine.

"Something nice, that's for sure," said Dahlia.

"I hope it will be something in gold," Favorite contributed.

They were soon distracted by the commotion at the water's edge, which they could make out through the branches of the great trees and which absorbed their attention completely. It was the hour when the mail coaches and diligences set out. Nearly all the stagecoaches heading for the south and the west took the Champs-Élysées in those days. Most of them followed the quai and went out through the barrière Passy. Every minute some great hulking carriage painted yellow and black and heavily loaded, harnesses jingling noisily, deformed by all the chests and luggage packed under tarpaulins, bristling with heads that swiftly vanished, grinding along the road surface jarring all the cobblestones and bricks, hurtled past the crowd in a shower of sparks, like a mobile forge, billowing dust like smoke in a fit of frenzy. This racket delighted the girls. Favorite exclaimed: "What a din! Sounds like a heap of chains flying off."

It so happened that one of these carriages, which could only just be made out through the thick foliage of the elms, stopped for a moment and then set off again at a gallop. This amazed Fantine.

"That's strange!" she said. "I didn't think the diligence ever stopped."

Favorite shrugged her shoulders.

"That Fantine is amazing! I never cease to marvel. She's dazzled by the simplest things. Here's an idea for you: Suppose I'm a traveler and I say to the diligence: 'I'm going ahead, you pick me up on the quai on your way.' The diligence comes along, sees me, stops, and picks me up. It happens every day. My darling, you know nothing of life."

Some time passed in this way. Suddenly Favorite sat up, alert, as though she'd just woken up.

"Well, now," she said, "what's happened to this surprise?"

"Now you mention it, yes," said Dahlia, "the famous surprise!"

"They're taking their time!" said Fantine.

Just as Fantine's sigh died, the waiter who had served dinner came in. He was holding what looked like a letter.

"What's that?" asked Favorite.

The waiter replied: "It's a note that the gentlemen left for the ladies."

"Why didn't you bring it right away?"

"Because the gentlemen ordered me not to give it to the ladies until an hour was up."

Favorite tore the note from the waiter's hands. It was, indeed, a letter.

"Well, well, well!" she said. "There's no address. But here's what it says on the outside: THIS IS THE SURPRISE!"

She swiftly broke the seal, opened it out and read (for she could read):

O, lovers of ours!

Know that we have parents. Parents are not something you know much about. They are called mothers and fathers in the civil code, which is puerile but honest. Now, these parents are moaning, these old men want to claim us, these good old men and women call us prodigal sons; they want us to return and offer to kill fatted calves for us. Being virtuous, we obey them. By the time you read this, five fiery steeds will be bringing us back to our mamas and papas. We are packing up our tents, as Bossuet would say. We are leaving, we have left. We are fleeing in the arms of Laffitte and on the wings of Caillard. The Toulouse diligence[1] is tearing us away from the abyss and the abyss is you, O, our beautiful little darlings! We are returning to society, to duty and to order, at a great clip, at the rate of three leagues an hour. It is important for the homeland that we be, like everyone else, police commissioners, fathers of families, council employees, and members of the Council of State. Venerate us. We are sacrificing ourselves. Mourn us rapidly and replace us pronto. If this letter tears you apart, tear it apart back. Adieu.

For nearly two years, we have made you happy. Don't hold it against us.

*Signed:* BLACHEVELLE
FAMEUIL
LISTOLIER
FÉLIX THOLOMYÈS

*Post-Scriptum.* The meal is paid for.

The four girls looked at each other.

Favorite was the first to break the silence.

"Well!" she cried. "That's a pretty good joke, I'll give them that."

"Very droll," said Zéphine.

"It must have been Blachevelle's idea," Favorite went on. "It makes me feel quite in love with him. No sooner lost than loved. That's the way it goes."

"No," said Dahlia, "it's Tholomyès's idea. You can tell."

"In that case," retorted Favorite, "down with Blachevelle and long live Tholomyès!"

"Long live Tholomyès!" cried Dahlia and Zéphine.

And they burst out laughing.

Fantine laughed with them.

An hour later, when she was back in her room, she cried. He was, as we said, her first love; she had given herself to this Tholomyès as to a husband, and the poor girl had a child.

# BOOK FOUR

# TO ENTRUST IS SOMETIMES
# TO ABANDON

### I. ONE MOTHER MEETS ANOTHER

There was, during the first quarter of the current century, in Montfermeil, near Paris, a kind of greasy spoon that no longer exists today. This greasy spoon was run by people by the name of Thénardier, husband and wife. It was located in the ruelle du Boulanger. Above the door was a board nailed flat against the wall. There was something painted on the board that looked like a man piggyback-ing another man wearing a general's big gold epaulets with big silver stars; red splotches represented blood; the rest of the tableau was of smoke and probably represented a battle. At the bottom you could read the inscription: AU SER-GENT DE WATERLOO.

There is nothing commoner than a wagon or a cart outside the door of an inn. But the vehicle, or to be more precise, the remnant of a vehicle, that was blocking the street in front of the Sergent de Waterloo, on a night in the spring of 1818, would certainly have attracted the attention of any passing painter by its sheer bulk.

It was the front-axle section of one of those log carriers used in lumber country to cart sawn timber and tree trunks. This section was composed of a swiveling front axle into which a heavy shaft was slotted, supported by two enormous wheels. The whole array was squat, overwhelming, deformed. You would have thought it was the mount of a giant cannon. Rust had coated the wheels, rims, hubs, axle, and shaft with a layer of mud—a hideous yellowish distemper not unlike the color wash deliberately applied to cathedrals. The wood had disappeared under the mud and the iron under the rust. Underneath the axle a huge chain fit for a Goliath of the galleys hung like drapery. This chain made you think, not of the beams it was meant to haul, but of the mastodons and mammoths it could have harnessed; there was the whiff of the lockup about it, but of some colossal, superhuman lockup, and it looked as if it had yanked away some monster. Homer would have tied up Polyphemus with it, Shakespeare, Caliban.[1]

Why was this partial front axle of a log carrier where it was, sitting there in the street? First, to obstruct passage; then, to complete the rusting process. In the old social order there were a host of institutions that you stumbled across on your path out in the open air, which had no other reason for being there.

The middle part of the chain hung under the axle quite close to the ground, and where it curved, two little girls were sitting together that night as if on a swing, exquisitely entwined, one of them about two and a half years old, the other eighteen months, the smaller in the arms of the bigger. A cleverly knotted handkerchief prevented them from falling off. Some mother had spotted the gruesome chain and said to herself: Now, there's a nice toy for the kids to play with!

To top it off, the two little girls were dressed gracefully and with some refinement and they were radiant; they were like two roses on a scrap heap, their eyes triumphant; their fresh cheeks blooming with laughter. One had chestnut hair, the other, brown. Their innocent faces shone in ravishment; perfume wafting from a flowering shrub nearby sent fragrant emanations out to passersby, but it seemed to come from the little girls. The one who was eighteen months old showed her lovely little bare tummy with the chaste indecency of the toddler. Above and around the two delicate heads, molded in happiness and dipped in light, the gigantic front axle, black with rust, almost shocking, all tangled up with curved bits and vicious sharp corners, arched like the mouth of a lair. A few feet away, squatting on the doorstep outside the inn, the mother, a woman whose appearance was not particularly attractive but rather touching at that precise moment, was swinging the two little girls by means of a long string, watching over them anxiously at the same time for fear of some accident, with that expression, both animal and angelic, that is peculiar to motherhood; at each movement, the grisly chain let out a screeching noise that sounded like a cry of fury; the little girls squealed in ecstasy, the setting sun glowed over their joy, and nothing could be as enchanting as this caprice of chance that had turned a Titan's chain into a swing for cherubim.

While rocking her two children, the mother tunelessly crooned a romantic ballad then all the rage:

You must, said a soldier . . .

Singing and watching her girls prevented her from hearing and seeing what was happening in the street.

Yet someone had approached her as she began the first lines of the ballad and suddenly she heard a voice say in her ear: "You have two pretty little girls there, Madame."

To the soft and beautiful Imogine,

replied the mother, continuing the song before turning round.

A woman stood a few feet away from her. This woman, too, had a child, which she was carrying in her arms.

She was also carrying a rather big overnight bag that looked extremely heavy.

This woman's child was one of the most divine creatures you could ever hope to see, a little girl two or three years old. She was more than a match for the other two little girls for the stylishness of her outfit; she had a fine linen bonnet trimmed with Valenciennes lace and a little chemise with ribbons. Her pleated skirt was hitched up, showing her chubby, firm little white legs. She was wonderfully rosy and in fine fettle and so beautiful she made you want to bite the apples of her cheeks. Nothing could be said of her eyes, except that they were probably very big and that they had magnificent eyelashes, for she was sleeping.

She was sleeping that sleep of absolute trust peculiar to her age. Mothers' arms are made for tenderness; children sleep deeply in them.

As for the mother, she looked poor and sad. She had the look of the urban working woman reverting to being a peasant. She was young. Was she beautiful? Maybe, but in that getup it was hard to tell. A single strand of her blond hair which looked as though it would be very thick, had escaped the extremely severe peasant's headdress that clamped her hair in, ugly, tight, narrow, and tied under the chin. Laughter reveals lovely teeth if you have them, but she did not laugh. Her eyes looked as though they hadn't been dry in a long while. She was pale; she seemed extremely listless and somewhat sick; she looked at her child asleep in her arms with the special look of a mother who has breast-fed her baby herself. A big blue handkerchief of the kind invalids use to blow their noses was tied like a shawl around her waist and largely concealed it. She had brown hands, dotted all over with freckles, the index finger calloused and jagged from sewing needles, a brown cloak of rough wool, a cotton dress, and heavy shoes. It was Fantine.

It was Fantine. Barely recognizable. Yet, if you looked closely, you could see she still had her beauty. A sad line, which looked like the beginnings of irony, marred her right cheek. As for her finery, that airy toilette of muslin and ribbons put together so gaily, with such whimsy and poetry, full of tinkling baubles and the scent of lilacs—it had evaporated like the lovely sparkling frosts that you can mistake for diamonds in the sun and that melt, leaving only the black branches behind.

Ten months had passed since "the great practical joke."

What had happened in those ten months? We can well imagine.

After abandonment came general embarrassment. Fantine had immediately lost sight of Favorite, Zéphine, and Dahlia—the bond, broken on the men's side, came undone on the women's. You would have truly amazed them, a fortnight later, if you'd said they'd ever been friends; they no longer had any reason to be. Fantine was left on her own. The father of her child was gone—alas! such splits are irrevocable—and she found herself absolutely alone, minus the habit of working and plus the acquired taste for pleasure. Encouraged by her liaison with Tholomyès to look down on the menial work she knew how to do, she had neglected any opportunities for employment, and they had soon slipped away. Nothing to fall back on. Fantine could not write, could scarcely read; as a child, she had only been taught to sign her name; she had paid a public letter-writer to write one letter to Tholomyès, then a second and a third. Tholomyès did not answer any of them. One day, Fantine had overheard some old crones in the street saying as they eyed her daughter: "Does anyone take these brats to heart? You wash your hands of brats like that!" So then she thought of Tholomyès, who had washed his hands of his own child and did not take this innocent being to heart; and her heart hardened toward that man. But what could she do about it? She did not know who to turn to anymore. She had sinned, but as you know, she was fundamentally decent and virtuous. She felt vaguely that she was on the brink of tumbling into destitution, of sliding down skid row. She had the courage she needed, and bore up bravely. The idea occurred to her to go back to her native village, to Montreuil-sur-mer. There, someone would perhaps remember her and give her work. Yes, but she would have to hide the evidence of her sin. And she had a clouded glimpse of another possible separation, even more painful than the first. Her heart ached, but she made her decision. Fantine, as we will see, was fiercely courageous in the face of life.

She had already valiantly renounced finery, dressing in cotton and putting all her silks, all her glad rags, all her ribbons and lace on her daughter's back—the sole vanity that remained to her, this one sacred. She sold everything she had, which gave her two hundred francs; her minor debts paid, all she had left was about eighty francs. At twenty-two years of age, on a fine spring morning, she left Paris, carrying her child on her back. Anyone who had seen them going past together would have taken pity on them. The woman had only that child in the whole wide world, and the child had only the mother. Fantine had breast-fed her baby herself; this had weakened her chest and she now had a bit of a cough.

We will have no further occasion to speak of Monsieur Félix Tholomyès. We will say here only that, twenty years later, under King Louis-Philippe,[2] he was a fat provincial attorney, influential and rich, a shrewd voter and a most severe jurist; and still a man of pleasure.

Around noon, after having got some rest by traveling now and then in what were known at the time as the *petites voitures*, or little cabs, of the Paris region, Fantine found herself in Montfermeil, in the ruelle du Boulanger.

As she was passing Thénardier's inn, the two little girls, so excited on their monster swing, had sort of dazzled her, and she had stopped in her tracks before this vision of joy.

There are such things as magic spells. Those two little girls cast theirs over this poor mother.

She stared at them, quite overcome. The presence of angels heralds paradise. She thought she could see, above the inn, the mysterious HERE of Providence. Those two little creatures were so obviously happy! She watched them, she admired them, so very moved that, the second their mother took a breath between two lines of her song, she couldn't help herself from saying what we have just read: "You have two pretty little girls there, Madame."

The most ferocious beasts are disarmed by any tenderness shown to their young. The mother looked up at the stranger and thanked her, and invited her to take a seat on the bench by the door, while she remained squatting on the doorstep. The two women chatted.

"I'm Madame Thénardier," said the mother of the two little girls. "We keep this inn."

Then, still caught up in her ballad, she sang through clenched teeth:

You must, I am a knight,
And I'm leaving for Palestine.

This Madame Thénardier was a redhead, fleshy, yet bony; the soldier's-wife type in all its ghastliness, and with an odd bent look acquired from devouring romantic novels. She was mannish, yet simpering. Old novels that play out in the imaginations of women running fleapit hotels have that effect. She was still young; had only just turned thirty. If the woman squatting had stood up, her height and her bearing, which were those of an ambulatory colossus fit for the fairground freak show, might very well have frightened off the traveler, derailed her confidence, and caused what we are about to relate to vanish into thin air. Whether a person sits or stands—fate hangs by threads like these.

The traveler told her tale, a slightly edited version: how she had been a working woman; how her husband had died; how she couldn't find work in Paris and was now looking elsewhere, in her own part of the country; how she had left Paris, on foot, that very morning; how, since she was carrying her child, she had got tired and, having come across the Villemomble coach, had hopped on;

how from Villemomble she had reached Montfermeil on foot; how her little girl had walked a bit, but not far, she was so little, and so she had had to carry her and her treasure had fallen asleep.

As she said this, she gave her daughter a passionate kiss that woke her up. The little girl opened her eyes, great big blue eyes like those of her mother, and looked at . . . what? Nothing, everything, with that grave and sometimes stern look little children have, which is one of the mysteries of their luminous innocence in the face of our waning virtues. You would think they knew they were angels and that we were mere human beings. Then the little girl began to laugh and, though her mother held her back, slid to the ground with the indomitable energy of a small being who wants to run. Suddenly she spotted the other two on their swing, stood stock-still and poked her tongue out, a sure sign of admiration.

Mother Thénardier unstrapped the children and took them down off the swing and said: "Go and play, the three of you."

Children make friends easily at that age and after a minute or two the Thénardier girls were playing with the newcomer, digging holes in the ground to their immense delight.

The newcomer was a very gay little girl; the mother's goodness was reflected in her gaiety; she had picked up a piece of wood, which she was using as a spade, and she was busily digging a ditch fit for a fly. What a gravedigger does becomes cheery when done by a child.

The two women went on chatting.

"What's your kid's name?"

"Cosette."

For Cosette read Euphrasie.[3] The little girl was called Euphrasie. But the mother had turned Euphrasie into Cosette through that sweet and gracious instinct of mothers and the common people, changing Josefa into Pepita and Françoise into Sillette. This is the kind of derivation that disturbs and disconcerts the whole science of etymology. We once knew a grandmother who managed to turn Théodore into Gnon.

"How old is she?"

"She'll soon be three."

"Same as my eldest."

Meanwhile, the three little girls were huddled in positions of deep anxiety and bliss; an event had taken place, a fat worm had just come out of the ground and frightened them and now they were in ecstasy.

They had their gleaming heads together, touching; for all the world like three heads in the one halo.

"Kids!" cried mother Thénardier. "See how well they get on already! You'd swear they were three sisters!"

This, no doubt, was the cue the other mother had been waiting for. She grabbed Madame Thénardier's hand, looked into her eyes, and said: "Would you keep my little girl for me?"

Mother Thénardier gave one of those starts of surprise that express neither consent nor refusal.

Cosette's mother continued: "You see, I can't take my little girl back home. Work won't allow it. If you have a child, you can't get a job. They are so ridiculous where I come from. It's the good Lord who's guided me to your inn. When I saw your little girls so pretty and clean and happy, I was quite overcome. I thought: Now, there's a good mother for you. That's exactly it: They would be like three sisters. And then again, it won't be long before I'm back. Would you look after my child?"

"I'd have to see," said mother Thénardier.

"I'd give you six francs a month."

At this point a man's voice boomed from the depths of the fleapit:

"Nothing less than seven francs. And six months up front."

"Six times seven is forty-two," said mother Thénardier.

"I'll pay," said the mother.

"And fifteen francs on top of that for initial expenses," added the man's voice.

"Total, fifty-seven francs," said Madame Thénardier. And in the middle of her calculations she went on softly crooning:

You must, said a warrior.

"I'll pay," said the mother. "I've got eighty francs. I'll have enough left over to get back home. If I walk. I'll earn money down there and as soon as I have a bit, I'll come back for my darling girl."

The man's voice resumed: "Does the little one have a supply of clothes?"

"That's my husband," said mother Thénardier.

"Of course she has some clothes, poor little treasure. I knew it was your husband. And beautiful clothes, too! Lovely things. Dozens of everything; and silk frocks like a lady's. They're in my overnight bag, there."

"You'll have to hand them over," the man's voice sounded again.

"Well, naturally I'll hand them over!" said the mother. "Wouldn't that be something if I left my daughter without a stitch!"

The master's face appeared.

"Right," he said.

The deal was done. The young mother spent the night at the inn, handed over her money and left her little girl behind, buckled up her overnight bag, emptied of its bundle of clothes and now light, and set out the following morning, counting on returning soon. These sorts of partings are arranged so smoothly, but they are full of despair.

One of the Thénardiers' neighbors met the young mother as she was setting out and he came back with the tale: "I've just seen a girl sobbing her heart out in the street."

When Cosette's mother was out of the way, the husband said to his wife: "This will fix up that bill for a hundred and ten francs that's due tomorrow. I was fifty francs short. You know, I would have had the bailiff on me and a caution. You're not a bad mousetrap with your two little ones."

"I didn't realize," said the wife.

## II. Initial Sketch of Two Shady Characters

The mouse caught in the trap was pretty puny; but the cat rejoiced even over a meager little mouse.

What were the Thénardiers?

We'll just say one thing for the moment. We can finish the sketch later.

These creatures belonged to that mongrel class composed of commoners who have risen and intelligent people who have fallen, which lies somewhere between the class known as middle and the class known as lower, and which combines some of the defects of the second with almost all the vices of the first, without having the generous impulse of the worker or the honest respectability of the bourgeois.

They had those stunted runtlike natures that easily turn monstrous if something sinister happens to fire them up. The woman was basically a brute and the man had all the makings of a complete scoundrel. Both were in the highest degree capable of the kind of odious progress that aims for evil. There exist cramped souls that are always darting backward into the shadows, like crayfish, regressing in life rather than advancing, employing experience to aggravate their deformity, going from bad to worse and getting more encrusted with a deepening blackness. This man and this woman were among such people.

Old man Thénardier in particular was a challenge for the physiognomist. You only have to look at certain men to be wary of them; you can sense that they are foul, through and through. They are anxious after the event and menacing ahead of it. There is some unknown quantity in them. We can no more account for what they have done than for what they will do. The shifty black look in their eyes gives them away. You only have to hear them utter a word or see them make a move and you get a glimpse of the dark secrets in their past and the dark mysteries in their future.

This Thénardier, if you took him at his word, had been a soldier—a sergeant, he claimed; he had probably taken part in the campaign of 1815, and even acquitted himself quite bravely, so it would seem. We will see down the track what this really entailed. The sign for his tavern was an allusion to one of his feats of arms. He had painted it himself, for he could turn his hand to anything—badly.

Those were the days when the early "classical" novel, which had started off as *Clélie*, had become nothing more than *Lodoïska*, ever aristocratic but increasingly vulgar, having tumbled from the lofty heights of Mademoiselle de Scudéri to the level of Madame Bournon-Malarme, and from Madame de Lafayette to Madame Barthélémy-Hadot,[1] inflaming the loving hearts of the concierges of Paris and wreaking havoc even farther afield in the suburbs. Madame Thénardier was just smart enough to read that kind of book. She crammed herself full of them. She drowned what little brains she had in them. This had given her, while she was still very young, and even a bit later on, a sort of wondering attitude toward her husband, who was a dyed-in-the-wool rotter with a certain depth, a thug who knew his grammar, almost, a man both gross and refined at once, but who, when it came to sentimentalism, read Pigault-Lebrun[2] and who, when it came to "anything to do with sex," as he so quaintly put it, was a thorough and unmitigated lout. His wife was some twelve or fifteen years younger than he was. Later, when the novelistically sweeping hair began to go gray, when Megaera, the harridan, emerged from Pamela,[3] mother Thénardier was nothing more than a nasty fat witch who had reveled in mind-numbing novels. Now, you don't read rubbish with impunity. The result was that her elder daughter was named Éponine. As for the younger one, the poor little girl was nearly named Gulnare;[4] owing to some happy diversion provided by a novel by Ducray-Duminil,[5] she merely collected the name Azelma.

And yet, we might just say in passing, not everything was superficial and ridiculous in what we might term the anarchy of Christian names characteristic of that curious age to which we are here alluding. Apart from the influence of romantic novels just mentioned, it was also a social symptom. Today it is not rare for a little cowherd to be called Arthur, Alfred, or Alphonse, or for a vicomte—if vicomtes still exist—to be called Thomas, Pierre, or Jacques. This displacement—switching the "elegant" name and the "plebeian" name around, turning the rustic aristocratic and the aristocrat rustic—is nothing more nor less than equality's backwash. The winds of change blow there as irresistibly as everywhere else. Beneath the apparent contradiction lies something great and profound: the French Revolution.

## III. The Lark

Being evil is not enough for a person to prosper. The greasy spoon was doing badly.

Thanks to the traveler's fifty-seven francs, Thénardier was able to avoid a caution[1] and to honor his signature. The following month, they were short of money again; the woman took Cosette's clothes to Paris and pawned them at the Mont-de-la-Piété, the pawnshop, for the sum of sixty francs. As soon as that sum was spent, the Thénardiers began seeing the little girl simply as a child they'd taken in out of charity and they treated her accordingly. Since she no longer had her own supply of clothes, they dressed her in the cast-off shirts and skirts of the little Thénardier girls, in other words, in rags. She was fed everyone else's leftovers, which was a step up from the dog but a step down from the cat. The dog and the cat were habitual table companions; Cosette ate with them, under the table, from a wooden bowl just like theirs.

Her mother, who, as we will later see, had settled in Montreuil-sur-mer, wrote, or to be more precise, got someone to write, every month in order to have news of her daughter. The Thénardiers invariably wrote back: Cosette is in perfect health.

When the first six months were up, the mother sent seven francs for the seventh month and continued to send funds from month to month with fairly constant regularity. The year was not yet out when Thénardier said: "A bloody lot of good that is! What does she expect us to do with her seven francs?" And he wrote to demand twelve francs. The mother, who had been persuaded that her little girl was happy and "coming along nicely," buckled and sent the twelve francs.

Certain natures can only love someone when they hate someone else. Mother Thénardier loved her own two daughters with a passion, which meant she loathed the outsider. It's sad to think that a mother's love can have a vile side. However tiny the space Cosette took up in her home, it seemed to her that it was being taken from her own and that the little girl reduced the very air her own girls breathed. This woman, like many women of her ilk, had a set store of cuddles and a set store of wallops and foul language to dispense each day. If she hadn't had Cosette, her own daughters, thoroughly idolized as they were, would certainly have received the lot, but the outsider did them the favor of diverting the wallops onto herself. The daughters got only the cuddles. Cosette did not make a move without causing a storm of violent and unmerited punishments to rain down upon her head. Sweet and fragile creature as she was, knowing nothing of this world or of God, she found herself endlessly punished, scolded, chastised, beaten, as she watched the two little creatures beside her, who were just like her, thrive in radiant sunlight.

Mother Thénardier being purely malevolent toward Cosette, Éponine and Azelma were malevolent, too. Children at that age are mere copies of their mothers. The format is smaller, that's all.

A year went by, then another.

In the village they would say: "They're good people, those Thénardiers.

They don't have much money and yet they're bringing up a poor kid someone dumped on their doorstep!"

It was thought that Cosette had been forgotten by her mother.

Yet old man Thénardier, having learned by some obscure means that the child was probably a bastard and that the mother was forced to disown her, demanded fifteen francs a month, saying that "the creature" was growing and "ate like a wild thing" and threatening to send her back. "She better not complain!" he cried. "I'll shove her brat in her face and that'll give the game away on her. I need more money." The mother paid the fifteen francs.

From year to year the child grew, and her misery grew, too.

While Cosette was still tiny, she was the whipping boy, so to speak, of the other two girls; as soon as she began to grow, that is, even before she was five, she became the drudge for the entire household.

Five, you will say, that's hardly likely. Alas, it's true. Social oppression can begin at any age. Did we not see, recently, the trial of a man named Dumolard, an orphan-*cum*-crook, who, according to the official record, being all alone in the world, from the age of five "worked for a living and stole."

Cosette was made to run errands, sweep the rooms, the courtyard, the street, wash up, even carry loads. The Thénardiers felt all the more authorized to act in this way because the mother, who was still in Montreuil-sur-mer, had begun not to pay on time. She was some months behind.

If the mother had returned to Montfermeil at the end of those three years, she would not have recognized her daughter. Cosette had been so pretty and so fresh when she arrived at the inn and now she was thin and pasty. There was a strangely anxious look about her. Sly! said the Thénardiers.

Injustice had made her sullen and misery had made her ugly. The only thing she still had were her beautiful eyes, and they were painful to look at because, being so big, they seemed to magnify the sadness she'd been dealt.

In winter it was a harrowing sight to see the poor child, who was not yet six, shivering in the scanty castoffs riddled with holes, sweeping the street before daybreak with an enormous broom in her little red hands and a tear in her great big eyes.

In those parts she was known as Alouette, the Lark. Ordinary people like metaphors and enjoyed calling by this name the tiny creature no bigger than a bird, trembling, frightened, and shivering, the first up every morning in the house and in the village, always on the street or in the fields before dawn.

Only, this poor Lark never sang.

BOOK FIVE

# THE DESCENT

## I. A HISTORY OF PROGRESS IN BLACK GLASS BEADS

But what had become of the mother who, according to the people of Montfermeil, seemed to have abandoned her child? Where was she? What was she doing?

After leaving her little Cosette with the Thénardiers, she had continued on her way and come to Montreuil-sur-mer.

This was, as you will recall, in 1818.

Fantine had left her province about twelve years before and Montreuil-sur-mer had changed. While Fantine had been slowly sinking deeper and deeper into destitution, her native town had prospered.

About two years previously one of those industrial feats had been accomplished that are major events in small country communities.

This detail is critical, so we feel it might be useful to enlarge on it—we would almost go so far as to say, to dwell on it.

From time immemorial, the special industry of Montreuil-sur-mer had been the reproduction of English jet beads and the black glass beads of Germany. This industry had always been sluggish because of the high cost of the raw materials, which had a trickle-down effect on labor. At the time of Fantine's return to Montreuil-sur-mer, an unheard-of transformation had occurred in the production of these "black goods." Toward the end of 1815, a man, a stranger, had blown into town and set up shop, and this newcomer had had the idea of substituting Japanese gum lac, or shellac, for resin in the manufacturing process and of using metal clasps that were simply bent rather than soldered, on bracelets in particular. This tiny change had amounted to a revolution.

This tiny change had in fact reduced the cost of the raw materials so considerably that it made it possible first, to raise wages, a benefit for the whole district; second, to improve the manufacture, an advantage for the consumer; and third, to sell them more cheaply while trebling the profits, a gain for the manufacturer.

Three outcomes from one idea.

In less than three years, the author of this process had become rich, which is good, and made everyone around him rich, which is even better. He was from outside the *département*. No one knew where he had come from, how he had got his start, or anything much at all about him.

The story went that he had come to town with very little money in his pockets, a few hundred francs at most.

It was from this measly capital, placed in the service of one ingenious idea, made fruitful by organization and thought, that he had made his fortune and the fortune of the whole surrounding country.

When he turned up in Montreuil-sur-mer, his clothes, manners, and turn of phrase were those of a mere laborer.

It seems that, the very day he made his obscure entry into the small town of Montreuil-sur-mer, as night was closing in on a cold December day, with a knapsack on his back and a thorn stick in his hand, a great fire had just broken out in the community hall. The man had thrown himself into the blaze and, at the risk of his own life, had saved two children who turned out to belong to the captain of the gendarmerie—which meant that no one thought to ask him for his passport. From that moment on, his name was known. He called himself father Madeleine.

## II. MADELEINE[1]

He was a man of about fifty, who had an absentminded air and who was good. That was all there was to say about him.

Thanks to the rapid expansion of the industry he had so impressively restructured, Montreuil-sur-mer had become a sizable business center. Spain, which consumes masses of black jet, placed huge orders with him every year. Montreuil-sur-mer was soon almost on a par with London and Berlin in the volume of trade. Father Madeleine's profits were such that, from his second year in business, he was able to build a huge factory, with two vast workshops, one for men and the other for women. Anyone who was hungry could show up and was sure of finding work and something to eat there. Father Madeleine required goodwill of the men and pure morals of the women and honesty of everyone. He had designed the workshops in order to keep the sexes separate so the women and girls could remain virtuous. On this point, he was inflexible. It was the only point on which he was more or less intolerant. He was all the more resolutely severe because the town of Montreuil-sur-mer was a garrison town and the opportunities for moral corruption there were rife. In every respect, his coming had been a blessing and his continued presence was the town's salvation. Before father Madeleine came along, the whole district had been going to the dogs; now, everything had come alive with the invigorating life of work. A high level of trade got everything moving and affected every corner of the region. Unemployment and poverty were now unknown. No pocket was so dingy it did not hold a bit of money, no abode so poor it did not enjoy a bit of joy.

Father Madeleine gave everyone a job. He demanded only one thing: that you be an honest man! That you be an honest woman!

As we said, out of all this activity, of which he was both cause and fulcrum, father Madeleine had made his fortune, but, rather strangely in a simple businessman, that did not seem to be his main concern. It looked as though he worried a lot about others and very little about himself. In 1820, he was known to have the sum of six hundred and thirty thousand francs in an account in his name with the bank of Laffitte; but before setting aside these six hundred and thirty thousand francs, he had spent more than a million on the town and on the poor.

The hospital had been poorly endowed; he had provided ten extra beds. Montreuil-sur-mer is divided into the upper town and the lower town. The lower town, where he lived, had only one school, a nasty shack that was falling to ruins; he had built two schools, one for girls, the other for boys. From out of his own pocket, he paid the two teachers twice their paltry official salary, and one day when someone was expressing amazement over this, he said: "The two most important civil servants are the nurse and the schoolteacher." At his own expense he had created a refuge, something then almost unknown in France, and had set up a relief fund for old and infirm workers. His manufacturing business was a hub of activity, and a new quartier with a good number of poor families had rapidly sprung up around it; he had established a free pharmacy there.

In the early days, when he was seen to be starting out, the old biddies of the town said: "There's a man who wants to get rich quick." When he was seen to be making the countryside rich before becoming rich himself, the same old biddies said: "That man is ambitious." This seemed all the more likely as he was religious, and even something of a practicing Catholic, which was highly regarded in those days. He went to hear low mass every Sunday. The local deputy, who could smell competition everywhere, started to fret about this religiousness before too long. The deputy had been a member of the legislative body under the empire and shared the religious notions of an Oratorian father named Fouché,[2] duc d'Otrante, whose puppet and friend he had been. Behind closed doors, he gently poked fun at God. But when he saw the wealthy manufacturer Madeleine going off to the seven o'clock mass, he smelled a potential future candidate and resolved to outdo him; he took on a Jesuit confessor and went to high mass and to vespers. Ambition in those days was, almost literally, a race to the altar. The poor, as well as the good Lord, benefited from the man's fears, for the honorable deputy also funded two beds at the hospital—which made twelve new beds in all.

But in 1819, a rumor spread around town one morning that, on the recommendation of the prefect, and in consideration of the services rendered the district, father Madeleine was to be named mayor of Montreuil-sur-mer by the king. Those who had declared the newcomer an ambitious man eagerly seized the opportunity everyone longs for to say: "There! I told you so!" All Montreuil-sur-mer was abuzz with the rumor. It was well founded. A few days later the nomination appeared in the *Moniteur.*[3] The following day, father Madeleine declined the offer.

In that same year of 1819, the products of the new process invented by father Madeleine were featured at the Industrial Exhibition; acting on the jury's report, the king named the inventor a chevalier of the Légion d'Honneur[4]—thereby providing a new rumor for the small-town mill. "Well, well! So, it was the cross he was after!" Father Madeleine declined the cross.

No doubt about it, the man was an enigma. The old biddies gave up the ghost, saying: "After all, he's a sort of adventurer."

As we've seen, the whole place owed him a great deal; the poor owed him everything; he was so useful that you had to end up honoring him and he was so sweet that you had to end up loving him; his workers, especially, adored him and he bore this adoration with a sort of melancholy gravity. When he was declared to be rich, those who comprised "society" saluted him and about town he began to be called Monsieur Madeleine; his workers and the children continued to call him father Madeleine and that was the thing that most made him smile. As he became more successful, invitations rained down on him. "Society" clamored for him. The posh little salons of Montreuil-sur-mer, which, of course, had been closed to the artisan in the early days, flung their doors open wide to the millionaire. Dozens of overtures were made to him. He declined.

Again the old biddies were not at a loss for words: "The man's a clod, quite uneducated. No one knows where he comes from. He wouldn't know how to conduct himself in polite society. It is by no means certain that he can read."

When they saw him making money hand over fist, they said: "The man's a trader." When they saw him throwing his money around, they said: "The man's ambitious." When they saw him rejecting honors, they said: "The man's an adventurer." When they saw him rejecting polite society, they said: "The man's a brute."

In 1820, five years after he first bobbed up in Montreuil-sur-mer, what he had done for the district was so spectacular, the desire of the whole population so unanimous, that the king again named him mayor of the town. He declined once more, but the prefect resisted his refusal, all the notables came to plead with him, the people in the street implored him, everyone made such a fuss about it that he wound up accepting. It was noted that what seemed to bring him round more than anything else was the almost cranky taunt of an old woman of the people who called out to him from her front doorstep with some verve: "A good mayor is a useful thing. A person doesn't shirk the good they can do, do they?"

That marked the third phase of his rise. Father Madeleine had become Monsieur Madeleine, and Monsieur Madeleine had become Monsieur le maire.

### III. Sums Deposited with Laffitte[1]

Yet, he had remained as unaffected as on his first day there regardless. He had the gray hair, the serious eyes, and the rugged complexion of a laborer and the thoughtful face of a philosopher. He normally wore a broad-brimmed hat and a long redingote of coarse woolen cloth buttoned up to the chin. He fulfilled his official duties as mayor, but beyond that, he lived a solitary life. He spoke to very few people. He shunned small talk, would offer a sidelong greeting and swiftly push on, smiled to get out of having to talk, gave to get out of having to smile. Women said of him: "What a gentle giant of a man—a real bear!" What he liked to do was roam through the fields.

He always ate alone, with a book open in front of him, reading. He had a small but well-stocked library. He loved books; books are remote but reliable friends. The more leisure he enjoyed as he grew wealthy, the more he took advantage of it to cultivate his mind, it would seem. Since he had been in Montreuil-sur-mer, it was noted that, from year to year, his language grew more refined, more discerning, and softer.

He liked to carry a gun on his walks but he rarely used it. When he did so, his aim was infallible and it frightened people. He never killed an animal that wasn't dangerous. He never fired at any small bird.

Although he was no longer young, he was reported to be phenomenally strong. He offered to lend a hand to anyone who was in need of it, pulled up a fallen horse, freed a wheel stuck in mud, grabbed an escaped bull by the horns to stop it. His pockets were always full of coins when he went out and always empty when he returned. Whenever he passed through a village, ragged little urchins would gleefully run after him and surround him like a cloud of flies.

It was thought that he must once have enjoyed the country life, for he had all kinds of useful secrets to teach the peasants. He taught them how to destroy grain moth by spraying the granary and soaking the cracks in the floor with a solution of common salt, and how to drive away weevils by hanging flowering orviot everywhere, from the walls and rafters, in all the sheds and throughout the house. He had "recipes" for eradicating from a field rust, blight, vetches, gorse, love-lies-bleeding, and all the various parasitical herbs and grasses that live on wheat. He could defend a rabbit hutch from rats just with the smell of a little Barbary pig that he'd put in.

One day he saw the people of the district madly pulling up nettles. He looked at the heap of uprooted plants and said: "That stuff's dead; but it'd be good if we knew how to put it to use. When nettles are young, the leaves make an excellent vegetable; when they get older, nettles produce filaments and fibers like hemp and flax. Cloth made from nettles is every bit as good as cloth made from hemp. Chopped up, nettles are good for poultry; ground, they're good for horned animals. Nettle seeds mixed in with fodder add luster to the animals' coats; the root mixed with salt produces a lovely yellow dye. And it also makes excellent hay that you can reap twice. And what do nettles need? Very little soil, no maintenance, no cultivation; the only thing is, the seeds fall as they ripen and it's hard to gather them. That's all. With a tiny bit of effort, the nettle would be useful; if you neglect it, it becomes a pest. So then we kill it. How many men are like nettles!" After a pause, he added: "My friends, remember this: There is no such thing as a weed and no such thing as a bad man. There are only bad cultivators."

The children loved him even more because he could make fabulous little things to play with out of straw and coconut.

Whenever he saw the door of a church draped in black, he would enter; he sought out a funeral the way others seek christenings. The bereavement and suffering of others attracted him because of his great compassion; he mingled with friends in mourning, with families dressed in black, with priests wailing around a coffin. He seemed glad to take as meditative texts those funereal psalms that are full of visions of another world. With his eyes raised to the heavens, he would listen, in a sort of yearning toward all the mysteries of infinity, to those sad voices that sing on the edge of the dark abyss of death.

He performed a whole host of good deeds as secretly as other people conceal bad deeds. He would steal into houses at night and furtively climb the stairs. Some poor devil, coming back to his hovel later, would find that his door had been opened, sometimes even forced open, in his absence. The poor man would cry out: "An evildoer's been here!" He'd go in and the first thing he would see would be a gold coin left lying on a piece of furniture. The "evildoer" who had been in was, of course, father Madeleine.

He was affable and sad. People would say: "Now there's a rich man who doesn't give himself airs. There's a lucky man who doesn't look happy."

A few claimed he was a bit of a mystery man and asserted that no one had ever been into his room, which was a real anchorite's cell, furnished with winged hourglasses and titivated with death's-heads and crossbones. There was so much talk of the kind that a group of sleek and cheeky young Montreuil-sur-mer girls teamed up one day and called on him, and asked him: "Monsieur le maire, do show us your room. They say it's quite a grotto." He smiled and showed them into this "grotto" without further ado. They soon got their come-uppance for being so curious—curiosity killed the cat, after all. It was a room furnished quite sparely with mahogany furniture, as ugly as all furniture of the kind usually is, with walls covered in cheap wallpaper. The only thing they noticed especially was two candlesticks of an old-fashioned shape standing on the mantelpiece, which looked like they were made of silver "since they bore hall-marks." An observation replete with that small-town spirit.

This didn't stop it being said that no one was ever allowed into the room and that it was a hermit's cave, a sleazy den where he slept it off, a bolt-hole, a tomb.

It was also whispered that he had "immense" sums of money deposited at Laffitte, with one peculiar stipulation, which was that the money was always immediately available, so that, it was added, Monsieur Madeleine could turn up any morning at Laffitte's, sign a receipt, and cart off his two or three million in ten minutes flat. In reality, the "two or three million" were reduced, as we mentioned, to six hundred and thirty or forty thousand francs.

## IV. Monsieur Madeleine in Mourning

At the beginning of 1821, the newspapers announced the death of Monsieur Myriel, bishop of Digne, "nicknamed Monseigneur Bienvenu," who passed away in the odor of sanctity at the age of eighty-two.

The bishop of Digne, to add a detail here that the papers left out, had been, by the time he died, blind for some years, and happy to be blind, since he had his sister with him.

We might just say in passing that, on this earth where nothing is perfect, being blind and being loved is one of the most strangely exquisite forms of happiness. To constantly have at your side a woman, an unmarried woman, a sister, a wonderful person who is there because you need her and because she can't do without you, to know that you are indispensable to the one you need, to be endlessly able to measure her affection by the amount of presence she grants you and to say to yourself, "since she devotes all her time to me, that means I have her whole heart"; to see her thoughts, if not her face, to weigh one being's faithfulness when the rest of the world has been eclipsed, to detect the rustling of her dress as though it were the sound of wings, to hear her coming and going, going out, coming back, talking, singing, and to know you are the center of every step she takes, of every word, of every song, to manifest your own gravitational pull every minute of the day, to feel yourself all the more powerful for your infirmity, to become in darkness, and through darkness, the star around which this angel revolves—few forms of bliss come anywhere near it! The ultimate happiness in life is the conviction that one is loved; loved for oneself—better still, loved in spite of oneself. And this conviction is what the blind have. In such distress, to be waited on is to be hugged and kissed. Is there anything the blind man is deprived of? No. Having love means not losing the light. And what love! Love entirely pure. Blindness does not exist where there is certainty. The soul gropes for another soul—and finds it. And this soul found and tried and tested is a woman. A hand supports you, it is hers; lips brush your forehead, hers; you hear breathing right next to you, it is her breathing. To have all of her, from her devotion to her sympathy, never to be abandoned, to have that sweet frailty that succors you, to lean on such an unshakable reed, to touch Providence with your own hands and hold it in your arms. God made palpable—what rapture! The heart, that dark celestial flower, bursts into mysterious bloom. You would not trade such shade for all the light in the world. The angel of the house is there, is always there; if she goes away, it is only to return; she fades like a dream only to reappear like reality. You sense her approaching, and there she is. Your cup runs over with serenity, gaiety, ecstasy; you are a beacon of light in the night. And the countless little shows of thoughtfulness! Little things that are enormous in the void. The most heavenly tones of the female voice are employed to soothe you and make up to you for the vanished universe. You are stroked with soul. You may see nothing, but you feel adored. It is a paradise of darkness.

It is from this paradise that Monseigneur Bienvenu passed into the other.

The announcement of his death was reprinted in the local Montreuil-sur-mer paper. Monsieur Madeleine appeared the next day all in black and with a black crepe band around his hat.

Monsieur Madeleine's mourning was noted in town and chins began wagging, since it seemed to throw some light on his background. It was concluded that he must have had some connection to the venerable bishop. "He's wearing black for the bishop of Digne," said the drawing rooms; it elevated Monsieur Madeleine enormously and gave him, suddenly and immediately, a certain standing in the noble world of Montreuil-sur-mer. The place's microscopic faubourg Saint-Germain[1] considered ending Monsieur Madeleine's quarantine, now that it looked as though he could very well be related to a bishop. Monsieur Madeleine realized he had been promoted by the increased curtsying on the part of the old ladies and the smiles bestowed upon him by the young ladies. One night, a doyenne of that special small world of high society, curious by right of seniority, ventured to ask: "Monsieur le maire is doubtless the cousin of the late bishop of Digne?"

He said: "No, Madame."

"But," the dowager persisted, "you are wearing mourning for him?"

He replied: "That's because I was one of his family's lackeys when I was young."

It was also noted that whenever any little homeless Savoyard came to town as he tramped around the countryside looking for chimneys to sweep, Monsieur Madeleine would send for him, ask him his name, and give him money. The little Savoyards spread the word among themselves and quite a few of them passed that way.

## V. Dim Flashes of Lightning on the Horizon

Little by little, with time, all who resisted were won over. At first Monsieur Madeleine had been vilified by slander and calumny, according to a sort of universal law that all those who better themselves are subject to; then these were reduced to spiteful cracks, then they became mere malicious jokes, and then that entirely evaporated. Respect was complete, unanimous, warm, and friendly, and there came a moment, around 1821, when the words *monsieur le maire* were spoken in Montreuil-sur-mer in the same tone as the words *monseigneur the bishop* had been spoken in Digne in 1815. People came from thirty miles around to consult Monsieur Madeleine. He settled differences, prevented lawsuits, reconciled enemies. Everyone accepted him as a judge as though that were his right by innate authority. It was as though he had the book of natural law for a soul. The veneration was contagious, and in six or seven years it had spread throughout the region from one person to the next.

One man alone, in all the town and the surrounding district, was completely immune to the infection and, no matter what father Madeleine did, refused to succumb, as if a kind of instinct, incorruptible and unflinching, aroused him and gnawed at him. It does seem, indeed, that certain people are endowed with a real animal instinct, pure and intact like all instincts, that creates antipathies and affinities, that fatally divides one personality from another, that does not hesitate, that is never in doubt, is never silenced and never flags, clear in its obscurity, infallible, imperious, resistant to all the counsels of intelligence and all the solvents of reason and that, whatever their fates may be, secretly alerts the dog-man to the presence of the cat-man, and the fox-man to the presence of the lion-man.

Often, when Monsieur Madeleine was walking down the street, serene, amiable, enveloped by the blessings of all, it would happen that a tall man dressed in an iron gray redingote, armed with a big cane and wearing a hat pulled down over his face, would abruptly turn round and follow him with his eyes until he had disappeared from view, standing with crossed arms, slowly shaking his head and pushing his top lip up practically to his nose in a sort of meaningful grimace that might be translated as: "What is it about that man, I wonder? . . . I'm sure I've seen him somewhere before . . . In any case, he still doesn't fool me."

This character, grave with an intense gravity that was practically a threat, was one of those people who worry the observer, even if you only catch sight of them for a few seconds.

His name was Javert and he was with the police.

He performed, in Montreuil-sur-mer, the unpleasant but useful job of inspector. He had not seen Madeleine's debut. Javert owed the position he occupied to the protection of Monsieur Chabouillet, the secretary of the minister of state, Comte Anglès, then prefect of police in Paris. When Javert arrived in Montreuil-sur-mer, the fortune of the great manufacturer had already been made and father Madeleine had become Monsieur Madeleine.

Certain police officers have a special physiognomy made complex by the blend of apparent meanness with apparent authority. Javert had such a physiognomy, minus the meanness.

It is our conviction that if souls were visible to the naked eye, we would clearly see the strange phenomenon whereby every individual member of the human race corresponds to one of the species of the animal kingdom; and we would easily recognize this truth, scarcely entertained by the theorists, that from the oyster to the eagle, from the pig to the tiger, all animals are in man and each of them is in a man—sometimes even several of them simultaneously.

Animals are nothing more than the forms our virtues and our vices take, trotting around before our very eyes, the visible phantoms of our souls. God reveals them to us to give us pause for thought. Only, since animals are mere shadows, God has not made them educable in the complete sense of the word. What would be the point? On the contrary, our souls being what is real and having a purpose unique to themselves, God has endowed them with intelligence, that is, the possibility of being educated. Public education, when it is good, can always bring out the latent usefulness of a soul, no matter what it is like to start with.

This is said, of course, from the limited point of view of life on earth as we know it, and without wishing to prejudge the profound question of the past and future personalities of beings that are not human. The visible self in no way gives the theorist authority to deny the latent self. These reservations having been made, we can now move on.

But if you will just bear with us a moment longer and accept that there is in every human being one of the species of the animals of creation, it will be easy for us to say exactly what this officer of the peace, Javert, was.

The Asturian peasants are convinced that in every litter of wolves there is one pup who is killed by the mother because otherwise it would grow up to devour all the other pups.

Give that male wolf puppy a human face, and you'd have Javert.

Javert was born in prison to a fortune-teller who read the cards and whose husband was serving time in the galleys. As he was growing up, he felt as though he were on the outside of society and despaired of ever getting in. He noticed that society kept at bay two classes of men, those who attack it and those who guard it; his only choice was between those two classes. At the same time, he felt in himself some kind of basic rigidity, steadiness, honesty, clouded by an inexpressible hatred for that race of bohemians to whom he belonged. He joined the police.

He did well there. At the age of forty, he was an inspector.

As a young man he had been stationed as a warden in the galleys of the south.

Before moving on to better things, let's be clear about the term *human face*, which we applied a moment ago to Javert.

The human face of Javert consisted of a pug nose, with two wide nostrils toward which two enormous sideburns climbed across his cheeks. You felt disconcerted the first time you set eyes on these two forests flanking those two cavernous holes. When Javert laughed, which was rare and terrible, his thin lips parted and revealed not only his teeth but his gums, and a line appeared around his nose that was as flat and feral as on the muzzle of one of the big cats. When Javert was serious, he was a mastiff; when he laughed, he was a tiger. For the rest, not much of a skull, a lot of jaw, hair that hid his forehead and fell into his eyes, a permanent frown line between his eyes like a star of anger, a dark glance, a pinched and formidable mouth, a ferocious air of command.

This man was composed of two sentiments, very simple and very good in themselves, relatively speaking, but which he made almost bad by exaggeration: respect for authority, and hatred of revolt; and in his eyes, theft, murder, all crimes, were just different forms of revolt. He wrapped up in a sort of blind and deep faith anyone serving some kind of function within the state apparatus, from the prime minister to the village cop. He heaped contempt, aversion, and disgust on anyone who had once crossed the legal divide into wrongdoing, who even once overstepped the bounds of the law. He was an absolutist and would brook no exceptions. On the one hand, he would say, "A public servant can't be deceived; a magistrate is never wrong." On the other, he would say, "That other lot are irredeemably lost. No good can come of them." He fully shared the opinion of those extremists who attribute to human law some kind of power to damn or, if you prefer, to record the damned, and who place a kind of Styx[1] at the bottom of society. He was stoical, serious, austere, a gloom-filled dreamer; humble and haughty like all fanatics. His stare was a corkscrew. It was cold and piercing. His whole life was expressed by two words: watching and waiting. He had drawn a straight line through what is most tortuous about the world; his conscience was completely bound up with his usefulness, his public role was his religion, and he was a spy by vocation the same way others are priests. Woe to anyone who should fall into his clutches! He would have arrested his own father if the man were breaking out of jail and denounced his own mother if she were returning illegally from banishment. And he would have done it with the sort of inner satisfaction virtue provides. On top of all that, a life of deprivation, isolation, self-denial, chastity, never a moment's fun. It was all implacable duty, policing seen the way the Spartans saw Sparta, with a merciless vigilance, a ferocious honesty—a snitch carved in marble, Brutus meets Vidocq.[2]

Javert's whole person screamed spy—and an underhand spy at that. The mystical school of Joseph de Maistre,[3] which, at the time, spiced up what were known as the "ultra"—ultra-royalist—newspapers[4] with highfalutin cosmogony, would not have failed to claim Javert as a symbol. You could not see his forehead, which was hidden under his hat, you could not see his eyes, which were buried under his eyebrows, you could not see his chin, which was plunged into his cravat, you could not see his hands, which were retracted into his sleeves, you could not see his walking stick, which he carried under his redingote. But when the occasion arose, you would suddenly see springing out of all that shadow, as though from an ambush, a bony narrow forehead, a forlorn gaze, a threatening chin, enormous hands, and a monstrous knobby cudgel.

In his rare spare time, although he hated books, he would read; the result was that he was not altogether illiterate. This could be gauged by a certain emphasis in his speech.

He had no vices whatsoever, as we said. When he was pleased with himself, he allowed himself a pinch of tobacco. That is the thread by which he hung on to humanity.

No wonder Javert was the terror of that whole class of people listed in the annual statistics of the Ministry of Justice under the heading: *Gens sans aveu*— "People of no fixed abode"—vagrants. They scuttled at the mere mention of the name Javert; Javert's face appeared to petrify them.

So that is the formidable man we are dealing with.

Javert was like an eye forever fixed on Monsieur Madeleine. An eye full of suspicion and conjecture. Monsieur Madeleine ended up becoming aware of this, but it seemed beneath his notice. He never questioned Javert, neither sought him out nor avoided him; he simply endured this annoying and almost heavy scrutiny, without appearing to give it a moment's thought. He treated Javert like everyone else, with courtesy and kindness.

From something Javert let slip, it was clear he'd done some secret research, with an inquisitiveness in keeping with the breed and having as much to do with instinct as with any deliberate intention, sniffing out any former traces that father Madeleine might have left behind elsewhere. He appeared to know, and sometimes covertly suggested, that someone had gathered certain information in a certain part of the country about a certain family that had disappeared.

Once he happened to say while talking to himself: "I think I've got him!" After which he sat brooding for three days without saying a word. It seems the thread he thought he held had snapped.

However—and this is a necessary qualification regarding the meaning certain words might convey in too absolute a manner—there can be nothing truly infallible in a human being, and the peculiarity of instinct is precisely its capacity for being clouded, thrown off scent, led astray. And if this were not the case, instinct would be superior to intelligence and the beast would turn out to be more enlightened than man.

Javert was obviously somewhat disconcerted by Monsieur Madeleine's complete insouciance and tranquillity.

But one day, his own strange manner appeared to attract Monsieur Madeleine's attention. And this was the occasion.


## VI. Father Fauchelevent

Monsieur Madeleine was walking along an unpaved alleyway one morning in Montreuil-sur-mer. He heard a noise and saw a group some distance away. He went over to them. An old man known as father Fauchelevent had just fallen under his cart when his horse fell.

This Fauchelevent was one of the rare enemies Monsieur Madeleine still had at the time. When Madeleine had popped up in the area, Fauchelevent, a former scrivener and peasant who was almost literate, had a business that was going bad. Fauchelevent watched this simple laborer getting rich while he, a legal professional, was going broke. The sight filled him with jealousy and he had done everything he could to hurt Madeleine. Then the old man had gone bankrupt and he no longer had anything but a horse and a cart to his name; being without family and without children, he had turned himself into a cart driver in order to survive.

The horse had broken both hind legs and could not get up. The old man was stuck between the wheels. The fall was such a bad one that his chest was taking the whole weight of the cart. The cart was loaded to the brim. Father Fauchelevent was letting out awful rattling noises. They tried to pull him out from under, but in vain. Any badly thought-out attempt, any clumsy bid to assist, any wrong move could easily finish him off. It was impossible to extricate him other than by lifting the cart from below. Javert, who had surged up out of nowhere the moment the accident occurred, had sent for a jack.

Monsieur Madeleine arrived on the scene. People made way for him out of respect.

"Help!" shrieked old Fauchelevent. "Who's the good lad who'll save an old man's life?"

Monsieur Madeleine turned to the onlookers: "Anyone got a jack?"

"Someone's gone to get one," replied a peasant.

"How long will it take?"

"They went to the nearest place, at Flachot's corner, where there's a smithy. But it'll still take a good quarter of an hour."

"A quarter of an hour!" cried Madeleine.

It had rained the day before, the ground was soaked, the cart was sinking deeper into the ground every second and crushing the old cart driver's chest more and more. It was obvious that his ribs would crack before another five minutes were up.

"We haven't got a quarter of an hour," said Madeleine to the peasants looking on.

"Nothing else for it!"

"But we don't have time! Can't you see the cart's sinking fast?"

"Jesus!"

"Listen," Madeleine went on. "There's still enough space under the cart for a man to slide under and lift it on his back. It'll only take half a minute and we'll pull the poor man out. Is there anyone here who's got the back and the heart for it? Five gold louis to be gained!"

No one in the group moved.

"Ten louis,"[1] said Madeleine.

The crowd stared at the ground. Someone murmured: "You'd have to be as strong as the devil. And you'd risk being crushed to a pulp, to boot!"

"Come on!" said Madeleine. "Twenty louis."

Same silence.

"It's not that they don't want to," a voice piped up.

Monsieur Madeleine wheeled round and recognized Javert. He had not seen him when he arrived. Javert continued: "It's the strength. You'd have to be a monster of a man to lift a cart like that on your back."

Then, not taking his eyes off Madeleine for a second, he went on, stressing each and every word he uttered: "Monsieur Madeleine, I have only ever known one man capable of doing what you're asking here."

Madeleine flinched.

Javert persisted with an air of indifference but still not taking his eyes off Madeleine.

"He was a convict."

"Ah!" said Madeleine.

"From the jail in Toulon."

Madeleine went pale. But the cart went on slowly sinking. Father Fauchelevent gasped and screamed:

"I can't breathe! It's breaking my ribs! A jack! Something! Aaagh!"

Madeleine looked around.

"So no one here wants to earn twenty louis and save this poor old man's life?"

Not one of the bystanders stirred. Javert repeated: "I've only ever known one man who could stand in for a jack. And it was that convict."

"Ah! It's crushing me!" screamed the old man.

Madeleine raised his head, met the falcon eye of Javert still fixed on him, looked at the paralyzed peasants and gave a sad little smile. Then, without saying a word, he fell on his knees, and before the crowd even had time to let out a cry, he was underneath the cart.

There was a frightening moment of suspense and silence.

Madeleine, lying almost flat on his stomach, was seen trying twice, in vain, to bring his elbows and knees closer together. The crowd shouted at him: "Father Madeleine! Get out of there!" Old Fauchelevent himself said to him: "Monsieur Madeleine! Get away! The jig's up for me, you can see that! Let me be! You'll get yourself crushed, too!" Madeleine did not respond.

The onlookers were breathless with emotion. The wheels had continued to sink, and it was already almost impossible for Madeleine to get out from under the carriage.

All of a sudden the enormous mass was seen to wobble, the cart slowly rose up, the wheels came halfway out of the rut. A strangled voice was heard crying out: "Hurry up! Help me!" Madeleine made one last supreme effort.

Everyone rushed forward. One man's devotion had given courage and strength to all. The cart was lifted by ten pairs of arms. Old Fauchelevent was saved.

Madeleine straightened up. He was white, though dripping with sweat. His clothes were torn and covered in mud. Everyone was in tears. The old man kissed his knees and called him the good Lord. The man himself had the strangest expression on his face, a kind of deliriously happy pain, and he fixed his gaze calmly on Javert, who was still watching him like a hawk.

## VII. FAUCHELEVENT BECOMES A GARDENER IN PARIS

Fauchelevent had thrown his kneecap out of joint in his fall. Father Madeleine had him carried to an infirmary that he had set up for his workers in the same building as his factory and that was serviced by two Sisters of Charity. The following morning, the old man found a thousand-franc note on the night table by his bed, with these words written in father Madeleine's hand: "I'm buying your horse and cart." The cart was smashed and the horse was dead. Fauchelevent recovered but his knee remained stiff. Monsieur Madeleine, through the recommendations of the sisters and his priest, found the old codger a job as a gardener in a convent in the Saint-Antoine quartier of Paris.[1]

A little while after this, Monsieur Madeleine was appointed mayor. The first time Javert saw Monsieur Madeleine sporting the sash that conferred all authority over the town, he felt a shudder run through him the way a bull mastiff would do if he scented a wolf underneath his master's clothing. From that moment on, he avoided him as much as he could. When the requirements of the job made it absolutely necessary and there was no way he could avoid finding himself face-to-face with the mayor, he addressed him with profound respect.

Apart from the visible signs we've mentioned, the prosperity father Madeleine had created in Montreuil-sur-mer had another symptom that, though not visible, was no less significant. This one is absolutely unmistakable. When the populace is hurting, when there isn't enough work, when business drops off, the taxpayer balks at paying taxes out of penury, exhausts and exceeds deadlines, and the government spends a lot of money on the legal costs of tax collection and recovery. When there is abundant work, when a region is happy and rich, taxes are easily paid and cost the government very little to collect. We might say that public poverty and wealth have an infallible barometer—the cost of tax collection. In seven years, the cost of tax collection had gone down by 75 percent in the arrondissement of Montreuil-sur-mer, which caused this arrondissement to become a general reference point, frequently cited by Monsieur de Villèle,[2] the then minister of finance.

So this was the situation when Fantine went back to her hometown. No one remembered her anymore. But happily the door of Monsieur Madeleine's factory was like the face of a friend. She applied and was accepted in the women's workshop. The work was entirely new to Fantine, she could not be expected to be particularly good at it, and she made very little as a result for a day's work, but it was enough in the end, the problem was solved, she was earning her living.

## VIII. Madame Victurnien Spends Thirty-five Francs on Morality

When Fantine saw she was making a living, she had a moment of sheer exhilaration. To live honestly by your labor, that was a blessing from above! A genuine love of work came back to her. She bought a mirror, delighted in gazing in it at her youthfulness, her beautiful hair and her beautiful teeth, forgot much, dreamed only of Cosette and of the possibilities the future held, and was very nearly happy. She rented a small room and furnished it on credit from her future labor—a vestige of her old spendthrift habits.

Not being able to say she was married, she was very careful, as we have already hinted, not to mention her little girl.

At the start, as we saw, she paid the Thénardiers punctually. As she only knew how to sign her name, she was obliged to use a public letter-writer to write to them.

She wrote often. This did not go unnoticed. They began to whisper in the women's workshop that Fantine "wrote letters" and that she was "stuck-up."

No one pries as effectively into other people's business as those whose business it most definitely is not. "Why does that gentleman only ever come at dusk?" "Why doesn't what's-his-name ever hang his keys on the hook on Thursdays?" "Why does she always take the backstreets?" "Why does Madame always get out of her fiacre before it drives into her yard?" "Why does she send someone out for a block of writing paper when she has loads of stationery in the house?" And so on and so forth. There are beings who, to find the answer to such teasing riddles, about which, furthermore, they don't actually give a fig, spend more money, devote more time, go to much more trouble than ten good deeds would require; and do so gratuitously, just for the hell of it, without being rewarded for their curiosity except by curiosity itself. They will follow this or that person for days at a time, while away the hours loitering on sundry street corners, under the arches of passageways, at night, in the cold and the rain, bribe desk attendants, get coach drivers and lackeys roaring drunk, buy off a chambermaid, put a porter in their pocket. What for? For nothing. For the sake of finding out, knowing, penetrating the mystery. Out of an itching need to be able to tell. And often, once these secrets are out, the mysteries broadcast, the enigmas exposed to the light of day, they lead to catastrophe, duels, bankruptcies, ruined families, shattered existences—to the great joy of those who "got to the bottom of it all" for no apparent reason and through sheer instinct. Sad.

Some people are malicious out of a simple need to have something to say. Their conversation, parlor talk, antechamber gossip, is reminiscent of those fireplaces that swiftly go through the wood—they need a lot of fuel, and the fuel is their neighbor.

So Fantine was observed.

On top of that, there was more than one woman who was jealous of her blond hair and her white teeth.

It was noted that in the middle of the workshop floor, she would often turn away and wipe a tear. Those were moments when she was thinking of her child; perhaps also of the man she had once loved.

Breaking the mournful ties of the past is hard and painful work.

It was noted that she wrote, at least twice a month, always to the same address, and that the postage was prepaid. The address was finally gleaned: *Monsieur Thénardier, Innkeeper, Montfermeil.* The public letter-writer, an old geezer who could not get his fill of red wine without emptying secrets out of his pockets, was made to spill the beans down at the tavern. In a word, Fantine was known to have a child. "It seems to be a daughter of some kind." One old crone did the trip to Montfermeil, spoke to Thénardier, and crowed on her return: "It may have cost me thirty-five francs but I got my money's worth. I saw the child!"

The windbag who did this was a gorgon known as Madame Victurnien, guardian and keeper of universal virtue. Madame Victurnien was fifty-six years old and wore the mask of age over her mask of ugliness. Her voice was querulous and her mind leaped about like a flea. This old woman had once been young, unbelievable as that was. In her youth, smack bang in the middle of '93, she had married a monk who'd escaped from the cloister in a red cap and switched from the Bernardins to the Jacobins.[1] Dried-up, bitter, cantankerous, shrill, prickly, virtually poisonous, she lived off memories of her monk, who was now dead, and who had ruled her with an iron fist and broken her. She was a nettle that you could see had been trampled by the passing monk. When the Restoration came, she turned herself into a bigot[2] and with such verve that the priests forgave her her monk. She had a small property, which she had made a great song and dance about bequeathing to some religious community or other. She was highly regarded by the bishop of Arras. So this Madame Victurnien went to Montfermeil and came back telling anyone who'd listen: "I saw the child."

All this took time. Fantine had been at the factory for over a year when, one morning, the overseer of the workshop handed her fifty francs on behalf of Monsieur le maire, told her that she was no longer part of the factory, and requested her, on behalf of Monsieur le maire, to kindly leave the district.

This was precisely the same month that the Thénardiers, having demanded twelve francs instead of six, had just upped it to fifteen francs instead of twelve.

Fantine was floored. She couldn't leave the district, she owed money for her rent and her furniture. Fifty francs was not enough to pay back her debts. She stammered some words of entreaty. The overseer indicated to her that she had to clear out of the workshop pronto. In any case, Fantine was a fairly average worker. Overwhelmed with shame even more than despair, she left the workshop and went back to her room. Her sin, clearly, was now known to all!

She no longer felt she had the strength to say a word in her own defense. She was advised to go and see Monsieur le maire but she did not dare. Monsieur le maire had given her fifty francs because he was good, he was driving her away because he was just. She bowed to that ruling.

## IX. Madame Victurnien's Success

So, the monk's widow was good for something.

Monsieur Madeleine had known nothing of all this. It was one of those combinations of events life is full of. Monsieur Madeleine virtually never set foot in the women's workshop. He had put an old maid the curé had passed on to him in charge of it and had complete confidence in this overseer, an impeccably respectable person, firm, fair, full of the charity that consists in giving, but not so full of the charity that consists in understanding and forgiving. Monsieur Madeleine left everything up to her. The best of men are sometimes forced to delegate their authority. It was in this absolute capacity and with the conviction that she was doing the right thing that the overseer had prepared the case for the prosecution, tried, condemned, and executed Fantine.

As for the fifty francs, she had taken them from a fund Monsieur Madeleine had entrusted to her for alms for the poor and for the relief of workers and which she did not have to account for.

Fantine offered her services as domestic help, going from house to house. Nobody wanted her. She had not been able to leave town. The secondhand dealer she owed money to for her furniture—some furniture!—had said to her: "If you try to sneak off, I'll have you arrested as a thief." The landlord she owed money to for her rent had said to her: "You're young and pretty, I'm sure you can pay." She divided the fifty francs between the landlord and the secondhand dealer, gave the dealer back three quarters of the furniture, keeping only what was strictly necessary, and found herself without a job, without social standing, with nothing more than her bed and still owing about a hundred francs.

She began to sew heavy-duty shirts as piecework for the soldiers in the garrison and made twelve sous a day.[1] Her daughter cost her ten. It was at this point that she began to fall behind in payments to the Thénardiers.

But an old woman who lit her candle for her when she came home at night taught her the art of living in destitution. Beyond living on little, there is living on nothing. These are two rooms; the first is dark, the second is black.

Fantine learned how you go completely without heat in winter, how you get rid of a bird who eats a farthing's worth of millet every other day, how you turn your petticoat into your blanket and your blanket into your petticoat, how you save your candle by eating by the light of the window across the way. No one knows how much certain enfeebled beings, who have grown old in deprivation, and honest deprivation at that, can get out of a sou. It ends up being a skill. Fantine acquired this sublime skill and with it got back a bit of her old courage.

At that time, she said to a neighbor: "Bah! I tell myself that by only sleeping five hours a day and working the rest of the time on my sewing, I'll always just about earn my daily bread. And then again, when you're sad, you don't eat as much. So, misery, worry, a bit of bread here, a bit of heartache there, it all keeps me going."

In such distress, to have had her little girl with her would have been a strange joy. She thought of sending for her. Christ! Make her share in her destitution! And then, she still owed the Thénardiers money! How could she pay? And what about the trip! How could she pay for that?

The old woman who had given her what we might call lessons in the art of poverty was a pious old maid named Marguerite, who was devout in the good sense of the term, poor and charitable toward the poor and even toward the rich, and who knew just enough to be able to sign "Margeritte," and believed in God, which is the trick.

These virtuous souls exist abundantly here below; one day they will be on high. Their lives have a sequel.

At first, Fantine was so ashamed, she didn't dare leave the house.

Whenever she was in the street, she felt people looking back at her and pointing her out; everyone stared at her and no one greeted her; the sour and chilling contempt of those she passed cut into her flesh and into her soul, cut her to the quick like an icy blast.

In small towns, a woman down on her luck is naked before the sarcastic remarks and curiosity of all and sundry. In Paris, at least, no one knows who you are and this anonymity cloaks you. Oh, how she wished she could get to Paris! Not possible.

Obviously she would have to get used to disrespect just as she had gotten used to poverty. Little by little she learned how to make the most of it. After two or three months she managed to shake off the shame and started going out again as though she thought nothing of it.

"I don't give a damn," she said.

She came and went, head held high, with a bitter smile on her lips as she felt herself becoming shameless.

Madame Victurnien sometimes saw her going by her window, noticed the distress of "that creature," "put in her place" thanks to her, and was very pleased with herself. Nasty people enjoy a grim satisfaction.

Fantine was working herself into the ground and the slight dry cough she suffered from got worse. She sometimes said to her neighbor Marguerite: "Just feel how hot my hands are."

Yet of a morning, when, with an old broken comb, she combed her beautiful hair that streamed down like threads of silk, she would enjoy a moment of happy vanity.

## X. CONTINUED SUCCESS

She had been fired toward the end of winter; summer came and went and winter returned. Short days mean less work. In winter, no heat, no light, no midday, night meets day, fog, twilight, the window is gray, you can't see out properly. The sky is a basement window. The whole day is a cellar. The sun looks like a pauper. Ghastly season! Winter turns the water of the heavens and the heart of man to stone. Her creditors were harassing her.

Fantine did not earn enough. Her debts had mushroomed. The Thénardiers, not getting regular payments, bombarded her with letters the contents of which distressed her and the postage costs of which were ruining her.[1] One day they wrote to tell her that her little Cosette was quite naked in the freezing cold they were having, that she needed a woolen skirt and that the mother would have to send at least ten francs to cover the cost. She accepted the letter and carried it around in her hand all day, screwed into a ball. That evening she went to a barber's shop at the end of the street and took the comb out of her hair. Her wondrous blond locks tumbled down to the small of her back.

"What beautiful hair!" the barber cried.

"How much will you give me for it?" she asked.

"Ten francs."

"Cut it off."

She bought a knitted skirt and sent it to the Thénardiers.

The skirt made the Thénardiers furious. It was the money they wanted. They gave the skirt to Éponine. The poor little Lark went on freezing.

Fantine thought: "My little girl is warm now. I've dressed her with my hair." She wore little round caps that hid her shaved head and still looked pretty.

A gloomy travail was being accomplished in Fantine's heart. When she saw that she no longer had hair to do up, she began to hate everything and everyone around her. She had long shared the universal veneration for father Madeleine; yet, by dint of repeating to herself that it was he who had sent her packing and that he was the cause of her plight, she wound up hating him, too, especially him. Whenever she passed by the factory at times when the workers were hanging around the doors, she would put on an act, laughing and singing.

An old factory woman who saw her laughing and singing like this one day said: "There's a girl who's headed for the rocks."

She picked up a man, the first man who happened along, a man she did not love, out of bravado, with rage in her heart. He was a miserable wretch, some sort of mendicant street musician, a lazy thug who beat her up and dumped her just as she had picked him up, in disgust.

She worshipped her daughter.

The lower she sank, the bleaker everything around her became, the more this sweet little angel shone in her heart of hearts. She would say: "When I'm rich, I'll have my Cosette with me." And she would laugh. The cough never left her and she had terrible night sweats.

One day she received a letter from the Thénardiers that went like this: "Cosette is sick from an epidemic that's going round the countryside. They call it miliary fever. She needs expensive drugs. It's costing us a fortune. If you don't send forty francs before the end of a week, the little one will be dead."

She burst out laughing hysterically and said to her old neighbor: "Hah! They're too much! Forty francs! That's all! That's two napoléons!² Where do they think I'm going to get them? Are they crazy, these damned peasants?"

Yet she climbed up the stairs to where there was a bull's-eye window and reread the letter. Then she came back downstairs and ran out of the house leaping and laughing still. Someone who ran into her said: "What have you got to be so happy about, then?"

She replied: "Some hayseeds just sent me a tremendous joke. They're asking for forty francs. What peasants!"

As she was crossing the square, she saw a crowd gathered around a weird-looking carriage on the top of which a man dressed entirely in red was holding forth. He was a tumbler and traveling dentist on tour and he was offering the public complete sets of dentures, opiates, powders, and elixirs. Fantine mingled with the crowd and started laughing like everyone else at the man's harangue, which combined slang for the rabble and jargon for the better class of person. The tooth-puller spotted this beautiful girl laughing and suddenly belted out: "You have very nice teeth, you, that girl laughing there. Sell me your two cutters and I'll give you a gold napoléon for each one."

"What's that, my two cutters?" asked Fantine.

"Cutters," said the professor of dentistry, "that's your two front teeth, the upper ones."

"How horrible!" cried Fantine.

"Two napoléons," growled an old toothless hag who was there. "It's all right for some!"

Fantine fled and covered her ears so she wouldn't hear the hoarse voice of the man shouting at her back: "Think about it, sweetheart! Two napoléons, that could come in handy. If your heart says yes, be there tonight at the Tillac d'Argent Inn; that's where you'll find me."

Fantine went home. She was furious and told her kind neighbor Marguerite all about it.

"Can you imagine? What kind of creep would say a thing like that? How can they let men like that travel around the country? Pull out my two front teeth! But I'd look hideous! Your hair grows back, but your teeth! Ah, what a monster of a man! I'd rather throw myself headfirst onto the pavement from the fifth floor! He reckoned he'd be at the Tillac d'Argent tonight."

"And what was he offering?" asked Marguerite.

"Two napoléons."

"That's forty francs."

"Yes," said Fantine, "that's forty francs."

She thought for a moment and resumed her sewing. After fifteen minutes, she dropped the sewing and went to reread the Thénardiers' letter on the stairs.

When she came back, she said to Marguerite, who was working next to her: "So what is miliary fever, anyway? Do you have any idea?"

"Yes," replied the old maid, "it's a disease."

"Do you need to take a lot of drugs for it?"

"Oh, terrible drugs."

"Where does it affect you?"

"It just happens, like that."

"Do children get it?"

"Children especially."

"Do you die of it?"

"Very often."

Fantine left the room and went to read the letter one more time on the stairs.

That night she went downstairs and could be seen heading off down the rue de Paris where the inns are.

The next morning, as Marguerite came into Fantine's room before daybreak, for they always worked together and so could share the one candle between the two of them, she found Fantine sitting on her bed, pale, icy cold. She had not been to bed. Her cap had fallen to her knees. The candle had been burning all night and was very nearly burned out.

Marguerite stopped at the door, petrified by the sight of this overwhelming chaos, and cried out: "Lord! The candle's all burned! Something terrible's happened!"

Then she looked at Fantine, who turned her hairless head toward her.

Fantine had aged ten years overnight.

"Jesus!" said Marguerite. "What's wrong with you, Fantine?"

"There's nothing wrong with me," replied Fantine. "On the contrary, now my little girl won't die of that terrible disease, for lack of help. I'm happy."

As she spoke, she showed the old maid two napoléons gleaming on the table.

"Oh, Jesus Christ!" said Marguerite. "But that's a small fortune! Where did you get these gold louis?"

"I got them," replied Fantine.

And with that, she smiled. The candle lit her face. It was a bloody smile. Reddish saliva besmirched the corners of her mouth and inside her mouth was a black hole.

The two teeth had been ripped out. She sent the forty francs to Montfermeil. But it was only a trick of the Thénardiers to get more money. Cosette was not sick at all.

Fantine threw her mirror out the window. Long before this she had vacated her cell on the second floor for an attic beneath the roof that had a simple latch for a lock; one of those garrets where the ceiling forms an angle with the floor and you bang your head on it every time you move. A poor person can only get to the back of their room, as to the end of their destiny, by stooping lower and lower. She no longer had a bed, all she had left was a rag she called her bedspread, a mattress on the floor, and a chair with the cane seat missing. A small rosebush sat dried out in a corner, forgotten. In the other corner was a butter pot for water—which froze in winter, the different levels of water remaining for a long time marked by rings of ice. She had already lost all sense of shame, she now lost all vanity. A sure sign of the end. She went out with filthy caps. Either from lack of time or from indifference she no longer mended her linen. When she wore holes in the heels of her stockings, she would simply stuff the stockings down into her shoes. You could tell by the perpendicular wrinkles. She patched her old, worn corset together with pieces of calico that tore at the slightest movement. The people she owed money to made scenes and never let her alone. She would stumble across them in the street, she would stumble into them again on her stairs. She spent nights crying and worrying. Her eyes were very glassy yet she felt a persistent pain in her shoulder, near the top of the left shoulder blade. She coughed a lot. She hated father Madeleine from the depths of her heart and never complained—about him or to him. She sewed seventeen hours a day; but a prison contractor who was putting female prisoners to work for a pittance suddenly dropped the prices, which reduced the day's pickings for free laborers to nine sous. Seventeen hours of work for nine sous a day! Her creditors were even more merciless than ever. The secondhand dealer, who had taken back nearly all the furniture, kept plaguing her: "When are you going to pay me, you tart?" What did they expect her to do, for God's sake? She felt hounded and something of the wild beast took shape inside her. At about the same time, old man Thénardier wrote to her that, really, he had waited far too long out of the goodness of his heart and that he must have a hundred francs immediately; otherwise, he'd show little Cosette the door, convalescing as she still was from her great illness—throw her out on the street, in the cold, let her fend for herself and she could drop dead if that's what she wanted to do. "A hundred francs," mused Fantine. "But is there anywhere on earth where you can earn a hundred sous a day?"

"Get on with it, then!" she said. "Let's sell what's left."

The poor girl made herself a whore.

## XI. CHRISTUS NOS LIBERAVIT[1]

What is this story of Fantine all about? It is about society buying itself a slave. Who from? From destitution.

From hunger, from cold, from loneliness, from abandonment, from dire poverty. A painful bargain. A soul for a bit of bread. Destitution makes an offer, society gives the nod.

The sacred law of Jesus Christ governs our civilization, but it has not yet managed to permeate it. They say slavery has vanished from European civilization. That is wrong. It still exists, but it now preys only on women, and it goes by the name of prostitution.

It preys on women, meaning on grace, on weakness, on beauty, on the maternal. It is not the least of man's shameful secrets.

At the point we have reached in this doleful drama, there is nothing left of the Fantine of the past. In becoming trash she turned to marble. Whoever touches her feels cold. She wafts into view, she goes along with you yet knows nothing about you; she is the face of dishonor and severity. Life and the social order have had their final say. All that can happen has happened to her. She has felt everything, accepted everything, experienced everything, suffered everything, lost everything, cried over everything. She is resigned with a resignation that resembles indifference just as death resembles sleep. Nothing is too awful for her now. She fears nothing. Let the sky fall on her head, let the whole ocean crash over her! What does she care? She is a sponge already completely soaked.

That, at least, is what she believes, but it is a mistake to imagine that you can exhaust fate or that you ever hit rock bottom—in anything.

Alas! What are all these lives driven willy-nilly? Where are they going? Why are they like this?

He who knows the answer to that, sees the darkness as a whole.

He is alone. His name is God.

## XII. The Idleness of Monsieur Bamatabois

In all small towns, and in Montreuil-sur-mer in particular, there is a class of young men who eat into their fifteen hundred livres in provincial income with the same cavalier attitude with which their peers in Paris devour two hundred thousand francs a year. These are beings from the great neutered species; geldings, parasites, nonentities, who have a bit of land, a bit of giddiness, and a bit of wit, who would be hicks in a salon and think themselves gentlemen in a barroom, who talk about "my acreage, my woods, my peasants," hiss and boo actresses at the theater to prove they are men of taste, pick fights with officers of the garrison to show they are men of war, hunt, smoke, yawn, drink, sniff tobacco, play billiards, ogle travelers alighting from the coach, live at the café, dine at the inn, have a dog who gobbles up the bones under the table and a mistress who slaps down dishes on top of it, hang on to their loose change for dear life, go overboard for whatever is in fashion, admire tragedy, despise women, wear out their old boots, ape London via Paris and Paris via Pont-à-Mousson, lose their marbles with age, never lift a finger to work, don't do any good and don't do much harm, either.

Monsieur Félix Tholomyès, if he had remained in his neck of the woods and never seen Paris, would have been such a man.

Any richer and you'd call them dandies; any poorer and you'd call them layabouts. They are quite simply the idle. Among the idle, there are those who are bores, those who are bored, daydreamers, and a few jokers.

In those days, a dandy was put together with a big collar, a big cravat, a watch dangling charms, three different colored waistcoats worn one on top of the other, with the red and blue on the inside, and then an olive-colored short-waisted jacket with tails and with a double row of silver buttons tightly buttoned right up to the shoulder, and lighter olive trousers, decorated at both seams with ribs of a random, but always odd, number, ranging from one to eleven, that limit never being exceeded. Add to that little boots with little iron caps on the heels, a narrow-brimmed top hat, hair worn in a tuft, an enormous cane, and conversation spiced with the puns of Potier. Crowning all, spurs and a mustache. In those days, a mustache was the mark of a man about town and spurs signified a pedestrian.

The provincial dandy wore longer spurs and a friskier mustache.

Those were the days of the struggle of the South American republics against the king of Spain, of Bolívar against Morillo.[1] Narrow-brimmed hats were worn by royalists and were known as *morillos;* the liberals wore wide-brimmed hats called *bolivars.*

And so, eight or ten months after what was narrated in the previous pages, around about the first days of January 1823, on a night of snow, one of these dandies, one of these idlers—obviously a true conformist, for he wore a *morillo,* and was snugly wrapped up in one of those huge greatcoats that then completed the cold-weather fashion plate—was getting his kicks harassing a creature on the prowl in front of the window of the officers' café in a very low-cut ball gown and with flowers wreathed around her head. The dandy was smoking, for smoking was very much in vogue.

Every time the woman passed in front of him, along with a puff of smoke from his cigar, he would toss her a bunch of insults that he found terribly witty and amusing, like: "God, you're ugly!" or, "Go and crawl under a rock!" or, "You've got no teeth!" and so on. This gentleman's name was Monsieur Bamatabois. The woman, a sad bejeweled specter in a dress, kept walking backward and forward in the snow and did not answer him, did not even glance at him, but continued pacing in silence and with a dismal regularity that brought her back within range of his sarcasm every five minutes, like the condemned soldier going back for the birch. Not making any impression doubtless stung the fop into action and so, taking advantage of a moment when the woman's back was turned, he snuck up behind her as stealthily as a wolf and, choking back a laugh, swooped down to the ground, scooped up a handful of snow, and swiftly thrust it down her back between her naked shoulder blades. The girl let out a howl of rage, spun round, and, springing like a panther, hurled herself at the man, digging her nails into his face as she swore like a trooper in the foulest language that ever spilled into the gutter from some backroom brawl. These obscenities, spewing out in a voice made husky by eau-de-vie, were truly hideous coming from a mouth in which the two front teeth were, indeed, missing. It was Fantine.

The racket brought all the officers running out of the café; passersby gathered, and a great circle, laughing, jeering, and clapping, formed around this whirlwind composed of two beings hard to recognize as a man and a woman, the man thrashing around, his hat on the ground, the woman kicking and punching and screaming, bareheaded, toothless and hairless and livid with rage, truly horrible.

Suddenly a tall man darted out of the crowd, seized the woman by her mud-spattered satin bodice, and barked: "Follow me!"

The woman looked up; her furious voice died at once. Her eyes glazed over, from being merely pale, she turned white and began shaking with terror. She had recognized Javert.

The dandy took advantage of the incident to sneak away.

### XIII. THE ANSWER TO SOME OF THE MUNICIPAL POLICE'S QUESTIONS

Javert broke up the circle, moved the bystanders along, and began to stride off forcefully toward the police station, which is at the far end of the square, dragging the wretched woman along after him. She let herself be dragged like a rag doll. Neither he nor she uttered a word. The swarm of onlookers, jumping for joy, followed behind, slinging taunts. Unmitigated wretchedess being a great source of obscene jokes.

They arrived at the police station, which was a low-ceilinged room heated by a potbellied stove and guarded by a sentinel; it had a door with a wire mesh window giving onto the street. Javert pulled the door open, entered with Fantine in tow, and shut the door behind him, to the great disappointment of the gawking horde who stood on tiptoe, craning their necks at the grimy guardroom window in an effort to get an eyeful. Curiosity is a form of greed. To see is to devour.

Fantine went in and flopped in a heap in a corner, motionless and mute, cowering like a frightened dog.

The desk sergeant brought over a burning candle and put it on the table.

Javert sat down, took a sheet of stamped paper[1] from his pocket, and began to write.

This class of women is placed by our laws completely at the mercy of the police's discretion. The police do what they like with them, punish them however they see fit, and confiscate at will those pathetic things they call their industry and liberty. Javert was imperturbable; his grave face betrayed no emotion. And yet he was seriously and profoundly troubled. This was one of those moments when he exercised without restraint, but with all the scruples of a strict conscience, his formidable discretionary power. In that instant, he knew, his policeman's stool was a court bench. He was conducting a trial. He was conducting a trial and handing down a sentence. He summoned all the notions his mind could contain to come to the aid of the mighty thing he was doing. The more he examined the conduct of this girl, the more he was revolted. It was clear he had just witnessed a crime. He had just seen, out there in the street, society, represented by a property owner and voter,[2] physically and verbally abused and vilified by a creature who was beyond the pale, an outcast. A prostitute had assaulted an upright citizen. He, Javert, had seen it. He wrote in silence.

When he had finished, he signed the letter, folded it, and said to the desk sergeant as he handed it to him: "Take three men and put this girl in the lockup." Then he turned to Fantine and said: "You're up for six months."

The poor woman shuddered.

"Six months! Six months' jail!" she wailed. "Six months making seven sous a day! But what will happen to Cosette? What about my daughter! My daughter! God, I still owe the Thénardiers over a hundred francs, Monsieur l'inspecteur, you know that?"

She dragged herself across the flagstones, wet from the muddy boots of all those men, without getting up, joining her hands together, taking great steps on her knees.

"Monsieur Javert," she said, "I beg your mercy. I swear to you I was not in the wrong. If you'd been there when it started you would have seen! I swear to you by the Lord above that I was not in the wrong. It was that swell, whoever he is, who shoved snow down my back. Do they have the right to shove snow down our backs when we're just going past like that, minding our own business, not causing anyone any harm? I saw red. I'm not very well, as you can see! And then, he'd been goading me for some time already. 'God, you're ugly! You've got no teeth!' I know very well I haven't got my teeth anymore. I did nothing, I didn't. I said: 'He's just a gentleman out for a bit of fun.' I was straight with him, I didn't say boo. And that was when he put snow on me. Monsieur Javert, my good Monsieur l'inspecteur! Isn't there anyone here who saw what happened and can tell you that it's perfectly true? Maybe I was wrong to get annoyed. You know, in the heat of the moment, you lose your head. You get a bit carried away. And then, when someone puts something so cold down your back when you're not expecting it! I was wrong to wreck the gentleman's hat. Why did he run off? I'd beg his pardon. Oh, my God! It wouldn't cost me anything to beg his pardon. Let me off just this once, Monsieur Javert. Listen, you don't know this, but in prison they only let you earn seven sous a day, and, just think, I've got to pay a hundred francs—otherwise they'll send back my little girl. Oh, good God! I can't have her with me. What I do is so vile! Oh, my Cosette, oh, my little angel sent by the good Holy Virgin, what will happen to her, poor little bunny! Let me tell you. It's the Thénardiers, they're innkeepers, peasants, you can't reason with them. They want money. Don't put me in jail! You see, she's just a little girl and they'll dump her on the highway; you're on your own, then, in the middle of winter; you must have pity on her, good Monsieur Javert. If she was older, she could earn her own living, but she can't, not at that age. I'm not a bad woman at heart. It's not being lazy or greedy that's made me what I am. I've drunk eau-de-vie, but only out of misery. I don't like it, but it makes you light in the head. In better days, you'd only have had to look in my cupboards and you'd have seen for yourself that I wasn't some slut living in a pigsty. I had linen, lots of linen. Have pity on me, Monsieur Javert!"

On and on she went, broken in two, racked by sobs, blinded by tears, her throat bare, wringing her hands, coughing with a short dry cough, and babbling so very softly in the voice of agony. Great pain is a divine and terrible ray of light that transforms the wretched. At that moment, Fantine was beautiful once more. Every so often, she paused and tenderly kissed the hem of the spook's frock coat. She would have caused a heart of stone to melt; but there is no melting a heart of wood.

"That's enough!" said Javert. "I've heard you out. Haven't you said everything you can say? Now get going! You've got your six months. The Eternal Father himself could do nothing more."

At those solemn words, "the Eternal Father himself could do nothing more," she realized the sentence had been handed down. She slumped in a heap, murmuring: "Mercy!"

Javert turned his back on her.

The soldiers grabbed her by the arms.

A few minutes before this, a man had come in unnoticed. He had shut the door behind him and stood with his back against it and had listened to Fantine's desperate pleas.

The moment the soldiers laid hands on the poor woman, who refused to get up, he stepped out of the shadows and said: "Just a moment, please!"

Javert looked up and recognized Monsieur Madeleine. He took off his hat and greeted him with a sort of exasperated awkwardness: "Pardon me, Monsieur le maire—"

Those words, *monsieur le maire,* had a strange effect on Fantine. She shot to her feet like a ghost clambering out of the grave, shoved the soldiers aside with both hands, walked straight up to Monsieur Madeleine before anyone could hold her back, and staring at him with wild eyes, cried:

"Ah! So you're the man they call Monsieur le maire!"

Then she burst into a cackle and spat in his face.

Monsieur Madeleine wiped his face and said: "Inspector Javert, let this woman go."

Javert felt his mind was about to snap. At that instant, he experienced the most violent emotions he had ever felt in his life, one after the other and almost all at once, in a jumble. To see a streetwalker spit in the face of a mayor, well, that was something so monstrous that he would never have imagined such a thing possible, not in his wildest dreams. On the other hand, at the back of his mind, he made a confused and hideous connection between what this woman was and what the mayor might be and then he glimpsed with horror something unutterably simple in this prodigious assault. But when he saw the mayor, this magistrate, calmly wipe his face and say "Let this woman go," he was thunderstruck; thought and speech both failed him; his capacity for amazement had been exceeded. He remained speechless, utterly lost for words.

Those words had also struck Fantine just as strangely. She lifted a bare arm and clung to the damper handle of the stove as though feeling not too steady on her feet. Yet her eyes danced all around her and she began to speak in a barely audible voice as though talking to herself: "Set me free! Let me go! Don't make me go to jail for six months! Who said that? It isn't possible that someone said that. I must have heard wrong. It couldn't have been that bastard of a mayor! Was it you, my good Monsieur Javert, who said to let me go? Oh, listen! I'll tell you and then you'll set me free. That bastard of a mayor, that mongrel of a mayor, he's the cause of all this. Can you imagine, Monsieur Javert, he sent me packing, because of a pack of old harlots who tell tales and stab you in the back in the workshop. If that isn't vile, I don't know what is! To turn away a poor girl who's just doing her job honestly! So then, I couldn't earn enough and that's when all the bad luck started happening. The first thing these gentlemen from the police could do to improve things is to see to it that the prison contractors don't cripple poor people. I'll tell you how it works, listen. Say you make twelve sous in shirts; if that drops to nine sous, you can't live. So you have to do what you can. Me, I had my little Cosette, I was forced to become a bad woman. So now you know it was that swine of a mayor who did all the damage. After that, I trampled on the hat of that respectable gent outside the officers' café. But him, he'd wrecked my whole dress with his snow. The likes of us, we only have one silk dress, for evening. You know, I never meant to do anything wrong. I really didn't, Monsieur Javert. Everywhere I look I see women much worse than me and they're much better off. Oh, Monsieur Javert, you're the one who said to let me go, aren't you? You ask around, talk to my landlord, I pay the rent on time now, they'll tell you I'm straight down the line. Oh, my God! I'm sorry, I'm so sorry. I didn't realize—I knocked the damper of the stove and now it's smoking."

Monsieur Madeleine listened in rapt attention. While the woman was talking, he fumbled in his jacket, pulled out his wallet and opened it. It was empty. He put it back in his pocket. He said to Fantine: "How much did you say you owed?"

Fantine, who had not taken her eyes off Javert, wheeled around: "Did I say anything to you?!"

Then, addressing the soldiers: "So, you lot, tell me, did you see how I spat in his face for him? Ah, you wicked old pig of a mayor, you came here to frighten me, but I'm not frightened of you. I'm frightened of Monsieur Javert. I'm frightened of my good Monsieur Javert!"

As she said this she turned back to the inspector: "Now you know all that, you know, Monsieur l'inspecteur, you've got to be just. I know you're just, Monsieur l'inspecteur. In fact, it's very simple: a man has a bit of fun shoving snow down a woman's back, that gives them a laugh—the officers, they've got to have some fun somehow; the likes of me, we're just there to keep them happy, of course we are! And then, you, you come along, you have to keep the peace, you cart off the woman in the wrong, but now you've thought about it, being good as you are, you say to let me go; it's for the little one, because six months in jail, that would stop me being able to feed my little girl. Only, don't ever come back again, you tart! Oh, I won't come back again, Monsieur Javert! Let them do what they like with me, I won't raise a finger. Only, today, you know, I made a racket because it hurt, I just wasn't expecting that snow that man had; and then, like I told you, I'm not very well, I've got a cough, it's like I've got a ball in my chest that burns me, and the doctor told me to look after myself. Here, feel that, give me your hand, don't be frightened, there it is."

She was no longer crying, her voice was caressing, she pressed Javert's big hairy hand over her delicate white bosom and watched him with a smile on her lips.

Suddenly she rearranged her clothes, smoothed out the wrinkles in her dress, which was hitched up almost to her knees as she crawled across the floor, and walked to the door, saying in a whisper to the soldiers with a friendly nod of the head:

"Boys, Monsieur l'inspecteur said to release me, so I'm off."

She placed her hand on the door handle. One more step and she'd be in the street.

Until that moment, Javert had stood stock-still, his eye boring a hole in the ground, all wrong in the middle of this scene like a misplaced statue waiting to be put in the right spot.

The noise of the door jolted him. He raised his head with an expression of sovereign authority, an expression always all the more frightening, the lower down power is vested, ferocious in a wild beast, atrocious in a nobody.

"Sergeant!" he shouted. "Can't you see this hussy is making off! Who told you to let her go?"

"I did," said Madeleine.

At the sound of Javert's voice, Fantine had flinched and let go of the door handle the same way a thief caught in the act drops the stolen object. At the sound of Madeleine's voice, she spun round, and from that moment, without saying a word, without even daring to breathe freely, her eyes flitted in turn from Madeleine to Javert and from Javert to Madeleine, whoever happened to be speaking.

It was obvious that Javert had been "knocked for a loop," as they say, to have allowed himself to say what he did to the sergeant after the mayor's invitation to set Fantine free. Had he actually reached the point of forgetting the mayor's very presence? Had he wound up telling himself that it was not possible for any person of authority to have given such an order and that Monsieur le maire must certainly have said one thing when he meant another altogether? Or else, confronted by the outrageous things he had witnessed for the last two hours, did he tell himself that it was necessary to resort to extreme measures, that it was time for the little man to assert himself, time that the informer turned into a magistrate, that the policeman became a man of the law, and that, in this dire extremity, law and order, morality, governance, society as a whole, were personified in himself, Javert?

Whatever the case, when Monsieur Madeleine let out that "I did" we heard a moment ago, the inspector of police was seen to turn toward Monsieur le maire, pale, cold, his lips blue, his eyes desperate, his whole body shaking with a barely perceptible tremor, and he was heard to say something unprecedented: "Monsieur le maire, that can't be done."

"How's that?" said Monsieur Madeleine.

"This wretched woman insulted a gentleman."

"Inspector Javert," Monsieur Madeleine replied in a calm, conciliatory tone, "listen. You are an honest man, so I don't mind spelling things out clearly for you. It's like this. I happened to be crossing the square as you were carting this woman away. There were still people milling around, I asked a few questions and I found out the truth: it is the gentleman who was in the wrong, and if the police were doing their job, he should have been arrested."

Javert could not stop himself: "This miserable creature just insulted Monsieur le maire."

"That's my business," said Monsieur Madeleine. "My insult is mine, if you like. I can do what I like with it."

"I beg Monsieur le maire's pardon. The insult is not his, it belongs to the system of justice."

"Inspector Javert," replied Monsieur Madeleine, "the highest form of justice is one's conscience. I've heard the woman out. I know what I'm doing."

"And I, Monsieur le maire, don't know what I am seeing."

"Then make do with obeying."

"I'm obeying my duty. My duty tells me that this woman should do six months behind bars."

Monsieur Madeleine responded gently: "Listen to me carefully. She will not do a single day."

At those decisive words, Javert risked a glare at the mayor and said to him, though in a tone of voice that was still scrupulously respectful: "It causes me despair to go against Monsieur le maire; this is the first time in my life, but he will deign to permit me to observe to him that I am within the bounds of my responsibilities. I will confine myself, since Monsieur le maire wishes it, to the case of the citizen in question. I was there. This girl threw herself at Monsieur Bamatabois, who is a voter and the owner of the magnificent house with a balcony on the corner of the esplanade, three stories, all in hewn stone. At the end of the day, some things count for something in this world! Anyhow, Monsieur le maire, this matter is a case for the street patrol and so it concerns me, and I am holding this woman, Fantine."

At these words, Monsieur Madeleine folded his arms and said in a harsh voice that no one in the town had ever yet heard: "The case you are talking about is a matter for the municipal police. By the terms of articles nine, fifteen, and sixty-six of the code of criminal law, I am the judge of it. I order this woman to be set free."

Javert struggled to make one last stand.

"But, Monsieur le maire—"

"Let me refer you to article eighty-one of the law of December 13, 1799, on arbitrary detention."

"Monsieur le maire, allow—"

"Not another word."

"But—"

"Get out," said Monsieur Madeleine.

Javert took the blow standing, full on and bang in the chest like a Russian soldier. He bowed practically to the ground to Monsieur le maire and left.

Fantine moved away from the door and watched in stupefaction as he went past her.

Yet she too was in the grip of a strange upheaval. She had just watched herself being in a way argued over by two opposing forces. She had seen before her very eyes the battle between two men who held in their hands her liberty, her life, her soul, her child; one of the men pulled her into the darkness, the other lifted her back into the light. In this struggle, glimpsed through the magnifying glass of terror, the two men seemed to her like giants; one spoke like her demon, the other spoke like her good angel. The angel had triumphed over the demon, and, something that made her shiver from head to toe, this angel, this liberator, was precisely the man she abhorred, this mayor that she had so long considered the author of all her ills, this Madeleine! And at the very moment when she had just insulted him in the most heinous way, he had saved her! So, had she got it all wrong? Did she therefore need to transform her whole soul? . . . She did not know, she was trembling. She listened, bewildered, she watched, alarmed, and at each word that Monsieur Madeleine uttered, she felt the awful blackness of hate dissolving and evaporating inside her and she felt something indescribably warm and wonderful well up in her heart; it was joy, trust, and love.

When Javert had gone, Monsieur Madeleine turned to her, and said in a careful voice, struggling to sound as though he were in control and not on the verge of breaking down: "I have heard you. It's all news to me. I believe it's true and I feel it's true. I didn't even know you had left my workshop. Why didn't you come and see me in person? But here's how it will be: I will pay your debts, I will have your child come to you, or you will go to her. You will live here, or in Paris, or wherever you like. I will look after your child and you. You will never have to work again, if you don't want to. I will give you all the money you need. You will go back to being an honest woman by being happy again. And, listen, I tell you here and now, if all is as you say, and I don't doubt it for a second, you have never stopped being virtuous and holy in the eyes of God. Oh, you poor, poor woman!"

This was more than poor Fantine could bear. To be with Cosette again! To leave this ignoble life behind! To live free, rich, happy, honest, with Cosette! To suddenly see blossoming in the middle of all her misery the fruits of paradise! She gazed, stunned, at the man speaking to her and could only let out two or three sobs: oh! oh! oh! Her legs gave way, she fell on her knees before Monsieur Madeleine, and before he could stop her, he felt her take his hand and press it to her lips.

Then she fainted.

# BOOK SIX

# JAVERT

## I. THE BEGINNING OF REST

Monsieur Madeleine had Fantine carried to the infirmary he had set up in his own home. He put her in the hands of the sisters, who put her to bed. A burning fever had come on. She spent part of the night ranting deliriously but ended up getting off to sleep.

The next day at around noon, Fantine woke up and heard someone breathing very close to her bed; she pulled the curtain aside and saw Monsieur Madeleine standing gazing at something above her head. His gaze was full of pity and anguish and supplication. She followed its direction and saw that he was addressing a crucifix nailed to the wall.

Monsieur Madeleine was from that moment transfigured in the eyes of Fantine. He seemed to her enveloped in light. He was absorbed in a kind of prayer. She watched him for a long time without daring to interrupt. Finally she spoke timidly to him: "What are you doing here, then?"

Monsieur Madeleine had been on the spot for an hour. He was waiting for Fantine to wake up. He took her hand, felt her pulse, and answered: "How are you?"

"Good, I slept," she said. "I think I'm getting better, it's nothing."

He went on, answering the first question she had asked him as though he had just heard it: "I was praying to the martyr up above."

And he added in his thoughts: "For the martyr here below."

Monsieur Madeleine had spent the night and the morning gathering information. He knew everything now. He knew Fantine's story in all its poignant details. He went on: "You have suffered very greatly, you poor woman. Oh, but don't complain, you now share the lot of the chosen ones. This is the way men turn into angels. It's not their fault; they don't know how else to go about it. You see, this hell you've just come out of is the first step to heaven. You had to start there."

He gave a deep sigh. She, however, smiled at him with that sublime smile in which two teeth were missing.

That same night Javert had written a letter. He himself took the letter to the post office in Montreuil-sur-mer the following morning. It was destined for Paris and was addressed: *Monsieur Chabouillet, secretary to the prefect of police.* As the business at the police station was the talk of the town, and the woman who ran the post office and a few others who saw the letter before it was whisked away, recognizing Javert's handwriting from the address, thought he was sending in his resignation.

Monsieur Madeleine promptly wrote to the Thénardiers. Fantine owed them a hundred francs. He sent them three hundred francs, telling them to pay themselves from out of this sum and to bring the child immediately to Montreuil-sur-mer, where her sick mother was calling for her.

This knocked old man Thénardier out. "Christ!" he said to his wife. "We better hang on to that kid. The little mouse looks like turning into a money-spinner after all. I think I get it. Some sucker's fallen for the mother."

He responded with a bill for over five hundred francs meticulously drawn up. This bill featured two incontestable memoranda for more than three hundred francs' worth of fees, one from a doctor, the other from an apothecary, who had both looked after and medicated Éponine and Azelma during two protracted bouts of illness. Cosette, as we've said, had not been sick. It was a matter of a little name change. At the end of the bill Thénardier had put: "Received in part payment three hundred francs."

Monsieur Madeleine immediately sent off another three hundred francs and wrote: "Hurry up and bring Cosette."

"Like hell we will!" said old man Thénardier. "We're not letting go of that kid."

Fantine, meanwhile, was not getting any better. She was still in the infirmary.

At first the sisters had taken in and cared for "that girl" only with repugnance. Anyone who has seen the bas-reliefs at Rheims[1] will remember the pouting bottom lips of the levelheaded virgins as they glare at the dizzy virgins. This antique scorn of the vestals for the flute-playing courtesans, their fallen sisters, is one of the deepest instincts of feminine dignity; the nuns had had a double dose of it, thanks to religion. But in a few days Fantine had disarmed them completely. She spoke so humbly and sweetly and the mother in her was so very moving. One day the sisters overheard her talking in her feverish delirium: "I have been a sinner, but when I have my child back with me, that will mean God has forgiven me. While I was still in sin, I wouldn't have wanted to have my Cosette with me, I wouldn't have been able to bear her sad, bewildered eyes. And yet it was for her that I did wrong, and that's why God forgives me. I'll feel the good Lord's blessing when Cosette is here. I'll feast my eyes on her, it'll do me good to see that innocent little girl. She knows nothing at all. She is an angel, you see, my dear sisters. At that age, the wings haven't yet fallen off."

Monsieur Madeleine went to see her twice a day and each time she would ask him: "Will I see Cosette soon?"

He would reply: "Maybe tomorrow morning. She'll arrive any moment, I'm expecting her."

And the mother's pale face would brighten.

"Oh!" she would say. "How happy I will be!"

We just said that she was not getting any better. On the contrary, her state seemed to worsen from one week to the next. That handful of snow applied to the bare skin between the shoulder blades had caused a sudden suppression of perspiration as a result of which the disease she had been incubating for several years finally broke out with a vengeance. At the time people were just beginning to follow the innovative practices of Laënnec[2] in the study and treatment of chest diseases. The doctor listened to Fantine's chest with his stethoscope, accordingly, and shook his head.

Monsieur Madeleine said to the doctor: "Well?"

"Doesn't she have a little girl she's keen to see?"

"Yes."

"Well, hurry up and get her here."

A shiver ran down Monsieur Madeleine's spine.

Fantine asked him: "What did the doctor say?"

Monsieur Madeleine forced a smile.

"He said to get your little girl here good and quick. That will get you back on your feet."

"Oh!" she said, "too right! But what can the Thénardiers be doing keeping my Cosette from me! Oh, but she'll come. At last I see happiness close by me!"

The Thénardiers, however, "hung on to the kid" and dished out a hundred poor excuses. Cosette was a bit too off-color to travel in winter. And then there were a number of pressing little debts run up all over the district and he was busy gathering the bills for them, and so on and so forth.

"I'll send someone to go and get Cosette," said father Madeleine. "If I have to, I'll go myself."

He wrote the following letter under Fantine's dictation and got her to sign it:

Monsieur Thénardier,
    You will hand Cosette over to the bearer.
    All small debts will be paid.

Yours faithfully,<br>FANTINE

At this juncture a serious incident occurred. We chip away as best we can at the mysterious block of marble our lives are made of—in vain; the black vein of destiny always reappears.

## II. How *Jean* Can Turn Into *Champ*

One morning, when Monsieur Madeleine was in his office, busy settling some pressing mayoral matters ahead of time in case he did decide to travel to Montfermeil himself, someone popped in to tell him that police inspector Javert wished to speak to him. At the sound of that name, Monsieur Madeleine could not help but have a bad feeling. Since the incident at the police station, Javert had avoided him more than ever and Monsieur Madeleine had not set eyes on him again.

"Send him in," he said.

In stepped Javert.

Monsieur Madeleine remained seated near the fireplace, a quill pen in his hand, his eye on a file he was flicking through and annotating, which contained police reports on infringements of the traffic regulations. He did not get up for Javert. He could not prevent himself from thinking of poor Fantine and he felt it was appropriate for him to be cool.

Javert respectfully saluted the mayor, who turned his back on him and, without taking any notice of him, went on making notes in his file.

Javert took two or three steps into the office and stopped without breaking the silence.

A physiognomist familiar with Javert's nature, one who had long studied this savage at the service of civilization, this bizarre composite of Roman, Spartan, monk, and corporal, this spy who could not lie, this virgin snitch, a physiognomist who knew of his secret and long-standing aversion to Monsieur Madeleine, of his conflict with the mayor over Fantine, and who could study Javert at this moment, would have wondered: "What on earth has happened to the man?" It was evident to anyone familiar with the man's straight, clear, sincere, righteous, austere, and ferocious conscience that Javert was emerging from some huge inner struggle. There was nothing in Javert's soul that wasn't written all over his face. He was, like all violent people, subject to abrupt mood swings. But his physiognomy had never been more bizarre or more startling. On entering, he had bowed before Monsieur Madeleine with a look completely devoid of bitterness, anger, defiance; he had stopped a few feet behind the mayor's chair; and now he just stood there in an almost military pose, with the naïve and cold cloddishness of a man never soft but always patient. He waited, without a word, without a movement, in genuine humility and quiet resignation, until it should please Monsieur le maire to turn around; calm, grave, hat in hand, eyes lowered, with an expression exactly halfway between that of a soldier facing his officer and a guilty party facing his judge. All the feelings and all the recollections you would imagine him to have had evaporated. Now there was nothing more on that impenetrable and simple granitelike face than a mournful sadness. His whole person exuded abasement and steadfastness and an inexpressibly courageous dejection.

Finally Monsieur le maire put down his pen and half turned round:

"Well, what? What's up, Javert?"

Javert remained silent for a moment as though gathering his wits; then he spoke up with a sort of sad solemnity, which was nonetheless straightforward: "What's up, Monsieur le maire, is that a criminal act has been committed."

"What act?"

"An inferior agent of the government has shown lack of respect for a magistrate in the most serious fashion. I come, as is my duty, to bring this fact to your attention."

"Who is this agent?" asked Monsieur Madeleine.

"Me," said Javert.

"You?"

"Me."

"And who is the magistrate who has something to complain about in this agent?"

"You, Monsieur le maire."

Monsieur Madeleine sat bolt upright in his chair. Javert went on, his manner serious, his eyes still cast down.

"Monsieur le maire, I have come to beg you to be so kind as to see to it that the authorities dismiss me."

Monsieur Madeleine, flabbergasted, started to open his mouth. Javert interrupted him.

"You're going to say that I could have tendered my resignation, but that is not enough. To tender your resignation is the honorable thing to do. I failed, I must be punished. I must be discharged."

And, after a pause, he went on: "Monsieur le maire, you were unjustly severe with me the other day. Be justly so today."

"So that's it! Why?" cried Monsieur Madeleine. "What is all this garbage? What are you trying to say? How has a criminal act been committed against me by you? What have you done to me? What wrong have you done me? You accuse yourself, you wish to be replaced—"

"Discharged."

"Discharged, all right. I just don't get it."

"You will, Monsieur le maire."

Javert released a sigh from deep in his chest and went on in the same sad, frigid manner: "Monsieur le maire, six weeks ago following the episode with that woman, I was furious and I denounced you."

"Denounced me!"

"To the prefecture of police in Paris."

Monsieur Madeleine, who laughed scarcely more often than Javert did, began to let loose.

"As a mayor encroaching on police turf?"

"As an ex-convict."

The mayor went very white.

Javert, who had not looked up, forged on:

"That is what I thought. For a long while I'd had my suspicions. A physical resemblance, information obtained in Faverolles, your amazing strength, the episode with old Fauchelevent, your skill as a marksman, the way you limp a little in one leg, I don't know! Rubbish like that! Whatever it was, I took you for a man who went by the name of Jean Valjean, that's all."

"Went by the name of? . . . What did you say his name was?"

"Jean Valjean. He was a convict I saw twenty years ago when I was the auxiliary guard in the hulks of Toulon. When he came out of jail, this Jean Valjean, it seems, robbed a bishop's, then went on to commit another armed robbery in a public thoroughfare, on a little Savoyard. He got away eight years ago, no one knows how, though they kept looking for him. Me, I fancied . . . In a word, that's what I did! Anger made up my mind for me, and I denounced you to the prefecture."

Monsieur Madeleine, who had taken up his file again a few moments before, said in a tone of perfect indifference: "And what was their reply?"

"That I was mad."

"So?"

"So, they were right."

"Just as well you recognize the fact!"

"I have no choice, since the real Jean Valjean has been found."

The sheet of paper Monsieur Madeleine was holding slipped out of his hands, he looked up and, firmly holding Javert's eyes, he said in an indescribable tone: "Ah!"

Javert went on: "This is the story, Monsieur le maire. It seems that down there, out Ailly-le-Haut-Clocher way, there was a fellow known as old man Champmathieu. He was very poor. Nobody took any notice of him. People like that, no one knows what they live on. Recently, this autumn, old man Champmathieu was arrested for stealing apples for cider, an act committed at . . . Never mind! There was a theft, a wall scaled, branches of a tree broken. My Champmathieu was arrested. He still had the apple branch in his hand. The cur was put behind bars. Up to that point, it wasn't much more than petty larceny—a matter for the magistrate. But that's where Providence comes in. The lockup was in a bad state, so the examining magistrate feels it only right to transfer Champmathieu to Arras where the departmental prison is. In this prison in Arras there's an old ex-con named Brevet who's being held for I don't know what reason and who has been made a gatekeeper at the barracks for good behavior. Monsieur le maire, Champmathieu no sooner turns up than this Brevet cries: 'Well, I never! I know that man! He's an old crim. Come on, look at me, mate! You're Jean Valjean!' 'Jean Valjean? Who the hell is Jean Valjean?' Old Champmathieu plays dumb. 'Don't come the innocent with me,' says Brevet. 'You're Jean Valjean! You were in the clink in Toulon. Twenty years ago we were in together.' Champmathieu won't have it. Hell! You can understand why. They dug deeper. They dug deeper into the whole business for me. And this is what they came up with: This Champmathieu, about thirty years ago, worked as a tree pruner all around the country and especially in Faverolles. There, we lose all trace of him. A long while later, we see him in the Auvergne, then in Paris, where he reckons he was a wheelwright and that he had a daughter who was a washerwoman, but there's no proof of that; finally, he shows up in this neck of the woods. Now, before he went to jail for aggravated theft, what was Jean Valjean? A pruner. Where? In Faverolles. Another fact. This Valjean was called Jean as his Christian name and his mother's maiden name was Mathieu. What could be more natural, when he got out of jail, than taking his mother's name to hide behind and pass himself off as Jean Mathieu? He heads for the Auvergne. There, they pronounce *Jean* as *Chan,* so he's known as Chan Mathieu. Our man goes along with this and suddenly he's transformed into Champmathieu. You follow my drift, don't you? Inquiries are made in Faverolles. Jean Valjean's family no longer lives there. No one knows where they are now. You know, in the lower classes, families often vanish from sight like that. We look, we can't find a thing. Those sorts of people, when they're not mud, they're dust. Then again, as the start of the story goes back thirty years, there's no one left in Faverolles who knew Jean Valjean. We make inquiries in Toulon. Besides Brevet there are only two convicts who ever clapped eyes on Jean Valjean. Their names are Cochepaille and Chenildieu[1] and they are now serving life sentences. We take them out of jail and bring them here. We confront them with this so-called Champmathieu. They don't hesitate. For them, same as for Brevet, it's Jean Valjean. Same age—he's fifty-four, same height, same look, same man, in a word, it's him. It was at that very moment that I sent my denunciation to the prefecture in Paris. They answered that I'm losing my mind and that Jean Valjean is in Arras in the hands of the law. You can imagine how amazed I was, since I thought I had this same Jean Valjean right where I wanted him—here! I write to the examining judge. He sends for me, they bring me Champmathieu—"

"And?" Monsieur Madeleine broke in.

Javert replied, his face incorruptible and sad: "Monsieur le maire, the truth is the truth. I don't like the fact, but that man is Jean Valjean. I, too, recognized him."

Monsieur Madeleine's voice was barely a whisper when he went on: "Are you sure?"

Javert began to laugh with that painful laugh that springs from deep conviction: "Oh, I'm sure!"

He remained reflective for a moment, mechanically taking pinches of the wood powder for drying ink from the little blotting-bowl on the table, then he added: "And more than that, now that I've seen the real Jean Valjean, I can't understand how I could have thought otherwise. I beg your forgiveness, Monsieur le maire."

In addressing this grave plea to the man who, six weeks before, had humiliated him in front of the whole police station and who had told him to "get out!" Javert, that arrogant man, was unwittingly full of guilelessness and dignity. Monsieur Madeleine answered his prayer only with this abrupt question: "And what does the man say?"

"Ah, heavens, Monsieur le maire, the whole thing's a mess. If it is Jean Valjean, we're dealing with a repeat offender. Leaping over a wall, breaking a branch, pinching apples, for a child, it's a bit of mischief; for a man, it's a misdemeanor; for a convict, it's a crime. Scaling a wall and theft, it's all there. It's not the examining magistrate anymore, it's the criminal court. It's not a few days in the lockup anymore, it's the galleys in perpetuity. And then, there's the business with the little Savoyard, who I hope will turn up. Lord! There's plenty to fight against, don't you think? Yes, for anyone other than Jean Valjean. But Jean Valjean is a sly dog. And that's also how I know him. Anyone else would feel that things were getting too hot; he'd go to great lengths to deny everything, he'd make a real song and dance, the kettle sings on top of the fire, he'd claim he wasn't Jean Valjean, and so on, and so forth. But him, he acts like he doesn't know what's going on, he says: 'I'm Champmathieu and that's all there is to it.' He acts amazed—even better, he acts dumb. Oh, the bastard's cunning as a sewer rat. But it makes no difference, the evidence is there. He's been identified by four people; the old scoundrel will be condemned. It's gone to the criminal court, in Arras. I'll be going there to testify. I've been called."

Monsieur Madeleine had sat back at his desk, taken up his file again, and was leafing through it quietly, reading and making notes, like a man with a lot on his plate. He wheeled round to Javert: "That's enough, Javert. I'm really not interested in all the details, to tell you the truth. We are wasting our time and there are urgent matters to attend to. Javert, you will go instantly to the good woman Buseaupied who sells herbs over on the corner of the rue Saint-Saulve. You will tell her to lodge her complaint against the cart driver, Pierre Chesnelong; that man is a thug who nearly crushed the woman and her child to death. He must be punished. You will then go to Monsieur Charcellay's, rue

Montre-de-Champigny. He's complaining that the house next door's gutter overflows into his place when it's raining and that it's eroding the foundations of his house. After that you will look into the offenses against police regulations that have been brought to my attention in the rue Guibourg at the widow Doris's place and rue du Garraud-Blanc at Madame Renée le Bossé's, and you will file reports. But I'm loading you up with work. Aren't you going to be away? Didn't you say you were going to Arras for that business in eight to ten days . . . ?"

"Sooner than that, Monsieur le maire."

"What day, then?"

"But I think I told Monsieur le maire that it was going to be tried tomorrow and that I was setting out by stagecoach tonight."

Monsieur Madeleine gave an imperceptible start.

"And how long will the trial last?"

"A day at the most. The sentence will be handed down tomorrow night at the latest. But I won't wait for the sentence, which is not in any doubt. As soon as my testimony is given, I'll come back here."

"Fine," said Monsieur Madeleine.

And he waved Javert out of the room.

Javert did not budge.

"Pardon me, Monsieur le maire."

"What else?" asked Monsieur Madeleine.

"Monsieur le maire, there is one thing I must remind you of."

"What?"

"It's that I have to be relieved of my duties."

Monsieur Madeleine rose.

"Javert, you are a man of honor, and I value you. You exaggerate your mistake. Besides, it is one more offense that concerns me alone. Javert, you deserve to rise, not fall. I want you to keep your job."

Javert looked at Monsieur Madeleine with his candid eyes, in whose depths you felt you could see his conscience, unenlightened but inflexible and unsullied and he said in a calm voice: "Monsieur le maire, I can't agree to that."

"I'll say it again," replied Monsieur Madeleine. "This matter is my business."

But Javert in his single focus was not about to be sidetracked, and persisted: "As for exaggerating, I'm not. This is how I look at it. I suspected you unjustly. That's nothing. It's anyone's right to be suspicious, even if there may be some abuse involved in suspecting people above your station. But without proof, and in a fit of rage, with only revenge in mind, I denounced you as a convict—you, a respectable man, a mayor, a magistrate! That is serious. Most serious. I offended authority in your person, I, an agent of authority! If one of my subordinates had done to me what I've done to you I would have declared him unworthy of the service and sent him packing. So, what are you waiting for?

Listen, Monsieur le maire, one more thing. I have often been hard in my life. On others. It was just. I did the right thing. So now, if I weren't hard on myself, everything I've ever done right would be wrong. Am I supposed to go softer on myself than on others? No. Heavens! If I was only good for chastising others and not myself, I'd be a miserable swine, indeed! And those who call me 'that mongrel Javert' would be right! Monsieur le maire, I don't want you to treat me with goodness, your goodness to others has made my blood boil. I don't want it for myself. The goodness that consists of ruling in favor of the strumpet against the bourgeois citizen, the policeman against the mayor, the underdog against the top dog, is what I call bad goodness. It's that sort of goodness that brings society down. God, it's as easy as winking to be good, the hard thing is to be just. Listen! If you had been what I thought you were, I wouldn't have been good to you! Not me! You'd have copped it! Monsieur le maire, I must deal with myself the way I'd deal with anyone else. Whenever I sent wrongdoers down, whenever I locked up scoundrels, I would often say to myself: 'You, if you ever slip up, if I ever catch you in the wrong, just look out!' I did slip up, I did catch myself in the wrong. Too bad! So let's go: booted out, cashiered, dismissed! Only right. I have arms, I'll work the land. I don't mind. Monsieur le maire, for the good of the service, make an example of me. I simply request the dismissal of Inspector Javert."

All this was said in a tone that was humble, proud, desperate, and convinced, which gave this strangely honest man an indescribably weird grandeur.

"We shall see," said Monsieur Madeleine.

And he held out his hand.

Javert recoiled and said in a fierce voice: "Forgive me, Monsieur le maire, but that is not right. A mayor does not give his hand to a snitch."

He added between clenched teeth: "A snitch, yes; the moment I misuse my powers as a policeman, I am nothing more than a snitch."

On that note, he bowed deeply and headed for the door.

At the door, he turned and, eyes still downcast, said: "Monsieur le maire, I will continue to perform my duties until a replacement is found."

He left. Monsieur Madeleine sat musing, listening to the firm and measured tread receding down the stone corridor.

# BOOK SEVEN

# THE CHAMPMATHIEU AFFAIR

## I. SISTER SIMPLICE

Not all the incidents you are about to read of were ever known in Montreuil-sur-mer, but the few stories that did make it there had such an indelible impact that it would be a serious gap in this book if we were not to narrate them in their minutest details.

Among these details, the reader will come across two or three improbable circumstances that we are keeping out of respect for the truth.

During the afternoon that followed Javert's visit, Monsieur Madeleine went to see Fantine as usual.

Before going in to Fantine, he asked for Sister Simplice. The two nuns who staffed the infirmary, Lazarist sisters[1] like all the Sisters of Charity, were called Sister Perpetua and Sister Simplice.

Sister Perpetua was an ordinary village lass, a Sister of Charity only in the broadest sense of the term, who had entered the house of God as someone else might enter domestic service. She was a nun the way others are cooks. This species is not rare. Monastic orders gladly accept this chunky peasant clay, so easily molded into a Capuchin nun or an Ursuline.[2] Such rustics are used for the tougher chores of the religious life. The transition from cowherd to White Friar[3] is not drastic in the least—the one turns into the other without too much effort; the common denominator of ignorance, whether of the village or of the cloister, is all the groundwork required and immediately places the country bumpkin on equal footing with the monk. Let the peasant smock out a little at the seams and you have your monk's frock. Sister Perpetua was a sturdy nun from Marines, near Pontoise, given to patois, psalm singing, whining, sweetening herbal concoctions according to the bigotry or hypocrisy of the bedridden invalid, rough with the sick, gruff with the dying, practically throwing God in their faces, bombarding their death throes with furious prayers, rash, honest, and red-faced.

Sister Simplice was white, with a waxy whiteness. Set beside Sister Perpetua, she was the beeswax altar candle next to the household candle made of tallow. Vincent de Paul[4] has divinely portrayed the Sister of Charity in words that vividly paint the combination of a high degree of freedom with a high degree of humility: His sisters were to spend their time nursing the sick in their homes, "having no monastery but the homes of the sick, no cell but a hired room, no chapel but the parish church, no cloister but the streets of the city or wards of the hospital, no fence but obedience, no gate but the fear of God, no veil but holy modesty." This ideal had been kept alive in Sister Simplice. No one could tell how old Sister Simplice was; she had never been young and seemed never to grow old. She was a person—we don't dare use the word *woman*—who was calm, austere, good company yet detached, and who had never told a lie. She was so gentle she seemed fragile, but was actually the opposite, solid as a rock. She touched the miserable lightly, with lovely, fine, pure fingers. There was silence, so to speak, in her words; she said only what was necessary, no more, and she had a voice that would have been edifying in a confessional and enchanting in a drawing room. This fineness adapted itself to the homespun nun's habit, providing a constant reminder of God and heaven in the rough contact. We might insist on this detail. Never to have lied, never to have told, out of whatever interest, or even disinterestedly, anything other than the truth, the sacred truth—this was the distinctive feature of Sister Simplice; it was the mark of her virtue. She was virtually famous in the congregation for this imperturbable truthfulness. Abbé Sicard speaks of Sister Simplice in a letter to the deaf-mute Massieu.[5] However sincere, however loyal and incorruptible we may be, we each have at least one crack in our candor formed by the innocent white lie. She did not. A white lie, a little white lie, does such a thing really exist? To lie is the absolute of evil. To lie a little is not possible; one who lies, lies wholly; the lie is the very face of the devil. Satan has two names—he is called Satan and he is called Lying. That is the way she looked at it. And she practiced what she preached. The result was the whiteness we mentioned, a whiteness that bathed even her lips and eyes in its radiance. Her smile was white, her gaze was white. There was not a single cobweb, not a single speck of dust on the window of that conscience. In vowing obedience to the Order of Saint Vincent de Paul, she had specially chosen the name of Simplice. Simplice of Sicily, as we know, was the saint who preferred to have both breasts ripped off rather than say that she was born in Segesta, when she was born in Syracuse—a lie that would have saved her. Such a patron saint suited this soul perfectly.

When she entered the order Sister Simplice had two faults, which she managed to correct slowly over time; she had a sweet tooth and she loved getting letters. She only ever read a prayer book in big letters and in Latin. She did not understand Latin but she understood the book.

The pious old maid had really taken to Fantine, probably sensing the latent virtue in her, and she had devoted herself to caring for her almost exclusively. Monsieur Madeleine took Sister Simplice aside and commended Fantine to her with a singular insistence that the sister would later recall. When he left the sister, he approached Fantine.

Every day Fantine waited for Monsieur Madeleine to appear as you might await a wave of heat or a ray of joy. She would tell the sisters: "I only feel alive when Monsieur le maire is there."

That day she had a high fever. As soon as she saw the mayor she asked him: "Cosette?"

He replied with a tight smile: "Soon."

Monsieur Madeleine was the same as ever with Fantine. Only, he stayed for an hour instead of half an hour, to Fantine's great delight. He badgered everyone in an effort to ensure that the sick woman had everything she needed, lacked nothing. It was noted that there was a moment when his face clouded over. But this was explained by the fact, soon learned, that the doctor had bent close to his ear and said to him: "She's going down fast."

He then returned to the *mairie* and was seen by the office boy there to examine carefully a road map of France that was hanging in his room. He jotted down a few figures in pencil on a scrap of paper.

## II. The Perspicacity of Master Scaufflaire

He set out from the *mairie* for the outskirts of town to see a Flemish man, Master Scaufflaër, Scaufflaire in French, who hired horses and "cabriolets upon request."

To get to this Scaufflaire's place, the shortest route was along a generally deserted backstreet where the presbytery of the parish Monsieur Madeleine resided in lay. The priest was, so they said, a worthy and respectable gent, one who gave good advice. When Monsieur Madeleine reached the presbytery there was only one other person in the street and this fellow pedestrian noticed the following: that Monsieur le maire, after having gone past the priest's place, had stopped, stood motionless for a moment, and then retraced his steps as far as the presbytery door, which was a motley affair with an iron door-knocker. He promptly seized the door-knocker and raised it; then stopped himself again and stayed that way, thinking, for a few seconds; and then, instead of letting the door-knocker fall with a loud rap, he gently brought it down and continued on his way, suddenly in a hurry as it seemed.

Monsieur Madeleine found Master Scaufflaire at home busy fixing a harness.

"Master Scaufflaire," he said, "you wouldn't happen to have a good horse, would you?"

"Monsieur le maire," said the Fleming, "all my horses are good. What do you mean by a good horse, anyway?"

"I mean a horse that can do twenty leagues in a day."

"Christ!" the Fleming exclaimed. "Twenty leagues!"

"Yes."

"Hitched to a cabriolet?"

"Yes."

"And how much time would he have to rest after the run?"

"He'd have to be able to set out again the next day."

"To do the same trip?"

"Yes."

"Jesus Christ! And that's twenty leagues?"

Monsieur Madeleine pulled out of his pocket the note on which he had penciled his figures. He showed it to the Fleming. The figures were the numbers five, six, and eight and a half.

"You see," he said. "That makes nineteen and a half, so we might as well say twenty leagues."

"Monsieur le maire," the Fleming went on, "I have just the ticket. My little white horse. You must have seen him going by sometimes. He's a little thing from Bas-Boulonnais. Full of fire. They tried to make a saddle horse of him to start with. Hah! He kicked like crazy and threw everyone to the ground. They thought he must have been vicious and no one knew what to do with him. I bought him. I put a cabriolet on him. Monsieur, that's what he was angling for; he's as gentle as a lamb and he rides like the wind. Ah, but mind you, you mustn't hop on his back. He has no intention of being a saddle horse. To each his ambition. Pull, yes, carry, no; you'd swear that's what he told himself."

"And he'll go the distance?"

"Your twenty leagues. At a brisk trot all the way, and he'll do it in under eight hours. But these are the conditions."

"Tell me."

"First, you let him get his breath back for an hour when you're halfway; he can eat then and someone has to be standing by while he's eating to stop the boy from the inn from stealing his oats, for I've noticed at inns that the oats get drunk by the stable boys more than they get eaten by the horses."

"I'll look after that."

"Second . . . is the cabriolet for Monsieur le maire?"

"Yes."

"Well then, Monsieur le maire will travel alone and without luggage so as not to overload the horse."

"Agreed."

"But Monsieur le maire, not having anyone with him, will be obliged to see to the oats himself."

"That's right."

"I'll need thirty francs a day. Days off paid for too. Not a penny less, and what the horse eats is at Monsieur le maire's expense."

Monsieur Madeleine drew three napoléons out of his purse and put them on the table.

"There's two days in advance."

"Fourth, for a trip like this, a cabriolet will be too heavy and will wear out the horse. Monsieur le maire will have to agree to travel in a little tilbury I happen to have."

"I'll go along with that."

"It's light but it's open."

"That's all the same to me."

"Has Monsieur le maire considered that it's winter?"

Monsieur Madeleine stayed silent. Master Scaufflaire continued: "That it could rain?"

Monsieur Madeleine raised his head and said: "The tilbury and the horse will be out in front of my place at four-thirty tomorrow morning."

"Say no more, Monsieur le maire," Scaufflaire replied before scratching away with his thumbnail at a mark on the wooden table and adding in the offhand way the Flemish soften their shrewdness: "While we're at it, I've just realized! Monsieur le maire hasn't told me where he's headed. Where is Monsieur le maire off to?"

He had thought of nothing else from the moment the conversation began, but for some reason hadn't dared bring the subject up.

"Does this horse have good strong forelegs?" asked Monsieur Madeleine.

"Yes, Monsieur le maire. You just have to hold him back a little going downhill. Are there are lot of ups and downs from here to where you're going?"

"Don't forget to be at my door at four-thirty sharp in the morning," replied Monsieur Madeleine, and with that he spun on his heel.

The Fleming stood there with his mouth open—"like an idiot," as he himself put it some time later.

Monsieur le maire had been gone two or three minutes when the door swung open again; it was Monsieur le maire. He had the same unflappable preoccupied look.

"Monsieur Scaufflaire," he said, "what value would you put on your horse and your tilbury, the ones you're renting out to me, with the one pulling the other?"

"The one dragging the other, more like, Monsieur le maire," guffawed the Fleming.

"However you like to put it. So?"

"Does Monsieur le maire want to buy them from me?"

"No, but in any event I'd like to insure them. When I return you can give me my money back. How much do you reckon your horse and cabriolet are worth?"

"Five hundred francs, Monsieur le maire."

"Here you are."

Monsieur Madeleine placed a banknote on the table, went out again, and this time did not come back.

Master Scauffaire could have kicked himself for not saying a thousand francs. In any case, the horse and tilbury together weren't worth more than a hundred écus.

The Fleming called his wife and told her all about it. Where the hell could Monsieur le maire be off to? They conferred.

"He's off to Paris," said the wife. "I don't think so," said the husband. Monsieur Madeleine had left the note with the numbers on it behind on the mantelpiece. The Fleming grabbed it and studied it. "Five, six, eight and a half? That must refer to the post houses." He turned to his wife. "I've got it." "What?" "It's five leagues from here to Hesdin, six from Hesdin to Saint-Pol, and eight and a half from Saint-Pol to Arras. He's off to Arras."

In the meantime, Monsieur Madeleine had gone home.

To return home from Master Scauffaire's he had taken the long way round, as though the presbytery door was some kind of temptation for him, one he wished to avoid. He had gone up to his room and shut himself in, which in itself was fairly unremarkable since he usually went to bed early. But the factory concierge, who was at the same time Monsieur Madeleine's only servant, noted that the light went out at as early as eight-thirty, and she said as much to the cashier when he came back, adding: "Is Monsieur le maire sick? I thought he looked a bit peculiar."

The cashier lived in the room exactly below Monsieur Madeleine's room. He took no notice of the concierge's words, went to bed and went to sleep. Around midnight, he woke with a start; he had heard a noise overhead in his sleep. He listened. It was the sound of feet coming and going as though someone were pacing up and down in the room above. He listened more carefully and recognized Monsieur Madeleine's tread. That struck him as strange; usually there was not a sound from Monsieur Madeleine's room before it was time to get up. A moment later the cashier heard what sounded like a wardrobe door being opened and shut. Then a piece of furniture was moved, then there was a silence, and then the pacing began again. The cashier sat up in bed, shook himself wide awake, looked out, and through his casement window saw the reddish reflection of light from a window on the wall opposite. From the direction of the light, it could only have been the window of Monsieur Madeleine's room. The reflection flickered as if it came from a blazing fire and not from a lamp. There was no trace of the shadow of the framed panes—which indicated that the window was wide open. In the freezing cold, that open window was startling. The cashier went back to sleep. An hour or so later, he woke again. The same tread, pacing to and fro, could still be heard directly overhead.

The reflection still graced the wall, but it was now pale and peaceful like the reflection from a lamp or a candle. The window was still open.

This is what was happening in Monsieur Madeleine's bedroom.

### III. A Storm on the Brain

The reader has no doubt worked out that Monsieur Madeleine was none other than Jean Valjean.

We have already delved into the depths of that man's conscience; the moment has come to delve a little deeper. We do not do so lightly, without emotion or without trembling. There is nothing more terrifying than this kind of contemplation. The mind's eye can find nothing more dazzling or dark anywhere outside mankind; it cannot fix on anything more fearful, more complex, more mysterious, or more infinite. There is a spectacle greater than the sea, and that is the sky; there is a spectacle greater than the sky, and that is the human soul.

To write the poem of the human conscience, were it only that of a single man, were it only that of the most insignificant man, would be to meld all epics into one superior epic, the epic to end all. Conscience means the chaos of chimeras, of lusts and temptations, the furnace of dreams, the den of ideas we are ashamed of; it is the pandemonium of sophisms, it is the battlefield of passions. Pierce through the livid face of a human being at certain moments as they ponder, look behind the façade, look into the soul, look into the darkness. There, beneath the outer silence, titanic struggles are taking place as in Homer, mêlées of dragons and hydras and swarms of phantoms as in Milton, visionary spirals as in Dante. What a somber thing is this infinity that each man carries within him and against which he measures in despair what his brain wants and what his life puts into action!

Dante Alighieri came upon a sinister door[1] one day and hesitated before it. Here stands another door before us, on the threshold of which we hesitate. Let's go in anyway.

We have very little to add to what the reader already knows about what happened to Jean Valjean since the Petit-Gervais episode. From that moment, as we saw, he was a different man. What the bishop had wanted him to become, he became. This was more than a transformation, it was a transfiguration.

He managed to vanish, sold the bishop's silver, keeping only the candlesticks as mementos, crept from town to town, traveled across France, turned up in Montreuil-sur-mer, had the bright idea we've mentioned above, achieved what we've outlined, managed to make himself unassailable and inaccessible and from then on, well established in Montreuil-sur-mer, happy to feel his conscience burdened by his past and the first half of his existence belied by this new phase, he lived a quiet life, reassured and hopeful, having only two concerns: to hide his name and to sanctify his life; to escape the clutches of men and to return to God.

These two concerns were so closely linked in his mind that they were inseparable; they were both equally absorbing and imperious and governed his every act. Normally they were in harmony, regulating the way he led his life; they turned him toward a life lived in the shadow; they made him benevolent and true; they gave him the same counsel. But sometimes there was a conflict between them. When this happened, as you will recall, the man the whole countryside called Monsieur Madeleine did not waver in sacrificing the first to the second, his security to his virtue. And so, in spite of all reservations and all prudence, he had kept the bishop's candlesticks, worn mourning for him, sent for and questioned all the little Savoyards coming through, made inquiries about the families of Faverolles, and saved old Fauchelevent's life despite the disturbing insinuations of Javert. It seems, as we have already remarked, that he thought, along with all those who have ever been wise, holy, and just, that his first duty was not to himself.

But, we have to say, nothing like this had ever come up before. Never had the two notions that ruled this unhappy man, whose sufferings are the subject of our tale, locked horns within himself in such a serious battle. He realized this dimly but deeply as soon as Javert had opened his mouth the day he came into his office. The instant that name, which he had buried under so many layers, was so weirdly voiced, he was struck dumb and sent reeling as though intoxicated by the sinister grotesqueness of his fate, and, through the daze, he felt the shudder that heralds huge quakes; he bent low like an oak about to be battered by a storm, like a soldier about to be assailed. He felt darkness full of thunder and lightning directly overhead. While he was listening to Javert speak, he had had an initial impulse to dash out, to run, to denounce himself, to drag Champmathieu out of jail and put himself in; this had been painful and heartrending like an incision in live flesh, and then it had passed and he had said to himself: "Let's wait and see! Let's wait and see!" He got this initial generous impulse under control and recoiled before such heroics.

No doubt it would have been very nice if, after the sacred words of the bishop, after so many years of repentance and self-denial, in the middle of a penance so nobly undertaken, the man had not batted an eyelid for an instant, even when faced with such a terrible situation, and had gone on walking at the same pace toward the yawning chasm at the bottom of which lay heaven; that would have been very beautiful, but it is not what happened. It is, of course, our job to make known exactly what was going on in this man's soul and we can only tell it the way it was. What won out at first was the instinct of self-preservation; he swiftly gathered his wits about him, stifled his emotions, considered that great peril, the presence of Javert, postponed any decision with the firmness of terror, felt dizzy with all there was to do, and resumed his outward calmness as a gladiator picks up his shield.

He remained in this state for the rest of the day, a tornado whirling within, profound calmness without; he took only what we might call "precautionary measures." Everything was still confused and in turmoil in his brain; his brain was still so troubled that he could not latch on to any idea clearly and he himself would have been hard-pressed to describe what was happening to him except to say that he had just suffered quite a blow. He took himself off as usual to Fantine's sickbed and stayed longer than usual out of an instinctual goodness, telling himself that this was how he should behave, and commended her earnestly to the sisters in case he should have to absent himself. He felt vaguely that he might be compelled to go to Arras and, without being in the least determined to make the trip, he told himself that being above all suspicion as he was, there was no harm in witnessing what would happen there, and so he retained Scaufflaire's tilbury, in order to be ready for any eventuality.

He dined with a fairly good appetite.

When he got back to his room, he gathered his wits about him again.

He examined the situation and found it quite incredible; so incredible that in the middle of his reflections he was moved by some mysterious and virtually inexplicable impulse of anxiety to get up from his chair and bolt the door. He was afraid something else might slip in and so barricaded himself against the possibility.

A moment later, he blew out his light. It was getting on his nerves.

It seemed to him that somebody could see him.

Who could that be?

Alas! The very thing he wanted to keep outside had entered; what he wanted to blind was looking at him. His conscience.

His conscience, meaning, God.

Yet at first he deluded himself. He felt safe and alone; with the bolt in place, he felt impregnable. With the candle out, he felt invisible. And so he pulled himself together. He sat with his elbows on the table, held his head in his hands, and began to meditate in the darkness.

"Where am I? Am I sure I'm not dreaming? What was said? Is it true I saw that Javert and that he said what I think he said? Who can this Champmathieu be? Someone who looks like me? How can that be? When I think that only yesterday I was happy and so far from having the faintest inkling! What was I doing this time yesterday? What is this all about? How will it turn out? What am I going to do?"

You can see what torment he was in. His brain had lost all power to retain ideas, they rushed through like waves and he grabbed his forehead in both hands to try and stop them.

This raging tumult shattered his will and his reason; he tried to extract some clarity and resolution from it, but all he came up with was anguish.

His head was on fire. He went to the window and threw it wide open. There were no stars in the sky. He went and sat back down at the table.

The first hour flew by.

Little by little, however, dim outlines began to form and hold their shape in his mind and he could perceive with the precision of reality, not the situation in its entirety, but some of the details.

He began by recognizing that, as extraordinary and critical as the situation was, he was completely in control of it.

His bewilderment only grew.

Independent of the strict religious goal his actions were directed toward, everything he had ever done till that day was nothing but a hole he had been digging in order to bury his name. What he had always most dreaded in his hours of turning on himself, during his nights of insomnia, was ever to hear that name spoken; he told himself that this would, for him, be the end of everything; that the day that name reappeared, it would cause his new life to vaporize around him, and, who knows, perhaps inside of him, his new soul? He shuddered at the very idea that this was possible. Certainly, if anyone had told him in those moments that a time would come when that name would resound in his ears again, when those hideous words, *Jean Valjean,* would shoot out of the dark and rear up before him, when that fearsome bolt from the blue fated to dispel the mystery he had wrapped himself in would suddenly turn into a circle of light and shine over his head; and that the name would not threaten him, that the light would produce only deeper darkness, that the torn veil would only intensify the mystery, that this earthquake would consolidate his edifice, that this prodigious event would have only the effect, if that's what he himself wished, of making his existence at once clearer and more impenetrable, and that, from his confrontation with the phantom of Jean Valjean, the good and worthy bourgeois Monsieur Madeleine would emerge more honored, more at peace, and more respected than ever—if anyone had told him that, he would have shaken his head and dismissed such words as garbage. Well! All that was precisely what had just happened, this piling on of impossible events was a fact, and God had allowed such insanities to turn into realities!

His musings grew clearer and clearer. He was able to take in his situation more and more.

He felt as though he had just woken up from some strange sleep, to find himself sliding down a slope in the middle of the night, on his feet, shivering, scrabbling backward in vain, on the extreme brink of an abyss. He could distinctly make out in the shadow a stranger that fate mistook for him and pushed into the gulf in his place. For the gulf to close up again, someone had to fall in—himself or the other man.

He had only to leave things alone.

Suddenly everything became clear, and he admitted this: that his place in the galleys was empty, that no matter what he did, it was still waiting for him, that robbing Petit-Gervais led him straight back there, that the empty place was waiting for him and would pull at him until he was back in it, that this was inevitable and fatal. And then he said to himself: that at that moment he had a substitute, that apparently a man named Champmathieu had the bad luck to be this substitute, and that, as for himself, present in jail from now on in the person of this Champmathieu, present in society under the name of Monsieur Madeleine, he had nothing more to fear, as long as he did not prevent people from sealing upon Champmathieu's head the stone of infamy that, like the stone over the grave, falls once, never to rise again.

All of this was so intensely violent and so strange that it created an indescribable commotion inside him that no one ever experiences more than two or three times in a lifetime, a sort of convulsion of your conscience that stirs up all the murky dubious things the heart contains, which are composed of irony, joy, and despair—what we might call an inner burst of laughter.

He promptly relit his candle.

"Well, so what!" he said. "What am I so afraid of? Why go over it all again? I'm saved. It's over. There was only one door still ajar through which my past could erupt into my present life. That door is walled up now! Forever! This Javert who has been on my tail for so long, with his appalling instinct that seemed to have sniffed me out, that did sniff me out, for Christ's sake! the way he followed me everywhere, this ghoulish hound always nipping at my heels, now he's been thrown off the scent, he's sniffing around elsewhere, absolutely off the track! Now he's satisfied, he'll let me alone, he's got his Jean Valjean! Who knows? He probably even wants to leave town! And it all came about without my doing a thing! I had nothing to do with it! So then, what? What's so miserable about that? Anyone who saw me now would think something terrible had happened, for heaven's sake! After all, if anyone has come to grief, it's not my fault. It's all the work of fate. Apparently that's what fate wants! Do I have the right to undo the work of Providence? What am I after now? Why am I sticking my oar in? It's none of my business. Lord! I'm not happy! What's missing? The goal to which I've been aspiring for so many years, the one great dream that rules my nights, the object of my prayers to heaven above, safety—now I've got it! It's God's will. I've got no business interfering with God's will. And why does God will it? So I can carry on what I started, so I can do good, so that one day I can be a great and inspiring example, so that it can be said that there was at last a bit of happiness involved in this penance that I've undergone and in this virtue that I returned to! Really, I don't know why I was afraid just now to go and spill my guts to the good curé as my confessor, and to ask his advice; this is obviously what he would have told me. So that's decided! Let things alone! Let God's will be done!"

He talked to himself in the depths of his conscience in this way, leaning over what we might call his own abyss. Then he got up from his chair and began to pace the room.

"So," he said, "that's enough of that. A decision has been reached and that settles that!"

But he felt no joy. Just the opposite.

You can't stop your mind returning to an idea any more than you can stop the sea returning to shore. For the sailor, it is known as the tide; for the person with a guilty conscience, it is known as remorse. God lifts the soul as well as the ocean.

After a few moments, try as he might, he was forced to resume the grim dialogue in which he was the one who both spoke and listened, saying what he wanted to keep quiet, listening to what he did not want to hear, yielding to that mysterious power that said to him: "Think!" Just as it said two thousand years ago to another condemned man: "Walk!"

Before we go any further, and in the interests of being fully understood, we must insist on an essential observation.

It is incontestable that we talk to ourselves, there is no thinking being who does not do so. We could even say that talk is never more of a magnificent mystery than when it travels, within a person's inner life, from mind to conscience—and back again, from conscience to mind. It's only in this sense that we should understand the words often used in this chapter: he said, he cried out. We say to ourselves, we talk to ourselves, we cry out inside ourselves, without the outer silence being broken. There is a great tumult; everything in us speaks, except our mouths. The realities of the soul are no less real for not being visible and tangible.

So he asked himself where he stood. He put himself through the third degree over this "decision reached." He confessed to himself that everything he had just managed to get into order in his mind was monstrous, that "to let things alone," "to let God's will be done," was quite simply horrible. To let this mistake of fate and of men be perpetrated, not to stop it, to have a hand in the process through his silence, in a word, to do nothing, was to do everything! It was the final degree of hypocritical vileness! It was a crime—a low, cowardly, sly, abject, hideous crime!

For the first time in eight years, the poor man felt the bitter taste of wrongfulness.

He spat it out in disgust.

He continued to quiz himself. He asked himself sternly what he meant by the following phrase: "My goal has been achieved!" He declared to himself that his life did, indeed, have a goal. But what goal? To hide his name? To hoodwink the police? Was it for something so petty that he had done all he had done? Didn't he have another goal, a big one, the true one? To save, not his body, but his soul. To become honest and good again. To be a just man! Isn't that—especially that, uniquely that—what he had always wanted, what the bishop had demanded of him? To close the door on his past? But he wasn't closing it, for God's sake! He was opening it again by doing something despicable! He was reverting to being a thief again, and the most odious of thieves! He was robbing another of his existence, of his life, his peace of mind, his place under the sun! He was becoming a murderer! He was murdering some poor bastard, morally speaking, he was inflicting this ghastly living death on him, this being buried alive, known as jail! On the contrary, to give himself up, to save this man struck by such a ghastly mistake, to take his name back, to become once more, out of duty, the convict, Jean Valjean—that was truly to complete his resurrection and close forever the hell he had come from! To fall into it again in appearance was to leave it behind in reality! He had to do it! He would have done nothing if he didn't do that! His whole life would have been useless, all his penitence wasted, and there would be only one thing left to say: What is the point? He felt that the bishop was there, with him, that the bishop was even more present now that he was dead, that the bishop was watching him, faithfully, that from now on the mayor Madeleine and all his virtues would be abhorrent to him and that the galley slave Jean Valjean would be noble and pure in his sight. He felt that most people saw his mask, but that the bishop saw his face. That ordinary men saw his life, but the bishop saw his conscience. So he had to go to Arras, free the false Jean Valjean, denounce the true one! Alas! That was the greatest of sacrifices, the most moving of victories, the final step to take; but it had to be done. Painful fate! He would only enter into sanctity in the eyes of God if he reentered infamy in the eyes of men!

"So," he said, "my mind's made up! Let's do our duty! Let's save the man!"

He practically shouted those words, quite unaware that he was talking out loud. He gathered his books, checked them and put them in order. He threw on the fire a bundle of letters of credit that he held[2] over some small traders who had their backs to the wall. He wrote a letter which he then sealed, and wrote an address on the envelope that you could have read, had you been in the room at the time: *To Monsieur Laffitte, Banker, rue d'Artois, at Paris.*

From a *secretaire* he pulled a wallet that held some banknotes and the passport he had used that same year to go to the elections. Anyone who had seen him perform these various actions, which had such a serious meditative underpinning, would not have had any idea what was going on inside him. Only, at times, his lips began to move; at other times, he looked up and focused on some point on the wall as though it was precisely there that there was something he hoped to clear up or question.

The letter to Monsieur Laffitte dealt with, he pocketed it along with the wallet and began pacing again.

His reverie had not deviated. He continued to see his duty clearly written in luminous letters flaming before his very eyes and following his eyes around: *Get going! Name yourself! Give yourself up!*

He also saw, as if they moved in front of him in perceptible form, the two ideas that, till then, had been the twin rules of his life: to hide his name, to sanctify his soul. For the first time, these imperatives seemed to him to be absolutely distinct, and he saw the difference that separated them. He recognized that one of these ideas was necessarily good, while the other could turn out to be bad; that the good idea was devotion and the other, the cult of personality; that one idea said *your neighbor* and the other said *yourself;* that one came from the light and the other came from the darkness.

They struggled with each other, he could see them fighting. The more he thought about it, the larger they grew in his mind's eye; they had now grown to colossal size, and it seemed to him that he was watching the titanic struggle, inside himself, within that infinity we spoke of earlier, in the midst of darkness and light, between a god and a giant.

He was full of horror, but it seemed to him that the good thought was winning. He felt that he was reaching the other decisive moment of his conscience and his fate; that the bishop had marked the first phase of his new life and that this Champmathieu was marking the second. After a great crisis, a great test of strength.

Yet the fever, for an instant quelled, gradually came over him again. A thousand thoughts flitted through him, but they only strengthened him in his resolve.

One moment he told himself that he was perhaps taking things too hard, that after all, this Champmathieu was of no interest, that he was, at the end of the day, a thief. He answered himself that if the man was, in fact, a thief and had stolen a few apples, it meant a month in jail. That was a long way from the galleys. And who knows, anyhow? Did he actually steal? Was there any proof? The name Jean Valjean had battened down on him, seeming to dispense with any need for proof. Don't the king's prosecutors usually act in similar fashion? The man is believed to be a thief because he is known to be a convict.

In another instant, the idea came to him that if he gave himself up, perhaps they would take into account the heroism of his action and his honest upstanding life of the last seven years and all he had done for the region, and pardon him.

But this supposition evaporated pretty swiftly and he smiled bitterly at the thought that the theft of those forty sous from Petit-Gervais made him a recidivist, that that business would certainly raise its ugly head again and, in the precise terms of the law, would make him a candidate for forced labor for life.

He turned away from all delusion, detached himself more and more from earthly things and sought consolation and strength elsewhere. He told himself he had to do his duty; that he might even be no more unhappy after having done his duty than after having eluded it; that if he let well enough alone, if he remained in Montreuil-sur-mer, his standing, his good reputation, his good works, the deference, the veneration, his charity, his wealth, his popularity, his virtue, would all be tainted by a crime; and what a taste all those sacred things would leave, tainted by something so vile! Whereas, if he went ahead with his sacrifice and landed in jail, shackled to a post, in an iron collar, with a green cap, doing hard labor till the end of his days, in relentless shame, there would be a touch of paradise involved!

Lastly he told himself that it was essential, that this was his fate, that it was not for him to disturb the way things were arranged up above, that in any case he had to choose: either virtue without and abomination within or holiness within and disgrace on show without.

In stirring up so many gloomy notions, his courage never failed him but his brain hurt, and he began to think of other things in spite of himself, meaningless things.

His blood was pounding violently in his temples. He was still pacing to and fro. First midnight rang out from the parish church, then from the *mairie*. He counted the twelve strokes from the two clocks and compared the sound of the two bells. He remembered as he did so that only a few days before he had seen at a scrap merchant's an old clock for sale on which this name was written: *Antoine Albin de Romainville.*

He was cold. He lit a small fire. It didn't occur to him to shut the window. Even so, he fell once more into a stupor. He had to make a huge effort to recall what on earth he'd been thinking before midnight sounded. He finally remembered.

"Ah, yes!" he said to himself. "I'd decided to give myself up."

All of a sudden he thought of Fantine.

"Wait a minute!" he said. "What about that poor woman!"

At this juncture, a new crisis erupted.

Fantine, appearing suddenly in his inner debate, was like a ray of light shining where it was least expected. It seemed to him that everything around him looked different suddenly and he cried out: "Of course! Till now, I've been thinking only of myself! I've only considered what suits me! It suits me either to keep quiet or to give myself up, to hide myself or to save my soul, to be a magistrate, despicable but respected, or a galley slave, disgraced but noble, it's all about me, me, me, me, nothing but me! But good God! Talk about sheer egotism! Different forms of egotism, but egotism just the same! How about thinking of others for a change? The first sacred duty is to think of one's neighbor. Let's see, let's have a closer look. Myself excepted, myself eliminated, myself left out of the picture, what happens with all of this? If I give myself up? They nab me, they let this Champmathieu go, they stick me back in the galleys. Right. And then what? What happens here? Ah! Here there is a region, a town, factories, a whole industry, workers, men, women, old grandfathers, children, poor people! I created all that, I keep all that going; wherever there's a chimney smoking, I'm the one who puts the log in the fire and the meat in the pot; I've created ease of living, movement, credit; before me there was nothing; I got things going again, brought things to life, put some spark back into things, invigorated, stimulated, enriched the whole place; with me gone, the soul is gone. If I take myself off, everything will die. And that woman who has suffered so much, who was so noble in her fall from grace . . . I was the cause of her downfall, albeit unwittingly! And what about the child I was about to go and get, I promised her mother! Don't I also owe something to this woman by way of reparation for the harm I've done her? If I disappeared, what would happen? The mother would die. The little girl would have to fend for herself. So that's exactly what would happen if I give myself up. What if I don't give myself up? Let's see, if I don't give myself up?"

After putting this question to himself, he stopped; he experienced a momentary hesitation and trembling, but the moment was soon over, and he answered himself calmly: "Well, that man goes to the galleys, that's true, but, what the hell! He did steal! There's no point in my pretending he didn't steal, he stole, all right! Me, I stay here, I carry on. In ten years, I'll have earned ten million, I give it back to the community, I keep nothing myself, what's it to me? It's not for myself that I do what I do! The prosperity of all grows, old industries crank up and expand, new manufactures and workshops mushroom, families—a hundred families, a thousand families!—are happy; the countryside gets peopled; villages spring up where there are only farms, farms spring up where there's nothing; poverty disappears, and with poverty, debauchery, prostitution, theft, murder, all the vices, all the crimes, disappear, too! And that poor mother can bring up her daughter! And the whole region is rich and honest! For heaven's sake, I must have been mad, I must have been completely brainsick, why on earth would I talk about giving myself up? I really had better pull myself together, this demands careful reflection, I really mustn't do anything hasty. Good Lord! Just because I fancied playing the great and the generous man—talk about melodrama, for God's sake!—because I was only thinking of myself, myself alone, good Lord! And all to save—who knows who? Some thief, obviously a scoundrel. And from a punishment that might be a tad excessive but is no doubt justified, at bottom. And for such a man, the whole region must go to the dogs! A poor woman must croak in the hospital! A poor little girl must croak by the roadside! Like dogs! Ah, now that's abominable, if you want abominable! Without the mother even sighting her child again! Without the child even knowing a thing about her mother! And all for this old bastard of an apple thief who, beyond any doubt, deserves the galleys for something else, if not for that! What fine scruples—to save a man who's guilty and sacrifice the innocent, to save some old vagrant, who's only got a few more years left in him when all's said and done and who wouldn't be any worse off in the galleys than he would be at home in his hovel, to sacrifice a whole population, mothers, women, children! Poor little Cosette who has only me in the world and who is no doubt at this very moment completely blue with cold in the glorified shack of those Thénardiers! There's some more riffraff for you, that lot! So I'm supposed to fail in my duty of care toward all those poor creatures! And I'm supposed to go and turn myself in! Imagine doing anything so damned stupid! Let's look at the worst that can happen. Let's suppose that in all this there is a bad deed on my part and that my conscience holds it against me one day, all we have to do is accept, for the good of others, such disapprobation as burdens me alone, this bad deed that compromises my soul alone—that's what devotion is, that's where virtue lies."

He got to his feet and began pacing again. This time it seemed to him that he was happy.

Diamonds are found only in the bowels of the earth; truths are found only in the depths of reflection. It seemed to him that having descended into those depths, after groping in the blackness of the shadows for so long, he had finally found one of those diamonds, one of those truths, and that he held it in his hand; and it blinded him to look at it.

"Yes," he thought, "that's it. I'm on the road to the truth. I've found the solution. You have to end up holding on to something. I've made my choice. Let well enough alone! No more vacillating, no more retreating! This is in everyone's interest, not just mine; I am Madeleine, and Madeleine I remain. Too bad for the fellow who is Jean Valjean! He is no longer me. I don't know the man, I don't know what he is anymore; if there is someone who is Jean Valjean at this moment, let him fend for himself! It's nothing to do with me. It's a fateful name that floats in the night; if it stops and falls on someone's head, too bad for that person!"

He looked at himself in the little mirror over the mantelpiece and said: "See! What a relief to come to a decision! I look completely different now."

He took another few steps and then stopped short: "Wake up to yourself!" he said. "You can't go back no matter what the consequences of the decision you've made. There are still a few ties that bind me to this Jean Valjean. They must be cut! Here, in this very room, there are a few objects that would point the finger at me, dumb things that would accuse me; make no bones about it, they have to go."

He felt around in his pocket, pulled out his purse, opened it and took out a small key. He fitted the key into a lock, though the keyhole was barely visible, lost as it was in the darkest shades of the design of the wallpaper on the wall. A little secret space opened, a sort of false cupboard set between the wall and the mantelpiece. There was nothing in this little hidden space but junk—a smock made of blue cloth, an old pair of pants, an old haversack, and a big thorn stick tipped with metal at both ends. Those who had seen Jean Valjean in the days when he was passing through Digne, in October 1815, would easily have recognized all the components of this miserable fancy dress.

He had kept them just as he had kept the silver candlesticks, to remind himself always of where he had come from. Only, he hid what had come from jail and left out in the open the candlesticks that had come from the bishop.

He cast a furtive glance at the door as though he feared it might open despite the bar that held it shut tight; then with an abrupt and violent move, he grabbed in a single armful, without so much as a quick glance at them, these things he had so religiously and perilously hoarded for so many years, and took the lot, rags, stick, haversack, and threw them on the fire.

He shut the false cupboard again and, taking further precautions, now rather pointlessly since the thing was empty, he hid the door behind a heavy piece of furniture, which he pushed in front of it.

After a few seconds, the room and the wall opposite were lit by a great flickering red reflection. It was all going up in flames. The thorn stick crackled and threw out sparks right to the middle of the room.

The haversack, as it went up along with the awful rags it held, exposed something gleaming in the ashes. If you bent over, you would easily have recognized a silver coin. No doubt the forty-sou piece stolen from the little Savoyard.

He did not watch the fire; he walked, pacing to and fro in the same steady rhythm. All of a sudden his eyes fell on the two silver candlesticks that the light set gleaming faintly on the mantelpiece.

"Hang on!" he thought. "The whole of Jean Valjean is there, still, in them. They must be destroyed too."

He grabbed the two candlesticks. There was enough of a fire to swiftly deform them and melt them down into a sort of unrecognizable ingot.

He bent down to the hearth and warmed himself there for a moment. "Nice and hot!" he said.

He stirred the coals with one of the candlesticks. A minute more and they'd have been in the fire.

At that instant, he seemed to hear a voice crying out inside him: "Jean Valjean! Jean Valjean!"

His hair stood on end, he froze as though he'd heard something terrible.

"Yes! That's it! Finish the job!" said the voice. "Finish what you've started! Destroy the candlesticks! Obliterate the memory! Forget the bishop! Forget everything! Sink this Champmathieu character! Go on, that's right. Give yourself a round of applause! That way, it's fixed, it's resolved, it's done. Here's a fellow, an old man, who doesn't know what they've got against him, who has possibly done nothing, an innocent, whose undoing is entirely due to your name, your name is weighing on him like a crime, and he will be taken for you, he will be condemned, he will end his days in utter humiliation and in horror! Never mind. You be an upright man, you keep on being Monsieur le maire, keep on being honorable and honored, play the hero, make the town rich, feed the poor, bring up orphans, live happily ever after, virtuous and admired, and during that time, while you're here living in joy and in the light, someone else will have your red shirt on, someone else will bear your name in ignominy and drag your chain in jail! Yes, that's all settled nicely, then! Ah! Miserable bastard!"

Sweat trickled down his forehead. He fixed wild eyes on the candlesticks. But whatever was talking inside him had not yet done with him. The voice went on: "Jean Valjean! There will be many voices around you that will make a lot of noise, that will clamor and shout, that will bless you, and one voice that no one will hear and that will curse you in the darkness. So then, hear this, you vile creature! All the blessings will fall away before they reach heaven, and only the curse will rise as far as God!"

This voice, at first quite weak and coming from the darkest recess of his conscience, had gradually become strident and frightening, and he now heard it in his ear. It seemed to him that it had come from inside him but that it was now talking from outside him. He felt he heard those last words so distinctly that he looked around the room in a sort of terror.

"Is there someone there?" he asked out loud, perfectly distraught.

Then he went on with a laugh that sounded like the laugh of a half-wit:

"What an idiot I am! There can't be anybody there."

There was someone there; but that someone was not among those the human eye can see.

He put the candlesticks back down on the mantelpiece.

Then he began the monotonous and grim pacing that troubled the dreams of the man below him and woke him with a start from his sleep.

Walking calmed him and excited him at the same time. It seems that in extreme situations we often move around to ask the advice of all we might encounter in our travels. After a few moments, he no longer knew where he was.

He now recoiled in equal horror from each of the decisions he had in turn made. The two ideas counseling him both seemed as disastrous as each other. What a fatal coincidence! What a turn of events, this Champmathieu being taken for him! To be mown down by the means Providence seemed to have used initially to bolster him!

There was a moment when he considered the future. Give himself up, great God! Turn himself in! He saw with immense despair all that he would have to leave, all that he would have to go through again. He would, then, have to say goodbye to this existence that was so good, so pure, so radiant, to the respect of all, to honor, to freedom. He would go no more into the fields to stroll, he would no longer hear the birds singing in the month of May, he would no longer hand out alms to the little children! He would no longer feel the looks of gratitude and love that settled on him! He would leave this house he had built, this room, this sweet little room! Everything looked lovely to him at that moment. He would no longer read from these books, he would no longer write from this little whitewood table! His old concierge, the only servant he had, would no longer bring up his coffee in the morning. Great God! Instead of that, the galley slaves, the shackles, the red shirt, the iron chain on his foot, the exhaustion, the dungeon, the camp bed, all the old familiar horrors! At his age, after having been what he was! If only he were still young! But, fancy being old and insulted by the first person to come along, to be searched by the galley guard, to be belted by the guard with a truncheon! To have his bare feet in ironclad shoes! To hold out his leg morning and night for the hammer of the geezer who does the rounds testing the fetters! To have to put up with the curiosity of strangers to whom they would say: "That one there, that's the famous Jean Valjean who used to be mayor of Montreuil-sur-mer!" At night, dripping with sweat, shattered by fatigue, the green cap over his eyes, to mount two by two, under the sergeant's whip, the gangway of that floating prison! Oh, what misery! Can destiny, then, be malevolent like an intelligent being and turn monstrous like the human heart!

Do what he might, he kept returning to this thorny dilemma at the back of his mind: whether to remain in paradise and turn into a demon there, or to return to hell and there become an angel!

What to do, great God! What to do?

The torment he'd struggled so painfully free of unleashed itself once more inside him. His ideas began to get tangled up again. They assumed that indefinably dazed, mechanical quality peculiar to despair. The name Romainville kept endlessly recurring, along with two lines of a song he'd once heard. He thought that Romainville was a small wood close to Paris where young lovers went to gather lilacs in the month of April.

He tottered without as within. He stumbled around like a toddler finally allowed to walk on its own two feet.

Now and then, fighting off his weariness, he made an effort to think straight. He struggled to put into words, finally and once and for all, the problem over which he now stumbled with exhaustion. Should he give himself up? Should he keep quiet? He couldn't manage to see anything clearly. The vague outlines of all the arguments he'd sketched in his mind trembled and broke up, one after the other, all went up in smoke. Only, he felt that, whatever side he opted for, necessarily and without his being able to escape it, something of himself would die; that he was entering a tomb, and whether he took the left turn or the right, he would undergo the final agony of death, the demise of his happiness or the demise of his virtue.

Alas! He was in the grip once more of a total lack of resolve. He was right back to square one.

And so this sorry soul went on debating with himself in anguish. Eighteen hundred years before this poor wretched man, the mysterious being in whom all the holiness and all the suffering of humanity are gathered, had also, while the olive trees were shivering in the wild wind of infinity, long pushed away with his hand the fearsome chalice that appeared to him, streaming shadow and running over with darkness in the star-filled depths.

## IV. FORMS SUFFERING TAKES DURING SLEEP

Three o'clock in the morning had just rung out and he had been pacing up and down for five hours, almost without letup, when he let himself sink into his chair.

There, he fell asleep and had a dream.

This dream, like most dreams, was only connected to the actual situation by something mysteriously forlorn and poignant, but it made an impression on him. The nightmare struck him so forcefully he later wrote it down. It is one of the notes written in his own hand that he left behind. We believe we should transcribe the thing verbatim here.

Whatever the dream, the story of that night would be incomplete if we left it out. It is the somber adventure of a sick soul.

Here it is. On the envelope we find written this line: "The dream I dreamed that night."

I was in the countryside somewhere. Wide open gloomy country where there was no grass. It didn't look like day or night as far as I could tell.

I was having a walk with my brother, the brother I had in my childhood, the brother I have to say I never think of and whom I hardly remember anymore.

We were chatting and we met others out walking. We were talking about a neighbor we once had who, ever since she'd moved into the street, used to always work with her window open. While we were chatting we got cold because of the open window.

There were no trees in the countryside.

We saw a man go past completely naked, the color of ash, mounted on a horse the color of dirt. The man had no hair; you could see his skull and the veins on his skull. He was holding a stick in his hand that was as flexible as a vine shoot and as heavy as iron. This horseman rode past and didn't say a thing to us.

My brother said to me: "Let's take the sunken lane."

There was a sunken lane where you never saw a single bush or patch of moss. Everything was the color of dirt, even the sky. After a few steps, no one answered me when I spoke. I realized my brother was no longer with me.

I walked into a village I saw. I thought it must be Romainville (why Romainville?).

The first street I went into was deserted. I took a second street. At the corner where the two streets met, a man was standing with his back against a wall. I said to this man: "What is this place? Where am I?" The man didn't answer. I saw the door of a house open and I went in.

The first room was deserted. I went into the second. Behind the door of this room, there was a man standing against the wall. I asked this man: "Whose house is this? Where am I?" The man didn't answer. The house had a garden.

I went out of the house and into the garden. The garden was deserted. Behind the first tree, I found a man standing. I said to this man: "What is this garden? Where am I?" The man didn't answer.

I wandered about the village and I saw that it was a town. All the streets were deserted, all the doors were open. Not one living being passed in the streets, or walked in the rooms, or strolled about the gardens. But behind every corner of wall, behind every door, behind every tree, there was a man standing who held his tongue. You never saw more than one of them at a time. These men watched me going past.

I left the town and began to walk through the fields.

After a while, I turned round and I saw a great crowd coming behind me. I recognized all the men that I'd seen in the town. They had strange heads. They didn't seem to be in any hurry and yet they were walking faster than I was. They didn't make a sound as they walked. In an instant, the mob had caught up with me and surrounded me. The faces of the men were the color of dirt.

Then the first man I saw and questioned when I entered the town said to me: "Where are you going? Don't you know you've been dead a long time?"

I opened my mouth to reply and realized there was no one around me.

He woke up. He was freezing. A wind as cold as the early morning was causing the window, which was still open, to rock and rattle in its frame. The fire had gone out. The candle was burned virtually to the bottom. It was still the dead of night.

He got up and went to the window. There were still no stars in the sky.

From his window he could see the courtyard in front of the house and the street. A hard dry sound that rang out suddenly from the ground made him look down.

He saw below him two red stars whose rays flickered long and then short, long and short, bizarrely, in the dark.

As his mind was still submerged in the fog of his dream:

"Hang on!" he thought. "There aren't any stars in the sky. Now they're on the ground."

But this confusion swiftly cleared and a second noise like the first managed to wake him up; he peered out and he recognized that the two stars were the lanterns of a carriage. In the light they threw out, he could make out the shape of the carriage. It was a tilbury attached to a small white horse. The noise he had heard was the horse's hooves stamping on the pavement.

"What the hell is that carriage doing here?" he wondered. "Who's turned up so early in the morning?"

At that moment someone knocked gently on the door of his room.

He shivered from head to toe and cried out in a frightening voice: "Who's there?"

Someone answered: "Me, Monsieur le maire."

He recognized the voice of the old woman, his concierge.

"Well," he said, "what's wrong?"

"Monsieur le maire, it's just on five o'clock."

"What do I care?"

"Monsieur le maire, the cabriolet is here."

"What cabriolet?"

"The tilbury."

"What tilbury?"

"Didn't Monsieur le maire ask for a tilbury?"

"No," he said.

"The driver says he's come for Monsieur le maire."

"What driver?"

"Monsieur Scaufflaire's driver."

"Monsieur Scaufflaire?"

The name made him flinch as though a streak of lightning had flashed in his face.

"Ah, yes!" he said. "Monsieur Scaufflaire."

If the old woman could have seen him at that moment, she would have been terrified.

There was a rather long silence. He studied the flame of the candle with his mouth hanging open like an imbecile and he pinched some of the molten wax around the wick and rolled it in his fingers. The old woman waited. Then she took the risk of raising her voice a little: "Monsieur le maire, what am I supposed to say?"

"Say everything's fine and I'll be right down."

## V. A Spoke in the Wheels

The postal service between Arras and Montreuil-sur-mer was still conducted at that time by little mail coaches dating from the days of the Empire. These mail coaches were two-wheeled cabriolets upholstered inside in tawny buckskin; they were suspended on pump-springs and had just two seats—one for the mailman, the other for the traveler. The wheels were fitted with those offensive long hubs that keep other cabs at a distance and that you can still see on the roads of Germany today. The chest for the mail was a huge oblong box stuck behind the carriage and coupled with it. This chest was painted black and the carriage, yellow.

You don't see anything like those carriages these days; there was something deformed and humped about them, and whenever you saw them trundling by in the distance or crawling along some road on the horizon, they looked like those insects known, I think, as termites, which have skinny thoraxes that drag great abdomens along behind them. Yet they got along at quite a clip. The mail coach left Arras every night at one, after the mail from Paris had passed, and arrived in Montreuil-sur-mer a bit before five in the morning.

That particular night, just as the mail coach that went down into Montreuil-sur-mer by the Hesdin road was turning the corner and coming into town, it ran into a little tilbury pulled by a white horse going in the opposite direction and with just one person in it, a man wrapped up in a coat. The tilbury's wheel took quite a shock. The mailman shouted to the man to stop, but the traveler wouldn't hear of it and went on his way at a rapid trot.

"There's a man with only a minute to live!" said the mailman to himself.

The man hurrying away was the same man we've just seen wrestling with himself in convulsions surely worthy of pity.

Where was he going? He could not have said. Why was he in such a hurry? He did not know. He was moving forward—aimlessly. Where to? To Arras, no doubt; but maybe he was going somewhere else, too. At times, he thought so, and he shuddered.

He sank into the darkness as though sliding down into a yawning chasm. Something was pushing him, something was pulling him. What was going on inside him, no one could have said, yet anyone could understand. What man has not, at least once in his life, plummeted into that dark cave of the unknown?

Besides, he had resolved nothing, decided nothing, stopped nothing, done nothing. None of his acts of conscience had been definitive. More than ever, he was back where he began.

Why was he going to Arras?

He went back over what he had already told himself when he booked the cabriolet from Scaufflaire: that, whatever the consequences might be, it wouldn't hurt to see things with his own eyes, judge things for himself; that this was only prudent, in fact, that he had to know what would happen; that he couldn't make any decision without having observed and scrutinized; that a person made mountains out of molehills at a distance; that, at the end of the day, when he'd seen this Champmathieu, whatever the poor bastard was, his conscience would probably be only too relieved to see him carted off to the clink in his stead; that, in all likelihood, Javert would be there and Brevet, and Chenildieu, and Cochepaille, ex-convicts who had known him, but that they would certainly not recognize him—Ha! The very idea!; that Javert was way off the scent; that all conjectures and suppositions were pinned on this Champmathieu, and that nothing could be harder to shift than suppositions and conjectures; and so, that there was no real danger.

He also thought that it was undoubtedly a dark hour, but that he would get through it; that, after all, he held his fate, however bad it might be, in his hands; that he was the master of it. He clung to that thought.

At bottom, if the truth be known, he'd have preferred not to go to Arras.

Yet that's where he was going.

Churning things over all the while, he whipped the horse, which was trotting along at a strong and steady pace that enabled them to make two and a half leagues an hour. The further the cabriolet went, the more he felt something inside him shrink.

At daybreak he was in the open countryside; the town of Montreuil-sur-mer was far enough behind him. He watched the horizon whiten; he watched, without seeing, all the chilling features of a winter dawn passing before his eyes. Morning has its ghosts just as night does. He did not see them but, unwittingly, and through almost a kind of physical osmosis, the black silhouettes of trees and hills added something inexpressibly mournful and sinister to the convulsive state of his soul.

Every time he passed one of those secluded houses that sometimes sit right next to the road, he said to himself: You wouldn't credit it, and yet, there are people in there sleeping!

The horse's trot, the harness bells, the wheels on the pavement, made a soft monotonous sound. Such things are lovely when you are full of joy and forlorn as can be when you are downhearted.

It was broad daylight by the time he reached Hesdin. He pulled up in front of an inn to let the horse get his breath and get him some oats.

The horse was, as Scaufflaire had said, one of the small-sized Boulonnais breed with too much of a head, too much of a gut, and not enough of a neck, but with an open chest, a good wide rump, a fine, neat leg, and a firm foot; an ugly breed, but a robust and healthy one. The excellent beast had done five leagues in two hours and there was not a drop of sweat on his rump.

He did not get down from the tilbury. The young stable hand who brought the oats knelt down suddenly and examined the left wheel.

"Have you got a long trip ahead of you in this?" the boy said. He responded, almost as though he were still lost in thought: "Why?"

"Have you come a long way?" the boy plowed on.

"Five leagues."

"Ah!"

"Why do you say 'ah'?"

The boy bent down again, said nothing for a moment, his gaze riveted on the wheel, then stood up and said:

"It's just that if that wheel's just done five leagues—and it's possible at a pinch—it won't do another quarter of a league, that's for sure."

He leaped down from the tilbury.

"What are you saying, my friend?"

"I'm saying that it's a miracle you went five leagues without taking a tumble, you and your horse, into a ditch on the highway. Have a look."

The wheel was, indeed, seriously damaged. The shock of the mail chest had split two spokes and loosened the hub so that the nut had worked its way out.

"My friend," he said to the stable hand, "is there a wheelwright around here?"

"Naturally, Monsieur."

"Do me a favor and go and get him."

"He's just there, two feet away. Coo-ee! Master Bourgaillard!"

Master Bourgaillard, the wheelwright, was standing on his doorstep. He came and examined the wheel and made a grimace like a surgeon looking at a broken leg.

"Can you fix the wheel right away?"

"Yes, Monsieur."

"When can I get going again?"

"Tomorrow."

"Tomorrow!"

"There's a full day's work there. Is Monsieur in a hurry?"

"In a great hurry. I have to get going again in an hour at the latest."

"Not possible, Monsieur."

"I'll pay whatever you want."

"Not possible!"

"Well, then! Two hours."

"Not possible today. There're two spokes and a hub to repair. Monsieur can't set off again before tomorrow."

"My business can't wait till tomorrow. What if you don't repair the wheel and replace it instead?"

"How can I do that?"

"You're a wheelwright, aren't you?"

"I certainly am, Monsieur."

"Haven't you got a wheel you could sell me? I could start out again at once."

"A replacement wheel?"

"Yes."

"I don't have a wheel ready-made for your cabriolet. Two wheels don't just fit together willy-nilly."

"In that case, sell me a pair of wheels."

"Monsieur, all wheels don't just fit all axles."

"Give it a try, anyway."

"There's no point, Monsieur. I've only got cartwheels for sale. This is the sticks, here."

"Would you have a cabriolet I could hire?"

The master wheelwright had seen at a glance that the tilbury was a hire-car. He shrugged his shoulders.

"You certainly know how to look after the cabriolets you hire! Even if I had one, I wouldn't let you rent it."

"Well then, sell it to me."

"I haven't got one."

"What! Not even a cariole? I'm not hard to please, as you can see."

"This is the sticks, here. I do have an old barouche under cover over there," the wheelwright added. "It belongs to a burgher in town who gave it to me to look after; he only uses it once in a blue moon. I'd let you have that for hire, what's it to me? But the burgher mustn't see it going past; and then again, it's a barouche, you'd need two horses."

"I'll take two post-horses."

"Where is Monsieur off to?"

"Arras."

"And Monsieur wants to get there today?"

"I certainly do."

"With post-horses?"

"Why not?"

"Does Monsieur mind if he gets there overnight—at four in the morning?"

"No, of course not."

"It's just that, you see, there's something that has to be said about taking post-horses ... Does Monsieur have his passport?"

"Yes."

"Well, then, if Monsieur takes post-horses, he won't get to Arras before to-morrow. We're a crossroads, here. The relays aren't manned, the horses are in the fields. The plowing season's starting, you need good strong teams under yoke and they're grabbing horses left, right, and center, from the post just the same as anywhere else. Monsieur will have to wait for three or four horses at every relay. And then, they'll only go pretty slowly. There are so many uphill stretches to climb."

"All right, I'll go on horseback. Unhitch the cabriolet. Surely someone in this place can sell me a saddle."

"Of course, but will this horse let you saddle him?"

"That's right, you've just reminded me: he won't."

"Well ..."

"But surely I can find a horse for hire in the village?"

"A horse to do the trip to Arras in one go!"

"That's right."

"You'd need a better horse than you'll see in this neck of the woods. You'd have to buy it first, because we don't know you from Adam. But there's nothing for sale, nothing for hire, not for five hundred francs, and not for a thousand, neither. You won't find one!"

"What can I do?"

"The best thing, if you're going to be sensible about it, is for me to fix the wheel and for you to put your trip back till tomorrow."

"Tomorrow will be too late."

"Jesus!"

"Isn't there a mail coach that goes to Arras? When does it come through?"

"Tomorrow night. Both the mail coaches run at night, the one going up as well as the one going down."

"And it will really take you a day to fix the wheel?"

"A day, and a full day at that!"

"What if you put two workers on it?"

"It'd take ten!"

"What if we tied the spokes with rope?"

"The spokes, all right; the hub, no go. Then again, the rim's in a bad way, too."

"Is there a car-hire place in town?"

"No."

"Is there another wheelwright?"

The stable boy and the wheelwright answered at the same time, shaking their heads.

"No."

He felt a great rush of joy.

It was obvious Providence had a hand in this. It was Providence that had busted the wheel of the tilbury and stopped him en route. He had not given up at the first sign of trouble; he had just done all he could to continue on his way. He had faithfully and scrupulously exhausted every means; he had not shrunk either before the season or before fatigue or before the expense; he had nothing to reproach himself with. If he were to go no further, it would not worry him. It was no longer his fault; it was not an act of his own volition but an act of God.

He breathed. He breathed freely and filled his lungs for the first time since Javert's visit. It felt as if the iron fist that had squeezed his heart for the last twenty hours had just let go.

It felt as if God was now on his side, and was making it known.

He told himself he'd done everything he could and that now all he had to do was go back the way he'd come, quietly.

If his conversation with the wheelwright had taken place in a room at the inn, there would have been no witnesses, no one would have heard it, things would have been left at that, and it is quite likely that we would not have to relate any of the events you are going to read about. But this conversation took place in the street. Any talk in the street inevitably gathers a circle of people. There are always people crying out to be spectators. While he was questioning the wheelwright, a few passersby had stopped around them. After listening in for a few minutes, one young lad, whom no one had taken any notice of, broke away from the group and ran off.

The very moment the traveler ended the inner debate we have just detailed and decided to go back the way he had come, the boy returned. He was accompanied by an old woman.

"Monsieur," said the woman, "my boy tells me you're after a cabriolet to rent."

Those simple words, uttered by an old woman shepherded by a child, caused sweat to trickle down his back. He felt as if he could see the hand that had just released him reappear in the gloom behind him, ready to grab him again.

He answered: "Yes, my good woman, I am looking for a cabriolet to rent." And he hastened to add: "But there aren't any around here."

"Yes there are," said the old woman.

"Where's that, then?" the wheelwright chipped in.

"At my place," replied the old woman.

He shivered. The fatal hand gripped him once more.

The old woman did, in fact, have a kind of wicker cariole in her shed. The wheelwright and the stable boy from the inn, sorry to see the traveler escape their clutches, stepped in. It was a dreadful old boneshaker, just a box plonked on top of the bare axle—no springs; the seats were actually hung inside from strips of leather, the rain got in, the wheels were rusty and eaten away with damp, it wouldn't go much farther than the tilbury, a real rattletrap! The monsieur would be making a dreadful mistake to set out in it. And so on and so forth.

All the above was true, but this boneshaker, this rattletrap, this thing, whatever it was, rolled along on its two wheels and could make it to Arras.

He paid the asking price, left the tilbury at the wheelwright's for repair to be picked up on his return trip, had the white horse harnessed to the cariole, hopped up and went on his way, following the road he'd been on since early morning.

The moment the cart lurched forward, he confessed to himself that a minute before he had felt a certain joy at the thought that he would not get where he was going. He examined this joy with a sort of fury and found it absurd. Why rejoice at going backward? After all, he was making this trip of his own free will. No one was forcing him to do it. And, naturally, nothing would happen that he didn't want to happen.

As he was leaving Hesdin, he heard a voice shouting: "Stop! Stop!" He pulled the cart up with a sharp jerk that still had something strangely feverish and convulsive about it resembling hope.

It was the little boy who belonged to the old woman.

"Monsieur," he said, "I'm the one who got you this cart."

"Right!"

"You didn't give me anything."

He who gave to everyone, and so easily, found this claim exorbitant and almost vile.

"Ah! So it was you, you little rascal?" he said. "You won't get a thing!"

He whipped the horse and galloped off hard.

He had lost a lot of time in Hesdin and wanted to make it up. The little horse was brave and pulled like two; but they were in the month of February, it had rained and the roads were bad. And then, it was not the tilbury now. The cart was hard and very heavy. On top of this, there were lots of hills.

It took him nearly four hours to get from Hesdin to Saint-Pol. Four hours to do five leagues.

At Saint-Pol he unharnessed the horse at the first inn he came to and had the horse taken to the stable. Just as he had promised Scaufflaire, he stayed close to the hayrack while the horse was eating. His mind was on sad and confused things.

The wife of the innkeeper came into the stable.

"Wouldn't Monsieur like something to eat?"

"Heavens, it's true," he said, "I've actually worked up quite an appetite."

He followed the woman, who had a fresh, happy face. She led him into a low room where there were tables with oilskins for tablecloths.

"Please be quick," he said. "I have to set out again. I'm in a hurry."

A fat Flemish servant promptly set the table for him. He watched the girl with a feeling of well-being.

"That was what was wrong with me," he thought. "I didn't have anything to eat."

He was served. He fell on the bread, bit a great mouthful off, then slowly put the bread back on the table and did not touch it again.

A cart driver was eating at another table. He said to the man: "Why is the bread here so bitter?"

The cart driver was German and didn't understand.

He went back to the stable and over to the horse.

An hour later, he was out of Saint-Pol heading for Tinques, which is only five leagues from Arras.

What did he do during this part of the trip? What was he thinking? Just as he had done that morning, he watched the trees go by, the thatched roofs, the fields under cultivation, and the vanishing stretches of the landscape shifting at every bend in the road. This is a kind of contemplation that sometimes satisfies the soul and almost allows it to dispense with thinking. To see a thousand things for the first time and for the last—what could be more melancholy or more profound! To travel is to be born and to die at every instant. Perhaps, in the most shadowy part of his mind, he was making connections between those shifting horizons and human existence itself. Everything in life is constantly fleeing in a headlong rush ahead of us. Things cloud over and clear as part and parcel of the same process: first dazzlement, then eclipse; you look, you rush around, you hold out your hands to seize what is passing; every event is a bend in the road; and then, all of a sudden, you're old. You feel a sort of jolt, everything is black, you make out a dim doorway, that somber horse of life that was dragging you along stops and you see someone veiled and unknown unharness it in the shadows.

Twilight was falling just as children coming out of school saw the traveler driving into Tinques. For it was, of course, still that time of year when the days are short. He did not stop in Tinques. As he was driving out of the village, a road-mender laying stones on the road raised his head and said: "That's a tired horse for you."

The poor creature was, in fact, going no faster than a walk.

"Are you headed for Arras?" the road-mender added.

"Yes."

"If you keep going at that pace you won't get there too early."

He stopped the horse and asked the man: "How much further is it from here to Arras?"

"A good seven leagues, just about."

"How do you work that out? The post book has it down as five and a quarter leagues."

"Ah!" the road-mender went on. "So you don't know the road is under repair? You'll find it cut off a quarter of an hour from here. No way you can go any further."

"Really?"

"You take the left, the road that goes to Carency, you cross the river; and, when you get to Camblain, you turn right; that's the Mont-Saint-Éloy road that goes to Arras."

"But night's coming. I'll get lost."

"You're not from around here?"

"No."

"And they're all back roads, too. Wait a minute, Monsieur," the man went on, "do you want my advice? Your horse is weary, go back to Tinques. There's a good inn there. Have a sleep. You'll go to Arras tomorrow."

"I have to be there tonight."

"That's different. Well, go back all the same to the inn and take a fresh horse. The boy that comes with the horse will guide you through all the back roads."

He followed the road-mender's advice and went back the way he'd come, and half an hour later he was going past the same spot again, but at quite a gallop, with a good fresh horse. A stable boy who styled himself a postilion was perched on the shaft of the cart.

Yet he felt he was losing time. It was now completely dark.

They turned off into the back roads. The road surface was terrible. The cart fell into one rut after another. He said to the postilion: "Keep up the pace and you get double the tip."

During one of the shudders, the singletree broke.

"Monsieur," said the postilion, "the singletree's gone and broken, I don't know how to hitch up my horse. This road is pretty awful at night; if you'd like to come back and sleep in Tinques, we could be in Arras early tomorrow morning."

He replied: "Have you got a bit of rope and a knife?"

"Yes, Monsieur."

He cut off the branch of a tree and turned it into a singletree.

It meant losing another twenty minutes; but then they set out again at a gallop.

The plain was in darkness. Low thick black mists crept up the hillsides and tore away from them like smoke. There were pale streaks of light in the clouds. A great wind coming in from the sea made a noise like someone moving furniture around all along the horizon. Everything that you could make out in the darkness looked to be terror-stricken. So many things shudder under the blast of the immense breaths of night!

The cold cut him to the bone. He hadn't eaten since the day before. He dimly remembered his other nocturnal trip on the great plain not far from Digne. That was eight years ago; yet it seemed to him only yesterday.

A distant bell struck the hour. He asked the boy: "What time is it?"

"Seven o'clock, Monsieur. We'll be in Arras by eight. We've only got three leagues to go."

At that instant something occurred to him for the first time and he found it odd that he hadn't thought of it before: that it was perhaps pointless, all this trouble he was going to; that he didn't even know what time the trial was on; that he might, at least, have found out about that; that it was mad to go on like this without knowing if it would serve any purpose. Then he made a few calculations in his head: that normally the sessions of the circuit courts began at nine o'clock in the morning; that this particular matter would probably not take long; that a case of apple stealing would be over in a jiffy; that it would be just a question of identity after that; four or five statements, nothing much the lawyers could say; that he was going to get there when it was all over!

The postilion whipped the horses. They had crossed the river and left Mont-Saint-Éloy behind them.

Night grew deeper and deeper.

## VI. Sister Simplice Is Put to the Test

Meanwhile, at that very moment, Fantine was delirious with joy.

She had had a very bad night. Hideous cough, galloping fever; and she had had dreams. In the morning, when the doctor dropped in, she was delirious. She seemed alarmed and asked them to tell her as soon as Monsieur Madeleine arrived.

The whole morning she was distraught, said little, and made pleats in the sheets while murmuring figures softly to herself that sounded like they were calculations of distance. Her eyes were hollow and staring. They seemed almost to have gone out and then, at times, they lit up again and shone like stars. It would seem that at the approach of a certain dark hour, the brightness of the sky fills those who are leaving the brightness of the earth.

Every time Sister Simplice asked her how she felt, she invariably answered: "Good. I'd like to see Monsieur Madeleine."

Some months previously, at the time that Fantine had lost what was left of her modesty, what was left of her shame, what was left of her happiness, she had been a shadow of her former self; now she was a ghost of her former self. Physical suffering had finished the job of moral suffering. This creature only twenty-five years old had a forehead covered in wrinkles, flaccid cheeks, pinched nostrils, receding gums, a grayish complexion, a skinny neck, protruding collarbones, withered limbs, sallow skin, and her blond hair showed gray at the roots. Alas! That's how suffering improvises on old age!

At midday, the doctor came back, wrote out a few prescriptions, inquired as to whether Monsieur le maire had turned up yet at the infirmary, and shook his head.

Monsieur Madeleine usually came at three o'clock to see the sick woman. As punctuality was part of goodness, he was punctual.

Close to two-thirty, Fantine began to get agitated. In the space of twenty minutes, she asked the nun more than ten times: "Sister, what time is it?"

The clock struck three. At the third stroke Fantine sat bolt upright, she who normally could barely move in her bed; she joined her two bony yellowed hands together in a sort of convulsive clasp, and the nun heard one of those deep sighs issue from her chest that seem to lift a great weight, release despair. Then Fantine turned and looked at the door.

No one came in; the door did not open.

She stayed in this position for a quarter of an hour, her eye fixed on the door, not moving and as though holding her breath. The sister didn't dare speak to her. The church struck a quarter past three. Fantine let herself fall back on the pillow.

She didn't say a word and began to pleat the sheet again.

The half hour went by, then the hour. No one came. Every time the clock struck, Fantine pushed herself up and looked toward the door, then fell back again.

It was obvious what she was thinking, but she did not utter a name. She did not complain, she did not accuse. Only, she coughed, horribly. You would have said something dark was battening down on her. She was livid and her lips were blue. At times, she smiled.

Five o'clock struck. The sister then heard her say, very softly and sweetly:

"But since I'm going away tomorrow, it's wrong of him not to come today!"

Sister Simplice herself was surprised that Monsieur Madeleine hadn't yet turned up.

Meanwhile Fantine was gazing at the canopy over her bed. She looked as though she were trying to remember something. Suddenly she began to sing in a voice as weak as a breath. The nun listened. This is what Fantine sang:

We'll buy some beautiful things
As we stroll down the boulevards.
Roses are red, violets are blue,
Violets are blue and my love is true.

The Virgin Mary next to my stove
Came to see me yesterday in a brocade coat
And said: Here, hidden beneath my veil
The little one you once asked me for.
Run to town, get some cloth,
Buy some thread, buy a thimble.

We'll buy some beautiful things
As we stroll down the boulevards.

Good Holy Virgin, next to my stove
I've done a cradle up with ribbons.
God could give me his brightest star,
I prefer the baby you gave me by far.
"My Lady, what will I do with the cloth?"
"Make a trousseau for my newborn babe."

Roses are red, violets are blue,
Violets are blue, my love is true.

"Wash the cloth." "But where?" "In the river.
Make it, without spoiling it or dirtying it,
Into a pretty skirt with a chemise
Which I'll embroider all over with flowers."
"The baby's gone, My Lady, what will I do?"
"Make it into a shroud to bury me in."

We'll buy some beautiful things
As we stroll down the boulevards.
Roses are red, violets are blue,
Violets are blue, my love is true.[1]

This song was an old nursery rhyme she used to sing in bygone days to rock her little Cosette to sleep, and it hadn't sprung to mind in all the five years she no longer had her baby with her. She sang it in a voice so sad and so sweet that it would make even a nun weep. The sister, accustomed to austerity, felt a tear well in her eye.

The clock struck six. Fantine didn't seem to hear. She didn't seem to notice anything around her anymore.

Sister Simplice sent a servant girl off to ask the concierge at Monsieur le maire's workshop if he had returned and if he would not shortly come to the infirmary. The girl was back in a flash.

Fantine still had not moved and seemed to be absorbed in her own thoughts.

The servant told Sister Simplice in a whisper that Monsieur le maire had left that same morning before six o'clock in a little tilbury harnessed to a white horse, freezing as it was, that he had set out alone, without even a driver, that no one knew what road he'd taken, that some people said they saw him take the Arras turn, that others reckoned they passed him on the road to Paris. That, as he went off, he was very sweet as usual and that all he said to the concierge was not to wait up for him that night.

While the two women were whispering with their backs turned to Fantine's bed, the sister asking questions and the servant speculating, Fantine, with the feverish vivacity certain organic diseases produce, combining vigorous healthy motion with the dreadful cadaverousness of death, had got to her knees on the bed, with her two clenched fists pressed into the bolster for support, and poking her head through the gap in the curtains, she strained to hear. Suddenly she yelled: "You're talking about Monsieur Madeleine there! Why are you whispering? What's he doing? Why isn't he coming?"

Her voice was so harsh and so hoarse that the two women felt they were hearing a man's voice; they whirled around, frightened.

"Well, answer me!" cried Fantine.

The servant stammered: "The concierge told me he couldn't come today."

"My child," said the sister, "stay calm, lie back down."

Fantine didn't move a hair, but only yelled loudly and in a tone at once imperious and harrowing: "He can't come? Why not? You know the reason. You were whispering it amongst yourselves. I want to know."

The servant hastened to whisper in the nun's ear: "Say he's busy with the municipal council."

Sister Simplice went a bit red; what the servant was suggesting was that she tell a lie. On the other hand, it did seem to her that telling the sick woman the truth would no doubt be dealing her a tremendous blow and that that would be dangerous in the state Fantine was in. Her blush did not last long. The sister turned her steady, sad eyes on Fantine, and said: "Monsieur le maire has gone away."

Fantine shot up and sat on her heels. Her eyes were glittering. An incredible sense of joy shone out of that painful face.

"Gone away!" she cried. "He's gone to get Cosette!"

Then she raised her hands to the heavens and her whole face expressed ineffable happiness. Her lips moved; she was softly praying.

When her prayer was done, she said: "Sister, I would like to lie down again now; I'll do whatever you like. A moment ago, I was bad, please forgive me for shouting, it's very bad to shout, I'm well aware of that, my good sister, but as you see, I'm very happy now. God is good, Monsieur Madeleine is good. Just think—he's gone to get my little Cosette in Montfermeil."

She lay down again, helped the nun arrange her pillow, and kissed a little silver cross that she had round her neck and that Sister Simplice had given her.

"My child," said the sister, "try to rest now, don't talk anymore."

Fantine took the sister's hand in hers, which were so clammy it hurt the sister to feel the sweat.

"He left this morning to go to Paris. You don't even need to go through Paris, actually. Montfermeil is a bit to the left on the way there. Do you remember how he said to me yesterday when I was talking to him about Cosette: *Soon, soon?* He wants to give me a surprise. You know, he got me to sign a letter to get her away from the Thénardiers. There's nothing they can do, is there? They'll hand Cosette over. Since they've got their money. Sister, don't tell me I mustn't talk. I am so happy, I feel very well, I don't feel any more pain at all, I'm going to see Cosette again, I even feel quite hungry. It's nearly five years since I've seen her. *You* can't imagine what a hold children have over you! And then, she'll be so nice, you'll see! If you only knew, she has such pretty little pink fingers! First thing, she's going to have very beautiful hands. When she was a year old, her hands were ridiculous. So! . . . She must be big now. She's seven years old. She's a young lady. I call her Cosette, but her real name is Euphrasie. Listen, only this morning, I was looking at the dust on the mantelpiece and I had a feeling I'd see Cosette again soon. My God! It's so wrong to let years go by without seeing your children! A person ought to realize that life is not forever! Oh, how good of Monsieur le maire to have gone himself! It's true, it's very cold! Did he have his coat, at least? He'll be here tomorrow, won't he? Tomorrow we'll have a party. Tomorrow morning, sister, remind me to put on my little cap with the lace on it. Montfermeil is in the country. I did that road on foot, once upon a time. For me it was a long way. But coaches go so fast! He'll be here tomorrow with Cosette. How far away is Montfermeil from here?"

The sister, who had no idea of distances, replied: "Oh, I'm sure he can be back here tomorrow."

"Tomorrow! Tomorrow!" said Fantine. "I'll see Cosette tomorrow! You see, my good sister who belongs to our good Lord, I'm not sick anymore. I'm mad with joy. I'd get up and dance if anyone wanted me to."

Anyone who had seen her a quarter of an hour earlier would not have believed their eyes. She was not quite so flushed, she spoke in a natural, lively voice, her whole face was one big smile. At times she laughed as she muttered to herself. A mother's joy is almost the same as a child's joy.

"Well," said the nun, "look how happy you are now, so do as I say and don't talk anymore."

Fantine laid her head on the pillow and said in a tiny voice: "Yes, lie down again, be good since you're going to see your little girl. She's right, Sister Simplice. All of them here are right."

And then, without moving a muscle, without shifting her head, she looked all around her with her eyes wide open and an air of joy and she said nothing more.

The sister closed the curtains hoping she would doze off.

Between seven and eight, the doctor came. Not hearing any sound, he thought Fantine was sleeping, so he tiptoed quietly in and silently approached the bed. He pulled the curtains back a little and by the light of the rushlight he saw Fantine's great calm eyes watching him.

She said to him: "Monsieur, they will, won't they, let me put her to bed beside me in a little cot, won't they?"

The doctor thought she was delirious. She added: "Just look, there's just enough room."

The doctor took Sister Simplice aside and she explained the situation to him—how Monsieur Madeleine was away for a day or two, and how, in their doubtfulness, they had not thought it necessary to disillusion the poor sick woman who believed Monsieur le maire had gone off to Montfermeil; how it was just possible, in a word, that she had guessed right. The doctor approved.

He went back to Fantine's bed and she went on: "It's just that, you see, in the morning, when she wakes up, I can say hello to the poor little bunny, and at night, since I don't sleep, I can listen to her sleeping. Her breathing is so faint and sweet, it'll do me good."

"Give me your hand," said the doctor.

She held out her arm and laughed out loud as she cried: "Ah, heavens, that's right! You don't know! The thing is, I'm cured. Cosette'll be here tomorrow."

The doctor was startled. She was better. Her breathing was lighter. Her pulse was stronger again. This poor worn-out creature suddenly had a new lease on life.

"Doctor," she went on, "did sister tell you that Monsieur le maire's gone to get my little scallywag?"

The doctor advised silence and avoidance of any painful emotion. He prescribed an infusion of pure quinine and, if she became feverish again overnight, a soothing potion. As he was leaving, he said to the sister: "She's better. If by some happy chance Monsieur le maire does turn up tomorrow with the child, who knows? There are some amazing recoveries, great joy has been seen to put an end to disease. I know this one is an organic disease and fairly well advanced, but it's all such a mystery, all that! Perhaps we will save her, after all."

## VII. The Traveler Arrives Only to Get Ready to Leave Again

It was nearly eight o'clock at night when the cart we left on the road drove through the carriage entrance of the Hôtel de la Poste in Arras. The man we followed up to this moment hopped down, responded absentmindedly to the eager attentiveness of the inn people, sent back the extra horse and led the little white horse to the stable himself; then he pushed open the door of a billiard room on the ground floor, took a seat there, and propped his elbows on a table. He had taken fourteen hours to do a trip he had counted on doing in six. To be fair to himself he admitted that it was not his fault; but in his heart of hearts, he was not sorry.

The hotel landlady came in.

"Does Monsieur need to sleep? Will Monsieur have supper?"

He shook his head in the negative.

"The stable boy says Monsieur's horse is extremely tired!"

Here he broke his silence.

"Won't the horse be able to set off again tomorrow?"

"Oh, Monsieur! He needs at least two days off."

He asked: "The post office is here, isn't it?"

"Yes, Monsieur."

The hostess took him to the office; he showed his passport and asked if it was possible for him to go back to Montreuil-sur-mer by mail coach that same night; as luck would have it, the seat next to the mailman was free; he reserved it and paid for it.

"Monsieur," said the post office clerk, "make sure you're back here ready to leave at one o'clock sharp in the morning."

That taken care of, he left the hotel and began to walk around the town.

He did not know Arras, the streets were dingy, and he wandered around aimlessly. Yet he seemed determined not to ask directions from any passersby. He crossed the little river Crinchon and found himself in a maze of narrow streets where he got lost. A bourgeois was making his way with a lantern. After some hesitation, he decided to speak to this man, but not without first looking in front and behind, as though he were frightened someone might overhear the question he was about to ask.

"Monsieur," he said, "the Palais de Justice, please?"

"You're not a local, Monsieur?" replied the burgher, who was a fairly old man. "Well now, follow me. I just so happen to be going close to the law courts, actually, to the prefecture building next door. They're doing some work on the law courts at the moment, so the hearings are being held temporarily in the prefecture."

"Is that," he asked, "where the circuit court is sitting?"

"No doubt, Monsieur. You see, what is now the prefecture used to be the bishop's palace before the Revolution. Monsieur de Conzié,[1] who was bishop in '82, had a big reception room built there. It's in that room that the court is sitting."

As they walked along, the burgher said to him: "If Monsieur is hoping to sit in on a trial, he's a bit late. Normally sessions finish at six."

But as they reached the big square, the burgher pointed out four tall windows lit up along the façade of a huge gloomy building.

"Well, blow me down, Monsieur, if you haven't got here in time. You're in luck. You see those four windows? That's the circuit court. The light's on. So it's not over. The thing must have dragged on and they're having an evening session. Are you interested in this case? Is it a criminal trial? Are you a witness?"

He replied: "I haven't come for any case, I'm only here to speak to a lawyer."

"That's different," said the burgher. "Look, Monsieur, there's the door. Where the guard is. All you have to do is go up the main staircase."

He stuck to the man's directions and a few minutes later he was in the room that was jammed with people and where lawyers in their robes were huddled together here and there among the crowd, whispering.

It always causes your heart to lurch, seeing these clusters of men in black murmuring among themselves sotto voce on the threshold of courts of law. It is rare that charity and pity emerge from all those words. What emerges most often is sentences handed down in advance, foregone conclusions. To the casual observer who lets his imagination run, all these men in groups huddled together look like so many sinister beehives where certain kinds of mind buzz away, building all kinds of bleak constructions together.

The room, though spacious, was illuminated by a single lamp; it had once been the bishop's antechamber but was being used as a waiting room for prisoners. A double door, closed at that moment, separated it from the great chamber where the circuit court was sitting.

It was so dark that he wasn't frightened of addressing the first lawyer he came to.

"Monsieur," he said, "where are we up to?"

"It's over," said the lawyer.

"Over!"

This word had been repeated in such a tone that the lawyer turned around.

"Forgive me, Monsieur, you are, perhaps, a relative?"

"No. I don't know anyone here. And was there a sentence?"

"Naturally. It could scarcely be otherwise."

"Hard labor?"

"In perpetuity."

He went on in a voice so weak, he could barely be heard: "So his identity was confirmed?"

"Whose identity?" demanded the lawyer. "There was no identity to confirm. It was an open-and-shut case. The woman had murdered her child, infanticide was proven, the jury ruled out premeditation, she was sentenced to life."

"It's a woman, then?" he said.

"But of course. The Limousin girl. What are you getting at?"

"Nothing. But since it's over, how come the light's still on in the room?"

"It's for the other case that started about two hours ago."

"What other case?"

"Oh! This one's clear too. Some poor swine, a recidivist, a galley slave, who committed some kind of robbery. I can't quite remember his name. But I tell you, if anyone looked like a proper bandit, this one does. I'd send him to the galleys on the strength of his face alone."

"Monsieur," he said, "is there any way of getting into the room?"

"I really don't think so. It's pretty packed. But they're taking a break just now. A few people have stepped out, so you could see what happens when the hearing resumes."

"How do you get in?"

"Through the main door there."

With that, the lawyer left him. In a few moments, he had experienced, almost at the same time, almost in the same breath, the whole gamut of possible emotions. The words of that coldhearted man had pierced his heart like needles of ice or knives of fire. When he found out that nothing was finished, he breathed again; but he could not have said whether what he felt was satisfaction or pain.

He stood next to several groups of people and eavesdropped. The court list was very full, the presiding judge had indicated that two straightforward, short matters were scheduled for that same day. They had started with the infanticide and now they had moved on to the convict, the recidivist, the "homing pigeon." This man had stolen some apples, but that did not seem to have been proven; what was proven was that he had already been in the galleys in Toulon. That is what ruined his case. The man's examination was already over and the witness statements had been taken, too; but still to come were the speech for the defense and the closing arguments of the public prosecutor's department; it would hardly be over before midnight. The man would most likely be found guilty; the counsel for the prosecution—a wit who made up rhymes—was good. He never missed "his" defendants.

An usher stood by the door that led to the courtroom. He asked this usher: "Monsieur, will the door be opened soon?"

"It will not be opened," replied the usher.

"What! Won't be opened again after the break? Isn't the court in recess?"

"The court has just resumed," replied the usher. "But the door will not be opened again."

"Why not?"

"Because the room is full."

"How's that! Aren't there any more seats?"

"Not a one. The door is closed. No one can get in now."

After a pause, the usher added: "There are actually two or three seats behind Monsieur le président, but the judge only allows public servants in there."

That said, the usher turned his back to him.

He withdrew with his head down, crossed the antechamber, and slowly went back down the stairs, as though hesitating at every step. It is likely he was holding counsel with himself. The violent struggle unleashed in him since the day before was not yet over, and at every moment it took a new turn. When he reached the landing, he leaned back against the rails and folded his arms. Suddenly he fished inside his redingote, took out his pocketbook, pulled out a pencil, ripped out a page, and swiftly wrote the following line: "Monsieur Madeleine, mayor of Montreuil-sur-mer." Then he flew back up the stairs, pushed through the crowd, went straight up to the usher, and said to him in the voice of authority: "Give this to Monsieur le président."

The usher took the sheet of paper, glanced at it, and did what he asked.

## VIII. Preferential Admission

Unbeknown to him, the mayor of Montreuil-sur-mer enjoyed a kind of celebrity. For seven years his reputation for virtue had spread throughout Lower Boulonnais, and it had ended up jumping over the borders of a small country enclave and spreading into two or three neighboring *départements*. Apart from the considerable service he had rendered to the main town by getting the jet bead industry back on its feet, there was not one of the hundred and forty-one communes in the arrondissement of Montreuil-sur-mer that did not owe some benefit to him. He had even been able to boost and assist the industries of other arrondissements to prosper, as the need arose. He had at times, accordingly, sustained with his own credit and his own funds the tulle factory in Boulogne, the mechanized flax mill in Frévent, and the hydraulic textile manufacturing of Boubers-sur-Canche. Everywhere the name of Monsieur Madeleine was uttered in veneration. Arras and Douai envied the happy little town of Montreuil-sur-mer its mayor.

The judge of the royal court of Douai, who was presiding over this session of the circuit court in Arras, like everybody else, knew this name, so thoroughly and universally honored. When the usher discreetly opened the door between the council chamber and the courtroom, leaned down behind the judge's chair, and handed him the piece of paper on which the line we have just read was written, he added: "This gentleman would like to sit in on the proceedings." The judge made a sharp gesture of deference, grabbed a pen, jotted a few words at the bottom of the note, and handed it back to the usher, saying to him: "Let him in."

The unfortunate man whose story we are relating had remained by the door of the hall at the same spot and in the same position as when the usher had left him. He heard someone say in the middle of his daydream: "Would Monsieur do me the honor of following me." It was this same usher who had turned his back on him a moment before and who now bowed and scraped so low before him he practically swept the ground. At the same time, the usher handed him the note. He unfolded it and, as he happened to be near the lamp, he was able to read: "The president of the circuit court would like to pay his respects to Monsieur Madeleine."

He screwed the note up in his hand as though those few words left him with a strange and bitter aftertaste.

He followed the usher.

A few minutes later, he found himself alone in a kind of paneled chamber that looked very spartan, lit by two candles standing on a table covered in green baize. The final words of the usher who had just left him were still buzzing in his ears: "Monsieur, you are now in the council chamber; you have only to turn the brass knob of this door and you will be in the courtroom behind the chair of Monsieur le président." Those words mingled in his thoughts with a dim memory of the narrow corridors and black stairs he had just traversed.

The usher had left him on his own. The supreme moment had arrived. He tried to collect himself but failed. It is especially at those moments when you most need to secure them to the poignant realities of life that all the loose threads of thought snap in your brain. He stood in the very spot where judges deliberate and sentence. In a calm daze he gazed at that peaceful and fearful chamber where so many existences had been broken, where his name would soon ring out and his destiny be decided. He gazed at the wall, then he gazed at himself, marveling that it was this particular chamber and that it was he, himself.

He hadn't eaten for more than twenty-four hours, he was shattered by the jolting of the cariole, but he didn't feel it; it seemed to him that he didn't feel a thing.

He went up to a black frame hanging on the wall, which contained, behind glass, an old autographed letter of Jean-Nicolas Pache, mayor of Paris and minister, dated, no doubt by mistake, *June 11, Year II,*[1] in it Pache was sending the Commune the list of ministers and deputies placed under house arrest. An onlooker able to see him and observe him in that instant would no doubt have imagined that the letter seemed most curious to him, for he couldn't take his eyes off it and read it over and over again. He read it without taking it in and without knowing what he was doing. He was thinking of Fantine and Cosette.

While he was lost in thought, he turned round and his eyes fell on the brass knob of the door that separated him from the courtroom. He had almost forgotten about that door. His gaze, at first steady, stopped there, remained fixed on this brass knob; then it turned wild and staring and little by little was tinged with horror.

Beads of sweat broke out on his scalp and streamed down his temples. At a certain point, he made a gesture with a sort of defiant authority, that indescribable movement perfectly embodying the meaning: *For God's sake! Who's forcing me to do this?* Then he swung back again sharply, saw the door through which he had come, went to it, opened it and went out. He was no longer in that room, he was outside, in a corridor, a long, narrow corridor, punctuated with steps and gates, which created all kinds of nooks and crannies, lit here and there by lamps similar to night-lights for sick people; it was the corridor by which he had come. He took a deep breath, cocked his ear—not a sound behind him, not a sound in front of him; he began to run as though someone were chasing him.

When he had gone back round several of the sharp turns in the corridor, he listened again. There was still the same silence and the same gloaming all around him. He was out of breath, he was tottering, he leaned against the wall. The stone was cold, his sweat was icy on his forehead, he straightened up with a shiver.

Then and there, alone in the darkness, standing trembling with cold and perhaps something else, he thought long and hard.

He had thought long and hard the whole night, he had thought long and hard the whole day; the only thing he could still hear inside him was a voice that said: Woe is me!

A quarter of an hour went by. Finally, he hung his head, sighed in anguish, dropped his arms to his side and retraced his steps. He walked slowly as if utterly overcome. It felt as though someone had collared him as he fled and brought him back.

He went back into the council chamber. The first thing he saw was the doorknob. This doorknob, round and of polished brass, gleamed, in his eyes, like some awful star. He gazed at it the way a lamb would gaze into the eyes of a tiger. He could not take his eyes off it.

Now and then he took another step toward the door.

Had he listened, he would have heard a confused buzz, the noise of the room next door; but he didn't listen and he didn't hear.

All of a sudden, without knowing how, he found himself right next to the door. He seized the knob convulsively; the door opened.

He was in the courtroom.

## IX. A Place Where Convictions Are About to Shape Up

He stepped inside, closed the door behind him mechanically, and remained stock still, considering what he saw.

It was a rather vast dimly lit enclosure, now full of din, now full of silence, where the whole apparatus of a criminal trial unfolded in all its mean and mournful gravity before the multitude.

At one end of the room, where he found himself, worried-looking judges in worn-out robes were biting their nails or closing their eyes; at the other end, the rabble in rags, lawyers in every possible pose, soldiers with hard, honest faces; tarnished old wainscoting, a dirty ceiling, tables covered in serge that was rather more yellow than green, doors blackened by hands; nails planted in the paneling, small tavern-style oil lamps providing more smoke than light; on the tables, candles in brass candlesticks; gloom, ugliness, sadness; and from all this a sense of the austere and the august emanated, for you could feel that great human thing known as the law and that great divine thing known as justice in that room.

No one in the crowd paid the slightest attention to him. All eyes converged on a single point, a wooden bench backing onto a small door, along the wall to the left of the presiding judge. On this bench, which was lit by several candles, there was a man between two gendarmes.

This man was the man. He did not look for him, he saw him at once. His eyes gravitated toward him of their own accord, as though they had known in advance where he was.

He felt as if he was looking at himself, older, not of course absolutely the same in the face, but alike in attitude and general look, with that hair sticking up, with those wild anxious eyes, with that smock—himself as he was the day he walked into Digne, full of hate and hiding in his soul that hideous store of frightening thoughts he had spent nineteen years hoarding on the paving stones of jail. He said to himself with a shiver: "My God! Is this what I'd come to again?"

This creature appeared to be at least sixty years old. There was something indefinably coarse, stupid, and scared about him.

At the sound of the door, people had stood aside to make room for him, the presiding judge had turned his head round, and realizing that the personage who had stepped in was Monsieur le maire of Montreuil-sur-mer, had nodded to him. The counsel for the prosecution, who had seen Monsieur Madeleine in Montreuil-sur-mer, where the duties of his office had called him more than once, also greeted him. He scarcely registered them. He was in the grip of a sort of hallucination; he stared.

Judges, a clerk, gendarmes, a sea of heads viciously curious—he had seen all that already, once, twenty-seven years ago. These deadly things had caught up with him once more; there they were, in front of him; they stirred once more, they existed. It was no longer an effort of memory, a mirage of his mind; those were real gendarmes and real judges, a real horde and real flesh-and-blood men. It had happened, it was all over; he saw all the monstrous aspects of his past come to life again, reappearing all around him, with all the frightening force of reality.

This was all gaping before him. He was horrified by it, he closed his eyes, and cried out from the bottom of his soul: Never!

And by a tragic twist of fate that caused all his notions to totter and almost caused him to lose his mind, it was another self who was there! This man they were trying—they all called him Jean Valjean!

He had before his eyes an unheard-of vision, a sort of reenactment of the most horrible moment of his life, played by his ghost.

It was all there, it was the same apparatus, the same time of night, almost the same faces on the judges, soldiers, and members of the audience. Only, above the president's head there was a crucifix, something that was missing from the courtrooms at the time he was convicted.[1] When he was tried, God had not been there.

There was a chair behind him; he dropped into it, terrified at the idea that he could be seen. When he was seated, he took advantage of a pile of files sitting on the judge's desk to hide his face from the whole room. He could now see without being seen. Little by little he recovered. He fully entered into a sense of reality; he attained that state of calmness that allows you to listen.

Monsieur Bamatabois was one of the jurors.

He looked for Javert, but couldn't see him. The witness bench was hidden from him by the clerk's table. Then again, as we've said, the room was barely lit.

When he entered, the defense counsel was winding up his speech for the defense. Everyone's attention was roused to its highest pitch; the matter had been going on for three hours. For three hours, this crowd had watched as a man, an unknown man, some kind of miserable specimen, either profoundly stupid or profoundly clever, gradually buckled under the weight of a terrible probability. This man, as we already know, was a tramp who had been found in a field, carrying a branch laden with ripe apples, torn off an apple tree in a neighboring enclosure known as Pierron Close. Who was this man? An investigation had been conducted, witnesses had just been heard, they had been unanimous; sure knowledge had shone forth out of the whole sorry deliberations. The prosecution was saying: "We are not only holding a fruit thief, a poacher; we are holding here, in our hands, a crook, a backslider at odds with the world who has broken parole, an ex-convict, a villain of the most dangerous kind, a criminal called Jean Valjean, wanted by the law for a long time and who, eight years ago, when he came out of jail in Toulon, committed highway robbery under force of arms against the person of a young boy from Savoy called Petit-Gervais, a crime under article 383 of the criminal code, for which we reserve the right to pursue him further, when his identity is legally established. He has just committed a fresh theft. This is a case of recidivism. Convict him for the new crime; he will be tried for the old crime later."

Faced with such an accusation, faced with the unanimity of the witnesses, the accused seemed above all amazed. He made gestures and signs that meant no! or else he examined the ceiling. He scarcely spoke, gave awkward answers, but from head to toe, his entire person screamed that he was not guilty as charged. He was like the village idiot in the presence of all these fine minds ranged in battle around him—or like a foreigner in the midst of this society that had him by the throat. Yet it meant the most menacing future for him; the probability of his conviction was growing every minute, and the whole crowd was looking, more anxiously than he was, at the disastrous sentence that was hanging over him more and more ominously. One possibility opened up the prospect, beyond jail, of the death penalty, if his identity was established and if the Petit-Gervais matter were to end up resulting in a conviction. What was this man? What was the nature of his apathy? Was it imbecility or a ruse? Did he understand only too well or did he not understand at all? Questions that divided the crowd and seemed to split the jury. There was something frightening and something intriguing in this trial; the drama was not only sinister, it was obscure.

The defense counsel had given a pretty good summing up in that provincial lingo that had long constituted the eloquence of the bar and that lawyers used to use in days gone by, every bit as much in Romorantin as in Paris or Montbrison, which today, having become classic and therefore old hat, is scarcely spoken anymore other than by the official orators at the bar, for whom it is most useful in its grave sonority and its majestic tone; a language in which a husband or a wife is called a *spouse,* Paris, *the center of the arts and of civilization,* the king, *the monarch,* my lord bishop, *the holy pontiff,* the counsel for the prosecution, *the eloquent interpreter for the prosecution,* the speech for the defense, *the strains we have just heard,* the century of Louis XIV, *the grand siècle,* a theater, *a temple of Melpomene,*[2] the reigning royal family, *the august blood of our kings,* a concert, *a solemn celebration of music,* the general in command, *the illustrious warrior who,* etc., theology students, *those gentle Levites,*[3] mistakes imputed to newspapers, *the imposture that distills its venom in the columns of these organs,* etc., etc. The lawyer had accordingly begun by expatiating on the theft of the apples—something difficult enough to do in the grandiloquent manner, but Bénigne Bossuet[4] himself was once forced to refer to a hen in the middle of a funeral oration and he carried it off with alacrity. The defense attorney had established that the theft of the apples had not been materially proved.

His client, whom, in his role as defense counsel, he insisted on calling

Champmathieu, had not been seen by anyone scaling the wall or breaking off the branch. He had been arrested in possession of said branch (which the lawyer happily dubbed a *bough*); but he claimed to have found it on the ground and to have picked it up. Where was the proof to the contrary? Undoubtedly the branch had been broken off and concealed after he had scaled the wall and then thrown away by the alarmed poacher; undoubtedly there had been a thief. But what proved that this thief was Champmathieu? A single thing—his status as an ex-convict. The attorney did not deny that this status appeared, unfortunately, to be clearly proved: The accused had resided in Faverolles; the accused had been a pruner there; the name Champmathieu could well have started out as Jean Mathieu; all that was true; finally, four witnesses recognized Champmathieu positively and without hesitation as being the galley slave Jean Valjean. To these points and to this testimony the attorney could only oppose his client's denial, a self-interested denial; but supposing he were the convict Jean Valjean—did that prove that he was the stealer of the apples? That was an assumption, at most; not proof. The defendant, it was true—and the defense counsel had to agree "in good faith"—had adopted "a bad defense strategy." He persisted in denying everything, both the theft and his status as an ex-convict. Admission on this last point would certainly have been better, and would have earned him the judges' indulgence; the defense counsel had advised him to take this course, but the accused had obstinately persisted in refusing to do so, no doubt thinking he'd save the whole situation by not admitting anything. It was a mistake; but was it not necessary to consider the limited nature of the man's intelligence? The man was obviously a cretin. A horrible long stretch in jail and a miserable long stretch out of jail had brutalized him, etc., etc. He defended himself badly, but was that a reason to convict him? As for the Petit-Gervais matter, it was not the job of the defense counsel to discuss it, it was not under consideration. The attorney summed up by beseeching the jury and the court, if the identity of Jean Valjean seemed evident to them, to apply police penalties to him that addressed the issue of breaking parole and not the appalling punishment that smites the repeat offender.

The counsel for the prosecution responded to the defense counsel. He was bad-tempered and floridly red-faced, like most prosecutors.

He congratulated the defense counsel on his "loyalty" and cleverly took advantage of this loyalty. He attacked the accused using all the points the defense had conceded. The defense seemed to agree that the accused was Jean Valjean. He noted this. The man was therefore Jean Valjean. This fact was now an established fact for the prosecution and could no longer be contested. Here, through a cunning bit of antonomasia,[5] going back to the sources and the causes of criminal behavior, the counsel for the prosecution thundered against the immorality of the Romantic school,[6] then dawning under the name Satanic school, which had been bestowed upon it by the critics of the *Oriflamme* and the *Quoti-*

*dienne*,[7] not without credibility, he attributed to the influence of this perverse literature the crime of Champmathieu, or rather Jean Valjean. These considerations exhausted, he moved on to Jean Valjean himself. What was Jean Valjean? Description of Jean Valjean. A monster spewed out, etc. The model for these sorts of descriptions is provided by the tale of Théramènes,[8] which is not much use for tragedy but serves legal eloquence brilliantly every day. Audience and jury quaked. The description over with, the counsel for the prosecution launched into an oratorical movement intended to excite the greatest possible enthusiasm on the part of the *Journal de la Préfecture* the following morning: "And it is a man like this, etc., etc., a vagrant, a beggar, with no means of support, etc., etc.; accustomed by his past life to culpable actions and barely checked by his time in jail, as the crime committed against Petit-Gervais proves, etc., etc.; it is a man like this who, caught on the public highway in the very act of theft, a few feet from a wall he'd scaled, still holding in his hand the object he'd stolen, denies being caught in the act, denies the theft, the scaling of the wall, denies everything, denies even his name, denies even his identity! Apart from a hundred other proofs we need not go back over, four witnesses recognize him, Javert, upstanding inspector of police, Javert, as well as three of his old companions in ignominy, the convicts Brevet, Chenildieu, and Cochepaille. What does he offer against this devastating unanimity? Denial. Talk about hard! You will take the law into your hands, gentlemen of the jury, etc., etc."

While the counsel for the prosecution spoke, the accused listened, his mouth hanging open, in a sort of amazement that was colored with a little admiration. He was obviously surprised that a man could talk like that. From time to time, at the most energetic moments of the prosecutor's speech, in those instants when eloquence cannot contain itself and spills over in a flow of withering epithets, enveloping the accused like a storm, he slowly shook his head from right to left and from left to right, a sad and mute sort of protest that he'd contented himself with since the beginning of the debates. Two or three times the spectators closest to him heard him say under his breath: "This is where it's got us, not asking Monsieur Baloup!"

The counsel for the prosecution remarked to the jury on this stunned, obviously calculated attitude which denoted, not imbecility but skill, ruse, the habit of misleading the law, and that showed "the profound perversity" of the man in its true light. He ended by expressing reservations about the Petit-Gervais affair and by calling for a severe sentence.

That was, as you will recall, hard labor in perpetuity.

The defense counsel rose, began by complimenting "Monsieur, the counsel for the prosecution" on his "admirable speech," then responded as best he could, but he tailed off feebly; the ground was evidently giving way beneath him.

## X. The Strategy of Denial

The moment for closing the proceedings had come. The presiding judge asked the accused to stand and put the usual question to him: "Have you anything to add to your defense?"

The man stood twirling a grubby cap in his hands and didn't seem to have heard. The judge repeated the question.

This time the man heard. He seemed to understand, he gave a start as though he'd just woken up, cast his eye all around him, looked at the public, the gendarmes, his lawyer, the jury, the court, placed his monstrous fist on the rim of the bar standing in front of his seat, gave everything the once-over again and suddenly, fixing his gaze on the counsel for the prosecution, broke into speech. It was like an eruption. The words seemed to escape from his mouth, incoherent, impetuous, jumbled, as though they were all rushing to get out at once. He said:

"I've got this to say. I used to be a wheelwright in Paris—and that was with Monsieur Baloup, too. It's a hard slog. If you're a wheelwright, you have to work outdoors all the time, in yards, under open sheds if you've got good masters, never in closed workshops, because you've got to have room, you see. In winter, you get so cold you have to flap your arms to keep warm; but the masters don't like that, they reckon that wastes time. Handling iron when there's ice on the pavement—that's tough. It wears a man out pretty quick. You're old before your time in this line of work. At forty, a man's finished. Me, I was fifty-three, I was really pushing it. And then, workers are a nasty lot! When a poor bugger's no longer young, they call you an old nitwit, an old noodle! I wasn't making more than thirty sous a day, they paid me as little as they could, the masters took advantage of my age. On top of that, I had my daughter, who was a washerwoman down by the river. She made a bit to put in. That way, with the two of us, we got by. She had it hard, too. All the livelong day in a tub up to your waist, come rain, come snow, with the wind whipping your face; even if it's freezing, doesn't matter, you got to get the washing done. There are some who don't have a lot of linen, so they're waiting on it; if you don't get their washing done, you lose the business. The planks aren't joined right and water drips on you from all sides. You get your skirts all wet, top and bottom. You get soaked to the bone. She also worked in the laundry at the Enfants-Rouges,[1] where the water comes through taps. You're not in a tub. You do your washing in front of you at the tap and you do your rinsing behind you in a trough. Because it's indoors, your body doesn't get so cold. But there's the steam from the hot water and it's something shocking and it ruins your eyes. She'd get home at seven at night and she'd get to bed quick she'd be so beat. Her husband hit her. She died. We weren't very happy.

She was a good sort who never went to dances,[2] who kept herself to herself. I remember one Shrove Tuesday[3] when she went to bed at eight o'clock. That's it. I'm not kidding. You've only got to ask. Oh, ask, fat chance! What an idiot I am! Paris is a bottomless pit. Who knows father Champmathieu there? But, like I was saying, there's Monsieur Baloup. Go and see Monsieur Baloup. I don't know what else you want me to say."

The man stopped speaking but stayed on his feet. He had said what he had to say in a voice that was loud, fast, raucous, hard, and hoarse, with a sort of irritated and savage naïveté. At one point he broke off to greet someone in the crowd. The sorts of affirmations he seemed to be casting to the winds before him came to him like hiccups, and he added to each of them the gesture of a woodcutter splitting wood. When he had finished, the audience burst out laughing. He looked at the public, saw that they were laughing, and though he didn't understand, started to laugh himself.

That was ominous.

The presiding judge, an attentive and benevolent man, spoke out.

He reminded the "gentlemen of the jury" that old Monsieur Baloup, the former master wheelwright the accused claimed to have worked for, had been summonsed to no avail. He had gone bankrupt and was nowhere to be found. Then he turned to the accused and advised him to listen to what he was about to say, adding: "You are in a situation where you must think carefully. The most serious assumptions weigh against you and may have critical consequences. As the accused and in your own interest, I must ask you again to explain yourself clearly one last time on two counts: First, did you, yes or no, climb over the wall of Pierron Close, break off the branch, and steal the apples, that is to say, commit the crime of theft, aggravated by illegal entry? Second, yes or no, are you the freed convict Jean Valjean?"

The accused shook his head with a competent look, like a man who has understood and knows what he is going to say in reply. He opened his mouth, turned to the judge and said: "First off . . ."

Then he looked at his cap, he looked at the ceiling, and was silent.

"Would the accused," the counsel for the prosecution went on in a stony voice, "please be very careful. You have not answered the questions put to you. Your distress condemns you. It is obvious that your name is not Champmathieu, that you are the convict Jean Valjean, first disguised under the name Jean Mathieu, which was his mother's name, that you have been in the Auvergne, that you were born in Faverolles, where you were a pruner. It is obvious that you stole ripe apples from Pierron Close after illegal entry. The gentlemen of the jury will take this into account."

The accused had ended up sitting back down; he shot to his feet again when the counsel for the prosecution was finished and cried out: "You're a nasty piece of work, you are! That's what I wanted to say. It wouldn't come to me at first. I didn't steal anything. I'm a man who doesn't eat every day. I was coming from out Ailly way, I was walking through the countryside after a shower that made the land all yellow, even the ponds were overflowing and all that was sticking up out of the sand was little grass shoots along the roadway, I found a broken branch lying on the ground with apples on it, I picked the branch up without knowing the trouble that would get me into. I've been in prison for three months now and I've been knocked around. More than that, I can't say. They say things against me, they tell me: Answer! The gendarme, who's a good lad, he nudges my elbow and whispers to me: Go on, answer. I don't know how to explain; me, I didn't have any schooling, I'm a poor man. That's where you go wrong, not seeing that. I didn't steal, I picked up what was lying on the ground. You talk about Jean Valjean, Jean Mathieu! I don't know those people. They must be village people. I worked for Monsieur Baloup, boulevard de l'Hôpital. My name's Champmathieu. You must be pretty clever to tell me where I was born. Me, I have no idea. Not everybody has a house to come into the world in. That'd be too easy. I think my father and my mother were people who worked the roads. But I don't know. When I was a kid they called me Little, now they call me Old. That's my Christian names for you. Take that however you like. I have been to the Auvergne, I have been to Faverolles, sure! So what? Can't a man go to the Auvergne or to Faverolles without having been in the clink? I tell you I never stole and that I am old man Champmathieu. I was with Monsieur Baloup, he put me up in his house. You're really starting to get my goat with all this garbage, you know! Why's everybody after me, trying to bring me down!"

The counsel for the prosecution had remained standing; he addressed the presiding judge: "Monsieur le président, in the presence of the confused but extremely cunning denials of the accused, who is clearly trying to pass himself off as an idiot, but who will not succeed—we warn him—we request that it please you and that it please the court to once again call to the bar the convicts Brevet, Cochepaille, and Chenildieu, and police inspector Javert, and to interrogate them one last time about the identity of the accused as the convict Jean Valjean."

"I must remind Monsieur, the counsel for the prosecution," said the presiding judge, "that police inspector Javert was called by his duties to the administrative center of a neighboring district, and left the court and left the town itself the moment his testimony was given. We gave him permission to do so, with the consent of Monsieur, the counsel for the prosecution, and the accused's defense counsel."

"That's right, Monsieur le président," the counsel for the prosecution chimed in. "In the absence of Inspector Javert, I believe I should remind the gentlemen of the jury what he said in this very place a few hours ago. Javert is an esteemed police officer who, through his strict and rigorous probity, does honor to his subordinate but important duties. This is his statement: "I do not even need moral assumptions and material proofs to refute the denials of the accused. I recognize him perfectly. This man's name is not Champmathieu; he is a former convict named Jean Valjean, who is very dangerous and very much feared. It was only with the utmost regret that he was released after serving his sentence. He did nineteen years' hard labor for aggravated theft. He tried to escape five or six times. Apart from the Petit-Gervais and Pierron robberies, I suspect him of having further committed theft at the home of His Grace, the late bishop of Digne. I often saw him in the days when I was assistant warden at Toulon jail. I repeat that I recognize him perfectly."

This very precise statement appeared to produce a rousing impression on the public and the jury. The counsel for the prosecution wound up by insisting that in the absence of Javert, the three witnesses Brevet, Chenildieu, and Cochepaille be heard again and solemnly cross-examined.

The presiding judge gave an order to an usher, and a moment later the door of the witness chamber opened. The usher, accompanied by a gendarme ready to come to his aid, escorted the convict Brevet into the courtroom. The audience was breathless with suspense and all hearts beat as one.

The former convict Brevet was wearing the black and gray jacket of the state penitentiaries. Brevet was a character sixty years old or so who had the face of a businessman and the look of a shyster. They sometimes go together. In prison, where fresh misdemeanors had led him once more, he had become some sort of gatekeeper. He was a man of whom his superiors said: He is trying to make himself useful. The chaplains spoke highly of his religious habits. You must not forget, this happened under the Restoration.

"Brevet," said the president, "you were sentenced for a heinous crime and you cannot take the oath . . ."

Brevet lowered his gaze.

"However," the president went on, "even in the man the law has degraded, there may remain, when divine pity allows, a feeling of honor and fairness. It is to this feeling that I appeal at such a decisive moment. If such a feeling still exists in you, and I hope it does, reflect before you answer me, consider, on the one hand, this man whom a word from you may destroy, and on the other hand, justice, which a word from you may clarify. The moment is a solemn one and there is still time for you to retract, if you think you have made a mistake. Would the accused please stand? Brevet, look carefully at the accused, gather your recollections and tell us, on your soul and conscience, if you still recognize this man as your former prison mate Jean Valjean."

Brevet looked at the accused, then turned to the court.

"Yes, Your Honor. I was the first to recognize him and I still do. This man is Jean Valjean. Entered Toulon in 1796 and came out in 1815. I came out the year after. He looks like a real brute now, that'd be age that's done that to him; in jail he was sly. I'm positive I recognize him."

"Go and sit down," said the president. "The accused will remain standing."

Chenildieu was brought in, a convict for life, as his red jersey and green cap indicated. He was serving his sentence at Toulon jail and had been removed from there for this matter. He was a small man of fifty or so, lively, weathered, puny, yellow, cheeky, frantic, whose limbs and whose whole person exhibited a sort of sickly feebleness and whose eyes expressed immense strength. His prison mates had nicknamed him *Je-nie-Dieu*—I deny God.

The president addressed almost identical words to him as to Brevet. The minute he reminded him that his infamy deprived him of the right to take the oath, Chenildieu raised his head and looked straight at the audience. The president invited him to gather his thoughts and asked him, as he had asked Brevet, if he still recognized the accused.

Chenildieu burst out laughing.

"By God! Recognize him! We were attached to the same chain for six years. Aren't you talking to me anymore, old fella?"

"You may sit down," said the judge.

The usher wheeled in Cochepaille. This other "lifer," who had come straight from jail and who was dressed in red like Chenildieu, was a peasant from Lourdes, half man, half Pyrenees bear. He had guarded flocks in the mountains and had gone downhill from shepherd to thief. Cochepaille was no less savage and seemed even stupider than the accused. He was one of those luckless men that nature churns out as wild animals to start with and that society turns into galley slaves in the end.

The president tried to prod him with a few pathetic and solemn words and asked him, as with the other two, whether he still, without hesitation and without any trouble, recognized the man standing before him.

"It's Jean Valjean," said Cochepaille. "We even called him Jean-the-Jack, he was so strong."

Each of the affirmations of these three men, obviously sincere and made in good faith, had stirred up a murmur that boded ill for the accused, a murmur that grew and lasted longer each time a new declaration was added to the preceding one. The accused, for his part, listened to them with the stunned look that, according to the prosecution, was his principal defense. At the first, the gendarmes next to him heard him mutter between clenched teeth: "Well! I'll be buggered!" After the second, he said a bit louder, with an almost gratified air: "Terrific!" At the third, he shouted: "Marvelous!"

The president addressed him: "The accused has heard the testimony. What do you have to say?"

He answered: "I say, Marvelous!"

A rumble broke out in the crowd and almost reached the jury. It was obvious the man was finished.

"Ushers," said the president, "call the room to order. I am about to close the case."

At that moment, a movement was made right next to the judge. A voice was heard, crying out: "Brevet, Chenildieu, Cochepaille! Look over here."

All who heard this voice froze, it was so harrowing and so terrible. All eyes turned to the spot from whence it had come. A man, placed among the privileged spectators sitting behind the judge and jury, had just stood up, had pushed the door at elbow height that separated the bench from the well of the courtroom, and was now standing in the middle of the room. The judge, the counsel for the prosecution, Monsieur Bamatabois, twenty people recognized him and cried out in unison: "Monsieur Madeleine!"

## XI. CHAMPMATHIEU MORE AND MORE AMAZED

It was, indeed, him. The clerk's lamp lit up his face. He was holding his hat in his hand, there was nothing out of place in his attire, his redingote was carefully buttoned up. He was pale and shaking slightly. His hair, still gray when he arrived in Arras, was not yet completely white when he first stepped into the courtroom. It had gone white in the hour he had been there.

All heads looked up. The sensation was indescribable. There was a moment of hesitation in the auditorium. The voice had been so poignant, the man standing there looked so calm, that at first nobody could work out what was going on. Everybody wondered who had cried out. Nobody could believe that it was this serene-looking man who had let out that hair-raising cry.

The confusion lasted only a few seconds. Before the presiding judge and the counsel for the prosecution could say a word, before the gendarmes and the ushers could make a move, the man everyone still called Monsieur Madeleine at the time had advanced toward the witnesses Cochepaille, Brevet, and Chenildieu.

"Don't you recognize me?" he said.

All three sat stunned and signaled by a shake of the head that they did not know him. Cochepaille was intimidated and gave a military salute. Monsieur Madeleine turned toward the jurors and toward the court and said in a soft voice: "Gentlemen of the jury, let the accused go. Monsieur le président, arrest me. The man you are looking for is not this man, it is me. I am Jean Valjean."

No one breathed. The initial commotion caused by amazement gave way to a sepulchral silence. You could feel in the room that kind of religious terror that takes hold of the crowd when something great is being enacted.

But the judge's face was stamped with sympathy and sadness; he had exchanged a quick sign with the counsel for the prosecution and a few words under his breath with the counsel assessors. He addressed the public and asked in a tone that was understood by all: "Is there a doctor in the house?"

The counsel for the prosecution took the floor: "Gentlemen of the jury, this very strange and unexpected incident that has disturbed this hearing inspires in us, as in you, only a feeling we have no need to express. You all know, at least by reputation, the honorable Monsieur Madeleine, mayor of Montreuil-sur-mer. If there is a doctor in the audience, we join Monsieur le président in begging him to please come to Monsieur Madeleine's assistance and to take him home."

Monsieur Madeleine did not let the counsel for the prosecution finish. He interrupted him in a tone full of indulgence and authority. Here are the words he spoke; we record them verbatim, such as they were immediately written down after the hearing by one of those who witnessed this scene, such as they are still ringing in the ears of those who heard them, now nearly forty years ago.

"Thank you, Monsieur, the counsel for the prosecution, but I am not mad. You will see. You were on the point of committing a grave mistake; let this man go. I am performing a duty, I am the sorry convict. I am the only one who can see clearly here and I am telling you the truth. What I am doing at this moment, God, who is on high, looks down upon, and that is enough. You can take me, for here I am. And yet, I did my best. I hid under another name, I became rich, I became mayor; I wanted to fit in with honest people. It seems that this is not to be. To be brief, there are a lot of things I can't tell you, I am not going to tell you the story of my life, one day you'll know. I did rob Monseigneur the bishop, it's true; I did rob Petit-Gervais, it's true. They were right when they told you Jean Valjean was a mean wretch of a man. He is not perhaps entirely to blame. Listen, Your Honors, a man as humbled as I am has no business remonstrating with Providence or giving society advice; but, you see, the infamy I tried to put behind me is a damaging thing. The galleys make the galley slave. Think about that, if you will. Before jail, I was a poor peasant, not too bright, a sort of dimwit; jail changed me. I was stupid, I became mean; I was a great lump, I became a firebrand. Later, goodness and compassion saved me, just as severity had once sunk me. Sorry, forgive me, you can't understand what I'm saying here. You will find at my place, in the ashes in the fireplace, the forty-sou coin I stole seven years ago from Petit-Gervais. I have nothing further to say. Take me. My God! Monsieur, the counsel for the prosecution, is shaking his head, you say, Monsieur Madeleine has lost his mind, you don't believe me! I tell you, that is appalling. Do not condemn this man, at least! How's that! These men don't recognize me! I wish Javert were here. He'd recognize me, that's for sure!"

Nothing could convey the somber and melancholy tone in which these words were spoken.

He turned to the three convicts: "Well, I recognize you, I certainly do, Brevet! Do you remember—"

He broke off, hesitated for a moment, and then said: "Do you remember those checked wool braces you used to have in jail?"

Brevet gave a start of surprise and studied him from head to toe with a frightened look. He continued: "Chenildieu, you gave yourself the nickname of Je-nie-Dieu, you have a terrible burn over the whole of your right shoulder from lying down one day with your shoulder on a chafing dish full of smoldering embers to erase the three letters T.F.P.,[1] which can still be seen even so. Answer me, is that true?"

"It is true," said Chenildieu.

He addressed Cochepaille: "Cochepaille, close to the crook of your left arm you have a date carved in blue letters with burnt powder. This date is the day the emperor landed in Cannes, March 1, 1815. Roll up your sleeve."

Cochepaille rolled up his sleeve, as all eyes around him were riveted to his bare arm. A gendarme brought a lamp closer; the date was there.

The poor man turned toward the audience and toward the judges with a smile that still, to this day, breaks the hearts of those who saw it when they think of it. It was a smile of triumph and it was also a smile of despair.

"So you see," he said, "I am Jean Valjean."

There were no longer in the ring either judges or accusers or gendarmes; there were only staring eyes and hearts that were deeply moved. No one any longer remembered the role that each one might be assigned to play; the counsel for the prosecution forgot he was there to prosecute, the presiding judge that he was there to preside, the defense counsel that he was there to defend. The striking thing is that no question was asked, no authority intervened. The peculiarity of sublime spectacles is to seize all souls and make all witnesses spectators. Perhaps none of them realized what he was experiencing; no doubt none of them told himself he was seeing a great light shining there in all its splendor; but all felt inwardly dazzled.

It was obvious that they had Jean Valjean before their very eyes. That shone out clear as the light of day. This man's emergence had been enough to completely illuminate an episode so completely obscure just a moment before. Without there being any need for any further explanation now, the entire crowd, as by a sort of electric revelation, understood at once and at a single glance the simple and magnificent story of a man giving himself up so that another man was not condemned in his place. The details, the hesitations, the possible niggling reluctance, were lost in this vast luminous fact.

The impression swiftly passed, but for the moment it was irresistible.

"I don't want to disturb the proceedings any further," Jean Valjean went on. "I'll be off, since no one wants to arrest me. I have several things to do. Monsieur, the counsel for the prosecution, knows who I am, he knows where I am going, he will have me arrested when he is ready."

He headed for the exit door. Not a voice rose, not an arm shot out to stop him. Everyone moved aside. He had something divine about him at that moment, a quality that forces the multitudes to draw back and make way before a man. He moved through the crowd slowly. No one ever knew who opened the door, but it is certain that the door was found open when he reached it. Having gotten that far, he turned round and said: "Monsieur, the counsel for the prosecution, I remain at your disposal."

Then he addressed the audience: "All of you, all who are here, you find me worthy of pity, don't you? My God! When I think what I was on the point of doing, I find myself worthy of envy. Yet I'd have preferred none of this happened."

He went out and the door shut as it had opened, for those who do certain supremely good and mighty things are always sure of being served by someone in the crowd.

Less than an hour later, the jury's verdict unburdened the man named Champmathieu from all accusation; and Champmathieu, immediately set free, walked away stunned, believing all men mad and not understanding a thing about the vision he'd beheld.

# BOOK EIGHT

# AFTERSHOCK

### I. IN WHAT MIRROR MONSIEUR MADELEINE
### LOOKS AT HIS HAIR

Day was beginning to dawn. Fantine had had a night of fever and insomnia—full of happy images, though; in the morning, she fell asleep. Sister Simplice, who had watched over her, took advantage of her sleep to go and prepare a fresh solution of quinine. The worthy sister had been in the dispensary only a few minutes, hunched closely over her drugs and her vials so as to see them in the mist that dawn spreads over things. Suddenly she turned her head and let out a low cry. Monsieur Madeleine stood before her. He had come in without a sound.

"It's you, Monsieur le maire!" she cried.

He replied in a low voice: "How is the poor woman doing?"

"Not bad just now. But we were very anxious, I can tell you!"

She explained what had happened, how Fantine had been very bad, indeed, the day before, and how now she was doing better, because she believed Monsieur le maire had been to get her little girl from Montfermeil. The sister did not dare question Monsieur le maire, but she could see very well from his look that that was not where he had been.

"That's all good," he said, "you were right not to disabuse her."

"Yes," the sister replied, "but now, Monsieur le maire, when she sees you and she does not see her child, what will we tell her?"

He remained pensive for a moment.

"God will inspire us," he said.

"But we can't lie to her," murmured the sister under her breath.

Bright sunshine streamed into the room. It struck Monsieur Madeleine's face head on. Luck would have it that the sister looked up right then.

"My God, Monsieur!" she cried. "What's happened to you? Your hair is all white!"

"White!" he exclaimed.

Sister Simplice did not have a mirror; she rummaged through a chest and pulled out a little mirror the infirmary doctor used to check if a patient was dead, no longer breathing. Monsieur Madeleine took the mirror, studied his hair, and said: "Look at that!"

He tossed those words off casually, as though his mind was on something else.

The sister felt chilled by something unfamiliar that she detected in all this. He asked: "Can I see her?"

"Isn't Monsieur le maire going to go and get her child back for her?" said the sister, scarcely daring to risk a question.

"Of course, but it will take at least two or three days."

"If she does not see Monsieur le maire before then," she went on timidly, "she won't know Monsieur le maire is back; it will be easy to make her be patient and when the child arrives she will naturally think Monsieur le maire has arrived with the child. We won't have to tell any lies."

Monsieur Madeleine appeared to be turning this over for a few moments, but then he said with his customary calm gravity:

"No, sister, I must see her. I may not have much time, perhaps."

The nun didn't seem to notice that word *perhaps*, which lent an obscure and odd meaning to Monsieur le maire's words. She replied, lowering her eyes and her voice respectfully: "In that case, she is resting, but Monsieur le maire may go in."

He commented on a door that wouldn't shut properly and the noise it made, which was enough to wake the patient up; then he went into Fantine's room, went over to the bed, and pulled back the curtains a fraction. She was sleeping. Her breath was coming out of her chest with that tragic wheezing sound characteristic of such diseases, which breaks the hearts of poor mothers staying up all night watching over their doomed and sleeping children. But this labored breathing scarcely ruffled the ineffable serenity that was spread over her face, transfiguring her in her sleep. Her pallor had turned to whiteness; her cheeks were rosy. Her long blond eyelashes, the sole remnant of beauty that had stayed with her from the days of her virginity and her youth, fluttered while remaining closed. Her whole body trembled as if from some indescribable deployment of wings ready to fan out and carry her away, which you could feel quivering, but which you could not see. To see her like this, you would never have thought that she was so sick they despaired of her. She looked more like she was about to fly away than about to die.

When a hand approaches the stem to pluck a flower, the stem shivers and seems both to shrink back and to offer itself at once. The human body undergoes something of this quivering as the moment arrives when the mysterious fingers of death are about to gather the soul.

Monsieur Madeleine stayed motionless for a while close to the bed, letting his eyes wander over the patient and the crucifix, looking from one to the other in turn, as he had done two months earlier when he came to see her in this refuge for the very first time. They were both still there in the same position, she sleeping, he praying; only now, two months later, her hair was gray and his hair was white.

The sister had not come in with him. He stayed standing close by the bed, a finger over his mouth, as though there were someone in the room who had to be hushed.

She opened her eyes, saw him, and said with a peaceful smile: "And Cosette?"

## II. FANTINE HAPPY

She did not jump with surprise, or with joy; she was joy itself. That simple question, "And Cosette?" was made with a faith so profound, with so much certainty, with such a total lack of anxiety and doubt, that he could find no words. She continued: "I knew you were there, I was sleeping, but I could see you. I've been able to see you for a long time. I followed you with my eyes all night. You were in a cloud of glory and you had all kinds of heavenly figures all around you."

He raised his eyes to the crucifix.

"But, tell me," she went on, "where is Cosette? Why haven't you put her in my bed so that I'd see her the moment I opened my eyes?"

He trotted out something he could no longer recall later. Luckily the doctor, who had been alerted, stepped in and came to Monsieur Madeleine's rescue.

"My child," said the doctor, "calm down. Your little girl is here."

Fantine's eyes lit up and covered her face in brightness. She brought her hands together with an expression that held all the violence and all the gentleness that prayer can hold.

"Oh!" she cried. "Carry her in!"

Touching maternal illusion! In Fantine's eyes, Cosette was still a baby that you carry.

"Not yet," the doctor went on, "not just now. You still have a bit of fever. The sight of your child will agitate you and set you back. You have to get better first."

She cut him off anxiously.

"But I am better! I tell you I'm better; is he all there, this doctor? I want to see my child right now! Now!!"

"You see," said the doctor, "how carried away you get. As long as you're like this, I won't let you have your daughter. It's not enough just to see her, you've got to live for her. When you behave yourself, I'll bring her in to you myself."

The poor mother hung her head.

"Monsieur le docteur, I beg your pardon, I really do beg your pardon. Once, I would never have spoken like I just did, so many bad things have happened to me that I don't know what I'm saying anymore, at times. I understand, you're worried about the emotion, I'll wait as long as you like but I swear to you that it would not have set me back to see my daughter. I have seen her, I haven't taken my eyes off her, since last night. Do you know? If you brought her in to me now, I'd simply speak to her very softly. That's all. Isn't it perfectly natural for me to want to see my little girl after they went and got her for me in Montfermeil? I'm not angry. I know very well that I'm going to be happy. All night I saw white things and people smiling at me. When Monsieur le docteur wants to, he'll bring me my Cosette. I don't have a fever anymore, because I'm better; I can feel that there's nothing wrong with me anymore at all. But I'll act like I'm still sick and I won't budge, to please the ladies here. When they see I'm perfectly calm, they'll say: We must give her her little girl."

Monsieur Madeleine had sat down on a chair beside the bed. She turned to him; she was visibly making an effort to appear calm and "well behaved," as she said, in this stage of the disease that resembles infancy, the patient is so weak, so that, seeing her so peaceful, they would not make a fuss about bringing her Cosette. Yet, though restraining herself, she could not prevent herself from firing a whole host of questions at Monsieur Madeleine.

"Did you have a good trip, Monsieur le maire? Oh, how good you are to have gone and got her for me! Just tell me how she is. Did she cope well with the travel? Alas! She won't recognize me! After all this time, she will have forgotten me, poor little mite! Kids! They have no memory. They're like birds. Today it sees something and tomorrow something else, and it doesn't think about anything anymore. Only, did she have clean clothes? Did those Thénardiers look after her properly? How did they feed her? Oh, how I've suffered, if you only knew! Asking myself all those questions in the days when I was so poor! Now it's over! I'm so happy! Oh, how I long to see her! Monsieur le maire, do you think she's pretty? She's beautiful, isn't she, my daughter? You must have been cold as anything in that coach. Couldn't they bring her in just for a second? They can take her away again straight after that. Tell me! You're the mayor, you can do it!"

He took her hand: "Cosette is beautiful," he said. "Cosette is doing well, you'll see her soon, just be quiet now. You're talking too fast and you've taken your arms out from under the covers, and it's making you cough."

Indeed, coughing fits were interrupting Fantine at very nearly every word.

Fantine didn't even murmur, she feared that she had overstepped the mark with her few overimpassioned pleas and compromised the confidence she hoped to inspire, and she suddenly changed tack.

"It's quite pretty, Montfermeil, isn't it? In summer, people go there for picnics. What about the Thénardiers? Is their business going well? They don't get a lot of people passing through in those parts. That inn is just a fleapit."

Monsieur Madeleine held her hand and watched her with anxiety; it was clear he had come to tell her things he was now hesitant to say. Having paid his visit, the doctor had now withdrawn. Only Sister Simplice remained with them.

But in the middle of the silence, Fantine yelled: "I can hear her! My God! I can hear her!"

She shot her arm up to demand silence around her. Held her breath and strained to listen, rapt.

There used to be a little girl who played in the courtyard; the child of the concierge or of one of the women from the workshop. It was one of those coincidences that are always cropping up and that seem to be part of the mysterious staging of funereal events, that this little girl was, right then, running up and down outside to keep herself warm and laughing and singing out loud as she did so. Alas! There is nothing the games of children do not get caught up in! It was this little girl that Fantine could hear singing.

"Oh!" she squealed. "It's my Cosette! I recognize her voice!"

The little girl vanished as she had come, the voice died, Fantine strained to hear a little longer, then her face clouded and Monsieur Madeleine heard her mutter: "Fancy that lousy doctor not letting me see my daughter! He's got a mean face, that man!"

But the laughing thought at the back of her mind pushed to the fore once more. She went on talking to herself, her head on the pillow: "How happy we will be! We'll have a small garden, to start with! Monsieur Madeleine promised me one. My daughter will play in the garden. She must know her letters by now. I'll teach her how to spell. She'll chase butterflies in the grass. I'll watch her. And then she'll make her first communion. As for that—when will she make her first communion?"

She began to count on her fingers.

"... One, two, three, four ... She's seven. In five years. She'll have a white veil, the latest stockings, she'll look like a proper little lady. Oh, my good sister, you don't know what an idiot I am, here's me thinking about my daughter's first communion!"

And she began to laugh.

He had let go of Fantine's hand. He listened to her words the way you listen to the wind blowing, eyes on the ground, mind plunged into unfathomable thoughts. Suddenly she stopped talking and her head shot up from the pillow. Fantine had become frightening.

She no longer spoke, she no longer breathed; she half sat up in bed, one thin shoulder poking out of her nightgown, her face, radiant only a moment before, was livid, and she seemed to be staring at something horrifying in front of her, at the back of the room, her eyes grown huge with terror.

"My God!" he cried. "What's the matter, Fantine?"

She did not reply, she did not take her eyes off whatever the object was that she seemed to see; she touched his arm with one hand and, with the other, signaled to him to look behind him.

He turned round and saw Javert.

### III. JAVERT SATISFIED

This is what had happened.

Half past midnight was ringing out when Monsieur Madeleine left the circuit courtroom in Arras. He had gone back to his inn just in time to leave again by the mail coach in which, you'll remember, he had booked a seat. A bit before six o'clock in the morning, he arrived in Montreuil-sur-mer, and his first concern had been to mail his letter to Monsieur Laffitte, then to get to the infirmary and see Fantine.

But scarcely had he left the courtroom of the circuit court than the public counsel for the prosecution, having recovered from the initial shock, had taken the floor to deplore the crazy action of the honorable mayor of Montreuil-sur-mer and to declare that his convictions were in no way altered by this bizarre incident, which would be illuminated forthwith, and that he, meanwhile, called for the condemnation of this Champmathieu, obviously the real Jean Valjean. The persistence of the prosecutor clearly went against the feeling of all— public, judges, and jury. The defense counsel had little trouble refuting his harangue and establishing that, following the revelations of Monsieur Madeleine, that is, of the real Jean Valjean, the whole case had been turned on its head and that the jury no longer had anyone under their noses but an innocent man. The counsel for the defense had drawn from this a few epiphomena, unfortunately not new, on judicial errors, etc., etc.; the presiding judge, in his summing up, had joined the defense counsel and the jury and in a few minutes had put Champmathieu out of the running, fully acquitting him.

But the counsel for the prosecution needed a Jean Valjean and, not having Champmathieu anymore, latched onto Madeleine.

Immediately after the release of Champmathieu, the counsel for the prosecution shut himself up with the judge. They conferred on "the necessity of seizing the person of Monsieur le maire of Montreuil-sur-mer." This phrase, in which there are a lot of *of*s, is from Monsieur, the counsel for the prosecution,

entirely written in his hand in the minutes of his report to the public prosecutor. The first wave of emotion having subsided, the presiding judge made little
objection. Justice must indeed take its course. And then, to tell the truth, although the judge was a good man and smart enough, he was at the same time a
committed and almost ardent royalist, and he had been shocked that the mayor
of Montreuil-sur-mer, in speaking of the landing in Cannes, had used the word
*emperor* and not *Buonaparte*.

The order for the arrest was thus promptly dealt with. The counsel for the
prosecution sent word to Montreuil-sur-mer via a courier, who was not to spare
the horses, tasking Inspector Javert with the job.

We know that Javert had immediately returned to Montreuil-sur-mer after
having given his testimony.

Javert got to his feet the moment the courier handed him the order for the
arrest and the summons. The courier was himself a policeman and very much
in the know and he quickly brought Javert up to speed with what had happened
in Arras. The order for the arrest, signed by the counsel for the prosecution, was
couched in these terms: "Inspector Javert will apprehend Sieur Madeleine,
mayor of Montreuil-sur-mer, who, in the hearing of this day, was recognized as
being the convict Jean Valjean."

Anyone who did not know Javert and who had seen him as he marched into
the antechamber of the infirmary would not have had an inkling of what was
afoot and would have thought he looked perfectly normal. He was cold, calm,
grave, wore his gray hair plastered down flat against his temples, and had just
mounted the stairs at his usual slow pace. Anyone who knew him well and had
studied him closely would have quivered in their boots. The buckle of his
leather collar, instead of lying flat on his neck, was curled up over his left ear.
This revealed an agitation never before seen.

Javert was the genuine article: He never allowed a wrinkle to ruffle his duty
or his uniform; methodical with crooks, rigid with the buttons of his coat. For
him to have done his collar buckle up incorrectly, he had to have been experiencing one of those emotions we might call internal earthquakes.

He had simply come, had grabbed a corporal and four soldiers from the
neighboring police station. Had left the soldiers in the courtyard and had himself directed to Fantine's room by the concierge, who did not smell a rat, accustomed as she was to seeing armed men asking for Monsieur le maire.

Once he reached Fantine's room, Javert turned the key, pushed the door as
gently as any male nurse, or spook, and walked in.

To tell the truth, he did not walk in. He stood in the half-open doorway, his
hat on his head, his left hand over his redingote, which was buttoned up to his
chin. In the crook of his elbow you could see the lead knob of his enormous
walking stick, which disappeared behind him.

He stood there for a minute without anyone's being aware of his presence. Suddenly Fantine looked up, saw him, and made Monsieur Madeleine look round.

The instant Madeleine's eyes met Javert's, Javert, without moving, without stirring, without coming a step closer, became truly terrible. No human feeling ever manages to be quite as appalling as gloating joy.

His was the face of a demon who has come to collect his doomed victim. The certainty of at last holding Jean Valjean in his hands, captive, sent all that he had in his soul rushing over his physiognomy. The murky bottom had been stirred up and rose to the surface. The humiliation of having lost the scent somewhat and of having been mistaken momentarily about this Champmathieu was wiped out by the pride of having been so right to start with and having so long had the right instinct. Javert's satisfaction exploded in his superior attitude. A contorting triumph rippled and bloomed across that narrow forehead. There, revealed, was the full panoply of ghastliness that only the smuggest of faces can offer.

Javert was at that moment in seventh heaven. Without being fully aware of it, yet with a confused intuition of his own indispensible status and of his success, he personified—he, Javert—justice, enlightenment, and truth in their heavenly function of crushing evil. He had behind him and around him, at infinite depth, authority, reason, precedent, the conscience of the law, the vengeance of the law, all the stars in the firmament; he protected order, he called forth the thunder of the law, he avenged society, he came to the aid of the absolute; he stood erect in a blaze of glory; there was in his victory a trace of defiance and of combat; standing tall, arrogant, resplendent, he displayed, out in the open, for all the world to see, the superhuman bestiality of a bloodthirsty archangel, the fearful shadow of the act he was performing made visible in his clenched fist with the dull flashing of the social sword; happy and outraged, he held crime, vice, revolt, perdition, hell, pinned beneath his heel; he shone, he exterminated, he smiled . . . and there was an incontestable grandeur in this monstrous Saint Michael.[1]

Javert, though horrifying, had nothing of the ignoble about him.

Probity, sincerity, candor, conviction, a sense of duty, are things that, when they go wrong, can become hideous, but that, even hideous, remain grand; their majesty, peculiar to the human conscience, persists even in horror. They are virtues that have a vice, error. The pitiless but honest joy of a fanatic in the middle of perpetrating an atrocity still preserves some mysterious radiance that is both funereal and noble. Without realizing it, Javert, in his formidable happiness, was to be pitied like any other ignoramus who triumphs. Nothing was as poignant and terrible as this face in which what we might call all the bad of good was exposed.

## IV. Authority Takes Back Its Rights

Fantine had not seen Javert since the day the mayor had snatched her out of the man's clutches. Her sick brain could not make head or tail of it. Only, she did not doubt that he had come back to get her. She could not bear that ghastly face, she felt as if she were dying, she hid her face in her hands and cried out in anguish: "Monsieur Madeleine, save me!"

Jean Valjean—we will call him nothing else from now on—had gotten to his feet. He told Fantine in his gentlest and calmest voice: "Stay calm. It is not for you that he has come."

Then he addressed Javert: "I know what you're after."

Javert answered: "Move it!"

There was in the tone that accompanied those two words something wild and frenzied. Javert did not say "Move it!" he said "Mout!" No spelling could render the tone in which this was uttered; it was no longer human speech, it was an animal roar.

He did not do what he usually did; he did not go into details, he did not show a summons. For him, Jean Valjean was a sort of mysterious and elusive combatant, a slippery fighter with whom he had been wrestling for five years without being able to pin him down. This arrest was not a starting point, but an endpoint. The only thing he could say was: "Move it!"

In speaking, he did not make a move; he shot Jean Valjean a look that he threw like a grappling iron, the kind he was used to tugging violently to pull poor miscreants in to him. It was this look that Fantine had felt penetrate her to the very marrow of her bones two months before.

At Javert's yowl, Fantine had opened her eyes again. But Monsieur le maire was there. What was there for her to fear? Javert advanced to the middle of the room and shrieked: "You! Are you coming?"

The poor woman gazed all around her. There was no one in there but the nun and Monsieur le maire. To whom could this arrant familiarity be addressed? Only to her. She shuddered.

Then she saw something the like of which she had never seen even in the darkest days of her fever. She saw that slimy spook, Javert, grab Monsieur le maire by the collar; she saw Monsieur le maire bow his head. It seemed to her as though the world was falling apart.

Javert had, in fact, seized Jean Valjean by the collar.

"Monsieur le maire!" cried Fantine.

Javert burst out laughing, with that frightening laugh that showed all his gums.

"There's no Monsieur le maire here anymore!"

Jean Valjean did not try to dislodge the hand that held the collar of his coat. He said: "Javert—"

Javert broke in: "Monsieur l'inspecteur, to you."

"Monsieur," Jean Valjean continued, "I'd like a word with you in private."

"Speak up! Speak so we can hear you!" replied Javert. "People speak up when they're talking to me!"

Jean Valjean continued, keeping his voice down: "I have a favor to ask you—"

"Speak up, I tell you."

"But it's something only you should hear."

"I couldn't care less. I won't listen!"

Jean Valjean turned to face the man and said quickly in a voice no louder than a whisper: "Give me three days! Three days to go and get this poor woman's child! I'll pay whatever I have to. You can come with me, if you want to."

"You're joking!" cried Javert. "Well! I didn't think you were stupid! You're asking me for three days so you can take off! And you reckon it's to go and get this tart's brat! Ha, ha! That's a good one! Talk about rich!"

Fantine began to shake.

"My child!" she yelled. "Go and get my child! So she's not here! Sister, answer me, where is Cosette? I want my little girl! Monsieur Madeleine! Monsieur le maire!"

Javert stamped his foot.

"There goes the other one now! Shut up, you slut! What a godforsaken place, where the galley slaves are magistrates and tarts are looked after like countesses! Well, that's all going to change, and high time, too!"

He glared at Fantine and added, grabbing a fistful of Jean Valjean's cravat, shirt, and collar: "I'm telling you there is no Monsieur Madeleine and there is no Monsieur le maire. There is a thief, there is a crook, there is a convict named Jean Valjean! He's the one I've got hold of! So that's what there is!"

Fantine sat bolt upright, leaning on both hands with her arms stiff, she looked at Jean Valjean, she looked at Javert, she looked at the nun, she opened her mouth to speak, a rattle came out from deep in her chest, her teeth began to chatter, she stretched her arms in anguish, convulsively opening her hands and groping all around her like someone drowning; then she suddenly sank back on her pillow. Her head hit the headboard and fell forward onto her chest, with her mouth gaping, her eyes open and glazed.

She was dead.

Jean Valjean placed his hand on the hand with which Javert held him and prized it open as easily as he would have opened the hand of a child; then he said to Javert: "You have killed this woman."

"That's enough of that!" Javert shouted, furious. "I'm not here to argue. You can save all that. The guard's below. Get cracking right now or I'll get out the handcuffs."

There was in a corner of the room an old iron bed in a pretty poor state that served the sisters as a camp bed when they were keeping watch. Jean Valjean went over to the bed and wrenched off in a flash the already extremely dilapidated iron bar at the head of the bed, a feat that was easy with muscles like his, grabbed the rod in his clenched fist and studied Javert. Javert leaped back toward the door.

Jean Valjean, the iron bar in his fist, walked slowly over to Fantine's bed. When he reached it, he wheeled round and said to Javert in a voice that could hardly be heard: "I advise you not to disturb me right now."

One thing is certain and that is that Javert was shaking.

He thought of running to call the guard but Jean Valjean could take advantage of that moment to get away. So he stayed put, grabbed his walking stick by the small end, and leaned against the doorjamb without taking his eyes off Jean Valjean.

Jean Valjean leaned his elbow on the bedpost at the head of the bed, his forehead in his hand, and began to contemplate Fantine, motionless and distended. He stayed there in this position, absorbed, silent, and apparently no longer thinking about a thing in this life. There was no longer anything in his face or in his attitude other than a pity beyond words. After a few moments' reverie, he leaned over Fantine and spoke to her in a low voice.

What did he say to her? What could this outcast of a man say to that woman who was now dead? What were such words? No one on this earth heard them. Did the dead woman hear them? There are touching illusions that are perhaps sublime realities. What is beyond doubt is that Sister Simplice, sole witness to what was happening, has often recounted that the moment Jean Valjean whispered in Fantine's ear, she distinctly saw a heavenly smile form on those pale lips and in those dull pupils, full of the wonder of the grave.

Jean Valjean took Fantine's head in both his hands and arranged it on the pillow the way a mother would do for her child, he did up the ribbon at the neck of her nightgown and tucked her hair gently under her bonnet. That done, he closed her eyes.

Fantine's face in that moment seemed strangely luminous. Death is entry into the light everlasting.

Fantine's hand was dangling from the bed. Jean Valjean knelt before this hand, gently raised it and kissed it.

Then he got to his feet and turned to Javert: "Now," he said, "I'm all yours."

## V. A Suitable Grave

Javert placed Jean Valjean in the town prison.

The arrest of Monsieur Madeleine caused a sensation in Montreuil-sur-mer, or, more precisely, an extraordinary commotion. We are sad not to be able to conceal the fact that when they heard the words "he was a galley slave,"[1] almost everyone abandoned him. In less than two hours, all the good he had done was forgotten, and he was "nothing but a galley slave." We should add, in all fairness, that the details of the Arras episode were not yet known. The whole day conversations like the following could be heard all over town:

"Don't you know? He was a convict who'd been freed!" "Who was?" "The mayor." "Come on! Monsieur Madeleine?" "Yes." "Really?" "His name wasn't Madeleine, it's something awful, Béjean, Bojean, Boujean." "Ah, heavens above!" "He's been arrested." "Arrested!" "Locked up in the town prison, waiting to be transferred." "To be transferred! To be transferred! Where are they going to transfer him to?" "He's going to appear in the circuit court for some highway robbery he did before." "Well, I did have my suspicions! That man was too good to be true, too perfect, too sickly sweet. He refused the cross, he handed out sous to all the little beggars he met. I always thought there was something bad at the bottom of all that."

The drawing rooms especially were all frantically touting this view. One old lady, a subscriber to the *Drapeau blanc*,[2] made this unfathomably deep observation: "I can't say I'm sorry. That'll teach the Buonapartists!"

This is how that phantom once known as Monsieur Madeleine broke up and evaporated at Montreuil-sur-mer. Three or four people alone in all the town remained faithful to his memory. The old concierge who had served him was one of them.

The evening of the same day, this worthy old woman was sitting in her lodge, still quite bewildered and reflecting sadly. The factory had been shut all day, the carriage entrance was locked, the street was deserted. There were only two nuns in the house, Sister Perpetua and Sister Simplice, who were watching over Fantine's body.

Round about the time that Monsieur Madeleine normally came home, the good old caretaker automatically rose, took the key to Monsieur Madeleine's room out of a drawer along with the candlestick he always used to mount the stairs to his room; then she hung the key from the nail where he would normally get it and placed the candlestick to one side, as though she were waiting for him. After that she sat down again in her chair and went back to her musings. The poor old woman had done all this in her goodness, without being remotely aware of what she'd done.

It was only after a couple of hours that she snapped out of her reverie and cried: "Heavens! Lord Jesus Christ! Look at me, hanging his key on his nail!"

At that moment, the window of the lodge opened, a hand moved through the opening, grabbed the key and the candlestick, and lit the candle by the light of a burning taper. The caretaker lifted her eyes and her mouth fell open, but she managed to stifle the cry that rose in her throat. She knew that hand, that arm, the sleeve of that coat.

It was Monsieur Madeleine.

It was a few seconds before she could speak, "gripped as she was," as she herself later put it when she told her story.

"My God, Monsieur le maire," she cried at last, "I thought you were—"

She stopped, for the end of her sentence would have been lacking in respect for the beginning. Jean Valjean was still, for her, Monsieur le maire.

He completed her thought.

"In prison," he said. "I was. I broke a bar at the window, I dropped down from a rooftop, and here I am. I'm going up to my room. Go and get Sister Simplice for me. She is, no doubt, with that poor woman."

The old woman rushed to comply.

He did not caution her at all, knowing perfectly well that she would protect him better than he could protect himself.

No one ever knew how he managed to get into the courtyard without going through the carriage entrance. He had, and still carried on him, a master key that opened a small side door; but he should have been searched and the master key taken from him. This point has never been cleared up.

He mounted the stairs that led to his room. When he got to the top, he left his candlestick on the top step, opened his door virtually without a sound and groped his way to the window, which he then closed along with the shutter; then he came back for the candle and went back into the room.

It was just as well to take such a precaution; you'll remember that his window could be seen from the street.

He ran his eyes around the room, over his table, his chair, his bed, which had not been slept in for three days. No trace of the chaos of the night before last remained. The caretaker had "made up the room." Only, she had picked out of the ashes and placed carefully on the table the two ends of the iron-tipped club and the forty-sou coin blackened by the fire.

He took a sheet of paper and wrote: "Here are the two ends of my iron-tipped club and the forty-sou coin stolen from Petit-Gervais of which I spoke at the circuit court," and he put the silver coin on the piece of paper along with the two bits of iron, so that it would be the first thing anyone saw when they entered the room. He took one of his old shirts out of a wardrobe and tore it up. This provided strips of cloth in which he wrapped up the two silver candlesticks. He didn't seem to be in any hurry or in any agitation, and while he was wrapping up the bishop's candlesticks, he munched on a lump of black bread. It was most likely the bread they'd given him in prison and which he'd taken with him when he escaped.

This was observed by the bread crumbs that were found on the tiled floor when the law later ordered a search.

Two soft raps sounded at the door.

"Come in," he said.

It was Sister Simplice.

She was pale, her eyes were red, the candle she was holding wobbled in her hand. The violent jolts of fate have this peculiar feature, which is that, however perfectly controlled or detached we may be, they drag human nature out of the depths of our entrails and force it to reappear on the surface. In all the emotional upheavals of that day, the nun had become a woman again. She had wept and she had been shaken.

Jean Valjean had just written a few lines on a piece of paper, which he handed to the nun, saying: "Sister, you will give this to Monsieur le curé."

The note was not folded. She glanced at it.

"You may read it," he said.

She read: "I beg Monsieur le curé to take care of all that I leave here. He will pay the costs of my trial out of it as well as the burial of the woman who died today. The rest is for the poor."

The sister tried to speak, but she could barely stutter a few inarticulate sounds. Yet she did manage to say: "Wouldn't Monsieur le maire like to see the poor unfortunate woman one last time?"

"No," he said, "they're after me, they would simply arrest me in her room and that would upset her."

He had barely finished his sentence when a loud noise was heard on the stairs. They heard the clamor of feet ascending and the old caretaker say in a voice as loud and piercing as she could make it: "My good man, I swear to God that no one has been in here the whole day or the whole evening, I haven't once left my door!"

A man replied: "But there's a light on in this room."

They recognized the voice of Javert.

The room was laid out so that the door hid a corner of the wall on the right when it opened. Jean Valjean blew out the candle and stood in this corner.

Sister Simplice fell to her knees by the table.

The door opened. Javert marched in.

The whispering of several men could be heard along with the protests of the caretaker in the corridor. The nun did not look up. She prayed.

The candle was on the mantelpiece and gave only a very dim light.

Javert noticed the sister and stopped in his tracks.

You will recall that the very basis of Javert, his element, the air that he breathed, was veneration for any and all authority. He was absolutely consistent and could brook no objection, no exception. For him, naturally, ecclesiastical authority was the highest of all. He was religious, superficial and correct on this point as on all others. In his eyes, a priest was a mind that could never make a mistake, a nun was a creature that never commits a sin. They were souls inured to this world with a single door open to them, one that only ever opened to let truth out.

As soon as he clapped eyes on the sister, his first impulse was to withdraw.

Yet there was also another duty that held him in its grip and drove him imperiously in the opposite direction. His second impulse was to remain where he was and to hazard at least one question.

It was the same Sister Simplice who had never lied in her life. Javert knew this and venerated her especially because of it.

"Sister," he said, "are you alone in the room?"

There was a horrible moment when the poor caretaker felt her legs were about to buckle. The sister looked up and replied: "Yes."

"In that case," said Javert, "forgive me if I insist—it is my duty—you have not seen this evening a person, a man. He has escaped, we are looking for him— the man named Jean Valjean, you haven't seen him?"

The sister answered: "No."

She lied. She lied twice in a row, one swipe after the next, without hestitating, speedily, like an old hand.

"Forgive me," said Javert, and he withdrew, bowing low.

Oh, holy child! You are no longer of this world—have not been for many years now; you have caught up with your virgin sisters and your angel brothers in the light; may these lies be chalked up to you in paradise!

The sister's affirmation was so decisive for Javert that he did not even notice the oddness of the candle's having just been blown out and smoking away on the table.

An hour later, a man walking through the trees and the mists had swiftly put distance between himself and Montreuil-sur-mer in the direction of Paris. The man was Jean Valjean. It has been established, by the testimony of two or three drivers who passed him, that he was carrying a bundle and that he was dressed in a smock. Where did he get the smock from? No one ever knew. But an old laborer had died a few days before at the factory infirmary, leaving only his smock. This was, perhaps, the one.

One last word about Fantine.

We each have a mother, the earth. Fantine was given back to this mother.

The priest thought that he was doing the right thing in keeping as much of the money as possible for the poor out of what Jean Valjean had left—and maybe he was. After all, who was involved here? A convict and a prostitute. This is why he simplified Fantine's burial and reduced it to the bare necessity known as the potter's field.

So Fantine was buried in this free corner of the cemetery that is open to everyone and no one, where the poor are lost without a trace. Happily, God knows where the soul is. They laid Fantine in the dark earth among the first bones they stumbled across; she suffered the promiscuity of ashes. She was thrown in the common grave. Her final resting place was just like her bed.

PART TWO

# COSETTE

# BOOK ONE

# WATERLOO

## I. WHAT YOU MEET WITH WHEN YOU COME FROM NIVELLES

Last year, 1861, on a lovely morning in May,[1] a wanderer, the man telling this tale, arrived from Nivelles heading for La Hulpe. He was on foot. He was following a broad paved roadway between two rows of trees, which undulated over hills that rolled along, one after the other, lifting the road up and letting it fall, like enormous waves. He had gone past Lillois and Bois-Seigneur-Isaac. In the west he could see the slate church tower of Braine-l'Alleud, which is in the shape of an upended vase. He had just left a wood behind him on a rise, and at a crossroad, next to a worm-eaten signpost bearing the inscription *Former tollgate no. 4*, he came to a tavern with this sign hanging on the outside: *Aux Quatre Vents. Echabeau, privately owned café.*

A bit farther down the road from this tavern, he reached the bottom of a small valley where water flows under an arch built into the embankment of the road. The cluster of trees, sparse but very green, that covers the valley on one side of the roadway, thins out into meadows on the other side before meandering off gracefully and haphazardly toward Braine-l'Alleud.

At that point, by the roadside to the right, was an inn with a four-wheel cart outside the door, along with a great bundle of hop poles, a plow, a pile of dry brushwood near a quickset hedge, some lime smoking in a square hole, and a ladder lying along an old shed with straw walls. A young girl was hoeing and pulling up weeds in a field where a big yellow poster, probably for some fairground show, fluttered and flapped in the wind. At the corner of the inn, next to a pond where a flotilla of ducks was sailing, a roughly cobbled pathway plunged into the scrub. This wanderer followed it in.

After about a hundred paces, having walked alongside a fifteenth-century wall surmounted by a sharp gable of contrasting bricks, he came to a great arched doorway made of stone, with a rectilinear impost in the heavy style of Louis XIV and two flat medallions mounted on either side. A severe façade dominated this doorway; a wall perpendicular to the façade came right up to the door, almost touching it, and flanked it with an abrupt right angle. Over the meadow in front of the door lay three old harrows through which all the flowers of May were growing pell-mell. The door was shut. It was held shut by a pair of decrepit double doors adorned with a rusty old knocker.

The sun was lovely; the branches of the trees were shivering gently in that May way that seems to come from nests more than from the breeze. A brave little bird, probably in love, was singing its heart out in a great big tree.

The wanderer bent down and peered at a rather large circular crater like the impact of a sphere, in the stone to the left of the door near the bottom of the right-hand abutment. At that moment the door panels were folded back and a peasant woman came out.

She saw the wanderer and realized what he was looking at.

"That was a French cannonball that did that," she said.

And she added: "What you can see there, higher up in the door, next to the nail, is the hole made by a Biscay musket. The ball didn't go through the wood."

"What's this place called?" the wanderer asked.

"Hougoumont," said the peasant woman.

The wanderer straightened up. He walked over to the hedge for a look at the view. On the horizon, he could see a sort of grassy knoll through the trees and on this grassy knoll something that, at that distance, looked like a lion.[2]

He was on the battlefield of Waterloo.


## II. HOUGOUMONT

Hougoumont[1]—this was the fatal spot, the first hurdle, the first resistance met with by that great lumberjack of Europe known as Napoléon; the first knot to go under the ax.

It was a château, it is now nothing more than a farm. Hougoumont, for the antiquarian, is *Hugomons*. This manor was built by Hugo, sire of Somerel, the same man who endowed the sixth chaplaincy in the abbey of Villers.

The wanderer pushed the door, elbowed his way past an old calash, and walked into the courtyard.

The first thing that struck him in this yard was a sixteenth-century doorway that looks like an archway, everything having collapsed around it. Ruins often look monumental. In a wall next to the archway, another door with keystones dating from the days of Henri IV[2] opens to allow a glimpse of trees in an orchard. Next to this door a manure pit, some picks and shovels, a few carts, an old well with its flagstone and its iron pulley, a foal leaping about, a turkey fanning its tail, a chapel surmounted by a small bell tower, a pear tree in flower espaliered against the wall of the chapel—that was the yard whose conquest was one of Napoléon's dreams. This patch of dirt would perhaps have brought him the world, if only he had been able to take it. Hens were scattering dust with their beaks. A growl was heard, the growl of a big dog baring its teeth, standing in for the English.

The English were admirable here. The four companies of Cooke's Guards held their ground for seven hours against the furious assault of an entire army.

Hougoumont, as seen on the map in geometric plan with its buildings and enclosure included, forms a sort of irregular rectangle with one of its corners cut off. It is at this corner that the southern gate stands, guarded by the wall that commands it at point-blank range. Hougoumont has two gates: the south gate, which is that of the château, and the north gate, that of the farm. Napoléon sent his brother Jérôme[3] against Hougoumont; the divisions of Guilleminot, Foy, and Bachelu[4] pitted themselves against it, practically the whole of Reille's corps was deployed there and crumbled, and Kellermann's cannonballs ran out along this heroic stretch of wall. It was too much for the Bauduin brigade to force Hougoumont to the north, and the Soye brigade could only make a hole in it to the south without taking it.

The farm buildings border the yard to the south. A piece of the north gate, broken by the French, hangs where it has been fixed to the wall. It consists of four planks nailed to two crosspieces where the scars of battle can clearly be seen.

The north gate, smashed by the French, and on which a patch has been stuck to replace the panel hanging from the wall, stands half open at the back of the yard; it is cut squarely into a wall, stone at the bottom, brick at the top, which closes the yard on the north side. It is a simple cart entrance such as are found on all leasehold farms, two big swing doors made of rustic planks; beyond, meadows. The battle over this entrance was furious. For a long time you could see all kinds of bloody handprints on the door pillar. It is here that Bauduin was killed.

The storm of battle still lingers in this courtyard; the horror is visible there, the reversal of the fray has turned to stone; it lives, it dies, it was yesterday. The walls are in agony, stones fall, breaches scream; holes are wounds; the buckled and shuddering trees are trying to get away.

The courtyard in 1815 was more built up than it is today. Structures that have since been pulled down formed redans, corners, and sharp right angles.

The English barricaded themselves in there; the French got in but could not maintain their position. Next to the chapel, a wing of the château, the sole remains of the manor of Hougoumont, stands crumbling, you might say disemboweled. The château served as a dungeon, the chapel served as a blockhaus. They exterminated people there. The French, shot down with harquebuses on all sides, from behind the walls, from on top of the barns, from down in the cellars, through every casement window, through every basement window, through every loophole in the stones, brought kindling and set fire to walls and men; the volleys of shot were answered by conflagration.

In the ruined wall, you can glimpse through windows garnished with iron bars the dismantled rooms of the main brick building. The English Guards lay in ambush in these rooms; the spiral staircase, split from the ground floor right up to the roof, looks like the inside of a broken shell. The staircase has two sections; the English, besieged on the stairs and huddled on the steps at the top, cut away the lower steps, and these big slabs of bluestone form a heap in among the nettles. A dozen steps still cling to the wall; on the first of them, the image of a trident is chiseled. These inaccessible steps are still firmly attached to their sockets. All the rest looks like a toothless jawbone. Two old trees stand there; one is dead, the other is wounded in the foot and grows young again every April. Since 1815, it has begun to grow through the staircase.

They massacred one another in the chapel. The interior, calm again, is strange. Mass has not been said here since the carnage. Yet the altar remains, a rough wooden altar backing on a wall of rough-hewn stone. Four walls washed with lime, a door opposite the altar, two small arched windows, on the door a great wooden crucifix, above the crucifix a square window stuffed with a bale of hay, in a corner, on the ground, an old glazed windowframe all broken—that is the chapel for you. Near the altar is nailed a wooden statue of Saint Anne dating from the fifteenth century; the head of baby Jesus was taken off by a Biscay musket. The French, managing to gain control of the chapel for a moment before being dislodged, set fire to it. The flames filled the place; it turned into an oven. The door burned, the floor burned. The wooden Christ did not burn. Fire lapped at his feet, which can now only be seen as blackened stumps, then it stopped. A miracle, according to the people of these parts. The decapitated baby Jesus, though, was not as lucky as Christ.

The walls are covered in writing. Near Christ's feet this name can be read: *Henquinez.* Then these others: *Conde de Rio Maïor. Marques y Marquesa de Almagro (Habana).*[5] There are French names with exclamation marks, signs of rage. The wall was whitewashed again in 1849. The nations were trading insults on it.

It is at the door of this chapel that a body was picked up holding an ax in its hand. This cadaver was Sous-Lieutenant Legros.

You come out of the chapel and on the left you see a well. There are two in the courtyard. You ask: Why isn't there a bucket and a pulley at this one? It is because water is no longer drawn from it. Why isn't water drawn from it anymore? Because it is full of skeletons.

The last one to be pulled out of the water of this well was called Guillaume Van Kylsom. He was a peasant who lived in Hougoumont and was a gardener there. On June 18, 1815, his family took flight and hid in the woods.

For several days and several nights, the forest surrounding the abbey of Villers harbored all the wretched scattered locals. Even today, certain recognizable vestiges, such as the old trunks of charred trees, mark the place where these poor bivouacs trembled in the depths of the scrub.

Guillaume Van Kylsom stayed in Hougoumont "to guard the castle" and hunkered down in a cellar. The English found him there. He was pulled out of his cubbyhole and given a good hiding with the flats of their swords before the enemy combatants forced the frightened man to wait on them. They were thirsty; Guillaume brought them something to drink. It was from this well that he drew the water. For many, it was the last mouthful of water they would ever drink. This well, where so many dead men drank, was also to die.

After the fighting, one thing needed to be done in a hurry and that was to bury the bodies. Death has its own way of harassing victory, sending pestilence hot on the heels of glory. Typhus is a footnote to triumph. The well was deep, it was turned into a tomb. Three hundred dead were thrown into it. Perhaps in too much haste. Were all of them actually dead? Legend says no. It seems that, the night after the burial, feeble voices could be heard calling out from down in the well.

The well stands alone in the middle of the courtyard. Three walls, half-stone and half-brick, folded like the leaves of a screen and simulating a square turret, surround it on three sides. The fourth side is open. This is where the water used to be drawn. The back wall has a sort of misshapen bull's-eye, perhaps a hole made by a shell. The turret had a roof of which all that remains are the beams. The iron supports for the right wall are in the form of a cross. If you bend over, your eye becomes lost in a deep brick cylinder filled with a densely layered darkness. All around the well the bottom of the walls disappear in nettles.

This well is not fronted by the broad blue flagstone that serves as an apron for all the wells of Belgium. The blue flagstone has been replaced here by a crossbar on which rest five or six deformed stumps of gnarled stiffened wood that look like great big bones. There is no longer any bucket, any chain, any pulley; but there is still a stone basin that was used for wastewater. Rainwater collects in it and from time to time a bird from the neighboring forests comes and drinks out of it and then flies off.

One house among these ruins, the farmhouse, is still inhabited. The door of this house opens onto the courtyard. Next to a pretty Gothic keyhole plate the door has a slanting iron handle in the shape of a clover leaf. The moment the Hanoverian lieutenant Wilda took hold of the handle to seek refuge inside the farmhouse, a French sapper chopped his hand off with an ax.

The grandfather of the family that now occupies the house was the old gardener Van Kylsom, long since dead. A gray-haired woman will tell you: "I was there. I was three years old. They carted us off into the woods. I was in my mother's arms. You glued your ears to the ground to listen. I used to imitate the cannon, I'd go *boom, boom*."

A courtyard door, on the left, as we said, opens on to the orchard.

The orchard is shocking.

It is divided into three parts, you might almost say three acts. The first part is a garden, the second is the orchard, and the third is a wood. These three parts are all enclosed, on the entrance side, by the buildings of the castle and the farm, on the left by a hedge, on the right, by a wall, at the back, by a wall. The wall on the right is made of brick, the back wall is made of stone. First you enter the garden. It is below street level, planted with currant bushes, overgrown with wild vegetation, closed off by a monumental terrace in stone slabs with balusters that have double bulbs. It was a seigneurial garden in the first French style that preceded Le Nôtre;[6] today, nothing but ruins and brambles. The pilasters are topped with globes that look like stone cannonballs. You can still count forty-three balusters in place on their bases; the rest are lying in the grass. Almost all of them show scuff marks from musketry. One broken baluster stands on its shaft like a broken leg.

It is in this garden, which is lower than the orchard, that six *voltigeurs* of the 1st Light Company, having broken through and not being able to get out again, were tracked down and taken like bears in a pit, and decided to stand and fight two Hanoverian companies, one of which was armed with rifles. The Hanoverians were ranged along the balustrade and fired from above. The light infantrymen, riposting from below, six against two hundred, intrepid, having only the currant bushes as cover, took fifteen minutes to die.

You mount a few steps and pass from the garden into what is properly called the orchard. Here, in these few square yards, fifteen hundred men fell in less than an hour. The wall seems ready to recommence the fighting. The thirty-eight loopholes cut by the English at irregular heights are still there. In front of the sixteenth lie two English graves in granite. The loopholes are only in the south wall; the main attack came from there. This wall is hidden outside by a great quickset hedge; the French arrived, thinking they had only the hedge to tackle, leaped over it, and found the wall, an obstructive hurdle and an ambush, the English guards entrenched behind it, thirty-eight loopholes all firing at once, a storm of grapeshot and cannonballs; and Soye's brigade was smashed against it. That is how Waterloo kicked off.

The orchard was taken, though. Since there were no ladders, the French used their fingernails to climb. They fought hand to hand beneath the trees. All this grass was sopping wet with blood. A battalion from Nassau, seven hundred men, was blasted to smithereens there. On the other side, the wall, against which Kellermann's two batteries trained their weapons, is bitten into by grapeshot.

This orchard is as responsive as any other to the month of May. It has its buttercups and its daisies, the grass is high there, cart horses graze there, horsehair ropes on which clothes are drying are slung between the trees and make anyone passing by duck their heads, you can walk through this wasteland and your feet sink in mole holes. In the middle of the grass you notice an uprooted tree trunk, recumbent, covered in green shoots. Major Blackman leaned up against it to expire. Beneath a great tree nearby fell the German general Duplat, from a French family who went into exile at the revocation of the Edict of Nantes. Right next to this a diseased old apple tree leans wrapped in a bandage of straw and clay. Nearly all the apple trees are falling down from old age. There is not one that does not have its cannonball or its Biscay musket ball. The skeletons of dead trees abound in this orchard. Crows fly among the branches and at the back there is a wood full of violets.

With Bauduin killed, Foy wounded, the fire, the massacre, the carnage, a stream made of English blood, German blood, and French blood furiously intermingled, a well crammed with cadavers, the Nassau regiment and the Brunswick regiment annihilated, Duplat killed, Blackman killed, the English Guards mutilated, twenty French battalions out of the forty of Reille's corps decimated, three thousand men, in this godforsaken hole of Hougoumont alone, run through with swords, torn to pieces, butchered, their throats cut, shot, burned to death; and all that just so some peasant today can say to a traveler: "Monsieur, give me three francs and, if you like, I'll tell you all about Waterloo!"

### III. JUNE 18, 1815[1]

Let's go back in time—it's one of the prerogatives of the narrator—and put ourselves back in the year 1815, and even a bit before the period when the action narrated in the first part of the book begins.

If it hadn't rained during the night of June 17–18, 1815, the future of Europe would have been different. A few drops of water, more or less, brought Napoléon to his knees. So that Waterloo could be the end of Austerlitz, Providence needed only a bit of rain,[2] and a cloud crossing the sky out of season was enough for a whole world to disintegrate.

The battle of Waterloo—and this gave Blücher[3] time to get there—could not begin until half past eleven. Why? Because the ground was too wet. They had to wait for it to firm up a little before the artillery could maneuver.

Napoléon was an officer of the artillery, and he felt it. In his heart of hearts, this prodigious captain was the man who, in his report on Aboukir[4] to the Directoire, had said: "This cannonball of ours killed six men." All his battle plans are for projectiles. To get the artillery to converge on a given point—that was his key to victory. He treated the strategy of the enemy general like a citadel and demolished it. He overwhelmed the weak point with grapeshot; he set battles up and dissolved them with cannons. There was marksmanship in his genius. To hammer square formations, pulverize regiments, smash lines, grind and scatter massed formations—this was what it was all about for him, strike, strike, strike without letup, and he entrusted this task to the cannonball. A fearsome method, and one that, allied with genius, made this somber athlete of the pugilism of war invincible for fifteen years.

On June 18, 1815, he was counting more than ever on the artillery because he had the numbers in his favor. Wellington[5] had only a hundred and fifty-nine pieces of ordnance; Napoléon had two hundred and forty.

Suppose the ground had been dry; the artillery could have rolled, the action would have begun at six in the morning. The battle would have been fought by two o'clock, three hours before the Prussian episode.

How much is Napoléon to blame for the loss of the battle? Is the shipwreck imputable to the pilot?

Was Napoléon's obvious physical decline coupled with a certain inner diminution by that stage? Had twenty years of war worn out the blade along with the sheath, the soul along with the body? Did the veteran make his inconvenient presence felt in the captain? In a word, was this genius, as many historians of note have thought, on the wane? Did he act so frenetically to disguise his enfeeblement from himself? Was he beginning to waver, in bewilderment, over a touch of adventure? Had he become oblivious to danger, which is a serious thing in a general? Within that class of material men we might call giants of action, is there an age at which genius becomes myopic? Old age has no hold on geniuses of the ideal; for the Dantes and the Michelangelos, to age is, on the contrary, to grow in stature; for the Hannibals and the Bonapartes, is it to shrink? Had Napoléon lost the feeling for victory? Had he got to the point where he could no longer make out the reef, no longer sniff out the trap, no longer see the crumbling edge of the abyss? Had he lost his scent for catastrophe? Was the man who once knew all the roads to triumph and pointed them out with a magisterial finger from the height of his chariot of lightning, now in such a sinister daze that he was leading his tumultuous team of legions to the brink? Had he, at the age of forty-six, been gripped by some supreme madness? Was this titanic driver of destiny now no more than a monster daredevil?

We do not think so.

His battle plan was, in the opinion of all, a masterpiece. To go straight to the center of the allied line, make a hole in the enemy, cut him in two, push the British half to Hal and the Prussian half to Tongres, turn Wellington and Blücher into two separate segments, take Mont-Saint-Jean, seize Brussels, chuck the Germans into the Rhine and the English into the sea. All that, for Napoléon, was involved in this battle. After that, we would see.

It goes without saying that we are not claiming to do the history of Waterloo here. One of the scenes that gave rise to the drama we are relating is connected to this battle, but this history is not our subject; this history, moreover, has been told and told in masterly fashion, both from Napoléon's point of view and from the opposite point of view[6] by a glittering array of historians. As for us, we'll leave the historians to it; we are just a distant witness, a traveler wandering through the plain, a seeker crouched over this ground molded with human flesh, perhaps mistaking appearance for reality; we have no right to tackle head-on, in the name of science, a whole raft of facts in which there is no doubt something of the mirage, we have neither the military experience nor the skills in strategy that would authorize such a scheme; in our view, a chain of accidents governed the two captains at Waterloo, and when it comes to destiny, that mysterious defendant, we judge as do the people, that guileless judge.

## IV. A

Those who would like to get a clearer idea of the battle of Waterloo have only to make the letter *A* on the ground in their mind. The left downstroke of the letter *A* is the road from Nivelles, the right downstroke is the road from Genappe, and the horizontal stroke is the sunken road from Ohain to Braine-l'Alleud. The apex of the A is Mont-Saint-Jean and that is where Wellington is; the lower left-hand point is Hougoumont and that is where Reille is with Jérôme Bonaparte; the lower right-hand point is La Belle-Alliance and that is where Napoléon is. A bit below the point where the horizontal stroke of the *A* meets and divides the right downstroke is La Haie-Sainte. In the middle of this horizontal bar is the exact point where the last word of the battle was said. That is where they put the lion, an involuntary symbol of the supreme heroism of the Imperial Guard.

The triangle consisting of the apex of the *A* between the two downstrokes and the horizontal stroke is the Mont-Saint-Jean plateau. The struggle for this plateau is what the whole battle revolved around.

The wings of the two armies extended to right and left of the two roads from Genappe and Nivelles, with d'Erlon facing Picton and Reille facing Hill.

Behind the tip of the *A,* behind the Mont-Saint-Jean plateau, is the forest of Soignes.

As for the plain itself, imagine a vast undulating terrain; each fold dominates the next fold and all the undulations rise toward Mont-Saint-Jean and end in the forest there.

Two enemy troops on a battlefield are like two wrestlers in a headlock. Each tries to make the other slip. They clutch at anything to hand: A bush is a fulcrum; the corner of a wall is a shoulder brace. For want of some shack to lean against, a regiment loses its footing; some shift in the plain, a movement of the terrain, a handy cross-path, a wood, a ravine, can snag the heel of this colossus we call an army and prevent it from retreating. Anyone who quits the field is mown down. Hence, for the commander in chief, the necessity of examining the slightest tuft of vegetation and of digging into the slightest contour.

The two generals had carefully studied the plain of Mont-Saint-Jean, known today as the plain of Waterloo. Since the previous year, Wellington, in his clairvoyant wisdom, had examined it as a possible site for a great battle. On this terrain and for this duel, on June 18, Wellington had the good side, Napoléon, the bad, the English army being on top, the French army below.

To sketch here Napoléon's appearance on horseback, his glasses in his hand, on the heights of Rossomme, at dawn on June 18, 1815, is almost too much. Before anyone pointed him out, everyone had spotted him. That calm profile beneath the little hat of the College of Brienne,[1] the green uniform, the white lapel hiding the insignia, the gray greatcoat hiding the epaulets, the diagonal slash of the red sash underneath the waistcoat, the leather pants, the white horse with its purple velvet cloth displaying crowned *N*s and eagles at the corners, the riding boots over silk stockings, the silver spurs, the Marengo sword[2]—the whole figure of the last Caesar stands in everyone's imagination, acclaimed by some, frowned upon by others.

This figure has long been in blazing light—which has to do with a certain legendary fog that most heroes give off and that always veils the truth for a more or less lengthy period of time; but today the real story has dawned with the light of day.

This bright light, history, is pitiless; what is strange and divine about it is that, completely luminous as it is, and precisely because it is light, it often casts shadow where there used to be rays of sunlight; it makes two different phantoms of the same man, and one attacks the other and proves him false, and the darkness of the despot does battle with the dazzling splendor of the captain. This allows a truer measure in the final evaluation of the peoples of the world. Babylon sacked diminishes Alexander; Rome in chains diminishes Caesar; Jerusalem massacred diminishes Titus.[3] Tyranny dogs the tyrant. It is a sorry thing for a man to leave behind him a pall that has his shape.

## V. THE QUID OBSCURUM OF BATTLES

Everyone knows what happened in the first stage of the battle; a bad start, confusing, tentative, threatening for both armies, but more for the English than the French.

It had rained all night; the ground had been pummeled by the downpour; water had collected here and there in the hollows of the plain as though in basins; at certain points the army service equipage were in it up to the axles; the girths of the harnessed teams of horses were dripping with liquid mud. If the wheat and rye flattened by this throng of advancing carts had not filled the ruts and made a bed under the wheels, all movement, particularly in the little valleys next to Papelotte, would have been impossible.

The business kicked off late; Napoléon, as we explained, was in the habit of holding all the artillery in his hand like a pistol, now aiming at this point, now at some other point of the battle, and he wanted to wait until the batteries could roll and move freely at a gallop; for that, the sun needed to come out and dry the ground. But the sun did not come out. This was no longer the meet at Austerlitz. When the first cannonball was launched, the English general Colville looked at his watch and noted that it was thirty-five minutes past eleven.

The action kicked off with fury, more fury perhaps than the emperor would have liked from the French wing at Hougoumont. At the same time, Napoléon attacked the center by hurling the Quiot brigade at La Haie-Sainte, and Ney[1] drove the right French wing against the left English wing that was bearing down on Papelotte.

The attack on Hougoumont was partly a feint; to lure Wellington there, to get him to draw to the left—that was the plan. And the plan would have succeeded if the four companies of the English Guards and the brave Belgians of Perponcher's division had not solidly held the position, and if Wellington, instead of massing troops there, had been able to limit himself to sending only four other companies of Guards and one of Brunswick's battalions as reinforcement.

The attack of the French right wing on Papelotte was a no-holds-barred one; to overwhelm the English left, cut off the Brussels road, bar passage to any Prussians who might turn up, carry Mont-Saint-Jean, push Wellington back on Hougoumont, and from there to Braine-l'Alleud, from there to Hal, nothing could be neater. And apart from a few snags, the attack succeeded. Papelotte was taken; La Haie-Sainte was won.

One noteworthy detail. In the English infantry, especially in Kempt's brigade, there were lots of new recruits. These young soldiers were valiant when confronted by our fearsome foot soldiers; in their inexperience, they stood up to the business fearlessly. They were especially useful as skirmishers; when a soldier becomes a skirmisher, to some extent left to his own devices, he becomes to all intents and purposes his own general; these recruits showed something of the inventiveness and fury of the French. This novice infantry had nerve. And Wellington did not like it one bit.

After the capture of La Haie-Sainte, the battle wavered.

During the day, there was an obscure interval, from noon to four; the middle of the battle is almost hazy and is part of the somberness of the mêlée. Twilight gathers there. You can see vast fluctuations in this fog, a dizzying mirage, the military tackle of the day almost unknown today, flaming busbies, floating sabretaches, leather cross-belts, grenade pouches, the dolmans of the hussars, red boots with hundreds of creases, heavy shakos festooned with torsades, the almost black infantry of Brunswick merged with the scarlet infantry of England, the English soldiers with great white circular rolls around the armholes for epaulets, the Hanoverian light horse with their oblong leather helmets with copper bands and plumes of red horsehair, the Scots with their bare knees and tartan plaids, the great white gaiters of our grenadiers—tableaux, not strategic lines, something for Salvator Rosa, not for Gribeauval.[2]

A certain amount of storminess is always mixed up in a battle. *Quid obscurum, quid divinum.*[3] Every historian sees what he wants to see in this free-for-all. Whatever the combination of generals, the clash of the armed masses has unpredictable surges; in action, the plans of the two chiefs overlap and are distorted by each other. Some point on the battlefield devours more combatants than some other point, the way more or less spongy soils suck up the water you throw on them at different rates. You are forced to pour more soldiers there than you would like. Such expenditures make up the unforeseen. The battle line wiggles and snakes around like a thread, trails of blood stream illogically, the fronts of the armies undulate, regiments coming in or leaving form capes and gulfs. All these reefs are continually shifting in front of each other; where the infantry was, the artillery arrives; where the artillery was, the cavalry comes rushing in; battalions are mere wisps of smoke. There was something there, but go and look and it's gone; clearings move around; dark folds advance and retreat; a sort of sepulchral wind pushes, sucks back, swells and disperses these tragic multitudes. What is a mêlée? An oscillation. The immobility of a mathematical plan expresses a minute, not a day. To paint a battle, we need those powerful painters whose brushes are dipped in chaos; Rembrandt would be better than Van der Meulen.[4] Van der Meulen was accurate at midday but lies at three o'clock. Geometry deceives; only the hurricane is true. This is what gives Folard the right to contradict Polybius.[5] We might add that there is always a certain moment when the battle degenerates into combat, individualizes itself, and dissolves into innumerable detailed events that, to borrow the phrase from Napoléon himself, "belong to the biography of the regiments rather than to the history of the army." In which case, the historian obviously has the right to simplify. He can only seize the main outlines of the struggle, and it is not given to any narrator, no matter how conscientious they may be, to absolutely fix the form of this horrible cloud we know as a battle.

This, which is true of all great armed clashes, is particularly applicable to Waterloo.

Yet that afternoon, at a certain moment, the battle took a definite shape.

## VI. Four O'clock in the Afternoon

By about four o'clock, the situation for the English army was serious. The prince of Orange commanded the center, Hill the right wing, Picton the left wing. The prince of Orange, frantic and fearless, yelled out to the Belgian Dutch: "Nassau! Brunswick! Never retreat!" Hill, exhausted, was falling back on Wellington. Picton was dead, for the very same instant that the English had taken the colors of the 105th regiment of the line from the French, the French had killed General Picton on the English side with a bullet through the head. The battle, for Wellington, had two pivotal points, Hougoumont and La Haie-Sainte; Hougoumont was still holding steady, but was in flames; La Haie-Sainte was taken. Of the German battalion defending it, only forty-two men survived; all the officers, minus five, were dead or taken. Three thousand combatants had been massacred in this barn. A sergeant of the English Guards, the foremost boxer of England, reputed by his comrades to be invulnerable, had been killed there by a little French drummer. Baring had been dislodged, Alten put to the sword. Several colors had been lost, one belonging to Alten's division, and one from the Lunebourg battalion, carried by a prince of the Deux-Ponts family. The Scottish Greys no longer existed; Ponsonby's heavy dragoons had been cut to pieces. That valiant cavalry had folded under Bro's lancers and Travers's cuirassiers; of their twelve hundred horses, six hundred remained; of the three lieutenant colonels, two were on the ground, Hamilton was wounded, Mater killed. Ponsonby had fallen, stabbed seven times with a lance. Gordon was dead, Marsh was dead. Two divisions, the fifth and the sixth, were wiped out.

With Hougoumont shaken, La Haie-Sainte taken, all that remained was one knot, the center. That particular knot still held. Wellington reinforced it. He called in Hill, who was at Merbe-Braine, he called in Chassé, who was in Braine-l'Alleud.

The center of the English army, somewhat concave, very dense and very compact, held a strong position. It occupied the plateau of Mont-Saint-Jean, with the village behind it and the slope in front of it, which at the time was pretty steep. It had its back to a strong stone house, which in those days was a property of the estate of Nivelles and marked the intersection of the roads, a sixteenth-century pile so robust that the cannonballs ricocheted off it without making a dent. All around the plateau the English had cut through the hedges here and there, made gun ports in the hawthorns, stuck the muzzle of a cannon between two branches, crenellated the bushes. Their artillery was waiting in ambush under the shrubbery. This Punic labor, incontestably authorized by war, which allows for traps, was so well performed that Haxo, sent by the emperor at nine o'clock in the morning to reconnoiter the enemy batteries, did not notice a thing and returned to tell Napoléon that there was no obstacle apart from the two barricades barring the roads from Nivelles and Genappe. It was that time of year when the harvest is high; on the clearing of the plateau, a battalion of the Kempt brigade, the 95th, armed with rifles, was lying hidden in the tall wheat.

Thus assured and shored up, the center of the Anglo-Dutch army was in a good spot.

The danger of the position was the forest of Soignes, then right alongside the battlefield and cut off by the ponds of Groenendael and Boitsfort. The only way an army could retreat into it would be by breaking up; the regiments would have been immediately disbanded. The artillery would have got lost in the swamp. Retreat, in the opinion of several military professionals—an opinion contested by others, it is true—would have meant a stampede.

Wellington added to the center one of Chassé's brigades, taken from the right wing, and one of Wincke's brigades, taken from the left wing, plus the Clinton division. To his English, to Halkett's regiments, to Mitchell's brigade, to Maitland's guards, he gave as supports and buttresses the infantry of Brunswick, the Nassau contingent, Kielmansegge's Hanoverians and Ompteda's Germans. That gave him twenty-six battalions at hand. "The right wing," as Charras says,[1] "was pulled back behind the center." An enormous battery was hidden by sacks of dirt at the spot that is today known as the Waterloo Museum. On top of this, Wellington had Somerset's Horse Guards, fourteen hundred horses, in a dip in the terrain. This was the other half of the English cavalry, so justly celebrated. Ponsonby wiped out, Somerset remained.

The battery, which would almost have been a redoubt had it been finished, was ranged behind a very low garden wall, hastily covered in sandbags, and a large bank of earth. The work was not yet completed; there had been no time to stockade it.

Wellington, anxious but impassive, sat on his horse and stayed there the whole day in the same position, a bit farther along from an old Mont-Saint-Jean mill, which still exists, under an elm that an Englishman, an enthusiastic vandal, has since bought for two hundred francs, sawn up, and carted away. Wellington sat there, icily heroic. Cannon shot rained down. His aide-de-camp, Gordon, had just fallen by his side. Lord Hill, pointing a bursting shell out to him, said: "Milord, what are your instructions and what orders do you leave us if you get yourself killed?" "To do as I do," replied Wellington. To Clinton, he said laconically: "Hold this spot to the last man." The day was clearly going badly. Wellington shouted to his old companions of Talavera, Vitoria, and Salamanca:[2] "Boys! Don't even think of giving way! Think of old England!"

At around four o'clock, the English line moved backward. Suddenly all you could see on the crest of the plateau was the artillery and the skirmishers, the rest had disappeared; the regiments, driven back by the French shells and musket balls, fell back into the valley still crossed today by the access road to the Mont-Saint-Jean farm. A retrograde movement took place, the battlefront of the English slipped away, Wellington backed off. "Beginning of retreat!" shouted Napoléon.

## VII. Napoléon in a Good Mood

Though ill and uncomfortable in the saddle due to a painful medical condition, the emperor had never been in such a good mood as he was that day. Since morning, he had smiled in all his impenetrability. On June 18, 1815, that deep soul, masked in marble, shone blindly. The man who had been so forlorn at Austerlitz was as gay as a lark at Waterloo. The greatest of the chosen ones misread things in this way. Our joys are shadows. The ultimate smile is God's alone.

*Ridet Caesar, Pompeius flebit,*[1] as the legionnaires of the Fulminatrix legion used to say. Pompey this time did not have to weep, but it is certain that Caesar laughed.

Since the previous night, at one in the morning, Napoléon had been galloping around with Bertrand[2] on horseback in the storm and the rain, exploring the hills around Rossomme, satisfied to see the long line of English fires lighting up the whole horizon from Frischemont to Braine-l'Alleud. It had seemed to him that destiny, with whom he had made a date on this field of Waterloo, was punctual; he had pulled up his horse and had remained sitting motionless for a few minutes, watching the lightning, listening to the thunder, and this fatalist had been heard to throw these mysterious words into the darkness: "We are agreed." Napoléon was wrong. They were no longer agreed.

He had not taken a minute's sleep, every moment of that night had been marked for him by joy. He had passed all along the entire line of the Grand Guards, stopping here and there to talk to the sentinels. At two-thirty, near the Hougoumont wood, he had heard the tread of a column on the move; for a moment he thought Wellington was falling back. He had said to Bertrand: "That's the English rear guard getting ready to decamp. I'll make prisoners out of the six thousand Englishmen who have just arrived in Ostend." He chatted volubly; he had recovered the excitement of the disembarkation of March 1, when he pointed out to the grand maréchal the enthusiastic peasants of the Juan Gulf, shouting: "There you go, Bertrand, here's some reinforcements, already!" The night of June 17–18, he poked fun at Wellington. "That little British git needs to be taught a lesson," said Napoléon. The rain fell harder, it bucketed down; thunder rolled as the emperor spoke.

At three-thirty in the morning, he had shed one illusion; the officers sent out as reconnaissance had told him that the enemy was not making a single move. No one was stirring; not one bivouac fire had been put out. The English army was sleeping. The silence was profound on the ground; the only sound was coming from the sky. At four o'clock, a peasant had been brought to him by the scouts; this peasant had served as a guide for an English cavalry brigade, probably Vivian's brigade, which was about to take up position in the village of Ohain, on the far left. At five o'clock, two Belgian deserters reported to him that they had just left their regiment and that the English army was expecting a battle. "Good for them!" Napoléon had cried. "I'd rather roll over them than drive them back."

In the morning, on the bank that forms a corner with the road at Planchenoit, he had stepped down into the mud; he had a kitchen table and a peasant's chair brought to him from the Rossomme farm, had sat down, with a bale of straw for a rug, and had spread out on the table the map of the battlefield, saying to Soult: "Not a bad chessboard!"

As a result of all the rain in the night, the convoys of supply wagons got bogged down in the churned-up roads and had not been able to make it there by morning; the soldiers had not slept, were soaked to the bone, and had not eaten; this had not stopped Napoléon from shouting gleefully to Ney: "We've got ninety chances in a hundred. Nine out of ten." At eight o'clock, the emperor was brought his breakfast. He had invited several generals. While they were eating, the story was told of how Wellington had been at a ball in Brussels the night before the last, at the home of the duchess of Richmond, and Soult,[3] roughneck man of war that he was, with the face of an archbishop, said: "The ball is today." The emperor had joked with Ney, who said: "Wellington would not be so silly as to wait for Your Majesty." That was the way he spoke. "He liked to tease," says Fleury de Chaboulon.[4] "His nature was basically cheerful," says Gourgaud.[5] "He was full of jokes, not so much witty as bizarre," says Benjamin Constant.[6] These jests of the giant are worth emphasizing. It was he who called his grenadiers *les grognards,* the whiners; he would pinch their ears, he would pull their mustaches. "All he ever did was play practical jokes on us"—so said one of them. During the mysterious trip from the isle of Elba to France,[7] on February 27, on the open seas, the French warship *Zéphir,* having encountered the brig *Inconstant,* on which Napoléon was hidden, and having asked for news of Napoléon from the *Inconstant,* the emperor, who was at the time still wearing the white cockade[8] on his hat and the amaranth strewn with bees[9] he had adopted on the isle of Elba, had grabbed the megaphone, chortling, and himself replied: "The emperor is doing well." Whoever can laugh like that is on good terms with events. Napoléon had several similar jolly outbursts over that Waterloo breakfast. After breakfast he collected his thoughts for a quarter of an hour; then two generals came and sat on the bale of hay, plume in hand, a sheet of paper each on their knees, and the emperor dictated the order of battle to them.

At nine o'clock, at the instant the French army, echeloned and set in motion in five columns, was deployed, the divisions in two lines, the artillery between the brigades, music at the head, belting out marches, with drumrolls and trumpet blasts, powerful, vast, jubilant, a sea of helmets, swords and bayonets all the way to the horizon, the emperor, much moved, cried out twice: "Magnificent! Magnificent!"

Between nine o'clock and half past ten, incredible as it seems, the whole army took up position and lined up in six rows, forming, to borrow an expression of the emperor's, "the figure of six Vs." A few moments after the formation of the battlefront, amid that profound silence that is the calm before the storm of a fray, seeing the three batteries of twelve-pounders file past, detached by his orders from the three corps of d'Erlon, Reille, and Lobau, and intended to begin the action by battering Mont-Saint-Jean at the intersection of the roads from Nivelles and Genappe, the emperor clapped Haxo on the shoulder and said to him: "There's twenty-four beauties for you, general."

Sure of the outcome, he smiled encouragement as he watched pass in front of him the company of sappers of the first corps, which he had designated to set up barricades at Mont-Saint-Jean once the village was won. All this serenity was marred only by a word of arrogant pity; when he saw, on his left, at a spot that is today the site of a great tomb, the admirable Scottish Greys massing with their superb horses, he said: "What a shame."

Then he hopped on his horse, rode out from Rossomme and chose his observation post, a small grassy knoll on the right of the road from Genappe to Brussels, which was his second station during the battle. The third station, the one from seven o'clock in the evening, between La Belle-Alliance and La Haie-Sainte, is frightening; still there today, it is a rather high mound behind which the Guards had massed on a reverse slope of the plain. Around this mound, cannonballs ricocheted over the paved roadway right up to Napoléon. As at Brienne, cannonballs and bullets whistled over his head. Almost at the very same spot where his horse's feet were, scarred balls, old saber blades, and warped projectiles eaten with rust have been collected. *Scabra rubigine.*[10] A few years back, a sixty-pound shell was disinterred, still loaded; its fuse had broken off flush with the bomb. It was at this last station that the emperor said to his guide, Lacoste, a frightened, hostile peasant tied to a hussar's saddle, turning round at every volley of shots and trying to hide behind him: "Idiot! This is shameful. You'll get yourself shot in the back." He who writes these lines himself found in the friable slope of the mound, by digging in the sand, the remains of the neck of a bomb decomposed by the oxide of forty-six years, along with some old bits of iron that snapped like elderberry twigs between his fingers.

As everybody knows, the varying undulations of the plains where the encounter between Napoléon and Wellington took place are no longer what they were on June 18, 1815. In taking from that deadly field what was needed to make a monument to it, they took away its contours, and history, aghast, no longer recognizes itself there. In order to glorify it, they disfigured it. When

Wellington saw Waterloo again, two years later, he cried: "They've changed my battlefield on me." Where today there is the great pyramid of earth surmounted by a lion, there was a ridge sloping down toward the Nivelles road in a negotiable ramp; but on the Genappe roadway side, this ridge was almost an escarpment. The elevation of the escarpment can still be measured today by the height of the two great burial mounds that hem in the Genappe-to-Brussels road; one of these, the English grave, is on the left; the other, the German grave, is on the right. There is no French grave. For France, the entire plain is a sepulchre. Thanks to the thousands and thousands of cartloads of dirt used in the knoll, which is one hundred and fifty feet high and five hundred feet in circumference, the plateau of Mont-Saint-Jean is today accessible by means of a gentle incline; on the day of battle, especially on the La Haie-Sainte side, it was tough going, steep and sheer. The slope there was so steep that the English cannon could not see the farm below them at the bottom of the valley that was the center of the action. On June 18, 1815, the runoff from the heavy rain accentuated the steepness further, the mire making the climb even harder; they not only struggled up but got stuck in the mud. All the way along the plateau ridge ran a sort of ditch that an observer could not possibly make out at any distance.

What was this ditch? We'll tell you. Braine-l'Alleud is a village in Belgium, Ohain is another. These villages, both hidden in the curves of the terrain, are joined by a path about one and a half leagues long that cuts across an undulating plain and often dips into and buries itself in among the hills like a furrow, which means that at various points the road becomes a ravine. In 1815, as now, the road cut across the ridge of the Mont-Saint-Jean plateau between the Genappe and Nivelles roads; but while today it is on a level with the plain, it was then a sunken road. They have taken away both its embankments for the knoll monument. This road was and still is a trench for most of its length; a trench sometimes twelve feet deep, whose too steep embankments would collapse here and there, especially in winter, in the rain. Accidents happened there. The road was so narrow at the entrance to Braine-l'Alleud that a traveler was crushed there by a wagon, as attested by a stone cross standing near the cemetery that gives the name of the dead man as *Monsieur Bernard Debrye, merchant of Brussels,* and the date of the accident as February 1637.* It was so deep along the Mont-Saint-Jean plateau that a peasant, Mathieu Nicaise, was flattened

*Here is the inscription:

> DOM
> CY. WAS CRUSHED
> THROUGH MISADVENTURE
> UNDER A CART
> MONSIEUR BERNARD
> DE BRYE MERCHANT
> AT BRUSSELS ON (illegible)
> FEBRUARY 1637.

there in 1783 by a landslide when the embankment collapsed, as is attested by another stone cross, the crown of which has disappeared in all the clearing, but whose overturned pedestal is still visible today on the grass-covered verge on the left side of the road between La Haie-Sainte and the Mont-Saint-Jean farm.

On the day of battle, this sunken road, which nothing gave away, bordering the Mont-Saint-Jean ridge, a ditch at the top of the escarpment, a rut hidden in the terrain, was invisible, that is, treacherous and terrible.

## VIII. THE EMPEROR PUTS A QUESTION TO LACOSTE, THE GUIDE

And so, on the morning of Waterloo, Napoléon was happy. He had reason to be; the battle plan he had designed, as we have seen, was, indeed, admirable.

Once the battle was under way, its extremely various episodes, the resistance of Hougoumont, the tenacity of La Haie-Sainte; Bauduin killed, Foy put out of action; the unexpected wall against which Soye's brigade was smashed; Guilleminot's fatal blunder in having neither explosives nor sacks of powder; the bogging down of the batteries; the fifteen guns without an escort toppled by Uxbridge along a sunken path; the underwhelming effect of the bombs falling on the English lines and burrowing into the rain-soaked ground, succeeding only in creating volcanoes of mud so that the hail of shot turned into spattering; the uselessness of Piré's performance at Braine-l'Alleud, all that cavalry, fifteen squadrons, virtually annihilated; the right wing of the English hardly turning a hair, the left wing barely grazed; Ney's strange misunderstanding that saw him massing—instead of echeloning—the four divisions of the first corps, causing men in rows twenty-seven deep and in fronts of two hundred to be delivered up to the hail of shot accordingly, the awful hole cut in these masses by the cannonballs, the attacking columns split up, the supporting battery suddenly uncovered along their flank, Bourgeois, Donzelot, and Durutte compromised, Quiot pushed back; Lieutenant Vieux, that Hercules who had sprung from the École Polytechnique, wounded at the very moment he was hoeing into the La Haie-Sainte gate with an ax under the plunging fire of the English barricade blocking the bend in the Genappe-Brussels road; Marcognet's division caught between infantry and cavalry, gunned down at point-blank range in the wheat by Best and Pack, cut down by Ponsonby, his battery of seven pieces pinned; the prince of Saxe-Weimar holding and keeping Frischemont and Smohain, despite the comte d'Erlon; the colors of the 105th taken, the colors of the 45th taken; this Prussian Black Hussar, brought in by the scouts of the flying column of three hundred chasseurs scouring the countryside between Wavre and Planchenoit and the disturbing things the prisoner had said; Grouchy's delay;[1] the fifteen hundred men killed in less than an hour in the orchard of Hougoumont, the eighteen hundred men mown down in even less time around La Haie-Sainte—all these storm-filled incidents, passing like battle clouds before Napoléon, had scarcely troubled his gaze and had not dimmed the certainty in that imperial face. Napoléon was used to staring hard at war; he never did the poignant sums of details, figure by figure; figures mattered little to him, as long as they amounted to this total: victory. If the beginnings went wrong, he did not get alarmed, for he believed himself master and possessor of the ends; he knew how to bide his time, supposing himself outside the equation, and he dealt with destiny as an equal. He seemed to say to fate: You wouldn't dare.

Half light, half shadow, Napoléon felt himself protected when things were going well and tolerated when they were going badly. He had on his side, or thought he did, a collusion, you might almost say a complicity, on the part of events, equivalent to antique invulnerability.

Yet when you have Beresina, Leipzig, and Fontainebleau[2] behind you, it seems you might not take Waterloo on trust. A mysterious frown becomes visible high overhead in the sky.

The moment Wellington fell back, Napoléon quivered. He suddenly saw the plateau of Mont-Saint-Jean laid bare and the front of the English army disappear. It rallied, but kept out of sight. The emperor half-rose in his stirrups. The lightning of victory flashed in his eyes.

Wellington driven back to the forest of Soignes and destroyed, that was the final overthrow of England by France; that was Crécy, Poitiers, Malplaquet, and Ramillies avenged. The man from Marengo was canceling out Agincourt.[3]

Musing on the terrible episode to come, the emperor then ran his field glasses one last time over every point of the battlefield. His guard, their weapons at their feet behind him, observed him from below with a sort of religious fervor, something close to worship. He was thinking: He was studying the hillsides, noting the slopes, scrutinizing the clumps of trees, the square patch of rye, the track; he seemed to be counting every bush. He looked for some time at the English barricades on both roadways, two broad abatis of felled trees, the one on the Genappe road above La Haie-Sainte equipped with two cannons, the only ones in the whole of the English artillery trained on the battlefield, and the one on the Nivelles road where the Dutch bayonets of Chassé's brigade glinted. He noticed, close by this barricade, the old white chapel of Saint-Nicolas, which stands next to the track to Braine-l'Alleud. He leaned over and spoke in a half whisper to Lacoste, the guide. The guide shook his head to say no, probably treacherously.

The emperor straightened up and gathered himself together.

Wellington had backed off. All that remained was to finish off this retreat with a crushing defeat.

Napoléon suddenly turned round and sent off a courier at full gallop to Paris to announce that the battle was won.

Napoléon was one of those geniuses that release thunder.

He had just found his thunderbolt.

He gave the order to Milhaud's cuirassiers to take the plateau of Mont-Saint-Jean.


## IX. THE UNEXPECTED

They were three thousand five hundred strong. They made a front half a mile long. They were giant men on colossal horses. They were twenty-six squadrons; and they had behind them, to lend them support, the division of Lefebvre-Desnouettes, the one hundred and six elite gendarmes, the chasseurs of the Guard, eleven hundred and ninety-seven men, and the lancers of the Guard, eight hundred and eighty lances. They wore plumeless helmets and cuirasses of beaten iron, with cavalry pistols in their holsters and long sabers. In the morning, the whole army had been filled with admiration for them when, at nine o'clock, with bugles blaring, all the bands playing "Veillons au salut de l'empire"—"Let's see to the salvation of the Empire"—they had come in a dense column, one of their batteries at their flank, the other at their center, to fan out over two rows between the Genappe road and Frischemont, and take up their battle position in this powerful second line, so wisely drawn up by Napoléon, which, with Kellermann's cuirassiers at its left end and Milhaud's cuirassiers at its right, had, so to speak, two wings of iron.

The aide-de-camp, Bernard, delivered the emperor's order to them. Ney drew his sword and placed himself at the helm. The enormous squadrons began to move.

Then a formidable spectacle was seen.

This whole cavalry, sabers raised, standards and trumpets to the wind, formed into a column by division, descended in unison and as one, with the precision of a bronze battering ram opening a breach, the hill of La Belle-Alliance, sank into the dreadful depths where so many men had already fallen, vanished there in the smoke, then, emerging from the shadows, reappeared on the other side of the valley of shadow, still compact and serried, rising at full trot, through the cloud of gunshot bursting overhead, up the awful mud slope of the Mont-Saint-Jean plateau. They rose, grave, menacing, imperturbable; in the lulls in the shooting and artillery fire, you could hear the colossal sound of shuffling. Being two divisions, they were in two columns; Wathier's division had the right, Delord's the left. From a distance they looked like two immense steel snakes stretching out toward the crest of the plateau. They passed through the battle like a miracle.

Nothing like it had been seen since the taking of the great redoubt of the Moskowa[1] by the heavy cavalry; Murat was missing,[2] but Ney had popped up again. It seemed as though the mass had become a monster with only one soul. Each squadron undulated and swelled like the rings of a polyp. They could be seen through a vast cloud of thick smoke, torn here and there. A jumble of helmets, shouting, sabers, the tumultuous bouncing of horses' rumps among the cannon and the fanfare, a disciplined and terrible commotion; over all, the cuirasses, like the scales over a hydra.

These tales seem to belong to another age. Something like this vision appeared no doubt in the old Orphic sagas[3] telling of centaurs, antique hippanthropes, those titans with human faces and equine chests who scaled Olympus gamboling, horrible creatures, invulnerable, sublime; gods and beasts, both.

In a bizarre coincidence of numbers, twenty-six battalions were to be joined by these twenty-six squadrons. Behind the crest of the plateau, under cover of the masked battery, the English infantry formed into thirteen squares, two battalions to a square, and in two lines, seven in the first, six in the second, rifle butts at the shoulder, taking aim at whatever happened along, waiting, calm, mute, unmoving. They could not see the cuirassiers and the cuirassiers could not see them. They listened to the tide of men rising. They heard the growing noise of three thousand horses, the alternating and symmetrical knocking of their shod hooves at full trot, the rattling of the cuirasses, the clang of sabers, and a sort of great fierce murmur. There was a fearful silence, then suddenly, a long line of raised arms brandishing sabers appeared above the crest, along with helmets and trumpets and standards and three thousand heads with gray mustaches, all crying: "Long live the emperor!" The entire cavalry poured out onto the plateau and it was like the start of an earthquake.

All of a sudden, tragically, to the left of the English, to our right, the head of the column of cuirassiers reared up with a frightening clamor. Having reached the culminating point of the crest, frantic, full of fury and hell-bent on exterminating the squares and cannons, the cuirassiers had just seen a ditch, a pit, between them and the English. It was the sunken road of Ohain.

The moment was horrifying. There was the ravine, unexpected, yawning, right at the horses' hooves, two fathoms deep between its twin banks. The second row pushed the first in and the third pushed the second; the horses reared, threw themselves backward, fell on their rumps, slid with their four feet in the air, knocking off and crushing their riders, no way of turning back. The entire column was now no more than a projectile, the force gathered to crush the English crushed the French, the inexorable ravine could not surrender until it was filled, riders and horses rolled into it pell-mell, grinding each other, forming one flesh in this gulf, and when the pit was full of men still alive, they marched over them and the remainder followed suit. Almost a third of Dubois's brigade toppled into this abyss.

This was the beginning of the end of the battle.

A local tradition, obviously exaggerated, has it that two thousand horses and fifteen hundred men were buried in the sunken road of Ohain. This figure probably includes all the other corpses that were thrown into the ravine the day after the fighting.

We might note in passing that it was the same brigade, Dubois's brigade, so fatally tested, that had charged separately an hour earlier and taken the colors of the Lunebourg battalion.

Napoléon, before ordering this charge of Milhaud's cuirassiers, had carefully examined the terrain, but had not been able to see the sunken road, which did not create so much as a wrinkle on the surface of the plateau. Warned, however, and put on his guard by the little white chapel that marks its junction with the Nivelles road, he had put a question to Lacoste, the guide, probably about the possibility of any obstacle. The guide had replied in the negative. You might go so far as to say that catastrophe came to Napoléon from that shake of a peasant's head.

Further bad luck was to ensue. Could Napoléon possibly have won the battle? We say no. Why? Because of Wellington? Because of Blücher? No. Because of God. Bonaparte as the victor at Waterloo—this was no longer in the law of the nineteenth century. A different series of feats was gearing up, in which there was no more room for Napoléon. The bad grace of events had announced itself long before. It was high time this mighty man fell.

The excessive weight of this man in human destiny upset the balance. This one individual alone weighed more than the population of the world. This plethora of all human vitality concentrated in a single head, the world going to the brain of one man, would be mortal to civilization if it were to go on. The moment had come for the incorruptible supreme equity to sort things out. Most likely the principles and elements, on which the regular movements in both the moral order and the material order depend, were beginning to groan. The fuming blood, the overflowing cemeteries, the mothers in tears—these are powerful pleas for the defense. When the earth is surfeited, there are mysterious wailings from the shadows that the abyss picks up.

Napoléon had been impeached before the Infinite, and his fall had been decreed. He was embarrassing God.

Waterloo is not a battle; it is a shift in the world's front.

## X. THE PLATEAU OF MONT-SAINT-JEAN

At the same time as the ravine, the artillery showed itself.

Sixty cannon and the thirteen squares blasted the cuirassiers at point-blank range. The intrepid general Delord gave the military salute to the English battery.

The whole of the English mobile artillery slammed into the squares at a gallop. The cuirassiers did not have time to pause for breath. The disaster of the sunken road had decimated, but not discouraged, them. They were the kind of men who, diminished in number, grew in heart.

Wathier's column alone had been cobbled by the disaster; Delord's column, which Ney had sent veering off to the left as though he had divined the trap, had arrived intact.

The cuirassiers hurled themselves at the English squares. Galloping furiously, reins let loose and flying, sabers in their teeth, pistols in their fists—such was the assault. There are moments in battle when the soul hardens the man to the point of turning a soldier into a statue and when all that flesh converts to granite. The English battalions, wildly beset, did not budge. So it was truly frightening.

All sides of the English squares were attacked at once. A frenetic swirl enveloped them. That cold-blooded infantry remained impassive. The first row, on their knees, received the cuirassiers on the ends of their bayonets, the second row gunned them down; behind the second row the cannoneers loaded their pieces, the front of the square opened up, made way for an eruption of firepower and then closed again. The cuirassiers responded by crushing them. Their great horses reared up, leaped over the ranks, jumped over the bayonets, and fell, gigantic, in the middle of those four living walls. The cannonballs made holes in the cuirassiers. The cuirassiers made breaches in the squares. Files of men disappeared, ground to a pulp underneath the horses. The bayonets sank into the guts of those centaurs. Creating, perhaps, the most monstrous wounds perhaps ever seen, anywhere. The squares, eaten into by the frenzied cavalry, dwindled without flinching. Scattering shot without letup, they exploded amid their assailants. The combat was a monstrous sight. The squares were no longer battalions, they were craters; the cuirassiers were no longer a cavalry, they were a shocking storm. Each square was a volcano attacked by a swarming cloud; lava did battle with lightning.

The square on the far right, which was the most exposed of all, being out in the open, was almost annihilated in the first few clashes. It was made up of the 75th regiment of Highlanders. The bagpipe player in the center, paying absolutely no attention while everyone was busy exterminating each other all around him, cast down his melancholy eyes full of the reflection of forests and lakes and played Highland ditties, sitting on a drum with his bagpipes under his arm. Those Scots died thinking of Ben Lothian as the Greeks died remembering Argos. A cuirassier's saber, smiting the bagpipe and the arm that held it, stopped the song by killing the player.

Relatively few in number, reduced by the disaster of the ravine, the cuirassiers had the whole English army arrayed against them there, but they were everywhere at once, each man suddenly finding the strength of ten. Meanwhile, some of the Hanoverian battalions buckled. Wellington noticed and remembered his cavalry. If Napoléon, even at that moment, had thought of his infantry, he would have won the battle. This forgetfulness was his great, his fatal mistake.

All of a sudden the attacking cuirassiers realized they were being attacked in turn. The English cavalry were upon them. In front of them, the squares; behind them, Somerset. Somerset meant the fourteen hundred dragoons. Somerset had Dornberg on his right, with the German light horse and, on his left, Trip, with the Belgian carabiniers; the cuirassiers, attacked head and flank, front and rear, by the infantry and the cavalry, had to square up on all sides. What did they care? They were a whirlwind. Their bravery was beyond words.

They had behind them the relentlessly booming battery, to boot. They had to have, for these men to be wounded in the back. One of their cuirasses, with a bullet hole through the left shoulder plate, is in the collection of the so-called Waterloo Museum. For such Frenchmen, nothing less than such Englishmen would do.

It was no longer a mêlée, it was a squall, a rampage, a dizzying fit of courageous hearts and souls, a hurricane of swords flashing. In an instant the fourteen hundred dragoons were down to no more than eight hundred; Fuller, their lieutenant colonel, fell, dead. Ney rushed in with the lancers and chasseurs of Lefebvre-Desnouettes. The plateau of Mont-Saint-Jean was taken, taken back, taken again. The cuirassiers left the cavalry to return to the infantry or, more accurately, all this formidable throng wrestled with each other without letting go their hold. The squares were still holding. There were twelve attacks. Ney had four horses killed under him. Half of the cuirassiers stayed on the plateau. The struggle lasted two hours.

The English army was profoundly shaken. There is no doubt that, if the cuirassiers hadn't been crippled in their first clash by the disaster of the sunken road, they would have overwhelmed the center and carried the victory. This extraordinary cavalry petrified Clinton, who had seen Talavera and Badajoz. Wellington, three-quarters vanquished, was struck with heroic admiration. He said in a half whisper: "Splendid!"

The cuirassiers annihilated seven out of thirteen squares, took or spiked sixty cannon pieces, and captured six colors from the English regiments, which three cuirassiers and three chasseurs of the Guard brought to the emperor out in front of the farm at La Belle-Alliance.

Wellington's situation had deteriorated. This strange battle was like a duel between two determined wounded men who, both fighting and fending off all the while, lose all their blood. Which of the two would drop first?

The battle of the plateau raged on.

How far did the cuirassiers get? No one can really say. What is certain is that, the day after the battle, a cuirassier and his horse were found dead in the framework of the machine for weighing vehicles at Mont-Saint-Jean, at the very point where the four roads from Nivelles, Genappe, La Hulpe, and Brussels come together and cut across each other. This cavalier had got through the English lines. One of the men who carted away the body still lives in Mont-Saint-Jean. His name is Dehaze. He was eighteen years old at the time.

Wellington felt himself buckling. The end was near.

The cuirassiers had not succeeded in the sense that the center was not overrun. Since everyone had the plateau, no one had it and, in a word, it remained for the greater part to the English. Wellington had the village and the crowning plain; Ney only had the ridge and the slope. On both sides they seemed rooted to this deathly soil.

But the English looked irremediably weakened. The hemorrhage of that army was horrible. Kempt, on the left wing, called for reinforcements. "There aren't any," Wellington replied. "Let him get himself killed!" Almost at the same instant, in an odd coincidence that shows how exhausted both armies were, Ney asked Napoléon for infantry and Napoléon shouted: "Infantry! Where does he want me to get them from? Would he like me to pull them out of a hat?"

Yet the English army was the sicker. The furious onslaughts of these great squadrons with their iron cuirasses and chests of steel had ground up the infantry. A few men around a flag marked the place of one regiment, another battalion was now commanded only by some lieutenant's captain; Alten's division, already so badly battered at La Haie-Sainte, was almost destroyed; the intrepid Belgians of Van Kluze's brigade were strewn over the fields of rye all along the Nivelles road; there were almost none left of the Dutch grenadiers who joined our ranks in Spain in 1811 to fight against Wellington and who rallied to the English in 1815 in their fight against Napoléon. The loss among officers was considerable. Lord Uxbridge, who the next day buried his leg, had a fractured knee. On the side of the French, in this battle of the cuirassiers, Delord, L'Héritier, Colbert, Dnop, Travers, and Blancard were out of action, but on the side of the English, Alten was wounded, Barne was wounded, Delancey was killed, Van Meeren was killed, Ompteda was killed, Wellington's entire staff was decimated, and England came off worse in this bloody juggling act. The 2nd regiment of foot guards had lost five lieutenant colonels, four captains, and three ensigns; the 1st battalion of the 30th infantry had lost twenty-four officers and one hundred and twelve soldiers; the 79th Highlanders had twenty-four officers wounded, eighteen officers dead, and four hundred and fifty soldiers killed. Cumberland's Hanoverian Hussars, an entire regiment, led by Colonel Hacke, who would later be court-martialed and cashiered, had turned tail at the sight of the mêlée and were fleeing through the forest of Soignes, sowing panic all the way to Brussels. Carts, gun carriages, supply and baggage wagons, wagons full of the wounded, seeing the French gaining ground and closing in on the forest, rushed there; the Dutch, cut down by the French cavalry, gave the alarm: Get out now! From Vert-Coucou right up to Groenendael, over a length of nearly six miles in the direction of Brussels, the road was jammed with people running for their lives, according to witnesses still alive today. The panic was so great that it reached the prince de Condé at Malines and Louis XVIII at Ghent.[1] With the exception of the paltry reserve echeloned behind the ambulance station set up in the Mont-Saint-Jean farm and the brigades of Vivian and Vandeleur that flanked the left wing, Wellington had run out of cavalry. A number of batteries were scattered around unhorsed. These facts have been admitted by Siborne; and Pringle, exaggerating the disaster, even goes so far as to say that the Anglo-Dutch army was reduced to thirty-four thousand men. The Iron Duke remained calm, but his lips were white. The Austrian commissary, Vincent, the Spanish commissary, Alava, who watched the battle with the English staff, thought the duke was finished. At five o'clock, Wellington pulled out his watch and was heard to murmur these somber words: "Blücher, or night!"

It was at about that point that a distant line of bayonets flashed on the heights around Frischemont.

This was the turning point in this colossal tragedy.

## XI. BAD GUIDE FOR NAPOLÉON, GOOD GUIDE FOR BÜLOW

We all know about Napoléon's heartbreaking mistake; how Grouchy was expected, while Blücher turned up—death instead of life.

Destiny makes such about-faces. You were hoping to sit on the world's throne and instead you spy Saint Helena looming.

If the little shepherd who served as a guide to Bülow, Blücher's lieutenant, had advised him to come out of the forest above Frischemont rather than below Planchenoit, the shape of the nineteenth century would perhaps have been different. Napoléon would have won the battle of Waterloo. By any other road than below Planchenoit, the Prussian army would have ended up at a ravine the artillery could not have crossed and Bülow would not have got there.

Just an hour's delay, as the Prussian general Müffling said, and Blücher would not have found Wellington standing; "the battle would have been lost."

It was high time, as we have seen, that Blücher turned up. He had been delayed for a considerable while. He had bivouacked at Dion-le-Mont and set out at dawn. But the roads were inaccessible and his divisions got stuck in the mud. The cannons were bogged right up to their hubs. On top of this, they had to cross the Dyle over the narrow bridge at Wavre; the road leading to the bridge had been set on fire by the French, and the ammunition caissons and artillery wagons, not being able to pass between two rows of burning houses, had had to wait for the fire to be put out. It was midday before Bülow's advance guard could get even as far as Chapelle-Saint-Lambert.

Had the action begun two hours earlier, it would have been over by four, and Blücher would have fallen in the battle won by Napoléon. Such are the immense strokes of luck, good or bad, that are calibrated by an infinity that escapes us.

As early as midday, the emperor was the first, with his telescope, to notice something on the horizon that caught his attention. He had said: "I see a cloud over there that looks to me like troops." Then he had asked the duc de Dalmatia:[1] "Soult, what do you see over toward Chapelle-Saint-Lambert?" The maréchal, training his field glasses that way, had answered: "Four or five thousand men, sire. Obviously it's Grouchy." Yet they remained motionless in the mist. The glasses of the whole staff studied the "cloud" signaled by the emperor. Some said: "They're columns taking a break." Most said: "Those are trees." The truth is that the cloud did not stir. The emperor sent Domon's division of light horse off to reconnoiter that dark spot.

Bülow had not, in fact, moved. His vanguard was very weak and could do nothing. He had to wait for the bulk of his army corps and he had been given the order to mass his forces before entering into battle; but at five o'clock, seeing the peril Wellington was in, Blücher ordered Bülow to attack and said this remarkable thing: "We must give the English army time to come up for air."

A little later, the divisions of Losthin, Hiller, Hacke, and Ryssel fanned out in front of Lobau's corps, the cavalry of Prince William of Prussia came out of the Paris wood, Planchenoit was in flames, and the Prussian cannonballs began to rain down as far as the rows of the reserve guard behind Napoléon.

## XII. The Guard

We know the rest: the irruption of a third army, the disintegration of the battle, eighty-six fire-breathing maws suddenly thundering; Pirch the First surging forward with Bülow, Zieten's cavalry led by Blücher in person, the French driven back, Marcognet swept off the Ohain plateau, Durutte dislodged from Papelotte, Donzelot and Quiot beating a retreat, Lobau sideswiped; a new battle gearing up as night fell over the dismantled regiments, the whole English line taking the offensive once again and driven forward, the gigantic hole made in the French army, the hail of English bullets and the hail of Prussian bullets lending each other support; the extermination, disaster along the front, disaster along the flank, the Guard falling into line under this horrifying collapse.

As though they sensed they were about to die, the Guards cried out: "Long live the emperor!" History has nothing more moving than this death rattle bursting out into acclamation.

The sky had been covered the whole day. Suddenly, at that very moment—it was eight o'clock at night—the clouds on the horizon parted and through the elms on the Nivelles road the great sinister redness of the setting sun streamed in. At Austerlitz, the sun had been rising.

Each battalion of the Guard, for this final scene, was commanded by a general. Friant, Michel, Roguet, Harlet, Mallet, Poret de Morvan, were there. When the high black bearskin hats of the grenadiers, decorated with the wide eagle plate, emerged from the fog of war, symmetrical, aligned, tranquil, superb, the enemy felt respect for France; it felt as if they were watching twenty Victories entering the battlefield, wings spread, and those who were victors, considering themselves vanquished, shrank back; but Wellington shouted: "On your feet, Guards, and aim straight!" The red regiment of the English Guards, lying behind the hedges, rose, a cloud of canister shot riddled the tricolor flag fluttering around our eagles, everyone lunged forward, and the final carnage began. The Imperial Guard could feel the army slipping away around them in the gloom and the vast shock of the rout; they heard the "Every man for himself!" that had replaced the "Long live the emperor!" and, despite all the men fleeing behind them, they continued to advance, more and more of them mauled and dying at every step they took. Not one of them hesitated or weakened. Every soldier in the troop was as much a hero as the general. Not one man baulked at the suicide.

Ney, in despair, grand with all the arrogance of acceptance of death, offered himself up to any and all blows in this torment. His fifth horse was killed under him there. Streaming with sweat, eyes aflame, foaming at the mouth, uniform unbuttoned, one of his epaulets half ripped off by the saber slash of a horse guardsman, his great eagle plate dented by a bullet, bleeding, covered in mud, magnificent, a broken sword in hand, he said: "Come and see how a maréchal of France dies on the field of battle!" In vain, for he did not die. He was crazed and filled with outrage. He hurled this question at Drouet d'Erlon: "Aren't you going to get yourself killed, then, eh?" He shouted in the middle of all this artillery fire that was mashing a cluster of men: "Isn't there anything for me, then? Oh, I'd love all those English bullets straight in the guts!" You were reserved for French bullets, poor man!

## XIII. THE CATASTROPHE

The rout behind the Guard was awful.

The army suddenly caved in on all sides at once—Hougoumont, La Haie-Sainte, Papelotte, Planchenoit. The cry "Treason!" was followed by the cry

"Every man for himself!" A disintegrating army is a thaw. Everything buckles, splinters, cracks, floats, rolls, tumbles down, crashes around, darts, rushes headlong. The disarray is unbelievable. Ney borrows a horse, hops up, and, without a hat, without a cravat, without a sword, plants himself sideways across the Brussels road, stopping both the English and the French at once. He tries to retain the army, he calls them back, he insults them, he dogs the rout. He is overwhelmed. The soldiers flee from him crying: "Long live Maréchal Ney!" Two of Durutte's regiments come and go, bewildered and as though tossed between the sabers of the Uhlans[1] and the fusillade of the brigades of Kempt, Best, Pack, and Rylandt. A rout is the worst kind of mêlée; friends kill each other in their bid to get away, squadrons and battalions smash and send each other flying, sending up a sea foam of battle. Lobau at one end and Reille at the other are rolled in the torrent. In vain Napoléon builds ramparts with what remains of the Guard; in vain he expends his reserve squadron in a last-ditch effort. Quiot shrinks back before Vivian, Kellermann before Vandeleur, Lobau before Bülow, Morand before Pirch, Domon and Subervic before Prince William of Prussia. Guyot, who led the charge of the emperor's squadrons, falls under the feet of the English dragoons. Napoléon gallops all the way along the rows of fugitives, haranguing them, pressuring them, threatening them, imploring. All those mouths that only that morning were shouting "Long live the emperor" are hanging open now; he is barely acknowledged. The Prussian cavalry, freshly arrived, darts in, flies, hacks, lops, kills, exterminates. Yoked teams hurtle off, the cannoneers take to their heels; the soldiers belonging to the train unhitch the ammunition caissons and take their horses to escape; overturned wagons, their four wheels in the air, block the way and are accessories to massacre. People are crushed to death, trampled, others walk over the dead and over the living. Arms are lost. A dizzying flood of men pours onto the roads, paths, bridges, plains, hills, valleys, woods, which are choked with this deluge of forty thousand men fleeing for their lives. Shrieks, despair, sacks and fusils thrown into the rye, paths hacked out with swords, no more comrades in arms, no more officers, no more generals, just unspeakable horror. Zieten comfortably hacking through France. Lions turned to deer. That is what the flight was like.

At Genappe, people tried to turn back, to form a united front, to create a roadblock. Lobau rallied three hundred men. They barricaded the entry to the village; but at the first volley of grapeshot from the Prussians, everyone took to their heels again and Lobau was taken. You can still see the mark left by the volley of shot today on the old gable of a brick hovel on the right-hand side of the road, a few minutes before you enter Genappe. The Prussians charged into Genappe, furious no doubt at having so little opportunity to play the conquerors. The pursuit was monstrous. Blücher gave the order for extermination. Roguet had set a grim example in threatening to kill any French grenadier who brought him a Prussian prisoner. Blücher outdid Roguet. The general of the Young Guard, Duhesme, nabbed at the door of an inn in Genappe, handed over his sword to a hussar of Death, who took the sword and killed the prisoner. Victory was completed by the assassination of the vanquished. Let us punish, since we are history: Old Blücher disgraced himself. The ferocity took the disaster to dizzying limits. The desperate rout passed through Genappe, passed through Quatre-Bras, passed through Gosselies, passed through Frasnes, passed through Charleroi, passed through Thuin, and stopped only at the border. Alas! Who was it that was fleeing so desperately? The Grande Armée.[2]

Was this craziness, this terror, this collapse in a heap, of the greatest bravery that has ever confounded history, without cause? No. The shadow of an enormous right hand looms over Waterloo. It is the day of destiny. The might beyond man made that day. Hence the heads bowed in horror; hence all those great souls yielding up their swords. Those who had conquered Europe fell to the ground, mown down, with nothing more to say or do, sensing a terrible presence in the shadows. *Hoc erat in fatis.*[3] That day, the perspective of the human race shifted. Waterloo is the event the nineteenth century hinges on. The disappearance of the great man was necessary to the coming of the great century. Someone whom you do not answer back saw to it. The panic of those heroes can be explained. In the battle of Waterloo, there was more than a cloud, there was a meteor. God passed.

As night fell, in a field near Genappe, Bernard and Bertrand seized by the lapels of his redingote and stopped a haggard, pensive, sinister man who, dragged that far by the current of the rout, had just dismounted, slipped his horse's reins under his arm, and, wild-eyed, turned back alone to Waterloo. It was Napoléon still trying to make headway, immense somnambulist of this shattered dream.

## XIV. THE LAST SQUARE

A few squares of the Guard, immobile in the streaming of the rout like rocks in running water, held till nightfall. When night came on, and death with it, they waited for that double darkness and let themselves be enveloped by it, unshakable. Each regiment, cut off from the others and with no further communication with the army that had entirely disintegrated, died in its own manner. They had taken up position to fight the final fight, some on the heights of Rossomme, others on the plain of Mont-Saint-Jean. There, abandoned, vanquished, terrible, the solemn squares stood dying tremendously. Ulm, Wagram, Jena, Friedland,[1] died with them.

At dusk, around nine in the evening, at the bottom of the plateau of Mont-Saint-Jean, one square remained. In this deathly valley, at the foot of the slope the cuirassiers had scaled, now flooded by the masses of the English, under the converging fire of the artillery of the victorious enemy, under a frightening rain of projectiles, this square fought on. It was commanded by a little-known officer named Cambronne.[2] At each discharge, the square diminished but riposted. It met grapeshot with gunfire, constantly contracting its four walls. In the distance the fugitives, stopping now and then, out of breath, listened in the darkness as the mournful thunder grew fainter.

When this legion was no more than a handful, when their flag was no more than a rag, when their fusils had run out of bullets and were no more than batons, when the heap of corpses was bigger than the group left alive, there was among the victors a sort of holy terror over these sublime dying men, and the English artillery, pausing for breath, fell silent. It was respite of a kind. The combatants were surrounded by what seemed like teeming ghosts, the silhouettes of men on horseback, the black outlines of their cannons, the white sky seen through wheels and gun carriages; the colossal death's head that heroes always see in the depths of the fog of war was closing in on them and looked at them. They could hear in the crepuscular gloom that cannons were being loaded, wicks were being lit and gleamed like the eyes of tigers in the night, making a circle around their heads; all the shot-firers of the English batteries approached the cannons, and then, deeply moved, holding the moment of reckoning hanging over these men, an English general—Colville according to some, Maitland according to others—cried out to them: "Brave Frenchmen, give yourselves up!" Cambronne replied: "Shit!"[3]

## XV. CAMBRONNE

Out of respect for the French reader, the most beautiful word perhaps that a Frenchman has ever uttered cannot be repeated to them. There is a ban on dropping the sublime into history.

At our own risk, we are violating that ban.

So, we say, among all these giants, there was a Titan,[1] Cambronne.

To say that word and then die. What could be more grand!? For to want death is to die and it is not this man's fault if, though shot, he survived.

The man who won the battle of Waterloo is not Napoléon routed, it is not Wellington buckling at four o'clock, desperate at five, it is not Blücher who did not fight; the man who won the battle of Waterloo is Cambronne.

To strike down the thunderbolt that kills you with such a word—that is to conquer.

To answer catastrophe back with that, to say that to fate, to give the lion of the future such a firm footing, to slam down that reply at the night's rain, at the treacherous wall of Hougoumont, at the sunken path of Ohain, at Grouchy's delay, at Blücher's arrival, to come up with irony with one foot in the grave, to manage to stay on your feet after you've fallen, to drown the European coalition in one syllable, to offer kings the lavatories already familiar to the Caesars, to make the last of words the first by fusing it with the lightning of France, to insolently bring Waterloo to a close with a Mardi Gras, round off Leonidas with Rabelais,[2] sum up the victory in one supreme word that cannot be uttered, to lose ground but keep history, after all the carnage to have the last laugh—this is huge.

It is an insult to the thunderbolt. It is to attain the greatness of Aeschylus.[3]

Cambronne's word has the effect of a fracture. It means fracturing a breast with scorn; it is overflowing agony exploding. Who won? Wellington? No. Without Blücher he was sunk. Blücher? No. If Wellington hadn't begun, Blücher could not have finished. This Cambronne, this man who pops up at the final hour, this unknown soldier, this infinitely small cog of war, feels that there is a lie in there, a lie in a catastrophe, a poignant doubling up, and at the instant he is about to burst with rage over this, he is offered this paltry joke—life! How can he not hit the roof?

There they are, all the kings of Europe, the happy generals, the thundering Jupiters, there are one hundred thousand victorious soldiers and behind the hundred thousand, a million; their cannons, wicks lit, are gaping; they have the Imperial Guard and the Grande Armée under their heels; they have just crushed Napoléon and there is only Cambronne left; there is no one left to protest except this earthworm. Protest he will. So he gropes for a word the way you grope for a sword. He foams at the mouth and this foam is the word. Faced with this miraculous and mediocre victory, faced with this victory without victors, the desperado holds his head high; he takes the whole enormous calamity on the chin but he sees its meaninglessness, and he goes one better than spitting on it; and under the overwhelming pressure of numbers, strength, and material circumstances, he finds in his soul an expression: excrement. We repeat it. To say that, to do that, to come up with that—this is to be the victor.

The spirit of past glory entered into this unknown man at that fatal moment. Cambronne comes up with the word for Waterloo the way Rouget de l'Isle comes up with the "Marseillaise,"[4] being visited with inspiration from on high. A whiff of the divine whirlwind breaks loose and wafts through such men, and they shudder, and one of them sings the ultimate song, and the other lets out this terrible cry. Cambronne not only slams down this word of titanic scorn at Europe in the name of the Empire—that would be a small thing; he slams it down at the past in the name of the Revolution. You hear it and you recognize in Cambronne the old soul of the giants. It sounds like Danton talking or Kléber roaring.[5]

To this word of Cambronne's, the English voice replied: "Fire!" The batteries blazed, the hill shook, from all those mouths of bronze one last vomit of shot spewed forth, appalling; one vast plume of smoke, vaguely whitened by the rising moon, rolled in, and when the smoke cleared, there was nothing left. This formidable remnant was annihilated; the Guards were dead. The four living walls of the redoubt were lying prone, you could barely make out a tremor here and there among the corpses. And this is how the French legions, greater than the Roman legions, expired at Mont-Saint-Jean on ground soaked with rain and blood, in the gloomy wheatfields, at the place where, these days, at four in the morning, whistling and cheerily whipping his horse, Joseph trots past on his rounds for the Nivelles mail coach service.

## XVI. Quot Libras in Duce?[1]

The battle of Waterloo is an enigma. It is as mysterious for those who won it as for the man who lost it. For Napoléon, it was pure panic.* Blücher sees nothing in it but excitement; Wellington can't make head or tail of it. Look at the reports. The bulletins are confused, the commentaries muddled. Some stammer, others stutter. Jomini divides the battle of Waterloo into four moments; Müffling carves it into three episodes; Charras[2] alone, although on some points our appreciation differs from his, grasped with his proud glance the characteristic features of this catastrophe of human genius grappling with divine chance. All other historians are dazzled and in their dazzled state they are left groping. A blinding day, indeed, the downfall of the military monarchy which, to the great stupor of the kings, dragged every kingdom down with it, the fall of might, the routing of war.

In this event, bearing the marks of superhuman necessity, the role men played is nothing.

Does taking Waterloo away from Wellington and Blücher mean taking something away from England and Germany? No. Neither this illustrious England nor that august Germany is in question in the problem of Waterloo. Thank heavens, peoples are great beyond the sorrowful adventures of the sword. Neither Germany nor England nor France fit into a scabbard. In these times when Waterloo is a mere clinking of sabers, above Blücher Germany has Goethe and above Wellington England has Byron.[3] A vast dawning of ideas marks our

---

* "A battle over, a day over, wrong steps corrected, greater successes assured for the next day, all was lost by a moment of panic-stricken terror." Napoléon, *Dictées de Sainte-Hélène*.

century and in this dawn England and Germany have their magnificent glow. They are majestic in what they think. The raising of the bar they have brought to civilization is intrinsic to them; it comes from themselves and not from some accident. The way they opened up the nineteenth century does not begin with Waterloo. Only barbarians experience sudden spurts of growth after a victory. That is nothing more than the passing vanity of torrents swollen by a storm. Civilized peoples, especially in our day, are not raised up or brought down by the good or bad luck of a captain. Their specific weight in the human race comes from something more than a fight. Their honor, thank God, their dignity, their radiance, their genius, are not numbers that those gamblers known as heroes and conquerors throw into the lottery of battle. Battle lost, progress is often won. Less glory, more liberty. When the drum shuts up, reason has its say. This is the game of loser wins. So let us keep our calm, on both sides, when we speak of Waterloo. Let us give to chance what is chance's and to God what is God's. What is Waterloo? A victory? No. A game of poker. A game of poker won by Europe, paid out by France. It really wasn't worth the trouble of sticking a lion there.

Besides, Waterloo is the strangest encounter in history. Napoléon and Wellington—they aren't enemies, they are opposites. Never has God, who likes an antithesis,[4] produced a more striking contrast or a more extraordinary confrontation. On one side, precision, foresight, geometry, prudence, an exit plan assured, supplies well managed, a stubborn sangfroid, an imperturbable approach, strategy that makes the most of the terrain, tactics that counterbalance battalions, carnage laid out like a map, war regulated by the clock, nothing deliberately left to chance, good old traditional courage, absolute correctness; on the other side, intuition, divination, military idiosyncrasy, a superhuman instinct, the flamboyant eye of a hawk, which watches and strikes like lightning, prodigious skill wedded to a contemptuous impetuosity, all the mysteries of a deep soul, a close connection to destiny, the river, the plain, the forest, the hill, marshaled and in some amazing way forced to obey, with the despot going as far as to tyrannize the battlefield. Faith in the stars melded to the science of strategy, expanding it but also muddying it. Wellington was the Barrême of the war, Napoléon was its Michelangelo;[5] and this time genius was beaten by arithmetic.

On both sides, they were waiting for someone. It was the one who was best at sums who succeeded. Napoléon was waiting for Grouchy; he did not turn up. Wellington was waiting for Blücher; he did.

Wellington is classic warfare getting its revenge. In his heyday, Bonaparte had come across this in Italy and defeated it superbly. The old owl had fled before the young vulture. Age-old tactics had not only been roundly trounced but outraged. Who was this twenty-six-year-old Corsican? What did this splendid ignoramus mean when, with everyone against him, no one for him, without provisions, without munitions, without cannons, without shoes, almost without an army, with a handful of men against masses, he ran at allied Europe and carried absurd—impossible—victories against all the odds? Where did he come from, this thundering maniac who, almost without stopping for breath, and with the same pack of combatants as the only hand he could play had pulverized one after another the five armies of the emperor of Germany, hurling Beaulieu back at Alvinzi, Wurmser at Beaulieu, Mélas at Wurmser, Mack at Mélas?[26] Who was this newcomer to war, this little upstart with the effrontery of a star? The military academe excommunicated him as it went under. Hence the implacable rancor of the old Caesarism against the new, of the ordinary saber against the flamboyant sword, and of the chessboard against sheer genius. On June 18, 1815, this rancor had the last word, and below Lodi, Montebello, Montenotte, Mantua, Marengo, Arcola,[7] it wrote: Waterloo. The triumph of mediocrity that the majority loves. Destiny let the irony pass. At his decline, Napoléon found himself facing another young Wurmser.[8]

For to get Wurmser all you have to do, in fact, is to whiten Wellington's hair.

Waterloo is a battle of the first order won by a captain of the second.

What has to be admired in the battle of Waterloo is England—English steadfastness, English resolution, English blood. The superb thing that England had going for it there, whether it likes it or not, was itself—not its captain, its army.

Wellington, oddly ungrateful, declares in a letter to Lord Bathurst[9] that his army, the army that did battle on June 18, 1815, was a "despicable army." What does that grisly pile of mixed bones buried beneath the furrows of Waterloo make of that, I wonder?

England has been too modest in relation to Wellington. To make so much of Wellington is to make too little of England. Wellington is just a hero like any other. The Scottish Greys, the Horse Guards, the regiments of Maitland and of Mitchell, the infantry of Pack and of Kempt, the cavalry of Ponsonby and of Somerset, the Highlanders playing bagpipes under fire, the battalions of Rylandt, the fresh-faced recruits who barely knew how to handle a musket holding out against the old hands of Essling and Rivoli[10]—that is what is great. Wellington was tenacious, that was his merit, and we don't want to take that away from him, but the least of his foot soldiers or horsemen was every bit as rock-solid as he was. The iron soldier is worth every bit as much as the Iron Duke. As for us, we attribute all glory to the English soldier, to the English army, to the English people. If there is to be a trophy, it is to the English people that it should go. The Waterloo Column would be more just if, instead of the figure of a man, it raised to the skies the statue of a people.

But this mighty England would be offended by what we are saying here.

Even after its 1688 and our 1789,[11] it still has feudal illusions. It believes in heredity and in hierarchy. This people, whom no one else surpasses in power and glory, esteems itself a nation, not a people. As a people, it willingly knuckles under and accepts a lord as its leader. A workingman lets himself be treated with contempt; a soldier lets himself be bludgeoned. We recall that at the battle of Inkermann a sergeant who, apparently, had saved the army could not be mentioned by Lord Raglan, the English military hierarchy not allowing any hero below the grade of officer to be cited in a report.

What we admire above all in an encounter of the kind that took place at Waterloo is the tremendous cunning of chance. Overnight rain, the wall of Hougoumont, the hollow road of Ohain, Grouchy deaf to cannonfire, Napoléon's guide deceiving him, Bülow's guide enlightening him; the whole cataclysm was conducted with consummate skill.

On the whole, we have to say, Waterloo was more of a massacre than a battle.

Of all pitched battles, Waterloo is the one with the smallest front in relation to the number of combatants. Napoléon, two miles, Wellington, a mile and a half; seventy-two thousand combatants on each side. The carnage stems from such density.

The sums have been done and this ratio established; loss of men, at Austerlitz: French, 14 percent; Russians, 30 percent; Austrians, 44 percent. At Wagram: French, 13 percent; Austrians, 14. At Moscow: French, 37 percent; Russians, 44. At Bautzen:[12] French, 13 percent; Russians and Prussians, 14. At Waterloo: French, 56 percent; allies, 31. Average for Waterloo, 41 percent. One hundred and forty-four thousand men; sixty thousand dead.

The field of Waterloo today looks like any other plain; it has that calm that belongs to the earth as mankind's impassive support.

At night, though, a sort of visionary mist emanates from it and if a traveler should stroll around there, and look, and listen, and dream like Virgil before the fatal plain of Philippi,[13] he is seized by a hallucination of the disaster. That terrible June 18 lives on; the artificial hill monument fades from view, the nondescript lion evaporates, the battlefield resumes its reality; lines of infantry snake across the plain, furious galloping stirs up the horizon; the startled dreamer sees the lightning flash of sabers, the glint of bayonets, the blazing of bursting shells, the monstrous crossfire of thunderbolts; he hears the dim clamor of the phantom battle, like a death rattle from the depths of the grave; these shades are the grenadiers; these gleams are cuirassiers; this skeleton is Napoléon; that skeleton is Wellington; all this is no more and yet the slaughter continues; and the ravines run red with blood and the trees shiver and the fury rises up to the skies, and in the darkness, all these wild and wind-blasted heights, Mont-Saint-Jean, Hougoumont, Frischemont, Papelotte, Planchenoit, appear crowned by blurry whirlpools of specters exterminating each other.

## XVII. Do We Have to Think Waterloo Was a Good Thing?

There exists a very respectable liberal school that does not abhor Waterloo. We do not subscribe to it. For us, Waterloo is merely the amazing birth of liberty. That such an eagle should emerge from such an egg is surely unexpected.

Waterloo, if you look at it in terms of its ultimate outcome, is a deliberate counterrevolutionary victory. It is Europe versus France, it is Petersburg, Berlin, and Vienna versus Paris, it is the status quo versus initiative, it is July 14, 1789, attacked via March 20, 1815,[1] it is the pandemonium of the monarchies versus the indomitable French riot. To finally extinguish this vast people that had been in eruption for twenty-six years—that was the dream. Solidarity of the Brunswicks, the Nassaus, the Romanoffs, the Hohenzollerns, the Hapsburgs, with the Bourbons.[2] Waterloo carries divine right in the passenger seat. It is true that, the Empire having been despotic, royalty, as a natural reaction, had no choice but to be liberal, and that a reluctant constitutional order has sprung from Waterloo, to the great regret of the victors. The fact is that revolution cannot really be defeated and that, being providential and absolutely inevitable, it always reappears—before Waterloo, in Bonaparte's tearing down the old thrones; after Waterloo, in Louis XVIII's granting the Charter[3] and abiding by it. Bonaparte places a coachman on the throne of Naples and a sergeant on the throne of Sweden,[4] using inequality to demonstrate equality; Louis XVIII at Saint-Ouen[5] countersigns the Declaration of the Rights of Man. If you want to understand what revolution is, call it Progress; and if you want to understand what progress is, call it Tomorrow. Tomorrow does its work irresistibly and it does it starting today. It always achieves its aim, strangely. It puts Wellington to work to turn Foy, who was a mere soldier, into an orator.[6] Foy falls wounded at Hougoumont and gets back on his feet at the rostrum. That is how progress works. No tool is wrong for this particular laborer. It adapts to its divine labor, without being put off, both the man who bounded over the Alps and the poor doddering old invalid of father Élysée.[7] It makes use of the gout sufferer as it does of the conqueror; the conqueror outside France, the gout sufferer inside. In cutting short the demolition of the European thrones by the sword, Waterloo had no other effect than to keep up the work of revolution by other means. The swordsmen have finished, it is the thinkers' turn. The century that Waterloo tried to put an end to walked all over it and went on its way. This sinister victory has been defeated by liberty.

Briefly, and incontestably, what triumphed at Waterloo, what smiled behind Wellington, what brought him all the batons of the marshals of Europe, including, they say, the baton of the maréchal de France,[8] what gleefully wheeled in barrows of dirt and bones to build the lion's knoll, what triumphantly wrote on the pedestal the date June 18, 1815, what encouraged Blücher as he hacked into the rout, what from the height of the plateau of Mont-Saint-Jean looked down over France as though looking down over some prey, was the counterrevolution. It was the counterrevolution that mumbled that infamous word: dismemberment. Reaching Paris, it saw the crater from close up, it felt the ashes burning its feet and had second thoughts. It reverted to stammering about a charter.

Let us see Waterloo for what it is and nothing more. A deliberate bid for liberty—not at all. The counterrevolution was unintentionally liberal the same way that, through a corresponding phenomenon, Napoléon was unintentionally revolutionary. On June 18, 1815, Robespierre on horseback was thrown from the saddle.

## XVIII. A Fresh Bout of Divine Right

It was the end of the dictatorship. And with it, a whole European system fell apart.

The Empire faded to a shadow that resembled that of the dying Roman world. An abyss opened up again as in the days of the barbarians. Only the barbarism of 1815, which should be called by its pet name, the counterrevolution, lacked stamina, soon ran out of puff and pulled up short. The Empire, we must admit, was cried over, and cried over by heroic eyes. If there is glory in the sword turned scepter, the Empire had been glory itself. It had spread over the earth all the light that tyranny can provide. A somber light. We might even go so far as to say, a dark light. Compared to the light of day, it is night. The disappearance of the night had the effect of an eclipse.

Louis XVIII returned to Paris. The going round in circles of July 8 obliterated the zeal of March 20. The Corsican became the antithesis of the man from the Béarn.[1] The flag on the dome of the Tuileries was white.[2] Exile sat in state on the throne. Hartwell's[3] pinewood card table took up position in front of Louis XIV's fleur-de-lis-patterned armchair. People talked about Bouvines and Fontenoy[4] as yesterday's news, Austerlitz being entirely out of date. The altar and the throne fraternized majestically. One of the most uncontested forms of salvation of nineteenth-century society set itself up in France and on the Continent. Europe wore the white cockade.[5] Trestaillon[6] became a celebrity. The saying *non pluribus impar*[7] cropped up again in the stone rays representing a sunburst on the façade of the quai d'Orsay barracks. Where there had been the Imperial Guard, there was now a Maison Rouge.[8] The arc du Carrousel, completely loaded with ill-gotten victories, feeling out of place among all these novelties and a bit ashamed, perhaps, of Marengo and Arcola, saved face with a statue of the duc d'Angoulême.[9] The cemetery of the Madeleine, that terrible potter's field of '93,[10] was covered over with marble and jasper, since the bones of Louis XVI and Marie Antoinette were in that dust. In the moat of Vincennes, a monumental pillar rose out of the ground recalling the fact that the duc d'Enghien[11] had died in the very same month Napoléon had been crowned. Pope Pius VII,[12] who performed this coronation hot on the heels of that death, calmly blessed the fall as he had blessed the rise. There was in Schönbrunn Castle a little shadow four years old whom it was seditious to call the king of Rome.[13] And these things were done and those kings took their thrones back and the master of Europe was thrown in a cage and the old regime became the new regime and all the light and all the shadow of the earth swapped places all because, one summer afternoon, a shepherd boy had said to a Prussian in a wood: "Go this way, not that!"

This 1815 was a gloomy sort of spring. The old unhealthy and poisonous realities decked themselves out in new appearances. Dishonesty espoused 1789, divine right hid itself behind a charter, fictions made themselves constitutional, prejudices, superstitions, and ulterior motives, taking Article 14[14] to heart, cloaked themselves in liberalism. The snakes shed their skins.

Man had been both aggrandized and belittled at once by Napoléon. The ideal, under this reign of material splendor, went by the strange name of ideology that was bestowed upon it. It was serious recklessness on the part of a great man to scoff at the future. Yet the people, that cannon fodder so in love with the cannoneer, looked around for him. Where is he? What is he doing? Napoléon is dead, said a passerby to one of the war wounded from Marengo and Waterloo. "Him, dead!" cried the soldier. "That's how well you know him!" People's imaginations[15] defied this man struck down. The heart of Europe, after Waterloo, was black. Something enormous remained empty for a long time when Napoléon vanished.

The kings threw themselves into the vacuum. Old Europe took advantage of it to reform itself. There was a Holy Alliance[16]—the Belle-Alliance that the fatal field of Waterloo foretold.

In the face of this antique Europe reformed, the outlines of a new France took shape. The future, scorned by the emperor, made its entrance. It had plastered on its forehead that star, Liberty. The ardent eyes of the younger generations turned toward it. What was strange was that they fell in love with both the future, Liberty, and the past, Napoléon, at the same time. The defeat had magnified the defeated out of all proportion. Bonaparte fallen seemed taller than Napoléon on his feet. Those who had triumphed took fright. England had him guarded by Hudson Lowe and France had him spied on by Montchenu.[17] His folded arms became the terror of thrones. Alexander[18] called him "my insomnia." This fear stemmed from the whiff of revolution he had about him. Which explains and excuses Bonapartist liberalism.[19] This phantom made the Old

World quake in its boots. The kings reigned uncomfortably, with the rock of Saint Helena on the horizon.

While Napoléon lay dying at Longwood, the sixty thousand men fallen in the field of Waterloo quietly rotted away and something of their peacefulness spread over the world. The Congress of Vienna[20] made the treaties of 1815 out of it and Europe called this the Restoration.

So that is what Waterloo is.

But what does that matter to eternity? That whole tempest, that whole cloud, the war and after it the peace, the whole shadow-play, did not darken for a moment the gleam of the immense eye before which an aphid hopping from one blade of grass to another is equal to the eagle flying from spire to spire among the towers of Notre-Dame.

### XIX. THE BATTLEFIELD BY NIGHT

Let's go back—it is a requirement of this book—to that fatal field of battle.

On June 18, 1815, there was a full moon. The brightness favored Blücher's ferocious pursuit, gave away the traces of those fleeing, delivered that hopeless mass to the bloodthirsty Prussian cavalry, and aided and abetted the massacre. Night sometimes enters into such tragic collaboration with disasters.

When the last cannonball had been fired, the plain of Mont-Saint-Jean remained deserted.

The English occupied the French camp, it being the usual observance of victory to sleep in the bed of the vanquished. They set up their bivouac on the other side of Rossomme. The Prussians, let loose on the fugitives, drove on. Wellington went into the village of Waterloo to draft his report to Lord Bathurst.

If ever the *sic vos non vobis*[1] was applicable, it surely is to the village of Waterloo. Waterloo did not do a thing and it was two miles from the action. Mont-Saint-Jean was shelled, Hougoumont was set on fire, Papelotte was set on fire, Planchenoit was set on fire, La Haie-Sainte was stormed, La Belle-Alliance saw the two victors embrace; yet these names are scarcely known and Waterloo, which played no role in the battle, takes all the credit for it.

We are not among those who flatter war; when the occasion arises, we say what we think of it to its face. War can be appallingly beautiful and we have not tried to hide this; it can also be, I think we all agree, somewhat ugly. One of its surprisingly ugly aspects is the prompt stripping of the dead after victory. The dawn that follows a battle always rises over bare corpses.

Who does this? Who so tarnishes triumph? Whose is the vile hand that furtively slips into victory's pocket? Who are these crooks on the job behind glory's back? Some philosophers, Voltaire among them, assert that it is precisely these people who make glory what it is. They are the same people, they say, there are no extras, those still standing loot those lying on the ground. The hero by day is the vampire by night. After all, a person has the right to rob a corpse he has made. As for us, we do not think so. For the same hand to gather laurels and steal a dead man's shoes seems inconceivable to us.

What is certain is that, normally, after the victors come the thieves. But let's exonerate the soldier, particularly the contemporary soldier, from such a charge.

Every army has a rear end and that is where the accusation should lie. Beings like bats, part brigand, part valet, every species of rodent engendered by this twilight we call war: wearers of uniforms who do not fight, would-be malingerers, dreadful walking wounded; shady canteen attendants, trotting along on little carts, sometimes with their wives, stealing things they later sell on; beggars offering themselves as guides to officers; scum, marauders ... Once upon a time—we are not speaking of the present day—armies on the march dragged all that straggling along, so much so that these camp followers were known in the trade as "stragglers." No army or nation was responsible for these creatures; they spoke Italian and followed the Germans; they spoke French and followed the English. It was by one of these miserable wretches, a Spanish camp follower who spoke French, that the marquis de Fervacques,[2] hoodwinked by the man's Picard gobbledygook and so taking him for one of ours, was treacherously killed and robbed on the battlefield itself, on the night that followed the victory of Cerisoles. From looting the looter was born. The hateful maxim "Live off your enemy" produced that leper that only strong discipline could cure. There are reputations that deceive; we don't always know why certain generals, and great ones at that, have been so popular. Turenne was adored by his soldiers because he tolerated pillaging; allowing wrongdoing is part of being good-hearted; Turenne was so good-hearted he let the Palatinate[3] be put to the fire and to the sword. You used to see more or fewer marauders tagging along behind armies depending on whether the chief was more or less strict. Hoche and Marceau[4] had no camp followers; Wellington, we gladly do him this justice, had few.

But on the night of June 18–19, they stripped the dead clean. Wellington was firm, and the order was to put to death anyone caught in the act; but plunder is tenacious. The marauders flew off to one corner of the battlefield while they were being shot in another.

The moonlight was sinister on that particular plain.

Around midnight, a man was prowling or, rather, creeping along the sunken Ohain road. To all appearances, he was one of those people we have just described, neither English nor French, neither peasant nor soldier, less man than ghoul, attracted by a nose for the dead, having theft for victory and coming to raid Waterloo. He was dressed in a smock that looked a bit like a greatcoat, he was both anxious and audacious, he crept forward but kept looking around behind him as he went. What was this man? The night probably knew more about him than the day. He didn't have any kind of bag, but obviously had big pockets under his greatcoat. Now and again, he stopped, studied the plain around him as though to see if he were being observed, suddenly crouched down, poked around something quiet and motionless on the ground, then stood up again and scuttled away. His slithering, his bearing, his mysterious darting movements caused him to resemble those crepuscular specters that haunt ruins and that old Norman legends call *Alleurs*—goers.

Certain nocturnal wading birds make similar silhouettes in the wetlands.

A gaze attentively probing all the mist might have noticed at a distance, standing still and as though hidden behind a shack alongside the Nivelles road where it meets the road from Mont-Saint-Jean to Braine-l'Alleud, a sort of small sutler's wagon with a tarred wickerwork cover, hitched to a starving nag grazing on nettles through her bit, and in this wagon a woman of some kind sitting on top of trunks and parcels. Maybe there was some connection between the wagon and the prowler.

The darkness was serene. Not a cloud in the sky. Too bad if the earth was red, the moon remained white regardless. Such is the indifference of the heavens. In the meadows, branches of trees broken by gunfire but not broken off, were hanging on by their bark and swaying gently in the night breeze. A breath, almost like sighing, stirred the undergrowth. There were ripples in the grass like souls departing.

You could dimly hear in the distance the coming and going of patrols and the circling watchmen of the English camp.

Hougoumont and La Haie-Sainte continued to burn, sending up two great flames, one in the west, one in the east, to which the ring of fires of the English bivouac, laid out in an immense semicircle over the hills along the horizon, had just linked up like a loosened ruby necklace with two red garnets at each end.

We've talked about the disaster of the Ohain path. What that death was like for so many brave men, the heart is too appalled to dwell on.

If anything is terrifying, if there is a reality that surpasses dream, it is this: to live, to see the sun, to be in full possession of manly vigor, to be full of health and joy, to laugh valiantly, to run toward the glory in front of you, dazzling, to feel in your chest lungs that breathe, a heart that beats, a will that reasons, to speak, to think, to love, to have a mother, to have a wife, to have children, to have the light, and all of a sudden, in the time it takes to let out a cry, in less than one minute flat, to tumble into an abyss, to fall, to roll, to crush, to be crushed, to see the blades of wheat, flowers, leaves, branches, and yet not to be able to stop yourself by grabbing any of them, to feel your saber useless, men underneath you, horses on top of you, to flail about in vain, your bones broken by some kick in the dark, to feel a heel making your eyes pop out of your head, to bite into horseshoes with rage, to suffocate, to howl, to twist yourself in knots, to be at the bottom of all this and tell yourself: Just now I was one of the living!

Where this lamentable disaster had resounded with its death rattle, everything was now silent. The cutting made by the sunken road was filled up with horses and riders all inextricably jumbled. Horrific entanglement. The embankment was no more; dead bodies made the road level with the plain right to the very edge, like a perfectly measured bushel of barley. A pile of dead men on the top, a river of blood on the bottom; that is what the road was like on the night of June 18, 1815. The blood ran right up to the Nivelles road and welled up there in a huge pool in front of the felled trees that blocked the road at a spot still marked today. It is, as you will recall, at the opposite spot, going toward the Genappe road, that the cuirassiers collapsed. The density of corpses was in proportion to the depth of the sunken road. Round about the halfway mark, at the spot where it became a plain, where Delord's division had passed, the layer of dead men thinned out a bit.

The night prowler the reader has just caught a glimpse of was headed that way. He was ferreting through that vast grave. He looked around. We don't know what hideous review of the dead he passed. He was walking with his feet in the blood.

All of a sudden, he stopped in his tracks.

A few feet in front of him, in the sunken road, at the spot where the mound of the dead ended, from underneath this heap of men and horses, an open hand emerged, lit up by the moon.

The hand had something on its finger that shone; it was a gold ring.

The man bent down, stayed crouching a moment, and when he stood up again, there was no more ring on the hand.

He didn't exactly stand up again; he stayed in a half-crouching position like that of a scared wildcat, turning his back on the heap of dead, scrutinizing the skyline, on his knees, the whole top part of his body being supported by his two index fingers on the ground, his head peering over the rim of the sunken road. The four paws of the jackal are just right for certain purposes.

When he had set his course, he stood up.

At that instant he nearly jumped out of his skin. He could feel someone grab him from behind.

He wheeled round; the open hand had closed again, seizing the lapel of his greatcoat.

An honest man would have taken fright. This man burst out laughing.

"I'll be damned," he said, "it's only the dead man. I'd prefer a ghost to a gendarme any day."

But the hand relaxed and released him. Effort is quickly exhausted in the grave.

"God!" the prowler went on. "Can this dead man be alive? Let's have a closer look."

He bent down again, fumbled in the heap, removed whatever was in the way, took the hand, grabbed the arm, freed the head, pulled out the body, and a few seconds later dragged into the darkness of the sunken road a man who was inanimate—or at least senseless. It was a cuirassier, an officer, even an officer of some rank; a big gold epaulet poked out from beneath his cuirass; this officer no longer had a helmet. A furious cut of the sword had slashed his face and you could not see it for blood. Yet it didn't look like he had any broken limbs, and by a stroke of luck, if we may use such a term here, the bodies had arched above him in such a way as to prevent him from being crushed. His eyes were closed.

He had on his cuirass the silver cross of the Légion d'Honneur.

The prowler ripped the cross off and it disappeared into one of the gaping holes of his greatcoat.

After that, he felt around in the officer's fob pocket, felt a watch in it and took it. Then he fumbled in the waistcoat, found a purse there and pocketed it.

As he reached this phase in the assistance he was offering the dying man, the officer opened his eyes.

"Thank you," he said feebly.

The roughness of the man handling him, the freshness of the night, the fact of being able to breathe freely, had brought him to his senses.

The prowler did not answer. He raised his head. The sound of footfalls could be heard on the plain, probably some patrol approaching.

The officer murmured, for there was still agony in his voice: "Who won the battle?"

"The English," replied the prowler.

The officer went on: "Look in my pockets. You'll find a purse and a watch. Take them."

This had already been done.

The prowler pretended to do what he was told and said: "There's nothing there."

"I've been robbed," the officer went on. "I'm so sorry. You could have had them."

The tread of the patrol was becoming more and more distinct.

"Someone's coming," said the prowler, making a move as though to go.

The officer, painfully raising his arm, held him back.

"You saved my life. Who are you?"

The prowler replied fast and low: "I was, like you, in the French army. I must leave you. If they catch me, they'll shoot me. I've saved your life. Now you're on your own."

"What's your rank?"

"Sergeant."

"What's your name?"

"Thénardier."

"I won't forget that name," said the officer. "And you, you remember mine. My name is Pontmercy."

BOOK TWO

# THE SHIP *ORION*

## I. NUMBER 24601[1] BECOMES NUMBER 9430

Jean Valjean was nabbed again.

You will be grateful to us for passing rapidly over these painful details. We will restrict ourselves to transcribing two short pieces published in the newspapers of the day, a few months after the surprising events that occurred in Montreuil-sur-mer.

These articles are a little perfunctory. You will recall that there was no *Gazette des Tribunaux* yet at the time.

We have taken the first from the *Drapeau blanc*.[2] It is dated July 25, 1823:

An arrondissement of the Pas-de-Calais has just seen an event out of the ordinary. Some years back, a stranger to that *département,* a man named Monsieur Madeleine, had revived an old local industry, the manufacture of jet and black glass beads, thanks to new processes. He made his fortune doing so and, we must say, that of the district. In recognition of his services, he was appointed mayor. The police have discovered that this Monsieur Madeleine was none other than an ex-convict in breach of ban, sentenced in 1796 for robbery, and named Jean Valjean. Jean Valjean has been sent back to jail. It seems that prior to his arrest he had managed to withdraw from Monsieur Laffitte's bank a sum of more than half a million which he had invested there and which he had earned, furthermore, perfectly legitimately, they say, through his business. It is not known where Jean Valjean has hidden this sum since his return to Toulon jail.

The second article, a bit more detailed, is taken from the *Journal de Paris,* same date.

A freed ex-convict named Jean Valjean has just appeared before the circuit court of the Var in circumstances made to attract attention. This rogue had managed to outwit the vigilance of the police; he had changed his name and succeeded in getting himself appointed as mayor of one of our little northern towns. He had set up in that town a fairly considerable business. He was at last unmasked and arrested, thanks to the indefatigable zeal of the public prosecutor's department. He had as concubine a streetwalker who died of shock at the moment of his arrest. This miserable wretch, who is endowed with herculean strength, found the means to escape; but, three or four days after said escape, the police once more got their hands on him, in Paris itself, just as he was climbing up into one of those little cabs that ply between the capital and the village of Montfermeil (Seine-et-Oise). They say he took advantage of the interval of those three or four days of freedom to withdraw a considerable sum placed by him with one of our leading bankers. This sum is estimated at six or seven hundred thousand francs. According to the bill of indictment, he has buried it in a place known only to himself and it has not been possible to seize it. Whatever the case may be, the said Jean Valjean has just been brought before the circuit court of the *département* of the Var charged with committing highway robbery under arms, about eight years ago, on the person of one of those honest children who, as the patriarch of Ferney[3] has written in immortal verse,

... Arrive every year from Savoy,
Their hands lightly wiping
Long chimneys thick with soot.

This bandit renounced any self-defense. It has been proved, through the able and eloquent mouthpiece of the public prosecutor's office, that the robbery was committed in collaboration and that Jean Valjean was part of a gang of thieves in the Midi. Consequently, Jean Valjean, being found guilty, has been given the death sentence. This criminal refused to take his case to the final court of appeal. The king, in his inexhaustible clemency, has deigned to commute his sentence to that of hard labor in perpetuity. Jean Valjean was immediately sent to Toulon jail.

It was not forgotten that Jean Valjean had religious habits at Montreuil-sur-mer. A few newspapers, among others the *Constitutionnel*,[4] presented this commutation as a triumph for the clerical party.

Jean Valjean changed numbers in jail. He became known as 9430.

For the rest, we might as well get it off our chests now once and for all that, along with Monsieur Madeleine, the prosperity of Montreuil-sur-mer disappeared; all he had foreseen during his long dark night of the soul came to pass;

with him gone, the soul was gone, in fact. After his fall, what happened at Montreuil-sur-mer was the usual self-interested divvying up of what is left when great men fall, that fatal carving up of flourishing enterprises that takes place, out of sight, daily, in the human community and that history has noted only once because it happened to occur after the death of Alexander the Great. Lieutenants have themselves crowned kings; foremen play at being manufacturers. Envious rivalries rear their ugly heads. The vast workshops of Monsieur Madeleine were shut down; the buildings fell into ruin, the workers scattered. Some left the area, others left the trade. From that day forth, everything was done on a small scale instead of on a large scale—for the lucre, instead of for the common good. No more center, everywhere competition and ruthlessness. Monsieur Madeleine used to dominate everything and provide direction. With him fallen, it was every man for himself; the fighting spirit took over from the spirit of organization, harshness from cordiality, the hate of each against all from the benevolence of the founder of all; the bonds knitted by Monsieur Madeleine became tangled and broke; processes were rigged, products debased, confidence killed off; markets diminished, fewer orders were placed; wages dropped, workshops stopped work, bankruptcy ensued. After that, nothing left for the poor. Everything fell apart.

Even the state realized that someone had been crushed somewhere. Less than four years after the circuit court decree establishing, for the benefit of the galleys, that Monsieur Madeleine and Jean Valjean were one and the same, taxes were doubled in the district of Montreuil-sur-mer, and Monsieur de Villèle addressed the House to that effect in the month of February 1827.

## II. In Which You Will Read Two Lines of Verse That Are Perhaps the Devil's

Before we go any further, it would be appropriate to recount in some detail a weird incident that happened at Montfermeil around the same time and that may not be purely coincidental to certain conjectures of the public prosecutor's department.

There is in the region of Montfermeil a very ancient superstition, all the more curious and all the more precious since a popular superstition in the Paris environs is like an aloe vera plant in Siberia. We are among those who respect anything that smacks of the rare plant. So here is the Montfermeil superstition. The locals believe that the devil has, from time immemorial, chosen the forest to hide his treasures in. The good women there claim that it is not rare, at the end of day, in remote places in the woods, to meet a black man with the look of a carter or a woodcutter, shod in clogs, decked out in breeches and a frock of coarse canvas cloth, who is recognizable in that, instead of a cap or hat, he has two immense horns on his head. This would, indeed, make him fairly recognizable. This man is usually busy digging a hole. There are three ways of dealing with coming across him. The first is to approach the man and speak to him. Then you realize the man is nothing more than a peasant, that he looks black because it is dusk, that he is not digging a hole at all but cutting the grass for his cows, and that what you took for horns is nothing more than a manure fork he carries on his back, whose prongs only seemed to sprout out of his head because of the perspective offered by the fading light. You go back home and you die before the week is out. The second approach is to observe him, wait till he has dug his hole, till he has covered it over and gone on his way; then to run quickly to the ditch, open it up again and take out the "treasure" that the black man has obviously put there. In this case, you die before the month is out. Lastly, the third approach is to not speak to the black man, to not even look at him, and to take off as fast as your legs will carry you. You die before the year is out.

As all three methods have their drawbacks, the second, which offers at least some advantages, among others that of owning a treasure, if only for a month, is the one generally adopted. Hardy types, who can't resist a gamble, have thereby often enough, we are assured, opened up the holes dug by the black man and tried to rob the devil. It seems the operation is fairly hopeless. At least, if we are to believe the tradition and, in particular, the two enigmatic lines in barbaric Latin that a bad Norman monk named Tryphon,[1] who was a bit of a wizard, has left us on the subject. This Tryphon is buried in the abbey of Saint-Georges de Bocherville near Rouen, and toads breed on his grave.

So, you go to enormous trouble, for these particular holes are normally very deep, you sweat, you root around, you toil away all night, for this is done at night, your shirt gets soaked, your candle burns out, you damage your pickax, and when at last you get to the bottom of the hole, when you lay your hand on the "treasure," what do you find? What is the devil's treasure? A sou, sometimes an écu, a stone, a skeleton, a bloody corpse, sometimes a ghost folded in four like a sheet of paper in a wallet, sometimes nothing. This is what Tryphon's couplet seems to announce to the indiscreetly curious:

> Dig, and in the hole find dark treasure buried,
> Paltry coins, stones, corpses, ghosts, worthless things.[2]

It seems that these days you also find there either a powder horn with bullets or an old pack of greasy scorched cards that has obviously been used by devils. Tryphon does not record the two last findings, given that Tryphon lived in the twelfth century, and it does not appear that the devil had the wit to invent gunpowder before Roger Bacon[3] or cards before Charles VI.[4]

For the rest, if you play with these cards, you are sure to lose everything you own; and as for the powder in the powder horn, it has the property of making your gun go off in your face.

Well, very shortly after the period when the public prosecutor's department decided the freed convict Jean Valjean had been prowling around Montfermeil during the few days he was on the run, it was remarked in this same village that a certain old road-mender named Boulatruelle was "taken with" the woods. People in the area claimed to know that this Boulatruelle had been in jail; he was subject to occasional police surveillance and, as he could not find work anywhere, the local council employed him at a pittance as a road-mender on the crossroad from Gagny to Lagny.

This Boulatruelle was looked down on by the people of the district—too respectful, too humble, too quick to doff his cap at everyone, quivering and smiling in front of the gendarmes, probably affiliated with gangs of bandits, people said, suspected of ambushes at the edge of copses at nightfall. The only thing going for him was that he was a drunk.

This is what people thought they had noted:

For some little time, Boulatruelle had been leaving his job of stone-lining and road maintenance extremely early and going off into the forest with his pickax. You would come across him round about evening in the most deserted clearings, in the wildest thickets, looking for all the world as if he was searching for something, sometimes digging holes. The good women who passed by took him for Beelzebub, then they recognized Boulatruelle and were scarcely more reassured. These encounters seemed to really throw Boulatruelle. It was obvious that he was trying to hide and that there was some mystery in what he was up to.

They said in the village: "It's clear the devil has made an appearance. Boulatruelle saw him and he's searching. Truth is, he's just the man to get his hands on Lucifer's stash." The Voltaireans added: "Will Boulatruelle catch the devil or will the devil catch Boulatruelle?" The old women crossed themselves a lot.

But Boulatruelle's shenanigans in the woods stopped and he went back to his regular hours as a road-mender. People moved on to other things.

A few people, though, remained curious, thinking that what might be involved in the whole business was not the fabulous treasure of legend, but a real windfall, a lot more serious and substantial than the devil's banknotes, and whose secret Boulatruelle had half-gleaned. The most intrigued were the schoolmaster and Thénardier, the keeper of the low-class inn, who was everybody's friend but who had not deigned to make friends with Boulatruelle.

"He was in the galleys, eh?" said Thénardier. "Christ! A person doesn't know who's coming or going, when it comes to the clink."

One night the schoolmaster remarked that once upon a time the law would have looked into what Boulatruelle was up to in the woods, and he would have had to talk whether he liked it or not, that they would have used torture on him if need be, and that Boulatruelle would not have stood up to it if, for example, they'd used water torture.

"Give him the booze treatment," said Thénardier.

They got together and plied the old road-mender with drink. Boulatruelle drank enormously and said little. With admirable art and a masterly sense of proportion, he combined the thirst of a greedy pig with the discretion of a judge. Yet, by dint of returning to the charge and by piecing things together and wringing out of him the few obscure words he inadvertently let slip, this is what Thénardier and the schoolmaster thought they understood:

One morning Boulatruelle turned up for work at daybreak and was surprised to see, in a corner of the woods, under a bush, a shovel and a pickax that "you'd have to say had been hidden." But it seems he thought that it was probably the shovel and pickax of old Six-Fours, the water carrier, and thought no more about it. But the evening of the same day, he apparently saw, without himself being seen, as he was hidden by a big tree, heading off the road to the thickest part of the wood "an individual who was in no way from round these parts" and that he, Boulatruelle, "knew very well." Translation courtesy of Thénardier: "a pal from the clink." Boulatruelle had obstinately refused to say who the man was. This individual was carrying a bundle, something square like a big box or a small chest. Surprise on the part of Boulatruelle. Yet it wasn't for six or seven minutes, it seems, that the idea of following "the individual" came to him. By then it was too late, the individual was already in the thicket, night had fallen, and Boulatruelle wasn't able to get to him. So he decided to keep his eye on the edge of the woods. "There was a moon." Two or three hours later, Boulatruelle saw his individual emerge from the thicket, now carrying not the small chest but a pickax and a shovel. Boulatruelle had let the individual pass and it didn't occur to him to approach him, because he told himself the other man was three times as strong as he was and armed with a pickax and would probably whack him when he saw who he was and figured out that he'd been recognized. Touching effusions of two old chums who run into each other suddenly. But the shovel and pickax had been a flash of light for Boulatruelle; he ran off into the bushes the next morning, but he didn't find either the shovel or the pickax. He concluded that this individual, after entering the wood, had dug a hole with the pickax, had buried the chest in it, and had filled the hole in with the shovel. Now, the chest was too small to contain a dead body, so it had to contain money. Hence his investigations. Boulatruelle had explored, probed, and poked around the whole forest and rooted around wherever the ground looked freshly disturbed to him. In vain.

He hadn't dug up a thing. No one thought any more about it in Montfermeil. There were just a few die-hard rumormongers who said: "You can be certain that the road-mender from Gagny didn't root around like that for nothing. The devil's come, nothing surer."

### III. How the Chain on the Shackles Must Have Undergone Preparatory Treatment to Be Shattered Like That with One Whack of the Hammer

Toward the end of October of that same year, 1823, the inhabitants of Toulon saw the ship *Orion* sail back into their port to have some damage repaired, following a bout of rough weather. The *Orion* was later employed in Brest as a training ship, but at the time it was part of the Mediterranean squadron.

This vessel, disabled as it was, for the sea had treated it badly, made quite an impression when it limped into harbor. It was bearing some flag or other— I can't remember which—that earned it a regulation eleven-gun salute, returned by it blast for blast, making twenty-two in all. It has been estimated that in salvos, royal and military shows of politeness, exchanges of courteous din, signals of etiquette, formalities of harbor and citadel, sunrises and sunsets, saluted daily by all the fortresses and all the warships, openings and closings of gates, etc., etc., the civilized world all over the globe fires off 150,000 pointless cannon shots every twenty-four hours. At six francs a shot, that means that nine hundred thousand francs a day, or three hundred million a year, goes up in smoke. This is just a detail. And while this is going on, the poor are dying of hunger.

The year 1823 was what the Restoration called "the time of the war with Spain."[1]

This war was actually many events rolled into one, with plenty of singularities thrown in for good measure. A big family affair for the Bourbons, the French branch aiding and protecting the branch in Madrid—in other words, performing an act of seniority; an apparent return to our national traditions, complicated by subservience and cringing to the state cabinets of the north; Monsieur le duc d'Angoulême, dubbed by the liberal rags "the hero of Andujar,"[2] cracking down, with a triumphal attitude somewhat contradicted by his peaceful air, on the old and very real terrorism of the Holy Office[3] as it grappled with the chimerical terrorism of the liberals; the sansculottes resurrected, to the great alarm of the dowagers, under the name of *descamisados*;[4] monarchists striving to impede progress, which they called anarchy; the theories of '89 nipped in the bud suddenly, a European "whoa" putting a stop to the French idea making its world tour; alongside the generalissimo son of France,[5] the prince de Carignan,[6] subsequently Charles-Albert, enlisting in this crusade of kings against peoples as a volunteer with the red wool epaulets of a grenadier; the soldiers of the Empire again going on campaign, though after eight years off, aged, sad, and under the white cockade; the tricolor flag waved around by a heroic handful of Frenchmen just as the white flag had once been in Koblenz,[7] thirty years previously; monks blending in with our troops; the spirit of liberty and novelty made to see reason at the end of a bayonet; principles brought down by cannon shot; France undoing with its arms what it had done with its spirit; to top it off, the enemy chiefs sold out, the soldiers hesitant, towns under siege by the teeming millions; no military dangers and yet potential explosions, as with any mine surprised and invaded; little blood shed, little honor won, shame for some, glory for none—such was this war made by princes who were descended from Louis XIV and led by generals who sprang from Napoléon. It had the sad fate of recalling neither great war nor great politics.

A few feats of arms were serious; the taking of the Trocadero, for example, was a fine military campaign; but on the whole, we repeat, the trumpets of this war produced a tinny sound, the ensemble was suspect, and history backs France in her difficulty in accepting this false triumph. It seemed obvious that certain Spanish officers tasked with resisting yielded too easily, the whiff of corruption was given off by the victory; it felt as if it was more a case of the generals having been won than the battles, and the victorious soldier went home humiliated. A demeaning war, indeed, one in which you could read *Banque de France* between the folds of the flag.

The soldiers of the war of 1808, on top of whom Saragossa[8] had so alarmingly collapsed, frowned darkly in 1823 when confronted by the easy sacking of citadels and took to regretting Palafox.[9] It is in the nature of France to prefer facing Rostopchine rather than Ballesteros.[10]

From an even graver point of view—something it is only right to insist on—this war, which rubbed France's military spirit up the wrong way, outraged the democratic spirit. It was a bid for enslavement. In this campaign, the goal of the French soldier, that son of democracy, was to put others under the yoke. Nasty nonsense. France is made to stir people's souls, not smother them. Since 1792, all the revolutions of Europe have been the French Revolution; liberty shines out of France. It is a question of the sun. Anyone who does not see it is blind! Bonaparte said so.

The war of 1823, an attack on the generous Spanish nation, was thus at the same time an attack on the French Revolution. This monstrous assault and battery was committed by France—by force; for, aside from wars of liberation, all that armies do, they do by force. The term *passive obedience* says it all. An army is a strange compound masterpiece in which force results from an enormous sum of impotence. This explains war, made by humanity against humanity in spite of humanity.

As for the Bourbons, the war of 1823 was fatal for them. They mistook it for a success. They did not see the danger in killing an idea with a slogan. In their naïveté, they got things so wrong they introduced into their program, as an element of strength, the enormous weakness of a crime. The spirit of ambush entered into their policy making. The year 1823 sowed the seeds of 1830.[11] In their debates, the Spanish campaign became an argument for violent shows of strength and for the shenanigans of divine right. Having reestablished *el rey neto* in Spain, France could certainly reestablish the absolute monarch on home turf. They fell into the frightening error of mistaking the soldier's obedience for the nation's consent. That kind of confidence loses thrones. It doesn't do to fall asleep, either in the shade of the poisonous manchineel tree or in the shadow of an army.

But let's get back to the good ship *Orion.*

During the maneuvers of the generalissimo prince's army, a squadron was cruising the Mediterranean. As we have just said, the *Orion* was part of this squadron and it had been driven back into the port of Toulon by rough seas.

The presence of a warship in a port has something indefinable that pulls the crowds and fills them with wonder. This is because it's big and crowds love anything big.

A ship of the line is one of the most magnificent encounters between the power of nature and the genius of man.

A ship of the line is composed of both the heaviest and the lightest of materials, because it is tied to three forms of substance at once, solid, liquid, and gas, and has to fight against all three. It has eleven iron claws to seize granite at the bottom of the sea, and more wings and antennae than a winged arthropod to catch the wind in the clouds. Its breath comes out of its one hundred and twenty guns as if through enormous bugles and proudly answers thunder back. The ocean tries to lead it astray with the frightening sameness of its waves, but the vessel has its soul, its compass, which counsels it and always shows it true north. On black nights, its lanterns make up for the stars. And so, against the wind, it has rope and canvas, against water, wood, against rock, iron, copper, and lead, against the darkness, light, and against the vastness, a needle.

If you want to get an idea of all the gigantic proportions that come together to make up a ship of the line, you only have to duck under one of the covered slipways, six stories high, of the ports of Brest or Toulon. Ships being built there sit under a bell jar, so to speak. This colossal beam is a yard; that great wood column stretching along the ground as far as the eye can see is the mainmast. Measuring from its roots in the slipway to its crown in the clouds, it is sixty fathoms high, and it is three feet in diameter at its base. The English mainmast rises two hundred and seventeen feet above the waterline. The navy of our fathers' day used cables, nowadays we use chains. Just the simple coil of chains of a hundred-gun ship is four feet high, twenty feet wide, and eight feet deep. And to build such a ship, how much wood do you need? Three thousand steres, or cubic meters. It is a floating forest.

And then again, take note, what we are talking about here is merely a military craft of forty years ago, a simple sailing ship; steam, then in its infancy, has since added new miracles to this prodigy known as a warship. At the present day, for example, the hybrid ship with propeller is an amazing machine hauled along by sails three thousand square meters in surface and by a 2500-horsepower boiler.

Forgetting about these new marvels, the old ship of Christopher Columbus and of de Ruyter[12] is one of man's great masterpieces. It is as inexhaustible in power as the infinite is in gusts of wind, it stores the wind in its sails, it is a fixed point in the endlessly spreading waves, it floats and it reigns.

But the moment comes when a squall snaps this sixty-foot yard like a piece of straw, when the wind bends that four-hundred-foot-high mast like a reed, when that anchor, weighing ten thousand pounds, is twisted in the maw of the waves like an angler's hook in the jaws of a pike, when those monster guns let out plaintive and futile roars that the hurricane carries into the void and into the darkness, when all this power and all this majesty are engulfed by a superior power and majesty.

Every time immense strength is deployed only to end in immense weakness, it makes people think. This is why the curious abound in seaports, without themselves being all that clear why they are there, thronging around these marvelous machines of war and navigation.

Every day, then, from morning to night, the quais, piers, and jetties of the port of Toulon were crawling with idlers and people strolling about—polishing the pavement, as they say in Paris—whose business was to gawk at the *Orion.*

The *Orion* had been a sick ship for a long time. In its previous voyages, thick layers of shellfish had built up on its hull to such an extent that they slowed it down to half its speed; it had been put in dry dock the previous year for the crust of shells to be scraped off, and then had put out to sea again. But this scraping job had weakened the bolting on the hull. When it got up around the Balearic Islands, the planking became fatigued and came loose, and since planking was not in those days lined with metal sheeting, the ship took on water. A violent equinoctial gale had blown up and had stoved in the head and a porthole on the port side and damaged the foresail chainwales. Following this damage, the *Orion* had put back to Toulon.

It was moored near the Arsenal, and it was being fitted out and repaired. The hull had not been damaged on the starboard side, but a few planks had been pried open here and there, according to custom, to let air into the shell.

One morning the crowd looking on witnessed an accident.

The crew was busy bending sail. The sailor whose job it was to let down the starboard peak of the main topsail lost his balance. He was seen to reel, the throng gathered on the Arsenal quai let out a cry, the man tipped head over heels, he spun around the yard, hands outstretched toward the abyss; as he flew past, he grabbed hold of the loose footropes first with one hand, then with the other, and he remained there, dangling. The sea lay dizzingly far below him. The shock of his fall had jolted the footropes and set them rocking like a swing. The man swung backward and forward at the end of the rope like a stone in a slingshot.

To go to his aid was to run a terrifying risk. None of the sailors, all fishermen from the coast freshly pressed into service, dared to give it a go. But the unfortunate topman was getting tired; you couldn't see the anguish on his face, but you could see the exhaustion in all his limbs. His arms were horribly stiff from being pulled. Every effort he made to climb back up only served to increase the swinging of the loose footropes. He did not cry out for fear of losing strength. All that was left was to wait for him to let go of the rope and at moments all heads turned away so that they would not see him fall. There are times when a bit of rope, a pole, the branch of a tree, mean the difference between life and death, and it is awful to see a living being let go and drop like ripe fruit.

All of a sudden, a man was seen climbing up the rigging with the agility of a wildcat. This man was dressed in red, he was a convict; he had the green cap of a lifer. When he got to the top, a gust of wind ripped off his cap, revealing a head completely white; this was no young man.

A convict, in fact, employed on board on prison duty, had immediately run to an officer of the watch and in the middle of the confusion and hesitation of the crew, while all the sailors trembled and shrank back, he had asked the officer's permission to risk his life to save the topman. When the officer gave him the nod, he had used a hammer to break the chain riveted to the iron shackle at his ankle, then he had grabbed a rope and flung himself into the shrouds. No one at that instant noticed how easily the chain had been broken. It was only later that people remembered that.

In the blink of an eye he was over the yard. He stopped for a few seconds and seemed to be weighing it up. Those seconds, during which the wind swung the topman at the end of a thread, felt like centuries to those who watched. At last the convict raised his eyes to the heavens and took a step forward. The crowd breathed again. They saw him run along the yard. When he got to the far end, he tied one end of the rope he had brought to it and let the other end hang, then he started descending, hand over hand, down this rope, and the anguish became unbearable, for instead of one man dangling over the depths, there were two.

You would have said it looked like a spider coming to grab a fly; only here the spider was bringing life, not death. Ten thousand pairs of eyes were fixed on the two of them. Not a cry, not a word; the same quivering brought a frown to every face. Everyone held their breath, as though afraid of adding the slightest puff to the wind that was shaking the two poor wretches.

Yet the convict had managed to haul down next to the topman. Not a moment too soon; one minute more and the man, exhausted and desperate, would have plummeted into the deep; the convict firmly secured him with the rope which he held with one hand while he worked with the other. At last they saw him climb back up the yard, hauling the sailor behind him; he held him for a moment to let him get back his strength, then lifted him in his arms and carried him as he walked back along the yard to the crosstrees and from there to the top, where he left him in the hands of his mates.

At that moment the crowd broke into applause; hardened galley-wardens wept, women hugged each other along the quai, and everyone could be heard shouting in a sort of softened fury: "Give this man a pardon!"

The man, however, had made a point of descending immediately to rejoin his work team. To get there faster, he slid down the rigging and started to run along a lower fore yard. All eyes followed him. At a certain point, everyone felt afraid; either he was tired or he felt dizzy, for it looked as if he hesitated and lurched. Suddenly the crowd gave a great cry. The convict had fallen into the sea.

It was a perilous fall. The frigate *Algésiras* was moored next to the *Orion,* and the poor galley slave had fallen in between the two boats. There was a real danger he would slip under one or the other of the two. Four men swiftly leaped into a small boat. The crowd urged them on, anxiety again took hold of everyone. The man had not risen to the surface. He had disappeared in the sea without so much as a ripple, as though he had fallen into a vat of oil. They sounded, they dived. It was in vain. The search continued till nightfall; they did not even find the body.

The next day, the Toulon paper ran these few lines:

November 17, 1823: Yesterday a convict, on duty aboard the *Orion,* returning from rescuing a sailor, fell into the sea and drowned. His body was not recovered. He is presumed to have got stuck under the piles of the Arsenal pier. This man was jailed under the number 9430 and was called Jean Valjean.

# BOOK THREE

# KEEPING THE PROMISE MADE
# TO THE DEAD WOMAN

## I. THE ISSUE OF WATER AT MONTFERMEIL

Montfermeil is situated between Livry and Chelles, on the southern edge of the high plateau that separates the Ourcq from the Marne. Today it is a fairly sizable market town, embellished all year round with stucco villas and, on Sundays, with its bourgeois citizens in full bloom. In 1823, there were not so many white houses in Montfermeil nor so many self-satisfied bourgeois. It was just a village in the woods. You did find a handful of rural retreats from the past century dotted around, recognizable by their grand air, their wrought-iron balconies, and those long windows with small square panes that show up as all kinds of different greens against the white of the closed shutters. But Montfermeil was no less a village for all that. The retired drapers and certified holiday makers had not yet discovered it. It was a quiet charming place on the road to nowhere; you could live the incredibly bountiful and easy life of a peasant there, cheaply. Only water was scarce because the plateau was so high.

You had to go quite a way to get it. The part of the village on the Gagny side drew its water from the glorious ponds in the woods; but the other end, surrounding the church on the Chelles side, only found drinking water at a little spring halfway up a hill close to the Chelles road, about a quarter of an hour away from Montfermeil.

So it was pretty tough going for each household to get its water supply. The great houses, the aristocracy—and the Thénardier dive was part of this—paid a *liard*,[1] or a farthing, a bucket to a man whose profession it was and who pulled in about eight sous a day from this Montfermeil waterworks; but this man only worked till seven o'clock at night in summer and five o'clock in winter, and once night had come on, once the ground-floor shutters were shut, anyone who didn't have any water to drink went and looked for it elsewhere or went without.

This was the terror of that poor creature that the reader has perhaps not forgotten—little Cosette. You will remember that Cosette was useful to the Thénardiers in two ways. They got themselves paid by the mother and waited on by the child. So when the mother stopped paying entirely, and we have just learned why in the preceding chapters, the Thénardiers hung on to Cosette. She saved them a servant. In this capacity, it was she who ran after water when it was needed. And so the child, who was absolutely horrified at the idea of going to the spring at night, made very sure that the house was never without water.

The Christmas of the year 1823 was particularly sparkling at Montfermeil. The beginning of winter had been mild; so far, there had been no frost or snow. Some tumblers from Paris had obtained permission from the mayor to set up their stands in the main street of the village, and a bunch of street peddlers were also allowed, by the same token, to erect their stalls on the church square and round as far as the ruelle du Boulanger, where, as perhaps you will recall, the Thénardiers' pothouse was located. This filled the inns and taverns and shook the quiet little backwater up with a lot of joyful noise. We should, as faithful historians, also add that among the curiosities on show in the square, there was a menagerie in which hideous barkers, dressed in rags and from heaven only knows where, showed the peasants of Montfermeil in 1823 one of those dreadful vultures from Brazil that our Royal Museum only acquired in 1845 and that have a tricolor cockade for an eye. Naturalists, I believe, call this bird *Caracara polyborus*; it belongs to the Apicidae order and the vulture family. A few good old retired Bonapartist soldiers of the village went to see the bird religiously. The tumblers boasted that the tricolor cockade was a unique phenomenon, one made by God expressly for their menagerie.

On Christmas Eve itself, several men, carters and peddlers, were sitting at table, drinking, ranged around four or five candles in the low room of the Thénardiers' inn. This room looked like every other tavern room; tables, pewter pitchers, bottles, drinkers, smokers; not much light, lots of noise. The year 1823 was, however, indicated by two objects that were in vogue at the time with the middle class and were sitting on a table, to wit, a kaleidoscope and an iridescent tin lamp. Mother Thénardier was taking care of supper, which was roasting over a good strong fire; old man Thénardier was drinking with his customers and talking politics.

Apart from the political chitchat, the main topics of which were the Spanish War and Monsieur le duc d'Angoulême, you could hear in the racket perfectly local brackets such as these: "Around Nanterre and Suresnes they've had a good yield of wine. Where they were counting on ten casks, they're getting twelve. That's a lot of juice shooting out of the press." "But the grapes can't have been ripe?" "Over that way, you don't pick the grapes ripe. If you pick 'em ripe, the wine turns oily come spring." "It's all light wine, then?" "It's all even lighter wines than around here. You've got to pick 'em green." And so on.

Or else, some miller might be carrying on: "Are we responsible for what's in the sacks? We find a heap of tiny seeds in them and we haven't got time to amuse ourselves picking 'em out, so of course we have to let 'em go under the millstones; there's rye grass, there's alfalfa, corn cockle, common vetch, hempseed, foxtail, love-lies-bleeding, and a lot of other stuff, not counting the pebbles that collect in certain types of wheat, especially in Breton wheat. I don't like milling Breton wheat one bit, any more than carpenters like sawing boards with nails in 'em. Just think of all the nasty dust that adds to the yield. And then they complain about the flour. It's not right. The flour isn't our fault."

In a space between two windows, a reaper, sitting at a table with a landowner who was trying to get a good price for work to be done on a meadow in the spring, said: "There's nothing wrong with the grass being wet. It cuts better. Dew is good, Monsieur. It doesn't make any difference—that grass, your grass, is young and pretty hard to cut. 'Cause it's so tender, it bends under the scythe." And so on . . .

Cosette was in her usual spot, sitting on the crosspiece of the kitchen table next to the fireplace. She was in rags, her feet were bare in her clogs, and she was knitting woolen stockings intended for the little Thénardier girls by the light of the fire. A tiny kitten was playing under the chairs. Two fresh children's voices could be heard laughing and babbling in a neighboring room; that was Éponine and Azelma.

In the corner of the fireplace, a leather strap hung from a nail.

At intervals, the cry of a very young child, who was somewhere in the house, broke through the ambient noise of the tavern. This was a little boy mother Thénardier had had a few winters back—"heaven knows why," she said, "must have been the cold weather"—and who was now a little over three years old. The mother had fed him, but did not love him. When the little nipper's fierce clamor got too much: "Your son's squealing," Thénardier would say. "Go and see what he wants, then." "Bah!" mother Thénardier would reply. "I'm sick to death of him." And the abandoned little boy would go on crying in the dark.

## II. Two Portraits Completed

So far in this book we have only seen the Thénardiers in profile; the moment has come to circle the couple and look at them from all sides.

Thénardier had just turned fifty. Madame Thénardier was hitting her forties, which is the fifties for a woman, so husband and wife were evenly matched in age.

The reader has, perhaps, retained some image of this Thénardier woman, since she first appeared, tall, blond, ruddy, barrel-like, brawny, boxy, huge, and agile; she belonged, as we said, to that race of colossal wild women who arch their backs at fairs with cobblestones hanging from their hair. She did everything around the place, the beds, the rooms, the washing, the cooking, whatever, she ruled the roost and called all the shots. The only servant she had was Cosette, a mouse at the service of an elephant. Everything trembled at the sound of her voice, the windows, the furniture, people. Her broad face, covered in freckles, looked like a strainer. She had a bit of a beard. She was the ideal butcher's boy dressed up as a girl. She swore like a trooper; she boasted of being able to crack a nut with a single blow. If it hadn't been for the novels she had read, which, at times, bizarrely brought out the snooty little prude beneath the ogress, the idea of calling her a woman would never have occurred to anyone. Mother Thénardier was like a damsel grafted onto a fishwife. To hear her speak, you'd say a gendarme; to see her knock it back, you'd say a carter; to see the way she treated Cosette, you'd say a torturer. When she was resting, a tooth protruded from her mouth.

Old man Thénardier was a skinny little runt, pale, angular, bony, rickety, who looked sick but was as fit as a fiddle; his deceitfulness started there. He habitually smiled as a precaution and was polite with nearly everyone, even with the beggar to whom he would not give a whit. He had the eyes of a weasel and the mien of a man of letters. He looked a lot like the portraits of the abbé Delille.[1] He liked to show off by drinking with the carters. No one had ever been able to get him drunk—he could drink anyone under the table. He smoked a great big pipe. He wore a smock and under the smock an old black outfit. He had pretensions to literature and to materialism as a philosophy. There were names he often uttered to support whatever he happened to be saying—Voltaire, Raynal, Parny, and, oddly, Saint Augustine.[2] He claimed to have "a system." Otherwise, he was a real swindler. A *filousophe,* a fowlosopher, or a crook and a philosopher rolled into one. Such a nuance exists. You will recall that he pretended he had served in the army; with a good deal of embellishment, he would tell how, at Waterloo, being a sergeant in a 6th or a 9th Light something-or-other, he alone, against a squadron of Hussars of Death, had covered "a dangerously wounded general" with his body, saving him from grapeshot. Whence the blazing sign for his wall and, for his inn, throughout the region, the name of "the sergeant of Waterloo's tavern." He was liberal, traditional, and Bonapartist. He had put in for the Champ d'Asile fund.[3] They reckoned in the village that he had once studied to be a priest.

We believe he had simply studied in Holland to be an innkeeper. This mongrel of very mixed blood was, in all probability, some kind of Fleming from Lille in Flanders, French in Paris, Belgian in Brussels, conveniently straddling two borders, with a foot in both camps. His prowess at Waterloo, we know about. As we see, he exaggerated a little. Drifting with the current, meandering, randomly trying his luck, this was the element of his existence; a divided conscience leads to a disjointed life, and most likely, in those stormy days that came to a head around June 18, 1815, Thénardier belonged to that species of marauding camp followers we were talking about earlier, a two-bit hustler, selling to some, stealing from others, and rolling along with the family, man, woman, and children, in some boneshaker of a cariole, in the wake of troops on the march, with a nose for the victorious army, to which he never failed to latch on. That campaign over, having, as he said, made a bundle, he had opened a pothouse in Montfermeil.

This "bundle," composed of purses and watches, gold rings and silver crosses, harvested from among the furrows sown with corpses, did not amount to much and was not enough to take this sutler turned greasy-spoon-keeper all that far.

Thénardier had something stiff in his movements, which reminded you of the barracks when he swore or of the seminary when he made the sign of the cross. He was a good talker. He let people think he was well educated. Nonetheless, the schoolmaster had noticed that he made "howlers." He composed traveler's bills in a superior manner, but a practiced eye could spot the odd spelling mistake. Thénardier was sly, greedy, lazy, and cunning. He did not disdain servant girls and so his wife did not have any anymore. That giant of a woman was jealous. In her view this skinny sallow little runt was the object of universal desire.

Thénardier, above all a man of astuteness and balance, was a scoundrel of the mild-mannered kind. This breed is the worst, for in them hypocrisy joins in.

It was not that Thénardier was not just as capable of rage as his wife on occasion; but this was very rare, and at those moments, since he resented the whole human race and contained inside him a furnace of hate, being one of those people who are always getting revenge, who blame anyone in the vicinity for anything that befalls them and are always ready to throw the sum of all the disappointments, failures, and calamities of their life at the first comer as a legitimate grievance—as all this leavening rose in him and foamed out of his mouth and into his eyes, he was truly ghastly. Woe to anyone who happened to be within arm's reach then!

Apart from all his other qualities, Thénardier was watchful and sharp, silent or occasionally chatty, and highly intelligent at all times. He had something of the look of the mariner accustomed to squinting into a spyglass. Thénardier was a statesman.

Every newcomer who entered the greasy spoon said when they saw mother Thénardier: There's the master of the house; she's the one who wears the trousers. Wrong. She was not even the mistress; the husband was master and mistress. She performed, he directed. He directed everything by a sort of invisible and continual magnetic action. A word was enough, sometimes a sign; the mastodon obeyed. Thénardier the man was for Thénardier the woman, without her fully realizing it, a species of weird and wonderful being. She had the virtues of her order of creation; never would she have differed in any detail with "Monsieur Thénardier," nor—this was an unthinkable hypothesis— would she have disagreed with her husband in public over any matter whatsoever. Never would she have committed, "in front of strangers," the mistake women so often make and which in parliamentary parlance is known as "unmasking the crown." Although their accord resulted in nothing but evil, there was admiration in mother Thénardier's submission to her husband. This mountain of flesh and fury moved when that frail little despot wagged his little finger. From his stunted and grotesque perspective, it amounted to this great universal: the worship of mind by matter; for certain ugly deformities have their raison d'être in the very depths of eternal beauty. There was something unknowable about Thénardier the man, whence his absolute hold over the woman. At certain moments, she saw him as a burning candle; at others, she felt him as a claw.

That woman was a formidable creature who loved only her children and feared only her husband. She was a mother only because she was a mammal. Besides, her maternal feelings stopped at her girls, and, as we will see, did not extend to boys. As for the man, he had only one thought: how to get rich quick.

He did not succeed. This great talent lacked a worthy theater. In Montfermeil, Thénardier was ruining himself, if ruin is possible when you are starting from nothing; in Switzerland or the Pyrenees, this pauper would have become a millionaire. But wherever fate sets down the innkeeper, there must he graze.

You will understand that the term *innkeeper* is used here in a limited sense and does not extend to a whole class.

In this same year, 1823, Thénardier owed around fifteen hundred francs in pressing debts, which made him fretful.

However doggedly unjust fate may have been toward him, Thénardier was one of those men who most appreciated, most profoundly and in the most modern way, something that is a virtue among barbarians and an item of merchandise among civilized peoples—hospitality. On top of this, he was an impressive poacher and renowned as an excellent shot. He had a certain cold, quiet laugh that was particularly dangerous.

His theories as an innkeeper sometimes shot out of him in flashes. He had a stock of professional aphorisms that he drilled into the mind of his wife. "The duty of the innkeeper," he said to her one day, sotto voce but with considerable vehemence, "is to sell whoever happens to come along grub, rest, light, fire, dirty sheets, a bit of the servant, fleas, a bit of a smile; to stop passersby, to empty small purses and to honestly lighten big fat ones; to respectfully shelter families on the move, to fleece the man, pluck the woman, skin the child; to charge for an open window, a closed window, the fireside nook, the armchair, the chair, the stool, the kitchen steps, the feather bed, the horsehair mattress, and the bale of straw; to know how much the dark wears out the mirror and to charge for that, and, come hell or high water, to make the traveler pay for everything, right down to the flies his dog gobbles up!"

That man and that woman were cunning and rage wedded together, a hideous and terrible coupling.

While the husband plotted and schemed, mother Thénardier, for her part, did not give the absent creditors a thought, did not worry about the day before or the day after, living furiously entirely in the moment.

So much for those two creatures. Cosette was caught between them, suffering their double pressure as though at once ground by a millstone and torn to shreds by pincers. The man and the woman each had a different style. Cosette was beaten to a pulp, courtesy of the woman; she went barefoot in winter, courtesy of the man.

Cosette clambered upstairs, ran downstairs, washed, brushed, rubbed, swept, raced about, slaved away, puffed and panted, lifted heavy things, and, puny as she was, did all the rough work. Not a shred of pity; a savage mistress, a venomous master. The Thénardier dive was like a web in which Cosette was caught, trembling. The ideal of oppression had been achieved in this sinister domesticity. It was a bit like a fly serving spiders.

The poor little girl was passive and kept her mouth shut.

When little girls find themselves in such a situation, at the dawn of their lives, so small, so naked, among men, what goes on in their souls, so fresh from God?

### III. MEN MUST HAVE WINE AND HORSES WATER

Four new travelers had turned up.

Cosette was dreaming forlornly, for, although she was only eight years old, she had already suffered so much that she dreamed with the mournful air of an old woman.

She had a black eye from a punch she had collected from mother Thénardier, which caused mother Thénardier to say now and again: "Talk about ugly, with that poached egg over her eye!"

Cosette, then, was thinking that it was dark, very dark, that the glasses and carafes in the rooms of the travelers who had suddenly appeared had to be filled immediately and that there was no water left in the household urn.

She was somewhat reassured by the fact that not a lot of water got drunk in the Thénardier household. There was no shortage of thirsty people around, but it was the kind of thirst that reaches more readily for the bottle than the water jug. Anyone asking for a glass of water among all those glasses of wine would have looked like a savage to those men. Yet there was a moment when the child quaked: Mother Thénardier lifted the lid on a pot that was boiling away on the stove, then grabbed a glass and dashed off toward the water urn. She turned on the tap; the child had lifted her head and was following her every move. A thin trickle of water ran from the tap only to fill the glass half-full.

"Damn!" she said. "There's no more water!"

Then she was quiet for a moment. The child did not breathe.

"Bah!" mother Thénardier went on, examining the half-full glass, "this'll have to do."

Cosette resumed her work, but for more than fifteen minutes she felt her heart skipping in her chest like a great snowflake. She counted the minutes as they ticked away and wished for all she was worth that it was the next morning.

Now and again one of the drinkers would look out at the street and exclaim: "It's as black as an oven!" Or, "You'd have to be a cat to be out on the street tonight without a lantern!" And Cosette would shudder.

All of a sudden, one of the peddlers who lodged in the tavern came in and said in a hard voice: "No one's watered my horse."

"Of course we have," said mother Thénardier.

"I say you haven't, missus," retorted the merchant.

Cosette had come out from under the table.

"Oh, yes we have, Monsieur!" she said. "The horse drank, all right, he drank from the bucket, a full bucket, I know 'cause it was me who took him the water and I talked to him and everything."

This was not true. Cosette was lying.

"Here's a girl no bigger than my fist and who can tell a whopper as big as a house!" cried the merchant. "I tell you he hasn't had anything to drink, you little rascal. He has a way of snorting when he hasn't had anything to drink that I know only too well."

Cosette persisted, adding in a barely audible voice, hoarse with anguish: "But he even drank a lot!"

"Come, come," said the merchant, angry now, "that's enough of that, get my horse some water and there's an end to it!"

Cosette dived back under the table.

"Actually, that's right," said mother Thénardier. "If the beast hasn't had anything to drink, she's got to have a drink."

Then she looked around: "All right, where's that kid?"

She bent down and spotted Cosette huddled at the far end of the table, almost under the drinkers' feet.

"Come out of there!" cried mother Thénardier.

Cosette emerged from the nook in which she had been hiding. Mother

Thénardier went on: "Mademoiselle Dog-for-want-of-a-better-name, go and get the horse something to drink."

"But, Madame," Cosette said feebly, "it's just that there is no water."

Mother Thénardier flung the door to the street wide open.

"Well, then, you'll have to go and get some!"

Cosette hung her head and went to get an empty bucket sitting in the corner of the fireplace. The bucket was bigger than she was and the child could easily have sat in it with room to spare.

Mother Thénardier went back to her stove and tasted what was in the pot with a wooden spoon, grumbling all the while: "There's some at the spring. They don't come any slyer than that one. I think I'd have done better to skip the onions."

Then she fumbled about in a drawer where there were some coins, pepper, and shallots.

"Here, Little Miss Toad," she added. "On the way back you can get me a big loaf at the baker's. Here's a fifteen-sou piece."

Cosette had a small side pocket in her smock; she took the piece without a word and put it in her pocket.

Then she stood rooted to the spot, bucket in hand, the open door in front of her. She seemed to be waiting for someone to come to her rescue.

"Off you go!" cried mother Thénardier.

Cosette went out. The door shut behind her.

## IV. A DOLL MAKES ITS ENTRANCE

The row of shops exposed to the wind that started at the church extended, as you will recall, right to the Thénardiers' tavern. These shops, because of all the good burghers who would shortly be passing on their way to midnight mass, were all lit up with candles burning in funnel-shaped paper holders, which, as the schoolmaster of Montfermeil said as he sat at a table at the Thénardiers' at that very moment, created "a magical effect." On the other hand, not a star was to be seen in the sky.

The last of these stalls, set up exactly opposite the Thénardiers' door, was a fancy goods shop, all glittering with tinsel and flashy beading, glass trinkets and magnificent things made of tin. In the first row, out in front, against a backdrop of white towels, the merchant had placed a huge doll nearly two feet tall that was dressed in a pink crepe frock and had golden ears of wheat on its head and real hair and enamel eyes. All day this marvel had been on show to the great bedazzlement of passersby under ten, without there apparently being a mother rich enough or extravagant enough in Montfermeil to give it to her child. Éponine and Azelma had spent hours contemplating it and Cosette herself, furtively it is true, had dared to cast a glance at it.

As Cosette went out, bucket in hand, forlorn and stricken as she was, she could not help herself from lifting her eyes to this wonderful doll, "the lady," as she called it. The poor child stopped in her tracks, petrified. She had not yet seen the doll up close. The whole shop seemed like a palace to her; the doll was not a doll, it was a vision. It was joy, splendor, wealth, happiness that appeared in a kind of dreamlike radiance to this unhappy little being so deeply swamped by a cold and dismal misery. With that sad and naïve sagacity of childhood, Cosette measured the abyss that separated her from the doll. She told herself you'd have to be a queen or at least a princess to have a thing like that. She studied the beautiful pink frock, the beautiful silky hair, and she thought: "How happy she must be, that doll!" She could not take her eyes off the fabulous boutique. The more she looked, the more dazzled she was. She believed she was seeing paradise. There were other dolls behind the big one that looked to her like fairies and sprites. The merchant pacing back and forth at the back of his stall had a bit of the effect on her of the Eternal Father.

In her adoration, she forgot everything, even the job she had been landed with. All of a sudden, the harsh voice of mother Thénardier brought her back to reality: "You little twirp! Are you still here? Wait there, I'm on my way! I'd like to know what she thinks she's doing there! You little monster, get going!"

Mother Thénardier had glanced out at the street and seen Cosette in ecstasy.

Cosette ran off with her bucket as fast as her legs would carry her.

## V. A LITTLE GIRL ALL ON HER OWN

As the Thénardier inn was in the part of the village that was nearest the church, it was to the spring in the woods on the Chelles side that Cosette had to go to draw water.

She did not look at a single merchant's display on the way. As long as she was in the ruelle du Boulanger and in the vicinity of the church, the illuminated shops lit the way, but soon the last lights of the last stall disappeared. The poor child found herself in darkness. She plunged on. Only, as a certain emotion overcame her, she rattled the handle of the bucket for all she was worth as she walked. The noise this made kept her company.

The farther she went, the thicker the darkness became. There was no longer a soul anywhere on the street. And yet, she met a woman who turned round when she saw her go by and stopped, mumbling between her lips: "Where on earth can that child be going? Is it a baby werewolf?" Then the woman recognized Cosette. "Of course!" she said. "It's the Lark!"

Cosette walked down the labyrinth of crooked deserted streets that ends the village of Montfermeil on the Chelles side. As long as she had houses and even just walls on both sides of the road, she trotted along boldly enough. Now and again, she saw the light of a candle beaming through the crack in a shutter and that was light and life to her, it meant there were people there and this reassured her. But the farther she went, the more her pace slowed, as though by itself. When she had turned the corner of the last house, Cosette stopped dead. To go beyond the last shop had been hard; to go farther than the last house— that was becoming impossible. She put the bucket on the ground, stuck her hand in her hair and began to slowly scratch her head, a gesture peculiar to children who are terrified and undecided. It was no longer Montfermeil, it was the open country. Dark and deserted space lay before her. She looked in despair at the darkness where there was no one now, where there were animals, where there were perhaps ghosts. She looked hard, and she heard animals walking in the grass and distinctly saw ghosts stirring in the trees. So she picked up her bucket and fear made her reckless: "Bah!" she said. "I'll tell her there is no more water!"

And she returned resolutely to Montfermeil.

Scarcely had she gone a hundred paces when she stopped again and went back to scratching her head. Now it was mother Thénardier who appeared to her; hideous mother Thénardier with her hyena mouth and rage blazing in her eyes. The child cast a pitiful glance in front and behind. What could she do? What would become of her? Where could she go? Before her, the specter of mother Thénardier; behind her all the ghosts of the night and the woods. It was in the face of mother Thénardier that she shrank back. She turned back to the spring road and began to run. She ran out of the village and she ran into the woods, not looking anywhere, not hearing anything. She only stopped running when she ran out of breath but even then, she did not stop walking. She put one foot in front of the other and continued straight ahead, frantic.

As she was running, she wanted to cry.

The nocturnal rustling of the forest enveloped her completely. She could no longer think, she could no longer see. The vast night confronted this tiny being. On one side, endless shadow; on the other, an atom.

It was only seven or eight minutes from the clearing in the woods to the spring. Cosette knew the way from having done the trip fairly often during the day. What was strange was that she did not get lost. A residual instinct guided her vaguely. But she did not glance to left or right for fear of seeing things in the branches of the trees or in the bushes. And so she made it to the spring.

This was a narrow natural basin, carved by the water through soil thick with clay, about two feet deep, surrounded by moss and that tall crimped grass known as "Henri IV's ruffs," and it was paved with a few large stones. A stream trickled out of it with a tranquil sound.

Cosette did not pause for breath. It was very black, but she was used to coming to the fountain. She searched in the dark with her left hand for a young oak bent over the spring that normally served her as support, found a branch, hung from it, lunged down and plunged the bucket in the spring. She was so worked up at that moment that her strength was as the strength of three. While she was leaning over in this position, she did not notice that the pocket of her smock was emptying itself into the spring. The fifteen-sou coin fell into the drink. Cosette neither saw nor heard it fall in. She pulled the bucket out almost full to the brim and plonked it on the grass.

That done, she realized she was completely overcome with exhaustion. She would naturally have liked to take off immediately, but the effort of filling the bucket had been so great she simply could not take a step. She just had to sit down. She plopped on the grass and stayed there, squatting. She closed her eyes, then opened them again, without knowing why, but without being able to do otherwise.

By her side, the water swirling in the bucket made circles that looked like snakes of white fire.

Over her head, the sky was covered in huge black clouds that were like palls of smoke. The tragic mask of shadow seemed to imperceptibly lean over the child.

Jupiter was setting in the depths of the sky.

The child looked wild-eyed at that great star, which she did not know and which frightened her. The planet was, in fact, very close to the horizon at that moment and passed through a thick layer of mist that gave it a horrible red color. The mist, lugubriously flushed with crimson, made the star bigger. You would have said it was a luminous wound.

A cold wind blew off the plain. The woods were murky, without any rustling of leaves, without any of those soft fresh glimmers of summer. Great branches rose up hideously. Spindly warped bushes whistled in the glades. The tall grasses writhed beneath the icy gusts like eels. The brambles twisted like long arms trying to snatch their prey in their claws; dry heather, driven by the wind, whipped past as though fleeing in terror from something coming. On every side were gloomy expanses.

The dark is dizzying. Man needs light. Whoever burrows into the opposite of daylight feels their heart lurch. When the eye sees black, the mind sees trouble. In an eclipse, in the night, in sooty opacity, there is anxiety, even in the heartiest. No one can walk alone through the forest at night without trembling. Shadows and trees form two fearful densities. A chimerical reality appears in the indistinct depths. The inconceivable takes shape a few steps away from you with a spectral clarity. You see floating, in space or in your own mind, something as strangely vague and elusive as the dreams of sleeping flowers. Ferocious things lurk on the horizon. You breathe in the effluvia of the great black void. You both want, and are frightened, to look behind you. The gaping holes opening up in the night, things that now look crazed, flinty profiles that break up as you approach, murky unbridled movements, churned-up tufts, livid puddles, the mournful reflected in the funereal, the sepulchral immensity of the silence, possible unknown beings, weirdly leaning branches, frighteningly twisting trees, long fistfuls of shivering grass—you are defenseless against all of it. No one is so hardy they don't flinch and feel themselves on the verge of anguish. You feel a ghastly sensation as though your soul were mingling with the shadows. This penetration by the darkness is unspeakably sinister for a child.

Forests are apocalypses; and the beating of a little soul's wings makes an agonizing sound under their monstrous vault.

Without understanding what she was going through, Cosette felt gripped by the black enormity of nature. It was no longer merely terror that took hold of her but something even more terrible than terror. She was shivering. Words cannot describe the strangeness of the shiver that chilled her to the bottom of her heart. Her eyes had become wild. She had a feeling that she might not be able to stop herself from going back there at the same time the following night.

So, out of a sort of instinct, to snap out of this odd state that she did not understand but that terrified her, she began to count out loud, one, two, three, four, up to ten, and when she had finished, she started again. This brought her back to her senses so that she could see the things around her for what they really were. Her hands, which she had gotten wet drawing the water, felt cold. She stood up. Fear had returned to her, a natural and insurmountable fear. She had only one thought and that was to run; to run as fast as her legs would carry her, through the woods, through the fields, till she reached houses, windows, burning candles. Her gaze fell on the bucket in front of her. Such was the fright that mother Thénardier inspired in her that she dared not run without the bucket of water. She grabbed the handle with both hands. She could hardly lift the bucket.

She took a dozen steps like this, but the bucket was full, it was heavy, she was forced to put it down again. She got her breath back for a moment, lifted the handle again and started walking once more, this time for a little longer. But she had to stop again. After a few seconds' rest, she set off again. She walked bent forward with her head down like an old woman. The weight of the bucket strained and stiffened her skinny little arms. The iron handle numbed and froze her tiny wet hands; from time to time she was forced to stop, and each time she stopped cold water slopped out of the bucket and splashed over her bare legs. This was happening in the depths of a wood, at night, in winter, far from all human eyes; she was an eight-year-old child. Only God could see this sad sight at that moment.

And doubtless her mother, too, more's the pity! For there are some things that cause dead women to open their eyes in their graves.

She breathed with a kind of painful rasp; sobs choked her throat, but she dared not cry, she was so frightened of mother Thénardier, even at a distance. It was her habit at all times to imagine that mother Thénardier was there.

But she could not make much headway the way she was going and her progress was painfully slow. It was no use trying to shorten the breaks and to walk as far as possible between them; it would take her more than an hour to get back to Montfermeil this way, and mother Thénardier would give her a belting. This anguish melded with the horror she felt at being alone in the woods at night. She was worn out with exhaustion and not yet out of the woods. Having reached an old chestnut tree she knew, she made one last stop longer than the others to have a proper rest, then she gathered all her strength, grabbed the bucket and courageously set off walking again. But the poor little mite could not stop herself from crying out in her despair: "Oh, my God! My God!"

At that moment, she suddenly felt that the bucket no longer weighed a thing. A hand, which seemed to her enormous, had just seized the handle and lifted it vigorously. She raised her head. A big black shape, straight and tall, was walking beside her in the darkness. It was a man, who had come up behind her without her hearing him coming. This man, without saying a word, had grabbed hold of the handle of the bucket she was carrying.

There are instincts for all life's encounters. The little girl felt no fear.

## VI. WHICH PERHAPS PROVES BOULATRUELLE'S INTELLIGENCE

During the afternoon of this same Christmas Eve of 1823, a man had been strolling up and down the deserted part of the boulevard de l'Hôpital in Paris for quite some time. This man looked like someone looking for a place to stay and seemed to stop by choice at the most humble houses along this dilapidated outer reach of the faubourg Saint-Marceau.[1]

We will see below that the man did, in fact, rent a room in this isolated quartier.

In his dress as in his whole person, the man embodied the archetype of what we might call the genteel beggar, combining extreme poverty with extreme propriety. This is a rather rare mix that inspires, in intelligent hearts, the twin respect we feel for a person who is extremely poor and for one who is extremely dignified. He was wearing a very old and very much brushed round hat, a completely threadbare redingote made of coarse yellow ocher cotton, a color not too odd at the time, a big waistcoat with pockets in a thoroughly outmoded cut, black breeches that had gone gray at the knees, black wool stockings, and heavy shoes with copper buckles. You would have said he looked like an old private tutor from a good house back home from the emigration. Going by his completely white hair, his wrinkled forehead, his pale lips, his face, all of which conveyed dejection and world-weariness, you would have put his age at well over sixty. But going by his firm, if slow, gait, by the unusual virility that marked his movements, you would have put it at fifty, if that. The wrinkles on his forehead were in the right place and would have biased in his favor anyone paying him particular attention. His lips were contracted in a strange crease that looked severe but was actually humble. Deep in his eyes there was some indefinably grim serenity. In his left hand he was carrying a small parcel knotted into a handkerchief and with his right, he was leaning on a kind of stick cut from a hedge. The stick had been worked with some care and did not look too nasty; the knots had been turned into a feature and a coral knob had been made out of red wax; it was a cudgel, yet it looked like a cane.

There aren't many people out walking on this boulevard, especially in winter. The man appeared to steer clear of them rather than seek them out, though without making this too obvious.

In those days, King Louis XVIII went nearly every day to Choisy-le-Roi. It was one of his favorite promenades. At around two o'clock, almost invariably, you would see his carriage and the royal cavalcade stream past furiously on the boulevard de l'Hôpital.

This was as good as a watch and a clock for the poor women of the quartier who would say: "It's two o'clock, there he is heading back to the Tuileries."

Some would come running and others would line the roadside; for a passing king always creates a commotion. Besides, the appearance and disappearance of Louis XVIII created certain waves on the streets of Paris. It was fast, but majestic. This impotent king liked a good gallop; not being able to walk, he liked to run; that legless cripple would gladly have had himself pulled by lightning. He passed, pacific and stern, between bare sabers. His massive berlin,[2] gilded all over with big bundles of lilies painted on the sides, made a great racket as it rolled past. You hardly had time to catch a glimpse of it. You could just see, in the right-hand corner at the back, on padded white satin cushions, a broad face, firm and rosy, a forehead freshly powdered *à l'oiseau royal*, an eye proud, hard, and keen, a scholar's smile,[3] two great braided epaulets floating on a bourgeois frockcoat, the Golden Fleece, the cross of Saint Louis, the cross of the Légion d'honneur, the silver medal of the Holy Spirit, a fat gut, and a wide blue sash:[4] This was the king. Outside Paris, he kept his white feather hat on his knees, which were swaddled in high English gaiters; when he returned to town, he stuck his hat back on his head, greeting few. He looked on the people coldly and they returned his look. When he appeared for the first time in the quartier Saint-Marceau, all he succeeded in doing was to solicit these words from a local: "That fat pig runs the place."

This unfailing passage of the king at the same hour was thus the big daily event of the boulevard de l'Hôpital.

The rambler in the yellow redingote was clearly not from the neighborhood and probably not from Paris, either, for he was ignorant of this detail.

When at two o'clock the royal carriage, surrounded by a squadron of silver-trimmed guards of the royal corps, came into the boulevard after skirting around La Salpêtrière hospital, he appeared startled and almost alarmed. He was the only person in the side street and he leaped back behind a recess in the enclosure wall, though this did not prevent Monsieur le duc d'Havré from spotting him. Monsieur le duc d'Havré,[5] as captain of the guards on duty that day, was sitting in the carriage opposite the king. He said to His Majesty: "There's a man with a mean mug for you." The policemen who were clearing the king's passage also noticed him and one of them was given the order to follow him. But the man melted away into the lonely little backstreets of the faubourg and as the light was beginning to fade, the officer lost all trace of him, as is noted in a report addressed that same evening to Monsieur le comte d'Anglès,[6] minister of state, prefect of police.

When the man in the yellow redingote had shaken off the police officer, he doubled back, though not without turning round many times to make sure he was not being followed. At a quarter past four, that is, when night had fallen, he went past the Porte Saint-Martin theater, where the play they were putting on that day was *The Two Convicts.*[7] The poster, lit up by the lights of the theater, struck him even though he was walking fast, and he stopped to read it. An instant later, he was in the cul-de-sac of La Planchette and he went into the Plat d'étain—the Pewter Dish, where the office of the Lagny coach was then located. This coach left at four-thirty. The horses were hitched and the travelers, summoned by the coach driver, were busily clambering up the steep iron steps of the dilapidated crate.

The man asked: "Do you have a seat?"

"Just one, next to me, up on the box," said the driver.

"I'll take it."

"Climb up."

But before starting off, the driver shot a glance at the traveler's mediocre getup, at the smallness of his bundle, and made sure he got the money up front.

"Are you going as far as Lagny?" the driver asked him.

"Yes," said the man.

The traveler paid the Lagny fare.

Off they went. When they had passed the barrière, the driver tried to start up a conversation, but the traveler answered only in monosyllables. The driver decided to whistle and to swear at his horses instead.

The driver wrapped himself up in his coat. It was cold. The man did not appear to notice. And so they went through Gournay and Neuilly-sur-Marne.

At around six o'clock in the evening they had reached Chelles. The driver stopped to let his horses have a breather in front of an inn for carters set up in the old buildings of the royal abbey.

"I'll get down here," said the man.

He took his bundle and his stick and jumped down from the coach. An instant later he had disappeared. He had not gone into the inn.

When, a few minutes later, the coach set off again for Lagny, they did not meet up with him on the main street of Chelles.

The coach driver turned to the passengers inside the coach.

"Now, there's a man," he said, "who's not from around here—I certainly don't know him. He doesn't look like he has a sou to his name, yet money means nothing to him; he pays for Lagny and he only goes as far as Chelles. It's night, all the houses are shut, he doesn't go into the inn, and we don't set eyes on him again. He must have sunk into the ground."

The man had not sunk into the ground, but he had swiftly paced up and down the main street of Chelles in the dark; then he had swung to the left before going as far as the church and taking the back road that leads to Montfermeil, quite as though he had been there before and knew the area.

He moved quickly down this road. At the spot where it intersects with the old road bordered with trees that goes from Gagny to Lagny he heard footsteps coming his way. He swiftly hid in a ditch and waited till the people walking past were a long way off. This precaution was more or less superfluous in any case, since, as we have already said, it was a very black December night. You were lucky to make out two or three stars in the sky.

It is at this point that the hill starts to climb. The man did not return to the Montfermeil road; he turned right and bounded across the fields till he reached the woods.

When he was in the woods, he slowed his pace and began to look carefully at all the trees, taking one step at a time, as though he were searching for and following a path known only to himself. There was a moment when he seemed to lose his way and when he stopped, undecided. At last he arrived, groping all the way, at a clearing where there was a mound of big whitish stones. He hurried over to the stones and examined them attentively in the night fog, as though he were formally inspecting them. A huge tree, covered in those excrescences that are the warts of vegetation, stood a few feet away from the heap of stones. He went to the tree and ran his hand over the bark of the trunk as if he were trying to recognize and count all the warts.

Opposite the tree, which was an ash, there was a chestnut tree that was losing its bark through some disease and that had a strip of zinc nailed on as a bandage. He stood on tiptoe and touched the band of zinc.

Then he stamped for some little time on the ground in the space bounded by the tree and the stones, as though making sure the ground had not been freshly dug.

That done, he got his bearings and resumed walking through the woods.

It was this man who had just stumbled on Cosette.

As he weaved through the thicket in the direction of Montfermeil, he had spotted this little shadow, struggling along groaning, dumping its burden on the ground, then picking it up again and walking on. He had approached and registered that it was a very young child, loaded with an enormous bucket of water. So he had gone up to the child and silently taken the handle of the bucket.

### VII. Cosette Side by Side with the Stranger in the Dark

Cosette, as we have said, had not felt frightened. The man spoke to her. He spoke in a grave voice, almost a whisper.

"My child, that is quite a load you're carrying there, for you."

Cosette lifted her head and replied: "Yes, Monsieur."

"Give it to me," the man went on. "I'll carry it for you."

Cosette let go of the bucket. The man began to walk along by her side.

"It is incredibly heavy, actually," he said between clenched teeth. Then he added: "How old are you, little girl?"

"Eight, Monsieur."

"And have you come some distance with this?"

"I've come from the spring in the woods."

"And do you have far to go?"

"It's a good quarter of an hour from here."

The man didn't say anything more for a while, then he said suddenly: "Don't you have a mother, then?"

"I don't know," replied the little girl.

Before the man had time to say another word, she added: "I don't think so. Others have one. Me, I don't have one."

And after a pause, she went on: "I don't think I ever had one."

The man stopped, put the bucket on the ground, bent down and placed his hands on the little girl's shoulders, trying hard to look at her and see her face in the darkness. Cosette's thin and puny silhouette took shape in the livid light of the sky.

"What is your name?" the man asked.

"Cosette."

The man felt something like an electric shock. He looked at Cosette again, then took his hands off her shoulders, grabbed the bucket and resumed walking.

After a moment, he asked: "Where do you live, little girl?"

"In Montfermeil, if you know it."

"Is that where we are going?"

"Yes, Monsieur."

He paused again, then started off once more.

"So who is it who sent you off at this hour to get water in the woods?"

"It was Madame Thénardier."

The man continued in a tone of voice he hoped sounded casual, but in which there was an odd tremor he could not hide: "What does she do, your Madame Thénardier?"

"She's my old lady," said the child. "She keeps the inn."

"The inn?" said the man. "Well then, that's where I'm going to spend the night. Take me there."

"That's where we're going," said the child.

The man was walking fairly quickly. Cosette kept up with him without any trouble. She no longer felt tired. Now and then she lifted her eyes up to the man with a sort of inexpressible tranquillity and abandon. No one had ever taught her to turn to Providence and to pray. Yet she felt something inside that resembled hope and joy and that wafted upward to the heavens.

Some minutes went by. The man went on: "Isn't there some kind of servant at Madame Thénardier's?"

"No, Monsieur."

"Are you on your own?"

"Yes, Monsieur."

There was another silence. Cosette piped up: "That is, there are two little girls."

"What little girls?"

"Popine and Zelma."

That was how the child shortened the fabulously romantic names so dear to mother Thénardier.

"Who are Popine and Zelma?"

"They are Madame Thénardier's young ladies. You could say, her daughters."

"And what do they do, this pair?"

"Oh!" said the child. "They have beautiful dolls, things with gold in them, all sorts of stuff. They play, they have fun."

"All day long?"

"Yes, Monsieur."

"What about you?"

"Me, I work."

"All day long?"

The little girl raised her great big eyes where tears were forming invisibly in the night, and she replied softly: "Yes, Monsieur."

After an interval of silence, she went on: "Sometimes, when I've finished work and if they let me, I have fun, too."

"How do you have fun?"

"However I can. They leave me alone. But I don't have many toys. Popine and Zelma don't like me playing with their dolls. All I have is a little lead sword no bigger than that."

The little girl held up her little finger.

"And it doesn't cut?"

"Yes it does, Monsieur," said the little girl. "It cuts lettuce and the heads off flies."

They were coming to the village. Cosette guided the stranger through the streets. They passed the baker's, but Cosette forgot all about the bread she was supposed to bring back. The man had stopped asking her questions and now kept a mournful silence. When they had put the church behind them, the man, seeing all the shops out in the open under the stars, asked Cosette: "So the fair has come to town, has it?"

"No, Monsieur, it's Christmas."

As they were getting near the inn, Cosette touched his arm, gingerly.

"Monsieur?"

"What, little one?"

"We are quite close to the house now."

"Well, then?"

"Would you let me have the bucket again now?"

"Why?"

"Because, if Madame sees someone else carried it for me, she'll belt me."

The man gave her back the bucket. An instant later, they were at the door of the pothouse.

## VIII. Unpleasantness of Putting Up a Pauper Who Might Just Be Rich

Cosette could not stop herself from shooting a look at the great doll that was still on show in the fancy goods shop; then she knocked on the door. The door opened. Mother Thénardier appeared, candle in hand.

"Ah, it's you, you little twirp! Lord knows, you took your time! She's been dawdling again having fun, the little hussy!"

"Madame," said Cosette, all trembling, "here is a monsieur who would like a room."

Mother Thénardier swiftly replaced her scowl with an amiable grimace, a change of perspective peculiar to innkeepers, and avidly strained to get a look at the newcomer.

"You are the gentleman?" she asked.

"Yes, Madame," replied the man, raising his hand to his hat.

Rich travelers are not so polite. The gesture plus inspection of the stranger's getup and luggage, which mother Thénardier passed in review at a glance, wiped the amiable grimace off her face and caused the scowl to reappear. She resumed drily: "In you come, my good man."

The "good man" entered. Mother Thénardier threw him a second glance, examined in particular his redingote, which was absolutely worn out, and his hat, which was a bit knocked around, and consulted her husband, who was still drinking with the carters, with a nod and a wink and a shake of the head. The husband responded with that imperceptible wagging of the index finger that, backed by a pouting of the lips, signifies in such cases: broke. At that, mother Thénardier cried: "Ah, well! My dear man, I'm truly sorry, but I'm full up."

"You can put me wherever you like," said the man. "In the attic, in the stables. I'll pay the same price as a room."

"Forty sous."

"Forty sous it is."

"Marvelous."

"Forty sous!" a carter whispered to mother Thénardier. "But it's only twenty sous."

"It's forty sous for the likes of him," replied mother Thénardier in the same tone. "I don't put paupers up for any less."

"It's true," the husband added softly. "It lowers the tone of a place to have that lot hanging round."

But the man, after leaving his bundle and his stick on a seat, had sat down at a table, where Cosette rushed to put a bottle of wine and a glass. The peddler who had asked for the bucket of water had gone to take it to his horse himself. Cosette had resumed her place under the kitchen table and her knitting.

The man, who had hardly wet his lips with the wine he had poured himself, contemplated the little girl with a strange intensity.

Cosette was ugly. If she had been happy, she might have been pretty. We have already sketched that sad little figure. Cosette was thin and pale. She was nearly eight years old but you would have put her age at six. Her great big eyes, set deep in a sort of shadow, were almost lifeless because of all the crying they had done. The corners of her mouth had that curve of habitual anguish that you see in people on death row or in the terminally ill. Her hands were, as her mother had guessed, "covered in chilblains." The firelight that shone on her at that moment made her bones more prominent and her thinness alarmingly visible. As she was always shivering, she had gotten into the habit of pressing her knees together. All she had for clothes was an old rag that would have been pitiful in summer but that was truly horrifying in winter. All she had on was a bit of cotton riddled with holes; not a scrap of wool. Here and there you could see her skin, and everywhere you could make out black-and-blue bruises showing where mother Thénardier had thumped her. Her bare legs were red and rough. The hollow at her collarbone would have made you weep. The little girl's whole person, the way she moved, her demeanor, the sound of her voice, the gaps between one word and the next, her eyes, her silence, her slightest gesture, expressed and translated a single idea: fear.

Fear was written all over her; she was covered in it, so to speak; fear drew her elbows back against her sides, pulled her heels back under her skirts, made her take up the smallest possible space, only let her breathe as much as strictly necessary, and had become what we might call her body's habit, without any possible variation, except to intensify. In the depths of her irises there was a point of amazement where terror lurked.

This fear was so strong that when she arrived, soaked to the bone as she was, Cosette had not dared to go and dry off by the fire and had silently resumed her work.

The expression in the eyes of this eight-year-old child was normally so forlorn and sometimes so tragic that it seemed, at certain moments, that she was in the process of turning into an idiot or a demon.

Never, as we said, had she known what it was to pray, never had she set foot inside a church. "You think I've got the time?" mother Thénardier would say.

The man in the yellow redingote did not take his eyes off Cosette.

"Ah, yes! Where's the bread?"

Cosette, as was her custom every time mother Thénardier raised her voice, sprang out very fast from under the table.

She had completely forgotten about the bread. She resorted to the expedient of children who are always frightened; she lied.

"Madame, the baker was shut."

"You should have knocked."

"I did knock, Madame."

"Well, then?"

"He didn't open."

"I'll find out tomorrow if that's true," said mother Thénardier, "and if you're lying, I'll make you dance! Meanwhile, give me back the fifteen-sou piece."

Cosette plunged her hand into the pocket of her smock, and went green. The fifteen-sou coin was not there anymore.

"Come on!" said mother Thénardier. "Didn't you hear me?"

Cosette turned her pocket inside out. There was nothing there. What could have happened to the money? The poor little girl could not get a word out. She was petrified.

"Did you lose it, the fifteen-sou coin?" growled mother Thénardier. "Or are you trying to steal it from me?"

As she spoke she reached up to grab the strap hanging from the mantelpiece. This dreaded movement gave Cosette the strength to shout: "Have mercy, Madame! Madame, I won't do it again!"

Mother Thénardier took down the strap.

Meanwhile the man in the yellow redingote had been fumbling in the pocket of his waistcoat without anyone noticing. In any case, the other travelers were drinking or playing cards and paying no attention to anything else.

Cosette curled up into a ball of anguish in the corner of the fireplace, trying to gather up and conceal her poor half-naked limbs from view. Mother Thénardier raised her arm.

"Excuse me, Madame," said the man, "but a little while ago I saw something fall out of the little girl's pocket and roll away. It may be that."

As he spoke he bent down and appeared to be searching on the ground for a moment.

"I was right. Here it is," he said, getting up.

And he handed a silver coin to mother Thénardier.

"Yes, that's it," she said.

That was not it, for it was a twenty-sou coin, but mother Thénardier had made a profit. She pocketed the coin and contented herself with throwing the child a ferocious look, saying:

"Don't let it happen again, ever!"

Cosette went back to what mother Thénardier called her "hole" and her great big eyes, fixed on the unknown traveler, began to take on an expression they had never had. It was still mainly naïve amazement but now tinged with a kind of stunned trust.

"While I think of it, do you want something to eat?" mother Thénardier asked the traveler.

He did not reply. He seemed to be deep in thought.

"What kind of man is this fellow?" mother Thénardier hissed. "Some frightful pauper. He doesn't have enough cash to eat. Is he only going to pay me for his room? Luckily he didn't get it into his head to pinch the money that was on the ground, but—"

Meanwhile a door opened and in walked Éponine and Azelma.

They really were two pretty little girls, more bourgeois than peasants, incredibly charming, one with very shiny auburn plaits, the other with long black plaits that fell down her back, both so lively, clean, plump, fresh, and healthy that it was a pleasure to lay eyes on them. They were warmly bundled up, but with such maternal art that the layers of material did not detract in any way from the stylishness of the arrangement. Winter was catered for without erasing spring. The two little girls streamed light. What is more, they reigned supreme. In their outfits, in their gaiety, in the racket they made, there was supreme power. When they entered, mother Thénardier said to them in a scolding voice that was full of adoration: "Ah! So there you are, you two!"

She pulled them up onto her knees, one after the other, smoothed their hair, retied their ribbons, and then releasing them again and with that gentle sort of shake peculiar to mothers, she cried: "Aren't they a sight for sore eyes!"

They went and sat by the fire. They had a doll they were turning over and back on their knees, chirping away happily. From time to time Cosette lifted her eyes from her knitting and sadly watched them playing.

Éponine and Azelma did not look at Cosette. For them she was like the dog. These three little girls could not chalk up twenty-four years between them and yet they already represented all of adult society; on the one side, envy, on the other, scorn.

The Thénardier sisters' doll was very washed-out and very old and badly battered, but it did not look any less wonderful to Cosette, who had never had a doll in her life, "a real doll," to use an expression any child will understand.

Suddenly mother Thénardier, who was constantly moving back and forth about the room, noticed that Cosette was distracted and that instead of working she was busy watching the little girls play.

"Aha! I've caught you!" she cried. "That's your idea of work, is it! I'll make you work with the strap."

The stranger, without getting up from his chair, turned toward mother Thénardier.

"Madame," he said, smiling with an almost frightened look, "Bah! Let her play!"

On the part of any traveler who had eaten a slice of lamb and drunk two bottles of wine at supper and who did not look like "a frightful pauper," such a wish would have been a command. But for a man with a hat like that to allow himself to have a desire and for a man with a redingote like that to allow himself to have a wish, that was something mother Thénardier did not feel she should put up with. She retorted sharply: "She has to work, since she eats. I don't feed her for her to do nothing."

"So what is she making?" asked the stranger in that sweet voice that contrasted so strangely with his beggar's clothes and his porter's shoulders.

Mother Thénardier deigned to reply: "Stockings, if it's all the same to you. Stockings for my little girls who don't have any, none to speak of, and will soon be getting around barefoot."

The man looked at Cosette's poor red feet and continued: "When will she be through with this pair of stockings?"

"She's got a good three or four full days ahead of her, the lazy thing."

"And how much might this pair of stockings be worth, when they're done?"

Mother Thénardier threw him a scornful look.

"At least thirty sous."

"Would you take five francs for them?" the man went on.

"Christ!" guffawed a carter who was listening. "Five francs? You bet she'll take 'em! Five big ones!"

Old man Thénardier decided it was time to take matters in hand.

"Yes, Monsieur, if they take your fancy, we could give you these stockings for five francs. We never refuse travelers anything."

"You'd have to pay right away," said mother Thénardier in her usual short, peremptory manner.

"I will buy this pair of stockings," replied the man, "and," he added, taking a five-franc coin out of his pocket and laying it on the table, "I will pay for them."

Then he turned to Cosette.

"Now your work is mine. Go and play, my child."

The carter was so moved by the five-franc coin that he left his glass where it was and came running over.

"Damn if it isn't real!" he said, examining it. "A real rear wheel! Not a fake!"

Old man Thénardier went over and quietly slipped the coin in his waistcoat pocket.

Mother Thénardier had no comeback. She bit her lips and her face took on an expression of hate.

Yet Cosette was trembling. She took the risk of asking: "Madame, is it true? Can I go and play?"

"Play!" said mother Thénardier in a terrible voice.

"Thank you, Madame," said Cosette.

And while her mouth thanked mother Thénardier, her whole little heart thanked the traveler.

Old man Thénardier went back to his drinking. His wife said in his ear:

"What the hell can this yellow man be?"

"I have seen," replied old man Thénardier, in a haughty tone, "millionaires getting around in redingotes like that."

Cosette had left her knitting but she had not left her place. Cosette always moved as little as possible. She had taken out of a box behind her a few old rags and her little lead sword.

Éponine and Azelma paid no attention whatsoever to what was happening. They had just performed a most important operation; they had grabbed hold of the cat. They had thrown the doll on the ground and Éponine, who was the elder, was wrapping the little cat up despite its meowings and contortions, in a whole pile of old red and blue rags. While she was performing this grave and difficult work, she said to her sister in that sweet and adorable language of children whose gracefulness, like the splendor of a butterfly's wings, eludes us when we try to pin it down.

"See, sister, this doll is more fun than the other one. It moves, it cries, it's nice and warm. See, sister, let's play with it. It will be my little girl. I'll be a lady. I'll come to see you and you'll look at it. Little by little you'll see its whiskers and you'll get a shock. And then you'll see its ears and then you'll see its tail and you'll get a shock. And you'll say to me: 'Oh, my God!' And I'll say to you: 'Yes, Madame, that's my little girl and she's like that. Little girls are like that these days.'"

Azelma listened to Éponine in wonder.

Meanwhile the drinkers had started singing an obscene ditty and they were laughing so hard they shook the ceiling. Old man Thénardier egged them on and joined in.

Just as birds will make a nest out of anything, children can make a doll out of anything at all. While Éponine and Azelma were dressing up the cat, Cosette for her part had dressed up the sword. This done, she had laid it down in her arms and was softly singing to put it to sleep.

The doll is one of the most imperious needs and at the same time one of the most charming instincts little girls have. To look after, clothe, adorn, dress and undress, dress all over again, to teach, to scold a bit, to rock, cuddle, put to sleep, to imagine that some object is someone—this is the whole future of the woman in a nutshell. While dreaming and while chattering away, while putting together little trousseaux and little layettes, while sewing little frocks, little bodices, and little tops, the little girl becomes a young girl, the young girl becomes a big girl, the big girl becomes a woman. The first baby takes over from the last doll.

A little girl without a doll is more or less as miserable and just as impossible as a woman without a child.

So Cosette had made a doll of the sword.

Mother Thénardier, for her part, had gone over to the "yellow man."

"My husband's right," she thought. "Maybe it's Monsieur Laffitte[1] in person. Some rich geezers are quite crazy!"

She came and leaned on his table.

"Monsieur—" she said.

At the word *monsieur,* the man turned around. Mother Thénardier had only called him *dear fellow* or *good man* till that moment.

"You see, Monsieur," she said, putting on her sweetest look, which was even more annoying to look at than her ferocious look, "I don't mind the child playing, I'm not against it—but just this once, because you're generous. You see, it comes from nothing. It has to work."

"The child is not yours, then?" asked the man.

"Good God, no, Monsieur! It's a poor little thing that we took in just like that, out of charity. A kind of idiot child, a moron. She must have water on the brain. You see what a great big head she's got. We do what we can for her— we're not rich, after all. We've been writing to her people for nothing, it's been six months since anyone's answered. You'd have to think her mother's dropped dead."

"Ah!" said the man, and he fell back into his reverie.

"The mother was no good," added mother Thénardier. "She abandoned her kid."

During this conversation, Cosette, as though some instinct alerted her that they were talking about her, had not taken her eyes off mother Thénardier. She was vaguely listening. She picked up a few words here and there.

Meanwhile the drinkers, all three-quarters sozzled, were singing their dirty song again, jollier than ever. It was an off-color story in very bad taste in which the Holy Virgin and the Infant Jesus both featured. Mother Thénardier had wandered off to join in the outburts of hilarity. Cosette, under the table, was watching the fire, which was reflected in her staring eyes; she had again begun to rock the sort of swaddled doll she had made, and while she rocked it, she sang in a low voice: "My mother is dead! My mother is dead! My mother is dead!"

At the renewed insistence of the hostess, the yellow man, "the millionaire," finally consented to have supper.

"What would Monsieur like?"

"Bread and cheese," said the man.

"No doubt about it, he's a beggar," thought mother Thénardier.

The drunks were still singing their song, and the child under the table also sang hers.

All of a sudden, Cosette broke off. She had just turned round and seen the little Thénardiers' doll, which they had abandoned for the cat and left lying on the floor, a few feet from the kitchen table.

She dropped the swaddled sword, which only half satisfied her, and ran her eyes slowly around the room. Mother Thénardier was whispering to her husband and counting the money, Ponine and Zelma were playing with the cat, the travelers were eating or drinking or singing, no one was looking at her. She did not have a moment to lose. She crawled out from under the table on her hands and knees, made sure once more that no one was spying on her, then swiftly slid over to the doll and grabbed it. A second later she was back in her spot, sitting down, not moving, just turned in such a way as to cast a shadow over the doll, which she held in her arms. The happiness of playing with a doll was so rare for her that it had all the violence of rapture.

No one had seen her, except the traveler, who was slowly eating his meager supper.

This joy lasted almost a quarter of an hour.

But no matter how careful she had been, Cosette did not realize that one of the doll's feet was sticking out and that the fire in the grate was shining very brightly on it. This luminous pink foot emerging from the shadows suddenly struck Azelma, who said to Éponine: "Look, sister!"

The two little girls stopped what they were doing, stunned. Cosette had dared take the doll! Éponine got up and, without letting go of the cat, went to her mother and began to tug at her skirt.

"Leave me alone!" said the mother. "What do you want?"

"Mother," said the child. "Just look!"

And she pointed a finger at Cosette. Cosette, completely rapt in the ecstasy of possession, saw and heard nothing anymore.

Mother Thénardier's face took on that special expression that is composed of the terrible and the trivial combined and that is why such women are called shrews. This time, wounded pride aggravated her anger even further. Cosette had crossed all the boundaries, Cosette had violated the doll of "the young ladies." A czarina who had seen a moujik[2] trying on her imperial son's big blue sash would have exactly the same expression on her face.

She yelled in a voice made hoarse by outrage: "Cosette!"

Cosette jumped as though there had been an earthquake underneath her. She turned around.

"Cosette!" mother Thénardier yelled again.

Cosette took the doll and laid it gently on the ground in a sort of veneration mixed with despair. Then, without taking her eyes off it, she joined her hands together and—and it is frightening to say this of a child of her age—wrung them; then, something that none of the emotions of the day had forced from her, neither the expedition to the woods, nor the awful weight of the bucket of water, nor losing the money, nor the sight of the strap, nor even the dark words she had heard mother Thénardier mutter, she burst into tears. She sobbed.

Meanwhile, the traveler had gotten to his feet.

"What's the matter?" he asked mother Thénardier.

"Can't you see?" said mother Thénardier, pointing to the corpus delicti lying at Cosette's feet.

"Well, what of it?" the man went on.

"That little bitch," answered mother Thénardier, "has dared touch the girls' doll!"

"All this carrying on for that!" said the man. "So what if she did play with the doll?"

"She's touched it with her filthy hands!" pursued mother Thénardier. "With her hideous hands!"

At this point, Cosette sobbed even harder.

"Will you shut up!" screamed mother Thénardier.

The man went straight to the door to the street, opened it, and went out.

The moment he had gone, mother Thénardier took advantage of his absence to swiftly give Cosette a nasty kick under the table, which caused the little girl to howl.

The door opened again, the man reappeared; he was carrying in both hands the fabulous doll we mentioned and that the village kids had been ogling since morning, and he stood it before Cosette, saying: "Here, this is for you."

It seems that all the time he had been there—over an hour—lost in his thoughts, he had vaguely been aware of the fancy goods shop lit up with little lanterns and candles so splendidly that you could see it through the tavern window like an illumination.

Cosette looked up. She watched the man coming toward her with the doll the same way she'd have watched the sun approaching, she heard those unheard-of words: "This is for you"—she looked at him, she looked at the doll, then she slowly backed away and went and hid right at the back of the table next to the wall.

She no longer cried, she no longer howled, she looked like she no longer dared breathe.

Mother Thénardier, Éponine, Azelma were all so many statues. Even the drinkers stopped drinking. A solemn silence had fallen over the entire tavern. Mother Thénardier, petrified and dumb, started in on her conjectures again: "What the hell is this old codger? Is he a pauper? Is he a millionaire? Maybe he's both—meaning, a thief."

The face of Thénardier the husband offered that expressive line that accentuates the humanness of the human face every time the dominant instinct shows up in it in all its bestial power. The man who ran that sleazy dive studied the doll and the traveler in turn; he seemed to smell the man as he would smell a sack of money. It was all over in a flash. He went over to his wife and whispered to her: "That thing costs at least thirty francs. Don't do anything stupid. Start groveling."

Vulgar natures have one thing in common with guileless natures and that is that there is never any transition.

"Well, Cosette," mother Thénardier crooned in a voice that was dripping with the bitter honey of the spiteful woman, "aren't you going to take your doll?"

Cosette took the risk of coming out of her hole.

"My little Cosette," mother Thénardier went on in syrupy tones, "Monsieur is giving you a doll. Take it. It's yours."

Cosette stared at the wonderful doll in a sort of terror. Her face was still flooded with tears but her eyes began to fill up, like the sky at the break of day, with strange rays of joy. What she felt at that moment was something like what she would have felt if someone had suddenly said to her: Little girl, you are the queen of France.

It seemed to her that if she touched the doll, thunder would roll out of it. Which was true to some extent, for she told herself that mother Thénardier would roar at her—and belt her. Yet the attraction won out. She ended up coming closer and timidly murmured as she turned toward mother Thénardier: "Can I, Madame?"

No words could describe the look on her face, which was at once desperate, horror-stricken, and thrilled.

"For God's sake!" said mother Thénardier. "It's yours. Since Monsieur is giving it to you."

"True, Monsieur?" Cosette went on. "Is it true? It's mine, the lady?"

The stranger looked as though his eyes were full of tears. He seemed to have reached that emotional state where you can't speak for fear of breaking down. He nodded to Cosette and placed the hand of "the lady" in her little hand.

Cosette pulled her hand back as though the hand of "the lady" had burned it and began to study the floor. We are compelled to add that at that moment, she stuck her tongue out in a fairly extravagant manner. All of a sudden she wheeled round and furiously grabbed the doll.

"I'll call her Catherine," she said.

It was a truly bizarre moment, the moment Cosette's rags pressed against and embraced the ribbons and fresh pink muslins of the doll.

"Madame," she went on, "can I put her on a chair?"

"Yes, my child," said mother Thenardier.

Now it was Éponine and Azelma who watched Cosette with envy. Cosette put Catherine on a chair, then sat on the floor in front of her and stayed there without moving, without saying a word, in an attitude of contemplation.

"Go ahead and play, then, Cosette," said the stranger.

"Oh, I am playing," replied the little girl.

This stranger, this unknown quantity who seemed like a visitation from Providence to Cosette, was at that moment what mother Thénardier hated most in the world. But she had to restrain herself. It was more emotion than she could bear, even accustomed as she was to dissimulation in her effort to copy her husband in all things. She rushed to send her daughters to bed, then asked the yellow man for his "permission" to send Cosette to bed, too—"she's had such a big day today," she added, on a maternal note. Cosette went off to bed carrying Catherine in her arms.

Mother Thénardier went every so often to the other end of the room, where her man was, "to soothe her soul," as she put it. She exchanged with her husband a few words all the more furious for her not daring to utter them out loud: "Stupid old goat! What's got into him? Turning up here and upsetting us like this! Wanting that little monster to play! Giving her dolls! Giving dolls worth forty francs to that little mongrel that I'd give away for forty sous, myself! Any more of that and he'll be calling her Your Majesty like she was the duchesse de Berry![1] He must be off his rocker! You reckon he's got rabies, our old mystery man?"

"Why? It's pretty straightforward," old man Thénardier shot back. "If it makes him happy! You, you're happy if the little one's working, him, he's happy if she's playing. He's within his rights. A traveler can do what he likes if he's paying. If the old boy's a philanthropist, what's it to you? If he's a half-wit, it's none of your business. What are you interfering for, as long as he's got the money?"

Spoken like the king of the castle and reasoned like an innkeeper. In neither case was there any right of reply.

The man was leaning on the table and had resumed his dreamy attitude. All the other travelers, peddlers, and carters had moved off a bit and stopped singing. They observed him at a distance with a sort of respectful fear. This ordinary character so poorly dressed, who pulled five-franc pieces, "rear wheels," out of his pocket with such ease and who lavished gigantic dolls on little trollops in wooden clogs was certainly a magnificent and awesome fellow.

Several hours passed. Midnight mass had been said, Christmas Eve was over, the drinkers had gone, the bar had closed, the low room was deserted, the fire had gone out, the stranger was still in the same place and in the same position. From time to time, he shifted his weight from one elbow to the other. That was all. But he had not said a word since Cosette had left.

Only the Thénardiers, out of propriety and curiosity, remained in the room.

"Is he going to spend the night like that?" grumbled mother Thénardier.

When the clock struck two in the morning, she declared herself defeated and said to her husband: "I'm going to bed. You do what you like."

The husband sat down at a table in a corner, lit a candle, and began to read the *Courrier français*.[4]

A good hour passed in this way. The worthy innkeeper had read the *Courrier français* at least three times, from the date of the edition to the name of the printer. The stranger did not budge.

Thénardier shifted in his seat, coughed, spat, blew his nose, made his chair creak. The man didn't move a muscle. "Is he asleep?" Thénardier wondered. The man was not asleep, but nothing could rouse him. Finally Thénardier took off his cap, quietly went over, and ventured to say: "Won't Monsieur get some rest?"

*Bed down* would have seemed excessive and too familiar to him. *Get some rest* smacked of luxury and was nice and respectful. Words like those have the mysterious and marvelous property of inflating the sum on the bill to be paid the following morning. A room where you *bed down* costs twenty sous; a room where you *get some rest* costs twenty francs.

"Oh, yes!" said the stranger. "You're right. Where is your stable?"

"Monsieur," said Thénardier with a smile, "I will take Monsieur there."

He took the candle, the man took his bundle and his stick, and Thénardier led him to a room on the first floor, which was of a rare splendor, all furnished in mahogany, with a sleigh bed and curtains of red calico.

"What is this?" said the traveler.

"It's our own bridal chamber," said the innkeeper. "We live in another room, the wife and I. We only come in here three or four times a year."

"I'd have been just as happy with the stable," said the man bluntly.

Thénardier acted as though he had not heard this rather unkind remark.

He lit two brand-new beeswax candles that were on display on the mantelpiece. A reasonable fire was blazing away in the hearth. On the mantelpeice, under a glass jar, sat a woman's headdress worked with silver thread and orange blossom.[5]

"And this, what is this?" the stranger continued.

"Monsieur," said Thénardier, "that's my wife's bridal hat."

The traveler gave the object a look that seemed to say: So there was once a time when that monster was a virgin!

As it happened, Thénardier was lying. When he took on the lease of this shack to turn it into a pothouse, he had found the room done out like this and had bought the furniture and picked the orange blossom up at the junk dealer's, judging that it would put "the wife" in a gracious light and that the result for his house would be what the English call respectability.

When the traveler turned round, the host had vanished. Thénardier had discreetly snuck off, without daring to say good night, not wanting to show excessive cordiality to a man he was planning to fleece royally the following morning.

The innkeeper retired to his room. His wife was in bed but she was not asleep. When she heard her husband's step, she turned over and said: "You know I'm kicking Cosette out the door tomorrow."

Thénardier replied coldly: "That's what you think!"

They did not exchange another word and some minutes later their candle went out.

For his part, the traveler had put his bundle and stick in a corner. With the host gone, he sat in an armchair and stayed there thinking for a while. Then he took his shoes off, took one of the two candles, blew out the other one, pushed the door open and left the room, looking all around him as though he were searching for something. He went down a hallway and reached the stairs. There, he heard a very faint little sound that was like a child breathing. He followed the sound and came to a sort of triangular nook built under the staircase or, rather, formed by the staircase itself. The nook was quite simply the space beneath the stairs. Here, among all kinds of old baskets and old bits of broken glass and crockery, in the dust and the cobwebs, there was a bed—if you can call a bed a straw mattress so riddled with holes you can see the straw beneath and a blanket so riddled with holes you can see the straw mattress beneath. No sheets. The mattress was lying right on the tiles on the floor. In this bed Cosette slept.

The man went up to her and looked at her. Cosette was sleeping soundly. She was fully clothed. In winter she did not take her clothes off at all because of the cold.

She held the doll tightly to her; its big open eyes shone in the dark. From time to time, she let out a huge sigh as if she were about to wake up, and she squeezed the doll in her arms almost convulsively. Only one of her wooden clogs was lying next to the bed.

An open door near Cosette's cubbyhole allowed a glimpse of a fairly big dark room. The stranger went in. At the back, through a glass door, you could see two tiny, very white twin beds. These were the beds of Azelma and Éponine. Behind the beds a curtainless wicker cradle was half-hidden, where the little boy who had screamed all night was sleeping.

The stranger surmised that this room communicated with that of the Thénardier couple. He was about to withdraw when his gaze fell on the fireplace—one of those vast tavern fireplaces that always have such a minuscule fire, when there is a fire, and that are so chilling to see. In this one, there was no fire, there were no ashes, even; but what there was attracted the traveler's attention. There were two little child's shoes in stylish shapes and different sizes; the traveler remembered the sweet and immemorial custom of children putting their shoes in the fireplace on Christmas Eve to wait there in the dark in the hopes that some sparkling present would be put in them by their good fairy. Éponine and Azelma had made sure they did not forget to do so and had each put one of their shoes in the fireplace.

The traveler crouched down.

The fairy, that is, the mother, had already paid her visit, and gleaming in each shoe was a beautiful brand new ten-sou piece.

The man stood up and was about to walk away when he spotted another object, at the back to one side, in the darkest corner of the hearth. He peered and recognized a clog, a hideous clog made out of the roughest wood, half-broken and all covered in ash and caked-on mud. It was Cosette's clog. Cosette, with that touching childish trust that can be endlessly betrayed without ever being discouraged, had also placed her clog in the fireplace.

Hope in a child who has never known anything but despair is a sweet and sublime thing.

There was nothing in this wooden shoe. The stranger felt in his waistcoat, bent down, and placed a gold louis in Cosette's clog.

Then he padded back to his room as silently as a wolf.

## IX. Thénardier in Operation

Next morning, two hours at least before daybreak, Thénardier, the husband, was sitting by a candle at a table in the low room of the tavern, pen in hand, composing the bill for the traveler in the yellow redingote.

The wife was on her feet, half-bent over him, following him with her eyes. They did not exchange a word. On one side, it was all profound meditation, on the other, that religious admiration with which you watch some wonder of the human mind spring forth and blossom. A noise could be heard in the house; it was the Lark sweeping the stairs.

After a good quarter of an hour and a few mistakes scratched out, Thénardier produced this chef d'oeuvre:

BILL OF THE MONSIEUR IN NO. 1

| | |
|---|---:|
| Supper . . . . . . . . . . . . . . . . . . . . . . . . . . . . . . . . . . . . . . . . . . . . . . . . . . . . . . . . | 3 fr. |
| Room . . . . . . . . . . . . . . . . . . . . . . . . . . . . . . . . . . . . . . . . . . . . . . . . . . . . . . . . . . | 10 " |
| Candle . . . . . . . . . . . . . . . . . . . . . . . . . . . . . . . . . . . . . . . . . . . . . . . . . . . . . . . . . | 5 " |
| Fire . . . . . . . . . . . . . . . . . . . . . . . . . . . . . . . . . . . . . . . . . . . . . . . . . . . . . . . . . . . . | 4 " |
| Service . . . . . . . . . . . . . . . . . . . . . . . . . . . . . . . . . . . . . . . . . . . . . . . . . . . . . . . . . | 1 " |
| TOTAL . . . . . . . . . . . . . . . . . . . . . . . . . . . . . . . . . . . . . . . . . . . . . . . . . . . . . . . . . | 23 " |

Service was written *servisse.*

"Twenty-three francs!" cried mother Thénardier with enthusiasm marred by some hesitation.

Like all great artists, Thénardier was not satisfied.

"Pah!" he said.

It was the tone of Castlereagh, at the Congress of Vienna, drawing up the bill France would have to pay.

"Monsieur Thénardier, you are right, he definitely owes that," mumured the wife, who was thinking of the doll given to Cosette in front of her girls. "It's only right, but it's too much. He won't pay."

Old man Thénardier gave out his chilling laugh and said: "He'll pay."

This laugh was the ultimate expression of certainty and authority. What was said thus had to be. The wife did not try to press the subject. She started to tidy the tables; the husband paced up and down the room. A moment later he added: "I owe at least fifteen hundred francs, myself!"

He went and sat in the corner of the fireplace meditating, his feet on the hot ashes.

"As for that!" the wife went on. "Aren't you forgetting I'm chucking Cosette out today? That monster! It tears my heart out to see her with that doll! I'd rather marry Louis XVIII than keep her in the house another day!"

Old man Thénardier lit his pipe and answered between two puffs: "You'll give the man the bill."

Then he went out. Scarcely had he quit the room than the traveler came in.

Thénardier spun round at once and stayed motionless at the half-open door, visible only to his wife.

The yellow man was carrying his bundle and his stick in his hand.

"Up so early!" said mother Thénardier. "Is Monsieur leaving us so soon?"

As she spoke, she turned the bill round in her hands with an embarrassed look and folded it over, creasing it with her nails. Her hard face had shifted subtly to an expression of timidity and punctiliousness that was not normal for her.

To present such a bill to a man who looked every inch "the bum" did not come easy to her.

The traveler seemed worried and distracted. He answered: "Yes, Madame. I'm off."

"Monsieur," she went on, "did not have business in Montfermeil, then?"

"No. I'm just passing through. That's all . . . So, Madame," he added, "what do I owe?"

Mother Thénardier handed him the folded bill without answering.

The man unfolded the piece of paper, looked at it, but his mind was clearly elsewhere.

"Madame," he said, "do you do a brisk trade in this Montfermeil?"

"So-so, Monsieur," replied mother Thénardier, stunned at not seeing any explosion.

She followed this up in an elegiac and lamenting tone: "Oh, Monsieur! Times are certainly hard! And then, we don't get many well-heeled types out here! It's all small fry, no-hopers, if you know what I mean. If only we got travelers as rich and generous as Monsieur now and then! We've got so many outlays. Listen, that little thing eats us out of house and home."

"What little thing?"

"The little girl, of course—you know! Cosette! The Lark, as we say around here!"

"Ah!" said the man.

She continued: "They're a silly lot, they are, these peasants, with their nicknames! She looks more like a bat than a lark. You see, Monsieur, we don't ask for charity, but we can't give it, either. We earn nothing, and we have to fork out a fortune. There's the license, the taxes, doors and windows,[1] duties! As Monsieur knows, the government demands an awful lot of money. And then I've got my own girls, haven't I? I don't need to feed someone else's brat."

The man replied in a voice he was forcing himself to make indifferent but in which there was a quiver: "What if she was taken off your hands?"

"Who? Cosette?"

"Yes."

The woman's violent red face lit up with a hideous flush.

"Ah, Monsieur! My good Monsieur! Take her, keep her, take her away, cart her off, sprinkle her with sugar, stuff her with truffles, drink her, eat her, and may the Holy Blessed Virgin and all the saints in heaven bless you!"

"Agreed."

"True? You'll take her away?"

"I'll take her away."

"Right now?"

"Right now. Call the child."

"Cosette!" yelled mother Thénardier.

"Meanwhile," the man went on, "I still haven't paid what I owe. How much is it?"

He cast a glance at the bill and could not repress a start of surprise.

"Twenty-three francs!"

He looked at the innkeeper's wife and repeated: "Twenty-three francs?"

There had been in the utterance of that repeated sentence the tone that distinguishes the question mark from the exclamation mark. Mother Thénardier had time to prepare herself for the shock. She answered with assurance: "Heavens, yes, Monsieur! It's twenty-three francs."

The stranger placed five five-franc coins on the table.

"Go and get the little girl," he said.

At that moment, old man Thénardier strode into the middle of the room and said: "Monsieur owes twenty-six sous."

"Twenty-six sous!" cried the wife.

"Twenty sous for the room," resumed Thénardier coldly, "and six sous for supper. As for the little girl, I need to talk that over a bit with Monsieur. Leave us, missus."

Mother Thénardier had one of those radiant flushes that unexpected flashes of talent will spur in a person. She felt that the great actor was entering the stage, and wordlessly made herself scarce.

As soon as they were alone, old man Thénardier offered the traveler a chair. The traveler sat down; Thénardier remained standing and his face took on a peculiar expression of bonhomie and simplicity.

"Monsieur," he said, "listen, I'll tell you something. And that something is that I adore her myself, that child."

The stranger stared at him.

"What child?"

Thénardier continued: "It's funny! You get so attached. What's all that money for? Take your hundred-sou coins back. I adore that child."

"Which one?" the stranger demanded.

"Our little Cosette, of course! Aren't you wanting to take her from us? Well, then, I'm telling you frankly, true as it is that you're an honest man, I can't allow it. She'd be breaking her promise to me, that little girl would. I first set eyes on it when it was just a tiny mite. It's true that she costs us money, it's true that she has her faults, it's true that we aren't rich, it's true that I forked out over four hundred francs in medicine in one go once when she was sick! But a person's got to do something for the good Lord. It doesn't have a mother or a father, I brought her up. My bread is her bread. In fact, I'm truly attached to her, that child. You understand, you get to feel real affection. I'm a bit of a sucker, myself, I don't think about it, I love the little girl; my wife's sharp but she loves her, too. You see, she's like our child. I need to have it jabbering away about the place."

The stranger went on staring at him. He continued.

"Pardon, sorry, Monsieur, but you don't give your child to some passerby just like that. Eh? I'm not wrong, am I? Although, I can't say you're rich, you seem like a good sort of fellow, what if it would make her happy? But we'd have to be sure about that. You get me? Suppose I do let her go and sacrifice myself, I'd like to know where she's going, I wouldn't want to lose sight of her, I'd want to know who she's living with, so I could go and see her now and then, and for her to know that her good old foster father is there, that he's watching over her. In the end, some things just can't be done. I don't even know your name. If you took her off, I'd be saying: 'Well, then, what about the Lark? Where can she be?' I'd have to see some miserable scrap of paper at least, a tiny speck of a passport, something!"

The stranger, without ceasing to look at him with that look that goes straight to the bottom of the conscience, so to speak, answered him in a grave and firm tone: "Monsieur Thénardier, you don't need a passport to go five leagues from Paris. If I take Cosette, I will take her, and that's that. You will not know my name, you will not know where I live, you will not know where she is, and my intention is that she never sees you again in her life. I break the rope she has tied around her foot, and she flies away, free. Does that suit you? Yes or no."

Just as demons and spirits recognize by certain signs the presence of a superior god, Thénardier understood that he was dealing with someone very strong. It was like an intuition; he understood this with his clear and sagacious swiftness. The night before, while drinking with the carters and smoking and singing dirty ditties, he had spent the evening observing the stranger, watching him like a cat, studying him like a mathematician. He had at once both spied on him on his own account, for pleasure and out of instinct, and spied on him as though he were being paid to do so. Not a gesture, not a move that the man with the yellow coat made had escaped him. Even before the stranger had so obviously shown interest in Cosette, Thénardier had seen it coming. He had intercepted the old man's searching glances, which constantly returned to the child.

Why the interest? What kind of man was he? Why, with so much money in his purse, the miserable getup? Questions that he asked himself without being able to resolve them and that annoyed him. He had dwelt on them all night. The man couldn't be Cosette's father. Was he a grandfather? Then why not make himself known right away? When you're within your rights, you show your hand. This man obviously had no rights over Cosette. So what was he? Old man Thénardier was lost in suppositions. He glimpsed everything and saw nothing. Whatever was going on, when he began this conversation with the man, sure that there was some secret at the bottom of it all, sure that the man was keen to stay in the shadows, he felt himself to be in a strong position; at the stranger's clear and firm response, when he saw that this mysterious personage was so simply mysterious, he felt weak. He had not expected anything of the kind. All his conjectures were put to rout. He rallied his ideas. He weighed the whole thing up in a second. Old man Thénardier was one of those men who judge a situation at a glance. He gauged that this was the moment to get straight to the point. He behaved like the great captains at the decisive moment that they alone know how to recognize. He promptly unmasked his guns.

"Monsieur," he said, "I must have fifteen hundred francs."

The stranger took an old black leather wallet out of a side pocket, opened it, and took out three banknotes, which he placed on the table. Then he pressed his huge thumb down on the notes and said to the owner of the flophouse: "Get Cosette."

While this was happening, what was Cosette doing?

As soon as she had woken up, Cosette had run to her wooden clog. She found the gold coin there. It was not a napoléon, it was one of those spanking new twenty-franc pieces from the Restoration, on the face of which the little Prussian pigtail had replaced the crown of laurel.[2] Cosette was dazed. Her fate was beginning to intoxicate her. She did not know what a gold coin was, she had never seen one, she wasted no time in hiding it in her pocket as though she had stolen it. Yet she felt that it really was hers, she guessed where the gift had come from, but the joy she felt was mixed with fear. She was happy, but more than anything else, she was stupefied. These things, so magnificent and so lovely, did not seem real to her. The doll frightened her, the gold coin frightened her. She vaguely shook before such splendors. Only the stranger did not frighten her. On the contrary, he reassured her. Since the night before, in her amazement, in her sleep, she had thought in her little child's head about this man who looked old and poor and so sad, and who was so rich and so good. Ever since she had met the man in the woods, everything seemed to have changed for her. Less happy than the merest swallow in the sky, Cosette had never known what it was to take refuge in her mother's shadow, under her mother's wing. For five years, that is, for as long as she could remember, the poor child had been shivering and freezing. She had always been completely naked beneath the bitter kiss of misfortune, now it seemed to her that she was fully clothed. Before, her soul had been cold, now it was warm. She no longer felt so terrified of mother Thénardier. She was no longer alone; someone was there.

She had very quickly got down to her usual morning job. The louis, which she had on her in the same apron pocket the fifteen-sou coin had fallen out of the night before, kept distracting her. She did not dare touch it, but she spent five minutes at a time contemplating it, with her tongue hanging out, we must confess. As she swept the stairs, she stopped dead, forgetting her broom and the entire universe as she looked at this star shining at the bottom of her pocket.

It was in one of these dreamy moments of contemplation that mother Thénardier caught up with her.

On her husband's orders, she had gone in search of her. It was unheard-of, but for once she did not give her a slap or let fly some insult.

"Cosette," she said almost sweetly, "come quick."

An instant later, Cosette stepped into the low room.

The stranger took the bundle he had brought and untied it. This bundle contained a little woolen dress, a smock, a fustian vest, a petticoat, a fichu, woolen stockings, and proper shoes—a complete outfit for an eight-year-old girl. All of it was black.

"My child," said the man, "take this and go and get dressed quickly."

Day was dawning when those inhabitants of Montfermeil who were starting to open their doors saw walking by on the road to Paris a shabbily dressed man hand in hand with a little girl all in mourning and carrying a big pink doll in her arms. They were heading for Livry. It was our man and Cosette.

No one knew who the man was, and as Cosette was no longer in rags, many did not recognize her either.

Cosette was going away. Who with? She had no idea. Where? She did not know. All she understood was that she was leaving the Thénardier flophouse behind. No one had thought to say goodbye to her, nor had she thought to say goodbye to anyone. She was getting away from this hated and hateful house.

Poor sweet little creature whose heart had till that moment only ever been crushed!

Cosette walked gravely, opening wide her huge eyes and studying the sky. She had put her louis in the pocket of her new smock. From time to time she bent over and took a peek at it, then she looked at the man. She felt a bit like she was walking along next to God.

## X. Who Looks for the Best May Find the Worst

Mother Thénardier, as was her wont, had left her husband to it. She was expecting big things. When the man and Cosette had gone, old man Thénardier let a good quarter of an hour pass, and then he took her aside and showed her the fifteen hundred francs.

"Is that all?" she said.

It was the first time since they were married that she had dared criticize an act of the master. He reeled from the blow.

"Actually, you're right," he said, "I'm an idiot. Give me my hat."

He folded the three banknotes, shoved them in his pocket, and went out as fast as he could go, but he went the wrong way at first, off to the right. Some neighbors he questioned soon set him straight. The Lark and the man had been seen heading in the direction of Livry. He followed the sign, taking great strides and muttering to himself.

"That man's obviously a millionaire dressed up in yellow and I'm a damned idiot. First he hands over twenty sous, then five francs, then fifty francs, then fifteen hundred francs—just as easily every time. He'd have handed over fifteen thousand francs. But I'll catch up with him."

Then there was the bundle of clothes already put together in advance for the little girl, that was very strange—there had to be any amount of mystery behind that. You don't let go of a mystery once you've got hold of one. The secrets of the rich are sponges full of gold; you have to know how to squeeze them. All these thoughts swirled around in his brain. "I'm a damned idiot," he said.

When you leave Montfermeil and reach the bend in the road to Livry, you can see the road lying ahead of you along the plateau for a very long way. Having reached that point, he reckoned he should be able to spot the man and the little girl. He looked ahead as far as the eye could see and saw nothing. He made further inquiries. But he was losing time. Passersby told him the man and the child he was looking for were heading off toward the woods near Gagny. He sped off in that direction.

They had the jump on him, but a child can only go slowly and he was going fast. And then again, he knew the countryside backward.

All of a sudden, he stopped and smacked his forehead the way a man will when he has forgotten something fundamental and is ready to retrace his steps.

"I should have brought my gun," he said to himself.

Thénardier was one of those split personalities who sometimes pass among us without our knowledge and who disappear without our knowing them because fate has shown us only one side of them. The fate of many a man is to live half submerged in this way. In a quiet, humdrum situation, Thénardier had all it takes to play—we do not say to be—what passes for an honest tradesman, a decent burgher. At the same time, given certain circumstances, given the occurrence of certain jolts stirring up the underside of his nature, he had all it takes to be a real bastard. He was a shopkeeper with a monster inside him. Satan must at times have crouched in some corner of that hole in which Thénardier lived and marveled at his hideous masterpiece.

After a moment's hesitation: "Bah!" he thought. "They've got time to get away!"

But he continued on his way, hurtling ahead, almost as though he knew exactly where he was going, with the cunning of a fox scenting a flock of partridges.

Indeed, when he had passed the ponds and cut diagonally across the big clearing that lies to the right of the avenue de Belleville, just as he reached the grassy path that practically circles the hill and covers the arch of the old aqueduct of the abbey of Chelles, he spotted above a bush a hat on which he had already built so many conjectures. It was the man's hat. The bush was low. Thénardier could make out the man and Cosette, just sitting there. You couldn't see the child because she was so small but you could see the doll's head.

Old man Thénardier was not mistaken. The man had sat down there to let Cosette have a little rest. The innkeeper rounded the scrub and appeared to pop up out of nowhere in the eyes of the people he was looking for.

"Pardon me, sorry, Monsieur," he said, completely winded, "but here's your fifteen hundred francs back."

As he spoke those words, he held out the three banknotes to the stranger. The man raised his eyes.

"What does this mean?"

Old man Thénardier answered respectfully: "Monsieur, it means that I'm taking Cosette back."

Cosette shuddered and snuggled closer to the nice man.

He answered looking Thénardier straight in the eye and enunciating each syllable distinctly: "You are taking Cosette back?"

"Yes, Monsieur, I'm taking her back. I'll tell you something. I've thought about it. Actually, I don't have the right to give her to you. I'm an honest man, you see. This little girl doesn't belong to me, she belongs to her mother. It's her mother that entrusted her to me, I can only hand her over to her mother. You'll say to me: Her mother is dead. Fine. In that case, I can only hand the child over to a person who can bring me a written order signed by the mother to the effect that I should hand the child to that particular party. That much is clear."

Without replying, the man fumbled in his pocket and Thénardier watched as the wallet with the banknotes reappeared. The innkeeper felt a shiver of joy.

"Good!" he thought. "Stay with it. He's about to corrupt me!"

Before he opened the wallet, the traveler quickly looked around him. The place was absolutely deserted. There was not a soul in the woods or in the valley. The man opened the wallet and pulled out, not a fistful of banknotes as Thénardier had hoped, but a simple bit of paper, which he unfolded and presented, open, to the innkeeper, saying: "You're right. Read."

Thénardier took the piece of paper and read:

*Montreuil-sur-mer, March 25, 1823*

Monsieur Thénardier,
   You will hand Cosette over to the bearer. He will settle all small debts.

> Yours most faithfully,
> FANTINE

"You know this signature?" the man went on.

It was Fantine's signature. Old man Thénardier recognized it.

There was nothing to say. He felt doubly furious, furious at being forced to do without the bribe he was hoping for and furious at being beaten. The man added: "You can keep this note as your receipt."

Old man Thénardier retreated in good order.

"This signature has been forged quite well," he grumbled through his teeth. "Well, so be it!"

Then he made one last deperate bid.

"Monsieur," he said, "it's all right, since you are the bearer. But you have to pay me 'all small debts.' I'm owed quite a lot."

The man rose to his feet and, flicking off the dust from his threadbare sleeve, he said: "Monsieur Thénardier, in January the mother reckoned that she owed you a hundred and twenty francs; in February you sent her a bill for five hundred francs; you received three hundred francs in February and three hundred francs at the beginning of March. Since then, nine months have gone by, at fifteen francs a month, the agreed fee, that comes to a hundred and thirty-five francs. You have received a hundred francs too much. There remains thirty-five francs owing to you; I just gave you fifteen hundred francs."

Old man Thénardier felt what a wolf feels when he has been bitten and held by the steel jaws of a trap.

"Who the hell is this man?" he wondered.

He did what the wolf does. He gave a jerk. Audacity had already paid off for him once.

"Monsieur Whose-name-I-don't-know," he said resolutely, this time putting aside all marks of respect. "You'll give me a thousand écus or I'll take Cosette back."

The stranger said calmly: "Come, Cosette."

He took Cosette with his left hand and with the right picked up his stick from the ground. Old man Thénardier noted how enormous the cudgel was and how isolated the place.

The man plunged into the woods with the child, leaving the innkeeper motionless and speechless. As they walked off, old man Thénardier observed the man's broad shoulders, a little slumped, and his huge fists. Then his eyes returned to himself, falling on his puny arms and his bony hands.

"I really must be an idiot," he mused, "not to have brought my gun—since I was going hunting!"

Even so, the innkeeper would not let go.

"I wouldn't mind knowing where he's going, but," he said.

And he began to follow them at a distance. Two things remained in his hands, one, ironically enough, the note signed *Fantine,* and the other, some consolation, the fifteen hundred francs.

The man led Cosette in the direction of Livry and Bondy. He walked slowly, with his head down, in an attitude of reflection and sadness. Winter had stripped the leaves off the trees and turned the woods to a lattice of bare branches, so much so that Thénardier did not lose sight of them, though he kept his distance. From time to time, the man turned and checked whether he was being followed. Suddenly he spotted Thénardier. He swiftly darted into a thicket with Cosette and they both disappeared from view.

"Hell's bells!" said Thénardier. And he stepped up the pace.

The density of the undergrowth forced him to stick close to them. When the man was in the most overgrown spot, he turned round. Thénardier tried in vain to hide among the branches, but there was nothing he could do to stop the man from seeing him. The man threw him an uneasy glance, then shook his head and continued on his way. The innkeeper started following him again. This time the man gave him such a dark look that old man Thénardier decided it was pointless going any farther. Thénardier turned back.

## XI. The Number 9430 Comes Up Again and Wins Cosette the Lottery

Jean Valjean was not dead.

When he fell into the sea or, rather, when he threw himself in, he was, as we have seen, without leg irons. He swam underwater between two wakes out as far as a ship at anchor that had a boat tied fast to it. He found a way to hide in this boat till nightfall. When night came on he dived into the water again and swam away, reaching the coast a short distance from Cap Brun. There, as he wasn't short of money, he was able to buy himself some clothes. An open-air dive with a dance floor on the outskirts of Balaguier doubled at the time as a changing room for escaped convicts, a lucrative speciality. Then, like all those sad fugitives trying to throw the eyes of the law off the track and elude social doom, Jean Valjean followed an obscure and meandering itinerary. He first found asylum in the Pradeaux, near Beausset. Then he headed toward the Grand-Villard near Briançon in the Upper Alps. A groping and fretful flight, a mole's maze, where the twists and turns were completely unfamiliar. Later, they were able to find traces of his having been in the Ain in the area around Civrieux, in the Pyrenees, at Accons at the spot known as the Grande-de-Doumecq, close to the hamlet of Chavailles, and in the environs of Périgueux, at Brunies, a canton of the Chapelle-Gonaguet. He made it to Paris. We have just seen him in Montfermeil.

His first concern when he arrived in Paris was to buy mourning gear for a little girl of seven or eight, then to find a place to stay. That done, he got himself to Montfermeil.

You will remember that the last time he escaped, he had already been on a mysterious trip there or in the general environs, which the law got wind of. Otherwise he was thought to be dead and this further clouded the obscurity that enveloped him. In Paris, a newspaper recording this fact had fallen into his hands. He felt reassured and almost at peace, as though he really were dead.

On the night of the very same day that Jean Valjean had wrenched Cosette out of the Thénardiers' clutches, he was back in Paris. He walked back in at nightfall, with the child, via the barrière de Monceaux. There he hopped into a cabriolet that drove him to the esplanade de l'Observatoire. He got down, paid the driver, took Cosette by the hand, and together, in the black of night, through the deserted streets that border on L'Ourcine and La Glacière, they headed toward the boulevard de l'Hôpital.

The day had been strange and full of emotion for Cosette; they had sat behind hedges and eaten bread and cheese bought at remote inns, they had changed carriages often, they had traveled short distances on foot; she did not complain, but she was tired, and Jean Valjean realized this from the way she pulled more heavily on his hand as they walked along. He lifted her up on his back; Cosette, without letting go of Catherine, laid her head on Jean Valjean's shoulder and fell asleep.

# BOOK FOUR

# THE OLD GORBEAU SLUM

### I. Maître Gorbeau

Forty years ago, the solitary walker who ventured into the back of beyond around La Salpêtrière and took the boulevard as far as the barrière d'Italie[1] came to places where you could well have claimed Paris had disappeared. It was not isolation, there were people walking by; it was not the countryside, there were houses and streets; it was not a town, the streets were as rutted as highways and grass grew over them; it was not a village, the houses were too tall. So just what was it? It was an inhabited area where there was no one, it was a deserted area where there was someone; it was a big city boulevard, a Paris street, wilder at night than any forest, more dismal in the daytime than any cemetery.

It was the old quartier of the Marché-aux-Chevaux, the horse markets.

This walker, if he ventured beyond the four crumbling walls of the decommissioned Marché-aux-Chevaux, and even opted to go past the rue du Petit-Banquier, after leaving behind on his right a courtyard protected by high walls, then a meadow where stacks of tan bark stood looking like gigantic beavers' dams, then an enclosure full of timber with a heap of stumps, sawdust, and wood shavings on top of which a huge dog barked, then a long low wall all in ruins, with a little gate that was black and decrepit, groaning with moss covered with flowers in spring, and then, at the most deserted point, a horribly dilapidated building on which could be read the words POST NO BILLS, this dubious walker would come to the corner of the rue des Vignes-Saint-Marcel—little-known parts. Here, near a factory and between two garden walls, you could in those days see a slum that, at first glance, looked as small as a cottage but that was in reality as big as a cathedral. It stood with its gabled end to the public thoroughfare; whence the impression that it was small. Practically the whole house was hidden. All you could see of it was the door and one window.

This slum had only one story.

On closer examination, the detail that first leaped out at you was that the door could only ever have been the door of a slum, whereas the casement window, had it been set into hewn stone instead of rubble-stone, could have been the window of a mansion.

The door was nothing more than a motley collection of worm-eaten planks crudely tacked together with crosspieces that looked like roughly sawn logs. It opened directly onto a steep staircase with high treads covered in mud, plaster, and dust, which was the same width as the door and which seemed, from the street, to shoot straight up like a ladder only to disappear in the shadows between two walls. The top of the lopsided opening where the door swung was masked by a narrow board in the middle of which a triangular aperture had been hacked, both skylight and transom when the door was shut. On the inside of the door a brush dipped in ink had drawn the number 52 in a couple of strokes, and above the board the same brush had daubed the number 50; so that you hesitated. Where were you? Over the door it said, at number 50; the inside replied, no, at number 52. Indescribable rags the color of dust hung by way of curtains at the triangular transom.

The window was wide, quite high, furnished with louvered shutters and sash windows with large panes; only, these large windowpanes had various wounds, at once hidden and betrayed by ingenious paper bandages, and the shutters, coming off their hinges and hanging loose, threatened passersby more than they shielded the inhabitants. Horizontal slats were missing here and there and had been crudely replaced by boards nailed on vertically; so that what started out as venetians ended up as plain panels.

Seen together like this in the same house, the door, looking so sordid, and the window, looking so respectable, if dilapidated, had the effect of two mismatched beggars, meeting up and traveling along side by side, apparently completely different beneath the same tatters, one having been a derelict all his life, the other having once been a gentleman.

The stairs led up to the main body of the building, which was extremely spacious, like a warehouse that had been converted into a house. The bowels of the building consisted of a long corridor that opened, to left and right, onto apartments of various sizes, habitable at a pinch and closer to booths than prison cells. These rooms looked out on the surrounding wastelands. The whole setup was dark and distressing, washed out, melancholy, sepulchral; shot through by cold rays of sunlight or icy gusts of wind, depending on whether the cracks were in the ceiling or the door. An interesting and picturesque feature of this type of residence is the enormous size of the spiders.

To the left of the front door, on the boulevard, at the height of an average man, a small walled-up window made a square niche full of stones that children threw in passing.

Part of the building has recently been demolished. What remains of it today can still give you an idea of what it was like. The building as a whole is scarcely more than a hundred years old. A hundred years—that is young for a church and old for a house. It seems that man's abode partakes of his own brief existence and God's abode of His eternal life.

Postmen called the tumbledown building no. 50–52; but it was known in the neighborhood as the Gorbeau House. We should say how it got that name.

Trivia fiends, who collect anecdotes the way herbalists collect dried flowers and prick fleeting dates on their memories with a pin, know that in the last century, in Paris, around 1770, there were two public prosecutors at Châtelet,[2] one known as Corbeau, the Crow, the other, Renard, the Fox. Two names anticipated by La Fontaine.[3] The opportunity was too good for the legal fraternity attached to the law courts not to have a good laugh about it, and a parody immediately made the rounds of the galleries of the Palais de Justice, in somewhat lame verse:

> Maître Corbeau, perched on a file,
> Held a seizure of goods in his beak;
> Maître Renard, lured by the smell,
> Made trouble for him in a tweak:
> Hey, there! Hello! Hello! etc.[4]

The two respectable practitioners, embarrassed by the taunts and impeded in their dignified bearing by the roars of laughter that followed them, resolved to shed their names and decided to appeal to the king. The petition was presented to Louis XV the very same day that the papal nuncio, on one side, and Cardinal de La Roche-Aymon, on the other, both devoutly kneeling, had, in the presence of His Majesty, put one slipper each on the two naked feet of Madame Du Barry[5] as she climbed out of bed. The king, who was laughing, went on laughing, passing merrily from the two bishops to the two attorneys and agreeing to let these men of the robe off their names, or almost. It was granted to Maître Corbeau, in the name of the king, to add a tail to the first letter of his surname and so call himself Gorbeau; Maître Renard didn't come off so well, for he only received permission to put a *P* before the *R* and so call himself Prenard, the Taker, this second name being scarcely any less true to life than the first.

Now, according to local tradition, this Maître Gorbeau had been the owner of the building at no. 50–52, boulevard de l'Hôpital. He was even responsible for the monumental window. Hence the name Gorbeau House bestowed upon the place.

Facing no. 50–52, among the groves of trees planted along the boulevard, stands a great elm three-quarters dead; and almost directly opposite lies the rue

de la barrière des Gobelins, a street in those days with no houses and no cobblestones, planted with scrawny trees and covered in grass or mud according to
the season. It ended smack bang against the outer wall encircling Paris. A stench
of vitriol gusted out of the roofs of a neighboring factory.

The barrière was very close. In 1823, the outer wall of the city was still
standing.

This barrière itself filled the mind with gloomy images. It was on the way
to Bicêtre.[6] It was the road taken by those sentenced to death under the Empire
and the Restoration when they came into Paris on the day of their execution. It
is here that, somewhere around 1829, the mysterious homicide known as "the
murder of the barrière de Fontainebleau"[7] occurred, the perpetrators of which
the law has never found, a woeful issue that has never been cleared up, a terrible riddle that has never been solved. Just a bit farther on you come to that fateful street, the rue Croulebarbe, where Ulbach stabbed the girl from Ivry who
minded goats, as the thunder roared, just like in a melodrama. A few steps farther still and you come to the awful pollarded elm trees of the barrière Saint-
Jacques, that expedient of philanthropists for hiding the scaffold, the mean and
shameful place de Grève[8] dreamed up by a society of shopkeepers and bourgeois, who preferred to sweep capital punishment under the carpet, daring neither to abolish it with any greatness of spirit nor to maintain it with any
semblance of authority.

Thirty-seven years ago, leaving aside the place Saint-Jacques, which
seemed fated to be what it was and which has always been horrible, perhaps the
most mournful point of the whole mournful boulevard was the spot, still so unattractive today, where you came to the slum at 50–52.

Middle-class houses only came to be built there twenty-five years later.
The place was incredibly bleak. On top of the gloomy thoughts that seized you
there, you felt yourself caught between La Salpêtrière, whose dome you could
catch a glimpse of, and Bicêtre, whose barrière you could practically touch—
that is, between the madness of women and the madness of men. As far as the
eye could see there was nothing but abattoirs, the outer city wall, and a few rare
factory fronts looking like barracks or monasteries; everywhere, shanties and
mounds of rubble, old walls as black as shrouds, new walls as white as winding
sheets; everywhere, parallel rows of trees, perfectly aligned houses, flat structures in long, cold lines, and the grim misery of right angles. Not a single uneven patch of ground, not a single architectural caprice, not a single wrinkle. It
was a glacial, regular, and hideous array. Nothing is as harrowing as symmetry.
The reason is that symmetry spells boredom and boredom is the very essence
of grief. Despair yawns. It is possible to conceive of something more terrible
than a hell where one suffers and that is a hell where one is bored. If such a hell
were to exist, this stretch of the boulevard de l'Hôpital could well serve as its
approach.

Yet at nightfall, at the moment when the light went and in winter especially, at the hour when the icy evening breeze ripped the last red leaves off the elms, when the gloom was deep and starless, or when the moon and the wind punched holes in the clouds, the boulevard suddenly became terrifying. The straight lines fell apart and merged with the darkness like fragments of infinity. The person on foot could not prevent himself from thinking of the innumerable sinister traditions of the place. The solitude of a place where so many crimes had been committed had something awful about it. You felt you could sense traps laid in the darkness; every indistinct shadow seemed suspect and the long square gaps you could make out between each tree looked like graves. In the day, it was ugly; in the evening, it was gloomy; in the night, it was sinister.

In summer, at dusk, you usually saw a few old women sitting around under the elms on benches that had gone moldy in the rain. Those old crones would put their hands out for alms at any opportunity.

Otherwise the quartier, which looked more antiquated than ancient, was starting to change. From that point in time, anyone who wanted to see it needed to be quick about it. Every day some detail went, changing the overall picture. Today and for the past twenty years, the terminus of the Orléans railway line has been located there, alongside the old faubourg, and it has strained it. Wherever a railway station has been set on the edge of a capital city, it has spelled the death of a local neighborhood and the birth of a township. It seems that around these great centers of the movement of people, at the rolling of these powerful machines, at the breathing of these monstrous horses of civilization that eat coal and vomit fire, the seed-filled earth trembles and opens in order to swallow up the former dwellings of men and let the new ones out. The old houses crumble, the new houses sprout.

Since the Orléans railway station[9] has invaded the grounds of La Salpêtrière, the ancient narrow streets that line the fossés Saint-Victor and the Jardin des Plantes have started shifting, brutally traversed three or four times a day as they are by these streams of diligences, fiacres, and omnibuses that, in the course of time, push back the houses on either side; for there are things that sound bizarre and yet are strictly correct, and just as it is true to say that in big cities the sun causes the façades of houses facing south to vegetate and grow, it is a fact that the frequent passage of vehicles widens streets. The symptoms of new life are obvious. In this old provincial quartier, in the wildest nooks and crannies, cobblestones are showing themselves, the footpaths are beginning to creep and stretch, even where there are no pedestrians yet. One morning, a memorable morning in July 1845, black drums of asphalt were seen smoking that day, you could say that civilization had reached the rue de Lourcine and that Paris had come to the faubourg Saint-Marceau.

## II. NEST FOR OWL AND WARBLER

It was in front of the Gorbeau slum that Jean Valjean stopped. Like a wild bird, he had chosen the most deserted place to build his nest in.

He fumbled in his waistcoat, took out a sort of skeleton key, opened the door, went in, then carefully closed it behind him and mounted the stairs, still carrying Cosette. At the top of the stairs, he pulled another key from his pocket and opened another door with it. The room he entered, once more immediately shutting the door, was a kind of attic, spacious enough and furnished with a mattress on the floor, a table, and a few chairs. There was a stove in one corner burning away with glowing embers you could see. The streetlamp out on the boulevard cast a dim light over this wretched interior. At the back, there was a small room with a camp bed. Jean Valjean carried the child to this bed and laid her down on it without her waking up.

He struck a light using flint and steel and lit a candle; all these things had been set up in advance on the table, and he began to study Cosette, as he had done the night before, with a gaze full of ecstasy in which goodness and tenderness combined almost to the point of distraction. The little girl, with that quiet confidence that belongs only to extreme strength or extreme weakness, had fallen alseep without knowing who she was with and she went on sleeping without knowing where she was.

Jean Valjean bent down and kissed the little girl's hand. Nine months before, he had kissed the mother's hand when she, too, had just fallen asleep. The same feeling—painful, religious, poignant—filled his heart. He knelt close to Cosette's bed.

It was broad daylight and yet the child slept on. A pale ray of December sunlight came through the casement window of the attic and trailed long filaments of light and shade across the ceiling. All of a sudden a carrier's cart, heavily loaded, rattled past on the boulevard and shook the old hovel like a roll of thunder, causing it to shudder from top to bottom.

"Yes, Madame," cried Cosette, waking with a start from her sleep. "Here I am! Here I am!"

And she threw herself out of bed, her eyelids still half-shut with the heaviness of sleep, and shot her arm out toward the corner of the room.

"Oh, God! My broom!" she said.

She opened her eyes completely then and saw the smiling face of Jean Valjean.

"Oh, yes, that's right!" she said. "Hello, Monsieur."

Children accept joy and happiness instantly and intimately, being themselves, by nature, all happiness and joy.

Cosette spotted Catherine at the foot of the bed and grabbed her, and while she was playing, she asked Jean Valjean any number of questions: Where was she? Was it big, Paris? Was Madame Thénardier well out of the way? Would she come back again? And so on and so forth. Suddenly she let fly with this: "It's so nice here!"

It was a ghastly dump, but she felt free.

"Don't I have to sweep?" she finally asked.

"Play," said Jean Valjean.

And the day went by in this way. Cosette did not bother to try and understand a thing and was happy beyond words, between the doll and the man.

### III. Mix Two Unhappy People Together and You Get Happiness

At daybreak the next day, Jean Valjean was still by Cosette's bed. He stood waiting there, motionless, watching her wake up.

Something new entered his soul.

Jean Valjean had never loved anything. For twenty-five years he had been alone in the world. He had never been a father, lover, husband, friend. In jail, he had been rotten, glum, chaste, ignorant, and savage. The heart of this old convict was virginal in so many ways. His sister and his sister's children were merely a dim and distant memory to him, one that had ended up evaporating almost entirely. He had made all those efforts to find them again and then, not having been able to find them again, he had forgotten them. That is how it goes with human nature. The other tender emotions of his youth, if he had any, had been sucked into an abyss.

When he saw Cosette, when he had taken her, carried her away and saved her, he felt stirred to the depths of his soul. All that he possessed of passion and affection sprang to life and rushed toward that child. He went over to the bed where she was sleeping and he trembled with joy; he felt the pangs of a mother and he did not know what they were; for it is so extremely obscure and so extremely sweet, this grand and strange lurch of the heart when it begins to love.

Poor old heart, all new!

Only, as he was fifty-five years old and Cosette was eight, all of the love that he might have felt over his whole life melted into a sort of ineffable incandescence.

This was the second white apparition he had encountered: The bishop had caused virtue to dawn on his horizon; Cosette brought the dawning of love.

The first few days flowed by in this bedazzlement.

On her side, Cosette, too, had changed, unwittingly, poor little lamb! She was so little when her mother had left her that she no longer remembered her. Like all children who, like the young tendrils of a vine, cling to everything, she had tried to love. She had not succeeded. Everyone had pushed her away—the

Thénardiers, their children, other children. She had loved the dog, who had died. After that, nothing and no one had wanted her. It is an awful thing to say but, as we have already indicated, at eight her heart was cold. It was not her fault, it was not the capacity to love that was lacking; alas! it was the opportunity. And so now, from the first day, all that could feel and dream in her began to love this good man. She felt what she had never felt before, a sensation of blossoming.

The man no longer even seemed old to her, or poor. She found Jean Valjean handsome just as she found the dump nice.

Such are the effects of dawn, of childhood, of youth, of joy. The newness of the earth and of life has something to do with it. Nothing is as wonderful as the reflection of happiness coloring the attic. We all have a rose-colored garret in our past.

Nature had placed a huge gap between Jean Valjean and Cosette—fifty years' difference in age; but destiny had closed the gap. The irresistible force of destiny promptly plighted and united these two rootless existences, different in age, similar in loss. One in fact completed the other. Cosette instinctively sought a father and Jean Valjean instinctively sought a child. To meet was to find each other. At the mysterious moment their hands first touched, they were welded together. When these two souls saw each other, they knew that each was what the other needed and they hugged each other tight.

In the broadest and most absolute sense of the words, you could say that, cut off from everything by tomb walls, Jean Valjean was a widower just as Cosette was a little orphan girl. This situation meant that Jean Valjean became Cosette's father, heaven-sent. And, in truth, the mysterious impression produced on Cosette, deep in the Chelles wood, by Jean Valjean's hand grabbing her own in the dark, was not an illusion but a reality. The entry of that man into this child's life had been the coming of God.

On top of this, Jean Valjean had chosen a good safe refuge. It gave him a sense of security that seemed almost total.

The room with the little room off it that he occupied with Cosette was the one whose window looked out on the boulevard. This was the only window in the house, so there was no neighbor's gaze to fear, either to the side or directly opposite.

The ground floor of no. 50–52, a sort of dilapidated lean-to, was used by market gardeners as a shed and was not connected to the upper floor. It was separated from it by a solid floor that had neither trapdoor nor stairwell and which was like the building's diaphragm. The top floor, as we said, contained several rooms and a few attics, of which only one was occupied—by an old woman who did Jean Valjean's housework for him. All the rest were uninhabited.

It was this old woman, decorated with the title of "chief tenant" and in reality lumbered with the job of caretaker, who had let his place to him on Christmas Eve. He had passed himself off to her as a man of means ruined by the Spanish loan affair, who intended to move in there with his granddaughter. He had paid six months up front and gave the old woman the task of furnishing the room and side room as we have seen. It was this good woman who had lit the stove and gotten everything ready the night they arrived.

The weeks flew by. The pair led a happy existence in that miserable hole. From break of day, Cosette laughed, jabbered away, sang. Children are their own dawn chorus just like birds.

It sometimes happened that Jean Valjean took her little hand, all red and chapped with chilblains, and kissed it. Being used to being hit, the poor child did not know what to make of this and would run away covered in shame.

At times she would become serious and would study her little black dress. Cosette was no longer in rags, she was in mourning. She had left poverty behind and was embarking on life.

Jean Valjean had begun teaching her how to read. Sometimes, while getting the little girl to spell, he remembered that it was with the idea of doing wrong in mind that he had learned to read in jail. That idea had turned into showing a child how to read. At that the old galley slave would smile with the thoughtful smile of the angels.

In this, he could feel the impulse of premeditation from on high, the will of someone not man, and he would become lost in thought. Good thoughts have their bottomless pits just as bad ones do.

To teach Cosette to read, and let her play, was more or less the sum total of Jean Valjean's life. After that, he would tell her about her mother and get her to pray.

She called him *father,* knew him by no other name.

He spent hours watching her dress and undress her doll and listening to her chirping away. Life now seemed to him full of interest, people seemed good and just; in his mind he no longer held anything against anyone, he saw no reason not to live to a ripe old age now that this child loved him. He saw a whole future for himself lit up by Cosette as though by a magic lantern. The best are not exempt from selfish thoughts. At times he felt with a sort of joy that she would turn out ugly.

This is just a personal opinion, but to come completely clean, at the point Jean Valjean had reached when he began to love Cosette, we have no proof that he did not need this refueling to stay on the straight and narrow. He had just been given a new purchase on the meanness of men and the misery of society— an incomplete view that only showed one side of the truth, disastrously, with the fate of woman summed up in Fantine, public authority personified in Javert; he had gone back to jail, this time for having done good; fresh bitterness had swamped him, disgust and weariness took hold of him again; even the memory of the bishop was at certain moments eclipsed, only to reappear later luminous and triumphant; but in the end, this sacred memory was growing fainter. Who knows if Jean Valjean was not on the verge of losing heart and falling again? He loved, and he got his strength back. Alas! He was hardly any less shaky than Cosette. He protected her and she strengthened him. Thanks to him, she could hold her head up and walk into life; thanks to her, he could continue on the path of virtue. He was the child's support and the child was his fulcrum. O, unfathomable and divine mystery of the balancing of destiny.

## IV. WHAT THE CHIEF TENANT NOTED

Jean Valjean was careful never to go out in the daytime. Every evening at dusk, he would walk for an hour or two, sometimes on his own, often with Cosette, seeking out the most deserted side streets off the boulevard, or going into churches after nightfall. He liked to go to Saint-Médard, the nearest church. When he did not take Cosette, she stayed with the old woman; but nothing thrilled the little girl more than to go out with the man. She preferred an hour with him to her ravishing tête-à-têtes with Catherine. He walked along holding her by the hand and saying sweet things to her.

It turned out that Cosette was extremely spirited.

The old woman did the housework and the cooking and the shopping.

They lived modestly, as people do when they are in dire straits financially, although they always had a small fire. Jean Valjean made no changes to the furniture that was there the first day; only, he had replaced the glass door of Cosette's small side room with a solid door.

He still had his yellow redingote, his black breeches, and his old hat. In the street he was taken for a pauper. It sometimes happened that respectable women would turn round after him and give him a sou. Jean Valjean would take the sou and bow deeply. It also sometimes happened that he met some miserable wretch begging for charity, and when he did he would look around to see if anyone was watching, furtively go up to the poor derelict and thrust a coin in his hand, often a silver coin, before swiftly moving on. This had its drawbacks. They were beginning to know him in the quartier as "the beggar who gives alms."

The old "chief tenant," a crabby old bag, highly endowed with the nosiness of the envious in relation to her neighbor, studied Jean Valjean thoroughly, unbeknownst to him. She was a bit deaf, which made her talkative. All she had left from her past was two teeth, an upper one and a lower one, which she constantly knocked together. She had put some questions to Cosette, who could not say anything because she did not know anything, except that she came from Montfermeil. One morning, the old spy spotted Jean Valjean going, with a look that seemed shifty to the old busybody, into one of the uninhabited reaches of the building. She followed him as stealthily as an old cat and managed to see him, without being seen, through the crack in the door directly opposite. Jean Valjean had turned his back to the door, no doubt as an added precaution. The old woman saw him fumble around in his pocket and take out a sewing kit, scissors, and thread; he proceeded to unpick the lining of one of the tails of his redingote and pulled out of the opening a piece of yellowing paper, which he then straightened out. The old woman realized with horror that it was a one-thousand-franc note. It was only the second or third she had ever seen in her life. She took to her heels, very frightened.

A moment later, Jean Valjean approached her and begged her to go and change the thousand-franc note, adding that it was his half-yearly annuity that he had withdrawn the day before.

"Where?" the old woman wondered. "He didn't go out till six in the evening and the state bank's certainly not open at that hour."

The old woman went and changed the note and scratched her old head. This thousand-franc note, embroidered and multiplied, produced a welter of alarmed chatter among the gossips of the rue des Vignes-Saint-Marcel.

Some days later, Jean Valjean happened to be sawing wood in the hall in his shirtsleeves. The old woman was in the room doing the cleaning. She was on her own, since Cosette was busy admiring the wood being sawn; the old woman saw the redingote hanging on a nail and examined it: the lining had been sewn up again. The old biddy felt around carefully and thought she could feel wads of paper in the tails and around the armholes. More thousand-franc notes, no doubt!

She also noted that there were all sorts of things in the pockets, not just the needles, scissors, and thread that she had seen, but a fat wallet, a very big knife, and, a most suspect detail, several wigs of various colors. Every pocket of the redingote seemed to hold supplies for use in unexpected emergencies.

The residents of the slum thus came to the last days of winter.

## V. WHEN IT FALLS ON THE GROUND A FIVE-FRANC COIN MAKES A RACKET

By the side of Saint-Médard there was a poor man who would squat on the rim of a condemned communal well and to whom Jean Valjean liked to give charity. He hardly ever passed the man without giving him a few sous. Sometimes he spoke to him. Those who were envious of the beggar reckoned he was from the police. He was a former beadle, seventy-five years old, who was always mumbling prayers.

One evening when Jean Valjean was passing by that way, without Cosette, he saw the beggar at his usual spot under the lamp that had just been lit. As usual, the man seemed to be praying and was all hunched over. Jean Valjean went over to him and placed his usual alms in his hand. The beggar suddenly looked up, stared hard at Jean Valjean, then swiftly dropped his head. The movement was like a flash of lightning. Jean Valjean flinched. He felt as though he had just seen, by the light of the streetlamp, not the placid and blissful face of the old beadle, but a face that was frightening and familiar. He had the impression you would have if you had suddenly come face-to-face with a tiger in the dark. He leaped back, frightened stiff, not daring to breathe, or speak, or remain, or flee, and studied the beggar, who hung his rag-covered head and no longer seemed to register that he was there. In that strange moment, an instinct, perhaps the mysterious instinct of self-preservation, stopped Jean Valjean from uttering a sound. The beggar had the same shape, the same rags, the same appearance as every other day. "Bah!" Jean Valjean said to himself. "I must be going mad! I'm dreaming! It's not possible!" And he went home deeply disturbed.

He scarcely dared admit to himself that the face he thought he had seen was the face of Javert.

That night, as he thought about it, he regretted not questioning the man and forcing him to raise his head again.

The next day, at nightfall, he went back. The beggar was in position. "Hello, my good man," said Jean Valjean resolutely, handing him a sou. The beggar raised his head and answered in a doleful voice: "Thank you, my good sir." It was, indeed, the old beadle.

Jean Valjean felt completely reassured, and he started to laugh.

"Why in hell did I think it was Javert?" he asked himself. "Don't tell me I'm seeing things now!"

He thought no more about it.

A few days later, it might have been about eight at night, he was in his room getting Cosette to spell out loud, when he heard the street door open and then shut again. That seemed odd to him. The old woman, who was the only other person besides him in the house, always went to bed as soon as it was dark to save on candles. Jean Valjean signaled to Cosette to be quiet. Someone was coming up the stairs. At a pinch, it could be the old woman who might have felt sick and gone to the apothecary's. Jean Valjean listened. The tread was heavy and reverberated like a man's tread, but the old woman wore thick shoes and nothing sounds more like a man's tread than the tread of an old woman. Still, Jean Valjean blew out his candle.

He sent Cosette to bed, telling her in a very low voice: "Hop into bed without a sound," and as he was giving her a kiss on the forehead, the footsteps stopped. Jean Valjean remained silent and motionless, with his back to the door, sitting in his chair without moving, holding his breath in the dark. After quite a while, not hearing another sound, he turned round without making any noise and, just as he was raising his eyes to the door of his room, he saw a light through the keyhole. This light made a kind of sinister star against the blackness of the door and the wall. There was clearly someone there holding a candle in their hand and listening.

A few minutes passed and the light went away. But he did not hear any further sound of footsteps, which seemed to indicate that whoever had come to listen at the door had taken their shoes off.

Jean Valjean threw himself fully dressed onto his bed and did not sleep a wink all night.

At first light, just as he was dozing off from tiredness, he was jolted awake by the creaking of a door of some mansard at the end of the hall, and then he heard the same man's footsteps that had come up the stairs the night before. The footsteps got nearer. He leaped out of bed and put his eye to the keyhole, which was fairly large, hoping to catch a glimpse of whoever it was that had stolen into the building in the night and listened at his door. It was, indeed, a man who went past Jean Valjean's room, this time without stopping. The hall was still too dark to make out his face; but when the man reached the stairs, a ray of light from outside highlighted his silhouette and Jean Valjean got a complete view from the back. The man was tall, dressed in a long redingote, and he had a cudgel under his arm. He had Javert's bull neck.

Jean Valjean could have tried to get a good look at him from his window on the boulevard. But he would have had to open the window and he did not dare.

It was clear that the man had let himself in with a key, as though he were at home there. Who had given him this key? And what did it mean?

At seven o'clock that morning, when the old woman came to clean, Jean Valjean threw her a penetrating look, but he did not question her. The old woman's manner was the same as always.

While she was sweeping, she said to him: "Monsieur perhaps heard someone come in last night?"

At her age, and on this boulevard, eight o'clock in the evening was the dead of night.

"I did, as a matter of fact," he replied, in the most natural tone. "So who was it?"

"A new tenant," said the old woman, "that's moved in."

"And what's his name?"

"I can't really remember. Monsieur Dumont or Daumont. Something like that."

"And what is he, this Monsieur Dumont?"

The old woman studied him with her little weasel's eyes and answered: "He's a tenant, like you."

She may have intended nothing by this, but Jean Valjean thought he could detect that she did. When the old woman had gone, he made a roll of a hundred one-franc coins he had in a cupboard and stuffed it in his pocket. Despite the care he had taken so that the money would not be heard rattling around, a hundred-sou coin slipped out of his hands and rolled noisily across the tiles.

At dusk, he went downstairs and looked carefully up and down the boulevard. He saw no one. The boulevard seemed absolutely deserted. It was true that someone could be hiding behind a tree.

He went back upstairs.

"Come," he said to Cosette.

He took her by the hand and they both went out.

# BOOK FIVE

# A Mute Pack of Hounds for a Dirty Hunt

## I. The Zigzags of Strategy

Here, in relation to the pages you are about to read and others you will come across further in the story, an observation is necessary.

It has already been many years since the author of this book, who is forced, reluctantly, to speak about himself, has been absent from Paris.[1] Since he left town, Paris has been transformed. A new city has shot up that is to him in some ways unknown. Needless to say, he loves Paris; Paris is his spiritual home. But through all the demolitions and reconstructions, the Paris of his youth, that Paris that he has carted around religiously in his memory, is now a Paris of bygone days. Let him be allowed to speak of that Paris as though it still existed. It is possible that where the author will lead his readers with the words, "In that street there is this house," neither house nor street is there anymore today. Readers may check, if they wish to take the trouble. As for himself, he knows nothing about the new Paris and writes with the old Paris before his eyes, an illusion that he treasures. It is sweet for him to dream that there remains behind him something of what he used to see when he was in his homeland and that not everything has vanished. As long as you are busy bustling about in your native land, you imagine that you couldn't care less about these streets, that these windows, these roofs, these doors, are nothing to you, that these walls are foreign to you, that these trees are any old trees, that these houses that you never enter are useless to you, that these cobblestones you are walking on are just stones. Later, when you are no longer there, you realize that those streets are dear to you, that you miss those roofs, those windows, and those doors, that those walls are necessary to you, that those trees are beloved trees, that those houses you never entered you entered every day, and that you left your blood and guts and your heart on those cobblestones. All the places you no longer see, that you will perhaps never see again, though you have hung on to their image, take on a painful loveliness, come back to you with the melancholy of an apparition, make the Holy Land visible to you, and are, so to speak, the true face of France; and you love them and you evoke them as they are, as they were, and you cling to them, and you don't want anything to change, for you hold the face of your homeland in your heart as you would your own mother's face.

Allow us, then, to speak of the past in the present tense. That said, we beg the reader to bear it in mind, and so we move on.

Jean Valjean had turned off the boulevard immediately and dived into the backstreets, changing his direction as often as he could, sometimes suddenly doubling back to assure himself that he wasn't being followed.

This maneuver is peculiar to the hunted stag. On ground where footprints could be left, the maneuver has the advantage, among others, of confusing the scent for dogs and hunters, with one set of tracks covering another. In hunting, this is known as "a false return to cover."

It was a full moon that night. Jean Valjean did not mind. The moon was still very low in the sky and sliced the streets into great blocks of light and shadow. Jean Valjean could glide along the houses and walls on the dark side and keep his eye on the light side. Perhaps he failed to consider what that dark side might hide from him. But in the deserted alleys around the rue de Poliveau he felt reasonably sure no one was coming after him.

Cosette tagged along without asking any questions. The suffering of the last six years of her life had made her somewhat passive. Besides, and this is something we will have more than one occasion to come back to, she was already used to the man's odd ways and the bizarre ways of destiny, without actually realizing it. Then again, she felt safe, since she was with him.

Jean Valjean did not know where he was going any more than Cosette did. He trusted himself to God just as she trusted herself to him. It seemed to him that he, too, was holding someone greater than himself by the hand; he thought he could feel a being guiding him, invisible. In any case, he had no definite idea, no plan, no scheme. He was not even positive that the man he'd seen was Javert, and then again, it could be Javert without Javert's knowing that he was Jean Valjean. Wasn't he in disguise? Didn't people think he was dead? Yet for some days, things had been happening that were increasingly strange. He did not need any further signs. He was determined not to set foot in the Gorbeau house again. Like an animal driven out of its nesting place, he was looking for a hole to hide in, until he could find one where it was safe to stay.

Jean Valjean traced various labyrinthine paths through the Mouffetard quartier, which was already as sound asleep as if this were the Middle Ages and it was still under medieval regulations and the curfew was still in force; he tackled the rue Censier and the rue Copeau, the rue du Battoir-Saint-Victor and the rue du Puits-l'Ermite, mixing them up and scrambling his tracks in cunning strategic mazes. Around there, there are landlords offering furnished rooms, but he did not even go in, not finding anything that suited him. He could not be sure that if, by chance, they were on his trail, they had lost it.

As eleven o'clock rang out at Saint-Étienne-du-Mont,² he was crossing the rue de Pontoise in front of the office of the chief of police, which is at no. 14. A few seconds later, the instinct we were talking about earlier made him turn round. At that instant, he distinctly saw, thanks to the police chief's lantern giving them away, three men, who were following him quite closely and who filed past this lantern one after the other on the dark side of the street. One of the three men went down the path to the police chief's house. The one walking at the head looked decidedly suspect to him.

"Come, little one," he said to Cosette, and he quickly turned off the rue de Pontoise.

He took a circuitous route, went round the passage des Patriarches, which was closed at this late hour, went up the rue de l'Épée-de-Bois and the rue de l'Arbalète and plunged into the rue des Postes.

Here, where the Collège Rollin stands today, there is a square where the rue Neuve-Sainte-Geneviève joins the rue des Postes.

(It goes without saying that the rue Neuve-Sainte-Geneviève is an old street and that not a single post chaise goes down the rue des Postes any more than once every ten years. In the thirteenth century, the rue des Postes was inhabited by potters and its original name was the rue des Pots.)

The moon cast a bright light over this square. Jean Valjean dived into a doorway, calculating that if the men were still following him, he could not fail to see them very clearly as they crossed in the bright moonlight.

In fact, less than three minutes later, the men appeared. There were now four of them; all tall, decked out in long brown redingotes with round hats and carrying big truncheons. Their tall stature and their enormous fists were no less disturbing than their sinister stealth in the darkness. You would have said they were four ghosts disguised as bourgeois citizens.

They stopped in the middle of the square and formed a huddle as though conferring together. They seemed undecided. The one who looked like the leader turned round and strongly indicated with his right hand the direction Jean Valjean had taken; one of the others seemed to be pointing somewhat stubbornly in the opposite direction. The moment that the first man turned back, the moon shone full in his face. Jean Valjean recognized Javert perfectly.

## II. It Is a Good Thing the Austerlitz Bridge
## Takes Vehicles

Uncertainty was over for Jean Valjean; luckily for him, it went on for the men on his trail. He took advantage of their indecision; time lost for them, time gained for him. He came out from under the doorway where he had been hiding and pushed off into the rue des Postes in the general direction of the Jardin des Plantes. Cosette was beginning to tire, so he swept her up in his arms and carried her. There was nobody around and the lamps had not been lit because of the moon.

He picked up the pace.

In a few strides, he reached the Goblet pottery, on whose façade the old inscription was clearly legible by the light of the moon:

> THIS IS THE FACTORY OF GOBLET & SONS.
> COME AND CHOOSE PITCHERS AND JUGS,
> FLOWERPOTS, PIPES, AND BRICKS.
> TO ALL COMERS THE HEART SELLS TILES.[1]

He left the rue de la Clef behind him, then the fontaine Saint-Victor, skirted around the Jardin des Plantes via the streets on the lower side, and arrived at the quai. There, he looked around. The quai was deserted. The streets were deserted. No one behind him. He took a deep breath.

He reached the pont d'Austerlitz.

There was still a tollhouse there at the time.

He marched up to the tollhouse and handed the man a sou.

"It's two sous," said the bridge-keeper, a returned soldier disabled by the war. "You're carrying a child there who can walk. You pay for two."

He paid up, annoyed that his passage had attracted attention. All flight should be a smooth slide.

A huge cart was crossing the Seine at the same time he was, going over to the right bank just as he was. This was useful to him and he was able to cross the whole bridge in the shadow of the cart.

Halfway across, Cosette decided to walk since her feet had gone to sleep. He put her down on the ground and took her by the hand again.

Once over the bridge, he noticed a timber yard a little to the right and he headed for it. To get there, he had to risk crossing a fairly wide space that was open and well lit. He did not hesitate. Those who were hunting him had evidently been thrown off the scent and Jean Valjean felt he was out of danger. Searched for, yes; followed, no.

A little street, the rue du Chemin-Vert-Saint-Antoine, opened up between two yards enclosed by walls. This street was narrow and dark and looked made for him. Before he went down it he looked back behind him.

From the spot where he was standing, he could see the entire length of the pont d'Austerlitz.

Four shadows had just turned onto the bridge.

These shadows had their backs to the Jardin des Plantes and were heading for the right bank.

These four shadows were the four men.

Jean Valjean gave the shudder of an animal whose scent has been picked up again.

There remained one hope left to him; it was that the men had perhaps not yet stepped onto the bridge and so had not seen him as he crossed the big brightly lit square, holding Cosette by the hand.

In that case, if he dived into the little street in front of him and managed to make it to the yards, the marshes, the market gardens, the empty lots, he could get away.

It seemed to him that a person could trust himself to this silent little street. He took it.

## III. See the 1727 Map of Paris[1]

After about three hundred feet, he reached a point where the street forked. It divided into two streets, one veering off diagonally to the left, the other to the right. Jean Valjean had before him something resembling the two branches of a Y. Which one should he choose?

He did not dither, but took the right.

Why?

Because the left branch went toward the faubourg, meaning toward built-up areas, and the right branch toward the countryside, meaning toward uninhabited areas.

But they were no longer going at a good clip. Cosette's pace slowed Jean Valjean down.

He picked her up and carried her again. Cosette laid her head on the good man's shoulder and did not say a word.

He turned round now and then to have a look. He was careful to stick to the dark side of the street at all times. The street was straight behind him. The first two or three times he looked round he saw nothing, the silence was profound, and he went on walking somewhat relieved. All of a sudden, at a certain point, he turned round and he seemed to see something move, far off in the darkness, at the part of the street he had just come down.

He did not walk, he raced ahead, looking for some little lane he could escape through and so throw them off the scent once more.

He came to a wall.

This wall did not make it impossible to go any farther, though; it was a wall bordering an alley where the street Jean Valjean had taken came to an end.

Here again, he had to decide whether to take the right or the left.

He looked to the right. The alley ran past structures that were either sheds or barns, then petered out in a dead end. You could clearly see the back of this blind alley: a great white wall.

He looked to the left. The alley on this side was open, and about two hundred feet farther on it ran into a street of which it was a tributary. It was on that side that salvation lay.

Just as Jean Valjean was thinking of turning left to try to get to the street he glimpsed at the end of the alley, he saw at the corner where the alley met the street he was heading for, some kind of statue, black, immobile.

It was a person, a man, who had evidently just been posted there, barring the way, waiting.

Jean Valjean stepped back, startled.

The spot in Paris where Jean Valjean found himself, situated between the faubourg Saint-Antoine and La Rapée, is one of those that have been transformed from top to bottom by recent construction works, a desecration according to some, transfiguration according to others. The market gardens, the yards, and the old buildings are gone. There are now brand-new, great wide avenues and amphitheaters, circuses, racetracks, railway stations, a prison, Mazas: progress, as you can see, with its corrective.

Half a century ago, in ordinary everyday parlance, which is entirely made up of traditions and which persists in calling the Institut, *Les Quatre Nations,* and the Opéra-Comique, *Feydeau,* the precise point Jean Valjean had come to was called the *Petit-Picpus.* The porte Saint-Jacques, the porte Paris, the barrière des Sergents, the Procherons, the Galiote, the Célestins, the Capucins, the Mail, the Bourbe, l'Arbre-de-Cracovie, the Petite-Pologne, the Petit-Picpus—these are names from the old Paris, lingering on in the new. The memory of the people floats on this flotsam and jetsam, these wrecks of the past.

The Petit-Picpus, which scarcely existed in any case and was never more than a rough attempt at a quartier, almost had the monastic look of a Spanish town. Not many of the paths were paved, not many of the streets were built on. Except for the two or three streets we will be dealing with, it was all walls and vacant lots. Not a shop, not a vehicle; barely a candle burning in a window here and there; all lights out after ten o'clock, gardens, convents, timber yards, swamps; the odd low-lying little house and great walls as high as the house itself.

That is what the quartier was like last century. The Revolution had already treated it very badly. The republican bigwigs had demolished it, drilled into it, bored through it. Rubbish dumps had been set up in it. Thirty years ago, the quartier started to disappear under the new constructions, deleted. Today it has been completely erased. You won't find a trace of the Petit-Picpus in any current map of Paris, but it is shown clearly enough in the 1727 map, published in Paris by Denis Thierry, rue Saint-Jacques, opposite the rue du Plâtre, and in Lyon by Jean Girin, rue Mercière, in the arrondissement known as La Prudence. The Petit-Picpus had what we have just called a Y-shaped fork, formed by the rue du Chemin-Vert-Saint-Antoine splitting into two branches and taking the name of petite rue Picpus on the left and rue Polonceau on the right. The two branches of the Y were joined together at the top as though by a bar. This bar was known as the rue Droit-Mur. The rue Polonceau ended there; the petite rue Picpus went beyond it and climbed toward the Marché Lenoir. If you were coming from the Seine and reached the end of the rue Polonceau, you had the rue Droit-Mur on your left, turning sharply at a right angle, with the wall at the end of this street facing you, and on your right a truncated extension of the rue Droit-Mur that had no exit and that was known as the cul-de-sac Genrot.

This is where Jean Valjean was.

As we have just said, when he saw the black silhouette in the spotlight at the corner of the rue Droit-Mur and the petite rue Picpus, he leaped back. No doubt about it. This phantom was lying in wait for him.

What was he to do?

There was no time now to turn back. What he had spotted moving in the shadows some distance behind him a moment before was no doubt Javert and his squad. Javert had probably already reached the start of the street at the end of which Jean Valjean was standing. Javert, to all appearances, knew this little maze, and had taken the precaution of sending one of his men to guard the exit. These conjectures, virtually facts, immediately whirled, like a handful of dust whipped up by a sudden gust of wind, through Jean Valjean's sore brain. He studied the cul-de-sac Genrot; that way was blocked. He studied the petite rue Picpus; that way lay a sentry. He could see the dark shape standing out in black against the white pavement flooded with moonlight. To go forward was to fall upon that man. To go back was to fall into Javert's hands. Jean Valjean felt himself caught in a net that was slowly tightening. He looked up at the sky in despair.

## IV. Tentative Attempts at Escape

To understand what follows, you need to get an exact sense of the Droit-Mur lane and in particular, of the corner you used to turn on the left as you emerged from the rue Polonceau to go down the lane. The Droit-Mur lane was almost entirely bordered on the right as far as the petite rue Picpus by shabby-looking houses; on the left by a single sharply angular building composed of several parts that gradually rose a story or two the closer they got to the petite rue Picpus, so that the building was fairly high at that end and fairly low at the rue Polonceau end. There, at the corner we mentioned, it dipped down so low that there was nothing left to see but a wall. This wall did not squarely abut the street; it was canted, with a cut-off corner set well back and shielded by its two angles from any observer who might be either in the rue Polonceau or in the rue Droit-Mur.

From these two angles of the cut-off corner, the wall ran along the rue Polonceau as far as a house bearing the number 49 and along the rue Droit-Mur, where it was much shorter, extending as far as the grim building mentioned above, intersecting with its gable and thereby making another inward-facing angle. The gable had a forlorn look; you could see only a single window or, more precisely, two shutters covered with a sheet of zinc and permanently shut.

The inventory of fixtures we are drawing up here is rigorously exact and will certainly stir up very precise memories in the minds of former residents of the quartier.

The cut-off corner was entirely taken up by a thing that looked like the colossal wreck of a door. This was a vast shapeless set of horizontal planks, the top ones wider than the bottom ones, held together by long transverse iron bands. To one side there was a normal-sized porte cochère that appeared to have been cut there no more than fifty years or so before.

A linden tree showed its branches above the cut-off corner and the wall was covered with ivy on the rue Polonceau side.

In the imminent peril Jean Valjean found himself in, this grim building had something lonely and uninhabited about it that tempted him. He quickly looked it over. He told himself that if he managed to get inside, he would perhaps be saved. Hope came to him with the idea.

In the central part of the front of the building on the rue Droit-Mur, there were old lead drainpipes at all the windows of the various floors. The various branchings of the conduits that ran from a main pipe to end in all these sill-like troughs underneath the windows traced a sort of tree on the façade. These tubular offshoots with their dozens of joints did a fair imitation of those old denuded grapevines that twist around and up the façades of old farmhouses.

This bizarre espalier with branches of metal and iron was the first thing that struck Jean Valjean. He sat Cosette down with her back against a boundary stone, urging her to be quiet, then ran to the spot where the main pipe met the ground. Perhaps there was a way to shinny up from there and get into the house. But the pipe was rusted and out of commission and was only just held up by its brackets. Besides, all the windows of this silent abode had thick iron bars on them, even the dormer windows in the roof. And then again, the moon shone fully on the façade and the man keeping watch at the corner of the street would have seen Jean Valjean scaling the wall. And, lastly, what would he do with Cosette? How could he get her to the top of a three-story house?

He gave up the idea of climbing up the drainpipe and crept along the wall to the rue Polonceau.

When he reached the cut-off corner where he had left Cosette, he noticed that no one could see him there. He eluded all eyes, from all sides, as we have just explained. And he was in shadow. And then, there were two doors. Perhaps they could be forced. The wall above which he could see the linden tree and the ivy obviously enclosed a garden where he could at least take cover, even though there were still no leaves on the trees, and spend the rest of the night.

Time was ticking away. He had to act fast.

He tried the porte cochère and could immediately tell that it had been boarded up on both sides.

He went over to the other big door, which looked more hopeful. It was unbelievably decrepit, its very hugeness making it less solid; the planks were rotten, the iron bands were rusted, and there were only three of them. It seemed possible to break through this worm-eaten obstruction.

When he looked closer, he saw that the door was not a door at all. It didn't have any hinges, or braces, or a lock, or a slot in the middle. The iron bands crossed it without a gap. Through cracks in the planks he glimpsed the mounds of rubble and roughly cemented stones that passersby could still see there ten years ago. He was forced to admit to his dismay that what looked like a door was simply a wooden panel cladding a structure it backed onto. A person could easily tear off a plank, but you would only find yourself staring at a blank wall.

## V. WHICH WOULD BE IMPOSSIBLE BY GASLIGHT

At that moment a muffled and rhythmical noise began to make itself heard some distance away. Jean Valjean took the risk of sticking his nose out to look round the corner into the street. Seven or eight soldiers, in platoon formation, had just turned into the rue Polonceau. He saw their bayonets glinting. They were coming toward him.

These soldiers, at the head of whom he made out the tall form of Javert, were advancing slowly and carefully. They frequently stopped. It was clear that they were exploring all the nooks and crannies in the walls and all the doorways and alleyways.

It was, and here there was no guesswork involved, some patrol that Javert had met up with and requisitioned. Javert's two acolytes marched in their ranks.

At the pace at which they were moving, and with the stops they kept making, they would need a quarter of an hour to get to the spot where Jean Valjean was. It was an awful moment. A few minutes separated Jean Valjean from this terrifying precipice that was opening up before him for the third time. And now, jail was no longer merely jail, it meant losing Cosette forever; that is, a living death.

There was only one way out.

Jean Valjean had this peculiarity, which we might describe as carrying two bags: In one, he had the thoughts of a saint, in the other, the formidable talents of a criminal. He fumbled around in one or the other as the occasion required.

Among other skills, thanks to his innumerable breakouts from the jail in Toulon, he was, as you will remember, a past master in the amazing art of climbing—without any ladders, without any crampons, through sheer muscle power, supporting himself by the back of the neck, the shoulders, hips and knees, barely making use of the odd relief in the stone in the right angle of a wall—if need be as high as the sixth floor. This is an art that has made the corner of the courtyard of the Conciergerie in Paris, where the prisoner Battemolle escaped twenty years ago, so famous and feared.

Jean Valjean sized up the wall above which he could see the linden tree. It was roughly eighteen feet high. The bottom part of the angle it formed with the gable of the main building was filled by a triangular pile of masonry, probably designed to preserve this too convenient recess from the stops made by those dung beetles known as pedestrians. This preventive filling in of the corners of walls is very common in Paris.

The pile was roughly five feet high. From the top of the pile the space that had to be climbed to reach the top of the wall was only about fourteen feet, if that. The wall was capped by flat stone without any zigzagging chevrons.

The hard part was Cosette. Cosette did not know how to scale a wall. Abandon her? It never crossed Jean Valjean's mind. There was no way he could carry her. A man needs all his strength to carry off these tricky ascents. The slightest burden would throw off his center of gravity and he would fall.

A rope was what was needed. Jean Valjean didn't have one. Where would a person find a rope at midnight on the rue Polonceau? Certainly, at that moment, if Jean Valjean had had a kingdom, he would have given it for a rope.

All extreme situations have their lightning flashes that sometimes blind us, sometimes illuminate us. The desperate gaze of Jean Valjean lit on the lamppost in the cul-de-sac Genrot.

In those days there were no gaslights in the streets of Paris. At nightfall they used to light lamps placed on posts at regular intervals and these lamps were lifted and lowered by means of a rope that ran from one end of the street to the other and that fitted inside the groove of the lamppost. The reel on which the rope was wound was housed beneath the lantern in a little iron box. The lamplighter had the key and the rope itself was protected up to a certain level by metal casing.

Jean Valjean, with the energy of some supreme struggle, bounded across the street, went into the cul-de-sac, broke open the lock of the little box with the point of his knife, and was back by Cosette's side an instant later. With a rope. They don't muck around, these grim finders of expedients, grappling with fate.

We explained before that the lamps weren't lit that particular night. So the lantern in the cul-de-sac Genrot naturally was out like the rest and you could go past it without noticing that it was no longer in its place.

Yet the hour, the place, the darkness, Jean Valjean's preoccupation, his odd movements, his comings and goings, all this began to make Cosette anxious. Any other child would have started screaming ages before this. She merely tugged at the bottom of Jean Valjean's coat. The noise of the approaching patrol could be heard more and more distinctly.

"Father," she said in a voice barely above a whisper, "I'm frightened. Who's that coming down there?"

"Shoosh!" the poor man replied. "It's mother Thénardier."

Cosette gave a start. He added: "Don't say a word. Let me handle it. If you yell, if you cry, mother Thénardier will spot you. She'll come and take you back."

Then, without hurrying, but working deftly with a steady and rapid precision and swift movements all the more remarkable at such a time, when Javert and company could arrive at any second, he undid his cravat, wound it round Cosette's body under the arms, taking care it would not hurt the little girl, then tied the cravat to one end of the rope using the knot that seamen call a reef knot, took the other end of the rope in his teeth, took off his shoes and his stockings and threw them over the wall, climbed on the pile of masonry, and began to lift himself up in the corner made by the wall and the gable as surely and steadily as if he had rungs under his heels and his elbows. He was on his knees on top of the wall in less than half a minute.

Cosette watched him, stunned and speechless. Jean Valjean's request for silence and the name of mother Thénardier had chilled her to the bone.

All of a sudden she heard Jean Valjean's voice crying out to her, though in a whisper again: "Lean back against the wall."

She did as she was told.

"Don't say a word and don't be frightened," Jean Valjean went on.

And she felt herself being lifted from the ground. Before she had time to think, she was at the top of the wall.

Jean Valjean grabbed her, put her on his back, took both her little hands in his left hand, lay down flat and crawled along the top of the wall as far as the cut-off corner. As he had guessed, there was a building there and its roof sloped steeply downward from the top of the wooden cladding to just above the ground, on a fairly gentle inclined plane, just touching the linden tree. A stroke of luck, for the wall was much higher on this side than on the street side. Jean Valjean saw that the ground was far below him.

He had just reached the inclined plane of the roof and had not yet let go of the ridge of the wall when a violent uproar announced the arrival of the patrol. You could hear Javert's voice thundering: "Search the cul-de-sac! The rue Droit-Mur is guarded, so is the petite rue Picpus. I say he's in the cul-de-sac!"

The soldiers stormed into the cul-de-sac Genrot.

Jean Valjean let himself slide down the whole length of the roof, supporting Cosette as he did so, and when he reached the linden tree he jumped to the ground. Whether out of terror or out of courage, there had not been a peep from Cosette. Her hands were a little grazed.

## VI. Beginning of an Enigma

Jean Valjean found himself in an amazingly vast, weird-looking garden; one of those gardens that seem made to be viewed at night, in winter. The garden was an oblong shape, with an avenue of huge poplars at the back, stands of tall forest trees in the corners, and a space with no shade in the middle, where a very tall tree could be seen standing alone, then a few fruit trees gnarled and bristling like overgrown bushes, square vegetable beds, a melon patch where bell jars shone in the moonlight, and an old drainage well. There were stone benches here and there that looked black with moss. The paths were lined with stiff little dark shrubs that shot straight up. Grass had invaded half of them and green mildew covered the rest.

Jean Valjean had next to him the building whose roof he had used to get down, a heap of firewood, and behind the firewood, right against the wall, a stone statue whose mutilated face was now just a deformed mask that dimly appeared in the darkness.

The building was a sort of ruin where you could make out stripped rooms, one of which seemed to serve as a shed and was full of junk.

The main building on the rue Droit-Mur, which wound back to the petite rue Picpus, threw two outstretched wings into the garden. These inner walls were even more tragic than the outside ones. All the windows were grated. No light was to be glimpsed in any of them. On the upper floors there were hoods over the windows like the ones used in prisons. One of the double façades cast its shadow over the other one, and it fell over the garden like a huge black sheet.

No other house could be seen. The bottom of the garden was lost in mist and in darkness. Yet you could dimly make out walls that intersected as though other things were growing over there, as well as the low roofs of the rue Polonceau.

You could not imagine anything wilder or lonelier than this garden. There was no one there, which was hardly surprising, given how late it was; but it did not look as though the place had been made for anyone to walk in, not even in the middle of the day.

Jean Valjean's first concern had been to find his shoes and put them back on, then to get into the shed with Cosette. A person trying to escape can never be hidden enough for his own liking. The child, thinking always of mother Thénardier, shared his urgent impulse to curl up into as small a ball as possible.

Cosette was huddled against him, trembling. The tumultuous clamor of the patrol could be heard as they searched the cul-de-sac and the street, the noise of musket butts against the stones, Javert yelling to the spies he had planted, and his curses scrambled with words that could not be made out.

After a quarter of an hour or so, it sounded as if this approximation of a rumbling storm was beginning to move off. Jean Valjean did not breathe.

He had gently placed his hand over Cosette's mouth.

In any case, the solitude he found himself in was so strangely calm that this appalling racket, so furious and so near, did not ruffle it in the least. It seemed as if the walls were built with the deaf stones the scriptures speak of.

All of a sudden, in the middle of this deep calm, a new noise sounded; a noise that was heavenly, divine, ineffable, as ravishing as the other had been awful. It was a hymn that came from out of the darkness, a dazzling fusion of prayer and harmony in the dark and terrifying silence of the night; the voices of women, but voices composed at once of the pure tone of virgins and the unsophisticated tone of children, the kind of voices that are not of this world and that resemble what the newborn hear, still, and what the dying hear, already. This song came from the black edifice that towered over the garden. At the moment that the uproar of the demons was moving away, you would have said a choir of angels was coming closer in the dark.

Cosette and Jean Valjean fell to their knees.

They did not know what it was, they did not know where they were, but they both felt—man and child, penitent and innocent—that they ought to be on their knees.

What was strange about these voices was that they did not stop the building from seeming deserted. It was like unearthly song in an uninhabited abode. While the voices went on singing, Jean Valjean no longer thought anything. He no longer saw night, he saw blue skies. It semed to him that he could feel the spreading of the wings we all have inside us.

The song died out. It had perhaps gone on a long time. Jean Valjean could not tell. Hours of ecstasy are never more than a minute long.

Everything had fallen silent again. Nothing more in the street, nothing more in the garden. What had been threatening, what had been reassuring—all had faded away. The wind ruffled the dry grass on top of the wall and it made a soft and mournful sound.

## VII. The Enigma Goes On

The night breeze was up, which indicated that it had to be between one and two in the morning. Poor Cosette did not say a word. Since she was sitting down on the ground beside him and had leaned her head against him, Jean Valjean thought she had fallen asleep. He bent over and looked at her. Cosette's eyes were wide open and her thoughtful look gave Jean Valjean a stab of pain. She was still trembling.

"Are you sleepy?" said Jean Valjean.

"I'm very cold," she answered.

A moment later she went on: "Is she still there?"

"Who?" said Jean Valjean.

"Madame Thénardier."

Jean Valjean had already forgotten the means he had used to get Cosette to stay quiet.

"Ah!" he said. "She's gone. There's nothing to be frightened of now."

The little girl sighed as though a heavy weight had been lifted from her chest.

The ground was damp, the shed was open on all sides, the breeze got fresher by the second. The good man took off his redingote and wrapped Cosette up in it.

"Are you a bit warmer like that?" he said.

"Oh, yes, father!"

"All right then, wait for me a moment. I'll be back."

He left the ruin and walked along the big building, looking for a better place to shelter. He came across several doors but they were closed. All the ground-floor casement windows had bars on them.

As he passed the inner corner of the building, he noticed that he had come to some arched windows and he could see light through them. He rose on the balls of his feet and looked in at one of these windows. They all opened on a fairly vast room, paved with great big flagstones, broken up with arches and pillars, where all you could make out was a dim glow and great shadows. The glow came from a night-lamp burning in a corner. The room was deserted and nothing stirred in it. Yet the more he looked, the more he thought he saw on the ground, on the flagstones, something that looked as though it was covered in a shroud and that had a vaguely human shape. It was stretched out flat on its stomach, face to the stone, arms out forming a cross, as motionless as death. It looked for all the world, from a sort of snake trailing across the flagstones, as though this sinister figure had a rope around its neck.

The whole room was bathed in that mist peculiar to dimly lit places that adds to their horror.

Jean Valjean often said afterward that, though he had seen many mournful sights in his life, never had he seen anything more chilling and more terrible than this enigmatic figure accomplishing who knows what mysterious rite in this dismal place, only half-visible in the night. It was frightening to speculate that the thing might be dead, and even more frightening to imagine that it might be alive.

He had the courage to stick his forehead against the glass and watch to see if the thing moved. He stayed like that what seemed to him a long time, in vain; the prostrate figure made no movement. All of a sudden, he felt himself seized with an indescribable terror and he fled. He started to run toward the shed without daring to look back. It seemed to him that if he turned his head he would see the figure walking behind him with great strides, flapping its arms.

He reached the ruin, breathless. His knees gave way; sweat was running down his back.

Where was he? Who could ever have imagined anything like this sort of sepulchre in the middle of Paris? What was this strange house? A building full of nocturnal mysteries, calling souls in the shadows in the voice of angels and then, when they came, suddenly offering them this horrifying vision, promising to open the radiant gate of heaven and opening, instead, the horrible gate of the tomb! And it was indeed a building, a house that had its number in some street! It was not a dream! He needed to touch the stones it was made of to believe it was real.

The cold, the worry, the anxiety, the anguish of the night were giving him a real fever and all these ideas were crashing around in his brain.

He went over to Cosette. She was sleeping.

## VIII. The Enigma Intensifies

The child had laid her head on a stone and gone to sleep.

He sat down next to her and looked at her. Little by little, the more he looked, the more he calmed down, and he regained his ability to think.

He clearly saw this truth, which was the whole basis of his life from that moment on: that as long as she was there, as long as he had her next to him, he would need nothing except her, would fear nothing except on her behalf. He did not even feel that he was really cold, having taken off his coat to cover her with it.

Meanwhile, through the reverie into which he had fallen, he had heard a peculiar noise for some time. It was like a little bell someone was jingling. The noise was coming from the garden. You could hear it clearly, if faintly. It was like the soft tinkling of cowbells in pastures at night. This noise made Jean Valjean turn round. He looked and saw that there was someone in the garden.

A being that looked like a man was walking among the bell jars in the melon patch, getting up, bending down, stopping, with regular movements, as though he were dragging or stretching something out on the ground. This being seemed to be limping.

Jean Valjean shuddered with the unconquerable tremor of the wretched victims of fate. To such people, everything is hostile and suspect. They distrust the day because it allows them to be seen and the night because it allows them to be caught unawares. A bit before this, he had shivered to see the garden deserted, now he shivered to see that someone was there.

He tumbled once more from chimerical terrors to real terrors. He told himself that Javert and his spies might not have gone, that they had doubtless left people in the street to keep watch, that if this man found him in the garden, he would cry thief and hand him over. He gathered the sleeping Cosette gently in his arms and carried her to the farthest corner of the shed, behind a pile of old furniture that was no longer in use. Cosette did not stir.

From there he observed the movements of the person in the melon patch. What was bizarre was that the noise of the little bell chimed in with the man's every move. When the man came nearer, the noise came nearer; when he moved away, the noise moved away; if he made a sudden movement, a tremolo accompanied that movement; if he stopped, the noise stopped. It seemed clear that the bell was attached to the man; but, then, what could this mean? What was this man with a bell hung on him like some ram or ox? While he was posing these questions, he felt Cosette's hands. They were frozen.

"Oh, God!" he said.

He called out in a low voice: "Cosette!"

She did not open her eyes.

He gave her a good shake. She did not wake up.

"She can't be dead!" he said, and he sprang up, quivering from head to toe.

The most awful thoughts flashed through his mind in a jumble. There are times when hideous suppositions besiege us like a pack of furies, violently storming the compartments of our brains. When it comes to those we love, we come up with all kinds of mad things in our concern. He remembered that sleep could be fatal in the open on a cold night.

Cosette had fallen sprawling to the ground at his feet without stirring, white as a sheet. He listened for her breath; she was breathing, but her breathing seemed weak and fading fast.

How could he get her warm again? How could he rouse her? Everything else was banished from his thoughts. He hurtled out of the ruin, distraught. It was absolutely essential that before a quarter of an hour was up, Cosette be in bed in front of a fire.

## IX. THE MAN WITH THE BELL

He went straight up to the man he could see in the garden. He had in his hand the roll of money from his waistcoat pocket.

The man had his head down and did not see him coming. In a few bounds, Jean Valjean was at his side. Jean Valjean accosted him, shouting: "A hundred francs!"

The man gave a start and looked up.

"There's a hundred francs in it for you," Jean Valjean went on, "if you give me shelter for the night!"

The moon shone right on Jean Valjean's wildly frightened face.

"Good grief, it's you, father Madeleine!" the man said.

This name, spoken in this tone, at this dark hour, in this unknown place, by this unknown man, made Jean Valjean jump back.

He was ready for anything, except that. The man talking to him was an old man, stooped and lame, decked out more or less like a peasant and wearing a leather knee pad on his left knee with a fairly big bell hanging from it. You could not make out his face, which was in the shadows.

Meanwhile the man had taken off his cap and exclaimed, trembling all over: "Oh, my God! What are you doing here, father Madeleine? How in Christ's name did you get in? You must have fallen from the sky! It's no mystery, if ever you do fall, that's where you'll fall from, that's for sure. And just look at you! Where's your cravat? Where's your hat? Where's your coat! Don't you realize you'd have given anyone who didn't know you quite a fright? No coat! God in heaven, have all the saints gone mad these days! But just how did you get in here?"

The words tumbled out, one after the other. The old man spoke with the volubility of a man of the land and there was nothing disturbing about it. Everything he said was said with a mixture of amazement and simple good nature.

"Who are you? And what is this place here?" asked Jean Valjean.

"Hah! Hah! That's a good one!" cried the old man. "I'm the man you got a job for and this place is the place you got me a job in. Heavens! Don't tell me you don't recognize me?"

"No," said Jean Valjean. "And how come you know who I am?"

"You saved my life," said the man.

He turned and a shaft of moonlight lit his face side-on and Jean Valjean recognized old Fauchelevent.

"Ah!" said Jean Valjean. "It's you? Yes, I recognize you."

"That's lucky!" said the old man in a tone of reproach.

"And what are you doing here?" Jean Valjean went on.

"What do you think? I'm covering my melons, of course!"

When Jean Valjean had accosted him, old Fauchelevent had, indeed, had in his hand a corner of a straw mat that he was busy laying over the melon bed. He had already laid a number of them in the hour he had been in the garden. It was this operation that had caused him to make the peculiar movements Jean Valjean had observed from the shed.

He went on: "I said to myself: The moon's bright, there's going to be a frost. What if I put coats on my melons for them? And," he added, looking at Jean Valjean with a big guffaw, "it wouldn't have hurt you to do the same! But how in God's name did you get here?"

Jean Valjean, seeing this man knew him, at least by the name of Madeleine, dropped his guard. He fired off questions. What was bizarre was the way their roles seemed to be reversed now. It was he, the intruder, who was asking the questions.

"And what on earth is this bell you have on your knee?"

"That?" replied Fauchelevent. "That's so they can keep away from me."

Old Fauchelevent gave a cheeky wink.

"Hell's bells! There are only women in this house; lots of young girls. It appears I'd be dangerous to run into. The bell warns them. When I come, they go."

"What is this house, anyway?"

"Heavens! You should know."

"I don't."

"Since you got me the job of gardener here!"

"Tell me as if I knew nothing."

"All right, then, it's the convent of Petit-Picpus!"

It came back to Jean Valjean then. Chance, meaning Providence, had thrown him precisely into the convent of the quartier Saint-Antoine where old Fauchelevent, maimed by the fall from his cart, had been accepted on his recommendation two years previously. He repeated, as though talking to himself: "The convent of Petit-Picpus!"

"Ah, yes, but now," Fauchelevent went on, "how the hell did you manage to get in here, you, father Madeleine? You may well be a saint. I know you're a saint! But you're a man and men don't get in here."

"You're here."

"I'm the only one."

"But," Jean Valjean plowed on, "I must stay."

"Oh, my God!" cried Fauchelevent.

Jean Valjean moved closer to the old man and said to him in a grave voice: "Father Fauchelevent, I saved your life."

"I remembered that first!" Fauchelevent shot back.

"Well, then, today you can do for me what I once did for you."

Fauchelevent took Jean Valjean's two robust hands in his old trembling wrinkled hands and it was some seconds before he could speak. At last, he said: "Oh! It would be a blessing from the good Lord if I could do something for you in return! Me, save your life! Monsieur le maire, this old boy is at your disposal!"

A wonderful joy had seemingly transfigured the old man. Light seemed to stream from his face.

"What would you like me to do?" he went on.

"I'll tell you. Do you have a room?"

"I have a solitary shack, over there, behind the ruin of the old convent, tucked away in a corner no one sees. It has three rooms."

The shack was indeed so well hidden behind the ruin, and so unobtrusive in its design, that Jean Valjean had missed it.

"Good," said Jean Valjean. "Now I am asking two things of you."

"What are they, Monsieur le maire?"

"First, you won't tell anyone what you know about me. Second, you won't try to find out anything more."

"As you wish. I know you could never do anything that wasn't honest and that you have always been a man of God. And then again, anyway, it's you who got me a place here, it's your business. I'm yours."

"All right, then. Now come with me. We'll go and get the child."

"Ah!" said Fauchelevent. "There's a child!"

He did not say another word and followed Jean Valjean like a dog following its master.

Less than half an hour later, Cosette, all rosy once more in the glow of a good fire, was sleeping in the old gardener's bed. Jean Valjean had put his cravat and his coat back on; the hat hurled over the wall had been found and retrieved. While Jean Valjean was putting on his coat, Fauchelevent had taken off his knee pad with the bell and it now hung from a nail next to a shutter, decorating the wall. The two men were warming themselves, leaning on a table on which Fauchelevent had put a lump of cheese, some grayish-brown bread, a bottle of wine and two glasses, and the old man was saying to Jean Valjean, putting his hand on his knee: "Ah, father Madeleine! You didn't recognize me straight off! You save people's lives and then you forget all about them! Oh, that's bad! They remember you! You're an ungrateful bugger!"

## X. In Which It Is Explained How Javert Came Up Empty

The events we have just seen in reverse, so to speak, happened in the most straightforward way.

When Jean Valjean, the very night of the day Javert had arrested him by Fantine's deathbed, escaped from the municipal prison of Montreuil-sur-mer, the police assumed that the escaped convict would have headed for Paris. Paris is a maelstrom where anyone can lose themselves and everyone disappears in the world's great whirlpool just as they would do in the whirlpool of the sea. No forest can conceal a man the way the teeming multitude does. Fugitives of every stripe know this. They head for Paris in order to be swallowed up; you can be saved by being swallowed up. The police know this, too, and it is in Paris that they look for what they have lost elsewhere. They looked for the ex-mayor of Montreuil-sur-mer there. Javert was called to Paris to advise in the investigation. Javert was, in fact, of tremendous assistance in the recapture of Jean Valjean. Javert's zeal and intelligence on that occasion were noted by Monsieur Chabouillet, the secretary of the prefecture under the comte Anglès. Monsieur Chabouillet had, in any case, already taken Javert under his wing, and he had the inspector from Montreuil-sur-mer transferred to the Paris police. There, in various ways, Javert made himself what we might call honorably useful, though the expression might seem misplaced for such services.

He no longer thought about Jean Valjean. For these dogs who are always on the hunt, today's wolf eclipses yesterday's wolf completely. Then suddenly in December 1823, Javert found himself reading a newspaper. Javert never read newspapers, but he was nothing if not a monarchist and he was eager to hear the details of the triumphant entry into Bayonne[1] of the "generalissimo prince." As he was finishing the article that interested him, a name, the name of Jean Valjean, leaped out at him at the bottom of a page. The paper announced that the convict Jean Valjean was dead and published this fact in terms so categorical that Javert was left in no doubt. All he said was: "That's that, then. Good riddance to bad rubbish." Then he threw the paper down and thought no more about it.

Some little time later it happened that the Seine-et-Oise[2] prefecture sent the prefecture of police in Paris a notice about the kidnapping of a child, which had taken place, they said, in peculiar circumstances, in the commune of Montfermeil. A little girl, seven or eight years old, said the notice, who had been entrusted by her mother to an innkeeper of the district, had been stolen by a stranger; this little girl answered to the name of Cosette and was the daughter of a whore named Fantine, who had died in hospital, no one knew when or where. This notice passed under Javert's nose and set him thinking.

The name Fantine was well-known to him. He remembered that Jean Valjean had made him, Javert, laugh out loud by asking him for a stay of three days so he could go and look for that creature's offspring. He recalled that Jean Valjean had been arrested in Paris just as he was getting into the Montfermeil coach. A few things at the time seemed to indicate that this was the second time he had taken this coach and that he had already, the day before, made a trip to the outskirts of the village, for no one had spotted him in the village itself. What was he doing in the Montfermeil region? They had not been able to figure it out. Javert now understood. Fantine's daughter was there. Jean Valjean had gone to look for her. Now this child had been stolen by a stranger. Who could this stranger be? Could he be Jean Valjean? But Jean Valjean was dead. Javert, without saying anything to anyone, took the rattletrap of a coach from the Plat-d'étain, in the cul-de-sac of La Planchette, and made the trip to Montfermeil. He hoped to find enlightenment there, instead he found a complete muddle.

In the first few days, the Thénardiers, greatly riled, had told all. The story of the Lark's disappearance had done the rounds of the village. There were instantly several versions of the story, which had wound up being described as a case of child-snatching. Hence the police notice. But once his initial reaction was over, old man Thénardier, with his usual admirable instinct, swiftly realized that it is never helpful to stir up the crown prosecutor and that his complaints regarding the "kidnapping" of Cosette would have the immediate result of fixing the beady eye of the law on him, Thénardier, and on lots of shady dealings he had going. The thing owls most want not to see is a light shone in their faces. To start with, how could he explain the fifteen hundred francs he had received? He reined himself in, muzzled his wife, and acted amazed when they talked to him about a "stolen child." He had no idea what they were going on about; no doubt he had complained in the heat of the moment about someone "stealing" that dear little girl from him so soon—out of tenderness he'd have liked to hang on to her for another two or three days—but it was her "grandfather" who had come for her, the most natural thing in the world. He had added the bit about the grandfather for effect. This was the story Javert had stumbled onto when he arrived in Montfermeil. The grandfather caused Jean Valjean to evaporate.

Yet Javert sank a few questions, like probes, into Thénardier's story. What kind of man was this grandfather and what was his name?

Thénardier answered in a straightforward manner: "He's a rich farmer. I saw his passport. I believe his name is Monsieur Guillaume Lambert."

Lambert is a solid sort of name and most reassuring. Javert went back to Paris.

"Jean Valjean is well and truly dead," he said to himself, "and I am a mug."

He was beginning to forget the whole thing when, sometime in March 1824, he heard talk of an odd character living in the parish of Saint-Médard and nicknamed "the beggar who gives alms." This character was, it was said, a man with a private income whose name no one really knew and who lived alone with a little girl of eight, who herself knew nothing, except that she came from

Montfermeil. Montfermeil! That name kept coming back, and it made Javert prick up his ears. A snitch of an old beggar, a former beadle, to whom this character had given charity, added a few extra details: This man of means was an extremely antisocial character, who only showed himself at night, never spoke to anyone, except, sometimes, to the poor, and never let anyone anywhere near him. He wore a horrible old yellow redingote worth several millions, since the lining was stuffed with banknotes. This definitely piqued Javert's curiosity. So as to get a very close look at this fantastic millionaire without scaring him off, he borrowed the beadle's castoffs one day and took over the spot where the old snitch used to crouch every night whining prayers while he did his spying.

The "suspicious individual" did indeed come to Javert thus disguised and gave him alms. The moment he did, Javert looked up, and the shock that Jean Valjean had received thinking he recognized Javert was the same as the one Javert received thinking he recognized Jean Valjean.

But the darkness could have deceived him; Jean Valjean's death was official. Javert still had doubts, serious doubts; and when in doubt, Javert, scrupulous as he was, never collared any man.

He followed his man right to the Gorbeau house and got the old woman to talk, which was not too hard to do. The old woman confirmed the story about the redingote lined with millions, and she told him about the episode with the thousand-franc note. She had seen it! She had touched it! Javert paid for a room. That very evening, he set himself up in it. He went and listened at the door of the mysterious tenant, hoping to hear the sound of his voice, but Jean Valjean had seen his candle through the keyhole and thwarted the spy by keeping quiet.

The next day Jean Valjean had decamped. But the noise made by the five-franc coin he dropped was noted by the old woman who, hearing the movement of money, suspected he was about to make a run for it and rushed to warn Javert. That night, when Jean Valjean went out, Javert was waiting for him behind the trees in the boulevard with two men.

Javert had asked the prefecture for backup, but he had not told them the name of the individual he was hoping to nab. That was his secret, and he had kept it for three reasons: first, because the slightest indiscretion could put Jean Valjean on his guard; next, because getting your hands on an escaped convict reputed dead, a condemned man that the annals of justice have classified once and for all time as "among the most dangerous kind of malefactors," would be a glorious coup that the old boys on the Paris police would definitely never allow a newcomer like Javert to score, and he feared they would take his galley slave away from him; last, because Javert, being an artist, had a taste for surprise. He couldn't stand those much-trumpeted successes that are spoiled by being talked about long in advance. He like to work on his masterpieces in the shadows and then unveil them suddenly to a general gasping.

Javert had followed Jean Valjean from tree to tree, then from street corner to street corner, and had not lost sight of him for a single instant. Even in those moments when Jean Valjean felt most secure, Javert's eye was on him.

Why didn't Javert arrest Jean Valjean then and there? Because he was still in doubt.

It must be remembered that, at the time, the police were not exactly at ease; they were hampered by a free press. The song and dance over a few arbitrary arrests, denounced by the newspapers, had been heard all the way to the Chambers and made the prefecture timid. To attack the freedom of the individual was a grave matter. The officers were afraid of getting things wrong, for the prefect put the blame on them; a mistake meant dismissal. Imagine the impact that this short paragraph, reproduced in twenty newspapers, would have had throughout Paris: "Yesterday, an old white-haired grandfather, a respectable man of means, was out walking with his eight-year-old granddaughter when he was arrested and taken to the prefecture, where he was locked up as an escaped convict!"

We repeat that, on top of this, Javert had his own scruples; the dictates of his conscience were added to the strictures of the prefect of police. He really did have his doubts.

So Jean Valjean turned on his heel and walked off into the dark.

Sadness, anxiety, anguish, despair, the fresh burden of being forced to disappear into the night once again and search for a refuge willy-nilly throughout Paris for Cosette and himself, the necessity of adapting his pace to the pace of a child, all this, even without his realizing it, had changed Jean Valjean's gait and given his physical bearing such a stamp of senility that the police themselves, incarnated in Javert, could be fooled, and were fooled. The impossibility of getting too close, his getup as an old emigrant tutor, Thénardier's declaration that made him a grandfather, finally, the belief that he had died in custody, added further to the uncertainty that coagulated in Javert's mind.

He momentarily entertained the idea of asking him for his papers. But if the man was not Jean Valjean, and if the man was not a good old honest man of means, then he was probably some cunning old shyster up to his neck in the obscure web of Paris crime, some dangerous gang leader, giving alms to hide his other talents—the oldest trick in the book. He would have his accomplices, his sidekicks, his bolt-holes where he could no doubt go to ground. All the detours he was taking around the streets seemed to indicate that he was not a simple sort of man. To arrest him too soon would be "to kill the goose that laid the golden eggs." Was there any harm in waiting? Javert was perfectly certain that he would not get away. And so, he walked on, in some perplexity, putting dozens of questions to himself about this enigmatic character.

It was not until quite late, in the rue de Pontoise, that thanks to the very bright light streaming from a pothouse, he definitely recognized Jean Valjean.

In this world there are two beings who are thrilled to the marrow: a mother when she finds her child again and a tiger who catches up with its prey. Javert experienced that profound thrill.

As soon as he recognized Jean Valjean, the fearsome convict, beyond a doubt, he remembered that there were only three of them and he asked for reinforcements from the prefect of police in the rue de Pontoise.

Before you grab a stick with thorns, you put gloves on.

The delay and stopping at the place Rollin to consult with his officers made him lose the scent. But he quickly realized that Jean Valjean would want to put the river between himself and his pursuers. He bent his head and thought hard, like a bloodhound putting his nose to the ground to pick up the right trail. With his powerfully direct instinct, Javert went straight to the pont d'Austerlitz. A word with the toll-keeper brought him up to speed: "Have you seen a man with a little girl?" "I made him pay two sous," said the toll-keeper. Javert reached the bridge in time to see Jean Valjean on the other side of the water, leading Cosette by the hand across the space lit by the moon. He saw him go into the rue du Chemin-Vert-Saint-Antoine; he thought of the cul-de-sac Genrot laid out there like a trap and of the single way out of the rue Droit-Mur into the petite rue Picpus. He "put out beaters," as hunters say, and sent one of his men to run round by a detour to guard this exit. Since a patrol was going back to its post at the Arsenal, he requisitioned it and brought it along. In such games, soldiers are trumps. Besides, it is the rule that, to overcome a wild boar, you need both the science of the master of the hounds and the strength of the hounds themselves. These qualities being brought together, feeling that Jean Valjean was caught between the impasse of the cul-de-sac Genrot on the right, his officer on the left, and himself behind, Javert took a pinch of tobacco.

Then he began to amuse himself. He had a ravishing and diabolical moment when he let his man get ahead of him, knowing he had him but wanting to draw out the moment when he arrested him, happy to see him free, knowing that he was trapped, and gazing longingly at him with the rapture of a spider letting a fly flit about or of a cat letting a mouse run around free. Claws and talons have a monstrous sensuality; it is a terrible pleasure, the obscure struggle of the animal caught in their grip. How delicious to snuff them out!

Javert was in seventh heaven. The mesh of his net was foolproof. He was sure of success; all he had to do now was close his hand.

Reinforced as he was, the very idea of resistance was out of the question, no matter how energetic or vigorous or desperate Jean Valjean might be.

Javert advanced slowly, poking around and scouring every nook and cranny in the street, like the pockets of a thief, along the way.

When he reached the center of his web, the fly was gone.

You can imagine his frustration.

He questioned his sentinel guarding the rue Droit-Mur and the rue Picpus; this officer, who had remained steadfastly at his post, had not seen the man go by.

It sometimes happens that a stag crashes through cover headfirst, in other words, escapes, even though he has the pack at his heels, and then the most experienced hunters are lost for words. Duvivier, Ligniville, and Desprez are at a loss. In a disappointment of the kind, Artonge cried: "That's not a stag, it's a sorcerer." Javert could easily have uttered the same cry.

His disappointment had the taint of despair and fury for a moment.

It is certain that Napoléon made mistakes in the war on Russia, that Alexander made mistakes in the war on India, that Caesar made mistakes in the war on Scythia, and that Javert made mistakes in this campaign against Jean Valjean. He was perhaps wrong in hesitating to recognize the former galley slave. That first glance should have been enough for him. He was wrong not to apprehend him without further ado in the old slum. He was wrong not to arrest him when he recognized him positively in the rue de Pontoise. He was wrong to consult with his aides, in full moonlight, in the place Rollin; certainly, advice is useful, and it is good to know and to question those hounds that have credibility. But a hunter can't be too careful when he is hunting nervous animals like a wolf or a convict. Javert, by being too anxious to set the bloodhounds of the pack on the right trail, alerted the beast by giving him wind of the move and so caused him to bolt, and with a head start. He was wrong above all in playing this dreadful and puerile game of holding him by a thread at arm's length and keeping him dangling, once he had found the scent again on the pont d'Austerlitz. He thought he was stronger than he was, thought he could play the mouse with a lion. At the same time, he thought he was weaker than he was when he judged it necessary to team up with reinforcements. A fatal precaution, a loss of precious time. Javert committed all these mistakes, yet was no less one of the smartest and ablest spies who ever existed. He was, in the full force of the term, what is known in hunting as "a wise hound." But nobody is perfect.

The great strategists have their off days.

Great blunders are often made, like great ropes, out of numerous strands. You take the rope, thread by thread, take separately all the decisive little motives, and you break them one by one, and you say, "That's all it is!" Weave and twist them together and it is monumental; it is Attila hesitating between Marcian in the East and Valentinian in the West; Hannibal hanging back in Capua; Danton falling asleep at Arcis-sur-Aube.[3]

Whatever the case may be, even at the moment when he saw that Jean Valjean had eluded him, Javert did not lose his head. Certain that this convict who had broken out could not be far away, he posted watchdogs, he set traps and ambushes and combed the area all night long. The first thing he saw was the street-lamp that had been tampered with, its rope cut. A precious clue, it still led him astray by deflecting all the search efforts to the cul-de-sac Genrot. There are some pretty low walls in this cul-de-sac enclosing gardens that end in a vast tract of uncultivated land at the back. Jean Valjean obviously must have escaped that way. The fact is that, if he had only gone a bit further into the cul-de-sac Genrot, he probably would have—and he would have been finished. Javert went over the gardens and wastegrounds as though searching for a needle in a haystack.

At daybreak, he left two bright men to keep watch and went back to the prefecture of police, shamefaced as a snitch who has been caught out by a thief.

# BOOK SIX

# PETIT-PICPUS

## I. PETITE RUE PICPUS, NO. 62

No porte cochère could have been more ordinary, half a century ago, than the porte cochère of no. 62, petite rue Picpus. This door was normally half-open in the most inviting way, revealing two things that had nothing especially gloomy about them—a courtyard surrounded by vine-covered walls and the face of a porter lounging there. Over the back wall, great trees could be seen. When a ray of sunshine brightened up the courtyard or when a glass of wine brightened up the porter, it was difficult to pass by no. 62 petite rue Picpus without carrying away a cheery idea of it. And yet it was a grim place when you first caught a glimpse of it.

The threshold grinned; the house prayed and wept.

You had to get past the porter, which was not easy, which was even impossible for almost everyone, for there was an open sesame that you had to know; but if you did manage to get past the porter, you walked straight into a little vestibule that led to a staircase squeezed in between two walls and so narrow that only one person at a time could pass; if you did not let yourself be frightened off by the canary yellow distemper on the upper part of the stair wall and the chocolate color on the base, if you ventured to go up, you passed one landing, then a second, and you reached the upper floor in a hall where the yellow distemper and the chocolate base followed you with quiet relentlessness. Stairs and hall were lit by two beautiful windows. The hall then veered like a dog's leg and became dark. If you jumped that hurdle, after a few feet you came to a door all the more mysterious for not being shut. You pushed it and you found yourself in a small room about six feet square, tiled, washed and scrubbed, clean and neat, cold, and hung with nankeen wallpaper with little green flowers at fifteen sous a roll. Dull white light came from a big window with little panes on the left and ran the whole length of the room. You looked, but you did not see anyone; you listened, but you did not hear a footstep or the faintest murmur of a human voice. The wall was bare; the room was unfurnished, with not a single chair.

You looked again and you saw that, on the wall opposite the door, a quadrangular opening about a foot square had a grate over it, a grate of crisscrossing iron bars, black, knotted, solid, that formed squares—I nearly said mesh—less than an inch across. The little green flowers of the nankeen wallpaper went calmly and neatly right up to these iron bars, without being frightened off by such dismal contact and sent into a tizzy. Supposing that some living being had been so fabulously thin as to even be able to think about getting in or out through the square hole, the grate would have prevented them from doing so. It would not let a body through, but it let your eyes through, that is, your mind. It seems they had thought of that, for it had been lined with a sheet of tin inserted into the wall a bit to the back and punched with a thousand holes tinier than the holes of a colander. At the bottom of this tin plate an opening had been punched that was exactly like the mouth of a letter box. A cord attached to a bell hung to the right of the grate.

If you pulled this cord, a little bell tinkled and you would hear a voice right next to you, which made you jump.

"Who's there?" the voice asked.

It was a woman's voice, a sweet voice, so sweet it was spooky.

Here again there was a magic word that you had to know. If you did not know what it was, the voice shut up and the wall became silent again as though the bewildered darkness of the tomb had been on the other side.

If you did know the word, the voice went on: "Enter at the right."

You then noticed on your right, opposite the window, a glass door surmounted by a glass window painted gray. You lifted the latch, you walked through the door, and you had exactly the same impression as when you go to a show at the theater and enter a ground floor box protected by a grille, before the grille is lowered and the lights go up. You were in fact in a sort of theater box, barely lit by the dim daylight from the glass door, tiny, furnished with two old chairs and a frayed straw mat, a veritable box with a front just the right height to lean on and a black sill. This box had a grille, too, only it was not a grille of gilded wood as at the Opéra, it was a monstrous trellis of iron bars hideously enmeshed and fixed to the wall with enormous bolts that looked like clenched fists.

After the first few minutes, when your eyes began to adjust to the crepuscular half-light of this cave, you tried to look through the grille but could not see more than six inches in front of you. There, you saw a barrier of black shutters, secured and reinforced by wooden crossbars painted a gingerbread yellow. These shutters were jointed and divided into long thin slats and they masked the entire length of the grate. They were always shut.

After a few minutes, you heard a voice calling you from behind these shutters and saying to you: "I am here. What do you want of me?"

It was a loved voice, sometimes an adored voice. You saw no one. You scarcely heard the sound of breathing. It seemed that it was a disembodied evocation speaking to you from across the barrier of the grave.

If you met certain essential requirements—this was extremely rare—the narrow slat of one of the shutters opened directly in front of you and the evocation became an apparition. Behind the grille, behind the shutter, you saw, as far as the grille allowed you to see, a head, of which only the mouth and the chin were visible; the rest was covered in a black veil. You caught a glimpse of a black wimple and a shapeless form covered in a black shroud. This head spoke to you but did not look at you and never smiled at you.

The light that came in behind you was slanted in such a way that you saw the head as white and it saw you as black. This daylight was symbolic.

Yet your eyes plunged avidly through this aperture that had opened up, into this space shut off from all eyes. A profound vagueness enveloped this form dressed in mourning. Your eyes searched the vagueness and sought to fathom what surrounded the apparition. In a very short while you realized you saw nothing. What you saw was night, emptiness, the dark, a winter fog mingled with vapor from the grave, a sort of terrifying peace, a silence in which you took in nothing, not even a sigh, a shadowland where you could make out nothing, not even a phantom.

What you saw was the interior of a cloister.

It was the interior of that mournful and severe house known as the convent of the Bernadines of Perpetual Adoration. The box you were in was the visitors' parlor. The voice, the one that first spoke to you, was the voice of the sister in charge of external relations who was always seated, motionless and silent, on the other side of the wall, next to the square opening, defended by a grate of iron and by the tin plate with a thousand holes as though by a double visor.

The darkness in which the grated box was plunged came from the fact that the visitors' room, which had a window onto the outside world, had none on the convent side. Profane eyes were not supposed to see anything of this holy place.

And yet there was something beyond this darkness, there was a light; there was a life amid all this death. Even though this convent was the most walled-in of all, we are going to try to get in and to get the reader in, and, all restraint aside, tell things that storytellers have never seen and consequently have never told.

## II. The Rule of Martin Verga

This convent that, in 1824, had already existed for many long years in the petite rue Picpus was a community of Bernardines of the rule of Martin Verga.[1]

These Bernardines[2] were, consequently, not linked to Clairvaux, like the Bernadine monks, but to Cîteaux, like the Benedictine monks. In other words, they were subjects not of Saint Bernard but of Saint Benedict.

Anyone who has leafed through old folios knows that in 1425, Martin Verga founded a Bernardine-Benedictine congregation, with the headquarters of the order at Salamanca and a branch church at Alcala. This congregation had grown sub-branches in all the Catholic countries of Europe.

Such grafts of one order onto another are not at all unusual in the Latin Church. To take only the order of Saint Benedict that we are dealing with here as an example, and without counting the rule of Martin Verga, four congregations are connected to this order: two in Italy, Monte Cassino and Santa Giustina of Padua, and two in France, Cluny and Saint-Maur; as well as nine orders, Vallombrosa, Grammont, the Celestines, the Camaldolese, the Carthusians, the Humiliati, the Olivetans, the Sylvestrines, and lastly Cîteaux, for Cîteaux itself, the trunk of other orders, is just an offshoot of Saint Benedict. Cîteaux was founded by Saint Robert, abbé de Molesme, in the diocese of Langres in 1098. Now, it was in 529 that the devil, who had retired to the desert of Subiaco—he was old and had perhaps become a hermit[3]—was driven out of the temple of Apollo, where he dwelt, by Saint Benedict, then seventeen years old.

After the rule of the Carmelites, who go barefoot, wear a bit of willow at their throats, and never sit down, the harshest rule is that of the Bernardine-Benedictines of Martin Verga. They are dressed in black and wear a wimple that, according to the express command of Saint Benedict, comes right up under the chin. A robe of serge with wide sleeves, a big woolen veil, the wimple worn right up to the chin and cut square across the chest, with the band coming down over the forehead to the eyes—this is their habit. Everything is black except the band, which is white. Novices wear the same habit, but all in white. Professed nuns also have a rosary at the side.

The Bernardine-Benedictines of Martin Verga practice Perpetual Adoration, as do the Benedictines known as Ladies of the Blessed Sacrament,[4] who, at the turn of the century, had two houses in Paris, one at the Temple and the other in the rue Neuve-Sainte-Geneviève. But the Bernardine-Benedictines of Petit-Picpus that we are concerned with were a completely different order from the Ladies of the Blessed Sacrament cloistered in the rue Neuve-Sainte-Geneviève and the Temple. There were numerous differences in their rule as well as in their attire. The Bernardine-Benedictines of Petit-Picpus wore the black wimple and the Benedictines of the Blessed Sacrament and the rue

Neuve-Sainte-Geneviève wore the white wimple and also wore a blessed crucifix about three inches long in gilded silver or gilded copper at their breasts.
The Petit-Picpus nuns did not wear this crucifix. Though the Perpetual Adoration was common to the Petit-Picpus house and the Temple house, the two orders remained perfectly distinct. Their only resemblance lies in this shared
practice of the Ladies of the Blessed Sacrament and the Bernardines of Martin
Verga, just as there was a similarity in the study and glorification of all the mysteries concerning the infancy, life, and death of Jesus Christ and the Blessed
Virgin Mary, between another pair of orders that were very distinct and on occasion even hostile: the Oratory of Italy, set up in Florence by Philip di Neri,
and the Oratory of France, set up in Paris by Pierre de Bérulle.[5] The Oratory in
Paris claimed precedence, Philippe di Neri being only a saint, whereas Bérulle
was a cardinal.

Let's get back to the harsh Spanish rule of Martin Verga. The Bernardine-
Benedictines of this order abstain from meat all year round, fast during Lent
and on plenty of other days that have special meaning for them, get up out of
their first sleep to say the breviary and chant matins from one o'clock till three
o'clock in the morning, sleep in serge sheets and on beds of straw whatever the
season, do not have baths, never light fires, scourge themselves every Friday, observe the rule of silence, only talking to each other during recreation periods,
which are extremely short, and wear hair shirts for six months of the year, from
September 14, which is the Exaltation of the Holy Cross, to Easter. These six
months are pretty moderate—the rule says all year, but hair shirts are unbearable at the height of summer and produce fevers and nervous spasms, so their
use had to be restricted. Even with this softening of the rule, on September 14,
when the nuns first put on the shirts, they have three or four days of fever. Obedience, poverty, chastity, perseverance in their seclusion—those are their vows,
made considerably more rigorous by the rule.

The prioress is elected for three years by the mother superiors, who are
called "vocal mothers" because they have a say in the matter. A prioress can be
reelected only twice, which means the longest possible reign for a prioress is
fixed at nine years.

They never see the officiating priest, who is always hidden from them by a
serge curtain nine feet high. During the sermon, when the priest is in the
chapel, they lower their veils over their faces. They must always speak softly
and walk with their eyes on the ground and the head bowed. Only one man may
ever enter the convent and that is the archbishop of the diocese.

There is actually one other man, and that is the gardener; but he is always
an old man, and to ensure that he is perpetually alone in the garden and the
nuns can be warned to avoid him, a bell is attached to his knee.

They are subject to the prioress with a submissiveness that is absolute and passive. This is canonical enslavement in all its self-abnegation. As at the voice of Christ, *ut voci Christi,* at the movement, at the first sign, *ad nutum, ad primum signum,* right away, with joy, with perseverance, with a certain blind obedience, *prompte, hilariter, perseveranter et caeca quadam obedientia,* like a file in the hand of a laborer, *quasi limam in manibus fabri,* not being able to read or write anything whatsoever without express permission, *legere vel scribere non addiscerit sine expressa superioris licentia.*

Taking turns, each nun makes what they call atonement. Atonement is prayer for all the sins, all the faults, all the disturbances, all the violations, all the iniquities, all the crimes that are committed on this earth. For twelve consecutive hours, from four o'clock in the late afternoon to four o'clock in the morning, or from four o'clock in the morning to four o'clock in the late afternoon, the sister making atonement remains on her knees on the stone floor before the Blessed Sacrament, her hands joined in prayer and a rope around her neck. When fatigue becomes unbearable, she prostrates herself flat on her stomach, her face to the floor, her arms out in a cross. That is the only relief she gets. In this attitude she prays for all the guilty of the universe. This is greatness that achieves the sublime.

As this act is accomplished in front of a pole with a burning candle on top of it, they call it, indiscriminately, "to make atonement" or "to be at the pole." Out of humility, the nuns even prefer the latter expression, which contains the idea of torture and abasement.

To make atonement is a process in which the whole soul is absorbed. The sister at the pole would not turn round even if a bolt of lightning were to strike right behind her.

Moreover, there is always a nun on her knees before the Holy Sacrament. This station lasts an hour. They relieve each other like soldiers on guard duty. This is Perpetual Adoration.

Prioresses and mother superiors almost always bear names impregnated with a particular gravity, recalling not the saints and martyrs but moments in the life of Jesus Christ, like Mother Nativity, Mother Conception, Mother Presentation, Mother Passion. Yet the names of saints are not prohibited.

When you see them, you only ever see their mouths. They all have yellow teeth. Never has a toothbrush entered the convent. To brush your teeth lies at the top of a slippery slope at the bottom of which lies: losing your soul.

They never say of anything "my" or "mine." They have nothing of their own and are supposed not to be attached to anything. They say of everything "our," so: our veil, our rosary; if they were referring to their shirt they would say "our shirt." Sometimes they become attached to some little object, to a book of hours, a relic, a holy medal. As soon as they realize that they are starting to become attached to this object, they must give it away. They recall what Saint Theresa replied when a grande dame who was about to enter into her order said, "Allow me, Mother, to send for a Holy Bible I'm very attached to." "Ah! You're attached to something! In that case, do not enter our house."

No one is allowed to shut herself away and have a home of her own, a room. They live in open cells. When they approach one another, one of them says: "Praised and adored be the most Blessed Sacrament of the altar!" The other one answers: "Forever." Same ceremony when one knocks on another's door. The door has hardly been touched before a sweet voice on the other side is heard to blurt out: "Forever!" Like all practices, this becomes mechanical through habit; and one of them will sometimes say "Forever" before the other one has the time to say "Praised and adored be the most Blessed Sacrament of the altar!" It is a bit of a mouthful after all.

Among the Visitandines, the nun entering says *"Ave Maria"* and the nun whose place is being entered says *"Gratia plena."* That is their greeting and it is, indeed, "full of grace."

At every hour of the day, three additional strokes ring out from the chapel bell of the convent. At this signal, the prioress, vocal mothers, professed nuns, converts, novices, postulants, interrupt what they are saying, what they are doing, what they are thinking, and they all say in unison, if it is five o'clock, for example: "At five o'clock and at any hour, praised and adored be the most Blessed Sacrament of the altar!" If it is eight o'clock: "At eight o'clock and at any hour," etc., according to whatever hour it is.

This custom, which aims to break the chain of thought and bring the mind back to focus always on God, exists in many communities; only the formula varies. Thus, at the Infant Jesus, they say: "At this hour and at any hour may the love of Jesus inflame my heart!"

The Benedictine-Bernardines of Martin Verga, cloistered fifty years ago in Petit-Picpus, sang the services to a solemn psalmody, pure plainchant, and always at full voice for the whole length of the service. Wherever there was an asterisk in the missal, they would pause and say in a low voice: "Jesus-Mary-Joseph." For the Service of the Dead they adopted such a low register, it was hard for women's voices to reach it. The effect produced was thrilling and tragic.

The nuns of Petit-Picpus had had a burial chamber made beneath the main altar for the burial of their community. The government, as they called it, did not allow this burial chamber to receive coffins, did not allow corpses to be put there. So they had to leave the convent when they died. This upset them and appalled them as a violation of the rules.

As a mediocre consolation, they had obtained the right to be buried at a special hour and in a special corner of the old Vaugirard Cemetery, in ground that once belonged to their community.

On Thursdays, the nuns heard high mass, vespers, and all the offices the same as on Sundays. They also scrupulously observed all the little feast days almost unknown to people in the outside world, feast days the Church was once very big on in France and still is in Spain and Italy. Their attendance in the chapel was interminable. As for the number and length of their prayers, the best we can do to give some idea of this is to cite the guileless words of one of the nuns: "The prayers of the postulants are frightening, the prayers of the novices are even worse, and the prayers of the professed nuns are worse still."

The chapter assembled once a week; the prioress presided, the vocal mothers attended. Each sister took a turn kneeling on the stone floor and confessing out loud, before all, the faults and sins she had committed that week. The vocal mothers conferred together after each confession and inflicted the penance out loud.

Apart from this loud and clear public confession, for which all remotely serious sins were stored up, they had what they called *la coulpe,* from *mea culpa,* for venial sins. To do your *culp* you prostrated yourself flat on your face in front of the prioress until she, who was never referred to as anything other than "our mother," alerted the culprit, by a little rap on the wood of her stall, that she could get up. You did your culp for pretty trivial things. Breaking a glass, tearing a veil, being a few seconds late unintentionally for a service, singing a wrong note in church, and so on, was enough for you to have to do your culp. The culp is completely spontaneous; it is the culprit herself (the word is here etymologically in its place) who judges herself and inflicts it on herself. On feast days and Sundays, four cantor mothers sang the offices before a great rostrum with four lecterns. One day a cantor mother intoned a psalm that began with the word *Ecce* and, instead of *Ecce,* she said out loud these three notes: *do, si, sol;* for this bit of absentmindedness she underwent a culp that lasted for the rest of the service. What made the fault so enormous was the fact that the chapter had laughed.

When a nun was called to the visitors' parlor, even if she was the prioress, she dropped her veil in such a way that, as you will recall, only her mouth could be seen.

The prioress alone could communicate with strangers. The others could only see their immediate family, and that very rarely. If by chance someone from outside turned up to see a nun they once knew or loved in the outside world, it was a matter for serious negotiation and a whole round of talks was required. If this person was a woman, authorization would sometimes be granted; the nun would come and talk to her through the shutters, which were only opened for a mother or a sister. It goes without saying that permission was never granted to men.

Such is the rule of Saint Benedict, aggravated by Martin Verga.

These nuns are not lighthearted, rosy, fresh girls the way the daughters of other orders often are. They are pale and serious. Between 1825 and 1830, three of them went mad.

## III. The Austerities

You are a postulant for at least two years, often four; a novice for four years. It is rare that the final vows can be taken before you reach the age of twenty-three or twenty-four. The Bernardine-Benedictines of Martin Verga do not admit widows into their order.

They deliver themselves up in their cells to secret mortifications of the flesh that they must never talk about.

The day a novice makes her profession she is decked out in all her finery, her head adorned with white roses and her hair washed and brushed till it shines and then curled, and after this, she prostrates herself; a great black veil is spread over her and the service of the dead is sung. Then the nuns split into two lines; one line files past her, saying in a plaintive tone, "Our sister is dead!" and the other file responds in a resounding voice, "Alive in Jesus Christ!"

At the time this story takes place, a boarding school was attached to the convent. A boarding school for young girls from the nobility, most of them rich, among whom the mademoiselles de Sainte-Aulaire and de Bélissen[1] and an English girl bearing the illustrious Catholic name of Talbot[2] stood out. These young girls, brought up by the nuns between four walls, grew up in horror of the outside world and of the age in which they lived. One of them told us one day: "To see the cobblestones on the street made me shiver from head to toe." They were dressed in blue with a white bonnet and wore a Holy Spirit medal in gilded silver or copper pinned to their breasts. On certain major feast days, particularly on the feast day of Saint Martha, they were allowed, as a special favor and supreme thrill, to dress up as nuns and to perform the offices and rituals of Saint Benedict for the entire day. In the early days, the nuns lent them their black habits. But this seemed profane and the prioress eventually banned it. Such a loan was only allowed on the part of novices. It is remarkable that these shows, tolerated no doubt and encouraged in the convent due to a secret spirit of proselytism and to give the girls a foretaste of the holy habit, were a real joy and a true recreation for the boarders. Quite simply, they had fun. "It was new, it was a change." A frankly childish rationale that can't quite explain to us men and women of the world, in a way that we can understand, the felicity of holding an aspergillum, or a sprinkler for holy water, in our hand and standing for hours at a stretch singing in a quartet in front of a whopping great rostrum.

The pupils conformed to all the practices of the convent, the austerities excepted. There are young women who, having entered the world and after several years of marriage, never quite managed to shed the habit of saying swiftly whenever anyone knocked on the door: "Forever!" Like the nuns, the boarders only saw their families in the visitors' room. Even their mothers were not allowed to hug or kiss them. Listen to just how far severity on this point could go: One day a young girl had a visit from her mother, accompanied by a little sister three years old. The young girl cried, for she really would have liked to give her sister a kiss and a hug. Not a chance. She begged for the child to at least be allowed to put her little hand through the bars so that she could kiss it. This was refused as virtually scandalous.

## IV. Fun

These young girls managed to fill this grave house with delightful memories in spite of everything.

At certain times, childhood sparkled in this cloister. The bell would ring for recreation. A door would turn on its hinges. The birds chirped: "Good! Here come the girls!" An eruption of young life flooded this garden that had a cross cut into it like a shroud. Radiant faces, white foreheads, innocent eyes full of happy light, all kinds of auroras would scatter into the shadows. After chanting, bell ringing, chime ringing, the knells, the services, the noise of little girls would suddenly burst out, sweeter than the humming of bees. The hive of joy opened and each one of them brought their honey. They played, they yelled at each other, they formed huddles, they ran around; pretty little white teeth chattered away in corners; the veils, from afar, surveyed the laughter, the shadows spied on the rays of sunshine, but what did it matter! They shone on and they laughed. These four gloomy walls had their dazzling moments. They stood there, vaguely brightened up by the reflection of so much joy, by this sweet whirling of swarms. It was like a shower of roses pelting down through the mourning. The young girls frolicked under the eyes of the nuns; the gaze of flawlessness does not bother innocence. Thanks to these children, there was an hour of simple fun among so many austere hours. The little girls leaped about, the big ones danced. In the cloister, games were heavenly. Nothing could be more ravishing and noble than all these fresh souls blossoming. Homer would have dropped in there for a laugh with Perrault, and there was enough youth, health, noise, yelling and screaming, giddiness, pleasure, happiness in that dark garden, to bring a smile to the lips of all the grandmothers, those of the epics every bit as much as those of the fairy tales, those on the throne every bit as much as those in the thatch-roofed hovel, from Hecuba to Mother Goose.

In this house, perhaps more than anywhere else, those children's sayings that are always so delightful and that always make people laugh with a laughter full of reverie, were said to each other. It is between these four gloomy walls that a little girl of five cried one day: "Mother, a big girl just told me I only have nine years and ten months to go here. Isn't that wonderful!"

It is also here that this memorable conversation took place:

A vocal mother: "Why are you crying, my child?"

The child (six), sobbing: "I told Alix I knew my history of France. She said I don't, and I do."

Alix (the big girl, nine): "No, she doesn't."

The mother: "How so, my child?"

Alix: "She told me to open the book anywhere and to ask her any question that was there in the book and she'd answer."

"Well?"

"She didn't answer."

"Let's have a look. What did you ask her?"

"I opened the book anywhere, just like she said, and I asked her the first question I found."

"And what was the question?"

"It was: 'What happens next?' "

It was at that juncture that the profound observation about a rather greedy parrot who belonged to a lady boarder was made: "Isn't it cute! She licks the jam off her toast just like a person!"

It is on one of the flagstones of this cloister that this confession was put together, written ahead of time so as not to be forgotten by a sinner seven years old: "Father, I confess I have been avaricious. Father, I confess I have been adulterous. Father, I confess I have raised my eyes to the gentlemen."

It is on one of the lawns of the garden that this tale was improvised by a rosy mouth of six and told to blue eyes of four or five: "Once upon a time there were three little chickens who lived in the countryside where there were lots of flowers. They picked the flowers and put them in their pockets. After that, they picked the leaves and put them in their toys. There was a wolf in the countryside and there were lots of woods; and the wolf was in the woods; and he ate the little chickens."

And again, this poem:

There was a blow with a stick.
It was Punchinello who hit the cat.
That didn't do him any good, it hurt him.
So a lady put Punchinello in prison.[1]

It was there that these sweet and heartrending words were spoken by a little abandoned girl, a foundling that the convent was bringing up out of charity. She heard the others talking about their mothers and she murmured in her corner: "My mother wasn't there when I was born!"

There was a fat sister there in charge of external relations who was always seen running down hallways with her bunch of keys and whose name was Sister Agatha. The big big girls—those over ten—called her Agathokeys.

The refectory, a big squared-off oblong that received light only from cloister arches on a level with the garden, was dark and damp and, as the children say, full of creepy-crawlies. All the neighboring rooms provided their contingent of insects. Each of the four corners had its own particular and expressive name bestowed upon it accordingly, in the language of the boarders. There was Spider Corner, Caterpillar Corner, Wood-louse Corner, and Cricket Corner. Cricket Corner was next to the kitchen and highly prized. You weren't as cold there as elsewhere. From the refectory the names had passed to the boarding school in general and served to distinguish four nations there, as at the old Mazarin College. Every pupil was from one of these four nations according to the corner of the refectory where she sat for meals. One day, the archbishop, on his pastoral rounds, saw a pretty little girl, all rosy-cheeked and with fabulous blond hair, skip into the classroom as he was passing, and he asked another boarder, a charming fresh-faced brunette, standing nearby: "What is that little girl?"

"She's a spider, Monseigneur."

"Bah! And that other one?"

"She is a cricket."

"And this one?"

"She is a caterpillar."

"Really, and what are you?"

"I'm a wood louse, Monseigneur."

Each house of this kind has its peculiarities. At the beginning of this century, Écouen was one of these lovely yet strict places where young girls spent their childhoods in shade almost august. At Écouen, to join the procession of the Blessed Sacrament in the proper rank, they distinguished between "virgins" and "florists." There were also "canopies" and "censers," the former carrying the cords of the canopy and the latter swinging censers around during the Blessed Sacrament. The flowers fell to the florists as of right. Four "virgins" walked out in front. The morning of the big day, it was not rare to hear someone in the dormitory asking: "Who's a virgin?"

Madame Campan quotes what a little girl of seven had to say to a big girl of sixteen, who took the head of the procession while she, the little girl, remained at the back: "You may be a virgin, but I'm not."

## V. ENTERTAINMENT

Over the refectory door was written in big black letters this prayer that they called the White Paternoster, whose virtue was to lead people straight to paradise:

"Little white Paternoster, that God made, that God said, that God put in paradise. At night, going to bed, I finded [*sic*] three angels lying on my bed, one at the foot, two at the head, the good Virgin Mary in the middle, who said to me to be going to bed, and don't worry about nothing. The good Lord is my father, the good Virgin is my mother, the three apostles are my brothers, the three virgins are my sisters. The shirt where Christ was born, my body is wrapped in; the cross of Saint Marguerite is written on my breast! Madame Virgin ranned away over the fields, God crying, ranned into Monsieur Saint John. Monsieur Saint John, where've you been? I've been at *Ave Salus*. You haven't seen the good Lord, have you? He's in the tree of the cross, his feet is dangling, his hands is nailed, a little hat of white thorns is on his head. Whoever says this three times at night, three times in the morning, will get to paradise in the end."

In 1827, this typical prayer had disappeared from the wall under three layers of paper. It is fading as we speak from the memory of a few women who were young girls back then, old ladies now.

A big crucifix stuck on the wall completed the décor of the refectory, whose only door, as I think I might have said, opened onto the garden. Two narrow tables, both flanked by wooden benches, made two long parallel lines from one end of the refectory to the other. The walls were white, the tables were black; these two colors of mourning are the only choices convents have. The meals were sour and even the children's food was strict. A single dish, meat mixed with vegetables, or salty fish, this was luxury. This limited everyday fare, reserved for the boarders alone, was, however, the exception rather than the rule. The children ate in silence under the watchful eye of the mother for the week, who, from time to time, if a fly got it into its head to buzz around in contravention of the rule, would noisily open and shut a wooden book. This silence was seasoned with the *Lives of the Saints*,[1] read aloud from a rostrum placed at the foot of the crucifix. The reader was one of the big girls, chosen for the week. All along the bare table at intervals there were enamel basins in which the pupils themselves washed their metal cups and their plates, sometimes chucking out scraps, a tough bit of meat or rotten fish—an act that was punished. These basins were known as "water bowls."

Any child who broke the silence had to make a "cross" with her tongue. Where? On the floor. She licked the tiles. Dust, that end of all delight, was meant to chastise these poor little rosebuds of girls, guilty of chattering.

There was in the convent a book that is the *only copy* ever printed and which it was forbidden to read. This is the Rule of Saint Benedict—illicit material that no profane eye must ever dip into. *Nemo regulas, seu constitutiones nostras, externis communicabit.*[2]

One day the boarders managed to steal this book and began to race through it avidly, their reading often interrupted by fear of being caught, which made them keep swiftly banging the volume shut. They did not get much pleasure from this exciting danger, though. A few unintelligible pages on the sins of young boys was what was "most interesting" for them.

They played on one of the allées in the garden, lined with a few skinny fruit trees. Despite the extreme surveillance and the severity of the punishments meted out, when the wind shook the trees they sometimes managed to furtively grab a green apple or a half-rotten apricot or a worm-riddled pear. I will let a letter take over at this point, a letter I have before me, written twenty-five years ago by a former boarder, today a duchess and one of the most elegant women of Paris. I quote verbatim: "You hide your pear or your apple as best you can. When you go up to put the coverlet on the bed while waiting for supper, you stuff them under your pillow and you eat them in bed at night, and if you can't do that, you eat them in the toilets." This was one of their most intense pleasures.

Once, on the occasion of another visit to the convent by the same archbishop, one of the young girls, Mademoiselle Bouchard, who was related to the Montmorencys,[3] bet that she would ask him for a day off, an outrage in a community so austere. The bet was accepted but none of the girls betting believed she would do it. When the moment came, as the archbishop was walking past the boarders, Mademoiselle Bouchard, to the unutterable horror of her companions, broke rank and said: "Monseigneur, a day off." Mademoiselle Bouchard was tall and delectably fresh, with the prettiest little rosy face in the world. Monseigneur de Quélen[4] smiled and said: "What do you mean, my dear child, a day off! Three days, please. I grant you three days." The prioress was powerless, the archbishop had spoken. Scandal for the convent but joy for the boarding school. Just imagine the effect.

This tough, gruff cloister was not so immured, however, that the life of the outside world, with its passions, its drama, and even its novels, did not penetrate. For proof, we will limit ourselves to briefly noting here a real and incontestable fact, though it is one that bears no relation in itself to our story and is not connected to it in any way, not by even a thread. We only mention this fact to complete the picture of the convent in the reader's mind.

Around this time there was a mysterious person in the convent who was not a nun, who was treated with great respect and who was known as Madame Albertine. Nothing was known about her except that she was mad and that in the world she had been given up for dead. Behind this story, it was said, there were makeshift arrangements that had been made for a magnificent marriage.

This woman, a rather beautiful brunette barely thirty years old, gazed out vaguely from big black eyes. Did she see anything? It was doubtful. She glided rather than walked; she never spoke; you couldn't be entirely sure that she breathed. Her nostrils were pinched and as pale as if she had heaved her last sigh. Touching her hand was like touching snow. She had a strange spectral grace. Wherever she went, you felt the chill. One day a sister, seeing her go by, said to another sister: "She looks dead." "Maybe she is," the other replied.

Any number of stories made the rounds about Madame Albertine. She was the object of the boarders' endless curiosity. There was a gallery in the chapel that was known as the Bull's-Eye. It was in this gallery, which only had a circular opening, a bull's-eye, that Madame Albertine would attend services. She was usually on her own there, because from this gallery, which was up some stairs, you could see the priest or the officiant and that was prohibited to the nuns. One day the pulpit was occupied by a high-ranking young priest, Monsieur le duc de Rohan,[5] peer of France, who had been an officer of the Red Musketeers in 1815, when he was prince de Léon, and who died later in 1830, a cardinal and archbishop of Besançon. It was the first time Monsieur de Rohan had preached in the convent of Petit-Picpus. Madame Albertine normally attended sermons and services in a state of profound calm and complete immobility. That particular day, as soon as she spotted Monsieur de Rohan, she half-rose and called out loudly in the silence of the chapel: "Lord! Auguste!" The whole community turned their heads, stunned, the priest looked up, but Madame Albertine had sunk into immobility once more. A breath of fresh air from the outside world, a glimmer of life had for a moment passed over that dead and frozen figure, then everything vanished and the madwoman became a cadaver again.

Those two words, though, set the tongues wagging in the convent—of those who were allowed to speak, at least. So much was packed into that *Lord! Auguste!* So many revelations! Monsieur de Rohan's name was, in fact, Auguste. It was obvious that Madame Albertine came from high society, since she knew Monsieur de Rohan, that she was herself from the upper echelons even, since she was on such intimate terms with such a great lord, and that she had some connection to him, was perhaps related, but in any case was close to him, since she knew his first name.

Two very severe duchesses, mesdames de Choiseul and de Sérent, often visited the community, where they gained access no doubt by virtue of the privilege of their status as *grandes dames,* to the great terror of the boarders. Whenever the two old ladies went by, all the poor young girls would tremble and lower their gaze.

Monsieur de Rohan was, in any case, unbeknownst to him, an object of interest for the boarders. At the time he had just been made grand-vicar of the archbishop of Paris, while biding his time waiting for the episcopacy. He was in the habit of coming often to sing the offices in the chapel of the nuns of Petit-Picpus. None of the young recluses could get a look at him because of the serge curtain, but he had a soft and slightly reedy voice that they had come to recognize and distinguish. He had been a musketeer and, then again, he was said to be extremely good-looking, with a fine head of beautiful chestnut hair arranged in a roll around his head, and with a magnificent wide black belt and a black cassock cut in the most elegant style in the world. He took up a lot of space in sixteen-year-old imaginations.

No sound from outside penetrated the convent. Yet there was one year when the sound of a flute made it through. This was an event, and the boarders of the day still talk about it.

It was a flute someone in the neighborhood was playing. This flute always played the same tune, a tune long since forgotten: "My Zétulbé, come and rule over my soul," and you heard it two or three times a day.

The young girls spent hours listening to it, the vocal mothers were incensed, brains became overwrought, punishments rained down. This went on for several months. The boarders were all more or less in love with the unknown musician. Every one of them dreamed they were Zétulbé. The sound of the flute came from the direction of the rue Droit-Mur; they would have given anything to see, to catch a mere glimpse, if only for a second, of the "young man" who played the flute so deliciously and who, without a shadow of a doubt, was playing at the same time with all those hearts. A few girls escaped by the service door and climbed up to the third floor on the rue Droit-Mur to try to get a look on delivery days when the door was left open. It could not be done. One girl went as far as sticking her arm above her head through the grate and waving her white hankie. Two were bolder still. They found a way to climb up onto the roof and took the risk and finally managed to sight "the young man." He turned out to be an old émigré gentleman, blind and ruined, who played the flute in his garret to while away the time.

## VI. THE LITTLE CONVENT

Within the Petit-Picpus enclosure, there were three perfectly distinct buildings, the big convent where the nuns lived, the boarding school where the schoolgirls lodged, and lastly what was known as the little convent. This was a separate building with a garden where all kinds of old nuns of different orders lived together, remnants of cloisters destroyed by the Revolution; a gathering of every shade of black, gray, and white, of every possible community and every possible stripe and that we might call, if such a coupling of words is permissible, a sort of harlequin convent.

From the days of the Empire, all these poor scattered and disoriented old maids had been allowed to take refuge under the wings of the Benedictine-Bernardines. The government paid them a small pension; the ladies of Petit-Picpus had rushed to take them in. It was a bizarre assortment. Each one followed her own rule. Sometimes the boarders were allowed, as a major excursion, to go and visit them, which means that those young minds have retained, among other memories, the memory of Mother Saint Basil, Mother Saint Scolastique, and Mother Jacob.

One of these refugees virtually found herself at home. This was a nun from Sainte-Aure, the only one of her order to have survived. At the beginning of the eighteenth century, what was the convent of the Ladies of Sainte-Aure[1] had occupied precisely the house in Petit-Picpus that later belonged to the Benedictines of Martin Verga. This holy old maid, too poor to wear the magnificent habit of her order, which was a white robe with a scarlet scapular, had piously decked out a little doll in it, and she showed this doll off smugly and bequeathed it to the house at her death. In 1824, there was only one nun left of the whole order; today, the only thing left is a doll.

Apart from these worthy mothers, a few old women of the world had obtained the prioress's permission, as had Madame Albertine, to withdraw to the little convent. This number included Madame de Beaufort d'Hautpoul and Madame la marquise Dufresne.[2] Another was only ever known in the convent by the alarming noise she made when she blew her nose. The schoolgirls called her Madame Racketini.

Around 1820 or 1821, Madame de Genlis,[3] who was editing a little periodical at the time called the *Intrépide,* asked if she could enter as an independent lady and have a room at the Petit-Picpus convent. Monsieur le duc d'Orléans gave her good references. Buzzing in the hive; the vocal mothers were all atremble; Madame de Genlis had produced novels. But she declared that she was the first to detest them, and then again, she had reached her ferociously devout phase. With God's help, and the prince's too, she entered. But she only stayed six or eight months, giving as the reason for leaving that the garden had no shade. The nuns were in raptures having her there. For although she was very old, she still played the harp and very well at that.

When she left, she left her mark on her cell. Madame de Genlis was superstitious and a Latin scholar. Those two words give a pretty good image of her. Up until a few years ago, you could still see, stuck on the inside of a small cupboard in her cell where she locked up her money and her jewels, these five lines of Latin written in her handwriting in red ink on yellow paper and which, in her opinion, had the virtue of warding off thieves:

> *Imparibus meritis pendent tria corpora ramis:*
> *Dismas et Gesmas, media est divina potestas;*
> *Alta petit Dismas, infelix, infima, Gesmas;*
> *Nos et res nostras conservet summa potestas.*
> *Hos versus dicas, ne tu furto tua perdas.*[4]

These lines, in the Latin of the sixth century, raise the question of whether the two robbers of Calvary were called Dismas and Gestas,[5] as is commonly thought, or Dismas and Gesmas. The latter spelling would put paid to the pretensions entertained, last century, by the vicomte de Gestas[6] of being a descendant of the unrepentant robber. Whatever the case, the practical virtue attached to these lines was gospel in the Hospitaller order.[7]

The house chapel, built in such a way as to separate the convent from the boarding school, splitting them as though actually sundering them, was, naturally, common to the school, the big convent, and the little convent. Even the public were admitted through a sort of quarantine entrance provided on the street. But everything was arranged in such a fashion that none of the inhabitants of the cloister could see a face from the outside world. Imagine a church whose choir was seized by a gigantic hand and twisted so as to form, not, as in ordinary churches, an extension behind the altar, but a sort of hall or dark cavern to the right of the officiant; imagine this hall shut off by the nine-foot-high curtain we mentioned earlier; heap together, in the shadow of this curtain, on wooden stalls, the nuns of the choir on the left, the boarders on the right, the lay sisters and the novices at the back, and you will have some idea of the nuns of Petit-Picpus attending divine service. This cavern, which was known as the choir, was connected to the cloister by a corridor. The church received light from the garden. When the nuns attended services where the rule of their order commanded silence from them, the public was alerted to their presence only by the crack of the stalls' hinged seats, or *miséricordes,* noisily going up or down.

## VII. A Few Silhouettes in the Shadows

During the six years that separated 1819 from 1825, the prioress of Petit-Picpus was Mademoiselle de Blemeur, whose religious name was Mother Innocent. She was from the family of Marguerite de Blemeur,[1] the author of *Lives of the Saints of the Order of Saint Benedict.* She had been reelected to a second term. She was a woman of sixty or so, short and fat, who sang "like a cracked pot," according to the letter we have already quoted; otherwise excellent, the sole cheery soul in the whole convent, and for that, adored.

Mother Innocent took after her ancestor Marguerite, the Dacier of the Order.[2] She was well-read, erudite, learned, competent, a historian out of curiosity, stuffed with Latin, crammed with Greek, full of Hebrew and rather more Benedictine monk than Bernardine nun.

The deputy prioress was an old Spanish nun who was almost blind, Mother Cineres.

The most esteemed among the vocal mothers were Mother Saint Honorine, treasurer, Mother Saint Gertrude, first mistress of the novices, Mother Saint Ange, second mistress, Mother Annunciation, sacristan, Mother Saint Augustin, nurse, and the only one in the whole convent who was mean; then

Mother Saint Mechthilde (Mademoiselle Gauvin), quite young, with a wonderful voice; Mother of the Angels (Mademoiselle Drouet, who had been in the Filles-Dieu convent and in the Trésor convent between Gisors and Magny); Mother Saint Joseph (Mademoiselle de Cogolludo); Mother Saint Adelaide (Mademoiselle d'Auverney); Mother Miséricorde (Mademoiselle de Cifuentes, who could not resist the austerities); Mother Compassion (Mademoiselle de la Miltière, admitted at sixty, in spite of the rule, very rich); Mother Providence (Mademoiselle de Laudinière); Mother Presentation (Mademoiselle de Siguenza),[3] who was prioress in 1847; and, lastly, Mother Saint Célinge (the sister of the sculptor Ceracchi), who has since gone mad; and Mother Saint Chantal (Mademoiselle de Suzon), who has since gone mad.

There was also among the prettiest a charming girl of twenty-three who was from the Isle of Bourbon and a descendant of the chevalier Roze,[4] whom the world knew as Mademoiselle Roze and who was known inside as Mother Assumption.

Mother Saint Mechthilde, in charge of singing and the choir, was only too happy to use the boarders. She usually grabbed a whole array of them, meaning, seven girls, from ten to sixteen years old, with graded voices and sizes, and made them sing standing side by side in a row, ranged according to age from the smallest to the biggest. This presented onlookers with a vision not unlike a pipe of young girls, a sort of living Pan's pipe made up of angels.

Those of the lay sisters that the boarders liked the most were Sister Saint Euphrasia, Sister Saint Marguerite, Sister Saint Martha, who was in her second childhood, and Sister Saint Michel, whose long nose made them hoot with laughter.

All these women were as sweet as pie to all those children. The nuns were hard only on themselves. Fires were lit only in the boarding school and the food there, compared to that of the convent, was choice. And there were all kinds of little treats on top of that. Only, when a child passed near a nun and spoke to her, the nun never replied.

This rule of silence had had the result that, throughout the entire convent, speech had been withdrawn from human creatures and given to inanimate objects. Sometimes it was the church bell that spoke, sometimes the gardener's bell. A very sonorous bell, placed next to the sister in charge of external relations, could be heard everywhere in the house, indicating by different rings, which were a kind of acoustic telegraph, all the actions of material life to be accomplished and calling to the visitors' room, if need be, this or that inhabitant of the house. Each person and each thing had its special ring. The prioress was one and one; the deputy prioress was one and two. Six-five announced classes, so that the students never said they were going back to their classes but going to six-five. Four-four was the ring for Madame de Genlis. It was heard very often. "There goes that devil of a four," as those who were not charitable would say. Nineteen rings announced a great event. It meant the opening of the main gate, a ghastly iron plate bristling with bolts that only turned on its hinges before the archbishop.

## VIII. Post Corda Lapides[1]

Having sketched the moral design of the place, it might not be pointless to indicate in a few words its material configuration. The reader already has some idea of this.

The convent of Petit-Picpus-Saint-Antoine almost entirely filled the vast trapezoid created by the intersection of the rue Polonceau, the rue Droit-Mur, the petite rue Picpus, and the condemned alley listed in old maps as the rue Aumarais. These four streets surrounded this area like a moat. The convent was composed of several buildings and a garden. The main building, taken as a whole, was a jumble of hybrid structures that, seen in bird's-eye view, outlined fairly exactly an L-shaped gallows laid on the ground. The long arm of the gallows occupied the entire slice of the rue Droit-Mur between the petite rue Picpus and the rue Polonceau; the small arm was a high, gray, grim grated façade that looked out on the petite rue Picpus; the porte cochère at no. 62 marked one end of it. Around the middle of this façade the dust and ash had bleached white an old low arched door where spiders spun their webs and which only opened for one or two hours on Sundays and on rare occasions when the coffin of a nun left the convent. This was the public entrance to the church. The elbow of the gallows was a square room that served as a pantry and that the nuns called the dispensary. In the long arm were the cells of the mothers and sisters and the novices; in the short arm the kitchens, the refectory backed by the cloister, and the church. Between the door at no. 62 and the corner of the closed-off Aumarais alleyway was the boarding school, which you could not see from the outside. The rest of the trapezoid formed the garden, which was much lower than the rue Polonceau level, and this made the walls a lot higher inside than outside. In the middle of the slightly convex garden, on top of a grassy knoll, there was a beautiful fir tree, pointed and conical, from which four great allées radiated, as from the pointed hub of a shield; arranged in pairs between the spokes of the broader walkways, eight small paths radiated, so that if the enclosure had been circular, the geometric plan of the garden paths would have looked like a cross laid on a wheel. The paths all ended at the extremely irregular walls of the garden and so were of uneven lengths. They were bordered by gooseberry bushes. At the bottom of the garden, an avenue of great poplars ran from the ruins of the old convent at the corner of the rue Droit-Mur to the house of the little convent at the corner of Aumarais lane. Just in front of the little convent was what was known as the little garden. Add to this array a courtyard, all sorts of nooks and crannies made by detached buildings inside, prison walls, no real views and no real neighborhood except for the long black line of roofs that bordered the other side of the rue Polonceau, and you can form a complete picture of what was, forty-five years ago, the house of the Bernardines of Petit-Picpus. This holy house had been built precisely on the site of a *jeu de paume*, a royal tennis court that was famous from the fourteenth to the sixteenth centuries and that had been known as the "den of the eleven thousand devils."[2]

All of these streets, furthermore, were the oldest in Paris. The names Droit-Mur and Aumarais are very old, the streets that bear them much older still. Aumarais lane was once called Maugout lane; the rue Droit-Mur was once called the rue des Églantiers—of dog roses—for God opened flowers before mankind cut stones.

## IX. A CENTURY UNDER A WIMPLE

Since we are in the process of giving details about what was once the convent of Petit-Picpus and have dared to open a window on this discreet refuge, we hope the reader will allow us a further small digression, one basically foreign to this book but typical and useful in showing us that even the cloister has its original characters.

There was in the little convent a centenarian who came from the abbey of Fontevrault.[1] Before the Revolution, she had even been in society. She talked a lot about Monsieur de Miromesnil,[2] keeper of the seals under Louis XVI, and about the wife of some presiding judge, a Duplat, whom she had known very well. It was her delight and her vanity to trot out those two names at every opportunity. She went on and on about the wonders of the abbey of Fontevrault, how it was like a town, and how there were streets within the monastery.

She spoke in Picardy dialect, to the great delight of the boarders. Every year she solemnly renewed her vows and, at the moment of taking the oath, she would say to the priest: "Monseigneur Saint Francis chucked it to Monseigneur Saint Julien, Monseigneur Saint Julien chucked it to Monseigneur Saint Eusebius, Monseigneur Saint Eusebius chucked it to Monseigneur Saint Procopius, etc., etc., just as I chuck it to you, father." And the boarders all chuckled, not up their sleeves, but under their veils; delightful little smothered chuckles that made the vocal mothers frown.

Another time, the centenarian was telling stories. She reckoned that when she was young, the Bernardines were right up there[3] with the Musketeers. That was a century talking, but it was the eighteenth century. She told about the custom of the four wines in Burgundy and Champagne. Before the Revolution, when an important personage, a maréchal de France, a prince, a duke, or a peer, passed through a town in Champagne or Burgundy, the city fathers would come and make him a speech and present him with four silver goblets, in which four different wines had been poured. On the first goblet you could read the inscription *monkey wine;* on the second, *lion wine;* on the third, *sheep wine;* on the fourth, *pig wine.* These four inscriptions expressed the four degrees of the drunk's descent: initial intoxication, which makes you merry; the second stage, which makes you irritated; the third, which stuns you; finally, the last, which turns you into a brute.

In a cupboard, under lock and key, she kept a mysterious object that she was very attached to. The rule at Fontevrault did not ban her from keeping it. She would not show this object to anyone. She shut herself away, which her rule allowed her to do, and hid every time she wanted to contemplate it. If she heard someone coming along the corridor, she would shut the cupboard again as fast as her old hands would let her. As soon as anyone spoke to her about it, she would shut up, though she was a real talker. The most curious faltered in the face of her silence and the most tenacious in the face of her obstinacy. This was also a topic of conversation for all the idle and bored in the convent. What on earth could this thing be that was so precious and so secret, what was the centenarian's treasure? Doubtless some holy book? Some unique rosary beads? Some certified relic? They would be lost in conjectures. On the poor old maid's death, they ran to the cupboard faster, perhaps, than was seemly and opened it. They found the object under three layers of linen, like a blessed communion plate. It was a faience plate representing cupids flying off pursued by apothecary boys armed with enormous syringes. The pursuit abounds with grimaces and comical postures. One of the charming little cupids is already completely run through. He struggles, flaps his little wings and goes on trying to fly, but the lad swaggering about laughs a satanic laugh. Moral of the story: love defeated by colic. This plate, a most curious piece in any case and one that, perhaps, had the honor of giving Molière an idea,[4] still existed in September 1845; it was for sale at a secondhand dealer's in the boulevard Beaumarchais.

This good old soul would not receive any visitors from outside, because, she said, the visitors' parlor was too "dreary."

## X. Origins of Perpetual Adoration

In any case, this virtually sepulchral visitors' parlor we have tried to give some idea of is a perfectly local feature not reproduced with the same strictness in other convents. In the convent of the rue du Temple, most notably—though it belonged, to be honest, to another order—the black shutters were replaced by brown curtains and the visitors' room itself was a salon with a parquetry floor and windows framed in *bonnes-grâces* drapes of white muslin and walls adorned with all kinds of framed pictures, including a portrait of a Benedictine nun with an unveiled face, painted flowers, and even a Turk's head.

It was in the garden of the convent of the rue du Temple that a chestnut tree from India, said to be the most beautiful and the tallest in France, stood; among the good folk of the eighteenth century it had the reputation of being "the father of all the chestnut trees in the realm."

As we said, the Temple convent was occupied by the Benedictines of Perpetual Adoration, Benedictines quite different from those that came from Cîteaux. This order of Perpetual Adoration is not all that old, going back no further than two hundred years. In 1649, the Blessed Sacrament was profaned twice, a few days apart, in two Paris churches, at Saint-Sulpice and at Saint-Jean en Grève, a frightening and rare sacrilege that shocked the whole town. Monsieur the prior—grand-vicar of Saint-Germain-des-Prés—ordered a solemn procession of all his clergy in which the papal nuncio officiated. But this expiation was not enough for two worthy women, Madame Courtin, marquise de Boucs, and the comtesse de Châteauvieux. This outrage done to the "most august sacrament of the altar," though short-lived, so troubled these two holy souls that it seemed to them the only possible atonement was through a "Perpetual Adoration" in some monastery for maidens. Both of them, one in 1652, the other in 1653, made sizable donations to Mother Catherine de Bar, a Benedictine nun called "of the Blessed Sacrament," to found a convent of the order of Saint Benedict with this pious aim;[1] initial permission was granted mother Catherine de Bar by Monsieur de Metz, abbé of Saint-Germain, "with the stipulation that no maiden can be admitted unless she brings three hundred livres in board which equals six thousand livres in principal." After the abbé of Saint-Germain, the king granted letters patent and the rest, the abbatial charter and royal license, was ratified in 1654 in the Chamber of Accounts and in parliament.

This is the origin and legal consecration of the establishment of the Benedictines of Perpetual Adoration of the Blessed Sacrament of Paris. Their first convent was "built new" in the rue Cassette with the funds provided by Mesdames de Boucs and de Châteauvieux.

This order, as we see, was nothing like the Benedictines from Cîteaux, known as the Cistercians. It derived from the abbé of Saint-Germain-des-Prés, the same way that the Ladies of the Sacred Heart derived from the general body of the Jesuits and the Sisters of Charity from the general body of the Lazarists.

It was also completely different from the Bernardines of Petit-Picpus, the interior of which we have just revealed. In 1657, Pope Alexander VII had issued a special bull authorizing the Bernardines of Petit-Picpus to practice Perpetual Adoration like the Benedictines of the Blessed Sacrament. But the two orders remained no less distinct.

## XI. END OF THE PETIT-PICPUS

The moment the Restoration began, the convent of Petit-Picpus went into decline, which is part and parcel of the general death of an order that went the way of all religious orders after the eighteenth century. Contemplation, like prayer, is a need of humanity; but like everything the Revolution has touched, it will transform itself and, though once hostile to social progress, it will become favorable to it.

The Petit-Picpus house rapidly emptied. By 1840, the little convent had disappeared, the boarding school had disappeared. The old women were no longer there and neither were the young girls; the former had died, the latter had gone on their way. *Volaverunt.*[1]

The rule of Perpetual Adoration is so very rigid that it alarms; vocations are in decline, the order is not taking on any new recruits. Forty years ago, the nuns numbered almost a hundred; fifteen years ago, there were no more than twenty-eight. How many are there today? In 1847, the prioress was young, a sure sign that the field of choice was shrinking. She was under forty. As the number went down, the fatigue increased, and the duty of each nun became more arduous; from that moment, you could see that the day was coming when there would be only a dozen shoulders left, sore and rounded, to bear the heavy burden of the rule of Saint Benedict. The burden is implacable and remains the same for the few as for the many. It weighs down, it crushes. So they die. Since the days when the author of this book still lived in Paris, two have died. One was twenty-five, the other twenty-three. This latter would agree with Julia Alpinula:[2] *Hic jaceo, vixi annos viginti et tres.* It is because of this decline that the convent gave up educating girls.

We could not pass by this extraordinary house, unknown and dark as it is, without going in and letting in the souls accompanying us on our journey and listening to us narrate, for the good of a few perhaps, the melancholy story of Jean Valjean. We have cast an eye over this community riddled with these old rites, which seem so novel today. It is a secret garden. *Hortus conclusus.* We have gone on about this singular place in some detail, but with respect, at least insofar as respect and detail are reconcilable. We do not understand everything, but we do not insult anything, either. We are equally distant from the hosanna of Joseph de Maistre, who winds up crowning and championing the executioner, and from the sneering of Voltaire,[3] who goes so far as to rail against the crucifix.

Lack of logic on Voltaire's part, by the way; for Voltaire would have defended Jesus as he defended Calas;[4] and, for the very people who deny super-human incarnations, what does the crucifix represent? The sage assassinated.

In the nineteenth century, religious notions are in turmoil. We are unlearning certain things and that is all to the good, as long as in unlearning this, you learn that. No vacuum in the human heart. Certain things are being torn down, and so they should be, but only on condition that all the demolition be followed by reconstruction.

Meanwhile, let's take a closer look at things that are no more. We need to know about them, if only to avoid them. The counterfeits of the past assume false identities and happily call themselves the future. That ghost, the past, tends to fake his passport. Let us be alert to such a trick. Let us be on our guard. The past has a face—superstition; and a mask—hypocrisy. Let us denounce that face and tear off the mask.

As for convents, they are a complex matter. A matter of civilization, which condemns them; a matter of liberty, which protects them.

# A PARENTHESIS[1]

## I. THE CONVENT AS AN ABSTRACT IDEA

This book is a tragedy in which infinity plays the lead.

Man plays a supporting role.

This being so, as a convent turned up on our path, we simply had to go in. Why? Because the convent, which belongs to the East as to the West, to antiquity as to modern times, to paganism, Buddhism, and Mohammedanism as to Christianity, is one of the optical devices man trains on infinity.

This is not the place to delve deeply into certain ideas; yet, while absolutely maintaining our reserve, our reservations, and even our feelings of outrage, we must say that, every time we come across the infinite[1] in man, whether properly or badly understood, we feel seized with respect. There is in the synagogue, in the mosque, in the pagoda, in the wigwam, a hideous side that we execrate and a sublime side[2] that we revere. What an object of contemplation for the mind, and what a source of endless reverie! The reflection of God on the human wall.

## II. THE CONVENT AS HISTORICAL FACT

From the point of view of history, reason, and truth, monasticism is doomed.

When monasteries abound within a nation, they are bottlenecks blocking the free flow of traffic, encumbrances, roadblocks, centers of indolence where centers of industry are needed. Monastic communities are to the broader social community what mistletoe is to the oak,[1] what warts are to the human body. Their prosperity and their corpulence mean bleeding the country dry. The monastic regime, good at the dawn of civilization, useful in reining in brutality through spirituality, is bad for the world in its maturity. On top of this, when it slackens and enters into a period of deregulation, it nonetheless goes on setting an example and in doing so becomes bad for all the reasons that made it salutary in its period of purity.

All this shutting oneself away in cloisters has had its day. Cloisters were useful in the preliminary education of modern civilization, but they have since cramped its growth and are harmful to its development. As an institution and a mode of training for man, monasteries were good in the tenth century, debatable in the fifteenth, and detestable in the nineteenth. The leprosy of monasticism has gnawed to the bone two wonderful nations, Italy and Spain, one the light, the other the splendor of Europe for centuries, and in our day these two illustrious peoples are only just beginning to heal, thanks to the wholesome and vigorous hygiene of 1789.

The convent, the age-old convent of women in particular, as it still appeared at the threshold of this century in Italy, Austria, and Spain, is one of the most somber sedimentations of the Middle Ages. That cloister, that particular cloister, is the point of intersection of unutterable horrors. The Catholic cloister, properly so called, is completely filled with the black radiance of death.

The Spanish convent is especially deadly. In it, massive Babel-like altars, as tall as cathedrals, rise in the darkness beneath vaults full of fog, beneath domes dim with dense shadow; in it, immense white crucifixes hang on chains in the gloom; great big ivory Christs spread out, naked on ebony, not just bloody but bleeding, hideous and magnificent, the elbows showing the bones, the kneecaps showing the cartilage, the wounds showing the raw flesh, crowned with thorns of silver, nailed with nails of gold, with drops of blood in rubies on the forehead and tears of diamonds in the eyes. The diamonds and rubies look wet and make the veiled ones cry, below in the shadows, veiled ones whose flanks are torn and bruised black-and-blue by cilices and by scourges with iron tips, whose breasts are crushed by wicker racks, whose knees are skinned by prayer; women who believe themselves to be brides of Christ, specters who believe themselves to be seraphim.[2] Do these women think? No. Do they desire? No. Do they love? No. Do they live? No. Their nerves have ossified; their bones have petrified. Their veils are knitted with night. Their breath beneath their veils is like some weird tragic exhalation of death. The abbess, a ghoul, sanctifies them and terrifies them. The immaculate is there, fierce. Such are the old monasteries of Spain. Lairs of terrible devoutness, caverns for virgins, savage places.

Catholic Spain was more Roman than Rome itself. The Spanish convent was the Catholic convent par excellence. You got a whiff of the East[3] there. There, the archbishop, aga khan of heaven,[4] locked up and spied on this seraglio[5] of souls reserved for God. The nun was the odalisque, the priest the eunuch. In their dreams, the fervent females were chosen by and possessed Christ. At night, the gorgeous naked young man came down from the cross and became the ecstasy of the cell. High walls protected from any living distraction the mystical sultaness who had the crucified one for a sultan. A glance outside was an act of infidelity. The *in pace* replaced the leather bag.⁶ What was hurled into the sea in the East was hurled into the ground in the West. On both sides, women flailed about madly; the waves for one lot, the pit for the others; there, they drowned, here, they were buried alive. Monstrous parallelism.

Today the defenders of the past, not being able to deny these things, have adopted the position of laughing at them. It has become the fashion, a convenient and strange fashion, to suppress the revelations of history, to invalidate the commentaries of philosophy, and to dodge all the embarrassing facts and all the somber questions. "The stuff of ranting," say the clever. Ranting, repeat the inane. Jean-Jacques,⁷ a ranter; Diderot,⁸ a ranter; Voltaire on Calas, Labarre, and Sirven,⁹ a ranter. I can't remember who it was who recently found that Tacitus, too, was a ranter, that Nero was a victim, and that one really had to feel sorry for "that poor Holofernes."¹⁰

The facts, however, are not so easily thrown off, and they persist. The author of this book has seen, with his own eyes, at about twenty miles from Brussels, a slice of the Middle Ages within everyone's reach, at the abbey of Villers, the hole of the *oubliettes*¹¹ in the middle of the meadow that was the cloister courtyard, and, on the banks of the Dyle, four solitary stone cells, half-underground, half-underwater. These were *in pace*. Every one of these cells has the remains of an iron door, a latrine, and a grated skylight, which is two feet above the river outside and six feet above the ground inside. Four feet deep, the river flows outside along the wall. The ground is always wet. The inhabitant of the dungeon had this wet ground for a bed. In one of the cells, there is the stump of a collar shackle bolted to the wall; in another, you can see a kind of square box made out of four slabs of granite, too short to lie down in, too low to stand up in. They used to put a living being in there, and then put a stone lid over it. It exists. You can see it. You can touch it. These *in pace,* these solitary cells, these iron hinges, these collar shackles, this high skylight on a level with the flowing river, this stone box sealed with a granite lid like a tomb, with this difference that here death was living, this floor that is mud, this shit-hole, these oozing walls—how they rant!

## III. On What Conditions We Can Respect the Past

Monasticism, as it existed in Spain and as it exists in Tibet, is a kind of consumption of civilization. It cuts life short. It depopulates, to put it simply. Claustration, castration. It has been the scourge of Europe. Add to that the violence so often done to conscience, forced vocations, the feudalism that props up the cloister, primogeniture pouring into the monastery the surplus of the family, the ferocities we have just been talking about, the *in pace*, the sealed lips, the walled-in minds, so many unlucky intellects placed in the solitary confinement of eternal vows, the taking of the habit, the burying of souls still very much alive. Add the individual tortures to the national degradations and no matter who you are, you will feel yourself shudder before the habit and the veil, those two shrouds of human invention.

And yet, on certain points and in certain places, despite philosophy and despite progress, the claustral spirit lives on, right into the middle of the nineteenth century, and a bizarre recrudescence in asceticism is stunning the civilized world at this very moment. The stubborn determination of old institutions to perpetuate themselves is like the obstinacy of rancid perfume in clinging to your hair, the claims of rotten fish to be eaten, harassment by children's clothes wanting grown-ups to wear them again, or the tenderness of corpses coming back to embrace the living.

"Ungrateful bastards!" say the children's clothes. "I protected you in bad weather. Why won't you have anything to do with me anymore?" "I come from the deep sea," says the fish. "I was a rose," says the perfume. "I loved you," says the corpse. "I civilized you," says the convent.

To that, there is only one response: Once.

To dream of the indefinite extension of defunct things and of the governing of men by embalming, to restore dogmas in lousy condition, to regild the shrines, replaster the cloisters, reconsecrate the reliquaries, revamp the superstitions, refuel the fanaticisms, put the handles back on the aspersoria and the sabers,[1] reconstitute monasticism and militarism, believe in the salvation of society through the proliferation of parasites, impose the past on the present, seems strange. Yet there are theorists for those very theories. These theorists, smart people in other respects, have a very simple method. They apply to the past a coat of what they call social order, divine right, morality, family values, respect for one's ancestors, time-honored authority, sacred tradition, legitimacy, religion, and so on; and they go around shouting: "Here! Take this, you respectable people." This tactic was known to the ancients. Haruspices[2] practiced it. They would rub a black heifer with chalk and say: She is white. *Bos creatus.*[3]

As for us, we respect the past here and there and spare it everywhere, provided it consents to be dead. Wherever it tries to be alive, we attack it and do our level best to kill it.

Superstitions, bigotries, hypocrisies, prejudices, these specters, as spectral as they are, cling to life, they have teeth and nails in their smoky trails; and they have to be grappled in hand-to-hand, head-to-head combat, in a war that must be waged without letup, for this is one of the things to which humankind is doomed—to be forever having to fight off phantoms. A shadow is difficult to grab by the throat and dash on the ground.

A convent in France, smack in the middle of the nineteenth century, is a college of owls peering out at daylight. A cloister, caught in the act of asceticism right in the heart of the city of 1789, of 1830, of 1848,[4] Rome flourishing in Paris—now, that is what I call an anachronism. In normal times, to dissolve an anachronism and make it vanish, you only have to get it to spell out the year of our Lord. But we are not living in normal times.

Let's fight.

Let's fight, but let's make distinctions. The thing about truth is never to overdo it. Why should it be exaggerated? There is what has to be destroyed and there is what simply has to be clarified and looked at. A benevolent and grave examination—what force! Let's not bring flame where light is enough.

And so, given that we are in the nineteenth century, as a general rule, and no matter what people are concerned, in Asia as in Europe, in India as in Turkey, we are against the seclusion of ascetics. When you say convent, you say swamp. Their tendency toward putrescence is obvious, their stagnation is unhealthy, their fermentation makes people feverish and enfeebles them; their proliferation turns into a biblical plague. We can only think with horror of those countries where fakirs, bonzes, santons, caloyers, marabouts, talapoins, and dervishes[5] pullulate like swarms of vermin.

That said, the religious issue abides. This issue has certain mysterious, almost formidable aspects; allow us to stare it straight in the face.

## IV. THE CONVENT FROM THE POINT OF VIEW OF PRINCIPLES

Men gather together and live in common. By virtue of what right? By virtue of the right of association.

They shut themselves up at home. By virtue of what right? By virtue of the right that every man enjoys of opening or shutting his door.

They don't go out. By virtue of what right? By virtue of the right to come and go, which implies the right to remain at home.

There, at home, what do they do?

They talk softly, they keep their heads down; they work. They turn their back on the world, the city, sensuality, pleasure, vanity, pride, interests. They are dressed in coarse wool and coarse cotton. Not one of them owns any property whatever. Once he enters there, he who was rich makes himself poor. Whatever he has, he gives to all. He who was what we call noble, a gentleman and a lord, is the equal of he who was a peasant. The cell is the same for all. All suffer the same tonsure, wear the same robe, eat the same black bread, sleep on the same straw, die on the same ash. With the same sack on the back, the same cord around the waist. If it is the rule to go barefoot, all go barefoot. There may well be a prince in there, but this prince is the same shadow as the rest. No more titles. Even family names have disappeared. They bear only Christian names. All buckle under the equality of baptismal names. They have dissolved the family of the flesh and set up the spiritual family within their community. They no longer have any relatives other than all mankind. They succor the poor, they tend the sick. They elect those they obey. They call each other: my brother.

You stop me and you cry out: But what you're talking about is the ideal convent!

It is enough that it is a potential convent for me to have to take it into account.

This is why, in the preceding book, I spoke of a convent in a tone of respect. The Middle Ages aside, Asia aside, the historic and political question left open, from a purely philosophical point of view, beyond the requirements of some militant polemics, on the condition that the monastery be absolutely voluntary and shut in only consenting adults, I will always look upon the cloistered community with a certain attentive and, in some respects, deferential gravity. Wherever there is a community, there is a commune; wherever there is a commune, there is law. The monastery is the outcome of the formula: Equality, Fraternity. Oh, how great Liberty is! And what a splendid transfiguration! Liberty is enough to transform the monastery into a republic.

Let's go on.

But these men, or these women, who are behind those four walls, dress in homespun, are equal, call themselves brothers or sisters. Which is all very well, but do they do anything else?

Yes.

What?

They stare at the dark, they get down on their knees and bring their hands together.

What does that mean?

## V. PRAYER

They pray.

Who to?

God.

To pray to God, what does that mean?

Is there an infinite outside ourselves? This infinite, is it one, immanent, permanent; necessarily substantial, since it is infinite and since, if it were devoid of matter, it would in that respect be limited; necessarily intelligent, since it is infinite and since, if it were devoid of intelligence, it would be in that respect finite? Does this infinite arouse in us the idea of an essence, whereas we can only attribute to ourselves the idea of existence? In other words, is it not the absolute of which we are the relative?

At the same time that there is an infinite outside us, isn't there also an infinite inside us? These two infinities (what a frightening plural!), do they not sit one on top of the other? Isn't the second infinite subjacent, so to speak, to the first? Isn't it the mirror of it, the reflection, the echo, a void concentric to another void? Is this second infinite also intelligent? Does it think? Does it love? Does it desire? If the two infinites are intelligent, each one of them has a desiring principle, and there is a self in the infinite above, just as there is a self in the infinite below. This self below is the soul; the self above is God.

To put the infinite below in touch with the infinite above, in thought—this is what we call prayer.

Let's not detract from the human mind; to repress is bad. We need to reform and transform. Certain of man's faculties are directed toward the Unknown: thought, meditation, prayer. The Unknown is an ocean. What is conscience? It is the compass of the Unknown. Thought, meditation, prayer: These are great radiant mysteries. Let's respect them. Where do these majestic rays of the soul go? Into the shadows; that is, into the light.

The greatness of democracy is that it denies nothing and renounces nothing for humanity. Next to the Rights of Man, or at least alongside them, there are the Rights of the Soul.

To crush fanaticisms and venerate the infinite, that is the rule. Let's not restrict ourselves to prostrating ourselves under the tree of Creation and to contemplating the immense branches full of stars. We have a duty: to work on the human soul, to defend mystery as opposed to miracle, to worship the incomprehensible and reject the absurd, to accept of the inexplicable only what is necessary, to clean up faith, to remove superstition from on top of religion; to rid God of worms.

## VI. Absolute Goodness of Prayer

As for methods of praying, all of them are good as long as they are sincere. Turn your book face down and be in the infinite.

There is, as we know, a philosophy that denies the infinite. There is also a philosophy, classified as pathological, that denies the sun; this philosophy is called blindness.

To set up a sense that we lack as a source of truth is a real blind man's ploy.

And what is truly curious is the haughty, superior, and sympathetic airs that this groping philosophy gives itself in relation to the philosophy that sees God. It makes you think of a mole crying out: I pity them, with their sun!

There are, as we know, illustrious and powerful atheists. When all's said and done, these people are brought back to the truth by their very power, are not really sure of being atheists; the whole thing is little more than a matter of definitions to them, and, in any case, even if they don't believe in God, being great minds, they prove God's existence.

We salute the philosopher in them, while at the same time inexorably qualifying their philosophy.

Let's move along.

What's wonderful, too, is the ease with which people spout hot air. A northern metaphysical school, somewhat impregnated with fog, thought it was causing a revolution in human understanding by replacing the word *force* by the word *will*.

To say "the plant wills" instead of "the plant grows" would, in fact, be fruitful if you added: "the universe wills." Why? Because this would flow from that: The plant wills, so it has a self; the universe wills, so there is a God.

As far as we're concerned, though unlike this school we reject nothing a priori, the idea of a will in a plant, which this school promotes, seems harder to accept than a will in the universe, which the school denies.

To deny the will of the infinite, that is, God, can happen only on condition of denying the infinite. This we have shown.

The negation of the infinite leads straight to nihilism. Everything becomes "a figment of the imagination."

With nihilism no discussion is possible. For the logical nihilist doubts that his interlocutor exists and is not all that sure of existing himself.

From his point of view, it is possible that he himself is only "a figment of the imagination."

Only, he does not see that everything that he has denied, he admits as a whole just by pronouncing that word *imagination.*

In sum, no window is opened for thought by a philosophy that makes everything end in the monosyllable "No."

To "No" there is only one answer: "Yes."

Nihilism has nowhere to go.

There is no nothingness. Zero does not exist. Everything is something. Nothing is nothing.

Man lives on affirmation even more than on bread.

To see and to show—even this is not enough. Philosophy has to be an energy, with the aim and effect of improving man. Socrates has to enter Adam and produce Marcus Aurelius.[1] In other words, make the man of wisdom emerge from the man of bliss. Change Eden into a lyceum.[2] Science should be a tonic. Pleasure—what a sad goal, what a puny ambition! The brute feels pleasure. To think—that's the real triumph of the soul. To hold out thought to quench people's thirst, to hand everyone the notion of God as an elixir, to cause conscience and science to fraternize inside them, make them more just through such a mysterious confrontation—that is the purpose of real philosophy. Morality is the blossoming of sundry truths. To contemplate leads to action. The absolute has to be put into practice. What is ideal has to be breathable, drinkable, edible to the human mind. It is the ideal that has the right to say: "Take of this, this is my body, this is my blood." Wisdom is Holy Communion. It is on this condition that it ceases to be a sterile love of science and becomes the one, almighty method of human rallying, and is promoted from philosophy to religion.

Philosophy should not be a simple ivory tower built over mystery so that it can gaze at it at its leisure, with no other consequence than being at curiosity's beck and call.

For us, postponing the development of our thinking for some other occasion, we will just say here that we do not understand either man as a starting point, nor progress as an end, without these two forces that are the two engines: faith and love.

Progress is the end; the ideal is the model.

What is the ideal? God.

Ideal, absolute, perfection, infinity—these are all words for the same thing.

## VII. PRECAUTIONS TO TAKE IN LAYING BLAME

History and philosophy have eternal duties that are at the same time simple duties: to oppose Caiaphas as bishop, Draco as judge, Trimalcion as lawmaker, Tiberius as emperor;[1] this is clear, direct, and transparent and presents no obscurity whatsoever. But the right to live apart, even with its drawbacks and its abuses, needs to be noted and carefully handled. Cenobitism[2] is a human problem.

When we speak of convents, those seats of error, but also of innocence; of befuddlement, but also of good intentions; of ignorance, but also of devotion; of torture, but also of martyrdom, you almost always have to say "yes and no."

A convent is a contradiction. As a goal, salvation; as a means, sacrifice. The convent is supreme selfishness resulting in supreme self-abnegation.

To abdicate in order to reign seems to be the motto of monasticism.

In the cloister, you suffer to achieve pleasure. You take out a mortgage on death. You bank terrestrial night on celestial light. In the cloister, hell is accepted as advance payment on paradise.

The taking of the veil or the habit is suicide reimbursed by eternity.

It seems to us that such a subject should not be treated with mockery. Everything about it is serious, the good along with the bad.

The just man frowns, but never sneers. We can understand anger, but not malevolence.

## VIII. Faith, Law

Bear with me a bit longer.

We blame the Church when it is riddled with intrigue, we scorn the spiritual when it is hard on the temporal; but we honor the meditative man wherever he appears.

We bow to anyone on their knees.

A faith is for man a necessity. Woe betide the person who believes in nothing!

You are not idle because you are absorbed. There is visible labor and invisible labor.

To contemplate is to toil; to think is to act. Crossed arms are at work, joined hands are doing something. Raising eyes to heaven is an opus.

Thales[1] did not move for four years. He founded philosophy.

To our mind, cenobites are not loafers, recluses are not slobs.

To think about the Dark is a serious thing.

Without undermining in any way what we have just said, we believe that a perpetual remembrance of the grave is only right for the living. On this score, the priest and the philosopher are in agreement. "We have to die." The abbé of La Trappe goes through Horace's lines with him.[2]

To mix a bit of the sepulchre into your life is the law of the sage; and it is the law of the ascetic. In this regard, the ascetic and the sage converge.

There is such a thing as material growth; we want that. There is also such a thing as moral greatness; we cling to it.

People who rush in without thinking say: "What's the good of these immobile figures who side with mystery? What purpose do they serve? What are they doing?"

Alas! Faced with the darkness that surrounds us, that awaits us, not knowing what the vast scattering will do to us, we reply: There is, perhaps, no work more sublime than the work these souls do. And we would add: There is, perhaps, no travail more useful.

We need those who forever pray for those who never pray.

For us, the whole question lies in the amount of thought that gets mixed in with the prayer.

Leibniz at prayer is a great thing; Voltaire at worship[3] is beautiful. *Deo erexit Voltaire.*[4]

We are for religion as opposed to religions.

We are of those who believe in the paltriness of sermons and the sublimeness of prayer.

Besides, in the times we are living through, times that hopefully won't leave their mark on the nineteenth century, at this hour when so many men have low brows and souls almost as low, among so many living beings who have pleasure as their morality and who are busy with the short term and the mangled things of matter, anyone going into exile strikes us as venerable. The monastery is a renunciation. Sacrifice that is misdirected is still sacrifice. There is something grand about making a serious mistake a duty.

Taken in itself, ideally—to circle around the truth to the point of impartially exhausting every aspect of it—the monastery, and the convent of women especially, for in our society it is women who suffer the most and their protest is evident in this exile of the cloister, the convent of women has, incontestably, a certain majesty.

This cloistered existence, so austere and so mournful, a few features of which we have just outlined, is not life, for it is not liberty; it is not the grave, for it is not fullness; it is a strange place from which you see, as though you were on a high mountaintop, the abyss where we are on one side and, on the other, the abyss where we will be; it is a thin and hazy border dividing two worlds, at once illuminated and obscured by both, where the feeble light of life mingles with the dim light of death; it is the half-light of the grave.

As for us, who do not believe what these women believe but live, like them, through faith, we have never been able to consider, without a kind of tender religious terror, without a sort of pity full of envy, those devout, quivering, and trusting creatures, those humble and august souls who dare to live on the very brink of mystery, waiting there between the world that is closed and the sky that is not yet open, turned toward the light you can't see, having only the happiness of thinking they know where it is, aspiring to the void and the unknown, their eye fixed on the unmoving darkness, on their knees, overcome, stunned, shivering, half lifted up at certain moments by the deep breaths of eternity.

# BOOK EIGHT

# CEMETERIES TAKE WHAT THEY ARE GIVEN

## I. IN WHICH THE WAY TO ENTER A CONVENT IS DEALT WITH

It is into this house that Jean Valjean had, as Fauchelevent said, "fallen from the sky."

He had climbed over the garden wall at the rue Polonceau corner, the hymn of angels that he had heard in the middle of the night was the nuns singing matins; the room he had glimpsed in the dark was the chapel; the ghost he had seen stretched out on the ground was a sister making atonement; the little bell whose ringing had so strangely startled him was the gardener's bell tied around father Fauchelevent's knee.

Once Cosette had been put to bed, Jean Valjean and Fauchelevent had, as we saw, made a meal of a glass of wine and a lump of cheese in front of a good blazing fire; then, the only bed in the shed being occupied by Cosette, they had each thrown themselves on a bale of straw. Before shutting his eyes, Jean Valjean had said: "I have to stay here from now on."

Fauchelevent had not been able to get those words out of his head all night. To tell the truth, neither of them got any sleep.

Jean Valjean, feeling that he'd been seen and that Javert was on his trail, realized that Cosette and he were finished if they went back to Paris. Since this latest blast of wind to blow over him had just swept him into this cloister, Jean Valjean had only one thought, to stay put. Now, for an unhappy man in his position, the convent was at once the most dangerous and the safest place to be; the most dangerous, because no man could get into it, so if he were discovered there, it would be in flagrante delicto, and being caught in the act for Jean Valjean meant just a skip and a jump from the convent to the clink; the safest, because if he managed to get himself accepted and to stay, who would think of

looking for him there? To live in a place that was out of bounds—that was salvation.

Fauchelevent also racked his brains. He started out by telling himself he
just didn't get it. How come Monsieur Madeleine had managed to get in, with
the walls that were there? You don't just step over cloister walls. How come he
managed to get in with a kid? You don't just scale a high wall with a kid in your
arms. Who the hell was this kid, anyway? Where had they both sprung from?

Since Fauchelevent had been at the convent, he hadn't heard another
word about Montreuil-sur-mer and he knew nothing about what had happened. Father Madeleine had that look that discourages questions and, anyway,
Fauchelevent told himself that you don't question a saint. For him Monsieur
Madeleine had kept all his prestige. Only, from a few words Jean Valjean had let
slip, the gardener thought he gathered that Monsieur Madeleine had gone
bankrupt on account of the hard times and that he was being pursued by his
creditors, or else that he had been compromised in some political affair and had
gone into hiding; which did not at all worry Fauchelevent who, like a lot of our
northern peasants, was an old Bonapartist at heart. Being in hiding, Monsieur
Madeleine holed up in the convent and it was only natural that he wanted to
stay there. But the thing Fauchelevent couldn't explain, and that he kept going
back to and was racking his brains over, was that Monsieur Madeleine was
there, and that he was there with this little girl. Fauchelevent saw them,
touched them, spoke to them, and didn't believe it. The incomprehensible had
just made its entrance in Fauchelevent's shack. Fauchelevent was madly groping around in surmise and there was only one thing he could see clearly anymore: "Monsieur Madeleine saved my life." This single certainty was enough
and made up his mind for him. He took himself aside and said to himself: "Now
it's my turn." In his conscience, he added: "Monsieur Madeleine didn't spend
much time making up his mind when it was a question of getting under the cart
to pull me out." So he decided he'd save Monsieur Madeleine.

And yet he put various questions to himself and gave himself various answers.

"After all he's meant to me, if he was a thief, would I save him? I would. If
he was a murderer, would I save him? I would. Since he's a saint, would I save
him? I would."

But to somehow keep him in the convent, now that was a problem! Faced
with this almost fantastic prospect, Fauchelevent did not back down; this poor
peasant from Picardy, with no ladder other than his devotion, his goodwill, and
a bit of good old country cunning placed, for once, at the service of a generous
intention, undertook to scale the impossibilities of the cloister and the craggy
escarpments of the rule of Saint Benedict. Father Fauchelevent was an old man
who had been selfish all his life but who, at the end of his days, lame, infirm, and
with no further interest in the world, found it sweet to be grateful, and seeing a

virtuous deed to be done, threw himself into it like a man about to die who suddenly sees a glass of good wine he's never tasted within reach and tosses it back with relish. We might add that the air he had been breathing for the past few years in the convent had already destroyed his personality and ended up making a good deed necessary to him, whatever it might be.

So he formed his resolution; to devote himself to Monsieur Madeleine.

We have just described him as a poor peasant from Picardy. The description is fair, but incomplete. At the point in the story where we now are, a glimpse of father Fauchelevent's makeup might come in handy. He was a peasant, but he had been a *tabellion*,[1] a scrivener, which added a bit of chicanery to his cunning and perspicacity to his gullibility. Having for various reasons failed in his affairs, he had fallen from being a scrivener to a carter and laborer. But despite the cursing and cracks of the whip that horses need, it seems he remained something of a lawyer deep down. He had some natural wit; he did not say "I is," or "I has" either; he spoke well, which was a rare thing in the village; and the other peasants said of him: "He talks just like a gent with a hat." Fauchelevent belonged, in fact, to that breed that the impertinent and flippant vocabulary of last century termed "half burgher, half boor," and that metaphors raining down from the château onto the humble thatched cottage labeled, in the pigeonhole of commoner, "a bit of a hick, a bit of a city slicker"; or "salt and pepper." Though badly used and abused by fate and showing the wear and tear, Fauchelevent was nevertheless an impulsive man and incredibly spontaneous—a precious quality that stops you from ever being bad. His defects and his vices, for he had a few, were entirely superficial; in short, his physiognomy was of the kind that passes the test up close to the observer. That old face had none of those unfortunate wrinkles at the top of the forehead that signify meanness or stupidity.

At daybreak, having racked his brains, father Fauchelevent opened his eyes and saw Monsieur Madeleine sitting on his bale of straw watching Cosette sleep. Fauchelevent sat up and said: "Now you're here, how are you going to get in?"

This question summed up the situation and woke Jean Valjean out of his reverie.

The two good old codgers put their heads together.

"First," said Fauchelevent, "you'll begin by not setting foot outside this room. Neither the little girl nor you. One step in the garden and we've had it."

"Fair enough."

"Monsieur Madeleine," Fauchelevent went on, "you arrived at a good moment, I mean a very bad moment, one of the ladies is very sick. That means no one will be taking much notice of what's going on over our way. It appears she's dying. They're saying the forty-hour prayers. The whole community's worked up. It keeps them busy. The one who's about to fly off is a saint. Actually, they're all saints here. The whole difference between them and me is that they say 'our cell' and I say 'my digs.' There's going to be the prayer for the dying and then the prayer for the dead. For today we'll be all right here; but I can't say what'll happen tomorrow."

"But," observed Jean Valjean, "this old shack is in the recess in the wall, it's hidden by a kind of ruin, there are trees, you can't see it from the convent."

"And I might add that the nuns never come near it."

"Well, then?" said Jean Valjean.

The question mark that underlined that "well, then?" signified: It seems to me that a person could live hidden here. It is to this question mark that Fauchelevent responded: "There are the little girls."

"What little girls?" asked Jean Valjean.

As Fauchelevent opened his mouth to explain what he meant, a bell rang suddenly.

"The nun's dead," he said. "That's the death knell."

And he signaled Jean Valjean to listen.

The bell rang for the second time.

"That is the death knell, Monsieur Madeleine. The bell will go on tolling every minute on the dot for the next twenty-four hours until the body's taken from the church. You see, they come out to play. At playtime, all it takes is for a ball to roll over this way and over they come, despite the ban, to look for it and they poke around here everywhere. They're little devils, those cherubs."

"Who?" asked Jean Valjean.

"The little girls. You'd be spotted in no time, you know. They'd sing out: 'Look! A man!' But there's no danger today. There won't be any playtime. The day'll be all taken up with prayers. You hear the bell. As I told you, one ring a minute. That's the death knell."

"I understand, father Fauchelevent. There are boarders."

And Jean Valjean thought to himself: "Look no further for Cosette's education."

Fauchelevent cried out: "Lord! You wouldn't believe how many little girls there are! Twittering all around a person! And then skedaddling! Here, being a man is like having the plague. You see how they've stuck a bell on my shank as if I was some kind of wild beast."

Jean Valjean was more and more pensive.

"This convent will be our salvation," he murmured. Then he raised his voice: "Yes, the hard thing is staying in."

"No," said Fauchelevent, "it's getting out."

Jean Valjean felt the blood rush to his heart.

"Getting out!"

"Yes, Monsieur Madeleine, to come back in, you have to get out."

And after waiting while the knell sounded again, Fauchelevent went on: "They can't find you here like this. Where did you come from? For me, you fell out of the sky, because I know you; but the nuns, they need you to come through the door."

All of a sudden, they heard the rather complicated ringing of another bell.

"Ah!" said Fauchelevent. "They're ringing for the vocal mothers. They're going in to the chapter. They always hold a chapter when someone's died. She died at daybreak. It's usually daybreak that you die. But can't you get out the way you got in? Look, I don't mean to ask, but where did you get in?"

Jean Valjean went white. The very idea of going back down into that dreadful street made him shudder. Imagine getting out of a forest full of tigers and then, once you are out, a friend advises you to steel yourself and go back in. Jean Valjean conjured up all the police still swarming over the area, officers on the lookout, sentries all over the place. Hideous fists reaching for his collar, maybe Javert at the corner of the square.

"Not possible!" he said. "Father Fauchelevent, let's just say I fell from on high."

"But I believe you, I believe you," Fauchelevent replied. "You don't need to tell me that. The good Lord would've taken you in hand to get a closer look at you and then let go his hold. Only, he meant to put you in a convent for men and he got it wrong. There, another ring. This one's to alert the porter to go and notify the *mairie* so they can go and alert the doctor of the dead and he can come and see that there is a dead woman. All that, that's the ceremony of dying. They don't much like that visit, these good ladies. A doctor, he doesn't believe in anything. He lifts the veil. Sometimes he even lifts something else. They've certainly been in a hurry to notify the doctor this time! What's up, I wonder? Your little girl is still asleep. What's her name?"

"Cosette."

"Is she your little girl? What I mean is, are you her grandfather?"

"Yes."

"For her, getting out of here will be easy. I've got my tradesman's entrance that opens onto the courtyard. I knock. The porter opens. I have my basket on my back, the little one's inside. Out I go. Father Fauchelevent's off with his basket, it's as simple as that. You tell the little one to stay nice and quiet. She'll be under the lid. I'll drop her off as fast as I can at a good old friend of mine's, a woman who sells fruit in the rue du Chemin-Vert, who's hard of hearing and who's got a little bed at her place. I'll shout in the fruit seller's ear that it's one of my nieces and to mind her for me till tomorrow. Then the little one can come back with you. For I'll get you back in. I have to. But what about you, how are you going to get out?"

Jean Valjean nodded.

"No one must see me. That's the rub, father Fauchelevent. Find a way of getting me out like Cosette in a basket and under a lid."

Fauchelevent scratched his earlobe with the middle finger of his left hand, a sure sign of serious confusion.

A third ring of the bell offered a diversion.

"That's the death doctor leaving," said Fauchelevent. "He's looked and he's said: 'She's dead, too right.' When the doctor has stuck a visa for paradise in the passport, the undertakers send in a coffin. If it's a mother, the mothers lay her out; if it's a sister, the sisters lay her out. After that, I nail it up. It's all part of my gardening. A gardener is a bit of a gravedigger. They put her in a low room in the church where there's a connecting door with the street and where the only man who can go in is the doctor of the dead. I don't count the undertaker's assistants or myself as men. It's in that room that I nail the coffin. The undertaker's assistants come and pick it up and Bob's your uncle! That's how you go off to heaven. They bring a box with nothing in it and they take it away with something in it. That's what a funeral's all about. *De profundis.*"

A horizontal ray of sunlight brushed the face of the sleeping Cosette, who opened her mouth a little and looked like an angel drinking the light. Jean Valjean was watching her again. He had stopped listening to Fauchelevent.

Not being listened to is no reason to keep quiet. The good old gardener went on calmly repeating himself: "They dig the hole at the Vaugirard Cemetery. They say they're going to get rid of it, this Vaugirard Cemetery. It's an old cemetery that's in breach of the regulations, it doesn't have the uniform and it's going to take retirement. It's a shame because it's nice and handy. I've got a friend there, old father Mestienne, the gravedigger. The nuns from here have a special privilege, which is being carted off to the cemetery at nightfall. There is a decree of the prefecture, just for them. But what a lot has happened since yesterday! Mother Crucifixion is dead and father Madeleine—"

"Is buried," said Jean Valjean, with a sad smile.

Fauchelevent made the word ricochet.

"Buried—! Christ! If you were here for good it would be a real burial."

The bell rang out for the fourth time. Fauchelevent swiftly grabbed the knee pad with the little bell and buckled it round his knee again.

"This time, it's me. The mother prioress is asking for me. Don't move, Monsieur Madeleine. Wait for me. Something's happened. If you're hungry, there's wine and bread and cheese."

And he beetled out of the shack, saying: "I'm coming! I'm coming!" Jean Valjean saw him running across the garden, as fast as his bad leg would let him, all the while casting sidelong glances at his melon beds.

Less than ten minutes later, father Fauchelevent, whose bell put the nuns to flight as he passed, knocked softly on a door and a soft voice answered: "Forever. Forever." That is, "Come in."

The door was the one in the visitors' room reserved for the gardener in the course of his duties. The visitors' room was adjacent to the chapter hall. The prioress was sitting on the only chair in the visitors' room, waiting for Fauchelevent.

## II. FAUCHELEVENT CONFRONTED WITH A PROBLEM

To look both agitated and grave in critical situations is peculiar to certain personalities and certain professions, notably priests and nuns. The moment Fauchelevent came in, this dual sign of preoccupation was stamped on the physiognomy of the prioress, who was the charming and learned Mademoiselle de Blemeur, Mother Innocent, normally so gay.

The gardener gave a frightened bow and remained standing at the threshold of the cell. The prioress, who was saying her rosary, looked up and said: "Ah, it's you, father Fauvent."

This abbreviation had been adopted in the convent.

Fauchelevent began to bow once more.

"Father Fauvent, I had you called."

"Here I am, Reverend Mother."

"I need to talk to you."

"And I, for my part," said Fauchelevent with a recklessness that frightened him inside, "I have something to say to the most reverend mother."

The prioress looked at him.

"Ah, you have some communication to make to me."

"A request."

"Well, then, speak."

The good Fauchelevent, ex-scrivener, belonged to that category of peasants who have aplomb. A certain canny ignorance is a strength; you don't suspect it and it grabs you. For a little over two years, since he had lived in the convent, Fauchelevent had done well in the community. Always on his own, even while he went about his business in the garden, he scarcely had anything else to do but be curious. At a remove as he was from all these veiled women coming and going, he scarcely saw anything before him but bustling shadows. By dint of attention and perspicacity, he had managed to put some flesh back into all these phantoms, and for him these dead women were alive. He was like a deaf man whose sight is enhanced or like a blind man whose hearing is sharpened. He had applied himself to unraveling the meaning of all the different bells and he had managed to do so, to the point where this enigmatic and glum cloister held no secrets for him; it was a sphinx that blurted out all its secrets in his ear. Knowing everything, Fauchelevent hid everything. That was his art. The whole convent thought he was stupid. A great merit in religion. The vocal mothers prized Fauchelevent. He was a curious mute. He inspired confidence. On top of this, he was regular in his habits, and went out only for the demonstrable necessities of the orchard and the vegetable garden. This discretion in his conduct was chalked up to his credit. Though that had not stopped him from getting two men to spill the beans: in the convent, the porter, who knew all about the peculiarities of the visitors' room; and, in the cemetery, the gravedigger, who knew all about the singularities of the sepulchre; accordingly, when it came to the nuns, he was doubly informed, about their lives, on the one hand, and on the other, about their deaths. But he did not abuse this knowledge in any way. The congregation thought a lot of him. Old, lame, blind as a bat, probably a bit deaf—so many good qualities! He'd have been hard to replace.

So, with the assurance of a man who feels himself to be appreciated, the dear old man stood before the reverend prioress and launched into a bucolic address that was fairly rambling and extremely deep. He went on at length about his age, his infirmities, the weight of the years now bearing down on him. The growing demands of his work, the size of the garden, nights to be spent, like last night for instance, when he had had to put straw mats over the melon beds because of the moon . . . And he finished off by saying: that he had a brother (the prioress gave a start)—a brother who was not young (second start of the prioress, but a reassured start)—that, if they liked, this brother could come and move in with him and help him, that he was an excellent gardener, that the community would get good work out of him, much more than he himself could give; and that, otherwise, if his brother was not accepted, as he, the eldest, felt himself to be broken down and no longer up to the job, he would be obliged, with much regret, to pack up and go . . . And that his brother had a little girl he would bring with him, who would be raised in God here in the house and who might, who knows? one day make a nun.

When he had finished speaking, the prioress interrupted the slipping of her rosary beads through her fingers and said to him: "Can you, between now and this evening, get hold of a strong iron bar?"

"What for?"

"To be used as a lever."

"Yes, Reverend Mother," answered Fauchelevent.

The prioress got up without saying another word and walked into the neighboring room, which was the chapter hall where the vocal mothers were probably assembled. Fauchelevent was left to his own devices.

### III. Mother Innocent

About a quarter of an hour elapsed. The prioress came back and resumed her seat.

Both parties seemed preoccupied. We have copied down the exchange between them as best we could.

"Father Fauvent?"

"Reverend Mother?"

"You are familiar with the chapel?"

"I've got a little box there to hear mass and the offices in."

"And you've gone into the choir for your work?"

"Two or three times."

"There's a stone there that has to be lifted up."

"Heavy?"

"The flagstone from the pavement next to the altar."

"The stone over the burial chamber?"

"Yes."

"This is one time when it'd be good to have two men."

"Mother Ascension is as strong as a man—she'll help you."

"A woman is never a man."

"We only have a woman to help you. Everyone does what they can. Because Dom Mabillon gives four hundred and seventeen epistles of Saint Bernard and Merlonus Horstius gives only three hundred and sixty-seven, I do not look down on Merlonus Horstius."

"Me neither."[1]

"Merit consists in working according to your strength. A cloister is not a building site."

"And a woman is not a man. My brother's the strong one!"

"And then, you'll have a lever."

"That's the only sort of key that fits that sort of door."

"There is a ring in the stone."

"I'll put the lever through it."

"And the stone is set up to pivot."

"That's good, Reverend Mother. I'll open up the vault."

"And the four cantor mothers will assist you."

"And when the vault is open?"

"It will have to be shut again."

"Will that be all?"

"No."

"Give me your orders, most Reverend Mother."

"Fauvent, we have confidence in you."

"I'm here to take care of everything."

"And to keep quiet about everything."

"Yes, Reverend Mother."

"When the vault is open—"

"I'll shut it again."

"But before that—"

"What, Reverend Mother?"

"Something has to be lowered into it."

There was a pause. The prioress thrust out her lower lip in a pout that looked like hesitation, then broke the silence.

"Father Fauvent?"

"Reverend Mother?"

"You know that a mother died this morning."

"No."

"Didn't you hear the bell, then?"

"You can't hear a thing down at the bottom of the garden."

"Really?"

"I can hardly make out my own ring."

"She died at daybreak."

"And then, this morning the wind wasn't blowing my way."

"It was Mother Crucifixion. One of the blessed."

The prioress stopped talking, moved her lips for a moment as though mouthing a mental sermon, and resumed: "Three years ago, a Jansenist, Madame de Béthune,[2] only had to see Mother Crucifixion praying and she turned orthodox."

"Ah, yes, I can hear the knell now, Reverend Mother."

"The mothers have carried her to the room of the dead that opens into the church."

"I know."

"No man other than you can or should enter that room. You make sure of that. That would be a pretty sight, to see a man go into the room of the dead!"

"More often!"

"What!"

"More often!"

"What do you say?"

"I say more often."

"More often what?"

"Reverend Mother, I don't say more often what, I say more often."

"I don't understand you. Why do you say more often?"

"To say what you say, Reverend Mother."

"But I didn't say more often."

"You didn't say it, but I said it to say what you say."

Just then, the clock struck nine.

"At nine o'clock in the morning and at any hour, praised and adored be the most Blessed Sacrament of the altar," said the prioress.

"Amen," said Fauchelevent.

The hour had sounded in the nick of time. It cut short that "more often." Without it is likely that the prioress and Fauchelevent would never have got out of this tangle.

Fauchelevent wiped his forehead.

The prioress gave another little interior murmur, probably holy, then spoke up.

"While she was alive, Mother Crucifixion made conversions; after her death, she will make miracles."

"She will, at that!" replied Fauchelevent, following her lead and making an effort to stick with it from now on.

"Father Fauvent, the community has been blessed in Mother Crucifixion. No doubt it is not given to everyone to die like Cardinal de Bérulle, saying the holy mass and exhaling his soul toward God, uttering these words: *Hanc igitur oblationem.*[3] But without attaining such happiness, Mother Crucifixion had a most beautiful death. She was conscious right up until the last. She talked to us, then she talked to the angels. She gave us her last commands. If you had a bit more faith, and if you had been able to be in her cell, she would have cured your leg for you just by touching it. She was smiling. You could feel that she was being born again in God. There was a touch of paradise in that death."

Fauchelevent felt that this was a sermon gearing up.

"Amen," he said.

"Father Fauvent, we must do what the dead want us to do."

The prioress counted a few beads on her rosary. Fauchelevent kept quiet. She went on.

"I have consulted on this question several ecclesiastics working in Our Lord who are engaged in the exercise of the clerical life and who have produced wonderful fruit."

"Reverend Mother, you can hear the knell much better from here than in the garden."

"Besides, she is more than a dead woman, she is a saint."

"Like you, Reverend Mother."

"She slept in her coffin for twenty years, with the express permission of our holy father, Pius VII."

"The one who crowned the emp—Buonaparte."[4]

For a clever man like Fauchelevent, the memory was untoward. Luckily the prioress was lost in thought and did not hear him. She continued: "Father Fauvent?"

"Reverend Mother?"

"Saint Diodorus, archbishop of Cappadocia, wanted this single word to be written on his tomb: *Acarus,* which means earthworm. This was done. Is that not true?"

"Yes, Reverend Mother."

"The blessed Mezzocane, abbé of Aquila, wanted to be buried beneath the gallows; that was done."

"That is true."

"Saint Terence, bishop of Ostia, where the Tiber meets the sea, asked that his tombstone be engraved with the sign that used to be put on the graves of parricides, in the hope that passersby would spit on his grave. That was done. We must obey the dead."

"So be it."

"The body of Bernard Guidonis, born in France near Roche-Abeille, was, as he had ordered and in spite of the king of Castile, carried into the church of the Dominicans of Limoges, although Bernard Guidonis was bishop of Tuy in Spain. Can this be denied?"

"No, it cannot, Reverend Mother."

"The fact is testified to by Plantavit de la Fosse."

A few more rosary beads were silently said. The prioress went on: "Father Fauvent, Mother Crucifixion will be buried in the coffin in which she slept for twenty years."

"That is only right."

"Death is merely a prolongation of sleep."

"So I'll have to nail her in that particular coffin?"

"Yes."

"And we'll set aside the undertaker's coffin?"

"Exactly."

"I am at the orders of the most reverend community."

"The four cantor mothers will help you."

"To nail the coffin? I don't need them."

"No. To lower it down."

"Where?"

"Into the vault."

"What vault?"

"Under the altar."

Fauchelevent gave a start.

"The vault under the altar!"

"Under the altar."

"Yes, but—"

"You'll lever up the stone with the bar, using the ring."

"But—"

"We must obey the dead. To be buried in the vault under the altar of the chapel, not to go into profane ground, to remain in death where she had prayed in life, this was Mother Crucifixion's last wish. She asked us, that is, she ordered us."

"But it is forbidden."

"Forbidden by men, ordered by God."

"If word got out?"

"We have confidence in you."

"Oh, as for me, I'm a stone in your wall."

"The chapter has assembled. The vocal mothers, whom I have just consulted again and who are deliberating as we speak, have decided that Mother Crucifixion will be buried in her coffin under our altar, according to her wish. You'll see if there won't be miracles galore here, Father Fauvent! What glory in God for the community! Miracles spring from graves."

"But Reverend Mother, if the officer from the health department—"

"Saint Benedict II, on the question of burial, resisted Constantine Pogonatus."

"Yet the police commissioner—"

"Chonodemaire, one of the seven German kings who joined the Gauls in the reign of Constantius, expressly recognized the right of the religious to be buried in religion, that is, under the altar."

"But the inspector from the prefecture—"

"The world is nothing in the face of the cross. Martin, eleventh general of the Carthusians, gave his order his motto: *Stat crux dum volvitur orbis.*"[5]

"Amen," said Fauchelevent, who stuck imperturbably to this way of extricating himself whenever he heard Latin.

The most mediocre listener will do for someone who has been silent far too long. The day the rhetorician Gymnastoras got out of jail, having held inside so many dilemmas and syllogisms, he stopped at the first tree he came to and harangued it, making great efforts to win it over. The prioress, usually dammed up by silence, and now having a surplus in her reservoir, stood and shouted with the loquacity of an opened sluice gate: "On my right, I have Benedict and on my left, Bernard. Who is Bernard? He is the first abbé of Clairvaux. Fontaine in Burgundy is blessed for having been the place of his birth. His father's name was Técelin and his mother's Alèthe. He began at Cîteaux only to end up at Clairvaux; he was ordained an abbé by the bishop of Chalon-sur-Saône, Guillaume de Champeaux; he had seven hundred novices and founded one hundred and sixty monasteries; he brought down Abelard at the Council of Sens[6] in 1140, and Pierre de Bruys and Henry his disciple, and another lot of strays known as the Apostolicals; he confounded Arnaud de Bresce, dumbfounded the monk Raoul, the Jew-slayer, took over the Council of Rheims in 1148, had Gilbert de la Porée, bishop of Poitiers, condemned, had Éon de l'Étoile condemned, sorted out the disputes between the princes, enlightened King Louis the Young,[7] counseled Pope Eugenius III,[8] regulated the Temple, preached the Crusade, performed two hundred and fifty miracles in his lifetime and up to thirty-nine in one day. Who is Benedict? He is the patriarch of Monte Cassino;[9] he is the second founder of Claustral Holiness, he is the Basil of the West.[10] His order has produced forty popes, two hundred cardinals, fifty patriarchs, sixteen hundred archbishops, four thousand six hundred bishops, four emperors, twelve empresses, forty-six kings, forty-one queens, and three thousand six hundred canonized saints, and has existed for fourteen hundred years. On one side, Saint Bernard; on the other, the health inspector! On one side, Saint Benedict, on the other, the other inspector from the department of roads! The government, the department of roads, the funeral parlor, the regulations, the administration—what do we know of all that? No one worries about how we are treated. We don't even have the right to give our dust to Jesus Christ! Your sanitation is an invention of the Revolution. God subordinated to the police commissioner. That's the age we live in. Silence, Fauvent!"

Fauchelevent was not terribly comfortable under this barrage. The prioress continued.

"No one questions the right of a monastery to bury their dead themselves. Only fanatics and lunatics deny it. We are living in times of terrible confusion. People don't know what they should know and know things they should not. People are crass and ungodly. These days, there are those who can't distinguish between the mighty Saint Bernard and the Bernard known as "of the Catholic Poor," a certain good-hearted ecclesiastic who lived in the thirteenth century. Others blaspheme as far as to compare the scaffold of Louis XVI to the cross of Jesus Christ. Louis XVI was a mere king. Let us then watch out for God! There is no just or unjust anymore. Everyone knows Voltaire's name and no one knows the name of Caesar de Bus. And yet Caesar de Bus is one of the blessed and Voltaire is a sorry soul. The last archbishop, the cardinal de Périgord, did not even know that Charles de Condren succeeded Bérulle, and François Bourgoin, Condren, and Jean-François Senault, Bourgoin, and the father of Saint Martha, Jean-François Senault. People know the name of Father Coton, not because he was one of the three who pushed for the foundation of the Oratory, but because the Huguenot king Henri IV[11] swore at him. What makes Saint François de Sales popular with worldly types is that he cheated at cards. And then they attack religion. Why? Because there have been bad priests, because Sagittarius, bishop of Gap, was a brother of Salone, bishop of Embrun, and both were followers of Mommol. What does that matter? Does it stop Martin of Tours[12] from being a saint and from having given half the coat off his back to a pauper? They persecute the saints. They shut their eyes to the truth. They are used to getting around in the dark. The wildest beasts are blind beasts. No one takes hell seriously anymore. Oh, the wicked people! "In the name of the king" now means "in the name of the Revolution." No one knows anymore what they owe either to the living or to the dead. Dying a holy death is now forbidden. Burial is a civil affair. It is horrifying. Saint Leo II wrote two letters expressly, one to Pierre Notaire, the other to the king of the Visigoths, opposing and rejecting, in matters touching on the dead, the authority of the exarch and the supremacy of the emperor. Gautier, bishop of Châlons, stood up to Othon, duc de Bourgogne, on the matter. The former Bench agreed on it. Once we even voted in the chapter on worldly concerns. The abbé of Cîteaux, general of the order, was hereditary councillor to the parliament of Burgundy. We do what we like with our dead. Is the body of Saint Benedict himself not in France in the abbey of Fleury, known as Saint-Benoît-sur-Loire, even though he died in Italy at Monte Cassino, one Saturday, on the twenty-first day of the month of March in the year 543? All this is incontestable. I abhor the Psallants, I hate the priors, I loathe heretics, but I would detest even more anyone who tried to contradict what I say. You only have to read Arnoul Wion, Gabriel Bucelin, Trithemius, Maurolicus, or Dom Luc d'Achery."

The prioress took a breath, then turned to Fauchelevent: "Father Fauvent, is it agreed?"

"It is agreed, Reverend Mother."

"Can we count on you?"

"I will obey."

"Good."

"I am completely devoted to the convent."

"Enough said. You will close the coffin. The sisters will carry it into the chapel. They will say the funeral service. Then they will go back to the cloister. Between eleven o'clock and midnight, you will come with your iron bar. It will all be done in the greatest secrecy. There will be only the four cantor mothers, Mother Ascension, and you in the chapel."

"And the sister at the post."

"She will not turn round."

"But she'll hear."

"She will not listen. Besides, what the cloister knows, the world knows nothing about."

There was another pause. The prioress went on: "You will take off your bell. There is no point in letting the sister at the post know you're there."

"Reverend Mother?"

"What, father Fauvent?"

"Has the doctor of the dead been?"

"He's coming at four o'clock today. We rang the bell that calls the doctor of the dead. So you really don't hear any of the bells?"

"I only take notice of my own."

"A good thing, father Fauvent."

"Reverend Mother, the lever'll need to be at least six feet long."

"Where will you get it?"

"Where there's no shortage of iron gates, there's no shortage of iron bars. I've got my scrap heap at the bottom of the garden."

"About three quarters of an hour before midnight. Don't forget."

"Reverend Mother?"

"What?"

"If ever you have other work like this, my brother's the one who's strong. A real Turk!"

"You will do it as quickly as possible."

"I can't go all that fast. I'm none too steady on my pins; that's why I need help. I limp."

"There's nothing wrong with limping—it may even be a blessing. The emperor Henri II, who fought the antipope Gregory and reestablished Benedict VIII, has two nicknames: the Saint and the Limper."

"It's a good thing to have two surnames," mumbled Fauchelevent, who was, in fact, a little hard of hearing.

"Father Fauvent, now I think about it, let's take a whole hour. Be at the high altar with your iron bar at eleven o'clock. The service begins at midnight. Everything has to be over a good quarter of an hour beforehand."

"I'll do all I can to prove my zeal to the community. This is what we've agreed. I'll nail up the coffin. At eleven o'clock sharp I'll be in the chapel. The cantor mothers will be there, Mother Ascension will be there. Two of me would be better. But, never mind! I'll have my lever. We'll open the vault, we'll drop the coffin down into it, and we'll seal the vault up again. After which, there won't even be a trace. The government won't suspect a thing. Reverend Mother, does that about cover it?"

"No."

"What else is there?"

"There's still the empty coffin."

This gave them pause for thought. Fauchelevent pondered. The prioress pondered.

"Father Fauvent, what will we do with the empty coffin?"

"We'll put it in the ground."

"Empty?"

Another silence. Fauchelevent made the sort of gesture with his left hand that puts to rest any disturbing question.

"Reverend Mother, I'll nail the empty coffin in the back room of the church. No one else but me can get in, and I'll cover the coffin with the pall."

"Yes, but when the pallbearers put it in the hearse and when they lower it in the ground, they will certainly feel there's nothing in it."

"Ah, Chri—" cried Fauchelevent.

The prioress began to make the sign of the cross and stared hard at the gardener. The "-st" stuck in his throat.

He swiftly sought to come up with an expedient to make her forget his bout of blasphemy.

"Reverend Mother, I'll put some dirt in the coffin. Then it will seem like there's a person."

"You're right. Dirt is the same thing as man. So you'll fix up the empty coffin?"

"I'll make it my business."

The prioress's face, till then worried and dark, became once more serene. She waved him away, a superior dismissing an inferior. Fauchelevent headed for the door. As he was about to step out, the prioress gently raised her voice: "Father Fauvent, I am happy with you; tomorrow, after the funeral, bring your brother to me and tell him to bring his daughter."

## IV. IN WHICH JEAN VALJEAN LOOKS AS THOUGH HE HAS READ AUSTIN CASTILLEJO

The strides of the lame are like the winks of the one-eyed; they don't go straight to the point. Moreover, Fauchelevent was puzzled. It took him nearly a quarter of an hour to get back to the garden shed. Cosette was awake. Jean Valjean had sat her next to the fire. As Fauchelevent came in the door, Jean Valjean was showing her the gardener's basket hanging on the wall; he told her: "Listen carefully, my little Cosette. We have to leave this house and go away, but we'll be back and we'll be as happy as can be here. This good man here will carry you on his back in that. You'll wait for me at a lady's place. I'll come and get you there. Above all, if you don't want mother Thénardier to take you away again, do what you're told and don't say a thing!"

Cosette nodded, looking grave.

At the sound of Fauchelevent pushing the door, Jean Valjean whipped round.

"Well?"

"Everything's arranged—and nothing is," said Fauchelevent. "I've got permission to bring you in; but before I can bring you in, I've got to get you out. That's where we come unstuck. For the little one, it's as easy as pie."

"You'll carry her out?"

"Will she keep quiet?"

"I can vouch for that."

"But what about you, father Madeleine?"

After a silence that was a trifle anxious, Fauchelevent went on to exclaim: "I know! You go out the way you came in!"

Jean Valjean answered the same way he did the first time: "Not possible."

Fauchelevent, talking more to himself than to Jean Valjean, grumbled: "There's something else that's tormenting me. I said I'd put some dirt in it. Trouble is, I don't think dirt instead of a body inside is going to do the trick; it won't work, it'll move around, it'll shake. The men will feel it. You see, father Madeleine, the government will be onto it."

Jean Valjean looked him in the eye and decided he was delirious.

Fauchelevent went on: "How in Chri—stmas are you going to get out of here? Because everything has to be done tomorrow! It's tomorrow that I'll be bringing you in. The prioress is expecting you."

Then he explained to Jean Valjean that it was payment for a service that he, Fauchelevent, was doing for the community. That it was one of his duties to take part in burials, to nail coffins and assist the gravedigger at the cemetery. That the nun who had died that morning had asked to be buried in the coffin that served her as a bed and to be interred in the vault under the chapel altar. That this was prohibited by police regulations, but that she was one of those dead women who always get their way. That the prioress and the vocal mothers meant to carry out the deceased's wishes. That it was too bad for the government. That he, Fauchelevent, would nail the coffin in the cell, lift up the stone in the chapel, and lower the dead woman into the vault. And that, to thank him, the prioress would admit his brother into the house as a gardener and his niece as a boarder. That this brother of his was Monsieur Madeleine and his niece, Cosette. That the prioress had told him to bring his brother along tomorrow evening, after the sham burial in the cemetery. But that he couldn't bring Monsieur Madeleine in from outside if Monsieur Madeleine was not outside. That was the first hitch. And after, that there was another hitch: the empty coffin.

"What is this empty coffin?" Jean Valjean asked.

Fauchelevent replied: "The coffin from the administration."

"What coffin? What administration?"

"A nun dies. The municipal doctor comes along and says: There is a dead nun. The government sends in a coffin. The next day it sends a hearse and undertakers to pick up the coffin and take it to the cemetery. The undertakers will come and lift up the coffin and there won't be anything in it."

"Put something in it."

"A dead body? I don't have one."

"No."

"What then?"

"A live body."

"What live body?"

"Me," said Jean Valjean.

Fauchelevent, who had sat down, shot up as though a firecracker had gone off under his chair.

"You!"

"Why not?"

Jean Valjean gave one of those rare smiles that came over him like a ray of sunshine in a winter sky.

"You know, Fauchelevent, how you said, Mother Crucifixion is dead, and I added, and father Madeleine is buried. Well, that's how it's going to be."

"Ah, right, you're having a laugh. You're not serious."

"I'm perfectly serious. Don't I have to get out of here?"

"Of course."

"I told you to get a basket and a lid for me as well."

"Well?"

"The basket will be made of pine and the lid will be a black sheet."

"To start with, it's a white sheet. Nuns are buried in white."

"A white sheet, then."

"You're not like other men, father Madeleine."

To see such imagination at work, devising schemes that are nothing more than the wild and reckless inventions of the galleys, to surface from his peaceful surroundings and get mixed up in what he called the "quiet chugging along of the convent" was as amazing to Fauchelevent as it would be to a person out walking if he saw a seagull fishing in the gutter of the rue Saint-Denis.

Jean Valjean went on: "The question is how to get out of here without being seen. This is one way to do it. But first, give me the full picture. What happens? Where is this coffin?"

"The one that's empty?"

"Yes."

"Down in what they call the room of the dead. It's on two trestles under a pall."

"How long is the coffin?"

"Six feet."

"What is this room of the dead?"

"It's a room on the ground floor that has a grated window looking on the garden, which is shut from outside with a shutter, and two doors; one going to the convent, the other going to the church."

"What church?"

"The church on the street, the church for everyone."

"Do you have the keys to these two doors?"

"No. I have the key to the convent door; the concierge has the key to the church door."

"When does the concierge open that door?"

"Only to let the undertakers in when they come for the coffin. Once the coffin's out, the door is shut again."

"Who puts the nails in the coffin?"

"I do."

"Who puts the cloth over it?"

"I do."

"Are you alone?"

"No other man, apart from the police doctor, can go into the room of the dead. It's even written on the wall."

"Could you, tonight, when everyone in the convent is asleep, hide me in that room?"

"No. But I can hide you in a little dark cubbyhole that opens into the room of the dead, where I put my burial tools and which I look after and have the key for."

"What time will the hearse come to pick up the coffin tomorrow?"

"Around three in the afternoon. The burial takes place at the Vaugirard Cemetery just before nightfall. It's quite a way away."

"I'll stay hidden in your toolshed all night and all morning. What about food? I'll be hungry."

"I'll bring you something."

"You can come and nail me into the coffin at two o'clock."

Fauchelevent took a step back and cracked his knuckles.

"But I can't do that!"

"Bah! Just grab a hammer and hammer the nails in a floorboard!"

What struck Fauchelevent as unbelievable was, we repeat, simple for Jean Valjean. Jean Valjean had been in direr straits than this. Anyone who has ever been a prisoner knows the art of shrinking to fit the size of the escape hatch. The prisoner is prone to flight the same way a sick person is prone to the crisis that cures or kills him. An escape is a cure. What won't we do to be cured? To have yourself nailed in and carted away in a box like a parcel, to live in a box for some little time, to find air where there is none, to cut down your breathing for hours on end, to know how to suffocate without dying—this was one of the dark talents of Jean Valjean.

In any case, a coffin in which there is a living being, this expedient of the convict, is also the expedient of the emperor. If the monk Austin Castillejo is to be believed, this was the means Charles V, wanting to see the woman known as La Plombes again one last time after his abdication, employed to get her into the monastery of Saint-Just and get her out again.[1]

Fauchelevent, recovering a little, cried: "But how will you manage to breathe?"

"I'll breathe."

"In that box! I'm suffocating just thinking about it."

"Surely you must have a gimlet, you can put a few small holes here and there around the mouth and you can nail it without making the lid too tight."

"Right! And what if you should cough or sneeze?"

"An escapee never coughs or sneezes."

And Jean Valjean added: "Father Fauchelevent, I have to decide; either get caught here or take my chances going out in the hearse."

Everyone knows how cats like to stop and dawdle wherever a door is half open. Who has not said to a cat: "Well, come in, then!" There are men who, when faced with an opportunity cracking open in front of them, also have a tendency to waver between two different solutions, at the risk of being crushed by fate's suddenly closing the door again. The overly cautious, thorough cats that they are, and because they are cats, sometimes take more risks than the bold. Fauchelevent was of such a hesitant character. Yet Jean Valjean's coolness won him over in spite of himself. He grumbled: "Indeed, there is no other way."

Jean Valjean went on: "The only thing that worries me is what happens in the cemetery."

"That is just what doesn't bother me," cried Fauchelevent. "If you're sure you can get out of the coffin, I'm sure I can get you out of the grave. The gravedigger's a drunk and a friend of mine. Name of father Mestienne. A good old stick, one of the old school. The gravedigger puts the dead in the grave and I put the gravedigger in my pocket. I'll tell you what will happen. We'll arrive a bit before sundown, three quarters of an hour before they shut the gates of the cemetery. The hearse will drive right up to the grave. I'll follow behind it; that's my job. I'll have a hammer, a chisel, and some pliers in my pocket. The hearse stops, the undertakers tie a rope around your coffin for you and lower you down. The priest says the prayers, makes the sign of the cross, chucks some holy water in, and clears off. I remain alone with father Mestienne. He's my friend, like I told you. Either he'll be plastered or he won't be plastered—it's all the same. If he's not plastered, I say to him: 'Come and have a drink while the Bon Coing's still open.' I drag him away, I get him drunk—it doesn't take long to get father Mestienne drunk, he's always halfway there—I drink him under the table for you, I take his pass to get back into the cemetery, and I come back without him. Then you'll only have me to deal with. If he's plastered, I say to him: 'Off you go, I'll stand in for you.' Off he goes and I pull you out of the hole."

Jean Valjean put out his hand and Fauchelevent fell on it with touching peasant-style emotion.

"Agreed, father Fauchelevent. It will all be all right."

"Provided nothing goes wrong," thought Fauchelevent. "What if it all goes horribly wrong?!"

### V. IT'S NOT ENOUGH TO BE A DRUNK TO BE IMMORTAL

The next day, as the sun was going down, the people going up and down the boulevard du Maine took their hats off as an old-model hearse went by, decorated with death's-heads, crossbones, and teardrops. Inside the hearse was a coffin covered with a white sheet on which a huge black cross spread out like a great dead woman with her arms hanging out. A draped coach, in which a priest in a surplice and a choirboy in a red skullcap could be seen, followed behind. Two undertakers in gray uniforms with black trim were walking to the left and right of the hearse. Bringing up the rear came an old man in the clothes of a laborer, limping. This cortège was heading for the Vaugirard Cemetery.

You could see sticking out of the old man's pocket the handle of a hammer, the blade of a cold chisel, and the double handle of a pair of pliers.

Vaugirard Cemetery was an exception among the cemeteries of Paris. It had its own peculiar customs, just as it had its porte cochère and its double gate that the old people in the quartier, holding fast to the old words, called the bridle gate and the pedestrian gate. The Bernardine-Benedictines of Petit-Picpus had obtained, as we said, the right to be buried apart in a corner and at night, this ground having once belonged to their community. The gravediggers accordingly had to work in the evening in summer and at night in winter and were kept to a peculiar discipline. In those days the gates of the cemeteries of Paris were shut at sunset, and, since this was a regulation made by the municipality, Vaugirard Cemetery was subject to it like the rest. The bridle gate and the pedestrian gate were two iron gates standing side by side next to a gatehouse built by the architect Perronet, where the cemetery gatekeeper lived. These gates thus turned inexorably on their hinges the instant the sun disappeared behind the dome of the Invalides.[1] If any gravedigger was caught lagging behind at that moment, his only resort for getting out was his gravedigger's pass, provided by the administration of the funeral parlor. A kind of letter box had been cut into the shutter of the gatekeeper's window. The gravedigger dropped his pass into this box, the gatekeeper heard it fall, pulled the cord, and the pedestrian gate opened. If the gravedigger did not have his pass, he called out his name and the gatekeeper, who was sometimes in bed asleep, would get up, go to identify the gravedigger, and open the gate with his key; the gravedigger would then go out—after paying a fifteen-franc fine.

This cemetery, with its novel practices outside the general run of things, disturbed the symmetry of the administration. It was closed down soon after 1830. Montparnasse Cemetery,[2] known as the East Cemetery, has taken over from it, inheriting the famous watering hole bordering the Vaugirard Cemetery that used to have a wooden signboard over it with a quince painted on it; it had an L-shaped bar, with the tables of drinkers on one side and the graves on the other, and this sign: AU BON COING—At the Good Quince.

Vaugirard Cemetery was what we might describe as a cemetery that had lost its bloom. It was falling into decay. Mold was invading it, the flowers were departing. Well-heeled bourgeois didn't think much of being buried in Vaugirard; it reeked of poverty. Père-Lachaise, and don't spare the horses! To be buried at Père-Lachaise was like having mahogany furniture. It was a sign of elegance for all to see. Vaugirard Cemetery was a venerable paddock, planted in the style of an old French garden. Straight paths, box hedges, cedars, holly, old graves under old yews, very tall grass. Night there was dramatic. There were some very lugubrious shapes and shadows there.

The sun had not yet set when the hearse with the white sheet and the black cross turned into the avenue that led to the Vaugirard Cemetery. The lame old man who was following it was, of course, none other than Fauchelevent.

The burial of Mother Crucifixion in the vault under the altar, the removal of Cosette, the smuggling of Jean Valjean into the room of the dead—all had gone smoothly and without a snag.

We might note in passing that the inhumation of Mother Crucifixion under the convent altar is a perfectly venial sin to our way of thinking. It is one of those sins that look very much like a duty. The nuns had carried it off, not only without any qualms but to the applause of their consciences. In the cloister, what is known as "the government" is merely an interference with their authority, an interference that was always questionable. The rule comes first; as for the civil code, we'll see. Men, you can make as many laws as you like, but keep them to yourselves. Caesar's toll is never anything more than what is left over from God's toll. A prince is nothing next to a principle.

Fauchelevent limped along behind the hearse, happy as can be. His two mysteries, his two twin plots, one in league with the nuns, the other with Monsieur Madeleine, one for the convent, the other against, had succeeded together, one after the other. Jean Valjean's calmness was one of those powerful tranquilizers that are contagious. Fauchelevent was no longer worried about whether they would bring it off. What remained to be done was nothing. For the past two years, he had got the gravedigger, good old father Mestienne, drunk a dozen times. He could do what he liked with him. The man was putty in his hands. Mestienne's head changed shape to fit Fauchelevent's cap. Fauchelevent felt completely secure.

As the convoy entered the avenue leading to the cemetery, Fauchelevent looked at the hearse, happy, and rubbed his big hands together, muttering to himself: "Not a bad joke!"

Suddenly the hearse stopped; they had reached the gate. The burial permit had to be shown. The man from the funeral parlor went and had a word with the cemetery gatekeeper. During this conversation, which always involves a wait of one or two minutes, someone, a stranger, came and stood behind the hearse next to Fauchelevent. He was some sort of laborer in a jacket with big pockets and a pick under his arm.

Fauchelevent looked at the stranger.

"Who are you?" he asked.

The man replied: "The gravedigger."

If you'd survived a cannon blast full in the chest, you'd look like Fauchelevent.

"The gravedigger!"

"Yep."

"You!"

"Me."

"Father Mestienne is the gravedigger."

"Was."

"What do you mean, was?"

"He's dead."

Fauchelevent had been ready for anything, except that, that a gravedigger could die. And yet it is true; gravediggers themselves die. By dint of digging the graves of others, they open up their own.

Fauchelevent remained speechless. He barely had the strength to stammer: "But he can't be!"

"He is."

"But," he repeated feebly, "father Mestienne is the gravedigger."

"After Napoléon, Louis XVIII. After Mestienne, Gribier. Peasant, my name is Gribier."

Fauchelevent, white as a sheet, studied this Gribier.

He was a long, skinny, pallid man, perfectly dismal. He looked like a doctor who had missed his calling and turned to gravedigging.

Fauchelevent burst out laughing.

"Ah, it's funny, the things that happen! Father Mestienne is dead. Little father Mestienne is dead, but long live little father Lenoir! You know what little father Lenoir is? It's the small jug of red at six a shot. It's the jug of Suresnes, for heaven's sake! Real Paris Suresnes! Ah, old Mestienne's dead, eh! I'm sorry to hear that; he was a real bon vivant. But you're a bon vivant, too. Isn't that right, friend? We'll go and have a drink together, in a sec."

The man replied: "I've been to school; I've done third year. I never drink."

The hearse had started off again and was rolling along down the main path of the cemetery.

Fauchelevent had slackened his pace. He was limping, even more from anxiety than infirmity.

The gravedigger was walking ahead of him.

Fauchelevent was giving the unexpected Gribier the once-over again.

He was one of those men who look old when they're still young and who are skinny but very strong.

"Hey, friend!" cried Fauchelevent.

The man turned round.

"I'm the gravedigger from the convent."

"My colleague," said the man.

Fauchelevent was illiterate but sharp as a tack and he knew right away that he was dealing with a formidable species, a smooth talker.

He grumbled: "So father Mestienne died, just like that."

The man replied: "Exactly. The good Lord consulted his book of due dates. It was father Mestienne's turn. So father Mestienne died."

Fauchelevent repeated mechanically: "The good Lord . . ."

"The good Lord," said the man with authority. "For the philosophers, the Eternal Father; for the Jacobins, the Supreme Being."[3]

"Aren't we going to get to know each other?" stammered Fauchelevent.

"We already do. You're a peasant, I'm a Parisian."[4]

"We don't know each other until we've drunk together. The man who empties his glass, empties his heart. You'll come and have a drink with me. You can't refuse."

"The job comes first."

Fauchelevent thought: "I'm finished. We were only a few turns of the wheel from the little path that leads to the nuns' corner."

The gravedigger went on: "Peasant, I've got seven little nippers to feed. Since they have to eat, I can't drink."

And he added with the satisfaction of a serious soul, pontificating: "Their hunger is the enemy of my thirst."

The hearse turned past a stand of cypresses, left the main path, took a small path, drove into the grounds, and bored into a thicket. This indicated the immediate proximity of the sepulchre. Fauchelevent slowed down again but could not slow down the hearse. Luckily the ground was loose and wet with all the winter rains and it stuck to the wheels, bogging the wheels down and making the going hard.

He caught up with the gravedigger.

"They have such a good little Argenteuil wine," mumured Fauchelevent.

"Villager," the man resumed, "I really should not be a gravedigger. My father was a porter at the Prytanée.[5] He intended me for Literature. But he had a run of bad luck. He lost money on the stock exchange. I was forced to give up the profession of author. But I am still a public letter-writer."

"So you're not a gravedigger, then?" Fauchelevent shot back, clutching at straws, however weak.

"One doesn't rule out the other. I'm holding two jobs concurrently."

Fauchelevent did not understand this last word.

"Let's go and have a drink," he said.

Here, an observation is necessary. Fauchelevent, whatever his anguish, was proposing a drink but forgot to say who was paying. Normally, Fauchelevent made the proposal, and father Mestienne paid. The offer of a drink was obviously the result of the new situation created by the new gravedigger and this offer had to be made, but the old gardener, not unintentionally, had left the proverbial hour of reckoning in the dark. When it came down to it, he, Fauchelevent, however nervous he might be, was not keen to cough up the money.

The gravedigger went on with a superior smile: "You've got to eat. I agreed to take on father Mestienne's obligations. When you've almost finished school, you are a philosopher. On top of working with my hands, I have added working with my arms. I have my writer's stall in the market in the rue de Sèvres. You know? The Marché-aux-Parapluies. All the women who are cooks in the Croix-Rouge[6] turn to me. I tart up their declarations to their true loves. In the morning I write love letters, in the afternoon I dig graves. That's life, hayseed."

The hearse advanced. Fauchelevent, at the peak of anxiety, looked all around him. Great beads of sweat were running down his forehead.

"Yet," the gravedigger continued, "you cannot serve two mistresses. I have to choose between the pen and the pick. The pick is ruining my hands."

The hearse pulled up. The choirboy got down from the draped car, followed by the priest. One of the small front wheels was up a bit on a pile of dirt beyond which an open grave could be seen.

"Not a bad joke!" Fauchelevent repeated, aghast.

## VI. Between Four Planks

Who was in the coffin? We know. Jean Valjean.

Jean Valjean had arranged himself to stay alive in there and he was more or less still breathing.

It is a funny thing how a secure conscience makes everything else secure. The whole scheme Jean Valjean had cooked up beforehand was working, and working well, from the start the night before. He was counting, like Fauchelevent, on father Mestienne. He had no doubt about the end result. Never was there a more critical situation, never more complete calm.

The four planks of the coffin gave off a kind of terrible peace. It was as though something of the repose of the dead had entered into Jean Valjean's tranquillity. From the depths of this bier he had been able to follow and was following all the phases of the formidable drama that he was playing with death.

Not long after Fauchelevent had finished nailing on the top plank, Jean Valjean felt himself being carted out, then rolling along. At the decrease in jolts, he felt that they had gone from the cobblestones to hard ground, that is, that they were leaving the streets and getting onto the boulevards. At a dull thump, he guessed they were crossing the pont d'Austerlitz. At the first stop, he had understood they were going into the cemetery; at the second stop, he said to himself: "Here's the grave."

Suddenly he felt hands grabbing the coffin, then a harsh scraping against the planks; he realized that this was a rope being tied around the coffin to lower it down into the freshly dug hole. Then he had a kind of dizzy spell. The undertakers and the gravedigger had probably tipped the coffin and let it down headfirst. He swiftly got his bearings back, feeling himself to be horizontal again and immobile. He had just touched bottom. He felt a certain chill.

A voice rose above him, icy and solemn. He heard, so slowly he could grasp them one after the other, Latin words that he could not understand rising and falling away: *"Qui dormiunt terrae pulvere, evigilabunt; alii in vitam aeternam, et alii in opprobrium, ut videant semper."*[1]

A child's voice said: *"De profundis."*[2]

The grave voice started again: *"Requiem aeternam dona ei, Domine."*[3]

The child's voice responded: *"Et lux perpetua luceat ei."*[4]

He heard something like the gentle patter of a few drops of rain on the plank that covered him. It was probably holy water. He thought: "This will soon be over. Hang on a bit longer. The priest is going to go away. Fauchelevent will take Mestienne for a drink. They'll leave me alone. Then Fauchelevent will come back alone, and I'll get out of here. This will all take a good hour."

The grave voice resumed: *"Requiescat in pace."*[5]

And the child's voice said: *"Amen."*

Jean Valjean cocked an ear and heard something like footsteps receding.

"There they go," he thought. "I'm on my own."

Suddenly he heard over his head a noise that sounded like a clap of thunder. It was a shovelful of dirt falling on the coffin.

A second shovelful of dirt fell. One of the holes through which he was breathing blocked up. A third shovelful of dirt fell. Then a fourth. Some things are stronger than the strongest of men. Jean Valjean passed out.

## VII. IN WHICH WE FIND THE ORIGINS OF THE SAYING: DON'T LOSE YOUR PASS

Here is what happened above the coffin in which Jean Valjean lay.

When the hearse had driven away, when the priest and the choirboy had climbed back into the carriage and gone, Fauchelevent, who didn't take his eyes off the gravedigger, saw him bend down and grab hold of his shovel, which was sticking straight up in the pile of dirt.

So then Fauchelevent made an extreme resolution.

He stood between the grave and the gravedigger, crossed his arms, and said: "I'm paying!"

The gravedigger looked at him in amazement and replied: "What's that, peasant?"

Fauchelevent repeated: "I'm paying!"

"What for?"

"The wine."

"What wine?"

"The Argenteuil."

"Where is this Argenteuil?"

"Au Bon Coing."

"Leave it alone!" said the gravedigger.

And he threw another shovelful of dirt on the coffin.

The coffin made a hollow sound. Fauchelevent felt himself teeter and almost fell into the grave himself. In a voice in which the rattling sound of choking could be heard, he yelled: "Come on, friend, before the Bon Coing closes!"

The gravedigger filled his shovel with another load of dirt. Fauchelevent went on: "I'm paying!"

And he grabbed the gravedigger's arm.

"Listen to me, friend. I'm the convent gravedigger. I'm here to help you. It's a job that can be done at night. So let's start by having a drink."

And while he continued to talk, while he clung to this desperate gambit, he had a gloomy thought: "And what happens even if he does have a drink? Will he even get tipsy?"

"Provincial," said the gravedigger, "if you insist, I consent. We'll have a drink. After the work's done, not a moment before."

And he set his shovel in motion once more. Fauchelevent held him back.

"It's Argenteuil at six sous a pop!"

"For heaven's sake," said the gravedigger, "you're like a bell-ringer. Ding-dong, ding-dong; same thing over and over. Shove off, will you."

And he launched a second shovelful.

Fauchelevent had reached the point where you no longer have a clue what you are saying.

"Oh, come on! Come and have a drink," he yelled, "since I'm the one that's paying!"

"When we've put the baby to bed," said the gravedigger.

He chucked in the third shovelful.

Then he stuck the shovel in the ground and added: "You see, it's going to be a cold night tonight and the dead woman's going to give us a piece of her mind if we plant her here without a cover."

At that moment, while he loaded his shovel, the gravedigger bent down and the pocket of his jacket gaped wide open.

Fauchelevent's wild eyes went automatically to this pocket and stayed there.

The sun was not yet hidden below the horizon; there was enough light to make out something white at the bottom of this gaping pocket.

The entire load of lightning that the eyes of a peasant from Picardy can hold flashed in Fauchelevent's pupils. An idea had just occurred to him.

Without the gravedigger's noticing, busy as he was with his shovelful of dirt, he slipped his hand in the pocket from behind and withdrew the white thing at the bottom.

The gravedigger sent the fourth shovelful into the grave.

The moment he turned back to get a fifth shovelful, Fauchelevent gave him a profoundly calm look and said: "By the way, newcomer, have you got your pass?"

The gravedigger stopped in his tracks.

"What pass?"

"The sun's going down."

"Good for him, let him put his nightcap on."

"The cemetery gate's about to shut."

"So what?"

"Have you got your pass?"

"Ah, my pass!" said the gravedigger.

And he fumbled in his pocket.

When he'd fumbled in one pocket, he fumbled in the other. He went on to his watch pockets, explored the first, turned the second inside out.

"Oh, no!" he said, "I don't have my card. I must have forgotten it."

"Fifteen francs fine," said Fauchelevent.

The gravedigger turned green. Green is what pallid people turn when they go pale.

"Jesus wept!" he cried. "Fifteen francs fine!"

"Three hundred sous," said Fauchelevent.

The gravedigger dropped his shovel.

Fauchelevent's turn had come.

"Oh, well," said Fauchelevent, "despair not, conscript. No need to slit your wrists and put the grave to use. Fifteen francs is fifteen francs and besides, you can always not pay. I'm an old hand, you're new. I know the tricks of the trade, the traps, the ins and outs. Let me give you a word of friendly advice. One thing is clear, and that is that the sun's going down, it's hit the dome, the cemetery is going to close in five minutes."

"That's true," replied the gravedigger.

"Five minutes starting from now is not enough time for you to fill up the grave—it's as deep as the devil, this hole—and get out before they shut the gates."

"You're right."

"In which case, there's the fifteen-franc fine."

"Fifteen francs."

"But you have time—where do you live?"

"A stone's throw from the barrière. A quarter of an hour from here, rue de Vaugirard, number eighty-seven."

"You have time, if you run as fast as your pins will go, to get out now."

"Quite right."

"Once you're through the gate, you scurry home, grab your pass, come back, the cemetery gatekeeper'll open up for you and then you won't have to pay, because you'll have your pass. And then you can bury your dead. Me, I'll keep an eye on her for you to make sure she doesn't run away."

"I owe you my life, peasant!"

"Get cracking," said Fauchelevent.

The gravedigger, overcome with gratitude, shook his hand and turned on his heel and ran.

When the gravedigger had disappeared through the bushes, Fauchelevent listened until his footsteps died away, then he bent over the grave and said in a low voice: "Father Madeleine!"

No answer.

Fauchelevent gave a shudder. He rolled into the grave more than he scrambled down into it, threw himself at the head of the coffin and cried: "Are you there?"

Silence in the coffin.

Fauchelevent could no longer breathe he was shaking so hard; he took his cold chisel and his hammer and wrenched the top plank off. Jean Valjean's face appeared in the twilight, eyes closed, pale.

Fauchelevent's hair stood on end, he shot to his feet, then fell with his back against the wall of the grave, ready to collapse on top of the coffin. He looked at Jean Valjean.

Jean Valjean lay there lifeless, ashen and still.

Fauchelevent murmured in a voice so low it was barely a breath: "He's dead!"

He straightened himself up, crossed his arms so violently he whacked his shoulders with his clenched fists and cried: "This is how I save him!"

Then the poor man began to sob. Carrying on a monologue, for it is a mistake to think the monologue is not a natural phenomenon. Extreme emotions often speak out loud.

"It's all father Mestienne's fault. Why did he have to die, the idiot? Why did he croak the very moment we weren't expecting it? He's the one who's killed Monsieur Madeleine. Father Madeleine! He's in the coffin. He's already been carted here. It's all over . . . But, things like this just don't make any sense, do they? God Almighty! He's dead! And what about the little girl? What am I to do with her? What's the fruit-hawker woman going to say? How in Christ's name can a man like that die like this? When I think how he got under my cart! Father Madeleine! Father Madeleine! Of course, he suffocated, I told him he would.

He wouldn't listen. Here's a pretty turnup for you, indeed! He's dead, that good man, the best man there was of all the good ones God made! What about his little girl! Ah! To start with, I'm not going back there. I'm staying put. Imagine pulling a stunt like this! A lot of good it's done being two old men if all we are is two old lunatics. But to start with, how did he manage to get into the convent? That was how it all started. You're not supposed to do that sort of thing. Father Madeleine! Father Madeleine! Father Madeleine! Madeleine! Monsieur Madeleine! Monsieur le maire! He can't hear me. How are you going to get yourself out of this one, I ask you!"

And he tore his hair.

In the distance, a harsh grating sound could be heard. It was the cemetery gates closing.

Fauchelevent leaned over Jean Valjean, and suddenly he sort of bounced up and leaped back—as far as you can leap back in a grave. Jean Valjean had his eyes open and was looking at him.

To see a dead person is frightening, to see a person resurrected is almost as bad. Fauchelevent turned to stone, pale, wild-eyed, overwhelmed by all these extreme emotions, not knowing whether he was dealing with the living or the dead, looking at Jean Valjean who was looking back at him.

"I almost went to sleep," said Jean Valjean.

And he sat up.

Fauchelevent fell on his knees.

"Holy Mother of God! You gave me a fright!"

Then he stood up and shouted: "Thank you, father Madeleine!"

Jean Valjean had merely passed out. The open air had revived him.

Joy is the backward surge of terror. Fauchelevent had almost as much work to do as Jean Valjean to recover.

"So you're not dead! Oh, you've got your wits about you! I called out to you so much that you came back. When I saw your eyes closed, I said: 'That's it! He's suffocated.' I'd have gone stark raving mad, mad enough for a straitjacket. They'd have stuck me in Bicêtre. What was I supposed to do if you *had* died? What about your little girl! The barrow woman would never have been able to make head or tail of it! There is the kid, plonked in her arms, and then the grandfather ups and dies! What a turnup for the books! By all the saints above, what a turnup for the books! Ah, but you're alive—that's the best part about it!"

"I'm cold," said Jean Valjean.

Those words brought Fauchelevent completely back to reality, and to its urgency. Both these men, even when they had fully recovered, felt troubled in their souls without realizing it, along with something strange inside that was the sinister wildness of the place creeping in.

"Let's get out of here, and fast," said Fauchelevent.

He fumbled in his pocket and pulled out a flask he had packed.

"But first, a little drop!" he said.

The flask finished off what the unfettered air had started. Jean Valjean took a swig of brandy and felt thoroughly restored.

He climbed out of the coffin and helped Fauchelevent nail the lid back on. Three minutes later, they were out of the grave.

After that, Fauchelevent was calm. He took his time. The cemetery was closed. There was no need to fear that Gribier, the gravedigger, would pop up. That "conscript" was at home, busy hunting around for his pass and not very likely to find it, since it was in Fauchelevent's pocket. Without a pass, he could not get back into the cemetery.

Fauchelevent grabbed the shovel and Jean Valjean the pick and together they buried the empty coffin.

When the grave was filled in, Fauchelevent said to Jean Valjean: "Come on and we'll get going. I'll keep the shovel and you take the pick."

Night was falling.

Jean Valjean had some trouble moving and walking. He had gone stiff in the coffin and turned into a bit of a corpse. The numbness of death had taken hold of him between those four planks. He needed, so to speak, to thaw out of the sepulchre.

"You're stiff," said Fauchelevent. "What a shame I'm lame, we'd step up the pace, otherwise."

"Bah!" replied Jean Valjean, "I'll soon get my legs loosened up."

They walked off down the paths the hearse had taken. When they got to the closed gate and the gatekeeper's pavilion, Fauchelevent, who was holding the gravedigger's pass in his hand, dropped it into his box; the gatekeeper pulled the cord, the gate opened and they walked through.

"That was a breeze!" said Fauchelevent. "What a brainwave you had, father Madeleine!"

They got past the barrière Vaugirard without any trouble. In the neighborhood of a cemetery, a pick and a shovel are a couple of passports.

The rue de Vaugirard was deserted.

"Father Madeleine," said Fauchelevent as he trotted along, glancing up at the houses, "your eyes are better than mine. Show me where number eighty-seven is."

"Right here, actually," said Jean Valjean.

"There's no one around," Fauchelevent went on. "Give me the pick and let me have a couple of minutes."

Fauchelevent went into no. 87, climbed to the top of the stairs, guided by the instinct that always leads the poor man to the attic, and knocked in the gloom on the door of a garret. A voice answered: "Come in."

It was the voice of Gribier.

Fauchelevent pushed the door open. The gravedigger's dwelling was, like all such downtrodden abodes, a dump, unfurnished and cluttered. A packing case—perhaps a coffin—served as a console, a butter pot served as a drinking fountain, a straw mat served as a bed, the tiles served as table and chairs. In a corner, on top of a ragged scrap of old carpet, a thin woman and any number of children were huddled in a heap. The whole destitute interior showed traces of being turned inside out. You'd have said that it was the site of a one-man earthquake. Lids were thrown around, rags scattered, a pitcher broken, the mother had been in tears, the children had probably been beaten—traces of a furious and relentless search. It was clear that the gravedigger had desperately tried to track down his pass and had taken his frustration at losing it out on everything in the dump, including his pitcher and his wife. He looked utterly distraught.

But Fauchelevent was racing too fast toward the episode's denouement to notice this sad side to his triumph.

He stepped in and said: "I thought I'd bring back your pick and shovel."

Gribier watched him, stunned.

"And tomorrow morning at the cemetery gatekeeper's you'll find your pass."

With that, he put the pick and the shovel down on the tiles.

"What's the meaning of this?" asked Gribier.

"What the meaning of this is, is that you dropped your pass out of your pocket and I found it on the ground after you'd gone. I buried the dead woman, I filled in the grave, I did your work for you, the gatekeeper will give you back your pass, and you won't have to pay fifteen francs. There you go, conscript."

"Thank you, villager!" cried Gribier, dazed. "Next time, it's my treat."

## VIII. A SUCCESSFUL INTERROGATION

One hour later, in the dead of night, two men and a child presented themselves at no. 62, petite rue Picpus. The elder of the men lifted the door-knocker and knocked. This was Fauchelevent, Jean Valjean, and Cosette.

The two old men had gone and gotten Cosette from the fruit-hawker in the rue du Chemin-Vert, where Fauchelevent had dropped her off the night before. Cosette had spent the last twenty-four hours not knowing what to think and trembling silently. She trembled all the more as she had not wept. She hadn't eaten either, or slept. The worthy fruit-hawker had put a hundred questions to her without getting more for an answer than the same mournful glance. Cosette did not let on for a second anything of all she had heard and seen over the last two days. She gathered that they were going through a crisis. She felt to her marrow that she had "to be good." Who has not experienced the ultimate power of these three words delivered in a certain tone in the ear of a frightened child: "Not a word!" Fear is mute. Besides, no one can keep a secret the way a child can.

Only when, after this grim twenty-four hours, she clapped eyes on Jean Valjean again, did she let out a yelp of joy in which any thoughtful soul who had overheard her would have picked up the sense of an escape from a bottomless chasm.

Fauchelevent was from the convent and he knew the passwords. Every door opened. And thus the terrifying twin problem was solved: how to get out, how to get in.

The porter, who had his instructions, opened the little door of the tradesman's entrance that was connected to the garden courtyard and that you could still see from the street twenty years ago, standing opposite the porte cochère. The porter let all three of them in through this door, and from there they reached the inner private visitors' room where Fauchelevent had received the prioress's orders the night before.

The prioress was waiting for them, rosary beads in hand. One of the vocal mothers was standing by her side with her veil down. A discreet candle lit up, we might almost say pretended to light up, the visitors' room.

The prioress gave Jean Valjean the once-over. No eye can scrutinize as thoroughly as a downcast eye. Then she questioned him: "You are the brother?"

"Yes, Reverend Mother," replied Fauchelevent.

"What is your name?"

Fauchelevent answered: "Ultime Fauchelevent."

He had, in fact, had a brother named Ultime who was dead.

"What part of the country are you from?"

Fauchelevent answered: "From Picquigny, near Amiens."

"How old are you?"

Fauchelevent answered: "Fifty."

"What is your profession?"

Fauchelevent answered: "Gardener."

"Are you a good Christian?"

Fauchelevent answered: "Everyone in the family is."

"Is this little girl yours?"

Fauchelevent answered: "Yes, Reverend Mother."

"You are her father?"

Fauchelevent answered: "Her grandfather."

The vocal mother whispered to the prioress: "He answers well."

Jean Valjean had not uttered a word. The prioress examined Cosette closely and whispered to the vocal mother: "She will be ugly."

The two mothers chatted for a few minutes in voices barely above a whisper in a corner of the visitors' room, then the prioress turned back and said: "Father Fauvent, you will have another knee pad and bell. We need two now."

The next day, in fact, two little bells could be heard in the garden, and the nuns could not resist lifting a corner of their veils. At the bottom, under the trees, two men could be seen digging side by side, Fauvent and another man. Obviously an enormous event. The silence was broken long enough to say: "That's the assistant gardener."

The vocal mothers added: "He's one of father Fauvent's brothers."

Jean Valjean was in fact properly fitted out; he had the leather knee pad and the bell; he was now officially accepted. His name was Ultime Fauchelevent.

The strongest determining argument for admission had been the prioress's observation about Cosette: "She will be ugly." This prognostic declared, the prioress immediately took Cosette to her heart and gave her a place in the boarding school as a charity case.

The move was only strictly logical. A lot of good it has done not having any mirrors in a convent, when women are so conscious of their appearance. Now, girls who feel they are pretty do not readily become nuns; luckily vocations declare themselves in inverse proportion to beauty, so hopes are higher for the ugly than for the beautiful. Hence the keen preference for ugly ducklings.

The whole episode greatly enhanced Fauchelevent's standing. He had had a triple success: with Jean Valjean, whom he had saved and sheltered; with Gribier, the gravedigger, who said to himself, "He saved me that fine"; with the convent, which, thanks to him, kept Mother Crucifixion's coffin under the altar, thereby eluding Caesar and satisfying God. There was a coffin with a corpse in Petit-Picpus and a coffin without a corpse in Vaugirard Cemetery; no doubt public order was profoundly disturbed, but it did not know it. As for the convent, its gratitude to Fauchelevent was great. Fauchelevent became the best of its servants and the most treasured of gardeners. At the very next visit of the archbishop, the prioress told the story to His Grace, half by way of a confession, half by way of a boast. When he left the convent, the archbishop spoke of it, very quietly, with approval to Monsieur de Latil, confessor to Monsieur, brother to the king,[1] and, subsequently, to the archbishop of Rheims and a cardinal. Admiration for Fauchelevent traveled far and wide, for it got as far as Rome. We have actually seen a note addressed by the then-reigning pope, Leo XII,[2] to one of his relatives, a monsignor in the nuncio's residence in Paris with the same name as himself, Della Genga; in it can be read these lines: "It appears that in a convent in Paris there is an excellent gardener who is a saintly man, known as Fauvent." Not a whiff of this triumph reached Fauchelevent in his shed; he continued to graft cuttings, to weed, and to cover his melon beds, without being brought up to speed on his excellence and his saintliness. He had no more suspicion of his splendid reputation than has a steer from Durham or Surrey whose portrait is published in the *Illustrated London News* with this caption: "The steer that won first prize in the cattle show."

## IX. Enclosure

At the convent Cosette continued to keep silent.

Cosette quite naturally thought she was Jean Valjean's daughter. Besides, not knowing anything, she could not say anything and then, in any case, she would not have said anything. We have just noted that nothing teaches children silence like calamity. Cosette had been through so much that she was afraid of everything, even to open her mouth, even to breathe. A word had so often brought an avalanche down on top of her! She had only just begun to feel safe since she had been in Jean Valjean's hands. She got used to the convent quite quickly. Only, she longed for Catherine, but did not dare say so. One time, though, she said to Jean Valjean: "Father, if I'd known, I'd have brought her along."

In becoming a boarder at the convent, Cosette had to adopt the uniform worn by the students of the house. Jean Valjean obtained permission to keep the clothes she was stripped of. This was the same mourning outfit he had made her wear when she left the Thénardiers' pothouse. It had not yet had much wear. Jean Valjean packed this outfit, plus her woolen stockings and her shoes, with ample camphor and all the aromatics convents abound in, in a little suitcase that he managed to procure himself. He put the suitcase on a chair by his bed and he carried the key to it on him always. "Father," Cosette asked him one day, "what is that box over there, then, that smells so good?"

Father Fauchelevent, apart from the glory we have just recounted and of which he was completely ignorant, was rewarded for his good deed; first, he was glad he'd done it, it made him happy; and then, he had a lot less work to do now he was sharing the load. Last, he really loved tobacco, and he found Monsieur Madeleine's presence made it possible for him to take three times as much tobacco as in the past and with infinitely more relish, since Monsieur Madeleine paid for it.

The nuns did not adopt the name of Ultime; they called Jean Valjean "the other Fauvent."

If those holy old maids had had a fraction of Javert's perceptiveness, they would have wound up noticing that, whenever there was some errand to run outside for the maintenance of the garden, it was always the elder Fauchelevent, the old one, the infirm one, the lame one, who went out, and never the other man; but, either because eyes forever fixed on God don't know how to spy, or because they were, out of preference, busy watching each other, they noticed nothing.

And Jean Valjean did well to keep quiet and not to move. Javert watched the quartier for a good long month or more.

The convent was for Jean Valjean like an island surrounded by sheer cliffs.

Those four walls were now the world for him. He saw enough of the sky from there to be serene and enough of Cosette to be happy.

A very sweet life began for him once more.

He lived with old Fauchelevent in the shed at the bottom of the garden. This shack, built out of rubble and still standing in 1845, consisted, as we have already said, of three rooms, all of which were completely bare. Father Fauchelevent had insisted Monsieur Madeleine have the main room, and he was forced to accept it, for Jean Valjean had resisted in vain. The walls of this room, apart from two nails for hanging up the knee pad and the basket, were adorned only with an example of the royalist paper money of '93[1] stuck on the wall over the mantelpiece. Here is an exact replica:[2]

| × | × | × | × | *Catholic & Royal* | × | × | × | × |
|---|---|---|---|---|---|---|---|---|
| × | | *In the name of the King* | | | | | | × |
| × | | *Negotiable bond of* ten LIVRES | | | | | | × |
| × | | *for objects supplied to the army* | | | | | | × |
| × | | reimbursable in peacetime | | | | | | × |
| × | Series 3 | | * | | No. 10390 | | | × |
| × | | | * | * | *Stofflet.* | | | × |
| × | × | × | × | *Army* | × | × | × | × |

This assignat from La Vendée[3] had been nailed to the wall by the previous gardener, an old member of the Chouan party[4] who had died in the convent and been replaced by Fauchelevent.

Jean Valjean worked all day in the garden and was extremely useful there. He had once been a pruner, after all, and was glad to find himself a gardener again. You will recall that he was full of all kinds of agricultural secrets and recipes for growing things. He put them to good use. Nearly all the trees in the orchard were wildings; he budded them and got them to yield excellent fruit.

Cosette had permission to go and spend an hour each day with him. As the sisters were sad and he was good, the child compared him with them and worshipped the ground he walked on. At the appointed hour she would run to the shed. When she entered this hovel, she filled it with paradise. Jean Valjean flourished and felt his happiness growing from the happiness he gave Cosette. The joy we inspire has this wonderful feature, which is that, far from dimming like any reflection, it comes back to us more radiant. At playtime, Jean Valjean would watch Cosette playing and running around from a distance and he could distinguish her laughter from the laughter of the other girls.

For Cosette now laughed.

Even the way Cosette looked had changed to a certain extent. All gloominess had vanished. Laughter is like sunshine; it chases winter away from the human face.

Cosette was still not pretty, but she had become charming regardless. She had a way of coming out with quite grown-up little notions in her sweet infantile voice.

When playtime was over and Cosette had gone back in, Jean Valjean would watch the windows of her classroom and at night he would get out of bed to watch the windows of the dormitory where she slept.

Besides, God has His ways; the convent, like Cosette, contributed to keeping up and completing the work of the bishop inside Jean Valjean. There is no doubt that one side of virtue leads to pride. There lies a bridge built by the devil. Jean Valjean had perhaps been, without knowing it, fairly close to both that side and that bridge, when Providence threw him into the Petit-Picpus convent. While he had compared himself only to the bishop, he had found himself unworthy and he had stayed humble; but for some little time he had been comparing himself to other men and pride had reared its ugly head. Who knows? He might well have ended up quietly returning to hate.

The convent stopped him on that slippery slope.

This was the second place of captivity he had seen. In his youth, in what had been for him the beginning of life, and then later, still only recently, he had seen another, an appalling and terrible place, whose austerities had always struck him as the iniquity of justice and the crime of the law. Today, after the galleys, he was seeing the cloister and thinking how he had been part of the prison system and was now a spectator, so to speak, of the cloister, and he compared them anxiously in his mind.

Sometimes he would lean on his spade and slowly descend the endless spirals of his thoughts.

He remembered his old companions and how miserable they were: they'd get up at the crack of dawn and work till nightfall; they were scarcely left enough time to shut their eyes; they slept on camp beds where mattresses no more than two thumbs thick were the only ones allowed in rooms that were only heated in the rawest months of the year; they were dressed in hideous red smocks; they were allowed, as a favor, to wear burlap pants in heatwaves and had a scrap of wool to slap on their backs in the coldest days of winter; they only drank wine and only ate meat when they were "on hard labor." They lived without names, designated only by numbers and in some way reduced to mere figures, their eyes lowered, their voices lowered, their hair shorn, under the rod, in shame.

Then his mind reverted to the creatures he now had before his eyes.

These beings, too, lived with their hair shorn, their eyes lowered, their voices lowered, not in shame but in the full force of the world's scorn, their backs not bruised by the rod but their shoulders lacerated by discipline.[5] Their names had also vanished from among men and they only existed now under the most austere appellations. They never ate meat and never drank wine; they were dressed, not in red vests, but in black shrouds made of wool, heavy in summer, light in winter, without being able to take anything off or put anything on, without even being able to resort to cotton clothing or a woolen overcoat, according to the season; and for six months of the year they wore hair shirts that gave them fever. They lived not in rooms heated only in the worst days of winter, but in cells where fires were never lit; they slept not on mattresses only two inches thick but on straw. Last, they were not even allowed to sleep; every night, after a day of toil, as they sank with exhaustion into first sleep, the very moment when they were dozing off, scarcely warming up a little, they had to wake up, get up, and go and pray in the icy dark chapel, with both knees on the stone.

On certain days, every one of these beings took a turn putting in twelve hours at a stretch kneeling on the flagstones or prostrate face down on the ground, arms out on both sides like a cross.

The first lot were men; these were women.

What had these men done? They had stolen, raped, looted, killed, murdered. They were bandits, forgers, poisoners, arsonists, murderers, parricides. What had these women done? They had done nothing.

On one side, armed robbery, fraud, theft, violence, lechery, homicide, every known form of sacrilege, every variety of assault; on the other, one thing only: innocence. Perfect innocence, almost lifted aloft in some mysterious assumption, still tethered to the ground through virtue, already tethered to heaven through holiness.

On one side, the whispered mutual avowal of crimes; on the other, the confession of sins said out loud. And what crimes! And what sins!

On one side, primeval sludge; on the other, an ineffable perfume. On one side, a moral pestilence, kept in custody, penned in under cannon and slowly devouring the plague-addled victims; on the other, a chaste kindling of all souls at the same hearth. There, darkness; here, shadow, but shadow full of flashes of light, and flashes of light full of radiance.

Two places of slavery; but in the first, deliverance is possible, a legal limit is always in sight, and there's always escape. In the second, perpetuity; the only hope, in the extremely distant future, that glimmer of freedom mankind calls death.

In the first, you were chained up in mere chains; in the other, you were chained by your faith.

What emerged from the first? Endless malediction, the gnashing of teeth, hate, a desperate depravity, a cry of rage against human association, utter contempt for heaven. What issued from the second? Benediction and love. And in these two places, so similar and yet so different, these two species of being, so very different, accomplished the same duty, atonement.

Jean Valjean understood perfectly well the atonement involved in the first, personal atonement, atonement for oneself. But he did not understand atonement for others, that suffered by these creatures, blameless and without stain, and he asked himself with a shudder: Atonement for what? What atonement?

A voice in his conscience answered him: the most divine form of human generosity, atonement for others.

Here we will refrain from adding our personal theories, we are merely the narrator, putting ourselves in Jean Valjean's shoes, seeing with his eyes and translating his impressions.

He had before his very eyes the sublime summit of self-abnegation, the highest peak of virtue possible—that innocence that forgives men for their sins and atones in their stead; servitude endured, torture accepted, torment sought out by souls who have not sinned in order to exempt from such torment souls that have faltered; the love of humanity losing itself in the love of God, yet remaining there, distinct and imploring; gentle weak creatures taking on the misery of those who are punished and the smile of those who are rewarded. And he remembered that he had dared to feel sorry for himself!

Often in the middle of the night, he would get up to listen to the grateful chanting of these innocent creatures overwhelmed by austerities, and he felt the blood run cold in his veins to think that those who were justly punished did not raise their voices to the heavens except to blaspheme and that he, miserable bastard, had shaken his fist at God.

One thing was striking and gave him pause for profound thought, like a warning whispered by Providence itself: The walls scaled, fences hurdled, luck tried to the death, the long hard climb uphill, all these same efforts he had made to get out of the other place of atonement, he had made to get into this one here. Was this an emblem of his fate?

This house was a prison, too, and looked horribly like the other abode he had fled, and yet he had never imagined anything remotely like it.

He saw, once more, grates, bolts, iron bars—to guard whom? Angels. These high walls that he had seen around tigers, he saw them once more around sheep.

This was a place of atonement and not of punishment; and yet it was even more austere, more mournful, and more merciless than the other one. These virgins were more savagely beaten down than the convicts. A cold, harsh wind, the wind that had frozen his childhood, swept through that grated, padlocked pit of vultures; an even more bitter and painful blast blew in this cage of doves. Why?

When he thought of these things, everything in him became deeply absorbed in this mystery of sublimeness. In these meditations, pride evaporated.

He circled himself, over and over again; he felt himself to be puny and he wept many times. All that had entered his life in the last six months brought him back to the holy injunctions of the bishop—Cosette, through love, the convent, through humility.

Sometimes, in the evening, at dusk, at the hour when the garden was deserted, he could be seen on his knees in the middle of the path that ran alongside the chapel, in front of the window he had looked in the night he arrived, turned to face the place where he knew that the sister making atonement lay in prostration and in prayer. He prayed, kneeling like this before this sister. It seemed that he did not dare kneel directly before God.

All that surrounded him, the peaceful garden, the fragrant flowers, the children letting out joyful cries, these grave and simple women, the silent cloister, slowly penetrated him, and little by little his soul filled with silence like the cloister, with perfume like the flowers, with peace like the garden, with simplicity like the women, with joy like the children. And then he reflected that it was two houses of God that had taken him in, one after the other, at the two critical moments of his life, the first when all doors had shut in his face and human society had pushed him away, the second at the moment when human society had set off after him again and when jail was once more opening its doors; and that without the first, he would have lapsed into crime again, and without the second, into torment.

His whole heart melted in gratitude and he felt more and more love.

Several years went by this way; Cosette was growing up.

# PART THREE

# MARIUS

# BOOK ONE

# PARIS STUDIED DOWN TO ITS MINUTEST ATOM

## I. PARVULUS[1]

Paris has a boy and the forest has a bird; the bird is called a sparrow and the boy is called a ragamuffin imp, a street urchin: *le gamin.*

Put these two ideas together, the one containing all the heat of a furnace, the other, all the light of dawn, strike these two sparks together—Paris, boyhood—and a small being will flare up as a result. *Homuncio,*[2] as Plautus would say.

This small being is bursting with joy. He doesn't eat every day but he goes to a show every night, if he feels like it. He doesn't have a shirt on his back, or shoes on his feet, or a roof over his head; he's like the flies in the air—they don't have any of that, either. He is somewhere between seven and thirteen years of age, lives in packs, wears his feet out walking, sleeps in the open, wears an old pair of pants of his father's that come down over his heels, an old hat from some other father that comes down over his ears, a single suspender with yellowing edges; he runs around, on the lookout, on the take, killing time; primes pipes, swears like one of the damned, haunts cabarets, knows thieves, is on intimate terms with the streetwalkers, talks slang, sings dirty ditties, and hasn't got a nasty bone in his body. This is because he has a pearl in his soul, innocence, and pearls do not dissolve in mud. As long as man is a child, God would like him to be innocent.

If you were to ask this vast city, "What on earth is that?" it would answer, "That's my boy."

## II. A Few of His Distinguishing Marks

The little tramp—the *gamin de Paris*—is the giant city's dwarf.[1]

Let's not get carried away. This cherub of the gutter[2] does sometimes have a shirt, but then only one; he does sometimes have shoes, but then they don't have soles; he does sometimes have a place to stay, and he loves it, for that is where he finds his mother, but he prefers the street, for that is where he finds his freedom. He has his own games, his own pranks basically fueled by hatred of the bourgeois; his own metaphors—he calls being dead "eating dandelions by the root"; his own occupations, such as hailing cabs, fiacres,[3] letting down carriage steps, collecting tolls for getting people from one side of the street to the other in heavy rains, which he calls "doing the *pont des arts*," crying out the speeches made by the powers that be in favor of the French people, scraping out the gaps between cobblestones; he has his own currency, which consists of all the tiny bits of beaten copper you can find on the public thoroughfare. This curious currency, which goes by the name of *loques,* or tatters, enjoys an invariable and highly regulated exchange rate within this little bohemia of children.

Last, he has his own fauna, which he studiously observes in corners: the ladybug, the death's-head plant louse, the daddy longlegs, a black insect known as "the devil," which has a tail armed with two horns that it twists when it wants to be menacing. He has his fabulous monster[4] that has scales on its belly but is not a lizard, that has pustules on its back but is not a toad, that lives in the holes of old lime kilns and dried-out cesspools, black, hairy, slimy, slithering, now slow, now fast, that does not cry but just looks, and is so terrible no one has ever seen it; he calls this monster "deafy." Looking for deafies among stones is a pleasure of the thrilling kind. Another pleasure is to suddenly lift up a cobblestone and see wood lice. Every part of Paris is famous for the interesting finds you can make there. There are earwigs in the Ursulines depots, there are millipedes at the Panthéon, there are tadpoles in the moats of the Champ de Mars.

As for words, this child is on a par with Talleyrand.[5] He is just as cynical, too, but more honest. He is endowed with an incredible and unpredictable cheerfulness; he stuns the shopkeeper with his fits of laughter. His range goes merrily from high comedy to farce.

A funeral passes. Among those accompanying the dead there is a doctor. "Hey!" cries a gamin. "Since when do doctors lug their work around?"

Another one is in a crowd. A grave-looking man, adorned with spectacles and a bracelet with lucky charms, whips round indignantly: "You little swine! You just pinched my wife's 'waist.'"

"Me, Monsieur! Search me."

### III. He Is Nice

Of an evening, thanks to the few sous he always manages to scrape together for himself, this *homuncio* steps into a theater. In crossing that magic threshold, he is transfigured; he was a guttersnipe, he becomes a cocky Parisian theatergoer. Theaters are like upside-down ships with the hold on top. It is up into this hold that this Artful Dodger piles. The cocky Parisian theatergoer is to the gamin what the moth is to the grub: the same creature taking wing and soaring. All he has to do is be there, with his radiant happiness, with his powerful enthusiasm and joy, with his hands clapping like beating wings, for this cramped, fetid, dark, sordid, insalubrious, awful, abominable hold to turn into paradise—the Gods.

Give a being what is useless and take away from him what is essential and you have the gamin.

The gamin is not without literary intuition. What he tends to go in for, and we say this with the proper dose of regret, is not in the classical taste. He is not, by nature, especially academic. Which is why, to give an example, the popularity of Mademoiselle Mars[1] among this little audience of stormy children was seasoned with a hint of irony. The gamin called her Mademoiselle Mache—lamb's lettuce.

This specimen heckles, jeers, sneers, likes a good brawl, wears a toddler's tatters and the rags of a philosopher, fishes in the sewer, hunts in the cesspool, digs gaiety out of muck, lashes the highways and byways with his verve, sniggers and bites, boos and sings, applauds and hurls abuse, tempers the Hallelujah with Tirralirra-by-the-river, belts out every tune from *De Profundis* to carnival numbers,[2] finds without having to look, knows what he does not know, is spartan to the point of fraud, is mad to the point of wisdom, is lyrical to the point of being foul. Would squat even on Olympus, wallows in dung and comes out of it covered in stars. The *gamin de Paris* is Rabelais[3] as a boy.

He isn't happy with his pants unless they have a fob pocket.

Nothing much fazes him, still less frightens him, he derides superstition, deflates exaggeration, makes a mockery of mysteries, pokes his tongue out at ghosts, knocks people off their high horses, caricatures epic aggrandizement. Not that he's prosaic, far from it; but he swaps the solemn vision for comical fantasies. If Adamastor,[4] the giant, were to pop up in front of him, the gamin would say: "Well, well! A little nipper!"

### IV. He Can Be Useful

Paris begins with the dawdling onlooker and ends with the gamin, two beings that no other town is capable of; the passive acceptance that makes a person happy just to look on, and inexhaustible initiative; Prudhomme and Fouillou.[1]

Paris alone boasts such native fauna. The monarchy begins and ends in the ambulatory onlooker. Anarchy begins and ends in the gamin.

This wan child of the working-class faubourgs of Paris lives and grows, ties himself in knots and "pulls through" in suffering, a thoughtful witness to social realities and human affairs, and he doesn't miss a trick. He believes that he himself is unconcerned; but he is not. He watches, ready to have a laugh; ready for other things, too. Whoever you are, you who go by the name of Prejudice, Abuse, Ignominy, Oppression, Iniquity, Despotism, Injustice, Fanaticism, Tyranny, watch out for the wide-eyed gamin.

This little kid will grow up.

What clay is he made of? Of the first lump of muck that turns up in the gutter. A handful of mud, a breath of air and voilà, Adam. All that is needed is for a god to pass. A god has always passed over the gamin. Fortune plays a hand in this small creature. By that word *fortune* we mean there is an element of luck. Will this pygmy, kneaded in nothing but common dirt, pig ignorant, illiterate, dim-witted, vulgar, crude, grow into an Ionian or a Boeotian?[2] Wait, *currit rota!* The wheel turns. The spirit of Paris, that demon that creates children of chance and men of destiny, unlike the Latin potter, turns the common or garden-variety jug into an amphora.

## V. His Boundaries

The gamin loves the city, he also loves solitude, having something of the sage in him. *Urbis amator,* like Fuscus; *ruris amator,* like Flaccus.[1]

Wandering around musing, in other words dawdling, is a good way to spend time for a philosopher; particularly in that funny, rather ugly semi-rural landscape, with its odd, dual nature, that surrounds certain big cities, notably Paris. To observe the urban outskirts is to observe the amphibian. End of trees, beginning of roofs, end of grass, beginning of pavement, end of furrows, beginning of shops, end of ruts, beginning of passions, end of divine murmuring, beginning of human racket; whence the extraordinary interest.

And whence the seemingly aimless promenades of the thinker, in these rather uninviting places forever branded by passersby with the epithet *sad.*

The person writing these lines was for a long time a prowler of the barrières of Paris and for him that prowling is a source of indelible memories. The bald turf, the rocky paths, the chalk, the limy clay, the rubble, the harsh monotony of fallow land and uncultivated land, the early fruit and vegetable crops of the market gardeners suddenly appearing under cover somewhere, that blend of the wild and the primly bourgeois, the vast deserted recesses where the garrison drums hold noisy lessons, reproducing the stammering staccato of battle, these places that are solitary retreats during the day, death traps at night, the spindly mill turning in the wind, the excavation wheels of the stone quarries, the open-air bars on cemetery corners, the mysterious charm of the great dark walls that cut through vast wastelands flooded with sunlight and full of butterflies—all this drew him.

There is hardly anyone on earth who knows these singular places, Glacière, Cunette, the hideous Grenelle wall riddled with bullet holes, Montparnasse, the Fosse-aux-Loups, the Aubiers on the banks of the Marne, Montsouris, the Tombe-Issoire, the Pierre-Plate de Châtillon,[2] where there is an old exhausted quarry that only serves now to push up mushrooms and is shut off at ground level by a trapdoor of rotten boards. The campagna around Rome is one thing, the suburbs of Paris another; to see nothing in what a horizon offers us but fields, houses, or trees is to stick to the surface, for all aspects of things are God's thoughts. The place where a plain meets a town is always impregnated with some indefinable but penetrating melancholy. Nature and humanity speak to you there at the same time. Local peculiarities flourish.

Anyone who has wandered around as we have through these lonely spots on the fringe of our faubourgs, and that we might lump together as the limbo of Paris, would have glimpsed here and there, dotted about in the most abandoned spots, at the most unexpected moments, behind a scrawny hedge or in the angle of some grimy wall, boisterous groups of children, whey-faced, covered in mud, covered in dust, scruffy, disheveled, playing jacks, crowned with cornflowers. Little as they are, they are all runaways from poor families. Outside on the boulevard is where they can breathe; the suburban fringe belongs to them. That is where they skip school all day, permanently. It is where they innocently belt out their repertoire of dirty songs. It is where they are, or better still, where they exist, far from all eyes, in the delicious May or June sun, kneeling around a hole in the ground, flicking marbles with their thumbs, squabbling over worthless coins, carefree, carried away, unbridled, happy. But as soon as they spot you, they remember they have a trade and that they have to make a living and they offer to sell you an old woolen stocking full of cockchafers or a clump of lilac. These encounters with strange children are one of the charms of the outskirts of Paris, lovely and poignant at the same time.

Sometimes, in the heaps of boys, there are a few little girls—their sisters?—who are almost big girls, skinny, feverish, covered in sunburn, dusted with freckles, with spikes of rye and poppies in their hair, gay, wild-eyed, barefoot. You see them eating cherries in the wheat fields. At night, you hear them laughing. These groups, warmly lit in the full blaze of noon or half-glimpsed at twilight, keep the dreamer busy for a long while and such visions find their way into his dreams.

Paris, center; outskirts, circumference—to these children this is the whole world. They never risk going beyond it. They can no more live out of the atmosphere of Paris than fish can live out of water. For them, there is nothing two leagues past its gates. Ivry, Gentilly, Arcueil, Belleville, Aubervilliers, Ménil-montant, Choisy-le-Roi, Billancourt, Meudon, Issy, Vanves, Sèvres, Puteaux, Neuilly, Gennevilliers, Colombes, Romainville, Chatou, Asnières, Bougival, Nanterre, Enghien, Noisy-le-Sec, Nogent, Gournay, Drancy, Gonesse[3]—this is where the world ends.

## VI. A Bit of History

At the time when the action of this book occurred, which is, after all, virtually contemporary, there was not, as there is today, a police officer on every street corner (an advantage there is no time to discuss here); Paris was crawling with stray children. Statistics show an average of two hundred and sixty homeless children were picked up annually by police on the beat in open terrain, in houses under construction, and under the arches of bridges. One such nest that has remained famous produced "the swallows of the pont d'Arcole."[1] This is, of course, the most disastrous social symptom. All the crimes of the man begin in the straying of the child.

We should except Paris, though. Relatively speaking, and notwithstanding the memories just called to mind, the exception is only fair. Whereas in any other big city a child vagabond means a lost man, whereas almost everywhere the child left to his own devices is practically dedicated and abandoned to a kind of fatal immersion in out-and-out vices that eat away at his honesty and even at his conscience, the *gamin de Paris,* we must insist, no matter how rough and damaged on the surface, is more or less intact on the inside. Something that is wonderful to note, and that bursts out in the splendid probity of our popular revolutions, is that a certain incorruptibility results from ideas that are in the air of Paris the way salt is in the ocean. To breathe Paris preserves the soul.

What we are saying here in no way detracts from the pang you feel every time you run into one of these children who seem to have the cut ties of the broken home floating all around them. In today's civilization, still so incomplete, it is not so unusual to see such breakdowns, with families falling apart in the shadows, parents having little idea of what has become of their children and spilling their guts on the public highway. Hence dark destinies. This is known, for this sad business has led to the coining of a phrase, "to be thrown out on the streets of Paris."

We should just say in passing that such abandonment of children was not discouraged by the erstwhile monarchy. A touch of Egypt and Bohemia in the lower orders accommodated the upper spheres and suited the purposes of the high and mighty. Hate-filled opposition to the education of lower-class children was a dogma. What was the good of "a little learning"? That was the catchcry. Well, the stray child is the corollary of the ignorant child.

Besides, the monarchy sometimes needed children, and when it did, it skimmed the street.

Louis XIV, to go no further back in time, wanted to build a naval fleet.[2] For very good reason—nothing wrong with the idea. But let's just look at the way they went about it. No fleet can exist unless, alongside the sailing ship, which is a plaything of the wind, you have a ship that can go wherever it likes, either by means of oars or by means of steam, in order to tow this sailing ship if need be. In those days, galleys were to the navy what steamers are today. So there had to be galleys; but a galley can only be moved by galley slaves; so there had to be galley slaves. Colbert made sure as many galley slaves as possible were churned out by provincial intendants and the parliaments.[3] The judges were more than happy to oblige. If a man kept his hat on his head before a procession, as the Huguenots did, he was sent to the galleys. If a boy was caught on the street, as long as he was at least fifteen years old and had nowhere to lay his head, he was sent to the galleys. Great reign; great age.

Under Louis XV, children disappeared in Paris, kidnapped by the police for no one knows what mysterious purpose. People whispered in horror of monstrous possibilities involving the king's blood-red baths. Barbier[4] speaks naïvely of these matters. It sometimes happened that the press-gangs, known as the exempt-gangs, when they were short on children, took some that had fathers. The fathers ran after the exempt-gangs in desperation. In such cases the parliament intervened and hanged—who? the exempt-gangs? No. The fathers.

## VII. THE GAMIN WOULD HAVE HIS PLACE IN THE CASTE SYSTEM OF INDIA

The *gaminerie* of Paris—the Parisian order of gamins—is almost a caste. You could say, not everyone can get in.

The word *gamin* was printed for the first time, thereby passing from the vernacular into the language of literature, in 1834. It is in a little work entitled *Claude Gueux*[1] that the word makes its appearance. It created a real scandal. But the word was adopted.

The things that attract esteem for a gamin among his cohorts are very varied. We knew and had dealings with one who was very much respected and very much admired for having seen a man fall from the top of one of the towers of Notre-Dame; another, for having managed to get into a rear courtyard where the statues from the dome of the Invalides had been temporarily deposited and having "swiped" a bit of the lead off one; a third, for having seen a coach tip over; yet another, because he "knew" a soldier who had almost knocked out some bourgeois gent's eye.

This explains that exclamation of the Parisian gamin, a profound epiphenomenon that the vulgar laugh at without understanding: "Hell's bells! Talk about unlucky! To think I still ain't seen anyone falling out of a fiff floor!" (*Haven't* pronounced *"ain't"* and *fifth* pronounced *"fiff."*)

There is such a thing as fine peasant talk and the following is an example: "Father So-and-so, your wife has died of her illness; why didn't you send for a doctor?"

"Why d'yer think, Monsieur? We poor people have t' die fer ourseln." But if all the taunting passivity of the peasant is packed into that expression, all the freethinking anarchy of the cheeky suburban nipper is packed, indubitably, into this other. A man in the cart taking him to the gallows is listening to his confessor. The child of Paris shouts a protest: "He's talking to his sacristy rat. God, what a scaredy-cat!"

A certain boldness in religious matters enlivens the gamin. Being strong-minded is important.

Attending executions constitutes a duty. You point out the guillotine to each other and laugh. You have all kinds of pet names for it: Bottom of the Soup, Crankypants, The Mother in the Blue Yonder (in the sky), The Last Mouthful, etc., etc. So as not to miss anything, you scale walls, hoist yourself up onto balconies, climb trees, hang off railings, cling to chimneys. The gamin is a born roofer just as he is a born sailor. A roof doesn't frighten him any more than a mast. No festival comes near La Grève.[2] Sanson and the abbé Montès[3] are the true stars. You boo the victim to encourage him. Sometimes you admire him. Lacenaire as a gamin saw the awful Dautun die bravely and came out with this expression that was to have quite a future: "I was jealous of him." In the order of gamins, you don't know Voltaire, but you know Papavoine. You put "politicals" in the same basket as murderers. You have traditions based on the last clothes worn by all of them. You know that Tolleron wore a driver's cap, Avril a cap of otter skin, Louvel a round hat, that old Delaporte was bald and bareheaded, that Castaing was all pink and pretty as a rose, that Bories had a romantic goatee, that Jean-Martin kept his braces on, that Lecouffé and his mother were arguing. "Don't fight over spilt milk," one gamin yelled at them. Another gamin, wanting to see Debacker[4] go past and being too little to see anything in the crowd, spotted a lamppost on the quai and started climbing it. A gendarme stationed there scowled at him. "Let me climb up, M'sieur Gendarme," said the gamin. And to soften up the authority figure he added: "I won't fall." "I couldn't care less if you fall or not," answered the gendarme.

In the *gaminerie*, a memorable accident is highly prized. You attain the height of esteem if you manage to cut yourself badly, "to the bone."

The fist is not a bad way to achieve respect, either. One thing the gamin most likes saying is: "I'm as strong as all get-out, I am!" To be left-handed[5] makes you most enviable. To squint is highly rated.

## VIII. In Which You Will Read a Delightful Saying of the King's

In summer, he turns into a frog; and in the evening, at nightfall, down by the bridges of Austerlitz and Iéna, from the top of coal barges and the boats of washerwomen,[1] he plunges headfirst into the Seine—and into all possible infringements of the laws of modesty and of the police. But police officers are on the lookout and there ensues a highly dramatic situation, of the kind that once gave rise to a memorable fraternal cry. This cry, which was famous around 1830, was a strategic warning telegraphed from gamin to gamin; it scans like lines of Homer, with a notation almost as inexpressible as the Eleusinian lamentations of the Panathenaea,[2] and it brings the antique *"Evoe"* to mind. Here's how it goes: "Yoo-hoo! Joker! Yoooo-hooo! There's flatfoots about, there's cops, grab yer gear and beat it, cut through the sewer!"

Sometimes this kid—for that is what this midget likes to go by—can read, sometimes he can write; he can always scrawl. He doesn't hesitate to endow himself, by we know not what mysterious mutual instruction, with all those talents that can be so useful in public life: From 1815 to 1830, he imitated the call of the turkey; from 1830 to 1848, he scrawled pears on walls.[3] One summer evening, Louis-Philippe was coming home on foot and saw a gamin, a tiny little thing knee-high to a grasshopper, sweating away, stretching high up on tiptoe to charcoal in a gigantic pear on one of the pillars of the Neuilly gate; the king, with that easy good nature that he got from Henri IV, helped the little lad, finished the pear for him and gave the boy a gold louis, telling him, "The pear's on that, too."[4] The gamin loves uproar. A certain violent state pleases him. He loathes curés.[5] One day in the rue de l'Université,[6] one of these little rascals was making faces at the porte cochère of no. 69. "What are you doing that to the door for?" a passerby asked. The boy replied: "There's a curé in there." The papal nuncio does, in fact, reside at that address. Yet, whatever the gamin's Voltairean tendencies, if the occasion presents itself to become a choirboy, he may very well take it up, and if he does, he serves perfectly politely at mass. He is like Tantalus[7] when it comes to two overriding ambitions that constantly elude him: to overthrow the government and to patch up his pants.

The gamin at his best is on top of all the police constables of Paris and can always put a name to a face when he meets one. He ticks them off on his fingers. He studies their ways and keeps special tabs on every one of them. He can read the soul of a policeman like an open book and will tell you frankly and without batting an eyelid: "So-and-so is a traitor . . . so-and-so is a nasty piece of work . . . so-and-so is terrific . . . so-and-so is a joke"—all these terms, *traitor, nasty piece of work, terrific, a joke,* have a specific, accepted meaning in his mouth.

"This one thinks he owns the Pont-Neuf[8] and stops *society* strolling along the cornice outside the parapets"; "that one is always pulling a person's ears," and so on, and so forth.

## IX. The Old Soul of Gaul

There was something of this little urchin in Poquelin, son of Les Halles;[1] there was something of him in Beaumarchais.[2] *Gaminerie* is a tonal variation on the Gallic spirit. Mixed with common sense, it occasionally reinforces it, as alcohol fortifies wine. Sometimes it is a defect. Homer goes on and on, we know; and you could say Voltaire plays the gamin—he *gamines*. Camille Desmoulins[3] was from the suburbs. Championnet,[4] who abused miracles, was a child of the streets of Paris; when still very little, he flooded the porticoes of Saint-Jean-de-Beauvais and Saint-Étienne-du-Mont, and he was on such intimate terms with Saint Geneviève's shrine as to order about Saint Januarius's glass vial, causing the blood to suddenly liquefy at will.

The *gamin de Paris* is respectful, ironic, and insolent. He has horrible teeth because he is malnourished and his stomach suffers, but he has beautiful eyes because he has wit. Faced with Jehovah himself, he would hop up the steps of paradise. He is strong on French boxing. There is nothing he could not grow into. He plays in the gutter and rises up out of it in revolt; his effrontery persists in the face of grapeshot; he was once a little guttersnipe, he is now a hero; just like the Theban boy,[5] he shakes the lion's skin; the drummer Barra[6] was a *gamin de Paris;* he yells "Forward, march!" the way the warhorse in the Scriptures[7] says "Ha!" and in a second goes from a waif to a giant.

This child of the quagmire is also a child of the ideal. Just try and measure the range that can go from Molière to Barra.

At the end of the day, and to cut a long story short, the gamin is a specimen that amuses himself because he is unhappy.

## X. Ecce Paris, Ecce Homo[1]

To sum up once more, the *gamin de Paris* today, like the *graeculus* of Rome[2] in days gone by, is the man of the people as a child, with the wrinkles of the old world on his forehead.

The gamin is a national treasure and, at the same time, a disease. A disease that must be cured. How? By light.

Light purifies.

Light enlightens.

All the generous radiance society spreads stems from science, letters, the arts, learning. Make men, make real men. Enlighten them if you want them to warm you. Sooner or later the magnificent matter of universal education will come up with the irresistible authority of absolute truth; and when it does, those that rule under the watchful eye of the French ideal of enlightenment will have to make the following choice: the children of France or the street urchins of Paris; flames in the light of day or will-o'-the-wisps in the dark.

The gamin embodies Paris and Paris embodies the world.

For Paris is what it all adds up to. Paris is the ceiling over the human race. This whole prodigious city is a condensation of dead customs and creeds and living customs and creeds. Whoever sees Paris feels like they have seen the hidden side of the whole of history with the sky and the constellations in the gaps in between. Paris has its Capitol, the Hôtel de Ville; a Parthenon, Notre-Dame; an Aventine Hill, the faubourg Saint-Antoine; an Asinarium, the Sorbonne; a Pantheon, the Panthéon;[3] a Via Sacra, the boulevard des Italiens; a Tower of the Winds, public opinion, which has replaced the Gemoniae with public ridicule. Its majordomo is the vulgar dandy, its *transteverino* is the working-class suburbanite, its native bearer is the Les Halles market porter, its *lazzarone* is the underworld, its cockney is the fop. Everything found elsewhere is found in Paris. The fishwife of Dumarsais could hold her own with Euripides' herb-hawker, the discus thrower Vejanus is resurrected in Forioso the tightrope walker, Therapontigonus Miles would go arm in arm with the grenadier Vadeboncoeur, Damasippus the junk dealer would be happy among the curiosity shops, Vincennes would get stuck into Socrates, just as the Agora would put Diderot behind bars, Grimod de la Reynière came up with roast beef with Yorkshire pudding just the way Curtullis invented roast hedgehog; we see popping up once more under the Arc de Triomphe at L'Étoile the same trapeze that is in Plautus, the sword-eater of the Poecilium encountered by Apuleius is the saber-swallower on the Pont-Neuf, Rameau's nephew and Curculion the parasite[4] are a perfect match, Ergasilus would get himself introduced into Cambacérès's circle by d'Aigrefeuille; the four muscadins of Rome, Alcesimarchus, Phoedromus, Diabolus, and Argyrippe, go down to the Courtille in Labatut's post chaise; Aulus Gellius did not linger in front of Congrio any longer than Charles Nodier in front of Punch and Judy; Marton is not a tigress, but Pardalisca was not a dragon, either; Pantolabus the buffoon sends up Nomentanus the high roller at the Café Anglais,[5] Hermogenus is a tenor on the Champs-Élysées and, around him, Thrasius the beggar, decked out as Bobèche, the Empire theater clown lingering on in the Restoration, passes the hat around; the pest who buttonholes you in the Tuileries makes you repeat Thesprion's remark, two thousand years down the track: *Quis properantem me prehendit pallio?*[6] the wine of Suresnes parodies the wine of Alba, and Désaugier's red rim matches Balatron's balloon glass; the rain at night in Père-Lachaise gives off the same sheen as the Esquilies, and the pauper's grave leased for five years is the equivalent of the hired coffin of the slave.

Try and find something Paris does not have. Trophonius's vat holds nothing not found in Mesmer's tub; Ergaphilas is resurrected in Cagliostro; the Brahmin Vasaphanta is incarnated in the comte de Saint-Germain; Saint-Médard Cemetery supplies miracles every bit as good as those of the Umumiya mosque of Damascus.

Paris has an Aesop and it is Mayeux, and a Canidia and it is Mademoiselle Lenormand,[7] the fortune-teller. It takes fright like Delphos at the blinding realities of vision; it rocks tables around at séances[8] just as Dodona did using tripods. It puts a grisette on the throne[9] just as Rome did a courtesan; and, all things considered, if Louis XV was worse than Claudius, Madame Du Barry was better than Messalina.[10] Paris combines Greek nudity, Jewish rancor, and Gascon jeering and comes up with an unheard-of character, who is real enough; indeed, we have rubbed shoulders with him. He is a blend of Diogenes, Job, and Paillasse, the clown, dresses a specter in old numbers of the *Constitutionnel* and does a Chodruc Duclos.

Though Plutarch says "the tyrant hardly ever ages," Rome, under Sulla as under Domitian, resigned itself and happily added water to its wine. The Tiber turned into a Lethe, if we are to believe the somewhat doctrinaire praise Varus Vibiscus heaped on it: *Contra Gracchos Tiberim habemus. Bibere Tiberum, id est seditionem oblivisci.*[11] Paris drinks a million liters of water a day, but that does not stop it from sounding the call to arms and ringing the tocsin on occasion.

Apart from that, Paris is easygoing. It regally accepts everything, and it doesn't make trouble when it comes to Venus. Its Callipygian is Hottentot; as long as it is laughing, it will grant amnesty: Ugliness cheers it up, deformity has it in stitches, vice entertains it; be funny and you can get away with murder. Even hypocrisy, the ultimate cynicism, does not put it off; it is so literary that it won't hold its nose when faced by Basilius, and it is no more scandalized by Tartuffe's posturing than Horace was shocked by Priapus' "hiccups."[12] No feature of the universal face is lacking in Paris's profile. The bal Mabille may not be the Polyhymnian dance on the Janiculum, but the toilet scalper devours the strumpet there with her eyes exactly the way the procuress Staphyla eyed the virgin Planesium. The barrière du Combat may not be a Coliseum, but they are as ferocious there as if Caesar were looking on. The Syrian hostess is more graceful than mother Saguet, but if Virgil haunted the Roman watering holes, David d'Angers, Balzac, and Charlet[13] have sat down in the greasy spoons of Paris. Paris reigns supreme. Geniuses blaze away there, red tails prosper. Adonaïs passes through on his twelve-wheeled chariot of thunder and lightning; Silenus makes his entrance on his donkey. For Silenus, read Ramponneau.

Paris is synonymous with the cosmos. Paris is Athens, Rome, Sybaris,

Jerusalem, Pantin. All civilizations are there in condensed form—and all the barbarisms with them. Paris would be really furious if it didn't have a guillotine.

A bit of a place de Grève is a good thing. What would this whole endless feast be without such seasoning? Our laws have wisely provided for it, and thanks to them, the blade drips over the Mardi Gras.

## XI. RAILING, REIGNING

Paris knows no bounds. No other city has enjoyed the kind of domination that sometimes scoffs at those it subjugates. "To please you, O Athenians!" cried Alexander.[1] Paris does more than lay down the law, it dictates the fashion; Paris does more than dictate the fashion, it lays down the routine. Paris can be stupid if it sees fit; it sometimes offers itself that luxury—in which case, the world is stupid with it. Paris wakes up, rubs its eyes, and says: "What an idiot I am!" and bursts out laughing in the face of the human race. What a wonderful town! How strange that such grandiosity and such burlesque get on so well together, that all the majesty is not ruffled by all the parody, and that the same mouth that blows the bugle of the Last Judgment today can blow the fife tomorrow! Paris has inimitable good cheer. Its gaiety is like lightning and its farce holds a scepter. Its hurricanes sometimes blow up from a grimace. Its explosions, its bad days, its masterpieces, its wonders, its epics spread to the ends of the earth—and so do its cock-and-bull skits. Its laugh is the mouth of a volcano that spatters the whole world. Its wisecracks are flying sparks. It imposes its caricature on the people as much as its ideals; the most noble monuments of human civilization accept its sarcastic comments and lend their eternity to its risqué remarks. It is superb; it has a wondrous Bastille Day that sets the entire globe free; it sees to it that all the nations take the Tennis Court Oath;[2] its night of August 4[3] dissolves a thousand years of feudalism in three hours; it makes its logic the muscle of universal will; it proliferates in all forms of the sublime; it fills with its light Washington, Kościuszko, Bolívar, Botzaris, Riego, Bem, Manin, López, John Brown, Garibaldi;[4] it is everywhere that the future flares up, in Boston in 1779, on the isle of Léon in 1820, in Pesth in 1848, in Palermo in 1860;[5] it whispers that potent watchword *Liberty* in the ear of the American Abolitionist gathered below Harper's Ferry, and in the ear of the patriots of Ancona assembled in the dark at the Archi, outside Gozzi Inn, along the seafront; it inspires Canaris; it inspires Quiroga; it inspires Pisicane; it beams greatness over the globe; it is by going where its breath drives them that Byron dies at Missolonghi[6] and Mazet dies in Barcelona;[7] it is a rostrum under Mirabeau's feet and a crater under the feet of Robespierre;[8] its books, its theater, its art, its science, its literature, its philosophy, are the manuals of the whole human race; it has Pascal, Régnier, Corneille, Descartes, Rosseau, Voltaire, for every moment,

Molière[9] for every age; it causes its language to be spoken by the world's mouth and that language becomes the Word; it sets up the idea of Progress in all minds; the dogmas of liberation that it forges are for whole generations bedside swords, and it is with the soul of its thinkers and its poets that all the heroes of all the peoples of the world have been made since 1789. But this does not prevent it from playing the gamin, for this huge genius that we call Paris, even while transfiguring the world by its light, draws Bouginier's nose in charcoal on the wall of Theseus' temple and scrawls *Crédéville is a thief*[10] on the Pyramids.

Paris always bares its teeth; when it's not rousing, it's laughing.

Such is Paris. The smoke from its rooftops is the ideas of the universe. A pile of mud or stones, if you like—but, above all else, a moral entity. It is more than great, it is immense. Why? Because it dares.

To dare—progress comes at this price.

All the sublime conquests are more or less the rewards of daring. For the Revolution to happen, it is not enough for Montesquieu to see it coming, for Diderot to preach it, for Beaumarchais to announce it, for Condorcet to plan it, for Arouet to pave the way for it, for Rousseau to premeditate it. Danton[11] has to dare it.

The cry, "Daring!" is a *fiat lux*.[12] The onward march of the human race requires that proud lessons in courage sit permanently on the peaks. Daring deeds dazzle history and are guiding lights for mankind. Dawn dares when it rises. To attempt, to brave, to persist, to persevere, to be true to oneself, to tackle destiny in hand-to-hand combat, to flummox catastrophe by fearlessness before it, to now confront unjust power, now deride intoxicated victory, to hold steady, to stand firm—that is the example the people need, and the light that galvanizes them. The same formidable lightning flashes from the torch of Prometheus to Cambronne's stunted pipe.[13]

## XII. THE FUTURE LATENT IN THE PEOPLE

As for the people of Paris, the grown man always remains, at heart, a gamin. To paint the portrait of the child is to paint the portrait of the city, and it is for this reason that we have studied the eagle in this candid little sparrow.

It is especially in the faubourgs, we must insist, that the Parisian race appears. This is where the thoroughbred is; this is where the true features of the breed are to be found; this is where the people work and suffer, and this suffering and work are the two faces of the man. The place is teeming with heaps of unknown beings, the strangest specimens from the stevedore of La Rapée to the knacker of Montfaucon. *Fex urbis*, cries Cicero;[1] *mob*, adds Burke,[2] indignant. Riffraff, mob, rabble—those words are easily said. But so be it. What does it matter? What do I care if they go about barefoot? Too bad if they can't read. Are you going to abandon them for that? Are you going to turn their distress into a curse? Can't the light penetrate the teeming masses? Let's get back to that cry: Let there be light! And let's stick to it! Light! Light! Who knows if these opaque walls won't become transparent? Aren't revolutions transfigurations? Off you go, philosophers—teach, enlighten, fire up, think out loud, speak out loud, go on joyful romps in broad daylight, fraternize in public places, bring glad tidings, spray alphabets lavishly all over the place, proclaim rights, sing Marseillaises, sow enthusiasm, rip green branches off the oaks. Whip up ideas into a whirlwind. The hordes can be made sublime. Let's learn how to use this vast blaze of principles and virtues that crackles and flames out and occasionally sputters. These bare feet, these bare arms, these rags, this ignorance, this abjectness, this darkness, can be put to work in the conquest of the ideal. Look through the people and you will see the truth. This vile sand that you trample beneath your feet, throw it into the furnace, and if it melts there and boils, it will become sparkling crystal. And it is thanks to this that Galileo and Newton will discover the stars.

## XIII. PETIT-GAVROCHE

About eight or nine years[1] after the events recounted in the second part of this story, people noticed, on the boulevard du Temple and in the area around the Château-d'Eau, a boy of eleven or twelve who would have matched the perfect gamin as sketched above if only, despite the laughter of his age that was on his lips, his heart had not been absolutely dark and empty. This child was indeed decked out in a pair of men's trousers, but he did not get these from his father, and a woman's camisole, but he did not get that from his mother. Perfect strangers had dressed him in rags out of charity. And yet he did have a father and a mother. But his father never gave him a thought and his mother did not love him. Of all the children with fathers and mothers, he was one of those who most deserve pity, for they are actually orphans.

This boy never felt as good as when he was on the streets. The pavement was not as hard to him as his mother's heart.

His parents had thrust him at life with a good swift kick in the pants. He had quite simply taken wing. He was a boisterous, wan, agile, bright, cocky boy, with a lively yet sickly look. He came and went, sang, played pitch and toss, scratched about in the gutter, did a bit of stealing—only, like cats and sparrows, gaily—laughed when people called him a little scallywag, got cross when people called him a lout. He had no roof over his head, no bread, no fire, no love, but he was jubilant because he was free.

When these poor beings have grown into men, the millstone of the social order almost always catches up with them and grinds them to a pulp, but while they are still children, they escape, being little. The tiniest hole saves them.

Yet, as abandoned as this child was, every two or three months or so he would say: "Hey, I think I'll go and see Maman!" He would then quit the boulevard, the Cirque, the Porte Saint-Martin,[2] and duck down to the quais, cross over the bridges, reach the faubourgs, get as far as La Salpêtrière, and arrive—where? Precisely at that double no. 50–52 that the reader is familiar with—the Gorbeau slum.

In those days, the slum at 50–52, normally deserted and permanently decorated with the sign ROOMS TO LET, found itself in the rare situation of being occupied by several individuals who, as always happens in Paris, what is more, bore no connection and no relationship to each other. All belonged to that indigent class that starts with the petit bourgeois struggling to make ends meet, and keeps spiraling down all the rungs of poverty to the very dregs of society, right down to the two specimens in whom all the material things of civilization end—the sewer worker who sweeps up the muck and the rag-and-bone merchant who picks through the trash.

The "chief tenant" from the days of Jean Valjean had died and been replaced by another woman exactly the same. I can't remember which philosopher it was who said: There is never any shortage of old women.

This new old woman was called Madame Burgon and there was nothing remarkable about her life except for a dynasty of three parrots which had successively ruled her heart.

The most wretched of those who lived in the slum were a family of four, father, mother, and two girls already fairly grown up, all four sleeping in the same garret, one of those cells we have already discussed.

This family did not stand out in any way at first except by its extreme destitution; in renting the room, the father had said his name was Jondrette. Some time after moving in, a process that looked strangely like "nothing at all moving in," to borrow the memorable expression of the chief tenant, this Jondrette had told the woman, who, like her predecessor, acted as concierge at the same time and swept the stairs: "Mother So-and-so, if anyone happens to turn up and asks for a Pole or an Italian, or maybe a Spaniard, that'll be me."

This family was the family of the cheeky little barefoot tramp. Whenever he went there, he was greeted by poverty, distress, and, sadder still, never a smile; cold hearth, cold hearts. Whenever he stepped inside, they would ask him: "Where the hell've you come from?" He would answer: "The street." Whenever he turned to go, they would ask him: "Where the hell do you think you're going?" He would answer: "The street." His mother would say to him: "What the hell'd you come here for?"

The boy lived in this lack of affection like pale grass that crops up in cellars. He did not suffer by being in this situation and he did not blame anybody. He had no idea what a father and mother should be like.

Besides, his mother loved his sisters.

We forgot to say that on the boulevard du Temple, the boy was known as Petit-Gavroche. Why did he call himself Gavroche—meaning urchin? Probably because his father called himself Jondrette.

To cut ties seems to be an instinct with certain dirt-poor families.

The room the Jondrettes lived in at the Gorbeau slum was the last one at the end of the corridor. The cell next door was occupied by a very poor young man named Monsieur Marius.

Let's see who Monsieur Marius was.

# BOOK TWO

# THE GRAND BOURGEOIS

## I. NINETY YEARS OLD AND ALL THIRTY-TWO TEETH

In the rue Boucherat, rue de Normandie, and rue de Saintonge, there are still a few old residents around who remember a gentleman called Monsieur Gillenormand and who speak of him favorably. This gentleman was already old when they were young. For those who look with melancholy at that vague swarming of shadows that we call the past, this silhouette has not yet entirely vanished from the labyrinth of streets around the Temple,[1] to which, under Louis XIV, the names of all the provinces of France were attached, just as in our day the streets of the new Tivoli quartier[2] have been given the names of all the capitals of Europe—a progression, let it be said in passing, in which progress is visible.

Monsieur Gillenormand, who was as alive as it was possible to be in 1831, was one of those men who have become a curiosity solely because they have lived a long while, and who are odd because once upon a time they looked like everyone else and now they don't look like anyone. He was a peculiar old bird and a genuine specimen from another age, a true and complete bourgeois,[3] a trifle haughty, from the eighteenth century, wearing his good old bourgeois-ness as marquises wear their marquisates. He was past ninety, walked tall, spoke loudly, saw clearly, knocked back his drink, ate, slept, and snored. He had every one of his thirty-two teeth and he wore glasses only to read. He was the amorous kind, although he maintained that he had definitely and completely given up women for over ten years. He could "no longer please" was how he put it; he did not add, "I'm too old" but, "I'm too poor." He would say: "If only I weren't ruined, ha!" All he had left, in fact, was an income of around fifteen thousand livres. His dream was to come by some windfall of an inheritance and to have a hundred thousand francs in income in order to have mistresses. He did not belong, as we see, to that variety of malingering octogenarians who, like Monsieur de Voltaire, have been dying their whole lives; his was not the longevity of a chipped plate—this randy old blade had always been in the pink of health. He was superficial, quick, hot-tempered. He would blow his stack at the slightest provocation, most often completely inappropriately. If anyone contradicted him, he would raise his stick; he beat people just as they did in the *grand siècle*. He had a daughter over fifty years old, unmarried, whom he thrashed whenever he got into a rage and whom he would happily have whipped. For him, she was about eight years old. He abused his servants with gusto and would say: "Ah, vermin!" One of his favorite curses was: *"Par la pantoufloche de la pantouflochade!"* Something like: "By the hair on my chinny-chin-chin!" In some respects he was curiously unflappable; he had himself shaved every day, for instance, by a barber who had once been insane and who couldn't stand Monsieur Gillenormand, being furiously jealous on account of his wife, a pretty tease of a woman and a barber herself. Monsieur Gillenormand admired his own discernment in all things and declared himself to be most sagacious. One of his favorite sayings was: "I do, in all honesty, have some perspicacity; I can tell, when a flea bites me, what woman it comes from." The words he most often uttered were *a sensible fellow* and *Nature.*[4] He did not use the latter in its general sense according to the meaning our age has assigned to it. But he would work it in his own way into his little fireside spoofs: "Nature," he would say, "offers civilization even the most hilariously barbaric specimens, so that it may have a bit of everything. Europe has samples from Asia and Africa, but in a smaller format. The cat is a drawing-room tiger, the lizard a pocket-size crocodile. The Opéra *danseuses* are rose-pink cannibals.[5] They don't eat men, they bleed them dry. Or, rather, those little enchantresses turn them into oysters and swallow them whole. The Caribbeans[6] leave nothing but the bones, the dancers leave nothing but the shells. Such are our customs. We don't devour, we gnaw; we don't exterminate, we claw to death."

## II. LIKE MASTER, LIKE ABODE

He lived in the Marais, rue des Filles-du-Calvaire, no. 6.

The house was his. This house has been torn down and rebuilt since and the number has probably changed in these numbering revolutions the streets of Paris undergo. He occupied an old and vast apartment on the first floor, between the street and the gardens, furnished right up to the ceilings with huge Gobelin and Beauvais tapestries representing pastoral scenes; the subjects on the ceilings and the wainscoting were repeated in miniature on the armchairs. He wrapped his bed round with a vast paravent in Coromandel lacquer that had nine panels. Long billowing curtains hung at the casement windows in great broken folds that were truly magnificent. The garden immediately below his windows was reached via the corner window by means of a flight of stairs of twelve or fifteen steps that the good old blade ran up and down most blithely. As well as a library next to his bedroom, he had a boudoir[1] he was very much attached to, a real rake's cubbyhole, which featured a magnificent straw wallhanging with a pattern of fleurs-de-lis and flowers made in the galleys of Louis XIV and commissioned from his galley slaves by Monsieur de Vivonne[2] for his mistress. Monsieur Gillenormand had inherited it from a ferocious great-aunt on his mother's side who was a hundred when she died. He had had two wives. His manners steered a course between the man of the court he had never been and the man of the robe[3] he might have been. He was chirpy and gentle when he wanted to be. When he was young, he had been one of those men who are always betrayed by their wives but never by their mistresses because they are at once the most dismal husbands and the most wonderful lovers in the world. When it came to painting, he was a connoisseur. In his room he had a wonderful portrait of someone-or-other by Jordaens,[4] painted with great big bold brushstrokes and a maze of detail all jumbled up seemingly at random. Monsieur Gillenormand's garb was not the attire of Louis XV, or even the attire of Louis XVI; it was the flamboyant getup of the Incroyables,[5] those young dandy reactionaries of the Directoire. He'd thought of himself as quite young till then and had followed the fashions. His coat was made of a light fabric, had wide lapels and a long swallowtail and big steel buttons. Add to this, short breeches and shoes with buckles. He always stuck his hands in his fob pockets. He would say with authority: "The French Revolution was a bunch of rotters."

## III. LUC-ESPRIT

One night at the Opéra when he was sixteen, he had had the honor of being ogled by two beauties at the same time, both then ripe and celebrated and sung by Voltaire—La Camargo and La Sallé.[1] Caught in the crossfire, he had beat a heroic retreat toward a little dancing girl named Nahenry, who was sixteen like him, as inscrutable as a cat, and with whom he was in love. The reminiscences spilled out of him. He would cry: "She was so pretty, that Guimard[2]-Guimardini-Guimardinette, the last time I saw her at Longchamp,[3] bursting with barely restrained feelings, with her garish turquoise baubles and her dress the color of arrivistes, waving her muff around!" In his adolescence he had sported a jacket made of light wool fabric known as nain Londrin, which he never tired of talking about, effusively. "I dressed like a Turk of the Levantine Levant," he would say. Madame de Boufflers,[4] having stumbled across him by chance when he was twenty, had described him as "a charming madman."

He was scandalized by all the names he saw in politics and in power, finding them crass and bourgeois. He read the papers, "the new newspapers, the gazettes," as he would say, choking with fits of laughter. "Oh!" he would say. "Who are these people? Corbière! Humann! Casimir Périer!⁵ That's your minister for you. Imagine this in the paper: Monsieur Gillenormand, minister! What a joke that would be. But then again, they're so stupid, it'd go over!" He cheerfully called all things by their true names, proper or improper, and did not hold back in front of women. He would come out with all manner of crude, obscene, and filthy remarks with wondrous calm and an unflappable air of elegance. It was the offhandedness of his century. Interesting that those days of euphemism in verse were the days of bluntness in prose. His godfather had predicted that he would be a man of genius and had given him these two momentous Christian names: Luc-Esprit.⁶

## IV. An Aspiring Centenarian

He had won prizes in his childhood at the college in Moulins, where he was born, and had been handed those prizes by the duc de Nivernais, whom he called the duc de Nevers. Neither the Convention nor the death of Louis XVI, nor Napoléon, nor the return of the Bourbons—nothing had been able to erase the memory of this crowning achievement. The duc de Nevers¹ was for him the great figure of the age. "What a charming grand seigneur," he'd say, "and he looked so distinguished in his blue sash."²

In the eyes of Monsieur Gillenormand, Catherine II³ had atoned for the crime of partitioning Poland by buying the secret of the gold elixir from Bestuchef for three thousand rubles. Over this, he would grow animated. "The gold elixir," he would shout, "Bestuchef's yellow dye, Général Lamotte's drops,⁴ were, in the eighteenth century, one louis for a half-ounce vial, the great remedy for the catastrophes of love, the panacea against Venus. Louis XV sent two hundred vials of it to the pope." He would have been extremely aggravated, in a real flap, if you'd told him that the gold elixir was nothing more than iron perchlorate.

Monsieur Gillenormand adored the Bourbons and held 1789 in horror; he never tired of recounting how he had saved himself in the Terror and how much gaiety and wit he had needed not to get his head lopped off. If any young man dared sing the praises of the Republic in front of him, he would go blue in the face and practically keel over with apoplexy.

Sometimes he would allude to his ninety years and say: "I do hope I won't see ninety-three twice." At other times he let people know he intended to live to a hundred.

## V. BASQUE AND NICOLETTE

He had his theories. This is one: "When a man loves women with a passion, and he has a wife of his own he doesn't think much of—ugly, grumpy, legitimate, full of her so-called rights, sitting like a hawk on the Civil Code and jealous whenever the occasion arises—there is only one way he can extricate himself and have a bit of peace and that is to let his wife hold the purse strings. This abdication makes him a free man. The wife then has something to keep herself occupied, becomes crazy about handling cash, stains her fingers green in the process, takes on the disciplining of the sharecroppers and the breaking in of the farmers, hauls in attorneys, presides over notaries, harangues scriveners, visits pettifoggers, follows lawsuits, draws up leases, dictates contracts, feels herself supreme, sells, buys, regulates, wheels and deals, promises and compromises, binds and resiles, cedes, concedes, and retrocedes, arranges, disarranges, hoards and squanders; she makes silly mistakes, that magisterial and personal pleasure, and this consoles her. While her husband scorns her, she has the satisfaction of ruining her husband." Monsieur Gillenormand had applied this theory in practice and it had become the story of his life. His wife, the second one, had managed his fortune in such a way that all that was left to Monsieur Gillenormand, when one fine day he found himself a widower, was just enough to live on, and that, only by turning virtually the whole amount into an annuity,[1] fifteen thousand francs in income, three quarters of which would expire with him. He had not hesitated, so little was he concerned with leaving an inheritance. Besides, he had seen for himself that personal assets had their ups and downs, turning, for example, into "national property"[2] and being confiscated; he had witnessed the vicissitudes of the *tiers consolidé*,[3] the consolidated third policy of 1797, and he did not have much faith in the ledger. "It reeks of the rue Quincampoix, all that!" he reckoned. His house in the rue des Filles-du-Calvaire, as we said, belonged to him. He had two servants, "a male and a female." Whenever a domestic entered his service, he would rebaptize them. He called the men after their original province: Nimois, Comtois, Poitevin, Picard.[4] His last valet was a fat, burnt-out, wheezy man of fifty-five, incapable of running twenty feet, but, because he was born in Bayonne, Monsieur Gillenormand called him Basque.[5] As for female servants, in his house all of them were called Nicolette—even La Magnon, whom we will hear more about later. One day an arrogant cook, a *cordon bleu*,[6] of the noble race of concierges, presented herself. "How much do you hope to earn a month in wages?" Monsieur Gillenormand asked her. "Thirty francs." "What's your name?" "Olympie." "You will be paid fifty francs and you will be called Nicolette."

## VI. In Which We Catch a Glimpse of La Magnon and Her Two Little Boys

With Monsieur Gillenormand pain was translated as rage; despair made him furious. He had every prejudice and took every possible liberty. One of the things he boasted of to buoy himself and that gave him intimate satisfaction was, as we have just indicated, having remained a young blade and passing emphatically for one. He called this having "a right royal reputation." This right royal reputation occasionally attracted some strange godsends. One day someone left him a wicker hamper, like an oyster basket, with a big newborn baby boy in it, duly swaddled in baby blankets and bawling his head off. A servant girl that he had sent packing six months previously claimed the baby was his. Monsieur Gillenormand was at the time eighty-four if he was a day. Indignation and clamor all around. Just who did that brazen hussy think would believe that? What gall! What outrageous calumny! Monsieur Gillenormand, however, was not the least bit upset. He gazed at the blanketed bundle with the amiable smile of a man flattered by such calumny and said for all to hear: "Well, what? What is it? What's the matter? What can the matter be? You seem mightily impressed—like true ignoramuses, I might add. Monsieur le duc d'Angoulême,[1] one of his majesty Charles IX's bastards, got married when he was eighty-five to a ninny of fifteen; when Monsieur Virginal, marquis d'Alluye, brother of the cardinal de Sourdis, archbishop of Bordeaux, was eighty-three, he had a son with a chambermaid attached to President Jacquin's wife, a real love child who became a knight of Malta[2] and a knighted councillor of state; one of the great men of the century, the abbé Taranbaud, is the son of a man who was eighty-seven years old at the time. These sorts of things are nothing if not normal. And what about the Bible! I swear on it that this little fellow is not mine. Look after him. He can't help it." This behavior was most debonair. The hussy in question, the one who called herself Magnon, sent him a second bundle the following year. That one was a boy, too. This time, Monsieur Gillenormand capitulated. He handed the two brats back to the mother, committed himself to paying eighty francs a month for their upkeep on condition that said mother did not try that one again. He added: "I want the mother to treat them well. I'll pop in and check on them from time to time." And he was as good as his word.

He had a brother who was a priest and who, after having been the rector of the Académie de Poitiers, had died at the age of seventy-nine. "He died young on me," he said. This brother, who has all but disappeared from memory, was a peaceable skinflint who, being a priest, felt obliged to give alms to any poor he happened to come across, but he only ever gave them coins that were out of commission, thereby finding the way to hell by the path to paradise. As for

Monsieur Gillenormand the elder, he did not barter when it came to giving alms and gave willingly and generously. He was benevolent, brusque, charitable, and if he had been rich, he would have tended to the lavish. He wanted everything that he had anything to do with to be done on a grand scale, even practical jokes. One day, having been swindled in a vulgar and patently obvious manner by a businessman in an inheritance matter, he let fly with this solemn exclamation: "Lord! Talk about dirty tricks! I'm appalled by such petty theft. Everything has gone downhill in this century, even the scoundrels. Heavens! That's no way to fleece a man of my stature. I've been robbed like a man in the woods, but pathetically robbed. *Sylvae sint consule dignae!*"[3]

He had had, as we said, two wives; from the first, a daughter who remained unmarried and from the second, another daughter who had died at around thirty years of age and who had married out of love or chance or something of the sort a soldier of fortune[4] who had served in the armies of the Republic and the Empire, had earned the cross at Austerlitz and been made colonel at Waterloo. "He is the disgrace of the family," said the old bourgeois. He took a lot of snuff and had a particularly graceful way of dusting off his lace ruffle with the back of his hand. He did not much believe in God.

## VII. Golden Rule: Only Receive Visitors in the Evening

And that is about it for Monsieur Luc-Esprit Gillenormand, who had not lost any of his hair, which was more gray than white and was always worn dog-ear style.[1] In short, and all in all, he was venerable. Very eighteenth century: frivolous and grand.

In the early years of the Restoration, Monsieur Gillenormand, who was still young at the time, being only seventy-four in 1814, lived in the faubourg Saint-Germain, rue Servandoni, near Saint-Sulpice. He had only retired to the Marais[2] after withdrawing from society, well after he turned eighty.

In withdrawing from the world, he had immured himself in his habits. The main one, which was immutable, was to keep his door shut during the day and to only ever receive in the evening, no matter what the business. He dined at five o'clock, then his door was thrown open. This was the fashion of his century and he was not about to budge from it. "Daytime is for the rabble," he would say, "and merits only a closed shutter. Everybody who is anybody turns on their wit when the firmament turns on its stars." And he barricaded himself away from everybody, the king included, if it came to that. The old elegant way of his day.

## VIII. Two Do Not Make a Pair

As for Monsieur Gillenormand's two daughters, whom we have just mentioned, they were born ten years apart. As children they had not resembled each other much at all and were as little like sisters as it is possible to be, either in character or in feature. The younger one was a charming soul attracted by all that is bright, interested in flowers, poetry, and music, off with the fairies in glorious places, enthusiastic, ethereal, engaged since childhood to some vague heroic figure in an ideal world. The elder one also had her dreamboat; she saw a purveyor of some kind written in the skies, some good fat munitions contractor who was filthy rich, a husband who was splendidly stupid, a million francs made man, or else a prefect; prefecture receptions, an antechamber usher with a chain around his neck, official balls, speeches at the *mairie,* being Madame la préfète, the prefect's wife—all this whirled around in her imagination. The two sisters thus lost themselves, each in her own dream, in the days when they were young girls. They both had wings, one the wings of an angel, the other of a goose.

No ambition is fully realized, not in this world, at least. There is no heaven on earth in the age in which we live. The younger one had married the man of her dreams, but she had died. The elder one had not married.

At the point at which she makes her entrance in the story we are telling, she was a pious old biddy, an incombustible prude, one of the sharpest beaks and dullest minds you could come across. A characteristic detail: Outside her immediate family, no one had ever known her first name. She was called Mademoiselle Gillenormand the elder.

When it came to cant, Mademoiselle Gillenormand could have held her own against a governess. She was modesty taken to a bleak extreme. She had one awful memory in her life: One day, a man had seen her garter.

Age had only intensfied this merciless modesty. Her bodice was never opaque enough, never climbed high enough. She multiplied hooks and pins where nobody would have thought of looking. The peculiar thing about prudery is that, the less the fortress is under threat, the more it puts sentries around.

And yet, explain if you can these age-old mysteries of innocence, she let herself be kissed without displeasure by an officer of the lancers who happened to be her great-nephew and whose name was Théodule.

Despite this favored lancer, the label *prude,* under which we have classified her, suited her to a tee. Mademoiselle Gillenormand was a kind of crepuscular soul. Prudery is half virtue and half vice.

To prudery she added bigotry,[1] the perfect double. She was of the Confraternity of the Virgin,[2] wore a white veil on certain feast days, mumbled special prayers, revered the Holy Blood, venerated the Sacred Heart, remained for hours in contemplation before a rococo Jesuit altar in a chapel closed to the majority of the faithful, and let her soul soar there among little marble clouds and along great shafts of gilded wood.

She had a chapel friend, an old virgin like herself, called Mademoiselle Vaubois, an absolute numskull next to whom Mademoiselle Gillenormand had the pleasure of being an eagle. Beyond the Agnus Deis and the Ave Marias,[3] the only thing Mademoiselle Vaubois had an inkling about was the different ways of making jams. Mademoiselle Vaubois, a perfect example of her kind, was the very picture of stupidity without a single blot of intelligence.

We should say that, in growing old, Mademoiselle Gillenormand had actually gained more than she had lost. That is how it goes with passive natures. She had never been nasty, which is a relative good; and then again, the years wear away any sharp angles and the softening that endurance brings had come to her. She was sad with an obscure sadness that baffled even the woman herself. Her whole being was full of the torpor of a life that is over before it has begun.

She kept her father's house. She was to Monsieur Gillenormand what we saw Monseigneur Bienvenu's sister was to him, always by his side. These households consisting of an old man and an old maid are not rare and always have the touching feel of two feeble people leaning on each other, propping one another up.

On top of the old maid and the old man, there was one other person in the household—a child, a little boy who was always trembling and mute in front of Monsieur Gillenormand. Monsieur Gillenormand never spoke to this boy except in a harsh voice, sometimes with his stick raised: "Here, Monsieur! You little duffer, you ninny, come here! Answer me, you nincompoop! Let me look at you, you good-for-nothing pipsqueak!" And so on and so forth. He idolized him.

The boy was his grandson. We will meet up with him again.

# BOOK THREE

# GRANDFATHER AND GRANDSON

## I. AN OLD-WORLD SALON

When Monsieur Gillenormand lived in the rue Servandoni, he haunted several very good and very noble salons. Although bourgeois, Monsieur Gillenormand was accepted. As he was doubly witty, first with the wit he actually had and then with the wit attributed to him, he was even sought after and lionized. He never went anywhere except on condition that he dominate proceedings. There are people who will go to great lengths to have influence and to be made a fuss of; where they can't be oracles, they turn themselves into buffoons. Monsieur Gillenormand was not that kind of man; his dominance in the royalist salons he frequented did not cost him an iota of self-respect. He was an oracle everywhere he went. He sometimes held his own with Monsieur de Bonald and even Monsieur Bengy-Puy-Vallée.[1]

Around 1817, he invariably spent two afternoons a week in a house in his neighborhood, rue Férou, at Madame la baronne de T——,[2] a worthy and respectable eminence whose husband had been ambassador of France in Berlin under Louis XVI. The baron de T——, who had been a passionate devotee of ecstasies and magnetic visions in his lifetime, had died ruined in the Emigration, leaving, as sum total of his fortune, very curious memoirs on Mesmer and his tub, in ten manuscript volumes bound in red morocco with gilt edging. Madame de T—— had not published the memoirs out of a sense of dignity and supported herself on a small income that had lingered on unaccountably. Madame de T—— lived far from the court, "a very mixed bag,"[3] she reckoned, in splendid isolation, proud and poor. A few friends gathered twice a week around her widow's fireside and this constituted an unadulteratedly royalist salon. They took tea there and gave out groans or cries of horror, according to whether the wind was blowing in favor of the elegy or the dithyrambic, over the age, over the Charter, over the Buonapartists, over the prostitution of the blue sash to the bourgeois, or over the Jacobinism of Louis XVIII,[4] and they discussed in very low voices their hopes for Monsieur, later Charles X.[5]

They greeted with transports of joy vulgar songs in which Napoléon was nicknamed Nicolas. Duchesses, the most delicate and the most charming women in the world, went into raptures there over couplets like the following, addressed to "the federates":[6]

> Pull up your breeches
> Your shirts are hangin' out.
> Don't let 'em say patriots
> Hung the white flag![7]

They had tremendous fun with puns they thought were fantastic, with plays on innocent words they considered deadly, with quatrains and even distiches; thus on the Dessolles ministry, a cabinet of moderates of which messieurs Decazes and Deserre[8] were members:

> To shore up the throne shaken to its foundations,
> You need a change of soil, greenhouse and pot.[9]

Or else they reworked the list of the Chamber of Peers, "an abominably Jacobin chamber," and joined names together from this list to make, for example, phrases like this one: *Damas, Sabran, Gouvion-Saint-Cyr*.[10] All this, gay as larks.

In that world they liked to parody the Revolution. For some reason, they seemed to feel the need to put the same anger to use, but the other way round, and sharper. They sang their own little "Ça ira."[11]

> Ah! It'll be all right! it'll be all right! it'll be all right!
> Let the Buonapartists string from the lampposts![12]

Songs are like the guillotine; they chop indifferently, today this head, tomorrow, that one. All just variations on the same theme.

In the Fualdès affair,[13] which dates from around that time, 1816, they sided with Bastide and Jausion because Fualdès was "a Buonapartist." Liberals were described as "the brothers and friends,"[14] which was the greatest possible insult.

Like certain church towers, the salon of Madame la baronne de T—— had two cocks. One was Monsieur Gillenormand, the other was the comte de Lamothe-Valois, of whom it was whispered in somewhat awed tones: "Did you know? He's the Lamothe of the Necklace Affair." Parties have strange amnesties.[15]

We might add this: In the bourgeoisie, honorable positions are diminished by too easy relations; you have to be careful who you let in, for just as there is a loss of heat in the vicinity of those who are cold, so there is a dwindling of respect in being approached by people who are frowned upon. The old world of high society held itself above that particular rule as above all others. Marigny, brother of La Pompadour,[16] had privileged access to the home of Monsieur le prince de Soubise.[17] Even though? No, because. Du Barry, godfather of La Vaubernier,[18] is more than welcome at Monsieur le maréchal de Richelieu's.[19] That world is Olympus. Mercury[20] and the prince de Guéménée are at home in it. A thief is accepted, as long as he is a god.

Le comte de Lamothe, who was an old man of seventy-five in 1815, had nothing remarkable about him except for his silent and sententious air, his angular and cold face, his perfectly polished manners, his coat buttoned right up to his cravat, and his great long legs, always crossed in long, loose trousers the color of burnt sienna. His face was the color of his trousers.

This Monsieur de Lamothe was "somebody" in this salon because of his "celebrity" and, strange but true, because of the name of Valois.

As for Monsieur Gillenormand, respect for him was absolutely genuine. He was an authority because he was an authority. As unashamedly light as he was and without detracting in any way from his gaiety, he had a certain way of being, imposing, dignified, honest, and arrogant in a bourgeois sort of way; and his great age added to the effect. You are not an entire era for nothing. The years end up giving a head a windswept look that is most distinguished.

He also had a way with words, the kind of words that put the sparkle in old rock. And so, when the king of Prussia, after seeing to the restoration of Louis XVIII, came and paid him a visit under the assumed name of the comte de Ruppin, he was received by Louis XIV's descendant somewhat like a marquis de Brandenburg[21] and with the most refined impertinence. Monsieur Gillenormand approved. "Any king who is not the king of France is a provincial king." One day this exchange occurred in his hearing: "What was the editor of the *Courrier français*[22] sentenced to?" "To being hung up for a spell." "*Up* is superfluous," observed Monsieur Gillenormand. Bons mots of the kind stand a man in good stead. At an anniversary Te Deum celebrating the return of the Bourbons, seeing Monsieur de Talleyrand[23] go by, he said: "There goes His Excellency, Evil."

Monsieur Gillenormand usually went accompanied by his daughter, that elongated mademoiselle who had just turned forty and looked fifty, as well as by a beautiful little boy of seven, white, rosy, fresh-faced, with happy, trusting eyes, who never appeared in the salon without hearing voices buzzing around him: "What a beautiful boy!" "What a shame!" "Poor child!" This child was the one we mentioned a moment ago. They referred to him as "poor child" because he had "a brigand of the Loire" for a father.

This brigand of the Loire[24] was Monsieur Gillenormand's son-in-law mentioned above, whom Monsieur Gillenormand described as "the disgrace of the family."

## II. ONE OF THE RED GHOSTS OF THE TIME

Anyone passing through the small town of Vernon¹ in those days and taking a stroll over the beautiful monumental bridge that will soon be replaced, let's hope, by some hideous wrought-iron affair, would have been able to see, if they looked down from the parapet, a man of about fifty wearing a leather cap and dressed in pants and a jacket of coarse gray woolen cloth, to which something yellow was sewn which had once been a red ribbon, shod in clogs, weathered by the sun, his face almost black and his hair almost white, with a large scar across his forehead that ran on down his cheek, bent, buckled, old before his time, strolling around virtually all day, with a spade or a billhook in hand, inside one of those walled plots of land right next to the bridge that line the left bank of the Seine like a chain of terraces—lovely enclosures full of flowers that you would describe as gardens if they were a lot bigger, and, if they were a lot smaller, as bouquets. All these enclosures end in the river at one end and in a house at the other. The man with the jacket and clogs lived around 1817 in the tiniest of the enclosures and the humblest of the houses. He lived there alone, single and solitary, silently and in poverty, except for a woman who was neither young nor old, neither beautiful nor ugly, neither peasant nor bourgeoise, who waited on him. The patch of dirt he called his garden was famous in town for the beauty of the flowers he grew there. Flowers were his stock-in-trade.

By dint of hard work, perseverance, attention, and buckets of water, he had managed to create, following in the Creator's footsteps, and he had invented certain tulips and certain dahlias that nature seemed to have left out. He was ingenious; he was ahead of Soulange-Bodin² in building up small flowerbeds of peaty soil for the cultivation of rare and precious shrubs from America and China. At the crack of dawn in summer he would be out on one of his paths, digging, pruning, weeding, watering, walking among his flowers with an air of sad, gentle goodness, sometimes daydreaming without moving a muscle for hours on end, listening to a bird singing in a tree, a baby babbling in a house somewhere, or else with his eye fixed on a drop of dew at the tip of a blade of grass, which the sun was turning into a precious gem. His table was extremely frugal and he drank more milk than wine. Any rogue could get the better of him and his servant scolded him. He was timid to the point of seeming fierce, rarely went out, and saw no one but the poor who knocked on his window and his priest, the abbé Mabeuf, who was a good old sort. Yet if any townspeople or strangers of whatever stripe came and rang the bell at his house, curious to see his tulips and roses, he would open his door with a smile. This was the brigand of the Loire.

Anyone who, in that same period, read military memoirs, biographies, the *Moniteur,* and the bulletins of the Grande Armée would have been struck by a name that cropped up regularly, the name Georges Pontmercy.[3] When he was very young, this Georges Pontmercy had been a soldier in the Saintonge regiment. Then the Revolution broke out. The Saintonge regiment was part of the Army of the Rhine, for the old regiments of the monarchy kept their provincial names, even after the fall of the monarchy, and were not dragooned into the army until 1794. Pontmercy fought at Spires, Worms, Neustadt, Turkheim, Alzey, and Mayence,[4] where he was one of the two hundred who made up Houchard's rear guard. He was one of the twelve men who held their ground against the prince of Hesse's entire corps behind the old ramparts of Audernach[5] and who did not fall back on the main body of the army until the enemy cannon fire opened a breach from the line of the parapet to the submerged embankment. He was under Kléber at Marchiennes and in the battle of Mont-Palissel, where he got his arm broken by a musket ball. He then went on to the Italian front and was one of the thirty grenadiers to defend the Col di Tende with Joubert.[6] Joubert was made adjutant general and Pontmercy second lieutenant. Pontmercy was by Berthier's side in the thick of the storm of grapeshot on that day at Lodi[7] that moved Bonaparte to say: "Berthier was canoneer, cavalier, and grenadier rolled into one." He saw his old general Joubert fall at Novi just as he raised his sword and cried "Forward!". Having been embarked with his company according to the requirements of the campaign in a barge, which went from Genoa to who knows which little port on the coast, he fell into a hornets' nest of seven or eight English clippers. The Genoese captain wanted to throw the cannon overboard, hide the soldiers in the hold, and slip away into the darkness like a merchant ship. Pontmercy had the red, white, and blue[8] hoisted to the halyards of the flag mast and passed proudly under the cannon of the British frigates. Fifty miles farther on, growing bolder than ever, with his barge he attacked and captured a large English transport ship ferrying troops to Sicily, so loaded up with men and horses that the vessel was full to the hatches. In 1805, he was in the Malher division that took Günzburg from the archduke Ferdinand. At Wettingen,[9] under a shower of balls, he held in his arms Colonel Maupetit, mortally wounded at the head of the 9th Dragoons. He distinguished himself at Austerlitz in that wonderful march in echelon under enemy fire. When the cavalry of the Russian Imperial Guard crushed a battalion of the 4th of the Line, Pontmercy was among those who took revenge and overwhelmed the Guard. The emperor gave him the cross. One after the other, Pontmercy saw Wurmser taken prisoner in Mantua, Mélas in Alexandria, Mack in Ulm.[10] He was part of the eighth corps of the Grande Armée that Mortier commanded and that captured Hamburg. Then he moved to the 55th of the Line, which was the old Flanders regiment. At Eylau,[11] he was in the cemetery where the heroic captain Louis Hugo,[12] uncle of the author of this book, alone with his company of eighty-three men, held out, for two hours, against the entire effort of the enemy army. Pontmercy was one of the three who came out of that cemetery alive. He was at Friedland. Then he saw Moscow, then the Beresina,[13] then Lützen, Bautzen, Dresden, Wachau, Leipzig, and the defiles of Gelenhausen;[14] then Montmirail, Château-Thierry, Craon, the banks of the Marne, the banks of the Aisne, and the redoubtable position of Laon.[15] At Arnay-le-Duc, being captain, he sabered ten cossacks and saved not his general but his corporal. He was badly wounded on that occasion and twenty-seven fragments of shot were taken out of his left arm alone. Eight days before the capitulation[16] of Paris, he changed places with a comrade and joined the cavalry. He was what was called in the ancien régime "two-handed," signaling equal dexterity in handling a saber or a musket as a soldier and a squadron or a battalion as an officer. It is this dexterity, perfected by military training, that has given rise to certain special units, the dragoons, for instance, who are both cavalry and infantry at once. He accompanied Napoléon to the island of Elba. At Waterloo, he led a squadron of cuirassiers in Dubois's brigade. He was the one who took the colors of the Lunebourg battalion. He went and threw the colors at the emperor's feet. He was covered in blood. In seizing the colors, he had received a saber cut across his face. The emperor, pleased, shouted to him: "You are a colonel, you are a baron, you are an officer of the Légion d'Honneur!" Pontmercy replied: "Sir, I thank you on my widow's behalf." One hour later, he fell into the Ohain gully . . . Now, what was this Georges Pontmercy? He was this same brigand of the Loire.

We have already seen something of his history. After Waterloo, having been pulled out of the sunken road of Ohain, Pontmercy had managed to get back to the army and had dragged himself from ambulance to ambulance as far as the billets of the Loire.

The Restoration put him on half pay,[17] then put him in a home—in other words, under surveillance—in Vernon. King Louis XVIII, considering as null and void anything that had been done in the Hundred Days, recognized neither his standing as officer of the Légion d'Honneur, nor his rank as colonel, nor his title as baron.[18] He, for his part, never missed an opportunity to sign himself *Colonel Baron Pontmercy*. He had only an old blue coat and never went out without pinning on it the rosette of an officer of the Légion d'Honneur. The crown prosecutor put him on notice that he would be prosecuted for "illegal wearing of said decoration." When this notice was handed to him by an officious intermediary, Pontmercy answered with a bitter smile: "I don't know if it is I who no longer understand French or you who no longer speak it, but the fact is, I don't understand a word." He promptly stepped out every day for a week with his rosette in place. No one dared rile him. Two or three times the war minister and the general commanding the *département* wrote to him, addressing him as Major Pontmercy. He sent the letters back, marked *Return to Sender,* unopened. At that same moment, Napoléon on Saint Helena was dealing similarly with the missives of Sir Hudson Lowe[19] addressed to General Bonaparte. Pontmercy had ended up with the same bile in his mouth, if you'll forgive the expression, as his emperor. In Rome, too, there were Carthaginian soldiers taken prisoner who had a little of Hannibal's soul and refused to salute Flaminius.

One morning he came across the crown prosecutor in a street in Vernon, went up to him and said: "Monsieur procureur du roi, am I allowed to wear my scar?"

He had nothing but his measly half-pay as squadron chief to live on and so he had rented the smallest house he could find in Vernon. He lived there alone—how, we have just seen. Under the Empire, between the wars, he had found time to marry Mademoiselle Gillenormand. The old bourgeois, outraged at heart, had consented with a sigh and this remark: "The greatest families are forced to do it."[20] In 1815, Madame Pontmercy, who was in all things admirable, in any case, high-minded and rare and worthy of her husband, had died, leaving a child. This child would have been the pride and joy of the colonel in his loneliness; but the grandfather had imperiously claimed his grandson, declaring that, if he was not handed over, he would disinherit him. The father had yielded in the little boy's interests and, not being able to have his son, had turned to flowers.

He had given up everything, anyway, neither aspiring nor conspiring. He divided his thoughts between the innocuous things he now did and the great things he had done. He passed his time either anticipating a carnation or remembering Austerlitz.

Monsieur Gillenormand had no contact with his son-in-law. The colonel was for him "a bandit" and he was for the colonel "an old codger." Monsieur Gillenormand never spoke of the colonel except occasionally to make some scathing allusion to "his barony." It was expressly agreed that Pontmercy would never try to see his son or to speak to him—or the boy would be handed back, driven out and disinherited. For the Gillenormands, Pontmercy was a leper. They intended to bring the child up as they pleased. The colonel was perhaps wrong to accept these conditions, but he bowed to them believing he was doing the right thing and hurting only himself. Old man Gillenormand's legacy was nothing much, but the legacy from Mademoiselle Gillenormand[21] the elder was considerable. This aunt, who had remained unmarried, was extremely rich on her mother's side and the son of her sister was her natural heir.

The child, who was called Marius, knew he had a father, but that's as far as it went. Nobody breathed a word to him about him. But in the social world his grandfather took him to, the whispers, hints, and winks finally ended up coming together in the little boy's mind; he wound up understanding something;

and as he naturally picked up, by a sort of slow trickle-down process like osmosis, the ideas and opinions that were, so to speak, the air he breathed, little by litle he came to think of his father only with a lump in his throat and a sense of shame.

While he was growing up in this fashion, two or three times a month, the colonel would escape and speed furtively to Paris like a fugitive from justice breaking his bans, and head for Saint-Sulpice, where he would take up his post at the hour when Aunt Gillenormand took Marius to mass. There, shaking for fear that the aunt would turn round, hiding behind a pillar,[22] motionless, hardly daring to breathe, he would watch his son. This battle-scarred hero was afraid of the old maid.

It was actually from this that his friendship with the curé de Vernon, Abbé Mabeuf, came about. This worthy priest was the brother of a Saint-Sulpice churchwarden who had several times noticed the man gazing at the child, and the scar on his cheek, and the fat tears in his eyes. This man, who looked so much the man and yet cried like a woman, had struck the churchwarden. The face stayed in his mind. One day, having gone to Vernon to visit his brother, he came across Colonel Pontmercy on the bridge and recognized the man from Saint-Sulpice. The churchwarden spoke to the curé about it and they both paid the colonel a visit on some pretext or other. This visit led to others. The colonel was at first very closed but finally opened up, and the priest and the churchwarden came to know the whole story, and how Pontmercy had sacrificed his own happiness to his son's future. This caused the curé to feel real veneration and tenderness for him and the colonel on his side took to the curé with affection. In any case, whenever both happen to be sincere and good, no one gets on as well or becomes as close as an old priest and an old soldier. Deep down, they are the same man. One has dedicated himself to the homeland here below, the other to the homeland up above; there is no other difference.

Twice a year, on the first of January and on Saint George's feast day, Marius wrote dutiful letters to his father that his aunt dictated and that you would have said were copied from some manual; this was all Monsieur Gillenormand would tolerate; and the father answered with overwhelmingly tender letters that the old man pocketed without reading.

### III. REQUIESCANT—R.I.P.

The salon of Madame T—— was all that Marius Pontmercy knew of the world. It was the sole opening through which he could look at life. This opening was grim and such a tiny window on the world brought him more cold than heat, more darkness than daylight. This child, who was all joy and light whenever he stepped into this strange world, became sad there in a very short space of time and, what is even more unusual at his age, grave. Surrounded by all these imposing and singular persons, he looked around him with serious amazement. Everything conspired to intensify his stupefaction. There were in Madame de T——'s salon noble and extremely venerable old ladies named Mathan, Noé, Lévis which was pronounced Lévi, Cambis which was pronounced Cambyse. These antique figures with their biblical names got mixed up in the little boy's mind with the Old Testament that he was learning by heart, and when they were all there together, sitting in a circle around a dying fire, scarcely illuminated by a lamp veiled in green, with their severe profiles, their gray or white hair, their long frocks from another age with their morbid colors that were barely discernible, dropping words at once majestic and savage at rare intervals, little Marius would study them with startled eyes believing that he saw, not real beings, but phantoms.

Blending in with these phantoms were several priests, habitués of the old salon, and a few gentlemen: the marquis de Sassenay, secretary-in-chief to Madame de Berry, the vicomte de Valory, who published monorhymed odes under the pseudonym of Charles-Antoine, the prince de Beauffremont, who, though still fairly young, was going gray and who had a pretty and witty wife whose extremely low-cut scarlet velvet frocks with gold trim scared off the gloom, the marquis de Coriolis d'Espinouse, the man in all France who best managed "measured politeness," the comte d'Amendre, a good old stick with a benevolent chin, and the chevalier de Port de Guy, pillar of the Bibliothèque du Louvre, which was known as "the king's study." Monsieur de Port de Guy, bald and more elderly than old, reckoned that in 1793, when he was sixteen years old, he had been thrown into jail as a recalcitrant and chained to an octogenarian, the bishop of Mirepoix, also a recalcitrant, only as a priest, whereas he was a recalcitrant soldier. This was in Toulon. Their job had been to go at night and collect from the scaffold the heads and bodies of those guillotined during the day; they then carried off these streaming trunks on their backs and their red convict smocks had a permanent crust of blood at the back of the neck, wet at night, dry in the morning. Such tragic tales abounded in the salon of Madame de T——;[1] and by dint of cursing Marat, they were forced to applaud the terrorist Trestaillon.[2] A few deputies of the kind that can't be pinned down played their whist there—Monsieur Thibord du Chalard, Monsieur Lemarchant de Gomicourt, and the celebrated right-wing comic Monsieur Cornet-Dincourt. The bailiff of Ferrette, with his short breeches and his skinny legs, occasionally breezed through the salon on his way to Monsieur de Talleyrand's.[3] He had been the boon companion in debauchery of the comte d'Artois[4] and in a move that was the complete reverse of Aristotle squatting under Campaspe, he had made La Guimard[5] walk around on all fours, thereby displaying for all the ages the image of a philosopher avenged by a bailiff.

As for the priests, these were the abbé Halma, the same to whom Monsieur Larose, his collaborator at the *Foudre*, said: "Bah! Who isn't at least fifty years old? A few whippersnappers, perhaps!"; the abbé Letourneur, preacher to the king; the abbé Frayssinous,[6] who was not yet a count or a bishop or a minister or a peer, and who wore an old soutane with the buttons missing; and the abbé Keravenant, curé of Saint-Germain-des-Prés; plus the pope's nuncio, at that time Monsignor Macchi, archbishop of Nisibis, later cardinal, remarkable for his long pensive nose; and another monsignor with the title Abbate Palmieri, domestic prelate, one of the seven participating protonotaries of the Holy See, canon of the Insignia of the Liberian Basilicate, advocate of the saints,[7] *postulatore di santi,* which deals with matters of canonization and more or less means master of requests for the paradise branch; and last two cardinals, Monsieur de la Luzerne and Monsieur de Clermont-Tonnerre. Monsieur le cardinal de Luzerne was a writer and was to have the honor, a few years later, of signing articles in the *Conservateur* alongside Chateaubriand;[8] Monsieur de Clermont-Tonnerre was archbishop of Toulouse and often came to Paris on holiday, staying with his nephew, the marquis de Tonnerre, who had been a minister of the navy and of war. The cardinal de Clermont-Tonnerre was a chirpy little old-timer who flashed a bit of a red stocking underneath a hitched-up soutane; his specialty was hating the Encyclopedia[9] and being mad about billiards, and anyone out and about on a summer evening who happened to stroll down the rue Madame, where the hôtel de Clermont-Tonnerre then was, would stop to listen to the clicking of billiard balls and the sharp voice of the cardinal yelling at his fellow conclavist, Monseigneur Cottret, bishop *in partibus* of Caryste: "See that, Abbé, I'm sending them crashing." The cardinal de Clermont-Tonnerre had been brought along to Madame de T——'s by his closest friend, Monsieur de Roquelaure, former bishop of Senlis and one of the famous *Quarante*—the forty members of the Académie Française. Monsieur de Roquelaure was impressive for his great height and his zeal at the Académie; through the glass door of the adjoining room of the library where the Académie Française then held its sessions every Thursday, the curious could contemplate the former bishop of Senlis, habitually on his feet, freshly powdered and in violet stockings and with his back turned to the door, apparently the better to show off his little cape. Though most were men of the court as much as men of the church, all these ecclesiastics added to the gravity of the T—— salon, whose seigneurial side was accentuated by five peers of France, the marquis de Vibraye, the marquis de Talaru, the marquis d'Herbouville, the vicomte Dambray, and the duc de Valentinois. This duc de Valentinois, though prince of Monaco, that is, a foreign sovereign prince, had such an elevated idea of France and of the peerage that he saw everything in terms of them. It was he who said: "Cardinals are the Roman peers of France; lords are the English peers of France." And the funny thing was—for in this century the Revolution has to muscle in everywhere—that this impeccably feudal salon was, as we have said, dominated by a bourgeois. Monsieur Gillenormand held sway there.

This, then, was the essence and quintessence of White—legitimist—Paris society.[10] People of renown were shunned there, even when they were royalists. There is always a bit of anarchy in renown. Had Chateaubriand set foot there, he would have had the same effect as Père Duchesne.[11] A few royalists who had rallied to the Republic managed to penetrate this orthodox world, though only under sufferance. Comte Beugnot[12] was received there as a matter of good manners.

The "noble" salons of today no longer bear any resemblance to those salons. The current faubourg Saint-Germain has a whiff of heresy about it. The royalists of the moment are demagogues—to their credit,[13] we might add.

In the superior world of Madame de T——'s salon, taste was exquisite and exalted, buoyed by the most flowery politeness. Little customs there involved all manner of unconscious refinements which were the ancien régime itself, buried but alive. Some of these customs, especially the linguistic ones, now seem bizarre. Superficial observers would have taken as provincial what was merely old-fashioned. A woman would be referred to as *Madame la générale,* and *Madame la colonelle* had not entirely fallen out of use. The charming Madame de Léon, no doubt in memory of the duchesses de Longueville and de Chevreuse,[14] preferred this form of address to her title of princesse. The marquise de Créquy, too, called herself Madame la colonelle.

It was this rarefied small world that invented the refinement of always, when speaking to the king in closed circles at the Tuileries, referring to him in the third person as *the king* and never *Your Majesty,* the term *Your Majesty* having been "besmirched by the usurper."[15]

Events and people were put on trial there. The age was mightily mocked, which exempted a person from trying to understand it. They bolstered each other's stunned amazement. They each passed on to the rest what little light they could shed. Methuselah informed Epimenides.[16] The deaf kept the blind up to speed. The time that had gone by since Koblenz[17] was declared nonexistant. Just as Louis XVIII was in the twenty-fifth year of his reign, by the grace of God, so the émigrés were, by rights, in the twenty-fifth year of their adolescence.

All was harmony; no one was too much alive, speech was barely a whisper, and a newspaper, in keeping with the salon, was like papyrus. There were young people there but they were all a bit dead. In the antechamber, the liveried attendants were dowdy; for those completely out-of-date characters were waited on by domestics of the same ilk. Everything had the air of having lived a long time ago and of holding out doggedly against the grave. Conserve, Conservation, Conservative—that was more or less the entire lexicon. *To smell good*—that was the thing. Indeed, aromatics entered into the opinions of these venerable bastions and their ideas reeked of violets. It was a mummified world. The masters were embalmed, the valets were stuffed. A worthy old marquise émigrée who had returned ruined, with only one maid left, went on saying: "My people."

What did they do in Madame de T——'s salon? They were Ultra—that is, ultra-royalists; this word no longer means anything today, although what it represents has not perhaps entirely disappeared. We should explain.

To be Ultra is to go one better. It is to attack the scepter in the name of the throne and the miter in the name of the altar; it is to maltreat the thing you trundle around; it is to kick over the traces; it is to quibble with the stake over the degree of cooking required for heretics; it is to attack the idol for lacking in idolatry; to insult through excessive respect; to find too little popery in the pope, too little royalty in the king, and too much light in night; it is to find alabaster, snow, the swan, and the lily sadly wanting when it comes to whiteness; to support things in a partisan spirit to the point where you become their enemy; it is to be so strongly for that you are against. The Ultra spirit is especially characteristic of the initial phase of the Restoration.

Nothing in history remotely resembles those fifteen minutes that begin in 1814 and end around 1820 with the advent of Monsieur de Villèle,[18] the pragmatist of the Right. Those six years were an extraordinary interlude, both noisy and grim, sunny and somber, luminous with the radiance of a new dawn and smothered in the gloom of the great catastrophes still choking the horizon, only slowly sinking into the past. In all that light and dark, a whole little world—new and old, comical and sad, juvenile and senile—stood there, rubbing its eyes. Nothing resembles an awakening so much as a return. This world regarded France with bad-tempered wistfulness and France regarded it with irony; the streets were full of marquises who looked like wise old owls, revenants,[19] and returned émigrés, *ci-devants*[20] stunned by everything, brave and noble gentlemen beaming at being back in France and weeping over it, too; thrilled to see their homeland again, and in despair not to find the monarchy still in place; the nobility of the Crusades[21] booing off the stage the nobility of the Empire, meaning the nobility of the sword; historic clans who had lost the thread of history; sons of the companions of Charlemagne looking down on the companions of Napoléon. Swords, as we said, batted insults back and forth; the sword of Fontenoy was laughable, nothing more than a stick of rust; the sword of Marengo[22] was base, nothing more than a saber. Yesteryear disowned Yesterday. The sense of what was great was lost along with a sense of the ridiculous. Someone called Bonaparte, Scapin the clown ... That world is no more. Nothing, we repeat, is left of it today. Whenever we happen to dredge up some feature of it and try to bring it to life again in imagery, it seems as strange to us as something from some antediluvian world. The fact is that it, too, has been engulfed by a deluge like the biblical Flood. It has disappeared beneath two revolutions. Ideas are such torrents! How swiftly they cover all they set out to destroy and bury, and how promptly they create terrifyingly fathomless depths!

Such were the features of the salons of those distant and candid times when Monsieur de Martainville[23] was considered wittier than Voltaire.

These salons had their very own literature and politics. They believed in Fiévée there. Monsieur Agier[24] ruled. They commented on Monsieur Colnet, the specialist in public law who was a secondhand bookseller—a bouquiniste—on the quai Malaquais. Napoléon came into his own as the Ogre of Corsica there; later on, the entry into history of Monsieur le marquis Buonaparté, lieutenant general of the king's armies, was a concession to the spirit of the age.

These salons did not stay pure for long. As early as 1818, a few doctrinaire types began to crop up in them, which was a disquieting development. The tactics these types employed were to carry on like royalists but apologize for it. Where the Ultras were extremely proud of who they were, the doctrinaires were a bit shamefaced. They were witty, but they were a little too silent; their political dogma was properly starched with arrogance, but they were a little too driven. They overdid the white cravats and buttoned-up coats, though this was effective. The mistake, or misfortune, of the doctrinaire party lay in creating old young people. They adopted the pose of sages. They dreamed of grafting moderate power on absolute and excessive principle. They opposed, sometimes with a rare intelligence, a destructive liberalism with a conservative liberalism. They could be heard saying: "Go easy on royalism! It hasn't done too badly. It has brought back tradition, worship, religion, respect. It is loyal, brave, chivalrous, loving, devout. It has come to infuse, however regretfully, the new splendors of the nation with the secular splendors of the monarchy. It is wrong not to understand the Revolution, the Empire, glory, liberty, new ideas, the younger generations, the age. But the wrong that it does us, don't we sometimes do the same wrong to it? The Revolution, whose heirs we are, ought to understand everything. To attack royalism is misdirected on the part of liberalism. What a mistake! And what blindness! Revolutionary France lacks respect for historic France, that is, its mother, that is, itself. After the fifth of September, the nobility of the monarchy was treated the same way as the nobility of the Empire was treated after the eighth of July.[25] They were unjust about the eagle, just as we are unjust about the fleur-de-lis. We always have to have something to outlaw! Removing the gilt from Louis XIV's crown, scratching Henri IV's coat of arms—is that really helpful? We laugh at Monsieur de Vaublanc[26] for effacing the *N*s from the pont d'Iéna! What on earth was he doing? Exactly what we are doing now. Bouvines is as much ours as Marengo. The fleur-de-lis belongs to us just as much as those *N*s. It is our heritage. What's the good of diminishing it? We should no more deny our homeland in the past than in the present. Why not embrace all of history? Why not love all of France?"

This is how the doctrinaires criticized and defended royalism, which did not like being criticized and was furious at being defended. The Ultras marked the first phase of royalism: The Congregation[27] characterized the second. Ardor was elbowed aside by cunning. Let's leave this sketch right there.

In the course of this tale, the author of this book has come across this curious moment in contemporary history on his travels; he could not help but cast a glance at it in passing and outline some of the singular features of that long-lost social world. But he does so rapidly and without a hint of bitterness or derision. Memories, fond and respectful since they touch on his mother, attach him to that past. Besides, let's admit it, this same small world had its grandeur. You can smile about it but you can't despise or hate it. It was the France of days gone by.

Marius Pontmercy, like all children, received some sort of education or other. Once he was off his aunt Gillenormand's hands, his grandfather put him in the care of a worthy professor of the purest classical innocence. This budding young soul changed hands from a prude to a pedantic prig. Marius had his years of college, then he entered law school. He was royalist, fanatical, and an aesthete. He had little love for his grandfather, whose frivolity and cynicism rubbed him the wrong way, and his heart was dark in relation to his father.

Apart from that, he was an ardent but aloof boy, noble, generous, proud, religious, exalted, dignified to the point of being hard, pure to the point of being savage.

## IV. END OF THE BRIGAND

The completion of Marius's classical studies coincided with Monsieur Gillenormand's exit from the world. The old man said goodbye to the fauboug Saint-Germain and to the salon of Madame de T—— and went and set up in the Marais, in his house on the rue des Filles-du-Calvaire. In addition to the porter, his servants included the particular Nicolette who had taken over from the Magnon woman as chambermaid and the huffing and puffing Basque we spoke of earlier.

In 1827, Marius had just turned seventeen. One night when he came home, he saw his grandfather with a letter in his hand.

"Marius," said Monsieur Gillenormand, "you will leave tomorrow for Vernon."

"Why?" said Marius.

"To see your father."

Marius gave a shudder. He had thought of everything but this, that the day might come when he would have to see his father. Nothing could have been more unexpected, more surprising, and, we have to say, more unpleasant. It was distance forced into proximity, compulsory intimacy. There was no chagrin, no; it was just a tiresome chore.

Apart from his feelings of political antipathy, Marius was convinced that his father, the swashbuckler, as Monsieur Gillenormand called him on his better days, did not love him; this was obvious, since he had clearly abandoned him, leaving him to the care of others. Feeling himself to be unloved, he did not feel love, either. As simple as that, he told himself.

He was so stunned that he did not question Monsieur Gillenormand. The grandfather went on: "It appears he is sick. He is asking for you."

After a silence, he added: "Go tomorrrow morning. I believe there is a coach that leaves from the cour des Fontaines at six o'clock and gets there in the evening. Take it. He says it's urgent."

He then screwed the letter up and shoved it in his pocket. Marius could have left that same night and been at his father's side the following morning. A coach from the rue du Bouloi made the trip to Rouen at night in those days and it passed through Vernon. But neither Monsieur Gillenormand nor Marius thought of inquiring.

The next day at dusk Marius arrived in Vernon. Candles were just being lit as he asked the first person he came across for "the home of Monsieur Pontmercy." For in his thoughts he was of the same view as the Restoration and he, too, did not acknowledge his father as either a baron or a colonel.

A building was pointed out to him. He rang the bell; a woman came and opened the door, a small lamp in hand.

"Monsieur Pontmercy?" said Marius.

The woman did not move.

"Is this the place?"

The woman gave an affirmative nod of the head.

"Could I speak to him?"

The woman gave a negative shake of the head.

"But I'm his son," Marius went on. "He's expecting me."

"Not anymore, he's not," said the woman.

It was then that he noticed she was in tears.

She pointed to the door of a low-ceilinged room. He went in.

In this room, which was lit by a tallow rushlight sitting on the mantelpiece, there were three men, one standing, one kneeling, one on the floor stretched out in his shirtsleeves on the tiles. The one on the floor was the colonel.

The other two were a doctor and a priest, who was busily praying.

The colonel had been struck down by brain fever three days before. At the onset of the disease, having a bad premonition, he had written to Monsieur Gillenormand to ask for his son. His condition had deteriorated. The very evening Marius arrived in Vernon, the colonel had had a bout of delirium; he had gotten out of bed in spite of the servant, crying: "My son hasn't arrived yet! I'll go and wait for him!" He promptly ran out of his room and fell on the tiled floor of the antechamber. He had only just died.

The doctor and the curé had been sent for. The doctor had got there too late, the curé had got there too late. The son, too, had got there too late.

By the crepuscular light of the candle, you could make out on the cheeks of the pale and prostrate colonel, the fat tears that had run from his death-stricken eyes. The eyes were extinguished but the tears had not yet dried. Those tears were the son's delay.

Marius gazed at this man, seeing him for the first, and the last, time—that noble manly face, the open eyes that did not see, the white hair, the robust limbs on which you could make out the brown lines of saber cuts and the red stars of bullet holes here and there. He gazed at the gigantic scar that stamped heroism on this face where God had imprinted goodness. He thought how this man was his father and the man was dead and he remained unmoved.

The sadness he felt was the sadness he would have felt confronted by any man he had seen lying there, dead.

Yet mourning, a poignant mourning, was in that room. The servant lamented in a corner by herself, the curé prayed and could be heard sobbing, the doctor dried his eyes; the corpse itself wept.

The doctor, the priest, and the woman looked at Marius in their affliction without saying a word; he was the stranger here. Marius, too little moved, felt awkward and ashamed of his attitude; he had his hat in his hand and so he let it drop to the floor to make them think he felt so much grief, he didn't have the strength to hold on to it.

At the same time, he felt something like remorse and he despised himself for acting this way. But was it his fault? So he didn't love his father—what of it?

The colonel left nothing. The sale of his furniture barely paid for his funeral. The servant found a scrap of paper, which she handed to Marius. It was written in the colonel's handwriting and this is what it contained:

*For my son.*—The Emperor made me a baron on the battlefield of Waterloo. Since the Restoration contests this title, which I have paid for with my blood, my son will take it and bear it. It goes without saying that he will be worthy of it.

On the back, the colonel had added:

At this same Battle of Waterloo, a sergeant saved my life. This man is named Thénardier. In recent times, I believe he was keeping an inn in a village on the outskirts of Paris, in Chelles or Montfermeil. If my son should meet up with him, he will do whatever he can for Thénardier.

Not from any sense of religious duty toward his father, but out of that vague respect for death which is always so imperious in the human heart, Marius took the note and held it tight.

Nothing else remained of the colonel. Monsieur Gillenormand had his sword and uniform sold to a secondhand clothes dealer. The neighbors raided the garden and made off with the rare flowers there. The other plants became bushy and straggly or died.

Marius had only stayed in Vernon for forty-eight hours. After the funeral, he went straight back to Paris and got stuck into law again, without giving his father another thought, as though his father had never lived. In two days, the colonel had been buried and in three days, forgotten.

Marius wore a band of crepe on his hat. That was all.

## V. THE USEFULNESS OF GOING TO MASS IF YOU WANT TO BE A REVOLUTIONARY

Marius had stuck to the religious habits of his childhood. One Sunday when he had gone to hear mass at Saint-Sulpice, in the same chapel of the Virgin that his aunt used to take him to when he was little, being even more absentminded and dreamy than usual that day, he took a seat behind a pillar and knelt, without paying it any attention, on a Utrecht velvet chair on the back of which was written the name *M. Mabeuf, churchwarden.* Mass had scarcely begun when an old man appeared and said to Marius: "Monsieur, that is my place."

Marius swiftly moved along and the old man took his chair.

When mass was over, Marius remained pensive as he moved along; the old man came up again and said to him: "I beg your pardon, Monsieur, for having disturbed you a moment ago and for disturbing you again now, but you must have found me most annoying and so I must explain."

"Monsieur," said Marius, "that is not necessary."

"Yes it is!" the old man pursued. "I don't want you to get the wrong idea about me. You see, that place means a lot to me. It seems to me that mass is better from there. Why? I'll tell you. It is from that place, there, that I used to watch, for years, regularly every two or three months, a poor brave father who had no other opportunity and no other way of seeing his son, because, for family reasons, he was prevented from doing so. He used to come at the time he knew that his son was brought along to mass. The little boy had no idea that his father was there. Perhaps he didn't even know he had a father, poor innocent babe! The father, well, he would stand behind that pillar so he couldn't be seen. He would watch his boy and he would cry. He adored the little fellow, that poor man! I could see that. That spot has become sort of sacred for me and I've got into the habit of going there to hear mass. I prefer it to the churchwarden's bench I have a right to as churchwarden. I even got to know the poor unfortunate gentleman a little. He had a father-in-law, a rich sister-in-law, relatives, I don't know exactly, who threatened to disinherit the boy if he, the father, saw him. He sacrificed himself so that his boy would be rich one day and happy. They kept him away from the boy because of his political opinions. Of course,

I approve of politial opinions, but some people just don't know where to draw the line. My God! Because a man was at Waterloo, that doesn't make him a monster; you don't separate a father from his son for that. He was one of Bonaparte's colonels. He is dead now, I think. He lived in Vernon, where I have a brother who is a curé, and his name was something like Pontmarie or Montpercy. He had a beautiful saber cut, incredible."

"Pontmercy?" said Marius, going white.

"Exactly. Pontmercy. Did you know him?"

"Monsieur," said Marius, "he was my father."

The old churchwarden joined his hands and cried: "Ah! You are the child! Yes, that'd be right, he'd have to be a man by now. Well! My poor child, you can say you had a father who loved you more than all the world."

Marius offered the old man his arm and walked him home. The next day, he said to Monsieur Gillenormand: "We've organized a hunting party with a few friends. Would you mind if I went away for three days?"

"Four!" replied the grandfather. "Go and enjoy yourself." And with a wink, he whispered to his daughter: "Some little minx!"

## VI. What It Is to Have Met a Churchwarden

Where Marius went, we will see a bit further on.

Marius was away for three days, then he returned to Paris, where he went straight to the law school library and asked for the collection of the *Moniteur*.

He read the *Moniteur*;[1] he read all the histories of the Republic and the Empire, the *Mémorial de Sainte-Hélène*,[2] all the memoirs, newspapers, bulletins, proclamations; he devoured the lot. The first time he came across his father's name in the bulletins of the Grande Armée,[3] he had a fever for a whole week. He went to see the generals under whom Georges Pontmercy had served, among others, the comte H——. Mabeuf, the churchwarden, whom he went to see again, had given him an account of life in Vernon, the colonel's retirement, his flowers, his loneliness. Marius ended up knowing very well this rare, sublime, and gentle man, this rather lamblike lion who had been his father.

Meanwhile, engrossed as he was in all this study, which took up all his time and all his waking thoughts, he almost never saw the Gillenormands anymore. At mealtimes, he appeared; then, when they looked for him, he was gone. The aunt grumbled. Old man Gillenormand smiled. "Bah! Bah! He's at the age when you become girl-crazy!" Sometimes the old man would add: "Good God! I thought it was just a fling, but it looks like it's real passion."

It certainly was real passion. Marius was beginning to worship his father.

At the same time, an extraordinary change took shape in his ideas. The phases of this change were numerous and sequential. As this is the story of many minds of our times, we believe it useful to follow these phases step by step and to flag each one. The history he had just cast his eyes on floored him. His initial reaction was dazzlement.

The Republic, the Empire, had been nothing but monstrous words for him till that moment. The Republic, a guillotine at dusk; the Empire, a saber at night. He had now looked into it and found that, where he was expecting only a chaos of darkness, he saw, in a sort of earth-shattering jolt mingled with fear and joy, bright shining stars, Mirabeau, Vergniaud, Saint-Just, Robespierre, Camille Desmoulins, Danton;[4] and he had seen a sun rise, Napoléon. He did not know where he was. He reeled back, blinded by so much light. Little by little, when amazement passed and he got used to this radiance, he gazed upon actions without feeling dizzy, he studied the characters involved without feeling terror. The Revolution and the Empire placed themselves luminously in perspective before his visionary eyes, and he saw how each of these two groups of men and events came down to two hugely momentous developments: the Republic's establishing the sovereignty of civil law and restoring it to the masses; the Empire's establishing the sovereignty of the French ideal and imposing it on Europe. He saw the great figure of the People emerge from the Revolution, and from the Empire, the great figure of France. He declared in his conscience that all that had been for the good.

What he neglected in his dazzlement in this initial, far too sweeping assessment, we feel no need to spell out here. We are describing the state of a mind on the move. Progress doesn't happen overnight. That said, once and for all, and for what precedes as well as what follows, we will plow on.

He then realized that until that moment he had not understood his country any more than he had understood his father. He had known neither one nor the other and he had deliberately kept himself in the dark. Now he could see and he admired the one and adored the other.

He was full of regret and remorse and he thought with despair how all that his heart held, he could now only say to a grave. Oh, if only his father were still alive, if he still had him, if God in his mercy and goodness had only allowed his father to go on living, how he would have run, how he would have flown, how he would have cried out to his father: "Father! Here I am! It's me! My heart is the same as yours! I am your son!" How he would have kissed his old white head, flooded his hair with tears, admired his scar, squeezed his hands, adored his clothes, kissed his feet! Oh, why had his father died so soon, before his time, before justice was done, before his son came to love him! Marius had a permanent sob in his heart that said at every moment: *alas!* At the same time, he became more genuinely serious, more genuinely grave, more sure of his faith and of his thinking. At every instant, glimmers of the truth carried his reasoning further. A sort of inner growth occurred in him. He felt a sort of natural expansion that these two things brought him, new as they were for him—his father and his country.

As though he had a key, everything opened; he could explain to himself what he had hated, he could fathom what he had abhorred; from that moment on, he could see clearly the providential, divine, and human meaning of great things he had been taught to detest and of great men he had been trained to curse. When he thought of his previous views, which only went back as far as the day before, though they seemed already so old, he felt furious with himself and he smiled.

From the rehabilitation of his father he naturally went on to the rehabilitation of Napoléon. Yet the latter, to be honest, was pretty hard work.

From infancy he had been imbued with the verdict of the party of 1814 concerning Bonaparte. Of course, all the prejudices of the Restoration, all its interests, all its self-serving instincts, tended to disfigure Napoléon. It execrated the man even more than Robespierre. It had exploited cleverly enough the nation's weariness and the hate mothers felt. Bonaparte had become an almost fabulous monster and in order to defile him in the popular imagination, which, as we pointed out a moment ago, is like the imagination of children, the party of 1814 whipped out every frightening mask it could marshal, one after the other, from the terrible that remains grandiose to the terrible that verges on the grotesque, from Tiberius to the bogeyman. Thus, in speaking of Bonaparte, you were free to sob or to gasp with laughter, provided your reaction was based on hate. Marius had never had—about "that man," as he was called—any other notions in his head. They matched the tenacity that was part of his nature. There was in him a stubborn little man who hated Napoléon.

By reading history and especially by studying documents and firsthand records, the veil that hid Napoléon from Marius's eyes was lifted bit by bit. He glimpsed something that was immense, and suspected that he had been wrong about Bonaparte till that moment as about all the rest; every day he saw better and he began to climb slowly, one by one, almost reluctantly at first, then with intoxication and as though drawn by an irresistible fascination, steps that started off dark then gradually became dimly illuminated, only to end in the luminous and splendid blaze of enthusiasm.

One night, he was alone in his little room under the eaves. His candle was burning and he was reading, leaning on the table beside his open window. All kinds of dreamy notions came to him from space and mingled with his thoughts. What a spectacle night is! You hear faint sounds without knowing where they come from, you see Jupiter, which is twelve hundred times bigger than earth, glowing red like embers; the skies are black, the stars shine, it is tremendous.

He was reading the bulletins of the Grande Armée, those Homeric stanzas written on the field of battle; now and again, he saw his father's name there, always, the name of the emperor; the whole great empire appeared to him; he felt as though a tide were swelling inside him and that it was rising; it seemed to him at times that his father brushed past him like a breath and spoke in his ear; he gradually became strange; he thought he could hear drums, cannon, trumpets, the measured tread of the battalions, the dull and distant gallop of the cavalries; from time to time, he lifted his eyes to the sky and looked at the colossal constellations glimmering in the limitless depths, then his eyes dropped back onto his book and he saw there other colossal things stir in the shadows. His heart was hammering. He was transported, trembling, panting; suddenly, without knowing himself what had gotten into him and what impulse he was obeying, he stood up, stretched both arms out the window, stared into the darkness, the silence, tenebrous infinity, the eternal immensity, and he shouted: "Long live the emperor!"

From that moment, it was all over. The Ogre of Corsica, the usurper, the tyrant, the monster who was his sisters' lover, the ham actor who took lessons from Talma, the poisoner of Jaffa,⁵ the tiger, Buonaparte—all that evaporated and made way in his mind for an indistinct and dazzling radiance where the pale marble phantom of Caesar shone out from an inaccessible height. For his father, the emperor had only been the beloved captain you admire and to whom you devote yourself; he was, for Marius, something more. He was the predestined builder of the French order succeeding the Roman order in world domination. He was the prodigious architect of a collapse, the heir of Charlemagne, of Louis XI, of Henri IV, of Richelieu, of Louis XIV, and of the Committee of Public Safety,⁶ doubtless having his blemishes, his faults, and even his crimes, for he was human, after all. But august in his faults, brilliant in his blemishes, mighty in his crimes. He was the foreordained man of destiny who had forced all nations to say: that great nation. He was more than this, even; he was the very incarnation of France, conquering Europe by the sword he held in his hand, and the world by the light he gave out. Marius saw in Bonaparte the dazzling specter that will always rise up at the frontier and watch over the future. Dictator, but despot; despot issuing from a republic and symbolizing a revolution. Napoléon became for him the man who was also the people, just as Jesus was the man who was also God.

As you can see, like all newcomers to a religion, he was intoxicated by his conversion, and, in his headlong rush to join, he went too far. That was his nature; once he was on an incline, it was almost impossible for him to hold back. A fanatical passion for the sword took hold of him and muddied his enthusiasm for the ideal. He did not realize that, along with the genius, what he admired—indiscriminately—was force; in other words, he was setting up, in the twin compartments of his idolatry, what is divine on one side and, on the other, what is brutal. In several respects, he began to deceive himself in other matters. He accepted everything. There is a way of falling into error on the road to truth. He had a kind of violent good faith that swallowed everything outright—lock, stock, and barrel. On this new path he had taken, in condemning the wrongs of the ancien régime as in measuring the glory of Napoléon, he neglected all extenuating circumstances.

Be that as it may, a mighty leap had been taken. Where he had once seen the fall of the monarchy, he now saw the emergence of France. His whole orientation had shifted. Sunset had turned into sunrise. He had turned around.

All these revolutions were accomplished in him without his family being any the wiser.

When, in this mysterious travail, he had completely shed his old Bourbon and Ultra skin, when he had stripped off the aristocrat, the Jacobin, and the royalist, when he was fully revolutionary, profoundly democratic, and almost republican, he went to an engraver on the quai des Orfèvres and ordered from him a hundred calling cards bearing this name: *Baron Marius Pontmercy.*[7]

Which was merely a perfectly logical consequence of the change that had been effected in him, a change in which everything revolved around his father. Only, as he knew no one and could not spray his cards around to any porters, he stuck them in his pocket.

By another natural consequence, the closer he came to his father, to his memory, and to the things for which the colonel had fought for twenty-five years, the further away he moved from his grandfather. As we said, for a long while Monsieur Gillenormand's outlook had rubbed him the wrong way. There was already between them all the friction there can be between an earnest young man and a frivolous old-timer. Géronte's gaiety shocks and exasperates the melancholy Werther.[8] For as long as they had shared the same political views and the same ideas, Marius had stood together with Monsieur Gillenormand as on a bridge. When the bridge fell, the gulf opened. And then, above all, Marius felt inexpressibly revolted in thinking that it was Monsieur Gillenormand who, for entirely stupid reasons, had torn him mercilessly from the colonel, thereby depriving the father of the son and the son of the father.

Out of piety for his father, Marius had almost come to feel aversion for his grandfather.

But, as we said, nothing of this was betrayed outwardly. Only, he grew colder and colder, was laconic at meals, and hardly ever home. When his aunt scolded him for this, he was very sweet and gave as an excuse his studies, courses, exams, symposia, and so on. The grandfather stuck to his infallible diagnosis: "In love! I know what I'm talking about."

Every so often, Marius stayed away from home.

"Where can he possibly have got to?" his aunt would ask.

On one of these excursions afield, which were always very short, he went to Montfermeil in compliance with his father's injunction and he had looked for the former sergeant of Waterloo, Thénardier, the innkeeper. Thénardier had gone bankrupt, the inn was closed, and nobody knew what had become of him. For this research, Marius was away from home for four days.

"Yes, indeed," said the grandfather, "he's going to a lot of trouble."

They thought they noticed that he was wearing something on his chest under his shirt and that was attached to his neck by a black ribbon.

## VII. A BIT OF SKIRT

We mentioned a lancer.

He was a great-grandnephew of Monsieur Gillenormand's on the paternal side, and he led the life of the garrison, away from the family and far from any domestic hearth. Lieutenant Théodule Gillenormand fulfilled all the desirable criteria of what is known as a good-looking officer.[1] He had "a girl's waist," a way of carelessly trailing his victorious saber, and a handlebar mustache. He only very rarely came to Paris, so rarely that Marius had never set eyes on him. The two cousins knew each other only by name. Théodule was, as I think we said, the favorite of dear old Aunt Gillenormand, who preferred him because she never saw him. Not seeing people allows you to think of them as perfect in all kinds of ways.

One morning, Mademoiselle Gillenormand the elder retired to her cubbyhole as excited as her placid temperament would allow. Marius had just asked his grandfather once more for permission to make another little trip away, adding that he counted on leaving that very night. "Go!" the grandfather had replied and then Monsieur Gillenormand had added an aside, lifting his eyebrows practically to his hairline: "When it comes to sleeping away from home, he's becoming a repeat offender." Mademoiselle had gone up to her room most intrigued and had thrown this exclamation mark at the stairs, "That's a bit rich!" and this question mark, "Where on earth does he get to?" She foresaw some affair of the heart, more or less illicit, a woman in the shadows, a rendezvous, a mystery, and she would not have minded sticking her beak in it. Savoring a mystery is like being first one in on a scandal; holy souls are not at all averse to such things. There is in the secret compartments of bigotry a certain taste for scandal.

So she was vaguely gripped by a need to know the whole story.

To distract herself from such prurient curiosity, which shook her up a bit more than was her wont, she had taken refuge in her talents and had sat down to embellishing, in cotton on cotton, one of those embroideries of the Empire and the Restoration that involve a lot of cabriolet wheels. Dreary work, crabby worker. She had been on her backside in her chair for several hours when the door swung open. Mademoiselle Gillenormand lifted her beak; Lieutenant

Théodule was before her, making her the standard salute. She let out a shriek of delight. You may be old, you may be a prude, you may be devout, you may be the aunt; but it is always nice to see a lancer step into your bedroom.

"There you are, Théodule!" she cried.

"Just passing by, Auntie."

"Well, give me a kiss, then."

"Here you go!" said Théodule.

And he kissed her. Aunt Gillenormand went to her secretaire and opened it.

"You'll be staying with us at least this week?"

"Auntie, I'm off again this evening."

"That's not possible!"

"Mathematically."

"Stay, my darling Théodule, please."

"My heart says yes, but my orders say no. It's a simple story. We're moving garrisons; we were in Melun, now they're putting us in Gaillon. To get from the old garrison to the new one, you have to go through Paris. So I said to myself: I know what I'll do. I'll go and see my auntie."

"And this is for your trouble."

She put ten louis in his hand.

"You mean for my pleasure, auntie dear."

Théodule kissed her a second time and she had the thrill of having her neck grazed a little by the braid of his uniform.

"And are you doing the trip on horseback with your regiment?" she asked him.

"No, Auntie. I so wanted to see you, I've got special leave. My groom's taking my horse; I'll be going by coach. Speaking of which, I have to ask you something."

"What?"

"My cousin Marius Pontmercy is traveling that way, too, is he not?"

"How should I know?" said the aunt, her curiosity suddenly violently piqued.

"As I was coming over, I went to the coach to reserve a seat in the coupé."

"And?"

"A traveler had already come and reserved a seat on top.[2] I saw his name on the sheet."

"What name?"

"Marius Pontmercy."

"That no-hoper!" cried the aunt. "Ah, your cousin is not a good steady boy like you. To think he'll be spending the night in a coach!"

"Like me."

"But you, it's out of duty; him, it's sheer dissipation."

"Goodness!" gulped Théodule.

Here, something happened to Mademoiselle Gillenormand the elder; she had an idea. If she had been a man, she would have slapped her forehead. She shouted at Théodule: "Do you know your cousin doesn't know who you are?"

"No. I've seen him, all right, but he has never deigned to notice me."

"So you'll be traveling together like that?"

"Him on top, me inside."

"Where's this coach going?"

"To Les Andelys."

"That's where Marius is going, then?"

"Unless, like me, he stops en route. I'll be getting out at Vernon to pick up the connection for Gaillon. I don't know anything about Marius's itinerary."

"Marius! What a horrible name! Why on earth did we call him Marius! Whereas you, at least, are called Théodule!"[3]

"I'd prefer to be called Alfred," said the officer.

"Listen, Théodule."

"I'm listening, Auntie."

"Listen carefully."

"I am listening carefully."

"Are you ready?"

"Yes."

"Well, then, Marius often stays away."

"Ha, ha!"

"He travels."

"Ah! Ah!"

"He sleeps away from home."

"Oh! Oh!"

"We'd like to know what's at the bottom of it."

Théodule answered with all the calm of a man in the artillery: "Some skirt."

And with that stifled chuckle that betrays certainty, he added: "Some little minx."

"Evidently!" cried his aunt, who could have sworn she was hearing Monsieur Gillenormand and who felt her own conviction firmed up by that word *minx* pronounced in almost the same way by the great-uncle and the grand-nephew. She went on: "Do us a favor. Follow Marius for a while. He doesn't know who you are, so it will be easy for you. Since there is some minx, try and see this minx. You can tell us all about it by letter. It will amuse his grandfather."

Théodule did not much like spying of the sort; but he was very much moved by the ten louis and thought he could see more of them lining up. He accepted the commission, saying: "Just as you like, Auntie." And he added to himself: "So now I'm a chaperone."

Mademoiselle Gillenormand kissed him.

"You're not one to get up to that sort of mischief, Théodule. You follow dis-cipline, you're a slave to orders, you're a man of scruple and duty; you'd never leave your family in the lurch to go gallivanting about with some shameless creature."

The lancer gave the complacent grin of a pickpocket praised for his pro-bity, Cartouche revered.

On the evening that followed this tête-à-tête, Marius hopped up on the coach without suspecting that he was under surveillance. As for the detective, the first thing he did was fall asleep. His sleep was sound and conscientious. Argus snored all night.[4]

At daybreak, the coach driver cried out: "Vernon! Vernon relay next stop! Passengers for Vernon!" And Lieutenant Théodule woke up.

"Right," he mumbled, still half-asleep. "This is where I get off."

Then his memory gradually unfogged, an effect of waking up, and he thought of his aunt, the ten louis, and the account he had agreed to give of Mar-ius's comings and goings. It made him laugh.

"Maybe he's not on the coach anymore," he thought, as he buttoned up his uniform jacket. "He might have stopped at Poissy; he might have stopped at Triel; if he didn't get out at Meulan, he might have got out at Mantes; unless he got out at Rolleboise, or unless he pushed on to Pacy, where you can either head left toward Évreux or right toward Laroche-Guyon. You run after him, Auntie. What the hell am I going to write to her, the dear old thing?"

At that moment a pair of black trousers clambered down from the top deck and appeared at the coach window.

"Could that be Marius?" the lieutenant wondered.

It was Marius.

A little peasant girl, at the back of the car, mixed up among the horses and the postilions, was offering flowers to the travelers. "Give your ladies flowers," she cried.

Marius approached her and bought the most beautiful flowers on her tray.

"Now that," said Théodule, jumping down from the car, "has got me going. Who the hell is he going to take those flowers to? It'd take a damned pretty woman for such a beautiful bouquet. I'd like to see that one."

And so, no longer by proxy now but out of personal curiosity, like a dog hunting on its own behalf, he began to trail Marius.

Marius paid no attention whatsoever to Théodule. Some elegant women got down from the coach but he did not even give them a glance. He seemed not to see anything around him.

"He's in love—and how!" thought Théodule.

Marius headed for the church.

"This gets better," Théodule said to himself. "The church! Of course.

Nothing like spicing up a rendezvous with a bit of a mass. What could be more exquisite than eyeing someone over the good Lord."

Marius reached the church, but did not go in; instead he turned and went behind the *chevet*. He disappeared around the corner of one of the buttresses of the apse.

"The rendezvous must be outside in the open," said Théodule. "Let's see the girl."

And he advanced on the tips of his boots toward the corner Marius had turned.

When he reached it, he was flummoxed.

Marius was kneeling in the grass over a grave, with his head in both hands. He had scattered his bouquet over it. At the far end of the grave, at a bulge that marked the head, there was a black wooden cross with this name in white letters: COLONEL BARON PONTMERCY. You could hear Marius sobbing.

The girl was a grave.

## VIII. Marble Versus Granite

This was where Marius had come the first time he had absented himself from Paris. This was where he returned each time Monsieur Gillenormand said: "He's sleeping away from home."

Lieutenant Théodule was absolutely floored by this unexpectedly close contact with a sepulchre; he experienced an unpleasant and odd sensation that he was incapable of analyzing, which had to do with respect for a grave combined with respect for a colonel. He backed away, leaving Marius alone in the cemetery, and there was something that smacked of military discipline in this backtracking. Death appeared to him with outsize epaulets and he almost gave it a military salute. Not knowing what to write to his aunt, he opted to write nothing at all; and perhaps nothing would have come of the discovery made by Théodule about Marius's love life if, through one of those mysterious coincidences that so frequently happen, the scene in Vernon had not had a sort of repercussion almost immediately in Paris.

Marius returned from Vernon early in the morning on the third day, got out at his grandfather's, and, weary after two nights spent in the coach, and feeling the need to make up for his lack of sleep by an hour at the swimming school, ran up to his room, took only enough time to remove his traveling coat and the black ribbon round his neck, and went off to the baths.

Monsieur Gillenormand had risen early, like all old men in the pink of health, and had heard him come in and had rushed as fast as his old pins would carry him upstairs to the rooftop landing where Marius's room was, to give him a hug—and ask him a few questions while he was at it in the hope of finding out a bit more about where he'd been.

But the young man had taken less time to go down than the octogenarian to climb up, and when old man Gillenormand stepped into the attic room, Marius was no longer there.

The bed had not been slept in and on the bed were laid out, trustingly, the coat and the black ribbon.

"I prefer that," said Monsieur Gillenormand.

And a moment later he made his entrance into the drawing room where Mademoiselle Gillenormand the elder was already in position, embroidering her cabriolet wheels.

His entrance was triumphant.

Monsieur Gillenormand held the coat in one hand and the neck ribbon in the other and he cried: "Victory! We are about to penetrate the mystery! We are going to find out how the story ends! We are going to put the finger on our sly little friend's debauchery. We're cutting straight to the romance! I have the portrait!"

Indeed, a black shagreen locket, similar to a medallion, was hanging from the ribbon. The old man grabbed this locket and studied it for a while without opening it, with the greedy, ravished, angry eyes of a poor starving wretch eyeing a sumptuous meal not meant for him as it passes under his nose.

"For obviously this is a portrait. I know what I'm talking about. It's worn tenderly over the heart. What dunderheads they are! Some ugly tart that'd make you shudder, I'll warrant! Young men have such bad taste these days!"

"Let's see, father," said the old maid.

The locket opened when you pressed a spring. All they found in it was a piece of paper, folded.

"The same old story," Monsieur Gillenormand said, bursting out laughing. "I know what this is. It's a love letter!"

"Ah, let's read it then!" said the aunt.

And she put her spectacles on. They unfolded the note and read the following: "*For my son.*—The Emperor made me a baron on the battlefield of Waterloo. Since the Restoration contests this title, which I have paid for with my blood, my son will take it and bear it. It goes without saying that he will be worthy of it."

What the father and daughter felt words can never tell. They felt themselves chilled to the marrow by the breath from a death's-head. They did not exchange a word. Only, Monsieur Gillenormand said in a low voice, as though talking to himself: "It's that swashbuckler's writing."

The aunt examined the note, turned it over and around, then put it back in the locket.

At the same moment, a tiny oblong parcel wrapped in blue paper fell from a coat pocket. Mademoiselle Gillenormand picked it up and undid the blue paper. It was Marius's set of one hundred calling cards. She passed one to Monsieur Gillenormand, who read: "Baron Marius Pontmercy."

The old man rang. Nicolette came. Monsieur Gillenormand took the ribbon, the locket, and the coat, threw the lot into the middle of the room, and said: "Take this trash away."

A good hour passed in the deepest silence.

The old man and the old maid were sitting with their backs to each other and were probably thinking, each on their own, the same things. At the end of the hour, Aunt Gillenormand said: "Lovely!"

A few minutes later Marius appeared. He came in through the front door. Before he had even put a foot in the door of the drawing room, he saw his grandfather, who was holding one of his calling cards in his hand and who, on seeing him, cried out with his crushing air of sneering bourgeois superiority: "Well, well! Well, well, well! You are a baron now? I present you with my compliments. What does this mean?"

Marius went slightly red and replied: "It means that I'm my father's son."

Monsieur Gillenormand stopped laughing and said in a harsh voice: "Your father? I am your father."

"My father," Marius went on, his eyes downcast and his manner stern, "was a humble and heroic man who served the Republic and France gloriously, who was great in the greatest history that men have ever made, who lived for a quarter of a century in a camp, under cannon fire and musket fire during the day, at night, in snow, in mud, in rain, who captured two standards, who received twenty wounds, who died forgotten and abandoned, and who only ever did one thing wrong, which was to love two ungrateful wretches too much—his country and me!"

This was more than Monsieur Gillenormand could bear to hear. At that word *Republic,* he had got to his feet, or rather, shot to his feet. Every one of the words that Marius had just uttered had inflicted on the face of the old royalist the effect of blasts of forge bellows on a burning brand. He went from black to red, from red to purple, and from purple to a dangerous flare.

"Marius!" he yelled. "You abominable child! I don't know what your father was! I don't want to know! I don't know anything about him and I don't know him! But what I do know is that there has never been anything but miserable bastards among all those sorts of scum! They are all, every one of them, rogues, cutthroats, red caps, thieves![1] Every one of them, I tell you! Every one of them, I tell you! I don't know anyone! I say every one of them! You hear me, Marius! Don't you see, you're as much a baron as my slipper! They were all bandits who worked for Robespierre! Doing his dirty work! All the brigands who served Bu-o-na-parte! All traitors who betrayed, betrayed, betrayed! Their legitimate king! All cowards who ran away from the Prussians and from the English at Waterloo!

There you have what I know. If Monsieur your father is among them, I don't know, I'm sorry, too bad, I am your servant!"

It was Marius's turn to be the brand and Monsieur Gillenormand the bellows. Marius was shaking all over, he did not know where to look, his head was on fire. He was the priest who sees all his hosts thrown to the wind, the fakir who sees some passerby spit on his idol. Such things could not be said with impunity in front of him. But what could he do? His father had just been trampled underfoot and stamped on in his presence, but by whom? By his grandfather. How could he avenge one without outraging the other? He couldn't possibly insult his grandfather and it was equally impossible not to stand up for his father. On the one hand, a sacred tomb, on the other, white hair. For a moment or two he stood, drunk and tottering, with this whirlwind swirling around in his head; then he looked up, stared hard at his grandfather and shouted in a thundering voice: "Down with the Bourbons and that fat pig of a Louis XVIII!"

Louis XVIII had been dead four years,[2] but he didn't care.

The old man, red as a beetroot as he was, suddenly went whiter than his hair. He turned toward a bust of the duc de Berry[3] on the mantelpiece and bowed deeply to it with a sort of singular majesty. Then he strode twice, slowly and in silence, from the fireplace to the window and from the window to the fireplace, crossing the whole length of the room, causing the parquet to creak, like a stone statue on the move. The second time, he bent over his daughter, who was bearing up under this shock with the stupor of an old sheep, and said to her with an almost calm smile: "A baron like monsieur and a bourgeois like me cannot remain under the same roof."

And suddenly standing erect again, wan, trembling, terrible, his forehead swelling with the frightening radiance of anger, he stretched his arm toward Marius and shouted: "Get out."

Marius left the house.

The next day, Monsieur Gillenormand said to his daughter: "You will send that bloodsucker sixty pistoles[4] every six months and never speak to me of him again."

Having an immense reserve of fury to vent and not knowing what to do with it, he continued to address his daughter coldly as *vous* for over three months.

Marius, for his part, had stormed out in outrage. One circumstance we must mention further aggravated his exasperation. Such piddling coincidences always complicate domestic dramas. Grievances are intensified by them, even though in reality they don't make anything any worse. In swiftly carting Marius's "trash" to his room on his grandfather's orders, Nicolette had, without realizing, dropped the medallion of black shagreen with the note written by the colonel in it, probably on the attic stairs, which were in darkness. Neither this note nor the medallion could ever be found. Marius was convinced that "Mon-

sieur Gillenormand"—from that day forth he never called him anything else—
had thrown his father's "will" into the fire. He knew by heart the few lines the
colonel had written and, consequently, nothing was lost. But the piece of paper
itself, the handwriting, that sacred relic, all this was his heart itself. What had
they done with it?

Marius had gone away without saying where he was going, without knowing where he was going, with nothing but thirty francs, his watch, and a few rags
in an overnight bag. He had climbed up into a cabriolet parked at the cab stand,
had rented it by the hour, and set out willy-nilly for the quartier Latin.

What was to become of Marius?

# BOOK FOUR

# FRIENDS OF THE ABC

## I. A GROUP THAT NEARLY BECAME HISTORY

In those days, outwardly so oblivious, a certain revolutionary frisson was vaguely felt around the place. Gusts of hot air rose up from the depths of '89 and '91 and floated about. The young were in the process of shedding their skins, if you'll forgive the expression. People were transformed, almost without suspecting it, by the very movement of time. The hands that march over the dial are also busy marching inside people's souls. Everyone took the step forward that they had to take. The royalists became liberals, the liberals became democrats.

It was like a rising tide chopped up by a thousand backward surges. The specialty of the backward surge is to churn things up as it ebbs; hence some very strange combinations of ideas; people worshipped Napoléon and Liberty at one and the same time. We are talking about history here. These were the mirages of those bygone days. Opinions go through phases. Voltairean royalism, that bizarre variation, had a counterpart no less strange in Bonapartist liberalism.

Other groups of leading lights were more serious. Some sought to define principles; others tackled the law. People were very keen on the absolute, imagining infinite forms it might take; the absolute, by its very rigidity, drives spirits upward into the blue and sets them floating in limitlessness. There is nothing like dogma to spawn dreams. And there is nothing like dreams to generate the future. Utopia today, flesh and blood tomorrow.

Advanced opinions, like suitcases, had false bottoms. The mysterious power emerging threatened "the established order," which was suspect and sly. This was a sign of revolution in the making, if ever there was one. The ulterior motives of power collide head-on with the ulterior motives of the people who undermine it. The incubation of insurrection is the rejoinder to the premeditated coup d'état.

At that time, France still did not have any of those vast underground organizations like the German Tugendbund or the Italian Carbonari; but here and there obscure underground cells were ramifying. The Cougourde[1] started up in Aix; in Paris, among other affiliations of the kind, there was the Society of the Friends of the ABC.

What were the Friends of the ABC? A society with the avowed aim of educating children, which, in reality, was designed to rehabilitate men.

They declared themselves the friends of the ABC—of the *abaissé*, the abased, the downtrodden, the people. They wanted to raise the people up, to set them on their feet. A pun you would be wrong to laugh at. Puns are sometimes serious in politics; witness the *Castratus ad castrata*, which made Narses an army general; witness *Barbari et Barbarini*; witness *Fueros y fuegos*; witness *Tu es Petrus et super hanc Petram*,[2] etc., etc.

The Friends of the ABC were not numerous. It was a secret society at the embryo stage; we would say virtually a clique, if cliques produced heroes. They met in Paris in two places, near Les Halles in a tavern named Corinthe that comes up again later, and near the Panthéon in a little café in the place Saint-Michel named the Café Musain,[3] today demolished; the first of these meeting places was close to the workers, the second, to the students.

The secret meetings of the Friends of the ABC were normally held in a back room in the Café Musain. This room was fairly removed from the café proper, with which it was connected by a very long corridor, and it had two windows and an exit onto the tiny rue des Grès via concealed stairs. They would smoke there, have a drink, play cards, have a laugh. They would carry on in very loud voices about everything and in very low voices about everything else. On the wall, an old map of France under the Republic was nailed up— enough of a clue for any passing police officer to smell a rat.

Most of the Friends of the ABC were students involved in an entente cordiale with a few workers. Here are the names of the main ones.[4] They belong to a certain extent to history: Enjolras, Combeferre, Jean Prouvaire, Feuilly, Courfeyrac, Bahorel, Lesgle or Laigle, Joly, Grantaire.

These young men formed a sort of family among themselves, they were such close friends. All of them except Laigle were from the south.

It was a remarkable group before it vanished into the invisible depths at our backs. At the point we have reached in our tale, it might perhaps be useful to shine a beam of light on those young heads before the reader sees them sink into the shadows of a tragic episode.

Enjolras, who comes first on our list—we will see why later—was an only son and rich.

Enjolras was a charming young man, capable of being terrifying. He was angelically beautiful. He was Antinous,[5] wild. To see the thoughtful light shining in his eyes, you'd have thought that he had already, in a previous life, lived through the apocalypse of the Revolution. He was familiar with its tradition as though he had been a witness to it. He knew every last detail of the broader canvas. His nature was both pompously dogmatic and warlike, which is strange in an adolescent. He was both officiant priest and militant; a soldier of democracy, in the immediate term, and, above and beyond the contemporary movement, a priest of the ideal. He had deep-set eyes, slightly red eyelids, a thick lower lip that could easily turn disdainful, a high forehead. A lot of forehead in a face is like a lot of sky over a skyline. Like certain young men at the end of last century and the beginning of this who were illustrious early, he had an excessively youthful look, as fresh as a young girl's, though with moments of pallor. Already a man, he seemed still to be a child. He was twenty-two years old but he looked seventeen. He was grave, he did not seem to know that there was on earth a creature known as woman. He had only one passion, justice, one thought, to overturn all obstacles. On the Aventine Hill, he would have been Gracchus; in the Convention, he would have been Saint-Just.[6] He barely saw the roses, ignored the spring, didn't hear the birds sing; Evadné's bare breast would not have moved him any more than Aristogeiton; for him, as for Harmodius,[7] flowers were good only for camouflaging swords. He was austere in his pleasures. Before all that was not the Republic, he lowered his eyes chastely, Liberty's marble lover. His words were fiercely inspired and had the trembling note of the hymn about them. He would suddenly spread his wings and take flight when you least expected it. Woe betide anyone who thought they could entice him into some casual fling! Had some grisette from the place Cambrai or the rue Saint-Jean-de-Beauvais clapped eyes on that college-escapee face, that page-boy neck, those long blond eyelashes, those blue eyes, that wild hair flying in the wind, those rosy cheeks, those fresh young lips, those exquisite teeth, and felt a violent stab of hunger for all that golden glow, and had she been bold enough to try and thrust her beauty on Enjolras, she would have promptly been shot a withering look from out of an unknowable abyss that would have taught her not to confuse the gallant cherubs of Beaumarchais with the awesome cherubim of Ezekiel.[8]

Alongside Enjolras, who represented the logic of the revolution, stood Combeferre, who represented its philosophy. Between the logic of the revolution and its philosophy, there is this difference—that its logic can logically lead to war, while its philosophy can only end in peace. Combeferre completed and corrected Enjolras. He was less high-minded and wider-ranging. He wanted them to fill hearts and minds with principles extrapolated into general ideas; he said, "Revolution, yes, but not without civilization"; and all around the mountain peak he opened up the vast blue horizon. This provided an accessible and pragmatic element in all Combeferre's views. The revolution was more breathable with Combeferre than with Enjolras. Enjolras maintained its divine-right side and Combeferre its natural right. The former sided with Robespierre; the latter confined himself to Condorcet. Combeferre lived a much more normal life than Enjolras. If it had been given to these two young men to step onto the stage of history, one would have played the righteous man, the other would have played the sage. Enjolras was more manly. Combeferre was more human. *Homo et Vir*[9]—that was, indeed, the difference between them. Combeferre was as gentle as Enjolras was severe, from native innocence. He liked the word *citizen* but he preferred the word *man*. He would gladly have said *hombre,* like the Spanish. He read everything, did the theaters, followed public lectures, learned about the polarization of light from Arago, was wildly inspired by a lecture in which Geoffroy Saint-Hilaire[10] explained the twin functions of the external carotid artery and the internal carotid artery, the one supplying the face, the other supplying the brain; he kept abreast of things, followed science every step of the way, compared Saint-Simon with Fourier,[11] deciphered hieroglyphs, broke open any stones he could get his hands on to sift through geology, would draw a silk moth from memory, point out the mistakes in French in the *Dictionnaire de l'Académie,* studied Puységur and Deleuze,[12] asserted nothing, not even miracles, denied nothing, not even ghosts, flipped through back issues of the *Moniteur,* daydreamed. He claimed that the future was in the hands of the schoolmaster and got involved in issues of education.[13] He wanted society to work tirelessly at raising intellectual and moral standards, popularizing science, circulating ideas and cultivating the minds of the young, and he feared that the current impoverishment of the methods employed, the dire narrowness of the teaching of literature, which was limited to two or three centuries said to be "classical," the tyrannical dogmatism of the official pedants, scholastic prejudices and routines, would wind up turning our colleges into artificial oyster farms. He was well-read, a purist, precise, polytechnical, hardworking, and at the same time imaginative "to the point of having hallucinations," as his friends liked to say. He believed in all these dreams: railroads, the elimination of suffering in surgical operations, the fixing of the image in the camera obscura, the electric telegraph, the use of steering in hot-air balloons. On top of this, he was not afraid of all the bulwarks thrown up everywhere you turn by the various forms of superstition, despotism, and prejudice, designed to shut out the human race. He was one of those who think that science will wind up turning the tables. Enjolras was a leader, Combeferre was a guide. You would have wanted to fight alongside one and walk alongside the other. It wasn't that Combeferre was not capable of fighting, he did not balk at taking an obstacle in hand-to-hand combat or grabbing it by brute force, explosively; but to bring the human race into harmony with its destinies, gradually, through the teaching of axioms and the promulgation of positive laws, was more to his liking; and between two bright lights, he tended toward illumination rather than conflagration. No doubt a raging fire can create light as bright as the light of day, but why not wait for daybreak? A volcano throws light, but sunrise throws even better light. Combeferre perhaps preferred the white purity of the beautiful to the flaming flash of the sublime. Clarity blurred by smoke, progress bought by violence, only half satisfied this tender and serious spirit. Any headlong plunge by a people into truth, any '93, frightened him; but stagnation revolted him even more—he smelled putrefaction and death in it. All in all, he liked sea spray better than miasma, preferred the torrent to the cesspool, and Niagara Falls to the lake of Montfaucon. In short, he wanted neither halt nor haste. While his boisterous friends, chivalrously in love with the absolute, worshipped and incited magnificent revolutionary adventures, Combeferre was inclined to let progress take its course—the right sort of progress, which was coolheaded, perhaps, but pure; methodical but irreproachable, phlegmatic but imperturbable. Combeferre would have fallen to his knees and prayed if it meant the future would arrive in all its candor, and for nothing to trouble the vast and virtuous evolution of the peoples of the world. "Good must be innocent," he never tired of repeating. And, in effect, if the great thing about revolution is that it keeps its eye on the dazzling ideal and flies to it through flashing lightning, with fire and blood in its talons, the beauty of progress is to be stainless; and there is between Washington, who represents the former, and Danton, who embodies the latter, the difference that divides the angel with the wings of a swan and the angel with the wings of an eagle.

Jean Prouvaire was a tad more mellow than Combeferre. He actually called himself Jehan,[14] due to the momentary touch of whimsy that got mixed up in the profound and powerful movement from which that most necessary study of the Middle Ages emerged. Jean Prouvaire was in love, cultivated a flower in a pot, played the flute, wrote poetry, loved the people, pitied womankind, wept for children, confused God and the future in the same trusting attitude, and blamed the Revolution for having caused a royal head to roll, that of André Chénier.[15] His voice was usually soft but would suddenly become manly. He was scholarly to the point of erudition and almost an orientalist. He was good, above all; and, in a way that is perfectly straightforward for those who know how closely goodness borders on greatness, he preferred the great in matters of poetry. He was fluent in Italian, Latin, Greek, and Hebrew; and this served him to read only four poets: Dante, Juvenal, Aeschylus, and Isaiah. In French, he preferred Corneille to Racine, and Agrippa d'Aubigné[16] to Corneille. He liked to stroll through fields of wild oats and cornflowers and was almost as involved with clouds as he was with events. His mind had two modes, one to do with man, the other to do with God; he was either studying or meditating. All day long, he pored over social questions: wages, capital, credit, marriage, religion, freedom of thought, freedom of choice in love, education, crime and punishment, poverty, freedom of association, property, production and distribution, the enigma of life here below that casts its shadow over the human anthill; and at night, he would gaze at those enormous beings, the stars. Like Enjolras, he was an only son and rich. He spoke softly, cocked his head to one side, kept his eyes downcast, smiled apologetically, dressed badly, looked a little gauche, blushed at nothing, was extremely shy. Otherwise, fearless.

Feuilly was a fan-maker, an orphan on both sides, who worked his fingers to the bone for his three francs a day and whose sole thought was to save the world. He had one other worry: to teach himself, which he also described as saving himself. He had taught himself to read and write; all he knew, he had learned on his own. Feuilly was very bighearted. He had a huge embrace. This orphan had adopted the whole world. Since he lacked a mother, he meditated on the motherland. He did not want there to be a single person on earth without a motherland. With the profound clairvoyance of the man of the people, he nurtured deep within what we now know as "the idea of different nationalities." He had learned history for the express purpose of being outraged with good reason. In this inner circle of young utopians, specifically focused on France, he represented the outside world. His specialty was Greece, Poland, Hungary, Romania, Italy.[17] He was always saying those names, appropriately or inappropriately, with the doggedness of those in the right. The rape of Crete and Thessaly by Turkey, of Warsaw by Russia, of Venice by Austria, these violations infuriated him. The great assault and battery of 1772,[18] when Poland was partitioned, got him going more than anything else. There is no more supreme eloquence than that derived from outrage based on truth, and he was eloquent with that kind of eloquence. He never tired of that infamous date, 1772, of that noble and valiant people put down by treachery, of that crime of three, of that monstrous ambush, the prototype and model of all the shocking acts of state repression committed since that have struck several noble nations and erased the records of their birth, so to speak. All contemporary social acts of terrorism derive from the partition of Poland. The partition of Poland is the theorem of which all current political crimes are the corollaries. There has been no despot, no traitor, for what will shortly be a century, who has not initialed, ratified, signed and countersigned, *ne varietur,*[19] the partition of Poland. When you consult the file of modern betrayals, that one appears at the top of the list. The Congress of Vienna consulted this crime before it perpetrated its own. The year 1772 sounds the mort, 1815 gives the hounds their quarry. Such was Feuilly's usual script. This poor workingman had made himself the guardian of justice, and justice rewarded him by making him great. The reason is that right is, in fact, indestructible. Warsaw can no more be Tartar than Venice can be Teutonic. Kings waste their time over such matters—and lose their honor. Sooner or later the submerged homeland floats to the surface and reappears. Greece goes back to being Greece; Italy goes back to being Italy. The protest of right against crime goes on forever. The theft of a people has no statutory limit. These top-level swindles have no future. You can't pick the initials off a nation the way you can off a handkerchief.

Courfeyrac had a father who was known as Monsieur *de* Courfeyrac. One of the false ideas the bourgeoisie of the Restoration held about the aristocracy and the nobility was to believe in that particle.[20] The particle, as we know, has no significance. But the bourgeoisie in the days of the *Minerve*[21] thought so highly of that poor little *de* that they felt obliged to surrender it. Monsieur de Chauvelin called himself Monsieur Chauvelin; Monsieur de Caumartin, Monsieur Caumartin; Monsieur de Constant de Rebecque, Benjamin Constant; Monsieur de Lafayette, Monsieur Lafayette. Courfeyrac did not want to be left behind so he called himself plain old Courfeyrac.

We could almost leave it there as far as Courfeyrac goes and just say, as for the rest: For Courfeyrac, see Tholomyès.

Courfeyrac did in fact have that youthful vim we might call the diabolical beauty of wit. Later on, this fades away like the sweetness of a kitten and all that grace ends, on two legs in the bourgeois, and on four legs in the tomcat.

This kind of wit is transmitted from generation to generation at school, in successive levies of young men who pass it along from hand to hand, *quasi cursores*,[22] more or less exactly the same; so that, as we have just noted, anyone hearing Courfeyrac in 1828 would have thought they were hearing Tholomyès in 1817. Only, Courfeyrac was a good lad. Beneath the apparent outward similarities of wit, there was a huge difference between him and Tholomyès. The latent man that existed in each was altogether different. In Tholomyès there was a prosecutor and in Courfeyrac a paladin.[23]

Enjolras was the leader, Combeferre the guide, and Courfeyrac the center. The others gave out more light, he gave out more heat; the fact is, he had all the properties of a center, being round and radiant.

Bahorel had featured in the bloody tumult of June 1822,[24] on the occasion of the funeral of the young student Lallemand.

Bahorel was the man to see for good humor and bad company; he was brave, hopeless with money, profligate verging on generous, chatty verging on eloquent, bold verging on provocative; he was the best bastard that ever there was; he wore loud waistcoats and flaming red opinions to match; he was a great one for noise, which is to say he liked nothing more than a good brawl except a riot, and nothing more than a riot except a revolution; always ready to throw a cobblestone through a window, then to tear up the whole street, then to tear down a government, just to see the effect; a student of the nursery school, always playing up. He sniffed around the law for a bit, but he never did it. He had taken as his motto: *never a lawyer be,* and for his coat of arms a night table on which a square cap[25] might be glimpsed. Every time he went past the law school, which was rarely, he would button up his redingote, the short jacket known as a *paletot* not having been invented yet, and he would take hygienic precautions. He said of the school portal: "What a fine old man!" and of the dean, Monsieur Delvincourt,[26] "What a monument!" For him, his courses were mere subjects for ditties and his professors, opportunities for caricatures. He ate up a fairly large allowance, something like three thousand francs, doing nothing. His parents were peasants he'd managed to teach to respect their son.

He used to say of them: "They're peasants, not bourgeois; that's why they're smart."

Bahorel was a capricious man and spread himself thin over several cafés; the others had habits, he had none. He strolled. To err is human, to stroll, Parisian. At bottom, a penetrating mind and more of a thinker than he let on.

He served as the connection between the Friends of the ABC and other groups that were still nebulous then, but would later take shape.

There was one bald member of this conclave of young heads.

The marquis d'Avaray, whom Louis XVIII had made a duke for having helped him to get up into a hackney cab the day he emigrated, told how in 1814, on his return to France, the king disembarked at Calais and a man presented him with a petition. "What are you after?" asked the king. "Sire, a post office." "What's your name?" "L'Aigle." The Eagle!

The king frowned, looked at the signature on the petition and saw the name written: *Lesgle.* This spelling, which was anything but Bonapartist, touched the king and he cracked a smile. "Sire," the man with the petition went on, "my grandfather was a whipper-in, a dog man, nicknamed Lesgueules, muzzles. That nickname became my name. I'm known as Lesgueules, Lesgle by contraction, and L'Aigle by corruption." This put the smile back on the king's face. Later on he gave the man the post office at Meaux—Mots—either by accident or design.

The bald member of the group was the son of this Lesgle or Lègle, and signed his name Lègle (de Meaux). His friends "shortened" this to Bossuet.[27]

Bossuet was a cheery boy who had bad luck. His specialty was not to succeed at anything. On the other hand, he laughed at everything. At twenty-five, he was as bald as a badger. His father had wound up with a house and a field; but he, the son, had wasted no time losing said house and field in a dodgy speculation. He had nothing left. He had erudition and wit, but he always misfired. Everything came to nothing on him, everything failed him; whatever he tried to achieve came crashing down on his head. If he tried to chop wood, he cut his finger. If he found a mistress, he very soon discovered he had also found a new male friend. At any given moment, some mishap would befall him; hence his joviality. He would say: "I live under a roof of falling tiles." Nothing surprised him, for accidents were only to be expected, as far as he was concerned; he took bad luck in his stride and smiled at fate's taunts as though they were terrific jokes. He was poor, but his fund of good humor was inexhaustible. He was very soon down to his last sou, never to his last laugh. When adversity came calling, he cordially greeted that old acquaintance; he was on very good terms with catastrophe; he was so familiar with the twist of fate that he called it by a nickname. "Hello, you old Spoilsport," he would say.

This relentless persecution by fate had made him inventive. He was endlessly resourceful. He had no money but, whenever the fancy took him, he always found the means to "damn the expense." One night he went so far as to gobble up a hundred francs dining with some scatterbrain, which inspired him to utter this memorable phrase in the middle of his orgy: "Five-gold-louis woman, pull off my boots!"

Bossuet was slowly making his way toward the legal profession; he did his law, in the manner of Bahorel. Bossuet didn't have much of a roof over his head; at times, none at all. He would camp for a while at one person's place, then at someone else's, most often at Joly's. Joly was studying medicine. He was two years younger than Bossuet.

Joly was the *malade imaginaire*,[28] the imaginary invalid, as a young man. What he had got out of medicine had made him more of an invalid than a doctor. At twenty-three, he believed himself to be chronically ill and spent his life looking at his tongue in the mirror. He asserted that man was magnetized like the needle of a compass and in his room he positioned his bed with the head facing south and the foot facing north so that at night the circulation of his blood would not be impeded by the great magnetic current between the two poles of the globe. In stormy weather, he would take his pulse. Otherwise, he was the cheeriest of the lot. All these inconsistencies—being young, fastidious, hypochondriacal, full of life—got on very well together, and produced an eccentric and likable person that his cronies, always free with winged consonants, called Jolllly. "You can take off with four *L*'s," Jean Prouvaire told him.

Joly was in the habit of rubbing his nose with the end of his cane, which is a sure sign of a sagacious mind.

All these young men, so diverse, and of whom, when it comes down to it, we should only speak seriously, shared the same religion: Progress.

All were the direct descendants of the French Revolution. The most lighthearted became solemn in pronouncing that date: 1789. Their flesh-and-blood fathers were, or had been, *feuillants*, royalists, doctrinaires;[29] it didn't matter much; this mishmash that came before them, the young, did not concern them; the blue blood of principles ran in their veins. They were directly related, without any intermediary link, to incorruptible right and absolute duty.

Associates and initiates, they drafted the ideal together in secret.

Among all these passionate hotheads and true believers, there was one skeptic. How did he get to be there? By juxtaposition. This skeptic's name was Grantaire and he normally signed with this rebus: *R*, for *grand R*, capital *R*. Grantaire was a man who took good care not to believe in anything. And he was one of the students who had got the most out of his studies in Paris; he knew that the best coffee was in the Café Lemblin and that the best billiard table was in the Café Voltaire; that you got good cakes and good girls at L'Ermitage on the boulevard du Maine, spatchcock chickens at mother Saguet's, excellent fish stews at the barrière de la Cunette, and a certain light white wine at the barrière du Combat. For everything, he knew all the best places; he also knew how to kickbox and make his way around a gymnasium and a dance floor, and he was a natural with a singlestick in stickfighting. A big drinker to boot. And unnaturally ugly. The prettiest boot-stitcher of the day, Irma Boissy, appalled by his ugliness, had come out with this sentence: "Grantaire is impossible." But Grantaire was so conceited he was not at all put off by this. He looked on all women tenderly and staringly, with an air of saying of all of them, *If I wanted to!* and hoping to persuade his friends that he was in general demand.

All these words: the right of the people, the rights of man, the social contract, the French Revolution, republic, democracy, humanity, civilization, religion, progress, were, for Grantaire, very close to being completely meaningless. He smiled at them. Skepticism, that dry rot of the intellect, had not left one intact idea in his head. He thrived on irony. This was his axiom: "There is only one certainty: my full glass." He derided any allegiance to any party, in the brother as much as in the father, in the young Robespierre as much as in Loizerolles.[30] "A fat lot of good it did them, dying," he would cry. He said of the crucifix: "Now there's a gibbet that worked." Womanizer, gambler, lecher, often drunk, he riled those young dreamers by endlessly crooning, "I loves the girls and I loves good wine," to the tune of "Long Live Henri IV."

Still, this skeptic was fanatical about one thing. This one thing he was fanatical about was neither an idea nor a dogma, neither an art nor a science; it was a man: Enjolras. Grantaire admired, loved, and venerated Enjolras. Who did this anarchic doubter rally to in this phalanx of absolutists? To the most absolute. In what way did Enjolras enthrall him? Through ideas? No. Through character. A phenomenon frequently observed. A skeptic sticking to a believer—it is as elementary as the law of complementary colors. What we lack attracts us. No one loves daylight more than the blind. The dwarf adores the drum major. The toad always has his eyes on the heavens. Why? To see the birds fly. Grantaire, in whom doubt lurked, loved to see faith soar in Enjolras. He needed Enjolras. Without really realizing it and without trying to explain it to himself, he was held spellbound by that chaste, healthy, firm, upright, hard, candid character. He admired, instinctively, his opposite. His limp, wavering, disjointed, sick, deformed ideas attached themselves to Enjolras as to a backbone. His moral spine leaned on that firm frame. Beside Enjolras, Grantaire became somebody again. He was himself, in any case, composed of two apparently incompatible elements. He was ironic and warmhearted. His indifference was loving. His mind dispensed with faith but his heart could not dispense with friendship. A profound contradiction—for an affection is a conviction. That was his nature. Some men seem born to be the verso, the reverse, the wrong side. They are Pollux, Patroclus, Nisus, Eudamidas, Hephaestion, Pechméja.[31] They can live only on condition of leaning on someone else; their name is a sequel and can only be written preceded by the conjunction *and;* their existence is not their own; it is the other side of a destiny that is not theirs. Grantaire was one of these men. He was the wrong side of Enjolras.

We could almost say that affinities begin with the letters of the alphabet. In the series, *O* and *P* are inseparable. You can say *O* and *P,* or Orestes and Pylades,[32] whichever you prefer.

Grantaire, as a true satellite of Enjolras, dwelt in this circle of young men; he lived there, he was only happy there, he followed them everywhere. His great delight was to see those silhouettes coming and going in the haze of wine. They put up with him because of his good humor.

The believer in Enjolras looked down on the skeptic and the teetotaler looked down on the drunk. He would dole out a dose of pity from on high. Grantaire was a Pylades who did not pass muster. Always treated roughly by Enjolras, pushed away harshly, rejected yet coming back for more, he would say of Enjolras: "Such a beautiful slab of marble!"

## II. Blondeau's Funeral Oration, by Bossuet

One particular afternoon that, as we are about to see, roughly coincided with the events related above, Laigle de Meaux was leaning back sensually in the doorway of the Café Musain. He looked like a caryatid on holiday, holding up nothing more than his reverie. He was watching the place Saint-Michel. Leaning back on something is a way of lying down standing up that dreamers don't mind at all. Laigle de Meaux was thinking, not too sorrowfully, of a bit of a mishap that had befallen him two days before at law school and that changed his personal plans for the future, plans that were, in any case, fairly vague.

Reverie does not stop a cabriolet from passing or the dreamer from noticing this cabriolet. Laigle de Meaux's eyes were wandering in a sort of leisurely stroll, and he saw, through the haze of his somnambulism, a two-wheeled vehicle making its way around the square at a very slow trot as though unsure where it was going. Who was this cabriolet after? Why was it going at such a slow trot? Laigle looked at it. Inside, next to the driver, there was a young man, and in front of this young man there was a fairly big overnight bag. The bag revealed to bystanders this name written in big black letters on a card sewed to the material: MARIUS PONTMERCY.

The name made Laigle shift position. He straightened up and called out to the young man in the cabriolet: "Monsieur Marius Pontmercy!"

The cabriolet thus hailed, stopped.

The young man, who also seemed deeply lost in thought, raised his eyes. "Pardon?" he said.

"You are Monsieur Marius Pontmercy?"

"I am."

"I've been looking for you," said Laigle de Meaux.

"How come?" asked Marius, for it was he, in fact, fresh from his grandfather's and setting eyes on this figure before him for the first time in his life. "I don't know you."

"I don't know you, either," answered Laigle.

Marius thought he'd run into a funny man, and that some sort of practical joke was being played in the middle of the street. He was not in a joking mood just then. He frowned. The unflappable Laigle de Meaux went on: "Weren't you at school the day before yesterday?"

"It's possible."

"It's a fact."

"Are you a student?" asked Marius.

"Yes, Monsieur. Like you. The day before yesterday, I just happened to turn up at school. You know how it is, you sometimes get these funny ideas. The professor was calling the roll. You're well aware how ridiculous they are about roll call. If you miss three calls, they take your name off the roll. Sixty francs down the drain."

Marius started to listen. Laigle continued: "It was Blondeau[1] who was calling the roll. You know Blondeau, he's the one with the very pointy, very spiteful nose who loves sniffing out absentees. He cunningly began with the letter *P*. I wasn't listening, not being implicated in that particular letter. The roll call wasn't going too badly. No one was struck off. Every man and his dog was present. Blondeau was disappointed. I said to myself: Blondeau, my love, you won't have even a hint of an execution today. Suddenly Blondeau calls out 'Marius Pontmercy.' No one answers. Blondeau gets his hopes up and repeats, louder: 'Marius Pontmercy.' And he grabs his pen. Monsieur, I'm not heartless. I swiftly told myself: Here's a brave lad who's about to be struck off. Careful. This one's a real live human being who is not punctual. This one's not a good boy. This is not some fat-arsed bookworm, a student who actually studies, some pimply pedant, strong in science, literature, theology, and sapience, one of those ninnies dressed to the nines, with a different outfit for each faculty. He's an honorable bludger who's ambling about the place somewhere, busy being on holidays, cultivating grisettes, courting beauties, who may, perhaps, at this very instant be with my mistress at her place. Let's save him. Death to Blondeau! At that moment, Blondeau dipped his pen, black with crossings out, in the ink, gave his audience the once-over with his catlike eyes, and repeated for the third time: 'Marius Pontmercy!' I answered: 'Present!' And that means you were not struck off."

"Monsieur—" said Marius.

"And that I was," added Laigle de Meaux.

"I don't understand," said Marius.

Laigle resumed: "Nothing simpler. I stood next to the rostrum to answer and next to the door to make my escape. The professor gave me a pretty steady stare. He'd have to be the cunning nose Boileau talks about, because suddenly Blondeau jumps to the letter *L. L,* that's my letter. I am from Meaux and my name's Lesgle."

"L'Aigle!" Marius interrupted. "What a beautiful name!"

"Monsieur, old Blondeau gets to that beautiful name and cries: 'Laigle!' I answer: 'Present!' So then Blondeau looks at me with the sweet smile of a tiger and he says: 'If you are Pontmercy, you are not Laigle.' A phrase that seems a bit insulting to you, but it was sinister only to me. And without further ado, he strikes me off."

Marius exclaimed: "Monsieur, I'm mortified—"

"Before anything else," Laigle broke in, "I ask to embalm Blondeau with a few phrases of heartfelt praise. I'm assuming he's dead. That wouldn't be much of a change, he's so skinny and pale and cold and stiff and smelly. And I say: *Erudimini qui judicatis terram.*[2] Here lies Blondeau, Blondeau the Nose, Blondeau Nasica, the bullock of discipline, *bos disciplinae,* the great watchdog of order, the angel of roll call, who was straight, square, punctual, rigid, honest, and awful. God struck him off just as he struck me off."

Marius went on: "I am so sorry—"

"Young man," said Laigle de Meaux, "let this be a lesson to you. In future, be on time."

"I am truly sorry."

"Never expose yourself again to having your fellow man struck off."

"I don't know what I can do—"

Laigle burst out laughing.

"I do: I'm thrilled! I was on the brink of becoming a lawyer. This being crossed out saves me. I renounce the triumphs of the bar. I will not defend the widow, nor will I attack the orphan. No more robe, no more professional training. My crossing out has already been achieved. I owe this to you, Monsieur Pontmercy. I intend to pay you a solemn visit of thanks. Where do you live?"

"In a cabriolet," said Marius.

"A sure sign of opulence," Laigle calmly shot back. "I congratulate you. You have there a rent of nine thousand francs a year."

At that moment Courfeyrac came out of the café.

Marius continued sadly: "I've been paying that rent for two hours now and I hope to get out of it; but, it's the usual story, I don't know where to go."

"Monsieur," said Courfeyrac, "come home with me."

"I should have priority," observed Laigle, "but I don't have a home to go to."

"Shut up, Bossuet," Courfeyrac went on.

"Bossuet," said Marius, "but I thought you said your name was Laigle."

"De Meaux," replied Laigle. "Bossuet, metaphorically speaking."

Courfeyrac climbed up into the cabriolet.

"Driver," he said, "Hôtel de la Porte Saint-Jacques."

And that very evening, Marius was installed at the Hôtel de la Porte Saint-Jacques in a room right alongside Courfeyrac.

### III. THE AMAZEMENT OF MARIUS

In a few days, Marius was friends with Courfeyrac. Youth is the season when bones are swiftly mended and wounds rapidly healed. Marius breathed freely by Courfeyrac's side, a fairly new sensation for him. Courfeyrac did not ask him any questions. He did not even think to. At that age faces say it all right away. Words are pointless. There is a kind of young man you could describe as having a face that talks. One look and you know each other.

One morning, though, Courfeyrac suddenly shot him this question: "By the way, do you have any political views?"

"Really!" said Marius, almost offended by the question.

"What are you?"

"A Bonapartist democrat."

"Ah, a nice gray shade of mousy," said Courfeyrac.

The next day, Courfeyrac introduced Marius to the Café Musain. Then he whispered in his ear with a smile: "I must gain your admission to the revolution." And he took him to the room of the Friends of the ABC. He introduced him to the other comrades, adding in an undertone this simple word that Marius did not quite get: "A novice."

Marius had fallen into a mental hornet's nest. But, although quiet and grave, he was just as quick on his feet and just as ready to sting as the best of them.

Till then solitary and given to monologues and private asides out of habit and inclination, Marius was a bit scared by this flock of young men flapping all around him. All these diverse initiatives demanded his attention and pulled him in all directions at once. The tumultuous give-and-take of all these minds at liberty and at work set his ideas in a whirl. Sometimes, in the confusion, they floated off so far away from him that he had trouble catching up with them again. He heard talk of philosophy, literature, art, history, religion, in the most unexpected ways. He glimpsed things from strange angles; and, as he could not put them into perspective, he wasn't sure whether he wasn't looking at chaos. In shrugging off the opinions of his grandfather to don the opinions of his father, he thought he was set; he now suspected, anxiously and without daring to admit it to himself, that he was not. The point from which he viewed all things was shifting once more. A certain oscillation was shaking up all the horizons of his brain. A bizarre inner commotion. It almost hurt him physically.

It looked like nothing was sacred to these young men. Marius had to listen to the most peculiar talk on every issue and this upset his still-timid mind.

A theater poster turned up, emblazoned with the title of a tragedy from the old, so-called classical, repertoire. "Down with tragedy, so dear to the bourgeois!" yelled Bahorel. And Marius heard Combeferre reply: "You're wrong, Bahorel. The bourgeoisie love tragedy and they should be left alone on that score. Bewigged tragedy[1] has its raison d'être and far be it from me to challenge its right to exist, as some do in the name of Aeschylus.[2] There are rough drafts in nature; there are, in creation, ready-made parodies. A beak that is not a beak, wings that aren't wings, fins that aren't fins, paws that aren't paws, a cry of pain that makes you want to laugh—there you have the duck in a nutshell. Now, since the domestic fowl exists alongside the bird, I can't see why 'classical' tragedy should not exist in the face of antique tragedy."

Another time, Marius happened to be going down the rue Jean-Jacques Rousseau between Enjolras and Courfeyrac.

Courfeyrac took his arm.

"Be careful. This is the rue Plâtrière, now called the rue Jean-Jacques Rousseau because of an odd couple that lived here about sixty years ago. That was Jean-Jacques and Thérèse.[3] From time to time, little creatures would be born there. Thérèse brought them into the world, Jean-Jacques booted them out into the world."

Enjolras then savaged Courfeyrac. "Silence in front of Jean-Jacques! I admire the man. He disowned his own children, admittedly; but he adopted the people."

None of these young men spoke the word *emperor*. Jean Prouvaire alone sometimes said Napoléon; all the others said Bonaparte. Enjolras pronounced it *Buonaparte*.

Marius was vaguely amazed. *Initium sapientiae.*[4]

## IV. THE BACK ROOM OF THE CAFÉ MUSAIN

One of the conversations these young men had, conversations that Marius sat in on and sometimes took part in, was a real eye-opener for Marius and shook him up quite badly.

It happened in the back room of the Café Musain. Just about all the Friends of the ABC were there that night. The oil lamp had been solemnly lit. They talked about this and that, noisily, passionlessly. Except for Enjolras and Marius, who kept silent, everyone joined in the aimless ranting. Talk among friends sometimes reaches this quietly tumultuous pitch. It was more random banter than conversation. Words were tossed around and caught. The talk was coming from all sides.

No woman was admitted into this back room except Louison, the café dishwasher, who passed through from time to time on her way from the laundry to the "laboratory."

Grantaire, perfectly plastered, was deafening everyone in the corner he'd taken possession of. He reasoned and raved at the top of his lungs, shouting: "I'm thirsty. Mortals, I have a dream: that the Heidelberg tun[1] has an attack of apoplexy and that I am among the dozen leeches they apply to it. I want to drink. I want to forget life. Life is a hideous invention of who knows who. It doesn't last two ups and it's not worth two ups. You break your neck trying to stay alive. Life is a stage set where nothing much actually works. Happiness is an old theater flat painted on one side only. Ecclesiastes says:[2] 'All is vanity.' I couldn't agree more with the poor bastard, if he ever existed. Zero, not wishing to get around in the nude, decked itself out in vanity. O vanity! The tarting up of everything in grand words! A kitchen is a laboratory, a dancer is a professor, an acrobat is a gymnast, a boxer is a pugilist, an apothecary is a chemist, a wig-maker is an artiste, a plasterer's helper is an architect, a jockey is a sportsman, a wood louse is a pterygobranchiate. Vanity has a back and a front: The front is stupid, it's the nigger decked out in his glass baubles; the back is silly, it's the philosopher in rags. One makes me cry and the other makes me laugh. What are called honors and dignities, and even real honor and dignity, are generally fake gold. Kings make a mockery of human pride. Caligula made a horse a consul; Charles II made a sirloin steak a knight. So now you can drape yourselves between the consul Incitatus and the baronet Roastbeef.[3] As for people's intrinsic worth, that's hardly any more respectable. Listen to the sort of praise a person heaps on their neighbor. White attacking white is ferocious; if the lily could talk, it'd make mincemeat of the dove! A bigot who tells tales about someone devout is more poisonous than an asp or a blue viper. It's a pity I'm an ignoramus or I would cite a whole host of examples for you, but I know nothing. For instance, I've always been a bit of a wit; when I was studying under Gros, the painter, instead of mucking about daubing piddling little paintings, I spent my time pilfering apples; *rapin*—dauber—is the masculine of *rapine*—plunder. So much for me; as for the rest of you, you're as bad as I am. I don't give a fig for your perfections, excellences, and good qualities. Every good quality ends in a defect; the man who looks after his money verges on the miser, the generous man borders on the wastrel, the brave man is pretty close to the braggart; when you say very pious you say holier-than-thou; there are just as many vices in virtue as there are holes in Diogenes' mantle.[4] Who do you admire, the one killed or the killer, Caesar or Brutus? Generally people are for the killer. Long live Brutus! He killed. That's virtue for you. Virtue? Very well, but madness too. Those great men, there, have some very strange blemishes. The Brutus who killed Caesar was in love with the statue of a little boy. This statue was made by the Greek sculptor Strongylion,[5] who also sculpted the figure of an Amazon called Beautiful Legs, Euknemos, which Nero took with him on his jaunts. This Strongylion has left only two statues that Brutus and Nero agreed about; Brutus was in love with one of them and Nero was in love with the other. The whole of history is just one long rehash. One century plagiarizes another. The battle of Marengo copies the battle of Pydna;[6] Clovis's Tolbiac[7] and Napoléon's Austerlitz are as alike as two drops of blood. I don't hold much store by victory. What could be stupider than winning? The real glory is in winning over. But just you try and prove anything! You're satisfied with succeeding—what mediocrity! And with conquering—how pathetic! Alas, nothing but vanity and cowardice everywhere you turn. Everything bows down before success, even grammar. *Si volet usus,*[8] says Horace. And so I despise the human race. Shall we descend from the whole to the part? Would you like me to admire the peoples of the world? Which particular people, if you please? Do you mean Greece? The Athenians, those Parisians of bygone days, killed Phocion, or Coligny[9] as we might say, and crawled to the tyrants to the point where Anacephoras said of Pisistratus:[10] 'His urine attracts bees.' The most important man in Greece for fifty years was the grammarian Philetas,[11] who was so tiny and thin that he was forced to put lead in his shoes so he didn't blow away in the breeze. In the biggest square in Corinth there was a statue sculpted by Silanion and catalogued by Pliny. This statue represented Episthates. What did Episthates do? He invented the wrestling move known as tripping someone up. That about sums up the glory of Greece. Let's move on to other peoples. Shall I admire England? Shall I admire France? France? What for? Because of Paris? I've just told you what I think of Athens. England? What for? Because of London? I hate Carthage. Then again, London, metropolis of luxury, is the capital of destitution. Every year, in the parish of Charing Cross alone, a hundred people die of starvation. So much for Albion. I add, to cap it off, that I once saw an Englishwoman dancing with a crown of roses and blue spectacles. So, a big hiss and a boo for England! If I don't admire John Bull, am I then to admire Brother Jonathan? I'm not too keen on this slave-owning brother. Take away 'time is money' and what's left of England? Take away 'cotton is king' and what's left of America? Germany is lymphatic; Italy is full of bile. Should we go into raptures over Russia? Voltaire admired it. He also admired China. I grant that Russia has its good points, among others a strong despotism; but I feel sorry for despots. Their health is delicate. An Alexis decapitated, a Peter stabbed, a Paul strangled, another Paul stomped on[12] and kicked to death by jackboots; sundry Ivans have had their throats cut, several Nicolases and Basils have been poisoned— all this indicates that the palace of the emperors of Russia was a flagrantly insalubrious place. All civilized peoples offer the thinker this little detail for his admiration: war. Now, war, civilized war, sums up and exhausts all forms of banditry, from the armed robbery of the Catalan bands in the gorges of Mount Jaxa to the marauding of the Comanche Indians in Doubtful Pass. Bah, you'll say to me, Europe is still better than Asia, surely? I agree that Asia is a joke; but I don't really see what you can afford to laugh about in the Great Lama, you peoples of the West who have blended with your fashions and your elegant ways all the ornate filth of majesty, from the dirty chemise of Queen Isabella to the dauphin's commode. Messieurs of the human race, I say: screw the lot of you! In Brussels they drink the most beer, in Stockholm the most eau-de-vie, in Madrid the most chocolate, in Amsterdam the most gin, in London the most wine, in Constantinople the most coffee, in Paris the most absinthe; that's it for all the most useful notions. In a word, Paris wins hands down. In Paris, even the rag-and-bone merchants are sybarites; Diogenes would have been just as happy as a rag-and-bone man in the place Maubert as he was as a philosopher in Piraeus. And there's something else you should know: The rag-and-bone-men's cabarets are called *bibines,* watering holes where they serve cheap booze; the most famous are the Casserole and the Abattoir.[13] And so, O open-air cafés, gin shops, little Lyon eateries, seedy dives, greasy spoons, pothouses, sleazy dance halls, smoky fleapit groggeries with your zink counters, dishwater bars of the rag-and-bone merchants, caravanserai of the caliphs, I swear to you I am a voluptuary, I eat at Richard's at forty sous a head, and I need a Persian carpet to roll Cleopatra[14] up in, naked! Where is Cleopatra? Ah! It's you, Louison. Hello."

And so the words streamed out of Grantaire, in his corner of the back room of the Café Musain as he buttonholed the dishwasher on her way past, Grantaire being more than drunk by then.

Bossuet put out his hand and tried to shut him up but Grantaire started up again even louder: "Aigle de Meaux, mitts off. You don't impress me, imitating the gesture of Hippocrates when he rejected Artaxerxes's hodgepodge.[15] I exempt you from calming me down. Besides, I'm sad. What do you want me to say? Man is bad, man is deformed; the butterfly is a success, man is a botched job. God bungled that particular animal. A crowd offers you a choice of ugliness. The first man that comes along is a miserable bastard. *Femme* rhymes with in-*fam*-y. Of course, I'm suffering from spleen, complicated with melancholy, nostalgia, plus hypochondria, and I rant and rage and yawn and bore myself, I bore myself to tears, I bore myself to death! God can go to hell!"

"Well, then, shut up, capital *R*!" said Bossuet, who was discussing a point of law with the company at large and was up to his neck in legal jargon, his closing remarks going like this: "As for me, although I'm barely a jurist, at best an amateur attorney, I maintain this: that according to the custom of Normandy, every year at Michaelmas, a token sum must be paid for the benefit of the seigneur, unless others are entitled, by each and every title-holder, whether by lease or right of succession, and this, for all long leases, allodiums, private estate and state contracts, mortgages and mortgagees—"

"Echo, plaintive nymph," hummed Grantaire.

Right next to Grantaire, at an almost silent table, a sheet of paper, an inkwell, and a plume between two small glasses announced that a vaudeville sketch was being drafted. This very serious matter was being tackled by two people talking in low voices with their heads together: "Let's start by finding the names. When we have the names, we have the subject."

"Right you are. You dictate. I'll write."

"Monsieur Dorimon?"

"Man of means?"

"Of course."

"His daughter, Célestine."

"—tine. Next?"

"Colonel Sainval."

"Sainval's a bit tired. I'd say Valsin."

Alongside these vaudeville aspirants, another group, which was also taking advantage of the racket to whisper together privately, was discussing a duel. An old-timer, thirty years old, was advising a young whippersnapper, eighteen years old, about the adversary he was dealing with.

"Christ! Be careful. He's a beautiful sword. He plays clean. He's got attack, no wasted feints, good wrist action, real sparkle, lightning fast, good parry, accurate cut and thrust, heavens! And he's left-handed."

In the corner opposite Grantaire, Joly and Bahorel were playing dominoes and talking about love.

"You're a happy man, you are," Joly was saying. "You've got a mistress who never stops laughing."

"That's a mistake on her part," replied Bahorel. "A man's mistress is wrong to laugh. It only encourages you to be unfaithful to her. Seeing her so gay takes away any remorse; if you see her sad, it pricks your conscience."

"Ungrateful bastard! A woman who laughs is a treasure! And you never ever fight!"

"That's because we've made a pact when we formed our little Holy Alliance. We drew lines we never cross. Anything on the wintry side belongs to Vaud, on the windy side to Gex.[16] Hence the peace."

"Peace is happiness digesting."

"But what about you, Joly? Where are you up to in your falling-out with what's-her-name—you know the one I mean?"

"She's still sulking—it's shocking how long she can sulk."

"Yet you're so lovesick you're wasting away."

"Alas!"

"If I were you, I'd dump her."

"Easy to say."

"Easy to do, too. Doesn't she call herself Musichetta?"

"Yes. Ah, my poor Bahorel! She's a wonderful girl, very literary, tiny feet, tiny hands, dresses well, white, plump; eyes of a fortune-teller. I'm mad about her."

"My dear man, in that case you have to sweep her off her feet, be elegant, bowl her over. Get yourself a pair of doeskin pants run up at Staub's.[17] They stretch."

"How much are they?" cried Grantaire.

The third corner was in the throes of a poetry discussion. Pagan mythology was going head-to-head with Christian mythology. The subject was Olympus, whose side Jean Prouvaire took, out of sheer romanticism. Jean Prouvaire was only timid at rest. Once he got excited, he erupted, a sort of gaiety accentuated his enthusiasm and he was both laughing and lyrical: "Let's not insult the gods," he was saying. "The gods have not perhaps left us. Jupiter doesn't strike me as being dead yet. The gods are mere dreams, you say. Yet now, when all these dreams have flown, the grand old pagan myths are still with us, even in nature such as it is today. A mountain like Vignemale, for instance, which looks like a fortress from the side, is still, for me, Cybele's headdress;[18] it has not, to my mind, been proven that Pan[19] doesn't come out at night to blow in the hollow trunk of a willow, stopping the holes with his fingers one by one; and I've always thought that Io had a hand in the waterfall of Pissevache."[20]

In the last corner they were talking politics. They were pulling apart the Charter that had just been granted. Combeferre was limply defending it. Courfeyrac was energetically demolishing it. There was an unfortunate copy of the famous Touquet Charter[21] on the table in front of them, and Courfeyrac grabbed it and was waving it around, supporting his arguments with the rustling of that sheet of paper.

"First, I want no kings. I'll have none of that, if only for economic reasons. A king is a parasite. Kings don't come free. Listen to this:—The High Cost of Kings. At the death of François I, the public debt in France was thirty thousand livres in revenue; at the death of Louis XIV,[22] it was two billion six hundred million, at twenty-eight livres a mark, which, according to Desmarets, was equivalent to four billion five hundred million in 1760, which is equivalent to twelve billion today. Second, whether Combeferre likes it or not, granting charters is not something civilization should resort to. To ease the transition, smooth the passage, dampen the shock, make the nation's shift from monarchy to democ racy imperceptible through the spinning of constitutional fictions—these are all despicable justifications! No! No! We must never light the people's way with false daylight. Principles wither and fade in your constitutional cave. No bastardization. No compromise. No grant from the king to the people. In all such grants there is an Article 14. Alongside the hand that feeds there is the claw that takes it all back. I reject your charter outright. A charter is a mask; underneath it is the lie. A nation that accepts a charter abdicates. Rights are only rights when they are whole. No! No charter!"

It was wintertime; two logs were crackling in the fireplace. It was tempting and Courfeyrac could not resist. He crumpled the poor Touquet Charter in his hand and tossed it on the fire. The paper caught fire. Combeferre watched philosophically as Louis XVIII's masterpiece burned and all he said was: "The charter has gone up in flames."

And the sarcastic gibes, the sallies, the taunts, the thing the French call wit and the English call humor, good taste and bad, good reasoning and bad, all the wild projectiles of repartee, flared up all at once and crossfired from all points of the room, creating a sort of joyous bombardment overhead.

## V. The Horizon Expands

The wonderful thing about the clash of young minds is that you can never predict the spark or foresee the lightning flash of the explosion it sets off. Anything could erupt at any moment. You have no idea what. A burst of laughter starts out as tender emotion. During a bout of buffoonery, seriousness makes its entrance. Stimulus is provided by the slightest chance word. The verve of each is at its peak. A quip is enough to open the field up to the unexpected. This is the kind of talk that takes sharp turns where the perspective suddenly changes completely. Chance is the scene-shifter in such conversations.

A harsh thought, oddly emerging from the clatter of words, suddenly pierced through the verbal free-for-all in which Grantaire, Bahorel, Prouvaire, Bossuet, Combeferre, and Courfeyrac were chaotically clashing swords.

How does a single phrase stand out in the middle of a conversation? How does it manage to suddenly stop everyone in their tracks? As we just said, nobody knows. In the middle of the din, Bossuet ended whatever he had been saying to Combeferre with this date: "June 18, 1815: Waterloo."

At the mention of Waterloo, Marius, who was leaning on the table beside a glass of water, took his hand away from under his chin and began to study the room in earnest.

"God Almighty!" cried Courfeyrac (*Good Lord* was by then falling into disuse). "The number eighteen strikes me as odd. It's Bonaparte's fatal number.[1] Put Louis in front and Brumaire behind and you have the man's entire destiny, with this amazing peculiarity, which is that the end follows hot on the heels of the beginning."

Enjolras, who had not said a word till then, broke his silence and addressed Courfeyrac: "You mean atonement follows hot on the heels of the crime."

That word *crime* exceeded the limits of what Marius could endure, deeply stirred as he already was by the sudden evocation of Waterloo.

He got up, walked slowly over to the map of France spread out on the wall, at the bottom of which you could see an island in a separate box, and he stuck his finger on this box and said: "Corsica. A tiny island that has made France truly great."

This was like a blast of arctic air. Everyone broke off—you could have heard a pin drop. Something was clearly about to take off.

Bahorel, about to retort to Bossuet, had been taking up a favorite pose. He dropped it to listen.

Enjolras, whose blue eyes were not fixed on anyone, seemingly staring into space, answered without looking at Marius: "France doesn't need any Corsica to be great. France is great because it is France. *Quia nominor leo.*"[2]

Marius did not feel even the vaguest desire to retreat; he turned toward Enjolras and he spoke in a voice ringing with emotion: "God forbid that I should diminish France! But it is not diminishing it by assimilating Napoléon to it. All right, so let's talk. I'm new here, but I have to confess you amaze me. Where are we at? Who are we? Who are you? Who am I? Let's be clear about the emperor. I hear you say Buonaparte, emphasizing the *u* the way the royalists do. I warn you that my grandfather goes one better still, he says Buonaparté. I thought you were young men. So where are you putting your enthusiasm, then? And what are you doing with it? Who do you admire if you don't admire the emperor? And what more do you need? If you don't want anything to do with that great man, what great men do you want? He had everything. He was complete. He had every human faculty in his brain—to the nth degree. He drew up codes like Justinian,[3] he ruled alone like Caesar, when he talked he mixed Pascal's lightning wit[4] with the thunder of Tacitus, he made history and he wrote it, his bulletins are Iliads, he combined Newton's mathematics[5] with Mohammed's metaphors, he left behind him in the Orient words as great as the pyramids; at Tilsit[6] he taught majesty to emperors, at the Académie des Sciences he had answers for Laplace,[7] at the Council of State he held his ground with Merlin,[8] he gave soul to the geometry of some and and to the chicanery of others, he talked law with attorneys and the stars with astronomers; like Cromwell, blowing out alternate candles, he took himself off to the Temple to haggle over a curtain tassel;[9] he saw everything, he knew everything, but that didn't stop him from laughing with joy like an ordinary man at his little baby's cradle; and all of a sudden Europe sat up and listened, armies went on the march, artillery parks rolled along, pontoon bridge trains stretched out over the rivers, clouds of cavalry galloped in the whirlwind, shouts, trumpets, everywhere the tottering of thrones, the borders of kingdoms wobbling on the map, you could hear the swoosh of a superhuman broadsword sliding out of its sheath, you could see him, the man himself, standing tall on the horizon with a blaze in his hand and a resplendent light in his eyes, deploying his two wings—the Grande Armée and the Old Guard—amid all the thunder, and there he was, the archangel of war!"

No one spoke. Enjolras hung his head. Silence always acts a bit like assent—or backing someone into a corner. Marius, almost without pausing for breath, went on with added exuberance: "Let's be fair, my friends! To be the empire of such an emperor—what more splendid destiny for a nation, when that nation is France and when its genius is added to the genius of the man! To come out of nowhere and take the reins, to march and to triumph, to have all the capitals of Europe as stops along the way, to take his grenadiers and turn them into kings, to decree the downfall of dynasties, to change the face of Europe as you charge on, for people to feel, when you threaten them, that you have your hand on the hilt of the sword of God, to follow Hannibal, Caesar, and Charlemagne in the person of one man, to be the nation of a man who greets you every dawn with the glorious announcement of a battle won, to have the cannon of the Invalides as your alarm clock, to hurl into the endless light mighty words that blaze out for all time, Marengo, Arcola, Austerlitz, Jena, Wagram! At every instant to cause constellations of victories to come out in the zenith of the centuries, to offer the French empire as a counterpart to the Roman empire, to be the grand nation that gives birth to the Grande Armée, sending its legions flying over the face of the earth the way a mountain sprays its eagles in all directions, to vanquish, dominate, crush, to be Europe's golden nation, ablaze with glory, to sound a Titanic fanfare down through history, to conquer the world twice over, by force of arms and by dazzlement—all this is sublime; what could possibly be greater?"

"To be free," said Combeferre.

It was Marius's turn to hang his head. That simple, chilling word had cut through his epic effusion like a steel blade and he felt it fall away inside him. When he raised his eyes, Combeferre was no longer there. Satisfied no doubt with pulling the rug from under Marius just as he reached his grand finale, he had simply left and everyone except Enjolras had followed suit. The room had emptied; Enjolras, left alone with Marius, looked at him gravely. Marius, though, having made an effort to rally his ideas, did not consider himself defeated; there was still something bubbling away inside him that would no doubt translate into syllogisms deployed against Enjolras. Then, all of a sudden, someone could be heard singing on the stairs as they went away. It was Combeferre, and this is what he sang:

If Caesar had offered me
   Glory and war,
But I had had to give up
   My mother's love,
I would say to great Caesar:
Take back your scepter and your chariot,
I love my mother more, hey nonny!
   I love my mother more.[10]

The tender and savage tone in which Combeferre was singing gave this verse a sort of strange grandeur. Marius, pensive and with his eyes on the ceiling, repeated almost mechanically: "My mother—"

At that moment, he felt Enjolras' hand on his shoulder.

"Citizen,"[11] said Enjolras, "my mother is the Republic."

## VI. RES ANGUSTA[1]

That soirée left Marius deeply shaken, with a sad darkness in his soul. He felt what the earth perhaps feels as it is being dug into by iron for seeds of wheat to be sown; it feels only the wound; the bursting of the wheat germ into life and the thrill of the wheat only come later.

Marius was forlorn. He had only just acquired a faith; did he have to reject it already? He told himself no. He resolved not to doubt, but he started to have doubts just the same. To be between two religions, one you have not yet emerged from, the other you have not yet embraced, is unbearable; and such gloomy half-light only appeals to batlike souls. Marius was open-eyed and he needed real light. The crepuscular light of doubt hurt him. Whatever his desire to stay put and to hold out, he was invincibly compelled to move on, to advance, to examine, to think, to go one step further. Where was all that going to lead him? He feared, after having taken so many steps that had drawn him closer to his father, to take steps now that would take him away from him. His uneasiness grew with every thought that came to him. High walls hemmed him in on all sides. He did not fit in with either his grandfather or his friends; he was reckless according to the one, backward according to the others; and he recognized that he was doubly cut off—from the old and from the young. He stopped going to the Café Musain.

In this troubled state of mind, he barely gave a thought to certain serious aspects of existence. But the realities of life do not let themselves be forgotten. They suddenly came and gave him a sharp nudge.

One morning the hotelkeeper sailed into Marius's room and said: "Monsieur Courfeyrac has vouched for you."

"Yes."

"But I need money."

"Ask Courfeyrac to come and speak to me," said Marius.

Courfeyrac came, the host left them to it. Marius now told him what he had not thought of telling him before this, which was that he was all alone in the world, not having any relatives.

"What's going to become of you?" said Courfeyrac.

"I have no idea," Marius replied.

"What are you going to do?"

"I have no idea."

"Have you got any money?"

"Fifteen francs."

"Would you like me to lend you some?"

"Not on your life."

"Have you got any clothes?"

"What you see."

"Any jewelry?"

"A watch."

"Silver?"

"Gold. Here it is."

"I know a secondhand-clothes dealer who'll take your redingote and a pair of pants."

"That's good."

"You'll only have one pair of pants, a waistcoat, a hat, and a morning coat left."

"And my boots."

"What! You mean you won't go barefoot? What luxury!"

"It'll do me."

"I know a watchmaker who'll buy your watch."

"That's good."

"No, it's not good. What are you going to do after that?"

"Whatever I have to—that's honest, at least."

"Do you know English?"

"No."

"Do you know German?"

"No."

"Too bad."

"Why?"

"It's just that one of my friends is a bookseller and he's doing a sort of encyclopedia and you could have translated articles from German or English for it. It's badly paid but you can live on it."

"I'll learn English and German."

"And in the meantime?"

"In the meantime, I'll eat my clothes and my watch."

They sent for the clothes dealer. He bought the castoffs for twenty francs. They went to the watchmaker's. He bought the watch for forty-five francs.

"That's not bad," said Marius to Courfeyrac on returning to the hotel. "With the fifteen francs I already have, that comes to eighty francs."

"What about the hotel bill?" observed Courfeyrac.

"Ah, yes! I forgot," said Marius.

"Christ!" went Courfeyrac. "You'll eat up five francs while you're learning English and five francs while you're learning German. You'll either have to swallow a language pretty fast or a hundred-sou piece pretty slowly."

Meanwhile Aunt Gillenormand, who was pretty good underneath it all in a crisis, wound up unearthing Marius's hideout. One morning, as Marius was coming back from the law school, he found a letter from his aunt and those "sixty pistoles," that is, six hundred francs, in gold, in a sealed box.

Marius sent the thirty louis back to his aunt with a respectful letter declaring he had the means to support himself and that he could now provide for all his needs on his own. At that point he had three francs left.

The aunt did not inform the grandfather about this rejection for fear of exasperating him further. Besides, hadn't he said: "Never speak to me of that bloodsucker again!"

Marius left the Hôtel de la Porte Saint-Jacques, not wanting to run up a debt there.

# BOOK FIVE

# THE VIRTUES OF ADVERSITY

## I. MARIUS DESTITUTE

Life became tough for Marius. Eating his clothes and his watch was nothing. He had to swallow something more galling, which was his pride, forced as he was to "live off the smell of an oily rag," as they say. A horrible thing that includes days without bread, nights without sleep, evenings without a candle, a fireplace without a fire, weeks without work, a future without hope, a coat worn through at the elbows, a hat so battered it makes girls giggle, a door you find closed at night because you can't pay the rent, the insolence of the porter and the pot-house proprietor, the snickering of neighbors, humiliation, dignity trampled underfoot, any odd jobs snapped up, disgust, bitterness, dejection. Marius learned how one devours all that and how these are often all there is to devour. At that stage of existence when a man needs pride because he needs love, he felt derided because he was badly dressed and ridiculed because he was poor. At an age when the sap rises in a young man's heart with overweening arrogance, he more than once looked down at his gaping boots and felt the unjust shame and heartrending embarrassment of destitution. A trial both awesome and terrible, out of which the weak emerge vile and the strong emerge sublime. Crucible into which fate hurls a man, whenever it wants to make a mongrel or a demigod.

For many great deeds are performed in the small struggles of life. There are dogged and unseen acts of bravery, which defend themselves every inch of the way behind the scenes against the deadly invasion of necessity and depravity. Noble and mysterious triumphs that no other eyes see, that no renown rewards, that no fanfare salutes.

Life, adversity, loneliness, abandonment, poverty are battlefields that have their heroes; obscure heroes, sometimes greater than the illustrious ones.

Steadfast and rare natures are forged this way; misery, almost always a stepmother, is sometimes a mother; deprivation begets strength of soul and mind; distress nurtures pride; adversity is just the milk the magnanimous need.

There was a moment in Marius's life when he swept his own doorstep, when he bought Brie by the sou at the grocer's, when he waited for dusk to fall to duck into the baker's and buy a loaf of bread, which he would then spirit away to the garret as though he had stolen it. Sometimes, slipping into the local butcher's in the thick of jeering cooks who jostled him, you would see an awkward young man with books tucked under his arm, looking timid and furious, who, when he came in, would take off his hat, the sweat beading on his forehead, bow deeply to the astonished butcher's wife, bow again to the butcher's boy, ask for a mutton chop, pay six or seven sous for it, wrap it in paper, stick it under his arm between a couple of books and be off. This was Marius. On this one chop, which he cooked himself, he could live for three days.

The first day he would eat the meat, the second day he would eat the fat, the third day he would gnaw the bone.

Several times, Aunt Gillenormand made overtures, sending him the sixty pistoles again. Marius always sent them back, saying he didn't need anything.

He was still in mourning for his father when the revolution that we have described occurred in him. From that day forth, he never abandoned black clothes. His clothes, however, abandoned him. The day came when he had no coat left. The pants were still all right. What was he to do? Courfeyrac, for whom he, on his side, had done a few good turns, gave him an old coat of his. For thirty sous, Marius had it turned by some porter or other, and it was as good as new. But the coat was green. So Marius only went out after dark. That turned the coat black. Wanting to remain in mourning at all times, he clothed himself in night.

Through all this, he got himself admitted to the bar. He was supposed to occupy Courfeyrac's chambers, which were decent and where a certain number of law books, bolstered and filled out by odd volumes of novels, made up the library required by the regulations. He saw to it that any correspondence was addressed to him care of Courfeyrac.

When Marius became a lawyer, he informed his grandfather of the fact in a letter that was cold but full of humility and respect. Monsieur Gillenormand took the letter in trembling hands, read it, ripped it in half and chucked it into the wastepaper basket. Two or three days later, Mademoiselle Gillenormand heard her father alone in his room talking out loud. This happened to him whenever he was really agitated. She cocked her ear; the old man was saying: "If you weren't such a noodle, you'd know you can't be a baron and a lawyer at the same time."

## II. Marius Poor

Misery is like anything else. It reaches the point where it is bearable. It ends up taking shape and assuming a form. You vegetate, meaning you evolve in a certain stunted fashion, but that is enough to live on. This is how the existence of Marius Pontmercy had arranged itself:

He had gotten through the worst of it; the defile was opening out a little before him. By dint of toil, courage, perseverance, and will, he had managed to get about seven hundred francs a year out of his work. He had learned German and English; thanks to Courfeyrac, who had put him in touch with his friend the bookseller, Marius played, in the literary section of the bookshop, the modest role of hack. He drew up prospectuses, translated journals, annotated editions, compiled biographies, etc. Net result, year in, year out: seven hundred francs. He could live off that. Not too badly. How? We'll tell you.

Marius occupied in the Gorbeau slum, at the annual rate of thirty francs, a rathole with no fireplace known as his "chambers," where there was nothing by way of furniture but what was strictly indispensable. This furniture was his. He gave the old chief tenant three francs a month to come and sweep out the rathole and bring him, every morning, a small supply of hot water, a fresh egg, and a little bread roll worth one sou. This bread roll and this egg were his breakfast. The cost of his breakfast varied from two to four sous, depending on whether eggs were cheap or dear. At six o'clock in the evening, he went down the rue Saint-Jacques to dine at Rousseau's,[1] opposite Basset's, the print dealer at the corner of the rue des Mathurins. He didn't eat any soup. He would have the meat dish for six sous, a half-serving of vegetables for three sous, and a dessert for three sous. For three sous, as much bread as he could eat. As for wine, he drank water. When he paid at the counter, where Madame Rousseau held sway, fat as ever but still fresh in those days, he gave a sou to the waiter and Madame Rousseau gave him a smile. Then he took himself off. For sixteen sous, he had a smile and a meal.

This restaurant Rousseau, where so few bottles and so many carafes were emptied, was a balm more than a restaurant. It no longer exists today. The proprietor had a great nickname; they called him Rousseau, the Aquatic.

So, at four sous for breakfast and sixteen sous for dinner, his food cost him twenty sous a day, which came to three hundred and sixty-five francs a year. Add the thirty francs rent and the thirty-six francs for the old girl, plus a few minor expenses, and for four hundred and fifty francs, Marius was fed, housed, and waited on. His clothing cost him a hundred francs, his linen fifty francs, his laundry fifty francs. The whole did not exceed six hundred and fifty francs. This left him fifty francs. He was rich. He occasionally lent a friend ten francs; Courfeyrac was once able to borrow sixty francs from him. As for heating, not having a fireplace, Marius had "simplified" things.

Marius always had two complete suits; one of them was old, "for everyday," the other was brand-new, for special occasions. Both were black. He only had three shirts, one on his back, one in his chest of drawers, and the third at the laundry. He replaced them as they wore out. They were usually frayed, which meant he buttoned his coat right up to his chin.

For Marius to reach this state of prosperity had taken years. Tough years, some hard to get through, others hard to get out of. Marius had never faltered for a single day. He had endured every kind of deprivation; he had done everything except get into debt. He paid himself this tribute, that never had he owed anyone a sou. For him, owing money was the beginning of slavery. He even told himself that a creditor was worse than a boss; for a boss only owns your person, but a creditor owns your dignity and can slap it around. Rather than borrow, he went without eating. There had been many days of fasting. Feeling that all extremes meet and that, if you are not careful, abasement of fortune may lead to baseness of soul, he jealously watched over his pride. A phrase or an approach that in any other situation would have looked like respect to him, struck him as obsequious, and he would brace himself against it. He took no risks, not wanting to take a backward step. His face was covered in angry red blotches. He was so shy he was rude.

In all these trials and tribulations he felt heartened and sometimes even buoyed by a secret force within. The soul assists the body and at certain moments uplifts it. It is the only bird that can lift up its cage.

Alongside his father's name, another name was engraved in Marius's heart, the name Thénardier. With his passionate and grave nature, Marius surrounded the man to whom he owed his father's life, or so he thought, that fearless sergeant who had saved the colonel as the cannonballs and bullets of Waterloo were raining down, in a sort of glory. He never separated the memory of this man from the memory of his father and in his veneration he connected them together. It was a sort of worship on two levels, with the big altar for the colonel and the little one for Thénardier. What intensified the tenderness of his gratitude was the notion of the misfortune that had befallen Thénardier and engulfed him. Marius had learned in Montfermeil of the ruin and bankruptcy of the hapless innkeeper. Since then he had made unbelievable efforts to pick up the scent and track him down in the black pit of misery where Thénardier had disappeared. Marius had combed the countryside; he had gone to Chelles, Bondy, Gournay, Nogent, Lagny. For three years he had been hard at it, spending what little money he had saved in these explorations. Nobody had been able to give him any news of Thénardier; he was thought to have gone abroad. His creditors had looked for him, too, with less love than Marius, but with just as much keenness, and had not been able to get their hands on him. Marius blamed himself and almost hated himself for not getting anywhere in his searches. It was the sole debt that the colonel had left to him and Marius considered it a point of honor that he should pay it. "Heavens!" he thought. "When my father lay dying on the battlefield, Thénardier managed to find him through all the smoke and the grapeshot and he carried him on his shoulders, and yet he owed him nothing, and I, I who owe so much to Thénardier, can't manage to reach him in this darkness where he lies in agony and bring him back, in my turn, from death to life! Oh, I'll find him all right!" To find Thénardier, indeed, Marius would have given his right arm, and to rescue him from misery, all his blood. To see Thénardier, to do something, anything, for the man, to say to him: "You don't know me but I know you! I'm here! Do what you will with me!"—this was the sweetest and the most glorious of Marius's dreams.

### III. MARIUS GROWN UP

Marius was now twenty years old. It was three years since he had left his grandfather. They had remained on the same terms on both sides, without any attempt at reconciliation or at seeing each other again. Besides, what was the point of seeing each other again? To get into a tussle? Which one would have come off best? Marius was a bronze vase, but old man Gillenormand was an iron pot.

We must say, Marius was wrong about his grandfather's heart. He imagined that Monsieur Gillenormand had never loved him and that this abrupt, hard, derisive old man, who swore, yelled, stormed, and raised his cane, at most felt for him that affection at once slight and severe that the Gérontes of comedy felt. Marius was mistaken. There are fathers who do not love their sons; there is no grandfather in the world who does not love his grandson. At the end of the day, as we have said, Monsieur Gillenormand idolized Marius. He idolized him in his own way, to the accompaniment of shoves and even the odd slap; but with the boy gone, he felt a black emptiness in his heart. He insisted that no one mention him in front of him again, regretting to himself quietly that he should be so perfectly obeyed. At first he hoped that this Buonapartist, this Jacobin, this terrorist, this Septembrist,[1] would come crawling back. But the weeks went by, the months went by, the years went by; to Monsieur Gillenormand's great despair, the bloodsucker never reappeared. "Yet I could hardly have done anything other than kick him out," the grandfather told himself, and he asked himself, "If it were to happen again, would I do it all over again?" His pride promptly answered yes, but his old head, which he shook in silence, sadly answered no. He had his hours of dejection. He missed Marius. Old men need affection like the sun. It means heat. However strong his nature, the absence of Marius had changed something inside him. He wouldn't for all the world have taken a step toward the "little bastard," but he suffered. He never inquired about him but he thought about him constantly. He lived more and more like a recluse in the Marais. He was gay and violent yet, as before, but his gaiety had a convulsive hardness about it as though it contained pain and anger, and his violent outbursts always ended in a sort of sweet and gloomy exhaustion. He sometimes said: "Oh, if he turned up here again, I'd give him such a hiding!"

As for the aunt, she thought too little to love a lot; Marius was no longer anything more to her than a kind of blurred black outline; and she had wound up busying herself with him a good deal less than with the cat or the parrot she probably kept.

What increased the secret suffering of old man Gillenormand is that he kept it completely bottled up inside and never let any of it show. His chagrin was like those newly invented furnaces that burn their own smoke. Sometimes it happened that some blundering officious person would speak to him of Marius and ask him: "What is Monsieur, your grandson, doing now, what's become of him?"

The old bourgeois would answer, with a sigh if he was too sad, or giving his cuff a flick if he wanted to appear casual: "Monsieur le baron Pontmercy is pettifogging in some hole."

While the old man was having his regrets, Marius was rejoicing. As with all good hearts, adversity had taken away his bitterness. He thought of Monsieur Gillenormand only with kindness, but he was determined never to receive anything more from the man "who had been rotten to his father." This was now the toned-down translation of his initial expressions of outrage. Furthermore, he was happy to have suffered and to suffer still. It was for his father. His hard life satisfied and pleased him. He told himself with a sort of joy that "it was the very least he could do"; that it was atonement; that, without that, he would have been punished, in a different way and later on, for his unholy indifference to his father, and to such a father; that it would not have been right for his father to have had all the suffering and for him to have none; and that, in any case, his travails and his deprivation were nothing next to the heroic life of the colonel; that, in the end, the only way he could get closer to his father and to be like him was to be valiant in the face of poverty just as his father had been brave in the face of the enemy; and that that was no doubt what the colonel had meant by the words "he will be worthy of it." Words that Marius continued to carry around with him, not on his breast, the colonel's note having disappeared, but in his heart.

Then again, when his grandfather had kicked him out, he was still a child; now he was a man. He felt it. Misery, we will say again, had been good for him. Poverty in youth, when it succeeds, has this magnificent effect: It turns the whole will toward effort and the whole soul toward aspiration. Poverty immediately pares down material life and makes it hideous; hence those inexpressible yearnings for the ideal life. The rich young man has a hundred brilliant and vulgar distractions, the horse races, hunting, dogs, smoking, gambling, wining and dining, and the rest; occupations for the nether regions of the soul at the expense of the higher and more delicate regions. The poor young man has to toil for his daily bread; he eats, and when he has eaten, all he can do is dream. He gets in for nothing to the shows God puts on for him; he looks at the sky, space, the stars, the flowers, children, humanity among whom he suffers, creation in which he shines. He looks so hard at humanity, he sees its soul; he looks so hard at creation, he sees God. He dreams and he feels grand; he dreams on and he feels full of love. He goes from the self-obsession of the suffering man to the compassion of the meditative man. A wonderful feeling grows inside him, self-forgetfulness and pity for all. In thinking of the numberless pleasures nature offers, gives, and lavishes on those with open hearts—and refuses to closed hearts—he ends up feeling sorry for the millionaires of money, for he is a millionaire of the mind. All hatred goes out of his heart as all light enters his mind. Anyway, is he unhappy? No. The misery of a young man is never miserable. Any young man whatever, no matter how poor he may be, with his health, his strength, his lively step, his shining eyes, his blood racing through his veins, his black hair, his fresh cheeks, his rosy lips, his white teeth, his pure breath, will always be the envy of an aged emperor. Then again, every morning he sets out to earn his bread again; and while his hands are gaining his bread, his backbone is gaining firmness, his brain is gaining ideas. When his job is done, he returns to ineffable ecstasies, to contemplations, to sheer delights; he lives with his feet in affliction, in impediment, on the cobblestones, in the brambles, sometimes in the mud, but with his head in the light. He is strong, serene, gentle, peaceful, attentive, serious, content with little, benevolent; and he praises God for having given him these two riches that are lacking in many of the rich: work, which makes him free, and thought, which makes him worthy.

This is what had happened to Marius. He had even erred on the side of contemplation, if the truth be known. The day he managed to earn his living more or less securely, he had stopped there, finding it good to be poor and cutting back on work to give more time to thought. Which meant he sometimes spent whole days daydreaming, lost and absorbed like a visionary in the mute ravishment of ecstasy and inner radiance. This is how he posed the problem of his life: to work as little as possible at material work in order to work as much as possible at intangible work; in other words, to give a few hours to real life and to pour the rest into infinity. He could not see, thinking that he lacked for nothing, that contemplation thus interpreted ends up becoming a form of laziness; that he had been content to master the primary necessities of life and was resting on his laurels too soon.

It was obvious that, for such an energetic and generous nature, this could only be a transitory phase and that at the first collision with the inevitable complications of fate, Marius would snap out of it.

Meanwhile, although he was a lawyer and whatever old man Gillenormand might think, he was not busy pleading, he was not even busy pettifogging.

Reverie had turned him away from the practice of law. Hanging around with attorneys, following the courts, looking for causes—boring! What was the point? He could see no reason for boosting his livelihood that way. The obscure commercial bookshop had ended up providing him with secure work, work that didn't involve much labor, and this, as we have just explained, was enough for him.

One of the booksellers for whom he worked, Monsieur Magimel,[2] I think, had offered to put him up at his place, to give him a decent room, furnish him with regular work, and pay him fifteen hundred francs a year. To have a decent room! Fifteen hundred francs! All very well. But to give up his freedom! To be a wage earner! A kind of lettered clerk! To Marius's mind, if he accepted this offer, his position would be both better and worse at once; he would gain material well-being and lose his dignity; it was complete and beautiful adversity turned into ugly and absurd inconvenience, something similar to a blind man's gaining sight in one eye. He turned the offer down.

Marius lived a solitary life. Through his inclination to stay on the outside of everything, and also because he had been really scared off, he quite deliberately did not throw himself into the group presided over by Enjolras. They had stayed good friends; they were ready to help each other out in every possible way should the occasion arise; but nothing more. Marius had two true friends, one young, Courfeyrac, and one old, Monsieur Mabeuf. He leaned toward the old one. For a start, he was indebted to him for the revolution that had occurred inside him; he was indebted to him for having known and loved his father. "He removed my cataracts," he said to himself.

Certainly, the churchwarden had been decisive.

But in that particular instance Monsieur Mabeuf had not been anything more than the imperturbable and calm agent of fate. He had enlightened Marius by chance and unwittingly, like a candle that someone happens to be carrying; he had been the candle and not the someone.

As for Marius's inner political revolution, Monsieur Mabeuf was wholly incapable of understanding it, of wanting it, or of directing it.

Since we will come across Monsieur Mabeuf later, a few words are not out of place here.

## IV. Monsieur Mabeuf

The day Monsieur Mabeuf said to Marius: "Of course, I approve of political opinions," he was expressing his true frame of mind. All political opinions were indifferent to him and he approved of all of them without distinguishing between them, so that they would leave him in peace, much the way the Greeks called the Furies "the beautiful, the good, the charming," the Eumenides![1]

Monsieur Mabeuf's own political stance was to love plants with a passion, and books more than anything in the world. Like everyone else, he was an -ist, without which no one in those days could have survived, but he was neither a royalist nor a Bonapartist, nor a Chartist, nor an Orléanist, nor an anarchist; he was a *bouquiniste*, devoted to old books.

He did not understand how men could waste their time hating each other over such poppycock as the Charter, democracy, legitimism, the monarchy, the Republic, and so on, when there were in this world all sorts of mosses, grasses, and shrubs that they could look at, and heaps of folios and even thirty-twomo editions that they could leaf through. He took good care not to be useless; having books did not stop him from reading, being a botanist did not stop him from being a gardener. In the days when he knew Pontmercy, there had been this sympathy between the colonel and himself, which was that what the colonel did for flowers, he did for fruit. Monsieur Mabeuf had managed to produce seedling pears as tasty as the pears of Saint-Germain; one of these hybrids gave birth, it would seem, to the early autumn mirabelle plum so celebrated today and no less fragrant than the summer mirabelle. He went to mass more out of goodness than devoutness and also because, though he loved people's faces, he hated their noise and it was only in church that he found them gathered together in silence. Feeling that he ought to be something in government, he had chosen the career of churchwarden. Apart from this, he had never loved any woman as much as a tulip bulb or any man as much as an Elzevir typeface. He was way past sixty when someone asked him one day: "Haven't you ever been married?"

"I forget."

When he occasionally let loose—and who doesn't?—with an: "Oh, if only I were rich!"—it was not ogling some young filly, like old man Gillenormand, but gazing at a book. He lived alone with an old housekeeper. He was a bit gouty and when he slept his old fingers, stiff with rheumatism, clutched at the sheets. He had produced and published a *Flora of the Environs of Cauteretz* with colored plates, a fairly highly regarded work of which he owned the copperplates and which he sold himself. People came two or three times a day to ring the bell of his home in the rue Mézières to buy it. He made a good two thousand francs a year from it; that was more or less the sum total of his fortune. Although he was poor, he had had the talent to amass, through patience, self-denial, and time, a precious collection of rare editions in all genres. He never went out without a book under his arm and he often came home with two. The only decoration in the four rooms on the ground floor that, along with a garden, comprised his dwelling, were framed herbariums and old master engravings. The sight of a saber or a gun froze him. He had never gone near a cannon in his life, not even at the Invalides. He had a reasonably strong stomach, a brother who was a curé, completely white hair, no more teeth left either in his mouth or in his mind, a tremor that shook his whole body, a Picardy accent, a boyish laugh, a propensity to frighten easily, and the look of an old woolly sheep. With all that, no other friend or intimate acquaintance among the living than an old bookseller of the porte Saint-Jacques called Royol. His dream was to adapt and grow indigo in France.

His housekeeper, too, was a permutation on innocence. The poor old soul was a virgin. Sultan, her tomcat, who could have meowed Allegri's *Miserere* in the Sistine Chapel, had filled her heart and been enough for the quota of passion she had in her. None of her dreams had gone as far as a man. She had never been able to get beyond her cat. Like him, she had whiskers. Her glory lay in her bonnets, which were always white. She whiled away her time on Sundays after mass counting the linen in her trunk and spreading out on her bed all the dress material she bought piecemeal and had never run up. She could read. Monsieur Mabeuf had nicknamed her Mother Plutarch.

Monsieur Mabeuf had taken to Marius because Marius, being young and gentle, warmed up his old age without stirring up his timidity. Gentleness in the young is like the sun without the wind to old people. When Marius was saturated with military glory, with cannon powder, marches and countermarches, and all the fabulous battles in which his father had given and received such great saber slashes, he went to see Monsieur Mabeuf and Monsieur Mabeuf would tell him about his hero from the flowers' point of view.

Around 1830, his brother the curé died and almost immediately, as at nightfall, the whole horizon darkened for Monsieur Mabeuf. A bankruptcy—of a notary public—stripped him of ten thousand francs, which was all the money he possessed of his brother's or his own. The July Revolution[2] ushered in a crisis in the book trade. In times of tightening belts, the first thing that does not sell is a *Flora*. The *Flora of the Environs of Cauteretz* stopped selling altogether. Weeks went by without a single buyer. Sometimes Monsieur Mabeuf would jump up at the sound of a bell.

"Monsieur," Mother Plutarch would say to him sadly, "it's only the water carrier."

In short, one day Monsieur Mabeuf left the rue Mézières, abdicated his duties as churchwarden, gave up Saint-Sulpice, sold not his books but part of his prints—what he prized least—and set himself up in a little house in the boulevard Montparnasse, where he only stayed three months, in any case, for two reasons: first, the ground floor and the garden cost three hundred francs and he did not dare put more than two hundred francs aside for his rent; second, being next to the Fatou shooting range, he had to listen to pistol shots all day long, which he found unbearable.

He carted off his *Flora,* his copperplates, his herbariums, his portfolios, and his books and set up near La Salpêtrière in a kind of cottage in the village of Austerlitz,[3] where he had three rooms and a hedged-in garden with a well for fifty écus a year. He took advantage of the move to sell nearly all his furniture. The day he stepped into the new place, he was very lighthearted and himself hammered in the nails required to hang the engravings and herbariums; he dug up his garden the rest of the day and, that evening, seeing Mother Plutarch down in the dumps and brooding, he clapped her on the shoulder and said to her with a smile: "Now then! We still have the indigo!"

Only two visitors, the bookseller from the porte Saint-Jacques and Marius, were allowed in to see him in his cottage in Austerlitz—a flash name which, if the truth be known, he didn't much like.

Be that as it may, as we have just pointed out, brains caught up in either wisdom or madness, or, as often happens, in both at the same time, only very slowly open up to the business of living. Their own destiny is far removed from them. This kind of concentration results in a passivity that, when it is thought through, resembles philosophy. You decline, you descend, you dwindle, you even drop without being particularly aware of it. This always finishes, it is true, in an awakening, but a tardy one. Meanwhile, it seems that you are neutral in the game being played out between your happiness and your unhappiness. You are the stakes, yet you look on the match with indifference.

And so, through all the dark clouds gathering around him, with all his hopes being snuffed out one by one, Monsieur Mabeuf remained serene, a little childishly, but profoundly. His mental habits had the swing of a pendulum. Once wound up by an illusion, he went for a long time, even when the illusion had vanished. A clock doesn't suddenly stand still the exact moment you lose the key that winds it.

Monsieur Mabeuf had innocent pleasures. These pleasures were cheap and unlooked for; the slightest accident provided them. One day Mother Plutarch was reading a novel in a corner of the room. She was reading out loud, as she found she could follow better that way. To read out loud is to assure yourself of what you are reading. There are those who read very loudly as though they are giving themselves their word of honor about what they are reading.

Mother Plutarch was reading with that kind of energy the novel she held in her hands. Monsieur Mabeuf could hear her but was not listening.

As she read, Mother Plutarch came to this sentence. It was about an officer of dragoons and some belle: ". . . The belle was brooding, and the dragoon . . ."

Here she broke off to wipe her glasses.

"Buddha and the dragon," mused Monsieur Mabeuf sotto voce. "Yes, that's right, there was once a dragon who, from deep in its lair, spewed flames out of its maw and burned the sky. Several stars had already been set alight by this monster who, on top of that, had the claws of a tiger. Buddha went into its den and managed to convert the dragon. You've got yourself a good book there, Mother Plutarch. There is no more beautiful legend."

And Monsieur Mabeuf fell into a delicious reverie.

## V. Poverty, Misery's Good Neighbor

Marius was genuinely fond of this open old man who saw himself slowly going under and yet managed to be amazed by it without yet being depressed. Marius ran into Courfeyrac, he ran to Monsieur Mabeuf. Very rarely, though, once or twice a month at most.

Marius's great pleasure was to take long walks alone along the outer boulevards or in the Champ de Mars or along the less frequented allées of the Luxembourg gardens. He sometimes spent half a day at a time gazing at a market garden, square beds of lettuce, hens scratching in the dung, and a horse turning the chain of a waterwheel. Passersby would study him with surprise and a few found he had a suspicious demeanor and a sinister face. He was just a young man with no money, dreaming aimlessly.

It was on one of these promenades that he had discovered the Gorbeau slum, and its isolation and low rent tempted him, so he moved in. There, everyone knew him only as Monsieur Marius.

Some of his father's old generals and old comrades had invited him, when they found out who he was, to come and see them, and Monsieur Marius had not refused. These were opportunities to talk about his father. And so from time to time he went to see Comte Pajol, General Bellavesne, and General Fririon,[1] at home in the Invalides. There was music there and dancing. On those evenings, Marius would put on his good coat. But he never went to these parties or balls except on days when it was cold and dry enough to split stone, for he could not afford a cab and he did not want to turn up unless his boots were polished to a mirror finish by the frost.

He sometimes said, though without bitterness: "Men are so made that, in a salon, you could be caked with mud all over, except for your shoes. In a salon, to be welcomed with open arms, you are asked to be irreproachable in one thing only. Your conscience? No. Your boots."

All passions, other than those of the heart, are dissipated by daydreaming. Marius's political fevers had evaporated. The revolution of 1830 had satisfied him and calmed him down and so had helped on this score. He had stayed the same, minus his anger. He still held the same views, only, they had mellowed. Actually he no longer had views as such, he had sympathies. Whose side was he on? On the side of humanity. Within humanity, he chose France; within the nation, he chose the people; within the people, he chose women. It was to women especially that his heart went out. He now preferred an idea to a deed, a poet to a hero, and he admired a book like Job[2] even more than an event like Marengo. And then again when, after a day of meditation, he strolled home in the evening along the boulevards and saw, through the branches of the trees, the endless space, the nameless lights, the void, the dark, the mystery, all that is merely human seemed pretty paltry to him.

He felt that he finally understood, and perhaps he did finally understand, what life was all about, and what human philosophy was all about, and he ended up scarcely looking at anything but the heavens, the only thing that truth can see from the bottom of its well.

This did not prevent him from making plan after plan, devising schemes, erecting scaffoldings, elaborating projects for the future. In this state of reverie, an eye that could see inside Marius would have been dazzled by the purity of his soul. In fact, if it were given to our eyes of flesh to see inside other people's minds, we would judge a man a great deal more accurately by his dreams than by his thoughts. There is something deliberate about thought, but there is no such thing in dreams. Even when it involves immensity and the ideal, a dream that is entirely spontaneous takes on and keeps the shape of our mind. Nothing emerges more directly and more genuinely from the very depths of our soul than our unthinking untamed aspirations toward the splendors of destiny. In such aspirations, much more than in composed, reasoned, and ordered ideas, we see every man's true character. Our fantasies are what most closely resemble us. Each of us dreams of the unknown and the impossible according to his nature.

Toward the middle of that year, 1831, the old woman who served Marius told him that his neighbors, the miserable Jondrette family, were going to be shown the door. Marius, who spent almost all his days away, hardly knew he had neighbors.

"Why are they kicking them out?" he asked.

"Because they didn't pay the rent. They owed six months."

"How much is that?"

"Twenty francs."

Marius had thirty francs in reserve in a drawer.

"Here," he said to the old woman, "here's twenty-five francs. Pay for these poor people, give them the extra five francs and don't say it's from me."

## VI. The Substitute

As luck would have it, the regiment Lieutenant Théodule belonged to came to be garrisoned in Paris. This was the occasion for Aunt Gillenormand to have a second idea. Initially she had imagined having Marius spied on by Théodule; now she plotted to have Marius supplanted by Théodule.

At all events, and in case the grandfather should feel a vague need to have a young face about the place—these rays of dawn are sometimes soft to ruins— it was expedient to come up with another Marius. "Yes," she thought, "it's just a printing error such as I sometimes see in books. For Marius, read Théodule."

A grandnephew is almost a grandson; for want of a lawyer, they could take a lancer.

One morning, as Monsieur Gillenormand was in the process of reading some rag like the *Quotidienne*,[1] his daughter came in and said to him in her sweetest voice, since it concerned her favorite: "Father, dear, Théodule is coming over this morning to pay you his respects."

"Who's that? Théodule?"

"Your grandnephew."

"Ah!" said the great-uncle.

At which he resumed his reading without giving his grandnephew another thought, as he was just another Théodule after all; soon he was in a very excited mood, which almost always happened when he read. The "broadsheet" he was holding, which was of course royalist—that goes without saying—announced for the following day, most ungraciously, one of the little daily occurrences of the Paris of the time: The students of the faculties of law and medicine would gather at the place du Panthéon at twelve noon—to deliberate. At issue was one of the questions of the moment, namely the artillery of the National Guard and a conflict between the minister of war[2] and "the citizen militia" over some cannons parked in the courtyard of the Louvre. The students were to "deliberate" over this. It didn't take much more to get Monsieur Gillenormand going.

He thought of Marius, who was a student and who, probably, would go, like the others, "to deliberate, at twelve noon, at the place du Panthéon."

As he was dwelling on this painful thought, Lieutenant Théodule came strutting in dressed like a bourgeois, which was a clever move, and he was discreetly introduced by Mademoiselle Gillenormand. The lancer had reasoned as follows: "The old troglodyte hasn't yet put all his money into buying an annuity. That's worth the trouble of disguising myself as a civilian from time to time."

Mademoiselle Gillenormand said, loudly, to her father: "Théodule, your grandnephew."

And, softly, to the lieutenant: "Agree with everything he says."

And with that, she withdrew.

The lieutenant, little accustomed to encountering such venerable personages, stammered rather timidly, "Hello, Uncle," and performed a mixed salutation consisting of an involuntary and mechanical attempt at a military salute finishing in a bourgeois bow.

"Oh, it's you! Right, right, sit down," said the old man.

That said, he forgot all about the lancer.

Théodule sat down and Monsieur Gillenormand stood up.

Monsieur Gillenormand began to pace up and down, his hands in his pockets, talking out loud and tormenting with his agitated old fingers the two watches he had in the two fob pockets of his waistcoat.

"That bunch of snotty-nosed upstarts! Calling a meeting at the place du Panthéon! I'll be a monkey's uncle! Cheeky little twirps! They're only just out of the nursery! If you squeezed their noses, milk would come running out! And that's what's deliberating at twelve noon tomorrow! What is the world coming to? What is the world coming to? It's clear we're headed for the abyss. That's where those *descamisados*³ have led us! Citizen artillery! Deliberate about the citizen artillery! Fancy going and jabbering in the open air about the farting of the National Guard! And who are they going to find themselves among there? Just see where Jacobinism gets you. I bet you all the money you like, a million to one, that the only people there will be fugitives from justice and freed convicts. Republicans and galley slaves go together like a nose and a handkerchief. Carnot said: 'Where do you want me to go, traitor?' Fouché answered:⁴ 'Wherever you like, you moron!' That's republicans for you."

"Hear, hear," said Théodule.

Monsieur Gillenormand turned his head half round, spotted Théodule and went on: "When I think that that little bastard has had the audacity to turn himself into a Carbonaro! Why did you leave my house? To go and make yourself a republican. Aaagh! To start with, the people don't want anything to do with your republic, they don't want it, they've got common sense, they know very well that there have always been kings and there always will be, they know very well that the people, after all, are just the people, they laugh at it, your republic, do you hear, you little dimwit! Is it horrible enough for you, this little whim of yours? To fall for Père Duchesne, make eyes at the guillotine, sing romances and play the guitar under the balcony of '93, it's enough to make you want to spit on all those young men, they are such dunderheads! They're all at it. Not one has escaped. All it takes is to breathe the air blowing down the street and you go stark raving mad. The nineteenth century is poison. The first little squirt that comes along grows his little goatee, thinks he's a genuine rogue, and leaves his old relatives in the lurch. That's republican, that's romantic. What the hell is romantic about that? Have the goodness to tell me, what the hell is that? Every crazy notion that pops into your head. A year ago, you all went to *Hernani*.⁵ I ask you, *Hernani*! Nothing but antitheses, abominations not even written in French! And then they stick cannons in the courtyard of the Louvre. That's the sort of dastardly deed they go in for these days."

"Too right, Uncle," said Théodule.

Monsieur Gillenormand went on: "Cannons in the courtyard of the museum! What for? Cannons, I tell you! So you want to blast the Apollo Belvedere? What have cartridge pouches to do with the Venus de Médicis? Oh, the young people of today, they're scoundrels, every one of them! What a nobody their Benjamin Constant[6] is! And those that aren't little rotters are nincompoops! They all do their level best to be ugly, they're badly dressed, they're frightened of women, around a bit of skirt they have the air of begging, which makes the fillies laugh in their faces; my word of honor, you'd think they were paupers, ashamed of love. They're grotesque, and they top it off by being morons; they trot out old puns of Tiercelin's and Potier's, they have coats that look like sacks, jockey's waistcoats, coarse cotton shirts, coarse cotton trousers, coarse leather boots, and all they manage to achieve is to look as if they're wearing feathers. You could resole their old clodhoppers with the jargon they use. And all these hopeless runts reckon they have political opinions. It ought to be strictly forbidden to have political opinions. They fabricate systems, they rebuild society, they dismantle the monarchy, they trample all laws underfoot, they put the attic where the cellar is and my porter where the king is, they turn Europe on its head, they remake the world, and what they get out of it all is to slyly peek at the washerwomen's legs when they climb up into their carts! Ah, Marius! Ah, you little beggar! Go and pontificate in the public arena! Discuss, debate, take measures! They call those measures, for God's sake! Disorder gets diminished and becomes inane. I've seen chaos, I see the damage done. Schoolboys deliberating about the National Guard, you won't see that among the Ojibways or the Cadodaches! Savages getting about stark naked, their noggins tizzed up like shuttlecocks, with clubs in their paws, aren't as savage as these gay young blades! Marmosets worth four sous apiece, making innuendos and pathetic wisecracks! It deliberates and ratiocinates! It's the end of the world. It's obviously the end of this miserable terraqueous globe. All it needed was some final hiccup and France has come up with it. Deliberate, you little turds! This sort of thing will keep happening as long as they go off and read the newspapers under the arches of the Odéon. It costs them a sou—and their common sense, and their intelligence, and their heart, and their soul, and their mind. Then they clear out and go home to their families. All newspapers are a scourge; all of them, even the *Drapeau blanc!* At bottom, Martainville[7] was a Jacobin. Ah, heavens above! You can certainly boast that you've caused your grandfather to despair, you can certainly do that!"

"Obviously," said Théodule.

And, taking advantage of Monsieur Gillenormand's pausing for breath, the lancer added magisterially: "There should be no other newspaper apart from the *Moniteur* and no other book apart from the *Annuaire militaire.*"

Monsieur Gillenormand went on: "He's like their Sieyès![8] A regicide winding up as a senator! For that's the way they always end up. They slash at each other with their 'citizen this' and 'citizen that' only to wind up getting about as Monsieur le comte. Monsieur le comte, my eye! The butchers of September! The philosopher Sieyès! I'll say this for myself: At least I have never taken any more notice of the philosophies of those particular philosophers than of the goggles of the clown who pulls faces at the Tivoli! One day I saw some senators passing along the quai Malaquais in mantles of violet velvet strewn with bees and wearing hats like Henri IV.⁹ They were hideous. You'd have said they were monkeys from the court of a tiger. Citizens, I tell you that your progress is lunacy, that your humanity is a dream, that your revolution is a crime, that your republic is a monster, that your young virginal France comes straight from the brothel, and I maintain it to all of you, whoever you may be, whether you are publicists, whether you are economists, whether you are legal experts, whether you are more connoisseurs of liberty, equality, and fraternity than of the blade of the guillotine! That's what I say, my good fellows!"

"Good Lord!" cried the lieutenant. "Not a truer word was spoken."

Monsieur Gillenormand broke off a gesture he had begun to make, wheeled round, looked the lancer Théodule straight in the eye and said to him: "You are a moron."

# BOOK SIX

# THE CONJUNCTION OF TWO STARS

## I. THE NICKNAME AS A WAY OF FORMING FAMILY NAMES

Marius was now a handsome young man of medium height, with thick, jet black hair, a high, intelligent forehead, passionate flaring nostrils, a candid and calm look, and with something hard to define that was at once arrogant, thoughtful, and innocent shining from every pore. His profile, whose every line was rounded without ceasing to be strong, had that Germanic softness that made its way into French physiognomy via Alsace and Lorraine and that complete absence of angles that made the Sicambri[1] so recognizable among the Romans and that distinguishes the leonine race from the aquiline. He was at that stage in life when the minds of thinking men are made up of almost equal proportions of depth and naïveté. Given a serious situation, he had all it took to be stupid; one turn of the screw more, and he could be sublime. His manners were reserved, frigid, polite, not particularly open. As his mouth was alluring, his lips the most rosy red and his teeth the whitest in the world, his smile made up for what was severe in his whole physiognomy. At certain moments, the contrast between his chaste forehead and that sensual smile was quite strange. His eyes were small, his gaze grand.

In the period when he was most desperately destitute, he noticed that young girls turned around when he passed and, with a heavy heart, he fled or hid. He thought they were looking at him because of his old clothes and that they were laughing at him; the fact is that they looked at him because of his grace, which set them dreaming.

This mute misunderstanding between himself and the pretty passersby had made him fierce. He did not choose any one of them for the very good reason that he took off when faced with any of them. He lived like this indefinitely—stupidly, said Courfeyrac.

Courfeyrac also told him, "Don't try and be honorable"—for they were on familiar terms; familiarity is a tendency early in a friendship when you are young. "My dear boy, a word of advice. Take your nose out of books for a while and look at the talent. There's something to be said for the girls, O Marius! The way you run away blushing, you'll end up a brute."

At other times, Courfeyrac would say when he ran into him: "Hello, Monsieur l'abbé."

Whenever Courfeyrac said something of the kind to him, Marius spent the week avoiding women more than ever, young or old, and he would avoid Courfeyrac into the bargain.

There were, though, two women, in all the immensity of creation, that Marius did not flee and that he was not on his guard with. If the truth be known, you would have amazed him by pointing out that these two were actually women. One was the old bearded woman who swept out his room and who made Courfeyrac say: "Since his servant wears her beard, Marius doesn't wear his." The other was a little girl whom he saw regularly and never looked at.

For more than a year, Marius had noticed in a deserted walk of the Luxembourg gardens, the walk that runs alongside the parapet of the plant nursery, a man and a very young girl, almost always seated side by side on the same bench at the most solitary end of the path, on the rue de l'Ouest side. Every time that fate, which gets mixed up in the promenades of people whose eyes are turned inward, took Marius into this path, which was practically every day, he would find this couple there. The man might have been sixty or so; he looked sad and serious; his whole person radiated that robust yet weary feel of the soldier retired from active service. If he had worn a decoration, Marius would have said: That's a former officer. He looked like a good man, but unapproachable, and he never met anyone else's gaze. He wore blue trousers, a blue redingote, and a broad-brimmed hat, all of which looked new, a black tie, and a Quaker shirt, meaning, dazzlingly white but made of coarse material. A young working girl passing close by one day said: "Now there's a widower who's nice and neat." His hair was as white as snow.

When the young girl who accompanied him first came and sat with him on the bench that they seemed to have adopted, she was just a bit of a girl, about thirteen or fourteen years old, thin to the point of being almost ugly, gauche, mousy, though promising to have rather beautiful eyes one day. Only, they were always looking up with a sort of off-putting assurance. She was dressed the way convent boarders are, in clothes both infantile and too old for her, in a badly cut dress of coarse black merino wool. They looked like father and daughter.

For two or three days, Marius studied this aging man who was not yet old and this little girl who was not yet a person, then forgot about them completely. They, for their part, did not seem to have even seen him. They chatted between themselves in a quiet, oblivious sort of way. The girl babbled endlessly and cheerily. The old man didn't say much, and at times would gaze at her with eyes filled with fatherly adoration.

Marius had got into the habit of walking down this path without thinking. He invariably found them there. This is how it went:

Marius preferred to come from the other end of the path to the one where their bench was. He would walk the whole length of the path, pass by them, then turn back and go as far as the end at which he had come in, then do it all again. He came and went this way five or six times on his walk and he did the walk five or six times a week without their reaching the point of exchanging greetings. Though they seemed, and perhaps because they seemed, to want to avoid people's eyes, the old gentleman and the young girl had naturally attracted the attention of the five or six students who occasionally strolled past the nursery, the studious ones after their courses, the others after their game of billiards. Courfeyrac, who was in the latter category, had observed them for a while, but he found the girl ugly and so had swiftly and carefully given them wide berth. He had fled like some Parthian,[2] firing a nickname at them as he did so. Struck solely by the girl's frock and the old man's hair, he had called the girl "Mademoiselle Lanoire"—Miss Black—and her father "Monsieur Leblanc"— Mr. White—so aptly that, as no one knew them from Adam in any case, in the absence of a name, the nickname stuck. The students would say: "Ah, Monsieur Leblanc's on his bench!" and Marius, like the others, had found it convenient to call this unknown gentleman Monsieur Leblanc. We will do as they did and use Monsieur Leblanc to simplify this tale.

So Marius saw them practically every day, at the same time, for the first year. He found the man to his liking, but the girl rather dismal.

## II. Lux Facta Est[1]

The second year, at the exact point in the story the reader has reached, it happened that this little Luxembourg habit was broken, without Marius himself really knowing why, and it was nearly six months before he set foot in his walk again. The day finally came when he went back. It was a blissful summer morning, Marius was full of joy as you are on a beautiful day. He felt as though his heart was bursting with all the birdsong he could hear and all the bits of blue sky he could see through the leaves of the trees.

He headed straight for "his" walk and when he got there he spotted the familiar pair, still on the same bench. Only, when he came closer, though it was definitely the same man, it seemed to him that it was not the same girl. The person he now saw was a tall and beautiful creature with the full array of womanly charms at that precise moment when these are still combined with all the utterly artless graces of the child; a fleeting and pure moment that these words alone can translate: fifteen years old. Wonderful chestnut hair streaked with gold, a forehead that looked made of marble, cheeks that looked made of rose petals, a pale incarnadine, a flushed whiteness, an exquisite mouth with a smile like a flash of light and a voice that was sheer music, a head that Raphael would have given Mary, placed on a neck that Jean Goujon[2] would have given Venus. And, so that nothing was missing from this ravishing face, the nose was not beautiful, it was pretty; neither straight nor curved, neither Italian nor Greek; it was a Parisian nose par excellence, that is, somewhat witty, fine, irregular, and pure, enough to drive painters to despair and to charm poets.

When Marius passed close by her, he could not see her eyes, which were constantly downcast. He could only see her long chestnut eyelashes dipped modestly in shadow.

This did not prevent the beautiful child from smiling while listening to the man with the white hair talking to her, and nothing was as ravishing as that fresh smile that went with her downcast eyes.

Initially Marius thought the man must have another daughter, that this girl was no doubt a sister of the first. But when the invariable habit of the walk had brought him close to the bench a second time, and he had studied her carefully, he recognized that it was the same one. In six months, the little girl had become a young girl; that's all. Nothing could be more normal than such a phenomenon. There is an instant, the blink of an eye, when girls blossom suddenly into roses. Yesterday when you left them they were still children, today you find them downright disturbing.

This one had not only grown, she had been perfected. Just as three days in spring are enough for certain trees to cover themselves with flowers, six months had been enough for her to deck herself out with beauty. Her very own spring had come.

You sometimes see people, poor and mean people, who seem to wake up out of destitution and suddenly hurtle headlong into wild extravagance; they go on a spending spree and suddenly become stunning, lavish, resplendent. This comes from income pocketed; yesterday an interest payment came through. The young girl had received her half-yearly dividend.

And then again, she was no longer the school boarder with her felt hat, her merino wool frock, her school shoes, and her chapped hands; taste had come to her with beauty; she was now dressed well with a sort of simple, rich, unmannered elegance. She had on a dress of black damask, a short hooded cape of the same fabric, and a white crepe hat. Her white gloves showed off the fineness of her hand as she played with the Chinese ivory handle of her umbrella, and her silk lace-up boots emphasized the smallness of her foot. When you passed close by, her whole toilette gave off a fresh, green, penetrating perfume.

As for the man, he was exactly the same.

The second time Marius veered close to her, the young girl looked up. Her eyes were a deep celestial blue, but this veiled azure still held only the gaze of a child. She looked at Marius with indifference, as she would have looked at a toddler running around under the sycamores or at the marble vase that was casting a shadow over the bench; and Marius for his part continued his promenade thinking of something else.

He passed close by the bench where the young girl was another four or five times but without even turning his eyes her way.

On the following days, he returned as usual to the Luxembourg; as usual, he found "the father and daughter" there, but he no longer took any notice of them. He thought no more of the girl now that she was beautiful than he had thought of her when she was ugly. He always passed close by the bench where she sat simply because that was his habit.

### III. THE EFFECT OF SPRING

One day the air was mild, the Luxembourg was flooded with sun and shade, the sky was as pure as if angels had rinsed it that morning, the sparrows were twittering deep in the chestnut trees, Marius had opened his whole soul to nature, he was not thinking anything, he lived and breathed, he passed close by the bench, the young girl glanced up at him and their eyes met.

What was there this time in the young girl's gaze? Marius could not have said. It was nothing and everything. It was a strange lightning flash.

She dropped her gaze and he went on his way.

What he had just seen was not the unaffected and simple eye of a child, it was a mysterious gulf that had cracked open a fraction, then promptly shut again. There comes a day when every young girl peeks out like this. Woe to the man who happens to be there!

This first glance of a soul that does not yet know itself is like dawn in the sky. It is the awakening of something radiant and new. Nothing can convey the dangerous charm of this unexpected gleam that dimly shines its light on lovely expanses of shadow and that is made up of all the innocence of the present and all the passion of the future. It is a sort of vague tenderness, lying in wait, and sparked by the merest chance. It is a trap that innocence sets unknowingly as it goes about collecting hearts unwittingly and unwillingly. It is a virgin with the glance of a woman.

Only very rarely does that look, wherever it falls, fail to send its object into a profound spin. All pure feeling, all yearning, all ardent longing, is concentrated in that heavenly yet fatal ray of light, which, more than the most practiced ogling of the flirt, has the magic power to suddenly cause that dark flower we call love, full of perfume and poison, to bloom deep in the soul.

That evening, when he got back to his garret, Marius ran his eyes over his clothes and realized for the first time that he had the sordidness, the indecency, and the unbelievable stupidity to go walking in the Luxembourg in his everyday attire, that is, in a hat that was ripped near the band, great walloping carter's clodhoppers, black pants that were shiny at the knees, and a black coat threadbare at the elbows.

## IV. BEGINNING OF A GREAT SICKNESS

The next day at the usual time, Marius dug his new coat out of his wardrobe, along with his new pants and his new boots; he donned the complete panoply, pulled on gloves, an extravagant luxury, and took himself off to the Luxembourg.

On the way there he ran into Courfeyrac and pretended not to see him. Courfeyrac, when he got home, told his friends: "I've just seen Marius's new hat and new coat, and Marius in them. No doubt he was off to sit for some exam. He looked a complete ninny."

When he got to the Luxembourg, Marius circled the pond and gazed at the swans, then stood for a long time contemplating a statue the head of which was black with mold and which was missing a hip. Near the pond a potbellied bourgeois in his forties was holding the hand of a little boy of five and quietly lecturing him: "Beware of extremes, son.[1] Maintain an equal distance from despotism and anarchy." Marius heard the bourgeois out, then circled the pond one more time. Finally, he headed for "his" walk, slowly and apparently with great reluctance. You would have said that he was both forced to go and hindered from doing so. He was unconscious of all this and believed he was behaving as he did every other day.

When he stepped into the walk, he immediately caught sight of Monsieur Leblanc and the young girl on "their" bench at the other end. He buttoned his coat right up to the top, carefully smoothed out the wrinkles, examined the lustrous sheen of his pants somewhat complacently and marched up to the bench. There was something of the attack in this approach and certainly a desire to conquer. I say, then, that he marched up to the bench the way I'd say: Hannibal marched on Rome.

Otherwise all his movements were completely mechanical and he did not for a second deviate from his usual concerns, either with work or matters of the mind. He was thinking at that moment that the *Manuel du Baccalauréat* was an idiotic book and that it must have been written by rare cretins for it to analyze, as masterpieces of the human spirit, three of Racine's tragedies but only one of Molière's comedies. There was a high-pitched ringing in his ear. As he came up to the bench, he smoothed the wrinkles out of his coat again and planted his gaze firmly on the young girl. It seemed to him that she filled the entire end of the walk with a vague blue light.

As he came closer, his pace slowed more and more. At some distance from the bench, well before he had come to the end of the walk, he stopped altogether and, though he himself did not know how it happened, he spun on his heel and turned back. He had not even told himself that he wasn't going to the end. The young girl would hardly have a chance to make him out from so far away—she would not see how handsome he looked in his new clothes. Yet he held himself perfectly erect, so that he would look good in case anyone behind him should happen to be watching.

He reached the opposite end, then came back, and this time he got a bit closer to the bench. He got as close as three trees away, in fact, but once there he felt for some reason that he could not possibly go on, and he hesitated. He thought he'd seen the young girl's face poke forward toward him. In any case, he made a virile and violent effort, overcame his hesitation, and continued his advance. A few seconds later, he passed the bench, straight and firm, his face red to the ears, without daring to dart so much as a glance either to left or right, his hand shoved stiffly in his coat like a statesman. The moment he passed—under the cannon standing in the square—his heart fluttered with palpitations. She was wearing the damask dress and crepe hat of the day before. He heard a heavenly voice that had to be "her voice." She was chatting away happily. She was indeed pretty. He could tell, even though he didn't try to get a look at her. "Yet," he thought to himself, "she couldn't help but hold me in high esteem if she knew it was I who am the real author of the dissertation on Marcos Obregon de la Ronda, which Monsieur François de Neufchâteau has claimed as his own and stuck at the beginning of his edition of *Gil Blas*!"[2]

He went past the bench, went right to the end of the walk a few steps farther on, then retraced his steps and went past the beautiful girl once more. This time he was very pale. Besides, he felt nothing but enormous discomfort. He walked away from the bench and from the young girl and, once his back was turned to her, he imagined her watching him and that made him stumble.

He did not try to approach the bench again but stopped about halfway down the walk and there he did something he never did, he sat down, casting sidelong glances and thinking, in the most hidden recesses of his mind, that after all it was pretty tough that persons whose white hat and black dress he admired could be so absolutely insensible to his lustrous trousers and his brandnew coat.

After a quarter of an hour, he got up, as though he were about to begin walking toward the bench again, surrounded as it was in glory. But, instead, he stood rooted to the spot. For the first time in fifteen months he told himself that the gentleman who sat there every day with his daughter must have noticed him and probably found his zeal rather strange.

For the first time, too, he felt some irreverence in giving this unknown man the nickname of Monsieur Leblanc, even if only in his secret thoughts.

He stood there for a few minutes with his head down, drawing in the sand with a stick. Then he promptly turned in the direction opposite to the bench and to Monsieur Leblanc and his daughter, and went home.

That day he forgot to have dinner. At eight o'clock in the evening he realized this and, since it was too late to go down to the rue Saint-Jacques, he said "Well!" and chewed on a bit of bread.

He went to bed only after he had carefully brushed his coat and folded it away.

## V. SUNDRY THUNDERBOLTS FALL ON MA BOUGON

The next day, Ma Bougon—or Grumpypants, as Courfeyrac called the old concierge–chief tenant–cleaning lady of the Gorbeau slum; her real name was Madame Burgon, but, as we have observed, that vandal Courfeyrac respected nothing—Ma Bougon, stupefied, noticed Marius going out again in his new coat.

He returned to the Luxembourg, but he did not get farther than his usual seat halfway along the walk. He sat down on it as he had the day before, gaping from a distance and distinctly seeing the white hat, black dress, and especially the blue light. He did not budge from his seat and only went home when the gates of the Luxembourg were closing. He did not see Monsieur Leblanc and his daughter leave and decided that they must have gone out through the rue de l'Ouest gate. Later, some weeks afterward, when he thought about it, he had no idea where he had dined that particular evening.

The next day, this was the third day, Ma Bougon was dumbstruck once more to see Marius going out again in his new coat.

"Three days in a row!" she cried.

She tried to follow him, but Marius walked briskly, with huge strides; it was like a hippopotamus trying to keep track of a chamois. She lost sight of him in two minutes flat and went home out of breath, half choking from asthma and fury.

"What a donkey," she grumbled, "putting on his best clothes every day and making people chase after him like that!"

Marius had taken himself to the Luxembourg. The young girl was there with Monsieur Leblanc. Marius got as close as he could while pretending to be reading his book, but he remained a long way off again, then he returned to plop himself down on his bench, where he spent four hours watching frank little sparrows hopping about on the path, seemingly poking fun at him.

A fortnight went by in this way. Marius no longer went to the Luxembourg to stroll, but to sit in the same place always without knowing why. Once he got there, he would not stir again. Every morning, he would put on his new outfit only to avoid showing himself off and the next day he would begin all over again.

She was definitely wondrously beautiful. The only slightly critical thing you could say perhaps was that the contradiction between her gaze, which was sad, and her smile, which was jubilant, gave her face a somewhat wild look, which meant that at times that sweet face became strange without ceasing to be lovely.

## VI. Taken Prisoner

On one of the last days of the second week, Marius was sitting as usual on his seat holding an open book, which he had not turned a page of for two hours. Suddenly he gave a start. An event was in train at the end of the walk. Monsieur Leblanc and his daughter had just left their bench, the daughter had taken her father's arm, and they were making their way together, slowly, to the middle of the walk, where Marius was. Marius closed his book, then opened it again and forced himself to read. He was trembling. The glory was heading straight for him. "Oh, my God!" he thought. "I'll never have time to strike a pose."

But the man with white hair and the young girl were coming closer. It seemed to him to be taking either a century or only a second. "What are they coming this way for?" he wondered. "Help! She's going to walk past! Her feet are going to walk on this sand, along this path, two feet away!"

He was overcome, he would have liked to be stunningly handsome, he would have liked to be wearing the cross of the Légion d'Honneur. He heard the soft measured tread of their footfalls as they approached. He imagined that Monsieur Leblanc was throwing him angry looks.

"Is this monsieur going to speak to me?" he wondered. He bowed his head; when he raised it again, they were almost upon him. The young girl went past and as she passed she looked at him. She looked straight at him, with a thoughtful sweetness that made Marius shiver from head to toe. It seemed to him that she reproached him for sitting there for so long without coming to her and that she was saying: "I'll come to you if you won't come to me."

Marius remained dazzled by the play of light and shadow in those eyes. He felt as though his brain was on fire. She had come to him, what ecstasy! And then, the way she had looked at him! She seemed to him more beautiful than he had ever seen her. Beautiful with a beauty both entirely womanly and angelic at once, with a complete beauty that would have made Petrarch sing and brought Dante[1] to his knees. He felt as if he were swimming in the wide blue sky. At the same time, he was horribly thrown because he had a speck of dust on his boots.

He felt sure that she had also looked at his boots.

He followed her with his eyes until she disappeared out of sight. Then he began to bound around the Luxembourg like a madman. At times, he probably actually laughed to himself and talked out loud. He mooned around nannies with their little charges so much that each one of them thought he was in love with her.

Finally he left the Luxembourg, hoping to come across her again in a street somewhere.

He crossed paths with Courfeyrac, instead, under the arcades of the Odéon and said to him: "Come and have dinner with me."

They went and had dinner at Rousseau's and spent six francs. Marius ate like a horse. Over dessert, he said to Courfeyrac: "Did you read the paper? What a great speech Audry de Puyraveau[2] gave!"

He was hopelessly in love. After dinner, he said to Courfeyrac: "Come and I'll take you to a show."

They went to the Porte Saint-Martin to see Frédérick[3] in *L'Auberge des Adrets*. Marius enjoyed himself enormously.

At the same time, he became twice as unsociable. As they left the theater, he refused to look at the garter of a pretty milliner who was leaping over a gutter and when Courfeyrac said, "I wouldn't mind adding that piece to my collection," he was very nearly appalled.

Courfeyrac had invited him to have lunch at the Café Voltaire the next day. Marius went and ate even more than the night before. He was quite pensive and very lighthearted. You'd have said he was seizing every opportunity to laugh his head off. He tenderly embraced some provincial who was introduced to him. A circle of students had gathered around the table and they had discussed the mindless poppycock, subsidized by the state, peddled at the Sorbonne; then the conversation had turned to the mistakes and gaps in the dictionaries and prosodies of Quicherat.[4] Marius cut into the discussion to shout: "But it's very nice, all the same, to get the cross!"

"That's a funny one, for you!" said Courfeyrac softly to Jean Prouvaire.

"No, it's not," replied Jean Prouvaire, "it's serious."

It was, in fact, serious. Marius was in the first violent and deliriously wonderful phase grand passions start with. Just one look was all it had taken. When the mine is loaded with explosives, when the fuse is ready to run, nothing could be simpler. A look is a spark.

The jig was up. Marius was in love with a woman. His destiny was entering the realm of the unknown.

The looks women throw out are like the moving parts of certain machines that look innocuous enough but are deadly. You go past the machinery every day quietly and with impunity and without suspecting a thing. There even comes a time when you forget the thing is there. You come and go, you daydream, you talk, you laugh. Then, suddenly, you feel yourself caught. It's all over. The machinery has you in its grip, you have been seized by a glance. It has caught you, no matter how or by what means, latching on to some trailing thought or some momentary distraction. You are lost. You will be sucked in, body and soul. A train of mysterious forces takes possession of you. You struggle in vain. No one can help you now. You are going to drop from one cog to the next, from one trap to the next, from one anguish to the next, from one torture to the next, you, your mind, your fortune, your future, your soul; and, depending on whether you are in the power of a nasty piece of work or a noble creature, you will not emerge from this terrifying machine except disfigured by shame or transfigured by passion.

## VII. Adventures of the Letter *U* Open to Conjecture

Isolation, detachment from everything, pride, independence, a love of nature, lack of any daily physical activity, living for himself, the secret struggles of chastity, benign rapture before all creation—all had prepared Marius for this possession we call passion. His worship of his father had gradually become a religion, and, like all religions, had withdrawn to the nether regions of his heart. He needed something in the foreground. Love came along.

A good long month went by during which Marius went to the Luxembourg every day. When the moment came, nothing could keep him away.

"He's out on the job," said Courfeyrac.

Marius lived in raptures. It was undeniable that the young girl now looked at him.

He had finally plucked up the courage to go closer to the bench. But he no longer passed directly in front of it, obeying at once the instinctive timidity and the instinctive prudence of lovers. He thought it was better not to attract "the father's attention." He worked out positions behind trees and the pedestals of statues with consummate Machiavellianism, so as to be seen as much as possible by the young girl and as little as possible by the old gent. Sometimes he would stand for half an hour at a stretch without moving in the shadow of some Leonidas or Spartacus,[1] holding a book while his eyes, gently raised, sought the beautiful girl over the top of it and she, for her part, would turn her lovely head toward him with a vague smile. Chatting away perfectly naturally and quietly all the while, she pressed on Marius all the longings of a virginal and passionate gaze. An antique and immemorial little game that Eve knew by heart from the day the world began and that every woman knows by heart from the day her life begins! Her lips responded to one man and her eyes responded to the other.

We must assume, though, that Monsieur Leblanc ended up catching on, for often when Marius arrived he would stand and start walking. He had abandoned their customary spot and had adopted the seat next to the Gladiator at the other end of the walk as though testing to see if Marius would follow. Marius did not understand and made the mistake of falling for it. The "father" began to be less punctual and no longer brought his "daughter" every day. Sometimes he came on his own. In which case Marius did not stay. Another mistake.

Marius took no notice of these symptoms. He had gone from the timid phase to the blind phase, a natural and fatal progression. His love was growing. He dreamed of the one he loved every night. And then something unexpectedly wonderful happened to him, to add fuel to the fire—and add to the haze covering his eyes. One evening, at dusk, he had found, on the bench that "Monsieur Leblanc and his daughter" had just left, a hankie. A very simple hankie with no embroidery, but fine and white and seemingly giving off heavenly scents. He snapped it up, over the moon. The hankie was marked with the letters *U.F.* Marius knew nothing about the beautiful child, nor about her family, nor her name, nor her address. Those two letters were the first thing about her that he had picked up, those adorable initials on which he immediately began building his castles in the air. *U* was obviously the first name. "Ursula!" he thought. "What a gorgeous name!" He kissed the hankie, inhaled its perfume, placed it over his heart, on his bare skin, during the day and slept with it under his lips at night.

"I can smell her whole soul in it!" he cried.

This hankie belonged to the old monsieur, who had quite simply dropped it out of his pocket. The days following the find, Marius no longer showed at the Luxembourg without pressing the hankie to his lips and holding it to his heart. The beautiful girl had no idea what was going on and indicated as much by barely perceptible signs.

"Such modesty!" sighed Marius.

## VIII. EVEN WAR INVALIDS CAN BE HAPPY

Since we have used the word *modesty*, and since we are hiding nothing, we should say that at one point, in the middle of all his ecstasy, "his Ursula" committed a grievous offense against him. It was one of those days where she managed to get Monsieur Leblanc to leave the seat and stroll down the walk. A fresh Prairial breeze[1] was blowing, stirring the tops of the plane trees. Father and daughter, arm in arm, had just passed in front of Marius's seat. Marius had stood up behind them and followed them with his eyes, as is only right for a lost soul in this situation.

All of a sudden a particularly lively gust of wind, probably specially tasked with going about the business of spring, flew up from the plant nursery, swooped down the path, enveloped the young girl in a ravishing shiver worthy of the nymphs of Virgil and the fauns of Theocritus,[2] and lifted her dress, that dress that was more sacred than the dress of Isis,[3] almost up to her garter. A leg of exquisite shape was revealed. Marius saw it. He went into a spin, furious.

The young girl had swiftly pulled her dress down in a divinely demure, indeed horrified, movement, but he was no less outraged. True, he was alone in the walk. But someone else could easily have been there. And what if there had been someone else there! The very thought! What she had done was terrible! Alas, the poor child had done nothing; there was only one culprit—the wind; but Marius, in whom the Bartholo who lurks in every Cherubino[4] was vaguely stirring, was determined to be unhappy and was even jealous of her shadow. For that is indeed how the bitter and bizarre jealousy of the flesh is awakened in the human heart and has its way there, no matter how unfairly. And quite apart from this jealousy, the sight of that gorgeous leg did not thrill him one bit; the white stocking of the first woman passing by would have given him more pleasure.

When "his Ursula," having reached the end of the path, turned and retraced her steps with Monsieur Leblanc, passing by the seat Marius had sat back down on, Marius threw her a gruffly savage look. The young girl tilted backward slightly and raised her eyebrows as if to say: "What's got into you?"

That was their "first tiff."

Marius had barely finished making a scene with his eyes when someone crossed the path. It was a disabled ex-serviceman, all bent over, all wrinkled and white, in a Louis XV uniform,[5] with the little oval patch of red cloth with crossed swords on his chest, the Saint-Louis Cross for soldiery; to cap it off, he was decorated with a coat sleeve that had no arm inside, a silver chin, and a wooden leg. Marius thought he sensed that the man looked extremely pleased. It even seemed to him that, as he hobbled past, the old cynic had given him an extremely gleeful conspiratorial wink, as though luck had put them in cahoots and they had enjoyed some windfall together. What did he have to be so happy about, this reject of Mars?[6] What possible connection was there anyway between this wooden leg and that other leg? Marius spiraled off into a paroxysm of jealousy. "Maybe he was there!" he said to himself. "Maybe he saw!" And he felt like exterminating the disabled ex-serviceman there and then.

In time every point loses its edge. Marius's fury at "Ursula," as right and just as it was, blew over. He ended up forgiving her; but it was quite an effort and he sulked for a whole three days.

Yet, through all that and because of all that, his passion only grew—to the point of becoming insane.

## IX. ECLIPSE

We have just seen how Marius discovered that She was called Ursula—or thought he had.

Appetite comes with loving. To know that her name was Ursula was already a lot, and not much. Marius would have devoured this crumb of happiness in three or four weeks. He wanted another crumb. He wanted to know where she lived.

He had made an initial mistake, falling into the ambush involving the move to the Gladiator's seat. He had made a second mistake, not staying in the Luxembourg when Monsieur Leblanc came there on his own. He now made a third. A whopper. He followed "Ursula" home.

She lived in the rue de l'Ouest, at the most deserted end, in a new three-story house that looked fairly unassuming.

From that moment on, Marius added the happiness of following her home to his happiness at seeing her in the Luxembourg. His hunger increased. He knew her name, her first name at least, and it was a lovely name, a beautifully feminine name; he knew where she lived; now he wanted to know who she was.

One night after he had followed her home and seen the two of them disappear behind the porte cochère, he went in after them and brazenly said to the porter: "Was that the gentleman from the first floor¹ who just came in?"

"No," answered the porter. "It was the gentleman from the third floor."

Another fact. This success made Marius even more reckless.

"At the front?" he asked.

"Heavens!" said the porter. "The whole house faces the street."

"And what does the gentleman do for a living?" Marius went on.

"He has a private income, Monsieur. And a very good man he is, too; he does a lot for the less fortunate, even though he's not rich himself."

"What is his name?" Marius went on.

The porter lifted his head and said: "Is Monsieur with the police?"

Marius took off at that, rather sheepishly, but also thrilled. He was finally getting somewhere.

"Good," he thought. "I know she's called Ursula, that she's the daughter of a man of private means, and that she lives here in the rue de l'Ouest, on the third floor."

The next day, Monsieur Leblanc and his daughter put in only a brief appearance at the Luxembourg and left while it was still broad daylight. Marius followed them into the rue de l'Ouest as was now his custom. When he got as far as the porte cochère, Monsieur Leblanc let his daughter pass ahead of him, then he stopped, turned round, and glared at Marius.

The day after that, they did not come to the Luxembourg at all. Marius waited in vain all day. At nightfall, he went to the rue de l'Ouest and saw a light in the third-floor windows. He strolled beneath these windows until the light went out.

The following day, no one at the Luxembourg. Marius waited all day, then went on night duty beneath the windows again. That took him till ten o'clock. He ate whatever he could garner for dinner. Fever feeds the sick, the lovesick feed on love.

He spent a week at this caper, Monsieur Leblanc and his daughter having given up the Luxembourg altogether. Marius engaged in sad conjecture; he did not dare keep watch over the porte cochère during the day. He made do with night forays to contemplate the reddish glow of the windowpanes. Now and again he saw shadows flit past, and his heart beat faster. On the eighth day when he arrived beneath the windows, there was no light.

"Oh!" he said. "The lamp hasn't been lit yet. Though it's dark already. I wonder if they've gone out?"

He waited. Ten o'clock came and went. Midnight. One in the morning. No light was lit in the windows of the third floor and no one came home. He went away very gloomy.

The next day—for he lived only from one next day to the one after that, there were no more todays, so to speak, for him—the next day, as expected, he found no one in the Luxembourg; at dusk, he went to the house. No light at the windows; the shutters were shut; the third floor was in total darkness.

Marius knocked on the porte cochère, went in, and asked the porter: "The gentleman on the third floor?"

"Moved," replied the porter.

Marius tottered, and bleated feebly: "Since when?"

"Yesterday."

"Where does he live now?"

"No idea."

"Didn't he leave his new address?"

"No."

And the porter looked up and recognized Marius.

"Well, well, it's you!" he said. "So you really are a snitch, then?"

# PATRON-MINETTE

## I. MINES AND MINERS

Every human society has what is known in the theater as "the third substage," the lowest level below stage. The social soil is everywhere mined, for better or for worse. This honeycomb of underground tunnels is layered. There are the upper mines and the lower mines. There is a top and a bottom in this dark basement that sometimes caves in under civilization and which we in our careless indifference stomp around on and trample underfoot. The Encyclopedia, in the last century, was virtually an open-cut mine. The darkness, that murky incubator of primitive Christianity, was just waiting for the chance to set off an explosion under the Caesars and flood the human race with light. For in the thickest darkness there is latent light. Volcanoes are full of darkness capable of bursting into flame. All lava begins in blackness. The catacombs, where the first mass was said, were not only the caves of Rome, they were the underground of the world.

Underneath the social structure, that marvel saddled with a ramshackle slum, all kinds of shafts have been bored. There is the religious mine, the philosophical mine, the political mine, the economic mine, the revolutionary mine. One person digs with an idea, another digs with numbers, yet another digs with rage. There is calling and answering from one catacomb to the next. Utopias make their way underground in tunnels that branch out in every direction. They sometimes run into each other there and fraternize. Jean-Jacques lends his pick to Diogenes, who lends him his lantern.[1] Sometimes they do battle. Calvin grabs Socin by the hair.[2] But nothing stops or interrupts the straining of all these energies toward their goal, and this vast simultaneous activity comes and goes, goes up and down and up again in the darkness, slowly transforming what lies above from below and the outside from the inside, in an immense teeming infestation. Society barely suspects this burrowing and undermining that changes its very guts, leaving its surface untouched. So many subterranean levels, so many different works, so many diverse yields. What comes out of all this deep delving? The future.

The deeper down you go, the more mysterious the workers become. Down to a level that social philosophy is still able to recognize, the work is good; beyond this level, it is dubious and mixed; deeper still, it becomes appalling. At a certain depth, the excavation work becomes impenetrable to the spirit of civilization, the limit at which mankind can breathe is exceeded; it is here that monsters may crop up.

The ladder going down is strange; and each of its rungs corresponds to a level where philosophy can get a foothold and where you meet one of the workers, sometimes divine, sometimes deformed. Below John Huss is Luther; below Luther is Descartes; below Descartes is Voltaire; below Voltaire is Condorcet; below Condorcet is Robespierre; below Robespierre is Marat; below Marat is Babeuf.[3] And on it goes. Lower still, murkily, at the line that divides the indistinct from the invisible, you catch sight of other somber men who perhaps do not yet exist. Those of yesterday are ghosts; those of tomorrow are spectral larvae. The mind's eye dimly makes them out. The embryonic labor of the future is one of the visions of the philosopher.

A limbo world in fetal state, something never before seen!

Saint-Simon, Owen, and Fourier[4] are there, too, in side saps.

Of course, although unbeknownst to them an invisible divine chain connects all these pioneers of the underground, who almost always believe themselves to be alone but are not, their work is extremely varied and the light of some contrasts with the blazing of others. Some are heavenly, others tragic. Yet, whatever the contrast, all these workers, from the uppermost to the most nocturnal, from the wisest to the most unhinged, have one thing in common and it is this: disinterestedness. Marat, like Jesus, forgets about himself. They put themselves completely to one side, leave themselves out, do not think about themselves. They see something other than themselves. They have a look in their eyes and this look is trained on the absolute. The very uppermost among them has the whole sky in his eyes; the lowest, no matter how enigmatic he may be, still has the pale glow of infinity in his sights. So no matter what he does, venerate whoever bears the sign of starry eyes.

Dead eyes—that is the opposite sign.

Evil starts with dead eyes. Faced with someone whose eyes see nothing, think carefully and be afraid. The social order has its starless miners.

There is a point where digging any deeper means being entombed and where the light is completely extinguished.

Below all these mines that we have described, below all these galleries, below all this vast network of the underground veins of progress and utopia, far deeper in the earth, deeper than Marat, deeper than Babeuf, deeper, far deeper way beyond any connection to the upper levels, there is the final sap. A dreadful place. This is what we have called the third substage—the dregs, rock bottom. It is the pit of darkness. It is the repository of the blind. *Inferi.*[5]

This is the way to the bottomless abyss.

## II. THE DREGS

Here, disinterestedness vanishes. The fiend dimly takes shape; it is every man for himself. The eyeless self howls, hunts, gropes and gnaws. Society's cannibals, the Ugolinos,[1] are found in this abyss.

The savage figures that prowl around this pit, half beast, half phantom, do not bother themselves with universal progress; they have never heard of the idea or the word, all they care about is individual satisfaction. They are barely conscious, and inside them there is a sort of terrifying blankness. They have two mothers, both stepmothers: ignorance and misery. They have one guide only, want; and only one craving, for all forms of gratification. They are brutally voracious, that is, ferocious, not in the manner of the tyrant, but in the manner of the tiger. These ghouls start out as larvae in dire poverty and then move on to crime—a fatal line of descent, a dizzying begetting, the logic of the dark. What grovels in this third social substage is no longer the stifled demand for the absolute; it is the protest of matter. Man turns into dragon there. Going hungry or thirsty is the point of departure, turning into Satan is the point of arrival. From this underground repository, Lacenaire[2] emerges.

A moment ago, in Book Four, we saw one of the chambers of the upper mine, of the great sap of politics, revolution, and philosophy. There, as we said, all is noble, pure, dignified, honest. Of course, you can make mistakes there, and do make mistakes; but error is venerable there, for it involves so much heroism. The whole of the work done there has a name: Progress.

The time has come to take a peek at depths below this, hideous depths.

Underneath society there is, and we must insist, until the day ignorance is dispelled, there always will be, the great cavern of evil.

This repository is below all the rest and is the enemy of all the rest. It is hate without exception. This cavernous hold knows no philosophers; its daggers have never whittled quills. Its blackness bears no relation to the sublime sable blackness of the writing case. Never have the fingers of night that clench beneath that suffocating ceiling leafed through a book or unfolded a newspaper. Babeuf is an exploiter for Cartouche;[3] Marat is an aristocrat for Schinderhannes.[4] The aim of this dark hold is to bring everything crashing down.

Everything. Including the upper galleries, which it loathes. In its hideous pullulation, it not only undermines the current social order, it undermines philosophy, it undermines science, it undermines law, it undermines human thought, it undermines civilization, it undermines revolution, it undermines progress. It is called quite simply theft, prostitution, murder, and assassination. It is darkness and it desires chaos. Its vaulted roof is made of ignorance.

All the others, those above, have but one goal and that is to do away with it. It is to this end that philosophy and progress tend, through all their organs at once, through the improvement of the real as well as contemplation of the absolute. Destroy the dark hold, Ignorance, and you destroy the mole, Crime.

To sum up in a few words part of what we have just said: The sole social peril is Darkness.

Humanity is identity. All men are made of the same clay. No difference, here below at least, in predestination. The same darkness before, the same flesh during, the same ashes after. But when ignorance is mixed with human dough, it blackens it. This incurable blackness takes over man's insides and there turns into Evil.

### III. Babet, Gueulemer, Claquesous, and Montparnasse

A quartet of crooks, Claquesous, Gueulemer, Babet, and Montparnasse, ruled the dregs of Paris from 1830 to 1835.

Gueulemer was a lowlife Hercules. His hideout was the Arche-Marion sewer. He was six feet tall, had pectorals of marble, biceps of bronze, cavernous lungs, the torso of a colossus, and the skull of a bird. You would think you were looking at the Farnese Hercules[1] decked out in drill trousers and a velveteen jacket. Built along such sculptural lines, Gueulemer could have broken monsters; he had found it easier to become one. With a low forehead, broad temples, a mass of crow's-feet though not yet forty years old, wiry short hair, bushy cheeks, the beard of a wild boar—you can see the man from here. His muscles cried out for work, his stupidity wouldn't hear of it. He was a huge lazy force. He was a killer out of nonchalance. He was thought to be a Creole.[2] He had probably had a bit of a brush with Maréchal Brune[3] at one time, having done a stint as a porter in Avignon in 1815. After that lesson, he moved up in the world and graduated as a crook.

Babet's diaphanousness was in stark contrast to Gueulemer's meatiness. Babet was skinny and smart. He was transparent, yet impenetrable. You could see daylight through his bones, but nothing in his eyes. He claimed to be a chemist. He had been a buffoon at Bobèche's and a clown at Bobino's.[4] He had played vaudeville at Saint-Mihiel. He was a man full of hot air, a good talker who put his smiles in italics and his gestures in inverted commas. His business was selling plaster busts and portraits of "the head of state" out on the street. On top of this, he pulled teeth. He had shown freaks at fairs and owned a booth with a trumpet and this advertisement: "Babet, dental artist, member of the academies, conducts physical experiments on metals and metalloids, extracts teeth, tackles stumps abandoned by his colleagues. Price: one tooth, one franc fifty centimes; two teeth, two francs; three teeth, two francs fifty centimes. Take advantage of this opportunity." (That "Take advantage of this opportunity" meant: Get as many pulled out as possible.) He had been married and he had had children. He did not know what had become of his wife or his children. He had lost them the way you lose your hankie. A noteworthy exception in the obscure world he lived in, Babet read the newspapers. Once, in the days when he had his family traveling with him in his booth-on-wheels, he had read in the *Messager* that a woman had given birth to a child with the muzzle of a calf who was likely to survive, and he had cried: "That's worth a fortune! Why can't my wife have the wit to give me a child like that!"

Since then he had left everything to "tackle" Paris. His words.

What was Claquesous? He was night. He would wait till the sky had painted itself black before showing himself, crawling out from some hole after dark and crawling back into it again before daybreak. Where was this hole? Nobody knew. When it was pitch black, he would speak, though only to his accomplices and only with his back turned. Was his name really Claquesous? No. He would say: "My name is Not-at-all." If a candle appeared, he slapped on a mask. He was a ventriloquist. Babet would say: "Claquesous is a night bird with two calls." Claquesous was blurry, restless, terrible. You couldn't be sure he had a name, Claquesous being only a nickname meaning blow-your-dough; you couldn't be sure he had a voice, his stomach having more to say than his mouth; you couldn't be sure he had a face, nobody having seen anything but his mask. He would vanish like an apparition and then reappear as though popping up out of the ground.

A lugubrious creature, that was Montparnasse. Montparnasse was a mere boy, less than twenty years old, with a pretty face, lips like cherries, lustrous black hair, the brightness of spring in his eyes; he had all the vices and aspired to all the crimes. Digesting what was bad gave him a craving for what was worse. He was the street kid turned lout and the lout turned killer. He was cute, effeminate, graceful, wiry, lethargic, cruel. He wore his hat turned up on the left to make room for a tuft of hair in the vogue of 1829. He lived off armed robbery. His redingote was of the best cut, but worn. Montparnasse was a fashion plate who had fallen on hard times, living in misery and committing murder and mayhem. The cause of all of this adolescent's assaults was the desire to look slick and expensive. The first hussy who had said to him, "You're easy on the eye," had flung the stain of darkness into his heart and turned this Abel into a Cain.[5] Finding himself pretty, he had wanted to be elegant, and, well, the first form elegance takes is idleness; and the idleness of a pauper means crime. Few prowlers were as feared as Montparnasse. At eighteen, he already had several corpses to his name. More than one passerby, with their arms outstretched and their face in a pool of blood, lay dead in the shadow of this miserable wretch. With his crimped and pomaded hair, his pinched waist, his womanly hips, and the bust of a Prussian officer, surrounded by the murmur of admiration of the girls on the boulevard, his tie suavely knotted, a club in his pocket and a flower in his buttonhole; such was this fop of the house of death.

## IV. Composition of the Troupe

Together these four crooks formed a single entity, a sort of Proteus,[1] snaking through and around the police and strenuously avoiding the indiscreet gaze of the great Vidocq[2] by taking on, like the ancient Greek sea god, "various guises, tree, flame, fountain," lending each other their names and tricks, disappearing into their own shadows, each one a secret bolt-hole and refuge for the others, throwing off their personalities as you take off a false nose at a masked ball, sometimes simplifying themselves to the point of being just one person, sometimes multiplying themselves to the point where Coco-Lacour[3] himself took them for a crowd.

These four men were not four men; they were a sort of single four-headed mystery thief working Paris in a big way; they were a single monstrous polyp of evil living in the crypt of society.

Thanks to their offshoots and to the underlying network of their contacts, Babet, Gueulemer, Claquesous, and Montparnasse ran the general ambush business of the entire *département* of the Seine.[4] They performed the coups d'état of the underworld on unsuspecting passersby. Men with ideas in this line, men of nocturnal imagination, came to them to get the job done. People came to these four rogues with the outline and they took care of the stage management. They worked up the script. They were always able to provide the right number and type of personnel for any crime that needed a hand and was sufficiently lucrative. If a crime was shorthanded, they subcontracted accomplices. They had a troupe of shady extras at their disposal for any secret underworld drama.

They usually gathered together at nightfall, which is when they woke up, in the wasteland next to La Salpêtrière. This was where they conferred. That way they had twelve hours of darkness ahead of them and they worked out how to put them to use.

Patron-Minette was the name in circulation in the underground for this four-man society. In the old popular whimsical parlance disappearing a little more each day, Patron-Minette refers to early morning, just as *entre chien et loup*—between dog and wolf—refers to early evening. The name Patron-Minette probably derived from the time their work usually finished, dawn being the moment phantoms fade and the crooks break up. It is the name these four men were known by. When the chief justice of the circuit court visited Lacenaire in jail, he questioned him over a felony that Lacenaire denied committing. "Who did it, then?" the judge demanded. Lacenaire gave this reply, puzzling to the magistrate but clear as day to the police: "Could be Patron-Minette."

Sometimes you can tell what a play is like from the list of the characters; similarly, you can more or less appreciate a gang by the list of gangsters. There follows, for these particular names linger on in special memoirs, a list of the names the principal affiliates of Patron-Minette answered to:

Panchaud, alias Printanier, alias Bigrenaille,
    or Hotwhack, Springlike, Golightly.
Brujon. (There was a whole dynasty of Brujons; we can't promise
    not to say more about this later.)
Boulatruelle, the road-mender we have already met.
Laveuve, or the Widow.
Finistère.
Homère Hugu, a black man.
Mardisoir, or Tuesday night.
Dépêche, or Dispatch.
Fauntleroy, alias Bouquetière, or the Flowergirl, that is, prostitute.
Glorieux, or Glorious, a freed convict.
Barrecarrosse, or Coachrod, alias Monsieur Dupont.
Lesplanade-du-Sud, or South-Esplanade.
Poussagrive, or Pushathrush.
Carmagnolet.
Kruideniers, alias Bizarro.
Mangedentelle, or Eatlace.
Les-pieds-en-l'air, or Feet-in-the-air.
Demi-liard, alias Deux-milliards, or Half-a-liard; Two Billion.
Etc., etc.

We pass over the rest, and not the worst. These names have faces. They express not only beings, but species. Each one of these names corresponds to a variety of those deformed toadstools that grow underneath civilization.

These beings were by no means happy showing their faces, though; they were not among those you see getting about the streets. During the day, tuckered out by the turbulent nights they put in, they went off to sleep, sometimes in plaster kilns, sometimes in the abandoned quarries of Montmartre or Montrouge, at times even in the sewers. They went to ground.

What's become of these men? They still exist. They have always existed. Horace talks about them: *Ambubaïarum collegia, pharmacopolae, mendici, mimde;*[5] and, for as long as society is what it is, they will be what they are. Under the dark roof of their holds, they are forever reborn out of the slime society oozes. Like ghosts, they return, always the same; only, they no longer bear the same names and no longer get about in the same skins.

The individuals may be eradicated, but the tribe lives on.

They always have the same skills. From the truant to the prowler, the race maintains its purity. They can divine purses in pockets, they can smell watches in fobs. Gold and silver have a distinct smell for them. There are guileless bourgeois who look as though they were just born to be robbed. These men patiently follow such bourgeois. When a foreigner or a provincial goes by, they quiver like spiders.

Men like that, when you run into them or merely catch a glimpse of them on a deserted boulevard around midnight, are terrifying. They don't look like men at all but like shapes made of living mist; you'd say they were one with the darkness, that they can't be distinguished from it, that they have no soul other than the gloom, and that it is only momentarily, just to live a monstrous life for a few minutes, that they break away from the night.

What is required to dissolve these ghouls? Light. Floods of light. No bat can brave the dawn. Light up the dregs of society.

# BOOK EIGHT

# THE BAD PAUPER

## I. MARIUS LOOKS FOR A GIRL IN A HAT AND MEETS A MAN IN A CAP

Summer passed, then autumn; winter came. Neither Monsieur Leblanc nor the young girl had set foot in the Luxembourg again. Marius now had only one thought, to see that sweet, adorable face again. He looked endlessly, he looked everywhere; he found nothing. He was no longer Marius the keen dreamer, the man who was resolute, ardent, and strong, the reckless provocateur of fate, the brain full of schemes for the future, the fresh mind full of plans, projects, points of pride, ideas, and desires; he was a lost dog. He fell into a black well of sadness. It was all over. Work disgusted him, walking wearied him, solitude bored him; the whole wide world of nature, once filled with shapes, limpid revelations, voices, counsel, perspectives, horizons, teachings, was now empty in his eyes. It seemed to him that everything had evaporated.

He went on thinking still, for he could hardly do otherwise; but he no longer took any pleasure in his thoughts. To everything that they suggested to him, gently but persistently, he would reply: What's the use?

He chided himself many times over. "Why did I have to go and follow her? I was so happy just seeing her! She looked at me, didn't that mean the world to me? She looked as though she loved me. Wasn't that everything? What more did I want? There's nothing more after that. I was a fool. It's all my fault." And so on and so forth. Courfeyrac, to whom he confided nothing—that was his nature—but who guessed just about everything—which was *his* nature—started off congratulating him for being in love, though he was utterly amazed; then, when he saw Marius plunged into the depths of melancholy like this, he wound up confronting him: "I see you're human after all. So, come to the Chaumière!"[1]

Once, lulled by the beautiful September sunshine, Marius had let himself be dragged off to the Sceaux Ball by Courfeyrac, Bossuet, and Grantaire, hoping against hope—what a dream!—that he might, perhaps, find her there. Naturally, he did not see the girl he was looking for. "But this is the place, if you're looking for lost women," Grantaire growled behind his back. Marius left his friends at the ball and returned home on foot, alone, weary, feverish, his eyes sad and cloudy in the night, stunned by the racket and the dust kicked up by the riotous old rattletraps full of carousing people that rolled past him, coming back from the party, while he, downhearted, breathed in the acrid scent of the walnut trees along the road to clear his head.

He reverted to living more and more on his own again, distraught, stricken, totally ruled by his inner anguish, crashing around in his pain like a wolf in a trap, searching everywhere for the missing girl, punch-drunk with love.

Another time, he had an encounter that had a powerful effect on him. In one of the little streets in the neighborhood of the boulevard des Invalides, he had come across a man dressed like a workman and wearing a cap with a long peak from which strands of very white hair escaped. Marius was struck by the beauty of this white hair and studied the man carefully as he trudged slowly along as though absorbed in painful meditation. The strange thing was that he thought he recognized Monsieur Leblanc. It was the same hair, the same profile, as far as you could tell with that cap, the same pace, only sadder. But why the workman's getup? What was that about? What did this disguise mean? Marius was truly astounded. When he snapped out of it, his first impulse was to follow the man; who knows if he would not then at last stumble on the trail he was looking for? In any case, he needed to see the man again up close and clear up the enigma. But he hit on the idea too late, the man was already nowhere to be seen. He had taken some tiny side street and Marius could not find him again. This encounter worried him for a few days, then faded. "After all," he told himself, "it's probably just a resemblance."

## II. A FIND

Marius had not stopped living at the Gorbeau slum. He paid no attention to anyone there.

At the time, it is true, there were no other residents in the slum apart from himself and the Jondrettes, whose rent he had once paid without ever having actually spoken either to the father or the mother or the daughters. The other tenants had either moved or died, or had been evicted for not paying the rent.

One day that winter the sun had shown itself a little in the afternoon, but it was February 2, that ancient feast of Candlemas whose treacherous sun, harbinger of six weeks of cold, inspired in Mathieu Laensberg these two lines that have rightly become classic:

Whether it gleams or it glimmers,
The bear goes back to its lair.[1]

Marius had just emerged from his. Night was coming down. It was time for dinner; for he was forced to eat once more, alas! Oh, the weakness of ideal passions! He had just stepped outside his door, where Ma Bougon was at that moment sweeping the doorstep while delivering this memorable monologue: "What's cheap these days? Everything's dear. The only thing that's cheap is the world's troubles; they come for nothing, the world's troubles!"

Marius ambled slowly up the boulevard toward the barrière on the way to the rue Saint-Jacques. He was thinking as he walked, his head down.

All of a sudden he felt himself elbowed in the gathering gloom; he wheeled round and saw two young girls in rags, one tall and thin, the other a bit shorter, running past fast, out of breath, scared; they looked as though they were running from something; they had been heading his way, had not seen him and had run into him in passing. In the twilight, Marius could just make out their livid faces, their thin matted hair, their awful bonnets, their tattered skirts and bare feet. They were talking to each other as they ran. The taller one said in a very low voice: "The cops came. They nearly nabbed me."

The other one replied: "I saw. Did I make a run for it!"

Marius understood by this sinister slang that the two girls had just missed being apprehended by gendarmes or police officers and that they had escaped.

They dived under the trees in the boulevard behind him and were a dim white smudge in the darkness for a few seconds before vanishing altogether.

Marius had stopped for a moment. But just as he was about to continue on his way, he saw a small grayish packet on the ground at his feet. He bent down and picked it up. It was a sort of envelope that felt like it contained papers.

"Right," he said to himself, "those poor girls must have dropped this!"

He turned back after them and called out, but he knew he'd never find them now; he reckoned they were already a fair way off and so he put the packet in his pocket and went to dinner.

On his way, he saw in an alley off the rue Mouffetard a child's coffin covered in a black cloth, placed on three chairs and lit by a candle. The two girls in the gloaming came back to him.

"Poor mothers!" he thought. "There's only one thing sadder than seeing your children die and that's seeing them go bad."

Then these shadows that shifted his sadness for a moment vanished from his mind and he lapsed into his usual woes. He set to thinking once more of his six months of love and happiness out in the open air under the beautiful trees of the Luxembourg, in the sun.

"How gloomy my life has become!" he said to himself. "Young girls still appear to me. Only, once upon a time they were angels; now they are ghouls."

### III. Quadrifrons[1]

That evening, as he was undressing for bed, he felt in his coat pocket and came across the packet he had picked up on the boulevard. He'd forgotten all about it. He thought it might be useful to open it, for it might well contain the girls' address, if in fact it belonged to them, or at least the information necessary to restore it to whoever had lost it.

He opened the envelope, which was not sealed; it contained four letters, all addressed, but also not sealed. All four reeked of cheap tobacco.

The first letter was addressed: *To Madame, Madame la marquise de Grucheray, square opposite the Chamber of Deputies,*[2] *no.* ——

Marius told himself that he would probably find the clues he was looking for inside and that in any case the letter was not sealed, so it was likely that it could be read without impropriety.

This is how it went:

Madame la marquise,
    The virtue of clemency and piety is what most tightly binds society. Give your Christian feeling an airing and look with compassion upon this unfortunate Spaniard, victim of loyalty and attachment to the sacred cause of legitimacy, which he has paid for with his blood, to which he has consecrated his fortune, holey, to defend this cause, and today finds himself in the greatest missery. He has no doubt that your honorable person will grant him sucur to preeserv an existence extreemly painful for a miltary man of educashon and honor, riddled with wounds. Count in advance on the humanity that move you and on the interest that Madame la marquise bears such an unhappy nation. Their prayer will not be in vain and their gratitude will preeserv her charming memry.
    Of my respeckful sentiments which I have the honnor to be,
    Madame,

        DON ALVAREZ, Spanish captain of cavallery, royalist refugee in France that finds himself on a voyage for his homeland and lack in funds to continue his voyage.

No address followed the signature. Marius hoped to find the address in the second letter, whose formal address was set out as: *To Madame, Madame la contesse de Montvernet, rue Cassette, no. 9.*

This is what Marius read in this one:

Madame la contesse,

This is an unforttunat muther of a family of six children, the last one being only eight months old. Am sick since my last lye-in, abandoned by my husband for five months not haveing any ressorse in the world in the most awfull indigance.

In the hope of Madame la contesse, she has the honnor to be, madame, with deep respect.

Wife BALIZARD.

Marius went on to the third letter, which was a begging letter like the preceding; it read:

Monsieur Pabourgeot, elector,[3] hosery holesaler, rue Saint-Denis, at the corner of the rue aux Fers.

I take the liberty of addressing this letter to you to beg you to grant me the preshous favor of your simpathies and to interest you in a man of letters who has just sent a play to the Théâtre-Français. The subject of it is historic and the action happens in Auvergne in the days of the Empire. The style, I think, is natural in it, pithie, and may have some merit. There are verses to sing in four places. The comic, the serious, the unpredictable, blend in it with the variety of the characters and with a tinge of romantisism lightly spred all threw the plot which works misteriously and goes, by striking twists and terns, to come to a head amid several wunderful stage coups.

My main aim is to satisfie the desire that is progressivly driving the man of our century, that is to say THE FASHION, that caprishous and bizarre wether vane that changes at each new wind almost.

Despite these qualities I have grownds to fear that jelousy and the selfishness of privilidged authors, obtain my exclusion from the theare, for I am well aware of the difficultees new comers are bombarded with.

Monsieur Pabourgeot, your just reputation as enlightened patron of literary fokes emboldens me to send you my daughter who will revel our indigant situation, lacking bread and fire in this wynter season. To tell you that I beg you to accept the hommage I desire to make you of my play and all those that I will do, is to prove to you how ambishous I am of the honnor of sheltering under your eegis, and of adorning my writings with your name. If you daine to honnor me with the most modest offering, I'll get bisy straight away and do a piese in verss to pay you my tribut of gratitude. This piese, that I will try and make as perfeck as possible, will be sente to you before being inserted at the beginning of the play and reeled off on stage.

To Monsieur,<br>And Madame Pabourgeot,<br>My most respeckful hommages,<br>GENFLOT, man of letters.

P.S. If only forty sous.
Pardon me for sending my daughter and for not presenting myself myself, but sad grownds of dress do not permit me, alas! to go out ...

Finally Marius opened the fourth letter. The address ran: *To the benevolent gentleman of the church of Saint-Jacques-du-Haut-Pas.*[4] It contained these few lines:

Benevolent man,
If you daine to accompany my daughter, you will see a misserable calamity and I will show you my certificates.
At the site of these writings your generous soul will be moved by a feeling of markt benevolence, for true philosophers always experience lively emotions.
Agree, compashionate man, that you have to experience the crullest want and that it is truly painfull, to obtain some releef, to have it attested by the authorities as if we wernt free to suffer and to die of starvashion waiting for someone to releev our missery. The fates are truly fatal for some and too profliget or too protectiv for others.
I await your presance or your offering, if you daine make one, and I beg you to accept the respeckful feelings with which I honnor myself to be,

truly magnanimus man,
your very humble
and very obediant servant,
P. FABANTOU, dramatic artiste.

After reading these letters, Marius did not find himself any the wiser. First, none of the signatories gave their address. Then they seemed to come from four different individuals, Don Alvarez, wife Balizard, the poet Genflot, and the dramatic artiste Fabantou, but the letters had one strange feature in common and that was that they were all four written in the same handwriting. What could you conclude from that except that they came from the same person?

On top of that, and this made the conjecture even more convincing, the paper, which was coarse and yellowed, was the same for all four, the smell of tobacco was the same, and even though efforts had been made to vary the style, the same spelling mistakes recurred with profound complacency, Genflot the man of letters being no more exempt than the Spanish captain.

There was no point trying to unravel this little mystery. If he hadn't found the bundle of letters by accident, it would have looked like a hoax. Marius was too sad even to laugh at a random joke or join in some game the streets of Paris apparently wanted to play with him. He felt like the blind man in a game of blind man's buff with the four letters poking fun at him.

Besides, nothing indicated that the letters belonged to the girls Marius had run into on the boulevard. After all, they were obviously worthless bits of paper. Marius shoved them back in the envelope, threw the bundle into a corner, and went to bed.

At around seven o'clock the next morning, he had just gotten up and had breakfast and was trying to get down to work when someone knocked gently on his door.

As he owned nothing, he never took his key out of the door, except some-times, very rarely, when he was working on some urgent job. And anyway, even when he wasn't there, he left the key in the door.

"You'll get yourself robbed," Ma Bougon used to say.

"What of?" Marius would reply.

The fact is that one day someone did take an old pair of boots, to Ma Bougon's great triumph.

There was a second knock, as gentle as the first.

"Come in," said Marius.

The door opened.

"What do you want, Ma Bougon?" Marius said, without taking his eyes off the books and manuscripts on his table.

A voice, which was not that of Ma Bougon, answered: "Pardon me, Mon-sieur—"

It was a dull, broken, strangled, rasping voice, the rough voice of an old man made husky by brandy and spirits.

Marius turned round and saw a young girl.

## IV. A ROSE IN MISERY

A very young girl was standing in the half-open doorway. The garret's dormer window, where daylight now appeared, was directly opposite the door and lit up this figure with a wan light. She was a haggard, sickly, emaciated creature, with nothing but a chemise and a skirt over shivering, freezing nakedness. A bit of string for a belt, a bit of string for a hair band, bony shoulders poking up out of the chemise, a blond lymphatic pallor, collarbones covered in dirt, red hands, a slack and depraved mouth, missing teeth, dull, defiant, mean eyes in which a corrupt old woman looked out of the body of an aborted young girl; fifty years were packed into fifteen, in one of those beings that are both weak and repul-sive together and that make you shudder when they don't make you weep.

Marius had stood and was studying her in a sort of stupor, this being so very like the shadows that flit through our dreams.

What was especially harrowing was that the girl had not come into the world to be ugly. In early infancy, she must even have been pretty. The grace of a child was still struggling with the ghastly premature aging brought on by debauchery and poverty. A trace of lingering beauty was dying in this sixteen-year-old face, like pale sunlight smothered by grim clouds at dawn on a winter's day.

The face was not absolutely unfamiliar to Marius. He thought he remembered seeing it somewhere.

"What do you want, Mademoiselle?" he asked.

The young girl answered in her drunken galley slave's voice: "There's a letter for you, Monsieur Marius."

She called Marius by his name; he could not doubt that her business was with him; but who was this girl? How did she know his name?

Without waiting for an invitation, she sauntered in, giving the room and the unmade bed the once-over with an assurance that made your heart sink. Her feet were bare. Big rips in her skirt gave a glimpse of her long skinny legs and her bony knees. She was shivering.

She did in fact have a letter in her hand and she handed it to Marius.

Marius opened the letter and noticed that the enormous blob of sealing wax was still wet. The message could not have come far. He read:

> My very kind naybor, young man!
>
> I have learned of your good deeds on my behalf, that you paid my rent six months ago, I bless you, young man. My elder daughter will tell you that we have been without a scrap of bred for two days, four persons, and my missus crook. If I'm not deceeved in my thinking, I beleeve I can hope that your generous heart will melt at this report and you will be overcome with the desire to smile upon me by daining to bestowe a small kindness upon me.
>
> I am, with the distinguished consideration that we owe the benefactors of humanity,
>
> > JONDRETTE.
>
> P.S. My daughter will await your orders, dear Monsieur Marius.

This letter, cropping up in the middle of the obscure episode that had been worrying Marius since the night before, was a candle in a cave. Everything was suddenly clear as day. This letter had come from the same place as the other four. It was the same writing, the same style, same spelling, same paper, same reek of tobacco.

There were five missives, five tales, five names, five signatures, and a single signatory. The Spanish captain Don Alvarez, the unhappy Balizard, the dramatic poet Genflot, the aging actor Fabantou were all four named Jondrette, if indeed Jondrette's name really was Jondrette.

As we might have mentioned, in all the fairly long time that Marius had lived in the building so far, he had only rarely had occasion to see, or even glimpse, what neighbors there were. His mind was elsewhere and where your mind is, your eyes follow. He must have crossed paths with the Jondrettes in the hallway or on the stairs; but for him they were mere silhouettes; he had taken so little notice of them that, the night before, he had knocked into the Jondrette girls on the boulevard without recognizing them. For it was obviously them; but even now, when this one had come into his room, it was only with great difficulty that he vaguely recalled, through the pity and disgust she aroused in him, having run into her somewhere else.

Now he saw it all clearly. He understood that the business his neighbor Jondrette was in, in his distress, was to exploit the charitable, that he procured the addresses of people he had sized up as rich and compassionate and wrote them, under assumed names, letters that the girls delivered by hand, at their peril, for this father had sunk so low as to put his own daughters at risk; he was playing a game with fate and they were the pawns. Marius understood that probably, judging by their flight the night before, their breathlessness, their terror, and the words of slang that he had heard, these sorry girls were also practicing all sorts of dark trades—and that the net result of the whole sordid business was two miserable beings who were neither children nor girls nor women, monsters of a sort at once foul and innocent, produced by dire poverty, smack in the middle of human society as we know it.

Sad creatures, without name, without age, without sex, already beyond good and evil, emerging from childhood into the world already stripped of everything, with neither liberty, nor virtue, nor any responsibility left. Souls blossoming only yesterday, but today faded like flowers fallen in the street, spattered by mud from all directions before being crushed under a wheel.

Yet while Marius pinned her with a stunned and sorrowful look, the young girl was pacing up and down the garret as though she owned the place, with the audacity of a revenant. She thrashed about completely oblivious to her nakedness. At times her unbuttoned and torn chemise nearly fell down to her waist. She moved the chairs around, she rearranged the toiletries on the chest of drawers, she felt Marius's clothes, she fumbled through the pockets.

"Well, well!" she said, "you have a mirror!"

And quite as if she were alone, she hummed snatches of vaudeville tunes, playful refrains that her raucous, guttural voice turned sinister. Beneath the daring, something forced, anxious, and abashed broke through. Effrontery is a form of shame.

Nothing could be more mournful than to see her frolicking and flitting, so to speak, about the room, like a bird with a broken wing, frightened by daylight. You felt that in different circumstances, with an education and a different life, the girl's carefree, chirpy manner might have been sweet and charming. Never in the animal kingdom does a creature born to be a dove turn into a rapacious white-tailed eagle. This only happens among men.

Marius was thinking his thoughts and let her carry on. She went to the table. "Ah!" she said. "Books!"

A light flashed in her glassy eyes. As she went on, her tone expressed the joy of being able to boast about something no human being is immune to: "I can read, you know!"

She swiftly grabbed the book that lay open on the table and read fairly fluently: ". . . General Bauduin received the order to take the five battalions of his brigade and capture the château of Hougoumont, which is in the middle of the plain of Waterloo—"

She broke off: "Ah! Waterloo! I know about that. It was a battle long ago. My father was there. My father served in the army. We are Bonapartist as all get-out at home, you know! It was against the English, Waterloo."

She put the book back down, took a pen and cried: "And I can write, too!"

She dipped the pen in the ink and turned to Marius: "Do you want to see? Look, I'll write something to show you."

And before he had time to answer, she wrote on a blank sheet of paper that was lying on the table: "The cops are here."

Then she tossed the pen aside: "There are no spelling mistakes. You can see for yourself. We've had education, my sister and me. We haven't always been what we are. We weren't made to—"

Here she stopped, fixed her lackluster eye on Marius and burst out laughing before saying, in a tone that contained extreme anguish smothered by extreme cynicism: "Gah!!"

And she began to croon these words to a very merry tune:

I'm hungry, father.
No stew.
I'm cold, mother.
No woolies.
    Shiver,
    Lolotte!
    Sob,
    Jacquot![1]

She had barely finished this verse when she cried:

"Do you sometimes go to shows, Monsieur Marius? I do. I've got a little brother who's friends with the artists and he sometimes gives me tickets. For one thing, I don't like balcony seats. You don't have any room and it's uncomfortable. There's sometimes real riffraff there and there's also a lot of smelly people."

She studied Marius, then adopted an odd look and said: "You know, Monsieur Marius, you are a very good-looking boy?"

The same thought struck them both at the same time, which made her smile and made him blush. She walked over to him and placed a hand on his shoulder.

"You never notice me, but I know you, Monsieur Marius. I run into you here on the stairs and then I see you visiting a man named Father Mabeuf who lives over Austerlitz way, sometimes, when I'm out walking around there. It suits you, you know, your hair sticking up like that."

Her voice struggled to sound soft and sweet but only managed to go very low. Some of her words were lost in the journey from larynx to lips as on a keyboard that is missing some notes.

Marius had quietly backed away.

"Mademoiselle," he said with cold gravity, "I have here a packet that is, I believe, yours. Allow me to give it back to you."

And he held out to her the envelope containing the four letters.

She clapped her hands together and cried: "We looked everywhere!"

Then she swiftly grabbed the packet and opened the envelope, prattling away as she did so: "God in heaven! We looked high and low, did we ever, my sister and me! And *you* found them! On the boulevard, I bet? It must have been on the boulevard? You see, they fell when we were running. It's my brat of a sister who slipped like an idiot. When we got home we couldn't find them anywhere. Since we didn't want to get the strap, there's no point, I mean, what for? whatever for? we told them at home that we'd taken the letters to the people and they told us, nothing doing! And here they are, the poor old letters! How could you tell they were mine—but, ah, of course! The writing! So it was *you* we bumped into last night when we were going past. We couldn't see, naturally! I said to my sister: Was that some sort of gent? My sister said: I reckon!"

She had by now unfolded the begging letter addressed to "the benevolent gentleman of the church of Saint-Jacques-du-Haut-Pas."

"Look!" she said. "This one's for the old geezer who goes to mass. Actually, it's on right now. I think I'll take it to him. Maybe he'll give us something so we can have breakfast."

Then she started laughing again and added: "You know what it'll mean if we have breakfast today? It'll mean we'll have had our breakfast for the day before yesterday, our dinner for the day before yesterday, our breakfast for yesterday, our dinner for yesterday—all in the one meal, this morning! Well, so what? Like it or lump it, or drop dead, dogs!"

This reminded Marius of what the poor sorry creature had come to his room for. He fumbled in his jacket, and found nothing. The young girl went on regardless, talking as though she were no longer conscious of Marius's being there.

"Sometimes I take off at night. Sometimes I don't come back. Before we were here, last winter, we lived under the arches of bridges. We huddled together so as not to freeze. My little sister cried. Water, God it's sad! I thought of drowning myself, but then I thought: No, it's too cold. I go off on my own when I feel like it, sometimes I sleep in a ditch. You know, at night, when I'm walking on the boulevard, I see trees like forks, I see houses all black and as big as the towers of Notre-Dame, I pretend that the white walls are the river, and I say to myself: Look, there's water here! The stars are like little paper lanterns all lit up, you'd say they were smoking and that the wind then snuffs them out, it gives me the shivers, as if I had horses breathing in my ear all of a sudden. Even though it's night, I can hear Barbary organs and the machines in the mills spinning, I don't know. I feel like they're people and they're throwing stones at me. I run for it, I don't even know I'm doing it, everything's spinning, it's all a whirl. When you haven't eaten, you feel funny."

And she stared at him, wild-eyed.

After digging deep into his pockets, Marius finally got five francs sixteen sous together. It was, at that moment, all he had in the world.

"This will do for my dinner today," he thought. "Tomorrow, we'll see."

He kept the sixteen sous and gave the five francs to the girl. She ripped it out of his hand.

"Hooray!" she said. "The sun's out!"

And as if this sun had the property of causing avalanches of slang to melt in her brain, she went on: "A fiver! A shiner! A monarch! In this joint! I'll be blowed! Knock me down with a feather! You beauty! You're not a bad sort. Hats off. Never say die! Two days of pine cones! Muck for meat and slosh for grub! We'll stuff our faces, don't think we won't!"

She hitched her chemise back onto her shoulders, gave Marius a deep bow, then a cheeky wave of the hand and tripped to the door: "I'm on my way, Monsieur. Hell's bells. I'm off to find the old man."

As she passed, she spotted a crust of dry bread gathering mold in the dust on top of the chest of drawers and she fell upon it and bit into it, muttering: "Good! Nice and hard! I can cut my teeth on it!"

And with that, she left.

## V. THE JUDAS OF PROVIDENCE

For five years Marius had lived in poverty, in deprivation, even in distress, but he realized he had never known real misery. Real misery, he had just seen. It was the specter that had just passed before his very eyes. Actually, anyone who has seen the misery of men only, has seen nothing, you have to see the misery of women; anyone who has seen the misery of women only, has seen nothing, you have to see the misery of a child.

When a man has hit rock bottom and death is not far off, he comes to the end of his tether, his wit's end, at the same time. Woe to the defenseless beings around him! Work, wages, bread, heat, courage, goodwill—he lacks everything at once. The light of day seems to go out without, the moral light goes out within; in the these dark shadows, men come up against the weakness of women and children, and bend them brutally to ignominious ends.

Then all horrors may break loose. Despair is penned in by the flimsiest walls, all of them opening onto vice or crime.

Health, youth, honor, the sacred and fierce fragility of still-fresh young flesh, the heart, virginity, modesty, that skin of the soul, are sinisterly twisted and misused by this groping in the dark after resources, which comes up against infamy and accommodates it. Fathers, mothers, children, brothers, sisters, men, women, girls, cling together and form a mass almost like some mineral outcrop, in this murky promiscuity of sexes, relationships, ages, foul deeds, innocent acts. They squat down on their haunches, back to back, in a kind of slum destiny, eyeing each other miserably. O, the poor unfortunates! Look how pale they are! See how cold they are! They seem to be on a planet a lot farther away from the sun than we are.

This young girl was for Marius a sort of emissary from the darkest depths. She revealed to him a whole dreadful side of the night.

Marius almost reproached himself for being so absorbed in the daydreams and passion that had kept him from casting so much as a glance at his neighbors until that day. To have cobbled together their rent was a mechanical gesture, anyone would have done the same thing; but he, Marius, should have done more. For God's sake! A mere wall separated him from these abandoned beings that lived groping around in the dark, beyond the land of the living. He rubbed shoulders with them, he was in a way the last link in the chain of the human race that they touched, he could hear them living or, rather, groaning in agony, right next to him and he had taken no notice! Every day, at every moment, through the wall, he could hear them walking, coming and going, talking, and he hadn't even listened! And among those words there were moans, and he hadn't even registered! His thoughts were elsewhere, lost in dreams, in wild fantasies, in love in the open air, in giddy delusions, and yet these human beings, his brothers in Jesus Christ, his brothers in the common people, were dying in agony right next to him! Dying pointlessly! He even contributed to their misfortune, and he exacerbated it. For, if they had had a different neighbor, a less fanciful and more attentive neighbor, a normal, charitable man, obviously their destitution would not have gone unnoticed, their distress signals would have been seen, and for a long time already, perhaps, they would have been rescued and saved! Of course, they seemed utterly depraved, utterly corrupt, utterly vile, utterly odious even, but they are rare, those who have fallen without being damaged on the way down; besides, there is a point where the unfortunate and the ignominious mingle and fuse, poor bastards, in a single word, a deadly word, outcasts, *les misérables,* and whose fault is that? And then again, shouldn't charity be the greater, the deeper the fall into darkness?

While he lectured himself in this vein, for there were times when Marius, like all truly honest souls, was his own schoolmaster, chastising himself more than he deserved, he studied the flimsy partition that separated him from the Jondrettes, as though he could drill his deeply compassionate gaze through it and warm those poor people up. The wall was nothing more than a thin layer of plaster supported by laths and joists and which, as we have just heard, allowed words and voices to be made out perfectly clearly. Only a dreamer like Marius could have failed to realize this already. There was no wallpaper pasted over the wall, either on the Jondrettes' side or on Marius's; the crummy construction was laid bare for all to see. Almost without being aware of it, Marius examined the partition; sometimes reverie examines, observes, scrutinizes much the same as thought would. Suddenly he bolted upright; almost at the very top, near the ceiling, he spotted a triangular hole where three laths had left a gap between them. The rubblework that should have filled up this gap was not there and by standing on the chest of drawers you could see through the hole into the Jondrettes' garret. Commiseration has, and should have, its curiosity. This hole created a sort of judas—a peephole. You are allowed to spy on misfortune as a traitor if you are going to relieve it.

"Let's take a bit of a peek at what these people are like," thought Marius, "and see how bad things really are."

He hopped up on the chest of drawers, put his eye to the crevice, and looked.

## VI. Feral Man in His Lair

Towns, like forests, have their dens where the nastiest and most terrifying creatures they harbor hide. Only, in towns, what hides like this is ferocious, filthy, and small, in other words, ugly; in forests, what hides is ferocious, wild, and big, that is, beautiful. As lairs go, those of beasts are preferable to those of men. Caves are better than ratholes.

What Marius saw was a rathole.

Marius was poor and his room was fairly bare; but, just as his poverty was noble, his attic was clean. The pigsty he had a bird's-eye view of at that moment was abject, dirty, fetid, putrid, dark, sordid. All it had for furniture was a straw chair, a rickety table, a few old shards of pottery, and, in two of the corners, two straw mattresses that defy description; all it had for light was a dormer window with four panes, draped in cobwebs. There was just enough light coming in through this window for a man's face to appear like the face of a phantom. The walls had a leprous look and were covered in cuts and scars like a face disfigured by some horrible disease. They oozed a kind of rheumy damp. Obscene drawings could be made out on them, roughly drawn in charcoal.

The room Marius occupied was tiled with dilapidated used bricks; this one had neither tiles nor floorboards; you walked straight on top of the tenement's undressed antique plaster, which had gone black from all the feet. On this uneven ground, where the dirt was more or less encrusted, and which was virgin soil only as far as the broom went, constellations of old shoes, ratty slippers, and awful rags were bunched willy-nilly; but the room had a fireplace and so it was rented at forty francs a year. There was a bit of everything in this fireplace, a stove, a cooking pot, some broken boards, rags hanging on nails, a birdcage, ashes, and even a bit of a fire. A tiny handful of embers was smoking away sadly.

One thing added further to the garret's horror and that was that it was big. It had projections, corners, black holes, recesses where the roof dipped down, bays, and ridges jutting out. Hence the frightening, unfathomable nooks and crannies where it seemed spiders as fat as your fist, wood lice as broad as your foot, and even, perhaps, some unspeakable human monsters had to be curled up snugly.

One of the pallets was close to the door, the other close to the window. Both of them touched the hearth at one end and were facing Marius.

In a corner next to the opening Marius was looking through, hanging on the wall in a black wooden frame, was a colored engraving at the bottom of which was written in capital letters THE DREAM. This represented a sleeping woman and a sleeping child, the child on the woman's knee, an eagle in a cloud with a crown in its beak, and the woman taking the crown off the child's head, and without its waking up, too; in the background, Napoléon in a blaze of glory was leaning on a fat blue column with a yellow capital adorned with this inscription:

MARINGO

AUSTERLITS

IENA

WAGRAMME

ELOT[1]

Below the framed engraving a sort of wooden panel that was taller than it was wide had been placed on the floor leaning against the wall at an angle. This looked to be a painting turned round back to front, a stretcher probably daubed with paint on the other side, some kind of pier glass taken down from a wall and forgotten there, waiting to be hung back up again.

At the table, on which Marius spotted a pen and ink and some paper, a man about sixty was sitting; he was small, thin, livid, haggard, with a cunning, cruel, and fretful look about him; a grisly evildoer.

If Lavater[2] had been able to study the man's face he would have found in it the vulture mingled with the prosecutor, the bird of prey and the pettifogging shyster bringing the worst out in each and completing each other, the shyster making the bird of prey ignoble, the bird of prey making the shyster appalling.

The man had a long gray beard. He was dressed in a woman's chemise that exposed his hairy chest and his bare arms bristling with gray hair. Under the chemise you could make out mud-caked pants and boots with his toes sticking out. He had a pipe clamped in his mouth and was puffing on it. There may have been no bread left in the rathole but there was still some tobacco. He was writing, probably a letter like the ones Marius had read.

On one corner of the table was an old odd volume with a reddish cover; its format, which was the old duodecimo of reading rooms, revealed a novel. On the cover the title spread in bold capital letters: GOD, THE KING, HONOR AND THE LADIES, BY DUCRAY-DUMINIL.[3] 1814.

While he wrote, the man talked out loud and Marius heard what he said: "To think there's no equality, not even when you're dead! You've only got to look at Père-Lachaise! The bigwigs, the nobs, are at the top, along the pathway where the acacias are, where it's paved. They get to arrive in a carriage. The little people, the poor people, the unlucky, in a word! they're stuck at the bottom, where there's mud up to your knees, in holes, in the muck. They put them there so they'll rot faster! You can't go and see them without getting stuck in the ground."

Here he stopped, banged the table with his fist, and added, grinding his teeth: "Oh! I could eat the whole rotten world!"

A big woman who could have been anywhere between forty and a hundred was squatting on her bare heels close to the fire. She, too, was dressed in a chemise as well as a knitted woolen skirt patched with bits of old sheeting. An apron of coarse canvas hid half the skirt. Although this woman was bent double, crouching and hugging herself, you could see that she was very tall. Next to her husband, she was a kind of giant. She had awful hair, a rusty blond going gray, and she pushed it back now and again with her enormous shiny flat-nailed hands.

Lying next to her on the floor, wide open, was a volume of the same format as the other one and probably of the same novel.

On one of the pallets, Marius glimpsed a sort of skinny whey-faced girl sitting, almost naked, with her feet dangling, looking as though she couldn't hear or see, and was not, in fact, alive. No doubt the younger sister of the one who had come to his room.

She looked eleven or twelve. If you studied her more closely, you would see that she was, in fact, fifteen. This was the child who had said, the night before on the boulevard: "Did I make a run for it!"

She was of that sickly species that remains backward for a long time, then suddenly grows up fast. It is destitution that produces these sad human plants, creatures who don't have a childhood or an adolescence, either. At fifteen, they look twelve, at sixteen, they look twenty. Today little girls, tomorrow mature women. It is as though they bounded through life to get it over with faster. At that moment, this being still looked like a child.

Whatever the case, nothing in the room pointed to any kind of work whatever; no tools of a trade, no loom, no spinning wheel, no implement. In one corner, there were a few dubious-looking bits of scrap iron. It was full of the forlorn indolence that follows despair and precedes the last gasp.

Marius gazed for some time at this funereal interior, more terrifying than the inside of a tomb, for you could feel the human soul stirring there and life pulsating still.

The garret, the cellar, the dungeon where certain of the destitute crawl at the bottom of the social edifice, is not yet quite the sepulchre. It is its antechamber; but, like rich people who display their greatest riches at the entrance to their palace, it seems that death, which is close at hand, puts its greatest miseries in this, its vestibule.

The man had shut up, the woman wasn't speaking, the young girl seemed not to be breathing. You could hear the pen scratching, screeching, screaming, across the page.

The man grumbled without ceasing to write: "Mongrels! Mongrels! They're all mongrels!"

This variation on Solomon's cry got a sigh from the woman.

"Calm down, pet," she said. "Don't upset yourself, dear heart. You're too good to write to all these people, treasure."

In misery, bodies huddle together against the rest, just as they do in the cold, but hearts grow distant. This woman, as far as anyone could tell, must once have loved this man with whatever quotient of love was in her; but most likely, in the daily mutual rage provoked by the awful distress that ground the family down, that love had died. There was nothing left in her for her husband except the cold ashes of affection. But terms of endearment, as so often, had survived. She called him *pet, dear heart, treasure,* etc., with her lips. Her heart said nothing.

The man had returned to his writing.

## VII. STRATEGIES AND TACTICS

Marius, with heavy heart, was about to climb back down from this observatory he had improvised, when a noise attracted his attention and made him stay right where he was.

The garret door had just swung open violently. The elder daughter appeared on the landing. She had a man's outsize clodhoppers on her feet and they were caked in mud, which had been spattered right up her reddened ankles, and she was cloaked in an old tattered mantle that Marius had not seen on her an hour ago, but that she had probably unloaded at his door in order to inspire more pity and then picked up again when she left. She came in, shut the door behind her, stopped to catch her breath, for she was quite winded, then shouted with an expression of triumph and joy: "He's coming!"

The father turned his eyes to her, the mother turned her head, the little sister did not stir.

"Who?" asked the father.

"The gent!"

"The philanthropist?"

"Yep."

"From the Saint-Jacques church?"

"Yep."

"The old geezer?"

"Yep."

"He's coming?"

"He's right behind me."

"Are you sure?"

"I'm sure."

"Just like that, you mean, he's coming?"

"He's coming in a cab."

"In a cab. Must be Rothschild!"[1]

The father got up.

"How can you be so sure? If he's coming in a cab, how come you got here first? You did give him the address, at least? You did tell him the last door on the right at the end of the hall? Let's hope he doesn't get it wrong! So you found him at the church? Did he read my letter? What did he say?"

"Tut, tut, tut!" said the girl. "God, you do go on, old man! Here's the story: I go into the church, he's at his usual place, I give him a curtsy and I hand him the letter, he reads it and he says: 'Where do you live, my child?' I say: 'Monsieur, I'll take you there.' He says: 'No, give me your address, my daughter has some shopping to do, I'll take a carriage and I'll get to your place the same time as you.' I give him the address. When I told him which house, he looked surprised and he hesitated for a second, then he said: 'It doesn't matter, I'll come anyway.' When mass was over, I saw him walk out of the church with his daughter and I saw them hop in a cab. And I did tell him the last door on the right at the end of the hall."

"And what makes you think he'll come?"

"I just saw the cab turning into the rue du Petit-Banquier. That's why I came running."

"How do you know it's the same cab?"

"Because I noted the number, that's how!"

"What's the number?"

"Four hundred and forty."

"Good, you're a smart girl."

The girl gave her father a defiant look and, showing the shoes she had on her feet, she said: "A smart girl, maybe. But I'm telling you now I'm never putting these shoes on again and I won't have anything more to do with them, for health reasons, to start with, and then for decency's sake. I don't know what could be more annoying than soles that ooze and go swish, swish, swish, all the way down the street. I'd rather go barefoot."

"Right you are," replied the father in a gentle tone that contrasted with the young girl's abrasiveness. "But then, they won't let you set foot in a church. The poor have to have shoes. You don't go to the house of the Lord barefoot," he added bitterly. Then he returned to the subject on his mind: "But you're sure, then, you're sure he's coming?"

"He's hot on my heels," she said.

The man straightened up. His face lit up with a strange inner glow.

"Woman!" he cried. "You hear that. The philanthropist's coming. Put the fire out."

The stupefied mother didn't budge. The father, with the agility of an acrobat, grabbed a jug with a broken neck that was sitting on the hearth and threw water on the embers. Then he turned to his elder daughter: "You! Strip the straw off the chair!"

His daughter didn't know what he meant. He took hold of the chair and with a swift thrust of his heel, kicked the straw out. His leg went right through it. As he pulled his leg out, he asked his daughter: "Is it cold out?"

"Bitterly cold. It's snowing."

The father turned to the younger daughter who was on the pallet by the window and bellowed at her in a thundering voice: "Quick! Off the bed, you good-for-nothing lump! Can't you do something for a change! Smash a bloody windowpane!"

The little girl hopped off the bed, shivering.

"Smash a windowpane!" he repeated.

The child was speechless.

"You heard me!" the father yelled. "I told you to smash a windowpane!"

In a sort of terrified act of obedience, the child stood on tiptoe and punched her fist into a windowpane. The glass shattered and fell with a crash.

"Good," said the father.

He was grave and abrupt. He ran his eyes rapidly over all the nooks and crannies of the garret, like a general making his final preparations as the battle was about to begin.

The mother, who had not yet uttered a word, got to her feet and asked in a slow, thick voice, in words that seemed to come out congealed: "Darling, what do you want to do?"

"You hop into bed," replied the man.

His tone did not admit of any deliberation. The mother obeyed and threw herself heavily onto one of the pallets. Meanwhile a sob was heard in a corner.

"What's that?" shouted the father.

The younger daughter, without coming out of the shadows she had sought refuge in, showed her bleeding fist. She had hurt herself breaking the glass and now she was at her mother's bed, quietly crying.

It was the mother's turn to stand up and yell: "Now look what you've done! God, you think up some stupid things! She's cut herself, breaking your stupid window for you!"

"Well and good!" said the man. "That was the idea."

"What do you mean, well and good?" the mother shot back.

"Quiet!" replied the father. "I suppress the freedom of the press!"[2]

Then, ripping the woman's chemise he was wearing, he tore off a strip and promptly wrapped the little girl's bleeding hand tightly with it. That done, he glanced down at his torn chemise with satisfaction.

"The chemise, while we're at it," he said. "It all looks pretty good."

An icy wind whistled at the window and swept into the room. The fog outside rolled in and spread out like whitish cotton wool vaguely pulled apart by invisible fingers. Through the broken window, you could see snow falling. The cold promised the day before by the Candlemas sun had arrived with a vengeance.

The father ran his eye one last time around him as though to reassure himself that he had not forgotten anything. He took an old shovel and spread the ash over the wet embers so as to hide them completely.

Then he stood up again and leaned back against the fireplace: "Now," he said, "we're ready to receive the philanthropist."

## VIII. A RAY OF LIGHT IN THE RATHOLE

The big girl went over and put her hand on her father's hand.

"Feel how cold I am," she said.

"Bah!" the father responded. "I'm a lot colder than that."

The mother cried impetuously: "You always have to go one better than everyone else, don't you! Even when it comes to pain."

"Down!" said the man.

At a certain look from the man, the mother shut up. There was a moment of silence in the rathole. The elder daughter was scraping the mud off the hem of her mantle, the younger sister went on sobbing; the mother had taken the girl's head in both hands and was covering it with kisses, whispering to her: "Now, now, my treasure, it's nothing, don't cry, you'll make your father angry."

"No!" cried the father. "On the contrary! Bawl your eyes out! Sob! That's just the ticket."

Then, turning back to the elder girl: "Well, then! He's not coming! What if he's not coming! I will have put out my fire, kicked in my chair, ripped my chemise, and broken my window all for nothing!"

"And hurt the little one," the mother murmured.

"Do you know," the father went on, "it's as cold as a nun's nasty in this dump of a place! If this bastard doesn't show up! He's said to himself: 'Well, then, let them wait! That's what they're there for!' Oh, how I hate them, how I would love to strangle every one of them, gleefully, joyfully, enthusiastically, happily, the bleeding rich! Every last one of them! These so-called charitable types, who make chutney, go to mass, go in for the priesthood, preach this, preach that, churchy types who think they're above us, and come to humiliate us and bring us their castoffs! That's what they call them! Togs not worth four sous, and bread! That's not what I want, you pile of steaming turds! I want money! Ah, money! Never! Because they say we'll just go and drink it all, we're nothing but drunks and layabouts! What about them! What are they, then, and what were they in their day? Thieves! They wouldn't have got rich otherwise! Oh, we ought to take society by the four corners of the tablecloth and toss the whole lot in the air! Everything would smash to smithereens, most likely, but at least then no one'd have anything, and that'd be something! But what can he be doing, then, your boor of a benevolent gent? Is he going to come? The stupid bastard's probably forgotten the address! I bet that old idiot . . ."

At that moment there was a gentle rap at the door, the man lunged toward it and opened it, offering smiles of adoration, as he scraped and bowed: "Come in, Monsieur! Deign to come in, my respectable benefactor, along with your charming young lady."

A man of mature age and a young girl appeared in the doorway of the garret. Marius had not left his place. What he felt at that moment is beyond the power of human language to tell.

Her.

Anyone who has ever loved knows all the radiant meaning packed into the three letters of that word: Her.

It really was her. Marius could barely make her out through the luminous haze that suddenly spread over his eyes. It was that sweet absent being, that star that had shone for six months, those eyes, that forehead, that mouth, that beautiful vanished face that had brought down the night in vanishing. The vision had been eclipsed, she reappeared!

She reappeared in this darkness, in this garret, in this diseased dump of a place, in this horror!

Marius shuddered uncontrollably. What? Her! His heart was beating so hard, he could hardly see. He felt he was about to burst into tears. What? He was finally seeing her again after searching for her for so long! It felt as if he'd lost his soul and had now suddenly found it again.

She was the same as ever, a bit paler only; her delicate face was framed by a hat of violet velvet. Her figure was hidden under a pelisse of black satin. Under her long frock, you could see her tiny feet, shod in silk brodequins.

She was still accompanied by Monsieur Leblanc. She had taken a few steps into the room and had placed a fairly large parcel on the table.

The elder Jondrette girl had retreated behind the door and eyed the velvet hat darkly, along with the silk mantle and the lovely, happy face.

## IX. JONDRETTE VERY NEARLY WEEPS

The rathole was so dark that anyone coming in from outside felt like they were entering a cellar. The two new arrivals accordingly advanced somewhat tentatively, barely making out the dim shapes around them, while being seen and examined perfectly well by the garret residents, whose eyes were accustomed to this eternal twilight.

Monsieur Leblanc approached with his kind sad eyes, and said to father Jondrette: "Monsieur, you will find new clothes, woolen stockings, and blankets in this parcel."

"Our angelic benefactor overwhelms us," said Jondrette, bowing to the floor.

Then, bending down to whisper in his elder daughter's ear while the two visitors were examining the lamentable interior, he added swiftly: "See? What did I tell you? Rags! No money. They're all the same! Speaking of which, how was the letter to this old codger signed?"

"Fabantou," she replied.

"The dramatic artiste, right!"

Lucky Jondrette had asked, for at that very moment Monsieur Leblanc turned to him and said, as though searching for his name: "I see that you really are to be pitied, Monsieur—"

"Fabantou," Jondrette quickly cut in.

"Monsieur Fabantou, yes, that's right, I remember."

"Dramatic artiste, Monsieur, one who has had his successes."

Here Jondrette evidently felt the moment had come to close in on "the philanthropist." He shouted in a voice combining the vainglory of the fairground tumbler with the humility of the high street beggar, all in one: "Student of Talma,[1] Monsieur! I am a student of Talma. Fortune once smiled on me. Alas! Now it's Misfortune's turn. You see, my benefactor, no bread, no fire. My poor kiddies have no fire! My only chair has the bottom out of it! A broken window-pane! In this weather! My missus in bed! Sick!"

"Poor woman!" said Monsieur Leblanc.

"My child hurt!" Jondrette added.

The child, distracted by the arrival of the strangers, was busy staring at "the young lady" and had stopped her sobbing.

"Go on, cry! Bawl!" Jondrette hissed at her.

At the same time, he pinched her sore hand. All with the skill of a conjurer. The little girl let out a few loud shrieks.

The adorable young girl whom Marius in his heart called "his Ursula" ran over: "You poor dear child," she said.

"You see, my beautiful young lady," Jondrette went on, "her bleeding wrist! It was an accident that happened while she was working away on a machine—just to make six sous a day. They may be forced to cut her arm off!"

"Really?" said the old gentleman, alarmed.

The little girl, taking this remark seriously, began to wail again, louder than ever, quite beautifully.

"Alas, yes, my benefactor!" the father replied.

For some moments, Jondrette had been studying "the philanthropist" in a bizarre way. Even as he spoke, he was scrutinizing the man with intense attention, as though he were trying to gather his memories together. All of a sudden, taking advantage of a moment when the newcomers were keenly questioning the little girl about her injured hand, he went over to the bed where his wife was, looking dopey and out of her depth, and he quickly whispered to her:

"Take a good look at that man, will you!"

Then he turned back to Monsieur Leblanc and continued his lament: "You see, Monsieur! All I have, myself, for clothes is one of my wife's chemises! And it's all torn! In the middle of winter! I can't go out without a coat. If I had a coat of some sort, I'd go and see Mademoiselle Mars,[2] who knows me and who is really fond of me. Doesn't she still live in the rue de la Tour-des-Dames? Do you know, Monsieur? We used to tour together in the country. I shared her laurels. Célimène would come to my aid, Monsieur! Elmira would give alms to Belisarius![3] But no, nothing! And not a sou in the house! My wife sick and not a sou! My daughter dangerously injured and not a sou! The missus has coughing fits. It's her age and, then again, the nervous system's got something to do with it. She needs help, and my daughter, too! But we can't afford doctors! Or chemists! How can we pay? Not a centime! I'd go down on my knees for a ten-centime piece, Monsieur! You see what the arts have been reduced to! And do you know, my charming young lady, and you, Monsieur, generous patron of mine, do you know, you who breathe virtue and goodness, and who perfume the church where my poor daughter goes to say her prayers and sees you every day? . . . For I bring my daughters up in the church, Monsieur. I didn't want them to take to the theater. Ah, the little scamps! If I see them batting an eyelid! I'm not kidding, no sir! I hit 'em with a bit of sound and fury about honor, and morality, and virtue! Ask them. They have to stick to the straight and narrow. They've got a father. They're not like those poor unfortunate girls who start off not having a family and end up taking on all comers. When you're Mamselle Nobody, you become Madame Everybody. Jumping Jehovah! None of that in the Fabantou family! I mean to educate them virtuously, and for 'em to be honest, and for 'em to be nice, and for 'em to believe in God! Good God! . . . Well, then, Monsieur, my worthy Monsieur, do you know what is going to happen tomorrow? Tomorrow is the fourth of February, that fatal day, the last day my landlord has given me; if I haven't paid by this evening, tomorrow my eldest daughter, me, my missus with her fever, my little girl with her injury, we will all four be evicted, kicked out, thrown on the street, on the boulevard, without shelter, in the rain, in the snow. There you have it, Monsieur. I owe four quarters, a whole year! That is, sixty francs."

Jondrette was lying. Four quarters would have meant only forty francs, and he could not owe four quarters since only six months ago Marius had paid two.

Monsieur Leblanc pulled five francs out of his pocket and put them on the table.

Jondrette had time to mumble into his big girl's ear: "Bastard! What does he want me to do with his five francs? That won't pay for my chair and my window! All that for nothing!"

But Monsieur Leblanc had taken off the big brown greatcoat he had been wearing over his blue redingote and thrown it over the back of the chair.

"Monsieur Fabantou," he said, "I have only those five francs on me, but I'm going to take my daughter home and I'll return this evening; it's this evening, isn't it, that you have to pay?"

Jondrette's face lit up with a strange expression. He quickly answered: "Yes, my estimable gentleman. At eight o'clock I have to be at my landlord's door."

"I'll be here at six o'clock, and I'll bring you the sixty francs."

"My benefactor!" cried Jondrette, overcome.

And he added in a whisper: "Take a good look at him, woman!"

Monsieur Leblanc had taken the arm of the beautiful young girl again and turned toward the door: "Till this evening, my friends," he said.

"Six o'clock?" said Jondrette.

"Six on the dot."

At that moment the greatcoat left on the chair caught the eye of the elder Jondrette girl.

"Monsieur," she said, "you've forgotten your overcoat."

Jondrette looked daggers at his daughter and gave a fearful shrug of the shoulders. Monsieur Leblanc turned round and answered with a smile: "I haven't forgotten it, I'm leaving it."

"O, my patron," said Jondrette. "My august benefactor. I am dissolving into tears! Please allow me to take you back to your cab."

"If you go out," rejoined Monsieur Leblanc, "put this overcoat on. It is very cold."

Jondrette did not need to be told twice. He swiftly threw the brown greatcoat on. And the three of them went out, Jondrette ahead of the two strangers.

## X. Rates for Cabs: Two Francs an Hour

Marius had missed nothing of this whole scene and yet in reality he had seen nothing. His eyes had remained glued to the young girl, his heart had, so to speak, seized her and enveloped her from head to toe the moment she stepped into the garret. The whole time she was there, he had lived that life of ecstasy that suspends material perceptions and causes the whole soul to rush to one point. He contemplated, not the girl, but the light, which wore a satin pelisse and a velvet hat. If Sirius, the star, had entered the room, he could not have been more dazzled.

While the young girl was opening the parcel and unfolding the clothes and the blankets, or questioning the sick mother so kindheartedly and the little injured girl so tenderheartedly, he was watching her every move very closely, and straining to hear what she said. He knew her eyes, her forehead, her beauty, her figure, her gait, but he did not know the sound of her voice. He thought he'd caught a few words once at the Luxembourg, but he was not absolutely sure. He'd have given ten years of his life to hear it, to be able to carry a bit of that music in his soul. But it was lost in all these lamentable performances and Jondrette's trumpeting. This added rage to Marius's rapture. He gazed longingly at her. He could not quite believe that it really was this divine creature that he was seeing amid these depraved beings in this monstrous hole. It was like seeing a hummingbird among toads.

When she left, he had only one thought, to follow her, to hug her tracks, not to let her go until he'd found out where she lived, not lose her again, at least, after having so miraculously found her again! He jumped down from the chest of drawers and grabbed his hat. Just as he placed his hand on the doorknob and was about to go out, a thought made him stop short. The hall was long, the staircase narrow, Jondrette was a talker, Monsieur Leblanc had no doubt not yet stepped back up into his carriage; if he turned round in the hall, or on the stairs, or at the doorstop, and saw Marius in this house, obviously he would be alarmed and would find a way of escaping yet again and it would all be finished yet again. What could he do? Wait a while? But while he was waiting, the cab might take off. Marius didn't know what to do. Finally he took the risk and left his room.

There was nobody in the hall now. He ran to the stairs. There was nobody on the stairs, either. He rushed downstairs and reached the boulevard just in time to see a fiacre turning the corner of the rue du Petit-Banquier to go back to Paris.

Marius hurried in that direction. When he reached the corner of the boulevard, he saw the same cab going at quite a clip down the rue Mouffetard; the cab was already a long way off, there was no way he could catch up with it; what did he imagine? That he'd run after it? Hardly. Besides, inside the cab they would surely notice this individual running for all his might in hot pursuit of them and the father would recognize him. Just then, an unbelievable and marvelous stroke of luck, Marius saw a cab for hire going past on the boulevard, empty. There was only one thing to do and that was to hop in this cab and follow the other one. This was safe, effective, and free of danger.

Marius signaled the driver to stop and shouted at him: "By the hour!"

Marius didn't have a cravat on, he was in his shabby old work coat which had buttons missing, and his shirt was torn along one of the folds at the front.

The driver pulled up, winked, and held out his left hand to Marius, gently rubbing his index finger with his thumb.

"What?" said Marius.

"Pay up front," said the driver.

Marius remembered he had only sixteen sous on him.

"How much?" he asked.

"Forty sous."

"I'll pay you when I get back."

The driver, by way of response, simply whistled the tune of "La Palisse" and whipped his horse into action.

Marius watched the cabriolet driving away, distraught. For want of twenty-four sous, his joy, his happiness, his love, was slipping through his fingers! He was sliding back into the gloom! He had seen and now he would be blind again! He thought bitterly and, it must be said, with deep regret of the five francs he had given that pig of a girl that very morning. If he had had those five francs, he would be saved, he would be born again, he would emerge from limbo and darkness, he would shed his loneliness, and his spleen, and his mourning for his lost love; he would have tied the knot once more between the black thread of his destiny and this beautiful gold thread that had just floated before his very eyes only to snap once more. He went back into the crumbling slum in despair.

He could have told himself that Monsieur Leblanc had promised to return that evening and that he only needed to be better prepared this time to follow him; but in his gloomy contemplation he had hardly registered this.

Just as he was going upstairs, he saw on the other side of the boulevard, walking along by the deserted wall of the rue de la Barrière-des-Gobelins, Jondrette wrapped up in the coat of "the philanthropist," talking to one of those disturbing-looking men who are appropriately known as "prowlers of the barrières"; rough men with ambiguous faces, given to dubious monologues and evil schemes, who routinely sleep during the day, from which you have to assume they work at night.

The two men, chatting away standing-stock still in the snow that was swirling down, formed an association that a police sergeant would definitely have kept his eye on but that Marius barely noticed.

Yet, whatever his painful preoccupation, he could not help remarking to himself that the barrière prowler Jondrette was talking to looked very like a certain Panchaud, alias Printanier, alias Bigrenaille, whom Courfeyrac had once pointed out to him and who passed in the quartier for a pretty dangerous night rambler. We saw this man's name in the preceding book. This Panchaud, alias Printanier, alias Bigrenaille, later featured in several criminal proceedings and has since become a celebrity crook. At the time he was still only a notorious crook. Today he is a part of the tradition among gangsters and murderers. He had a real following toward the close of the last reign. And in the evening, at nightfall, at the hour when groups huddle together and speak in hushed voices, they used to talk about him in the exercise yard called the Lions' Den at La Force.[1] At that fabled prison, at the exact spot under the covered way where the sewer runs that was used in the incredible breakout in broad daylight of thirty detainees in 1843, you could even read, above the flagstones over the toilets, his name, PANCHAUD, boldly carved by the man himself on the parapet wall in one of his attempts at escape. In 1832, the police already had him under surveillance, but he had not yet seriously made his début.

## XI. MISERY OFFERS PAIN ITS SERVICES

Marius climbed upstairs slowly; the moment he was about to go back to his cell, he saw in the hallway behind him the elder Jondrette girl following him. This girl was odious in his sight; she was the one who had his five francs and it was too late to ask her to give them back, the cabriolet was no longer there, the fiacre was far away. She wouldn't give them back to him, anyway. As for quizzing her about where the people who had come a moment ago lived, that was pointless, it was obvious she didn't know, since the letter signed Fabantou was addressed *to the benevolent gentleman of the church of Saint-Jacques-du-Haut-Pas.*

Marius stepped into his room and slammed the door shut behind him. It did not close; he turned round and saw that a hand was keeping it open.

"What is it?" he asked. "Who's there?"

It was the Jondrette girl.

"It's you?" said Marius, almost harshly. "You again! What do you want this time?"

She seemed pensive and did not answer. She had lost the morning's confidence. She did not come in but stood in the shadows in the hall, where Marius saw her through the half-open door.

"Come on, spit it out!" said Marius. "What do you want?"

She lifted her forlorn eyes to him, a spark of life seeming to ignite in them, and said: "Monsieur Marius, you look sad. What's wrong?"

"Me!" said Marius.

"Yes, you."

"Nothing's wrong."

"Yes, it is!"

"No, it's not."

"I'm telling you it is!"

"Leave me alone!"

Marius tried to shut the door again, but she continued to hold it open.

"Listen," she said, "you're wrong. Even though you're not rich, you were kind this morning. Be kind again now. You gave me something to eat with, tell me now what's the matter. You're upset, anyone can see that. What can be done to help? Can I do something? Put me to use. I'm not asking you for your secrets, you don't need to tell me, but, well, I can be useful. I can help you, I help my father. When someone has to carry letters, go into houses, go from door to door, find an address, follow someone, well, I'm the one that does it. So then, you can tell me what's wrong. I'll go and talk to certain persons. Sometimes a body just has to speak to certain persons and that's enough to find out things, and everything's set right. Use me."

An idea came to Marius. Is there a straw we won't clutch at when we feel ourselves drowning? He went over to the Jondrette girl.

"Listen," he said.

She promptly cut in, with a flash of joy in her eyes.

"Oh, yes! Tell me. That's better!"

"Well, then," he went on, "you know that old gentleman that you brought here with his daughter—"

"Yes."

"Do you know their address?"

"No."

"Find out for me."

The Jondrette girl's eyes had gone from forlorn to joyful and from joyful to grim.

"So that's what you're after?"

"Yes."

"Do you know them?"

"No."

"So what you're saying is," she went on sharply, "you don't know her, but you'd like to know her."

That shift from *them* to *her* was dripping with innuendo and bile.

"Well, can you do it?" said Marius.

"Get you the address of the lovely young lady?"

There was again in those words "the lovely young lady" a tone that irritated Marius. He went on:

"Does it matter! The address of the father and the daughter. *Their* address, no?!"

She glared at him.

"What'll you give me?"

"Whatever you like!"

"Whatever I like?"

"Yes."

"You'll get the address."

She looked down, then promptly pulled the door shut.

Marius found himself alone again.

He dropped onto a chair and leaned forward with both elbows on the bed and his head in both hands, sunk in thoughts he could not grasp as though he were having a dizzy spell. Everything that had happened since that morning, the appearance of the angel, her disappearance, what this creature had just said to him, which was like a ray of hope bobbing on an ocean of despair—his brain was filled with this giddy jumble.

Suddenly he was jolted violently out of his reverie. He heard the high, hard voice of Jondrette utter these words full of strangely intense interest for him: "I tell you I'm sure of it. I recognized him."

Who was Jondrette talking about? He recognized who? Monsieur Leblanc? The father of "his Ursula"? What! Did Jondrette know him? Was Marius about to have all the information, without which his life was meaningless to him, through this sudden and unexpected channel? Was he about to find out at last who it was he loved? Who this young girl was? Who her father was? Was that incredibly dense shadow that cloaked them about to be dispersed by light? Was the veil about to be lifted? Ah, heavens above!

He sprang rather than climbed up on the chest of drawers and resumed his place by the hole in the wall.

Once more the interior of the Jondrette rathole came into view.

## XII. Use of Monsieur Leblanc's Five-Franc Piece

Nothing had changed in the family's appearance except that the woman and the girls had thrown themselves on the parcel and pulled on stockings and woolen camisoles. Two brand-new blankets had been thrown over the two beds.

Old man Jondrette had evidently just got back. He was still winded by his trip outside. His daughters were by the fireside, sitting on the ground, the elder bandaging the younger's hand. His wife was slumped on the pallet next to the fireplace with amazement written all over her face. Jondrette paced up and down the garret, taking great strides. His eyes were crazed.

The woman, who seemed timid and dumbstruck in front of her husband, risked a question: "Is that right? Are you sure?"

"Sure! It was eight years ago! But I recognize him! Ah, I recognize him, all right! I recognized him right off! What, didn't it hit you in the face?"

"No."

"Yet I told you to pay attention! But it's the height, the face, he hasn't aged a bit, there are people who don't age, I don't know how they do it, it's the sound of his voice. He's better turned out, that's all! Ah, you old devil of a mystery man, I've got you now, all right!"

He stopped and said to his daughters: "Get lost, you two! . . . It's funny it didn't hit you right in the face."

The girls got up to do as they were told. The mother stammered: "With her sore hand?"

"The air'll do her good," said Jondrette. "Go on."

It was clear that this man was one of those you do not answer back. The two girls left. Just as they were going out the door, the father grabbed hold of the elder's arm and said in a very peculiar tone: "You be back here at five o'clock sharp. Both of you. I'll be needing you."

Marius's attention intensified.

Now that he was alone with his wife, Jondrette resumed pacing the room and he circled it two or three times in silence. Then he spent a few moments tucking the woman's chemise he was wearing into his pants and doing them up tighter.

All of a sudden he spun around to mother Jondrette, folded his arms and yelled: "And another thing! That young lady—"

"What about her?" the woman shot back, "what about the young lady?"

Marius could be in no doubt, they were clearly talking about Her. He listened with ardent anxiety. His whole life was throbbing in his ears.

But Jondrette had bent down and practically whispered to his wife. Then he straightened up and said very loudly: "It's her!"

"*That?*" said the wife.

"That!" said the husband.

Words could not express all that was packed into the mother's *that*. There was surprise, rage, hate, anger, mixed and blended in a monstrous intonation. All that it took was a few words uttered by her husband, the name no doubt that her husband had whispered in her ear, for this big sleepy woman to wake up and shift from repulsive to appalling.

"Can't be!" she cried. "When I think that my girls go barefoot and don't have a dress between them! You've got to be kidding—a satin pelisse, a velvet hat, silk brodequins, the works! More than two hundred francs' worth! Like she was a blasted princess! No, you've got it mixed up! To start with, that other thing was a fright, this one isn't too bad! Not too bad at all! It can't be her!"

"I tell you it is her. You'll see."

In the face of such absolute assertion, mother Jondrette lifted her big ruddy blond head and looked up at the ceiling with a twisted expression. At that moment, she struck Marius as even more frightening than her husband. She was a sow with the eyes of a tigress.

"You've got to be kidding!" she went on. "That horrible beautiful young lady who looked at my girls with pity in her eyes, you reckon she's that little frump! Oh, I'd like to kick her guts in with hobnailed boots!"

She leaped out of bed and stood there for a moment, hair in a tangle, nostrils flaring, mouth gaping, fists clenched and drawn up. Then she dropped back onto the pallet. The man paced up and down without paying the slightest attention to his female. After a few seconds' silence, he went over to mother Jondrette and stood facing her with his arms folded, as he had done a moment before.

"And you know what else?"

"What?" she asked.

He answered in a short, low voice: "My fortune's made."

Mother Jondrette studied him with a look that said: Has this man talking to me gone stark raving mad?

He continued: "Holy hell! I've been a member of the down-and-out club a bit too long now! I've had a gut full of misery! I've had my share—more than my share! I'm not joking around anymore, I don't find it funny anymore, enough wordplay, for Christ's sake! No more farces, Heavenly Father! I want to eat my fill, I want to drink my fill! Wolf it down! Sleep! Laze around doing nothing! I want my turn, do you get it! Before I croak, I'd like to be a bit of a millionaire, too!"

He circled the rathole before adding: "Like other people."

"What do you mean?" the woman asked.

He shook his head, winked, and raised his voice in the manner of a roving medicine man about to give a demonstration in the street: "What do I mean? I'll tell you what I mean!"

"Shoosh!" growled mother Jondrette. "Not so loud! This isn't something anyone else should hear about."

"Bah! Who? The neighbor? I saw him go out a while ago. Besides, do you think he listens in, that great booby? And anyway, I told you, I saw him go out."

Yet out of a sort of instinct, Jondrette lowered his voice, though not enough for his words to escape Marius. A favorable circumstance that allowed Marius not to lose any of this conversation was that the fallen snow muffled the noise of carriages on the boulevard.

Here is what Marius heard: "Listen carefully. We've got him, this Croesus![1] As good as. It's in the bag. It's all arranged. I saw some people. He's coming here at six o'clock tonight. Bringing his sixty francs, the mongrel! Did you see how I pulled that out of the bag for you, my sixty francs, my landlord, my fourth of February! It's not even a quarter yet![2] Talk about stupid! So he'll be here at six o'clock! That's when the neighbor goes out to dinner. Mother Bougon goes and does the dishes in town. There's no one in the house. The neighbor never gets back before eleven. The girls can keep a lookout. You'll help us. He'll go along—and hang himself."

"And what if he doesn't go along?" asked the woman.

Jondrette made a sinister gesture and said: "We'll do it for him."

With that, he burst out laughing.

It was the first time Marius had seen him laughing. His laugh was faint and chilling and gave Marius goosebumps.

Jondrette opened a cupboard next to the fireplace and pulled out an old cap, which he slapped on his head after whacking it on his sleeve to dust it.

"Now," he said, "I'm off. I've still got people to see. Good people. You'll see how it all works out. I won't stay out any longer than I have to. It's quite a hand to play. Look after the house for us."

And, with his fists thrust in the pockets of his pants, he stood there thinking for a moment, then cried: "You know it's pretty damned lucky that he didn't recognize me, though! If he'd recognized me on his side, he wouldn't be back. He'd escape our clutches. It's my beard that saved me! My romantic little goatee! My sweet romantic little goatee!"

And he started to laugh again. He went to the window. The snow was still falling, streaking the gray of the sky.

"Lousy weather!" he said.

Then he crossed the overcoat over in front: "The coat's too big, of course . . . Never mind," he added. "Just as well he left it for me, though, the old bastard! If he hadn't, I would never have been able to go out in this and the whole thing would've come to naught! Such a near thing, but look how it's worked out!"

On that note, he jammed his cap down over his eyes and turned on his heel.

He had hardly had time to take a few steps outside when the door opened again and his cunning feral profile reappeared.

"I forgot," he said. "You're to get a charcoal fire going in the stove."

And he threw into his wife's apron the five-franc piece that "the philanthropist" had left him.

"A charcoal fire?" the woman asked.

"Yes."

"How many bushels of charcoal?"

"Two good ones."

"That'll come to thirty sous. With the rest, I'll buy something for dinner."

"Like hell you will!"

"Why not?"

"Don't you go spending that hundred-sou piece."

"Why not?"

"Because I've got something else to buy with it instead."

"What?"

"Something."

"How much will you need?"

"Where's there an ironmonger's around here?"

"Rue Mouffetard."

"Ah, yes, on the corner of whatsit street, I can see the shop."

"But how much is this thing going to cost, then?"

"Three francs fifty sous."

"There won't be much left for dinner."

"Today's one day we won't be eating. We've got better things to do."

"Whatever you say, treasure."

At this word from his wife, Jondrette closed the door again, and this time Marius heard his footsteps receding down the tenement hallway and quickly down the stairs.

At that moment the bells of Saint-Médard struck one.

## XIII. Solus cum Solo, in Loco Remoto, Non Cogitabantur Orare Pater Noster[1]

However much of a dreamer, Marius was, as we know, a strong and active person. The habits of solitary living, by developing sympathy and compassion in him, had perhaps diminished his capacity for irritation, but left intact his capacity for outrage; he had the benevolence of a Brahmin[2] and the severity of a judge; he might feel sorry for a toad, but he could easily crush a viper underfoot. Now, he had just looked down into a vipers' hole; it was a nest of monsters and it was right under his nose.

"I'll have to stamp on these miserable bastards," he said.

None of the puzzles he'd hoped would be cleared up had been illuminated; on the contrary, they had all, perhaps, become even more opaque; he knew nothing more about the beautiful girl from the Luxembourg gardens or about the man he called Monsieur Leblanc, except that Jondrette knew who they were. Through the black words delivered, he glimpsed only one thing at all clearly and that was that an ambush was being set up, an obscure but terrible ambush; that they were both in serious danger, she probably, her father for sure; that they had to be saved, that the hideous schemes of the Jondrettes had to be undone and the web of these spiders torn down. He observed mother Jondrette for a moment. She'd pulled an old cast-iron stove from out of a corner and was rummaging round in the scrap.

He got down from the chest of drawers as quietly as he could, being careful not to make a sound.

In his dread of what was being set up and in the horror into which the Jondrettes had plunged him, he felt a kind of joy that it might perhaps be given to him to do a great service to the one he loved.

But what could he do? Warn the people under threat? Where would he find them? He didn't have an inkling of their address. One minute they were there, before his very eyes, the next minute they were gone again, driven back into the unfathomable depths of Paris. Wait for Monsieur Leblanc at the door at six o'clock, when he was supposed to turn up, and warn him about the trap? But Jondrette and his cronies would see him keeping watch, the place was deserted, they would be stronger than he was, they would find a way of nabbing him and carting him off, and the man Marius wanted to save would be sunk. One o'clock had just sounded, the ambush was to take place at six. Marius had five hours ahead of him.

There was only one thing for it.

He put on his presentable coat, tied a scarf around his neck, grabbed his hat and went out, without making any more noise than if he had been walking barefoot on moss.

In any case, mother Jondrette was still rattling around in her iron scrap.

Once he was out of the house, he headed for the rue du Petit-Banquier.

He was about halfway down the street, level with a very low wall that you could step over in certain places and that bordered a patch of wasteland, and he was walking along slowly, preoccupied as he was, the snow muffling his footfalls, when, all of a sudden, he heard voices talking quite close by. He turned his head, the street was deserted, there was nobody, it was broad daylight, and yet he could distinctly hear voices.

It occurred to him to look over the wall. There were in fact two men there leaning against the wall, squatting in the snow and talking in whispers to each other. These two figures were not known to him. One was a bearded man in a smock and the other was a long-haired man in rags. The bearded one had a Greek skullcap, the other was bareheaded and there was snow in his hair. By leaning over them, Marius could hear what they said. The long-haired one dug the other one in the ribs and said: "With Patron-Minette, you can't go wrong."

"You think so?" said the bearded one, and the long-haired one replied: "It'll mean five hundred big ones each, and the worst that can happen? Five years, six years, ten at the most!"

The other man replied with some hesitation, scratching his head under his Greek cap: "That sounds pretty solid. A person can't turn down a job like that."

"I tell you, the deal can't fail," the long-haired one resumed. "Old man What's-his-name. He'll make sure the chaff-cutter's hitched and hot to trot."

Then they started talking about a melodrama they'd seen the night before at the Gaîté. Marius continued on his way.

It seemed to him that the obscure words of these men, so strangely hidden behind the wall, crouching in the snow, were perhaps not unrelated to the abominable plans of Jondrette. That must be "the deal" they were referring to.

He headed for the faubourg Saint-Marceau and asked at the first shop he came to where he could find the prefect of police. He was directed to the rue de Pontoise, no. 14. Marius went straight there.

As he passed a baker's, he bought a bread roll for two sous and ate it, fore-seeing that he would not eat dinner.

On the way, he gave Providence its due. He thought how, if he had not handed over his five francs that morning to the Jondrette girl, he would have followed Monsieur Leblanc's cab and as a result been completely in the dark. Then nothing would have stood in the way of the Jondrettes' ambush and this Monsieur Leblanc would have been lost and, doubtless, his daughter with him.

## XIV. Where a Police Officer Gives a Lawyer a Couple of Punches

When he got to no. 14, rue de Pontoise, he went up to the first floor and asked for the prefect of police. "The police chief isn't in," said an office boy. "But there's an inspector standing in for him. Would you like to speak to him? Is it ur-gent?"

"Yes," said Marius.

The office boy took him to the commissioner's room. A tall man was stand-ing there behind a metal gate, leaning toward a stove and holding up with both hands the tails of a vast coachman's overcoat with a triple cape. He had a square face, with a thin mouth and strong, wild, bushy graying sideburns and a gaze that could turn your pockets inside out. You would have described this gaze as not so much penetrating as boring right through you.

The man did not look all that much less ferocious or frightening than Jon-drette; a mastiff is occasionally no less alarming to run into than a wolf.

"What do you want?" he barked at Marius, without adding *monsieur*.

"Monsieur, the prefect of police?"

"He's not here. I'm standing in for him."

"It concerns a very confidential matter."

"Go on, then, speak."

"And it's extremely urgent."

"Then speak fast."

The man was calm and brusque, both frightening and reassuring at once. He inspired awe and confidence. Marius told him the story—that a person he only knew by sight was to be led that very evening into an ambush; that, living in the room next door to the lair in question, he, Marius Pontmercy, lawyer, had heard the whole plot through the wall; that the rogue who had thought up the trap was one Jondrette by name; that he would have accomplices, probably the barrière prowlers, among others a certain Panchaud, alias Printanier, alias Bigrenaille; that Jondrette's daughters would be on the lookout; that there was no way to warn the man threatened, given that no one even knew his name; and that, finally, all this was to be carried out at six o'clock that very evening at the most deserted point on the boulevard de l'Hôpital, in the house at no. 50–52.

At that number, the inspector raised his head and said coldly: "So it's the room at the end of the hall?"

"Exactly," said Marius, adding, "Do you know the house?"

The inspector remained silent for a moment, then he answered, warming the heel of his boot in the mouth of the stove: "Apparently."

He went on through his teeth, speaking less to Marius than to his cravat.

"Sounds like Patron-Minette's mixed up in this somewhere."

The name struck Marius.

"Patron-Minette," he said. "I did in fact hear that name mentioned."

And he told the inspector of the conversation between the long-haired man and the bearded man in the snow behind the wall of the rue du Petit-Banquier.

The inspector muttered: "The long-haired fellow would have to be Brujon, and the bearded fellow would have to be Demi-liard, alias Deux-milliards."

He dropped his eyes again and mused.

"As for father What's-his-name, I have an inkling who that is. There, I've singed my coat. They always make these stoves too hot. Number 50–52. The old Gorbeau building."

Then he looked at Marius: "You saw only this bearded fellow and the long-haired one?"

"And Panchaud."

"You didn't see a sort of godforsaken rodentlike little muscadin[1] of a fop getting about over that way by any chance, did you?"

"No."

"Or a great big lump that looks like the elephant at the Jardin des Plantes?"

"No."

"Or a sewer rat that looks like an old red-tail of an ex-convict?"

"No."

"As for the fourth, no one sees him, not even his adjutants, clerks, and employees, so it's not surprising you didn't see him."

"No. What is all this?" asked Marius. "Who are all these people?"

The inspector answered: "Anyway, it's not the time they come out."

He lapsed into silence, then went on: "Number 50–52. I know the building. Impossible for us to hide inside without the artists cottoning on. Then all they'd have to do is cancel the show. They're so modest! An audience embarrasses them. Can't have that, can't have that. I'd like to hear them sing and make them dance."

This monologue over, he turned toward Marius and asked him, pinning him with a stare: "Would you be frightened?"

"What of?" said Marius.

"Of these men?"

"No more than of you!" Marius replied rudely, now that he'd begun to notice that this police spy had still not had the courtesy to refer to him as *monsieur.*

The inspector stared even harder at Marius and then went on with a sort of sententious solemnity: "Spoken like a brave man and an honest man. Courage does not fear crime, and honesty does not fear authority."

Marius broke in: "That's all very well, but what are you going to do?"

The inspector merely answered:

"The tenants of that house have latchkeys to get in with at night. Have you got one?"

"Yes," said Marius.

"Have you got it on you?"

"Yes."

"Give it to me," said the inspector.

Marius took the key from his waistcoat and handed it to the inspector, adding: "If you take my advice, you'll come in force."

The inspector threw Marius the look Voltaire would have given a provincial academic who had suggested a rhyme to him; with a single movement, he plunged both hands, which were enormous, into the two vast pockets of his coachman's coat and pulled out two little steel pistols, the sort of pistols known as *coups de poing,* "punches." He presented them to Marius, with these sharp and short instructions: "Take these. Go back home. Hide yourself in your room. Let them think you've gone out. They're loaded. Each one has two bullets. Keep watch. There's a hole in the wall, you tell me. The men will come. Let them carry on for a while. When you think things are getting nice and hot and it's time to stop them, you fire a pistol shot. Not too early. The rest's my business.

One shot in the air, at the ceiling, it doesn't matter where. Above all, not too early. Wait till there's some action. You're a lawyer, you know what that means."

Marius took the pistols and put them in the side pocket of his coat.

"They stick out like that, you can see the bulge," said the inspector. "Better put them in your trouser pockets."

Marius hid the pistols in his other pockets.

"Now," the inspector went on, "there is not a minute to lose on anyone's part. What time is it?' Two-thirty. It's for seven o'clock?"

"Six o'clock," said Marius.

"I have time," the inspector went on, "but only just. Don't forget any of what I've told you. Bam! One pistol shot."

"Don't worry," answered Marius.

And as Marius was putting his hand on the door handle to go out, the inspector called: "By the way, if you need me between now and then, come round here or send someone. Ask for Inspector Javert."

## XV. JONDRETTE DOES HIS SHOPPING

A few moments later, at around three o'clock, Courfeyrac happened to be walking down the rue Mouffetard in Bossuet's company. The snow was falling twice as heavily and filled the air. Bossuet was just saying to Courfeyrac: "Seeing all these snowflakes falling you'd think there was a plague of white butterflies in the sky."

All at once, Bossuet spotted Marius coming up the street toward the barrière and looking a little strange.

"Look!" Bossuet exclaimed. "Marius!"

"I saw him," said Courfeyrac. "Let's not speak to him."

"Why not?"

"He's busy."

"Doing what?"

"Can't you see how he looks?"

"How does he look?"

"He looks like he's following someone."

"That's true," said Bossuet.

"Look at his eyes, will you!" Courfeyrac went on.

"But who the hell is he following?"

"Some cutie-pie-floral-bonnet-hussy! He's in love."

"But," Bossuet observed, "it's just that I can't see any cutie, or any hussy, or any floral bonnet in the street. There isn't a single woman."

Courfeyrac looked around and cried: "He's following a man!"

A man, with a cap on his head and a gray beard that could just be made out even though he had his back to them, was indeed walking twenty feet ahead of Marius.

This man was dressed in a brand-new overcoat that was far too big for him and a dreadful pair of pants in tatters, black with mud.

Bossuet burst out laughing.

"Who on earth can that man be?"

"That," Courfeyrac said, "is a poet. Poets love getting around in the trousers of rabbit-skin peddlers and the overcoats of the peers of France."

"Let's see where Marius is going," said Bossuet. "Let's see where the man's going, let's follow them, eh?"

"Bossuet!" cried Courfeyrac. "L'Aigle de Meaux! You are an extravagant eagle! Fancy following a man who's following a man!"

They turned back.

Marius had in fact spotted Jondrette in the rue Mouffetard and was keeping an eye on him.

Jondrette forged straight ahead without suspecting that he was already being watched. He turned off the rue Mouffetard and Marius saw him go into one of the most grisly dives in the rue Gracieuse, where he stayed for a quarter of an hour before heading back to the rue Mouffetard. He stopped at an iron-monger's that, in those days, was at the corner of the rue Pierre-Lombard, and a few moments later, Marius saw him come out of the shop holding a huge cold chisel with a beechwood handle, which he slipped under his overcoat. When he reached the rue du Petit-Gentilly, he turned left and headed swiftly for the rue du Petit-Banquier. Night was falling; the snow, which had stopped for a moment, was starting to fall thick and fast again. Marius stopped and hid at the corner of the rue du Petit-Banquier, which was deserted as always, and didn't follow Jondrette farther. This was lucky for him because, just as Jondrette reached the low wall where Marius had overheard the bearded man and the long-haired man talking, he turned round to make sure no one was following him or could see him, then hopped over the wall and vanished.

The wasteland the wall bordered was connected to the backyard of a carriage-hire business run by a man of ill repute who had gone bust but who still had a few old *berlingots* sitting around in sheds.

Marius thought it wise to take advantage of Jondrette's absence to go back home; besides, time was ticking away; every evening Ma Bougon was in the habit of locking the front door on her way out as she left to go and wash dishes in town, so the front door was always locked shut at dusk; Marius had given his only key to the police inspector, so it was vital that he hurry.

Evening had come; night had almost closed in; there was now only one small spot lit by the dying sun in all the endless sky, and that was the moon. It was rising, red, behind the low dome of La Salpêtrière.

Marius bounded back to no. 50–52. The door was still open when he got there. He tiptoed upstairs and slid along the wall of the hallway to his room. This hall, as you will recall, had garrets running off it on either side that were currently all empty and to let. Ma Bougon usually left their doors open. As he passed one of these doors, Marius thought he saw in one of the unoccupied cells the motionless heads of four men, which a faint glimmer of dying light, falling through a dormer window, lit up. Marius did not try to see, not wanting to be seen. He managed to make it back to his room without being spotted and without any noise. Just in the nick of time. A second later, he heard Ma Bougon going out and locking the front door of the house behind her.

## XVI. Where You Will Find the Words of an English Tune Fashionable in 1832

Marius sat on his bed. It might have been half past five. A mere half an hour separated him from what was to come. He could hear his arteries thumping the way you can hear the ticking of a clock in the dark. He thought of the double march that was going on at that moment in the shadows, crime advancing on one side, justice coming from the other. He wasn't frightened, but he could not think without a certain shudder of the things that were going to happen, like all who suddenly embark on an amazing adventure out of the blue. This whole day had the effect on him of a dream, and in order not to feel he was in the throes of a nightmare, he needed to feel the coldness of the two steel pistols in his pockets.

It had stopped snowing; the moon grew brighter and brighter, emerging from the mists, and its light mingled with the white reflection of the fallen snow, giving the room a twilight feel.

There was light in the Jondrette dungheap. Marius saw a red gleam shining through the hole in the wall, which looked like it was bleeding.

He was sure that this gleam could scarcely be produced by a candle. Otherwise, there was no movement at the Jondrettes', no one was stirring there, or talking, not a breath; the silence was glacial and profound, and without the red light you would have thought you were next to a tomb.

Marius quietly took off his boots and pushed them under the bed.

A few minutes went by. Marius heard the door below turn on its hinges, a heavy quick tread mounted the stairs and came along the hallway, the latch of the rathole clicked open; Jondrette was back.

Immediately, several voices rose. The whole family was in the garret. They simply kept quiet in the absence of the master the way wolf cubs do in the absence of the wolf.

" 'Tis I," he said.

"Good evening, Pappy," yelped the daughters.

"Well?" said their mother.

"It's all coming along nicely," replied Jondrette, "but my feet are frozen. Ah, good, that's it, I see you're all dolled up. You have to be able to inspire trust."

"All ready to go."

"You won't forget anything I told you? You'll do everything right?"

"Don't you worry about that."

"It's just that—" Jondrette started to say. But he didn't finish his sentence.

Marius heard him put something heavy on the table, probably the chisel he'd bought.

"Ah, right!" Jondrette said. "Have you had something to eat?"

"Yes," said the mother, "I had three big potatoes with salt. I made use of the fire to cook 'em."

"Good," said Jondrette, "Tomorrow I'll take you out to dinner. We'll have duck with all the trimmings. You'll dine like Charles X. Things are going well."

Then he added in a lowered voice: "The mousetrap's set. The cats are ready to pounce."

He lowered his voice further still: "Put this on the fire."

Marius heard the clatter of charcoal being knocked by tongs or some other iron instrument and Jondrette continued:

"Did you oil the door hinges so they won't make a noise?"

"Yes," said the mother.

"What time is it?"

"Getting on for six. It's just struck the half hour at Saint-Médard."

"Jesus!" said Jondrette. "It's time for the girls to get going if they're going to keep watch. Over here, you two, listen carefully."

There was a bout of whispering, then Jondrette spoke up again: "Has mother Bougon gone?"

"Yes," said the woman.

"Are you sure there's no one home next door?"

"He hasn't come back all day, and you know this is the time he has his dinner."

"Are you sure?"

"Yes, I'm sure."

"All the same," said Jondrette, "no harm going round to check. Girlie, take the candle and pop next door."

Marius dropped to his hands and knees and crawled silently under the bed. He had only just curled up under it when he saw a light through the cracks in his door.

"Pa," a voice cried, "he's out."

He recognized the voice of the elder daughter.

"Did you go in?" asked the father.

"No," answered the girl, "but his key's in the door, so he's out."

The father yelled: "Go in just the same."

The door opened and Marius saw the big Jondrette girl come in, candle in hand. She was the same as she had been that morning, but even more frightening by candlelight.

She went straight to the bed. Marius had a moment of horrible panic, but by the bed there was a mirror nailed to the wall and that was where she was headed. She stretched up on tiptoes and looked at herself. You could hear the noise of scrap iron being moved around in the room next door as she smoothed her hair with the palm of her hand and smiled in the mirror, softly crooning in her deathly broken voice:

> Our love lasted one whole week of heaven,
> But how short such moments of bliss!
> It was well worth it, joy times seven!
> Love should last forever, like this!
> Should last forever! should last forever![1]

Marius was shaking all the while. He could not believe that she could not hear him breathing.

She went to the window and looked out, talking to herself out loud with that half-mad look of hers: "God, Paris is ugly when it puts on its white chemise!" she said.

She returned to the mirror and made faces once more, studying herself first face-on, then in profile.

"Hey!" yelled the father. "What the hell are you doing?"

"I'm looking under the bed and behind the furniture," she answered, continuing to arrange her hair. "There's nobody here."

"Half-wit!" shrieked the father. "Get in here this minute! We've got no time to waste."

"I'm coming! I'm coming!" she said. "A girl doesn't have time to scratch herself in this dump!"

She hummed:

> You leave me to find fame one day,
> My sad heart will follow you all the way.[2]

She cast a last glance in the mirror and left, shutting the door behind her.

A moment later, Marius heard the noise of the two girls padding down the hallway in their bare feet and Jondrette's voice shouting after them: "Be very careful! One over at the barrière, the other at the corner of the rue du Petit-

Banquier. Don't lose sight of the front door for a second, and if you see anything at all, I want you back here on the double! Hop to it! You've got a key to get back in."

The elder daughter grumbled: "Fancy keeping watch barefoot in the snow!"

"Tomorrow you'll have little scarab-colored silk ankle boots!" yelled the father.

They went downstairs, and a few seconds later the front door banged shut, announcing that they were now outside.

There was no one left in the house except Marius and the Jondrette couple and probably also the mysterious beings glimpsed by Marius in the gloom behind the door of the vacant garret.

## XVII. MARIUS'S FIVE-FRANC PIECE PUT TO USE

Marius judged that the moment had come to resume his place at his observation post. In the blink of an eye and with all the suppleness of a young man, he was back at the hole in the wall.

He peered in.

The interior of the Jondrette dwelling looked weirdly different. Marius could now see what was causing the strange light he had noticed. A candle was burning in a candlestick green with verdigris, but that was not what was really lighting the room. The whole rathole was lit up by the glare from a big cast-iron stove parked in the fireplace and filled with burning charcoal—the stove that mother Jondrette had worked on that morning. The charcoal was burning and the stove was red hot, with a blue flame dancing inside. By its light, you could pick out the shape of the chisel Jondrette had bought in the rue Pierre-Lombard, thrust into the burning coals and now glowing red. In a corner near the door, arranged as for some anticipated use, there were two mounds, one a heap of old scrap iron, the other a heap of ropes. Anyone who didn't know what was in the works would have been in two minds at seeing all this, and would have wavered between a very sinister interpretation and a perfectly straightforward one. Lit up the way it was, the dump looked more a forge than the mouth of hell. But in this light, Jondrette looked more like a demon than a blacksmith.

The heat of the burning coals was so great that the candle on the table was melting fast and had burned right down on the side nearest the stove. An old Chinese lantern made of copper, worthy of a Diogenes turned housebreaker like Cartouche,[1] had been placed on the mantelpiece.

The stove had been placed on the hearth itself, next to the mostly extinguished embers, and it was sending its steam straight up through the chimney flue without spreading any odor.

The moon came in through the four panes of the window, throwing its whiteness into the flaming crimson garret, and to the poetic mind of Marius, dreamer that he was even at the moment of action, it was like a beam from heaven spilling into the grotesque fantasies of earth.

A gust of air whooshed in through the broken pane and helped disperse the smell of burning coal and hide the stove.

The Jondrette lair was, if you recall what we said earlier about the old Gorbeau building, admirably well chosen to serve as the theater of a very dark and dirty deed, and for staging a crime. It was the most remote room in the house, the one farthest away from the most deserted boulevard in Paris. If this ambush had not already been planned, someone would have invented it there.

The whole thickness of a house and a host of vacant rooms separated this rathole from the boulevard, and its only window looked out on vast wastelands blocked off behind walls and paling fences.

Jondrette had lit his pipe and was sitting on the chair with the straw seat kicked out, smoking. His wife was talking to him in a voice just above a whisper.

If Marius had been Courfeyrac, that is, one of those people who laugh at every occasion life throws up, he'd have burst out laughing when his eye lit on mother Jondrette. She was wearing a black hat with feathers not unlike one of the hats of the heralds-at-arms at Charles X's consecration,[2] an immense tartan shawl over her woolknit skirt, and the man's shoes her daughter had turned her nose up at that morning. It was this getup that had caused Jondrette to let out his exclamation: "Good, that's it, I see you're all dolled up. You have to be able to inspire trust."

As for Jondrette, he had not quit the overcoat, new and far too big for him, that Monsieur Leblanc had given him, and his outfit continued to offer that contrast between overcoat and trousers that constituted the ideal of the poet in Courfeyrac's view.

All of a sudden, Jondrette raised his voice: "Hang on! I've just thought of something. In this lousy weather, he'll come in a cab. Light the lantern, and go down with it. Stay there behind the front door. The moment you hear the cab stop, open up straightaway, he'll come up, you'll light the stairs and the hall, and when he comes in here, go straight back down again and pay the driver and send the cab on its way."

"What about the money?" asked the woman.

Jondrette fumbled in his pants and handed her five francs.

"What's that?" she cried.

Jondrette replied with dignity: "It's the monarch the neighbor gave us this morning." And he added: "Know what? We need two chairs in here."

"What for?"

"To sit on."

Marius felt a shiver run down his spine when he heard mother Jondrette answer calmly:

"Christ! I'll go and get the neighbor's for you."

And she swiftly opened the door of the rathole and went out into the hall.

Marius did not physically have the time to get down off the chest of draw-ers, run to the bed, and hide.

"Take the candle!" yelled Jondrette.

"No," she said, "I've only got two hands and I've got two chairs to carry. The moon's out."

Marius heard mother Jondrette's heavy hand groping for his key in the dark. The door opened. He remained rooted to the spot in shock and astonish-ment.

Mother Jondrette came in.

The dormer window let in a ray of moonlight between two great blocks of shadow. One of the blocks of shadow covered the whole wall that Marius was leaning against in such a way that he disappeared.

Mother Jondrette looked up, did not see Marius, took the two chairs, the only ones Marius owned, and went out again, letting the door shut with a bang behind her.

She resurfaced in the rathole: "Here're the two chairs."

"And here's the lantern," said the husband. "Go down, quick."

She rushed to obey and Jondrette was left on his own.

He arranged the two chairs on either side of the table, turned the chisel in the fire, put an old screen in front of the fireplace to hide the stove, then went over to the corner where the pile of ropes was and bent down as though to ex-amine something there. Marius then saw that what he had taken for a shapeless heap was a rope ladder, very well made, with wooden rungs and two large hooks for hanging.

This ladder and a few large tools, veritable iron clubs, which were jumbled in with the scrap iron heaped behind the door, had not been in the Jondrette hole that morning and had evidently been brought in during the afternoon, while Marius was out.

"Those are edge-tool maker's tools," thought Marius.

If Marius had been a bit better informed in this line, he would have recog-nized that what he took for the stock-in-trade of the edge-tool maker was ac-tually either instruments able to force a door or pick a lock or ones able to cut and slice—the two families of sinister implements that thieves know as *juniors* and *reapers*.

The fireplace and the table with the two chairs sat exactly facing Marius. With the stove hidden, the room was now illuminated by the candle alone and the tiniest object on the table or mantelpiece cast a huge shadow. A water jug with a broken neck covered half a wall. There was a heavy menacing calm in the room. You could feel that something appalling beyond words was building.

Jondrette had let his pipe go out, a serious sign of intense preoccupation, and had come and sat back down again. The candle brought out the sharp angles of his face in all their savageness. He kept frowning furiously and abruptly opening his right hand as though responding to the final counsel of some somber inner monologue. In one of these obscure replies he was giving himself, he swiftly pulled out the table drawer, took out a long kitchen knife that was hidden there, and tested the blade on a fingernail. That done, he put the knife back in the drawer and pushed it shut.

Marius himself took hold of the pistol that was in his right fob pocket, pulled it out and cocked it. As he cocked it, the pistol made a small, clear, sharp sound. Jondrette jumped and half rose from his chair: "Who's there?" he shouted.

Marius held his breath, Jondrette listened for a second, then started to laugh: "What an idiot I am! It's only the wall creaking."

Marius kept the pistol in his hand.

## XVIII. THE FACE-OFF OF MARIUS'S TWO CHAIRS

All of a sudden, the distant and melancholy ringing of a bell rattled the windows. Six o'clock rang out at Saint-Médard.

Jondrette marked each stroke with a nod of the head. At the sixth stroke, he snuffed out the candle with his fingers. Then he began to circle the room, listened in the hall, walked a bit, listened again: "He'd better turn up!" he growled, before returning to his chair.

He had only just sat down again when the door opened. Mother Jondrette had opened it but remained in the hall, her face frozen in a hideous grimace of hospitality that one of the slits in the Chinese lantern lit from below.

"Come in, Monsieur," she said.

"Come in, my benefactor," Jondrette repeated, shooting to his feet.

Monsieur Leblanc appeared. He had an air of serenity that made him strangely venerable. He laid four louis on the table.

"Monsieur Fabantou," he said, "that is for your rent and your immediate needs. We'll see to the rest later."

"May God reward you, my generous benefactor!" said Jondrette; before rushing to his wife and whispering in her ear: "Send the cab away!"

She slipped away while her husband was bowing extravagantly and offering Monsieur Leblanc a chair. A moment later, she returned and whispered in his ear: "Done."

The snow that had not stopped falling all day was now so thick that none of them had heard the fiacre arrive, and they did not hear it leave.

Meanwhile, Monsieur Leblanc had taken a seat. Jondrette had taken possession of the other chair opposite Monsieur Leblanc.

Now, to truly grasp the scene that is about to unfold, the reader needs to get a clear picture of the freezing cold night, the vast expanses of La Salpêtrière covered in snow and looking as white, in the moonlight, as immense winding-sheets, the dim light of the streetlamps creating fuzzy reddish pools of light here and there along the mournful boulevards, and the long rows of black elms, not a living being out perhaps for a mile around, the old Gorbeau slum at its most intense pitch of silence, horror, and blackness, and inside this slum, in the middle of those expanses, in the middle of that darkness, the cavernous Jondrette garret lit by a single candle, and inside this dump, two men seated at a table, Monsieur Leblanc calm and tranquil, Jondrette smiling and terrifying, mother Jondrette, the she-wolf, in a corner, and on the other side of the dividing wall, Marius, on his feet, invisible, not missing a word, not missing a movement, his eye at the peephole, his pistol firmly in his grip.

Marius, in fact, felt only the emotion of horror, not fear. He held the butt of the pistol tightly and felt reassured. "I'll stop this miserable bastard when I'm good and ready," he thought.

He could sense that the police were there somewhere, lying in ambush, waiting for the agreed signal and ready to leap into action.

He hoped, too, that from this violent encounter between Jondrette and Monsieur Leblanc some light would be shed on all it was in his interests to find out.

## XIX. Dealing with the Darkest Depths

No sooner had Monsieur Leblanc sat down than he turned his eyes toward the pallets, which were empty.

"How is the poor little injured girl faring?" he asked.

"Badly," answered Jondrette, with a terribly distressed and grateful smile, "very badly, my worthy monsieur. Her older sister has taken her to the hospital in the rue Bourbe to be bandaged. You will see them, they will be back shortly."

"Madame Fabantou looks to me to be much better?" Monsieur Leblanc pursued, casting his eyes over the bizarre getup of mother Jondrette, who was standing between him and the door as though already guarding the exit, and studying him in a threatening, almost a fighting, stance.

"She is dying," said Jondrette. "But what can you do, Monsieur? She has so much courage, that woman! She's not a woman, she's an ox."

Mother Jondrette, touched by the compliment, protested with the affected simpering of a flattered monster: "You are too kind, Monsieur Jondrette!"

"Jondrette?" said Monsieur Leblanc. "I thought your name was Fabantou."

"Fabantou alias Jondrette!" the husband hastened to reply. "My stage name!"

And, giving his wife a shrug that Monsieur Leblanc did not see, he continued in a histrionic yet oily voice: "Ah, it's just that we have always gotten on so well together, that poor old darling and yours truly! What would we have left, if it weren't for that? Ours is a sorry lot, my estimable sir! We've got the hands, but no labor! We've got the heart, but no work! I don't know how the government does it, but, on my word of honor, Monsieur, I'm no Jacobin, Monsieur, I'm no troublemaker, I don't wish them any harm, but if I were the ministers, on my most sacred word, it'd be a very different story. Listen, here's an example: I wanted my girls to learn packing as a trade. You'll say to me: 'What! A trade?' Yes! A trade, a simple trade! A living! What a fall, my benefactor! What degradation, when you've been what we were! Alas, nothing's left of our days of prosperity! Nothing but one thing, a painting I'm very fond of, which I'd part with if I had to, though, for a person's got to live! I say again, a person's got to live!"

While Jondrette was rabbiting on incoherently in a way that sat oddly with the cool, calm, and collected expression on his face, Marius looked up and saw someone he had not yet seen at the back of the room. A man had come in, so quietly no one had heard the door turning on its hinges. This man had on a violet knitted waistcoat that was old, worn through, stained, cut off at the bottom, and gaping at the seams, baggy corduroy pants and, on his feet, soft-soled slippers; he had no shirt, his neck was bare, his arms were bare except for tattoos, and his face was daubed in black. He had sat down in silence with his arms folded on the nearest bed, and as he was sitting behind mother Jondrette, you could only dimly make him out.

The kind of magnetic instinct that alerts the eye made Monsieur Leblanc turn round almost at the same time as Marius. He could not help but give a start of surprise that did not escape Jondrette.

"Ah, I see!" cried Jondrette, buttoning himself up with an air of complacency. "You've noticed your overcoat? It suits me! My faith, it suits me down to the ground!"

"Who is that man?" said Monsieur Leblanc.

"That?" said Jondrette. "He's one of the neighbors. Don't take any notice."

The neighbor had a most peculiar appearance. But factories producing chemicals abound in the faubourg Saint-Marceau and a lot of factory workers get their faces blackened. Monsieur Leblanc's whole person, moreover, gave off a frank and fearless confidence. He went on: "Pardon me, what were you saying, Monsieur Fabantou?"

"I was saying, Monsieur, dear patron," Jondrette resumed, leaning on the table and contemplating Monsieur Leblanc with steady and tender eyes not unlike the eyes of a boa constrictor, "I was saying that I had a painting for sale."

A slight noise sounded at the door. A second man came in and sat on the bed, behind mother Jondrette; he, like the first, had bare arms and a mask of ink or soot. Although the man had, literally, slipped into the room, he could not prevent Monsieur Leblanc from spotting him.

"Don't mind them," said Jondrette. "They live in the place. So, as I was saying, I still have a painting, one precious painting, left . . . Look, Monsieur, see."

He got up, went to the wall where the panel we mentioned before was leaning, and turned it round the right way, though leaving it standing against the wall. The thing did actually resemble a painting, which the candle vaguely revealed. Marius couldn't see much, Jondrette having come between him and it; all he could make out was a splotchy background and a sort of central character colored in with the garish crudeness of fairground banners and screen paintings.

"What on earth is that?" asked Monsieur Leblanc.

Jondrette exclaimed: "An old master, a very valuable picture, my benefactor! I'm as fond of it as I am of my two daughters, it brings back such memories! But, I said it before and I'll say it again, I'm down on my luck at present, so I'm willing to part with it . . ."

Either by chance or because he was beginning to smell a rat, Monsieur Leblanc's gaze went to the back of the room while he examined the painting. There were now four men there, three sitting on the bed, one standing by the door, all four bare-armed, motionless, their faces painted black. One of the three on the bed was leaning against the wall with his eyes closed, and you would have sworn he was asleep. This particular man was old, the sight of his white hair on top of his black face was shocking. The other two seemed young. One of them had a beard, the other, long hair. None had shoes; those who didn't have socks were barefoot.

Jondrette noticed that Monsieur Leblanc was staring at the men.

"They're friends. They live around here," he said. "They're all black because they work in coal. They're chimney specialists. Don't you worry about them, my benefactor, but do buy my painting. Take pity on me in my misery. I'll give you a good price. What do you reckon it's worth?"

"But," said Monsieur Leblanc, staring hard at Jondrette now, as though he was beginning to be on his guard, "it's just some cabaret sign. It's worth all of three francs."

Jondrette replied sweetly: "Do you have your wallet with you? I'll be happy with a thousand écus."

Monsieur Leblanc got to his feet, put his back to the wall, and swiftly ran his eye around the room. He had Jondrette on his left on the window side and mother Jondrette and the four men on his right on the door side. The four men did not move a muscle and looked as though they hadn't even seen him; Jondrette had begun talking in a whining tone again, with such a clouded look in his eyes and in such a woeful manner that Monsieur Leblanc could believe that the man he had before him had, quite simply, gone mad with misery.

"If you don't buy my painting, dear benefactor," Jondrette wailed, "I'll be without resources, there'll be nothing left for me to do but throw myself in the river. When I think I wanted my two girls to go into the packing industry, making cardboard gift boxes for New Year's Day. All very well! But you have to have a table with a special panel at the bottom so the glass jars don't fall on the floor, you have to have a specially built stove, a pot with three compartments for heating the glue to the different degrees of strength it has to be depending on whether it's used for wood, paper, or fabric, you have to have cutters to cut the cardboard, molds to shape it, hammers to nail in the bits of steel, chisels, and pincers, heaven knows what else! And all that just to earn four sous a day! For fourteen hours' work! And every box passes through the worker's hands thirteen times! And you've got to keep the paper wet! And you can't get anything dirty! And you've got to keep the glue hot! It's hell, I tell you! All for a lousy four sous a day! How do you expect them to live?"

While he spoke, Jondrette was looking away from Monsieur Leblanc, who was watching him closely. Monsieur Leblanc's eyes were riveted on Jondrette and Jondrette's eyes were riveted on the door. Marius's breathless attention swung from one to the other. Monsieur Leblanc appeared to be wondering if the man was a cretin. Jondrette repeated two or three times, using all sorts of tonal variations within the same imploring, drawling style: "There's nothing left for me to do but throw myself in the river! The other day I went down three steps over by the pont d'Austerlitz with that in mind!"

Suddenly his dull eyes blazed with a hideous fire, the little man straightened up and became terrifying; he took a step toward Monsieur Leblanc and bellowed at him in a thundering voice: "But never mind all that! Don't you recognize me?"

## XX. The Ambush

The door of the garret had just swung open abruptly and revealed three men in blue canvas smocks wearing masks of black paper. The first was skinny and had a long cudgel with an iron tip, the second was a sort of colossus, carrying a poleax for slaughtering cattle, holding it by the middle of the handle with the hatchet part pointing downward. The third, a man with big broad shoulders, was bigger than the first but not as massive as the second, and he was holding an enormous key stolen from some prison or other in his clenched fist.

It looked as if it was the arrival of these men that Jondrette had been waiting for. A rapid dialogue broke out between him and the man with the cudgel, the skinny one.

"Everything ready?" asked Jondrette.

"Yes," answered the thin man.

"Where's Montparnasse, then?"

"The juvenile lead stopped for a bit of a chin-wag with your daughter."

"Which one?"

"The big one."

"Is there a cab down below?"

"Yes."

"The old rattletrap's hitched?"

"It's hitched."

"Two good horses?"

"The best."

"Waiting where I said to wait?"

"Yes."

"Good," said Jondrette.

Monsieur Leblanc was very pale. He looked everything over in the dump around him like a man who has finally realized where he has landed, and as he slowly turned his head to study the faces of all the men surrounding him, his movement showed alert amazement, but there was nothing in his manner that remotely resembled fear. Using the table as a makeshift entrenchment, this man who, only a moment before, looked like nothing more than a nice old gent, suddenly became a sort of athlete as he gripped the back of his chair with his powerful fist in a surprising and frightening gesture.

This old man, so strong and so brave in the face of such danger, looked to be one of those people who are as courageous as they are good—easily and simply. The father of a woman that we love is never a stranger for us. Marius felt proud of this man he didn't know.

Three of the bare-armed men Jondrette had described as "chimney specialists" had delved into the pile of scrap iron, one extracting some very large shears, another a pair of weighing tongs, the third a hammer, and they had then ranged themselves across the doorway without a word. The old one stayed where he was on the bed and merely opened his eyes. Mother Jondrette was sitting next to him.

Marius knew that the moment to intervene would arrive in a matter of seconds and he raised his right hand toward the ceiling, in the direction of the hall, ready to let fly with a pistol shot.

Jondrette had finished his confabulation with the man with the cudgel, and he now turned once more to Monsieur Leblanc and repeated his question, this time to the accompaniment of that awful low choking laugh of his: "So you really don't recognize me, then?"

Monsieur Leblanc looked him in the face and answered: "No."

Jondrette then bounded over to the table, leaned over the candle, folded his arms, and thrust his fierce angular jaw at the calm face of Monsieur Leblanc as closely as he could without Monsieur Leblanc's stepping back, and in this posture of a feral animal about to bite, he shouted: "My name is not Fabantou, my name is not Jondrette. My name is Thénardier! I'm the innkeeper of Montfermeil! Do you hear me? Thénardier! Now do you recognize me?"

An imperceptible flush passed over Monsieur Leblanc's face but he answered with his usual placidity, in his usual soft, steady voice: "No more than before."

Marius did not hear this reply. Anyone seeing him at that moment, in the dark, would have seen how wild-eyed, staggered, and stunned he had become. The moment Jondrette said: "My name is Thénardier," Marius's whole body had started shaking and he had fallen back against the wall as though he'd felt the cold blade of a sword run through his heart. Then his right arm, raised ready to release the signal shot, slowly dropped, and the moment Jondrette shouted, "Do you hear me? Thénardier!" Marius's failing fingers had nearly let go of the pistol. Jondrette, by revealing who he was, had not shaken Monsieur Leblanc, but he had shattered Marius. The name Thénardier, which Monsieur Leblanc did not seem to know, was known to Marius. Remember what the name meant to him! He had worn it over his heart, written as it was in his father's will! He wore it at the back of his mind, in the depths of his memory, in the form of this sacred command: "A man named Thénardier saved my life. If my son should meet him, he will do all he can for him." This name, as you will recall, had become an article of faith for him, engraved in his soul; he associated it with his father's name in religious worship. And now! Here he was! Here was this Thénardier, here was this innkeeper from Montfermeil he had searched for, high and low, in vain, for so long! He had at last found him—and how? This, his father's savior, was a crook! This man, to whom he, Marius, burned to dedicate himself, was a monster! This, Colonel Pontmercy's liberator, was in the process of committing some crime whose actual form Marius could not yet make out clearly but which looked like murder! And murder of whom? Good God! What a cursed fate! What a bitter mockery of fate! His father commanded him from beyond the grave to do everything he could for Thénardier. For four years, Marius had thought of nothing but how to acquit himself of his father's debt. And now, at the very moment he was about to deliver a brigand, in the middle of perpetrating a crime, to the legal authorities, destiny screamed at him: *But it's Thénardier!* When, at last, he could pay back the man who had saved his father's life, on the heroic field of Waterloo, in a storm of grapeshot, he was going to pay him back by delivering him to the scaffold! He had promised himself that, if ever he were to find this Thénardier, he would simply throw himself at his feet. And now, he had actually found him, but only to hand him over to the executioner! His father said to him: Help Thénardier! And he was to answer this adored and saintly voice by destroying Thénardier! His father would turn in his grave at the spectacle of the man who had snatched him from the jaws of death, at his own peril, executed in the place Saint-Jacques through the intervention of the son to whom he had bequeathed the man! What a mockery, to have so long worn over his breast his father's last wishes, written in his own hand, just to do the complete opposite so vilely! But, on the other hand, how could he witness this ambush and not stop it? Hell! How could he condemn the victim and spare the assassin? Could you be bound in any shape or form of gratitude to such a miserable bastard?

All the ideas Marius had entertained for the last four years were smashed to smithereens by this unexpected blow. He shuddered. It all depended on him. He held all these people in the palm of his hand, unbeknownst to them, as they jerked about, under his nose. If he fired a shot, Monsieur Leblanc would be saved and Thénardier sunk; if he didn't shoot, Monsieur Leblanc would be sacrificed and, who knows? Thénardier might get away. To send one down, or drop the other? Remorse either way. What was he to do? Which should he choose? To fail his most imperious memories, all those deep commitments he had made to himself, the most sacred duty, the most venerated text! To fail his father's will . . . Or let a crime go ahead! It seemed to him that, on one side, he could hear "his Ursula" imploring him to save her father and, on the other, the colonel commending Thénadier to his care. He felt as if he were going mad. His knees were buckling under him. And there was no time to decide, anyway, for the drama was racing ahead furiously, even as he looked on. It was like a whirlwind, which he thought he controlled but which was suddenly sweeping him away. He was on the point of passing out.

Meanwhile Thénardier—we will call him that and nothing else from now on—was pacing up and down in front of the table in a sort of panicky triumphant frenzy.

He wrapped his fist round the candle and plunked it down on the mantelpiece with such a violent thud that the wick nearly went out and hot wax flew over the wall.

Then he wheeled round on Monsieur Leblanc, frightening, and spat out these words: "The jig's up! Your goose is cooked! I'll have you for dinner!"

With that, he started pacing again, erupting like a volcano as he did so: "Ah!" he cried. "At last I've caught up with you again, Monsieur, the philanthropist! Monsieur, the threadbare millionaire! Monsieur, the giver of dolls! Old numskull! Ah, so you don't recognize me! No, I suppose you're not the one who came to Montfermeil, to my inn, eight years ago, the night before Christmas, 1823! You're not the one who took Fantine's kid, the Lark, from us! You're not the one who used to go around in a yellow coachman's greatcoat! Oh, no, not you! You even had a parcel of clothes in your hand just like here, this morning! Tell me, now, woman! It's a mania with him, it looks like, to carry parcels stuffed with blasted woolen stockings to other people's houses! Charitable old bastard, aren't you? Are you in the hosiery business, by any chance, Monsieur millionaire? You palm off the stuff you can't sell on the poor, saintly man! What a charlatan! Ah, you don't recognize me? Well, I recognize you! I recognized you right off, as soon as you stuck your nose in the door. Ah, at last you're about to see that it's not all roses, poking around other people's places like that, just because they happen to be inns, decked out in lousy old clothes, looking like such a pauper that you'd have given him a coin, pulling the wool over a person's eyes, acting the generous one, and then taking their livelihoods away, and making threats out in the woods. You'll see it's not enough that you come back later, when the people are ruined, bringing a dirty great overcoat that's too big for a person and a couple of flea-bitten hospital blankets, you old rogue, you old child-snatcher!"

He stopped and appeared to be talking to himself for a moment. You would have said his fury was subsiding, like the Rhône, rushing down some hole; then, as he finished off out loud the things he had been muttering to himself under his breath, he brought his fist down on the table and shouted: "And he looks so easygoing, too!"

And he yelled at Monsieur Leblanc: "Jesus wept! You had a good laugh at me back then, eh! You're the cause of all my woes! For fifteen hundred francs, you got hold of a girl I had who certainly had wealthy connections—she'd already brought me in a lot of cash. And when I was supposed to make enough out of her to live on all my life! A girl who would have paid me back for all I lost in that lousy fleapit of a pothouse where they made such a royal racket and where I ate up all my assets like a fool! Oh, I wish all the wine they drank in that dive was poison to the swine who drank it! But never mind! So tell me! You must have thought I was a real idiot when you went off with the Lark! You had your cudgel tucked away in the forest! You were the strongest, then. Well, it's time for revenge. I hold the winning cards today! You're done for, my good man! Oh, but I have to laugh. I do have to laugh. Look how he fell into the trap! I told him I was a performer, that my name was Fabantou, that I'd been onstage with Mamselle Mars, and Mamselle Muche, that my landlord wanted to be paid tomorrow, the fourth of February, and he didn't even twig that it's the eighth of January and not the fourth of February that's the last day of the quarter! Brainless goose! And what about the four lousy philippes he brings me! Louse! He wasn't even big enough to go up to a hundred francs! And the way he went along with my platitudes! I enjoyed that bit. I said to myself: Silly old goat! Go on, I've got you by the short and curlies now. I was licking your arse this morning! But I'm going to be chomping on your heart tonight!"

Thénardier stopped. He was out of breath. His narrow little chest was heaving like a smithy's bellows. His eyes were full of the ignoble jubilation of a weak, cruel, and cowardly creature, when it finally manages to bring to ground what it has feared, and insult what it has flattered—the joy of a dwarf stamping on Goliath's head, the joy of a jackal as it tucks into a sick bull, dead enough not to defend itself, alive enough to suffer still.

Monsieur Leblanc did not cut him off, but when he cut himself off, he said: "I don't know what you are talking about. You are mistaken. I am a very poor man, anything but a millionaire. I don't know you. You have me mixed up with someone else."

"Ah!" groaned Thénardier. "What garbage! You're sticking to your little story, are you! You're talking hogwash, old man! You don't remember, eh? You don't see who I am!"

"Pardon me, Monsieur," answered Monsieur Leblanc in a polite tone that, at such a moment, had a strange and powerful effect, "I see that you are a crook."

As we have all noticed, even the vilest beings have their susceptibilities; monsters are touchy. At the word *crook,* mother Thénardier shot up from the bed, Thénardier grabbed his chair as though he was about to break it in two with his bare hands. "Don't you move!" he yelled at his wife; then he turned to Monsieur Leblanc: "A crook! Yes, I know that's what you call us, you rich folk! Listen! It's true, I went bust, I'm now in hiding, I don't have a crust of bread, I don't have a sou, I'm a crook, all right! It's three days since I've eaten, I'm a crook! Ha! You keep your feet warm, you lot, you've got your fancy Sakoski loafers,[1] you've got your padded overcoats, like archbishops, you live on the first floor of houses that have porters, you eat truffles, you eat whole bunches of asparagus at forty francs a bunch in the month of January, green peas, you stuff your faces, and, when you want to know if it's cold out, you look in the newspaper to see what it says on the thermometer of Chevalier the engineer. Us lot, we're our own thermometers! We don't need to go and stand on the quai at the corner of the Tour de l'Horloge to see how many degrees below zero it is, we feel our blood freeze in our veins and ice bite into our hearts, and we say: There is no God! And you come creeping into our sties, yes, our sties, and call us crooks! But we will eat you! You poor little things, we will devour you! Monsieur millionaire! Let me tell you this: I was once set up in business, I was licensed, I was a voter, I'm a respectable citizen! I am! You, perhaps, are not!"

Here Thénardier took a step toward the men near the door and added, shaking: "When I think he's got the nerve to come here and speak to me as if I was a cobbler!"

Then he rounded on Monsieur Leblanc in a fresh burst of frenzy: "And let me tell you this, too, Monsieur philanthropist! I'm no sleazy sluggard, that I am not! I'm not some nonentity without a name who slinks into other people's houses and kidnaps children! I was once a French soldier, I'm a blasted veteran, I ought to be decorated! I was at Waterloo, you hear! And in that battle I saved a general called Count Someone-or-other! He told me his name; but his lousy voice was so weak I didn't catch it. All I heard was *mercy—merci!* I'd have preferred his name to this *merci* caper. Thanks, but no thanks. His name would have helped me find him again. This painting you see here, which was painted by

David at Bruqueselles,[2] do you know who it's a painting of? Yours truly. David wanted to immortalize that feat of arms. I've got the general on my back and I'm carrying him through the grapeshot. That's the story. He never even did anything for me, that particular general, never; he was no better than the rest of you! It didn't stop me from saving his life, but, at the risk of losing my own, and I've got documents to prove it coming out my pockets! I am a soldier of Waterloo, for crying out loud! And now that I've had the goodness to tell you all that, let's get it over with: I need money, I need a lot of money, I need an enormous amount of money, or I'll exterminate you, come hell or high water!"

Marius had managed to subdue his anguish and was listening hard. The last shred of doubt had now evaporated. This was indeed the Thénardier of the will. Marius winced at the man's attack on his father for ingratitude—which he had come fatally close to denying out loud. His confusion spiraled. Besides, in all Thénardier's words, in his tone, in his gestures, in his crazily flashing eyes, flaring at every word, in the whole explosion, an evil nature was on show, parading openly in a mix of bravado and abjectness, pride and pettiness, rage and silliness, in this whole chaotic jumble of real grievances and sham emotions, in the shamelessness of a vicious criminal savoring the voluptuous pleasure of violence, in this brazen nakedness of an ugly soul exposed to view, this conflagration of extreme suffering combined with extreme hate—in all of this, there was something hideous like evil yet poignant like truth.

The masterwork, this painting by David that he had proposed Monsieur Leblanc buy, was nothing other, as the reader will have guessed, than the sign from his old pothouse, painted, as you will recall, by the man himself, the sole bit of flotsam that he had saved from his shipwreck in Montfermeil.

As he had stopped blocking Marius's line of sight, Marius could now study the thing and in this mess of paint, he actually could make out a battle, a background of smoke and a man carrying another man. It was the group formed by Thénardier and Pontmercy—the savior-sergeant and the colonel he had saved. Marius more or less went into a delirium. The painting somehow restored his father to life and it suddenly stopped being the sign from the Montfermeil tavern to become a resurrection; in it a grave cracked open, a phantom rose to its feet, Marius could hear his blood thumping at his temples, he had the cannon of Waterloo in his ears, his bleeding father dimly painted on that sinister panel terrified him, he felt as though that amorphous blob was staring straight at him.

When Thénardier had gotten his breath back, he trained his bloodshot eyes on Monsieur Leblanc and said to him in a tight, low voice: "What have you got to say before we get to work on you?"

Monsieur Leblanc said nothing. In the middle of this silence, a hoarse voice threw in a grimly sarcastic remark from the hallway: "If you need any wood chopped, don't forget I'm here!"

It was the man with the poleax, having fun.

656 • *Les Misérables*

At the same time, an enormous dirty bristly face bobbed up at the door with a hideous grin that showed, not teeth, but fangs. It was the face of the man with the poleax.

"Why'd you take your mask off?" Thénardier barked at him in fury.

"So's I could laugh," the man replied.

For some moments, Monsieur Leblanc had apparently been closely following every move Thénardier made, while the latter, blinded and dazed as he was by his own rage, confidently stomped up and down the lair, knowing that the door was guarded and that nine armed men held one unarmed man captive, assuming mother Thénardier counted as only one man herself. As he shouted at the man with the poleax, he turned his back on Monsieur Leblanc.

Monsieur Leblanc seized the moment. He kicked the chair away with his foot, pushed the table away with his fist and, in a single bound, with wonderful agility, before Thénardier had time to turn round, he was at the window. It took him only a second to open it, hop onto the sill and step over. He was halfway out when six powerful fists grabbed him and yanked him violently back into the hole. The three "chimney specialists" had hurled themselves at him. At the same time, mother Thénardier had grabbed hold of his hair.

At the sound of a scuffle, the other thugs came running from the hallway. The old man on the bed, apparently half-drunk, got off the pallet and staggered over with a road-mender's hammer in his hand.

One of the "chimney specialists" whose candle lit up his smeared face and in whom Marius, despite the smear of paint, recognized Panchaud, alias Printanier, alias Bigrenaille, raised over Monsieur Leblanc's head a sort of club consisting of an iron bar with a knob of lead at each end.

Marius could hold out no longer. "Father," he silently prayed, "forgive me!" And his finger sought the trigger of the pistol. He was just about to fire a shot when Thénardier's voice rang out: "Don't hurt him!"

The victim's desperate bid to escape, far from exasperating Thénardier, had calmed him down. There were two men in Thénardier, the vicious thug and the crafty intriguer. Till that moment, in the first flush of triumph, with the prey brought down and no longer moving, the vicious thug had dominated; when the victim resisted and seemed to want to fight back, the crafty intriguer reappeared and took over.

"Don't hurt him!" he repeated. He didn't know it, of course, but the first positive result for him of this shift was to stop the cocked pistol from going off and to paralyze Marius, for whom the urgency disappeared. Faced with this new development, Marius could not see what was wrong with waiting a bit longer. Who was to say that some stroke of luck would not intervene and save him from the ghastly alternatives of letting Ursula's father perish or sinking the savior of his own father, the colonel?

A herculean struggle had begun. With a direct punch in the guts, Monsieur

Leblanc had sent the old man flying to the middle of the room, then with two backhanders he knocked two other assailants to the ground and pinned them, one under each of his knees; the poor scoundrels groaned under the pressure as though they were being squashed by a granite millstone; but the four others had seized the formidable old man by both arms and by the neck and were holding him hunched over the two flattened "chimney specialists." And so, mastering some and mastered by others, crushing those below and suffocating under those above, vainly endeavoring to shake off the blows raining down on him, Monsieur Leblanc disappeared beneath this horrible pile of thugs like a wild boar under a howling pack of mastiffs and bloodhounds.

They managed to throw him onto the bed next to the window and hold him at bay there. Mother Thénardier had not let go of his hair.

"You," Thénardier said to her, "stay out of it. You'll rip your shawl."

Mother Thénardier obeyed as the she-wolf obeys the wolf, with a growl.

"The rest of you," said Thénardier, "search him."

Monsieur Leblanc seemed to have abandoned the idea of resistance. They searched him. He had nothing on him except a leather purse that contained six francs and his handerkerchief. Thénardier shoved the hankie in his pocket.

"Jesus! No wallet?" he asked.

"No watch, either," answered one of the "chimney specialists."

"Just what you'd expect," murmured the masked man who held the big key, in the voice of a ventriloquist. "This one's an old bruiser from way back!"

Thénardier went over to the corner by the door, grabbed a bundle of ropes from the floor, and threw it to them.

"Tie him to the foot of the bed," he said. Then, seeing the old man was still sprawled across the floor from the punch Monsieur Leblanc had given him and was not moving, he said: "Boulatruelle's not dead, is he?"

"No," answered Bigrenaille, "he's drunk."

"Sweep him into a corner," said Thénardier.

Two of the "chimney specialists" pushed the drunk with their feet over to the heap of old scrap iron.

"Babet, what did you bring so many men for?" Thénardier said in a low voice to the man with the cudgel. "There's no point."

"What's a man to do?" replied the man with the cudgel. "They all wanted to be in on it. The season's slow. Business is bad."

The pallet Monsieur Leblanc had been thrown onto was a kind of hospital bed supported by four big, rough, uneven posts. Monsieur Leblanc did not struggle. The brigands tied him up good and tight, standing upright with his feet on the floor, to the bedpost farthest from the window and closest to the fireplace.

When the last knot had been tied, Thénardier pulled up a chair and sat almost facing Monsieur Leblanc. Thénardier was a different man now. Within a few seconds, his expression had shifted from unbridled violence to a calm and relaxed cunning. Marius hardly recognized, in this polite office clerk's smile, the almost bestial maw foaming away in a frenzy only a moment before. He studied this fantastic and alarming metamorphosis in amazement, feeling what any man would feel on seeing a tiger change into an attorney.

"Monsieur—" Thénardier began.

Waving away the brigands who still had their hands on Monsieur Leblanc, he said: "Back off a bit and let me have a chat with the gentleman."

They all stepped back toward the door.

"Monsieur, you were wrong to try and jump out the window. You could have broken a leg. Now, if you don't mind, we're going to have a quiet little chat. To start with, I must tell you something I've noticed and that is that you haven't yet let out the slightest protest."

Thénardier was right, this detail was accurate, though it had escaped Marius in his distress. Monsieur Leblanc had hardly uttered more than a few words, and that without raising his voice; even in his struggle with the six brigands by the window, he had kept profoundly, and strangely, silent. Thénardier went on: "My God! If you'd cried 'thief' for a bit, I wouldn't have found it out of place. 'Murder!' The word is used on occasion, and, for my part, I wouldn't have taken it amiss. It's only natural that a man make a bit of a racket when he finds himself with individuals who don't exactly inspire sufficient confidence. If you'd done that, we wouldn't have touched you. We wouldn't even have muzzled you. And I'll tell you why. It's because this room here is soundproof. That's all it's got going for it, but at least it has that. It's like a cellar. You could let a bomb off in here and all they'd hear at the nearest guardhouse would be a sound like a drunk snoring. In here a cannon would just go fizz and a roll of thunder would go puff. It's a handy little dive. But you didn't cry out, which was nice of you, my compliments; and I'll tell you what I conclude from that fact: My dear monsieur, when a man cries out, who comes? The police. And after the police? The law. So, as I say, you didn't let out a peep; and that's because you don't want to see the police and the law turn up here any more than we do. And that is because—I suspected as much a long time ago—you're hiding something and you want to keep it hidden. It looks like we've got a common interest. So surely we can come to some sort of an understanding."

While he spoke, Thénardier kept his eyes fixed on Monsieur Leblanc, looking daggers at him, for all the world as though he was trying to bore into his prisoner's very conscience. Moreover his language, though colored with a sort of mild, sly insolence, was reserved and very nearly refined and, in this miserable wretch who had been nothing but a thug a moment before, you now sensed the man who "once studied to be a priest."

The silence that the prisoner had maintained, the wariness he had shown that went as far as completely disregarding his own safety, the way he had resisted the natural impulse of anyone whose life is in danger, which is to cry for help—all this, we have to say, since it had now been called to his attention, posed a real problem for Marius and came as a painful shock.

Thénardier's observation, well founded as it was, further deepened for Marius the dense mystery in which this grave and strange figure to whom Courfeyrac had given the nickname of Monsieur Leblanc, concealed himself. But whatever he was, now when he was tied up with ropes, surrounded by homicidal maniacs and half-buried, so to speak, in a grave that was getting deeper under him at every instant, faced with both the fury and the calm of Thénardier, the man remained imperturbable; and Marius could not help but admire, at such a moment, that superbly melancholy face.

The man was evidently beyond the reach of horror or desperation. He was one of those men who can master shock in desperate situations. No matter how extreme the crisis, no matter how inevitable the disastrous outcome, there was no sense here of a drowning man opening startled eyes underwater as he went down for the last time.

Thénardier stood up quietly, went to the fireplace, removed the screen and stood it against the nearby pallet, thereby revealing the stove full of burning charcoal, in which the prisoner could see perfectly clearly the white-hot chisel, dotted here and there with little bright red stars.

Then Thénardier went back and sat very close to Monsieur Leblanc.

"To continue," he said, "we can come to an understanding. Sort things out amicably. I was wrong to fly off the handle a while ago, I don't know what I was thinking, I got carried away, I said things I should not have said. For instance, since you're a millionaire, I told you I demanded money, a lot of money, enormous amounts of money. But that would not be reasonable. My God, you could be as rich as you like, but you've still got your expenses, as who has not? I don't want to ruin you, after all I'm no bloodsucker. I'm not one of those people who make ridiculous demands, just because they have the advantage of the situation. Listen, I'll meet you halfway, I'll make a sacrifice on my side. All I need is two hundred thousand francs."

Monsieur Leblanc did not say a word. Thénardier went on: "You see I'm prepared to mix quite a bit of water with my wine. I don't know the state of your fortune, but I do know that you don't care too much for money, and an openhanded almsgiving man such as yourself can easily spare two hundred thousand francs for a family man who's not so lucky. Certainly you are reasonable, too, and you don't imagine that I'd go to all the trouble I've gone to today to organize this evening's little event, which is nice work in the opinion of all these gentlemen, just to wind up asking you for what it takes to go and get plastered on red wine at fifteen sous a glass and eat veal at Desnoyers.[3] Two hundred thousand francs, that's what this is worth. Once that trifle has been removed from your pocket, I assure you that'll be the end of it, we won't harm a hair on your head. You'll tell me: But I don't have two hundred thousand francs on me. Oh, I'm not excessive. I don't demand that. I ask you for one thing only. To be so good as to write what I will now dictate to you."

Here Thénardier broke off, then he added, emphasizing every word and throwing a smile in the direction of the stove: "I warn you that I won't accept that you don't know how to write."

A grand inquisitor would have envied that smile.

Thénardier pushed the table in toward Monsieur Leblanc, took the inkwell, a pen, and a sheet of paper from the drawer, which he left slightly open, and where the long blade of a knife gleamed. He placed the sheet of paper in front of Monsieur Leblanc.

"Write," he said.

The prisoner spoke at last: "How do you expect me to write? My hands are tied."

"That's true, sorry!" said Thénardier. "You're right there."

He turned to Bigrenaille: "Untie Monsieur's right hand."

Panchaud, alias Printanier, alias Bigrenaille carried out Thénardier's order. When the prisoner's right hand was free, Thénardier dipped the pen in the ink and handed it to him.

"Don't forget, Monsieur, that you are in our power, at our discretion, that no human authority can get you out of here, and that we would be really sorry to be forced to resort to unpleasant extremes. I know neither your name nor your address, but I warn you that you will remain tied up until the person charged with delivering the letter you are about to write has returned. Now have the kindness to write."

"What?" asked the prisoner.

"I'll dictate."

Monsieur Leblanc took up the pen. Thénardier began to dictate: "My daught—"

The prisoner started and looked up at Thénardier.

"Put 'my dear daughter,'" said Thénardier. Monsieur Leblanc did as he was told. Thénardier continued: "Come right away—"

He broke off:

"You're on close terms, aren't you? You use *tu*?"

"Who with?" asked Monsieur Leblanc.

"For Christ's sake! The little one, the Lark."

Monsieur Leblanc answered without showing the slightest emotion: "I don't know who you mean."

"Go on, anyway," said Thénardier, and he resumed the dictation: "Come right away. I need you urgently. The person who hands you this note is charged with bringing you to me. I'll be waiting for you. Come in all confidence."

Monsieur Leblanc wrote it all down. Thénardier went on: "No! Scratch out 'come in all confidence'; that might make her suspect that things are not so simple and might not inspire confidence."

Monsieur Leblanc crossed out the four words.

"Now," Thénardier pursued, "sign. What is your name?"

The prisoner put down the pen and asked: "Who is this letter for?"

"You know very well," answered Thénardier. "For the little one. I just told you."

It was obvious that Thénardier was avoiding naming the young girl in question. He said "the Lark," he said "the little one," but he did not say her name. This was the precaution a cunning man takes to keep his secret to himself in front of his accomplices. To say the name would be to hand "the whole affair" over to them and tell them more than they needed to know.

He resumed: "Sign. What is your name?"

"Urbain Fabre," said the prisoner.

Thénardier, catlike, thrust his hand into his pocket and whipped out the handkerchief taken from Monsieur Leblanc. He held it up to the candle, looking for the initials.

"*U.F.* Right you are. Urbain Fabre. So then, sign *U.F.*"

The prisoner signed.

"Since you need two hands to fold the letter, give it to me, I'll fold it."

That done, Thénardier went on: "Put the address: *Mademoiselle Fabre*, at your place. I know you don't live all that far from here, somewhere near Saint-Jacques-du-Haut-Pas, since that's where you go to mass every day, but I don't know which street. I see you appreciate your situation. As you didn't lie about your name, you won't lie about your address. You write it yourself."

The prisoner remained thoughtful for a moment, then he took up the pen and wrote: "Mademoiselle Fabre, care of Monsieur Urbain Fabre, rue Saint-Dominique d'Enfer, no. 17."

Thénardier seized the letter in a sort of feverish convulsion.

"Woman!" he cried.

Mother Thénardier came running.

"Here's the letter. You know what you have to do. There's a fiacre down below. Get going pronto and come back ditto."

And addressing the man with the poleax: "You, since you took your face mask off, you can go with the good woman. You can hop up the back of the fiacre. You know where you left the old rattletrap?"

"Yes," said the man.

And he dropped his poleax in a corner and followed mother Thénardier out.

As they were leaving, Thénardier stuck his head out the half-open door and shouted into the hall: "Whatever you do, don't lose that letter! Just remember, you've got two hundred thousand francs on you."

Mother Thénardier's raucous voice came back: "Don't worry. I stuck it between my jugs."

A minute had not elapsed when the crack of a whip was heard, growing fainter and then quickly dying away altogether.

"Good!" growled Thénardier. "They're off at a clip. If they keep trotting along like that, the good woman will be back in three quarters of an hour."

He brought his chair closer to the fireplace and sat down, folding his arms and holding his muddy boots up to the stove.

"My feet are cold," he said.

There were now only five thugs left in the rathole besides Thénardier and the prisoner. These men, with their masks or with the black slime covering their faces and turning them into colliers, negroes, or fiends, whatever you feared most, looked numb and forlorn, and you could feel that they were carrying out a crime as they would a household chore, quietly, without anger and without pity, with a sort of weariness. They were huddled together in a corner like brutes and they did not make a sound. Thénardier was warming his feet. The prisoner had relapsed into his taciturn state. A somber calm had succeeded the wild tumult that had filled the garret a few minutes before.

The candle, spreading out like a giant mushroom, barely lit the cavernous vastness, the fire had died down, and all these monstrous heads made deformed shadows on the walls and ceiling. The only noise that could be heard was the peaceful breathing of the old drunk who was now fast asleep.

Marius waited in a state of anxiety that grew more intense by the second. The enigma was more impenetrable than ever. Who was this "little one" that Thénardier had called the Lark? Was it "his Ursula"? The prisoner had not seemed to be moved by the name Lark and had answered as naturally as could be: "I don't know who you mean." On the other hand, the two letters *U.F.* were explained, they stood for Urbain Fabre, and Ursula's name was no longer Ursula. That was the thing Marius saw most clearly. A sort of ghastly fascination nailed him to the spot from which he looked down on the whole scene. He stood there, almost incapable of thinking or moving, as though annihilated by the sight of such abominable things up close. He waited, hoping for some incident, no matter what, unable to gather his wits and not knowing whose side to take.

"In any case," he said to himself, "if she is the Lark, I'll soon see, since mother Thénardier is bringing her here. Then it will all come out, I'll lay down my life and spill every drop of my blood if I have to, but I will save her! Nothing will stop me."

Nearly half an hour passed. Thénardier looked to be absorbed in some murky meditation; the prisoner did not stir. Yet Marius thought he could hear, intermittently and only for the last few moments, a faint dull noise coming from where the prisoner was.

All of a sudden, Thénardier addressed the prisoner: "Monsieur Fabre, listen, I may as well tell you right now."

Those few words seemed to prelude clarification. Marius cocked his ear. Thénardier went on: "The missus will come back, don't you worry. I believe the Lark truly is your daughter, and it seems only natural that you should hold on to her. Only, bear with me. With your letter, the wife is going to find her. I told the wife to get dolled up, as you saw, so the young lady will follow her without giving it a moment's thought. They'll hop in a cab together with my friend up behind. Somewhere beyond the barrière there is an old rattletrap hitched up to two very good horses. They'll take the young lady there. She'll get out of the fiacre. My friend will hop up in the rattletrap with her, and the wife will come back here and tell us: It's done. As for the young lady, they won't hurt her, the boneshaker will take her to a place where she'll be nice and cosy and, as soon as you've given me the paltry sum of two hundred thousand francs, she'll be handed back to you. If you have me arrested, my friend will finish off the Lark. There you have it."

The prisoner did not utter a word. After a pause, Thénardier went on: "It's simple, as you see. There'll be no harm done, if you don't want there to be any harm done. I'm just telling you how things stand. I'm warning you just so you know."

He stopped; the prisoner did not break the silence. Thénardier went on: "As soon as my missus comes back and tells me the Lark's on her way, we'll let you go and you'll be free to go home to bed. You see that we have no bad intentions."

Appalling images rolled across Marius's mind. Christ! So they weren't going to bring this girl they were kidnapping back here, then, after all? One of these monsters was going to cart her off into the darkness? Where?—And what if it was her! And it was clear that it was her! Marius felt his heart stop beating. What to do? Fire the pistol shot? Put all these miserable bastards into the hands of the law? But the hideous thug with the poleax would still be completely out of reach somewhere with the girl, and Marius thought about those words of Thénardier's whose murderous significance he had an inkling of: "If you have me arrested, my friend will finish off the Lark."

Now he felt himself held back not only by his father's will, but by his very love, by the danger she was in. This awful situation, which had already gone on for more than an hour, was changing every second. Marius had the strength to pass in review, one after the other, all the most distressing conjectures, searching for some hope and finding none. The tumult of his thoughts contrasted with the funereal silence of the lair.

In the middle of this silence, the sound of the stair door could be heard, opening, then shutting.

The prisoner jerked in his bonds.

"Here's the good woman now," said Thénardier.

He had barely finished when mother Thénardier, indeed, rushed into the room, flushed, winded, panting, her eyes ablaze, and shouted, whacking both her thighs at once with her huge hands: "False address!"

The thug that she had taken with her appeared behind her and came in to retrieve his poleax.

"False address?" repeated Thénardier.

She went on: "No one! Rue Saint-Dominique. No number seventeen, no Monsieur Urbain Fabre! No one's ever heard of him!"

She stopped, choking, then continued: "Monsieur Thénardier! This old geezer's put one over on you! You're too good, you see! Me, I'd have rearranged his mug for him, for starters! And if he turned nasty, I'd have roasted him alive! He would've had to talk then, and say where his daughter is, and say where the loot is! That's how I'd have gone about it, myself! No wonder they say men aren't as smart as women! No one there! No number seventeen! There's nothing but a great big porte cochère! No Monsieur Fabre, rue Saint-Dominique! And going flat out, and a tip for the driver, and everything! I spoke to the porter and his missus, who's a lovely stout woman, they don't know anything about him!"

Marius breathed again. She, Ursula, or the Lark, the one he no longer knew what to call, was safe.

While his exasperated wife stormed, Thénardier took a seat at the table; he stayed for a few moments without uttering a word, swinging his right leg which was dangling, and studying the stove with a look of savage concentration. Finally he said to the prisoner in a slow and oddly ferocious tone: "A false address? What were you hoping to gain?"

"Time!" cried the prisoner in an explosive voice.

And at the same time he shook off his bonds; they had been cut. The prisoner was no longer tied to the bed except by a leg.

Before the seven men had time to recover their wits and lunge at him, he ducked down under the mantel to the fireplace, extended his hand toward the stove, then straightened up, and now Thénardier, mother Thénardier, and the thugs, driven by the shock to the back of the rathole, watched in stupefaction as he raised the red-hot chisel, throbbing with a sinister glow, above his head, almost free and most menacing.

The judicial inquiry, to which the ambush in the old Gorbeau building eventually gave rise, revealed that a retooled one-sou coin, cut and worked in a particular way, was found in the garret when the police descended on it. This retooled sou was one of those marvels of patient industry that the galleys foster in the dark and for the dark, marvels that are nothing less than the instruments of escape. These dreadful yet delicate products of a prodigious art are to jewelry what the metaphors of slang are to poetry. There are Benvenuto Cellinis behind bars, just as there are Villons[4] in the local patois. The poor unfortunate wretch who aspires to deliverance finds the means, sometimes without any tools beyond a pocketknife or an old razor blade, to saw a sou into two thin sections, two discs, to then hollow out these two sections without touching the imprint of the mint, and to cut a screw thread along the edge of the sou in such a way that the sections screw back together again. This device can be screwed and unscrewed at will; it is a box. In this box, you can hide a watch spring, and this watch spring, properly handled, can cut through standard-size shackles and iron bars. You think this poor unfortunate convict has only a sou to his name; not so, he has liberty. It was a retooled sou of the kind that, in later police searches, was found lying open in two pieces in the rathole under the pallet next to the window. They also found a little blue steel saw that could be hidden in the retooled sou. It is likely that when the bandits were rifling through the prisoner's pockets, he had this retooled sou on him and managed to hide it in his hand, and that afterward, with his right hand free, he managed to unscrew it and used the saw to cut through the ropes tying him. This would explain the faint noise and barely perceptible movements Marius had picked up.

Not being able to bend down for fear of giving himself away, he had not cut the rope around his left leg.

The bandits had recovered from their initial surprise.

"Don't worry," said Bigrenaille to Thénardier. "We've still got him by a leg, he won't be going anywhere. Take my word for it. I'm the one who trussed up his paw for him."

But the prisoner spoke up: "You are poor worthless wretches, but my own life is not worth being so heavily guarded. As for imagining that you'll make me talk, that you'll make me write anything I don't want to write, that you'll make me say anything I don't want to say—"

He rolled up the sleeve of his left arm and added: "Watch this."

He instantly held out his arm and, holding the chisel by the wooden handle in his right hand, placed the burning chisel on his naked flesh.

You could hear the hiss of burning flesh; the smell peculiar to torture chambers spread through the sty. Marius tottered, faint with horror, the thugs themselves shuddered, the face of the strange old man barely contracted, and, while the red-hot iron dug deeper into the smoking wound, imperturbable and almost regal, he fixed his beautiful eyes on Thénardier. There was no hate there and pain had melted into a serene majesty.

In great and exalted natures, physical pain brings out the soul, through the revolt of the flesh and the senses against it. The soul appears on the face, just as mutinies of the soldiery force the captain to show himself in his true colors.

"Poor devils," he said. "Don't be any more afraid of me than I am of you."

And lifting the chisel off his wound, he hurled it out the open window; the horrible glowing tool disappeared, spiraling off into the night to fall in the distance and be extinguished by the snow.

The captive went on: "Do what you like with me."

He was unarmed.

"Grab him!" said Thénardier.

Two of the brigands clapped their hands on his shoulders and the masked man with the ventriloquist's voice stood facing him, ready, at the slightest movement, to smash his skull in with a blow of the giant key.

At the same time, Marius heard below him, at the foot of the dividing wall, but so close that he couldn't see them talking, this hushed exchange: "There's only one thing to do."

"Slit his throat!"

"That's it."

It was the husband and wife holding counsel. Thénardier walked slowly round the table, opened the drawer, and took out the knife.

Marius was tormenting the butt of the pistol. Unbearable dilemma. For an hour now, there had been two voices in his conscience, one telling him to respect his father's will, the other screaming at him to come to the prisoner's rescue. Those two voices continued to tear at him without letup, and he was in agony. He had vaguely hoped up to that point to find a way of reconciling the two duties, but nothing had occurred. Meanwhile, the danger was urgent, the point of no return had been reached while he dithered only feet away from the captive. Thénardier, knife in hand, was working out what to do.

Marius cast his eyes wildly around him; the last, automatic resort of despair. Suddenly he jumped.

At his feet, on the table, the full moon directed a bright beam right onto a piece of paper, as though pointing it out to him. On this sheet of paper he read this line written in capital letters that very morning by the elder of the Thénardier girls: "THE COPS ARE HERE."

An idea flashed through Marius's mind; this was the opportunity he had been waiting for, the solution to the ghastly dilemma torturing him: how to spare the assassin and save the victim. He knelt down on the chest of drawers, reached out and grabbed the note, quietly tore a bit of plaster from the dividing wall and threw the lot through the crevice into the middle of the rathole.

It was high time. Thénardier had overcome his last fears, or scruples, and was about to lunge at the prisoner.

"Something fell!" cried mother Thénardier.

"What is it?" asked Thénardier.

The woman had lurched forward and picked up the chunk of plaster wrapped in the note.

She handed it to her husband.

"Where'd this come from?" asked Thénardier.

"Lord spare us!" said the woman. "Where do you think it came from? It came through the window."

"I saw it go past," said Bigrenaille.

Thénardier rapidly unfolded the note and brought it over to the candle.

"It's Éponine's writing. Jesus!"

He signaled to his wife, who came running, and after he showed her the line written on the piece of paper, he added in a muffled voice: "Quick, the ladder! We'll leave the cheese in the mousetrap and clear out!"

"Without cutting that bastard's throat for him?" gasped mother Thénardier.

"We don't have time."

"Which way?" added Bigrenaille.

"Through the window," answered Thénardier. "Since Ponine threw the stone through the window, that means the house isn't covered on that side."

The mask with the ventriloquist's voice threw his giant key to the ground and lifted both arms in the air without a word. This was like the signal for the crew to clear the decks. The brigands holding the prisoner let go of him; in the blinking of an eye, the rope ladder was unfurled out the window and solidly attached to the sill by means of the two iron hooks.

The prisoner paid no attention to what was happening around him. He seemed to be either dreaming or praying. As soon as the ladder was in place, Thénardier yelled: "Come on, missus!"

And he rushed to the casement window. But just as he was about to climb over it, Bigrenaille grabbed him roughly by the collar.

"Oh, no you don't, you old joker! Us first!"

"Us first!" shouted the thugs.

"Now, now, children," said Thénardier, "we're losing time. The flatfeet are at our heels."

"Well, then," said one of the thugs, "let's draw lots to see who goes first."

Thénardier exploded:

"You're mad! You're insane! What a pack of mugs! You want to lose time? Why don't we draw lots while we're at it? Shall we use a wet finger! Or the short straw! Write our names down! Put 'em in a hat!—"

"Would you like my hat?" cried a voice from the door.

Everyone wheeled round. It was Javert.

He had his hat in his hand and held it out, smiling.

## XXI. YOU SHOULD ALWAYS ARREST THE VICTIMS FIRST

As night came down, Javert had posted himself and his men behind the trees on the rue de la Barrière-des-Gobelins, where they were hidden opposite the old

Gorbeau slum on the other side of the boulevard. He had begun by opening his "bag," hoping to drop in the two young girls who were supposed to be on surveillance outside the rat's nest of a building. But he only managed to bag Azelma. As for Éponine, she was not at her post, she had vanished, and so he was not able to nab her. Javert then went into pointer mode and stood listening for the agreed signal. The comings and goings of the fiacre had really stirred him up. Finally, he couldn't stand it any longer, and "since there was bound to be a nest there," since he was "bound to be in luck," having recognized several of the bandits who had gone in, he had finally decided to go up without waiting for the pistol shot.

You will recall that he had Marius's skeleton key.

He had come just in the nick of time.

The frightened bandits hurled themselves on the weapons they had dropped willy-nilly as they were about to make good their escape. In less than a second, these seven men, so dreadful to look at, had formed into a defensive position, one with his poleax, another with his key, another with his club, the others with chisels, pincers, and hammers, Thénardier with his knife in his hand. Mother Thénardier picked up an enormous cobblestone that was in a corner by the window and that served her daughters as a stool.

Javert clapped his hat back on his head and took two steps into the room, arms folded, cane under his arm, sword sheathed in its scabbard.

"Stop right there!" he cried. "You will not leave by the window, you will leave by the door. It's less dangerous to life and limb. There are seven of you, there are fifteen of us. Let's not get into a brawl like a lot of hayseeds from Auvergne. Let's be nice."

Bigrenaille grabbed a pistol that he kept hidden in his smock and put it in Thénardier's hand, whispering in his ear: "It's Javert. I don't dare shoot at that man. Do you?"

"For Christ's sake!" replied Thénardier.

"Well, then, shoot."

Thénardier took hold of the pistol and aimed at Javert. Javert, who was only three feet away, looked him steadily in the eye and merely said: "Don't shoot, please! You'll miss."

Thénardier pulled the trigger. He missed.

"What did I tell you!" said Javert.

Bigrenaille threw his club at Javert's feet.

"You're the devil's emperor! I surrender."

"And you?" Javert asked the other bandits. They answered: "We do, too."

Javert calmly went on: "That's it, that's good, as I was saying, we can be nice."

"There's just one thing I'd like to ask for," Bigrenaille went on, "and that is that I'm allowed tobacco when I'm inside in solitary."

"Granted," said Javert.

Then he turned round and called out behind him: "You can come in now!"

A squad of police constables with swords drawn and officers armed with clubs and cudgels rushed in at Javert's summons. They tied the bandits up. This horde of men, dimly lit by a single candle, filled the lair with shadows.

"Cuff all of them!" shouted Javert.

"Just you try it!" shouted a voice that was not the voice of a man but that no one could say was a woman's voice.

Mother Thénardier had taken refuge in a corner of the window and it was she who had let out this roar. The constables and officers shrank back. She had thrown off her shawl but kept her hat on; her husband, crouching behind her, almost vanished under the discarded shawl and she covered him with her body, holding the cobblestone with both hands above her head with the poise of a giant about to launch a rock.

"Stand back!" she roared.

They all backed off toward the hall. A large gap was left in the middle of the garret. Mother Thénardier threw a look at the bandits who had gotten themselves tied up and growled in a raucous gutteral voice: "Cowards!"

Javert smiled and stepped forward into the empty space that mother Thénardier had covered.

"Get back," she yelled, "or I'll knock your block off."

"What a trooper!" said Javert. "Listen, old duck! You may have a beard like a man but I've got claws like a woman."

And he continued to advance toward her.

Mother Thénardier, frantic and terrible, spread her legs, bent backward, and furiously hurled the cobblestone at Javert's head. Javert ducked, the cobblestone flew over him, hit the back wall, taking out a huge chunk of plaster, and then bounced back, ricocheting from corner to corner across the room, which was happily almost empty, to come to rest just behind Javert.

At the same moment, Javert made it to the Thénardier couple. One of his huge hairy hands came down on the wife's shoulder, the other on the husband's head.

"Cuffs!" he shouted.

The police officers returned in block formation and within a few seconds Javert's order had been executed. Mother Thénardier, broken, gazed at her bound hands and those of her husband, then dropped to the ground and howled through tears: "My daughters!"

"They're out of harm's way."

Meanwhile the officers had spotted the drunk asleep behind the door and were shaking him. He woke up, stammering: "Is it over, Jondrette?"

"All over," answered Javert.

The six manacled bandits were on their feet; but they still had their ghost faces on; three smeared with black, three masked.

"Leave your masks on," said Javert.

And, passing them in review with the eye of Frederick II on parade at Potsdam,[1] he said to the three "chimney specialists": "Hello, Bigrenaille. Hello, Brujon. Hello, Deux-milliards."

Then he turned to the three masks and said to the man with the poleax: "Hello, Gueulemer."

And to the man with the cudgel: "Hello, Babet."

And to the ventriloquist: "Hello, there, Claquesous."

It was only then that he noticed the bandits' prisoner who, since the police arrived on the scene, had just stood with his head down, not uttering a word.

"Untie monsieur!" said Javert. "And don't anyone leave!"

That said, he sat with sovereign authority at the table, where the candle and the writing set still stood, pulled out a stamped sheet of official letterhead from his pocket, and started on his report. When he had written the first few lines, standard formulae that never vary, he looked up: "Bring this gentleman they tied up over here."

The officers looked around.

"Well," said Javert. "Where's he got to?"

The bandits' prisoner, Monsieur Leblanc, Monsieur Urbain Fabre, the father of Ursula or the Lark, had vanished.

The door was guarded but the window was not. The very instant he found himself untied, while Javert was busy making out his report, he had taken advantage of the confusion, the clamor, the crowd, the darkness, and of a moment when attention was not fixed on him, to leap out the window. One of the officers ran over and looked. Not a soul could be seen outside. The rope ladder was still swinging.

"Christ!" Javert hissed between his teeth. "He must have been the best of the lot!"

## XXII. THE LITTLE BOY[1] WHO CRIED OUT IN PART THREE

The day after these events took place in the house on the boulevard de l'Hôpital, a child, who seemed to come from the pont d'Austerlitz, walked up the side path on the right heading for the barrière de Fontainebleau. Night had closed in. This child was pale, thin, dressed in rags, with only cotton pants in the middle of February, and he was singing at the top of his lungs.

At the corner of the rue du Petit-Banquier, an old crone was foraging around in a pile of rubbish by the light of a streetlamp; as he passed, the child bumped into her and leaped back saying: "Hey! And here's me thinking it was an enormous, ENORMOUS dog!"

He uttered the word *enormous* for the second time with an exaggerated snicker that only capital letters could do justice to.

The old woman straightened up, furious.

"Rotter of a kid!" she growled. "If I hadn't been bending over, I know where I'd've planted my foot!"

The child was already well out of reach.

"Kiss, kiss!" he said. "Anyway, I wasn't far off the mark!"

The old woman stood straighter, choking with indignation, and the red glare of the lantern brightly lit her livid face, bringing out all the hollows and sharp angles and lines and crow's-feet that ran all the way down to the corners of her mouth. Her body disappeared in the shadows and all that could be seen of her was her head. You would have said she was the very mask of Decrepitude, picked out by a glimmer of light in the night. The child studied her.

"Madame," he said, "is really not my type, as far as beauty goes."

He turned and went on his way again, singing this song:

King Get-the-boot-in
Went a' huntin',
A' huntin' crows . . .[2]

At the end of those three lines, he broke off. He had arrived at no. 50–52, and finding the door closed, had started battering it with kicks, kicks resounding and heroic, which owed rather more to the men's shoes he was wearing than the child's feet he was endowed with.

Meanwhile, the same old crone he had encountered at the corner of the rue du Petit-Banquier was running after him, shouting her head off and flailing her arms about frantically.

"What's going on? What's going on? Good Lord! Someone's breaking the door down! They're knocking the house down!"

The kicking continued. The old woman was yelling at the top of her voice.

"Look how they treat buildings nowadays!"

Suddenly she stopped short. She had recognized the gamin.

"So it's you, you little devil!"

"Well, well, if it isn't the old girl," said the child. "Hello, mother Burgonsky. I've come to see my ancestors."

The old woman responded with a complex grimace, an admirable improvisation of hatred that made the most of ugliness and decay, which was unfortunately lost in the dark: "There's no one there, you little lout."

"Bah!" the child replied. "So where's my father, then?"

"In the clink—at La Force."

"Well, well! And my mother?"

"At Saint-Lazare."[3]

"You don't say! And my sisters?"

"In Les Madelonnettes."[4]

The child scratched the back of his ear, looked at Ma Bougon, and said: "Ah!"

Then he spun on his heel, and a moment later the old woman, still standing on the doorstep, heard him singing in his clear young voice again as he dived under the elm trees swaying in the winter wind:

> King Get-the-boot-in
> Went a' huntin',
> A' huntin' crows,
> Mounted on stilts.
> You ducked under 'im,
> An' you paid 'im two sous.[5]

# PART FOUR

# The Idyll of the Rue Plumet and the Epic of the Rue Saint-Denis

# BOOK ONE

# A FEW PAGES OF HISTORY

## I. WELL CUT

The two years 1831 and 1832, following hot on the heels of the July Revolution,[1] make up one of the most peculiar and most striking moments in history. These two years, seen between those that came before and those that came after, are like two mountains. They have revolutionary grandeur. You can make out sheer precipices in them. The social masses, the very bedrock of civilization, the solid cluster of interests, layered yet sticking together, the secular strata of the ancient formation of France, all appear and disappear there at every instant through the stormy clouds of systems, passions, and theories. These appearances and disappearances have been named resistance and movement. At intervals we see truth, that sunshine of the human soul, glimmering away there.

This remarkable epoch is fairly circumscribed and is now far enough away from us for us to be able to seize the main outlines.

This, we will try to do.

The Restoration had been one of those intermediary phases that are hard to define, in which there is weariness, buzzing, murmuring, dozing, uproar all at once—phases that are nothing more or less than a great nation coming to a standstill. These epochs are singular and manage to baffle politicians who hope to exploit them. In the beginning, the nation demands only rest; there is only one thirst, for peace; there is only one ambition, to be small. Which is a translation for being quiet. People have had enough of great events, great risks, great adventures, and more than enough, Lord knows, of great men; they are sick and tired of them. They would swap Caesar for Prusias, and Napoléon for the king of Yvetot[2]—"What a good little king he was!" They have been marching since first light, they have come to the end of a long, hard day; they did the first stretch with Mirabeau, the second with Robespierre, the third with Bonaparte; they are absolutely worn to a frazzle. Everyone wants to go to bed.

Weary devotions, worn-out heroisms, sated ambitions, fortunes made, all search, clamor, beg, implore—for what? A place to rest. They have it. They take possession of peace, of tranquillity, of leisure, move in and are content. Yet at the same time certain facts crop up, make themselves known, knock on the door to be let in, too. These facts emerge from revolutions and wars, they exist, they are alive, they have the right to settle in to society and they do settle in; and most of the time the facts are sergeants and billeting officers simply getting the billet ready to accommodate principles.

So this is what appears to political philosophers:

At the same time that tired people demand rest, established facts demand guarantees. Guarantees are to facts what rest is to people.

That is what England demanded of the Stuarts after the Protector;[3] it is what France demanded of the Bourbons after the Empire.

These guarantees are a necessity of the times. They must be extended. Princes "grant" them but in reality it is the force of circumstances that gives them. This is a profound and useful truth to know, one the Stuarts did not have an inkling of in 1660 and the Bourbons did not have a clue about even in 1814.

The fated family that came back to France when Napoléon went down had the fatal naïveté to believe that they were the ones doing the giving, and that what they had given, they could take back; that the House of Bourbon had divine right, that France had nothing; and that the political rights conceded in Louis XVIII's Charter were nothing more than a branch of divine right, snapped off by the House of Bourbon and graciously given to the people until such time as it should please the king to grab it back. Yet, from the displeasure that the gift cost them, the House of Bourbon should have realized that it was not theirs to give.

The Bourbons were very bad-tempered in the nineteenth century. They pulled a sour face at every flourishing of the nation. To use a trite word, which is to say a popular and a true one, they balked. The people couldn't help but notice.

They thought they were strong because the Empire had been swept away before them like a theater set. They didn't see that they had themselves been swept onto the stage in the same way. They didn't see that they were in the same hands that had cleared Napoléon out.

They thought they had roots because they were the past. They were wrong; they were part of the past, but the whole of the past was France. The roots of French society did not lie in the Bourbons but in the nation. These obscure and vigorous roots did not constitute the right of one family, but the history of a people. They were everywhere—except beneath the throne.

The House of Bourbon was for France the illustrious and bloody heart of its history, but it was no longer the main element in its destiny or the essential basis of its politics. The Bourbons could be done without; the Bourbons had been done without for twenty-two years; there had been a break in continuity; this never occurred to them. And how could it occur to them, they who imagined that Louis XVII reigned on the ninth of Thermidor[4] and that Louis XVIII reigned on the day Marengo took place? Never, since the beginning of history, had princes been so blind in the face of the facts and of the portion of divine authority that the facts contain and promulgate. Never before had this pretention here below known as the right of kings denied to such an extent the right that comes from on high.

A capital error that led this family to lay its hand once more on the guarantees "granted" in 1814—concessions, as they called them. Sadly enough! What they called their concessions were actually our conquests. What they called our infringements were actually our rights.

When the time seemed ripe, the Restoration, assuming it had beaten Bonaparte and that it had roots in the nation, that is, believing itself to be strong and believing itself to run deep, suddenly came out and risked its coup. One morning it rose up and faced France head on, and, raising its voice, it disenfranchised the collective and the individual, it contested the sovereignty of the nation and the liberty of the citizen. In other words, it denied the nation what made it a nation, and the citizen what made them a citizen.

This is the essence of the famous decrees known as the July Ordinances.[5]

The Restoration fell.

And rightly so. But, we have to say, it had not been absolutely hostile to all forms of progress. Great things had been done while it sat on the sidelines.

Under the Restoration the nation had grown accustomed to calm discussion, something that was missing in the Republic; and to greatness in times of peace, something that was missing in the Empire. France, free and strong, had been an encouraging spectacle for the other peoples of Europe. The Revolution had had its say under Robespierre; the cannon had had its under Bonaparte; under Louis XVIII and Charles X it was intelligence's turn to hold the floor. The wind died down, the torch flared up again. The pure light of intellect was seen flickering on serene mountaintops. A magnificent spectacle, useful and lovely. For fifteen years, in complete peace and completely in public, these great principles, so old for the thinker, so new for the statesman—equality before the law, freedom of conscience, freedom of speech, freedom of the press, and equal accessibility to all positions for people at all levels of ability—were seen at work. This lasted until 1830. The Bourbons were an instrument of civilization that broke in the hands of Providence.

The fall of the Bourbons was full of greatness—not on their side, but on the side of the nation. They stepped down from the throne with gravity, but without authority; their descent into the night was not one of those solemn disappearances that leave history with a somber feeling; it did not have either the spectral calm of Charles I,[6] or Napoléon's eagle cry. They went, that's all. They laid down the crown and did not keep the aura. They were dignified, but they were not august. They failed to live up to the majesty of their misfortune. On the long trip to Cherbourg, Charles X, having a round table cut into a square table,[7] seemed more worried about imperiled etiquette than about the crumbling monarchy. This decline saddened the devoted men who loved them personally and the serious men who honored their race. But the people were wonderful. Attacked one morning by force of arms in a sort of royal insurrection, the nation felt so strong that it had no anger. It defended itself, restrained itself, put things back in their place—the government in the hands of the law, the Bourbons, alas! in exile—and stopped there. It removed old king Charles X from under the canopy that had sheltered Louis XIV and gently set him down on the ground. It handled royal persons only in sorrow and with care. It was not just one man, it was not just a few men, it was France, the whole of France, France victorious and intoxicated with its victory, that seemed to remember and put into practice before the eyes of the whole world these grave words of Guillaume du Vair after the Day of the Barricades:[8] "It is easy for those who are accustomed to skimming the favors of the great, and to flitting like birds from branch to branch, from a grievous to a flourishing fortune, to show themselves bold toward their prince in his adversity; but to me the fortune of my kings will always deserve reverence, especially in their grief."

The Bourbons took respect with them, but not regret. As we said, their misfortune was greater than they were. They sank out of sight below the horizon.

The July Revolution immediately had friends and enemies throughout the entire world. Some rushed to embrace it with enthusiasm and joy, others turned their backs on it, each according to their nature. At the outset, the princes of Europe, owls at this dawn, closed their eyes, hurt and stunned, and only opened them again to issue threats. Understandable fear, excusable rage. This strange revolution had scarcely amounted to a clash; it had never even paid vanquished royalty the honor of treating it as an enemy and shedding its blood. In the eyes of despotic governments, which are always counting on liberty slandering itself, the July Revolution made the mistake of being formidable but remaining mild. Nothing, moreover, was attempted or plotted against it. The most dissatisfied, the most irate, the most tremulous, embraced it. However selfish and bitter we may be, a mysterious respect attends events in which we feel the collaboration of someone working on a higher plane than man.

The July Revolution is the triumph of right bringing down might. A thing full of splendor.

Right bringing down might. Hence the brilliance of the 1830 revolution, hence its goodwill, too. Right that triumphs has no need to be violent.

Right is what is just and true.

The peculiarity of right is to remain eternally beautiful and pure. Might, even the most apparently necessary, even the most accepted by contemporaries, if it exists only as might and if it contains all too little right or no right at all, is infallibly doomed to become warped, vile, maybe even monstrous over time. If you want to gauge in a glance the degree of ugliness that might can achieve, viewed at a distance of centuries, just look at Machiavelli.[9] Machiavelli was not an evil genius, or a fiend, or a miserable coward of a writer; he is nothing but might. And not just Italian might, but European might, sixteenth-century might. He seems hideous, and so he is, in the light of nineteenth-century moral notions.

This struggle between right and might has been going on ever since society began. To end the duel, to meld the pure ideal with human reality, to peacefully rub right into might and might into right—this is the work of the wise.

## II. BADLY STITCHED TOGETHER

But the work of the wise is one thing, the work of the clever is something else again.

The revolution of 1830 rapidly came to a halt.

As soon as a revolution runs aground, the clever carve up the wreck.

The clever, in our century, have given themselves the title of statesmen, so much so that the term *statesman* has wound up being something of a slang word. We should not forget, in fact, that wherever there is only cleverness, there is necessarily pettiness. To say "the clever" is the same as saying "the mediocre."

Similarly, saying "statesmen" is sometimes the equivalent of saying "traitors."

And so, if you believe the clever, revolutions such as the July Revolution are like severed arteries; prompt ligature is required. Right, too grandly proclaimed, is disturbing. So once right has been asserted, the state must be shored up. Liberty being assured, power must be looked to.

Here the wise have not yet parted ways with the clever, but they have begun to smell a rat. Power, so be it. But, first, what is power? Second, where is it coming from?

The clever do not seem to hear this murmured objection and they carry on with their maneuvers.

According to these politicians, so ingenious at wrapping profitable fictions in the cloak of necessity, the first thing a nation needs after a revolution, when this nation is part of a monarchic continent, is to get itself a dynasty. In this way, they reckon, it can have peace after its revolution, that is, time to bandage its wounds and get its house in order. The dynasty hides the scaffolding and covers the ambulance.

Well, it isn't always easy to get yourself a dynasty.

At a pinch, the first man of genius or even the first man of fortune who happens along will do as a king. In the first case, you have Bonaparte and in the second, Iturbide.[1]

But the first family that happens along is not enough to make a dynasty. There is necessarily a certain amount of antiquity in a race and the wrinkles of centuries cannot be improvised.

If you look at it from the point of view of "statesmen," with, of course, all due reservations, after a revolution, what are the features of the king who emerges from it? He may be, and it is useful if he is, himself a revolutionary, meaning that he has taken part in this revolution in person, actively, that he has either compromised himself or distinguished himself in it, that he has either handled an ax or wielded a sword.

What are the features of a dynasty? It should be national, meaning remotely revolutionary, not because of any deeds performed, but because of ideas accepted. It should be made up of the past and so be historic, and made up of the future and so be sympathetic.

All this explains why the first revolutions were content just to find a man, a Cromwell or a Napoléon; and why the next revolutions insisted on finding a family, a House of Brunswick[2] or a House of Orléans.

Royal houses are like those Indian fig trees whose every branch hangs down all the way to the ground and takes root there to become itself a fig tree. Every last branch can turn into a dynasty. On the sole condition of reaching down all the way to the people.

That is the theory of the clever.

And this is the great skill of alchemy: to make a success look like a catastrophe so that those who benefit from it also quake in their boots over it, to season any step forward with fear, to increase the transition curve so much that progress is slowed, to make the dawn dull, to denounce and discount the bitter struggles of enthusiasm, to cut corners and fingernails, to dampen triumph, to muffle right, to wrap that giant, the people, in flannel and put them swiftly to bed, to impose a diet on such excessively good health, to put Hercules on a convalescent's regime, to water down the event with the expedient, to offer minds thirsty for the ideal this nectar diluted with herbal tea, to take all precautions against too much success, to stick a lampshade over the revolution.

The year 1830 put this theory into practice, as had already been done in England in 1688.[3]

The year 1830 is a revolution stopped midway. Half-progress, semi-right. But logic ignores the near miss as absolutely as the sun ignores the candle.

Who stops revolutions midway? The bourgeoisie.

Why?

Because the bourgeoisie is self-interest that has attained satisfaction. Yesterday there was appetite, today there is fullness, tomorrow there will be satiety.

The phenomenon of 1814 after Napoléon was reproduced in 1830 after Charles X.

People have tried, wrongly, to make the bourgeoisie a class. The bourgeoisie is quite simply the contented section of the people. The bourgeois is the man who now has time to sit down. A chair is not a caste.

But by being in too much of a hurry to sit down, you can even stop the march of the whole human race. This has often been the mistake of the bourgeoisie.

Making a mistake does not make you a class. Selfishness is not one of the categories of the social order.

But to be fair, even to selfishness, the state to which that part of the nation that we call the bourgeoisie aspired after the shake-up of 1830 was not inertia, which gets tangled up with indifference and laziness and contains a bit of shame; it was not sleep, which assumes a momentary forgetfulness accessible to dreams; it was a halt.

*Halt* is a word with a peculiar double sense that is very nearly contradictory: It implies troops on the march, that is, movement; and a stop, that is, rest.

A halt is for getting your strength back; it is rest, armed and awake; it is the *fait accompli* that posts sentinels and keeps itself on guard. A halt supposes combat yesterday and combat tomorrow.

It is the in-between of 1830 and of 1848.

What we call combat here can also be called progress.

And so the bourgeoisie, like the statesmen, needed to have a man who embodied this word *halt*. An Although-Because. A composite personality, signifying revolution and stability at once—in other words, shoring up the present by bringing out the compatibility between the past and the future.

This man was ready-made. His name was Louis-Philippe d'Orléans.

The 221[4] made Louis-Philippe king. Lafayette took on the coronation. He called it "the best of republics." The Hôtel de Ville of Paris replaced the cathedral of Rheims.[5]

This substitution of a half-throne for a full throne was "the work of 1830."

When the clever had finished the job, the immense flaw in their solution became apparent. All this was done without reference to absolute right. Absolute right cried out: I protest! Then a shocking thing happened: It sank back into the shadows.

## III. LOUIS-PHILIPPE

Revolutions have tremendous arms and lucky hands; they hit hard and choose their targets well. Even when they are incomplete, even when they are bastardized and crossbred and reduced to the state of junior revolutions, like the revolution of 1830, they nearly always retain enough providential lucidity not to come at the wrong time. Their eclipse is never an abdication.

Still, let's not crow too loudly; revolutions, too, can go wrong, and serious mistakes have been known to happen.

Let's go back to 1830. In its deviation, 1830 was lucky. In the establishment that called itself order after the revolution was cut short, the king was better than royalty. Louis-Philippe was a rare man.

Son of a father[1] to whom history will certainly grant extenuating circumstances, but just as worthy of esteem as that father had been worthy of blame; having every private virtue and several public virtues; mindful of his health, his fortune, his person, his affairs; knowing the cost of a minute and not always the cost of a year; sober, serene, peace-loving, patient, a good man and a good prince; sleeping with his wife and having lackeys in his palace whose job it was to show the conjugal bed to the bourgeois, an ostentation of regular intimacy that had become useful after the old illegitimate displays of the elder branch of the family; knowing all the languages of Europe and, what is rarer still, all the languages of all the interests, and speaking them fluently; admirable representative of the middle class, but outdistancing it and in every way greater than it; having the excellent sense, even while appreciating the blood from which he sprang, to esteem himself for his intrinsic worth, and on the very particular question of his race, declaring himself Orléans and not Bourbon; very much the first prince of the blood[2] as long as he had been only a Most Serene Highness, but an honest bourgeois the day he became Majesty; diffuse in public, concise at home; a declared, but not proven, miser, and at bottom, one of those economical types who are easily moved to extravagance when the whim or duty takes them; literate yet not too fussed about literature; a gentleman, but not a knight; simple, steady, and strong; adored by his family and by his household; a winning conversationalist; a savvy statesman, cold inside, ruled by the immediate interest, always sailing close to the wind, incapable of rancor or gratitude, pitilessly wearing out his superiority on mediocrities, skilled at proving wrong through parliamentary majorities, those mysterious unanimities that grumble quietly beneath thrones; expansive, sometimes imprudent in his expansiveness, but showing marvelous adroitness in this imprudence; rich in expedients, faces, masks; frightening France with Europe and frightening Europe with France; incontestably loving his country but preferring his family; prizing domination more than authority and authority more than dignity, a disposition that is disastrous in that, by turning everything toward success, it accepts ruse and does not absolutely repudiate baseness, but profitable in that it preserves politics from violent clashes, the state from fractures, and society from disasters; meticulous, proper, vigilant, attentive, sagacious, indefatigable; contradicting himself sometimes, and giving himself the lie; daring against Austria at Ancona, relentless against England in Spain, bombarding Antwerp and paying off Pritchard;[3] singing the "Marseillaise" with conviction; impervious to despondency, to world-weariness, to any yen for the beautiful and the ideal, to reckless generosity, to any utopia, to any chimera, to anger, to vanity, to fear; having every form of personal fearlessness, a general at Valmy, a soldier at Jemappes;[4] having had brushes with death by regicide eight times and still smiling; brave as a grenadier, courageous as a thinker; anxious only when faced with the chances of a European uprising, yet unfit for the great political adventures; always ready to risk his life, never his life's work; disguising his will as influence in order to be obeyed as an intelligent man rather than as king; endowed with powers of observation but not divination; taking little notice of minds but knowing a lot about men, that is, needing to see in order to judge; prompt and penetrating common sense, practical wisdom, ready speech, prodigious memory; delving endlessly into that memory, his sole point of resemblance to Caesar, Alexander, and Napoléon; knowing the facts, the details, the dates, the proper names; ignorant of the tendencies, the passions, the diverse genies of the teeming hordes, the inner aspirations, the hidden and obscure upheavals of souls, in a word, all that might be called the invisible currents of people's consciences; a bit out of touch with the France below the surface; getting by on finesse; ruling too much and not reigning enough; his own prime minister unto himself; excelling at making the pettiness of daily reality a bulwark against the immensity of ideas; adding to a real creative faculty for civilization, order, and organization some indefinable spirit of procedure and chicanery; founder and lawmaker of a dynasty; having something of Charlemagne about him and something of an attorney—all in all, a lofty and original character, a prince who knew how to govern with authority in spite of France's anxiety and how to hold on to power in spite of Europe's jealousy. Louis-Philippe will be classed among the eminent men of his century, and would be ranked among the most illustrious rulers in history, if he had only loved glory a little and had appreciated what is great to the same extent as what is useful.

Louis-Philippe had been handsome and he remained graceful even in old age; not always approved of by the nation, he was always approved of by the multitude; he was pleasing. He had this gift, charm. He lacked majesty; he did not wear the crown even though he was king and he did not wear white hair, either, even though he was old. His manners were those of the old regime and his habits those of the new, a blend of noble and bourgeois perfectly appropriate to 1830; Louis-Philippe was transition itself reigning; he had kept the old pronunciation and the old spelling, which he put to work in the service of modern opinions; he loved Poland and Hungary,[5] but he wrote *"les polonois"* and said *"les hongraïs."*[6] He wore the costume of the National Guard like Charles X, and the sash of the Légion d'Honneur like Napoléon.

He rarely went to church, did not go hunting, and never went to the opera. Incorruptible by sacristans, by whippers-in, or by dancers; this had something to do with his popularity with the bourgeoisie. He had no court. He went out with his umbrella tucked under his arm and this umbrella was part of his aura for a long time. He was something of a mason, something of a gardener, something of a doctor; he bled a postilion once when he fell off his horse; Louis-Philippe never went around without his lancet any more than Henri III did without his dagger.[7] The royalists scoffed at this ridiculous king, the first to have spilled blood as part of a cure.

In history's grievances against Louis-Philippe, there is a balance sheet to be drawn up: There is what is to be charged to royalty, what is to be charged to the reign, and what is to be charged to the king; three columns that each add up to something quite different. Democratic right having been confiscated, progress deflected, street protests violently put down, insurrections met with military force, riots resorting to arms, the rue Transnonain,[8] the war councils, the absorption of the real country by the legal country, the government sharing profits with three thousand privileged people—these are the acts of royalty. Belgium rejected,[9] Algeria conquered too brutally[10] and, like India by the English, with more barbarity than civilization, the breach of faith with Abd-el-Kader,[11] Blaye, Deutz bought off, Pritchard paid off—these are the acts of the reign. Policy more familial than national is the act of the king.

As you can see, once the sum is done, the king's load decreases.

His great mistake was this: He was modest in the name of France.

Where does this mistake come from?

We might as well spell it out.

Louis-Philippe as a king was too much a father; this incubation of a family that is supposed to hatch a dynasty is afraid of everything and has no intention of being disturbed; whence all the excessive timidity, a liability for a nation that has July 14 in its civilian tradition and Austerlitz in its military tradition.

Still, if we take away public duties, which demand to be carried out first, this profound tenderness of Louis-Philippe for his family,[12] the family deserved. As a domestic group, they were admirable. Their virtues sat well with their talents. One of Louis-Philippe's daughters, Marie d'Orléans,[13] placed the name of her race among the artists as Charles d'Orléans had placed it among the poets. She turned her soul into a block of marble that she called Joan of Arc. Two of Louis-Philippe's sons had wrung this demagogic praise from Metternich:[14] "Those are young men of a kind we rarely see and princes of a kind we never see."

There you have the truth about Louis-Philippe, without holding anything back, but also without aggravating anything.

To be "prince égalité," to get around bearing the internal contradiction between the Restoration and the Revolution, to have the disturbing look of the revolutionary who becomes reassuring as the ruler, that was Louis-Philippe's fortune in 1830; never has a man adapted more completely to an event; the one blurred into the other and the incarnation was carried off. Louis-Philippe is 1830 made man. On top of that, he had in his favor that great promotion to the throne, exile. He had been banned, errant, poor.[15] He had lived off his labor. In Switzerland, this monopoly-holder of the richest princely domains in France had sold an old horse to be able to eat. At Reichenau, he had given lessons in mathematics while his sister Adélaïde[16] did embroidery and sewing. Those memories associated with a king galvanized the bourgeoisie. He had torn down with his own hands the last iron cage[17] of Mont Saint-Michel, built by Louis XI and used by Louis XV. He was Dumouriez's[18] bosom companion, he was the friend of Lafayette; he had belonged to the Jacobin Club; Mirabeau had slapped him on the shoulder; Danton had said to him, "Young man!"[19] In '93, at twenty-four years of age, he had sat at the back of the Convention on an obscure bench as Monsieur de Chartres[20] and witnessed the trial of Louis XVI, so aptly dubbed "that poor tyrant." The blind clairvoyance of the Revolution, smashing royalty in the king and the king in royalty almost without noticing the man in its savage crushing of the idea, the vast storm of the assembly tribunal, the public wrath putting the questions, Capet[21] not knowing how to reply, the terrifying stunned vacillation of that royal head under that grim blast, the relative innocence of everyone in this catastrophe, of those who condemned as well as of the man who was condemned—he had looked on these things, he had contemplated these dizzy excesses; he had seen the centuries appear at the bar of the Convention; he had seen, behind Louis XVI, that poor hapless passerby who was held responsible, the formidable accused, the monarchy, rise up in the dark; and in his soul what had remained was a respectful horror of the immense justice of the people that is almost as impersonal as the justice of God.

The impact of the Revolution on him was tremendous. His memory was like a living impression of those great years, minute by minute. One day, in front of a witness beyond all possible doubt,[22] he corrected from memory the entire letter *A* of the alphabetic roll of the Constituent Assembly.

Louis-Philippe was a broad-daylight kind of king. With him reigning, there was freedom of the press, freedom of opinion, freedom of conscience, and freedom of speech. The laws of September[23] are as clear as day. Well aware of the corrosive power of light on privilege, he left his throne exposed to the light. History will take his loyalty into account.

Louis-Philippe, like all men of history who have left the stage, has today been put on trial by the conscience of humanity. His trial is still only at the first hearing.

The hour when history speaks in its venerable and free tone has not yet sounded for him; the moment has not yet come to deliver the final judgment on this king; the austere and illustrious historian Louis Blanc[24] himself recently softened his initial verdict; Louis-Philippe was the chosen representative of those two approximations known as the 221 and 1830, that is, a semi-parliament and a semi-revolution; and in any case, from the lofty vantage point at which philosophy should position itself, we could only judge him here, as you might have gathered from the above, with certain reservations in the name of the absolute principle of democracy; in the eyes of the absolute, beyond these two rights, the right of man first, the right of the people next, everything is usurpation. But what we can say at present, these reservations made, is that, all in all and however you look at it, Louis-Philippe, taken by himself and from the point of view of human goodness, will remain, to use the old language of ancient history, one of the best princes ever to sit on the throne.

What is there against him? That very throne. Take the king out of Louis-Philippe, there remains the man. And the man is good. He is sometimes good to the point of being admirable. Often in the middle of the most serious troubles, after a day of struggle against the entire diplomatic world of the Continent, he went back to his apartment in the evening and there, thoroughly exhausted, bowed down with the need to sleep, what did he do? He took a file and spent his night going over some criminal matter, feeling that it was one thing to stand your ground against Europe, but a greater thing still to snatch a man away from the executioner. He put up a strong show of resistance against his keeper of the seals; he disputed every inch of ground the guillotine stood on with the public prosecutor's department, "those windbags of the law," as he called them. Sometimes the piles of documents covered his table; he examined all of them; it was sheer anguish for him to abandon those miserable condemned heads. One day he said to the same witness we mentioned a moment ago: "Last night, I won back seven of them." During the early years of his reign, the death sentence was more or less abolished, and when the scaffold was rebuilt, it was a severe blow to the king. La Grève having disappeared with the elder branch, a bourgeois Grève was set up under the name of the barrière Saint-Jacques;[25] pragmatists felt the need for a quasi-legitimate guillotine; and that was one of the victories of Casimir Périer,[26] who represented the narrow-minded side of the bourgeoisie, over Louis-Philippe, who represented the liberal side. Louis-Philippe had annotated Beccaria[27] in his own hand. After the Fieschi plot,[28] he cried out: "What a pity I wasn't wounded! I could have pardoned him." Another time, alluding to his ministers' resistance, he wrote concerning a political prisoner, who is one of the most generous figures of our times: "His pardon is granted, all

I have left to do now is to obtain it." Louis-Philippe was softhearted like Louis IX[29] and good like Henri IV.

Now, to our mind, goodness is the rare pearl in history and the good almost come before the great.

Louis-Philippe was judged severely by some, perhaps harshly by others, and so it is only right that a man who knew the king and who is himself a phantom these days, come out and testify in the king's favor before history; this testimony, whatever else it may be, is clearly and above all disinterested; an epitaph written by a dead man is sincere, one shade may console another shade; the sharing of the same darkness gives right of praise; and there is little fear that it will ever be said of two tombs in exile:[30] This one flattered the other.

## IV. CRACKS BENEATH THE FOUNDATION

At the moment that the drama we are relating is about to pierce through one of the tragic clouds densely blanketing the beginnings of Louis-Philippe's reign, we had to be unambiguous, this book needed to explain itself in relation to the king.

Louis-Philippe had assumed royal authority without violence, without direct action of any kind on his part, simply by virtue of the fact that a revolutionary change of tack had occurred, evidently perfectly distinct from the real aim of the revolution, but in which he, the duc d'Orléans, had no personal initiative. He was born a prince and believed himself to be elected as king. He had not given himself this mandate; he had not seized it; it had been offered to him and he had accepted it, convinced as he was, wrongly, certainly, that the offer was consistent with right and that acceptance was consistent with duty. And so he held tenure in good faith. Now, we will say in all conscience, Louis-Philippe being in good faith in his tenure, and democracy being in good faith in its assault, the degree of horror that attaches to the social struggles cannot be charged either to the king or to the democracy. A clash of principles is like a shock in the elements. The ocean defends water, the hurricane defends air; the king defends royalty, democracy defends the people; the relative, which is the monarchy, resists the absolute, which is the republic; society bleeds under the conflict, but what is its suffering today will later be its salvation; and, in any case, there is no point here in blaming those who struggle; one of the two parties obviously got it wrong; right is not, like the colossus of Rhodes, able to straddle two shores at once, with one foot in the republic and one foot in royalty; it is indivisible, and all on one side; but those who get it wrong do so sincerely; a blind man is no more guilty of blindness than a Vendéen[1] is an outlaw. So let us then impute these fearsome collisions to the inevitable alone. Whatever such tempests are, human irresponsibility is mixed up in them.

Let's polish off this exposé without further ado.

The government of 1830 had a hard time of it from the outset. Born only yesterday, it was forced to fight today.

It had only just been set up when it already felt the apparatus of July, still so newly put in place and so unsteady on its feet, being beset on all sides in a general tug-of-war.

Resistance sprang up the day after; maybe it sprang up the very same night.

From month to month, the hostility grew and went from being hidden to being blatant.

The July Revolution, so little accepted by the kings outside France, as we've seen, had been variously interpreted inside France.

God delivers his will as visible in events, an obscure text written in a mysterious tongue. People toss off instant translations of it, hasty translations that are incorrect, full of faults, omissions, and misreadings. Very few minds understand the divine tongue. The wisest, the calmest, the deepest, set about slowly deciphering it, and when they finally turn up with their text, the job has long been done; there are already twenty translations in the marketplace. From each translation a party is born, and from each misreading a faction; and each party believes it has the only true text, and each faction believes it holds the light.

Often the government itself is a faction.

In revolutions, there are some who swim against the current; these are the old parties.

For the old parties, who hang on to heredity by the grace of God, revolutions stem from the right to revolt, and there is always the right to revolt against them. Wrong. For in revolutions, the party in revolt is not the people, it is the king. A revolution is precisely the opposite of a revolt. Every revolution, being an ordinary achievement, contains within itself its legitimacy, which false revolutionaries sometimes dishonor, but which persists, even when sullied, which survives, even when soaked with blood. Revolutions stem not from some accident, but from necessity. A revolution is a return from the false to the real. It happens because it has to happen.

The old legitimist parties nonetheless assailed the revolution of 1830 with all the violence that comes from false reasoning. Mistakes make excellent projectiles. They hit home cannily just where it was vulnerable; they attacked this particular revolution in its royalty. They shouted at it: "Revolution, why this king?" Factions are blind men with perfect aim.

This cry was also made by the republicans. But coming from them, the cry was logical. What was blindness on the part of the legitimists was clairvoyance on the part of the democrats. The year 1830 had gone bankrupt as far as the people were concerned. Indignant democracy reproached it on those grounds.

Between the attack of the past and the attack of the future, the July establishment thrashed about. It represented one tiny moment grappling with centuries of monarchy on the one hand and, on the other, eternal right.

On top of that, externally, not being the revolution anymore and turning into the monarchy, 1830 was obliged to keep step with Europe. Maintaining the peace was an added complication. An attempt at harmony, only going about it the wrong way. Going against the grain is sometimes more onerous than a war. From this muted conflict, always muzzled but always growling, armed peace was born, this ruinous expedient of a civilization that has begun to suspect itself. The July royalty reared and bucked, despite getting whipped, in the harness of the European cabinets. Metternich would happily have put it in kicking-straps. Spurred on in France by progress, in Europe it spurred on monarchies, those lazy sloths. Towed along, it towed in turn.

Yet internally, poverty, the proletariat, wages, education, sentencing laws, prostitution, the fate of women, wealth, misery, production, consumption, distribution, exchange, money, credit, the right of capital, the right of labor— all these issues were escalating and hanging over society; a frightening overhang.

Outside the political parties properly so-called, another movement popped up. The democratic ferment was answered by philosophical ferment. The elite felt troubled just as the teeming hordes did—in a different way, but every bit as much.

The thinkers pondered while the grass roots, meaning the people, run through by revolutionary currents, trembled beneath them with who-knows-what epileptic shocks. These dreamers, some isolated, some gathered in families and almost in communities, stirred up the social issues, peacefully but profoundly; imperturble miners that they were, quietly boring their tunnels deeper into a volcano, barely disturbed by the muted commotions and the half-glimpsed furnaces of lava.

This tranquillity was not the least beautiful spectacle of that stormy period.

These men left to the political parties the issue of rights; they busied themselves with the issue of happiness.

Man's well-being—that is what they wanted to extract from society.

They elevated material questions, the question of agriculture, industry, and commerce, almost to the level of a religion. In civilization as it is set up, a bit by God and a lot by man, interests combine, coalesce, and fuse in such a way as to form a veritable deposit of hard rock, according to a law of dynamics patiently studied by the economists, those geologists of politics.

These men, grouped together under various names but who could all go under the generic title of socialists, tried to drill through this rock and make the fresh running water of human felicity gush forth.

From the issue of the scaffold to the issue of war, their works embraced everything. To the rights of man[2] proclaimed by the French Revolution, they added the rights of women and the rights of children.

It will come as no surprise that, for various reasons, we won't delve too deeply into the theory behind the questions raised by socialism. We will limit ourselves to pointing those questions out.

All the problems that the socialists listed, aside from cosmogonic visions, dreams, and mysticism, can be reduced to two main problems:

First problem: how to produce wealth.

Second problem: how to distribute it.

The first problem contains the question of labor. The second contains the question of wages.

The first problem is about the use of force. The second is about the distribution of pleasure.

From the right use of force, public power results.

From the right distribution of pleasure, individual happiness results.

By right distribution, we mean not equal distribution but equitable distribution. The prime equality is equity.

From these two things combined, public power without, individual happiness within, social prosperity results.

Social prosperity means the human being happy, the citizen free, the nation great.

England solves the first of these two problems. It creates wealth to a wonderful degree; it distributes it badly. This lopsided solution, complete on one side only, inevitably leads it to these two extremes: monstrous opulence, monstrous misery. All the pleasure is for the happy few, all the deprivation is for the rest, that is, the people; privilege, favor, monopoly, feudalism, are born of labor itself. A false and dangerous situation that seats public authority on private misery, and that plants the greatness of the state in the suffering of the individual. A greatness that is badly constituted, in which all the material elements combine without a single moral element entering into the mixture.

Communism and agrarian law think they have solved the second problem. They are wrong. Their kind of distribution kills production. Equal parceling out abolishes emulation. And as a consequence, labor. It is a parceling out performed by the butcher, who kills what he carves up. It is thereby impossible to stop at these self-proclaimed solutions. To kill wealth is not to share it.

The two problems need to be solved together to be properly solved. The two solutions need to be combined to provide a single solution.

Solve only the first of the two problems and you will be Venice, you will be England. Like Venice, you will have an artificial power, or like England a material power; you will be the evil rich. You will perish by assault and battery, as Venice died,[3] or by bankruptcy, as England will one day fall. And the world will let you fall and die because the world lets everything fall and die that is nothing but self-interest, everything that does not represent for mankind some virtue or idea.

Naturally it is clear here that these words, Venice and England, designate not peoples but social constructions; the oligarchies superimposed on nations and not the nations themselves. The nations always have our respect and our sympathy. Venice, as a people, will rise again; England, as an aristocracy, will fall, but as a nation it is immortal. That said, we will plow on.

Solve these two problems, encourage the rich and protect the poor, eliminate misery, put an end to the unjust exploitation of the weak by the strong, curb the iniquitous jealousy of the man on the way up for the man who has arrived, adjust, in a manner that is both mathematical and fraternal, wages to work, add free and compulsory education to the growth of the child and make science the basis of manhood, develop the intelligence while keeping the hands busy, be at once a powerful nation and a family of happy people, democratize property ownership, not by abolishing it but by universalizing it, so that every citizen without exception is a property owner, which is easier to do than you think, in short, work out how to produce wealth and work out how to parcel it out, and you will have material greatness and moral greatness all in one—and you will be worthy of calling yourselves France.

And that, above and beyond a few sects that went off the rails, is what socialism was saying; that was what it was looking to put into action, that is what it was roughly sketching out in men's minds.

Admirable efforts! Sacred attempts!

These doctrines, these theories, these forms of resistance, the unexpected necessity for the statesman to consult the philosopher, blurry half-glimpsed evidence, the need to create new policy in accord with the old world without causing too much discord with the revolutionary ideal, a situation in which Lafayette had to be used to defend Polignac,[4] the hint of progress transparent in the riot, in the Chambers, and on the street, rivalries to balance all around him, his faith in the revolution, maybe some indefinable sense of resignation deriving from vague acceptance of a definitive and superior right, his desire to remain true to his race, his sense of family, his sincere respect for the people, his own honesty—all these preoccupied Louis-Philippe almost painfully at times, and as strong and courageous as he was, overwhelmed him with the difficulty of being king.

He felt a dreadful disintegration beneath his feet, though this was not a crumbling into dust, as France was more France than ever.

Dark clouds piled up on the horizon. A shadow came closer and closer and gradually spread over people, over things, over ideas; a shadow that came from anger and sundry systems. All that had swiftly been stifled was stirring and fermenting. At times, the honest man's conscience got its breath back, there was so much malaise in this air thick with sophisms and truths fused together. Minds trembled in the social anxiety like leaves at the approach of a storm. The electric tension was such that, at certain moments, the first person to happen along, a stranger, shone out. Then the crepuscular darkness fell again. At times, deep and muted rumblings gave an indication of the amount of thunder stored in the cloud.

Barely twenty months had gone by since the July Revolution, and the year 1832 had begun⁵ with a look of imminent menace. The distress of the people; laborers with no bread; the last prince de Condé vanishing into the shadows; Brussels chasing Nassau out⁶ the way Paris chased the Bourbons; Belgium offering itself to a French prince and handed over to an English prince; the Russian hatred of Nicholas; at our rear two demons from the south, Ferdinand in Spain, Miguel in Portugal; the earth quaking in Italy, Metternich extending his hand over Bologna; France manhandling Austria at Ancona; in the north the mysteriously sinister sound of a hammer nailing Poland⁷ back into its coffin; in all of Europe furious eyes on France; England, a suspect ally, ready to shove over whatever might bend and to throw itself on whatever might fall; the peerage taking refuge behind Beccaria just to keep four heads from the law; the fleur-de-lis scratched off the king's carriage, the cross torn down from Notre-Dame;⁸ Lafayette diminished, Laffitte ruined, Benjamin Constant dead in dire poverty, Casimir Périer dead in the exhaustion of power; the political disease and the social disease breaking out at the same time in the two capitals of the realm, the one the city of thought, the other the city of work: in Paris, civil war, in Lyon, servile war; in both cities, the same laval glare of the furnace; the crimson of the crater reflected on the forehead of the people; the south fanaticized, the west churned up; the duchesse de Berry in the Vendée;⁹ plots, conspiracies, uprisings, cholera, added to the grim noise of ideas the grim tumult of events.

## V. Deeds from Which History Emerges and Which History Ignores

Toward the end of April everything got worse. The ferment turned to boiling. Since 1830, there had been small halfhearted riots here and there, swiftly put down but breaking out again, a sign of a vast underlying conflagration. Something terrible was brewing. You could glimpse the makings, still fairly indistinct and shadowy, of a possible revolution. France had its eyes on Paris; Paris had its eyes on the faubourg Saint-Antoine.

The faubourg Saint-Antoine, silently stoked, was starting to boil.

The cabarets of the rue de Charonne were serious and stormy, though the conjunction of the two adjectives seems odd when applied to cabarets.

There, the government was purely and simply called into question. There, whether it was "the thing to fight or to remain calm" was debated in public. There were back rooms where workers were made to swear that they would be on the street at the first cry of alarm and "that they would fight without counting the enemy's numbers." Once this commitment was made, a man seated in a corner of the cabaret put on a ringing voice and boomed, "You know what you're saying! You've taken an oath!" Sometimes people went upstairs to a closed room, and there scenes occurred that were practically Masonic. Initiates were put under oath "to render service as they would to their own fathers." That was the formula.

In the lower rooms they read "subversive" pamphlets. "They crucified the government," a secret report of the day claimed.

There you could hear people saying things like the following: "I don't know the names of the leaders. The likes of us, we'll only know two hours beforehand on the day." A worker said: "There are three hundred of us, let's put in ten sous each, that makes a hundred and fifty francs to manufacture musket balls and powder." Another said: "I'm not asking for six months, I'm not asking for two. Before the fortnight's out, we'll be on a par with the government. With twenty-five thousand men, we can face them." Another said: "I don't go to bed because I'm up making cartridges all night." From time to time, men "decked out like bourgeois in good clothes" turned up, "making a fuss" and having an air "of command," shook hands with "the more prominent" and took off again. They never stayed more than ten minutes. They exchanged meaningful words in very low voices: "The plot is ripe, the thing is ready to go." "Everyone there was buzzing with it," to borrow the very expression of one of those taking part. The exultation was such that, one day, in the middle of the cabaret, a worker shouted: "We don't have any weapons!" One of his comrades replied, "The soldiers have got some!" thereby parodying, without realizing it, Bonaparte's proclamation to the Army of Italy.[1] "Whenever they had something more secret," adds one report, "they would not communicate it there." One can scarcely imagine what they could have to hide after saying what they did say.

Meetings were sometimes intermittent. At certain of them, there were never more than eight or ten—always the same eight or ten. At others, anyone could walk in off the street and the room was so full, people were forced to stand. Some were there out of enthusiasm and passion; others because it was on the way to work. As during the Revolution, there were patriot women in the cabarets who embraced the newcomers.

Other expressive deeds came to light.

A man went into a cabaret, had a drink, and went out again, saying: "Wine seller, what is owing will be paid by the revolution."

At one cabaret opposite the rue de Charonne, revolutionary agents were appointed. The ballots were collected in caps.

Workers gathered at a fencing master's who gave lessons in the rue de Cotte. There was a trophy of arms there made of wooden swords, canes, truncheons, and foils. One day the buttons were removed from the foils. One worker said: "There are twenty-five of us, but they don't count me because I'm regarded as a machine." That machine later became Quénisset.[2]

Any small thing that was premeditated gradually took on some strange notoriety. A woman sweeping her doorstep said to another woman: "We've been hard at it for a long time making cartridges." Proclamations addressed to the National Guard of the *départements* were read in the middle of the street. One of these proclamations was signed: *Burtot, wine seller*.

One day, at a liquor seller in the Lenoir market, a man with a thick collar of a beard and an Italian accent hopped up on a milestone and read out loud an odd text that seemed to emanate from some occult power. Groups of people had formed around him and they clapped. The passages that most stirred the crowd were taken in and noted. ". . . Our doctrines are trampled underfoot, our proclamations are ripped up, our bill posters are watched and thrown in jail . . ." "The debacle that has just taken place in the cotton industry has converted many moderates to our cause." ". . . The future of nations is taking shape in our obscure ranks." ". . . This is how it is: action or reaction, revolution or counter-revolution. For in our times no one believes in inertia anymore or in immobility. For the people or against the people, that is the question. There is no other." ". . . The day when we no longer suit you, crush us, but until then, help us to walk." All this in broad daylight.

Other acts, even more audacious, were suspicious to the people because of their very audacity. On April 4, 1832, a man strolling by suddenly got up on the milestone at the corner of the rue Sainte-Marguerite and shouted: "I am a Babouvist!" But behind Babeuf, the people could smell Gisquet.[3]

Among other things, this same passerby said:

"Down with property! The left-leaning opposition are cowards and traitors. When they want to be in the right, they preach revolution. They're democrats so they won't get beaten up and royalists so they won't have to fight. Republicans are two-faced. Watch out for republicans, citizen workers."

"Silence, citizen spy!" yelled a worker.

That yell put an end to the speech.

Mysterious incidents occurred.

At nightfall, one worker met "a well-heeled man" down by the canal who said to him: "Where are you going, citizen?" "Monsieur," the worker replied, "I don't have the honor of knowing you." "I know you, though," the man said, adding, "Don't be frightened. I'm the committee officer. You're suspected of not being fully convinced. You know that if you give anything away, we've got our eye on you." Then he shook the worker's hand and went on his way, saying: "We'll see each other again soon."

The police, ears to the ground, intercepted very odd conversations not only in the cabarets but also on the streets:

"Get yourself admitted quick," said a weaver to a cabinetmaker.

"Why?"

"There's a bit of shooting that needs to be done."

Two passersby in rags exchanged these remarkable lines, full of apparent jacquerie:[4]

"Who governs us?"

"It's Monsieur Philippe."

"No, it's the bourgeoisie."

You would be wrong to think we use the word *jacquerie* perjoratively. The Jacques were the poor. And those who are hungry are right.

Another time, as two men walked past each other, one was overheard saying to the other: "We've got a good plan of attack."

Of a private conversation between four men squatting in a ditch at the barrière du Trône roundabout, all that could be gleaned was this:

"Everything possible will be done to see he struts about Paris no more."

Who was *he*? Menacing obscurity.

"The main leaders," as they said in the faubourg, kept out of sight. It was thought they got together to thrash things out in a cabaret close to the point of Saint-Eustache.[5] A man named Aug——, head of the Tailors' Benevolent Society, rue Mondétour, was thought to act as principal intermediary between the leaders and the faubourg Saint-Antoine. However, there was always a fog hanging over these leaders, and no actual fact could shore up the odd pride of this response made later by a defendant before the Court of Peers:[6]

"Who was your leader?"

"I didn't know any and I didn't acknowledge any."

It was scarcely anything more than words, transparent, but vague; sometimes words floating in the air, as they say, hearsay. Other indices emerged.

A carpenter, busy in the rue de Reuilly nailing up posts for a fence around a lot where a house was going up, found on this lot a fragment of a torn-up letter in which the following lines were still legible: "... The committee must take measures to prevent recruiting in the sections for the different societies ..."

And this postscript: "We have learned that there were guns at no. 5a, rue du Faubourg-Poissonnière, in the number of five or six thousand, in a courtyard at an armorer's. The section does not have any weapons."

What moved the carpenter to show this to his neighbors was that, a few steps farther on, he picked up another note, also ripped up and even more interesting. We reproduce its layout below due to the historic interest of these strange documents:

Q   C   D   E      Learn this list by heart. Afterward, tear it up.
                  Men admitted will do likewise when you
                  have given them their orders.
                  Safety and fraternity.

                                                        L.

              u og a fe

Those who were let into the secret of this discovery at the time, only found out later what those four capital letters referred to: *quinturions, centurions, décurions, éclaireurs,* and the meaning of the letters *u og a fe,* which formed a date, namely, *this 15th April, 1832.* Under each capital letter, names were listed followed by perfectly typical indications. So: Q. *Bannerel.* 8 muskets. 83 cartridges. Solid. C. *Boubière.* 1 pistol. 40 cartridges. D. *Rollet.* 1 foil. 1 pistol. 1 pound of powder. E. *Teissier.* 1 saber. 1 cartridge-box. Exact. *Terreur.* 8 guns. Brave. Etc.

Finally this same carpenter found, in the same enclosed space, a third bit of paper on which was written, in pencil but very legibly, an enigmatic kind of list:

Unité. Blanchard. Arbre-sec. 6.
Barra. Soize. Salle-au-Comte.
Kósciuszko. Aubry the butcher?
J. J. R.
Caius Gracchus.
Right of revision. Dufond. Oven.
Fall of the Girondins. Derbac. Maubuée.
Washington. Pinson. 1 pist. 86 cart.
Marseillaise.
Souver. Of the people. Michel. Quincampoix. Saber.
Hoche.
Marceau. Plato. Arbre-sec.
Warsaw. Tilly, crier for the *Populaire.*[7]

The honest bourgeois in whose hands this list ended up knew its significance. It appears that the list was the complete nomenclature of the sections of the fourth arrondissement for the Society of the Rights of Man, with the names and the addresses of the section leaders. These days, when all these facts that remained in the shadows are no more than history, they can be published. It should be added that the Society of the Rights of Man seems to have been founded later than the date on this note. Perhaps it was just a draft.

Meanwhile, with all the talk and speeches and written clues, material facts began to emerge.

In a chest of drawers at an old curiosity shop in the rue Popincourt, seven sheets of gray paper were seized, all of them folded lengthwise and then in four.

These sheets of paper held twenty-six squares of the same gray paper folded in the form of cartridges, and a card on which the following could be read:

| | |
|---|---|
| Saltpeter | 12 ounces. |
| Sulfur | 2 ounces. |
| Charcoal | 2½ ounces. |
| Water | 2 ounces. |

The official report of the seizure observed that the drawer gave off a strong odor of powder.

A mason going home after a day's work left a small packet on a bench near the pont d'Austerlitz. This packet was taken to the guardhouse. It was opened and in it were found two printed dialogues signed *Lahautière,* a song called "Workers Unite," and a tin box full of cartridges.

A worker having a drink with a friend got him to pat him down to see how hot he was; the other man felt a pistol under his jacket.

In a ditch on the boulevard between Père-Lachaise and the barrière du Trône, at the most deserted spot, children playing discovered a bag under a heap of wood shavings and peelings that contained a bullet mold, a wooden mandrel for making cartridges, a begging bowl in which there were a few grains of gunpowder, and a small cast-iron pot the insides of which revealed obvious traces of molten lead.

Police officers turning up without warning at five in the morning at the home of one Pardon, who was later a member of the Barricade-Merry section and who got himself killed in the insurrection of April 1834,[8] found him on his feet by his bed, holding cartridges that he was in the process of making.

Around the time when workers take a break, two men were seen meeting between the barrière Picpus and the barrière Charenton in a little covered way between two walls near a barkeeper's who had a Siamese draught board on a card table out front. One pulled a pistol out from under his smock and showed it to the other one. Just as he was about to hand it over he noticed that the sweat from his chest had made the powder somewhat damp. He primed the pistol and added more powder to what was already in the pan. Then the two men went their separate ways.

A man named Gallais, later killed in the rue Beaubourg during the April affair, boasted of having seven hundred cartridges and eighty gun flints at home.

The government got word one day that weapons had just been handed out in the faubourg along with two hundred thousand cartridges. The following week, thirty thousand cartridges were distributed. What was amazing was that the police couldn't lay their hands on any of them. An intercepted letter went like this: "The day is not far off when, at four by the clock, eighty thousand patriots will be armed."

All this ferment was out in the open, public, you might almost say serene. The imminent insurrection was gathering momentum calmly as the government looked on. No weirdness was lacking in this crisis, as yet subterranean but already perceptible. The bourgeois talked peacably with the workers about what was ginnying up. They would say "How's the riot going?" in the same tone in which you might have said "How's your wife?"

A furniture dealer in the rue Moreau asked: "So, then, when do you attack?"

Another shopkeeper said: "We'll attack soon, I know. A month ago, there were fifteen thousand of you, now there are twenty-five thousand of you." He offered his gun, and a neighbor offered a small pistol that he was hoping to sell for seven francs.

Revolutionary fever was gaining, in any case. No part of Paris or France was exempt from it. The same artery was throbbing everywhere. Like those membranes that flare up in certain inflammations and spread through the human body, the network of secret societies began to spread throughout the country. From the Association of the Friends of the People, which was both public and secret at once, emerged the Society of the Rights of Man, which dated one of its orders of the day like this: *Pluviôse, Year XL° of the Republican Era*. This society was to survive even the decrees of the court of assizes pronouncing its dissolution. It did not hesitate to give its sections such loaded names as:

The Pikes.
Tocsin.
Alarm Gun.
Phrygian Cap.
21st January.
Beggars.
Vagrants.
Forward March.
Robespierre.
Level.
Ça ira.[10]

The Society of the Rights of Man engendered the Society for Action. This was a group of impatient types that broke away and hurtled ahead. Other associations sought to recruit from among the great parent societies. The sectionaries complained of being plagued by such touting, pulled in all directions. Thus the Gallic Society and the Organizing Committee of the Municipalities. Thus the associations for the freedom of the press, for the freedom of the individual, for the education of the people, against indirect taxes. And after that, the Society of Egalitarian Workers, which split into three factions: the Egalitarians, the Communists, and the Reformists. Then there was the Army of the Bastille, a sort of cohort organized along military lines, four men commanded by a corporal, ten by a sergeant, twenty by a second lieutenant, forty by a lieutenant; there were never more than five men who knew each other. An arrangement whereby precaution was combined with audacity and which smacked of the genius of Venice. The central committee, which was the brain, had two arms, the Society for Action and the Army of the Bastille. A legitimist association, the Faithful Knights, moved among these republican affiliations, but it was denounced and repudiated.

The Parisian societies grew branches in the other main towns. Lyon, Nantes, Lille, and Marseilles each had its own Society of the Rights of Man, the Carbonari, the Free Men. Aix had a revolutionary society known as the Cougourde. We have already mentioned that word.

In Paris, the faubourg Saint-Marceau was almost as hectic as the faubourg Saint-Antoine and the schools were buzzing just as much as the faubourgs. A café in the rue Saint-Hyacinthe as well as the Sept-Billards bar in the rue des Mathurins-Saint-Jacques served as rallying points for the students. The Society of the Friends of the ABC, an affiliate of the mutualists of Angers and the Cougourde of Aix, gathered, as we saw, in the Café Musain. These same young men also met up, as we said, in a cabaret-restaurant near the rue Mondétour that was called Corinthe. These meetings were secret. Others were as public as possible and you can judge how reckless this was by this fragment of a statement submitted in one of the subsequent trials: "Where was the meeting held?" "Rue de la Paix." "Whose place?" "In the street." "What sections were there?" "Only one." "Which one?" "The section Manuel." "Who was the leader?" "Me." "You are too young to have taken on the serious business of attacking the government on your own. Where did you get your instructions from?" "From the central committee."

The army was mined at the same time as the general population, as was later proved by the Belfort, Lunéville, and Épinal movements.[11] "They were counting on the 52nd regiment, on the 5th, on the 8th, on the 37th, on the 20th Light. In Burgundy and in the towns of the south they planted "the Tree of Liberty"[12]—a mast surmounted by a red cap.

Such was the situation.

And this situation was, as we said at the beginning, made more palpable and urgent by the faubourg Saint-Antoine than by any other part of the population. This was where the thorn in the side was.

This old faubourg, teeming with people like an anthill, industrious, brave, and angry as a beehive, quivered with anticipation and the desire for commotion. Everything was heating up there, though without the daily grind being interrupted for all that. Nothing can give a clear idea of the lively yet grim face of this district. The faubourg hides poignant cases of distress under mansard roofs; there are also people of rare and ardent intelligence there. When it comes to distress and intelligence it is especially dangerous for the two extremes to meet.

The faubourg Saint-Antoine had still other causes for excitement, for it takes the brunt of the commercial crises, bankruptcies, strikes, and unemployment inherent in great political conflagrations. In times of revolution, misery is both cause and effect at the same time. The blow it strikes comes back to haunt it. This population, full of proud virtue, capable of the highest degree of latent heat, always ready to take up arms, quick to explode, irritable, deep, ground down, seemed to be waiting only for a flying spark to fall. Every time certain sparks fly across the horizon, driven by the wind of events, you can't stop yourself thinking of the faubourg Saint-Antoine and of the dreadful fate that placed this powder keg of suffering and ideas at the gates of Paris.

The cabarets of the faubourg Saint-Antoine, which have been drawn more than once in the sketch you have just read, have a historic notoriety. In times of trouble, people there get more drunk on words than on wine. A sort of prophetic spirit and a whiff of the future wafts through them, swelling hearts and expanding souls. The cabarets of the faubourg Saint-Antoine are like those taverns of the Aventine Hill built over the sibyl's cave and communicating with deep and sacred spirits; taverns whose tables were virtually tripods and where they drank what Ennius[13] calls "sybilline wine." [14]

The faubourg Saint-Antoine is a reservoir of people. Revolutionary agitation opens up fissures there out of which popular sovereignty flows. This sovereignty can do damage; it can go wrong like any other; but, even when led astray, it remains great. You could say of it, as of the blind Cyclops, *Ingens*.[15]—Power!

In '93, depending on whether the idea floating around was good or bad, depending on whether it was the day for fanaticism or for enthusiasm, either legions of savages or heroic bands set out from the faubourg Saint-Antoine.

Savages. Let's explain what we mean by that word. What did they want, these bristling men who, in the Genesis-like days of revolutionary chaos, ragged, screaming, fierce, clubs raised, pikes held high, dashed all over old shattered Paris? They wanted an end to oppression, an end to tyranny, an end to the broadsword, work for men, education for children, social ease for women, liberty, equality, fraternity, bread for all, ideas for all, the Edenization of the world, Progress; with their backs to the wall, beside themselves, terrible, half-naked, maces in their fists and a roar in their mouths, they reclaimed that sacred thing, so good and so sweet, Progress. They were savages, yes; but savages of civilization.

They proclaimed justice with fury; though trembling with fear and horror, they wanted to force the human race into paradise. They looked like barbarians yet they were saviors. They reclaimed the light wearing the mask of night.

Opposite these men, wild, we admit, and frightening, but wild and frightening for the good, there are other men, smiling, prettily primped up, gilded, beribboned, spangled, in silk stockings, white feathers, yellow gloves, brightly polished shoes, who, leaning on velvet tables at the corners of marble fireplaces, gently insist on the maintenance and preservation of the past, of the Middle Ages, of divine right, of fanaticism, ignorance, slavery, the death penalty, war, politely glorifying in hushed voices the saber, the stake, and the scaffold. As for us, if we were forced to choose between the barbarians of civilization and the civilized representatives of barbarity, we would go for the barbarians.

But, thank heaven, another choice is possible. No sheer plummet is necessary, no more forward than backward. Neither despotism nor terrorism. We want progress that has a gentle incline.

God provides for this. The softening of inclines—that is God's whole policy.

## VI. Enjolras and His Lieutenants

Round about this time, Enjolras, in view of possible events, did a sort of mysterious stocktaking.

They were all at a conference in the Café Musain.

Throwing a few semi-enigmatic but meaningful metaphors together, Enjolras said: "It would be good to know where we stand and who we can count on. If we want fighters, we have to create them. Have the wherewithal to strike. That can't do any harm. Passersby always have more chance of being gored when there are bulls on the road than when there aren't any. So let's count the herd for a bit. How many of us are there? We can't put this work off till tomorrow. Revolutionaries have to always be in a hurry; progress has no time to lose. Look out for the unexpected. Let's not let ourselves be caught short. It's a matter of going back over all the seams we have sewn and seeing if they hold. We've got to get to the bottom of this business today. Courfeyrac, you go and see the polytechnic students.[1] It's their day off. Today, Wednesday. Feuilly, isn't it? You go and see the students at La Glacière. Combeferre promised me he'd go to Picpus. There's a whole excellent batch of them there. Bahorel will visit the Estrapade. Prouvaire, the Masons are cooling off; you go and bring us the latest from the lodge in the rue de Grenelle-Saint-Honoré. Joly will go to Dupuytren's[2] clinic and take the pulse of the school of medicine. Bossuet will make a little tour of the Palais de Justice and have a chat with the law students. As for me, I'll tackle the Cougourde."

"So everything's all set," said Courfeyrac.

"No."

"What's left?"

"Something very important."

"What?" asked Courfeyrac.

"The barrière du Maine," replied Enjolras.

Enjolras spent a moment lost in thought, then resumed: "At the barrière du Maine, there are marble cutters, painters, sculptors' assistants from the sculpture studios. They're an enthusiastic family, but subject to sudden chills. I don't know what's been up with them for some time. Their minds are on something else. They're losing heart. They spend their time playing dominoes. It's rather urgent to go and have a word with them—a firm word. They hang around Richefeu's place. They can be found there between twelve and one. Someone needs to go and blow on these particular embers. I was counting on the absent-minded Marius, who is pretty good on the whole, but he doesn't come here anymore. I need someone for the barrière du Maine. I haven't got anyone spare."

"What about me?" said Grantaire. "I'm here."

"You?"

"Me."

"You, indoctrinate republicans! You, warm cold feet in the name of principles!"

"Why not?"

"Can it really be that you're good for something?"

"Well, I have a vague ambition to be," said Grantaire.

"You don't believe in anything."

"I believe in you."

"Grantaire, do me a favor, would you?"

"Anything. I'll even polish your boots."

"No need, just keep your nose out of our business. Sleep off the absinthe."

"You're an ungrateful bastard, Enjolras."

"I can just see you at the barrière du Maine, ha! As if you were capable of it!"

"I'm perfectly capable of walking down the rue des Grès, crossing the place Saint-Michel, cutting through the rue Monsieur-le-Prince, taking the rue Vaugirard, going past the Carmes, turning into the rue d'Assas, reaching the rue du Cherche-Midi, leaving the Conseil de Guerre behind me, striding down the rue des Vieilles-Tuileries, bounding over the boulevard, following the chaussée du Maine and stepping into Richefeu's. I am perfectly capable of doing that. My shoes are capable."

"Are you at all familiar with our Richefeu friends?"

"Not really. Only to say hello to."

"What'll you say to them?"

"I'll speak to them of Robespierre, in faith. Of Danton. Of principles."

"You!"

"Me. But you don't do me justice. When I put my mind to it, I am daunting. I've read Prudhomme, I know the Contrat Social. I know my constitution for the Year II[3] by heart. 'The liberty of one citizen ends where the liberty of another citizen begins.' What do you take me for, a brute? I have an old assignat[4] in my drawer. The rights of man, the sovereignty of the people, heavens! I'm even a bit of a Hébertist.[5] I can jabber on for six hours at a stretch by the clock, watch in hand, about such wonders of the world."

"Be serious," said Enjolras.

"I am unflinching," answered Grantaire.

Enjolras thought for a few seconds before making the gesture of a man who has made up his mind.

"Grantaire," he said gravely, "I consent to trying you out. You will go to the barrière du Maine."

Grantaire lived in a furnished room quite close to the Café Musain. He ducked out and returned five minutes later. He had been home to put on a waistcoat in the style of Robespierre.

"Red," he said as he came in, eyeing Enjolras steadily.

Then, with an energetic sweep of his palm, he smoothed the two scarlet points of his waistcoat down flat against his chest.

And, going over to Enjolras, he whispered in his ear: "Don't worry."

He jammed his hat down resolutely and left.

A quarter of an hour later, the back room of the Café Musain was deserted. All the Friends of the ABC had gone, each on his way to his own task. Enjolras, who had kept the Cougourde all to himself, was the last to leave.

Those members of the Cougourde of Aix who were in Paris gathered at the time on the Issy plain, in one of the numerous abandoned quarries on that side of Paris.

As he made his way toward the meeting place, Enjolras went back over the situation in his head. The gravity of events was plain for all to see. When events, those early warning signs of a sort of latent social disease, move slowly, the slightest complication can stop them in their tracks and tangle them up. A phenomenon leading to collapse and revival. Enjolras glimpsed a luminous uprising beneath the dingy folds of the future. Who knows? Perhaps the moment was coming. The people grabbing back their rights, what a beautiful sight! The revolution majestically taking back possession of France and telling the world: to be continued tomorrow! Enjolras was happy. The furnace was heating up. At that very moment he had a powder trail of friends scattered all over Paris. He was putting together in his mind, using the penetrating philosophical eloquence of Combeferre, the cosmopolitan enthusiasm of Feuilly, the verve of Courfeyrac, the laughter of Bahorel, the melancholy of Jean Prouvaire, the science of Joly, the sarcasm of Bossuet, a sort of crackling electric fire more or less everywhere at once. Everyone on the job. The result would surely be worth the effort. All was well. This made him think of Grantaire.

"Wait," he said to himself, "the barrière du Maine is hardly out of my way. What if I went on as far as Richefeu's? Let's have a peek at what Grantaire is up to and how far he's got."

One o'clock rang out from the Vaugirard bell tower as Enjolras reached the Richefeu tobacconist's. He pushed the door open, went in, and stood, arms folded, letting the door swing shut and hit him in the shoulders, and peered around the room full of tables, men, and smoke.

A voice burst out in the smog, sharply cut off by another voice. It was Grantaire arguing with an adversary he had found.

Grantaire was sitting down opposite another figure at a table of Saint Anne marble, which was strewn with bran and dotted with dominoes; he was banging his fist on the marble and this is what Enjolras heard:

"Double six."

"Four."

"The swine! I'm out."

"You're finished. Two."

"Six."

"Three."

"Ace."

"My turn to put down."

"Four points."

"Only just."

"Your turn."

"I made a huge mistake."

"You're doing all right."

"Fifteen."

"Seven more."

"That brings me to twenty-two. [Musing.] Twenty-two!"

"You weren't expecting the double six. If I'd played it at the start, it would've changed the whole game."

"Two again."

"Ace."

"Ace! All right, five."

"I don't have any."

"You're the one who put down, aren't you?"

"Yes."

"Blank."

"Does he have a chance! Ah, you have one chance! [Long reverie.] Two."

"Ace."

"No five, no ace. Take that!"

"Domino."

"Of all the rotten luck!"

# BOOK TWO

# ÉPONINE

## I. The Lark's Field

Marius had witnessed the unexpected denouement of the ambush he had put Javert onto, but Javert had barely left the tumbledown building, hauling his prisoners away in three fiacres, when Marius, too, slipped out of the house. It was still only nine o'clock at night. Marius went to Courfeyrac's place. Courfeyrac was no longer the imperturbable local of the quartier Latin; he had gone to live in the rue de la Verrerie "for political reasons." This quartier was one of those that insurrection was only too happy to move to in those days. Marius told Courfeyrac: "I've come to sleep at your place." Courfeyrac pulled a mattress off his bed, which had two of them, laid it on the floor, and said: "There you go."

By seven o'clock the next day, Marius was back at the slum. He paid his rent and whatever else he owed Ma Bougon, loaded his books, his bed, his table, his chest of drawers, and his two chairs onto a wheelbarrow and trundled off without leaving his address, so that when Javert came back later that morning to question Marius about the events of the previous night, he found only Ma Bougon, who barked: "Gone!"

Ma Bougon was convinced that Marius was somehow in cahoots with the robbers seized in the night. "Who'd have thought it?" she cried, as she made the rounds of the neighborhood porters. "A young wisp of a thing like that, you'd have taken him for a girl!"

Marius had two reasons for clearing out so swiftly. The first was that he now had a horror of this house where he had seen, so very close and in all its most repulsive and its most ferocious variations, a social deformity perhaps even more awful than the evil rich: the evil poor. The second was that he did not want to feature in whatever trial would probably ensue and so be called on to testify against Thénardier.

Javert thought the young man, whose name he had not retained, had been frightened off or, perhaps, had not made it home when the ambush was taking place; he did make some attempts to find him, though, but he did not succeed.

A month went by, then another. Marius was still at Courfeyrac's. He had learned from a law student who regularly paced the *salle des pas perdus*[1] at the Palais de Justice that Thénardier was in solitary confinement. Every Monday, Marius had the clerk of La Force prison send five francs to Thénardier.

Having no money left, Marius borrowed the five francs from Courfeyrac. It was the first time in his life that he had borrowed money. Those regular five francs were a double enigma—for Courfeyrac, who gave them, and for Thénardier, who received them. "Who can it be going to?" Courfeyrac wondered. "Where can it be coming from?" Thénardier asked himself.

Marius was otherwise devastated. Everything had gone down the drain again. He could no longer see what was in front of him; his life had plunged back into this mystery in which he staggered along clutching at support. For a moment he had seen, once more, up close in the darkness, the young girl he loved and the old man who seemed to be her father, these unknown beings who were his only interest and his only hope in this world; and at the point where he thought he had them in his grasp, a blast of air had swept all these shadows away. Not one spark of certainty or truth had shot out even from the most horrifying shock. No conjecture was possible. He no longer even knew the name he had thought he knew. One thing for sure, it was not Ursula. And the Lark was a nickname. And what to make of the old man? Was he, in fact, hiding from the police? The worker with the white hair whom Marius had come across near the Invalides came back to him. He guessed now that this worker and Monsieur Leblanc were probably the same man. So he wore a disguise? This man had a heroic side and a shady side. Why didn't he call out for help? Why did he run away? Was he the young girl's father—yes or no? Was he, lastly, really the man Thénardier thought he recognized? Could Thénardier have been mistaken? So many unresolvable problems. All this, it is true, did not detract in any way from the angelic charm of the young girl from the Luxembourg. Poignant distress; Marius had passion in his heart and darkness over his eyes. He was driven, he was drawn, and yet he couldn't move. Everything had gone up in smoke, except love. But even there, he had lost love's instincts and sudden illuminations. Normally this flame that burns us also enlightens us a little, shedding a little helpful light around us. Marius could not even pick up the mute promptings of passion anymore. Never did he say to himself: "What if I went there? What if I tried that?" The girl he could no longer call Ursula was obviously somewhere, but nothing alerted Marius as to where he should look for her. His whole life now came down to two words: absolute uncertainty, in an impenetrable fog. He still yearned to see her again, but he no longer hoped to.

To cap it off, destitution returned. He felt its icy breath brush right up against him, at his back. For a long time already, with all his torment, he had stopped working, and nothing is more dangerous than stopping work; it means the habit goes. A habit that is easy to let go of, hard to get back.

A certain amount of daydreaming is good, like a narcotic in discreet doses. It sedates the sometimes high fevers of the overwrought brain at work and produces a soft fresh vapor in the mind that smooths out the oversharp points of pure thought, fills up the gaps and holes here and there, binds things together and blunts the jagged corners of ideas. But too much daydreaming drags you under and drowns you. Woe to the person who works with their brain who lets themselves sink completely from thinking to daydreaming! That person thinks they'll climb out again easily, and tells themself that it's the same thing, after all. Wrong!

Thinking is the labor of the intellect, daydreaming is its sensual pleasure. To replace thinking with daydreaming is to confound poison with food.

Marius, you will recall, had started off this way. Passion had reared its lovely head and had wound up plunging him headlong into bottomless and aimless fantasies. In that state, you no longer leave the house except to wander in a dream. A lazy childbirth. A tempestuous yet stagnant pit. And as work decreases, need increases. This is a law. Man, in this dreamy state, is naturally extravagant and limp; the slack mind cannot tightly embrace life. There is, in this way of living, some good mingled with the bad, for if enfeeblement is harmful, generosity is healthful and good. But the poor man, generous and noble, who does not work, is lost. Resources dry up, necessities loom.

A fatal slope, down which the strongest and most honest are dragged just like the weakest and most vicious. It ends in one of two holes, suicide or crime. By dint of going out every day to dream, there comes a day when you go out to throw yourself in the water. Too much dreaming produces men like Escousse and Lebras.[2]

Marius was walking slowly down this slope, his eyes fixed on someone he could no longer see. What we have just written seems strange and yet it is true. The memory of an absent being lights up the darkness of the heart; the longer they have been gone, the brighter they shine; the desperate and gloomy soul sees this light on its horizon; the star of inner night. All Marius could think about was Her. He dreamed of nothing else; he felt dimly that his old coat was becoming unacceptable and that his new coat was becoming an old coat, that his shirts were wearing out, that his hat was wearing out, that his boots were wearing out, in other words, that his life was wearing out, and he said to himself: "If only I could see her before I die!"

A single sweet idea remained to him and that was that She had loved him, that her eyes had told him so, that she might not know his name, but she knew his soul, and that, perhaps, wherever she was, whatever that mysterious place might be, she loved him still. Who knows if she wasn't dreaming of him the way he dreamed of her? Sometimes, in those unaccountable moments every heart that loves has, with reasons only to feel pain and yet feeling an obscure thrill of joy, he said to himself: "These thoughts are coming to me from her!" Then he added: "Perhaps my thoughts reach her, too."

This illusion, which he would shake his head at a moment later, still managed to cast a ray of light into his soul that sometimes resembled hope. From time to time, especially at that blue hour of the evening when dreamers are at their saddest, he would drop into a notebook devoted to the purpose the purest, the most impersonal, the most ideal of reveries that love filled his brain with. He called this "writing to her."

You must not think his reason was disturbed. Quite the contrary. He had lost the capacity to work and to move firmly toward a determined goal, but he was even more clear-sighted and honorable than ever. Odd as it may seem, Marius saw, in the calm light of reality, what was happening under his nose, even the most indifferent deeds of men; he always found the right word for everything in a sort of honest dejectedness and frank disinterestedness. His judgment, very nearly dissociated from hope, held its head high and soared.

In this state of mind nothing escaped him, nothing fooled him, and he saw to the bottom of life, of humanity, of destiny, at every instant. Happy, even in his anguish, is he to whom God has given a soul worthy of love and of calamity! Whoever has not seen the things of this world and the heart of men in this double light has seen nothing of the truth and knows nothing.

The soul that loves and that suffers has attained the sublime.

Otherwise, the days went by, one after the other, and nothing new cropped up. Only, it seemed to him that the gloomy time left to him was getting shorter by the minute. He thought he could already distinctly make out the brink of the bottomless pit.

"God!" he would say to himself over and over, "Won't I ever see her again before . . . I go?"

When you go up the rue Saint-Jacques, and cross over the barrière side and follow the old inner boulevard on the left for a while, you come to the rue de la Santé, followed by La Glacière and, shortly before you get to the little Gobelins stream, you find a sort of field that is, in the whole, long, monotonous belt of the boulevards around Paris, the only spot where Ruisdael[3] would be tempted to sit down.

That magic thing from which grace springs was there, a green meadow crisscrossed with taut ropes from which rags hung to dry in the wind, an old market-garden farmhouse built in the days of Louis XIII, with its great roof bizarrely punctuated with dormers, dilapidated paling fences, a tiny pond between the poplars, women, laughter, voices; on the horizon, the Panthéon, the tree of the Deaf-Mutes, the Val-de-Grâce, black, squat, fantastical, amusing, magnificent, and in the background the severe square crest of the towers of Notre-Dame.

As the place is worth seeing, nobody goes there. Barely a cart or a wagon every fifteen minutes.

Once it happened that Marius's solitary walks took him to this wasteland by this pond. That particular day there was something rare on the boulevard, a person. Marius was vaguely struck by the almost wild charm of the place and asked this person: "What's this place called?"

The person answered: "It's the Field of the Lark."

And he added: "It's here that Ulbach killed the shepherdess from Ivry."

But after the word *Lark,* Marius heard nothing. There are sudden crystallizations in the dream state that need only one word to be triggered. Suddenly all thought is condensed around an idea, and the mind is no longer capable of any other perception. The Lark was the name that, in the depths of Marius's melancholy, had replaced "Ursula." "Fancy!" he said, in the kind of irrational stupor peculiar to these mysterious asides. "This is her field. Now I'll find out here where she lives."

This was absurd but irresistible.

And he went every day to the Field of the Lark.

## II. EMBRYONIC DEVELOPMENT OF CRIMES
### IN PRISON INCUBATORS

Javert's triumph in the old Gorbeau slum had looked to be total, but was not.

In the first place, and this was his main worry, Javert had not taken the prisoner, prisoner. The victim of an assassination who gets away is more suspect than the assassin; and it is likely that this character, such a precious haul for the bandits, was no less a good catch for the authorities. After that, Montparnasse had eluded Javert.

He would have to wait for another opportunity to lay his hand once more on that "fiend of a fop." Montparnasse, in fact, had run into Éponine on the boulevard where she was keeping watch under the trees and had taken her with him, preferring to play Némorin to the daughter rather than Schinderhannes[1] to the father. Just as well for him that he did. He was free. As for Éponine, Javert saw to it that she was "nabbed" again. Not much of a consolation. Éponine had joined Azelma in Les Madelonnettes.

In the end, on the trip from the Gorbeau slum to La Force, one of the principal felons arrested, Claquesous, had been lost. No one knew how it could have happened, the officers and sergeants "didn't get it," the man had disappeared into thin air, he had slipped through the thumbscrews, he had poured through the cracks in the cab, the fiacre had leaked and he had fled; no one knew what to say, except that when they reached the prison, no Claquesous. Either the fairies or the police had something to do with this. Had Claquesous melted in the darkness like a snowflake in water? Was there some secret connivance on the part of the officers? Did this man belong to the twin enigma of disorder and order? Was he concentric to the felony and repression? Did this sphinx have his front paws in crime and his hind paws in authority? Javert could not accept those particular tricks and his hackles rose at the thought of such compromises; but his squadron included other inspectors besides himself, ones who, though his subordinates, were, perhaps, more experienced than he was in the secrets of the prefecture, and Claquesous was such a scoundrel that he would have made a very good policeman. To be on such intimate terms with the trick of vanishing into the night is an excellent thing for armed robbery and marvelously useful for the police. Such two-faced rogues exist. Whatever the case might be, Claquesous was mislaid and was not found again. Javert seemed more annoyed than surprised by this.

As for Marius, "that drip of a lawyer who probably took fright" and whose name Javert had forgotten, Javert didn't give two hoots about him. Besides, a lawyer can always be found. But was he just a lawyer?

The preliminary investigation was under way. The examining magistrate found it useful not to put one of the men from the Patron-Minette gang into solitary confinement, hoping he would reveal something while chatting. This man was Brujon, the hairy one from the rue du Petit-Banquier. He had been released into the Charlemagne yard and the prison guards' eyes were on him.

That name, Brujon, is still remembered in La Force. In the ghastly courtyard known as that of the New Building, which the administration used to call Saint-Bernard yard and the thieves called the Lions' Den, on the wall covered with scales and damp that rose on the left to the same level as the rooftops, next to an old rusty iron gate that led to the old chapel of the La Force ducal mansion, which had become a dormitory for crooks, you could still see even twelve years ago a sort of fortress roughly carved in the stone with a nail, and below it this signature:

BRUJON, 1811.

The Brujon of 1811 was the father of the Brujon of 1832. The latter, of whom we only caught a glimpse in the Gorbeau ambush, was a strapping young lad, extremely cunning and extremely adroit, with a stunned, mournful look. It is because of this stunned look that the examining magistrate let him go, thinking he would be more useful in the Charlemagne yard than in a cell in solitary.

Thieves don't cease operating because they are in the hands of justice. They are not so easily put off. Being in jail for a crime does not prevent a person from getting another crime off the ground. They are artists who already have a painting in the Salon[2] but who are nonetheless working on a new work in their studio.

Brujon seemed stupefied by prison. He could sometimes be seen for hours at a stretch in the Charlemagne yard, standing next to the canteen window staring like an idiot at that grimy notice that listed the canteen's prices, starting with *garlic, 62 centimes* and ending with *cigar, five centimes*. Or else he would spend his time shivering, his teeth actually chattering, claiming he had a fever and asking if one of the twenty-eight beds in the fever ward was vacant.

All of a sudden, about the second fortnight in February 1832, it was discovered that Brujon, this sleepwalking lump, had had, through brokers of the house, not in his name but in the names of three of his mates, three different commissions carried out, which had cost him in all fifty sous, an exorbitant expense that attracted the attention of the prison brigadier.

Inquiries were made and, after consulting the price list for errands posted in the detainees' visitors' room, it emerged that the fifty sous were broken down as follows: three errands; one for the Panthéon, ten sous; one for the Val-de-Grâce, fifteen sous; one for the barrière de la Grenelle, twenty-five sous. This one was the most expensive on the price list. Now, the Panthéon, the Val-de-Grâce, and the barrière de la Grenelle just happened to be the precise locales of three of the most dreaded barrière prowlers, Kruideniers alias Bizarro, Glorieux, a freed convict, and Barrecarrosse, all of whom now came under the surveillance of the police. It was thought that these men were somehow affiliated with the Patron-Minette gang, two of whose chiefs, Babet and Gueulemer, had been locked up. It was assumed that in Brujon's dispatches, delivered by hand not to residential addresses but to people waiting in the street, there must have been information to do with some planned felony. There were further indications still; the three prowlers were arrested and Brujon's scheme, whatever it was, was thought to have been nipped in the bud.

About a week after these measures were taken, a warden doing the rounds one night was inspecting the dormitory in the basement of the New Building, and just as he was about to drop his chestnut in the chestnut box—this was the method then employed to ensure that wardens performed their duties correctly: every hour a chestnut was supposed to fall into all the boxes nailed to the dormitory doors—this warden saw, through the dormitory peephole, Brujon sitting up in bed writing something by the light of the wall lamp. The warden stepped in. Brujon was thrown into the dungeon for a month but they could not find what he had written. The police had nothing to add, either.

What is certain is that the next day "a postilion" was lobbed from the Charlemagne yard into the Lions' Den over the five-story building that separated the two yards.

The detainees gave the name *postilion* to a tiny pellet of artfully kneaded bread which is sent *to Ireland,* that is, over a prison's roof, from one courtyard to another. Etymology: *over England;* from one territory to another; *to Ireland.* This small pellet falls into the courtyard. Whoever picks it up and breaks it open finds in it a note addressed to some prisoner in the courtyard. If a detainee finds it, he hands the note over to the person it is intended for; if it is a warden, or one of those prisoners who have secretly sold out, known as sheep in prisons and foxes in galleys, the note is taken to the clerk and delivered to the police.

This time, the postilion reached its address, though the person the message was meant for was at that moment in solitary. This addressee was none other than Babet, one of the four leaders of Patron-Minette.

The postilion contained a screwed up piece of paper on which there was nothing but these two lines: "Babet. There is something going down rue Plumet. A garden gate."

That was what Brujon had written in the middle of the night.

Despite the male and female officers carrying out body searches, Babet found a way of getting the note from La Force to La Salpêtrière to a "good friend" he had there—behind bars. This girl in turn transmitted the note to another woman she knew, a woman called Magnon, closely watched by the police but not yet arrested. This Magnon, whose name the reader has already come across, was linked to the Thénardiers in a way that will be clarified later, and could, by going to see Éponine, serve as a bridge between La Salpêtrière and Les Madelonnettes.

It happened that, just at that very moment, proof being lacking in the preliminary investigation into the daughters' involvement in Thénardier's case, Éponine and Azelma were released.

When Éponine came out, Magnon, who was watching for her at the doors of Les Madelonnettes, handed her Brujon's note to Babet, urging her to clarify the matter.

Éponine went to the rue Plumet, recognized the gate and garden, observed the house, spied, watched, and a few days later, took the Magnon woman, who lived in the rue Clocheperce, a biscuit that Magnon then transmitted to Babet's mistress at La Salpêtrière. A biscuit in the murky symbolism of prisons signifies *nothing doing.*

So that less than a week after that, Babet and Brujon ran into each other in the covered way that ringed La Force, as one was heading for "the preliminary" and the other was returning from it:

"Well, then," asked Brujon, "the rue P.?"

"A biscuit," answered Babet.

And so this fetus of crime conceived at La Force was aborted. But this abortion had repercussions completely foreign to Brujon's program. We will see what they were.

Often when we think we are tying a knot with a simple thread, we don't notice we've caught up another thread as well.

### III. FATHER MABEUF'S APPARITION

Marius no longer went to see anyone, but it did sometimes happen that he ran into Father Mabeuf.

While Marius was slowly going down the gloomy steps we might call the cellar stairs, which lead to places without light where you hear the happy walking over your head, Monsieur Mabeuf was also going down.

*The Flora of Cauteretz* was no longer selling at all—not a single copy. The experiments with indigo had not succeeded in the little Austerlitz garden so badly exposed. Monsieur Mabeuf could grow only a few rare plants that like rain and shade there. He was not discouraged, though. He had obtained a bit of ground in the Jardin des Plantes, in a good spot in terms of exposure, to conduct his indigo trials "at his own expense." For this, he had pawned the copperplates of his *Flora.* He had cut his breakfast down to two eggs and one of those he left to his old servant whose wages he had not paid now for fifteen months. And often this breakfast was his only meal. He no longer laughed his childlike laugh, he had grown morose and no longer received visitors. Marius was right not to think of calling anymore. Sometimes, at the hour at which Monsieur Mabeuf went to the Jardin des Plantes, the old man and the young man would cross paths on the boulevard de l'Hôpital. They would not stop to speak but would just nod to each other sadly. It is heartrending that there comes a time when misery undoes the ties that bind people! You were once two friends, you are now just two passersby.

The bookseller Royol had died. Monsieur Mabeuf now had only his books, his garden, and his indigo; these things were, for him, the three forms happiness, pleasure, and hope had taken. That was enough for him to live on. He said to himself: "When I've finished my balls of blue, I'll be rich, I'll get my copperplates out of hock, I'll get my *Flora* back on the shelves with a bit of charlatanism, some hefty handouts under the counter, and a few ads in the papers, and I'll buy, and I know exactly where, a copy of Pierre de Médine's *The Art of Sailing,* the edition of 1559, with woodcuts." Meanwhile, he worked all day on his patch of indigo and at night he went home to water his garden and read his books. Monsieur Mabeuf was very close to eighty at the time.

One night he saw a strange apparition.

He had gone home while the sun was still high in the sky. Mother Plutarch, whose health was not the best, was in bed sick. He had dined on a bone that still had a bit of meat on it and a bit of bread that he'd found on the kitchen table and he was sitting on an overturned block of stone that substituted for a bench in his garden.

Near this seat there rose, in the manner of old orchard gardens, a sort of large, extremely weathered hut made of boards and joists, a rabbit hutch on the ground floor, a storeroom for fruit upstairs. There were no rabbits in the hutch, but there were a few apples in the fruit storeroom, the remains of the provisions for winter.

Monsieur Mabeuf had begun to flick through a book and to read, with the aid of his spectacles, two books that fascinated him and even totally absorbed him, which is more serious at his age. His native timidity made him susceptible to a certain acceptance of superstitions. The first of these books was the famous treatise of president Delancre, *De l'inconstance des démons,* the other was the quarto of Mutor de la Rubaudière, *Sur les diables de Vauvert et les gobelins de la Bièvre.* This last book fascinated him even more because his garden had been one of the places once haunted by goblins. Twilight was starting to turn anything high up white and to turn whatever was down low black. As he read, Father Mabeuf was looking over the book in hand at his plants, among others a magnificent rhododendron that was one of his consolations; four days of dryness, of sun and wind, without a drop of rain, had just passed; the branches were hanging down, the buds drooping, the leaves dropping, everything needed watering; the rhododendron especially was sad. Father Mabeuf was one of those for whom plants have souls. The old man had toiled all day at his indigo patch, he was completely exhausted, and yet he got up, laid his books down on the seat, and walked over to the well, all hunched over and tottering; but when he grabbed the chain, he could not pull hard enough on it to unhook it and lower it down. He turned back and cast eyes full of anguish up at the sky that was filling with stars.

The evening had that serenity that rolls over the sorrows of man and buries them under some unfathomable joy, mournful yet eternal. The night promised to be as arid as the day had been.

"Stars everywhere!" thought the old man. "Not the merest wisp of a cloud! Not the tiniest drop of water!"

And his head, which he had held up for a moment, fell back on his chest.

He raised it again and looked at the sky once more, muttering: "The tiniest drop of dew! A dollop of pity!"

He tried again to disengage the chain from the well and could not do it.

At that moment, he heard a voice say: "Father Mabeuf, would you like me to water your garden for you?"

At the same time, a noise like a wild animal going by came from the hedge, and he saw a sort of tall, thin girl emerge from the bushes and stand before him, eyeing him boldly. This looked less like a human being than some sort of shade that the twilight had just hatched.

Before Father Mabeuf, who frightened easily and was, as we said, always ready to be scared, could get out a syllable in reply, this creature, whose movements in the dusk were weirdly brusque, had unhooked the chain, dropped the bucket in, and pulled it back out and filled the watering can, and the good man saw the apparition, which had bare feet and a skirt of rags, race through the flower beds distributing life all around it. The sound of the water on the leaves filled Father Mabeuf's soul with rapture. It seemed to him that the rhododendron was happy now.

When the first bucket was empty, the girl drew a second, then a third. She watered the whole garden.

Walking like this through the flowerbeds along paths where her silhouette appeared all black, shaking her badly torn shawl over her long bony arms, she looked somehow like a bat.

When she had finished, Father Mabeuf approached with tears in his eyes and placed his hand on her forehead.

"May God bless you," he said, "you are an angel, since you care for flowers."

"No," she replied, "I am the devil, but I don't care."

Without waiting for and without hearing her reply, the old man cried out: "What a pity I'm so poor and wretched and I can't do anything for you!"

"You can do something," she said.

"What?"

"Tell me where Monsieur Marius lives."

The old man didn't understand.

"What Monsieur Marius?"

He raised his rheumy eyes and seemed to be looking for something that had evaporated.

"A young man who used to come here once."

Meanwhile, Monsieur Mabeuf was foraging through his memory.

"Ah, yes!" he cried. "I know who you mean. Hang on! Monsieur Marius . . . Baron Marius Pontmercy, by Jove! He lives . . . Actually, he doesn't live there anymore . . . Ah, well, I don't know."

As he spoke, he had bent down to tie up a branch of the rhododendron and he went on: "Wait, I remember now. He passes by the boulevard all the time and he heads for La Glacière. Rue Croulebarbe. The Field of the Lark. Start there. He isn't hard to find."

When Monsieur Mabeuf stood up again, there was no one there anymore. The girl had vanished.

He definitely felt a little afraid.

"Really," he thought, "if my garden wasn't watered, I'd think it was a spirit."

An hour later, when he had gone to bed, this came back to him and, as he fell asleep, at that disturbing moment when thought, like that fabulous bird that turns into a fish to slide through the sea, gradually takes the form of dreaming to cross through sleep, he said to himself vaguely: "In fact, this is a lot like what Rubaudière says about goblins. Could it have been a goblin?"

## IV. Marius's Apparition

One morning, a few days after this visit by a "spirit" to Father Mabeuf—it was a Monday, the day on which Marius borrowed the hundred-sou piece from Courfeyrac for Thénardier—Marius had put this hundred-sou piece in his pocket and, before taking it to the prison clerk, had gone off "for a bit of a stroll," hoping that this would make him work on his return. This was what always happened, actually. As soon as he got out of bed, he would sit down in front of a book and a sheet of paper to hack away at some translation or other; at the time, he had the job of translating into French a celebrated quarrel between Germans, the controversy between Gans and Savigny;[1] he took up Savigny, he took up Gans, read four lines, tried to get one of them down, could not, saw a star between the paper and his eyes and rose from his chair, saying: "I'm going out. That'll put me in the right frame of mind."

And off he'd go to the Field of the Lark. There, more than ever, he would see that star and, less than ever, Savigny and Gans.

He would go back home, try to resume his labors, and not manage; there was no way to tie a single one of the broken threads in his brain; so then he would say: "I won't go out tomorrow. It stops me working." Yet out he would go, every day.

He spent more time in the Field of the Lark than he did in Courfeyrac's cubbyhole. His true address was this: boulevard de la Santé, seventh tree from the rue Croulebarbe.

That particular morning, he had quit the seventh tree and gone to sit on the parapet along the Gobelins stream. Cheery sunshine shone through the glossy green leaves, freshly unfurled.

He was dreaming of "Her." But his dreaming turned into reproof and then turned back on himself; he thought painfully of the laziness, the paralysis of the soul that was overcoming him and of that night which was growing darker from one moment to the next to the point where he could already no longer even see the sun.

Yet through this painful emanation of indistinct ideas that was not even a monologue—so much had action been stifled within him that he no longer even had the strength to want to grieve—through this melancholy absorption, sensations from the world outside came to him. He heard behind him, below him, on both riverbanks, the washerwomen of the Gobelins beating their washing, and, overhead, the birds twittering and singing in the elms. On one side, the sound of freedom, of happy insouciance, of spare time with wings; on the other, the sound of work. Both were joyful sounds—something that set him musing deeply, almost reflecting.

All of a sudden, in the middle of his overwhelming ecstasy, he heard a voice he knew saying: "Hey! Here he is!"

He looked up and recognized the unhappy waif who had come to his place one morning, the elder of the Thénardier girls, Éponine, for he now knew her name. The odd thing was that she looked both poorer and prettier; two steps you would not have thought possible for her to take. She had brought off a dual progress—toward the light and toward distress. She was barefoot and in rags like the day she strode so resolutely into his room, only her rags were two months older; the holes were bigger, the tatters more sordid. It was the same hoarse voice, the same forehead, browned and wrinkled by the sun, the same open, wild, and wandering gaze. She had in her countenance, more than before, that indefinably frightened and pathetic look that a stint in jail adds to misery.

She had bits of straw and hay in her hair, not like Ophelia[2] from having gone mad after catching Hamlet's contagious madness, but because she had slept in some stable loft.

Yet with all that, she was beautiful. What a star you are, O youth!

Meanwhile, she had planted herself in front of Marius with a trace of joy visible on her livid face and something that resembled a smile.

She looked for a few moments as though she couldn't speak.

"So, I've caught up with you!" she said at last. "Father Mabeuf was right, it was this boulevard here! I've looked everywhere for you! If you only knew! You know what? I've been in the clink. A fortnight! They let me go! Since they had nothing on me and, anyway, I hadn't reached the age of consent. I was underage. By two months. Oh, I've looked everywhere for you! For six weeks now. You don't live over there anymore, then?"

"No," said Marius.

"Oh, I understand. Because of that business. It's not nice, that sort of carrying-on. You moved. Listen! What are you getting about in an old hat like that for, then? A young man like you should have nice stuff. You know what, Monsieur Marius? Father Mabeuf calls you Baron Marius something-or-other. But you're not a baron, are you? Barons are old geezers, they go to the Luxembourg and sit in front of the château where there's more sun, they read the *Quotidienne* for a sou. Once I went and took a letter to a baron who was like that. He was over a hundred. So, tell me, where do you live these days?"

Marius did not answer.

"Ah!" she went on. "You've got a hole in your shirt. I'll have to sew that up for you."

She went on with an expression that gradually clouded over.

"You don't seem happy to see me?"

Marius said nothing; for a second she remained silent, too, then she cried: "If I wanted to, but, I could make you pretty happy!"

"What?" asked Marius. "What are you talking about?"

"Ah, you used to talk to me more friendly!" she said.

"Well, then, would you please tell me what you're talking about?"

She bit her lip; she seemed to hesitate as though in the grip of some sort of inner struggle. Finally she seemed to reach a decision.

"Never mind, it doesn't matter. You look sad and I want you to be happy. Just promise me you'll laugh. I want to see you laugh and see you say: 'Well, now, that's good.' Poor Monsieur Marius! You know! You promised me you'd give me anything I wanted—"

"Yes! But you have to tell me!"

She looked Marius straight in the eye and told him: "I have the address."

Marius went white. All his blood rushed to his heart.

"What address?"

"The address you asked me for!"

She added, as though making an effort: "The address—you know very well!"

"Yes!" Marius stammered.

"Of the young lady!"

That word out of the way, she sighed deeply.

Marius jumped down from the parapet he was sitting on and wildy clutched her hand.

"Oh! Well! Take me there! Tell me! Ask me for anything you like! Where is it?"

"Come with me," she answered. "I don't know the street or the number all that well. It's quite a way away from here, but I know the house real well, I'll take you there."

She pulled her hand away and went on, in a tone that would have broken the heart of any observer but that did not remotely move Marius, intoxicated, in raptures as he was: "Oh, how happy you are!"

A cloud passed over Marius's forehead. He seized Éponine by the arm.

"Swear to me one thing!"

"Swear?" she said. "What does that mean? Fancy wanting me to swear!"

And she laughed.

"Your father! Promise me, Éponine! Swear to me that you won't say anything to your father about this address!"

She turned toward him with a stunned look.

"Éponine! How did you know my name's Éponine?"

"Promise me what I say!"

But she didn't seem to hear him.

"I like that! You called me Éponine!"

Marius grabbed both her arms.

"Answer me, for Christ's sake! Listen carefully to what I'm saying, swear to me that you won't tell your father the address that you know!"

"My father?" she said. "Ah, yes, my father! Don't worry. He's in solitary. Anyway, do you think I care about my father!"

"But you haven't promised me!" Marius shouted.

"Let go of me, then!" she said, bursting out laughing. "Look how you're shaking me! All right! All right! I promise you! I swear to you! What's it to me? I won't tell my father the address. There! How's that? Is that it?"

"Or anybody else!" said Marius.

"Or anybody else."

"Now," said Marius, "take me there."

"Right away?"

"Right away."

"Come. Oh, look how happy he is!" she said.

After a few steps, she stopped.

"You're too close behind me, Monsieur Marius. Let me go ahead, and follow me like this, like you haven't seen me. A fine-looking young man like you shouldn't be seen with a woman like me."

No tongue could tell all that this word, *woman*, contained, uttered the way it was by that child.

She took a dozen steps and stopped again; Marius joined her. She spoke to him out of the corner of her mouth without turning round: "By the way, you know you promised me something?"

Marius fumbled in his pocket. All he had in the whole world was the five francs destined for father Thénardier. He took it and put it in Éponine's hand.

She opened her fingers and let it fall to the ground and shot him a dark look: "I don't want your money," she said.

# BOOK THREE

# THE HOUSE IN THE RUE PLUMET

## I. THE HOUSE WITH A SECRET ENTRANCE

Around the middle of the last century, a presiding judge who wore a magistrate's hat and sat on the parliament of Paris,[1] and who had a mistress and hid the fact, for in those days the *grands seigneurs* showed off their mistresses and the bourgeois hid them, had "a little house"[2] built in the faubourg Saint-Germain in the deserted rue Blomet, which is now called the rue Plumet, not far from the spot then known as the Combat des Animaux.

This house was a detached two-story villa with two rooms on the ground floor, two bedrooms upstairs, a kitchen downstairs, upstairs a boudoir, and an attic under the roof, the whole thing fronted by a garden with a large gate opening onto the street. This garden was on about an acre of land. It was all passersby could see; but at the rear of the house there was a small yard and at the back of the yard there was a low building consisting of two rooms over a cellar, a "little something" intended to conceal a child and a nursemaid, should the need arise. This building was connected, at the back, via a concealed door that opened with a secret key, to a long narrow passageway that was paved, winding, uncovered, bordered by high walls and hidden so incredibly artfully it was almost lost between the garden walls and the walls of the cultivated plots whose every twist and turn it followed before ending in another door, also with a secret key, that opened a quarter of a mile away, almost in another quartier, at the lonely end of the rue de Babylone.

Monsieur le président, the presiding judge, snuck in this back way so that even those who might have spied on him and followed him and observed that every day Monsieur le président went off somewhere mysteriously, could not have suspected that going off to the rue de Babylone actually meant going off to the rue Blomet. Thanks to the clever buying up of land, the ingenious magistrate was able to get this secret passage to his house built on his own land, and consequently without any monitoring. Later he sold off the plots of land bordering the passage in small allotments for gardens and crops, and the owners of these plots of land on both sides thought they were seeing a single common without for a moment suspecting the existence of this long ribbon of cobblestones snaking between two walls among their flowerbeds and their orchards. Only the birds could see this curiosity. The tits and warblers of last century no doubt gossiped a good deal together about Monsieur le président.

The villa, built in stone in the Mansart style, wainscoted and furnished in the Watteau[3] style, all loose rocaille inside, all fuddy-duddy periwig outside, walled about with a triple hedge of flowers, had something discreet, tizzy, and solemn about it, as befits a passing fancy of love and of the bench.

The house and the passageway, which have since disappeared, still existed fifteen years ago or so. In '93, a boilermaker bought the house to demolish it, but since he couldn't pay the asking price, the nation sent him into bankruptcy. So you could say the house demolished the boilermaker. Thereafter the house remained empty and slowly fell into ruin, like all dwellings bereft of people to lend them life. It had remained furnished with its old furniture and was always for sale or to let, and the ten or twelve people who passed through the rue Plumet in the course of a year were notified of this by an illegible yellow sign that had been hanging off the garden gate since 1810.

Toward the end of the Restoration, these same passersby might have noticed that the sign had disappeared and that the shutters on the first floor were even open. The house was, in fact, occupied. The windows had little curtains, a sure sign that there was a woman about.

In the month of October 1829, a man of a certain age had shown up and rented the house as it was, including, of course, the outbuilding at the back and the passageway that ended at the rue de Babylone. He had had secret locks fixed on the two passageway doors. The house, as we said, was still more or less furnished with the old furnishings of the presiding judge. The new tenant had ordered a few repairs, added what was missing here and there, replaced some cobblestones in the courtyard, some bricks on the floor, some steps on the stairs, some strips of wood in the parquet floor and panes of glass in the casement windows, and had finally moved in with a young girl and an old servant, noiselessly, more like someone stealing in than a man entering his own home. The neighbors did not gossip about him for the simple reason that there were no neighbors.

This tenant who created so little stir was Jean Valjean and the young girl was Cosette. The servant was an old maid called Toussaint, or All Saints, whom Jean Valjean had saved from the hospital[4] and destitution. She was ancient, provincial, and she stuttered, three qualities that had decided Jean Valjean to take her with him. He had rented the house under the name of Monsieur Fauchelevent, man of private means. In all that was recounted earlier, the reader no doubt recognized Jean Valjean even before Thénardier did.

Why had Jean Valjean left the Petit-Picpus convent? What had happened? Nothing had happened.

As you will recall, Jean Valjean had been happy in the convent, so happy that his conscience had wound up being troubled by it. He saw Cosette every day, he felt a sense of paternity stirring and growing inside him more and more, he protected that child with his soul like a brooding hen, he told himself that she was his, that nothing could take her away from him, that this was how it would be forever; that she would most certainly become a nun, being gently prodded in that direction every day, that accordingly the convent was now the world for her as for him, that he would grow old there and she would grow up there, that she would grow old there and he would die there, that in the end— ravishing hope!—no separation was thinkable. In reflecting upon this, he had ended up falling into a state of great confusion. He questioned himself. He asked himself if all that happiness really did belong to him, if it were not made up of somebody else's happiness, of the happiness that he was confiscating, that he was stealing, from this child—he, an old man. Wasn't it a case of theft? He told himself that this child had a right to know life before renouncing it, that cutting her off, in advance and in a sense without consulting her, from all the joys of life on the pretext of sparing her from all of its ordeals, to take advantage of her ignorance and her isolation to plant an artificial vocation in her, was to warp and damage another human being and to lie to God. And who knows if, one day realizing all this and regretting having become a nun, Cosette would not end up hating him for it? A final thought, this one less heroic than the others, almost selfish, but which he found unbearable. He resolved to leave the convent.

He resolved to do it; he recognized with great sorrow that he had to do it. As for objections, there weren't any. Five years' sojourn between those four walls as a disappeared man had necessarily vaporized or laid to rest any trace of fear. He could quietly return to live among men. He had aged and everything had changed. Who would recognize him now? And then again, if the worst came to the worst, there was no danger except for himself, and he did not have the right to condemn Cosette to the cloister for the reason that he had been condemned to penal servitude. Besides, what is danger in the face of duty? Lastly, nothing was stopping him from being careful and taking his precautions. As for Cosette's education, it was almost finished and complete.

Once his decision had been taken, he waited for the right opportunity. It was not long coming. Old Fauchelevent died.

Jean Valjean demanded an audience with the reverend prioress and told her that he had come into a small inheritance at the death of his brother that allowed him to live without working from that point on, and so he was leaving the service of the convent and would take his daughter with him; but that, as it was not fair that Cosette, now that she would not be taking her vows, should have been educated for free, he humbly beseeched the reverend prioress to approve his offer to the community of a sum of five thousand francs as indemnity for the five years that Cosette had spent there.

And that is how Jean Valjean emerged from the Convent of Perpetual Adoration.

On leaving the convent, he stashed under his arm the small suitcase whose key he still kept on him always, not wanting to entrust it to any carrier. This suitcase used to intrigue Cosette because of the smell of embalming that came from it.

Let us say immediately that from that day, this case never left him. He had it always in his room. It was the first and sometimes the only thing he took with him in his various moves. Cosette would laugh about it, calling the suitcase "the inseparable," and saying, "I'm jealous of it."

Jean Valjean, though, did not appear out in the open again without profound anxiety.

He discovered the house in the rue Plumet and dug in there. He was now in possession of the name Ultime Fauchelevent.

At the same time, he rented two other apartments in Paris, so that he would attract less attention than if he always stayed in the same quartier, so that he could absent himself, if need be, at the slightest concern he might have, and finally, so that he would not find himself caught short again like the night when he had so miraculously escaped from Javert. These two apartments were two extremely rickety run-down dwellings in two quartiers a fair distance apart, one in the rue de l'Ouest, the other in the rue de l'Homme-Armé.[5]

From time to time he would go either to the rue de l'Homme-Armé or to the rue de l'Ouest to spend a month or six weeks there with Cosette, leaving Toussaint behind. He had himself waited on by the porters there and passed himself off as a man of private means from the suburbs with a pied-à-terre in town. This man of lofty virtue had three domiciles in Paris solely for the purpose of evading the police.

## II. JEAN VALJEAN AS A NATIONAL GUARD

Still, strictly speaking, he lived in the rue Plumet, and he organized his life there in the following fashion:

Cosette occupied the main house along with the servant; she had the master bedroom with the painted window piers, the boudoir with the gilded mold-ings, the presiding judge's salon furnished with tapestries and vast armchairs; she had the garden. Jean Valjean had a four-poster bed put in Cosette's bedroom with a canopy of antique damask in three colors and a beautiful old Persian rug bought in the rue du Figuier-Saint-Paul at mother Gaucher's, and, to balance the severity of these magnificent old things, he had mixed these odds and ends with all the bright and lovely furnishings young girls like, a set of shelves known as a whatnot, a bookcase and some gilt-edged books, stationery, a blotter, a work table inlaid with mother-of-pearl, a silver-gilt sewing kit, a washstand of Japanese porcelain. Long damask curtains in three colors on a red background, matching the colors over the bed, hung from the upstairs windows. On the ground floor, tapestry curtains. All winter Cosette's little house was heated from top to bottom. As for him, he lived in the sort of porter's lodge at the back of the yard, with a mattress on a bed of webbing, a pinewood table, two straw-bottomed chairs, an earthenware water pitcher, a few books on a board, his precious suitcase in a corner, never a fire. He dined with Cosette and there would be a coarse whole-grain loaf for him on the table. He had said to Toussaint when she entered their service: "Mademoiselle is the mistress of the house." "What about you, M-m-monsieur?" Toussaint had replied, stunned. "Me, I'm much more than the master, I am the father."

Cosette had been taught housekeeping in the convent and she took care of expenses, which were extremely modest. Every day Jean Valjean took Cosette's arm and took her out for a stroll. He would walk her to the Luxembourg, to the least frequented allée, and every Sunday he took her to mass, always at Saint-Jacques-du-Haut-Pas because it was far away. As that is a very poor quartier, he was always giving alms there and the downtrodden would swarm around him in the church, which is what earned him the Thénardiers' epistle: *To the benevolent gentleman of Saint-Jacques-du-Haut-Pas church.* He liked to take Cosette along on visits to the needy and the sick. But no stranger ever entered the house in the rue Plumet. Toussaint brought back the groceries and Jean Valjean himself would go and fetch water from a water hydrant very close by on the boulevard. Wood and wine were kept in a kind of semi-subterranean recess lined with loose stones right next to the door on the rue de Babylone, a space that had once served as a grotto to the presiding judge; for in the days of follies and country cottages, no love affair was complete without a grotto.

In the once-illicit door on the rue de Babylone, there was one of those boxes that look like piggybanks and are designed for letters and newspapers; only, the three inhabitants of the house on the rue Plumet did not receive newspapers or letters, so the entire usefulness of the box, once upon a time a go-between in flings and confidant of a skirt-chasing gownsman, was now limited to the notices of the tax collector and to guard-duty rosters, for Monsieur Fauchelevent, man of means, was in the National Guard;[1] he had not been able to slip through the tightly woven net of the 1831 census. The municipal information gathered at the time went back as far as the convent of Petit-Picpus, a sort of impenetrable and holy cloud from which Jean Valjean had emerged venerable in the eyes of his local *mairie*,[2] and, as a result, worthy of mounting guard.

Three or four times a year, Jean Valjean donned his uniform and did his stint of guard duty, and very gladly, too; for him, it was the perfect disguise, which let him mingle with the world at large while leaving him alone. Jean Valjean had just turned sixty, the age of legal exemption, but he didn't look a day older than fifty; besides, he had no desire to evade his sergeant major or to cavil with the comte de Lobau;[3] he had no civil status; he was concealing his name, he was concealing his identity, he was concealing his age, he was concealing everything; and so, as we just said, he was a keen National Guard. To resemble the man in the street who pays his taxes, that was the sum total of his ambition. This man's ideal, within, was an angel; without, a bourgeois.

We note one detail, though. Whenever Jean Valjean went out with Cosette, he dressed as we have seen and looked very much the part of a retired officer. When he went out alone, and this was usually in the evening, he was always dressed in a worker's jacket and pants, with a cap on his head that hid his face. Was it a precaution, or humility? Both at once. Cosette was used to the enigmatic side of her destiny and scarcely noticed her father's odd ways. As for Toussaint, she venerated Jean Valjean and liked everything he did. One day her butcher, who had just caught sight of Jean Valjean, said to her: "That's a funny one." She answered: "That is a-a-a saint."

Neither Jean Valjean, nor Cosette, nor Toussaint ever came in or went out except through the door on the rue de Babylone. Unless you saw them through the garden gate, it would have been hard to guess that they lived in the rue Plumet. This gate always remained shut. Jean Valjean had left the garden wild so that it would not attract attention.

There, perhaps, he got it wrong.

### III. Foliis ac Frondibus[1]

The garden, thus left to itself for more than half a century, had become extraordinary and charming. Passersby of forty years ago would stop in the street to gaze at it, without suspecting the secrets it concealed behind its fresh green layers. More than one dreamer of the day had many times let his eyes and his thoughts stray indiscreetly through the bars of the antique gate, which was padlocked, warped, rickety, fixed to two pillars that had gone green with moss, and bizarrely crowned with a pediment of indecipherable arabesques.

There was a stone bench in one corner, one or two moldy statues, a few trellises, their nails loosened by time, rotting against the wall; otherwise, no paths or lawn, just couch grass all over the place. Gardening had gone out the door, nature had returned in all its glory. Weeds flourished, which is a wonderful adventure for a poor patch of dirt. The stocks there were having a field day, riotously splendid. Nothing in the garden opposed the sacred effort of things toward life; venerable growth was very much at home. The trees hung down toward the brambles, the brambles reached up toward the trees, the plant climbed, the branch bowed, what crawls on the ground had gone to look for what blossoms in the air, what floats on the wind had stooped toward what trails in the moss; trunks, limbs, leaves, twigs, tufts, tendrils, shoots, thorns mixed together, crossed, married, merged; in a close and powerful embrace, the vegetation had achieved and celebrated there, under the satisfied eye of the Creator, in this enclosure of three hundred square feet, the sacred mystery of His fraternity, a symbol of human fraternity. This garden was no longer a garden, it was a colossal thicket, that is, as impenetrable as a forest, as crowded as a town, as tremulous as a nest, as somber as a cathedral, as fragrant as a bouquet, as lonely as a tomb, as full of life as the teeming multitudes.

In Floréal,[2] this enormous bushland, free behind its gate and within its four walls, began to rut in the mute labor of universal germination, quivering in the rising sun almost like an animal gulping in the effluvia of cosmic love and feeling the April sap rise and boil in its veins; it shook its extravagant green hair in the wind, scattered over the wet ground, over the worn statues, over the crumbling steps of the villa and even over the pavement in the deserted street, flowers like stars, dew like pearls, fecundity, beauty, life, joy, perfume. At noon, a thousand white butterflies took refuge there, and it was a divine spectacle to see this living summer snow swirling there in flakes in the shade. There, in the jaunty gloom of the greenery, a host of innocent voices spoke softly to the soul, and what the warbling forgot to say, the humming completed. At night a dreamy vapor rose from the garden and enveloped it; a shroud of mist, a calm celestial sadness covered it; that intensely intoxicating smell of honeysuckle and wild morning glory wafted up on all sides like an exquisite and subtle poison; you could hear the final calls of the tree creepers and the wagtails dozing off under the branches; you could feel the sacred intimacy of bird and tree; of a day, the wings rejoice the leaves, of a night, the leaves protect the wings.

In winter the thicket was black, wet, bristling, shivering with cold, and it let the house be seen a little. Instead of flowers among the branches and dew on the flowers, you could see the long silver ribbons of slugs on the cold thick carpet of yellow leaves; but in every case, whatever the aspect, whatever the season, spring, winter, summer, autumn, this little enclosure breathed melancholy, contemplation, solitude, freedom, the absence of man, the presence of God; and the old rusty gate looked as if it were saying: This garden is mine.

In vain were the cobblestones of Paris all around, the classical and splendid mansions of the rue de Varenne two feet away, the dome of the Invalides so close, the Chamber of Deputies not much farther; in vain the coaches of the rue de Bourgogne and the rue Saint-Dominique rolled with pomp and circumstance through the neighborhood, in vain the yellow, brown, white, red omnibuses passed each other at the next intersection along. The rue Plumet was a desert; and the death of the former owners, the passing of a revolution, the collapse of ancient fortunes, absence, oblivion, forty years of abandonment and of widowhood, were all that had been needed to bring back into this privileged place the ferns, the common mullein, the hemlock, the yarrow, the foxglove, the tall grass, the great crinkled plants with broad leaves of pale green brocade, the lizards, the beetles, the anxious quick insects; to flush out from the depths of the earth and put on show between these four walls a magically wild and savage grandeur; and for nature, which upsets the stingy arrangements of man and always offers itself completely wherever it spreads, as much in the ant as in the eagle, came and flourished in a mean little Parisian garden with all the ruggedness and majesty of a virgin forest in the New World.

Nothing is small, actually; anyone who leaves themselves open to nature knows this. Even though no absolute satisfaction is given to philosophy, no more in circumscribing the cause than in limiting the effect, the contemplator falls into endless raptures at all these breakdowns of forces that end in unity. Everything works on everything else.

Algebra applies to the clouds; the radiance of the star benefits the rose. No thinker worth his salt would dare claim that the scent of the hawthorn is useless to the constellations. Who can calculate the trajectory of a molecule? How do we know the creation of worlds is not determined by the falling of grains of sand? Who, after all, knows the reciprocal ebb and flow of the infinitely big and the infinitely small, the reverberation of causes in the chasms of a being, the avalanches of creation? A cheese mite matters; the small is big, the big is small; everything is in equilibrium within necessity—a frightening vision for the mind. There are miraculous relationships between beings and things; in this inexhaustible whole, from sun to aphid, no one looks down on anyone else; everyone needs each other. Light does not carry off earthly perfumes into the blue without knowing what it does with them; night distributes stellar essence to the sleeping flowers. All the birds that fly hold the thread of infinity in their claws. Germination involves the hatching of a meteor and the peck of a swallow's beak breaking out of its egg, and it brings off at once the birth of an earthworm and the coming of Socrates. Where the telescope ends, the microscope begins. Which of the two has greater vision? You choose. A patch of mold is a pleiad of flowers; a nebula is an anthill of stars. There is the same promiscuity, only even more amazing, between things of the intellect and the facts of substance. Elements and principles mingle, combine, intermarry, multiply, each together, to the point of finally bringing the material world and the moral world to the same clarity. Phenomena are perpetually folded back on themselves. In the vast cosmic exchanges, universal life comes and goes in unknown quantities, rolling everything in the invisible mystery of effluvia, putting each thing to work, not losing a single dream, a single bout of sleep, sowing an animalcule here, breaking up a star there, wavering and winding, turning light into a force and thought into an element, one propagated and indivisible, dissolving everything except that geometric point, the self; bringing everything back to the atom of the soul; making everything blossom in God; entangling all activities, from the highest to the lowest, in the obscurity of a dizzying mechanism, linking the flight of an insect to the movement of the earth, subordinating, who knows? if only by the sameness of the law, the evolution of the comet in the firmament to the twirling of the infusoria in a drop of water. A machine made of spirit. Enormous gears whose primary motor is the gnat and whose ultimate wheel is the zodiac.

## IV. Gate Change

It seems that this garden, created in the days of yore to hide dirty secrets, had transformed itself till it was fit for harboring chaste secrets. It no longer had either arbors or lawns, bowers or grottoes; there was a magnificent disheveled gloom falling like a veil everywhere you looked. Paphos[1] had turned itself back into Eden. Some indefinable penance had purified the retreat. This particular flower girl now offered her flowers to the soul. The flirtatious garden once highly compromised had retrieved its virginity and modesty. A presiding judge assisted by a gardener, an old man who thought he was a second Lamoignon, and another old man who thought he was a second Le Nôtre,[2] had shaped it into complex curves, pruned it, worried it, bedizened it, fashioned it for gallantry; nature had snatched it back, had filled it with shade and straightened it out for love.

There was a heart close at hand in such solitude. Love only had to show its face; there was a temple there, built of foliage, grass, moss, birds' sighs, soft shadows, waving branches, and a soul made of gentleness, faith, candor, hope, longing, and illusion.

Cosette had emerged from the convent when she was still virtually a child; at little more than fourteen years old, she was "at the difficult age," as we've said. Apart from her eyes, she looked rather more ugly than pretty, and, though she didn't have any particularly unattractive feature, she was awkward, skinny, timid, and bold at once—in short, a big little girl.

Her education was finished; that is, she had been taught religion and even, and especially, devotion; then "history," or what passes for history in the convent, geography, grammar, the participles, the kings of France, a bit of music, how to draw a nose, and so on, but otherwise she was ignorant about everything, which is both an asset and a danger. The soul of a young girl should not be left in the dark; later, mirages that are too sudden and too alive spring up in it as in a camera obscura.³ It should be gently and discreetly enlightened, by the reflection of reality rather than by reality's direct hard light. A helpful and graciously austere half-light that dissipates childish fears and prevents falls from grace. Only maternal instinct, that admirable intuition into which the memories of the virgin and the experience of the woman enter, knows how and with what this half-light should be made. Nothing can replace this instinct. To shape the soul of a young girl, all the nuns in the world are not equal to one mother.

Cosette had never had a mother. She had only had a whole host of mothers, plural. As for Jean Valjean, there was certainly all manner of tenderness in him at once, and all manner of care; but he was just an old man who knew absolutely nothing. Now, in this work of education, in this grave business of preparing a woman for life, how much science you need to do battle with that great ignorance known as innocence!

Nothing prepares a young girl for the passions like the convent. The convent turns thoughts toward the unknown. The heart, thrown back on itself, grows bigger, not being able to pour itself out, and grows deeper, not being able to bloom. Hence visions, suppositions, conjectures, novels sketched out, adventures yearned for, fantastic constructions, whole edifices built in the inner darkness of the mind, somber and secret abodes where the passions immediately find their dwelling place as soon as the floodgates are opened and they are allowed inside. The convent is a compression chamber that has to keep working for an entire life, if it is to triumph over the human heart.

On leaving the convent, Cosette could not have found anything sweeter or more dangerous than the house in the rue Plumet. It was an extension of solitude coupled with the beginnings of freedom; a walled garden, but with nature sharp, rich, voluptuous, and fragrant; the same dreams as in the convent, but with glimpses of young men; a gate, but one on the street.

Yet, we repeat, when she first arrived, she was still just a child. Jean Valjean delivered to her this uncultivated garden. "Do whatever you like with it," he told her. This amused Cosette; she foraged around every tuft and every stone, looking for "beasties"; she played there, in anticipation of dreaming there; she loved the garden for the secrets she found in the grass under her feet, in anticipation of loving it for the stars she would see through the branches above her head.

And then again, she loved her father, that is, Jean Valjean, with all her heart, with a naïve filial passion that made of the old man a charming and welcome companion. You will recall that Monsieur Madeleine was an avid reader. Jean

Valjean had continued to read; through this he had come to speak well; he had the secret wealth and the eloquence of a genuine and humble intelligence that has cultivated itself spontaneously. There was just enough harshness left in him to season his goodness; he had a rough mind and a gentle heart. At the Luxembourg, in their tête-à-têtes, he gave elaborate explanations of everything, drawing on what he had read, drawing also on what he had been through. While she listened, Cosette's eyes vaguely wandered.

This simple man was enough for Cosette's mind, just as this wildly overgrown garden was enough for her eyes. Whenever she had been chasing butterflies, she would run up to him out of breath and say: "Ah! I ran and ran!" He would kiss her on the forehead.

Cosette adored the old man. She was always following at his heels. Wherever Jean Valjean was, there was well-being. As Jean Valjean did not live either in the villa or in the garden, she was happier in the cobbled courtyard out back than in the enclosure full of flowers, and in the little shed furnished with straw chairs than in the grand salon hung with tapestries where you could recline on padded armchairs. Jean Valjean sometimes said to her, smiling with happiness at being pestered: "Go home, for heaven's sake! Leave me alone for a bit!"

She would scold him tenderly in that way that is so lovely coming from the daughter to the father.

"Father, I'm extremely cold at your place. Why don't you put a rug and a stove in here?"

"Dear child, there are so many people better than I am who don't even have a roof over their heads."

"Well, why is there a fire at my place and everything else you could want?"

"Because you are a child and a woman."

"Bah! Men must all be cold and uncomfortable, in that case."

"Certain men."

"All right, I'll come here so often you'll be forced to have a fire."

And she would also say to him: "Father, why do you eat that awful bread?"

"Because, my girl."

"Well, then, if you eat it, I'll eat it."

Then, so that Cosette would not eat black bread, Jean Valjean would switch to white bread.

Cosette only dimly remembered her childhood. She prayed morning and night for the mother she had never known. The Thénardiers had remained for her like two hideous figures from out of a nightmare. She remembered that "one day, after dark" she had been out fetching water in a wood. She thought it was a long way from Paris. It seemed to her that she had begun her life in a black void and that it was Jean Valjean who had pulled her out of it. Her childhood seemed like a time when there was nothing around her but millipedes, spiders, and snakes. When she was musing at night before going off to sleep, as she did not have a very clear sense of being Jean Valjean's daughter or of his being her father, she imagined that her mother's soul had passed into this good man and had come to live close by her.

When he was sitting down, she would press her cheek against his white hair and silently shed a tear, telling herself: "He could well be my mother, this man here!"

Cosette, though this is strange to say, in her profound ignorance as a convent-bred girl, and maternity in any case being absolutely unintelligible to virginity, had ended up realizing that she had as little of a mother as it was possible to have, hardly any mother at all. She did not even know this mother's name. Whenever she happened to ask Jean Valjean, Jean Valjean would clam up. If she asked him twice, he would simply smile by way of reply. Once she had insisted; the smile had ended in a tear.

This silence of Jean Valjean's buried Fantine under a cover of night. Was it prudence? Was it respect? Was it fear of delivering that name to the hazards of a memory other than his own?

As long as Cosette was little, Jean Valjean had been happy to talk to her about her mother; when she became a young girl, he just could not do it anymore. It seemed to him that he no longer dared. Was this because of Cosette? Was it because of Fantine? He felt a kind of religious horror at letting that shade into Cosette's thoughts and wheeling in the dead woman as a third party in their shared destiny. The more sacred this shade was to him, the more fearful she seemed. He thought of Fantine and felt himself overwhelmed with silence. He saw dimly in the darkness something like a finger over someone's lips. Had all that modesty that had been in Fantine and that, during her life, had been forced out of her by violence, come back after her death to land on her and watch, outraged, over the dead woman's peace and, ferocious, keep her in her grave? Did Jean Valjean, without knowing it, feel its pressure? We who believe in death are not among those who would reject this mysterious explanation. Hence the impossibility of uttering, even for Cosette, the name: Fantine.

One day Cosette said to him: "Father, last night I saw my mother in a dream. She had two big wings. My mother must have come close to sanctity in her lifetime."

"Through martyrdom," answered Jean Valjean.

Otherwise, Jean Valjean was happy.

When Cosette went out with him, she leaned on his arm, proud, happy, her heart full to overflowing. Jean Valjean, at all these marks of a tenderness so exclusive and so satisfied with him alone, felt his thoughts melt into delight. The poor man shuddered inside, flooded with an angelic bliss; he told himself in a burst of joy that this would last all his life; he said to himself that he had not really suffered enough to deserve such radiant happiness and he thanked God, from the depths of his soul, for having allowed him to be so loved, he, miserable wretch, by this innocent being.

### V. The Rose Realizes She Is an Engine of War

One day Cosette accidentally looked at herself in the mirror and let out a cry: "Well!" It almost seemed to her that she was pretty. This threw her into a strange turmoil. Till that moment she had not thought about her looks. She saw herself in the mirror, but she did not look at herself. And then again, she had often been told she was ugly. Jean Valjean alone would softly say: "No, you're not! No, you're not!" Whatever the case may be, Cosette had always thought she was ugly and had grown up thinking so with the easy resignation of a child. And now suddenly her mirror was chiming in with Jean Valjean and telling her: "No, you're not!" She could not sleep that night. "What if I were actually pretty?" she thought. "Wouldn't it be funny if I were pretty!" And she remembered those of her school friends whose beauty had made an impression on the convent, and she said to herself: "Gosh! I'd be like Mademoiselle Thingummy!"

The next day she looked at herself, but not by accident, and she doubted: "What gave me that idea?" she said. "No, I'm ugly." She had quite simply slept badly, she had dark circles under her eyes and she was pale. She had not felt all that deliriously happy the night before in thinking she was beautiful, but she felt sad now that she no longer thought so. She did not look at herself anymore and for a fortnight tried to do her hair with her back to the mirror.

In the evening after dinner, she quite often worked on a tapestry in the salon, or on some other dainty work she'd been taught in the convent, while Jean Valjean sat reading beside her. Once she looked up from her work and was floored by the anxious way her father was looking at her.

Another time, she was walking down the street and it seemed to her that someone she did not see said behind her back: "Nice-looking woman! But badly dressed." "Bah!" she thought. "It's not me. I'm well dressed and ugly." She was wearing her fluffy plush hat and her merino wool dress at the time.

Finally, she was in the garden one day when she heard poor old Toussaint say: "Monsieur, have you noticed how pretty Mademoiselle is becoming?" Cosette did not hear what her father replied, Toussaint's words sent her into such a spin. She ran out of the garden, raced up to her room, ran to the mirror—she hadn't looked at herself for three months—and let out a cry. She had dazzled herself.

She was pretty, and beautiful, too; she couldn't help but agree with Toussaint and the mirror. Her figure was now perfect, her skin had become luminously white, her hair had become lustrous, an unfamiliar sparkle lit up her blue eyes. Her conviction that she was beautiful came to her whole, all at once, in a flash, like daylight suddenly dawning; others noticed it, too. Toussaint said so, and it was obviously her the passerby had been talking about, there could be no more doubt about it. She went back down to the garden, feeling like a queen, hearing the birds sing—this was in winter—seeing the sky all golden, the sun in the trees, flowers among the shrubs, bewildered, wild, giddy with inexpressible rapture.

For his part, Jean Valjean felt a profound and indefinable pang. He had for some little time, in fact, been contemplating with terror this beauty that grew more resplendent every day on Cosette's sweet face. A radiant dawn for everyone else, gloom for him.

Cosette had been beautiful for quite a while before realizing it. But from the very first day, that unexpected light that slowly rose and gradually enveloped the young girl's whole person had stung Jean Valjean's somber eyes. He felt it as a change in a life that was happy, so happy that he didn't dare poke about in it for fear of disturbing something. This man, who had been through every form of hardship known to man, who was still bleeding from the wounds of his fate, who had been very nearly vicious and had become very nearly saintly, who, after having dragged around the chain of the galleys, was now dragging around the invisible, but heavy, chain of indefinite infamy, this man whom the law had not been able to let go of, and who might at any moment be seized again and brought back from the obscurity of his virtue into the broad daylight of public opprobrium, this man accepted everything, excused everything, forgave everything, blessed everything, welcomed everything, and asked of Providence, of men, of justice, of society, of nature, of the world, one thing only—that Cosette love him!

That Cosette continue to love him! That God not stop the heart of that child from coming to him, and remaining his! Loved by Cosette, he felt himself healed, rested, soothed, fulfilled, rewarded, crowned. Loved by Cosette, he was happy! He asked for nothing more. If anyone had said to him, "Would you like to be better off?" he would have replied: "No." If God had said to him: "Would you like heaven itself in exchange?" he would have replied, "I would be the loser."

Anything that could ruffle this situation, if only on the surface, made him quail as if it were the start of something new. He had never really thought about what the beauty of a woman was, but he instinctively understood that it was devastating.

He watched this beauty that bloomed more and more triumphantly and superbly beside him, under his very eyes, on the frank and fearsome forehead of this child, from the depths of his ugliness, of his age, of his misery, of his reprobation, of his devastation, terrified.

He said to himself: "She is so beautiful! What will become of me?"

That, moreover, was the difference between his tenderness and the tenderness of a mother. What he watched in anguish a mother would have watched with joy.

The first symptoms were not long in presenting themselves. From the day after the day when she had said to herself, "No doubt about it, I am beautiful!" Cosette paid attention to her toilette. She recalled what that passerby had said—"Nice-looking but badly dressed"—a blast from an oracle that had whizzed past her and vanished after dropping in her heart one of the two seeds that later fill up a woman's whole life: coquetry. Love is the other.

With faith in her beauty, the whole soul of femininity blossomed in her. She was horrified by the merino wool frock and ashamed of the fluffy plush hat. Her father had never denied her anything. Right away she knew everything there was to know about the hat, the dress, the short cape, the brodequin, the cuff, the right fabric, the flattering color, that science that makes the Parisian woman so charming, so deep, and so dangerous. The term *captivating woman* was invented for the Parisienne.

In less than a month, in that solitary retreat on the rue de Babylone, little Cosette was not only one of the prettiest women in Paris, which is already saying something, but one of the best dressed, which is something else again. She would have liked to run into her passerby now to see what he had to say, and "to show him!" The fact is that she was ravishing in every way and that she had a breathtaking ability to distinguish between a hat by Gérard and a hat by Herbaut.[1]

Jean Valjean studied these ravages anxiously. He who felt that he could only crawl, at best walk, watched Cosette sprout wings.

Still, by a simple inspection of Cosette's finery, a woman would have been able to tell that she did not have a mother. Certain little proprieties, certain special conventions, were not observed by Cosette. A mother would have told her, for instance, that a young girl does not wear damask.

The first day that Cosette stepped out in her black damask frock and short hooded cape and her white crepe hat, she came to take Jean Valjean's arm, gay, radiant, rosy, proud, stunning.

"Father," she said, "how do you like me in this?"

Jean Valjean answered in a voice very like the bitter voice of envy.

"Charming!"

He was his normal self on the walk, but once they were back home again, he asked Cosette: "Aren't you going to wear your dress and your hat anymore, you know the ones?"

This occurred in Cosette's bedroom. Cosette turned to the rail in the wardrobe where her school castoffs were hanging.

"That ridiculous disguise!" she scoffed. "Father, what do you expect me to do with it? Oh, not on your life, no! I'll never put those horrors on again. With that thing on my head I look like a raving lunatic."

Jean Valjean sighed deeply.

From that moment, he noticed that Cosette, who used to always prefer staying home and would say, "Father, I have more fun here with you," was now always asking to go out. Indeed, what was the good of having a nice face and a delectable outfit if you don't show them off?

He also noticed that Cosette was no longer so fond of the backyard. Now, she seemed to want to stick to the front garden, and would stroll in front of the gate apparently quite happily. Jean Valjean, unshakable, never set foot in the garden. He stayed in his backyard, like the dog.

Knowing that she was beautiful, Cosette lost the grace that goes with ignorance; an exquisite grace, for beauty enhanced by artlessness is ineffable and nothing is as adorable as the blossoming innocent who walks along holding the key to paradise in her hand without knowing it. But what she lost in naïve grace, she gained in grave and pensive charm. Her whole person, pervaded by the joys of youth, by innocence and beauty, breathed a splendid melancholy.

It was at this time, when six months had gone by, that Marius saw her again at the Luxembourg.

## VI. THE BATTLE BEGINS

Cosette was standing in her own shadow, as Marius was in his, all ready to take fire and blaze. Destiny, with its mysterious and fateful patience, was slowly bringing together these two beings all fired up and languishing from the stormy electrical charges of passion; these two souls that carried love like two clouds carrying lightning were about to approach each other and fuse in a glance like clouds in a flash of lightning.

The glance has been so abused in love stories that we have ended up discounting it. Hardly anyone ever dares now say that two beings fell in love because their eyes met. And yet that is the way you fall in love and it is the only way you fall in love. The rest is simply the rest and comes after. Nothing is more real than those great seismic shocks that two souls give each other in exchanging that spark.

At the exact moment that Cosette unwittingly gave Marius the glance that so troubled him, Marius had no idea that he had given Cosette a glance that troubled her. It hurt her and thrilled her in the same way.

For a long time already she had seen and studied him the way girls see and study, looking elsewhere. Cosette had already begun to find Marius handsome when he still regarded her as ugly. But since he took no notice of her, she did not give two hoots about the young man.

Yet she could not help saying to herself that he had beautiful hair, beautiful eyes, beautiful teeth, a lovely voice when she heard him chatting with his friends, that he walked awkwardly, if you like, but with a grace all his own, that he didn't seem altogether stupid, that his whole bearing was noble, gentle, natural, and proud, and that, when all was said and done, he looked poor, yes, but he looked good.

The day their eyes first met and at last blurted out those first obscure and unspeakable things that a look stammers, Cosette did not at first understand. She went home in a daze to the rue de l'Ouest where Jean Valjean, as he was in the habit of doing, had just come to spend six weeks. The next day, when she woke up, she thought of the unknown young man, for so long icy and indifferent, and how he now seemed to pay attention to her; and his attention did not please her in the least. She was rather angry with this disdainful beau. The first deep rumble of war stirred in her. It seemed to her, and this caused her a feeling of glee still utterly childish, that she was about to get revenge at last.

Knowing that she was beautiful, she felt thoroughly, if indistinctly, that she had a weapon. Women play on their beauty as children play with their knives. And they hurt themselves on it, too.

You will recall Marius's hesitations, palpitations, terrors. He stayed on his seat and did not come near. Which really piqued Cosette. One day she said to Jean Valjean: "Father, let's take a stroll down there for a bit." Seeing that Marius wasn't coming to her, she decided to go to him. In such cases, every woman is like Mohammed. Then again, oddly enough, the first symptom of true love in a young man is timidity, in a young woman, daring. This never ceases to amaze people and yet nothing could be simpler. It is just the two sexes coming together and each taking on the characteristics of the other.

That particular day, Cosette's glance drove Marius wild, Marius's glance made Cosette tremble. Marius went away confident, and Cosette anxious. From that day forth, they adored each other.

The first thing Cosette felt was a confused and deep sadness. It seemed to her that, from one day to the next, her soul had turned black. She no longer recognized it. The whiteness of soul of young girls, which is made of frigidity and gaiety, is like snow. It melts in the glow of love, which is its sun.

Cosette did not know what love was. She had never heard the word uttered in its earthly sense. In the books of profane music that made their way into the convent, *amour*—love—was replaced by *tambour*—drum—or *pandour*—soldier. This made for riddles that exercised the imaginations of the big girls. For instance, "Ah! The *tambour* is so exciting!" or, "Pity is not a soldier!" But Cosette had left while she was still too young to worry too much about this *tambour*.

she did not know what to call what she was now feeling. Are you any less sick for not knowing the name of your sickness?

She loved with all the more passion for loving in ignorance. She did not know whether it was good or bad, useful or dangerous, necessary or deadly, eternal or ephemeral, allowed or prohibited—she loved. She would have been truly amazed if you had said to her: Aren't you sleeping? But that's forbidden! Aren't you eating? But that's really bad! Do you have flutterings and palpitations of the heart? But that's not done! Do you blush and go white when a certain being dressed in black appears at the end of a certain leafy path? But that's appalling! She would not have understood and she would have replied: "How can I be blamed for something I can't help and that I know nothing about?"

It turned out that the love that presented itself was exactly the love that best suited the state of her soul. It was a sort of adoration at a distance, mute contemplation, the deification of a stranger. It was adolescence appearing to adolescence, a nightly dream turning into a novel yet remaining a dream, the desired phantom at last realized and made flesh but not yet having a name, or any wrong, or any stain, or any demand, or any defect; in a word, the distant lover remaining ideal, a chimera given shape. Any closer, more physical encounter would have scared Cosette off at this initial stage, half-immersed as she still was in the magnifying mists of the convent. She had all the fears of a convent girl and all the fears of a nun combined. The spirit of the convent, with which she had been imbued for five years, was still only slowly evaporating from her whole person and made everything around her quiver. In this situation, it was not a lover she needed, it was not even an admirer, it was a vision. She began to worship Marius as something enchanting, luminous, and impossible.

As extreme naïveté verges on extreme coquetry, she would smile at him quite openly.

Every day she waited for the walk impatiently, she found Marius there, felt indescribably happy, and sincerely believed that she was expressing her whole thought by saying to Jean Valjean: "What a delicious garden the Luxembourg is!"

Marius and Cosette were in the dark in relation to each other. They did not speak to each other, did not greet each other, did not know each other; they saw each other; and like the stars in the sky that are separated by millions of miles, they lived on looking at each other.

This is how Cosette turned little by little into a woman and grew, beautiful and in love, aware of her beauty and ignorant of her love. Coquettish into the bargain—out of innocence.

## VII. Sadness, and More Sadness

Every situation has its instincts. Good old eternal mother nature secretly warned Jean Valjean of Marius's presence. Jean Valjean shuddered in the darkest recesses of his soul. Jean Valjean saw nothing, knew nothing, and yet he studied the darkness where he was with dogged acuity as though he could feel something building on one side and, on the other, falling apart. Marius was also warned, by that same good old mother nature, which is the profound law of God, and he did all he could to hide from "the father." But it happened that Jean Valjean sometimes caught sight of him. The way Marius behaved was no longer at all natural. He was full of sly caution and clumsy recklessness. He no longer walked close by them as he used to do before; he would sit far away and remain in ecstasy; he would have a book with him and pretend to read it; but who was he pretending for? Before, he came in his old redingote; now, he wore his new redingote every day; you couldn't say for sure that he didn't curl his hair, his eyes were all peculiar, he wore gloves. In short, Jean Valjean heartily detested the young man.

Cosette gave nothing away. Without really knowing what was wrong with her, she had the distinct feeling that there was something and that it had to be kept hidden.

Between Cosette's newly acquired taste for clothes and the habit of wearing new coats that had suddenly taken hold of this unknown young man, there was a worrying parallel for Jean Valjean. It was merely a coincidence, perhaps, no doubt, of course, but a threatening coincidence. He never opened his mouth to Cosette about this stranger. But one day, he could hold back no longer, and with that vague despair that suddenly sounds the depths of a person's pain, he said to her: "Now, there's a young man who looks like a real pedant, for you!"

A year before, as an oblivious little girl, Cosette would have replied: "No, he doesn't! He looks charming." Ten years later, with the love of Marius firmly in her heart, she would have replied: "A pedant and hard on the eyes! How right you are!" At this moment in her life and with her heart in such a state, she limited herself to replying with supreme calm: "That young man there?"

As though she were looking at him for the first time in her life.

"What a fool I am!" thought Jean Valjean. "She hadn't even noticed him yet. Now I've gone and pointed him out."

O, simplicity of the old! knowingness of the young!

It is also a law of these fresh years of torment and worry, of these bracing struggles of first love against first obstacles, that the young woman not let herself be caught in any trap and that the young man fall into every one of them. Jean Valjean had opened a silent war against Marius that Marius, with the sublime stupidity of his passion and his age, had no inkling of. Jean Valjean set out a whole series of snares for him; he changed times, he changed seats, he forgot his handkerchief, he came to the Luxembourg on his own; Marius fell headlong into every trap; and at every question mark planted along his path by Jean Valjean, he guilelessly answered: Yes. Meanwhile Cosette remained immured in her apparent insouciance and her imperturbable tranquillity—so much so that Jean Valjean came to this conclusion: This noodle is madly in love with Cosette, but Cosette doesn't even know he exists.

That did not make the heartache he felt any less painful, though. Cosette could fall in love from one moment to the next. Doesn't everything start off with indifference?

Only once did Cosette slip up and frighten him. He was getting up from the seat to leave, after sitting there for three hours, when she said: "So soon!"

Jean Valjean had not cut out the strolls to the Luxembourg, not wanting to do anything out of the ordinary and above all fearing to alert Cosette to what was going on; but during those hours that were so sweet for the two little lovebirds, while Cosette sent her smile to the intoxicated Marius, who saw nothing but that and now no longer saw anything else in this world but that one radiant and adored face, Jean Valjean fixed glittering and terrible eyes on Marius. For a man who had come to think he was now incapable of a malevolent feeling, there were moments, when Marius was there, when he thought he was reverting to his old ferocity, and he felt the old murky depths of his soul, where there had once been so much anger, opening again and rising up against this young man. It almost felt to him as though fresh new craters were forming in him.

What! He was here, that popinjay! What was he doing here? He was here to pirouette, to sniff out, to ogle, to try! He was here to say: Hmmm, why not? He was here to poke around his life, his, Jean Valjean's, own life! Poke around his happiness, just to take it and make off with it!

Jean Valjean went further: "Yes, that's it! What's he come looking for? An adventure! What does he want? A fling! A casual fling! What about me? Heaven forbid! Am I to have first been the most miserable of men and then the most unhappy, am I to have done sixty years of life on my knees, am I to have suffered all a person can suffer, am I to have grown old without ever having been young, am I to have lived without a family, without parents, without friends, without a wife, without children, am I to have left my blood on every stone, on every blackberry bush, on every landmark, along every wall, am I to have been soft even though they were so hard on me, and good even though they were so bad to me, am I to have become an honest man again in spite of everything, am I to have repented of the wrong I've done and to have forgiven the wrong done to me, just so that, the moment I'm finally rewarded, the moment it's all over, the moment I've reached the end, the moment I've got what I want—which is good, which is only right, I've paid for it, I've earned it—it all goes, it all evaporates into thin air, and I lose Cosette, and I lose my life, my joy, my soul, because some donkey feels like coming and strutting around the Luxembourg!"

Then his eyes filled with a strange and doleful flame. He was no longer a man watching another man; he was not an enemy watching an enemy. He was a mastiff watching a thief.

We know the rest. Marius continued to be careless. One day he followed Cosette to the rue de l'Ouest. Another day he spoke to the porter. The porter also spoke in turn and he spoke to Jean Valjean: "Monsieur, who is that nosy young man who's been asking after you, then?"

The next day Jean Valjean threw Marius the glance Marius finally caught. One week later, Jean Valjean had moved house. He swore to himself that he would never set foot in the Luxembourg again, or in the rue de l'Ouest, and he went back to the rue Plumet.

Cosette did not complain, she did not say a thing, she did not ask any questions, she did not seek any reason why; she had already reached the stage where you fear being found out or giving yourself away. Jean Valjean had no experience of these miseries, the only miseries that are sweet and the only ones that he did not know; this meant he did not understand the grave significance of Cosette's silence. He only noticed that she had become sad and he became forlorn. On both sides it came down to lack of experience grappling with lack of experience.

One time he set a test. He asked Cosette: "Would you like to go to the Luxembourg?"

A ray of sunshine lit Cosette's pale face.

"Yes," she said.

Off they went. Three months had gone by. Marius no longer went there, Marius was not there. The next day Jean Valjean asked Cosette again: "Would you like to go to the Luxembourg?"

She answered softly and sadly: "No."

Jean Valjean was crushed by this sadness and shattered by this softness.

What was going on in that mind, so young and already so impenetrable? What was coming to fruition there? What was happening to Cosette's soul? At times, instead of going to bed, Jean Valjean would go on sitting by his cot with his head in his hands. He spent whole nights wondering what was going on in Cosette's mind and thinking about the things she might be thinking.

Oh, at those times, what painful eyes he turned toward the cloister, that chaste summit, that dwelling place of angels, that inaccessible glacier of virtue! With what despairing ravishment he contemplated that convent garden, full of flowers blooming unseen and incarcerated virgins, where all the perfumes and all the souls wafted straight up to heaven! How he worshipped that Eden shut away forever, which he had left of his own free will and from which he had so foolishly descended! How he regretted his self-sacrifice and his insanity in bringing Cosette back into the world, poor hero of renunciation, seized and felled by his very devotion! How he whipped himself with that: What have I done?

But he didn't let Cosette see any of this. No bad humor, no rudeness. Always the same serene face full of goodness. Jean Valjean's manner was more tender and more fatherly than ever. If anything could have given away the fact that there was less joy, it was greater indulgence.

For her part, Cosette sank into black despond. She suffered from Marius's absence just as she rejoiced in his presence, strangely, without really knowing she did so. When Jean Valjean stopped taking her on the usual walk, a womanly instinct had vaguely murmured from the depths of her heart that she should not appear to set much store by the Luxembourg and that if she really didn't care about it, her father would take her back there. But days, weeks, months went by. Jean Valjean had tacitly accepted Cosette's tacit acceptance. She regretted it. It was too late. The day she went back to the Luxembourg, Marius was no longer there. Marius had vanished; it was over, what could she do? Would she ever find him again? She felt a pain in her heart that nothing could ease and that got worse every day; she no longer knew if it was winter or summer, sun or rain, if the birds were singing, if it was the season for dahlias or daisies, if the Luxembourg was lovelier than the Tuileries, if the linen the washerwoman brought back was too starched or not enough, if Toussaint had done her shopping well or badly, and she remained devastated, absorbed, intent on a single thought, her eye vague and staring, just as you look in the dark night at the deep black spot an apparition has vanished into.

But she didn't let Jean Valjean see any of this, either, except for her pallor. She always put on her sweet face for him. The pallor was more than enough to worry Jean Valjean, though. Sometimes he asked her: "What's the matter?"

She would answer: "Nothing's the matter."

And after a pause, as she sensed that he was sad, too, she would ask: "What about you, father, is something the matter?"

"Me? No, nothing," he would say.

These two beings who had loved each other so exclusively, and with such a touching love, and who had lived for each other for so long, now suffered alongside each other, because of each other, without saying so to each other, without resenting each other for it, and smiling all the while.

## VIII. The Chain Gang

Jean Valjean was the unhappier of the two. Youth, even in its heartaches, always has a luminosity of its own.

At certain moments, Jean Valjean suffered so much he became infantile. It is the province of pain to bring out the childish side of a man. He felt irresistibly that Cosette was escaping him. He would have liked to fight, to hang on to her, to get her excited about something external and dazzling. These ideas, which were infantile, as we said, and at the same time sterile, gave him, in their very childishness, a fairly just notion of the influence of showy trappings on a young girl's imagination. He once happened to see passing in the street a general on horseback in full dress, the comte Coutard, commandant of Paris. He envied this golden boy; he said to himself: What happiness it would be to be able to put on that uniform, which was something incontestable, that if Cosette saw him decked out like that, it would bowl her over, that if he were to give Cosette his arm and stroll by the Tuileries gate in that getup, they would present arms to him and that would be all Cosette needed and would put paid to this business of looking at young men.

An unexpected shock cut off these sad thoughts.

In the isolated life they led, and ever since they had come to live in the rue Plumet, they had developed a habit. They sometimes went to watch the sun come up just for the pleasure of it—a sort of gentle joy that suits those entering life and those leaving it.

To stroll around at the break of day, for whoever likes solitude, is the equivalent of strolling around at night, with the gaiety of nature as a bonus. The streets are deserted and the birds sing. Cosette, herself a bird, was happy to wake up so early. These morning trips were arranged the night before. He suggested, she accepted. It was all organized like a conspiracy; they stepped out before first light, and this made it all the merrier for Cosette. Such innocent foibles give the young a thrill.

Jean Valjean's tendency was, as we know, to head for little-frequented spots, solitary nooks and crannies, forgotten places. In those days, around the barrières of Paris, there were scrubby, stubbly fields that were almost part of the city, where reedy wheat grew thinly in summer and which, in autumn, after harvest, looked not so much harvested as stripped. Jean Valjean haunted them as a predilection. Cosette did not get bored there, either. It meant solitude for him, freedom for her. There, she was a little girl again, she ran around almost frolicking, she took her hat off, sat it on Jean Valjean's knees, and gathered bouquets of flowers. She looked at the butterflies on the flowers, but did not catch them; compassion and tenderness come with love and the young girl, who has inside her a quivering fragile ideal, takes pity on the butterfly's wing. She made a chain of poppies which she put on her head and which, shot through and lit up by the sun, turned a flaming dark red and made a crown of glowing embers around that fresh pink face.

Even after their life had taken such a sad turn, they had stuck to their habit of early morning walks.

And so, one October morning, tempted by the perfect serenity of the autumn of 1831, they had gone out and found themselves as day was dawning close to the barrière du Maine. It was not daybreak, it was dawn; a ravishing, wild moment. A few constellations here and there in the pale, deep sky, the earth all black, the sky all white, a shiver rippling through the blades of grass, everywhere the mysterious rush and sudden chill of dawn light. A lark that seemed to be caught up in the stars was singing at an incredible height, and you would have said that this hymn of smallness to the infinite calmed the vastness. In the east, the dark bulk of the Val-de-Grâce stood out, as sharp as steel, on the clear horizon; dazzling Venus was climbing up from behind the dome like a soul escaping from a gloomy building.

All was peace and silence; no one was on the causeway; on the verges, a few scattered workingmen, barely glimpsed, were going off to work.

Jean Valjean had sat down in a side track on some wood piled at the gate of a timber yard. He had his face turned to the road and his back turned to the light; he had forgotten about the sun coming up; he had fallen into one of those profoundly absorbing meditations where the whole mind is concentrated, where even your eyes are trapped—the equivalent of four square walls. There are meditative states that we might call vertical; when you are at the bottom, it takes time to come back up to the surface. Jean Valjean had plunged down into one of those sorts of reveries. He was thinking about Cosette, about the happiness possible if nothing came between her and him, about the light she filled his life with, a light that was the air his soul breathed. He was almost happy in this trance. Cosette, standing next to him, was watching the clouds turn pink.

All of a sudden, Cosette cried: "Father, it looks like someone's coming over there." Jean Valjean looked up.

Cosette was right.

The causeway that leads to the old barrière du Maine is an extension, as we know, of the rue de Sèvres, and it is intersected at a right angle by the inner boulevard. At the bend where the roadway turns away from the boulevard, at the point where they diverge, you could hear a sound hard to explain at such an early hour, and a sort of confused jumble appeared. Something amorphous came from the boulevard and turned into the causeway.

It was getting bigger, it seemed to move along in an orderly fashion, and yet it was all spiky and shuddering; it seemed to be a conveyance but you could not make out its load. There were horses, wheels, shouts, cracking whips. By degrees the outlines became more defined, although drowned in shadow. It was, indeed, a conveyance that had just turned off the boulevard and into the road, heading for the barrière where Jean Valjean was sitting; a second one, the same as far as one could see, followed, then a third, then a fourth; seven carts turned at the intersection, one after the other in tight procession, the heads of the horses behind touching the backs of the cars in front. Dark figures were flailing about in the carts; you could see glinting steel in the half-light as though there were drawn swords, you could hear a clanking sound like chains rattling; the whole thing was coming closer, the voices were getting louder, and it was frightening, like the sort of thing that rolls out of the caverns of our dreams.

As it came nearer it took shape, looming from behind the trees with the bleached-out look of an apparition; the bulk turned white; the dawning light pasted a pallid gleam over this swarming mass at once sepulchral and alive, the heads of the silhouettes turned into the faces of cadavers. This is what it was:

Seven vehicles were moving in single file along the road. The first six were weirdly built. They looked like coopers' drays, with long ladders laid over two wheels and forming shafts at the front ends. Each dray or, better still, each ladder was harnessed to four horses in tandem. Strange clusters of men were being drawn along on these ladders. In such light as there was, you couldn't see the men, you only guessed they were there. Twenty-four to a car, in two rows of twelve on either side sitting back to back, facing the pedestrians, with their legs dangling over the side, these men rolled along like this, and at their backs they had something that rattled and was a chain, and at their necks they had something that glinted and was a yoke, an iron collar, a shackle. Each man had his own shackle, but the chain was shared by everyone; so that if the twenty-four men got down from the dray to walk, they were seized by a sort of inexorable unity and had to snake along the ground with the chain as a backbone, a bit like a centipede. At the front and back of each car, two men, armed with guns, stood, each with one end of the chain underfoot. The collar shackles were square. The seventh car, a huge wagon that had side panels but no cover, had four wheels and six horses, and was carrying a rattling pile of iron boilers, cast-iron melting pots, stoves, and chains and, mixed up in all that, a few men, trussed and laid out flat, who looked to be sick. This wagon, entirely made of latticework, was equipped with dilapidated racks that looked like they might once have been used in torture.

The cars kept to the middle of the pavement. On either side a double row of guards marched, looking pretty scruffy under tricorn hats like those worn by the soldiers of the Directoire, stained, riddled with holes, dirty, decked out in the uniforms of the war disabled and the breeches of undertakers' assistants half gray, half blue, practically in tatters, with red epaulets, yellow cross-belts, sheath knives, muskets, and clubs; a ragtag lot of soldier-thugs. These henchmen seemed to combine the abjectness of beggars and the authority of hangmen. The one who looked to be the chief held a horsewhip in his hand. All these details, blurred by the half-light, stood out more clearly as day came on. At the head and rear of the convoy, gendarmes on horseback trotted along gravely, sabers at the ready.

This cortège was so long that the first car had already reached the barrière as the last one was just turning off the boulevard.

A crowd had surfaced from who knows where and gathered in the blink of an eye, as often happens in Paris, pressing in from both sides of the road to gape. You could hear people yelling at each other in the neighboring lanes and the wooden clogs of the market gardeners as they ran to get a look.

The men piled up on the drays let themselves be jolted along in silence. They were wan with the morning chill. They all had coarse cotton breeches and wooden shoes on their bare feet. The rest of their raiment was whatever dire poverty could devise. Their accessories were hideously ill-matched; nothing is more mournful than the harlequin in rags. Staved-in felt hats, tarred caps, awful woolen beanies, and, alongside a workman's smock, a black coat gone at the elbows; several of them had women's hats; others had clapped baskets on their heads; hairy chests were on show and through the tears in their clothing flashed tattoos—temples of love, burning hearts, little cupids. You could also see patches of red or scurfy skin that looked very unsavory. Two or three of them had a straw rope tied to the struts of the wagon, which hung down under them like a stirrup and supported their feet. One of them was holding something in his hand that he brought to his mouth and that looked like a black stone he appeared to bite into; this was bread and he was eating it. There were nothing but dry eyes among them, listless or shining with an ugly glint. The escort troops were grumbling; the men in chains did not breathe a whisper; from time to time you could hear the noise of a club coming down with a whack across shoulder blades or on a head; some of the men yawned; their rags were terrible; their feet dangled, their shoulders rocked; their heads banged together, their irons clanked, their eyes blazed fiercely, their fists clenched or opened, as inert as the hands of the dead; behind the convoy, a troop of children burst out laughing.

This file of cars, whatever it was, was doleful. It was obvious that the next day, in an hour's time, it might pour with rain, with one shower followed by another shower, and another, and that these ruins of clothes would be soaked through, and once they were wet the men would not dry off again, that once they were frozen, they would not thaw out again, that their canvas pants would stick to their bones with the rain, that the water would fill their shoes, that the lashes of the whip would not stop their teeth chattering, that the chain would go on holding them by the neck, that their feet would go on dangling over the side; and it was impossible not to shudder on seeing these human beings tied up like this and passive under the cold autumn clouds, and delivered up to the rain, to the icy wind, to all the furies of the air, like trees, like stones.

The whacks of the clubs did not even spare the sick, who groaned, trussed with ropes and motionless, on the seventh car, and who looked as though they'd been thrown there like sacks full of misery.

Suddenly, the sun came out; an immense shaft of sunlight shot out from the east and seemed to set fire to all these fierce heads. Tongues were loosened; a firestorm of jeering and swearing and singing erupted. The broad horizontal light cut the whole field in two, illuminating heads and torsos, leaving feet and wheels in darkness. Thoughts appeared on faces; that was an appalling moment, revealing demons with their masks off, visible, savage souls laid completely bare. Lit up, this mob remained dark. Some of them, the cheery ones, had quill pipes through which they blew vermin at the crowd, singling out the women; dawn exaggerated the lamentable profiles through the blackness of the shadows; there was not one being among them who was not disfigured by misery and this was so monstrous that you would have said it changed the brightness of the sun into a lightning flash. The wagonload that headed the convoy struck up a tune, which they began belting out at the top of their lungs, with frantic joviality; it was "La Vestale," one of Désaugiers's[1] medleys, famous at the time; the trees shivered forlornly; in the side alleys, the faces of the bourgeois throng were covered in moronic bliss as they listened, riveted, to these bawdy ditties sung by specters.

Every kind of distress was in that convoy in a tangled heap; every cut of head of all the beasts was there, old men, adolescents, bare skulls, gray beards, cynical monstrosities, aggressive resignation, savage grimacing, insane posturing, muzzles with caps on, heads a bit like young girls' with corkscrew curls over the temples, faces that were childish and, because of that, horrible, the fleshless faces of skeletons where only death was missing. On the first car, you could see a black man who had once, perhaps, been a slave and could compare chains. That terrifying lowest common denominator, shame, had passed over these foreheads; at this level of debasement, the final transformations were undergone by all in the final depths, absolute rock bottom; and ignorance turned to stupor was indistinguishable from intelligence turned to despair. No choice was possible between these men who appeared to onlookers to be the elite of the gutter, the scum of the earth. It was clear that whoever was in charge of this sordid procession had not bothered to sort them. These creatures had been bound and paired off willy-nilly, probably in alphabetic disorder, and loaded haphazardly onto the carts. But when horrors are lumped together, they always yield a result; every addition to the count of the miserable yields a total; from each chain a common soul emerged and each cartload had its distinctive countenance. Besides the one that was singing, there was one that was shouting; a third was begging; you could see one that was gnashing its teeth; another threatened bystanders, another railed against God in sheer blasphemy; the last kept as silent as the grave. Dante would have thought he was seeing the seven circles of hell on the march.

The march of the damned toward their damnation, undertaken sinisterly, not on the awesome flashing chariot of the Apocalypse but, more somber still, on the cart of the Gemoniae[2]—the hangman's cart.

One of the guards, who had a hook on the end of his club, made a show of stirring this pile of human refuse now and then. An old woman in the crowd pointed them out to a little boy of five and said to him: "That'll teach you to behave, you little rascal!"

As the singing and blaspheming got louder, the man who seemed to be the captain of the escort cracked his whip, and at that signal, a frightening muffled and blind bludgeoning fell on the seven carts with a noise like hail; many roared and foamed at the mouth; which only redoubled the joy of the urchins who had come running, a cloud of flies on these open wounds.

Jean Valjean's eyes had become frightening. They were no longer eyes; they were the deep window on the soul that replaces gazing eyes in certain long-suffering people; such a look seems oblivious to reality, reflecting past horrors and calamities in a blaze of fierce light. He was not looking at a spectacle; he was enduring a vision. He tried to stand, to run, to escape; he could not move a muscle. Sometimes the things you see grab you and hold you in place. He stayed nailed to the spot, petrified, dumbstruck, wondering, through a confused and inexpressible anguish, what this sepulchral persecution meant and where the pandemonium that was hounding him came from. All of a sudden, he clapped his hand on his forehead, which you usually do when your memory suddenly comes back to you; he remembered that this was in fact the route, that this was the customary detour to avoid royal encounters which were always possible on the Fontainebleau road, and that thirty-five years previously, he had passed by this very same barrière.

Cosette was just as horrified but in a slightly different way. She did not understand; she could not breathe; what she was seeing did not seem possible to her; she finally cried out: "Father! What is in those cars?" Jean Valjean answered:

"Convicts."

"Where are they going?"

"To the galleys."

At that moment, the bludgeoning, multiplied by a hundred hands, was reaching a crescendo and extended to include whacking with the flats of swords; the galley slaves crouched down, bent double, under this storm of whips and clubs; a ghastly obeisance was produced by the torture and all fell silent, with the look of chained wolves. Cosette was shaking from head to toe; she went on: "Father, are these men?"

"At times," said the wretched man.

It was in fact the chain gang, which had set out before daybreak from Bicêtre, and was taking the Mans road to avoid Fontainebleau, where the king was. This detour made the whole horrifying trip last three or four days longer; but, to spare the royal person the sight of such torture, it was certainly worth prolonging.

Jean Valjean went home shattered. Such encounters are a shock to the system and the memory they leave is like a convulsion.

Yet on the way back to the rue de Babylone with Cosette, Jean Valjean did not notice that she asked him other questions about what they had just seen; maybe he was too absorbed in his own utter dejection to register what she said and to respond. Only that evening, as Cosette was saying good night before going to bed, did he hear her say in a faint little voice as though to herself: "I think that if ever I ran into one of those men in a dark alley, my God! I'd die just seeing him up close!" Luckily chance would have it that the day after this tragic day, there was some kind of official celebration—I don't remember what was being celebrated exactly—and formal festivities took place all over Paris: a military review in the Champ de Mars, jousting on the Seine, theatricals along the Champs-Élysées, fireworks at L'Étoile, light shows everywhere. Jean Valjean, doing violence to his habits, took Cosette to see the festivities to distract her from the memory of the day before and to erase the abominable thing that had passed before her in the laughing tumult of *le Tout-Paris.* The review that enlivened the celebrations made the parade of uniforms completely natural; Jean Valjean donned his National Guard uniform with the vague inner feeling of a man taking refuge. But the goal of the outing seemed achieved. Cosette, who made it a rule to please her father and for whom, in any case, all spectacle was fresh and new, accepted the distraction blithely with the good grace of adolescence and did not pout too disdainfully at this joyful romp known as a fête; so much so that Jean Valjean could tell himelf he'd carried it off, and that no trace of the hideous sight remained.

One morning, several days later, they were both sitting on the garden steps in bright sunshine—another infringement of the rules Jean Valjean seemed to impose, and of the habit of keeping to her room that sadness had caused Cosette to adopt. Cosette was standing in her dressing gown, carefree in her early morning negligée, with a casualness that wraps young girls round as adorably as a cloud covering a star; her face all rosy from having slept so well, she stood in the light under the loving gaze of the tender old man, pulling the petals off a daisy. Cosette knew nothing of that delightful little riddle *He loves me, he loves me not, he loves me,* etc.; who would have taught her? She was handling the flower instinctively, innocently, without suspecting that pulling the petals off a daisy is to pluck a heart. If there had been a fourth Grace named Melancholy, who smiled, she would have looked like that Grace. Jean Valjean was spellbound by those little fingers working that little flower, forgetting everything else in the child's radiance. A red robin was twittering in the bushes beside them. White clouds were scudding across the sky as gaily as if they had just been released from captivity. Cosette continued to pluck her daisies attentively; she seemed to be thinking about something, but it must have been something lovely; all of a sudden she turned her head back over her shoulder as delicately and slowly as a swan and shot Jean Valjean a question: "Father, what are they, actually, these galleys?"

# BOOK FOUR

# HELP FROM BELOW MAY BE
# HELP FROM ABOVE

## I. WOUND WITHOUT, HEALING WITHIN

And so, their life gradually came under a cloud.

There was only one diversion left to them, one that had once been a joy, and that was to take bread to those who were hungry and clothes to those who were cold. On these visits to the poor, on which Cosette often accompanied Jean Valjean, they found once more some remnant of their old openhearted intimacy; and, sometimes, when it had been a good day, when many in distress had been relieved and many little children revived and made warm, Cosette would be almost lighthearted in the evening. It was at this time that they had paid a visit to the Jondrette pigsty.

The very day after that visit, Jean Valjean appeared in the villa in the morning, calm as usual but with a great big wound on his left arm. Highly inflamed, highly infected, it looked like a burn, but he brushed it off with some banal explanation. This wound meant he was housebound with fever for over a month. He would not see a doctor. When Cosette urged him to do so, he would say: "Send for the dog doctor."

Cosette dressed the wound morning and night with such a divine expression on her face and such angelic happiness at being useful to him, that Jean Valjean felt all his old joy return, his fears and anxieties evaporate, and he would gaze at Cosette saying: "Oh, what a blessed wound! Oh, what blessed pain!"

Cosette, seeing her father sick and wounded, had deserted the villa, regaining her taste for the little cottage and the backyard. She spent nearly all her time by Jean Valjean's side, reading whatever books he liked to him—in general, travel books. Jean Valjean was born anew; his happiness revived with ineffable radiance; the Luxembourg, the unknown young prowler, Cosette's cooling off, all these clouds in his soul dissolved. It got to the point where he said to himself: "I must have imagined all that. I'm such an old goose."

His happiness was such that the appalling discovery of the Thénardiers in the Jondrette hole, though so unexpected, was water off a duck's back to him now. He had managed to escape, his own tracks were covered, what did the rest matter to him! He only thought about it at all to feel sorry for those poor bastards. "They're all in jail now and can do no more harm," he thought, "but what a lamentable family in distress!" As for the hideous vision at the barrière du Maine, Cosette had not mentioned it again.

At the convent, Sister Saint Mechthilde had taught Cosette music. Cosette had the voice of a warbler with a soul and sometimes in the evening, in the invalid's humble cottage, she would sing sad songs that brought joy to Jean Valjean's heart.

Spring was coming, the garden was so beautiful at that time of year that Jean Valjean said to Cosette: "You never go into the garden anymore, I want you to walk around in it."

"As you like, father," said Cosette.

And just to obey her father, she resumed her walks in her garden, most often alone, for, as we pointed out, Jean Valjean, who possibly feared being seen through the gate, almost never set foot there.

Jean Valjean's wound had been a diversion.

When Cosette saw that her father was not in so much pain, that he was on the mend, that he seemed happy, she felt a contentment she didn't even realize, it came on so gently and so naturally. Then it was the month of March, the days were getting longer, winter was going, and winter always takes something of our sorrows with it; then April came, that summer's dawn, fresh like all dawns, gay like all childhoods; a little bit of a crybaby, in fact, like all newborns. Nature in the month of April is full of that glorious light that travels from the sky, the clouds, the trees, the meadows, and the flowers right into the heart of humankind.

Cosette was still too young for the joy of April—so like her—not to find its way into her heart. Insensibly, and without her suspecting a thing, the darkness lifted off her spirit. In spring, the light shines in sad souls just as it shines in caves at midday. Even Cosette was no longer so very sad. Anyway, that's how it was, and Cosette was not aware of it. In the morning, after breakfast, at about ten, when she had managed to drag her father out into the garden for fifteen minutes and was walking him in the sun at the bottom of the garden steps, supporting his wounded arm for him, she did not realize that she laughed at every turn and that she was happy.

Jean Valjean was deliriously happy to see her becoming all fresh and rosy again.

"Oh, what a blessed wound!" he repeated in a hushed voice.

And he was grateful to the Thénardiers.

As soon as his wound was healed, he resumed his solitary walks in the gloaming.

It would be a mistake to think you can walk around like this, on your own, in uninhabited areas of Paris, without meeting with some adventure.

## II. MOTHER PLUTARCH DOESN'T MIND EXPLAINING A PHENOMENON

One night Petit-Gavroche had not eaten; he remembered that he had not eaten the night before, either; this was getting tedious. He resolved to try and get himself some supper. He went on the prowl in the deserted no-man's-land beyond La Salpêtrière; that is where the windfalls are; where there is no one, you always find something. He got as far as a settlement that looked to him to be the village of Austerlitz.

On one of his previous reconnoiters, he had noticed an old garden there haunted by an old man and an old woman, and in this garden a passable apple tree. Beside the apple tree there was a sort of fruit shed where a person could land himself an apple. An apple is a meal in itself; an apple is life. What sank Adam might save Gavroche. The garden ran alongside a lonely unpaved laneway that was bordered with bushes for want of houses; a hedge separated the garden from the lane.

Gavroche headed for the garden. He came to the lane, recognized the apple tree, checked the fruit shed, examined the hedge; a hedge is a leg up. Day was dimming, there was not even a cat in the lane, the time was right. Gavroche began scaling the hedge, then suddenly stopped in his tracks. Someone was talking in the garden. Gavroche peered through a hole in the hedge.

Two feet away, at the base of the hedge and on the other side, exactly at the point where the gap he was considering would have dropped him, there was an overturned stone that made a kind of bench and on this bench the old man of the garden was sitting, with the old woman standing in front of him. The old woman was grumbling. Gavroche, who was anything but discreet, listened in.

"Monsieur Mabeuf!" the old woman was saying.

"Mabeuf!" thought Gavroche. "What a funny name."

The old man addressed did not stir. The old woman repeated: "Monsieur Mabeuf!"

The old man kept his eyes on the ground but decided to reply: "What, mother Plutarch?"

"Mother Plutarch!" thought Gavroche. "Another funny name."

Mother Plutarch went on and the old man was forced to join in the conversation.

"The landlord is not happy."

"Why's that?"

"He's owed three quarters."

"In three months, he'll be owed four."

"He says he'll turn you out."

"I'll go."

"The fruit-hawker woman wants to be paid. She won't let you have any more bundles of firewood. How will you keep yourself warm this winter? We won't have any wood."

"There's always the sun."

"The butcher's refusing credit, he won't give us any more meat."

"Well and good. Meat's bad for my digestion. It's too heavy."

"What will we have for dinner?"

"Bread."

"The baker's demanding an installment and says no money, no bread."

"Good-o."

"What are you going to eat?"

"There's always the apples from the apple tree."

"But, Monsieur, a person just can't live like that, without money."

"I don't have any."

The old woman beetled off, the old man remained alone. He set to thinking. Gavroche was thinking alongside him. It was almost night.

The first result of Gavroche's thinking was that instead of scaling the hedge, he decided to crawl under it. The branches separated a bit at the bottom of the bush.

"Look at that," cried Gavroche to himself, "an alcove!" And he crept in. He was now practically back-to-back with Father Mabeuf's bench. He could hear the octogenarian breathing.

So, for dinner, he tried to sleep.

A catnap, sleeping with one eye open. Even while he dozed off, Gavroche was on the lookout.

The whiteness of the twilight sky bleached the ground and the lane made a livid line between two rows of black bushes.

All of a sudden, on that whitish band, two silhouettes appeared. One was out in front, the other, some distance behind.

"Here's trouble," muttered Gavroche.

The first silhouette looked to be that of some old bourgeois gentleman, stooped and deep in thought, dressed remarkably plainly and walking slowly because of his age, out for an amble under the stars.

The second was straight, firm, slight. It was walking in step with the first; but in that deliberate snail's crawl, you could sense suppleness and coiled agility. This silhouette had something unspeakably mean and disturbing about it, the whole look was of what was then known as a fop; the hat was stylish, the redingote was black, well cut, probably of good fabric, and cinched at the waist. The head was held high with a sort of robust grace, and, beneath the hat, you caught a glimpse in the twilight of a pale adolescent's face. The face had a rose in its mouth. This second silhouette was well-known to Gavroche; it was Montparnasse.

As for the other, he really could not have said anything except that it was some old geezer.

Gavroche went into observation mode immediately.

One of the two out walking clearly had designs on the other. Gavroche was well placed to see what happened next. The alcove had very conveniently turned into a spy-hole.

Montparnasse on the hunt at such an hour, in such a place—this was menacing. Gavroche felt his little boy's heart lurch with pity for the old fellow.

What could he do? Intervene? That would amount to one weakling trying to rescue another! It would give Montparnasse a good laugh. Gavroche did not disguise the fact that this fearful cutthroat of eighteen would have them both for supper, the old man first, the child next.

While Gavroche was deliberating, the assault took place, abrupt and awful. A tiger attacking a wild ass, a spider attacking a fly. Without further ado, Montparnasse chucked the rose, lunged at the old man, collared him, grabbed hold of him and hung on tight, and it was all Gavroche could do not to let out a scream. A moment later, one of the men was under the other one, exhausted, panting, flailing about, with a knee of marble on his chest. Only, it wasn't exactly what Gavroche was expecting. The one on the ground was Montparnasse, the one on top was the old man.

All of this happened just a few feet from Gavroche.

The old man had had a shock and had given as good as he got, and so terribly that, in the blink of an eye, assailant and assailed had switched places.

"There's a proud old war veteran for you!" thought Gavroche.

And he couldn't stop himself from clapping. But the clap was lost. It did not reach the two combatants, absorbed and deafened by each other as they were, their breath mingled in the fray.

There was a silence. Montparnasse stopped struggling. Gavroche said to himself: "Is he dead?"

The old bloke had not uttered a sound, not a word or a cry. He picked himself up and Gavroche heard him say to Montparnasse: "Get up."

Montparnasse got up, but the old man held him tight. Montparnasse had the furious humiliated look of a wolf that has been snatched by a sheep.

Gavroche watched and listened, all eyes and ears. He was enjoying himself immensely.

He was rewarded for his conscientious anxiety as a spectator, for he was able to catch the following dialogue, which borrowed an indescribably tragic tone from the darkness. The old man asked the questions. Montparnasse answered.

"How old are you?"

"Nineteen."

"You're strong and fit. Why aren't you at work?"

"Work bores me."

"What is your occupation?"

"Layabout."

"Be serious. Can I do anything for you? What would you like to be?"

"A thief."

There was a silence. The old man seemed deep in thought. He stood stock-still but did not let go of Montparnasse.

Now and then the young villain, vigorous and deft, thrashed around like an animal caught in a trap. He gave a jerk, tried to trip the old man up, wildly writhing and twisting his limbs, attempted to break free. The old man didn't even seem to notice as he held both his arms with a single hand, with the sovereign indifference of unassailable strength.

The old man's trance lasted a while, then he fixed his eyes steadily on Montparnasse, gently raised his voice, and delivered him, from out of the shadows where they were standing, a sort of solemn address which Gavroche did not lose a syllable of: "My boy, you are embarking on one of the most laborious of existences, out of sheer laziness. Ah! You declare yourself a layabout! Get ready to work. Have you ever seen a very frightening machine called a rolling mill? You have to take great care with it, it's a sly and savage thing; if it catches a flap of your coat, the whole of you goes in. This machine is idleness. Stop, while there's still time and save yourself! Otherwise, it's all over for you; before too long, you'll be caught in the wheels. Once you're caught, don't hope for another thing again. Till you drop, lazybones, forget about rest! The iron hand of relentless work will have grabbed you. Earn your living, have a job, perform a duty—you won't have any of that! Being like everyone else bores you! Well, then! You will be different. Work is the rule; whoever rejects it as boring will have it as torture. You don't want to be a workingman, you will be a slave. Work only drops you now to pick you up again later; you don't want to be its friend, you will be its navvy. Ah! You don't want any of the honest weariness of men, you will have the sweat of the damned. Where others sing, you will moan. You will see from afar, from below, other men working; it will look to you like they are resting. The laborer, the reaper, the sailor, the blacksmith, will appear to you in the light as the blessed in some paradise. What radiance in the anvil! To drive a plow, to bind sheaves—sheer bliss. The boat, free in the breeze, what a holiday! You, lazybones, dig, drag, roll, march! Drag your yoke, there you go, you're a beast of burden in the harness from hell! Ah, to do nothing, that was your goal. Well, then! Not a week, not a day, not an hour goes by without shattering exhaustion. You can't lift a thing except in anguish. Every minute that passes will make your muscles crack. What is a mere feather for others will be a rock for you. The simplest things will overpower you. Life will turn into a monster around you. Coming and going, even breathing, will be so many terrible travails. Your lungs will feel like they are lifting a hundred-pound weight. To walk here rather than over there will be a problem to be solved. Any other man who wants to go out pushes his door open and, there, it's done, he's outside. You, if you want to go out, you'll have to bore through your wall. To go out into the street, what does everybody else do? Everybody else goes downstairs; you, you'll rip up your bedsheets, you'll tie them together, strip by strip, and make a rope, then you'll go out your window and you'll hang there by this thread over an abyss, and it will be at night, in a storm, in the rain, in a hurricane, and if the rope is too short, you'll only have one way left to get down and that will mean dropping. Dropping any which way, into the void, from whatever height, onto what? Onto whatever is below, onto the unknown. Or you'll climb up a chimney at the risk of getting burned; or you'll crawl along a sewer, at the risk of getting drowned. I won't mention the holes you'll have to cover up, the stones you'll have to take out and put back twenty times a day, the rubble you'll have to hide in your straw pallet. A lock presents itself; the bourgeois has his key made by a locksmith there in his pocket. You, if you want to get in, you're condemned to making an awesome masterpiece; you'll take a sou, you'll cut it into two sections. With what tools? You'll have to invent them. That's your problem. Then you'll hollow out the inside of these two sections, handling the outside very carefully, and you'll cut a screw thread all around the edge, so that they fit together perfectly, like a top and bottom lid. With the bottom and the top screwed together in this fashion, nobody would suspect a thing. To those watching you, for you will be watched, it will be a sou; to you, it will be a box. What will you put in this box? A tiny bit of steel. A watch spring that you'll have cut teeth into and which will become a saw. With this saw, as long as a pin and hidden in the sou, you'll have to cut the bolt of the lock, the slide of the bolt, the latch of the padlock, and the bar you'll have at your window, and the shackle you'll have on your leg. This masterpiece made, this marvel accomplished, all these miracles of art, skill, cleverness, patience executed, if it comes to be known that you are their author, what will be your reward? The dungeon. There's the future for you. Laziness, pleasure—what bottomless pits! To do nothing is a woeful choice to make, don't you know? To live idly off the substance of society! To be useless, that is, noxious! That leads straight to the direst misery. Woe to the man who wants to be a parasite! He will be vermin. Ah, you don't like the idea of working! Ah, there's only one thing on your mind: to drink well, to eat well, to sleep well. You'll drink water, you'll eat black bread, you'll sleep on a plank with irons riveted to your limbs and you'll feel how cold they are at night against your skin! You'll break this iron, you'll run away. Very well. You'll be crawling on your stomach through the scrub and you'll eat grass like the brutes of the woods. And you'll be nabbed again. And then you'll spend years in a dungeon, bolted to a wall, groping for a drink from your pitcher, gnawing on a horrible loaf of blackness even dogs wouldn't touch, eating beans the worms would have got to before you. You'll be a wood louse in a cellar. Ah, have pity on yourself, miserable child, so young you can't have been sucking at your nurse's tits more than twenty years ago, and doubtless you still have your mother! I implore you, listen to me. You want fine black fabric, patent leather shoes, you want your hair crimped, to run sweet-smelling oil through your curly locks, to please the ladies, to be a pretty boy. You'll be shaved bald and you'll wear a red smock and wooden clogs. You want a ring on your finger, you'll have an iron collar around your neck. And if you so much as look at a woman, a whack of the club. You'll go in at twenty and you'll come out at fifty! You'll go in young, rosy, fresh, with your sparkling eyes and your white teeth, and your beautiful adolescent head of hair, and you'll come out broken, stooped, wrinkled, toothless, horrible, with white hair! Ah! My poor boy, you're going the wrong way, laziness is giving you bad advice; the toughest of all work is theft. Believe me, do not take on the dreadful drudgery of being a layabout. To become a villain is not easy. It's easier to become an honest man. Go now, and think about what I've told you. Speaking of which, what did you want from me? My purse. Here it is."

And the old man let go of Montparnasse and put his purse in Montparnasse's hand. Montparnasse weighed it for a moment, after which, with the same mechanical precaution he'd have taken if he'd stolen it, he slipped it gently into the back pocket of his redingote.

When all this was said and done, the old man turned his back and quietly resumed his stroll.

"Silly old codger!" murmured Montparnasse.

Who was this old man? The reader has no doubt guessed.

Montparnasse stood, stunned, watching him disappear in the twilight. This contemplation was fatal to him.

While the old man was disappearing into the distance, Gavroche was stealing closer.

Out of the corner of his eye Gavroche had assured himself that Father Mabeuf was still sitting on the bench, though perhaps asleep now. Then the little urchin came out of his bush and began to creep along in the shadows behind the motionless Montparnasse. He reached Montparnasse accordingly without being seen or heard, gently insinuated his hand into the back pocket of the redingote of fine black fabric, grabbed the purse, withdrew his hand, and, creeping off again, made good his escape like a garter snake in the gathering gloom. Having no reason to be on his guard, and actually thinking for the first time in his life, Montparnasse didn't feel a thing. When he got back to the spot where Father Mabeuf was, Gavroche threw the purse over the hedge and ran away as fast as his legs would carry him.

The purse fell on Father Mabeuf's foot. The commotion woke him. He bent down and picked it up. He could not make head or tail of it; he opened it. It was a purse with two compartments; in one, there were a few small coins; in the other, there were six napoléons.

Monsieur Mabeuf was startled out of his wits and took the thing to his housekeeper.

"This has fallen from the sky," said mother Plutarch.

# BOOK FIVE

# Whose End Is Nothing
# Like Its Beginning

## I. Loneliness and the Barracks Combined

Cosette's pain, still so poignant and so acute four or five months before, had entered into the convalescent phase, without her even noticing. Nature, springtime, youth, her love for her father, the gaiety of the birds and the flowers, caused something almost like forgetting to trickle, little by little, day by day, drop by drop, into this soul so virginal and young. Was the fire dying out there completely? Or was a layer of ash simply forming? The fact is that she now hardly felt any of those sore spots once so burning.

One day, she suddenly thought of Marius: "Fancy!" she said. "I never think about him anymore."

That same week she noticed a very good-looking officer of the lancers going by the garden gate, a man with a wasp waist, a ravishing uniform, the rosy cheeks of a girl, a saber under his arm, a waxed mustache, and a polished lancer's cap. Add to that, blond hair, striking blue eyes, a round, vain, insolent, and pretty face; the absolute opposite of Marius. He even had a cigar in his mouth. Cosette thought this officer had to be in the regiments barracked in the rue de Babylone.

The next day, she saw him go by again. She noted the time. Dating from that moment, was it purely by chance? she saw him go by almost every day.

The officer's friends noticed that in that "badly kept" garden, behind that nasty rococo gate, there was a rather pretty creature who was almost always to be found dawdling about when the good-looking lieutenant went by, a man not unknown to the reader, going as he did by the name of Théodule Gillenormand.

"Wait!" they said to him. "There's a girl there giving you the eye—go on, look!"

"Do you think I have time," answered the lancer, "to look at all the girls who look at me?"

This was precisely the time that Marius was gravitating seriously toward death and telling himself: "If only I could see her one more time before I die!" If his wish had been granted, if he had at that moment seen Cosette ogling a lancer, he would have died of pain without being able to utter a word.

Whose fault was it? No one's.

Marius had the sort of temperament that sinks deep into sorrow and stays there, wallowing; Cosette was of those who dive in and resurface fairly fast.

Cosette, what's more, was going through that phase, so dangerous, so fatal to a woman's development, when she is left to her own devices, when her lonely young girl's heart is like the tendrils of the vine, clinging, willy-nilly, to the capital of a marble column or a cabaret signpost.

A quick and decisive moment, critical for every orphan, whether poor or rich, for wealth does not protect you from making a bad choice; misalliances are made very high up the ladder; the true misalliance is that of souls; and, just as more than one unknown young man, without name, without birth, without fortune, is a marble capital that supports a temple of grand feelings and grand ideas, so some other man of the world, self-satisfied and opulent, with polished boots and polished words, if you look, not at the outside, but at the inside, that is, at what is reserved for women, is nothing more than a crummy little dive dimly haunted by violent, sordid, and debauched passions—the cabaret signpost.

What was there in Cosette's soul? Passion that had calmed down or gone to sleep; love in a floating state; something limpid and shiny, murky at a certain depth, dark deeper down still. The image of the good-looking officer was reflected on the surface. Was there a memory at the bottom? At the very bottom? Perhaps. Cosette did not know.

Something strange happened.

## II. COSETTE'S FEARS

In the first two weeks of April, Jean Valjean went on a trip. This, we know, was something he did from time to time, at very long intervals. He stayed away one or two days at most. Where did he go? No one knew, not even Cosette. Only once, at one of these departures, had she accompanied him in a fiacre as far as the corner of a little cul-de-sac, where she read: Impasse de la Planchette. There, he had got down and the fiacre had taken Cosette back to the rue de Babylone. It was usually when the household money was running out that Jean Valjean went on these little trips.

So Jean Valjean was away. He had said: "I'll be back in three days."

That evening, Cosette was alone in the salon. To stop herself from being bored, she had opened her piano-organ and had started to sing, accompanying herself, the chorus from *Euryanthe*[1]—"Hunters lost in the woods!"—which is perhaps the most beautiful thing in all music. When she had finished, she remained pensive.

All of a sudden she thought she heard someone walking in the garden. It couldn't be her father, he was away; it couldn't be Toussaint, she was in bed. It was ten o'clock at night.

She went to the salon window, which was shut and shuttered, and pressed her ear against it. It seemed to her that it was a man's tread and that whoever it was was walking very softly.

She flew upstairs to her bedroom, opened a transom cut into her shutters, and looked out at the garden. There was a full moon that night. You could see as clearly as in broad daylight. There was no one there.

She opened the window. The garden was absolutely still, and all you could see of the street was deserted as always.

Cosette thought she must have imagined it. She had only thought she'd heard the noise. It was a hallucination brought on by Weber's somber and majestic chorus, opening up as it does bewildering depths before the mind and shimmering before your eyes like a dizzying forest, in which you hear the crackling of dead branches under the anxious feet of hunters glimpsed in the twilight.

She thought no more of it.

Besides, Cosette was not by nature easily frightened. There was in her veins the blood of the bohemian and the adventurer who goes about barefoot. As you'll recall, she was more of a lark than a dove. In her heart of hearts, she was wild and brave.

The next day, not so late, at nightfall, she was strolling around the garden. Amid the jumble of thoughts that were preoccupying her, she was fairly sure she could hear the same sound as the night before, now and again, the sound of someone walking in the dark under the trees pretty close by, but she told herself that nothing resembles the sound of footfalls in grass as much as two branches rubbing against each other, and she took no more notice. Besides, she couldn't see anything.

She emerged from "the bushes" and now only had to cut across a small green lawn to reach the steps. The moon, which had just risen behind her, cast her shadow in front of her on the lawn as she came out of the flowerbeds. Cosette stopped in her tracks, terrified.

Next to her shadow, the moon distinctly threw another shadow on the lawn, one strangely frightening and terrible, a shadow with a round hat. It was like the shadow of a man standing on the edge of the flowerbeds just a few feet behind Cosette.

For a moment she could not speak, or cry out, or call for help, or move, or turn her head. Finally she mustered all her courage and spun around resolutely. There was no one there. She looked at the ground. The shadow had disappeared.

She ducked back into the bushes, boldly ferreted around in all the nooks and crannies, went as far as the gate, and came up empty.

Her blood was like ice in her veins. Was it yet another hallucination? What! Two days in a row? One hallucination, all right, but two hallucinations? What was truly disturbing was that the shadow was assuredly not a ghost. Ghosts hardly ever wear round hats.

The next day Jean Valjean came back. Cosette told him what she thought she'd heard and seen. She expected to be reassured, that her father would just shrug his shoulders and tell her: "You are a silly little girl." Jean Valjean was worried.

"It can't be anything," he said.

He made some excuse to leave her and went into the garden and she saw him examining the gate very carefully.

That night, she woke up; this time she was sure, she distinctly heard someone walking quite close to the steps under her window. She ran to her transom and opened it. There in the garden there was, indeed, a man, holding a big stick in his hand. Just as she was about to cry out, the moon lit the man's profile. It was her father. She went back to bed, telling herself: "That means he's really worried!"

Jean Valjean spent that night in the garden, and the two nights that followed. Cosette could see him through the peephole in her shutters.

The third night, the moon was waning and starting to rise later; it might have been one o'clock in the morning, she heard a great guffaw and her father's voice calling her: "Cosette!"

She leaped out of bed, threw on her dressing gown and opened her window.

Her father was down below on the lawn.

"I'm waking you up to reassure you," he said. "Look. There's your shadow with a round hat."

And he pointed to a long shadow that the moon cast on the lawn and that did, indeed, bear a close resemblance to a man wearing a round hat. It was the silhouette produced by a metal chimney, with a capped pot, rising up above a neighboring roof.

Cosette started to laugh, too, all her ghoulish speculations fell away, and the next day, over breakfast with her father, she poked fun at herself over the sinister garden haunted by the shadows of chimney pots.

Jean Valjean became perfectly relaxed again; as for Cosette, she didn't much notice whether the chimney pot was actually in the right place to cast the shadow she had seen, or thought she had seen, or whether the moon was in the right spot in the sky. She didn't pose herself any questions about the weirdness of a chimney pot that is afraid of being caught in the act and darts back when you look at its shadow, for the shadow had leaped back when Cosette had turned round and Cosette had thought she was quite sure of that. Cosette became perfectly serene again. The demonstration struck her as complete; the idea that there could have been someone walking in the garden in the evening or at night went out of her head.

A few days later, though, a fresh incident occurred.

### III. Embellished by Toussaint's Comments

In the garden, near the gate on the street, there was a stone bench, which was protected from prying eyes by an arbor, but which a passerby could just reach, at a pinch, stretching an arm through the gate and the arbor.

One evening in this same month of April, Jean Valjean had gone out and Cosette had sat down on this bench after sunset. The wind was freshening in the trees, Cosette was in a trance; an aimless sadness was taking hold of her little by little, that invincible sadness that evening brings on and that stems, perhaps—who knows?—from the mystery of the half-open grave at that hour.

Fantine was, perhaps, lurking in the shadows.

Cosette rose to her feet, slowly circled the garden, walking on grass wet with dew. In the midst of this melancholy somnambulism in which she was immersed, she told herself: "You really need wooden clogs to be in the garden at this hour. I'll catch a cold."

She went back to the bench. As she sat down, she noticed, over where she had just been, a rather big stone that had definitely not been there a moment before.

Cosette studied the stone, wondering what this could mean. All at once the idea that the stone had not come and sat on the bench on its own, that someone had put it there, came to her and frightened her. No doubt about it; the stone was there; she did not touch it, she fled without daring to look back, taking refuge in the house and immediately closing the shutters on the French windows by the steps, and barring and bolting the windows. She asked Toussaint: "Is my father back yet?"

"Not yet, Mademoiselle."

(We have indicated Toussaint's stutter once and for all. Please permit us not to dwell on it any further. We draw the line at musical notation of a disability.)

Jean Valjean was a thoughtful man and a nocturnal wanderer, and he often came home quite late at night.

"Toussaint," Cosette went on, "you are careful to barricade the shutters properly with bars at night, aren't you?—at least on the garden side? Do you stick those little iron things in the little rings to lock them properly?"

"Oh, don't you worry, Mademoiselle."

Toussaint never failed in this, which Cosette knew very well, but she couldn't prevent herself from adding: "Because it's so deserted around here!"

"As for that," said Toussaint, "it's the honest truth. A body could be murdered in their bed before you could say Boo! And with Monsieur not sleeping in the house! But there's nothing to fear, Mademoiselle, I lock up the windows like it was the Bastille.[1] Women, on their own! It's enough to make you shudder, I know! Can you imagine? Seeing a man come into your room at night and telling you to shut up! and then setting about cutting your throat for you. It's not so much dying I worry about—we all die, that's all right, we know very well we have to die. It's the abomination of feeling those people pawing you. And then again, their knives, they can't be all that sharp! Oh, God!"

"That's enough," said Cosette. "Just lock everything nice and securely."

Cosette, horrified by the melodrama improvised by Toussaint and perhaps also by a recollection of the apparitions of the other week, which now came back to her, did not even dare say, "Go and have a look at the stone someone has put on the bench, then!" for fear of having to reopen the garden door and letting "those people" in. She had all the doors and windows carefully shut everywhere, got Toussaint to go over the entire house from cellar to attic, shut herself up in her room, shot the bolts, looked under her bed, got into bed, and slept badly. The whole night, she saw that stone as big as a mountain and full of caves.

At sunrise—the peculiarity of the sun rising is to make us laugh at all our terrors of the night, and the laugh we have is always in proportion to the fear we have had—at sunrise Cosette woke to dismiss her fright as a nightmare and said to herself: "What was I dreaming about? It's like those footsteps I thought I heard the other week in the garden at night! It's like the shadow of the chimney pot! Am I going to be a complete coward this time?" The sun, which was glowing red through the slits in the shutters, turned the damask curtains crimson and reassured her to such an extent that everything vanished from her thoughts, even the stone.

"There was no more a stone on the bench than there was a man with a round hat in the garden; I dreamed up the stone like the rest."

She got dressed, went downstairs to the garden, ran to the bench, and felt a cold sweat break out, for the stone was there. But this lasted only a moment. What is fright at night is curiosity by day.

"Bah!" she said. "Let's take a closer look."

She lifted up the stone, which was sizable. There was something underneath that looked like a letter. It was a white paper envelope. Cosette snatched it. There was no address on one side, no seal on the other. Yet the envelope, although open, was not empty. You could see sheets of paper inside.

Cosette fumbled inside. It was no longer fear she felt, it was not only curiosity; it was the beginning of anxiety.

Cosette pulled out the contents of the envelope—a small paper notebook, each page of which was numbered and bore a few lines written in a rather lovely hand, Cosette thought, and very fine.

Cosette looked for a name, there was none; a signature, there was none. To whom was this addressed? Probably to her, since a hand had deposited the packet on the bench. Who did it come from? An irresistible fascination took hold of her, she tried to turn her eyes away from these pages that trembled in her hand, she looked up at the sky, the street, the acacias all drenched in light, the pigeons flying over a neighboring rooftop; then all at once her eyes swiftly dropped to the manuscript and she told herself that she had to know what was inside.

This is what she read:

## IV. A HEART UNDER A STONE

*The reduction of the universe to one single being, the expansion of one single being into God: That is what love is.*

*Love is the angels' greeting to the stars.*

*How sad the soul when it is sad out of love!*
*What a void is the absence of the being who alone fills the world! Oh, how true it is that the loved being becomes God! You would understand God becoming jealous if the Father of all had not evidently made Creation for the soul, and the soul for love.*

*A glimpse of a smile down there under a white crepe hat with a lilac veil is enough for the soul to enter the palace of dreams.*

*God is behind all things, but all things hide God. Things are black, human beings opaque. To love someone is to make them transparent.*

*Certain thoughts are prayers. There are moments when, whatever the body's position, the soul is on its knees.*

*Lovers who are separated cheat absence by a thousand chimeras that, nonetheless, have their reality. They are prevented from seeing each other, they can't write to each other, yet they find a whole host of mysterious ways of communicating. They send each other birdsong, the perfume of flowers, the laughter of children, the sun's rays, the wind's sighs, starlight, all of Creation. And why not? All God's works are made to serve love. Love is powerful enough to load the whole of nature with its messages.*

*O spring, you are a letter I write to her.*

*The future belongs even more to hearts than to minds. Loving is the only thing that can occupy and fill eternity. The infinite requires the inexhaustible.*

*Love partakes of the soul itself. It is of the same nature. Like the soul, it is a divine spark, like the soul, it is incorruptible, indivisible, imperishable. It is a point of fire that is inside us, that is everlasting and infinite, that nothing can limit and that nothing can extinguish. You feel it burn right to the marrow of your bones and you see it shine out to the back of the sky.*

*O love! Adoration! Sensual joy of two minds that understand each other, of two hearts that are exchanged, of two glances that pierce each other through! You will come to me, won't you, happiness? Strolling together in lonely expanses! blessed sparkling days! I have sometimes dreamed that now and then the hours broke away from the life of the angels and came down here below to traverse the destiny of men.*

*God cannot add anything to the happiness of those who love each other except by giving them endless duration. After a life of love, an eternity of love is, indeed, an increase; but to increase the intensity itself of the ineffable felicity that love brings to the soul—that is impossible, even for God. God is the fullness of heaven; love is the fullness of mankind.*

*You look at a star for two reasons, because it is bright and because it is impenetrable. You have beside you a softer radiance and a greater mystery, a woman.*

*All of us, whoever we may be, have beings we breathe in like air. If they are lacking, air is lacking, we suffocate. Then we die. To die for lack of love is appalling. The suffocation of the soul!*

*When love has melted and blended two beings in an angelic and sacred unity, the secret of life is open to them; they are nothing more, then, than the two sides of a single destiny; they are nothing more than the two wings of a single spirit. Love, soar!*

*The day a woman who passes you by radiates light as she walks, you are lost, you love. There is only one thing left for you to do and that is to think of her so unwaveringly that she is forced to think of you.*

*What love starts only God can end.*

*True love feels despair or delight over a glove lost or a handkerchief found and it needs eternity for all its devotion and its hopes. It is composed at once of the infinitely big and the infinitely small.*

*If you are stone, be a magnet; if you are plant, be sensitive; if you are man, be love.*

*Nothing is enough for love. We have happiness, we want paradise; we have paradise, we want heaven.*

*O, you who love each other, all these things are contained in love. Know how to find them in it. Love entails contemplation, as much as the heavens, and, more than the heavens, sensual delight.*

*"Will she come again to the Luxembourg?" "No, Monsieur." "It's in this church that she hears mass, is it not?" "She no longer comes." "Does she still live in this house?" "She moved." "Where has she moved to?" "She didn't say."*
 *What a dismal thing not to know the address of one's soul!*

*Love has its childish side, the other passions have their petty side. Shame on passions that make man petty! Glory be to the passion that makes him a child!*

*It is a strange thing, you know? I am in darkness. There is a being that has taken the heavens with her in moving away.*

*Oh! To be lying down side by side in the same grave, hand in hand, and from time to time gently to stroke each other's fingertip in the dark, that will do for my eternity.*

*You who suffer because you love, love still more. To die of love is to live from it.*

*Love. A somber starry transfiguration is involved in this torture. There is ecstasy in agony.*

*O, joy of the birds! It's because they have a nest that they are able to sing.*

*Love is breathing in the heavenly air of paradise.*

*Deep hearts, wise spirits, take life the way God made it. It is a long ordeal, an unintelligible preparation for an unknown destiny. This destiny, the true one, begins for man at the first step inside the grave. Then something appears to him and he begins to discern finality. Finality, think about that word. The living see infinity; finality only lets itself be seen by the dead. Meanwhile, love and suffer, hope and contemplate. Woe, alas! to whoever has loved only bodies, forms, appearances! Death will take everything from him. Try to love souls and you will find them again.*

*I met in the street a very poor young man who loved. His hat was old, his coat was worn; there were holes at his elbows; the water got into his shoes and the stars got into his soul.*

*What a great thing, to be loved! What an even greater thing, to love! The heart becomes heroic through passion. It is no longer made up of anything but what is pure; it no longer relies on anything but what is elevated and grand. An unworthy thought can no more germinate in it than a nettle on a glacier. The lofty and serene soul, out of reach of vulgar passions and emotions, rises above the clouds and shadows of this world, the follies, the lies, the hatreds, the vanities, the miseries, and inhabits the endless skies and feels only the deep and subterranean rumblings of destiny, as the mountain peak feels earthquakes.*

*If there wasn't someone who loved, the sun would go out.*

## V. COSETTE, AFTER THE LETTER

While she read, Cosette gradually fell to daydreaming. The moment she lifted her eyes from the last line of the notebook, the good-looking officer—it was his hour—passed, triumphant, in front of the gate and Cosette found him repulsive.

She returned to contemplating the notebook. It was written in a ravishing hand, Cosette thought; the same hand, but different inks, sometimes very black, sometimes pale, as when you put water in the inkwell and write on different days. It was obviously a whole way of thinking that poured its heart out there, sigh by sigh, erratically, without order, without choice, without aim, randomly. Cosette had never read anything like it. This manuscript, in which she saw more clarity than obscurity, had the effect on her of a sanctuary whose door suddenly cracked open. Every one of these lines shone out resplendent in her eyes and flooded her heart with a strange glow. The education she had received had always spoken to her of the soul but never of love, which was like talking about a firebrand without mentioning the flame. This manuscript of fifteen pages suddenly and sweetly revealed to her all about love, pain, destiny, life, eternity, the beginning, the end. It was like a hand opening and suddenly throwing a fistful of sunbeams her way. She felt in these few lines a passionate, ardent, generous, honest nature, a sacred will, immense pain and boundless hope, an aching heart, ecstasy in full bloom. What was this manuscript? A letter. A letter without an address, without a name, without a date, without a signature, urgent and disinterested, an enigma composed of truths, a message of love made to be carried by an angel and read by a virgin, a rendezvous arranged for somewhere out of this world, a love letter from a phantom to a shade. It was a calm but shattered absent being, who seemed to be ready to take refuge in death and who was sending the absent woman the secret of destiny, the key of life, love. It had been written with one foot in the grave and a finger in heaven. These lines, falling one by one onto the paper, were what could be called soul drops.

Who could these pages come from? Who could have written them? Cosette did not hesitate for a second. There was only one man it could have come from.

Him!

The day looked brighter again to her mind. Everything was clear again. She felt unbelievable joy and profound anguish. It was him! He was writing to her! He was there! It was his arm that had passed through this gate! While she was busy forgetting him, he had found her once more! But had she forgotten him? No! Never! She was mad to have thought so for a moment. She had always loved him, always adored him. The fire had been covered and lay smoldering for a while, but she could see clearly that it had only gone deeper. Now it burst into flame again and fired every bit of her, body and soul. This notebook was like a flying spark that had fallen from this other soul into her own, and she felt the wild blaze rekindling. She took every word of the manuscript to heart. "Oh, yes!" she said. "How well I recognize all that! That's everything his eyes already told me."

As she finished reading it for the third time, Lieutenant Théodule waltzed back past the gate and made his spurs ring out on the pavement. Cosette was forced to look up. She found him insipid, silly, stupid, useless, conceited, offensive, impertinent—and extremely ugly. The officer thought he should smile at her. She turned away in shame and outrage. She would gladly have thrown something at his head.

She fled, went back inside the house and shut herself up in her room to reread the manuscript, learn it by heart, and daydream. When she had read it thoroughly, she kissed it and tucked it inside her corset.

That was it, Cosette had fallen once more in deep seraphic love. The abyss known as Eden had just opened up again.

All that day, Cosette was in a kind of haze. She could barely think, her ideas were scrambled like a tangled skein of wool in her brain, she couldn't manage any conjectures, she hoped, trembling all the while—what? vague things. She didn't dare promise herself anything and didn't want to deny herself anything, either. Her face went all pale and her body all shivery. It seemed to her at times that she was verging on the fanciful; she said to herself: "Is this real?" Then she patted the beloved bundle under her dress, she pressed it to her heart, felt its corners against her flesh, and if Jean Valjean could have seen her at that moment, he would have shuddered in the face of this luminous and unfamiliar joy that streamed from her eyes. "Oh, yes!" she thought. "It's him all right! This comes to me from him!"

And she told herself that an intervention of angels, some celestial chance, had restored him to her.

O, transfigurations of love! O, dreams! This celestial chance, this intervention of angels, was that little ball of bread hurled by one thief to another thief, from the Charlemagne yard to the Lions' Den, over the rooftops of La Force.

## VI. THE OLD ARE MADE FOR GOING OUT
### AT THE RIGHT MOMENT

When evening came, Jean Valjean went out; Cosette got dressed. She did her hair the way it most became her, and put on a dress whose bodice had had one snip of the scissors too many, and which, thanks to this low neckline, let the hollow of the neck show and was, as young girls say, "a bit indecent." It was not indecent in the slightest, but it was prettier than it otherwise would have been. She went to all this trouble with her toilette without knowing why.

Did she want to go out? No. Was she expecting a visit? No. At dusk, she went down into the garden. Toussaint was busy in her kitchen, which opened onto the rear courtyard.

She began to walk under the trees, parting the branches from time to time, since some were very low.

And so she reached the bench. The stone was still there. She sat down, and placed her soft hand on the stone as if she wanted to stroke it and thank it.

All of a sudden, she had that indefinable feeling you get when someone is standing behind you, even when you can't see them. She turned her head and shot to her feet.

It was him.

He was bareheaded. He looked pale and emaciated. You could scarcely see that his clothes were black. Twilight turned his beautiful forehead white and covered his eyes in shadow. Beneath a veil of incomparable sweetness, he had a whiff of death and of the night about him. His face was lit up by the brightness of the dying light and by the thoughts of a soul about to depart. It seemed that he was not yet a phantom but already no longer a man.

His hat had been tossed a few feet away in the bushes.

Cosette was ready to faint and did not let out a cry. She slowly backed away, for she felt herself drawn. He didn't budge. Something indefinably sad enveloped her; she could feel his eyes on her rather than see them.

As she backed away, Cosette hit a tree and leaned back on it. Without the tree, she would have fallen.

Then she heard his voice, that voice that she had never really heard, as it rose above the rustling of the leaves and murmured: "Forgive me, I'm here. My heart is bursting, I couldn't go on living the way I was, I've come. Did you read what I put there, on that bench? Do you recognize me a little? Don't be afraid of me. It's been a while already, do you remember the day you looked at me? It was in the Luxembourg, near the Gladiator. And the day you walked past me? That was the sixteenth of June and, then, the second of July. It will soon be a year ago. For a long while now, I haven't seen you. I asked the woman who rents chairs, she told me she didn't see you anymore. You were living in the rue de l'Ouest, on the third floor at the front of a new house, you see how I know? I followed you. What else could I do? And then you disappeared. I thought I saw you go past once when I was reading the paper under the arcade of the Odéon. I ran. But no. It was just someone who had a hat like yours. At night, I come here. Don't worry, no one sees me. I come and look at your windows as close as I can. I tread very softly so you won't hear me, for you would perhaps be frightened. The other night I was behind you, you turned around, I fled. Once I heard you singing. I was happy. Does it worry you if I hear you singing through the shutters? It can't hurt you. No, isn't that so? You see, you are my angel, let me come sometimes. I think I'm going to die. If you only knew! I adore you! I do! Forgive me, I'm talking to you, but I don't know what I'm saying, perhaps I'm annoying you, am I annoying you?"

"Oh, Mother!" she said.

And she slumped in a heap as though she were dying herself.

He caught her, she fell, he caught her in his arms, he squeezed her tight without knowing what he was doing. He tottered himself as he held her. He felt as if his head were full of smoke; he had flashes in his eyes; his thoughts vanished; it seemed to him that he was performing a religious act and that he was committing an act of profanation. Besides, he did not feel the slightest desire for this ravishing woman whose shapes he could feel against his chest. He was lost in love.

She took his hand and put it on her heart, he felt the notebook there. He stammered: "You love me?"

She answered in such a low voice that it was no more than a breath you could barely hear: "Be quiet! You know I do!"

And she hid her burning face against the proud and intoxicated young man's chest.

He fell on the bench, she flopped next to him. They had run out of words. The stars began to shine. How did it happen that their lips met? How does it happen that birds sing, snow melts, the rose opens, that May blossoms, that dawn comes on all white behind the black trees over the shivering hilltops?

One kiss, and that was everything.[1]

Both quivered, thrilled, and they looked at each other in the shadows with sparkling eyes. They did not feel either the freshness of the night, or the coldness of the stone, the dampness of the ground, or the wetness of the grass; they looked at each other and their hearts were full of thoughts. They had taken each other's hands without knowing it.

She did not ask him, she did not even wonder, where and how he had got into the garden. It seemed so natural to her that he should be there!

Now and then, Marius's knee touched Cosette's knee and both shivered. At intervals, Cosette stammered out a word. Her soul was trembling on her lips like a drop of dew on a flower.

By and by they began to talk. The outpouring succeeded the silence, which is bliss. The night was serene and splendid overhead. These two beings, pure as spirits, told each other everything, their dreams, their euphorias, their ecstasies, their fantasies, their weaknesses, how they had adored each other from afar, how they had longed for each other, their despair when they no longer saw each other. They each confided to the other, in an ideal intimacy that already nothing could add to, what was most hidden and most mysterious in themselves. They told each other, with a candid faith in their illusions, all that love, youth, and the vestiges of childhood that survived in them both, had put into their heads. These two hearts poured themselves out to each other and into each other, so that at the end of an hour, the young man had the soul of the young girl and the young girl had the soul of the young man. They entered each other, enchanted each other, dazzled each other.

When they had finished, when they had told each other everything, she laid her head on his shoulder and asked him: "What is your name?"

"My name is Marius," he said. "And you?"

"My name is Cosette."

# BOOK SIX

# PETIT-GAVROCHE

## I. NASTY TRICK OF THE WIND

Since 1823, while the greasy spoon of Montfermeil was gradually going under and sinking, not into the bottomless pit of bankruptcy, but into the cesspool of petty debt, the Thénardier couple had had two more children, both male. That made five: two girls and three boys. It was a lot.

Mother Thénardier ditched the last two, while they were still very young and little, through a singular stroke of luck.

*Ditched* is the right word. There was only a tiny fragment of maternal instinct in that woman. And she is not the only example of the phenomenon I can think of. Like the maréchale de la Mothe-Houdancourt,[1] mother Thénardier was a mother only as far as her daughters were concerned. Her maternity ended there, her hatred of the human race began with her sons. When it came to her sons, her viciousness knew no bounds and her heart was sealed off as though by a bleak stone wall. As we saw, she detested the eldest boy; she execrated the other two. Why? Because. The most terrible of motives and the most unarguable of answers: Because. "I don't need a pack of screaming brats," their mother would say.

We should explain how the Thénardiers managed to divest themselves of their youngest children and even to make a profit in so doing.

The Magnon woman we mentioned a few pages back is the same one who had managed to get good old Gillenormand to pay an allowance to the two children she had. She lived on the quai des Célestins, at the corner of that ancient rue du Petit-Musc, which has done what it could to come up smelling like roses despite the odor of its bad reputation. You will recall the great croup epidemic of thirty-five years ago, which devastated the quartiers bordering the Seine in Paris and which gave medical science the opportunity to conduct large-scale experiments testing the effectiveness of inhalations of alum, happily replaced today with tincture of iodine applied externally. In that epidemic, mother Magnon had lost her two boys the same day, one in the morning, the other in the evening, when they were still mere toddlers. It was a blow. Those children were precious to their mother; they represented eighty francs a month. Those eighty francs were paid most punctually, on behalf of Monsieur Gillenormand, by his rent collector, Monsieur Barge, a retired bailiff in the rue du Roi-de-Sicile. With the children dead, the endowment was buried. Mother Magnon sought an expedient. In that shady freemasonry of evil of which she was a part, everything is known, secrets are kept, and they all help each other out. Mother Magnon required two children; mother Thénardier had two. Same sex, same ages. Good arrangement for one, good investment for the other. The little Thénardier boys became the little Magnon boys. Mother Magnon left the quai des Célestins and went to live in the rue Clocheperce. In Paris, the identity that binds an individual to themselves snaps from one street to the next.

The registry office, not being tipped off, did not intervene, and the substitution was carried out as straightforwardly as could be. Only, Thénardier demanded, for this loan of the children, ten francs a month, which mother Magnon promised and even paid. It goes without saying that Monsieur Gillenormand continued to come up with the money. He went every six months to see the little boys, and did not see the change. "Monsieur," mother Magnon would say to him, "don't they take after you!"

Thénardier, to whom metamorphoses came easily, seized the opportunity to become Jondrette. His two daughters and Gavroche had barely had time to notice that they had two little brothers. At a certain level of misery a sort of spectral indifference comes over you and you regard other human beings as worms. Your nearest and dearest are often no more to you than vague shadows you can barely make out against the nebulous background of life and that easily slip back and disappear into invisibility.

The evening of the day she had delivered her two little boys to mother Magnon, with the firm intention of giving them up for good, mother Thénardier had, or pretended she had, a scruple. She said to her husband: "But this is abandoning your own children, this is!"

Thénardier, magisterial and phlegmatic, cauterized this scruple with this sentence: "Jean-Jacques Rousseau went one better!"

The mother went from scruple to anxiety: "But what if the police come pestering us? What we've done here, Monsieur Thénardier, tell me, then, is it allowed?"

Thénardier answered: "Everything is allowed. Everyone'll think it's for the good. Anyway, no one's interested in taking a close look at kids who don't have a single sou."

La Magnon was a sort of fashion plate of crime. She liked to tart herself up.

She shared her lodgings, furnished in a manner both lavish and wretched, with a skillful English thief who had gone French. This Englishwoman, who had been naturalized a Parisienne, and who was respectable through her extremely rich connections, was intimately acquainted with the medals of the Bibliothèque and the diamonds of Mademoiselle Mars, and was later famous in the judicial records. She was known as Mamselle Miss.

The two little boys who had accrued to mother Magnon had nothing to complain about. Recommended by the eighty francs, they were handled with care, like all that is exploited for money; not too badly turned out, not too badly fed, treated almost like "little gentlemen," better off with the false mother than with the real one. Mother Magnon played the lady and never spoke slang in front of them.

They spent several years in this way. Thénardier had high hopes for them. One day he was moved to say to mother Magnon, who was bringing him his monthly ten francs: "The 'father' should give them an education."

Suddenly, these two poor children, until then fairly well protected, even though it was by their sorry fate, were abruptly hurled at life and forced to start living it.

A mass arrest of miscreants like the arrest at the Jondrette garret, necessarily complicated by later searches and incarcerations, is a real disaster for this hideous occult subculture that lives beneath public society; an episode of the kind involves a whole chain of collapses in this gloomy netherworld. The Thénardier catastrophe produced the Magnon catastrophe.

One day, shortly after mother Magnon had handed Éponine the note about the rue Plumet, the police suddenly descended on the rue Clocheperce; mother Magnon was seized along with Mamselle Miss, and the entire household, which was suspect, was hauled in. The two little boys were playing in the backyard at the time and saw nothing of the raid. When they tried to get back in, they found the door locked and the house empty. A cobbler whose shop was opposite called them over and handed them a piece of paper that their "mother" had left for them. On the piece of paper was an address: *Monsieur Barge, rent collector, rue du Roi-de-Sicile, no. 8.* The man from the shop told them: "You don't live here anymore. Go there. It's very close. The first street on the left. Ask your way there using this note."

The two boys took off, the elder leading the younger and holding in his hand the note that was supposed to be their guide. He was cold and his little fingers were numb and had trouble hanging on to the bit of paper. At the bend in the rue Clocheperce, a gust of wind ripped it from him and, as night was falling, the boy could not find it again.

They began to wander aimlessly through the streets.

## II. IN WHICH PETIT-GAVROCHE PUTS NAPOLÉON THE GREAT TO GOOD USE

Spring in Paris is pretty often swept by bitterly cold and biting north winds that don't so much freeze you as chill you to the bone; these north winds, which mar the most beautiful days, have the exact effect of the drafts of cold air that rush into a warm room through gaps in a window or a door not properly closed. It feels like the gloom-laden door of winter has remained ajar and that that is where the wind is coming from. In the spring of 1832, a time when the first great epidemic of the century[1] broke out in Europe, the north winds were sharper and more piercing than ever. A door even more icy than winter's was ajar. The door of the sepulchre. You could feel the breath of cholera in those north winds.

From the meteorological perspective, the cold winds had the peculiarity of not excluding a high electrical pressure. Storms accompanied by thunder and lightning frequently broke at the time.

One evening when the north winds were whistling rudely, so much so that it felt like January was back and the bourgeois grabbed their coats again, Petit-Gavroche, shivering gaily as always in his rags, was standing in apparent rapture in front of a wigmaker's shop over l'Orme-Saint-Gervais way. He was decked out in a woman's woolen shawl, picked up who knows where, and had turned it into a muffler. Petit-Gavroche looked for all the world to be lost in admiration of a wax bride in a low-cut gown with orange blossoms in her hair, which was revolving in the window, flashing her smile at the passersby between two "peepers"—oil lamps; but in reality he was observing the shop in order to see if he couldn't "lift" a cake of soap from the front window, which he would then go and sell for a sou to a "fence"—who called himself a "hairdresser"—in the suburbs. He often breakfasted on such a cake. He called this type of work, for which he had real talent, "shaving the barbers."

While he was gazing at the bride, and eyeing the cake of soap, he was muttering between clenched teeth: "Tuesday . . . It can't be Tuesday . . . Is it Tuesday? . . . Maybe it is Tuesday . . . Yes, it's Tuesday."

No one ever knew what this monologue was about. If, by chance, it had to do with the last time he had eaten, then that was three days before, for it was now Friday.

The barber, in his shop heated by a good hot stove, was shaving a customer and throwing a look from time to time at this enemy, this cocky little kid frozen stiff, who may have had both hands in his pockets but had obviously unsheathed and sharpened his wits.

While Gavroche was studying the bride, the shop window, and the Windsor soaps, two children of different heights, fairly neatly dressed and even smaller than he was, one looking to be about seven, the other five, timidly turned the door handle and went into the shop asking for who knows what, charity perhaps, in a plaintive murmur more like a moan than a prayer. Both boys spoke at once and their words were unintelligible because sobs choked the younger one's voice and the cold made the elder one's teeth chatter. The barber wheeled around with a look of fury on his face and, without letting go of his razor, shoved the elder boy back with his left hand and the little one with his knee, pushing them out into the street; then he shut his door in a huff: "Letting in the cold for nothing!"

The two children went on their way again, crying. But a cloud had come up; it started to rain. Petit-Gavroche ran after them: "What's the matter, then, kids?"

"We've got nowhere to sleep," said the older one.

"Is that all?" said Gavroche. "That's nothing. Is that anything to cry about? What a pair of ninnies!"

And adopting a tone of tender authority and gentle protectiveness from the heights of his slightly grumpy superiority, he continued: "Little girls, come with me."

"Yes, Monsieur," said the elder.

And the two children followed him as they would have followed an archbishop. They had stopped crying. Gavroche took them up the rue Saint-Antoine in the direction of the Bastille.

As he headed off, Gavroche cast an indignant backward glance at the barber's shop.

"It's got no heart, that cold fish of a barber," he growled. "He's a Brit."

A girl, seeing them walking in single file, all three of them, with Gavroche in the lead, let out a great guffaw. This guffaw was wanting in respect for the group.

"Good day, Mamselle Back-of-a-Bus," Gavroche said to her.

A moment later, the wigmaker came back to him and he added: "I got the wrong beast; he isn't a cold fish, he's a snake. Wigmaker, I'll go and get a smithy and I'll have 'im put a rattle on your tail for you."

The wigmaker had made him aggressive. Leaping over a gutter, he shouted at a bearded woman porter worthy of meeting Faust on the Brocken,[2] with her broom in her hand.

"Madame," he said to her, "you've come out with your horse, then, have you?"

And on that note, he splashed the patent leather boots of a passerby.

"Little stinker!" yelled the passerby, furious.

Gavroche poked his nose out of his shawl.

"Monsieur has a complaint?"

"About you!" said the man.

"The office is closed," said Gavroche. "I can't receive any more complaints."

Meanwhile, as he continued up the street, he noticed a girl of about thirteen or fourteen, frozen stiff under a porte cochère and begging, her clothes so short you could see her knees. The little girl was beginning to be too big a girl for that. Growing plays such tricks on you. Your skirt becomes too short the moment your nakedness becomes indecent.

"Poor girl!" said Gavroche. "It doesn't even have any drawers. Here, take this at least."

And, unwinding all that fine wool he had around his neck, he threw it over the thin blue shoulders of the beggar girl and the muffler turned back into a shawl again. The girl looked at him in amazement and received the shawl in silence. At a certain level of distress, the poor, in their stupor, no longer bemoan the bad and are no longer thankful for the good.

That done:

"Brrrrr!" said Gavroche, shivering for all he was worth, for he was colder than Saint Martin, who at least managed to keep half his cloak.[3]

At that "Brrrrr!" the shower redoubled in fury and raged. Bad skies such as this one punish good deeds.

"Now what!" cried Gavroche. "What can this mean? It's raining again! God Almighty, if this continues, I'm cancelling my subscription."

And he set off again.

"Never mind," he went on, casting a glance at the beggar girl who was snuggling into the shawl. "At least one of us has a flash fur."

And, glaring at the cloud, he cried: "So put that in your pipe and smoke it!"

The two children fell in behind him.

As they were passing one of those thick grated trellises that indicate a baker's shop, for bread is placed like gold behind iron bars, Gavroche turned round: "Listen, kids, have we dined?"

"Monsieur," replied the elder boy, "we haven't eaten since early this morning."

"Are you without father or mother, then?" Gavroche pursued grandly.

"Begging your pardon, Monsieur, we have Papa and Maman, but we don't know where they are."

"Sometimes that's better than knowing," said Gavroche, who was a thinker.

"It's been two hours now," continued the elder boy, "that we've been walking, we've been looking everywhere for a snack but we can't find anything."

"I know," said Gavroche. "The dogs eat everything."

He went on after a pause: "So! We've lost our progenitors. We don't know what we've done with them. That won't do, kids. It's not too bright to lose the old folks like that. Ah, you've just got to swallow it."

Apart from this, he asked them no questions. To be homeless, what could be more natural? The elder of the two kids, who had almost completely reverted to the ready insouciance of childhood, let out this exclamation: "It's funny, all the same. Maman said she'd take us to get blessed palms on Palm Sunday."

"You don't say," replied Gavroche.

"Maman," the elder boy went on, "is a lady who lives with Mamselle Miss."

"I'll be blowed," Gavroche fired back.

Meanwhile he had stopped and for a few minutes had been feeling and fumbling in all kinds of recesses in his rags. Finally he raised his head trying to look merely satisfied but looking perfectly triumphant.

"Let's stay calm, little nippers. Here is enough for supper for three."

And he pulled a sou out of one of his pockets. Without giving the two little boys time to be impressed, he pushed them both ahead of him into the baker's shop and slapped his sou on the counter, shouting: "Garçon! Five centimes' worth of bread."

The baker, who was the master in person, took a loaf of bread and a knife.

"Cut it into three, garçon!" Gavroche went on, adding with dignity: "There are three of us."

And seeing that the baker, after carefully eyeing the three diners, had grabbed an unbleached loaf, he stuck his finger right up his nose with a snort as imperious as if he had a pinch of Frederick the Great's snuff at the end of it, and he flung this indignant yell right in the baker's face: "Whathahellsat?"

Those of our readers who may be tempted to interpret Gavroche's shouted question to the baker as a Russian or Polish word or one of those savage cries the Iowas and the Botocudos[4] hurl at each other from opposite banks of some river in the wilderness, are hereby warned that it is a word they say every day (they, our readers) and that it stands for the phrase: What the hell is that? The baker understood perfectly and replied: "Why, it's bread! Very good second-class bread."

"You mean rock-hard black dodger," Gavroche retorted, calmly and coldly contemptuous. "White bread, garçon! Fluffy white bread! It's my treat."

The baker could not help smiling, and as he cut the white loaf, he studied them in a compassionate way that riled Gavroche.

"Hey, baker's boy!" he shouted. "What are you giving us the once-over for like that?"

Placed end to end, the three of them would not have come to more than six feet.

When the bread was cut, the baker put the sou away and Gavroche said to the two little boys: "Tuck in."

The little boys looked at him, speechless. Gavroche chortled: "Oh, silly me, it's true they don't know yet, they're too little!"

And he translated: "Eat."

He handed each of them a chunk of bread at the same time.

And, thinking that the elder boy, who struck him as the more worthy of his conversation, merited some special encouragement and should be relieved of all hesitation in satisfying his appetite, he added as he gave him the biggest piece: "Shove this in your gob."

One piece was noticeably smaller than the other two; he took that one for himself.

The poor boys were starving, Gavroche included. While they were tearing into their bread, they were cluttering up the shop and the baker, now that he had been paid, was giving them cranky looks.

"Let's hit the street again," said Gavroche.

They headed once more toward the Bastille.

From time to time, as they passed shop windows all lit up, the littler one would stop to check the time on a lead watch hanging from his neck by a string.

"That one's a ninny, all right," said Gavroche.

Then, pensive, he muttered through his teeth: "All the same, if I had kids, I'd keep 'em on a tighter rein than that."

As they were polishing off their bread and coming to the corner of the dismal rue des Ballets at the end of which the low forbidding grated door of La Force could be seen, someone said: "Hey, Gavroche, is that you?"

"Hey, Montparnasse, is that you?" Gavroche replied.

It was a man who had accosted the kid and this man was none other than Montparnasse, disguised behind blue spectacles but recognizable to Gavroche.

"I'll be a monkey's uncle!" Gavroche went on. "You've got a coat the color of a flaxseed poultice and blue specs like a doctor. You've got class, cross my old man's heart!"

"Shhhh!" said Montparnasse. "Not so loud."

And he swiftly pulled Gavroche away from the shop lights.

The two little boys trotted along behind mechanically, holding each other by the hand.

When they were under the black archivolt of a porte cochère, out of sight and out of the rain, they spoke again: "You know where I'm goin'?" asked Montparnasse.

"To the Abbey of You'll-be-sorry-you-climbed-up-the-scaffold," said Gavroche.

"Joker!"

Montparnasse went on: "I'm goin' to find Babet."

"Ah!" said Gavroche. "So her name's Babet."

Montparnasse lowered his voice.

"Not her, him."

"Ah, Babet!"

"Yes, Babet."

"I thought he was locked up."

"He picked the lock," Montparnasse shot back.

And he quickly told the kid that, that same day, in the morning, Babet had been transferred to the Conciergerie[5] and had escaped by turning left instead of right in "the halls of justice."

Gavroche had to admire the man's cunning.

"What an artist!" he said.

Montparnasse added a few details about Babet's breakout and ended with: "Oh, but that's not all!"

Gavroche, though listening, had grabbed a walking stick that Montparnasse was holding in his hand; he had mechanically tugged the top bit and the blade of a dagger had appeared.

"Ah!" he said, swiftly shoving the dagger back in, "I see you brought your gendarme disguised as a bourgeois."

Montparnasse gave him a wink.

"Blast!" Gavroche said. "So you're going to have a brawl with the cops?"

"Hard to say," said Montparnasse, sounding indifferent. "It's always good to have a pin on you."

Gavroche insisted: "What are you up to tonight, then?"

Montparnasse again adopted a serious tone and, swallowing every consonant, he said: "Things."

And, brusquely changing the subject: "By the way!"

"What?"

"Something that happened the other day. Just think. I meet a bourgeois gent. He hands me a sermon and his purse as presents. I put the purse in my pocket. A minute later, I feel around and there's nothing there."

"But the sermon," quipped Gavroche.

"What about you?" continued Montparnasse. "Where are you off to right now?"

Gavroche showed his two protégés and said: "I'm going to put these children to bed."

"Bed? Where's that?"

"My place."

"Your place? Where's that?"

"My place."

"You got a place, then?"

"Yep, I've got a place."

"And where is this place of yours?"

"In the elephant," said Gavroche.

Montparnasse, although by nature not easily amazed, couldn't prevent himself from exclaiming: "In the elephant!"

"Why, yes, in the elephant!" Gavroche shot back. "Whaddovit?"

This is another word in that language that nobody writes but everybody speaks. *Whaddovit* means: What of it?

The kid's profound observation brought Montparnasse back to calm and common sense. He seemed to regard Gavroche's abode more highly.

"I see!" he said. "Of course, the elephant . . . Is it cosy?"

"Very cosy," said Gavroche. "Cosy as anything. There are no drafts like under bridges."

"How do you get in?"

"I get in."

"You mean there's a hole?" asked Montparnasse.

"For crying out loud! Yes! But you're not allowed to tell. It's between the front legs. The squealers haven't spotted it."

"And you climb up? Right, I get it."

"There's a knack, crick, crack, in no time at all, you're up and you're on your own."

After a pause, Gavroche added: "For the little ones I'll use a ladder."

Montparnasse started to laugh.

"Where the hell did you pick up these little pipsqueaks?"

Gavroche answered guilelessly: "They're little nippers a wigmaker gave me as a present."

Meanwhile Montparnasse had come over all pensive.

"You recognized me without too much trouble," he muttered.

He took two small objects out of his pocket that were simply two bits of quill wrapped in cotton and he introduced one into each nostril. This gave him a different nose.

"That changes you," said Gavroche. "You're not nearly as ugly. You ought to keep those things up your schnoz all the time."

Montparnasse was a pretty boy, but Gavroche was a scoffer.

"Joking aside," Montparnasse asked, "how do I look?"

The sound of his voice was also different. In the twinkling of an eye, Montparnasse had become unrecognizable.

"Oh! Do Punchinello for us!" cried Gavroche.

The two little boys, who hadn't been listening to anything till then, busy as they were picking their own noses, came closer at the sound of that name and gazed at Montparnasse with dawning joy and admiration.

Unfortunately Montparnasse had other things to worry about.

He clapped his hand on Gavroche's shoulder and spoke, emphasizing every word: "Listen to what I tell you, boy, if I was out in the square with my digger and my dagger and my dugs and you were to lavish ten sous on me I wouldn't mind singing for my supper, but it's not Mardi Gras yet."

This bizarre phrase had a strange effect on the boy. He spun on his heel, ran his small bright eyes all around him with keen attentiveness and spotted, a few feet away, a police constable with his back to them. Gavroche let out an "Ah, right!" that he immediately bit off, and shaking Montparnasse's hand: "Well, then, good night, I'm off to my elephant with my toddlers. Just supposing you need me one night, you know where to find me. I reside on the mezzanine level. There is no porter, you will ask for Monsieur Gavroche."

"Right you are," said Montparnasse.

And they went their separate ways, Montparnasse worming his way toward the place de Grève and Gavroche toward the Bastille. The little five-year-old, dragged along by his brother who was dragged along by Gavroche, turned his head several times to watch "Punchinello" walking away behind him.

The garbled sentence, by means of which Montparnasse had warned Gavroche of the presence of the police constable, contained no other talisman than the syllable *dig* repeated five or six times in different forms. That syllable *dig,* not voiced on its own but artfully combined with other words in a sentence, means: *Watch out, we can't talk freely.* There was as well in Montparnasse's sentence a literary beauty that was lost on Gavroche. "My digger, my dagger and my dugs" was a slang phrase from the Temple quartier that signifies *my dog, my knife, and my wife,* and was very much in use among the clowns and the commedia dell'arte red-tails of the *grand siècle,*⁶ when Molière wrote and Callot drew.

Twenty years ago, you could still see at the southeast corner of the place de la Bastille, near the dock of the canal dug out of the old moat of the prison-citadel, a bizarre monument that has already been wiped from the memory of Parisians yet that deserved to leave a trace there, for it was something that a member of the Institut, commander in chief of the Army of Egypt,⁷ no less, had come up with.

We say *monument* though it was only a model. But this model itself, a wondrous first draft, the grandiose carcass of an idea of Napoléon's that two or three successive gusts of wind had whisked away and deposited each time further away from us, had become historic and had taken on something indefinably final that contrasted with its provisional look. It was an elephant forty feet high, built out of plaster on a timber framework and carrying on its back a tower that resembled a house. It was once painted green by some dauber but was now painted black by the sun, the rain, the weather. In this deserted and open corner of the square, at night, the broad forehead of the colossus, its trunk, its tusks, its tower, its enormous rump, its four legs like columns, was startling and terrible, silhouetted against the starry sky. No one knew what it meant. It was a sort of symbol of the force of the people. It was grim, enigmatic, immense. It was a mysterious and mighty phantom, one visible, standing next to the invisible specter of the Bastille.

Few foreigners visited this edifice, no one walking by looked up at it. It fell into ruin; every season, bits of plaster broke off its flanks, leaving grisly wounds. The "aediles," as town councillors are called in elegant patois, had left it to rot since 1814. It stood there, in its corner, mournful, diseased, disintegrating, surrounded by a rotting paling fence pissed on at every turn by drunken coach-drivers; cracks zigzagged up its belly, a lath stuck out of its tail, weeds were pushing up between its legs; and as the level of the square had been rising all around for thirty years, due to that slow yet never-ending movement that imperceptibly raises the ground of great cities, it now stood in a dip as though the earth were subsiding under it. It was filthy, despised, repulsive, and superb, ugly in the eyes of the bourgeois, melancholy in the eyes of the thinker. It had a feel of garbage about to be swept out of the way and a feel of a royal majesty about to be decapitated.

It looked different at night, though, as we were saying. Night is the true medium for all that is shadowy. As soon as twilight fell, the old elephant was transfigured; it took on a peaceful yet awesome look in the formidable serenity of the darkness. Being a thing of the past, it was one with the night; and this obscurity suited its grandeur.

This monument, stiff, squat, heavy, harsh, austere, almost deformed, but most certainly majestic and stamped with a kind of magnificent wild gravity, has vanished, allowing to reign in peace the sort of gigantic stove, capped with its stovepipe, that replaced the somber fortress with its nine towers a bit the way the bourgeoisie has replaced the feudal system. It is only natural that a stove be the symbol of an era whose power is contained in a cooking pot. This era will pass, is already passing; we are beginning to understand that, if there may be some force in a boiler, there can only be power in a brain; in other words, that what leads and pulls the world along is not locomotives, it is ideas. Harness locomotives to ideas, by all means; but don't mistake the cart for the horse.

Be that as it may, to go back to the place de la Bastille, the architect of the elephant had managed to make something grand out of plaster; the architect of the stovepipe has succeeded in making something paltry out of bronze.

In 1832, this stovepipe,[8] since baptized with the sonorous name of the July Column, this failed monument of an aborted revolution, was still wrapped in a facing of tall scaffolding, which we, for our part, regret, and by a huge wooden fence that put the finishing touches on the elephant's isolation.

It was toward this corner of the square, so dimly lit by the reflection of a distant streetlamp, that the boy directed the two "toddlers."

Kindly allow us to stop here and remind you that we are within the bounds of reality, plain and simple, and that twenty years ago the criminal courts actually sentenced a child caught sleeping[9] inside the elephant of the Bastille for vagrancy and for trespassing on a public monument. This fact noted, we push on.

As they approached the colossus, Gavroche realized the effect that the infinitely big can have on the infinitely small and he said: "Nippers! Don't be frightened."

Then he slipped through a gap in the fence and entered the elephant's enclosure and helped the little ones to step over the breach. The two boys were a tad frightened, but they followed Gavroche without a word, trusting this little savior in rags who had given them bread and promised them a place to sleep.

There was a ladder lying along the fence, which workers on the nearby site used in the daytime. Gavroche lifted it with remarkable vigor and propped it against one of the elephant's front legs. Near the point where the ladder ended, you could see a sort of black hole in the colossus's belly. Gavroche pointed out the ladder and the hole for his guests and said to them: "Climb up and go in."

The two little boys looked at each other, terrified.

"Don't tell me you're frightened, little nippers!" cried Gavroche.

And he added: "Watch this."

He hugged the elephant's rough foot and in the twinkling of an eye, without deigning to use the ladder, he had shinnied up and reached the crevice. He slipped in the way a grass snake slides into a crack, kept going, and a moment later the two boys vaguely made out his whitish head as it popped out, a pale and wan disk, at the edge of the hole full of darkness.

"What are you waiting for!" he cried. "Up you come, kidlingtons! You'll see how cosy it is! You go first!" he said to the elder boy. "I'll give you a hand."

The little boys nudged each other; the urchin frightened them and reassured them at the same time and then, it was raining hard. The elder one decided to take the plunge. The younger one, seeing his brother climb up and himself left standing all alone between the paws of that huge beast, felt a great desire to cry but he didn't dare.

The elder boy climbed up the rungs of the ladder, wobbling away; Gavroche encouraged him all the way with the rallying cries of a fencing master to his students or of a mule driver to his mules:

"Don't be frightened!"

"That's it!"

"Put your foot there!"

"Your hand here."

"Keep going!"

And when he was within reach, he grabbed him swiftly and vigorously by the arm and pulled him up.

"One down!" he said.

The nipper slipped in through the hole.

"Now," said Gavroche, "wait for me. Monsieur, be good enough to take a seat."

And, coming out of the gap the way he had gone in, he let himself slide down the entire length of the elephant's leg, with the agility of a monkey, fell on his feet in the grass, grabbed the little five-year-old by the waist and planted him right in the middle of the ladder, then began to climb up behind him, calling out to the elder boy: "I'll push him, you pull him."

In a flash the little one had been lifted, pushed, dragged, pulled, crammed, stuffed into the hole before he had time to know what was happening, and Gavroche, coming in after him and kicking away the ladder with his heel so that it fell on the lawn, started clapping his hands and yelled: "Here we are, then! Long live General Lafayette!"

This explosion over, he added: "Welcome, little mites, this is my home."

This was, indeed, Gavroche's home.

O, the unforeseen usefulness of the useless! The charity of big things! The goodness of giants! This outsize monument that had once held an idea of the emperor's had become a poky home for a little street kid. The nipper had been accepted and sheltered by the colossus. The bourgeois in their Sunday best who passed in front of the Bastille elephant liked to say, looking it up and down derisively with their bulging bug-eyes: "What's the use of that?" Its use was to save from the cold, the frost, the hail, the rain, to protect from the winter wind, to keep from sleeping in the mud that brings fever and from sleeping in the snow that brings death, a little being with no father or mother, with no bread, with no clothes, with no refuge. Its use was to take in the innocent that society drove out. Its use was to lessen society's sin. It was a retreat open to one to whom all doors were closed. It seemed that the miserable old mastodon, invaded by vermin and oblivion, covered in warts, patches of mold and ulcers, tottering, worm-eaten, abandoned, condemned, a kind of colossal beggar asking in vain for the alms of a benevolent look in the middle of the crossroads, had alone taken pity on this other beggar, on this poor pygmy who went off with no shoes on his feet, with no roof over his head, blowing on his fingers to warm them, dressed in rags, fed by what everyone else throws out. That was the use of the elephant of the Bastille. This idea of Napoléon's, scorned by men, had been taken up by God. What would have been merely illustrious had become august. To achieve what he had in mind, the emperor would have needed porphyry, bronze, iron, gold, marble; to God, the old assemblage of boards, joists, and plaster was enough. The emperor had had an idea of genius; in this titanic elephant, armored, tremendous, holding up its trunk, carrying its tower and causing joyous invigorating water to spurt all around him, he wanted to embody the people; God had made something grander out of it, he had housed a child in it.

The hole Gavroche had slipped through was scarcely visible on the outside, hidden as it was, as we said, under the belly of the elephant and so small that hardly anything but cats and little nippers could have got through.

"Let's start," said Gavroche, "by telling the porter that we're not in."

And diving into the dark confidently like a man who knows his apartment, he took a board and blocked the hole with it.

Gavroche dived back into the dark. The children heard the sputtering of a matchstick thrust into a phosphorous bottle. The chemical match did not yet exist; the Fumade lighter was the height of progress in those days.

A sudden brightness made them blink; Gavroche had just lit one of those bits of string doused in resin that are known as "cellar rats." The cellar rat, which smoked more than it shed light, made the inside of the elephant dimly visible.

Gavroche's two guests looked around them and felt something of what a person would feel shut up in the great tun of Heidelberg[10] or, more to the point, what Jonas must have felt inside the belly of the biblical whale.[11] A whole gigantic skeleton appeared to them and wrapped them round. Above, a long dark wooden beam, from which massive curved beams shot out at regular intervals, represented the backbone with its ribs; stalactites of plaster hung down from it like viscera and from one rib to the next vast spiderwebs made dusty diaphragms. You could see here and there in the corners big blackish spots that looked like they were alive and that changed places quickly in sudden startled motion.

The debris that had fallen off the back of the elephant onto its belly had filled up the concave space so that you could walk around as though on a floor.

The smaller boy huddled close to his brother and said in a little voice: "It's dark."

This word made Gavroche shout out loud. The petrified look on the two nippers' faces made it necessary to give them a shock.

"What's gotten into you?" he yelled. "Are we complaining? Are we turning up our noses? Is it the Tuileries you're after? You're not a pair of snobs, are you? Tell me. I must warn you, I'm not part of that pack of ninnies. Heavens, don't tell me you two little nippers have grown too big for your boots?"

A bit of rough treatment is a good antidote to terror. It is reassuring. The two little boys moved in closer to Gavroche again.

Gavroche was moved in a fatherly way by such trust and shifted "from serious to soft" as he spoke to the smaller boy: "Silly!" he said to him, imparting a caressing nuance to the insult. "It's outside that it's dark. Outside it's raining, here it's not raining; outside it's cold, here there isn't a puff of wind; outside there's heaps of people, here there's no one; outside there isn't even a moon, here there's my candle, by jingo!"

The two little boys began to look at the apartment with less fright; but Gavroche did not give them a spare moment to think.

"Quick!" he said.

And he pushed them toward what we are very happy to be able to call the back of the room. That was where his bed was. Gavroche's bed had everything. Meaning, there was a mattress, a cover, and an alcove with curtains. The mattress was a straw mat, the cover was a fairly voluminous loose skirt of coarse gray wool that was very warm and almost new.

The alcove was like this:

Three fairly long poles, rammed into the rubble on the ground and solidly reinforced, that is, sunk into the elephant's belly, two in front, one at the back, and tied together by a rope at the top so as to form a pyramid. This pyramid supported brass wire netting that was simply hung over this structure, but artistically arranged and held in place by iron wire straps in such a way as to entirely wrap around the three poles. A ring of heavy stones pinned the netting to the ground all around in such a way as to let nothing through. This netting was nothing other than a bit of the copper mesh that is used for cladding aviaries in zoos. Gavroche's bed sat under the mesh as in a cage. The whole setup was like an Eskimo tent. It was this mesh that took the place of curtains.

Gavroche moved some of the stones that held the mesh down in front and the two overlapping panels of the trellis moved apart.

"Kids, down on all fours!" said Gavroche.

He got his guests into the cage carefully, then crawled in after them, put the stones back together and hermetically sealed the opening.

They were all three stretched out on the mat. Little as they were, not one of them could have stood up in the alcove. Gavroche was still holding the cellar rat in his hand.

"Now," he said, "get some shut-eye! I'm going to dim the candelabra."

"Monsieur," the elder of the brothers asked Gavroche, pointing to the mesh, "what is that?"

"That," said Gavroche gravely, "is for the rats. Get some shut-eye!"

Though he did feel obliged to add a few words by way of educating these beings of such tender age and so he went on: "All that's from the Jardin des Plantes. It's all used for the wild animals. Reckonairs [I reckon there's] a shopful of stuff. Allyaftado [all you have to do] is hop over a wall, climb through a window, and slide under a door. You can take as much as you like."

Talking all the while, he pulled the cover up over the tiny one who murmured: "Oh, that's nice! It's so warm!"

Gavroche looked with satisfaction at the cover.

"That's also from the Jardin des Plantes," he said. "I took it off the monkeys."

And showing the elder boy the mat on which he was lying, a good thick mat, beautifully made, he added: "This, this was the giraffe's."

After a pause, he continued: "The animals had all this. I took it off them. They didn't mind. I told them: It's for the elephant."

He was silent again and then he resumed: "We hop over walls and we don't give two hoots about the government. And that's that."

The two boys studied, with a shy and stunned respect, this intrepid and inventive being, a vagabond like them, on his own like them, puny like them, who had something both wretched and all-powerful about him, and who seemed to them supernatural, with his face that could pull all the grimaces of an old fairground entertainer and that was lit up by the most guileless and charming smile.

"Monsieur," the elder boy said bashfully, "aren't you afraid of policemen, then?"

Gavroche merely answered: "You baby! We don't say policemen, we say cops."

The tiny one had his eyes open, but he didn't say a word. As he was on the edge of the mat, the elder being in the middle, Gavroche tucked the cover round him the way a mother would have done and raised the mat under his head with old rags to make the little nipper a pillow. Then he turned to the elder boy: "Eh? We're pretty cosy in here!"

"Oh, yes!" answered the elder boy, gazing at Gavroche with the expression of a rescued angel.

The two poor little soaked children began to warm up.

"Ah, so," said Gavroche, "what was all that crying about?"

And jerking his thumb at the little one: "A little mite like that, that's different; but a big boy like you, crying, that's idiotic; it makes you look like a blubbering dumb cluck."

"But, golly," said the boy, "we didn't have a home to go to anymore."

"Little nipper!" Gavroche went on. "We don't say home, we say digs."

"And then, we were frightened of being all alone at night."

"We don't say night, we say curfew."

"Thank you, Monsieur," said the boy.

"Listen," Gavroche went on, "you mustn't whine about anything ever again. I'll look after you. We'll have such fun. You'll see. In summer, we'll go to La Glacière with Turnip, a mate of mine, we'll go swimming in the canal, we'll run stark naked over the tracks in front of the pont d'Austerlitz—that gets the washerwomen in a real lather. They yell and carry on, if you only knew what a scream they are! We'll go and see the skeleton man. He's alive. At the Champs-Élysées. He's as skinny as anything, that character. And then I'll take you to a show. I'll take you to see Frédérick Lemaître. I've got tickets, I know the actors, I even acted in a play once. We were nippers about so high, we ran around under a cloth—and that was the sea. I'll have you signed on at my theater. We'll go and see the savages. They're not real, these particular savages. They've got pink tights that get all wrinkled, and you can see that their elbows are darned with white thread. After that, we'll go to the Opéra. We'll go in with the hired claquers. The claque at the Opéra is most select. I wouldn't hang around with the claquers on the boulevards.[12] At the Opéra, can you imagine, there are people who pay twenty sous, but they're noodles. They're known as drips . . . And then we'll go and watch the guillotine in action. I'll take you to see the executioner. He lives in the rue des Marais. Monsieur Sanson. There's a letter box on his door. Ah, we'll have such a good time!"

At that moment, a drop of wax fell on Gavroche's finger and brought him back to life's realities.

"Ow!" he said. "That's it for the wick. Be careful! I can't put more than a sou a month into my lighting. When you go to bed, you've got to sleep. We don't have the time to read the novels of Monsieur Paul de Kock.[13] Anyway, the light could get under the cracks in the porte cochère and all the cops'd have to do is look."

"And then," timidly observed the elder boy, the only one who dared chat with Gavroche and answer him back, "a spark might fall on the straw, we have to be careful not to burn the house down."

"We don't say burn the house down," said Gavroche. "We say heat up the stew."

The storm got much worse. You could hear, through the rolls of thunder, the heavy downpour battering the colossus's back.

"Hammer away, rain!" said Gavroche. "I really like hearing the whole jugful running all the way down the legs of the house. Winter's a brute; it loses its load, it goes to all that trouble for nothing, it can't wet us, and that makes it grumble, that old water porter up there!"

This allusion to thunder, all of whose consequences Gavroche, in his capacity as a philosopher of the nineteenth century, accepted, was followed by a flash of lightning so dazzling that something of it came in through the crack in the elephant's belly. Almost at the same time the thunder growled—and furiously at that. The two little boys let out a howl and shot to their feet so fast that the netting was almost knocked over; but Gavroche turned his bold little face toward them and took advantage of the thunderclap to burst out laughing.

"Steady on, children. Let's not bring the house down. Now that's what I call thunder! Fantastic! That was no damp squib. Good for you, Lord! By jingo! It's almost as good as at the Théâtre Ambigu."[14]

That said, he put the netting right, gently pushed the two little boys back down on the bed, pressed down on their knees to stretch them out to their full length and cried out: "Since the good Lord's lighting his candle, I can blow mine out. Children, it's time to sleep, my young human beings. It's very bad not to sleep. It turns you into a smelly arse, or, as they say out there in the world of grown-ups, it makes your gob reek. Wrap yourselves up nice and tight in your fur coats! It's lights out. Everyone all right?"

"Yes," murmured the elder boy, "I'm all right. It's like I've got feathers under my head."

"We don't say head," cried Gavroche. "We say noggin."

The two boys cuddled up together. Gavroche finished arranging them on the mat and pulled the cover right up to their ears, then repeated for the third time the injunction in hieratic tongue: "Get some shut-eye!"

And with that, he blew out the candle.

Hardly was the light extinguished when a weird tremor began shaking the netting the three children were lying under. There was a series of muffled rubbing noises that gave out a metallic sound as though claws and teeth were grinding the copper wire. This was accompanied by all kinds of sharp little cries.

The little boy of five, hearing this racket above his head and frozen stiff with terror, gave his older brother a dig with his elbow, but the older brother was already "getting some shut-eye," as Gavroche had ordered him to do. So the little boy, frightened out of his wits, dared to address Gavroche, though in a barely audible voice, holding his breath in: "Monsieur?"

"Eh?" said Gavroche, who had just shut his eyes.

"What's that?"

"It's the rats," replied Gavroche.

And he laid his head back on the mat.

Actually, the rats, which congregated in the thousands in the carcass of the elephant and which were the live black spots we spoke of above, had been holding back out of respect for the flame of the candle while it was burning, but as soon as this cavern, which was like their city, had been returned to the night, smelling what the good storyteller Perrault calls "fresh meat,"[15] they had made a mad dash en masse for Gavroche's tent, had clambered to the top, and were biting into the mesh as though they were trying to break through this new style of mosquito net.

Still the little boy could not get to sleep: "Monsieur?" he started again.

"Eh?" said Gavroche.

"What are rats?"

"Mice."

This explanation reassured the little boy a bit. He had seen white mice in his lifetime and he hadn't been frightened of them. Yet he piped up again: "Monsieur?"

"Eh?" said Gavroche again.

"Why don't you have a cat?"

"I did have one," replied Gavroche. "I brought one back here, but they ate it on me."

This second explanation undid the work of the first and the little boy began to tremble again. The dialogue between him and Gavroche resumed for the fourth time.

"Monsieur!"

"Eh?"

"Who was it who got eaten?"

"The cat."

"Who was it who ate the cat?"

"The rats."

"The mice?"

"Yes, the rats."

The little boy, appalled at these mice that eat cats, persisted: "Monsieur, would they eat us, those mice there?"

"Naturally!" said Gavroche.

The little boy's terror reached a peak. But Gavroche added: "Don't be afraid! They can't get in. And anyhow, I'm here! Here, hold my hand. Now shut up and get some shut-eye!"

At the same time Gavroche reached out over his brother and took the little one's hand. The little boy pressed his hand against him, and felt reassured. Courage and strength have mysterious circuits. Silence once more settled in around them, the sound of voices had startled and scattered the rats; in just a few minutes they were back and made a mighty racket, but the three little nippers, deeply immersed in sleep, no longer heard a thing.

The hours of the night flew by; darkness covered the immense place de la Bastille, a winter wind joined the rain and blew in gusts, patrols ferreted around doorways, alleyways, enclosures, hidden corners, and looking for nocturnal vagrants, passed silently by the elephant; the monster, standing motionless, its eyes open in the dark, looked as though it were dreaming, satisfied with its good deed, and went on sheltering the three poor sleeping boys from the heavens and from men.

To understand what is about to follow, we have to remember that at this time the Bastille guardhouse was located on the other side of the square and that what happened near the elephant could not be seen or heard by the sentinel.

Toward the end of the hour just before dawn, a man came running out of the rue Saint-Antoine, crossed the square, ran round the big enclosure of the July Column, and slipped through the palings of the fence and up under the belly of the elephant. If any light, however dim, had shone on this man, you would have guessed he had spent the night in the rain—he was soaked through. Once he was under the elephant, he let fly with a bizarre cry that doesn't belong to any human tongue and that only a parakeet could reproduce. Twice he repeated this cry, which might be transcribed as follows, though this gives only the merest idea of how it sounded: "Kirikikiou!"

At the second cry, a bright cheery young voice answered from the belly of the elephant: "Yes."

Almost immediately, the board that closed the hole shifted, opening the way to a child who slid down the elephant's leg and dropped lightly by the man's side. This was Gavroche. The man was Montparnasse.

As for the cry, *kirikikiou*, that was doubtless what the boy meant when he said, "Just ask for Monsieur Gavroche."

On hearing it, he had woken up with a start. Had crawled out of his "alcove," parting the mesh a little before carefully closing it again, then opened the trapdoor and come down.

The man and the boy silently acknowledged each other in the night; all Montparnasse said was: "We need you. Come and give us a hand."

The gamin did not ask for further clarification.

"Here I am," he said.

And they both set off toward the rue Saint-Antoine, from which Montparnasse had emerged, quickly wending their way through the long line of carts belonging to the market gardeners who head for the markets at that hour.

The market gardeners, squatting in back of their carts among the lettuces and vegetables, half-asleep, buried up to their eyeballs because of the driving rain, didn't even look at this odd pair going past.

## III. THE UPS AND DOWNS OF ESCAPE

This is what took place that same night at La Force:

A breakout had been planned jointly by Babet, Brujon, Gueulemer, and Thénardier, even though Thénardier was in solitary. Babet had carried out his part of the business that same day, as we saw according to the story Montparnasse told Gavroche.

Montparnasse was supposed to help them from the outside.

Brujon, having spent a month in a correctional chamber, had had the time while he was there, first, to plait a rope, second, to perfect a plan. In days gone by these austere places where prison discipline leaves a prisoner alone with himself consisted of four stone walls, a stone ceiling, a flagstone floor, a camp bed, a barred window, and an iron-clad door, and was called a dungeon; but the dungeon was judged too horrible; now the cell consists of an iron-clad door, a barred window, a camp bed, a flagstone floor, a stone ceiling, and four stone walls and is called a correctional chamber. A streak of daylight comes in around noon. The problem with these chambers, which, as you see, are nothing like dungeons, is that they leave a body to ponder when they should be putting it to work.

So, Brujon had pondered, and he had emerged from the correctional chamber with a rope. As he had the reputation of being extremely dangerous in the Charlemagne yard, he was put in the New Building. The first thing he found in the New Building was Gueulemer, the second was a nail; Gueulemer meant crime, a nail meant liberty.

It's time we got a better purchase on Brujon. He looked delicate, with his pale complexion and his profoundly premeditated languor, but he was actually a lusty strapping lad, well-bred and intelligent, a thief with a melting look in his eyes and an atrocious grin. The melting look was a result of his will but the grin was a result of his nature. His initial studies in his art focused on roofs; he had caused great progress to be made in the industry of lead lifters, who strip off roofing and peel off guttering by means of the process known as "cooking with double the fat."

What wound up making the moment favorable for a breakout was that roofers were, at that very moment, repointing and relaying a section of the slate tiles on the prison roof. The Saint-Bernard yard was no longer absolutely cut off from the Charlemagne yard or from the Saint-Louis yard. There were scaffolding and ladders up there; in other words, bridges and stairways to deliverance.

The New Building, which was, in fact, the most decrepit and crack-riddled building in the world, was the prison's weak spot. Its walls were so eaten away by saltpeter that the vaults of the dormitories had had to be completely lined in wood because stones were breaking away and falling on the inmates as they lay in their beds. Despite its dilapidated state, they made the mistake of locking up in the New Building the most alarming of the accused, sticking what is known in prison parlance as "the hard cases" in there.

The New Building contained four dormitories, one on top of the other, and an attic on the very top known as the Bel-Air. A wide chimney, probably left over from some ancient kitchen of the ducs de La Force, started at ground level and passed through the next four floors, dividing all the dormitories in half, like a sort of flattened pillar, before boring through the roof.

Gueulemer and Brujon were in the same dormitory. They had been put on the bottom floor as a precaution. Chance would have it that the heads of their beds leaned against the chimney flue. Thénardier found himself precisely above them in the attic described as the Bel-Air.

The passerby who stops at the rue Culture-Sainte-Catherine, after the fire station, outside the porte cochère of the bathhouse, sees a courtyard full of flowers and shrubs in tubs, at the back of which sits a little white rotunda, with two wings, brightened up by green shutters, the bucolic dream of Jean-Jacques. Not more than ten years ago, towering above this rotunda, was an enormous black wall, bare and ghastly, which it rested against. This was the wall of the covered way that encircled La Force.

The wall behind the rotunda was like Milton glimpsed behind Berquin.[1]

High as it was, the wall was overshadowed by an even blacker roof that could be seen beyond it. This was the roof of the New Building. You could see four dormer windows there fitted with bars; these were the windows of the Bel-Air. A chimney poked through the roof; this was the chimney that passed through the dormitories.

The Bel-Air, the attic of the New Building, was a sort of great gallery with a steeply pitched roof, sealed with triple grilles and with metal-backed doors studded with enormous nails. When you entered by the north end, you had the four dormer windows on your left, and on your right, facing the dormer windows, four good-sized square cages, spaced apart and separated by narrow passageways, built out of masonry to elbow height and the rest out of iron bars right up to the roof.

Thénardier had been in solitary confinement in one of these cages since the night of February 3. They never did find out how, and through whose connivance, he had managed to procure for himself and hide a bottle of that wine invented, they say, by Desrues, which has a narcotic mixed in with it and which the Endormeurs gang,[2] the "dopers," made famous.

There are traitors employed in lots of prisons, half jailors, half thieves, who help in breakouts, who sell their disloyal services to the police and make a fair bit on the side out of the rotten eggs thrown in the police wagon.

So, the self-same night that Petit-Gavroche had picked up the two stray boys, Brujon and Gueulemer, who knew that Babet had escaped that very morning and was waiting for them in the street along with Montparnasse, quietly got out of bed and started to drill through the chimney flue that their beds touched with the nail Brujon had found. The rubble fell on Brujon's bed without a sound. The squalls combined with the thunder to rattle the doors on their hinges and made an appalling and very convenient racket inside the prison. Those of the inmates who woke up pretended to go back to sleep and let Gueulemer and Brujon get on with the job. Brujon was deft; Gueulemer was strong. Before any sound had reached the guard, who was lying in a grated cell that looked onto the dormitory, the wall was drilled through, the chimney scaled, the wire-mesh grille that shut off the upper opening of the flue forced, and the two fearsome villains were on the roof. The rain and the wind grew wilder, the roof was slippery.

"What a good night for a getaway!" said Brujon.

A chasm six feet wide and eighty feet deep lay between them and the encircling prison wall. At the bottom of this chasm they could see a sentry's fusil gleaming in the darkness. They tied one end of the rope Brujon had woven in his dungeon to the stumps of the chimney bars they had just twisted off, threw the other end over the encircling wall, leaped over the chasm in a single bound, hung on tight to the top of the wall, clambered over it, let themselves slide, one at a time, down the rope onto a little roof that abutted the bathhouse, pulled in their rope, jumped down into the bathhouse courtyard, crossed it, pushed open the porter's transom, next to which hung his cord, pulled the cord, opened the porte cochère, and found themselves in the street.

It was not yet three quarters of an hour since they had gotten out of bed in the gloom, their nail in hand, their scheme in mind.

A few seconds later, they had caught up with Babet and Montparnasse as they prowled the neighborhood.

In pulling in their rope, they had broken it and a bit had remained tied to the chimney on the roof. Otherwise they had sustained no real damage, apart from more or less entirely skinning their hands.

That night, Thénardier had been tipped off, they never could shed light on how, and he stayed awake. Toward one o'clock in the morning, the night being pitch black, he saw on the roof, in the rain and howling wind, two shadows flit past the dormer window opposite his cage. One of them stopped long enough for a quick look. It was Brujon. Thénardier recognized him and that was all he needed: he understood.

Thénardier, flagged as a killer and held for laying an ambush at night with force of arms, was kept under constant surveillance. A guard, who was relieved every two hours, strode with loaded fusil in front of his cage. The Bel-Air was lit by a wall lamp. The prisoner had a pair of irons on his feet weighing fifty pounds each. Every day at four in the afternoon a warder escorted by two mastiffs—this was still the practice in those days—entered his cage, deposited by his bed a two-pound loaf of black bread, a jug of water, and a bowl full of thin bouillon with a few broadbeans swimming in it, checked his irons, and banged on the bars. This man came back twice in the night, with his mastiffs.

Thénardier had obtained permission to keep a sort of iron dowel which he used to pin his bread to a crack in the wall, "so," he said, "the rats can't get it." As Thénardier was kept under constant surveillance, no one had raised any objection to this dowel. Yet later it was recalled that one of the warders had said: "It'd be better only letting him have a wooden dowel."

At two o'clock in the morning, the guard, who was an old soldier, was changed and replaced by a conscript. A few seconds later, the man with the dogs paid his visit and went off without noticing anything peculiar except that the "tenderfoot" was too young and looked like "a real hick." Two hours later, at four o'clock, when they came to relieve the conscript, he was found fast asleep, slumped on the ground in a heap next to Thénardier's cage. As for Thénardier, he was no longer there. His broken irons lay on the tiles. There was a hole in the top of his cage and, above that, another hole in the roof. A plank had been ripped off his bed and no doubt carted away, for it was never found. They also seized from the cell a half-empty bottle containing the remains of the laced wine with which the soldier had been knocked out. The soldier's bayonet had disappeared.

As all this was being discovered, Thénardier was believed to be well beyond all reach. The truth is that, while he was no longer in the New Building, he was still in grave danger. He had not yet made a clear getaway.

When he had gotten as far as the roof of the New Building, Thénardier had found the remains of Brujon's rope hanging from the bars of the chimney pot. But this remnant was far too short for him to be able to escape over the encircling wall as Brujon and Gueulemer had done.

When you turn out of the rue des Ballets and into the rue du Roi-de-Sicile, you run into a squalid recess almost immediately. There was a house there last century of which only the back wall remains, a genuine hovel wall rising to a height of three stories between the neighboring buildings. This ruin is recognizable by two big square windows that can still be seen there; the one halfway up, closest to the gable on the right, is barred by a worm-eaten joist propped against the wall like an upright beam. Through these windows you could once see a thick high dismal wall that was a section of the covered way that surrounded La Force.

The hole that the demolished house left in the street is half-filled by a rotten paling fence, propped up by five stone posts. Hidden in this enclosure is a small lean-to of a shack, propped against the fragment of the ruin that remains standing. The paling fence has a gate that, a few years ago, was shut only by a latch.

It was on top of this ruin that Thénardier lobbed a little after three in the morning.

How did he get there? That is what no one has ever been able to explain or work out. The lightning must have both hindered and helped him at once. Did he use the roofers' ladders and scaffolding to go from roof to roof, from enclosure to enclosure, from compartment to compartment, to the buildings of the Charlemagne yard, followed by the buildings of the Saint-Louis yard, the encircling wall, and from there, to the hovel on the rue du Roi-de-Sicile? But there were gaps in this route that seemed to rule it out as impossible. Did he lay down the plank from his bed as a bridge from the Bel-Air to the covered way of the encircling wall, and did he then set about crawling on his stomach along the top of the covered way, all the way round the prison as far as the ruin of a hovel? But the wall of the covered way of La Force followed a jagged and uneven line; it had ups and downs, it dipped down at the fire station, it rose up again at the bathhouse, it was intersected by buildings, it was not the same height at the Hôtel Lamoignon as on the rue Pavée, it had sudden drops and right angles everywhere; and then, the sentries would have seen the fugitive's black silhouette; on that score, the route taken by Thénardier still remains virtually inexplicable. Either way, flight is impossible. Thénardier, fired by that terrifying thirst for liberty that turns precipices into mere ditches, iron gates into willow fences, a legless cripple into an athlete, a gout sufferer into a bird, stupidity into instinct, instinct into intelligence, and intelligence into genius—had Thénardier invented and improvised a third way out? No one ever knew.

You can't always take in the wonders of escape. The man who breaks out, we repeat, is a man inspired; there is starlight and lightning in the mysterious glow of flight; the straining after deliverance is no less amazing than the flapping after the sublime; and we say of a thief who got away: How did he manage to scale that roof? just as we say of Corneille: How did he come up with the famous line in Horace, "He should have died!"—*"Qu'il mourut"?*[3]

Be that as it may, dripping with sweat, drenched with rain, his clothes in tatters, his hands skinned raw, his elbows bleeding, his knees torn to shreds, Thénardier had reached what children, in their figurative language, call "the sharp edge" of the wall of the ruin, he had lain on it stretched out to full length and there, at that point, his strength had failed him. A sheer escarpment three stories high separated him from the pavement in the street.

The rope he had was too short.

He waited there, pale, exhausted, despairing of any hope he had had, still covered by night but aware that day was about to dawn, horrified by the notion that in a few moments' time, he would be hearing the nearby clock of Saint Paul[4] chiming four, the hour when the sentry would be relieved and when he would be found sound asleep outside his cage under the hole punched through the roof. By the light of the streetlamps he gazed in stupefaction at the terrible depth of the drop, at the wet black pavement, that longed-for and appalling pavement that spelled both death and freedom.

He asked himself if his three accomplices in escape had succeeded, if they had waited, and if they would come to his aid. He listened. Apart from a patrol, no one had passed in the street while he had been there. Nearly all the market gardeners from Montreuil, Charonne, Vincennes, and Bercy descended on the markets via the rue Saint-Antoine.

Four o'clock rang out. Thénardier gave a start. A few moments later, the crazy and confused hubbub that follows the discovery of a breakout erupted in the prison. The noise of doors opening and shutting, the squeal of gates on their hinges, the tumult of the guards, the raucous shouts of the gatekeepers, the jarring of the butts of muskets on the courtyard pavements reached him. Lights bobbed up and down in the barred windows of the dormitories, a torch ran over the attic of the New Building, the firemen from the station next door had been called in. Their helmets, which the torch lit up in the rain, came and went all along the roofs. At the same time, Thénardier saw that a wan streak of light was turning the bottom of the sky mournfully white behind the Bastille.

He was on top of a wall ten inches wide, stretched out in the downpour, with two chasms to both left and right, unable to move, dizzy with the prospect of falling and horrified at the certainty of being arrested, and his thoughts, like the pendulum of a clock, swung from one of these notions to the other. "Dead if I fall, nabbed if I stay put."

In his anguish, he suddenly saw, the street being still completely dark, a man, who was sliding along the walls and who had come from the direction of the rue Pavée, stop in the hollow above which Thénardier was suspended, so to speak. This man was joined by a second man who walked with the same cautiousness, then by a third, then by a fourth. When these men had met up, one of them raised the latch on the gate in the fence and all four slipped into the enclosure where the shack was. They found themselves exactly below Thénardier. The men had obviously chosen the hollow so that they could talk without being seen by anyone going past or by the sentry guarding the gate of La Force a few feet away. We should add that the rain kept this sentry blockaded in his sentry box. Thénardier, not being able to make out their faces, cocked his ear at their words with the desperate attention of a luckless lowlife who feels he is sunk.

Suddenly Thénardier saw something like hope flash before his eyes, for the men were talking slang. The first man was saying, low but distinctly: "Let's beat it. What're we coolin' our 'eels in this 'ole *icigo* for?"

The second replied: "It's pissing down fit to put out the devil's bonfire. The cops are onto us, to boot, and there's a gunner on the lookout. We're gonna get ourselves put back in the slammer killin' time 'ere *icicaille*."

Those two words *icigo* and *icicaille*, which both mean *ici* (here), and which belong, the first to the argot of the *barrières*, the second to the argot of the Temple,[5] were beacons of light for Thénardier. At *icigo* he recognized Brujon, who was a prowler of the *barrières*, and at *icicaille*, Babet, who, among all his other trades, had been a junk dealer at the Temple.

The antique argot of the *grand siècle* is now spoken only at the Temple, and Babet was actually the only person who spoke it really purely. Without that *icicaille* Thénardier would not have recognized him, for he had completely disguised his voice.

Meanwhile, the third man piped up: "What's the hurry? Let's wait a bit. Who's to say he doesn't need us?"

At this, which was merely French, Thénardier recognized Montparnasse, whose elegance consisted in understanding all varieties of slang but speaking none.

As for the fourth, he kept quiet, but his vast shoulders gave him away. Thénardier did not hesitate. It was Gueulemer.

Brujon spat back almost impetuously, though still in a low voice: "What are you yammering on about? The innkeeper wasn't able to make a break for it. He hasn't got the knack, end of story! Rip up his shirt and carve up his sheets to twist himself a hangman's friend, belt a few portholes in the door, cook up some false dog tags, knock up a few open sesames, snip his fetters, chuck his twister outside, lie low, keep under cover, you've got to be smart to last! The old bugger can't 'a been up to it, he doesn't know how to use the old elbow grease!"

Babet added, sticking to the classic wisecracking slang Poulailler and Cartouche[6] used to speak, and which is to the bold, new, colored, and risqué slang Brujon used what the language of Racine is to the language of André Chénier:[7] "Your barkeep must've been caught in the act on the stairs. You gotta be one jump ahead. He's an amateur. He's let 'imself get played for a sap by some flatfoot, maybe even by a stool pigeon, and they've pulled a fast one on him. Cock an ear, Montparnasse, d'you hear all the yapping in the clink? You saw all those fireflies. He's been busted again! So now he'll be doing his twenty long ones. I don't want to get the wind up, I'm no chicken, that's a known fact, but we can't lounge around here all day—otherwise they'll have our hides. Don't blow a gasket, come with us, let's hit the bottle together."

"You don't leave your friends in the lurch," snapped Montparnasse.

"I'm telling you, he's been nicked!" Brujon persisted. "At the hour that jangles, the innkeeper isn't worth a bent sou! There's nothin' we can do about it. So let's make ourselves scarce. I keep thinkin' some cop's got me by the tail."

Montparnasse only put up a show of resistance after this; the fact is that the four men, with the loyalty of villains who never abandon each other, had prowled around La Force all night, regardless of the danger, in the hope that Thénardier would pop up on top of a wall somewhere. But the night really was becoming too much now, the rain was bucketing down so heavily it cleared the streets, the cold was creeping up on them, their clothes were soaked, their shoes had holes in them and were taking on water, the alarming uproar that had just broken out in the prison meant hope was fading, fear was returning. All this drove them to beat a retreat. Montparnasse himself, though in a way practically Thénardier's son-in-law, gave in. A moment more and they would have left. Thénardier gasped for breath on his wall like the shipwrecked survivors from the *Medusa*[8] on their raft, seeing the ship that had appeared vanish over the horizon.

He did not dare call out to them—a cry overheard would mean all would be lost. He had an idea, a last one, a flash of light; he grabbed the bit of Brujon's rope he had shoved in his pocket after having untied it from around the chimney of the New Building, and threw it into the fenced-off enclosure.

The rope fell at their feet.

"A widow!" said Babet, using the Temple slang for a rope.

"My twister!" said Brujon, using the barrières word.

"The innkeeper's here," said Montparnasse.

They looked up. Thénardier poked his head out a little.

"Quick!" said Montparnasse. "Have you got the other bit of rope, Brujon?"

"Yep."

"Tie the two bits together, we'll throw him the rope, he'll fix it to the wall, he'll have enough to get down with."

Thénardier risked raising his voice.

"I'm frozen stiff."

"We'll warm you up."

"I can't move."

"You only have to let yourself slide down, we'll catch you."

"My hands are numb."

"Just tie the rope to the wall."

"I couldn't."

"One of us has to climb up," said Montparnasse.

"Three stories!" cried Brujon.

An old plaster pipe that had served a stove once used to heat the shack crept all the way up the wall almost to the point where Thénardier could be seen. This stovepipe, at the time seriously damaged and split, has long since fallen off, but you can still see a few traces of it. It was extremely narrow.

"You could climb up there," said Montparnasse.

"Up that pipe?" cried Babet. "What a funnyman! Not on your life!" Using the Temple slang for child, he added, "It needs a shaver."

"It needs a nipper," Brujon chimed in with the barrières slang.

"Where'll we find a little mite?" said Gueulemer.

"Wait," said Montparnasse. "I know just the thing."

He gently opened the fence gate a fraction, checked to see if anyone was passing in the street, carefully stepped out, shutting the door behind him, and ran off in the direction of the Bastille.

Seven or eight minutes went by—eight thousand centuries for Thénardier; Babet, Brujon, and Gueulemer kept their mouths shut; finally the gate opened again and Montparnasse reappeared, out of breath and with Gavroche in tow. The rain continued to keep the street entirely deserted.

Petit-Gavroche stepped into the enclosure and looked at these crooks' faces calmly. Water was dripping off his hair. Gueulemer spoke to him: "Nipper, are you a man?"

Gavroche shrugged his shoulders and answered: "A kid like yours truly is a proper jock, and jocks like you lot are kids."

"This little shaver sure has the gift of the gab!" cried Babet.

"The Paris kid isn't knocked up out of damp chaff," added Brujon.

"What do you want me to do?" said Gavroche.

Montparnasse answered: "Climb up this pipe."

"With this widow," said Babet.

"Then tie the twister," continued Brujon.

"To the top of the perch," Babet finished, meaning the top of the wall.

"To the pole in the peephole," added Brujon, meaning the crosspiece of the window.

"And then?" said Gavroche.

"That's it!" said Gueulemer.

The kid examined the rope, the pipe, the wall, the windows and made that inexpressibly scornful sound with his lips that signifies: "Is that all?"

"There's a man up there you'll be saving," resumed Montparnasse.

"Will you do it?" Brujon added.

"Nitwit!" replied the child, as though the question was ridiculous; and, with that, he took off his shoes.

Gueulemer picked Gavroche up with one hand, dropped him on the roof of the shack, whose worm-eaten boards buckled under the boy's weight, and handed him the rope that Brujon had tied together again in Montparnasse's absence. The gamin headed for the stovepipe, which he could easily squeeze into thanks to a gaping hole level with the shack roof. Just as he was about to climb up, Thénardier, who saw salvation coming at him, bringing him life, leaned over the edge of the wall; the first glimmer of daylight lit up his brow, which was bathed in sweat, his livid cheekbones, his tapered savage nose, his bristly gray beard, and Gavroche recognized him: "Hang on!" he said. "That's my father . . . Oh, well! Can't be helped."

And carrying the rope in his teeth, he resolutely began the ascent.

He reached the top of the ruin, straddled the wall like a horse, and firmly knotted the rope to the upper crosspiece of the window frame.

A moment later, Thénardier was down on the street.

As soon as his feet hit the ground, as soon as he felt he was out of danger, he was no longer tired, or frozen stiff, or shivering; the horrible things he'd just been through evaporated like a puff of smoke, all that strange ferocious intelligence roused itself again and found it was on its feet and free, ready to forge ahead. And here is the first thing the man said: "Now, who are we going to eat?"

There is no point in explaining the meaning of this horribly transparent phrase that signifies at once to kill, to murder, and to rob. *To eat*, real meaning: *to devour*.

"Let's go to ground good and proper," said Brujon. "Let's wind up quick smart and go our separate ways. There was a bit of business in the rue Plumet that sounded good—deserted street, isolated house, rotten old gate on a garden, women on their own."

"Well, then! Why not?" asked Thénardier.

"Your fairy princess, Éponine, had a bit of a sniff around," Babet went on.

"And she took Magnon a biscuit!" Gueulemer chipped in. "Nothin' worth knockin' off there."

"The fairy princess is no dunce," said Thénardier. "But we should go and have a look."

"Too right," said Brujon. "We should go and have a look."

Meanwhile, none of the men seemed to see Gavroche, who, while this confabulation was taking place, had gone and sat on one of the fence posts; he waited a few moments, maybe for his father to look his way, then he put his shoes back on and said: "Is that it? You don't need me any more, men? There you are, then, you're out of the woods. I'll be off. I've got to go and get my nippers up."

And off he went. The five men filed through the fence, one after the other.

When Gavroche had disappeared at the turn of the rue des Ballets, Babet took Thénardier aside: "Did you get a good look at that shaver?" he asked him.

"What shaver?"

"The shaver who climbed up the wall and brought you the rope."

"Not really."

"Well, I don't know, but it seems to me that that's your son."

"Bah!" said Thénardier. "D'you think so?"

And off he went.

# BOOK SEVEN

# SLANG

## I. Origins

*Pigritia* is a terrible word. It brings a whole world to life; *la pègre*, the criminal underworld, for which read *theft*, and *la pégrenne*, hell, for which read *hunger*.

And so idleness is a mother. She has a son, theft, and a daughter, hunger. Where are we right now? In the world of slang.

What is slang? It is both nation and idiom at the same time; it is theft in its two different species, people and language.

When, thirty-four years ago,[1] the narrator of this grave and somber tale introduced a slang-speaking thief in the middle of a written work with the same aim as this one, there was amazement and uproar. "What! The very idea! Slang! But slang is ghastly! Why, it's the language of convicts, of galleys, of jails, of all that is most abominable in society!" and so on and so forth.

We have never understood this kind of objection.

Since then, two powerful novelists, one of whom is a profound observer of the human heart, the other a fearless friend of the people, Balzac and Eugène Sue,[2] having got crooks to talk in their native language just as the author of *Le Dernier Jour d'un condamné* had done in 1828, the same complaints were made. They kept repeating: "What are these writers trying to do to us with this revolting patois? Slang is vile! Slang makes you shudder!"

Who denies it? Of course it's all true.

When it comes to probing a wound, or sounding an abyss, or a society, since when has it been a crime to go too far, to descend to the very depths? We have always thought that this was sometimes an act of courage, and at the very least a simple and useful activity, worthy of the sympathetic attention that duty accepted and performed deserves. Not to explore everything, not to study everything, to stop en route, what for? Stopping is up to the probe and not the prober.

Certainly, to go poking about among the dregs of the social order, where the ground ends and the muck begins, to ferret around in these muddy waters, to pursue, seize, and dash on the pavement, still throbbing, this abject idiom streaming filth thus exposed to the light of day, this pustulous vocabulary each word of which seems like an obscene ring of some monster of the slimy deep, is not an attractive task nor an easy one. Nothing is more disheartening than contemplating the awful teeming of slang, thus laid bare, by the light of the mind. It does indeed feel like a sort of horrible animal of the night that has just been dragged out of its cesspool. You think you see some hideous bush, alive and thorny, rustling, stirring, whipping around, trying to crawl back into the shadows, menacing and watching. This word here is like a claw, this other one is like a dead eye, bleeding; this phrase seems to pinch like a crab's pincers. And all of it is alive with the awful vitality of things that have organized themselves in the midst of disorganization.

Now, since when has horror ruled out study? Since when has disease chased the doctor away? Just imagine a naturalist who refused to study the viper, the bat, the scorpion, the scolopendrid centipede, the tarantula, who chucked them back into their gloom with this: "Yeek! That's so ugly!" The thinker who turned his back on slang would be like a surgeon who turned his back on an ulcer or a wart. He would be like a philologist hesitating to examine a linguistic act, a philosopher hestitating to scrutinize an act of humanity. For, those who don't know it must be told, slang is both a literary phenomenon and a product of society all in one. What is slang, strictly speaking? Slang is the language of destitution.

Here, you might stop us; you might generalize the facts, which is sometimes a way of attenuating them; you might remind us that all trades, all professions, one might almost add all accidents in the social hierarchy and all forms of intelligence, have their slang. The shopkeeper who says: *Montpellier available, Marseilles*[3] *good quality;* the stockbroker who says: *carryover rate, premium, end current account;* the gambler who says: *a run of three sees you out, spades it is;* the bailiff of the Norman isles who says: *the enfeoffor who closes on his property cannot claim the fruits of this property during the seizure of the immovable property of the defaulting tenant;* the vaudevillian who says: *they baited the bear* (for they booed the play); the actor who says: *I was a flop;* the philosopher who says: *phenomenal triplicity;* the whale hunter who says: *there she blows, there she breaches;* the phrenologist[4] who says: *amativeness, combativeness, secretiveness;* the foot soldier who says: *my clarinette* (for his musket); the horseman who says: *my Indian chicken* (for his horse); the fencing master who says: *tierce, quarte, break;* the printer who says: *let's use boldface*—all of them, printer, fencing master, horseman, foot soldier, phrenologist, whale hunter, philosopher, actor, vaudeville writer, bailiff, gambler, stockbroker, shopkeeper, all of them are talking slang. The painter who says: *my dauber* (for one of his art students); the notary who says: *my puddle jumper* (for his office boy); the wigmaker who says: *my gofer* (for his assistant); the cobbler who says: *my tinker* (for his journeyman), are talking slang. At a pinch and if you really want to push it, all the various ways of saying left and right are slang, from the sailor's *portside* and *starboard* to the stagehand's *court side* (stage left) and *garden side* (stage right) and the beadle's *Epistle side* (of the altar) and *Gospel side*. There is the slang of stuck-up little mesdames just as there once was the slang of the *Pré-cieuses*. If you like, you could say the Hôtel de Rambouillet meets the Cour des Miracles.[5] Duchesses have their slang, too, as is attested by this sentence that occurs in a love letter written by a very great lady, and a very pretty one, of the Restoration: "You will find in such palaver a spate of reasons why I should want to fly the coop" (for: You will find in that gossip many reasons why I wish to free myself). Diplomatic ciphers are slang; the pontifical chancellery, in saying *26* for *Rome, grkztntgzyal* for dispatch and *abfxustgrnogrkzutuXI* for duke of Modena, talks slang. The doctors of the Middle Ages who, to say carrot, radish, and turnip, said: *opoponach, perfroschinum, reptitalmus, dracatholicum angelorum, post-megorem*, were talking slang. The sugar manufacturer who says: *low-grade beet, cone, refined, crushed, lumps, molasses, coarse, unrefined, overrefined, loaf,* this respectable manufacturer is talking slang. A certain school of criticism of twenty years ago used to say, "Half of Shakespeare is wordplay and puns"—and was thereby talking slang. The poet and the artist who, with profound significance, would label Monsieur de Montmorency a *bourgeois*[6] for not being au fait with verse and statues, are talking slang. The classics academician who calls flowers *Flora,* fruit *Pomona,* the sea *Neptune,* love *a flame,* beauty *charms,* a horse *a steed,* the white or tricolor cockade *the rose of Bellona,* the tricorn hat *the triangle of Mars*— that classics academician is talking slang. Algebra, medicine, and botany all have their slang. The language employed on board ship, that admirable language of the sea, so perfect and so picturesque, spoken by Jean Bart, Duquesne, Suffren, and Duperré,[7] and that blends with the whistling of the rigging, the noise of the bullhorns, the clang of the scuttling axes, with the rolling, with the wind, with the squalling, with the cannon, is one great heroic dazzling form of slang that is to the fierce unflinching slang of the underworld what the lion is to the jackal.

Granted. But, whatever you may say, this way of understanding the word *slang* is an extrapolation and one that not everybody would even accept. As for us, we hold to the old precise meaning of the word, which is circumscribed and specific, and we limit slang to slang. True slang, slang par excellence, if those two words can be coupled together, that immemorial slang that was once a whole realm to itself, is nothing else, we repeat, than the ugly, fretful, underhand, treacherous, venomous, cruel, sleazy, vile, profound, fatal language of misery. There is, at the extreme of all debasements and all personal disasters, one last form of misery that rebels and decides to do battle with the whole raft of happy facts and reigning rights; an appalling battle where, now cunning, now violent, at once morbid and wild, it attacks the social order through the pin-pricks of vice and through the club blows of crime. For the requirements of this battle, misery has invented a language of combat and that language is slang.

To keep afloat and hold above oblivion, above the abyss, if only a fragment of whatever language man has spoken and which would otherwise be lost, that is to say one of the elements, good or bad, which civilization consists of and which makes it complex, is to extend the scope of social observation, it is to serve civilization itself. This service Plautus[8] performed, whether he wanted to or not, by making two Carthaginian soldiers speak Phoenician; this service Molière performed by making so many of his characters speak Levantine[9] and all sorts of dialects. Here objections pick up again: Phoenician, marvelous! Levantine, well and good! Even dialect, all right! Those are languages that have belonged to nations or to provinces; but slang? What's the good of preserving slang? What's the good of "keeping afloat" slang?

To that we will answer in a word. Certainly, if the language spoken by a nation or a province is worthy of interest, there is something still more worthy of attention and study and that is the language spoken by any form of misery.

That is the language spoken in France, for example, for more than four centuries now, not only by a form of misery, but by misery itself, all the possible human misery in the world.

And then, we insist, studying social deformities and infirmities and identifying them in order to cure them is not a job where choice is allowed. The historian of customs and ideas has no less austere a mission than the historian of events. The latter has the surface of civilization, the struggles for crowns, the births of princes, the marriages of kings, the battles, the assemblies, the great public men, the revolutions in broad daylight, all the externals; the other historian has the internals, the background, the common people who work, suffer, and wait, the downtrodden woman, the child in its death throes, the muted one-on-one wars, obscure ferocities, the prejudices, the accepted iniquities, the hidden repercussions of the law, the secret revolutions of souls, the indistinct quiverings of the multitudes, those dying of hunger, the barefoot, the bare-armed, the disinherited, the orphans, the wretched, and the vile, all the spine-less worms that wander about in the dark. He has to descend, his heart full of charity and severity at the same time, like a brother and like a judge, right down to those impenetrable blockhouses where those who are bleeding and those who strike, those who are crying and those who curse, those who go without food and those who devour, those who endure wrong and those who do it, crawl and slither willy-nilly. Are the duties of these historians of hearts and souls lesser than those of the historians of external events? Do you think Dante has less to say than Machiavelli? Is the bottom of civilization, being deeper and darker, any less important than the top? Can you really know the mountain well if you don't know anything about the cave?

We must say, however, in passing that from some of the above you might infer that there is a clear-cut division between the two classes of historian that does not, to our mind, exist. Nobody can be a good historian of the patent, visible, dazzling, and public life of peoples if he is not at the same time, to a certain extent, a historian of their deep and hidden life; and nobody can be a good historian of the inner life if he can't manage to be, whenever necessary, a historian of the outer life. The history of customs and ideas bleeds into the history of events, and the other way round. They are two different orders of fact that match each other, that always follow on from one another and often generate each other. All the lines that Providence draws on a nation's surface have their somber but distinct parallels down below, and all the convulsions down below produce upheavals on the surface. True history involving everything, the true historian gets involved with everything.

Man is not a circle with a single center; he is an ellipse with two focal points. Deeds are one, ideas the other.

Slang is nothing more nor less than a changing room where language, having some dirty deed to do, disguises itself. It puts on word-masks and rag-metaphors.

In the process it turns ugly.

You can hardly recognize it. Is this really the French language, the great language of humanity? There it is ready to take to the stage and give crime its cues, apt to play every role in the repertoire of evildoing. It no longer walks, it hobbles; it limps on the crutch of the Cour des Miracles, a crutch that can metamorphose into a club; it goes by the name of vagrancy; all the specters, its dressers, have tarted it up with makeup; it drags itself along and rears its ugly head, twin attributes of the reptile. It is now primed for any role, made seedy by the forger, tarnished by the poisoner, blackened with soot by the arsonist; and the murderer applies its rouge.

When you listen, from the side of honest folk, at the gate of society, you catch the dialogue of those who are outside. You make out questions and answers. You pick up, without understanding it, a hideous murmur that sounds almost like the human voice but is closer to some kind of howling than to speech. This is slang. The words are deformed, stamped with some indescribable and fantastical bestiality. You think you are hearing hydras talking.

This is the unintelligible in the dark. It screeches and it whispers, rounding off the dying light with an enigma. It is dark in misfortune, it is darker still in crime; these two darknesses together compose slang. Obscurity in the atmosphere, obscurity in deeds, obscurity in voices. Abominable toad language that comes and goes, hops, crawls, dribbles, and wriggles monstrously in that endless gray mist made of rain, night, hunger, vice, lies, injustice, nakedness, suffocation, and winter, high noon for the outcast.

Let's have compassion for those so chastised. Alas! Who are we ourselves? Who am I, I who am talking to you? Who are you, you who are listening to me? Where have we come from? And can we be sure we didn't do anything before we were born? The earth is not unlike a jail. Who knows if man is not an ex-convict of divine justice?

Look closely at life. It is so made that you can sense punishment everywhere.

Are you what is known as a lucky man? Well, you are sad every day. Every day has its great chagrin or its small worry. Yesterday you were trembling for the health of someone dear to you; today you fear for your own; tomorrow it will be anxiety over money, the day after tomorrow the vicious attack of some slanderer, the day after that, the misfortune of a friend; then the weather, then something broken or lost, then some pleasure that both your conscience and your spinal column hold against you; another time, the course of public affairs. Without counting all the heartaches. And on it goes. One cloud disperses, another forms. Scarcely one day in a hundred of unbounded joy and unbounded sunshine. And you are among the happy few! As for other men, stagnant night is upon them.

Thoughtful people rarely use the terms, the happy and the unhappy. In this world, antechamber of another, evidently, there are no happy people.

The true division of humanity is this: those filled with light and those filled with darkness.

To reduce the number of those filled with darkness, to increase the number of those filled with light, that is the goal. That is why we cry: education! knowledge! science! To learn to read is to light a fire; every syllable spelled out sparkles.

But when we say light we do not necessarily say joy. We suffer in the light; too much of it burns. Flames are inimical to wings. To burn without ceasing to fly, that is the miracle of genius.

When you learn finally to know and when you learn finally to love, you will suffer still. The day begins in tears. Those filled with light weep, if only over those filled with darkness.

## II. Roots

Slang is the language of those filled with darkness.

Thought is moved in its gloomiest depths, social philosophy is spurred on to its most poignant meditations, in the presence of this enigmatic dialect at once blighted and defiant. It is here that chastisement is visible. Every syllable in it seems to be marked. The words of the vernacular appear in it as though wrinkled and withered under the red-hot brand of the executioner.[1] Some of them seem still to be smoking. A particular phrase hits you like the suddenly bared shoulder of a thief tattooed with fleurs-de-lis. Ideas almost refuse to allow themselves to be expressed by these ex-convict nouns. Its metaphors are sometimes so shameless you can feel they have been in shackles.

Yet, in spite of all that and because of all that, this strange patois is entitled to its pigeonhole in that great impartial filing cabinet, where there is room for the oxidized farthing as well as the gold medal, and which we call literature. Slang, whether we like it or not, has its syntax and its poetry. It is a language. If, by the deformity of certain terms, we recognize that it has been chewed up by the outlaw Mandrin,[2] by the splendor of certain metonyms we can feel it has been spoken by Villon.[3]

This line, so exquisite and so celebrated:

*Mais où sont les neiges d'antan?*

But where are the snows of yore?

is a line of slang. *Antan—ante annum—*is a word from the argot of Thunes that meant the past year and by extension the past. At the time of the departure of the great chain gang of 1827, thirty-five years ago, you could still read in one of the dungeons of Bicêtre this maxim dug into the wall with a nail by a king of Thunes sentenced to the galleys: *"Les dabs d'antan trimaient siempre pour la pierre du Coësre"*—The old men of yore always slaved away for the stone of the Grand Coësre. Which means: *In the past the kings always went off to be crowned.* In the mind of that particular king, the crown was jail.

The word *décarrade,* which expresses the departure at a gallop of a heavy carriage, is attributed to Villon and is worthy of him. This word, which blazes along on all four feet, sums up in masterly onomatopoeia the whole of La Fontaine's[4] wonderful line:

*Six forts chevaux tiraient un coche.*

Six strong horses pulled a coach.

From a purely literary point of view, few studies could be more fascinating and more fruitful than the study of slang. It is a whole language within a language, a sort of sickly excrescence, an unwholesome graft that has produced a vegetation of its own, a parasite with roots in the old Gallic trunk and whose sinister foliage creeps over the whole of one side of the language. This is what we might call the primary aspect, the vulgar side of slang. But, for those who study language as it should be studied, meaning, the way geologists study the earth, slang appears as a veritable alluvium. If you dig far enough, below popular old French, you find in slang Provençal, Spanish, Italian, Levantine, that language of the Mediterranean ports, English and German, the three Romance languages—French, Italian, and Norman—Latin, and, finally, Basque and Celtic. A deep-rooted and bizarre formation. A subterranean edifice built together by all the miserable outcasts. Every accursed race has laid down its deposit, every torment has dropped its stone, every heart has given its pebble. A host of souls, evil, vile, or bitter, who have passed through life and vanished into eternity are there, almost intact and in a way still visible in the form of a monstrous word.

Would you like some Spanish? The old gothic slang is crawling with it. There is *boffette*, bellows, which comes from *bofeton; vantane*, window (later *vanterne*), which comes from *ventana; gat*, cat, which comes from *gato; acite*, oil, which comes from *aceite*. Would you like some Italian? There is *spade*, sword, which comes from *spada; carvel*, boat, which comes from *caravella*. Would you like some English? There is *bichot*, bishop; *raille*, spy, which comes from *rascal, rascalion*, rapscallion, rogue; *pilche*, case, which comes from *pilcher*, sheath. Would you like some German? There is *caleur*, waiter, *Kellner; hers*, master, *Herzog* (duke). Would you like some Latin? There is *frangir*, to break, *frangere; affurer*, to rob, *fur; cadène*, chain, *catena*. There is a word that crops up in every language on the Continent with a sort of power and mysterious authority and that is the word *magnus;* Scotland turns it into *mac*, which designates the chief of the clan. MacFarlane, MacCallummore, the great Farlane, the great Callummore. (It should be noted, though, that *mac* means son in Celtic.) Slang turns *mac* into *meck* and later, *meg*, meaning God. Would you like some Basque? There is *gahisto*, devil, which comes from *gaïztoa*, bad; *sorgabon*, good night, which comes from *gabon*, good evening. Would you like some Celtic? There is *blavin*, handkerchief, which comes from *blavet*, gushing water; *ménesse*, woman (in a bad sense), which comes from *meinec*, full of stones; *barant*, stream, from *baranton*, fountain; *goffeur*, locksmith, from *goff*, blacksmith; *guédouze*, death, which comes from *guenn-du*, white-black. Would you like some history, finally? Slang calls the coins known as écus *les maltaises*, or Malteses, in a nod to the coinage that was current on the galleys of Malta.

Apart from the philological origins we just mentioned, slang has other even more natural roots that spring, so to speak, from the very mind of man:

First, the direct creation of words. This is where the mystery of languages lies. To paint with words that have, we know not how or why, images. This is the primitive foundation of every human language, what we might call the bedrock. Slang is riddled with words of this kind, words that are immediate, out-and-out inventions from we know not where nor by whom, without etymologies, without analogies, without derivations, solitary words, barbarous, sometimes hideous, that have a rare expressive power, that are alive. Executioner, *le taule;* forest, *le sabri;* fear, flight, *taf;* lackey, *le larbin;* general, prefect, minister, *pharos;* the devil, *le rabouin.* Nothing could be stranger than these words that both conceal and reveal. Some of them, *le rabouin,* for instance, are at once grotesque and terrible, and conjure up a colossal grimace.

Second, metaphor. The thing about a language that wants to say everything and to hide everything is that it abounds in images. Metaphor is a riddle in which the thief planning a job, the prisoner plotting a breakout, take refuge. No idiom could be more metaphoric than slang. *Dévisser le coco,* to unscrew the coconut—wring someone's neck; *tortiller,* to wolf down—to eat; *être gerbé,* to cop it—to be sentenced; *un rat,* a rat—a bread thief; *il lansquine,* to pelt down daggers—to rain, a striking age-old image that, in a way, bears its own date with it, assimilating the long slanting lines of rain with the thick angled pikes of the lansquenets, and capturing in a single word the popular metonymy: *it's raining pitchforks.* Sometimes, as slang passes from the first phase to the second, words pass from their wild and primitive state to the state of metaphor. The devil ceases to be *le rabouin* and becomes *le boulanger,* the baker, he who puts into the oven. This is wittier, but less grand; something like Racine after Corneille, like Euripides after Aeschylus. Certain slang phrases that belong to both generations and are both barbaric and metaphoric at once resemble phantasmagoria. *Les sorgueurs vont sollicer des gails à la lune,* the night owls are going to snitch nags by the moon—the rustlers are going to steal horses when night comes. This rolls past the mind's eye like a bevy of ghosts. It is hard to tell what we see.

Third, expediency. Slang lives off the language. It does whatever it likes with it, dips into it at random and is often content, when the need arises, to summarily and grossly distort it. Now and then, with common words thus deformed and jumbled up with words of pure slang, colorful expressions are created in which you can feel the melding of the two preceding elements, direct invention and metaphor: *Le cab jaspine, je marronne que la roulotte de Pantin trime dans le sabri,* the mutt's yapping, I have a hunch the Pantin buggy's slogging through the scrub—the dog is barking, I suspect the Paris diligence is passing through the woods. *Le dab est sinve, la dabuge est merloussière, la fée est bative,* the old man's thick, the old lady's slippery, the sprite's easy on the eye—the bourgeois gentleman is stupid, his lady wife is cunning, the daughter is pretty. Most often, to throw unwelcome listeners off track, slang is content to stick a sort of ignoble tail on all the words of the language, indiscriminately, such as an ending in *-aille, -orgue, -iergue,* or *-uche.* Accordingly: *Vousiergue trouvaille bonorgue ce gigot-muche?* Do you find this leg of lamb good? A question put by Cartouche to a prison gatekeeper in order to ascertain whether the sum offered for an escape was acceptable to him. The *-mar* ending is a fairly recent addition.

Being the idiom of corruption, slang is corrupted fast. On top of this, as it always seeks to conceal itself, as soon as it feels understood it transforms itself. In contrast to all other vegetation, every ray of light that falls on it kills what it touches. And so slang goes on decomposing and recomposing itself endlessly; a murky and swift labor that never stops. It covers more ground in ten years than the official language does in ten centuries. And so *le larton,* bread, becomes *le lartif; le gail,* nag, becomes *le gaye; la fertanche,* straw, *la fertille; le momignard,* brat, *le momacque; les figues,* clothes, *les frusques; la chique,* church, *l'égrugeoir; le colabre,* neck, *le colas.* The devil is first *gahisto,* then *le rabouin,* then *le boulanger;* the priest is *le ratichon,* little teeth-gnasher, then *le sanglier,* wild boar; a dagger is *le vingt-deux,* twenty-two (meaning watch out!), then *le surin,* knife, then *le lingre,* gold ingot; the police are *railles,* the crew, then *roussins,* partners in crime, then *rousses,* the fuzz, then *marchands de lacets,* lace merchants, then *coqueurs,* squealers, then *cognes,* coppers; the executioner is *le taule,* the slammer man, then Charlot, then *l'atigeur,* a man who goes too far, then *le becquillard,* the man with the crutches. In the seventeenth century, *se battre,* to have a fight, was *se donner du tabac,* to give each other tobacco—a hammering; in the nineteenth century, it has become *se chiquer la gueule,* to chew each other's mug. Twenty different versions have come and gone between these two extremes. Cartouche could be talking Hebrew to Lacenaire. All the words in this language are perpetually on the run like the people who utter them.

Yet, from time to time, and because of this very movement, the old slang reappears and becomes new again. It has its main centers where it holds steady. The Temple preserved the slang from the seventeenth century; Bicêtre, when it was still a prison, preserved the slang of Thunes. You could hear there the *-anche* ending of old Thuners. *Boyanches-tu (bois-tu),* are you drinking? *Il croyanche (il croit),* he believes. But perpetual movement still remains the rule.

If the philosopher manages to set aside a moment to observe this language that is endlessly evaporating, he lapses into painful yet useful meditation. No study is more effective and more fruitful in instruction. There is not one metaphor, not one etymological derivation of slang that does not contain a lesson. Among these men, *battre,* to beat but also to whip up, means *feindre,* to feign; you whip up an illness; ruse is their strong point.

To them the idea of man is inseparable from the idea of the dark. Night is called *la sorgue;* man, *l'orgue.* Man is a derivation of night.

These people have acquired the habit of regarding society as an atmosphere that kills them, like a deadly force, and they talk about their liberty as you would talk about your health. A man arrested is *malade,* sick, a man condemned is *mort,* dead.

The most terrible thing for the prisoner within the four stone walls that entomb him is a sort of icy chastity; he calls the dungeon, *le castus,* the castrator. In that funereal place, life outside always appears in its most deliriously happy aspect. The prisoner has iron shackles on his feet; perhaps you assume he dreams about how you walk with your feet? No, he dreams about how you dance with your feet; and so, if he somehow manages to saw through his irons, his first thought is that now he can dance and so he calls the saw a *bastringue*, a sleazy dance hall. A name is a *centre*, center—which is a profound association for you. A bandit has two heads, one reasons out his actions and guides him all his life, the other is what sits on his shoulders the day he dies, when it is on the block; he calls the head that counsels crime *la sorbonne*, and the head that expiates it *la tronche*, noggin. When a man has nothing left but the rags on his back and the vices in his heart, when he has reached that twin degradation, material and moral, that characterizes the two accepted meanings of the word *gueux*, beggar, he is ripe for crime; he is like a well-sharpened knife; he has a double edge, his distress and his malice; and so slang does not say "a beggar"; it says a *réguisé*, which sounds like a pun on *aiguisé*, sharpened. What is jail? An inferno of damnation, a hell. And so the convict is a *fagot*, a bit of firewood. Lastly, what name do felons give prison? *Le collège*, college. A whole penitentiary system could spring from that word.

The thief, too, has his cannon fodder, robbable material—you, me, whoever happens to be passing by, *le pantre*, sucker, the ordinary everyman. (*Pan*, everybody.)

Would you like to know where most prison songs come from, those refrains known in the specialized vocabulary as *les lirlonfa*? Then listen to this:

There used to be a great long cellar at Châtelet in Paris.

This cellar was eight feet below the level of the Seine. It had neither windows nor ventilators, the only opening was the door; people could go in, but not air. This cellar had a stone vault for a ceiling and ten feet of mud for a floor. It had been paved with flagstones, but under the oozing waters the flagstones had rotted and cracked. Eight feet above the floor, a massive beam went from one end of this underground passage to the other; from this beam, at regular intervals, hung chains three feet long, and on the end of these chains were collar shackles. Men condemned to the galleys were put in this cellar until the day of their departure for Toulon. They were shoved under this beam where each one of them had his iron brace swinging in the darkness, waiting for him. The chains, those hanging arms, and the collar shackles, those open hands, grabbed these poor bastards by the neck. They were riveted in and they were left there. The chain was too short, they could not lie down. They remained immobile in this cellar, in that pitch blackness, under that beam, very nearly hung by the neck, forced to make unbelievable efforts to reach the bread or the pitcher, the vault on top of their heads, mud up to their knees, their excrement running down their legs, shattered by exhaustion, sagging at the hips and the knees, hanging on to the chain by their hands for a rest, unable to sleep except standing, and woken up at every instant by the stranglehold of the iron collar; some did not wake up. To eat, they dragged their bread, which was thrown in the mud at their feet, up their shinbone with their heel until they could reach it with their hand. How long were they left like this? A month, two months, six months sometimes; one stayed a year. It was the antechamber to the galleys. You were put there for stealing a hare from the king. In this hell-like tomb, what did they do? What can be done in a tomb, they died, and what can be done in a hell, they sang. For when you have no more hope, you still have song. In the waters off Malta, whenever a galley was approaching, you could hear the singing before you heard the oars. The poor poacher Survincent,[5] who had been through the cellar prison of Châtelet, used to say: "It was the rhymes that kept me going." Useless poetry. What good is rhyme? It is in this cellar that nearly all the slang songs were born. It is from this dungeon of the Grand-Châtelet of Paris that the melancholy refrain of the galleys of Montgomery comes: *"Timaloumisaine, timoulamison."* Most of these songs are mournful, a few of them are gay; one of them is tender:

*Icicaille est le théâtre*
*Du petit dardant.*

Thisaway's the theater
Of Cupid, the little pricker

Try as you might, you will never annihilate that eternal remnant of the heart of man, love.

In this world of dark deeds, you keep your secrets to yourself. A secret is something anyone can have. A secret, for these poor bastards, is the unity that serves as a basis for union. To violate a secret is to tear something of himself from each member of this savage community. To inform on someone, in the vibrant language of slang, is known as *manger le morceau*, to eat the morsel, the pound of flesh. As though the informer pulled off a bit of the substance of all and fed himself with a morsel, a pound, of the flesh of each.

What is it to get a slap in the face? The ordinary everyday metaphor answers: *voir trente-six chandelles*, to see thirty-six candles—to see stars. Here slang intervenes and sums up: *Chandelle, camoufle.* In so doing, this idiomatic language makes *camouflet*, candlestick, a synonym for *soufflet*, a slap in the face. And so, through a sort of trickling upward from the bottom to the top, with the help of metaphor, that incalculable pathway, slang climbs from the cavern to the academy; and when Poulailler says, *"J'allume ma camoufle,"* I light my candle, he makes Voltaire write, *"Langleviel La Beaumelle[6] mérite cent camouflets,"* Langleviel La Beaumelle deserves a hundred slaps in the face.

Any dig into slang means discovery every step of the way. Studying and deepening our understanding of this strange idiom leads us to the mysterious point of intersection between regular society and the society of the damned.

Slang is the word made convict.

That the thinking principle of man can be trampled so low underfoot, that it can be dragged down to the pits and choked there by the obscure tyrannies of fate, that it can be tethered there we know not how at that brink of disaster— this is appalling.

O poor thinking of the down-and-out!

Alas! Will no one come to the rescue of the human soul in this shadowland? Is its destiny to wait forever there for the mind, the liberator, the towering rider of the pegasuses and the hippogriffs, the fighter the color of dawn who descends from out of the blue between two wings, the radiant knight in shining armor of the future? Will it always call out in vain for the lance of light of the ideal to rescue it? Is it condemned to the horror of hearing Evil approaching through the denseness of the abyss and of glimpsing, closer and closer to it, beneath the hideous water, that draconian head, that great maw chomping on foam, that serpentine undulation of claws, swellings, and rings? Must it stay there, without a glimmer of light, without a glimmer of hope, delivered up to that awful approach, dimly sniffed out by the monster, shaking, frantic, wringing its hands, forever chained to the rock of night, somber Andromeda, white and naked in the darkness!

### III. Slang That Cries and Slang That Laughs

As you see, slang as a whole, the slang of four hundred years ago as well as the slang of today, is pervaded by this grim symbolic spirit that gives all words a plaintive sound one moment, a threatening ring the next. You can feel in it the old wild sadness of those vagrants of the Cour des Miracles who used to play their own made-up card games with their own packs, some of which have come down to us. The eight of clubs, for instance, was a big tree bearing eight enormous clover leaves, a sort of fantastic personification of the forest. At the foot of this tree, there was a burning fire where three hares were roasting a hunter on a spit and in the background, over another fire, a smoking pot from which the head of a dog poked out. Nothing could be more lugubrious than these pictured reprisals, painted on a pack of cards, in the days when smugglers were still roasted at the stake and counterfeiters were still boiled in cauldrons. The various forms that thought assumed in the realm of slang, even song, even raillery, even threat, all had the same impotent and despairing quality. All the songs, some of the tunes of which have been anthologized, were so humble and lamentable they would make you weep. *La pègre,* the underworld, calls itself *la pauvre pègre*, the poor underworld, and it is always the hare hiding, the mouse running away, the bird flitting off. It hardly ever complains, restricting itself to sighing. One of its moans has come down to us: *"Je n'entrave que le dail comment meck, le daron des orgues, peut atiger ses mômes et ses momignards et les locher criblant sans être atigé lui-même"*—I can't make head or tail of the fact that Mack, the king of the heap, can knock his kids and his kids' kids around and cop them singing out without him being knocked around himself. (I don't understand how God, the father of men, can torture his children and his children's children and hear them crying out without being tortured himself.) Every time the poor miserable wretch has a moment to think, he makes himself small before the law and puny before society; he lies down flat on his stomach and he grovels, he implores pity; you feel that he knows he's in the wrong.

Toward the middle of last century a shift occurred. Prison songs, thieves' ritornellos took an insolent and jovial turn, so to speak. The plaintive *maluré* was elbowed aside by the *larifla*. In nearly all the songs from the galleys, penal colonies, and penitentiaries of the eighteenth century, you find a diabolical and puzzling gaiety. You hear this strident and bouncy refrain that has a kind of phosphorescent sheen to it, much like a will-o'-the-wisp playing the fife in some forest:

> *Mirlababi surlababo*
> > *Mirliton ribon ribette*
> *Surlababi, mirlababo*
> > *Mirliton ribon ribo.*

This was sung while you were cutting a man's throat in a cellar or in a spot in the woods.

A serious symptom. In the eighteenth century, the age-old melancholy of these mournful classes lifts. They start to laugh. They mock the great *meg*, the Lord, and the great *dab*, the devil. Louis XV being in power, they call the king of France "the marquis de Pantin" (Paris). They are very nearly chirpy. A sort of breezy lightheartedness wafts from these miserable wretches as though their consciences no longer weighed on them. These lamentable tribes of the shadows suddenly show not only desperate audacity in their actions, they show the insouciant audacity of wit. A sign that they are losing any sense of their criminality, and that they feel some kind of hidden unwitting support even among thinkers and dreamers. A sign that theft and pillage are even beginning to infiltrate doctrines and sophisms, in such a way as to shed a little of their ugliness by adding greatly to the ugliness of the sophisms and doctrines. A sign, in a word, of some prodigious and imminent eruption, if nothing intervenes in the meantime.

Let's stop there for a moment. Who are we accusing here? Is it the eighteenth century? Is it its philosophy? Of course not. The work of the eighteenth century is healthy and good. The Encyclopedists, led by Diderot, the physiocrats, led by Turgot,[1] the philosophers, led by Voltaire, the utopians, led by Rousseau, formed four sacred legions. The immense advance of humanity toward the light is due to them. Those are the four vanguards of the human race moving toward the four cardinal points of progress, Diderot toward the beautiful, Turgot toward the useful, Voltaire toward the true, Rousseau toward the just. But, beside and below the philosophers, there were the sophists, a poisonous weed blending with the healthy growth, hemlock in virgin forest. While the executioner was burning the great liberating books of the century on the steps of the Palais de Justice, writers now forgotten were bringing out, with the king's seal of approval, all kinds of weirdly subversive writings avidly read by the dregs.[2] A few of these publications, sponsored by a prince, amazingly, can be found in the *Bibliothèque secrète.* These facts, far-reaching yet unknown, were not perceptible on the surface. Sometimes it is the very obscurity of a fact that makes it dangerous. It is obscure because it is underground. Of all those writers, the one who perhaps bored the most unhealthy tunnel into the masses was Restif de la Bretonne.[3]

This labor was carried out over the whole of Europe but caused more havoc in Germany than anywhere else. In Germany, during a certain period summed up by Schiller in his famous play *The Robbers,*[4] robbery and plunder set themselves up as a protest against property and labor, absorbing certain elementary ideas, specious and false, apparently just but in reality absurd, wrapped themselves up in these ideas, disappeared into them in a way, took on an abstract name and became theory, and in this fashion circulated among the hardworking, long-suffering, and honest hordes, unbeknownst even to the reckless chemists who originally prepared the mixture, unbeknownst even to the masses who took it. Whenever something like this happens it is serious. Suffering begets rage; and while the prosperous classes turn a blind eye or nod off, which is always the same thing as shutting your eyes, the hate of the unprosperous classes has its torch lit by some malcontent or warped mind dreaming away in a corner somewhere, and it begins to examine society. Examination by hate is a terrible thing!

Whence, if the times are hard enough, those alarming commotions once known as jacqueries, peasants' revolts, next to which purely political turbulence is child's play. Jacqueries are no longer the struggle of the oppressed against the oppressor, but the revolt of deprivation against comfort. Everything then comes tumbling down.

Jacqueries are people-quakes—seismic shifts of the people.

It is this danger, imminent in Europe perhaps at the end of the eighteenth century, that was short-circuited by the French Revolution, that immense act of probity.

The French Revolution, which was nothing more or less than the ideal armed with the sword, got to its feet, and in the same sudden movement, shut the door of evil and opened the door of good.

It made the issue clear, promulgated truth, drove away miasma, cleaned up the century, crowned the people.

You could say that it created man a second time, by giving him a second soul, power.

The nineteenth century has inherited and profited by its work and today the social catastrophe we talked about a moment ago is simply impossible. Blind are those who put it down! Silly are those who dread it! Revolution is the vaccine for jacquerie.

Thanks to the Revolution, social conditions have changed. The diseases of feudalism and monarchism are no longer in our blood. There is no longer anything of the Middle Ages in our constitution. We have moved on from the days when those terrifying swarms of people erupted in France, when you could hear beneath your feet a muffled and obscure stirring, when molehills mushroomed mysteriously on the surface of society, when the ground cracked open, caves yawned, and you saw the heads of monsters suddenly rear up out of the ground.

The revolutionary sense is a moral sense. The sense of one's rights, when it is developed, develops the sense of duty. The law of all is liberty, which ends where the liberty of others begins, according to the admirable definition of Robespierre. Since 1789, the entire people has been expanding in the sublimated individual; there is no poor person who, having his rights, does not have his ray of light; the man dying of hunger feels within himself the integrity of France; the dignity of the citizen is internalized armor. Whoever is free is scrupulous; whoever votes, reigns. Whence incorruptibility; whence the aborting of unhealthy desires; whence eyes heroically averted in the face of temptations. Revolutionary purification is such that on a day of deliverance, a fourteenth of July, a tenth of August,[5] there is no more mob. The first cry of the enlightened and growing hordes is: Death to thieves! Progress is an honest man; the ideal and the absolute do not pick pockets. Who were the wagons that carried the riches of the Tuileries escorted by in 1848?[6] By the rag-and-bone men of the faubourg Saint-Antoine. The rag mounted guard over the treasure. Virtue made those ragged men resplendent. In among those wagons, in those chests stuffed so full they could hardly close, some even half-open, among those dazzling caskets of jewels, was the old crown of France, all diamonds, surmounted by the carbuncle of royalty, of the regent, which was worth thirty million. They guarded that crown, barefoot.

So no more jacquerie. I feel sorry for the clever. But that's one old fear that has had its day and just can't be used in politics anymore. The great mainspring of the red specter is broken. Everyone knows that now. The horrifying no longer horrifies. The birds take liberties with the scarecrow, the dung beetles sit on it, the bourgeois laugh at it.

## IV. The Two Duties: To Watch and to Hope

This being so, is all social danger dispelled? No, of course not. No jacquerie—society can rest assured on that score, the blood will no longer rush to its head. But let it worry about how it breathes. Apoplexy is no longer to be feared, but there is consumption about. Another word for social consumption is destitution.

You can die by wasting away as well as being struck by lightning.

As we never get tired of repeating, think, first and foremost, of the disinherited and hurting hordes, relieve them, give them air, give them light, love them, broaden their horizon magnificently, lavish all kinds of education on them, set them the example of toil, never the example of idleness, lighten the weight of the individual burden by giving more weight to the notion of the universal goal, limit poverty without limiting wealth, create vast fields of activity, public and popular, be like Briareus and have a hundred hands that can reach out on all sides to the downtrodden and the weak, put collective power to work at that great duty, which is to open workshops to all hands, schools to all aptitudes, and laboratories to all forms of intelligence, increase wages, decrease the struggle, balance debits and credits, that is, match pleasure to effort and gratification to need—in a word, make the social apparatus release more light and more comfort, for the benefit of the suffering and the ignorant. This is, let sympathetic souls not forget, the foremost of fraternal obligations; it is, let self-centered hearts be aware, the first and foremost of political necessities.

But, we have to say, this is just a start. The real issue is this: Work cannot be a law without being a right.

We won't insist, this is not the place.

If we think of nature as Providence, society should think of itself as provident.

Intellectual and moral growth is no less indispensable than material enrichment. Knowledge is a store of provisions; thought is a primary necessity; the truth is food the same as wheat is. An argument that abstains from science and wisdom loses weight. We should feel sorry for minds that don't eat the way we do for stomachs. If there is something more poignant than a body dying for want of bread, it is a soul dying starved of light.

The whole of progress strains toward the solution. One day we will be amazed. With the human race rising upward, the lowest levels will emerge quite naturally from the zone of distress. The eradication of destitution will occur through a simple rise in level.

This solution is blessed and we would be wrong to have doubts about it.

The past, it is true, is very strong at the point we have reached. It is reviving. This rejuvenation of a corpse is surprising. Here it is on its feet heading for us. It looks victorious; this dead body is a conqueror. It arrives with its legion, superstitions, with its sword, despotism, with its banner, ignorance; in a very short while it has won ten battles. It advances, it threatens, it laughs, it is at our door. As for us, let's not despair. Let's sell the field Hannibal is camped on.

We who believe, what do we have to fear?

Ideas can't flow backward any more than rivers can.

But let those who don't want anything to do with the future think carefully. By saying no to progress, it is not the future they condemn, it is themselves. They give themselves a fatal disease when they inoculate themselves with the past. There is only one way to reject Tomorrow and that is to die.

Now, no death, that of the body as late as possible, that of the soul never— that is what we would like.

Yes, the key to the riddle will be found, the sphinx will speak, the problem will be solved. Yes, the People, roughly sketched out by the eighteenth century, will be completed by the nineteenth. Whoever doubts that is a moron! The future blossoming, the imminent blossoming of universal well-being, is a divinely preordained phenomenon.

Immense broad upsurges govern human affairs and bring them all in any given time to their logical state, meaning equilibrium, meaning equity. A force consisting of heaven and earth results from humanity and rules it; this force is a miracle worker; fabulous outcomes are no harder for it to pull off than extraordinary episodes are. Aided by science, which derives from man, and events, which derive from someone else, it doesn't worry too much about those contradictions in the framing of problems, which seem to the vulgar to be impossible to solve. It is no less adept at getting a solution to spring out of the bringing together of ideas than at producing a lesson out of the bringing together of facts; and we can expect anything on the part of this mysterious power of progress which, one fine day, brings East and West face-to-face in the depths of a tomb and gets imams to converse with Bonaparte inside the great pyramid.[1]

Meanwhile, no halt, no hesitation, no pause in the grand forward march of minds. Social philosophy is essentially the science of peace. It has as its aim, and should have as its result, the dissolving of anger through the study of antagonisms. It examines, it scrutinizes, it analyzes; then it puts back together again. It proceeds by way of reduction, lopping hate off from everything.

That a society may founder in the winds that rage over mankind has been known to happen more than once; history is full of shipwrecks of peoples and empires; customs, laws, religions, are all swept away, one fine day, by that unknown entity, the hurricane, as it passes. The civilizations of India, Chaldea, Persia, Assyria, Egypt, have disappeared, one after the other. Why? We don't have a clue. What are the causes of these disasters? We don't know. Could those societies have been saved? Was it partly their own fault? Did they persist in some fatal vice that sank them? How suicidal were these terrible deaths of nations and races? Questions without answers. Darkness blankets those doomed civilizations. They took on water, for they were engulfed and sank; we have nothing more to say; and it is in a sort of bewildered daze that we watch, at the bottom of that ocean we call the past, behind those colossal waves, the centuries, the sinking of those immense ships, Babylon, Nineveh, Tarsus, Thebes, Rome, in the frightening blasts that shoot from all the mouths of the dark. But what is dark down there is light up here. We know nothing about the diseases of ancient civilizations, but we know the infirmities of our own. We have the right to shine the light all over it; we contemplate its beauties and we lay bare its deformities. Wherever it hurts, we probe; and, once we've diagnosed the trouble, studying the cause leads to discovery of the remedy. Our civilization, the work of twenty centuries, is both their monster and their crowning achievement at once; it is worth saving. And it will be. To relieve it, is already a lot; to enlighten it, is something else again. All the works of modern social philosophy must converge toward that end. The thinker of today has a great duty, which is to apply his stethoscope to civilization's chest and listen.

We repeat, this auscultation is encouraging; and it is in insisting on such encouragement that we would like to wind up these few pages, an austere entr'acte in a painful tragedy. Beneath the mortality of society, we sense the imperishability of humanity. The globe does not die, just because there are wounds like craters, here and there, and patches of scurf like sulfur-spewing vents on top of a volcano that erupts and shoots its pus. The maladies of a people do not kill mankind.

And yet, even so, whoever keeps an eye on the social clinic shakes their head at times. The strongest, the most tenderhearted, the most logical, have their moments of weakness.

Will the future ever arrive? It seems we might very well be justified in asking ourselves this question when we see such terrible darkness. Gloomy face-off of the egoists and the miserable. On the part of the egoists, prejudice, the glumness of a rich education, a growing appetite based on intoxication, the giddiness of a prosperity that deadens, a fear of suffering that, in some people, reaches the point of aversion for those who suffer, an implacable self-satisfaction, the ego so inflated that it blocks out the soul; on the part of the miserable, covetousness, envy, hate at seeing others having fun, the deep pull of the human animal toward personal gratification, hearts filled with fog, sadness, want, fatalism, ignorance impure and simple.

Must we continue to raise our eyes to the sky? Is the luminous dot that we make out there one of those that go out? The ideal is terrifying to see thus lost in the depths, small, isolated, imperceptible, brilliant but surrounded by all those great black threats monstrously banked up around it; yet no more in danger than a star in the gob of the clouds.

# BOOK EIGHT

# ENCHANTMENT AND DESOLATION

## I. BROAD DAYLIGHT

The reader will have worked out that Éponine, having recognized through the gate the girl living in the rue Plumet where Magnon had sent her, had begun by keeping the burglars away from the rue Plumet, then had taken Marius there; and that after several days of ecstasy in front of the gate, Marius, driven by that force that draws iron to the magnet and the man in love to the stones the beloved's house is made of, had ended up entering Cosette's garden much as Romeo had entered the garden of Juliet. This had been even easier for him than for Romeo; Romeo was forced to scale a wall; Marius had only to gently force the decrepit gate's bars that wobbled in their rusty sockets, like old people's teeth in theirs. Marius was thin and easily squeezed through.

As there was never anyone in the street and Marius only went into the garden at night in any case, he did not risk being seen.

From that blessed and sacred moment when a kiss sealed the betrothal of these two souls, Marius went there every evening. If, at this time in her life, Cosette had fallen in love with an unscrupulous philanderer, she would have been lost, for there are generous natures that give themselves and Cosette was of their number. One of a woman's magnanimous impulses is to yield. Love, at this height, where it is absolute, gets complicated with an inexpressibly heavenly blindness on the part of modesty. What dangers you run, O noble souls! Often, you give your heart, but we take only your body. Your heart is left to you and you look at it in the shadows and shudder. Love has no middle ground; either it destroys or it saves. All of human destiny lies in that particular dilemma. A dilemma, the choice between destruction or salvation, which no act of fate poses more inexorably than love does. Love is life—except when it is death. Cradle—coffin, too. The same emotion says both yes and no in the human heart. Of all the things that God has made, the human heart is the one that shines brightest—and blackest, alas!

God wanted the love that Cosette met with to be the kind that saves.

Right to the end of that month of May in the year 1832, every night, in that poor wild garden, under those daily more perfumed and more profuse bushes, were two beings, made up of every form of chastity and every form of innocence, overflowing with every kind of heaven-sent felicity, closer to archangels than to human beings, pure, honest, exhilarated, radiant, shining resplendent for each other in the darkness. It seemed to Cosette that Marius had a crown and to Marius that Cosette had a halo. They touched each other, they gazed at each other, they took each other's hands, they held each other tight; but there was a limit they did not overstep. Not that they respected it; they didn't know it existed. Marius felt a barrier, Cosette's purity, and Cosette felt a support, Marius's loyalty. That first kiss had also been the last. Since then Marius had gone no further than brushing Cosette's hand, or her fichu, or a lock of her hair, with his lips. Cosette was to him a perfume, not a woman. He breathed her. She refused nothing and he demanded nothing. Cosette was happy and Marius was satisfied. They lived in that ravishing state that we might describe as the bedazzlement of one soul by another soul. It was that ineffable first embrace of two pure virgin souls in the ideal. Two swans meeting on the Jungfrau.[1]

At that initial phase of love, a phase when sensual pleasure keeps absolutely still under the all-powerfulness of ecstasy, Marius, the pure and seraphic Marius, would have been rather more capable of visiting a streetwalker than lifting Cosette's gown up to ankle level. Once, in the moonlight, Cosette had bent down to pick something up off the ground, and her bodice gaped open to reveal a glimpse of her cleavage; Marius averted his eyes.

What went on between these two beings? Nothing. They adored each other.

At night, when they were there, the garden felt sacred and alive. All the flowers opened around them and sent them incense; they opened their souls and spread them out among the flowers. The lascivious and vigorous vegetation quivered, full of sap and euphoria, around these two innocents, and they spoke words of love that made the trees shiver.

What were these words? Breaths. Nothing more. But those breaths were enough to arouse and excite the whole of the natural world around them. A magic power you would hardly fathom if you were to read such babble in a book, for it is made to be blown away and dispersed like puffs of smoke by the wind under the leaves. Take away from the murmuring of two lovers that melody that comes from the soul and that accompanies them like a lyre, and all that is left is no more than shadow; you say: What! Is that all? Ah, yes, infantile drivel, needless repetition, laughing at nothing, useless information, inanities, all that is deepest and most sublime in this world! The only things worth the trouble of being said and of being listened to.

Those particular inanities, those particular sweet nothings—the man who has never heard them, the man who has never uttered them, is an imbecile and a nasty piece of work. Cosette was saying to Marius: "You know what?"

(In all this, through all this celestial virginity, and without either one of them being in the least able to say how, they had come to address each other with the familiar form of "you"—*tu*.)

"You know what? My name is Euphrasie."

"Euphrasie? No, it's not, your name is Cosette."

"Oh, Cosette is a pretty awful name they must have pulled out of a hat when I was little. But my real name is Euphrasie. Don't you like the name Euphrasie?"

"Yes . . . But Cosette isn't awful."

"Do you like it better than Euphrasie?"

"Er . . . yes."

"Well, then, I like it better too. It's true, it's quite pretty, Cosette. Cosette it is."

And the smile she added turned this dialogue into an idyll fit for some celestial grove.

Another time she looked him steadily in the eye and declared: "Monsieur, you're handsome, you're gorgeous, you're clever as can be and you're not at all dumb, you're a lot more knowledgeable than I am, but take this: I love you!"

And Marius, on cloud nine, imagined he had heard a verse sung by a star in the sky.

Or else, she would give him a little tap because he was coughing, and would say to him: "Don't cough, Monsieur. I don't want anyone to cough at my place without my permission. It's extremely mean to cough and worry me like that. I want you to be in fine fettle, first because if you are not in fine fettle, I will be most unhappy. What do you expect me to do?"

And this was quite simply divine.

Once Marius said to Cosette: "Just imagine, for a while I thought your name was Ursula."

This made them laugh all evening.

In the middle of another conversation, he was suddenly moved to exclaim: "Oh, one day, at the Luxembourg, I could happily have broken an old returned soldier's neck!"

But he pulled up short and went no further. It would have meant speaking to Cosette about her garter and there was no way he could do that. It would have meant contact with an unknown quantity, the flesh, before which, out of a sort of holy fright, this immense innocent love recoiled.

Marius imagined life with Cosette just like this, without anything else; coming every evening to the rue Plumet, shifting the obliging old bar of the presiding judge's gate, sitting on the bench, side by side, elbow to elbow, watching the falling night begin scintillating through the trees, reconciling the pleat in his trousers to the fullness of Cosette's frock, stroking her thumbnail, calling her *tu*, each smelling the same flower, one after the other, forever and ever, indefinitely. All that time the clouds passed over their heads. Every time the wind blows, it sweeps away more of humanity's dreams than clouds in the sky.

But this does not mean that this chaste and almost fierce love was absolutely without gallantry—no. To pay compliments to the woman you love is the first step toward caressing her, a half-daring testing of the waters. A compliment is something like kissing through a veil. Sensual pleasure sets its soft seal there, while staying well out of sight. Faced with sensual pleasure, the heart steps back, the better to love. Marius's sweet talk, dripping as it was with fantasy, was, so to speak, tinged with a celestial hue. When birds fly high above beside the angels, they must hear words like those. Tangled up in them, though, was life, humanity, the whole positive power of which Marius was capable. It was what is said in the grotto as a prelude to what will be said in the boudoir, a lyrical effusion, strophe and sonnet mixed up together, the sweet hyperbole of billing and cooing, all the refinements of adoration arranged in a bouquet and giving off a subtle heavenly perfume, the ineffable warbling of heart to heart.

"Oh!" Marius would murmur. "You are so beautiful! I don't dare look at you. That's why I contemplate you instead. You are so graceful. I don't know what's wrong with me. When the tip of your shoe peeks out from the hem of your dress, it bowls me over. Then there's that enchanted glow when your thoughts dawn. You speak such amazingly good sense. I sometimes feel you're a dream. Speak, I'm listening, I think you're wonderful. O, Cosette! It's so strange and wonderful. I've completely lost my head. You are wonderful, Mademoiselle. I study your feet with a microscope and your soul with a telescope."

And Cosette would reply: "I love you a little bit more with every passing minute this morning."

The call-and-answer did what it could in this dialogue, always coming back to the subject of love, like those weighted dolls made of elder wood that bounce back upright each time they're knocked down.

Everything about Cosette epitomized naïveté, ingenuousness, transparency, purity, candor, radiance. You could have described Cosette as cloudless. She had the effect of spring or first light on whoever saw her. There was dew in her eyes. Cosette was a condensation of dawn light in the form of a woman.

It was only perfectly natural that Marius admire her, adoring her as he did. But the truth is that this little boarding-school girl, fresh from the convent, chatted with an exquisite perspicacity and at times came out with all sorts of true and subtle things. Her very babble was conversation. She saw clearly and was never wrong about anything. Women feel and speak with the loving instinct of the heart, that infallible organ. No one knows better than a woman how to say things that are both sweet and profound at once. Sweetness and profundity, that is a woman in a nutshell; that is heaven in a nutshell.

In this state of complete happiness, tears sprang to their eyes at every instant. One of God's creatures crushed, a feather fallen from a nest, a broken branch of hawthorn, roused their pity, and their ecstasy, sweetly steeped in melancholy, seemed to want nothing more than to cry. The most imperious symptom of love is at times an unbearable compassion.

And alongside all this—all such contradictions are the lightning play of love—they liked to laugh and with such delightful abandon and such intimacy that they sometimes seemed almost like two boys. Yet, unbeknownst even to hearts drunk with chastity, nature, unforgettable, is always there. It is there, with its sublime and brutal end; and no matter how innocent souls may be, you can feel, in the most decorous tête-à-tête, the wonderful and mysterious difference that distinguishes a couple of lovers from a pair of friends.

They idolized each other.

The permanent and the immutable subsist. Two people love each other, they smile at each other, they laugh at each other, they pout at each other halfheartedly, they entwine their fingers, and none of this stops eternity. Two lovers hide in the evening, in the twilight, in the invisible, among the birds, among the roses, they fascinate each other in the shadows with their hearts which shine through their eyes, they murmur, they whisper, and all the time the immense wheeling of stars fills infinity.

## II. THE GIDDINESS OF COMPLETE HAPPINESS

They existed somehow, dazed with happiness, spellbound. They did not notice the cholera that decimated Paris that very month. They had swapped as many secrets as they could but that did not get them much further than their names. Marius had told Cosette he was an orphan, that his name was Marius Pontmercy, that he was a lawyer, that he made a living writing things for booksellers, that his father had been a colonel, that he was a hero, and that Marius had fallen out with his grandfather, who was rich. He had also said something about being a baron but that had not impressed Cosette. Marius, a baron? She did not understand. She did not know what the word meant. Marius was Marius. On her side, she had confided to him that she had been brought up in the Petit-Picpus convent, that her mother was dead just as his was, that her father was called Monsieur Fauchelevent, that he was a very good man, that he gave a lot to the poor but that he was poor himself, and that he deprived himself of everything while depriving her of nothing.

Oddly, in the kind of symphony in which Marius had been living since he started seeing Cosette, the past, even the most recent past, had become so confused and remote for him that what Cosette told him satisfied him fully. It did not even occur to him to speak to her about the episode that night in the old Gorbeau building, the Thénardiers, the burn, or her father's strange attitude and incredible escape. Marius had forgotten all that for the moment; he did not even know in the evening what he had done that morning, nor where he had eaten, nor whom he had spoken to; he had singing in his ears that made him deaf to all other thoughts, he existed only during the hours he saw Cosette. So, since he was in heaven, it was perfectly natural that he should forget earth. Both of them languidly carried the indefinable weight of unearthly pleasures. This is the way those somnambulists known as the lovesick live.

Alas! Who has not felt all these things? Why must the time come when you emerge from blue skies and why does life go on afterward?

Loving almost takes the place of thinking. Love is an ardent forgetting of the rest. So try asking passion to be logical. There is no more of an absolute logical sequence in the human heart than there is a perfect geometric figure in celestial mechanics. For Cosette and Marius nothing existed anymore except Marius and Cosette. The world around them had fallen down a hole. They lived inside a golden moment. There was nothing ahead, nothing behind. Marius scarcely even thought about the fact that Cosette had a father. He was so bedazzled that everything else had been wiped from his brain. So what did they talk about, these lovers? We know: the flowers, the swallows, the setting sun, the rising moon, all the things that matter. They had told each other everything, and nothing. The everything of those in love is nothing. But the father, the real world, that dump, those thugs, that episode, what was the point? And was he absolutely certain that that nightmare had really happened? They were together, they adored each other, that was all there was. Everything else was not. It seems likely that this vanishing of the hell behind us is part and parcel of arriving in paradise. Did we see demons? Do they exist? Did we tremble? Did we suffer? We no longer have a clue. A rose-colored cloud blankets all that.

So these two went on living like this, in this rarefied atmosphere, with all the improbability that is part of nature; neither at the nadir nor at the zenith, between humanity and the seraphim, above the mire, below the ether, in the clouds; barely flesh and blood, soul and rapture from head to toe; already too elevated to have their feet on the ground, still too loaded with humanity to disappear into the blue, in suspension like atoms awaiting precipitation; apparently outside fate; oblivious to that rut, yesterday, today, and tomorrow; filled with wonder, swooning, floating; at times light enough to soar into infinity; almost ready to vanish into eternity.

They were sleeping wide awake, rocking, cradled. O, splendid lethargy of the real, bowled over by the ideal! Sometimes, beautiful as Cosette was, Marius would close his eyes before her. Eyes closed—that is the best way to see the soul.

Marius and Cosette did not ask themselves where this was taking them; they looked on themselves as having arrived. It's one of man's strange conceits, to want love to take them somewhere.

### III. THE BEGINNING OF A SHADOW

Jean Valjean himself suspected nothing.

Cosette, not quite as dreamy as Marius, was gay and that was all Jean Valjean needed to be happy. The thoughts Cosette had, her tender preoccupations, the image of Marius that filled her soul, in no way detracted from the incomparable purity of her beautiful chaste and smiling face. She was at that age when a virgin carries her love the way an angel carries its lily. So Jean Valjean was at peace. Then again, when two lovers understand each other, it all goes very smoothly; any third party, no matter who, that might disturb their love, is kept completely in the dark by a few precautions that are always the same for all lovers. And so, Cosette never objected to anything Jean Valjean said. If he felt like a walk: Yes, my darling father. If he felt like staying home: Perfect. If he felt like spending the evening with her: She was thrilled. As he always retired at ten o'clock at night, Marius only ever turned up in the garden after ten, when he heard, from the street, Cosette opening the French windows onto the terrace by the garden steps. It goes without saying that Marius was never to be seen in the daytime. Jean Valjean forgot about Marius's existence. Only once, one morning, he happened to say to Cosette: "Why, you've got white all over your back!" The night before, Marius had got carried away and pressed Cosette against the wall.

Old Toussaint, who went to bed early, thought only of sleeping once her chores were finished and was as much in the dark as Jean Valjean.

Never did Marius set foot in the house. When he was with Cosette, they hid in a recess near the steps so that they could not be seen or heard from the street and they sat there, often contenting themselves, by way of conversation, with squeezing each other's hands twenty times a minute and gazing up at the branches of the trees. At those moments, a bolt of lightning could have fallen thirty feet away and they would not have noticed, so deeply absorbed were they in each other.

Endless limpid purity. Hours all white, almost all alike. This kind of love affair is a gathering of lilies and dove's feathers.

The whole garden lay between them and the street. Whenever Marius came or went, he carefully readjusted the bar of the gate so that no one could see it had been disturbed.

He usually dragged himself away around midnight and went back to Courfeyrac's. Courfeyrac said to Bahorel: "Would you believe it? Marius comes home these days at one in the morning!"

Bahorel answered: "What do you expect? There's a live wire in every seminarian."

At times, Courfeyrac would cross his arms, look serious, and say to Marius: "You're going to rack and ruin, young man!"

Courfeyrac was a pragmatist and did not take kindly to this reflected glow of some secret paradise that lay over Marius; he was not used to passions that didn't publicize themselves; he had no time for them and occasionally challenged Marius to return to the real world.

One morning he threw this rebuke at him: "My dear man, you strike me these days as living on the moon, in the kingdom of dreams, province of illusion, capital, Soap Bubble. Come on, be a good boy, what's her name?"

But nothing could induce Marius "to spill the beans." You could have ripped out his nails sooner than one of the two sacred syllables that made up that unspeakably wonderful name, *Cosette*. True love is as luminous as the dawn and as silent as the grave. But Courfeyrac could see this change in Marius, that even his taciturnity was now radiant.

In that sweet month of May, Marius and Cosette discovered what triggered even more immense happiness:

How to argue and use *vous* just to use *tu* with all the more relish afterward;

How to talk together at length and in the most minute detail about people who didn't interest them in the slightest; one more proof that, in this ravishing opera we call love, the libretto is virtually of no account;

For Marius, listening to Cosette talk fashion;

For Cosette, listening to Marius talk politics;

Sitting side by side, knees grazing, and listening to the carriages bowling along the rue de Babylone;

Gazing at the same planet in space or the same worm glistening in the grass;

How to be silent together, a sweetness even greater than talking;

And so on, and so forth.

Yet sundry complications were looming.

One evening, Marius was wending his way to their rendezvous along the boulevard des Invalides, walking with his head down as usual. Just as he was about to turn the corner into the rue Plumet, he heard someone say quite close to him: "Good evening, Monsieur Marius."

He lifted up his face and recognized Éponine.

This had a singular effect on him. He had not thought for single moment about the girl since the day she had taken him to the rue Plumet, he had not seen her again, she had completely gone out of his mind. He had every reason to be grateful to her, he owed her his present happiness and yet he was embarrassed at seeing her.

It is a mistake to think that passion, when it is happy and pure, leads a person to a state of perfection; it simply leads them, as we have observed, to a state of forgetting. In such a situation, a person forgets to be bad, but they also forget to be good. Gratitude, obligation, vital and troublesome recollections, evaporate. At any other time, Marius would have behaved differently toward Éponine. Absorbed by Cosette as he was, he didn't even clearly register that this particular Éponine was Éponine Thénardier, that she bore a name written down in his father's will and testament, that name to which, only a few months earlier, he would have been so ardently devoted. We show Marius as he was, without embellishment. His father himself was fading somewhat from his heart beneath the splendor of his love.

He answered rather awkwardly: "Ah! It's you, Éponine?"

"Why do you say *vous* to me? Have I done anything to you?"

"No," he replied.

Certainly, he had nothing against her. Far from it. Only, he felt that now that he called Cosette *tu*, he could only use *vous* on Éponine.

As he said no more, she burst out: "So, why—?"

Then she stopped. It seemed that words failed this creature once so insouciant and so bold. She tried to smile and could not. She stumbled on: "Well, then—"

Then she shut up again and stood there looking down.

"Bonsoir, Monsieur Marius," she said suddenly, brusquely, then turned and left.

## IV. A Cab Rolls in English and Yelps Like a Mutt in Slang

The next day was June 3, 1832, a date we must draw attention to because of the grave events that were at that time hanging over Paris like heavy black clouds. As night fell, Marius was walking along the same path as the day before with the same rapturous thoughts in his heart, when he saw, through the trees on the boulevard, Éponine coming toward him. Two days in a row was too much. He swiftly turned off the boulevard, changed direction, and headed for the rue Plumet by the rue Monsieur.

This prompted Éponine to follow him as far as the rue Plumet, something she had never yet done. Until that moment she had been happy just to see him go by on the boulevard without even trying to run into him. The night before she had tried to speak to him for the very first time.

So Éponine followed him, without his suspecting a thing. She saw him shift the bar on the gate and slip into the garden.

"Well I never!" she said. "He's going into the house!"

She went over to the gate, tested the bars one after the other and easily identified the one Marius had shifted. She muttered to herself on a forlorn note: "None of that, Lisette!"

She sat down at the bottom of the gate right beside the bar as though guarding it. This was exactly the point where the gatepost joined the neighboring wall. There was a dark corner there where Éponine disappeared entirely.

She stayed there for over an hour without moving, almost without breathing, a prey to her ideas. At around ten o'clock, one of the two or three people out and about in the rue Plumet, an old bourgeois out late who was racing to get through that deserted and ill-famed stretch, passed close by the garden gate and got as far as the corner the gate formed with the wall when he heard a muffled and menacing voice say: "I wouldn't be surprised if he came every night!"

The man looked all around him, saw no one, dared not peer into that black corner, and stepped up the pace, frightened out of his wits.

This passerby did well to hurry, for very shortly afterward, six men entered the rue Plumet, creeping along the walls, separately and at some distance from each other, looking for all the world like a drunken patrol.

The first to reach the garden gate stopped and waited for the others; a second later, all six were gathered together. The men began talking in low voices.

"It's *icicaille*," said one.

"Is there a mutt in the garden?" asked another.

"Don't know. Anyway, I've got a meatball we'll make him chew on."

"Have you got some putty to take out the porthole?"

"Yep."

"The gate's old," added a fifth man, who had the voice of a ventriloquist.

"All the better," said the second man to have spoken. "She won't sing as much under the fiddle [saw] and won't be so hard to mow down."

The sixth man, who had not yet opened his mouth, began to inspect the gate just as Éponine had done an hour earlier, gripping each of the bars in turn and jiggling them carefully. And so he came to the bar Marius had worked loose. As he was about to grab this bar, a hand shot out suddenly from the shadows and clapped itself on his arm. He felt himself shoved back hard from the middle of his chest and a voice, hoarse but restrained, said to him: "There *is* a mutt."

At the same time, he saw a pale girl standing in front of him.

The man felt that commotion that the unexpected always produces. He bristled hideously; nothing is as awful to see as a wild animal, startled; their frightened look is frightening. He staggered back and stammered: "Who's this hussy?"

"Your daughter."

It was, indeed, Éponine who was speaking to Thénardier.

As soon as Éponine popped up, the five others, that is, Claquesous, Gueulemer, Babet, Montparnasse, and Brujon, came over without a sound, without haste, without a word, with the sinister slowness peculiar to such men of the night.

You could see ghastly-looking tools in their hands. Gueulemer was holding the curved pliers that prowlers call *fanchons,* cutters.

"Jesus wept! What are you doing here? What're you trying to do to us? Are you off your rocker?" shouted Thénardier, insofar as you can shout keeping your voice down. "What are you doing, coming here and stopping us from getting on with the job?"

Éponine started to laugh and leaped up to kiss him.

"I'm here, daddy darling, because I'm here. Can't a girl sit on a stone these days? You're the one who shouldn't be here. What are you doing turning up here, since it's a no-go? I told Magnon. There's nothing doing here. Oh, come on, give me a kiss, my dear darling daddy! It's been so long since I last saw you! So you're out again, then?"

Old man Thénardier tried to get out of Éponine's arms and grumbled: "All right then. You've had your kiss. Yes, I'm out. I am not in. Now get lost."

But Éponine would not let go and kissed him all the harder.

"My dear darling daddy, how did you do it, then? You must be sharp as a tack to get out of that one. Tell me all about it! And what about my mother? Where's my mother? What's the latest on Mum?"

Thénardier answered: "She's doing all right, I don't know, leave me alone; I said, get lost."

"I don't want to get lost, though," said Éponine, simpering like a spoiled brat. "Fancy sending me packing when I haven't seen you for four months already and I've hardly had time to give you a kiss."

And she flew at her father's neck again.

"Come on now, this is ridiculous!" said Babet.

"Let's get a move on," said Gueulemer. "The cops could come past any minute."

The ventriloquist's voice sang this couplet:

It's not New Year's Day by heck
To hang off Mummy or Daddy's neck.[1]

Éponine turned to face the five crooks.

"Well, well, if it isn't Monsieur Brujon. Hello, Monsieur Babet. Hello, Monsieur Claquesous. Don't you recognize me, Monsieur Gueulemer? How are things, Monsieur Montparnasse?"

"Of course they recognize you!" yelled Thénardier. "But hello, goodbye, shove off! Leave us alone."

"It's the hour for foxes, not the hour for chicks," said Montparnasse.

"You can see for yourself we've got a joint to case *icigo*," added Babet.

Éponine took Montparnasse's hand.

"Watch out!" he said. "You'll cut yourself, I've got a blade out."

"My dear Montparnasse," Éponine replied very sweetly, "you must learn to trust people. I am my father's daughter, after all. Monsieur Babet, Monsieur Gueulemer, I'm the one who was asked to look into this business."

It is remarkable that Éponine did not speak a word of slang. Since she met Marius, that ghastly language had become anathema to her.

She squeezed Gueulemer's big rough fingers with her weak bony little skeleton's hand and went on: "You know very well I'm no fool. Normally people believe me. I've done you favors on more than one occasion. Well, then, I've gathered information, you'd be exposing yourselves for nothing, you know. I swear to you there's nothing doing in this house."

"There are women there on their own," said Gueulemer.

"No. The people have moved."

"The candles haven't, though!" said Babet.

And he showed Éponine, through the treetops, a light moving around in the attic of the villa. This was Toussaint, who had stayed up to hang the linen out to dry.

Éponine made a last-ditch effort.

"Well, anyway," she said, "these people are as poor as church mice and this is the kind of shack where there isn't a sou."

"Get the hell out of here!" cried Thénardier. "When we've turned the joint upside down and we've put the cellar up top and the attic down below we'll tell you what's inside and if it's francs, sous, or centimes."

And he pushed her aside to get past.

"My very dear friend, Monsieur Montparnasse," said Éponine, "please, you're a good boy, don't go in!"

"Be careful, you'll cut yourself!" replied Montparnasse.

Thénardier added in that decisive tone of his: "Beat it, fairy princess, and let the men go about their business."

Éponine let go of Montparnasse's hand, which she had grabbed again, and said: "So you want to get into this house?"

"Just for a bit!" said the ventriloquist, snickering.

She backed against the gate, faced the six bandits, though they were armed to the teeth and looked like demons in the night light, and in a firm low voice she said: "Sorry, I don't want you to."

They stopped in their tracks, dumbfounded. The ventriloquist, though, stopped snickering. She went on: "Friends! Listen carefully. It's not on. Now I'm doing the talking. First of all, if you enter this garden, if you touch this gate, I'll scream, I'll bang on the walls, I'll wake everyone up, I'll get you nabbed, all six of you, I'll call the police."

"She'd do it, too," said Thénardier in an undertone to Brujon and the ventriloquist.

She nodded and added: "Starting with my father!"

Thénardier went up to her.

"Not so close, little man!" she said.

He backed off, grumbling between his teeth. "What the hell's got into her?" And he added: "Bitch!"

She began to laugh with a terrible laugh.

"Whatever you say, you won't be going in. I can't be the daughter of a dog since I'm the daughter of a wolf. There are six of you, but what do I care? You are men. Well, I am a woman. You don't frighten me, not for a second. I'm telling you, you won't be going in that house, because I don't want you to. If you go near it, I'll bark. I told you, the mutt is me. I don't care what happens to you. On your way, you're boring me! Go wherever you like, but don't come here, I forbid you to! You've got your knives, I've got my fists, we're even. Come on, what are you waiting for!"

She took a step toward the crooks, she was terrifying, she started to laugh again.

"Good God! I'm not frightened. This summer, I'll be hungry, this winter, I'll be cold. How hilarious they are, these silly geese of men who think they can frighten a girl. Me, frightened? What of? Oh, yeah, that's right, terrified! Because you have stupid tarts for mistresses who hide under the bed every time you start yelling. That won't wash here! Not with me! I'm not frightened of anything!"

She pinned Thénardier with her steady stare and said: "Not even of you!"

Then she continued, raking her bitter flaming ghost's eyes over the rest of the crooks: "What's it to me if they scrape me off the pavement in the rue Plumet tomorrow, hacked to death by my own father—or if they find me in a year's time in a ditch in Saint-Cloud or on the Île des Cygnes[2] in among all the rotten old cork floats and drowned dogs!"

Here she was forced to break off, a dry cough took hold of her, her breathing came out like a rattle from her narrow, frail chest.

She went on: "All I have to do is scream, they'll come running, whoosh! There are six of you; but I am the rest of the world."

Thénardier made a move toward her.

"Get back!" she cried.

He stopped, and said to her gently: "All right, I won't come any closer, but there's no need to shout. So then, my girl, you want to stop us working? But we've got to earn our living. Aren't we friends anymore, then?"

"You annoy me," said Éponine.

"But we've got to live, got to eat—"

"Drop dead."

That said, she plonked down on the base of the gate, and began quietly singing:

My arms so plump
My legs so shapely,
And time won't come again.[3]

She was leaning with her elbow propped on her knee and her chin in her hand, and swinging her foot in an attitude of complete indifference. Her dress was full of holes and showed her sharp collarbones. The streetlamp nearby lit up her face and her body. Nobody could look more resolute and amazing.

The six assassins, dumbstruck and dark at being held in check by a mere girl, darted under the long shadow cast by the lamp and held a conference full of furious and humiliated shrugs.

She watched them, but with a calm and savage air.

"There's something up with her," said Babet, "some reason. D'you reckon she's fallen in love with the mutt? It'd be a shame to miss out on this, but. Two women, an old man who lives out the back; there are plenty of good curtains at the windows. The old boy'd have to be a Jew-bag. Looks like a safe bet to me."

"Well, then, in you go, the rest of you," cried Montparnasse. "Do the business. I'll stay here with the girl, and if she moves a muscle—"

He flashed the switchblade that he held open up his sleeve in the light of the streetlamp.

Thénardier did not say a word and seemed ready to be led.

Brujon, who was a bit of an oracle and who had, as we know, "set the job up," had still not spoken. He seemed to be thinking. He had the reputation of not backing away from anything and it was known that he had one day, out of sheer bravado, done over a police station. On top of that, he made up verses and songs, which gave him great authority.

Babet questioned him.

"You don't say anything, Brujon?"

Brujon remained silent a moment more; then he shook his head in several different ways and finally decided to speak: "This is the thing: I came across two sparrows fighting this morning. This evening, I bang into a woman arguing. All this is bad. Let's clear out."

They cleared out.

While clearing out, Montparnasse muttered: "All the same, if they'd wanted me to, I'd have finished her off."

Babet responded: "Not me. I don't touch women."

At the corner of the street they stopped and engaged in this puzzling dialogue in muted voices:

"Where are we going to sleep tonight?"

"Underneath Pantin."

"Have you got the gate key on you, Thénardier?"

"Ah, hell."

Éponine, who had not taken her eyes off them, saw them turn back the way they had come. She got up and started to creep behind them, hugging the walls and houses. She followed them in this fashion as far as the boulevard. There, they split up and she saw those six men sink into the darkness where they seemed to melt.

## V. THINGS OF THE NIGHT

After the crooks had gone, the rue Plumet resumed its quiet nocturnal appearance.

What had just happened in this street would not have amazed a forest. Timberland, thickets, ferns, heather, fiercely entangled branches, tall grasses, lead their own dark lives; wild teeming nature suddenly catches glimpses of the invisible there; what is below man makes out through the mist what is above man; and things we, the living, know nothing about, confront each other in the night. Bristling musky nature is startled by certain approaches in which it believes it gets a whiff of the supernatural. The forces of darkness know each other and have mysterious checks and balances among themselves. Teeth and claws dread the intangible. Bloodthirsty bestiality, starving voracious appetites in quest of prey, instincts armed with nails and jaws whose only source and goal is the stomach, anxiously watch and scent the imperturbable spectral shape prowling under a shroud, standing in its filmy rustling dress and seeming to them to live a dead and terrible life. These brutal things, which are merely matter, vaguely fear having to deal with the immense darkness condensed in an unknown being. A black figure barring the way stops the wild beast in its tracks. What emerges from the graveyard intimidates and disconcerts what emerges from the lair; the ferocious is frightened of the sinister; wolves back away when they come upon a ghoul.

## VI. MARIUS FALLS TO EARTH AND GIVES COSETTE
### HIS ADDRESS

While this species of bitch with a human face mounted guard against the gate and the six bandits were giving in, outmaneuvered by a girl, Marius was by Cosette's side.

Never had the sky been more starry and enchanting, the trees more tremulous, the smell of the grass more pungent; never had the birds gone to sleep in among the leaves with a sweeter twittering; never had all the harmonies of universal serenity better answered the inner music of love; never had Marius been more in love, happier, more enraptured. But he had found Cosette sad. Cosette had been crying. Her eyes were red.

This was the first cloud in this wonderful dream.

Marius's first words had been: "What's wrong?"

And she had replied: "This."

Then she had sat down on the bench by the steps and while he took his place all atremble beside her, she had expanded: "My father told me this morning to get ready, that he had business to attend to, and that we might perhaps be going away."

Marius shuddered from head to toe.

When you are at the end of life, dying means going away; when you are at the beginning of life, going away means dying.

For six weeks now, Marius had, little by little, slowly, by degrees, been taking possession of Cosette each day. An ideal but thorough possession. As we've already explained, with first love, you take the soul well before the body; later on you take the body well before the soul, sometimes you don't take the soul at all; the Faublases and the Prudhommes[1] add: because there isn't one; but happily this bit of sarcasm is blasphemy. Marius, then, possessed Cosette the way minds possess—in spirit; but he wrapped her round with all his soul and held her jealously to him with incredible conviction. He possessed her smile, her breath, her scent, the deep radiance of her blue eyes, the softness of her skin when he touched her hand, the lovely mark she had on her neck, her every thought. They had vowed never to sleep without dreaming of the other and they had kept their word. And so he possessed her every dream, too. He gazed endlessly at the tiny hairs on the back of her neck, which he sometimes brushed with his breath, and he told himself that there was not one of those tiny hairs that did not belong to him, Marius. He contemplated and adored the things she wore, her ribbons and bows, her gloves, her cuffs, her brodequins, as sacred objects of which he was master. He felt he was lord of the pretty tortoiseshell combs she wore in her hair and he even told himself, muffled and confused stammerings of dawning desire, that there was not a thread of her dress, not a stitch of her stockings, not a tuck of her corset, that was not his. By Cosette's side, he felt himself to be by his property, by his possession, by his despot and his slave. It felt as though their souls had so merged that, if they had wanted to take them back again, they could not possibly have distinguished between them. "This one is mine." "No, it's mine." "I assure you, you're mistaken. This is me all over." "What you take for you is me." Marius was part of Cosette and Cosette was part of Marius. Marius could feel Cosette living in him. To have Cosette, to possess Cosette, was no different for him from breathing. It was into the midst of this faith, of this intoxication, of this virginal possession, amazing and absolute, of this sovereignty, that these words, "We are going away," fell suddenly and the abrupt voice of reality cried out to him: "Cosette is not yours!"

Marius woke up. For six weeks he had lived, as we said, outside life; those words—*going away!*—brought him down to earth with a thud.

He was lost for words. Cosette felt only that his hand was cold. It was her turn to say: "What's wrong?"

He replied, so low that Cosette could hardly hear him: "I don't understand what you mean."

She recapitulated: "This morning my father told me to pack all my things and get ready, that he would give me his clothes to pack in a trunk, that he was obliged to go on a trip, that we were going away, that we needed a big trunk for me and a little one for him, and to get all that ready within a week from now, that we would perhaps go to England."

"But that's monstrous!" cried Marius.

It is certain that at that moment, to Marius's mind, no abuse of power, no violence, no abomination of the most extravagant tyrants, no act of Busiris,[2] Tiberius, or Henry VIII was equal in ferocity to this: Monsieur Fauchelevent's taking his daughter off to England because he had business to attend to.

He asked in a weak voice: "And when would you leave?"

"He didn't say when."

"And when would you come back?"

"He didn't say when."

Marius shot to his feet and said coldly: "Cosette, are you going?"

Cosette turned her beautiful eyes full of anguish toward him and answered in a baffled voice: "Where?"

"To England? Are you going?"

"Why are you talking to me in that tone?"

"I'm asking you whether you're going?"

"What do you expect me to do?" she said, clasping her hands together.

"So you'll go?"

"If my father goes?"

"So you'll go?"

Cosette took Marius's hand and squeezed it without answering.

"Fine," said Marius. "Then I'll go elsewhere."

Cosette felt the meaning of these words even more than she understood them. She went so pale that her face became white in the dark. She stammered: "What do you mean?"

Marius looked at her, then slowly raised his eyes to the sky and answered: "Nothing."

When he lowered his gaze again he saw that Cosette was smiling at him. The smile of the woman you love has a brightness you can see at night.

"What idiots we are! Marius, I've got an idea."

"What?"

"You go, too, if we're going! I'll tell you where! You can come and join me wherever I am!"

Marius was now wide awake. He had come back to reality. He shouted at Cosette: "Go with you! Are you mad? That'd take money and I don't have any! Go to England? But I now owe, I don't know, over ten louis to Courfeyrac— a friend of mine you don't know! I've got an old hat that's not worth three francs, I have a coat that has buttons missing in front, my shirt's all torn, I've got holes at the elbows, my boots let in water; for six weeks I haven't thought about all that and I haven't told you about it. Cosette, I'm a pauper! You only see me at night and you give me your love; if you saw me in daylight, you'd give me a sou! Go to England? How? I don't even have the money for a passport!"

He threw himself against a tree that happened to be there and stood with both arms above his head, his forehead against the bark, feeling neither the wood scraping his skin nor the fever hammering at his temples, motionless, ready to fall, like the very statue of despair.

He stayed in that position for a long time. A person could spend eternity in such bottomless pits. Finally he turned round. He heard a small stifled sound behind him, soft and sad.

It was Cosette sobbing.

She had been crying for close to two hours right next to Marius while he had been lost in thought.

He went to her, fell on his knees, and slowly prostrating himself, took the tip of her foot, which peeped out from under her dress, and kissed it. She let him do this in silence. There are moments when a woman accepts the religion of love like a gloomy and resigned goddess.

"Don't cry," he said.

She murmured: "But I might be going away and you can't come!"

He said: "Do you love me?"

She answered him sobbing these words straight from paradise that are never more thrilling than when said through tears: "I adore you!"

He went on in a tone of voice that was an inexpressible caress: "Don't cry. Tell me, will you do that for me and not cry?"

"Do you love me?" she said.

He took her hand: "Cosette, I have never given my word of honor to anyone because my word of honor frightens me. I feel that my father is there, looking over my shoulder. And yet, I give you my most sacred word of honor that, if you go away, I will die."

There was in the tone in which he uttered those words a melancholy so solemn and so calm that Cosette shook. She felt the chill that something somber and true gives off as it passes. She stopped crying from shock.

"Now listen," he said. "Don't expect me tomorrow."

"Why not?"

"Don't expect me until the day after tomorrow."

"Oh! Why not?"

"You'll see."

"A day without seeing you! I couldn't stand it."

"We can sacrifice one day if it means spending our whole lives together."

Then Marius added in a whisper as though to himself: "He is a man who never changes his habits and he has never received anyone except at night."

"What man are you talking about?" asked Cosette.

"Me? I didn't say anything."

"What are you hoping for, then?"

"Wait till the day after tomorrow."

"Is that what you want?"

"Yes, Cosette."

She took his head in both hands, stood on tiptoe to be at his height, and tried to see the hope in his eyes.

Marius went on: "I've been thinking, you should know my address, anything could happen, you never know; I live at that old friend of mine's, Courfeyrac, rue de la Verrerie, number sixteen."

He fumbled in his pocket, pulled out a penknife, and with the blade wrote on the plaster of the wall: *16, rue de la Verrerie*. Cosette meanwhile was looking intently into his eyes again.

"Tell me what you're thinking. Marius, you are thinking something. Tell me what it is. Oh, tell me so I can get to sleep tonight!"

"What I'm thinking is this: that God can't possibly want to separate us. Wait for me the day after tomorrow."

"What will I do till then?" said Cosette. "It's all right for you, you're out and about, you can come and go. Men are so lucky! Me, I'll be all on my own. Oh, I'll be so sad! What will you do tomorrow night, then, tell me?"

"I'm going to try something."

"Then I'll pray to God and I'll think of you all the time, from now till then, so you are sure to succeed. I won't ask you any more questions. You are my master. I'll spend tomorrow night singing that music from *Euryanthe* that you love—

you came and listened to it one night outside my shutters. But come early the day after tomorrow. I'll expect you at nine o'clock on the dot, I warn you. My God! How sad that the days are so long! Nine o'clock sharp, you hear me—I'll be in the garden."

"I will, too."

And without a word, moved by the same thought, driven by the same electric currents that put two lovers in perpetual contact, both of them dizzy with desire even in their misery, they fell into each other's arms, without realizing that their lips were joined while their uplifted eyes, overflowing with ecstasy and tears, were fixed on the stars.

When Marius left, the street was deserted. At that precise moment Éponine had tracked the burglars as far as the boulevard.

While Marius had been daydreaming, with his head against the tree, an idea had flashed through his mind; an idea, alas! that he himself judged outrageous and unthinkable. He had decided on a desperate course of action.

## VII. OLD HEART AND YOUNG HEART FACE-TO-FACE

Old man Gillenormand had now long since turned ninety-one. He was still living with Mademoiselle Gillenormand at no. 6, rue des Filles-du-Calvaire in the old house that belonged to him. He was, as you will recall, of that antique race of old men who await death perfectly erect, whom age burdens without buckling, and whom even sorrow does not bow.

Yet for some little time, his daughter had been saying: "My father is going downhill." He no longer slapped the servants; he no longer banged his cane with the same verve on the stair landing when Basque was slow to open the door for him. For the past six months, the July Revolution had hardly ruffled his feathers at all. He had seen in the *Moniteur* almost with tranquillity this coupling of words: Monsieur Humblot-Conté, peer of France.[1] The fact is that the old man was filled with despair. He did not sag, he did not surrender—that was no more in his physical makeup than in his moral makeup; but he felt himself inwardly disintegrating. For four years he had been waiting for Marius resolutely—that is indeed the right word—in the conviction that the naughty little rascal would ring at his door one of these days; now he had reached the point where, at certain mournful hours, he told himself that if Marius took his time even a little longer . . . It wasn't death that he found unbearable, it was the idea that he might never see Marius again. Never to see Marius again—that had never, even for a moment, entered his head until now; but now the idea was beginning to occur to him and it sent shivers down his spine. Absence, as always happens with emotions that are natural and true, only increased the love the grandfather felt for the ungrateful boy who had taken himself off like that. It is on nights in December, when the temperature drops below zero, that we most think of the sun. Monsieur Gillenormand was, or thought he was, utterly incapable of making a move, he the grandfather, toward his grandson. "I'd sooner croak," he said. He did not think himself in the wrong in any way, but he never thought of Marius except with deep affection and the mute despair of an old man with one foot in the grave.

He was beginning to lose his teeth, which added to his sadness.

Though he never admitted it to himself, for it would have made him furious and ashamed, Monsieur Gillenormand had never loved any mistress the way he loved Marius.

He had them hang in his bedroom, on the wall opposite his bed, as the first thing he would see when he woke up, an old portrait of his other daughter, the one who had died, Madame Pontmercy, a portrait done when she was eighteen years old. He never tired of looking at this portrait. One day while he was studying it, he happened to say: "I think it's a good likeness."

"Of my sister?" asked Mademoiselle Gillenormand. "Why, yes, it is."

The old man added: "And of him, too."

Once, as he was sitting with his knees pressed together and his eyes almost closed in an attitude of dejection, his daughter ventured to say to him: "Father, do you still bear as much of a grudge as ever toward—"

She broke off, not daring to go any further.

"Who?"

"That poor Marius."

He lifted his old head, slammed his bony wrinkled old fist on the table, and shouted in his crabbiest and most ringing voice: "Poor Marius, you say! That gentleman is a bounder, a nasty little rotter, an ungrateful upstart, with no heart, no soul, a puffed-up popinjay, a bad piece of work."

And he turned away so that his daughter could not see the tears that had welled up in his eyes. Three days later, he emerged from a silence that had lasted for four hours to tell his daughter point-blank: "I have the honor of beseeching Mademoiselle Gillenormand never to speak to me of him again."

Aunt Gillenormand gave up all attempts and arrived at this profound diagnosis: "My father never loved my sister much after her silly mistake. It is clear he detests Marius."

"After her silly mistake" meant: after she married the colonel.

Still, as you might well have surmised, Mademoiselle had failed in her attempt to substitute her favorite, the officer of the lancers, for Marius. Théodule had not taken as a replacement. Monsieur Gillenormand had not accepted the quid pro quo. A hole in the heart is not satisfied with a stopgap. Théodule, for his part, even with his nose on the inheritance, rebelled at the chore of pleasing. The old man bored the lancer and the lancer disgusted the old man. Lieutenant Théodule was doubtless cheery, but chatty; frivolous but common; a bon vivant, but one who mixed with a bad crowd; he had mistresses, it is true, and he talked about them a lot, also true, but he said nasty things about them. All his good points had their bad points. Monsieur Gillenormand was exasperated at his tales of casual amorous encounters near his barracks in the rue de Babylone. And then again, Lieutenant Gillenormand sometimes turned up in his uniform with the tricolor cockade. This made him quite simply insupportable. Old man Gillenormand had wound up telling his daughter: "I've had enough, of Théodule. You receive him if you like, I don't have much time for men of war in times of peace. I don't know if I don't prefer sabreurs to saber-draggers.² The clattering of blades in battle is less pathetic, after all, than the racket scabbards make tapping on the pavement. And then, arching his back like a swashbuckler and lacing himself up like a sissy! Fancy wearing a corset under a cuirass—it's too ridiculous for words. When you are a real man, you keep an equal distance from bravado and simpering affectation. Neither a braggart nor a pretty boy. You can keep your Théodule to yourself."

His daughter could try as she might to tell him, "But he is your grand-nephew, after all." It turned out that Monsieur Gillenormand, a grandfather to his fingertips, was no great-uncle at all.

Basically, as he was of sound mind and could make comparisons, Théodule only served to make him miss Marius all the more.

One evening—it was the fourth of June, though that did not stop old Gillenormand from having a roaring fire going in his fireplace—he had dismissed his daughter, who was quietly sewing in the next room. He was alone in his room with the pastoral scenes, his feet up on his firedogs, half wrapped round in his vast nine-panel Coromandel screen, leaning on his table where two candles burned under a green shade, swallowed up in his tapestry armchair, a book in his hand, but not reading. He was decked out, in his usual style, as an *incroyable*—a dandy—and he looked like an antique portrait of Garat.³ This would have caused him to be followed in the street, but his daughter always bundled him up whenever he went out in a vast quilted bishop's overcoat that hid his clothes. At home, except when he got up or went to bed, he never wore a dressing gown. "They make a man look old," he said.

Old Gillenormand was thinking of Marius lovingly and bitterly, and as usual, bitterness dominated. His embittered tenderness always ended up boiling over into outrage. He had reached the point where you try to come to grips with and accept what is tearing you apart. He was busy explaining to himself that there was no longer any reason for Marius to come back, that if he had needed to come back, he would have done so already, that he had to give up hoping for that. He tried to get used to the idea that it was over and that he would die without seeing "that gentleman" again. But his whole nature rebelled; his old paternal feelings could not allow it. "I don't believe it!" he said; it was his painful refrain. "I don't believe he's never coming back!" His bald head had sunk onto his chest and he vaguely leveled at the ashes in his hearth a woeful yet cranky glance.

As he was in the depths of this reverie, his old servant Basque came in and asked him:

"Is Monsieur able to receive Monsieur Marius?"

The old man jerked upright, ashen and like a corpse jumping under a galvanic shock. All his blood had rushed to his heart. He stammered: "Monsieur Marius what?"

"I don't know," answered Basque, intimidated and thrown by his master's look. "I didn't see him. It was Nicolette who came and told me that there is a young man and to say that it's Monsieur Marius."

Old Gillenormand stuttered in a voice just above a whisper: "Sh-ssh-ow him in."

And he remained in the same position, his head wobbly, his eyes riveted to the door. It opened again. A young man entered. It was Marius.

Marius stopped at the door as if waiting to be asked in.

His almost wretchedly shabby getup could not be seen in the obscurity created by the lampshade. Only his face could be made out, calm and grave, but strangely sad.

Old Gillenormand, overcome with amazement and joy, remained so dazzled for a few moments he was unable to see anything more than a bright light, as when you are confronted by an apparition. He was ready to pass out; he saw Marius through a blinding haze. It really was him, it really was Marius!

At last! After four years! He seized him, so to speak, sized him up, in a single glance. He found him handsome, noble, distinguished, grown-up, a mature man, with a correct demeanor and a charming air. He wanted to open his arms, to call him, to run to him, his heart was melting in ravishment, affectionate words welled up inside him and overflowed from his breast; finally, all this tenderness made itself felt and reached his lips, but out of that warring urge that was the very basis of his nature, harsh words came out. He said abruptly: "What have you come here for?"

Marius answered, embarrassed: "Monsieur . . ."

Monsieur Gillenormand would have liked Marius to throw himself into his arms. He was annoyed with Marius and with himself. He felt he was being brusque and that Marius was being cold. It was for the old man an unbearable and infuriating anxiety to feel himself so loving and so tearful inside yet not to be able to be anything but hard on the outside. His bitterness returned. He interrupted Marius in a gruff tone: "So why are you here?"

That "so" signified: *if you have not come to give me a hug and a kiss.* Marius looked at his grandfather, whose pallor had turned his face to marble.

"Have you come to say you're sorry? Do you admit now that you were wrong?"

He thought he was putting Marius on the right track and that the "boy" was about to give in. Marius flinched; he was being asked to disown his father. He looked at the floor and answered: "No, Monsieur."

"Well then," cried the old man impetuously with a pain that was poignant and full of anger, "what do you want with me?"

Marius clasped his hands, took a step forward, and said in a weak and quivering voice: "Monsieur, have pity on me."

These words stirred Monsieur Gillenormand; if they'd been said earlier, he would have relented, but they came too late. The grandfather got up, he leaned on his walking stick with both hands; his lips were white, his head wobbled, but he dominated the bowed Marius with his height.

"Pity on you, Monsieur! It's the adolescent asking for pity from the old man of ninety-one! You are just starting out in life, I'm about to leave it; you go off to shows, to balls, to cafés, to billiards, you're witty, you please the ladies, you're a good-looking boy; I, I sit there spitting on my embers in the middle of summer; you are rich with the only riches that count, I've got all the impoverishments of old age, infirmity, isolation! You've got all your thirty-two teeth, a good stomach, a keen eye, strength; I don't even have white hair now, I've lost my teeth, I'm losing my legs, I'm losing my memory, there are three street names I always get wrong, the rue Charlot, the rue du Chaume, and the rue Saint-Claude, that's where I'm at; you have the whole future before you, full of sunshine, while I can hardly see what's in front of my nose anymore, I've gone so far into the night; you are in love, that goes without saying, I'm not loved by anyone in the world, and you ask me for pity! By Jove, Molière overlooked this one.[4] If this is how you jest at the Palais, you lawyers, I offer you my sincere compliments. You are true comedians."

And the old man went on in a voice both wrathful and grave: "Right, then, what do you want from me?"

"Monsieur," Marius said, "I know that my presence annoys you, but I've only come to ask you for one thing, and then I will go at once."

"You are a noodle!" said the old man. "Who said you were to go?"

This was a translation of the tender words in his innermost heart: *Just say you're sorry, why don't you! Throw your arms around my neck!* Monsieur Gillenormand realized that Marius would leave him in a few moments, that his unpleasant welcome had put him off, that his harshness was driving him away, he told himself all that and his pain only intensified and, since pain for him turned immediately to anger, his harshness only intensified. He wanted Marius to understand, but Marius did not understand, which made the old man furious. He went on: "Really! You deserted me, me, your grandfather, you left my house to go God knows where, you upset your aunt, you've gone and led—one can very well guess, it's much more fun—the life of a bachelor, playing the fop, coming home at all hours, kicking up your heels, you haven't given me the slightest sign of life, you've run up debts without even telling me to pay them,[5] you've turned yourself into a smasher of windows and a rowdy hooligan and now, after four long years, you turn up on my doorstep and this is all you have to say to me!"

This violent way of pushing his grandson into a show of affection produced only silence with Marius; Monsieur Gillenormand folded his arms, a gesture that, with him, was particularly imperious, and he spat out bitterly at Marius: "Let's get it over with. You've come to ask me something, you say? Well then, what? What is it? Speak."

"Monsieur," said Marius, with the look of a man knowing he is about to plummet over a precipice, "I've come to ask your permission to marry."[6]

Monsieur Gillenormand rang. Basque cracked the door open.

"Send my daughter in."

A second later the door opened again, Mademoiselle Gillenormand did not come in, but showed herself at the doorway; Marius was standing, mute, his arms hanging, with the face of a criminal, Monsieur Gillenormand was pacing up and down the length of the room. He turned to his daughter and said to her: "Nothing. It's Monsieur Marius. Say hello. Monsieur wants to marry. That's all. Off you go."

The old man's clipped, hoarse tone of voice announced a strange fullness of feeling. The aunt threw Marius a bewildered look, seemed to scarcely recognize him, did not let a movement or a word escape her, and disappeared at a snort of fury from her father faster than a straw scuttled by a hurricane.

Meanwhile old Gillenormand had gone back to lean against the mantelpiece.

"Marry! At twenty-one! You've arranged it! You've nothing left to do now but to ask my permission! A mere formality. Do have a seat, Monsieur. Well now, you've been through a revolution since the last time I had the honor of seeing you. The Jacobins came out on top. You must have been happy about that. Aren't you a republican—since you are a baron? You are made for each other. The republic must be the icing on the cake of our barony. Were you decorated for July? Did you help storm the Louvre[7] a little, Monsieur? Very close to here, rue Saint-Antoine, opposite the rue des Nonnains-d'Hyères, there is a cannonball lodged in a third-story wall of a house with this inscription: July 28, 1830. Go and have a look at it. That makes a good impression. Ah, they do such nice things, don't they, your friends! Speaking of which, aren't they putting up a fountain to replace the monument of Monsieur le duc de Berry?[8] And so, just like that, you want to get married? To whom? May one ask, without being indiscreet, to whom?"

He paused, but before Marius had a chance to answer, he erupted violently: "For heaven's sake, do you have any standing? A fortune behind you? How much do you make in the legal profession?"

"Nothing," said Marius with an almost fierce firmness and resolve.

"Nothing? All you have to live on is the twelve hundred livres[9] I give you?"

Marius did not answer. Monsieur Gillenormand continued: "So, I take it the girl is rich?"

"Like me."

"What! No dowry?"

"No."

"Any expectations?"

"I think not."

"Not a rag on her back! And what does the father do?"

"I don't know."

"And what is her name?"

"Mademoiselle Fauchelevent."

"Fauchele-what?"

"Fauchelevent."

"Phh!" went the old man.

"Monsieur!" cried Marius.

Monsieur Gillenormand cut him off in the tone of a man talking to himself.

"That's right, twenty-one years old, no standing, twelve hundred livres a year, Madame la baronne Pontmercy will go and ask for two sous' worth of parsley at the fruit-seller's."

"Monsieur," Marius cut in wildly, now clutching at the last vanishing straw of hope, "I beg you! I beseech you, in heaven's name, I join my hands together in prayer, Monsieur, I throw myself at your feet, allow me to marry her."

The old man let out a laugh, shrill and grim, through which he coughed and spoke.

"Ha! Ha! Ha! You said to yourself: Damn it! I'll have to go and look up that doddering old fogy, that driveling old goat! What a pity I'm not twenty-five yet! What a nice respectable notice I'd chuck him then! How well I'd make do without him! Never mind, I'll say to him: Old noodle, you are only too happy to see me, I want to marry, I want to marry Mamselle Nobody, daughter of Monsieur Nothing, I have no shoes, she has no chemise, no matter, I want to throw my career to the dogs, my future, my youth, my life, I want to sink into destitution with a wife around my neck, that's what I have in mind, you must consent! And, just like that, the old fossil will consent . . . Go to it, my boy, as you will, tie your millstone round your neck, marry your Pousselevent, your Coupelevent . . . Never, Monsieur! Never!"

"Father!"

"Never!"

At the tone in which that *never* was uttered, Marius lost all hope. He rose and slowly crossed the room, head bowed, unsteady on his feet, more like a man about to die than one taking his leave. Monsieur Gillenormand followed him with his eyes and the moment the door opened and Marius was about to go out, he darted forward four steps with that senile vivacity imperious and spoiled old men have, grabbed Marius by the collar, marched him back energetically into the room, threw him into an armchair and said to him: "Tell me about it!"

It was that single word *father* escaping Marius's lips that had brought about this revolution. Marius stared at him, amazed. Monsieur Gillenormand's mobile face no longer expressed anything other than a rough and ineffable bonhomie. The stern ancestor had made way for the grandfather.

"Come on, let's talk, tell me about your love life, you chatterbox, tell all! Heavens! What geese these young men are!"

"Father!" said Marius once more.

The old man's whole face lit up with an indescribable radiance.

"Yes, that's the way! Call me father and you'll see!"

There was now something so good, so soft, so open, so paternal in this brusqueness that Marius was made dizzy and almost drunk by the sudden shift from discouragement to hope. He was sitting near the table; the light from the candles brought out the dilapidated state of his clothes and old father Gillenormand was studying them, flabbergasted.

"Well then, father," said Marius.

"For heaven's sake," Monsieur Gillenormand broke in. "You really haven't got a sou, have you?! You're rigged out like a thief."

He fumbled in a drawer and pulled out a purse, which he put on the table.

"Here, there's a hundred louis, buy yourself a hat."

"Father," Marius plowed on, "my good, dear father, if you only knew! I love her. You can't imagine, the first time I saw her was in the Luxembourg, she used to go there; in the beginning, I didn't pay her much attention and then I don't know how it happened, but I fell in love with her. Oh, how unhappy it made me! In the end, well, now I see her every day, at her place, her father doesn't know, imagine, they are about to go away, we see each other in the garden in the evening, her father wants to take her away to England, so I said to myself: I'll go and see my grandfather and tell him all about it. I'd go mad first, I'd die, I'd get sick, I'd throw myself in the river. I absolutely have to marry her, I'd go mad otherwise. So, well, that's the whole truth, I don't think I've left anything out. She lives in a garden where there's a gate, rue Plumet. That's over by the Invalides."

Old father Gillenormand had sat down next to Marius, beaming with joy. While listening to him and savoring the sound of his voice, he savored at the same time a good long pinch of snuff. At the words *rue Plumet,* he stopped inhaling and let the rest of his snuff fall on his knees.

"Rue Plumet? You say rue Plumet? Let me see, now! I'll be! Isn't there a barracks over that way? Yes, that's it. Your cousin Théodule has told me about her—You know, the lancer, the officer—A peach, my dear friend, a peach! Lordy, yes, rue Plumet. It's what used to be called the rue Blomet. Now it's coming back to me. I've heard talk about this lass at the gate of the rue Plumet. In a garden. A real Pamela.[10] Nothing wrong with your taste. They say she's nice and clean. Between you and me, I think that nincompoop of a lancer had a try at wooing her. I don't know how far it went. When it comes down to it, that's neither here nor there. Besides, you can't take him at his word, he's such a braggart. Marius! I think it's wonderful that a young man like you should be in love. You're the right age for it. I like you better in love than a Jacobin. I like you better smitten by a skirt—by Jove! by twenty skirts—than by Monsieur Robespierre. For my part, I must admit that the only sansculottes I've ever loved are the women. Pretty girls are pretty girls, for pity's sake! There's nothing wrong with that. As for this little lass, she sees you behind papa's back. That's how it should be. I've had affairs like that myself, too. More than one. Do you know what you do? You don't go in too hard; you don't go asking for trouble; no talk of a wedding and Monsieur le maire and his sash. You've got a head on your shoulders—use it. It's as simple as that. You have to show some common sense. Err by all means, mortals, but do not marry. You come and find the grandfather, who's not a bad old stick at heart, and who always has a few rolls of louis lying around in an old drawer, and you say to him: Grandfather, this is how it is. And the grandfather says: It's quite simple. Youth profits and old age provides. I was young once, and one day you will be old. Go to it, my boy, you'll hand this on to your grandson. Here are two hundred pistoles. Have fun, for heaven's sake. Nothing better! That's how the business should be conducted. Don't marry, but don't let that stop you. Do you get my meaning?"

Marius, absolutely dumbstruck, unable to articulate a single sound, shook his head to say no. The old man burst out laughing, gave him a wink of his tired old eye, and a rap on the knee, looked him straight in the eye, beaming mysteriously, and told him, with the most affectionate shrug of the shoulders: "Make her your mistress, you silly goose!"

Marius blanched. He had not been able to make head or tail of anything his grandfather had just been saying. That rigmarole about the rue Blomet, Pamela, barracks, lancers, had gone over his head. Nothing of such a fantasy could have any bearing on Cosette, who was as pure as a lily. The old man was rambling. But this rambling had ended in a word Marius understood only too well—a word that was a mortal insult to Cosette. That phrase "make her your mistress" stabbed the strict young man's heart like a sword.

He stood up, picked up his hat, which was on the floor, and walked to the door with firm and assured tread. There he turned round, bowed deeply to his grandfather, lifted his head high again, and said: "Five years ago, you insulted my father, today you insult my wife. I will never ask you for anything again, Monsieur. Adieu."

Old Gillenormand, stupefied, opened his mouth, reached out his arms, attempted to get up; but before he could utter a word, the door had shut again and Marius was gone.

The old man remained for a few moments without moving and as though thunderstruck; he could not talk or breathe, as though a fist was closing around his gullet. Finally, he tore himself out of his armchair, ran to the door as fast as a person can run at ninety-one, flung it open and yelled: "Help! Help!"

His daughter appeared, then the servants. He shouted at them, with a terrible rattle in his voice: "Run after him! Catch him! What did I do to him? He's gone mad! He's going! Oh, my God! Oh, my God! This time he won't come back!"

He rushed to the window that looked on the street, opened it with his shaky old hands, leaned out down to the waist while Basque and Nicolette held him from behind, and cried: "Marius! Marius! Marius! Marius!"

But Marius was already out of hearing, was at that very moment turning the corner of the rue Saint-Louis.

The old man clapped his hands on his temples two or three times in anguish, turned away from the window and flopped into an armchair, pulseless, speechless, tearless, nodding his head and moving his lips like a half-wit, with nothing left in his eyes or his heart but a deep mournful sensation that resembled night.

# BOOK NINE

# WHERE ARE THEY GOING?

## I. JEAN VALJEAN

That same day, at around four o'clock in the afternoon, Jean Valjean was sitting alone on the shady side of one of the most solitary slopes in the Champ de Mars. Either out of prudence or a desire to gather his thoughts, or quite simply as a result of one of those imperceptible changes of habit that creep little by little into all our lives, he now only went out with Cosette fairly rarely. He was wearing his workingman's jacket and trousers of coarse gray cotton, and his cap with the long peak hid his face. He was now easy and happy where Cosette was concerned; what had frightened and disturbed him for a while had blown over; but, for a week or two now, worries of a different kind had been plaguing him. One day, as he was strolling along the boulevard, he had caught sight of Thénardier. Thanks to his disguise, Thénardier had not recognized him; but since then Jean Valjean had seen him again several times and he now felt sure that Thénardier had adopted the quartier as his new hunting grounds. This had been enough for him to make a momentous decision. For Thénardier to be there, hanging around, meant every shade of peril at once.

On top of this, Paris was stirring; for anyone who had something in his life to hide, the political turmoil offered this disadvantage, the fact that the police had become extremely nervous and extremely jumpy, and that in their efforts to track down men like Pépin or Morey,[1] they could well uncover a man like Jean Valjean.

On all fronts, he had something to worry about.

Lastly, he had just stumbled across something inexplicable to add to his alarm and he was still reeling from it. The morning of that very day, being the only one up and about in the house and taking a stroll in the garden before

Cosette's shutters opened, he had suddenly spotted this line carved into the wall, probably with a nail: *16, rue de la Verrerie.*

It was quite recent, the nicks were white in the old black mortar and a clump of nettles at the foot of the wall was powdered with fine fresh plaster. It had probably been written there during the night. What was it? An address? A signal for others? A warning to him? Whatever the case, it was clear that the entry to the garden had been forced and that unknown people were getting in. He remembered the odd incidents that had already had the household on alert. While his mind kept working on this strange tapestry, he was careful not to mention to Cosette the line written on the wall with a nail for fear of frightening her.

After carefully considering and weighing all this up, Jean Valjean had decided to leave Paris, and even France, and go over to England. He had warned Cosette. Within a week, he wanted to be gone. He sat on the slope in the Champ de Mars, turning all sorts of ideas around in his mind, Thénardier, the police, this strange line written on the wall, the voyage, and the difficulty of getting himself a passport.

While he sat mulling over these concerns, he saw, from a shadow cast by the sun, that somebody had just stopped on the crest of the slope immediately behind him. He was about to turn round when a piece of paper folded in four landed on his knees as though a hand had thrown it over his head. He took the piece of paper, unfolded it, and read these two words written in capital letters in pencil: CLEAR OUT.

Jean Valjean shot to his feet, but there was no one now on the slope; he looked all around and saw a strange-looking creature, bigger than a child, smaller than a man, dressed in a gray smock and a pair of dun-colored velveteen trousers leaping over the parapet and sliding down into the ditch that ringed the Champ de Mars.

Jean Valjean went home immediately, deep in thought.

## II. MARIUS

Marius had left Monsieur Gillenormand's in desolation. He had gone there with pretty small hopes. He left with immense despair.

Still, and those who have observed the first stirrings of the human heart will understand this, the lancer, the officer, that nincompoop, good old cousin Théodule, had left no shadow in his mind. Not the slightest. A playwright might be tempted to hope for a few complications arising out of such a revelation made to the grandson by the grandfather, out of the blue. But what the drama would gain, the truth would lose. Marius was at that age when you believe nothing bad; the age when you believe everything you hear comes later. Suspicions are nothing more than wrinkles. Those in the first flush of youth don't have any. What devastates Othello is water off a duck's back to Candide.[1] Suspect Cosette! There was a whole host of crimes Marius would have committed more easily than that.

He began wandering the streets, the resort of those in pain, thinking of nothing he could later remember. At two in the morning he went home to Courfeyrac's and threw himself on his mattress, fully clothed. The sun was high in the sky when he fell into that awful heavy sleep where your brain goes on working. When he woke up, he saw Courfeyrac, Enjolras, Feuilly, and Combeferre standing in his room, hats on heads, all ready and raring to go.

Courfeyrac said to him: "Are you coming to General Lamarque's funeral?"[2]

Courfeyrac may as well have been speaking Chinese.

He left the house some time after they did, but not before putting in his pocket the pistols that Javert had entrusted to him at the time of the February 3 episode and that he had hung on to. The pistols were still loaded. It is hard to say what he was thinking, if anything, in taking them with him.

All day he prowled around without knowing where; it rained now and then, but he did not notice; for his dinner he bought a *flûte*, a skinny stick of bread, for a sou in a baker's, stuck it in his pocket and forgot about it. It appears he took a bath in the Seine without being aware of doing so. There are moments when your brain is like a furnace burning in your skull. Marius was in one of those moments. He no longer hoped for anything, he no longer feared anything; that is how far he had gone since the night before. He waited for night to fall with feverish impatience, he only had one clear idea left and that was that at nine o'clock he would see Cosette. This final happiness was now his whole future; beyond that, darkness. At intervals, even though he was taking the most deserted boulevards, he seemed to hear strange noises in Paris. He poked his head out of his reverie and wondered: Are they fighting?

At nightfall, at precisely nine o'clock, as he had promised Cosette, he was at the rue Plumet. As he approached the gate, he forgot everything. It was forty-eight hours since he had seen Cosette, he was about to see her again, all other thoughts faded leaving nothing but a deep unbelievable joy. Those minutes in which we live through centuries have this supremely and wonderful peculiarity, which is that while they go past, they fill our hearts completely.

Marius shifted the gate and rushed into the garden. Cosette was not in the spot where she normally waited for him. He made his way through the bushes to the recess near the steps. "She's waiting for me there," he said. But Cosette was not there. He looked up and saw that the house's shutters were all shut. He circled the garden, the garden was deserted. Then he went back to the house and, driven mad with love, giddy, terrified, wild with pain and worry, like a man who comes home at the wrong moment, he banged on the shutters. He banged, and he banged again, not caring if the window flew open and the solemn face of the father appeared, asking him "What do you want?" This was nothing now compared to what he was starting to dread. When he had finished banging, he called out to Cosette.

"Cosette!" he shouted. "Cosette!" he repeated imperiously.

No one answered. It was over. No one in the garden; no one in the house.

Marius fixed his desperate eyes on that gloomy house, as black and as silent as a tomb, and even emptier. He looked at the stone bench where he had spent so many wonderful hours by Cosette's side. Then he sat on the steps, his heart full of sweetness and resolve, he blessed his love from the bottom of his heart and he told himself that, since Cosette had gone, all that was left for him to do now was to die.

All of a sudden, he heard a voice that seemed to come from the street and that cried through the trees: "Monsieur Marius!"

He stood up.

"Eh?" said he.

"Monsieur Marius, are you there?"

"Yes."

"Monsieur Marius," the voice went on, "your friends are waiting for you at the barricade in the rue de la Chanvrerie."

This voice was not entirely unfamiliar to him. It resembled the rough gravelly voice of Éponine. Marius ran to the gate, pulled back the loose bar, poked his head through, and saw someone that looked to him like a young man disappearing into the twilight, running.

## III. MONSIEUR MABEUF

Jean Valjean's purse was useless to Monsieur Mabeuf. Monsieur Mabeuf, in his venerable childlike austerity, had not accepted this gift of the stars; he had not accepted that a star could convert itself into gold louis. He had not guessed that what fell out of the sky actually came from Gavroche. He had taken the purse to the local police chief as lost property placed by the finder at the disposal of any claimants. The purse was, in fact, lost. It goes without saying that no one claimed it and it did not help Monsieur Mabeuf one bit.

What's more, Monsieur Mabeuf had continued to go downhill.

His experiments with indigo had fared no better at the Jardin des Plantes than in his own garden at Austerlitz. The year before, he owed his housekeeper her wages; now, as we saw, he owed the rent. After thirteen months had elapsed, the pawnshop had sold the copperplates of his *Flora*. Some coppersmith had made saucepans out of them. With his copperplates gone, he was no longer able to complete even the odd copies of his *Flora* that he still owned, and so he had ceded his illustrations and text as "faulty sheets," at a giveaway price, to a sec-ondhand book and bric-a-brac dealer. He had nothing left now of his whole life's work. He lived for a while off the proceeds from these odd copies. When he saw that even that meager reserve was drying up, he gave up his garden and left it lying fallow. Before this, a long time before, he had given up the two eggs and piece of beef that he would occasionally treat himself to. He dined on bread and potatoes. He had sold his last sticks of furniture, then anything he had two of by way of bedding, clothing, and covers, followed by his herbaria and his prints. But he still had his most precious books, among which several that were extremely rare, including *Les Quadrains historiques de la Bible,* the 1560 edi-tion, *La Concordance des Bibles* by Pierre de Besse, *Les Marguerites de la Marguerite* by Jean de la Haye with a dedication to the queen of Navarre, the book *De la Charge et dignité de l'ambassadeur* by the old de Villiers Hotman, a *Florilegium rab-binicum* of 1644, a Tibulle of 1567 with this splendid inscription: *Venetiis, in œdibus Manutianis;* and finally, a Diogenes Laertius, printed in Lyon in 1644 and containing the famous variants of manuscript 411, thirteenth century, from the Vatican and those of the two manuscripts from Venice, 393 and 394, so fruit-fully consulted by Henri Estienne, and all the passages in the Doric dialect that are only found in the celebrated twelfth-century manuscript in the library of Naples. Monsieur Mabeuf never lit a fire in his bedroom and always went to bed while it was still light, to save candles. It was as if he had no neighbors any-more; people avoided him whenever he went out, and he noticed. The misery of a child is of interest to a mother, the misery of a young man is of interest to a young girl, the misery of an old man is of interest to nobody. Of all forms of distress, this is the coldest. Yet old Father Mabeuf had not entirely lost his child-like serenity. His eyes very nearly lit up whenever they settled on his books and he smiled when he thought about the Diogenes Laertius, which was the only copy extant. His glass bookcase was the sole piece of furniture that he had kept beyond what was indispensable.

One day mother Plutarch said to him: "I don't have anything to buy dinner with."

What she called dinner was a loaf of bread and four or five potatoes.

"What about credit?" said Monsieur Mabeuf.

"You know very well they won't give me any."

Monsieur Mabeuf opened his bookcase, studied all his books for a long while, one after the other, the way a father forced to slaughter his children would look at them before choosing among them, then swiftly grabbed one, shoved it under his arm, and left the house. He came back two hours later with nothing under his arm, put thirty sous on the table and said: "Now you can get dinner."

From that moment on, mother Plutarch watched a somber veil come down over the old man's candid face, and it never lifted again.

The next day, the day after that, every day, the whole thing had to be gone through again. Monsieur Mabeuf would go out with a book and come back with a piece of silver. As the secondhand book and bric-a-brac dealers could see that he was forced to sell, they bought off him for twenty sous what he had paid twenty francs for—sometimes to the same booksellers. Volume by volume, the whole library went south. At times he would say, "I'm eighty-four, though," as if he had some lingering hope of coming to the end of his days before coming to the end of his books. His sadness grew. Once, though, he had a burst of real joy. He went out with a Robert Estienne, which he sold on the quai Malaquais for thirty-five sous, and he came back with an Alde which he had bought for forty sous in the rue des Grès. "I owe five sous," he said to mother Plutarch, beaming.

That day, he did not eat.

He belonged to the Society of Horticulture. They knew about his destitution there. The president of the society came to see him, promised to speak to the minister of agriculture and commerce about him, and did so.

"Well I never!" cried the minister. "Is that so! An old savant! A botanist! A harmless old fellow! We must do something for him!"

Next day Monsieur Mabeuf received an invitation to dinner at the minister's. Trembling with joy, he showed the letter to old mother Plutarch.

"We're saved!" he said.

On the appointed day, he went to the minister's. He noticed that his crumpled cravat, his big old square-cut coat, and his shoes polished with egg white astounded the ushers. Nobody spoke to him, not even the minister. Getting on for ten o'clock in the evening, as he was still waiting for a word, he heard the minister's wife, a beautiful lady in a low-cut dress whom he had not dared approach, ask: "Who on earth is that old gentleman?" He went home on foot, at midnight, in driving rain. He had sold an Elzévir to pay for the cab there.

He had acquired the habit of reading a few pages from his Diogenes Laertius every night before going to bed. He knew enough Greek to savor the particularities of the text he possessed. This was his only pleasure now. A few weeks went by. All of a sudden, mother Plutarch fell ill. If there is one thing sadder than having nothing to buy bread with at the baker's, it is having nothing to buy drugs with at the apothecary's. One evening, the doctor had prescribed a very expensive potion. And then the illness got worse and a nurse was needed. Monsieur Mabeuf opened his bookcase, but there was nothing left there. The last volume was gone. All he had left was the Diogenes Laertius.

He put the only extant copy under his arm and went out. This was June 4, 1832. He went to the porte Saint-Jacques to Royol's successor and came back with a hundred francs. He placed the pile of five-franc coins on the old servant's night table and went back to his room without saying a word.

Next day, at the crack of dawn, he went and sat on the overturned stone post in his garden; from over the hedge, he could be seen sitting motionless all morning, his head down, his eyes vaguely staring at the withered flowerbeds. It rained at times, but the old man didn't seem to notice. In the afternoon extraordinary noises broke out in Paris. It sounded like musket shots and the clamor of a big crowd.

Old Mabeuf raised his head. He saw a gardener going past and he asked him: "What is that?"

The gardener answered, his shovel over his shoulder, and in the most placid tone: "It's the riots."

"What! Riots?"

"Yes. They're fighting."

"What are they fighting for?"

"Ah! That!" said the gardener.

"Whereabouts?" Monsieur Mabeuf continued.

"Round by the Arsenal."[1]

Old Mabeuf went back inside, took his hat, automatically looked around for a book to tuck under his arm, did not find any, muttered, "Ah! That's right!" and went off looking distraught.

# BOOK TEN

# JUNE 5, 1832

## I. THE ISSUE ON THE SURFACE

What makes a riot? Nothing and everything. Electricity released a little at a time, a flame suddenly shooting out, a roving force, a momentary breath of wind. This breath of wind meets beings that think, brains that dream, souls that suffer, passions that burn, howling torments, and carries them away.

Where?

Anywhere, willy-nilly. Regardless of the state, regardless of the laws, regardless of the prosperity and the insolence of others.

Inflamed convictions, embittered enthusiasms, agitated indignations, warlike instincts held back, exalted young spirits, blindly generous impulses, curiosity, the taste for change, the thirst for the unexpected, the feeling that gives us pleasure reading the bill for a new show and makes us thrill to the whistle of the stagehand at the theater; vague hatreds, resentments, disappointments, any vanity that feels that fate has failed them; discontentments, hollow dreams, ambitions hedged in by high walls; whoever hopes that collapse will provide a way out; finally, at the very bottom, the peat bog, that mud that catches fire—these are the elements that make up a riot.

The grandest and the most inconsequential; beings who roam on the fringes, beyond the pale, waiting for an opportunity, bohemians, vagrants, street-corner vagabonds, those who sleep at night in urban deserts with no roof over their head but the cold clouds in the sky, those who look to chance, not work, for their daily bread, those unknown inhabitants of destitution and nothingness, the bare-armed, the barefoot, belong to the riot.

Anyone who nurses in their soul a secret grudge against some act of the government, or of life or fate, lives on the brink of riot and as soon as it shows, begins to quiver and feel themselves lifted up by the vortex.

The riot is a sort of whirlwind of the social atmosphere that forms without warning when the temperature reaches a certain level and that rises as it swirls, runs, thunders, rips up, crushes, demolishes, uproots, dragging with it great natures and puny ones, manly men and the feebleminded, the tree trunk and the wisp of straw.

Woe to the one it carries away as much as to the one it comes to strike! It smashes them against each other.

It imparts to those it seizes some mysterious extraordinary power. It fills the first comer with the force of events; it turns everything into projectiles. It turns a bit of rubble into a cannonball and a street porter into a general.

If you believe certain oracles of under-the-table politics, from the authorities' point of view, a bit of a riot is desirable. How it works in theory: A riot shores up those governments it fails to overthrow. It tests the army; it focuses the bourgeoisie; it flexes the muscles of the police; it gauges the strength of the social backbone. It is a gymnastic exercise; it is almost hygiene. The government feels better after a riot like a man after a rubdown.

Thirty years ago, the riot was seen in a different light.

For everything there is a theory that proclaims itself "common sense"; Philinte versus Alceste;[1] the offer of a compromise between the true and the false; explanation, admonition, a somewhat arrogant mitigation that, because it is mixed with blame and excuse, believes itself to be wisdom yet is often only pedantry. An entire school of politics, known as the happy medium,[2] has emerged from this. Between cold water and hot water, it is the party of lukewarm water. This school, whose pseudoprofundity is all on the surface, dissects effects without going back as far as causes, and rails against the tumult of the marketplace from the height of its pseudoscience.

To hear this school: "The riots muddied the waters in 1830 and robbed that great event of part of its purity. The July Revolution had been a beautiful popular breath of fresh air, swiftly followed by blue skies. The riots brought the cloudy skies back, they made that revolution, initially so remarkable for its unanimity, degenerate into a brawl. In the July Revolution, as in all disjointed bouts of progress, there had been secret fractures; rioting made these more marked. It became possible to say: 'Ah! This is broken.' After the July Revolution, all you had was a sense of liberation; after the riots, you sensed catastrophe.

"Any riot shuts the shops, depresses funds, upsets the stock exchange, suspends commerce, hampers business, speeds up bankruptcies. Money runs dry; private fortunes are thrown into turmoil, public credit is rattled, industry is thrown out of whack, capital withdraws, labor is underpaid, fear is everywhere; aftershocks are triggered in all the towns. Fissures then open into chasms. They reckon the first day of rioting costs France twenty million, the second, forty, the third, sixty. A three-day riot costs a hundred and twenty million; in other words, looking only at the financial result, it is equivalent to a disaster, a ship-wreck or battle lost, one that wipes out a fleet of sixty ships of the line.

"Doubtless, historically, the riots had their beauty; the war of the cobble-stones is no less grandiose and no less pathetic than the war of the bushes; in one lies the soul of the forest, in the other the heart of the city; one has Jean Chouan, the other has Jeanne.[3] The riots lit up in red, garishly but splendidly, all the most prominent features of the Parisian character in its originality, gen-erosity, devotion, stormy gaiety, with students proving that bravery plays a part in intelligence, the National Guard unshakable, the bivouacs of shopkeepers, the fortresses of street kids, the contempt for death of the average man in the street. Schools and legions clashed. After all, there was only a difference in age between the combatants; they are the same race; the same stoical men die at twenty for their ideas, at forty for their families. The army, always sad in civil wars, pitted prudence against audacity. The riots, at the same time that they manifested the intrepidity of the people, were the making of bourgeois courage.

"That is all very well. But is all that worth the bloodshed? And to the blood shed add the future darkened, progress compromised, anxiety among the best, honest liberals despairing, foreign absolutism rubbing its hands with glee to see the revolution inflict such wounds on itself, the vanquished of 1830 triumphant and crowing, 'We told you so!' Add Paris made greater, perhaps, but France di-minished, for certain. Add, for we have to make a clean breast of it, the mas-sacres that too often dishonored the victory of order turned ferocious over liberty run amok. All in all, the riots have been catastrophic."

Thus speaks that approximation of wisdom with which the bourgeoisie, that approximation of the people, contents itself so readily.

As for us, we reject this too broad and consequently too convenient term: the riots. Between one popular movement and another popular movement, we make a distinction. We don't ask ourselves if a riot costs as much as a battle. For a start, why a battle? Here the question of war raises its ugly head. Is war less of a scourge than a riot is a calamity? And then, are all riots calamities? And what if the fourteenth of July did cost twenty million? The setting up of Philippe V in Spain[4] cost France two billion. Even if the cost was the same, we prefer July 14. Besides, we reject these figures that sound like arguments but are merely words. Given a riot, we look at it on its own. In all that the doctrinaire objection exposed above says, it is a question only of the effect; we look for the cause.

We try to be specific.


## II. THE HEART OF THE MATTER

There is the riot and there is the insurrection; they are two different forms of rage; one is wrong, the other is right. In democratic states, the only states based on justice, it sometimes happens that a fraction usurps power; then all rise up and the necessary vindication of rights can go as far as the taking up of arms. In all the issues that arise from collective sovereignty, the war of the whole against the fraction is an insurrection, the attack of the fraction against the whole is a riot; according to whether it is the king or the Convention that is holed up in the Tuileries, they are justly or unjustly stormed. The same cannon turned on the hordes is wrong on August 10 and right on Vendémiaire 14. Similar in appearance, different at bottom; the Swiss Guards defend the false, Bonaparte defends the true.[1] What universal suffrage has done in all its liberty and its sovereignty cannot be undone by the street. The same goes for the things of civilization pure and simple; the instinct of the masses, yesterday clear-sighted, may be cloudy tomorrow. The same fury is legitimate against Terray and absurd against Turgot.[2] The smashing of machines, the pillaging of warehouses, the tearing up of railway lines, the demolition of docks, the wrong turns taken by the multitudes, the people's denials of justice for progress, Ramus assassinated by schoolboys,[3] Rousseau driven out of Switzerland,[4] pelted with stones—that is rioting. Israel versus Moses, Athens versus Phocion, Rome versus Scipio—that is rioting. Paris versus the Bastille is insurrection. The soldiers versus Alexander, the sailors versus Christopher Columbus[5]—it is the same revolt; an ungodly revolt. Why? Because Alexander does for Asia with the sword what Christopher Columbus does for America with the compass; Alexander, like Columbus, discovers a world. These gifts of a world to civilization are such increments of light that any resistance to them is criminal. Sometimes the people twist fidelity to themselves. The mob is a traitor to the people. Is there anything more peculiar, for instance, than that long and bloody protest of the contraband saltmakers, a chronic legitimate revolt which, at the decisive moment, on the day of salvation, at the hour of popular victory, suddenly takes up the cause of the throne, turns into the Chouan uprising and goes from being an insurrection against to a riot for! Grim masterpieces of ignorance! The contraband saltmaker escapes the royal gallows and, with a remnant of rope still around his neck, sports the white cockade. "Death to the Salt Taxes"[6] gives birth to "Long Live the King." The Saint Bartholomew killers, September cutthroats, Avignon slaughterers, assassins of Coligny, assassins of Madame de Lamballe, assassins of Brune, Miquelet militia, followers of Verdet, Cadenette-wearing soldiers, Companions of Jesus, the Chevaliers du Brassard—that is riot for you. La Vendée is one big Catholic riot.[7]

The sound of justice in motion is recognizable and it doesn't always come from the quaking of the overburdened masses; there are crazy rages, there are cracked bells; not all tocsins ring out with the sound of bronze. The surging motion of passion and ignorance is not the same as the jolt of progress. Rise up, by all means, but only to grow. Show me where you are going. Insurrection can only ever forge ahead. Any other uprising is bad. Any violent step backward is riot; to recoil is an act of assault and battery against the human race. Insurrection is the truth's fit of fury; the cobblestones that the insurrection tears up throw off the spark of justice. These cobblestones leave riot only their mud. Danton versus Louis XVI is an insurrection; Hébert versus Danton[8] is a riot.

This is why, in given cases, an insurrection may be, as Lafayette claims, the most sacred of duties, but a riot may be the most deadly of violent attacks.

There is also some difference in the intensity of heat given off; an insurrection is often a volcano, a riot is often a flash in the pan.

Revolt, as we have said, sometimes occurs within the powers that be. Polignac is a rioter; Camille Desmoulins[9] is a ruler.

Sometimes insurrection is resurrection.

The solving of everything by universal suffrage being an entirely modern development, and all history prior to this development being filled for four thousand years with the violated rights and suffering of peoples, each era of history brings with it what protest is thinkable to it. Under the Caesars there was no insurrection—but there was Juvenal.[10]

The *facit indignatio*—anger writes poetry—replaces the Gracchi.[11]

Under the Caesars, there is the Syene exile; there is also the man of the *Annals*.[12]

We say nothing of the mighty exile of Patmos[13] who, too, shatters the real world with a protest in the name of the ideal world, turns vision into an enormous satire, and casts over Rome-Nineveh, over Rome-Babylon, over Rome-Sodom, the flaming reflection of the Apocalypse.

John on his rock is the sphinx on its pedestal: We may not understand him; he is a Jew and it is all in Hebrew; but the man who writes the *Annals* is a Latin; better still, a Roman.

Since the Neros[14] reign so blackly, they should be depicted accordingly. The work of the engraver's burin on its own would be too pale; we need to pour concentrated prose that bites into the engraved lines.

Despots have a hand in creating thinkers. Shackled words are terrible words. The writer doubly, triply intensifies his style when silence is imposed on the people by some master. A certain mysterious fullness swells up out of this silence and it filters thought and turns it to stone. Clamping down in history produces concision in the historian. The rock-solid compactness of whatever celebrated prose is nothing more than a tamping down by the tyrant.

Tyranny forces the writer to make cuts in diameter that are incremental increases in strength. The Ciceronian period,[15] barely adequate on the subject of Verres, would lose its edge on Caligula. Less scope in the phrase, more intensity in the punch. Tacitus thinks with his arm drawn back.

The honesty of a big heart, condensed into justice and truth, strikes like lightning.

We might note in passing that it is remarkable that Tacitus was not historically superimposed on Caesar. The Tiberii[16] were reserved for him. Caesar and Tacitus are two successive phenomena whose meeting seems to have been mysteriously avoided by the one who regulates entrances and exits in the mise-en-scène of the centuries. Caesar is great, Tacitus is great; God spares these two great men by not pitting them against each other. The righter of wrongs, striking Caesar, may strike too hard and be unjust. God does not want that. The great wars of Africa and Spain, the eradication of the Sicilian pirates, the introduction of civilization into Gaul, Britain, and Germany—all that glory spans the Rubicon.[17] There is a sort of delicacy in divine justice here, when it hesitates to let the formidable historian loose on the illustrious usurper, saving Caesar from Tacitus and allowing the genius extenuating circumstances.

Of course, despotism remains despotism, even under the despot of genius. There is corruption under illustrious tyrants, but moral pestilence is more hideous still under infamous tyrants. In those particular reigns nothing cloaks the shame; and the makers of examples, Tacitus as much as Juvenal, slap this unanswerable ignominy in the face more usefully with the human race looking on.

Rome smells worse under Vitellius than under Sulla.[18] Under Claudius and under Domitian[19] there is a deformed baseness corresponding to the ugliness of the tyrant. The vileness of the slaves is a direct product of the tyrant; a miasma is given off those foul consciences in which the master is reflected; public authorities are sleazy; hearts are cramped, consciences are shallow, souls are sluglike; this is how it is under Caracalla, this is how it is under Commodus, this is how it is under Heliogabalus,[20] while the only thing given off by the Roman Senate under Caesar is the pong of droppings peculiar to eagles' aeries.

Whence the coming, apparently late in the piece, of the Tacituses and the Juvenals; it is only when everything is obvious that the demonstrator pops up.

But Juvenal and Tacitus, just like Isaiah in biblical times, just like Dante in the Middle Ages, mean lone men; riot and insurrection mean the multitude, now wrong, now right.

In the most general cases, the riot springs from a material event; insurrection is always a moral phenomenon. The riot is Masaniello, insurrection is Spartacus.[21] Insurrection is limited to the mind, the riot to the stomach. Gaster gets cranky, but Gaster,[22] of course, isn't always wrong. In cases of famine, the riot, Buzançais,[23] for instance, has a real, pathetic, and perfectly just starting point. Yet it remains a riot. Why? Because, being right at bottom, it is wrong in form. Vicious, though right, violent, though strong, it lashed out in all directions; it crashed along like a blind elephant, crushing everything in its path, leaving the dead bodies of old men, of women and children behind it; it shed, without knowing why, the blood of the innocent and the inoffensive. To feed the people is a fine goal, massacring them is not a good way to go about it.

Every armed protest, even the most legitimate, even August 10, even July

14, kicks off with the same turmoil. Before right becomes clear, there is sound and fury. At the start, the insurrection is a riot, just as the river is a torrent. Normally it ends in the ocean that is revolution. Sometimes, though, having come from those high mountains that dominate the moral horizon, justice, wisdom, reason, right, made up of the purest snow of the ideal, after a long fall from rock to rock, after having reflected the sky in its transparency and being swollen by a hundred tributaries in the majestic pace of triumph, the insurrection suddenly loses itself in some bourgeois quagmire, like the Rhine in a swamp.

All that is in the past, the future is something else. Universal suffrage has a wonderful way of dissolving the riot's raison d'être, and by giving insurrection the vote, it takes away its weapons. The melting away of wars, the street war as much as the border war—such is inexorable progress. Whatever today may be, peace is Tomorrow.

But insurrection, riot, and how the first differs from the second—your so-called bourgeois really can't tell the difference. For him everything is sedition, rebellion, pure and simple, revolt of mastiff against master, a bid to bite that has to be punished with the chain and the doghouse, barking, yapping; until the day when the dog's head, suddenly much bigger, stands out dimly in the shadows with the face of a lion.

That's when the bourgeois shouts: Long live the people!

Given the above explanation, what is the movement of June 1832 in the eyes of history? Is it a riot? Is it an insurrection?

It is an insurrection.

We may at times, in this mise-en-scène of a fearsome event, happen to say riot, but only to describe surface events and always maintaining the distinction between riot as form and insurrection as foundation.

In its swift explosion and its bleak extinction, the movement of 1832 had so much grandeur that even those who see it as a mere riot do not talk about it without respect. For them it is like a hangover from 1830. Imaginations once fired, they say, do not calm down in a day. A revolution does not break off just like that. It always of necessity has a few ups and downs before returning to a state of peace, like a mountain shifting back down again onto the plain. There are no Alps without the Jura, nor Pyrenees without the Asturias.[24]

This pathetic crisis in contemporary history, which Parisians like to remember as "the days of the riots," is surely a typical moment in the stormy episodes of this century.

One last word before we tell the story of it.

The events we are about to relate belong to that dramatic and living reality that the historian sometimes neglects for want of space and time. But this is where, and we insist on this, this is where life is, the throbbing, the shuddering of humanity. Little details, as I think we may have said, are the foliage, so to speak, of big events and are lost in the remoteness of history. The era known as "the riots" abounds in details of the kind. The judicial investigations, for reasons other than history's, did not reveal everything, nor did they perhaps get to the bottom of everything. So we will bring to light, among the known and published particularities, things that were never made known, facts buried by the obliviousness of some, the death of others. Most of the actors in these gigantic scenes have disappeared; they kept their mouths shut from the very next day; but of what we are about to relate, we can say: We saw it with our own eyes. We will change a few names, for history recounts, it does not denounce, but we will be telling a true tale. Within the terms of the book we are writing, we will only show one side and one episode, and that certainly the least known, of the days of the fifth and sixth of June 1832; but we will do so in such a way that the reader will catch a glimpse of the real face of this terrible public incident, beneath the dark veil we are about to lift.

### III. A Burial: An Occasion for Rebirth

In the spring of 1832, although for three months cholera had turned Parisians cold and thrown some mysteriously morbid blanket over their turbulence, Paris had long been ready for some kind of strife. As we said, the big city is like a cannon; when it's loaded, all that's needed is a flying spark, and off it goes. In June 1832 that spark was the death of General Lamarque.

Lamarque was a man of action and of renown. Under both the Empire and the Restoration, one after the other, he had enjoyed the two forms of bravery necessary to the two epochs, bravery on the battlefield and bravery at the rostrum. He was as eloquent as he had been valiant; you could feel the sword in what he said. Like Foy, his predecessor,[1] he upheld liberty after having upheld command. He sat between the left and the extreme left, loved by the people because he accepted the chances the future offered, loved by the hordes because he had served the emperor well. He was, along with the comte Gérard and the comte Drouet,[2] one of Napoléon's maréchaux *in petto*.[3] The treaties of 1815[4] stirred him up like some personal offense. He hated Wellington with a straightforward hate that pleased the masses; and for seventeen years, scarcely paying any attention to intermediate events, he had magnificently maintained his sadness over Waterloo. In his death throes, at his final hour, he had hugged to his breast a sword that the officers of the Hundred Days had presented to him. Napoléon died uttering the word *armée*, Lamarque uttering the word *patrie*—homeland.

His death, which was foreseeable, was dreaded by the people as a loss and by the goverment as a galvanizing occasion. This death was a day of mourning. Like anything bitter, mourning can turn into revolt. That is exactly what happened.

The night before and the morning of June 5, the day set for Lamarque's funeral, the faubourg Saint-Antoine,[5] which the funeral procession was to skirt, took on a very formidable aspect. This turbulent network of streets filled with hubbub. People armed themselves with whatever they could lay their hands on. Joiners carted off the clamps and joining presses from their workbenches "to break down doors." One of them had made himself a dagger out of a shoemaker's hook by snapping the hook off and sharpening the stump. Another, in his feverish keenness to attack, had gone to bed for three days in a row fully dressed. A carpenter named Lombier ran into a comrade who asked him: "Where are you going?" "Well, I haven't got a weapon." "So?" "I'm going to the site to get a pair of compasses." "What for?" "Damned if I know," said Lombier.

A certain Jacqueline, a man in the transport business, accosted any worker who happened to go by: "Over here, you!" He stood them to ten sous' worth of wine and said: "You got a job?" "No." "Right. Go to Filspierre's, between the Montreuil barrière and the Charonne barrière, there's a job for you there."

At Filspierre's they found cartridges and weapons. Certain acknowledged leaders "collected the mail," meaning they ran from door to door rounding up their cohorts. At Barthélemy's, near the barrière du Trône, at Capel's, at the Petit-Chapeau, drinkers sang out to each other with heavy gravity. You could hear them say to one another: "Where've you got your pistol?" "Under my smock. What about you?" "Under my shirt." Rue Traversière, outside Roland's workshop, and in the courtyard of the Maison-Brûlée, outside Bernier the toolmaker's workshop, groups huddled, whispering. A certain Mavot stood out as the most ardent; he was a man who never spent more than a week in any one workshop, the masters sending him packing "because we had to argue with him every day." Mavot was killed the next day on the barricade in the rue Ménilmontant. Pretot, who was also to die in the struggle, seconded Mavot and to the question, "What is your goal?" answered: "Insurrection." Workers, gathered on the corner of the rue de Bercy, were waiting for a certain Lemarin, a revolutionary agent for the faubourg Saint-Marceau. Watchwords were exchanged almost out in the open, in public.

And so, June 5, on a day of mixed rain and sunshine, General Lamarque's funeral procession crossed Paris with all official military pomp and state, somewhat enhanced as a precautionary measure. Two battalions of infantry, drums draped, fusils inverted, ten thousand National Guards, their sabers at their sides, the batteries of the artillery of the National Guard, escorted the coffin. The hearse was drawn by young men. Disabled officers followed immediately behind carrying branches of laurel. Then came a motley crowd in countless numbers, excited, strange, the sectionaries[6] of the Friends of the People, the school of law, the school of medicine, refugees of all nations,[7] bearing Spanish, Italian, German, Polish flags, horizontal red-white-and-blue flags and every kind of banner imaginable, children waving branches of greenery, stonemasons and carpenters who were out on strike at that very moment, printers recognizable by their paper caps, walking two by two, three by three, letting out shouts, nearly all of them waving sticks, some sabers, in disarray and yet as one at heart, now a pushing and shoving crush, now a column. Packs chose leaders for themselves; one man, armed with a perfectly visible pair of pistols, seemed to be passing others in review as the files moved out of the way in front of him. On the side streets off the boulevards, in the branches of trees, on balconies, at windows, on rooftops, men, women, and children milled; their eyes were full of anxiety. An armed mob went by while a frightened mob looked on.

The government, for its part, observed. It observed, its hand on the hilt of its sword. In the place Louis XV,[8] you could see, ready and raring to march, with cartridge pouches full and muskets and carbines loaded, four squadrons of carabineers in the saddle, bugles at the head; in the quartier Latin and the Jardin des Plantes, the municipal guard was echeloned from street to street; at the Halles-aux-Vins there was a squadron of dragoons, at La Grève, one half of the 12th Light, the other half at the Bastille, the 6th Dragoons were at the Célestins, the courtyard of the Louvre was full of artillery. The rest of the troops were stationed in the barracks as reserves, without counting the regiments from the outskirts of Paris. The nervous authorities held hanging over the menacing hordes twenty-four thousand soldiers in the town itself and thirty thousand in the suburbs.

Sundry rumors rippled through the procession. There was talk of legitimist intrigues; there was talk of the duc de Reichstadt,[9] whom God marked down for death at the very moment the mob was singling him out for the Empire. A character who remained anonymous announced that, at the appointed hour, two foremen who had been won over would open the doors of an arms manufacture to the people. The dominant expression on the bared foreheads of most of those taking part was enthusiasm mingled with overweening woe. You could also see here and there among the multitude, gripped by so many violent but noble emotions, the faces of real miscreants and ignoble mouths saying: "Let's do some looting!" There are certain kinds of turbulence that stir up the bottom of the swamp, causing clouds of mud to rise up through the water. A phenomenon not altogether foreign to certain "well-organized" police.

The procession ambled along with a slowness that was febrile, from the house of the departed down through the boulevards as far as the Bastille. It rained now and again, but the rain meant nothing to that thronging crowd. Several incidents occurred, the coffin was trotted around the Vendôme column,[10] stones were thrown at the duc de Fitz-James,[11] spotted on a balcony with his hat on, the Gallic cock[12] was ripped off a popular standard and dragged through the mud, a police officer was wounded by a sword thrust at the porte Saint-Martin, an officer of the 12th Light was heard to say out loud, "I am a republican," the École Polytechnique popped up unexpectedly after its forced confinement, with shouts of "Long live the École Polytechnique! Long live the Republic!"

marking the progress of the cortège. At the Bastille, the long and awe-inspiring lines of curious onlookers going all the way down the faubourg Saint-Antoine ran into the procession and the crowd started to heave and boil over in a terrifying way.

One man was heard telling another: "You see that fellow with the red goatee? He's the one who says when its time to shoot." It would seem that the same red goatee popped up later with the same function in another riot, the Quénisset affair.

The hearse went past the Bastille, then along the canal, crossed the little bridge, and reached the esplanade of the pont d'Austerlitz. There it stopped. At that moment a bird's-eye view of the crowd would have revealed a sort of comet with its head in the esplanade and its tail fanning out over the quai Bourbon covering the Bastille and stretching all the way down the boulevard to the porte Saint-Martin. A circle was drawn around the hearse. The vast throng fell silent. Lafayette spoke and said farewell to Lamarque. It was a moving and majestic moment, every head was bared, every heart beat faster. Suddenly a man on horseback, dressed in black, appeared in the middle of the group with a red flag, though others claim it was a pike topped by a red cap.[13] Lafayette turned his head the other way. Exelmans[14] left the cortège.

This red flag kicked up a storm and disappeared into it. From the boulevard Bourdon to the pont d'Austerlitz, one of those commotions that are like rough swells stirred the crowd. Two almighty shouts rose over the racket: "Lamarque to the Panthéon!" "Lafayette to the Hôtel de Ville!"[15] Some young men, to the cheers of the crowd, harnessed themselves up and set about dragging Lamarque in the hearse via the pont d'Austerlitz and Lafayette in a fiacre via the quai Morland.

In the crowd surrounding and cheering Lafayette, people noticed a German named Ludwig Snyder and pointed him out to each other. Snyder, who has since died a centenarian, had also been in the war of 1776 and had fought at Trenton under Washington and at Brandywine under Lafayette.

Meanwhile, on the left bank, the municipal cavalry swung into motion and came to bar the bridge exit; on the right bank the dragoons emerged from the Célestins and deployed along the quai Morland. The crew dragging Lafayette suddenly saw them at the bend in the quai and shouted: "The dragoons! The dragoons!" The dragoons advanced at a walking pace, in silence, their pistols in their holsters, sabers in their sheaths, carbines in their rests, with an air of grim expectancy.

Two hundred feet from the little bridge, they halted. The fiacre with Lafayette in it wound its way over to them, they broke ranks to let him pass, then closed ranks again behind him. At that moment, the dragoons and the crowd came together, face-to-face. The women fled in terror.

What happened in that fatal minute? No one will ever know. It was that dark moment when two clouds merge. Some say a trumpet blast was heard sounding the charge from the direction of the Arsenal, others that a boy stabbed a dragoon with a dagger. The fact is that three shots were suddenly fired, the first killing the head of the Cholet squadron, the second killing an old deaf woman as she was shutting her window in the rue Contrescarpe, the third singeing the epaulet on an officer's uniform; a woman cried out, "They're starting too soon!" and all of a sudden, from the opposite side of the quai Morland a squadron of dragoons, who had stayed in the barracks, was seen debouching at a gallop, sabers drawn, via the rue Bassompierre and the boulevard Bourdon, sweeping all before them.

The die is cast, the tempest rages, stones rain down, gunfire erupts, many scuttle headlong down the bank and cross over the narrow arm of the Seine[16] that is now filled in; the building yards of the Île Louviers, that vast ready-made citadel, bristle with combatants; stakes are torn up, pistols are fired, a makeshift barricade is erected, young men driven back now race across the pont d'Austerlitz with the hearse and charge the Municipal Guard, the carabineers come running, the dragoons lash out with their sabers, the crowd scatters in every direction, talk of war flies around the four corners of Paris, people cry: "To arms!" They run, they tumble, they flee, they stay and put up a fight. Anger spreads the riot the way the wind spreads fire.

## IV. The Seething of Days Gone By

Nothing is more extraordinary than the initial swarming hustle and bustle of a riot. Everything breaks out everywhere at once. Was it predicted? Yes. Was it planned? No. Where does it spring from? From the cobblestones. What does it come out of? From out of the blue. Here the insurrection looks like a plot; there, like an improvisation. The first comer gets hold of a current from the crowd and takes it wherever he likes. It is a beginning full of horror mixed with a sort of tremendous gaiety. First there is the hubbub, the shops shut, merchants' displays disappear; then there are isolated shots; people flee; butts and clubs hammer portes cochères; you hear servants laughing in the courtyards of houses and saying: "There's going to be a hell of a dustup!"

Here is what happened almost at the same time at twenty different spots aound Paris before a quarter of an hour had elapsed.

At the rue Sainte-Croix-de-la-Bretonnerie, twenty or so young men, with beards and long hair, went into a bar and came out again a moment later carrying a horizontal tricolor flag covered in crepe; at their head were three armed men, one with a sword, the second with a fusil, the third with a pike.

At the rue des Nonnains-d'Hyères, a well-dressed bourgeois with a big gut, a deep ringing voice, bald head, high forehead, black beard, and one of those wiry mustaches that cannot be curled, was openly handing out cartridges to passersby.

At the rue Saint-Pierre-Montmartre, bare-armed men were parading a black banner on which this could be read in white letters: *Republic or Death*. At the rue des Jeûneurs, rue du Cadran, rue Montorgueil, rue Mandar, groups appeared waving flags on which you could make out the word *section* and a number in gold letters. One of these flags was red and blue with an imperceptible white stripe[1] in between.

An arms factory was ransacked on the boulevard Saint-Martin, and three armorers' shops, the first in the rue Beaubourg, the second in the rue Michel-le-Comte, the other in the rue du Temple. In just a few minutes, the mob with its thousand hands had seized and carried off two hundred and thirty fusils, nearly all double-barreled, sixty-four swords, and eighty-three pistols. So that more people would be armed, one grabbed a fusil, the other a bayonet.

Young men armed with muskets set themselves up among the women overlooking the quai de la Grève to shoot. One of them had a musket with a matchlock. They rang the bell, waltzed in, and started making cartridges. One of the women said: "I didn't know what a cartridge was until my husband told me."

A throng broke into a curiosity shop in the rue des Vieilles-Haudriettes and took some yataghans[2] and other Turkish weaponry.

The dead body of a mason killed by musket shot lay in the rue de la Perle.

And then, right bank, left bank, on the quais, along the boulevards, in the quartier Latin, in the quartier around Les Halles, breathless men, workers, students, sectionaries, read proclamations and cried: "To arms!" They smashed streetlamps, unhitched wagons, tore up the streets, battered down the doors of houses, uprooted trees, ransacked cellars, rolled out barrels, piled up paving stones, rubble, furniture, and timber and made barricades.

They forced the burghers to lend a hand. They broke into houses where the women were, made them hand over the absent husband's saber and fusil, and wrote over the door in Spanish white: "Weapons have been handed over." A few signed receipts for the fusils and sabers with their name, saying: "Send for them tomorrow at the Hôtel de Ville." They disarmed solitary sentinels and National Guards on their way to their *mairie*. They ripped officers' epaulets off. In the rue du Cimitière-Saint-Nicolas, an officer of the National Guard, pursued by a troop armed with clubs and foils, took refuge after much ado in a house where he was stuck until that night, and could then only leave it in disguise.

In the quartier Saint-Jacques, students scurried out of their hotels in droves and swarmed up the rue Saint-Hyacinthe to the Café du Progrès or down to the Café des Sept-Billards, rue des Mathurins. There, young men standing in the doorways on stone posts distributed weapons. The timber yard on the rue

Transnonain was ransacked for barricades. At a single point, the residents resisted—at the corner of rue Sainte-Avoye and the rue Simon-le-Franc, where they themselves destroyed the barricade. At a single point the insurgents buckled, abandoning a barricade begun in the rue du Temple after having fired on a detachment of the National Guard and fleeing down the rue de la Corderie. The detachment picked up a red flag, a packet of cartridges, and three hundred pistol bullets at the barricade. The National Guards tore up the flag and carried off the shreds on the points of their bayonets.

All that we are relating here slowly and sequentially occurred at all points over town at once amid an incredible and vast tumult, like a host of lightning flashes in a single roll of thunder.

In under an hour, twenty-seven barricades had sprung up out of the ground in the Les Halles quartier alone. At the center was the famous house at no. 50, once the fortress where the worker Jeanne and his one hundred and six companions³ holed up, and which, flanked on one side by a barricade at Saint-Merry and on the other by a barricade in the rue Maubuée, commanded three streets, the rue des Arcis, the rue Saint-Martin, and the rue Aubry-le-Boucher, which it fronted. Two barricades at right angles stretched out and ran from the rue Montorgueil to the Grande-Truanderie, and from the rue Geoffroy-Langevin to the rue Sainte-Avoye. This is without counting the innumerable barricades that went up in twenty other quartiers of Paris, in the Marais, on the montagne Sainte-Geneviève; one, in the rue Ménilmontant, even sported a porte cochère that had been torn off its hinges; another close to the little bridge of the Hôtel Dieu was made with the coach known as an *écossaise,* unhitched and upended, only three hundred feet from the prefecture of police.⁴

At the barricade in the rue des Ménétriers, a well-heeled man distributed money to the workers. At the barricade in the rue Greneta, a man appeared on horseback and handed something that looked to be a roll of silver to the man who seemed to be in charge of the barricade. "There you go," he said. "This is to cover your expenses, for wine and so on." A young blond man, without cravat, was going from one barricade to the next passing on watchwords. Another man, saber drawn, a blue police cap on his head, was posting sentries. Inside the barricades, wine bars and porters' lodges were converted into guardhouses. What's more, the riot was conducted according to the soundest military tactics. The narrow, uneven, winding streets full of twists and turns, had been impressively well chosen; the environs of Les Halles in particular, a network of streets more tangled than a forest. The Society of the Friends of the People had, they said, taken over the insurrection in the quartier Sainte-Avoye. A man killed in the rue du Ponceau was rumbled and found to have a map of Paris on him.

But what had really taken over the riot was a sort of unfamiliar recklessness that was in the air. The insurrection had suddenly thrown up barricades with one hand and, with the other, seized practically all the posts of the garrison. In under three hours, like a powder train that catches alight, the insurgents had invaded and occupied, on the right bank, the Arsenal, the *mairie* in the place Royale, all of the Marais, the Popincourt arms factory, the Galiote, the Château-d'Eau, all the streets close to Les Halles; on the left bank, the veterans' barracks, Sainte-Pélagie, the place Maubert, the Deux-Moulins powder store, all the barrières. At five o'clock in the evening they were masters of the Bastille, the Lingerie, the Blancs-Manteaux; their scouts had got as far as the place des Victoires and were threatening the Banque de France, the Petits-Pères barracks, the Hôtel des Postes. A third of Paris was rioting.

At all points the struggle was escalating on a gigantic scale and the outcome of all the disarming, the house-to-house visits, the brisk invasion of armorers', was that combat that had kicked off with stone-throwing moved on to an exchange of gunfire.

Toward six o'clock in the evening, the passage du Saumon became a battlefield, with the rioters at one end, the troops at the other, shooting each other from opposite gates. One observer, a dreamer, the author of this book, who had gone to see the volcano up close, found himself caught in the crossfire in the arcade. All he had to protect himself from bullets was the bulging half-columns that divide the shops; he remained pinned in this delicate situation for close to half an hour.

Meanwhile the drums were drumming up the troops, the National Guards dressed and armed themselves in hot haste, the legions poured out of the *mairies,* the regiments poured out of the barracks. Opposite the passage de l'Ancre, a drummer received a thrust of a dagger. Another drummer in rue du Cygne was assailed by thirty or so young men who punctured his drum and took his saber. Yet another was killed in the rue Grenier-Saint-Lazare. In the rue Michel-le-Comte, three officers fell down dead one after the other. Several Municipal Guards, wounded in the rue des Lombards, turned back.

In front of the Cour-Batave, a detachment of National Guards found a red flag bearing this inscription: *Republican Revolution No. 127.* Was it actually a revolution?

The insurrection had turned the center of Paris into a sort of colossal, impenetrable, labyrinthine citadel. This was where the focal point was, it was obviously where the outcome would be decided. Everything else was a mere skirmish. The proof that everything would be decided there was that they were not fighting there yet.

In some regiments the soldiers were undecided, which added to the terrifying amorphousness of the crisis. They remembered the popular ovation that greeted the neutrality of the 53rd regiment of the line in July 1830. Two intrepid men, whose mettle had been tested and proved in the great wars, the maréchal de Lobau and General Bugeaud, commanded, Bugeaud under Lobau. Huge patrols, composed of regular battalions of the line flanked by whole companies of National Guards and preceded by a police commissioner in full regalia, set off to reconnoiter the insurgent streets. On their side, the insurgents posted sentinels at the corners of crossroads and boldly sent patrols beyond the barrières. Both sides kept close watch on each other. The government, with an army in hand, hesitated; night would soon be coming on and the tocsin of Saint-Merry[5] had begun to sound. The war minister of the day, the maréchal Soult,[6] who had seen Austerlitz, watched it all with a somber air.

These old hands, used to the correct maneuver and having only that battle compass, tactics, as a resort and guide, are quite disoriented when faced with the immense fuming known as public wrath. The winds of revolution are not easily controlled.

The National Guards from the suburbs raced in swiftly and chaotically. A battalion of the 12th Light galloped in from Saint-Denis; the 14th of the line arrived from Courbevoie; the batteries of the École Militaire took up position at the Carrousel; the artillery came across from Vincennes.

The Tuileries were isolated. Louis-Philippe was perfectly serene.

## V. Originality of Paris

In the past two years, as we said, Paris had seen more than one insurrection. Outside the insurgent quartiers, nothing is more weirdly calm as a rule than the face of Paris during a riot. Paris very quickly gets used to everything—it's only a riot—and Paris is so busy that it does not trouble itself for so little. Only such colossal cities can offer such spectacles. Only such vast enclosures can contain civil war and an indescribably odd tranquillity at the same time. Usually, when an insurrection kicks off, when you hear the drums, the recall, the alarm call, the shopkeeper is content merely to say: "Looks like there's a bit of trouble, rue Saint-Martin."

Or: "Faubourg Saint-Antoine."

Often he adds, nonchalantly: "Somewhere over that way."

Later, when the harrowing and mournful din of musketry and the gunfire of platoons makes itself heard, the shopkeeper says: "So, things are heating up, eh? Well, well, well; they're heating up!"

A moment later, if the riot gets closer and bigger, he swiftly shuts up shop and throws on his uniform; in other words, he secures his merchandise and puts his person at risk.

People shoot at each other at street corners, in arcades, in dead-end streets; barricades are taken, lost, and taken back; blood flows, house fronts are riddled with grapeshot, bullets kill people in their beds, dead bodies choke the pavements. A few streets away, you can hear the clinking of billiard balls in the cafés.

The curious laugh and chatter two feet away from these streets full of war;

the theaters open their doors and perform vaudeville. The fiacres roll along; people go off to dine *en ville.* Sometimes in the very quartier where the fighting is going on. In 1831,[1] a fusillade was suspended to let a wedding party pass.

In the insurrection of May 12, 1839,[2] in the rue Saint-Martin, a rickety little old man dragging a handcart with a tricolor cloth over it and carrying carafes filled with some kind of liquid, came and went from the barricade to the troops and from the troops to the barricade, impartially offering glasses of licorice water now to the government, now to the anarchists.

Nothing could be weirder; and that is precisely the nature of the riots peculiar to Paris which you will not find in any other capital. Two things are needed for this, the greatness of Paris and its gaiety. You need the city of Voltaire and the city of Napoléon.

Yet this time, in the military parade of June 5, 1832, the great city felt something that was perhaps greater than it. It felt fear. Everywhere, in the most remote and "uninvolved" quartiers, you saw doors, windows, and shutters closed in the middle of the day. The brave armed themselves, cowards hid. The insouciant bustling man on foot disappeared. Many streets were as empty as they would be at four o'clock in the morning. Alarming details made the rounds, ominous news was spread like wildfire. It was said that *they* had gained control of the Banque de France; that, in the Saint-Merry cloister alone, there were six hundred of them, entrenched and fortified in the church; that the line was not secure; that Armand Carrel had been to see the maréchal Clauzel[3] and that the maréchal had said, "Get a regiment together first"; that Lafayette was sick, but had told them anyhow, "I am at your disposal. I'll follow you wherever there's room for a chair"; that everyone had to stay on their guard; that come nightfall, there would be people looting isolated houses in the deserted corners of Paris (here you could detect the imagination of the police at work—that Anne Radcliffe[4] embedded in the government); that a battery had been planted in the rue Aubry-le-Boucher; that Lobau and Bugeaud[5] were conferring and that at midnight, or at daybreak at the latest, four columns would march at the same time on the center of the riot, the first coming from the Bastille, the second from the porte Saint-Martin, the third from La Grève, the fourth from Les Halles; that perhaps the troops would also evacuate Paris and withdraw to the Champ de Mars; that no one knew what would happen but that one thing was for sure and that was that, this time, it was serious. Everyone was worried about Maréchal Soult's holding back. Why didn't he attack right away? One thing is certain and that was that he was deeply absorbed. The old lion seemed to scent some unknown monster in the shadows.

Evening came, the theaters did not open; the patrols did the rounds looking peevish; pedestrians were searched; suspects were arrested. By nine o'clock, more than eight hundred people had been arrested; the prefecture of police was packed, the Conciergerie was packed, La Force was packed. At the Conciergerie, in particular, the long underground tunnel known as the rue de Paris was strewn with bundles of straw on which a heap of prisoners lay, being harangued, valiantly, by Lagrange, the man from Lyon.[6] The rustling of all that straw, tossed around by all those men, made a noise like a shower of rain. Elsewhere prisoners lay in the open air in the prison yards, piled on top of each other. A feeling of foreboding was everywhere, and a certain tremulousness, most unusual for Paris.

People barricaded themselves in their houses; wives and mothers fretted; all you heard was: "Oh, my God! He hasn't come home!" In the distance, carriages were only very rarely heard bowling along. People listened, on their doorsteps, to the noise, the shouting, the commotion, the muted and indistinct sounds, things about which they said, "That's the cavalry," or, "That's the caissons galloping along," the bugles, the drums, the fusillades, and, especially, the mournful tocsin of Saint-Merry. Everyone was waiting for the first cannonball to be fired. Armed men surged up at street corners and then vanished, shouting: "Go home!" And everyone bolted their doors as fast as they could. They said: "How will it all end?" With each passing moment, as night came down and the twilight thickened, Paris seemed to redden ever more woefully with the fearful blaze of the riot.

# BOOK ELEVEN

# THE ATOM FRATERNIZES
# WITH THE HURRICANE

### I. SOME INSIGHTS INTO THE ORIGINS OF GAVROCHE'S POETRY—INFLUENCE OF AN ACADEMICIAN ON THIS POETRY

At the instant that the insurrection, arising from the clash between the people and the troops in front of the Arsenal, inspired a backing-off in the multitude who were following the hearse and who, all the way along the boulevards, weighed, so to speak, on the head of the convoy, there was a terrible backward surge. The crowd rocked, the rows broke up, everyone ran, took to their heels, escaped, some with battle cries, others with the pallor of flight. The great river that covered the boulevards split in the twinkling of an eye, overflowing to left and right and pouring in torrents down two hundred streets at once, streaming like water through opened sluice gates. At that moment a ragged little boy, who was coming down the rue Ménilmontant holding in his hand a branch of laburnum in bloom which he had just picked on the heights of Belleville, caught sight of an old horse pistol in the shopwindow of a bric-a-brac dealer's. He threw his flowering branch on the pavement and said: "Mother Whatsit, I think I'll just borrow your thingy."

And he ran off with the pistol.

Two minutes later, a flood of terrified bourgeois fleeing down the rue Amelot and the rue Basse ran into the boy brandishing his pistol and singing:

> You can't see a thing at night,
> Of a day, all's clear and bright,
> A spurious note
> Gets your burgher by the throat,
> So please be good
> Pointy-hatted hood![1]

It was little Gavroche going off to war.

It wasn't till he was on the boulevard that he saw that the pistol had no hammer.

Who wrote this refrain that helped him keep time as he walked along—and all the other songs that, on occasion, he liked to sing? We have no idea. Who knows? Maybe he did. In any case Gavroche was up with all the popular ditties in circulation and he put in his own babble to boot. An imp and a little devil, he made a medley of the voices of nature and the voices of Paris. He combined the repertoire of the birds with the repertoire of the workshops. He knew some artists' apprentices, a tribe closely related to his own. He had been, it seems, an apprentice printer for three months. One day he had done an errand for Monsieur Baour-Lormian,[2] one of the Forty. Gavroche was a gamin of letters.

Besides, Gavroche had no idea that on that horrible rainy night when he had offered two little mites the hospitality of his elephant, it was for his own brothers that he had played the part of Providence. His brothers in the evening, his father next morning; such had been his night. When he came out of the rue des Ballets just after dawn, he had rushed back to the elephant, had artfully extracted the two little boys, had shared whatever he was able to invent for breakfast, then gone off again, handing them over to that excellent mother, the street, who had more or less raised him. As he was leaving them, he arranged to meet them that same evening at the same place, and had left them with these words by way of goodbye: "I'm going to beat it, in other words, I'm taking off, or, as they say at court, I'll skedaddle. Kidlingtons, if you don't find Mummy and Daddy, come back this evening. I'll rustle up some tucker for you and put you up for the night." The two little boys, picked up by some police officer and parked at the station, or stolen by some traveling showman, or simply lost in the vast Chinese puzzle that is Paris, had not returned. The dregs of our current social world are full of such lost traces. Gavroche had not seen them again. Ten or twelve weeks had gone by since that night. More than once he had scratched his head and asked himself: "Where the devil are my two children?"

Meanwhile, pistol in hand, he had reached the rue du Pont-aux-Choux. He noticed that there was only one shop open in that street and, something that gave pause for thought, it was a patisserie. This was a heaven-sent opportunity to eat another apple turnover before launching into the unknown. Gavroche stopped, patted his sides, fumbled in his fob gusset, turned his pockets inside out, found nothing, not a sou, and began to shout: "Help!"

It is hard to miss out on the greatest cake there is.

Gavroche went on his way, anyway.

Two minutes later he was in the rue Saint-Louis. Crossing the rue du Parc-Royal, he felt the need to compensate himself for the impossible apple turnover and so gave himself the immense pleasure of tearing down the theater posters in broad daylight.

A bit farther along, seeing a group of well-heeled burghers go by who looked to him to be men of property, he shrugged his shoulders and randomly spat out this mouthful of philosophical bile: "These rich bastards, God they're fat! They stuff themselves. They wallow in fine dinners. Ask them what they do with their money. They haven't got a clue. They eat it, that's what they do with it! Gone with the wind of the gut."

## II. GAVROCHE ON THE MARCH

Waving a hammerless—"dogless"—pistol around in your hand in the middle of the street is such a public service that Gavroche felt his verve increasing with each step. He shouted, between the snatches of the "Marseillaise" that he was singing: "All's well. My left paw hurts like blazes, my rheumatism's killing me, but I am happy, citizens. All the bourgeois have to do is behave themselves, I'll belt out a few subversive lines for them. What are stool pigeons? They're dogs, by jingo! But let's have a bit of respect for dogs. I could use a dog myself on my pistol. I've come from the boulevard, my friends, it's getting hot, it's simmering along nicely, it's nearly on the boil. Time to give the pot a good skim. Forward, men! Let impure blood flood our furrows!¹ I give my life for the homeland, I'll never see my concubine again, hey nonny-nonny, all over, yes. Ninny! Gone! But who cares, long live joy! Let's have it out, damn it! I've had a gutful of despotism."

At that instant, the horse of a National Guard lancer riding past came crashing down, Gavroche laid his pistol on the ground and pulled the man up, then he helped pull up the horse. After which he picked up his pistol and continued on his way.

In the rue de Thorigny all was peace and quiet. This apathetic stillness, peculiar to the Marais, contrasted with the vast surrounding uproar. Four gossips were jabbering away on a doorstep. Scotland has its trios of witches,² but Paris has its quartets of gossips; and the "thou shalt be king hereafter," hurled at Macbeth on the heath at Armuyr, would be just as ominous hurled at Bonaparte in Baudoyer Square. The croaking would be more or less the same.

The gossips of the rue de Thorigny were exclusively caught up in their own affairs. Three of them were porters and the other one, with her sack and her hook, was the rag-and-bone dealer–*cum*–garbage collector that is known as a *chiffonnière*.

They seemed, all four of them, to be standing at the four corners of old age—decay, decrepitude, ruin, and sorrow.

The rag-and-bone woman was humble. In this all-weather world, the rag-and-bone woman greets, the porter protects. It all depends on where the concierge draws the boundary line, for the pickings may be big or small, according to the whim of whoever is sweeping the garbage into a pile. Even a broom can show goodwill.

This particular rag-and-bone woman was a grateful old sack and she smiled—what a smile!—to the three porter women. The talk ran along the following lines:

"Heavens, so your cat's still mean?"

"My God, cats, you know, are the natural enemy of dogs. It's the dogs that have something to complain about."

"People, too."

"And yet cat fleas don't go after people."

"That's not the trouble, dogs—dogs is dangerous. I remember one year when there was so many dogs they were forced to put it in the papers. It was the days when they had great big sheep in the Tuileries that used to pull the little carriage of the king of Rome. You remember the king of Rome?"

"Me, I was fond of the duc de Bordeaux."

"Me, I knew Louis XVII.³ I prefer Louis XVII."

"Meat's dear, Ma Patagon!"

"Ah, don't talk to me about meat, the butcher's is shocking. Truly shocking. All they've got now is tough old leftovers."

Here the rag-and-bone woman broke in: "Ladies, trade's poor. The garbage piles are lousy. No one's throwing anything away these days. They eat everything."

"There's poorer folks than you, Vargoulême."

"Well, that's true," replied the rag-and-bone woman deferentially. "Me, I've got a job."

There was a pause and the rag-and-bone woman, yielding to that need for display that is at the bottom of mankind, added: "In the morning when I get home, I go through the sack, I take me peck [probably pick], I do me sortie [probably sorting]. I end up with great heaps in me room. I put the rags in a basket, the scraps in a tub, the linen in me cupboard, the woolens in me chest of drawers, the old papers in a corner of the window, anything worth eating in me bowl, the bits of glass in the fireplace, the old shoes behind the door, and the bones under me bed."

Gavroche, who had stopped behind, was listening: "Hey, old girls," he said, "what business do you have talking politics?"

A volley assailed him, composed of a quadruple hissing and booing.

"There's another little stinker for you!"

"What's he got in his mitt, then? A pistol!"

"I ask you, a slip of a kid like that!"

"It's not happy unless it's knocking over authority."

Gavroche, contemptuous, restricted himself, by way of retort, to lifting his nose with his thumb while opening his hand completely.

The rag-and-bone woman cried: "Cheeky little tramp!"

The one who answered to the name of Patagon clapped her hands together, scandalized: "There's going to be trouble, that's for sure. That little shyster next door with his goatee, I see him go past every morning with a young thing in a pink cap on his arm, today I saw him go past and he was giving his arm to a musket. Ma Bacheux reckons there was a revolution just this last week at . . . at . . . at . . . Where's that cow of a place! Pontoise. And then, this look-at-me here, with his pistol, this horrible little twirp! Apparently there are cannons all over the Célestins. What do you want the government to do with little wastrels who've got nothing better to do than think of ways to upset everyone, just when things were starting to quiet down a bit again after all the troubles we've had. Lord Almighty, that poor queen I seen go by in the cart! And it's all going to send the prices up. It's a disgrace! No doubt about it, I'll be going to see you guillotined, you little swine!"

"You're sniffling, old girl," said Gavroche. "Blow your hooter, why don't you."

And he moved on. When he had got to the rue Pavée, the rag-and-bone woman came back into his mind and he uttered this soliloquy: "You are wrong to insult revolutionaries, mother Gutter-Sweep. This pistol here is to act on your behalf. It's so you have more stuff worth eating in your sack."

All of a sudden he heard a noise behind him; it was the porter woman, Patagon, who had followed him and who, from a distance, was showing him her fist and shouting: "You are nothing but a bastard!"

"As for that," said Gavroche, "I am—profoundly—indifferent."

Soon after, he was passing the Hôtel Lamoignon.[4] There, he let out this call: "En route for battle!"

And he was overcome by a fit of melancholy. He looked at his pistol with an air of reproach as though he was trying to soften it.

"I go off," he said, "but you can't go off."

One dog may distract attention from another. A very skinny poodle had just walked past. Gavroche was moved to pity.

"You poor little pooch," he said to it, "did you swallow a barrel, then, for your ribs to be sticking out everywhere like that."

Then he headed for the Orme-Saint-Gervais.

### III. A WIGMAKER'S JUST INDIGNATION

The worthy wigmaker who had chased away the two little boys to whom Gavroche had opened the elephant's paternal intestines was at this moment in his shop busy shaving an old legionnaire who had served under the Empire. They were chatting. The wigmaker had naturally spoken to the veteran about the riot, then about General Lamarque, and from Lamarque they had come to the emperor. Hence a conversation between a barber and a soldier which Prud-homme,[1] had he been there, would have embellished with a flourish or two and called "Dialogue of the Razor and the Saber."

"Monsieur," said the wigmaker, "how did the emperor mount his horse?"

"Badly. He didn't know how to fall. So he never did."

"Did he have beautiful horses? He must have had beautiful horses?"

"The day he gave me the cross, I noticed his nag. She was a racing mare, all white. She had wide-set ears, a deep saddle, a fine head with a black mark like a star, a very long neck, strongly jointed knees, protruding ribs, sloping shoulders, a powerful rump. A bit over fifteen hands high."

"A nice horse," said the wigmaker.

"It was His Majesty's animal."

The wigmaker felt that after those words a small pause was appropriate, which he observed, and then resumed: "The emperor was only ever wounded once, Monsieur, isn't that so?"

The old soldier replied in the calm and sovereign tone of one who was there: "In the heel. At Ratisbon.[2] I never saw him so spruced up as that day. He was as shiny as a pin."

"What about you, Monsieur le vétéran, you must have been wounded quite a bit?"

"Me?" said the soldier. "Ah, nothing much. At Marengo I caught a couple of saber slashes on the back of the neck, a bullet in my right arm at Austerlitz, another in my left hip at Jena, a jab with a bayonet at Friedland—here—in Moscow, seven or eight thrusts of a lance here, there, and everywhere, in Lutzen a shell burst and crushed a finger . . . Ah! and then at Waterloo a Biscay musket ball in the thigh. That's about it."

"What a beautiful thing," cried the wigmaker in a Pindaric[3] tone, "to die on the field of battle! Me, word of honor, rather than croak in the cot, of illness, slowly, a bit more every day, with drugs and poultices and syringes and the doctor, I'd rather catch a cannonball in the guts!"

"You're not squeamish," said the soldier.

He had only just finished when a dreadful crash shook the shop. One of the windowpanes in the shop front had suddenly been shattered. The wigmaker went white.

"My God!" he yelped. "There's one now!"

"What?"

"A cannonball."

"Here it is," said the soldier.

And he picked up something that was rolling on the ground. It was a pebble.

The wigmaker ran to the broken window and saw Gavroche running away as fast as his legs would carry him toward the Saint-Jean market. As he was going past the wigmaker's, Gavroche, who had the two little kids on his mind, had not been able to resist the desire to greet him and had thrown a stone through his window.

"You see that!" screamed the wigmaker, who had gone from white to purple. "He makes trouble for the heck of it. What did anyone ever do to that kid anyway?"

## IV. THE BOY MARVELS AT THE OLD MAN

Meanwhile Gavroche, at the Saint-Jean market, where the guards posted were already disarmed, had joined up with a gang led by Enjolras, Courfeyrac, Combeferre, and Feuilly. They were more or less armed. Bahorel and Jean Prouvaire caught up with them and swelled their number. Enjolras had a double-barreled fowling piece, Combeferre a National Guard fusil bearing the number of the legion, as well as two pistols in his belt that his unbuttoned overcoat revealed, Jean Prouvaire an old cavalry carbine, Bahorel a hunting rifle, and Courfeyrac was waving around an unsheathed sword cane. Feuilly, a drawn saber in his hand, was marching in front crying: "Long live Poland!"[1]

They were coming from the quai Morland, cravatless, hatless, breathless, soaked by the rain, lightning in their eyes. Gavroche calmly accosted them.

"Where are we going?"

"Come along," said Courfeyrac.

Behind Feuilly, Bahorel was marching, or rather, bounding, a fish in the water of the riot. He was wearing a crimson waistcoat and he was swearing like a trooper. One passerby was bowled over by his waistcoat and cried out, frantic: "Here come the reds!"

"The red, the reds!" replied Bahorel. "What are you frightened of, my good bourgeois. You won't see me trembling at the sight of a red poppy, Little Red Riding Hood does not inspire me with horror. Bourgeois, believe me, we ought to leave fear of red to horned beasts."

He eyed a bit of wall plastered with the most pacific sheet of paper in the world, an authorization to eat eggs, the pastoral letter for Lent from the archbishop of Paris to his "flock."

Bahorel shouted: "Flock—that's a polite way of saying sheep."

And he ripped the pastoral letter off the wall. This won Gavroche over. From that moment, Gavroche began to study Bahorel closely.

"Bahorel," observed Enjolras, "you're wrong. You should have left that pastoral letter alone, that's not what we're about, you're wasting your anger on nothing. Hold your fire. You don't shoot outside the ranks any more with your soul than you do with your gun."

"To each his own, Enjolras," Bahorel shot back. "This bishop's prose shocks me, I want to be able to eat eggs without someone authorizing me to do so. You, you're the burning-ice type; me, I have fun. Besides, I'm not wasting my anger, I'm just warming up; and if I rip up pastoral letters, by Hercules! it's only to work up an appetite."

That word, *Hercules,* struck Gavroche. He was always looking for any opportunity to educate himself and this ripper-upper of posters had gained his esteem. He asked him: "What does that mean, *Hercules?*"

Bahorel answered: "It means 'holy hell' in Latin."

Here Bahorel recognized a pale young man with a black beard at a window, watching them go past, probably a Friend of the ABC. He shouted to him: "Quick! cartridges! *para bellum.*"[2]

"*Bel homme*—handsome! It's true," said Gavroche, who now understood Latin.

A boisterous cortège accompanied them, students, artists, young men affiliated with the Cougourde d'Aix, workers, dockers, armed with clubs and bayonets, some like Combeferre with pistols stuck in their trousers. An old man, who looked really old, was marching with this band. He had no weapon and was rushing so as not to be left behind, although he looked lost in thought. Gavroche spotted him: "Whassat?" he said to Courfeyrac.

"Some old man."

It was Monsieur Mabeuf.

## V. The Old Man

Here's what had happened:

Enjolras and his friends were on the boulevard Bourdon near the grain warehouses just as the dragoons had charged. Enjolras, Courfeyrac, and Combeferre were among those who took to the rue Bassompierre shouting: "To the barricades!" In the rue Lesdiguières they had run into an old man walking along.

What got their attention was that this old man was zigzagging from one side of the street to the other as if he were drunk. On top of that, he had his hat in his hand even though it had rained all morning and it was raining pretty hard at that very moment. Courfeyrac had recognized old Mabeuf. He knew him from having seen him many times walking Marius to the front door. Knowing the peaceful and more than shy habits of the old churchwarden bookworm, and amazed to see him in the midst of all the mayhem, two feet from the cavalry charges, almost in the middle of a fusillade, bareheaded in the pouring rain and strolling among the bullets, he went over to him, and the twenty-five-year-old rioter and the octogenarian had exchanged this dialogue:

"Monsieur Mabeuf, go home."

"Why?"

"There's going to be some strife."

"Good."

"Sword thrusts and gunshot, Monsieur Mabeuf."

"Good."

"Cannon fire."

"Good. Where are you off to, you fellows?"

"We're off to overthrow the government."

"Good."

And he started to follow them. From that moment, he had not said a word. His stride suddenly became firm, a few workmen had offered him their arm but he had refused with a shake of the head. He had surged ahead practically to the front of the column, his movements both those of a man on the march and of a sleeping man, at once.

"There's a great old militant for you!" mumured the students. The rumor rippled through the crowd that he was a former member of the Convention, an old regicide.

The company had turned into the rue de la Verrerie. Little Gavroche marched at the head singing this song at the top of his lungs, like a kind of bugler. He sang:

> Here's the moon coming out
> Let's go to the forest round about.
> Charlot said to Charlotte.
>
>> Tou tou tou
>> For Chatou.
> I have only one God, one king, one sou, and one boot.
>> Early in the morning, having fasted,
>> Two sparrows drank the dew
>> On the thyme and got plastered.
>
>> Zi zi zi
>> For Passy.
> I have only one God, one king, one sou, and one boot.
>> And those two poor wolf cubs
>> Were stewed like two grubs;
>> In his lair a tiger had a good hoot.
>
>> Don don don
>> For Meudon.
> I have only one God, one king, one sou, and one boot.
>> One swore and the other cursed
>> We'll go to the forest or I'll burst.
>> Charlot said to Charlotte.

Tin tin tin
For Pantin.
I have only one God, one king, one sou, and one boot.[1]

They made their way toward Saint-Merry.

## VI. Recruits

The band was growing by the second. Near the rue des Billettes, a tall man, graying, whose rough and reckless mien Courfeyrac, Enjolras, and Combeferre remarked on, but whom none of them knew, joined them. Gavroche, busy singing, whistling, humming, charging ahead and banging shop shutters with the butt of his hammerless pistol, paid the man no attention.

As it happened, in the rue de la Verrerie, they went past Courfeyrac's door.

"This is a stroke of luck," said Courfeyrac. "I forgot my purse and I lost my hat." He peeled off from the crowd and bounded upstairs to his place four steps at a time. He grabbed an old hat and his purse. He also grabbed a fairly large square box the size of a big suitcase that was hidden in his dirty washing. As he was running back down again the concièrge hailed him.

"Monsieur de Courfeyrac!"

"Portress, what is your name?" Courfeyrac shot back.

The portress was baffled.

"Why, you know very well, I'm the concierge, my name is mother Veuvain."

"Well, then, if you call me Monsieur de Courfeyrac again, I'll call you mother de Veuvain. Now speak, what is it? What's up?"

"There's someone here who wants to talk to you."

"Who's that?"

"I don't know."

"Where are they?"

"In my lodge."

"Blast them!" said Courfeyrac.

"But he's been waiting for over an hour for you to come back!" the portress insisted.

At the same time, a sort of young workman, thin, pale, small, freckled, dressed in a torn smock and patched-up corduroy trousers, who looked more like a girl playing a boy than a man, came out of the lodge and told Courfeyrac in a voice that was certainly not in any way like a woman's voice: "Monsieur Marius, please?"

"He's not in."

"Will he be back this evening?"

"I haven't a clue."

Courfeyrac added: "As for me, I won't be back."

The young man looked him steadily in the eye and asked him: "Why's that?"

"Because."

"Where are you off to, then?"

"What's it to you?"

"Would you like me to carry your box?"

"I'm off to the barricades."

"Would you like me to go with you?"

"If you like!" answered Courfeyrac. "The street's free, the cobblestones belong to everyone."

And he ran off to catch up with his friends. When he caught up with them, he gave the box to one of them to carry. It was only a good fifteen minutes later that he saw that the young man had, indeed, tagged along behind.

A crowd that gathers does not exactly go where it would like. We explained that it is swept along by the wind. They passed Saint-Merry and found themselves, without really knowing how, in the rue Saint-Denis.

# BOOK TWELVE

# CORINTHE[1]

## I. HISTORY OF CORINTHE FROM ITS FOUNDATION

Parisians today who enter the rue Rambuteau coming from Les Halles and notice, on their right, opposite the rue Mondétour, a basket weaver's shop whose sign is a basket in the shape of the emperor, Napoléon the Great, with this inscription:

NAPOLÉON IS MADE
ENTIRELY OF WICKERWORK

have no inkling of the terrible scenes that this same spot saw barely thirty years ago.

This is the site of the rue de la Chanvrerie, which used to be spelled Chanverrerie in old deeds, as well as the famous tavern known as Corinthe.

You will recall all that has been said about the barricade put up on this spot and eclipsed, as it happens, by the barricade at Saint-Merry. It is over this famous barricade in the rue de la Chanvrerie, nowadays vanished into the mists of time, that we will now throw a little light.

I hope, for the sake of the tale's clarity, we may be allowed to resort to a simple device already used on Waterloo. Anyone wanting to get a pretty precise image of the jumble of houses that stood in those days near the tip of Saint-Eustache, at the northeast corner of Les Halles of Paris, where the rue Rambuteau comes out today, has only to imagine an N, joining the rue Saint-Denis at the top and Les Halles at the bottom. The two vertical strokes would be the rue de la Grande-Truanderie and the rue de la Chanvrerie and the horizontal stroke would be the rue de la Petite-Truanderie.[1] The old rue Mondétour cut the three strokes at the most tortured angles. So much so that the tangled maze of the four streets was enough to create, over a space of less than two hundred square yards between Les Halles and the rue Saint-Denis on one side, and between the rue du Cygne and the rue des Prêcheurs on the other, seven islands of houses, bizarrely shaped, of varying sizes, placed crookedly and apparently randomly and barely separated, like blocks of stone on a building site, by narrow crevices.

We say narrow crevices and we can't give a better idea of these dark, constricted, angular lanes, bordered by eight-story slums. These slums were so decrepit that, in the streets of la Chanvrerie and de la Petite-Truanderie, the façades were propped up by wooden beams that ran from one house to the next. The street was narrow and the gutters wide, so anyone walking along had to wend their way on a pavement that was always wet, alongside shops like cellars, great big iron-hooped curbstones, unbelievable mounds of garbage, alley gates fortified with enormous age-old grilles. The rue Rambuteau laid waste to all that.

The name Mondétour wonderfully conjures up the way the whole of this road network snaked around. A bit farther along, this was even better expressed by the rue Pirouette, which flowed into the rue Mondétour.

The pedestrian coming from the rue Saint-Denis and going into the rue de la Chanvrerie saw it gradually shrivel away in front of him as though he had stepped into an elongated funnel. At the end of the street, which was incredibly short, he found the way barred on the Les Halles side by a tall row of houses and he would have thought himself in a dead end if he did not see, to right and left, two black trenches down which he could escape. This was the rue Mondétour, which went off to join the rue des Prêcheurs on one side, and, on the other, the rue du Cygne and the rue de la Petite-Truanderie. At the bottom of this sort of dead end, at the corner of the right-hand trench, you noticed a house that was not nearly as tall as the rest and that formed a sort of promontory on the street.

It is in this house, only two stories high, that an illustrious tavern had been merrily chugging along for the past three hundred years. This tavern made a joyous racket on the very spot old Théophile[2] noted in these two lines:

Here bobs the horrible skeleton
Of a poor lover who hanged himself.[3]

The position was good and the tavern was handed down from father to son.

In the days of Mathurin Régnier[4] the tavern was called the Pot-aux-Roses and as plays on words were all the rage, the sign was a post—*poteau*—painted rose pink. In the last century, the worthy Natoire,[5] one of the masters of whimsy now scorned by the school of rigidity, having gotten tipsy several times in this tavern at the very table where Régnier got plastered, had painted a bunch of Corinth grapes on a rose pink post out of gratitude. The publican gleefully changed his sign and had these words done in gold letters below the bunch of grapes: *au Raisin de Corinthe*. Hence the name, Corinthe. Nothing comes more naturally to staggering drunks than elliptical expressions. The elliptical expression is the zigzagging phrase. Corinthe had gradually dethroned the Pot-aux-Roses. The last publican of the dynasty, old man Hucheloup, not even having a clue about the tradition anymore, had had the post painted blue.

A downstairs room where the bar was, a room on the first floor where the billiard table was, a wooden spiral staircase going through the ceiling, wine on the tables, soot on the walls, candles in broad daylight—that was what the tavern was like. A stairwell with a trapdoor in the basement room led to the cellar. On the second floor were the Hucheloups' rooms. You went up by a staircase, more like a ladder than a staircase, the only entrance being a door hidden in the main room on the first floor. Under the roof, two garrets with dormer windows, servants' nests. The kitchen shared the ground floor with the bar-room.

Old father Hucheloup may have been a born chemist; he was certainly a cook. You not only drank in his tavern, you ate there. Hucheloup had invented an excellent thing you could only get at his establishment and that was stuffed carp, which he called *carpes au gras*. This was eaten by the light of a tallow candle or an oil lamp from the days of Louis XVI on tables where an oilskin was nailed down as a tablecloth. People came from miles around. One fine day, Hucheloup decided the time had come to alert the passing trade to his "specialty"; he dipped a brush into a pot of black and as his spelling was peculiar to him, just like his cooking, he improvised on a wall outside this remarkable inscription:

CARPES HO GRAS

One winter the storms and squalls got it into their heads to wipe out the *s* at the end of the first word and the *g* at the start of the third, and this is what was left:

CARPE HO RAS

With the help of time and the rain, a humble gastronomical advertisement had become a profound piece of advice: Seize the hours.

And so it was that, not knowing French, old father Hucheloup had come up with Latin and brought philosophy out of the kitchen; wanting simply to erase

Lent, he had equaled Horace. And the striking thing was that this also meant: Come into my tavern.

Not a trace of all this exists today. The Mondétour maze was ripped up and largely opened up in 1847 and may well be no more at the present time. The rue de la Chanvrerie has disappeared, and Corinthe with it, under the pavement of the rue Rambuteau.

As we said, Corinthe was one of those places where Courfeyrac and his friends gathered, if not rallied. It was Grantaire who had discovered Corinthe. He had gone in because of the *Carpe horas* and had gone back because of the *Carpes au gras*. They drank there, they ate there, they spouted there; they paid little, they paid badly, they did not pay at all, yet they were always welcome. Old man Hucheloup was a good sport.

This good sport, Hucheloup, as we said, was a mustachioed keeper of the grittier sort of tavern; an amusing variety. He always looked as if he was in a bad mood, seemed bent on intimidating the clientele, growled at people coming into his place, and looked like he'd rather pick a fight with them than serve them soup. And yet, we say again, everyone was always welcome. This quirkiness ensured that the place was always full, and brought him young men who would say to each other: "Come and see old man Hucheloup blow his top." He had been a fencing master. He had a way of bursting out laughing all of a sudden. Big booming voice, but a good old fellow with it. He was at bottom a comedian behind a tragic mask; he liked nothing better than to scare you; a bit like those snuffboxes in the shape of a pistol. The shot is a sneeze. His wife, mother Hucheloup, was an uncommonly ugly bearded woman.

Around 1830, old man Hucheloup died. The secret of the *carpes au gras* died with him. His widow, who was barely consolable, kept the tavern going. But the cooking degenerated and became execrable, and the wine, which had always been bad, was now shocking. Courfeyrac and his friends continued to haunt Corinthe, though—out of pity, said Bossuet.

Widow Hucheloup was short-winded and misshapen, full of country memories. She relieved their tiresomeness by her pronunciation. She had her own way of saying things that spiced up these springtime village reminiscences of hers. Once upon a time it had been her delight, she claimed, to hear "the bread-breasts sing in the hawkthorns."

The room on the upper floor, where the "restaurant" was, was a great long well crammed with stools, stepladders, chairs, benches, and tables and with a rickety old billiard table. You reached it by the spiral staircase that came out in a corner of the room in a square hole like a ship's hatch.

This room, lit by a single narrow window and an oil lamp that was always burning, was a real shambles. All the furniture with four legs behaved as though they had three. As sole decoration, the whitewashed walls had this quatrain in honor of mother Hucheloup:

She passes at ten paces, she horrifies at two,
A wart lives up her nose, so risky—true;
You're worried all the time she'll blow down the house,
And that one fine day her nose will fall into her mouth.[6]

This was written in charcoal on the wall.

Ma Hucheloup, true to life, went back and forth morning and night in front of those four lines with perfect serenity. Two servants, called Matelotte, Fish Stew, and Gibelotte, Rabbit Stew, whose real names no one ever knew, helped Ma Hucheloup deck the tables with the carafes of dark rotgut wine and the various gruels that were served to the hungry in earthenware bowls. Matelotte, fat, round, ruddy, and loud, former favorite sultaness of the late Hucheloup, was uglier than any mythological monster you care to name; and yet, as it is only fitting that the servant should always trail behind the mistress of the house, she was not as ugly as Ma Hucheloup. Gibelotte, long, delicate, white with a lymphatic whiteness, with rings round her eyes, drooping eyelids, always exhausted and overwhelmed, suffering from what we might call chronic fatigue, first up, last to bed, served everyone, even the other servant, silently and sweetly, smiling beneath the fatigue with a sort of sleepy vague smile.

There was a mirror above the bar.

Before entering the restaurant room, you could read this line written in chalk over the door by Courfeyrac:

REVEL IF YOU CAN AND EAT IF YOU DARE.[7]

## II. PRELIMINARY GAIETIES

L'Aigle de Meaux, as we know, lived rather more with Joly than anywhere else. He had a room the way a bird has a branch. The two friends lived together, ate together, slept together. They shared everything, even Musichetta, a little. They were what the hooded friars call *bini*,[1] a pair. On the morning of June 5, they went off to have breakfast at Corinthe. Joly was all stuffed up with a bad head cold that Laigle was beginning to share. Laigle's coat was threadbare, but Joly was dapper.

It was about nine in the morning when they pushed open the door of Corinthe. They went up to the first floor. Matelotte and Gibelotte greeted them.

"Oysters, cheese, and ham," said Laigle.

And they sat down at a table. The tavern was empty; they were the only ones there. Gibelotte recognized Joly and Laigle and plunked a bottle of wine on the table.

As they were downing their first oysters, a head appeared at the stairwell hatch and a voice said: "I was just passing when I caught a heady whiff of Brie from the street. I'm coming in."

It was Grantaire. Grantaire took a stool and planted himself at the table. Gibelotte, seeing Grantaire, put another two bottles of wine on the table. That made three.

"Are you going to drink those two bottles?" Laigle asked Grantaire.

Grantaire answered: "Everyone else is ingenious, you alone are ingenuous. No one ever balked at two bottles."

The others had begun by eating, Grantaire began by drinking. Half a bottle was swiftly dispatched.

"Have you got hollow legs?" said Laigle.

"You obviously have," said Grantaire. He emptied his glass and added: "Dear me, Laigle of the funeral orations,[2] your coat has had it."

"I should hope so," Laigle retorted. "It means we get on well together, my coat and I. It's taken on all my wrinkles, it doesn't get in my way at all, it has molded itself to all my deformities, it goes along with all my movements, I only know it's there because it keeps me warm. Old coats are exactly the same as old friends."

"True," cried Joly, chiming in. "An old coat is an old goat."

"Especially," said Grantaire, "in the mouth of a man stuffed up with a cold."

"Grantaire," Laigle asked, "did you come from the boulevard?"

"No."

"We just saw the head of the procession go by, Joly and I."

"It is a barvelous sight," said Joly.

"This street is so quiet!" cried Laigle. "Who would ever suspect that Paris is in pandemonium? You can really tell it used to be all convents around here! Du Breul and Sauval list all of them and so does the abbé Lebeuf. They were all around here, the place was crawling with them, the shod, the unshod, the tonsured, the bearded, the grays, the blacks, the whites, the Franciscans, the Minimi, the Capuchins, the Carmelites, the Lesser Augustines, the Greater Augustines, the Old Augustines. The place was riddled with them."

"Don't talk to me about monks," Grantaire cut in. "It makes you want to scratch yourself."

Then he exclaimed: "Errk! I've just swallowed a bad oyster. Looks like my hypochondria's back. The oysters are off, the servants are dogs. How I hate the human race. I was in the rue Richelieu just now and I went past the big public library. That great mound of oyster shells[3] they call a library—it makes me sick just thinking about it. All that paper! All that ink! All that scribbling! Someone wrote all that! What moron once said that man was a biped without feathers? And then I ran into a pretty girl I know, lovely as springtime, a girl worthy of being called Floréal, and she was delighted, overjoyed, delirious, in seventh heaven, the poor silly goose, because yesterday some ghastly banker, pitted with smallpox, deigned to fancy her! Alas! A woman watches the quack treating her as keenly as her case of thrush; cats chase mice as well as birds. This little madam, not even two months ago, was sitting pretty in a garret, fitting the little copper rings in the eyeholes of corsets, what do you call those things? She sewed, she slept on a camp bed, she lived with a flowerpot for company, she was content. Now she's a lady banker. This transformation happened overnight. I met the victim this morning, jubilant. The awful part of it is that the brazen hussy was just as pretty today as she was yesterday. Her financier didn't show on her face. Roses are better or worse than women in that you can see when the grubs have been attacking them. Ah, there is no morality on this earth. I call as my witness the myrtle, symbol of love, the laurel, symbol of war, the olive, that ninny, symbol of peace, the apple that nearly choked Adam with its pips, and the fig leaf, ancestor of the petticoat. As to justice, do you want to know what justice is? The Gauls covet Clusium, Rome defends Clusium and asks them what wrong Clusium has done to them. Brennus replies: 'The wrong Alba did to you, the wrong Fidenae did to you, the wrong the Aequi, the Volsci, and the Sabines did to you.[4] They were your neighbors. The Clusians are ours. We understand neighborliness the same way you do. You stole Alba, we are taking Clusium.' Rome says: 'You will not take Clusium.' Brennus took Rome. Then he cried: *'Vae victis!'* Woe to the vanquished! That's what justice is! Ah, in this world, there are only beasts of prey! only eagles! only eagles! It makes my skin crawl."

He held his glass out to Joly, who refilled it, then he drank, and proceeded, almost without having been interrupted by this glass of wine which no one noticed, not even himself.

"Brennus, who takes Rome, is an eagle; the banker, who takes the little working girl, is an eagle. One is as shameless as the other. So we may as well believe in nothing. There's only one reality: drinking. Whatever your opinion, whether you are for the lean cock like the canton of Uri, or for the fat cock like the canton of Glaris,[5] it matters little, so drink. You talk to me about the boulevard, the procession, etc. Well, well, so there's going to be another revolution, is there? This poverty of means amazes me on the part of the good Lord. He has to keep on greasing the groove of events without letup. Things get stuck, they won't shift. Quick, a revolution. The good Lord's hands are black all the time from this dreadful dirty oil. In his place, I'd keep it simple, I wouldn't keep cranking up my machinery in an endless restaging, I'd promptly lead the human race by the horns, I'd knit events together stitch by stitch without breaking the thread, I wouldn't have any tricks up my sleeve, I wouldn't have any fancy repertoire. What you lot call 'progress' runs on two engines, people and events. But the sad thing is that, from time to time, something exceptional is called for. For events as for people, the stock company's not enough; there have to be geniuses among people, and among events, revolutions. Great accidents are the rule, the nature of things can't do without them, and going on the way comets appear, you could be forgiven for thinking that heaven itself needs star attractions. The moment you least expect it, God plasters a meteor across the wall of the firmament. Some bizarre star shoots out, emphasized by an enormous tail. And that's the reason Caesar dies. Brutus strikes him with a knife, and God strikes him with a comet.[6] Hey presto! Up pops an aurora borealis, up pops a revolution, up pops a great man; '93 in big letters, Napoléon in the starring role, the comet of 1811[7] at the top of the bill. Ah, and what a beautiful bill it is, blue and all studded with stunning flashing lights! Boom! Boom! What an amazing show! Look up, you gawking spectators. Everything's out of control, the star as well as the play. Good God, it's both too much and not enough. Such resources, plucked from the grab bag of the exceptional, seem magnificent, yet they are really rather poor. My friends, Providence is down to expedients. A revolution—what does that prove? That God is hard up. He stages a coup d'état, because there is a break in the connection between the present and the future and because, even being God, he can't make the two ends meet. In fact, this confirms my conjectures about the state of Jehovah's fortunes; and to see so much uneasiness up above as well as down below, so much meanness and stinginess and miserliness and distress in heaven as well as on earth, from the bird, who doesn't have a grain of millet, to little old me, who doesn't have a hundred thousand livres a year in income, to see the fate of humanity, which is pretty threadbare, and even the fate of royalty, which is showing its warp—witness the hanging of the prince de Condé,[8] to see winter, which is nothing more than a rip in the zenith that the wind blows through, to see all those streaks like tatters in the brand-new crimson of the morning over the hilltops, to see the dewdrops, those fake pearls, to see the frost, that jewelry paste, to see humanity coming apart at the seams and events patched up, and so many spots on the sun, and so many holes in the moon, to see so much misery everywhere, I suspect God is not rich. He keeps up appearances, it's true, but I sense the straits He's in. He throws a revolution the way a merchant whose coffers are empty throws a ball. We must not judge gods by appearances. Beneath the gilding of the heavens I glimpse a destitute universe. There is bankruptcy in creation. That's why I'm out of sorts. You see, it's June 5, it's almost night; I've been waiting for the day to come since morning. It hasn't come yet and I bet it won't come all day. That's like the lack of punctuality of a poorly paid clerk. Yes, everything's badly organized, nothing hangs together, this old world is a shambles, I'm going over to the opposition. Everything's going to rack and ruin; the world is a pain in the neck. It's like children: The people who want them don't have any, those who don't want them, do. Net result: I'm riled. On top of that, Laigle de Meaux, that baldy, hurts my eyes. It humiliates me to think I'm the same age as that cue ball. Otherwise, I criticize but I don't insult. The world is what it is. I'm talking here without any malice and to ease my conscience. Receive, Eternal Father, the assurance of my sincere esteem. Ah, by all the saints on Olympus and by all the gods in heaven, I was not made to be Parisian, meaning, to ricochet forever between two gangs, like a shuttlecock between two racquets, from the strutting flâneurs to the loudmouth louts! I was made to be a Turk gazing all the livelong day at oriental scatterbrains performing that exquisite Egyptian dancing, lewd as the dreams of a celibate, or a hick from Beauce, or a Venetian gentleman surrounded by gentle dames, or a German princeling,[9] providing half a foot soldier to the German Confederation and filling his spare time drying his socks on his hedge, that is, on his border! That's what I was born for! Yes, I say Turk, and I'm not about to unsay it. I don't understand why everyone's so hard on the Turks; Mohammed has his good side; let's have some respect for the inventor of seraglios full of houris and of paradises full of odalisques![10] Let's not insult Mohammedanism, the only religion that comes complete with a henhouse! On that note, I insist on drinking. The earth is one huge silly prank. And it seems they're going to fight, all these half-wits, bash each other's heads in, slaughter each other, in the middle of summer, in the month of Prairial,[11] when they could be going off to the countryside with some luscious creature on their arm to breathe in that great cup of tea of freshly mown hay! They really are too silly for words. An old broken oil lamp I saw just a moment ago in a junk shop prompts me to make this point: It's time to illuminate the human race. Yes, I've come over all sad again! What a thing it is to swallow an oyster or a revolution the wrong way! I'm getting gloomy again. Oh, this rotten old world! We vie against one another, we depose one another, we prostitute ourselves, we kill one another—and then we put up with it all in the end!"

Here Grantaire, after this fit of eloquence, had a well-earned fit of coughing.

"Speaking of revolution," said Joly, "it would appear that Barius is decibedly aborous."

"Who of, do we know?" asked Laigle.

"Do."

"No?"

"Do, I told you!"

"The love life of Marius!" cried Grantaire. "I can see it now. Marius is a mist and he will have found himself some vapor. Marius is a born poet. Say poet and you say madman. *Tymbraes Apollo.*[12] Marius and his Marie, or his Maria, or his Mariette, or his Marion, they must make pretty hilarious lovers. I can see it all. Ecstasies in which they forget to kiss. Chaste here below but going at it for all they're worth in infinity. They are souls with senses. They sleep together among the stars."

Grantaire was getting stuck into his second bottle and perhaps his second harangue when a new creature emerged from the square hole at the top of the stairs. This was a boy of under ten, in rags, tiny, sallow, with a sharp little muzzle of a face, bright-eyed and bushy-tailed, hair all over the place, soaked with rain, looking pleased.

Making his choice without hesitation from among the three even though he obviously didn't know any of them, the boy addressed Laigle de Meaux.

"Are you Monsieur Bossuet?" he asked.

"That's my nickname," answered Laigle. "What do you want?"

"All right. A big fair-headed fellow on the boulevard says to me: 'Do you know mother Hucheloup?' 'Yes,' I says, 'rue Chanvrerie, widow of the old geezer.' He says to me: 'Get yourself over there. You'll find Monsieur Bossuet there. Tell him from me: A—B—C.' They're pulling your leg, aren't they? He gave me six sous."

"Joly, lend me ten sous," said Laigle. Then he turned to Grantaire: "Grantaire, lend me ten sous."

That made twenty sous, which Laigle promptly gave the boy.

"Thank you, Monsieur," the boy said.

"What's your name?" asked Laigle.

"Turnip, Gavroche's friend."

"Stay here with us," said Laigle.

"Have breakfast with us," said Grantaire.

The child replied: "I can't, I'm in the procession, I'm the one crying, 'Down with Polignac.'"

And kicking his foot way out behind him, which is the most respectful of all possible bows, he took off.

Once the child was gone, Grantaire took the floor again: "That is pure gamin, pure Paris boy. There are many varieties in the gamin genus. The notary's boy is known as a gutter-leaper, a *saute-ruisseau,* the cook's boy is known as a pot-stirrer, a *marmiton,* the baker's boy is known as a pastry-puff, a *mitron,* the footman's boy is known as a groom, the sailor boy is known as a latherer, a *mousse,* the soldier boy is known as a drummer boy, a *tapin,* the painter's boy is known as an apprentice dauber, a *rapin,* the merchant's boy is known as an errand boy, a runner, a *trottin,* the boy courtier is known as a junior gentleman-in-waiting, a *menin,* the king's boy is known as a dauphin, the boy god is known as a bambino."

Laigle, meanwhile, was musing; he said in a small voice:

"ABC. That'd be: Lamarque's funeral."

"The big fair-headed fellow," observed Grantaire, "that'd be Enjolras alerting you."

"Will we go?" said Bossuet.

"It's raining," said Joly. "I swore I'd go through fire, not water. I do'd wad do catch a cold."

"I'm staying put," said Grantaire. "I prefer breakfast to a hearse."

"Conclusion: We're staying," Laigle summed up. "Well, then, we'd better drink. Anyway, you can miss the funeral without missing the riot."

"Ah, the riod! I'b all for it," cried Joly.

Laigle rubbed his hands together: "So we're going to go back to the revolution of 1830. Actually, it's a bit tight in the arms for the people now."

"I really couldn't care less about your revolution," said Grantaire. "I don't abhor this particular government. It's a crown tempered with a cotton cap. It's a scepter ending in an umbrella. In fact, today, I'm just reminded by the weather, Louis-Philippe could use his royalty at both ends, extend the scepter end against the people and open up the umbrella end against the skies."

The room grew dark, huge clouds now completely blotted out the sun. There was no one in the tavern or on the street, everybody having gone "to see the events."

"Is it midday or midnight?" cried Bossuet. "You can't see a bloody thing. Gibelotte, some light on the subject!"

Grantaire went on forlornly drinking.

"Enjolras looks down on me," he murmured. "Enjolras must have said: Joly is sick. Grantaire is drunk. So he sent Turnip for Bossuet. If he'd come to get me, I'd have gone with him. Too bad for Enjolras! I won't be going to his funeral!"

This resolution taken, Bossuet, Joly, and Grantaire did not budge from the tavern. At around two in the afternoon, the table they were leaning on was covered in empty bottles. Two candles were burning on it, one in a bright green copper candlestick, the other in the neck of a cracked carafe. Grantaire had led Joly and Bossuet to the wine; Bossuet and Joly had jollied Grantaire up again.

Speaking of Grantaire, since midday, he had progressed beyond wine, a mediocre source of dreams. Wine, with serious drunkards, has only a succès d'estime. When it comes to inebriety, there is black magic and white magic; wine is merely white magic. Grantaire was a daring drinker of dreams. The black hole of a fearful drunkenness gaping open before him, far from stopping him in his tracks, drew him in. He had abandoned the bottle and taken to the tankard. The tankard is a bottomless pit. Not having either opium or hashish to hand, and wanting to fill his brain with twilight dimness, he had resorted to that frightening mix of eau-de-vie, stout, and absinthe that produces such terrible sluggishness. It is from these three vapors, beer, eau-de-vie, and absinthe, that the soul is turned to lead. They are three forms of darkness, the celestial butterfly drowns in them; and, in a membranous smog vaguely condensed into a bat's wing, three mute furies, Nightmare, Night, and Death, form and flit over the sleeping Psyche.[13]

Grantaire had not yet reached that dismal point—far from it. He was wildly gay, and Bossuet and Joly kept pace with him. They clinked glasses. Grantaire added rambling gestures to the eccentric emphasis of his words and ideas; he sat straddling his stool, resting his left hand on his knee with dignity, his arm at a right angle, and, with his cravat loose and his glass full in his right hand, he tossed these solemn words to the fat servant, Matelotte: "Let the palace doors be opened! Let everyone belong to the Académie Française and have the right to kiss Madame Hucheloup! Let's drink to that."

Then he turned toward Ma Hucheloup and added: "Antique woman consecrated by use, approach, that I may contemplate you!"

And Joly shouted: "Batelotte and Bibelotte, dod't give Gradtaire ady bore to drik. He spedds crazy abouds of boney. Since this borning, he's already eaden up two francs nidety-five centibes in desperade extravagandce."

Grantaire went on: "Who the hell took the stars down without my permission only to put them on again, this time disguised as candles?"

Bossuet, completely plastered, had kept his cool.

He had gone and sat on the sill of the open window, getting his back wet with the falling rain, and he contemplated his two friends.

All of a sudden, he heard a racket behind him, the sound of running, cries of "To arms!" He turned round and saw, in the rue Saint-Denis, at the end of the rue de la Chanvrerie, Enjolras flying past, musket in hand, and Gavroche with his pistol, Feuilly with his saber, Courfeyrac with his sword, Jean Prouvaire with his carbine, Combeferre with his musket, Bahorel with his rifle, and the whole stormy armed mob that followed them.

The rue de la Chanvrerie was scarcely as long as the range of a rifle. Bossuet improvised a megaphone with both hands cupped around his mouth and shouted: "Courfeyrac! Courfeyrac! Ahoy there!"

Courfeyrac heard the call, spotted Bossuet, and took a few steps into the rue de la Chanvrerie, shouting a "What do you want?" that got crossed on the way with a "Where are you going?"

"To make a barricade," answered Courfeyrac.

"Why not here! This is the place for it! Make one here!"

"You're right, Laigle," said Courfeyrac.

And at a sign from Courfeyrac, the mob rushed into the rue de la Chanvrerie.

## III. Night Begins to Fall on Grantaire

The place was in fact exactly right with its funnel-shaped entrance from the street tapering at the bottom and ending in a dead end, where the Corinthe caused a bottleneck, the rue Mondétour easily blocked off both left and right, and no attack possible except via the rue Saint-Denis, that is, from the front and without cover. Bossuet on the turps had the sure eye of Hannibal on the wagon.

At the eruption of the gathering, horror took hold of the whole street. There was not a passerby who did not rapidly slip away. In a flash, from one end to the other, left, right, and center, shops, stalls, alleyway gates, windows, Persian blinds, attics, shutters of all shapes and sizes were slammed shut, from the ground floor to the rooftops. A frightened old woman had even stuck a mattress in front of her window on two clothesline poles, to cushion the musketry. The tavern was the only place open, and that for the good reason that that is where the crowd had rushed to.

"Oh, my God! Oh, my God!" sighed Ma Hucheloup.

Bossuet had gone down to meet Courfeyrac.

Joly, who had run to the window, shouted: "Courfeyrac, you should dave grabbed ad ubbrella. You're going to catch a colb."

Meanwhile, in a matter of minutes, twenty iron bars had been ripped off the grate over the shop front of the tavern, twenty yards of pavement had been ripped up, Gavroche and Bahorel had seized and tipped over the narrow dray of a lime manufacturer named Anceau, this dray containing three barrels full of lime, which they stashed under the piles of cobblestones; Enjolras had lifted up the trapdoor to the cellar and all the widow Hucheloup's empty kegs had gone to flank the barrels of lime; Feuilly, with his fingers accustomed to coloring the delicate blades of fans, had buttressed the barrels and the dray with two massive piles of rubble. Rubble improvised like everything else, obtained who knows where. Wooden support beams had been ripped off the front of a neighboring house and laid over the kegs. When Bossuet and Courfeyrac turned round, half the street was already barricaded with a rampart taller than a man. There is nothing like the hand of the people when it comes to throwing up by tearing down.

Matelotte and Gibelotte had joined the workers. Gibelotte came and went, loaded with debris. Her weariness was a help to the barricade. She served up cobblestones the way she would serve wine, looking half-asleep.

An omnibus drawn by two white horses went past at the end of the street.

Bossuet bounded over the pavement, ran, stopped the driver, made the passengers get down, gave his hand to the ladies, sent the conductor packing and returned, leading carriage and horses by the bridle.

"Omnibuses," he said, "do not pass by the Corinthe. *Non licet omnibus adire Corinthum.*"[1]

A second later, the unhitched horses were wandering off down the rue Mondétour and the omnibus was lying on its side, completing the roadblock.

Ma Hucheloup, shattered, had taken refuge upstairs.

Her eyes were glazed and she looked around without seeing, crying very softly. Her cries of horror didn't dare come out of her throat.

"It's the end of the world," she muttered.

Joly planted a kiss on Ma Hucheloup's fat red wrinkled neck and said to Grantaire: "My friend, I've always considered a woman's neck to be an infinitely delicate thing."

But Grantaire was climbing up to the highest reaches of the dithyramb. Matelotte had gone back upstairs, Grantaire had grabbed her by the waist and pushed her toward the window, with long peals of laughter.

"Matelotte is ugly!" he yelled. "Matelotte is a dream come true of ugliness! Matelotte is a pipe dream. Here's the secret of her birth: One fine day, a Gothic Pygmalion[2] making cathedral gargoyles fell in love with one of them, the most horrible one. He begged Love to give her life and Matelotte was the result. Look at her, citizens! She has chrome yellow hair like Titian's mistress[3] and she's a good girl. Take my word for it, she'll put up a good fight. Every good girl contains a hero. As for mother Hucheloup, she's a good old sort. Look at the mustache she's got! She inherited it from her husband. A real hussar, all right! She'll put up a fight, too. Between the two of them, they'll put fear into the place. Comrades, we will overthrow the government, true as it is that there are fifteen intermediate acids between margaric acid and formic acid. Anyhow, I couldn't care less. Gentlemen, my father always detested me because I was no good at mathematics. I am only good at love and liberty. I am the unflappable Grantaire! Never having had money, I've never become accustomed to it, which means I've never missed it; but if I had been rich, no one else would've been poor! I'd have shown 'em! Oh, if only good hearts had good big purses! How much better it would be! I can imagine Jesus Christ with Rothschild's fortune! How much good he'd do then! Kiss me, Matelotte! You are so shy and sensual! You've got cheeks that cry out for a sister's kiss and lips that cry out for the kiss of a lover!"

"Shut up, you wine cask!" said Courfyerac.

Grantaire replied: "I am Capitoul, municipal magistrate of Toulouse and master of flower games!"[4]

Enjolras, who was standing on top of the roadblock, fusil in hand, lifted up his handsome, austere face. Enjolras, we know, had something of the Spartan and the Puritan. He would have died at Thermopylae with Leonidas and would have burned Drogheda with Cromwell.[5]

"Grantaire!" he shouted. "Go and sleep off the booze away from here. This is the place for intoxication—not drunkenness. Do not dishonor the barricade!"

Those angry words had an incredible effect on Grantaire. You'd have sworn he'd just had a glass of cold water thrown in his face. He suddenly seemed sobered up. He sat down, leaned on a table near the window, looked at Enjolras with ineffable sweetness and said to him: "You know I believe in you."

"Go away."

"Let me sleep here."

"Go and sleep somewhere else," yelled Enjolras.

But Grantaire kept gazing steadily at him with loving, troubled eyes, and he replied: "Let me sleep here—until I die."

Enjolras gave him a disdainful glare: "Grantaire, you are not capable of believing, thinking, wanting, living, or dying."

Grantaire retorted in a grave voice: "You'll see."

He stammered out a few more unintelligible words, then his head fell heavily on the table, and, as commonly happens in the second stage of inebriety into which Enjolras had so rudely and brusquely pushed him, a moment later he was fast asleep.

## IV. An Attempt at Consoling Widow Hucheloup

Bahorel, in ecstasies over the barricade, cried: "There's the street nicely cropped off for you! Doesn't it look splendid!"

Courfeyrac, helping to demolish the tavern all the while, sought to console the widow who owned it.

"Mother Hucheloup, weren't you complaining just the other day that you'd been fined for breaking the law because Gibelotte had shaken a bedspread out your window?"

"Yes, my good Monsieur Courfeyrac. Oh, my God! Are you going to put that table on your horrible pile, too? And, as for the bedspread, and also for a flowerpot that fell onto the street from an attic, the government took a hundred francs off me in fines. Tell me that isn't an abomination!"

"Well, then, mother Hucheloup! We're avenging you!"

Mother Hucheloup did not seem to much appreciate the benefit of this compensation they were getting for her. She was satisfied in the manner of the Arab woman who, having received a slap from her husband, went off to complain to her father, calling for vengeance and saying: "Father, you owe my husband affront for affront." The father asked: "Which cheek did he slap?" "The left cheek." The father then slapped the right cheek and said: "Now you're happy. Go and tell your husband he slapped my daughter, but I slapped his wife."

The rain had stopped. Recruits arrived. Under their smocks, workers had smuggled in a powder keg, a basket containing bottles of vitriol, two or three carnival torches, and a wicker basket full of Chinese paper lanterns "left over from the king's birthday, *la fête du roi*." Which fête was quite recent, having taken place on the first of May. It was said that this ammunition came from a grocer named Pépin in the faubourg Saint-Antoine. They broke the only streetlamp in the rue de la Chanvrerie, the corresponding streetlamp in the rue Saint-Denis, and all the streetlamps in the surrounding streets of Mondétour, du Cygne, des Prêcheurs, and de la Grande- and de la Petite-Truanderie.

Enjolras, Combeferre, and Courfeyrac directed everything. Now two barricades were under construction at the same time, both leaning against the house of Corinthe at right angles; the bigger of the two closed off the rue de la Chanvrerie, the smaller closed off the rue Mondétour on the rue du Cygne side. This last barricade, which was extremely narrow, was built exclusively out of barrels and cobblestones. There were about fifty workers there, some thirty armed with muskets, for on their way over, they had borrowed wholesale from an armorer's shop.

You could not get a more odd and motley crew. One had a short coat, a cavalry saber, and two horse pistols, another was in shirtsleeves with a round hat and a powder horn dangling at his side, a third had padded his chest with a breastplate of nine sheets of gray packing paper and was armed with a saddler's awl. One of them cried: "Let's exterminate them to the last man and die on the point of our bayonets!" This man had no bayonet. Another displayed over his greatcoat a leather cross-belt and a cartridge pouch of the National Guard, the pouch cover adorned with this inscription in red wool: *Public Order.* Plenty of fusils bearing the numbers of legions, not many hats, no cravats, lots of bare arms, a few pikes. Add to that all the different ages, all the different faces, little pallid young men, suntanned dockworkers. All of them were rushing around frantically and while they gave each other a hand they talked about their prospects—how they would have help by three o'clock in the morning, how they were sure of one regiment, how Paris would rise up. Terrible words, delivered with a sort of cordial joviality. You'd have thought they were brothers, yet they did not know each other's names. The beautiful thing about great danger is that it brings out the fraternity of strangers.

A fire had been lit in the kitchen and they were melting down into a bullet mold pitchers, spoons, forks, all the cabaret's metalware, and drinking all the while. Caps and bits of buckshot lay around on the tables next to the glasses of wine. In the billiard room, Ma Hucheloup, Matelotte, and Gibelotte, variously changed by terror, one stupefied, one breathless, the third now actually awake, were tearing up old dishcloths and making lint; three insurgents were helping them, three great strapping lads with long hair, beards, and mustaches, who were going through the cloth with the nimble fingers of laundry supervisors and throwing them into a flutter.

The tall man that Courfeyrac, Combeferre, and Enjolras had noticed the moment he approached the crowd at the corner of the rue des Billettes was making himself useful working on the small barricade. Gavroche was working on the big one. As for the young man who had waited at Courfeyrac's place for him and had asked for Monsieur Marius, he had disappeared more or less at the same time the omnibus had been overturned.

Gavroche, radiant and completely airborne, had taken on the job of keeping things moving. He came and went, climbed up, clambered down, climbed back up, bustled, sparkled. He seemed to be there to goad everyone else on. Was there something spurring him on? Yes, of course there was, his misery. Did he have wings? Yes, of course he did, his exhilaration. Gavroche was a human whirlwind. He was to be seen constantly, he was to be heard never-endingly. He filled the air, being everywhere at once. He was almost annoyingly ubiquitous—no letup was possible with him around. The whole enormous barricade felt him on its rump. He vexed the loafers, roused the layabouts, revived the weary, annoyed the reflective, cheered up some, kept others on their toes, stirred others to fury, got everyone going; he stung a student, bit into a worker, he landed, stopped, took off again, flying above the mayhem and the effort, leaping from one group to the next, babbling, buzzing, and harassing the whole team; a fly on the vast revolutionary coach.

Perpetual motion was in his tiny arms and perpetual clamor in his tiny lungs: "Go to it! More cobblestones! More barrels! More thingummies! Where can we find some? A sack of rubble to block up that hole for me. It's too small, this barricade of yours. It needs to be higher. Pile everything on, chuck everything on, toss everything on. Break up the house. A barricade, it's child's play. Look, here's a glass door."

This made the workers snort: "A glass door! What do you want us to do with a glass door, pipsqueak?"

"Hercules yourselves, are you?" retorted Gavroche. "A glass door is an excellent thing in a barricade. Doesn't stop it being attacked, but makes it harder to take. Haven't you ever snitched apples over a wall that's got the bottoms of glass bottles stuck on it, then? A glass door'll cut the corns off the feet of the National Guard when they try to climb up on the barricade. Crikey! Glass is treacherous. Gosh, you haven't got unbridled imaginations, have you, my comrades!"

But what he was really furious about was his pistol's not having a "dog"—a hammer. He went from one man to the next demanding: "A musket! I want a musket! Why won't anyone give me a musket?"

"A musket, you!" said Combeferre.

"Listen!" said Gavroche. "Why not? I had one all right in 1830 when there was a bit of strife with Charles X!"

Enjolras shrugged his shoulders.

"When there are enough to go round the men, we'll start handing them out to boys."

Gavroche spun around proudly and shot back: "If you're killed before me, I'll take yours."

"Brat!" said Enjolras.

"Novice!" said Gavroche.

An elegant stray fop strolling at the end of the street became a diversion.

Gavroche called out to him: "Come and join us, young man! Aren't you going to do anything for this old homeland of ours, then?"

The fop fled.

## V. Preparations

The newspapers of the day that said the barricade in the rue de la Chanvrerie, that "almost impregnable structure" as they called it, reached a level as high as the second story, were mistaken. The fact is that it got no higher on average than six or seven feet. It was built in such a way that the combatants could, at will, either disappear behind the barrier or peer over it or even scramble up on top of it by means of four rows of cobblestones laid on top of each other and arranged in tiers on the inside like a flight of steps. From the outside the front of the barricade, composed of piles of cobblestones and barrels held together by beams and boards that interlocked with the wheels of Anceau's cart and the overturned omnibus, looked hideously tangled and impossible to get out of. But an exit big enough for a man to get through had been provided between the wall of the houses and the end of the barricade that was farthest away from the cabaret, so that there was a way out. The beam of the omnibus was set upright and held in place with ropes, and a red flag, tied to this beam, fluttered over the barricade.

The little Mondétour barricade, hidden behind the tavern, could not be seen. The two barricades together formed a real redoubt. Enjolras and Courfeyrac had not seen fit to barricade the other end of the rue Mondétour that offers a way to Les Halles through the rue des Prêcheurs, no doubt wanting to preserve a possible connection with the outside and having little fear of being attacked by the dangerous and difficult alleyway known as the rue des Prêcheurs.

Except for this passage remaining free, constituting what Folard, in his style of strategy, would have called an inner trench, and also taking into account the narrow exit provided on the rue de la Chanvrerie, the inside of the barricade, where the tavern formed a salient angle, presented an irregular quadrilateral closed on all sides. There was a gap of about twenty feet between the main barrier and the tall houses that formed the back of the street, so you could say that the barricade backed onto those houses, which were all inhabited but sealed tight from top to bottom.

All this labor was carried out without hindrance in under an hour and without this handful of daring men seeing one fur cap or one bayonet emerge.

The few bourgeois who still ventured into the rue Saint-Denis at that point in the riot shot a glance down the rue de la Chanvrerie, saw the barricade, and stepped lively on their way.

When the two barricades were finished and the flag run up, a table was dragged out of the tavern and Courfeyrac hopped up on this table. Enjolras brought over the square box and Courfeyrac opened it. This box had been filled with cartridges. When they saw the cartridges, there was a shudder among the bravest and a moment of silence. Courfeyrac distributed them with a smile.

Every man was issued with thirty cartridges; many of them had powder and set about making more of them with the bullets that were being cast. As for the powder keg, it was on a table by itself, near the door, kept in reserve.

The long rappel that rolled throughout Paris went on and on but in the end, it was merely a monotonous background noise which they paid no further attention to. At times, this noise moved away, at times it came closer, wavering mournfully.

The muskets and carbines were loaded, all together, unhurriedly, with solemn gravity. Enjolras went and positioned three sentinels outside the barricades, one in the rue de la Chanvrerie, the second in the rue des Prêcheurs, the third at the corner of la Petite-Truanderie.

Then, with the barricades built, the posts assigned, the guns loaded, the scouts positioned, alone in these fearsome streets where no one walked anymore, surrounded by these mute and seemingly dead houses where no human movement pulsed, enveloped in the darkling shadows of twilight, in the middle of this obscurity and this silence, in which they could feel something indescribably tragic and terrifying advancing, isolated, armed, resolute, and calm, they waited.

## VI. While Waiting

In those hours of waiting, what did they do?

We have to tell you, since this is history.

While the men were making cartridges and the women lint, while a large saucepan, full of molten pewter and lead destined for the bullet mold, was smoking on a burning stove, while the scouts were keeping watch over the barricades with their weapons on their arms, while Enjolras, whom nothing could distract, was watching over the scouts, Combeferre, Courfeyrac, Jean Prouvaire, Feuilly, Bossuet, Joly, Bahorel, and a few others besides sought each other out and came together as in their most tranquil schooldays when they would huddle together, chattering, and in a corner of the tavern that had been turned into a casemate, two feet from the redoubt they had put up, their primed and loaded carbines resting on the backs of their chairs, these beautiful young men, so near their final hour, began to recite a love poem.

Which poem? This one:[1]

Do you remember our sweet life,
When we were both so young,
And our hearts had but one desire
To look good and be in love!

When we added your age to mine
We did not have forty years between us,
And in our humble little home,
Everything, even winter, was spring to us!

Beautiful days! Manuel was proud and wise,
Paris sat down to sacred banquets,
Foy launched thunder, and your corsage
Had a pin that I pricked myself on.

Everyone looked at you. Lawyer without a cause,
When I took you to the Prado to dine,
You were so pretty the roses
Seemed to me to gaze after you.

I heard them say: How beautiful she is!
How good she smells! What flowing hair!
Under her cape she is hiding wings;
Her lovely bonnet is barely blooming.

I wandered with you, squeezing your soft arm.
Passersby thought that charmed love
Had married, in our happy couple,
The sweet month of April to gorgeous May.

We lived hidden, happy, behind closed doors,
Devouring love, that lovely forbidden fruit;
My mouth could not say a thing
Before already your heart answered.

The Sorbonne was a country retreat
Where I adored you from morning to night.
That's how a soul in love applies
The Tender card[2] to the quartier Latin.

O, place Maubert! O, place Dauphine!
When, in our fresh springtime hovel,
You ran your arms over your fine legs,
I could see a star at the back of the garret.

I've read a lot of Plato, but none of it has stuck;
Better than Malebranche and Lamennais[3]
You showed me heavenly bounty
In a flower you gave me.

I obeyed you, you submitted to me.
O golden garret! To enfold you! To see you
Come and go at dawn in a chemise,
Gazing at your fresh face in your old mirror!

And who, tell me, could lose the memory
Of those days of dawns and stars,
Of ribbons, of flowers, of gauze and moiré,
Where love stutters in such charming argot!

Our garden was a pot of tulips;
You cloaked the window with a petticoat;
I took the bowl of the clay pipe,
And I gave you the japanned cup.

And the great calamities that made us laugh!
Your burned muff, your lost boa!
And that dear portrait of the divine Shakespeare
That we sold so we could eat at night!

I was a beggar, you were charitable.
I kissed your fresh round arms on the wing.
Dante in folio served us as a table
To gaily munch through a hundred chestnuts.

The first time in my joyful hovel
That I took a kiss from your fiery lips,
When you went off disheveled and red,
I stayed all pale and believed in God!

Do you remember our endless happiness,
And all those fichus that turned to rags!
Oh! So many sighs, from our hearts full of shadow,
Soared up into the endless heavens!

The hour, the place, these memories of youth recalled, a few stars starting
to twinkle in the sky, the funereal repose of those deserted streets, the imminence of the inexorable adventure gearing up, gave a pathetic charm to these
lines murmured softly in the twilight by Jean Prouvaire, who, as we said before,
was a very gentle poet.

Meanwhile a paper lantern had been lit at the little barricade, and at the
big one, one of those wax torches you see at Mardi Gras in front of the carriages

loaded with masks heading for the Courtille. These torches, as we know, came from the faubourg Saint-Antoine.

The torch had been placed in a cage of cobblestones closed on three sides to shelter it from the wind, and positioned so that all the light fell on the flag. The street and the barricade remained plunged in darkness and nothing but the flag could be seen, wonderfully lit up as though by some enormous dimmed lantern.

This light added to the scarlet of the flag an indescribably terrible crimson.

## VII. THE MAN RECRUITED IN THE RUE DES BILLETTES

Night had well and truly fallen, but nothing happened. All that could be heard was dim muffled sounds and the odd volley of gunfire, but these were rare, not long sustained, and remote. This respite was dragging on, a sign that the government was taking its time and gathering its forces. These fifty men were expecting sixty thousand.

Enjolras felt himself seized by that impatience that takes hold of the headstrong on the threshold of awe-inspiring events. He went to find Gavroche, who had settled in to making cartridges in the downstairs room by the dubious light of two candles, placed on the bar out of harm's way as a precaution due to the powder spread over the tables. The insurgents had also been careful not to light any light in the upstairs rooms.

At that moment Gavroche was extremely preoccupied, though not exactly with his cartridges. The man from the rue des Billettes had just come into the downstairs room and had taken a seat at the table farthest from the light. A large-model infantry flintlock musket had fallen into his hands and he held it between his knees. Until that moment, distracted by a hundred "amusing" things, Gavroche had not even seen the man.

When he came in, Gavroche followed him mechanically with his eyes, admiring his musket, then, suddenly, just as the man sat down, the boy shot up. Anyone eyeing the man up to that point would have seen him taking everything in about the barricade and the band of insurgents with singular intensity, but from the moment he stepped into the barroom, he had fallen into a kind of meditative state and did not seem to see anything anymore of what was going on. The kid went over to this pensive character and began circling around him on tiptoe the way you walk when you're frightened of waking someone up. As he did so, his little boy's face, at once so cheeky and serious, so mobile and so deep, so chirpy and so harrowing, reproduced all the grimaces of an old man that signify: Ah, bah! Can't be! I'll be buggered! I must be seeing things! I must be dreaming! Can it be? . . . No, it's not! Yes, it is! No, it's not! and so on.

Gavroche rocked on his heels, balled his two fists in his pockets, bobbed his head on his neck like a bird, put all the sagacity of his bottom lip into one enormous pout. He was dumbstruck, doubtful, incredulous, convinced, dazzled. He had the facial expression of the head eunuch at the slave market discovering a Venus among all the lumps of lard, or the look of an amateur recognizing a Raphael in a stack of crummy paintings. Everything in him was at work, his instinct for sniffing out and his intellectual capacity for putting two and two together. It was obvious that something powerful was happening to Gavroche.

It was at the peak of this preoccupation that Enjolras came up and spoke to him.

"You're little," said Enjolras. "You won't be seen. Duck out of the barricades, slip along the houses, ferret around the streets, and come back and tell me what's happening."

Gavroche straightened up.

"So little 'uns are good for something, eh? That's lucky! I'll go. Meanwhile, trust the little 'uns, don't trust the big 'uns—"

Here Gavroche raised his head and lowered his voice and added, indicating the man from the rue des Billettes: "You see that big 'un over there?"

"What about him?"

"He's a stool pigeon."

"You sure?"

"Not even a fortnight ago, he pulled me by the ear off the ledge of the pont Royal where I was getting some fresh air."

Enjolras swiftly left the kid and murmured a few words in a whisper to a laborer from the wine docks who happened to be there. The laborer left the room and came back almost immediately with three others. These four men, four broad-shouldered porters, went and positioned themselves behind the table where the man from the rue des Billettes was leaning, without doing anything that might attract his attention. They were ready to throw themselves upon him.

Enjolras then approached the man and asked him: "Who are you?"

At this abrupt question, the man flinched. He looked Enjolras straight in his frank and open eyes and seemed to read what he was thinking there. He smiled a sneer of a smile that was the most disdainful, the most forceful, and the most resolute smile it was possible to smile and he answered with arrogant gravity: "I see what you're up to ... So, then, yes!"

"You're a spy?"

"I am a government official."

"What's your name?"

"Javert."

Enjolras signaled to the four men. In the twinkling of an eye, before Javert had time to turn round, he was collared, laid out, tied up, frisked.

They found on him a small round card stuck between two bits of glass and bearing, on one side, the engraved coat of arms of France, with this legend: *Surveillance et Vigilance* and, on the other, this information: JAVERT, Inspector of Police, aged fifty-two; and the signature of the prefect of police of the time, Monsieur Gisquet.

On top of this, he had on him his watch and his purse, which contained a few gold coins. They let him keep his purse and his watch. Under the watch, at the bottom of his fob pocket, they felt around and found a piece of paper in an envelope that Enjolras opened. He read these lines, written in the prefect's very own handwriting: "As soon as his political mission has been fulfilled, Inspector Javert will ascertain, by special investigation, whether it is true that malefactors have rallying points on the slope of the right bank of the Seine, near the pont d'Iéna."

The search over, they lifted Javert back onto his feet, tied his arms behind his back and bound him to that celebrated post that had once given the tavern its name, in the middle of the downstairs room.

Gavroche, who had witnessed the whole scene and approved it all with a quiet nod of the head, went up to Javert and said: "Looks like the mouse caught the cat."

All this was done so fast that it was over by the time anyone else in or around the tavern realized. Javert had not let out a single cry.

But when they saw Javert tied to the post, Courfeyrac, Bossuet, Joly, Combeferre, and the men scattered about the two barricades came running.

Javert had his back against the post and was so wound round with ropes that he couldn't move a muscle, yet he raised his head with the intrepid serenity of a man who has never lied.

"He's a spy," said Enjolras.

And he turned to Javert: "You'll be shot two minutes before the barricade is taken."

Javert replied in his most imperious tone: "Why not right away?"

"We're saving our powder."

"Well, you could get it over with with a knife."

"Spy," said the handsome Enjolras, "we are judges, not assassins."

Then he called Gavroche.

"You! Get about your business! Go and do what I told you."

"I'm going," cried Gavroche.

But he paused on the way out: "By the way, you'll give me his musket!"

And he added: "I leave you the musician, but I want the clarinet."

The kid gave a military salute and gaily bounded through the gap in the main barricade.

## VIII. Several Question Marks Regarding a Man Named Le Cabuc Who Was Perhaps Not Le Cabuc

The tragic picture we have begun to paint would not be complete, the reader would not see, in their exact and actual relief, these great moments of society in labor and giving birth to revolution, in which the convulsions are mixed with sheer hard work, if we leave out of the outline sketched here, an incident full of epic and savage horror that occurred almost immediately after Gavroche left.

Mobs, as we know, are like snowballs and gather as they roll a heap of rowdy men. These men do not ask each other where they come from. Among the passersby who attached themselves to the mob led by Enjolras, Combeferre, and Courfeyrac, there was a man in a porter's jacket worn at the shoulders, who was gesticulating and vociferating and flailing his arms around for all the world like a crazy drunk. This man, going by the name or nickname of Le Cabuc (Fathead) and otherwise completely unknown to those who claimed to know him, who was extremely drunk or pretending to be, had sat down with a few others at a table they had dragged outside the cabaret. This Le Cabuc, all the while encouraging those who were with him to drink, looked to be studying most thoughtfully the big house at the back of the barricade whose five stories dominated the whole street and faced the rue Saint-Denis. Suddenly he shouted: "Comrades, you know what? We should shoot from that house there. When we're up there at the windows, I'll defy any bastard to come down the street!"

"Yes, but the house is shut up," said one of his drinking mates.

"We'll knock!"

"They won't open."

"We'll break the door down!"

Le Cabuc runs to the door, which has an absolutely massive knocker, and knocks. The door does not open. He knocks a second time. No one answers. A third knock. Same silence.

"Is anyone there?" cries Le Cabuc.

Nothing stirs.

So then he grabs a gun and begins bashing the door with the butt. It was an old alley door, arched, low, narrow, solid, all in oak, lined on the inside with sheet metal and an iron brace, a regular fortress door. The banging made the house shake but did not shift the door.

Yet it is likely that the inhabitants were roused, for a small square dormer window on the third floor was finally seen to light up and open and an old man with gray hair was seen to appear at this window with a candle, openmouthed and frightened-looking—it was the porter.

The man hammering the door stopped.

"Messieurs," asked the porter, "what is it you want?"

"Open up!" roared Le Cabuc.

"Messieurs, that can't be done."

"Open up, right now."

"Impossible, messieurs!"

Le Cabuc got his gun and took a bead on the porter's head; but as he was below and it was very dark, the porter didn't see him.

"Will you open up, yes or no?"

"No, messieurs!"

"No, you say?"

"I say no, my good—"

The porter did not finish his sentence. The gun went off; the bullet entered just below his chin and exited at the back of his neck after cutting straight through the jugular. The old man slumped forward in a heap without a sigh. The candle fell and went out, and nothing more could be seen except an unmoving head sitting on the windowsill and a wisp of whitish smoke curling up toward the roof.

"That's that!" said Le Cabuc, letting the butt of his gun drop to the pavement again.

Hardly had he uttered those words than he felt a hand land on his shoulder with the weight of an eagle's talons and he heard a voice say to him: "On your knees."

The murderer turned and saw in front of him the cold white face of Enjolras. Enjolras had a pistol in his hand.

At the explosion, he had come running. He had grabbed Le Cabuc's collar, smock, and braces in his left hand.

"On your knees," he repeated.

And with a sovereign movement, the frail young man of twenty pushed the stocky and robust picklock onto his knees in the mud, bending him like a reed. Le Cabuc tried to resist but it was as though he'd been seized by a superhuman fist.

Pale and wan, with his neck bare, his hair wild, his perfectly womanly face, Enjolras looked amazingly like the Themis of antiquity.[1] His flaring nostrils and downcast eyes gave his implacable Greek profile that expression of fury and of chastity combined that, in the ancient world's view, belonged to justice.

The whole barricade had come running, then all had lined up in a circle at a distance, feeling it impossible to utter a word in the face of what they were about to see.

Le Cabuc, defeated, gave up trying to fight and trembled from head to foot. Enjolras let him go and and took out his watch.

"Pull yourself together," he said. "Pray or reflect. You've got one minute."

"Mercy!" murmured the murderer. Then he hung his head and stuttered out a few inarticulate oaths.

Enjolras did not take his eyes off his watch; he let a minute pass, then he put the watch back in his fob pocket. That done, he grabbed Le Cabuc, who was curled over at his knees, howling, by the hair, and pressed the muzzle of his gun to his ear. Many of those intrepid men, who had embarked on the most frightening of adventures without turning a hair, now turned their heads away.

They heard the explosion, the assassin hit the pavement face first, and Enjolras straightened up and ran his determined eagle eye around him.

Then he pushed the dead body away with his foot and said: "Throw that outside."

Three men lifted up the body of the poor miserable wretch, which was still juddering with the last mechanical convulsions of the life that had flown, and threw it over the small barricade into Mondétour alleyway.

Enjolras remained lost in thought. It was hard to know what imposing shadows were slowly spreading over his awsome serenity. Suddenly he raised his voice. Everyone fell silent.

"Citizens," said Enjolras, "what that man did is horrifying and what I did is horrible. He shot someone and that is why I killed him. I had to do it, for an insurrection must be disciplined. Murder is even more of a crime here than elsewhere; we are under the eye of the revolution, we are the priests of the Republic, we are the sacramental hosts of duty and no one must be able to vilify our struggle. So I judged that man and sentenced him to death. As for myself, forced to do what I did, but abhorring it, I have judged myself as well and you will soon see what I have sentenced myself to."

Those who were listening shuddered.

"We will share your fate," cried Combeferre.

"So be it," Enjolras went on. "One other thing. In executing that man, I obeyed necessity. But necessity is a monster of the old world, necessity is called Fatality. Now, the law of progress has it that monsters disappear in the face of angels, and that Fatality evaporates in the face of Fraternity. This is a bad moment to utter the word *love*. Never mind, I utter it, and I glorify it. Love, you hold the future in your hands. Death, I use you, but I hate you. Citizens, in the future there will be no darkness, no thunderbolts, no vicious ignorance, no bloody eye for an eye, blood for blood. Since there will be no more Satan, there will be no more Michael.[2] In the future no one will kill anyone, the earth will shine, the human race will love. It will come, citizens, the day when all will be peace, harmony, light, joy, and life, it will come. And it is so that it comes that we are going to die."

Enjolras was silent. His virgin lips closed; and he remained for some time standing at the spot where he had spilled blood, as still as a marble statue. His staring eyes made everyone drop their voices around him.

Jean Prouvaire and Combeferre quietly shook hands, and leaning on each other at the corner of the barricade, studied with an admiration that had a touch of compassion in it this grave young man, executioner and priest, made of light like crystal, and of rock, too.

We should say right now that later, after the action, when the bodies were taken to the morgue and searched, a police officer's card was found on Le Cabuc. In 1848, the author of this book held in his own hands the special report on this subject made to the prefect of police in 1832.

We should add that, if we are to believe a strange but probably well-founded police tradition, Le Cabuc was Claquesous. The fact is that, after the death of Le Cabuc, nothing more was ever heard of Claquesous. Claquesous left no trace of his disappearance; he seemed to have vanished into thin air. His life had been darkness, his end was invisible night.

The whole group of insurgents was still in the grip of the emotion of this tragic trial, so quickly set up and so quickly ended, when Courfeyrac spotted in the barricade the young man who had been looking for Marius at his place that morning.

This boy, who had a bold and reckless look, had come at night to join the insurgents.

# BOOK THIRTEEN

# MARIUS STEPS INTO THE SHADOWS

### I. FROM THE RUE PLUMET TO THE QUARTIER SAINT-DENIS

The voice that had called Marius through the dying light to the barricade in the rue de la Chanvrerie sounded to him like the voice of destiny. He wanted to die, the occasion presented itself; he knocked at heaven's door, a hand in the shadows held out the key to him. These dismal opportunities that open up in the darkness of despair are tempting. Marius pulled back the bolt that had let him pass through so many times, walked out of the garden, and said: "Let's go."

Mad with pain, no longer feeling anything steady or solid in his brain, incapable of accepting anything anymore that fate had to offer after these two months spent in the intoxications of youth and of love, overwhelmed by all the visions of despair coming all at once, he had only one desire left: to end it all, fast. He started to step up his pace. It just so happened that he was armed, having Javert's pistols on him.

The young man he thought he'd seen had vanished out of sight on the street.

Marius had come from the rue Plumet via the boulevard. He now crossed over the Esplanade and the pont des Invalides, the Champs-Élysées, the place Louis XV, and turned into the rue de Rivoli. The shops were open, the gas was burning under the arcades, women were buying up in the boutiques, people were having ice cream in the Café Laiter, they were eating little cakes in the English pastry shop. Only a few post chaises were setting out at a gallop from the Hôtel des Princes and the Hôtel Meurice.

Marius turned into the rue Saint-Honoré via the passage Delorme. The boutiques were closed, the merchants were chatting in front of their half-open doors, people were strolling around, the streetlamps were lit, all the windows were lit from the first floor up, as usual. There were cavalry on the place du Palais-Royal.

Marius followed the rue Saint-Honoré. The farther away he got from the Palais-Royal, the fewer lights there were in windows; the boutiques were completely closed, no one was chatting on their doorsteps, the street grew darker and at the same time the crowd grew denser. For the passersby were now a crowd. No one was seen to speak in this crowd, and yet a deep muffled hum was coming from it.

Near the fontaine de l'Arbre-Sec, there were "gatherings," motionless gloomy groups, standing amid the eddying hordes like stones in the middle of a running stream.

At the mouth of the rue des Prouvaires, the crowd had stopped moving. They formed a resistant block, massive, solid, compact, almost impenetrable, of people heaped together and talking in low voices. Black coats and round hats had virtually disappeared. Smock frocks, smocks, caps, bristling heads caked with dirt.[1] This mob undulated confusedly in the nocturnal fog. Its whisperings had the harsh sound of sighing. Although not one person was moving, you could hear shuffling in the mud. Beyond this dense mass, in the rue du Roule, in the rue des Prouvaires, and in the extended part of the rue Saint-Honoré, there was not a single window with a candle burning in it. In those streets, single files of solitary lanterns could be seen stretching away in thinning numbers. The lanterns of those days were like big red stars hanging from ropes and throwing shadows over the footpath in the shape of great spiders. Those streets were not deserted. You could make out stacks of muskets there, bayonets waving around, and troops bivouacking. Nobody curious stepped over that mark. There, the traffic stopped. There, the crowd ended and the army began.

Marius willed with the will of a man beyond all hope. He had been called, he had to go. He found a way of cutting through the crowd and cutting through the bivouac of troops, hiding from the patrols and avoiding the sentries. He took a detour, made it to the rue de Béthisy and headed for Les Halles. At the corner of the rue de Bourdonnais there were no more lanterns.

After cutting through the crowd belt, he passed beyond the fringe of troops and found himself in a frightening place in the middle of something terrible. Not one person walking by, not one soldier, not one light; no one. Solitude, silence, night; a mysterious chill that bit to the bone. Going into a street was like going into a cellar.

He continued on, tentatively. Someone ran right past him. Was it a man? A woman? Several people? He could not have said. It had passed and it had vanished.

By a roundabout way, he came to a little street that he thought must be the rue de la Poterie; about halfway along, he ran into an obstacle. He put his hands out. It was an overturned cart; his feet recognized puddles of water, potholes, scattered and piled-up cobblestones. A barricade had been started there and then abandoned. He climbed up the cobblestones and found himself on the other side of the barrier. He walked along, sticking close to the curbstones and guiding himself by the walls of houses. A little beyond the barricade, he thought he caught a glimpse of something white up ahead. He approached, it took on a shape. It turned into two white horses, the horses of the omnibus unhitched that morning by Bossuet and who had wandered about willy-nilly from street to street the whole day and had wound up stopping there, with the weary patience of brutes that don't understand the actions of men any more than men understand the actions of Providence.

Marius left the horses behind. As he came to a street that struck him as being the rue du Contrat-Social, a gunshot, coming from who knows where and shooting across the darkness randomly, whistled past him very close; the bullet went through a copper shaving dish hanging outside a hairdresser's shop. You could still see this shaving dish with a bullet hole in it in 1846, in the rue du Contrat-Social, at the corner where the pillars of Les Halles stand.

This gunshot meant life, still. From that moment on, though, he didn't come across another thing.

This whole excursion was like going down dark stairs.

But that didn't stop Marius pressing ahead.

## II. Paris as the Owl Flies

Anyone who could have soared over Paris at that moment with the wings of a bat or an owl would have had a grim spectacle beneath their eyes.

The whole of the old Les Halles quartier, which is like a city within a city, crossed by the rue Saint-Denis and the rue Saint-Martin, crisscrossed by a thousand little lanes, and which the insurgents had made their redoubt and their field of arms, would have appeared to them like an enormous black hole dug out in the center of Paris. There their gaze would have fallen into an abyss. Thanks to the broken streetlamps, thanks to the windows shut tight, any beam of light, any life, any sound, any movement, ceased there. The invisible riot police were watching everywhere and maintaining order, meaning darkness. To drown the smallness of their number in one vast obscurity, to beef up each combatant through the possibilities this obscurity offers, this is the essential tactic of insurrection. At nightfall, every window where a candle burned received a bullet. The light was put out, sometimes the inhabitant killed. And so nothing stirred. There was nothing there, inside the houses, but fear, mourning, stupor; in the streets, a sort of awestruck horror. You could not even see the long rows of windows and stories, the jagged lace of the chimneys and roofs, not even the dim reflections gleaming on the muddy, wet pavement. Any eye that could have looked down from above into that jumble of shadows might perhaps have glimpsed, here and there, in places, indistinct lights bringing out the broken and bizarre lines and shapes of weird constructions, something like ghostly glimmerings coming and going among ruins; that was where the barricades were. The rest was a lake of darkness, foggy, heavy, funereal, above which rose the motionless and gloomy silhouettes of the Tour Saint-Jacques, Saint-Merry church, and two or three other of those great edifices man turns into giants and the night turns into phantoms.

All around this deserted and ominous labyrinth, in the quartiers where the Paris traffic had not been brought to a standstill and where a few rare lamplights still shone, the aerial observer would have been able to make out the metallic scintillation of sabers and bayonets, the muffled rumbling of artillery, and the swarming of silent battalions swelling in number from one minute to the next; a daunting belt that slowly tightened and closed around the riot.

The besieged quartier was now no more than a sort of monstrous cavern; everything in it seemed to be asleep or motionless and, as we have just seen, each of the streets offering access was now nothing but shadow.

A fierce shadowland, full of traps, full of unknown and fearful things, where it was frightening to go and awful to stay, where those who went in shivered in the face of what was waiting for them there, where those who waited shuddered in the face of those who were about to come. Invisible combatants entrenched at every street corner; pitfalls of the grave hidden in the thick layers of the night. It was all over. No light to hope for from now on, other than the flash of guns, no encounter, other than the sudden swift appearance of death. Where? How? When? You did not know, only that it was certain and inevitable. There, in that place marked for battle, the government and the insurrection, the National Guard and the popular clubs, the bourgeoisie and the dissidents, were about to grope their way toward each other. For both sides, the essential requirement was the same. To come out of it slain or victorious, the only possible way out from that point on. Such an extreme situation, such powerful darkness—the most timid felt filled with resolution and the most daring, with terror.

Add to this, on both sides, fury, relentlessness, equal determination. For one side, to advance meant to die, yet no one thought of turning back; for the other side, to stay meant to die, yet no one thought of running away.

It was essential that everything be over by the next day, that triumph be on one side or the other, that the insurrection be a revolution or a mere skirmish. The government understood this and so did the different parties; the least significant bourgeois felt it. Whence a feeling of anguish that melded with the impenetrable shadow of this quartier where all would be decided; whence a redoubling of anxiety around this silence from which only a catastrophe would emerge. Only one sound could be heard there, a sound as heartrending as a death rattle, as menacing as a curse, the tocsin of Saint-Merry. Nothing was as bloodcurdling as the clamor of this wild and desperate bell, wailing in the dark.

As often happens, nature seemed to have come to terms with what men were about to do. Nothing disturbed the deadly harmonies of this whole. The stars had gone out; heavy clouds filled the horizon all around with their melancholy billowing. There was a black sky over those dead streets as though an immense pall had unfurled over that immense grave.

While a battle still entirely political was brewing in that same spot that had already seen so many revolutionary events, while youth, secret societies, schools, in the name of principles, and the middle class, in the name of vested interests, approached each other to go head to head, to tear into each other and knock each other down, while each one was rushing and calling the final decisive hour of the crisis, beyond that fatal quartier, far away, in the deepest depths of the unfathomable cavities of the old desperately down-and-out Paris that is disappearing under the splendor of the happy, opulent Paris, the somber voice of the people could be heard roaring dully.

A frightening and sacred voice combining the bellowing of the brute and the word of God, that terrifies the weak and warns the wise, coming both from below, like the voice of a lion, and from above, like the voice of thunder, at one and the same time.

### III. The Extreme Edge

Marius had reached Les Halles.

Everything here was even calmer, darker, and stiller than in the neighboring streets. You would have said that the icy peace of the tomb had seeped up from the ground and spread out under the sky.

A red glare, though, carved out against this black backdrop the high rooftops of the houses that blocked off the rue de la Chanvrerie on the Saint-Eustache side. This was the reflection of the torch burning in the Corinthe barricade. Marius headed for that red glare. It brought him to the Marché-aux-Poirées, and he could just see the dark mouth of the rue des Prêcheurs. He went in. The insurgents' scout keeping watch at the other end did not notice him. He felt himself to be very close to what he had come for and he tiptoed forward. In this way he reached the elbow of that short arm of the rue Mondétour which was, you will recall, the only connection to the outside that Enjolras had kept open. At the corner of the last house, on his left, he poked his head around and looked down this stretch of rue Mondétour.

A bit past the black corner where the little street met the rue de la Chanvrerie, which threw a broad patch of shadow in which he himself was buried, he saw a glimmer of light on the cobblestones, part of the tavern, and, behind it, a paper lantern twinkling in a sort of amorphous wall and men crouching down with guns resting on their knees. All this was only ten yards away. It was the inside of the barricade.

The houses lining the lane on the right hid from him the rest of the tavern, the main barricade, and the flag.

Marius had only one more step to take. So the unhappy young man sat down on a curbstone, folded his arms, and thought about his father.

He thought about the heroic colonel Pontmercy who had been such a proud soldier, who had defended the frontier of France under the Republic and reached the frontier of Asia under the emperor, who had seen Genoa, Alexandria, Milan, Turin, Madrid, Vienna, Dresden, Berlin, Moscow, who had left on all Europe's fields of victory drops of that same blood that he, Marius, had in his veins, who had gone gray before his time due to the rigors of discipline and command, who had lived with his sword-belt buckled, his epaulets falling on his breast, his cockade blackened by gunpowder, his forehead creased by his helmet, in barracks, in camps, in bivouacs, in ambulances, and who, twenty years later, had come back from the great wars with his cheek scarred, a smile on his face, unaffected, at peace, admirable, as pure of heart as a child, having given his all for France and done nothing against her.

He told himself that his day had come now, too, that his hour had finally sounded, that following in his father's footsteps, he, too, brave, fearless, bold, would run in front of bullets, offer his chest to bayonets, shed his blood, seek out his enemy, seek death, that he, in turn, would wage war and enter onto the field of battle—but that the field of battle he was about to enter was the street, and that the war he was about to wage was civil war!

He saw civil war yawning open like an abyss before him and he knew that it was there that he would fall. And a shiver ran down his spine.

He thought about his father's sword that his grandfather had sold to a secondhand dealer and that he himself had so sorely missed. He told himself that it had done the right thing, that chaste and valiant sword, in escaping from his clutches and going off in anger into the dark; that if it had fled like that, it was because it was smart and could foresee the future; it was because it had a foreboding of the riot, the war of the gutters, the war of the cobblestones, the fusillades through cellar windows, all the stabbing in the back; it was because, coming from Marengo and Friedland, it did not want to go to the rue de la Chanvrerie, it was because all that it had done with the father, it would not do with the son! He told himself that if he had collected that particular sword from his dead father's bedside and dared to bring it with him for this struggle between French compatriots, on a street corner, under cover of night, it would most certainly have burned his hands and burst into flame in front of him like the sword of the angel! He told himself that he was happy that it was not there, that it had disappeared, that this was good, that this was only right, that his grandfather had been the true keeper of his father's flame and that it was better that the colonel's sword had been sold to the highest bidder, sold to a junk dealer, tossed among old scrap iron, rather than to cause the flank of his homeland to bleed today.

And then he began to cry bitter tears.

It was horrible. But what could he do? Live without Cosette he could not. Since she had gone away, there was nothing left for him to do but die. Had he not given her his word of honor that he would die? She had gone away knowing that, which meant she liked the idea of his dying. And anyway, it was clear she no longer loved him, since she had gone away like that, without a word of warning, without a letter, even though she knew his address! What was the good of living, what was there to live for now? And anyway, for God's sake! How could he come this far, only to turn back! How could he come so close to danger, only to run away! How could he come to stare into the barricade, only to slink off all atremble saying: Actually, I've had enough of this, I've seen it, that's enough, it's civil war, I'll be on my way! How abandon his friends who were waiting for him! who perhaps needed him! who were a mere handful against an entire army! How drop everything at once, love, friendship, his word! To give his cowardice the excuse of patriotism! But this was impossible, and if his father's ghost were there in the shadows and saw him recoil, he would whip his backside with the flat of his sword and shout at him: On you go, coward!

In the grip of his seesawing thoughts, he hung his head.

All of a sudden, he lifted it again. A sort of dazzling adjustment had just been effected in his mind. The mind expands when you are close to the grave; to be close to death makes you see things as they really are. The vision of action that he perhaps felt he was about to throw himself into appeared to him no longer woeful, but superb. The street war was suddenly transfigured, by some unknowable interior labor of the soul, before the eye of his mind. All the tumultuous question marks of his reverie came thronging back to him, but without troubling him in the slightest. He did not leave one of them unanswered.

Let's see, why would his father be outraged? Aren't there any cases where insurrection achieves the dignity of duty? What would be demeaning, then, for the son of Colonel Pontmercy, in the impending fight? It was no longer Montmirail or Champaubert,[1] it was something else. It was no longer a matter of sacred ground, but of a holy idea. The country was groaning, true; but humanity was applauding. Besides, was it true that the country was groaning? France was bleeding, but liberty was smiling; and before the smile of liberty, France forgot her wounds. And then, to see things from an even higher perspective, what was all the talk of civil war about?

Civil war? What did that mean? Is there such a thing as a foreign war? Isn't every war between men a war between brothers? War can only be described by its aim. There is neither foreign war nor civil war; there is only unjust war and just war. Until the day the great human concordat should be concluded, war, the kind of war, at least, that is the striving of the future's headlong rush against the past's dragging the chain, may well be necessary. What was there to attack in such a war? War only becomes shameful, the sword only becomes a dagger, when it kills right, progress, reason, civilization, truth. Then, civil war or foreign war, it is iniquitous; its name is crime. Outside that sacred thing, justice, by what right does one form of war scorn another? By what right does Washington's sword disown Camille Desmoulins' pike? Leonidas versus the foreigner, Timoleon versus the tyrant[2]—who is the greater? One is a defender, the other a liberator. Are we to condemn, without bothering about its aim, any show of arms within the city? Then mark down as infamous Brutus, Marcel, Arnold of Blankenheim, Coligny.[3] Scrub warfare? Street warfare? Why not? That was the war waged by Ambiorix, by Artevelde, by Marnix, by Pelagius.[4] But Ambiorix fought against Rome, Artevelde against France, Marnix against Spain, Pelagius against the Moors; all of them against the foreigner. Well, then, the monarchy is the foreigner, here; oppression is the foreigner; divine right is the foreigner. Despotism violates the moral frontier just as invasion violates the geographic frontier. To drive out the tyrant or drive out the Englishman[5] is, in either case, to take back your territory. There comes a time when protest is no longer enough; philosophizing must be followed by action; the strong hand finishes what the idea has started; *Prometheus Bound* begins, Aristogeiton ends;[6] the Encyclopedia enlightens souls, August 10 electrifies them. After Aeschylus, Thrasybulus;[7] after Diderot, Danton. The multitudes have a tendency to accept whoever is master. Their very mass weighs them down with apathy. A mob easily adds up to obedience. You have to stir them up, push them, treat the men rough using the very advantage of their deliverance, hurt their eyes with the truth, throw light at them in terrible handfuls. They must themselves be rocked a bit by their own salvation; this dazzlement wakes them up. Hence the necessity of tocsins and wars. Great combatants must rise up, illuminate nations by their audacity, and shake up this sad humanity that is covered in darkness by divine right, Caesar-style glory, force, fanaticism, irresponsible power, and absolute majesty; a throng busy gazing idiotically at these dismal triumphs of the night in all their crepuscular splendor. Down with the tyrant! But wait a minute! Who are you talking about? Are you calling Louis-Philippe a tyrant? No, he's no more a tyrant than Louis XVI. Both men are what history is accustomed to calling good kings; but principles can't be broken up, the logic of truth is a straight line, the peculiarity of truth is to lack complacency; so no concessions, then; any encroaching on mankind must be put down; there is divine right in Louis XVI, there is the element of "because he is a Bourbon"[8] in Louis-Philippe; both represent a confiscation of rights to a certain extent, and in order to get rid of this universal usurpation, we must fight them; we French must, for

France always takes the initiative. When the master falls in France, he falls everywhere. In short, reestablish social truth, give liberty back its throne, give the people back to the people, give man back his sovereignty, remove the purple from the head of France, restore reason and equity in all their fullness, suppress all forms of antagonism by restoring each person to themself, do away with the obstacle that royalty constitutes to vast universal harmony, put the human race on equal footing with the law—what cause could be more just and, consequently, what war greater? Such wars as these build peace. An enormous fortress of prejudices, privileges, superstitions, lies, of exactions, abuses, acts of violence, of iniquities, of darkness, is still standing over the world with its towers of hate. It must be thrown down. This monstrous pile must be toppled. To conquer at Austerlitz is a great thing, to storm the Bastille is immeasurable.

There is not a person who hasn't noticed for themself that the soul—and this is what is so wonderful about its complex, ubiquitous unity—has the strange ability to reason almost coldly in the most desperate extremities, and it often happens that passionate sorrow and profound despair, in the very agony of their blackest monologues, address issues and develop arguments. Logic joins in the turmoil and the thread of a syllogism floats without breaking in the mournful storm of thought. This was Marius's state of mind.

While he was thinking along these lines, devastated but resolute, hesitant, though, and, in a word, shuddering in the face of what he was about to do, his gaze wandered about the interior of the barricade. The insurgents were chatting there in low voices, without stirring, and you could feel that half-silence there that marks the final phase of waiting. Above them, at a third-floor window, Marius could make out a sort of spectator or witness who seemed to him peculiarly attentive. It was the porter killed by Le Cabuc. From below you could dimly make out the head in the reflection from the torch stuck in the cobbles. Nothing could be stranger, in that dim and uncertain light, than this livid face, still, stunned, hair standing on end, eyes open and staring, mouth gaping, leaning over the street in an attitude of curiosity. You would have said that the man who had died was studying those who were about to die. A long trail of blood that had flowed from the head ran in reddish trickles from the dormer window down to the first floor, where it stopped.

# BOOK FOURTEEN

# THE GRANDEURS OF DESPAIR

## I. THE FLAG—ACT ONE

Still nothing happened. Ten o'clock had sounded at Saint-Merry, Enjolras and Combeferre had gone and sat, carbines in hand, near the opening in the main barricade. They were not talking; they were listening, trying to catch even the most muffled and most remote sound of marching feet.

Suddenly, in the middle of this gloomy calm, a clear, young, cheery voice, which seemed to come from the rue Saint-Denis, rose and began distinctly to sing to the tune of the old popular ditty "Au clair de la lune," these lines ending in a sort of cry similar to the crow of a cock:

> My nose is in tears,
> My dear friend Bugeaud,
> Lend me your gendarmes
> For a word or so.
> In their big blue jackets,
> Hens on their shakos
> Here come the suburbs![1]
> Cock-a-doodle-do![2]

They shook hands.

"It's Gavroche," said Enjolras.

"He's warning us," said Combeferre.

Running footsteps startled the deserted street, you could see a creature nimbler than a clown clambering over the omnibus, and Gavroche bounded into the barricade, all out of breath, saying: "My gun! Here they are."

An electric thrill ran through the entire barricade and the sound of hands fumbling for muskets could be heard.

"Would you like my carbine?" Enjolras asked the gamin.

"I want the big gun," replied Gavroche.

And he grabbed Javert's musket.

Two sentries had fallen back and returned almost at the same time as Gavroche. These were the sentinel at the end of the street and the scout at de la Petite-Truanderie; the scout at the rue des Prêcheurs lane had stayed at his post, which indicated that nothing was coming from the direction of the bridges or Les Halles.

The rue de la Chanvrerie, in which only a few cobblestones were dimly visible in the reflection of the light falling on the flag, looked to the insurgents like some grand black porch opening onto a cloud of smoke.

Everyone had taken up his battle station.

Forty-three insurgents, among them Enjolras, Combeferre, Courfeyrac, Bossuet, Joly, Bahorel, and Gavroche, were kneeling inside the main barricade, their heads level with the top of the barrier, the barrels of their muskets and their carbines positioned on the cobblestones as though through gun slits, alert, silent, ready to open fire. Six others, commanded by Feuilly, were stationed at the windows of both upper floors of the Corinthe, guns aimed.

A few more moments passed; then the sound of footfalls, measured, heavy, numerous, was distinctly heard coming from the direction of Saint-Leu. This sound, at first faint, then precise, then heavy and resonant, came nearer slowly, without stopping, without interruption, with a calm and terrible persistence. It was all that could be heard. It was altogether the silence and the sound of the statue of the Commendatore[3] in one, but this stony tread had such an indescribably enormous and multiple quality that it called up the notion of a crowd at the same time as the notion of a ghost. You would have thought you were hearing some frightening statue of a legion on the march. The footfalls came closer; closer still, and stopped. It felt as though you could hear a whole host of men breathing at the end of the street. They couldn't see a thing, though, only, right at the back, in the dense blackness, they could make out a multitude of metal wires, as fine as needles and almost imperceptible, waving around like the indescribable phosphorous networks we see on our closed eyelids just as we fall into the first mists of sleep. They were bayonets and musket barrels dimly lit by the distant reflection from the torch.

There was another pause, as though both sides were waiting. All of a sudden, from the depths of the shadows, a voice, all the more sinister because nobody could be seen and so it seemed that the darkness itself was speaking, cried: "Who's there?"

At the same time, they heard the clatter of guns being leveled.

Enjolras answered in a vibrant and haughty tone: "French Revolution."

"Fire!" said the voice.

A flash turned all the façades of the street crimson as though the door of a furnace had suddenly opened and shut.

A dreadful explosion burst over the barricade. The red flag fell. The shooting had been so heavy and so dense that it had cut the pole, that is, the very tip of the shaft of the bus. Bullets ricocheted off the cornices of the houses, bored into the barricade, and wounded several men.

The impression produced by this opening volley was chilling. The attack was rude, so rude as to give the boldest pause for thought. It was obvious that they were dealing with a whole regiment, at least.

"Comrades," cried Courfeyrac, "let's not waste powder. Let's wait for them to come into the street before we retaliate."

"And before we do anything else," said Enjolras, "let's hoist the flag back up!"

He picked up the flag which had fallen right at his feet.

They could hear outside the clang of ramrods in muskets; the troop was reloading their weapons. Enjolras went on: "Who here has the courage? Who will plant the flag back on the barricade?"

Not one responded. To climb onto the barricade at the moment they were undoubtedly aiming at it once more—that meant death, pure and simple. The bravest hesitate to condemn themselves. Enjolras himself gave a shudder. He repeated: "No volunteers?"

## II. THE FLAG—ACT TWO

Since they had arrived at the Corinthe and had begun building the barricade, no one had paid much attention anymore to old Father Mabeuf. Monsieur Mabeuf, however, had not left the group. He had gone into the ground floor of the tavern and sat behind the bar. There he had sunk into himself, so to speak. He seemed to stop looking or thinking. Courfeyrac and others had spoken to him once or twice, warning him of the danger, advising him to withdraw, but he didn't seem to hear them. When nobody was talking to him, his mouth moved as though he were answering someone, and as soon as someone did speak to him, his lips froze and his eyes no longer looked alive. A few hours before the barricade was assailed, he had adopted a position and he had not moved since, his two hands on his two knees and his head bent forward as though he were looking into a gorge. Nothing had been able to drag him out of this position; it did not look as though his mind was on the barricade. When everyone had gone to take their place for combat, no one was left in the downstairs room except Javert, tied to the post, an insurgent with his saber drawn, keeping watch over Javert, and Mabeuf himself. When the attack occurred, when the explosion erupted, the physical shock reached him and sort of woke him up; he swiftly got to his feet, crossed the room, and, the second Enjolras repeated his appeal, "No volunteers?" they saw the old man appear in the doorway of the tavern.

His presence created a sort of commotion in the ranks. A cry went up: "It's the voter! It's the Conventionist! It's the representative of the people!"

He probably did not hear.

He walked straight up to Enjolras, the insurgents parted in front of him with a religious fear, he ripped the flag from Enjolras, who stepped back, petrified, and then, since no one dared either to stop him or help him, this old man of eighty, his head shaky, his foot firm, slowly began to climb the stairway of cobblestones built into the barricade. This was so grim and so grand that everyone around him cried: "Hats off!" Every step he climbed was torture; his white hair, his decrepit face, his high forehead, bald and wrinkled, his hollow eyes, his mouth gaping open in amazement, his old arm holding up the red banner, emerged from the shadows and grew bigger in the bloodred glare of the torch; and it felt like they were seeing the ghost of '93 emerging from the ground, the flag of the Terror in his hand.

When he was on top of the last step, when this trembling and terrible phantom, standing on that mound of debris before twelve hundred invisible guns, straightened up, in the face of death and as though he were stronger than it, the whole barricade took on a supernatural and colossal look in the darkness. There was one of those silences that only happen in the face of feats of wonder.

In the midst of this silence the old man waved the red flag and cried: "Long live the Revolution! Long live the Republic! Fraternity! Equality! And Death!"

A low rush of whispering could be heard from the barricade, similar to the muttering of a hurrying priest whipping off a quick prayer. It was probably the police chief issuing the customary warnings at the other end of the street. Then the same booming voice that had shouted, "Who's there?" cried: "Get down!"

Monsieur Mabeuf, pallid, haggard, his eyes alight with the wild flames of madness, raised the flag over his head and repeated: "Long live the Republic!"

"Fire!" said the voice.

A second volley, like a shower of grapeshot, came raining down on the barricade.

The old man buckled at the knees, then straightened up, let go of the flag and fell flat on his back on the pavement, like a board, laid out full length with his arms stretched out to the sides like a man on a cross. Streams of blood ran out from under him. His old face, pale and sad, seemed to be looking at the sky.

One of those emotions that are bigger than man and that even make you forget to defend yourself, took hold of the insurgents and they approached the dead body with terror-stricken respect.

"What men these regicides are!" said Enjolras.

Courfeyrac bent down to Enjolras' ear: "This is for your ears only, and I don't want to dampen your enthusiasm. But he was anything but a regicide. I knew him. His name was Father Mabeuf. I don't know what got into him today. But he was a good old codger. Just look at his face."

"The face of an old codger and the heart of a Brutus," answered Enjolras.

Then he raised his voice: "Citizens! This is the example the old give to the young. We were hesitating, he came along! We were backing away, he came forward! This is what those trembling with old age teach those trembling with fear! This old man is august in the eyes of his country. He had a long life and a magnificent death! Now let's cover his corpse and let every one of us defend this old man dead the way he would defend his father alive, and let his presence in our midst make the barricade unassailable!"

A murmur of mournful and impassioned assent followed these words.

Enjolras bent down, lifted the old man's head, and fiercely kissed him on the forehead before folding his arms down; handling the dead man with loving care as though afraid to hurt him, he then took off the old man's coat, showed everyone the bleeding holes in it, and said: "This is our flag now."

### III. GAVROCHE WOULD HAVE DONE BETTER TO ACCEPT ENJOLRAS' CARBINE

They threw a long black shawl belonging to the widow Hucheloup over Father Mabeuf. Six men made a stretcher out of their muskets, placed the body on it and carried it, with their heads bared and with slow solemnity, to the big table in the downstairs room.

These men, completely absorbed as they were in the grave and holy thing they were doing, no longer gave a thought to the perilous situation they were in.

When the corpse passed close to the ever imperturbable Javert, Enjolras snapped at the spy: "You! Not long, now."

While this was happening, little Gavroche, who had remained at his post keeping watch, thought he saw men approaching the barricade, stealthy as wolves. Suddenly he yelled: "Look out!"

Courfeyrac, Enjolras, Jean Prouvaire, Combeferre, Joly, Bahorel, Bossuet, all bundled out of the tavern in turmoil. Already it was almost too late. They could see a sparkling hedge of bayonets rippling above the barricade. Tall Municipal Guards were coming in, some by leaping over the omnibus, the others via the opening, driving before them the gamin who fell back but did not run away.

The moment was critical. It was that first frightening minute of a flood, when the river rises to the level of the levee and the water begins to seep through the cracks in the dike. A second more and the barricade would have been taken.

Bahorel rushed at the first Municipal Guard to come in and killed him point-blank with a shot of his carbine; the second guard killed Bahorel with a thrust of his bayonet. Another had already brought down Courfeyrac who cried: "My turn!" The biggest of them all, a kind of colossus, marched on Gavroche with his bayonet thrust forward. The kid took Javert's enormous musket in his tiny arms, resolutely took aim at the giant, and pulled the trigger. Nothing happened. Javert had not loaded his gun. The Municipal Guard burst out laughing and raised his bayonet over the child.

Before the bayonet touched Gavroche, the gun slipped from the soldier's hands, a bullet had hit him in the middle of his forehead, and he fell on his back. A second bullet struck the other guard, who had assailed Courfeyrac, full in the chest and threw him onto the pavement.

Marius had just stepped into the barricade.

## IV. The Powder Keg

Still hidden in the crook of the rue Mondétour, Marius had watched the first phase of the battle, irresolute and shivering. But he could not resist that mysterious and imperious rush of blood to the head we might name the call of the abyss. Before the imminence of the danger, before the death of Monsieur Mabeuf, that bleak enigma, before Bahorel killed, Courfeyrac crying, "My turn!," this child threatened, his friends to help or to avenge, all hesitation melted away and he leaped into the fray, his two pistols in hand. With the first shot he had saved Gavroche, with the second freed Courfeyrac.

At the gunshots, at the cries of the guards who had been hit, the assailants had scaled the entrenchment, and a throng of Municipal Guards, soldiers of the line, and National Guards from the suburbs could now be seen over the top of it, more than waist-high, with guns in hand. They already covered two thirds of the barrier but they did not jump down into the enclosure, as though weighing things up, fearing some trap. They peered into the dark barricade as you would peer into a lion's den. The glare of the torch lit up only the bayonets, the fur caps, and the upper part of angry, anxious faces.

Marius now had no weapon; he had chucked his pistols once they were discharged, but he had spotted the powder keg next to the door in the downstairs room.

As he half turned round, looking in that direction, a soldier drew a bead on him. Just as the soldier aimed at Marius, a hand planted itself over the end of the gun barrel and blocked it. It was somebody who had rushed forward—the young workman in the velvet pants. The shot went off, the bullet passed through his hand and perhaps through the workman, too, for he fell, but the bullet did not reach Marius. In the smoke all this was glimpsed rather than seen.

Marius, who was stepping into the downstairs room, scarcely noticed. Yet he had dimly seen the gun barrel directed at him and the hand that had blocked it and he heard the shot. But at moments like these, the things you see waver and rush on and you stop for nothing. You feel yourself obscurely driven into even greater darkness and everything turns foggy.

Surprised but not frightened, the insurgents had rallied. Enjolras had cried: "Wait! Don't shoot at random!" In the initial confusion they might indeed have wounded each other with friendly fire. Most had gone up to the window on the first floor and to the dormer windows in the attic, from where they dominated the assailants. The most determined had joined Enjolras, Courfeyrac, Jean Prouvaire, and Combeferre, and had proudly backed against the houses at the end of the street, out in the open and facing the rows of soldiers and guards that crowned the barricade.

All this was achieved without any haste, with that strange and menacing gravity that precedes a mêlée. Both sides took aim, at point-blank range, so close they were within earshot and could talk without raising their voices. Just as sparks were about to fly, an officer in a gorget and with huge epaulets raised his sword and said: "Lay down your arms!"

"Fire!" said Enjolras.

The two sets of explosions went off at the same time and everything disappeared in smoke. Acrid suffocating smoke in which the dying and the wounded crawled with weak and muffled groans.

When the smoke cleared, you could see the combatants on both sides, a bit thinned out but still in the same places, reloading their weapons in silence. All of a sudden a thundering voice was heard, shouting: "Clear out or I'll blow up the barricade!"

Everyone turned to where the voice had come from.

Marius had gone down into the downstairs room, had taken the powder keg that was there, then had taken advantage of the smoke and the kind of black fog that filled the entrenched enclosure to slip along the barricade to the cage full of cobblestones where the torch was propped up. To pull out the torch, put the powder keg in its place, shove the pile of cobblestones under the keg, which had suddenly caved in with a terrible show of compliance—all this had taken Marius the time it took to bend down and straighten up again; and now every one of them, National Guards, Municipal Guards, soldiers, huddled together at the far end of the barricade, looked at him flabbergasted as he stood there with his foot on the cobblestones, the torch in his hand, his proud face lit up with a deadly resolve, tipping the flame of the torch toward the fearful pile where the broken powder keg could be made out, and letting out this terrifying cry: "Clear out or I'll blow up the barricade!"

Marius atop the barricade, following in the octogenarian's footsteps, was a vision of the young revolution after the apparition of the old.

"Blow up the barricade, then!" said a sergeant. "And yourself with it!"

Marius retorted: "And myself with it."

And he brought the torch closer to the powder keg.

But already there was no one left on the roadblock. The assailants, leaving their dead and their wounded behind them, were racing back toward the end of the street pell-mell in chaos, and were once more swallowed up by the night. It was a stampede.

## V. END OF JEAN PROUVAIRE'S POEM

Everyone surrounded Marius. Courfeyrac threw his arms around his neck.

"There you are!"

"Marvelous!" said Combeferre.

"You got here just in time!" said Bossuet.

"Without you I was dead!" continued Courfeyrac.

"Without you, I was a goner!" added Gavroche.

Marius asked: "Where's the chief?"

"You're it," said Enjolras.

Marius had had a furnace burning in his brain all day, now there was a whirlwind. This whirlwind inside him felt like it was outside him, carrying him away. He felt like he was already an immense distance away from life. His two luminous months of love and joy had suddenly ended at this terrifying precipice, Cosette lost to him, this barricade, Monsieur Mabeuf getting himself killed for the Republic, himself the leader of the insurgents—all these things seemed like some monstrous nightmare. He was forced to make a mental effort to remember that all that surrounded him was real. Marius had not lived enough yet to know that nothing is more inevitable than the impossible and that what you must always foresee is the unforeseeable. He was the spectator of his own drama, like a person at a play he doesn't understand.

In this fog where his thoughts were scrambled, he did not recognize Javert. Tied to his post, Javert had not even moved his head during the attack on the barricade. He watched the revolt going on around him with the resignation of a martyr and the majesty of a judge. Marius did not even see him.

Meanwhile the assailants made no further move; you could hear them stamping and swarming at the end of the street, but they did not venture forward, either because they were awaiting orders or awaiting reinforcements before charging at this impregnable redoubt again. The insurgents had posted sentinels and some who were students of medicine had started bandaging the wounded.

All the tables had been thrown out of the tavern except for two tables reserved for lint and cartridges and the table where Father Mabeuf lay dead; they had been added to the barricade and been replaced in the downstairs room by the mattresses from the beds of the widow Hucheloup and her servants. The wounded were laid out on these mattresses. As for the three poor things who inhabited Corinthe, nobody knew what had become of them. They found them in the end, though, hiding in the cellar.

A poignant emotion came to darken the joy of the redeemed barricade.

They called the roll. One of the insurgents was missing. Who was it? One of the most loved, one of the most valiant. Jean Prouvaire. They looked for him among the wounded, he wasn't there. They looked for him among the dead, he wasn't there. He had obviously been taken prisoner.

Combeferre said to Enjolras: "They've got our friend; but we have their agent. Have you got your heart set on the death of that spy?"

"Yes," answered Enjolras, "but not as much as on the life of Jean Prouvaire."

This took place in the downstairs room near Javert's post.

"Well, then," Combeferre went on, "I'm going to tie my handkerchief to my walking stick and go out and negotiate with them by offering to swap their man for ours."

"Listen," said Enjolras, laying his hand on Combeferre's arm.

At the end of the street there was an ominous clatter of arms.

A manly voice was heard to cry out: "Long live France! Long live the future!"

They recognized the voice of Prouvaire.

There was a sudden flash and an explosion.

Silence fell once more.

"They've killed him," cried Combeferre.

Enjolras looked at Javert and said to him: "Your friends have just shot you."

## VI. THE AGONY OF DEATH AFTER THE AGONY OF LIFE

A feature of this kind of warfare is that an attack on the barricades is almost always frontal and that, generally, the assailants refrain from rotating their posts, either because they are worried about ambushes or because they are frightened of committing themselves to the winding streets. All the insurgents' attention, therefore, was centered on the main barricade, which was obviously the point still under threat and where the battle would infallibly start up again. Marius, though, thought about the small barricade and went off there. It was deserted and guarded only by the paper lantern flickering between the cobblestones. Otherwise Mondétour lane and the side streets forking off it—the rue de la Petit-Truanderie and the rue du Cygne—were dead calm.

Just as Marius was withdrawing after his inspection, he heard someone calling his name softly in the dark: "Monsieur Marius!"

He gave a start, for he recognized the voice that had called him two hours earlier through the gate in the rue Plumet. Only, this voice now seemed no more than a breath.

He looked around him and couldn't see anything. Marius thought he'd dreamed it and that his mind was adding hallucinations to the extraordinary events that were piling up around him. He took a step away from the hidden recess where the barricade was tucked away.

"Monsieur Marius!" came the voice again.

This time there could be no doubt, he had distinctly heard it; he looked but still couldn't see anything.

"At your feet," said the voice.

He bent down and saw a shape in the shadows creeping toward him, crawling along the pavement. It was this that had spoken to him.

The paper lantern allowed him to make out a smock, torn pants of coarse velvet, bare feet, and something that looked like a pool of blood. Marius glimpsed a pale face looking up at him and this face said to him: "Don't you recognize me?"

"No."

"Éponine."

Marius swiftly crouched down. It was indeed that poor girl. She was dressed like a man.

"How did you get here? What are you doing here?"

"I'm dying," she told him.

There are words and incidents that wake up even those in the depths of despair. Marius cried with a start: "You're hurt! Wait, I'll carry you to the room. We'll get you bandaged up. Is it serious? How should I pick you up so as not to hurt you? Where does it hurt? Over here, help! My God! Whatever did you come here for?"

And he tried to pass his arm under her to lift her up.

As he lifted her up, he touched her hand.

She let out a feeble cry.

"Did I hurt you?" Marius asked.

"A bit."

"But I only touched your hand."

She raised her hand to Marius's eyes and Marius saw that the hand had a black hole in the middle.

"What's wrong with your hand?" he said.

"It's been ripped open."

"Ripped open!"

"Yes."

"What by?"

"A bullet."

"How?"

"Didn't you see a gun that was aimed at you?"

"Yes, and a hand that blocked it."

"That was my hand."

Marius gave a shudder.

"What madness! You poor girl! But so much the better, if that's all it is, it's nothing. Let me carry you to a bed. We'll get you fixed up, you don't die because your hand's been ripped open."

She murmured: "The bullet passed through my hand, but it came out my back. There's no point taking me anywhere. I'll tell you how you can fix me up, better than any surgeon. Sit next to me on that stone."

Marius did as he was told; she laid her head on his knees, and, without looking at him, she said: "Oh! This is so good! Isn't this cosy! See, I'm not in pain anymore."

She remained silent for a while, then she turned her head with effort and looked at Marius.

"You know, Monsieur Marius? It bothered me that you went into that garden, it was silly of me since it was me who showed you the house, and then, in the end, I should have known that a young man like you—"

She broke off and, leaping over the somber hurdles that were no doubt in her mind, she went on with a heartbreaking smile: "You found me ugly, didn't you?"

She went on: "You see, you're finished! Nobody's going to get out of the barricade alive now. I'm the one who led you here, ha! You're going to die, I should damn well hope so. And yet, when I saw they were aiming at you, I stuck my hand over the mouth of the gun barrel. Funny, isn't it! But it's only because I wanted to die before you did. When the bullet hit me, I crawled over here, no one saw me, no one picked me up. I was waiting for you. I said: Isn't he coming, then? Oh, if you only knew, I was chewing my shirt, it hurt so much! Now I'm fine. Do you remember the day I came into your room and I looked at myself in your mirror, and the day I ran into you on the boulevard near those women on the day shift? How the birds sang! Not all that long ago. You gave me a hundred sous, and I said to you: I don't want your money. Did you pick up your coin, at least? You're not rich. I didn't think to tell you to pick it up. The sun was shining bright, we weren't cold for once. Do you remember, Monsieur Marius? Oh, I'm so happy! Everyone's going to die."

She had a wild, grave, and harrowing air about her. Her torn blouse showed her bare throat. While she was talking, she rested her wounded hand on her chest where there was another hole and where a stream of blood spurted at intervals like a jet of wine from an open stopper.

Marius studied this unhappy creature with deep compassion.

"Oh!" she went on suddenly. "It's coming back. I can't breathe!"

She bunched her blouse and bit into it and her legs went stiff on the pavement.

At that moment the young cock's voice of little Gavroche rang out through the barricade. The boy had climbed up on a table to load his gun and was gaily singing the song so popular at the time:

At the sight of Lafayette,
The gendarme lost his head:
Run! Run! Run! he said.[1]

Éponine lifted herself up and listened, then she murmured: "It's him."

And she turned to Marius: "My brother's here. He mustn't see me. He'd only scold me."

"Your brother?" asked Marius, who was thinking in the bitterest and most painful recesses of his heart of the duties to the Thénardiers that his father had bequeathed to him. "Who is your brother?"

"The little one."

"The one singing?"

"Yes."

Marius made a move.

"Oh, don't go!" she said. "It won't be long now."

She was almost sitting upright, but her voice was very faint and broken by hiccups. At times a death rattle interrupted her. She brought her face as close as she could to Marius's face and added with a strange expression: "Listen. I don't want to play any dirty tricks on you. I have a letter in my pocket for you. I've had it since yesterday. I was told to put it in the post. But I kept it. I didn't want you to get it. But you'd hold it against me, maybe, when we see each other again in a little while. We will see each other again, won't we? Take your letter!"

She seized Marius's hand convulsively with her wounded hand, but she no longer seemed to feel pain. She stuck Marius's hand in the pocket of her smock. Marius felt a piece of paper there.

"Take it," she said.

Marius took the letter. She gave a sign of satisfaction and contentment.

"Now, for my pains, promise me . . ."

She stopped.

"What?" asked Marius.

"Promise me!"

"I promise you."

"Promise me you'll kiss me on the forehead when I'm dead . . . I will feel it."

She let her head fall on Marius's knees and her eyelids closed. He thought the poor soul had departed. Éponine remained motionless; then, all of a sudden, at the very moment when Marius thought she had gone to sleep forever, she slowly opened her eyes and death appeared in their gloomy depths, and she said to him in a tone whose sweetness seemed already to come from another world: "And then, you see, Monsieur Marius, I think I was a little bit in love with you."

She tried to smile again and died.

## VII. GAVROCHE A PROFOUND CALCULATOR OF DISTANCES

Marius kept his promise. He placed a kiss on that pale forehead beaded with ice-cold sweat. It was not an act of infidelity to Cosette; it was a thoughtful and sweet farewell to a poor unhappy soul.

He had not taken the letter Éponine had given him without a thrill. He had immediately felt that it was an event. He was longing to read it. Thus is the heart of man made—scarcely had the poor unhappy girl closed her eyes than Marius was thinking about opening the note. He laid her gently on the ground and moved away. Something told him he could not read the letter in front of that corpse.

He ran to a candle in the downstairs room. It was a little note, folded and sealed with a woman's elegant care. The address was in a woman's handwriting and ran: *To Monsieur, Monsieur Marius Pontmercy, care of Monsieur Courfeyrac, rue de la Verrerie, no. 16.*

He broke the seal and read:

My beloved, alas! My father wants us to leave right away. We will be at the rue de l'Homme-Armé, no. 7, this evening. In a week we will be in England. Cosette. June 4.

Such was the freshness of this love affair that Marius did not even know Cosette's writing.

What had happened can be told in a few words. Éponine had done it all. After the evening of June 3, she had dreamed up a twin plot, to undo the schemes of her father and his cohorts on the house in the rue Plumet, and to separate Marius and Cosette. She had swapped rags with the first young rogue to come along who had found it fun to dress up as a woman while Éponine disguised herself as a man. It was Éponine who, at the Champ de Mars, had given Jean Valjean that evocative warning: "Clear out!" Jean Valjean had in fact gone home and said to Cosette: "We're leaving this evening and we're going to the rue de l'Homme-Armé with Toussaint. Next week we will be in London." Cosette, floored by this unexpected blow, had dashed off a couple of lines to Marius. But how could she get the letter to the post? She did not go out alone and Toussaint, surprised by such an errand, would most certainly have shown the letter to Monsieur Fauchelevent. In her anxiety, Cosette had looked through the gate and spotted Éponine in her man's getup, now prowling endlessly about the garden. Cosette had called over this "young working lad" and given him five francs and the letter, with the instructions: "To carry this letter immediately to the address on it." Éponine had pocketed the letter. The next day, June 5, she had gone to Courfeyrac's to ask for Marius, not to hand him the letter but, something every jealous and loving heart will understand, "to see." There, she had waited for Marius, or, at least Courfeyrac—yet again, to see. When Courfeyrac had told her, "We're going to the barricades," she had had an idea. To throw herself into that very death just as she would have thrown herself into any other, and drag Marius in, too. She had followed Courfeyrac, had made sure exactly where the barricade was being built, and had made very sure, since Marius had had no notice and since she had intercepted the letter, that he would be at his usual evening rendezvous. And so she had gone to the rue Plumet, had waited for Marius there and sent him, on his friends' behalf, the appeal that should, she thought, send him to the barricade. She was counting on Marius's despair when he did not find Cosette, and she was not mistaken. She had gone back, for her part, to the rue de la Chanvrerie. We have just seen what she did there. She died with the tragic joy of jealous souls who drag the one they love down into death with them, telling themselves: No one else will have him!

Marius covered Cosette's letter with kisses. So she loved him after all! For a moment, he had the idea that he must not die now. Then he told himself: She is going away. Her father is taking her to England and my grandfather refuses to consent to the marriage. Nothing has changed fate. Dreamers like Marius feel such extreme devastation and only desperate measures result. When you are tired of living because life is unbearable, death is soon over with.

He then thought that there were two duties he had yet to perform: to inform Cosette of his death and send her one last farewell, and to save that poor boy, Éponine's brother and Thénardier's son, from the catastrophe that was coming.

He had a wallet on him; the same one that had contained the notebook in which he had written so many loving thoughts for Cosette. He ripped out a page from it and penciled these few lines:

Our marriage was impossible. I asked my grandfather and he refused; I have no money and neither do you. I ran to your place, but I did not find you there. You know the promise I made to you and I will keep it. I am dying. I love you. When you read this, my soul will be near you, and will smile at you.

Having nothing to seal this letter with, he merely folded the page in four and wrote this address out: *To Mademoiselle Cosette Fauchelevent, care of Monsieur Fauchelevent, rue de l'Homme-Armé, no. 7.*

The letter folded, he remained lost in thought for a moment, grabbed his wallet again, opened it, and wrote with the same pencil on the first page these four lines:

My name is Marius Pontmercy. Carry my body to my grandfather, Monsieur Gillenormand, rue des Filles-du-Calvaire, no. 6, in the Marais.

He put the wallet in his coat and then he called Gavroche. The gamin came running at the sound of Marius's voice, with his face full of joy and devotion.

"Would you like to do something for me?"

"Anything," said Gavroche. "God Almighty! Without you, hell, I'd have bitten the dust!"

"You see this letter?"

"Yep."

"Take it. Go out of the barricade as fast as you can"—Gavroche, anxious, started to scratch his ear—"and tomorrow morning, take it to the address on it, to Mademoiselle Cosette at Monsieur Fauchelevent's place, rue de l'Homme-Armé, number seven."

The heroic child answered: "Ah, well, but in that time, they'll storm the barricade and I won't be there."

"The barricade won't be attacked again before daybreak as far as I can tell, and it won't be taken before tomorrow afternoon."

The new respite that the assailants were allowing the barricade had indeed been extended. It was one of those intermissions, frequent in night combat, that are always followed by a redoubling of fury.

"In that case," said Gavroche, "suppose I go and take your letter tomorrow morning?"

"It will be too late. The barricade will probably be blocked off, all the streets will be guarded, and you won't be able to get out. Go now."

Gavroche was stuck for a reply, so he stayed there, undecided and scratching his ear sadly. All of a sudden, with one of those birdlike movements of his, he took the letter.

"All righty," he said.

And he ran off down Mondétour lane.

Gavroche had had an idea that had decided him, but he did not tell Marius for fear that he would object to it.

The idea was this: "It's not yet midnight, the rue de l'Homme-Armé isn't far, I'll take the letter there right away and I'll be back in plenty of time."[1]

# BOOK FIFTEEN

# THE RUE DE L'HOMME-ARMÉ

## I. A BLABBER OF A BLOTTER

What are a city's convulsions next to the riots of the soul? One man on his own is even deeper than the whole populace put together. Jean Valjean, at that very moment, was in the grip of a frightening upheaval. All the bottomless pits had opened up again inside him. He, too, shuddered, like Paris, on the brink of a mighty and obscure revolution. A few hours had been enough. His destiny and his conscience had abruptly clouded over. Of him, too, as of Paris, you could say that the two principles were having a face-off. The white angel and the black angel were about to go head to head on a bridge over an abyss. Which of the two will push the other over? Who will win?

The night before that same day, June 5, Jean Valjean, accompanied by Cosette and Toussaint, had moved to the rue de l'Homme-Armé. A twist of fate awaited him there.

Cosette had not left the rue Plumet without a show of resistance. For the first time since they had lived together, side by side, Cosette's will and Jean Valjean's will had revealed themselves to be distinct, and had, if not clashed, then at least been at variance. There had been objections on one side and inflexibility on the other. That abrupt advice, "Clear out," tossed at Jean Valjean by an unknown person, had alarmed him to the point of making him uncompromising. He believed himself to have been tracked down and pursued. Cosette had had to yield.

Both had arrived at the rue de l'Homme-Armé without opening their mouths or saying a word, each absorbed in their personal preoccupations; Jean Valjean so anxious he didn't see Cosette's sadness, Cosette so sad she didn't see Jean Valjean's anxiety.

Jean Valjean had brought Toussaint along, which he had never done in his previous absences. He anticipated that he would perhaps not return to the rue Plumet, and he could not leave Toussaint behind or tell her his secret. Besides, he felt that she was devoted and reliable. Between servant and master, treachery begins with curiosity. Now, Toussaint, as though predestined to be Jean Valjean's servant, was not curious. She stuttered in her Barneville peasant's talk: "I'm ever the same; I do whatever I do; the remainder is not my work." (That's how I am; I do my job; the rest is not my affair.)

In this departure from the rue Plumet, which had almost amounted to flight, Jean Valjean had taken nothing except the small embalmed case christened by Cosette "the inseparable." Packed trunks would have required carriers and carriers are witnesses. They called a fiacre to the gate on the rue de Babylone and off they went.

It was only with great difficulty that Toussaint had obtained permission to bundle up a bit of linen and clothing and a few toiletries. Cosette herself had only taken her stationery and her blotter.

To make doubly sure no one would see them disappear into the shadows, Jean Valjean had arranged things so as not to leave the villa on the rue Plumet until the close of day, which had left Cosette time to write her note to Marius. They had arrived at the rue de l'Homme-Armé after dark. They had gone to bed in silence.

The accommodation in the rue de l'Homme-Armé was located off a rear courtyard, on the second floor, and consisted of two bedrooms, a dining room, and a kitchen off the dining room, with a closet under the stairs where there was a camp bed that fell to Toussaint. The dining room doubled as an antechamber and divided the two bedrooms. The apartment was provided with all the necessary utensils.

We are reassured almost as crazily as we are alarmed; it's human nature. Hardly had Jean Valjean been in the rue de l'Homme-Armé five minutes than his anxiety lifted, and by degrees, blew over. There are places that have a calming effect that works more or less mechanically on the mind. A dark street, quiet residents, and Jean Valjean felt strangely infected by tranquillity in this laneway of old Paris, so narrow it was barred to carriages by a crossbeam placed across two posts, deaf and dumb in the middle of the noisy city, crepuscular in broad daylight, and incapable, so to speak, of emotion between its two rows of tall century-old houses that hold their peace like the old folk they are. There is stagnant oblivion in this street. Jean Valjean could breathe there. How could anyone find him there?

His first concern was to see that "the inseparable" was stowed by his side.

He slept well. Night counsels; we might add: Night pacifies. The next morning, he woke up almost lighthearted. He found the dining room charming when it was hideous, furnished with an old round table, a low sideboard surmounted by a slanting mirror, a worm-eaten armchair, and a few chairs stacked with Toussaint's bundles. Through an opening in one of these bundles you could see Jean Valjean's National Guard uniform.

As for Cosette, she had had Toussaint bring her a bouillon in her room and only put in an appearance in the evening.

At around five o'clock, Toussaint, who was bustling about, very busy with this little move, had laid out cold chicken on the dining table, which Cosette, out of deference to her father, had consented to look at.

That done, Cosette had pleaded a persistent migraine, said good night to Jean Valjean and shut herself up in her room. Jean Valjean had wolfed down a chicken wing and, with his elbows on the table, putting his mind gradually to rest, was regaining his sense of security.

While he was enjoying this sober meal, he had vaguely picked up, once or twice, Toussaint's stuttering as she said to him: "Monsieur, there is a row, they're fighting in Paris." But absorbed as he was in a whole host of inner thoughts, he had not paid much attention. To tell the truth, he hadn't really heard. He got up and started to pace from the window to the door and from the door to the window, calmer and calmer.

With this calmness, Cosette, his sole concern, came flooding back into his mind. Not that he was worried about this migraine of hers, a minor attack of nerves, a young girl's sulks, a momentary cloud that would disappear in a day or two; but he was thinking of the future, and as usual, he thought about it sweetly, with pleasure.

After all, he could see no obstacle to their happy life's resuming its normal course. At certain moments, everything seems impossible; at others, it all seems so easy; Jean Valjean was in one of those happy moments—they normally follow the bad ones, as day follows night, according to that law of succession and contrast that is the very basis of nature and that superficial minds call antithesis. In this peaceful street where he had taken refuge, Jean Valjean let go of all that had been troubling him for some time. Just because he had seen so many dark clouds, he could now begin to see a bit of blue sky up ahead. Having got away from the rue Plumet without any complications or incidents was already a step in the right direction.

Perhaps it would be wise to leave the country, if only for a few months, and go abroad to London. Well, then, they would go. Whether they were in France or England, what did it matter, as long as he had Cosette by his side? Cosette was his nation. Cosette was all he needed to be happy; the idea that he was perhaps not all Cosette needed to be happy, this idea that had once given him fever and insomnia, simply did not occur to him. He was enjoying the collapse of all his past pain and he was full of optimism. Cosette, being by his side, seemed to him to belong to him, an optical illusion that everyone has experienced. He arranged in his head, with the greatest possible ease, the trip to England with Cosette, and he saw his felicity rebuild itself, no matter where, from the standpoint of his waking dream.

While he slowly paced up and down, his gaze suddenly fell on something strange. He saw opposite him, in the slanting mirror on top of the sideboard, these four lines which he could distinctly read:

My beloved, alas! My father wants us to leave right away. We will be at the rue de l'Homme-Armé, no. 7, this evening. In a week we will be in England. Cosette. June 4.

Jean Valjean froze, aghast.

On arriving, Cosette had placed her blotter on the sideboard in front of the mirror and, completely lost in her painful anguish, had left it there, without even realizing that she had left it wide open, and open precisely at the page on which she had pressed, to dry them, those four lines written by her and which she had entrusted to the young workman passing by in the rue Plumet. The writing had left its imprint on the blotter. The mirror reflected the writing.

The result was what is known in geometry as a symmetrical image; the writing reversed on the blotter showed itself the right way round in the mirror and ran in the right direction. And Jean Valjean had before his eyes the letter written the night before by Cosette to Marius. It was simple and it was devastating.

Jean Valjean went to the mirror. He reread the four lines, but he did not believe it. They had the effect on him of an apparition seen in a flash of lightning. It was a hallucination. It was impossible. It was not.

Little by little his perception became more precise; he looked at Cosette's blotter and awareness of reality came back to him. He snatched the blotter and said: "That comes from this." He feverishly examined those four lines imprinted on the blotter, the reversal of the letters turning it into bizarre scribble that he couldn't make head or tail of. So he told himself: "But it doesn't mean anything, there's nothing written there." And he breathed deeply with inexpressible relief. Who has not felt ridiculous joy like that in moments of horror? The soul does not give in to despair without exhausting all possible illusions.

He held the blotter in his hand and contemplated it, stupidly happy, almost ready to laugh at the hallucination he'd been hoodwinked by. All of a sudden his eyes fell on the mirror again and again he saw the vision. The four lines stood out in the mirror with a sharpness that was inexorable. This time it was not a mirage. The second occurrence of a vision is a reality; it was palpable, it was writing corrected in a mirror. He finally understood.

Jean Valjean tottered, dropped the blotter, and fell into the old armchair next to the sideboard, his head down, his eyes glassy, half-crazed. He told himself it was all too clear and that the world's light was forever eclipsed and that Cosette had written that to somebody. Then he heard his soul, which had become black and terrible again, let out a muffled roar in the darkness. Try and take away the dog the lion has in its cage!

What was odd and sad was that, at that moment, Marius did not yet have Cosette's letter; chance had treacherously brought it to Jean Valjean before handing it over to Marius.

Until that day, Jean Valjean had never been defeated by any ordeal. He had been subjected to horrific trials and tribulations; not a single assault and battery of an ill-starred life had ever been spared him; the ferocity of fate, armed with every act of vengeance and every kind of social scorn, had taken him up and hounded him relentlessly. He had not backed down or flinched before any of it. He had accepted, when he had to, every violent blow; he had sacrificed his inviolability as a man redeemed, surrendered his freedom, risked his neck, lost everything, been to hell and back, and had remained disinterested and stoical, to the point where at times you might have thought him dissociated from himself in the manner of a martyr. His conscience, battle-hardened against all possible assaults by adversity, might seem forever impregnable. Well, then, anyone who had seen deep inside him at that moment would have been forced to admit that he had taken a terrible beating and was failing.

For, of all the tortures that he had suffered in this long testing that destiny had subjected him to, this one was the most awful. Never had such a vise had him in its grip. He felt the mysterious stirrings of all his latent sensibilities. He felt the tug of an unknown feeling. Alas, the supreme ordeal, better still, the only ordeal, is the loss of the one you love.

Poor old Jean Valjean, of course, loved Cosette only as a father; but, as we noted earlier, into this fatherly love his lonely single status in life had introduced every other kind of love; he loved Cosette as his daughter, and he loved her as his mother, and he loved her as his sister; and, as he had never had either a lover or a wife, as nature is a creditor that does not accept nonpayment, that particular feeling, too, the most indestructible of all, had thrown itself in with the rest, vague, ignorant, heavenly, angelic, divine; less a feeling than an instinct, less an instinct than an attraction, imperceptible and invisible but real; and love, truly called, lay in his enormous tenderness for Cosette the way a vein of gold lies in the mountain, dark and virginal.

We should bear in mind that state of the heart that we have already mentioned. Marriage between them was out of the question, even that of souls; and yet it is certain that their destinies had joined together as one. Except for Cosette, that is, except for a child, Jean Valjean had never, in all his long life, known anything about love. Serial passions and love affairs had not laid those successive shades of green over him, fresh green on top of dark green, that you notice on foliage that has come through winter and on men that have passed their fifties. In short, and we have insisted on this more than once, this whole inner fusion, this whole set, the result of which was lofty virtue, had wound up making Jean Valjean a father for Cosette. A strange father, forged out of the grandfather, son, brother, and husband that were all in Jean Valjean; a father in whom there was even a mother; a father who loved Cosette and worshipped her, and for whom that child was light, was home, was his homeland, was paradise.

So when he saw that it was all over, that she was escaping from him, that she was slipping through his fingers, that she was hiding, that she was a cloud, she was water, when he had this shattering evidence before his very eyes: "another is the one her heart yearns for, another is the hope of her life; there is the beloved, I am only the father; I no longer exist"; when he could no longer doubt, when he said to himself, "She's going away out of me!" the pain he felt was beyond endurance. To have done all he had done only to come to this! And, what! Be nothing! At that point, as we said, he gave a shudder of revolt. He felt even the roots of his hair stand on end with the rousing of egotism, and his ego howled in the abyss of his soul.

You can collapse inside. A despairing certainty does not penetrate a man without pushing aside and sundering certain deep features that are sometimes the man himself. When pain reaches that level, all the forces of a person's conscience stampede. Such crises are fatal. Not many of us emerge from them in our right minds and firm in our sense of duty. When the limit of suffering is exceeded, the most imperturbable virtue is rocked. Jean Valjean grabbed the blotter again and convinced himself once more. He stayed hunched, and as though turned to stone, over those four indisputable lines, his eyes staring; and such a heavy cloud formed inside him that you could believe that the man's entire innards were falling apart.

He studied this revelation, through the magnification of reverie, in apparent yet frightening calm, for it is a fearful thing when a man's calmness achieves the coldness of a statue.

He measured the appalling turn his fate had taken without his suspecting it; he recalled his fears of the previous summer, so crazily dispelled; he recognized the edge of the abyss; it was still the same; only Jean Valjean was no longer on the brink, he was at the bottom.

An unheard-of and heartrending thing, he had fallen in without realizing. The whole light of his life had gone out and he had believed he could still see the sun.

His instinct was swift and sure. He put together certain circumstances, certain dates, certain blushes and pallors of Cosette's, and he said to himself: "It was him." The divination of despair is a sort of mysterious bow that never misses the mark. In his first conjecture, he hit on Marius. He did not know the name, but he found the man immediately. He distinctly saw, at the bottom of the implacable evocation of memory, the unknown prowler of the Luxembourg, that miserable seeker of flings, that ne'er-do-well of romance, that lovelorn imbecile, that coward, for it is a form of cowardice to come and make eyes at girls who have by their side their father who loves them.

After he had fully decided that it was that young man who was at the bottom of this situation, and that it all stemmed from there, he, Jean Valjean, the regenerated man, the man who had done so much work on his soul, the man who had made so many efforts to resolve all life, all misery, and all unhappiness in love—he looked inside himself and saw there a specter, Hate.

Great pain brings great weariness with it. It dampens the will to live. The man it enters feels something go out of him. In youth its visit is gloomy; later, it is sinister. Alas, when your blood is hot, when your hair is black, when your head sits straight on your shoulders like a flame on a flare, when the scroll of destiny is still almost unrolled, when your heart, full of a love that is sanctioned, can still beat in a way that calls forth another's heartbeats, when you have all the time in the world ahead of you to mend, when all women are there, and all smiles and all the future, and the whole horizon, when the force of life is at its fullest—if despair is an appalling thing even so, what is it in old age, when the years hurtle on, bleaker and bleaker, to that twilight hour when you begin to see the stars of the grave!

While he was musing, Toussaint came in. Jean Valjean got up and asked her: "Whereabouts is it? Do you know?"

Toussaint, astonished, could only answer: "Sorry?"

Jean Valjean went on: "Didn't you tell me a moment ago that there was fighting?"

"Ah, yes, Monsieur!" replied Toussaint. "It's over by Saint-Merry."

There are certain mechanical motions that come to us, even unwittingly, from our deepest thoughts. It was no doubt under the impulse of such a motion of which he was barely aware that Jean Valjean found himself five minutes later on the street.

He was bareheaded, sitting on his doorstep. He seemed to be listening. Night had come.

## II. THE KID AS THE ENEMY OF THE ENLIGHTENMENT

How much time did he spend like this? What were the ebbs and flows of his tragic meditation? Did he straighten up? Did he remain slumped? Was he buckled so far as to break? Could he straighten up again and regain a foothold on something solid in his conscience? He himself probably could not have said.

The street was deserted. A few anxious bourgeois rapidly returning home scarcely looked his way in passing. It's every man for himself in times of peril.

The lamplighter came along as usual and lit the streetlamp that stood exactly opposite the door of no. 7, and went away again. Jean Valjean, to anyone examining him in the shadows, would not have looked like he was alive. He just sat there, on his doorstep, stock-still like a specter made of ice. Despair causes us to freeze. You could hear the tocsin and vague stormy noises. In the middle of all this convulsive clamor, with the bell and the riot sounding together, the clock at Saint-Paul struck eleven, gravely, taking its time, for the tocsin is man and the hour is God. The passing of the hour had no effect on Jean Valjean; Jean Valjean did not budge. Yet, almost at that very moment, a brusque explosion erupted over by Les Halles, followed by a second explosion, even more violent; it was most likely the attack on the barricade of the rue de la Chanvrerie which we just saw Marius repel. At this double detonation, whose fury seemed intensified by the stupor of the night, Jean Valjean came to his senses; he shot up in the direction the noise had come from; then he fell back down on the doorstep, folded his arms, and his head dropped slowly back down onto his chest.

He resumed his dark dialogue with himself.

All of a sudden he raised his eyes. Someone was walking in the street. He heard footsteps close by, he looked, and, by the light of the streetlamp, on the side of the street that ends in the Archives, he saw a face that was pale, young, and radiant.

Gavroche had just reached the rue de l'Homme-Armé. Gavroche was gazing up in the air as though looking for something. He saw Jean Valjean perfectly well, but he took no notice of him.

After looking up in the air, Gavroche looked down at the ground; he stood on tiptoes and groped around the doors and windows of the ground floors; they were all shut, locked and bolted. After checking five or six housefronts barricaded in this fashion, the kid shrugged his shoulders and tackled the matter with himself in these terms: "I'll be buggered!"

Then he started looking up in the air again.

Jean Valjean who, a moment before, in the state of mind he was in, would not have spoken to or even answered anyone, found himself irresistibly driven to address this child.

"Little one," he said, "what's the matter?"

"What the matter is, is that I'm hungry," answered Gavroche bluntly. And he added: "Little one yourself."

Jean Valjean fumbled in his fob pocket and pulled out a five-franc piece. But Gavroche, who was of the wagtail species and flitted from one move to the next fast, had just picked up a stone. He had noticed the streetlamp.

"Hey," he said, "you've still got your streetlamps over here. You're out of order, my friends. It's downright disorderly. Smash that for me."

And he threw the stone at the lamp whose glass fell with such a racket that the bourgeois huddled behind their curtains in the house opposite shrieked: "It's '93 all over again!"

The lamplight flickered wildly and went out. The street suddenly went black.

"That's it, old street," said Gavroche. "Put your nightcap on."

And turning to Jean Valjean: "What d'you call that gigantic monument you've got at the end of the street? It's the Archives, isn't it? I need you to knock off a bit of those silly great columns down there for me and be good enough to make me a barricade with 'em."

Jean Valjean went over to Gavroche.

"Poor boy," he said in a voice barely above a whisper, adding to himself, "he's hungry."

And he put the hundred-sou piece in the boy's hand.

Gavroche stuck his head up, amazed by the size of this *gros sou;* he looked at it in the dark, and the whiteness of the *gros sou* dazzled him. He knew about five-franc coins by hearsay; their reputation pleased him; he was enchanted to see one so close. He said: "Let's have a look at the tiger."

He studied it for a few moments in ecstasy; then he turned toward Jean Valjean and handed him back the coin, saying magisterially: "Bourgeois, I'd rather smash lanterns. Take your wild beast back. No one corrupts me. It's got five claws; but it won't scratch me."

"Do you have a mother?" asked Jean Valjean.

Gavroche replied: "Maybe more than you have."

"Well, then," Jean Valjean continued, "keep the money for your mother."

Gavroche felt stirred. Besides, he had just noticed that the man talking to him had no hat and that inspired his confidence.

"Say," he said, "it's not to stop me smashing streetlamps or anything?"

"Smash away."

"You're all right," said Gavroche.

And he put the five-franc piece in one of his pockets. His confidence growing, he said: "Are you from this street?"

"Yes, why?"

"Can you show me which one's number seven?"

"Why number seven?"

Here the boy stopped. He feared he might have said too much, he raked his hair hard with his nails and refrained from saying more than: "Ah, there it is."

A bright idea popped into Jean Valjean's head. Anguish produces such lucidity. He said to the boy:

"So it's you, is it? You've brought me the letter I'm waiting for?"

"You?" said Gavroche. "You're not a woman."

"The letter's for Mademoiselle Cosette, isn't it?"

"Cosette?" growled Gavroche. "Yes, I think it's some funny name like that."

"Well, then," Jean Valjean went on, "I'm the one who's supposed to hand her the letter. Give it to me."

"In that case, you must know I've been sent from the barricade?"

"Of course," said Jean Valjean.

Gavroche buried his fist in another of his pockets and pulled out a note folded in four.

Then he gave the military salute.

"Respect to the dispatch," he said. "It comes from the provisional government."

"Give it to me," said Jean Valjean.

Gavroche held the note up above his head.

"Don't go getting the idea that this is a love letter. It's for a woman, but it's for the people. We men, we're fighting men, and we respect the sex. We're not like in high society where there are nobs who send sweet nothings to slack cows."

"Give it to me."

"Actually," Gavroche continued, "you look to me to be a good sort of geezer."

"Give it to me quick."

"Take it."

And he handed Jean Valjean the note.

"And get a move on, Monsieur Thingummyjig, because Mamselle Thingummyjigette is waiting."

Gavroche was very pleased with himself for having come up with this line.

Jean Valjean went on: "Should the answer be sent to Saint-Merry?"

"If you do that," declared Gavroche, "you'd be making the bungle commonly known as a howler. That letter comes from the barricade in the rue de la Chanvrerie and I'm going back there now. *Bonsoir,* citizen."

And with that, Gavroche spun on his heel and went, or, to be more accurate, zoomed off in the direction he had come from like a bird that has escaped. He dived back into the darkness as though boring through it, with the rigid speed of a projectile; the little rue de l'Homme-Armé became silent and solitary once more; in the blink of an eye, that strange child, who had both shadow and dream in him, had sunk into the mist of those rows of black houses and been lost there like smoke in the dark; and you might well think he'd blown away and vanished if, a few minutes after he disappeared, a resounding noise of breaking glass and the splendid crash of a streetlamp shattering onto the pavement had not brusquely woken up the indignant bourgeois once more. It was Gavroche going down the rue du Chaume.

### III. WHILE COSETTE AND TOUSSAINT ARE SLEEPING

Jean Valjean went home with the letter from Marius.

He groped his way upstairs, pleased with the darkness like an owl holding his prey, opened and softly closed his door, listened to hear if there was any sound, assured himself that, as far as he could tell, Cosette and Toussaint were sleeping, plunged three or four matches into the bottle of the Fumade tinder-box before he could get the spark to ignite, his hand was shaking so much, for what he had just done smacked of stealing. Finally, his candle lit, he leaned on the table, unfolded the piece of paper, and read.

In the throes of violent emotions, you do not read, you wrestle to the ground, so to speak, the piece of paper you are holding, you strangle it like a victim, you crush it, you dig your nails into it with your anger or your delight; you race to the end, you jump to the beginning; attention is feverish; it understands the essential, overall, more or less; but then it seizes on a point and all the rest disappears. In Marius's note to Cosette, Jean Valjean saw only these words: "I am dying . . . When you read these lines, my soul will be near you . . ."

In the face of those two lines, he felt a horrible giddiness; he remained for a moment apparently crushed by the emotional shift that was happening inside him, he looked at Marius's note in a sort of drunken stupor; he had before his eyes that splendor, the death of the hated being.

He let out a hideous cry of inner joy. So it was over. The end had come sooner than he would have dared hope. The being in the way of his destiny was about to disappear. He was going away of his own accord, freely, in good faith. Without him, Jean Valjean, having to do anything to provoke it, without its being his fault in any way, "that man" was going to die. Perhaps he was already dead, even.—Here he started to calculate in his fever.—No. He is not dead yet. The letter was clearly written for Cosette to read first thing in the morning; since those two discharges went off between eleven and midnight, nothing has happened; the barricade will not be seriously attacked until daybreak; but that doesn't matter, from the moment "that man" gets mixed up in this war, he's lost; he's caught in the machinery.—Jean Valjean felt himself released. So he was going to find himself alone with Cosette again. The competition was about to end. The future was about to begin again. All he had to do was keep this note in his pocket. Cosette would never know what had happened to "that man." "All I have to do is let things take their course. That man can't escape. If he isn't dead yet, he soon will be, that's for sure. What happiness!"

All this gone over inside, he became gloomy. Then he went downstairs and woke up the porter.

About an hour later, Jean Valjean left in full National Guard regalia, and armed. The porter had easily been able to dig up in the neighborhood what he needed to complete his gear. He had a loaded musket and a cartridge pouch full of cartridges. He headed toward Les Halles.

## IV. Gavroche's Excessive Zeal

Meanwhile Gavroche had just had an adventure.

After conscientiously stoning the streetlamp in the rue du Chaume, he came to the rue des Vieilles-Haudriettes, and not seeing any "cat" there, thought it a good opportunity to strike up a song. Far from being slowed down by the singing, his pace picked up. He began sowing these incendiary couplets all the way along the sleeping or terrified houses:

> The bird sounds off in the bowers
> And reckons that yesterday Atala
> Went off with a Russian.
>
> > Where have all the beautiful girls gone,
> > Lon la.
>
> My friend Pierrot, you're babbling,
> Because the other day Mila
> Tapped her window and called me.
>
> > Where have all the beautiful girls gone,
> > Lon la.
>
> The hussies are very nice
> Their poison that bewitches me
> Would intoxicate Monsieur Orfila.
>
> > Where have all the beautiful girls gone,
> > Lon la.
>
> I love love and its tiffs,
> I love Agnes, I love Pamela,
> Lise will get burned if she stirs me up.
>
> > Where have all the beautiful girls gone,
> > Lon la.
>
> Once, when I saw the mantillas
> Of Suzette and of Zéila,
> My soul melted in their folds.
>
> > Where have all the beautiful girls gone,
> > Lon la.

Love shines in the shadows,
And dresses Lola's hair with roses,
I'd go down to hell for that.

> Where have all the beautiful girls gone,
> Lon la.

Jeanne, you get dressed at your mirror!
One fine day my heart will fly away;
I think it's Jeanne who has it.

> Where have all the beautiful girls gone,
> Lon la.

At night, as I leave the lancers
I show the stars Stella
And I tell them: look at her.

> Where have all the beautiful girls gone,
> Lon la.[1]

While he sang, Gavroche was lavish with pantomime. Gesture is the basis of the refrain. His face was an inexhaustible repertory of masks and he made grimaces more convulsive and more fantastic than the mouths that washing torn in a heavy wind makes. Unfortunately, as he was alone and it was night-time, all this was neither seen nor seeable. So many treasures are lost.

Suddenly he stopped in his tracks.

"Let's cut the romance," he said.

His catlike eyes had made out in the recess of a porte cochère what is known in painting as a group; that is, a being and a thing. The thing was a cart, the being was a peasant from Auvergne sleeping in it.

The handles of the cart were resting on the pavement and the head of the Auvergnat was leaning on the tailboard of the cart. His body was curled up on this inclined plane and his feet touched the ground.

Gavroche, with his experience of the things of this world, knew a drunk when he saw one. It was some carter from around there who had drunk too much and was now sleeping too much.

"This," said Gavroche, "is what summer nights are good for. The Auvergnat is dozing in his cart. We'll take the cart for the Republic and we'll leave the Auvergnat to his monarchy."

He had had a bright idea: "This cart will go nicely on our barricade."

The Auvergnat was snoring.

Gavroche gently pulled the cart by the rear end and the Auvergnat by the front end, that is, by the feet; and soon the imperturbable Auvergnat was lying flat on the ground. The cart had been freed.

Gavroche was used to confronting the unexpected at every turn and always had everything on him. He fumbled in one of his pockets and pulled out a scrap of paper and a stub of a red pencil nicked from some carpenter.

He wrote: "*French Republic.* Received your cart."

And he signed: "Gavroche."

That done, he stuck the piece of paper in the pocket of the still-snoring Auvergnat's velvet waistcoat, took hold of the shaft with both hands, and left, heading for Les Halles, steering the cart in front of him at a fast clip in a glorious triumphal breach of the peace.

This was perilous. There was a post at the Imprimerie Royale. Gavroche had forgotten about it. This post was occupied by National Guards from the suburbs. A certain alertness was beginning to rouse the squad, and heads were lifting from off camp beds. Two streetlamps broken one after the other, that song sung at the top of someone's lungs, was a lot for such lily-livered streets, full of people who just wanted to go to sleep at sundown and who clapped their snuffers over their candles so early. For an hour the kid had been making as much racket in this peaceful arrondissement as a fly in a bottle. The suburban sergeant listened. He waited. He was a prudent man.

The furious sound of the cart bowling along filled up the measure of waiting allowable and drove the sergeant to attempt a reconnaissance.

"There's a whole gang of them out there!" he said. "Let's tread carefully."

It was clear that the hydra of anarchy was out of the box and that it was wreaking havoc in the quartier. And the sergeant ventured out of the station soundlessly.

All of a sudden, just as Gavroche was about to turn out of the rue des Vieilles-Haudriettes wheeling his cart, he came face-to-face with a uniform, a shako, a plume, and a musket. For the second time, he stopped in his tracks.

"Say," said Gavroche. "If it isn't the man himself. Hello, law and order."

The moments when Gavroche was stumped for words were short and quickly thawed.

"Where are you going, you lout?" cried the sergeant.

"Citizen," said Gavroche, "I haven't called you a bourgeois yet. So why are you insulting me?"

"Where are you going, you tramp?"

"Monsieur," Gavroche went on, "you might have been a man of wit yesterday, but you were clearly relieved of duties today."

"I asked you where you're going, you scoundrel."

Gavroche replied: "You speak so nicely. Really, no one would guess your age. You should sell all your hair at a hundred francs apiece. That'd give you five hundred francs."

"Where are you going? Where are you going? Where are you going, you cur?"

Gavroche retorted: "What a vile way to talk. The next time someone gives you a suck on their tit, they should wipe your mouth cleaner."

The sergeant crossed his bayonet.

"For the last time, are you going to tell me where you are going, you miserable little bastard?"

"My dear general," said Gavroche, "I'm going to fetch the doctor for my wife who's in labor."

"To arms!" yelled the sergeant.

To save yourself by using what has sunk you, that is the masterpiece of a great man; Gavroche was able to sum up the whole situation at a glance. It was the cart that had compromised him, it was the cart that would protect him.

Just as the sergeant was about to swoop down on Gavroche, the cart, turned into a projectile and launched with all the kid's might, rolled furiously on top of him and hit him right in the guts; the sergeant fell over backward into the gutter while his gun went off in the air.

At the sergeant's cry, the men from the post swarmed out; the gunshot triggered a general random discharge, following which they reloaded their weapons and started all over again. This blindman's buff–style musketry went on for a good fifteen minutes and killed several panes of glass.

Meanwhile Gavroche, who had madly retraced his steps, stopped five or six streets away and sat down panting on the curbstone at the corner of the Enfants Rouges. He cocked his ear.

After getting his breath for a few minutes, he turned round to where the shooting was raging, brought his left hand up to his nose and thrust it forward three times while smacking the back of his head with his right hand; a sovereign gesture in which the Parisian gamin has condensed all French irony and which is obviously effective since it has already lasted half a century.

This gaiety was disturbed by a bitter reflection.

"Yes," he said, "here I am tittering and killing myself laughing and overflowing with mirth, but I've lost time, I'm going to have to make a detour. If only I make it to the barricade in time!"

Without further ado, he resumed his course. And as he ran: "Hang on, where was I?" he said.

He started singing that song again, hurtling headlong into the streets, and the song receded into the darkness:

> But there are more Bastilles left,
> And I'm going to put a stop
> To law and order, voilà.
>
> Where have all the beautiful girls gone,
> Lon la.

Anyone for a game of skittles?
This old world will collapse one day
When the big ball rolls.

> Where have all the beautiful girls gone,
>    Lon la.

Good ancient people, with thrusts of your crutches
We'll smash up this Louvre where
The monarchy pranced around in its flounces.

> Where have all the beautiful girls gone,
>    Lon la.

We've broken down the gates;
King Charles the Tenth that day
Held up badly and his head came off.

> Where have all the beautiful girls gone,
>    Lon la.[2]

The post's show of arms was not without results. The cart was conquered, the drunk taken prisoner. One was impounded; the other was later tried half-heartedly before a court-martial as an accomplice. The public administration of the day thereby proved its tireless zeal in defending society.

Gavroche's adventure, which remained in the traditons of the Temple quartier, is one of the most terrible memories of the old bourgeois of the Marais and is entitled in their reminiscences: "Night Attack on the Post of the Imprimerie Royale."

PART FIVE

# Jean Valjean

# BOOK ONE

# WAR BETWEEN FOUR WALLS

## I. THE CHARYBDIS OF THE FAUBOURG SAINT-ANTOINE AND THE SCYLLA[1] OF THE FAUBOURG DU TEMPLE

The two most memorable barricades that the observer of social ills might mention do not belong to the period in which the action of this book is set. These two barricades, symbols both, from two different angles, of a terrible situation, sprang up out of the ground during the fatal insurrection of June 1848,[2] the biggest street war history has ever seen.

It sometimes happens that, from the depths of their anguish, their discouragement, their privation, their feverishness, their distress, their rankness, their ignorance, their darkness, that great desperado, the rabble, protests—even against principles, even against liberty, equality, and fraternity, even against universal elevation, even against the rule of all by all—and the plebs do battle with the people.

The scum attack common law; mob rule rises up against the Demos.[3]

Those are dolorous days; for there is always a certain amount of justice even in such madness, there is suicide in such a duel; and these words that are intended as insults, scum, rabble, mob rule, plebs, alas! register the fault of those in power more than the fault of those who suffer; the fault of the privileged more than the fault of the dispossessed.

As for us, we never utter those particular words without pain and respect, for when philosophy probes the facts to which they correspond, it often finds plenty of greatness bound up with all the misery. Athens was ruled by the mob; the scum made Holland; the plebs saved Rome more than once; and the rabble followed Jesus Christ.

There is no thinker who has not at times contemplated the splendors down below among the dregs.

No doubt Saint Jerome was thinking of this rabble, and of all the poor people, all the vagabonds, all the miserable outcasts from whom the apostles and the martyrs emerged, when he uttered those mysterious words: *Fex urbis, lex orbis.*[4]

The angry seething of the hordes who suffer and bleed, their acts of violence in contravention of the principles that are their lifeblood, their acts of assault and battery against the law, are popular coups d'état and must be put down. The man of integrity devotes himself to the task, and for very love of those same hordes, he does battle with them. But how excusable he finds them, even while standing up to them! How he reveres them, even while resisting them! This is one of those rare times when, in doing what you have to do, you feel something disconcerting that almost puts you off going any further; you persist because you have to; but your conscience, though satisfied, is sad, and doing your duty is made hard by heartache.

June 1848, we hasten to say, was a unique event and almost impossible to place within the philosophy of history. Everything we have just said has to be set aside when we consider that extraordinary riot in which you felt the sacred anxiety of labor reclaiming its rights. It had to be fought, and that was a duty, because the riot was aimed at the Republic. But what was June 1848, when it all comes down to it? A revolt of the people against themselves.

When the subject is not lost sight of, there is no digression; so hopefully the reader will bear with us for a moment as we dwell on the two absolutely unique barricades that we have just been talking about, and that typified that insurrection.

One blocked the entrance to the faubourg Saint-Antoine; the other defended the approach to the faubourg du Temple. No one who saw those frightening masterpieces of civil war rise up before them, beneath the dazzling blue June sky, will ever forget them.

The Saint-Antoine barricade was monstrous. It was three stories high and seven hundred feet wide. It barred the vast mouth of the faubourg from one corner to the other, that is, across three streets. Ravined, jagged, serrated, snarled, crenellated by an immense rip, buttressed by piles that were themselves bastions, thrusting out jutting headlands here and there, and powerfully backed by the two great promontories of the faubourg houses, it loomed like a cyclopean levee at the far end of the fearful square that witnessed July 14.[5] Nineteen barricades rose up in tiers throughout the dense streets behind this mother barricade. Just to see it, you could feel that the immense suffering in the faubourg had reached that final moment of agony when distress tips over into catastrophe. What was this barricade made of? Of the rubble of three six-story houses, torn down for the purpose, said some. Of the wonders achieved by every kind of rage, said others. It had the woeful look of all constructions built by hate: It was a ruin. You could have asked: Who built that? You could equally have asked: Who destroyed that? It was an improvisation thrown up by ferment.

Hey! That door! That gate! That awning! That mantelpiece! That broken stove!
That cracked pot! Hand it all over! Throw it all on! Push, roll, dig, dismantle,
knock over, pull down the whole lot! It was the collaboration of the cobblestone,
of rubblework, of the beam, the iron bar, the rag, the broken windowpane, the
staved-in chair, the cabbage stump, the scrap, the piece of trash, and malediction. It was big and it was little. It was the bottomless pit parodied on the spot
by pandemonium. Mass alongside the atom; a bit of wall torn down and a bowl
smashed; a menacing fraternization of every kind of debris; Sisyphus had
tossed his rock on and Job his shard of pottery.[6] In a word, it was horrendous. It
was the acropolis of the barefoot tramps. Overturned carts made the talus haz-
ardous; a huge dray was piled on sideways, with the axle pointing up at the sky
and looking like a scar on that tumultuous façade; an omnibus, gaily hoisted up
to the very top of the pile by brute force, as though the architects of this sav-
agery had wanted to add a bit of cheek to the horror, offered its unhitched shaft
to invisible horses of the air. This gigantic jumble, the alluvial deposits of the
riot, suggested an Ossa heaped upon the Pelion[7] of all revolutions; '93 on top of
'89, Thermidor 9 on top of August 10, Brumaire 18 on top of January 21,
Vendémiaire on top of Prairial,[8] 1848 on top of 1830. The square was worth the
trouble, and the barricade worthy of appearing on the very spot where the
Bastille had disappeared. If the ocean went in for dikes, this is how it would
build them. The fury of the rising tide was stamped on that amorphous clutter.
What rising tide? The teeming hordes. You felt you were looking at mayhem
petrified. You felt you heard buzzing above the barricade, as though the enormous dark bees of violent progress were in their hive. Was that a clump of
bushes? Was it a drunken orgy? Was it a fortress? Vertigo seemed to have built
the thing with the flapping of wings. There was something of the open cesspit
about that redoubt and something Olympian in that tangle of junk. You could
see there, in a mishmash full of despair, roof rafters, chunks of attics with their
wallpaper attached, window frames with all the glass intact planted in the
wreckage, waiting for the cannon, ripped-out fireplaces, wardrobes, tables,
benches, all howling, topsy-turvy, and a thousand wretched things even beggars
reject as detritus, containing as they do both fury and nothingness. You would
have said it was the tatters of a whole populace, rags made of wood, iron,
bronze, stone that the faubourg Saint-Antoine had shoveled there at its
doorstep with one colossal sweep of the broom, turning its misery into a barricade. Chunks of wood like chopping blocks, broken chains, a framework with
brackets in the shape of gallows, wheels poking out of the rubble horizontally—
all this lumped together in one great monument to anarchy, the somber features
of the old tortures once suffered by the people. The Saint-Antoine barricade
turned everything into a weapon; everything that civil war can throw at society's head surfaced there; it was not combat, it was paroxysm; the guns that defended that redoubt, among which were a few blunderbusses, sprayed around

bits of crockery, knucklebones, coat buttons, and even bedside table casters, projectiles made dangerous because of the copper. This barricade was frenzied; it threw up into the clouds a crazy clamor; at certain times, provoking the army, it was seething with teeming throngs and squalling tempests; a mob of flaming heads crowned it; a swarm filled it; its crest was thorny with guns, sabers, clubs, axes, pikes, and bayonets; a vast red flag snapped in the wind there; you could hear cries of command, songs of attack, the rolling of drums, the sobbing of women, and the dark roars of laughter of the starving. It was outrageous and alive; and, as though from the back of some electric beast, lightning crackled out of it. The spirit of revolution spread its cloud over that summit where the voice of the people rumbled like the voice of God; a strange majesty emanated from that titanic sackload of rubble. It was a heap of garbage and it was Sinai.[9]

As we said above, in the name of the Revolution, it attacked . . . what? The Revolution. It, this barricade—chance, disorder, alarm, misunderstanding, the unknown—was faced with the Constituent Assembly, the sovereignty of the people, universal suffrage, the nation, the Republic—and it was the "Carmagnole" challenging the "Marseillaise."[10]

An insane but heroic challenge, for this old faubourg is a hero.

The faubourg and its redoubt lent each other a hand. The faubourg put its shoulder to the redoubt, the redoubt leaned back on the faubourg. The vast barricade displayed itself like a cliff face where the strategy of the generals of Africa[11] came to grief and was shattered. Its caves, its excrescences, its warts and humps, grimaced, so to speak, and snickered under the smoke. Grapeshot vanished there in the amorphous, shells sank into it, were swallowed up by it; cannonballs managed only to bore holes in it; what was the point of shelling chaos? And the regiments, accustomed to the most savage sights of war, looked on with anxious eyes at this wildcat of a redoubt, with its boarlike bristling and its mountainous enormity.

Less than a mile away, at the corner of the rue du Temple that debouches onto the boulevard near the Château-d'Eau, if you were game enough to poke your head out beyond the tip formed by Dallemagne's shop front, you saw way in the distance, beyond the canal, in the street that goes up the slopes of Belleville, at the highest point of the hill, a strange wall reaching the second story of the façades, a sort of hyphen linking the houses on the right and the houses on the left, as though the street had decided to fold its highest wall back in on itself to seal itself abruptly off. This wall was built with paving stones. It was upright, correct, cold, perpendicular, squarely leveled, straight as a die, aligned with the use of a plumb bob. No doubt it was lacking cement but, as with certain Roman walls, this did not disturb its rigid architecture. Its height gave you some idea of how thick it was. The molding at the top was mathematically parallel to the substructure. Here and there, over the gray surface, invisible arrow slits that looked like black threads could be made out. These arrow slits were spaced apart at equal intervals. The street was deserted as far as the eye could see. All the windows and all the doors were shut. At the end of it rose this roadblock that turned the street into a cul-de-sac, a still and tranquil wall. No one could be seen, nothing could be heard; not a cry, not a sound, not a breath. A sepulchre.

The dazzling June sun flooded that terrible thing with light.

This was the barricade of the faubourg du Temple.

As soon as you arrived in the vicinity and saw it, it was impossible, even for the heartiest, not to pause for thought in the face of such a mysterious apparition. It was tightly tailored, stacked, imbricated, rectilinear, symmetrical, and deadly. There was art and darkness in it. You felt that the chief of this barricade was either a geometer or a specter. As soon as you saw it, you dropped your voice to a whisper.

When anyone, soldier, officer, or representative of the people, ventured to cross the lonely roadway, which they did from time to time, a faint but sharp whistling would be heard and the person would fall, wounded or dead; or, if he escaped, a bullet would be seen sinking into some closed shutter, into a gap between rubble stones, into the plaster of some wall. Sometimes it was a big Biscay ball. For the men manning the barricade had turned two bits of cast-iron gas piping, each blocked at one end with oakum and fireclay, into two small cannons. No wasting gunpowder. Nearly every shot hit home. There were a few corpses here and there and pools of blood over the cobblestones. I remember a white butterfly that came and went, up and down the street. Summer does not abdicate.

In the surrounding area, portes cochères were obstructed with the wounded.

You felt there that you were in the sights of someone you could not see and you realized that the entire street was ready and aiming.

Massed behind the kind of humpback that the bridge forms at the entrance to the faubourg du Temple as it arches over the canal, the soldiers of the attacking column, grave and collected, observed the grim redoubt, the stillness, that death-delivering imperturbability. Some of them crawled on their stomachs right up to the top of the bridge, making sure their shakos did not show above it.

The valiant Colonel Monteynard admired the barricade with a shudder. "Look how it's built!" he said to a representative. "Not one cobblestone out of line. It's like porcelain." At that instant a bullet shattered the cross on his breast and he fell.

"The cowards!" people said. "Just let them show their faces, why don't they! Let us see them! They don't dare! They're hiding!" The faubourg du Temple barricade, defended by eighty men, attacked by ten thousand, held for three days. On the fourth day, the army did what was done at Zaatcha and Constantine:[12] They bored right through the houses, they came over the rooftops, and the barricade was taken. Not one of the eighty so-called cowards thought of fleeing; every one of them was killed on the spot except for the chief, Barthélemy, of whom we will have more to say below.

The Saint-Antoine barricade was the crashing of thunder and lightning; the barricade du Temple was silence. The difference between the two redoubts was the difference between the shocking and the sinister. One looked like a great gaping maw, the other a mask.

Accepting that the gigantic and tenebrous June insurrection was triggered by a bout of rage and a riddle, the dragon was palpable in the first barricade, the sphinx in the second.

These two walls had been built by two men, one named Cournet, the other Barthélemy.[13] Cournet made the barricade Saint-Antoine; Barthélemy the barricade du Temple. Each was the image of the man who built it.

Cournet was a very tall man; he had broad shoulders, a red face, powerful fists, a bold heart, a loyal soul, a sincere and terrible gaze. Fearless, energetic, irascible, stormy; the most affable of men, the most formidable of fighters. War, battle, the mêlée were the air he breathed and put him in good spirits. He had been a naval officer and from his movements and his voice, you could tell he was a sea dog who was at home on the ocean in a tempest; he brought the hurricane with him into battle. Except for genius, there was something of Danton in Cournet; except for divinity, there was something of Hercules in Danton.

Barthélemy, skinny, puny, whey-faced, taciturn, was a sort of tragic gamin who, when smacked around by some police constable, had kept an eye out for him, lay in wait for him, and killed him, and, at seventeen years of age, was thrown into jail. He came out and put up this barricade.

Later fate caught up with them both in London, where both men had gone into hiding as outlaws. Barthélemy killed Cournet, in a fateful duel. Some time after that, caught in the machinery of one of those mysterious adventures involving passion, disasters in which French justice sees extenuating circumstances and British justice sees only death, Barthélemy was hung. The somber social edifice is so constructed that, thanks to material deprivation, thanks to moral darkness, that poor hapless being, with his undoubtedly sound, perhaps even great, intellect, started out in the galleys in France and ended up on the gallows in England. Barthélemy, whatever the occasion, flew only one flag—and it was black.

## II. WHAT IS THERE TO DO IN A BOTTOMLESS PIT BUT TALK?

Sixteen years count in the underground education in rioting, and June 1848 knew a lot more about it than June 1830. And so the barricade in the rue de la

Chanvrerie was just a rough draft, an embryo, compared to the two colossal barricades that we have briefly described; but, for the time, it was pretty impressive.

The insurgents, under the watchful eye of Enjolras, for Marius no longer watched anything, had put the night to good use. The barricade had not only been repaired but enhanced. It had been raised two feet. Iron bars planted in between the cobblestones looked like lances at rest. All kinds of rubbish had been wheeled in from all directions and thrown on, making the exterior even more tangled. The redoubt had been cleverly rebuilt as a wall inside and as a thicket outside.

They had rebuilt the stairs of paving stones that allowed it to be mounted like a citadel wall.

They had tidied the barricade up, cleared the downstairs room of the tavern, taken over the kitchen as a field hospital, finished dressing the wounds of the wounded, collected the powder scattered over the floor and on the tables, cast bullets, made cartridges, scraped lint, distributed the arms of the fallen, cleaned up the interior of the redoubt, picked up debris, carted away the bodies.

They deposited the dead in Mondétour lane, which they still controlled. The pavement was red for a long while afterward at that spot. Among the dead there were four National Guards from the suburbs. Enjolras had their uniforms put to one side.

Enjolras had advised two hours' sleep. Any advice from Enjolras was an order. And yet, only two or three profited by it. Feuilly put those two hours to use engraving this inscription on the wall opposite the tavern:

LONG LIVE THE PEOPLE!

These four words, gouged out in the stone with a nail, could still be read on the wall in 1848.

The three women had taken advantage of the respite the night offered to vanish completely; which made the insurgents breathe easier. The women had managed to find refuge in some neighboring house.

Most of the wounded were able and willing to fight still. But on a bed consisting of a mattress and trusses of straw, in the kitchen–*cum*–field hospital, there were five seriously wounded men, two of whom were National Guards. The Municipal Guards were being treated first.

There was nothing left now in the downstairs room except Mabeuf under his black cloth and Javert tied to the post.

"This is the dead room," said Enjolras.

Inside the room, only very dimly lit by a tallow candle, at the very back, the mortuary table standing behind the post like a horizontal bar meant a sort of big cross was roughly formed by Javert standing and Mabeuf lying down.

The omnibus shaft, though truncated by the fusillade, was still standing upright enough to have a flag hung from it.

Enjolras, who had that trait of a born leader of always doing what he said he would do, lashed to this pole the torn and bloodstained coat of the old man killed.

A meal was now out of the question. There was no bread and no meat. The fifty men in the barricade had quickly exhausted the meager provisions of the tavern over the sixteen hours they had been there. At a given moment, any barricade that holds out inevitably becomes a raft of the *Medusa*. They had to resign themselves to going hungry. They were in the early hours of that spartan day of June 6 when, in the Saint-Merry barricade, Jeanne, surrounded by insurgents wanting bread, answered all the combatants clamoring for "Something to eat!" with, "What for? It's three o'clock. At four, we'll be dead."

Since they could no longer eat, Enjolras ruled out drinking. He banned wine and rationed eau-de-vie.

Some fifteen bottles, full and hermetically sealed, had been found in the cellar. Enjolras and Combeferre went down to examine them. Combeferre said when they came back up: "It's old stock of old man Hucheloup's—he started out as a grocer." "That'd have to be real wine," observed Bossuet. "It's a good thing Grantaire's asleep. If he was on his feet, we'd be hard-pressed to hang on to those bottles." In spite of the murmurs of protest, Enjolras put his veto on the fifteen bottles and, so that no one would touch them and to make them more or less sacrosanct, he had them put under the table where old father Mabeuf was lying.

At around two in the morning, they did a count. There were still thirty-seven of them.

Day was beginning to dawn. They had just snuffed out the torch, which had been put back in its socket of paving stones. The inside of the barricade, that small courtyardlike space enclosing part of the street, was drowned in darkness, and in the dim crepuscular horror, it looked like the deck of a disabled ship. The fighters came and went, moving around inside like black shapes. Above this frightening nest of shadow, the upper floors of houses stood out, livid; at the very top, the chimneys were turning white. The sky had that lovely undecided tone that might be white or might be blue. Birds were flying around letting out cries of happiness. The tall house that formed the back of the barricade, being turned toward the east, had a rose-colored reflection over its roof. At the dormer window on the third floor, the morning breeze was riffling through the gray hair on the dead man's head.

"I'm glad they put out the torch," Courfeyrac was saying to Feuilly. "I was getting sick of that torch being startled by the wind. It looked as though it was frightened. The light of a torch is like the wisdom of a coward; it's too busy trembling to shed much light."

Dawn wakes up minds just as it does birds; everyone was chattering away.

Joly saw a cat prowling around in a gutter and drew a lesson in philosophy from this.

"What is a cat?" he cried. "It is a rectification. The good Lord, having created the mouse, said: 'Oh dear, I've made a boo-boo.' And so he created the cat. The cat is the erratum of the mouse. The mouse plus the cat equals the revised and corrected proofs of Creation."

Combeferre, surrounded by students and workers, spoke of the dead, of Jean Prouvaire, of Bahorel, of Mabeuf, and even of Le Cabuc—and of Enjolras' stern sadness. He was saying: "Harmodius and Aristogeiton, Brutus, Chereas, Stephanus, Cromwell, Charlotte Corday, Sand[1]—all of them had their moment of anguish after the blow they struck. Our hearts are so shaky and human life is such a mystery that, even in a public-spirited murder, even in a liberating murder, if there is such a thing, remorse at having struck a man down exceeds joy at having served the human race."

And, words tossed out meandering along the way they do, a minute later, after a detour via Jean Prouvaire's poetry, Combeferre was comparing the translators of the *Georgics*[2] to one another, Raux to Cournand, Cournand to Delille, pointing out the few passages translated by Malfilâtre, particularly the bit on the miracles and wonders surrounding the death of Caesar; and, at that word Caesar, the conversation swung back to Brutus.

"Caesar," said Combeferre, "rightly fell. Cicero was tough on Caesar and he was right. That sort of toughness is no diatribe. When Zoïlus insults Homer, when Maevius insults Virgil, when Visé insults Molière, when Pope insults Shakespeare, when Fréron insults Voltaire,[3] it is the old law of envy and hate at work; geniuses attract abuse, great men are always more or less barked at. But Zoïlus and Cicero are two different people. Cicero is a righter of wrongs through his thinking, just as Brutus is a righter of wrongs through his sword. I condemn, for my part, the latter kind of justice, the blade; but antiquity accepted it. Caesar, that rapist of the Rubicon,[4] conferring as though they came from him honors that came from the people, and not being upstanding when the Senate came in, acted, as Eutropius[5] says, the part of a king and almost of a tyrant, *regia ac poene tyrannica*. He was a great man; so much the worse, or so much the better; the lesson is more to the point. His twenty-three wounds touch me less than the gob of spit on Jesus Christ's forehead. Caesar was stabbed by senators; Christ was slapped in the face by lackeys. We feel the god in the greater outrage."

Bossuet, lording it over the talkers from the top of a heap of paving stones, cried out, carbine in hand: "O Cydathenaeum, O Myrrhinus, O Probalinthus, O Graces of the Aeantides. Oh, who will say Homer's verses for me like a Greek from Laurium or from Edapteon!"[6]

### III. Brightening and Darkening

Enjolras had gone on reconnaissance. He had ducked out through Mondétour lane, winding his way along the houses.

The insurgents, we have to say, were full of hope. The way they had repelled the night attack made them almost scorn the dawn attack before the event. They waited for it, smiling. They did not doubt their success any more than they doubted their cause. Besides, help was evidently on the way. They were counting on it. With that penchant for prophetic triumphalism that is one of the strengths of the French fighter, they divided the day that was about to begin into three distinct phases: At six o'clock in the morning, a regiment that had been "worked on" would come over and join them; at midday, the insurrection of all Paris; at sundown, revolution.

They could hear the tocsin of Saint-Merry, which had not let up for a minute since the previous evening; proof that the other barricade, the main one, Jeanne's, was still holding out.

All these hopes were communicated from one group to the next in a sort of gay and grim whispering that was like the buzz of a hive of warring bees.

Enjolras reappeared, back from his somber eagle's promenade in the outer darkness. He listened for a moment to all this jubilation with his arms folded, one hand over his mouth. Then, fresh and rosy in the growing whiteness of the morning, he said: "The whole Paris army is in it. A third of the army is bearing down on the barricade where you are. On top of the National Guard. I made out the shakos of the Fifth of the Line and the colors of the Sixth Legion. You will be attacked in an hour. As for the people, they were boiling over yesterday, but this morning they're not budging. Nothing to expect, nothing to hope for. Not a single faubourg, not a single regiment. You have been abandoned."

These words fell on the buzzing groups with the effect of the first drops of a storm on a swarm of bees. No one said a word. There was a moment of utter silence in which you could have heard death taking wing.

That moment was brief. A voice, from the darkest depths, shouted to Enjolras: "So be it. Let's raise the barricade to twenty feet and let's all stay our ground. Citizens, let's offer the protest of dead bodies. Let's show them that though the people may desert the republicans, the republicans will not desert the people."

This speech released everyone's thinking from the painful cloud of individual anguish. It was greeted by enthusiastic applause.

No one ever knew the name of the man who had spoken; it was some smock-wearer without a name, an unknown man, a forgotten man, a passing hero, that great anonymous man who is always caught up in human crises and spurts of social evolution and who, at a given moment, says the decisive word supremely well, before melting back into the darkness after having represented, in a flash of lightning that is over in a second, God's people.

This inexorable resolution was so much in the air of June 6, 1832, that, almost at the same moment, in the barricade at Saint-Merry, the insurgents raised an uproar that has gone down in history, having been recorded at trial: "Whether they come to our aid or whether they don't—what does it matter! Let's get killed here to the very last man."

As we see, the two barricades, although physically isolated, were very much of one mind.

## IV. Five Fewer, One More

After this average unknown man, who decreed "the protest of dead bodies," had spoken, expressing how they all felt, a strangely satisfied and terrible cry arose from everyone's lips, deadly in meaning and yet triumphant in tone: "Long live death! Let's all stay here."

"Why all?" said Enjolras.

"All! All!"

Enjolras resumed: "The position's good, the barricade is beautiful. Thirty men are enough. Why sacrifice forty?"

They responded: "Because not one of us wants to leave."

"Citizens," cried Enjolras, and there was in his voice an almost angry tremor, "the Republic is not rich enough in men to incur unnecessary costs. Vainglory is squandering. If, for some of you, getting away from here is a duty, then that duty should be performed like any other."

Enjolras, the man as principle, had over his coreligionists the sort of all-powerfulness that emanates from the absolute. Yet notwithstanding this omnipotence, there was muttering.

A leader to his fingertips, Enjolras heard the muttering and put his foot down. He said haughtily: "Let those who are afraid of there only being thirty say so."

The muttering intensified.

"Anyway," observed a voice from one huddle, "as for getting away, that's easier said than done. The barricade's surrounded."

"Not on the Les Halles side," said Enjolras. "The rue Mondétour is free and through the rue des Prêcheurs you can get to the Marché-des-Innocents."

"And there," another voice in the group shot back, "you'll be caught. You'll fall on some great guard of the line or the guard from the suburbs. They'll see a man in a smock and a cap filing past. 'Hey you, where've you come from? You wouldn't be from the barricade by any chance, would you?' Then they look at your hands. You reek of gunpowder. The jig's up: You're shot."

Without answering, Enjolras gave Combeferre a tap on the shoulder and both of them went off into the downstairs room.

They resurfaced a moment later. Enjolras held in his outstretched hands the four uniforms he had had put aside. Combeferre followed him, carrying the leather gear and the shakos.

"With this uniform," said Enjolras, "you blend into the ranks and you can escape. There's enough here for four, anyway."

And he threw the four uniforms on the ground where the cobblestones had been ripped up.

No one moved a muscle in that stoical audience. Combeferre took the floor: "Listen," he said, "show a little pity. Do you know what's at stake here? What's at stake here are the women. Let's see. Do any of you have wives, yes or no? Do any of you have children, yes or no? Do any of you, yes or no, have mothers, rocking cradles with their foot, with a heap of little ones around them? Let any among you who has never seen the breast of a woman feeding her baby raise his hand. Ah, you want to get yourselves killed. Well, I do too, I who am talking to you, but I don't want to feel the phantoms of women wringing their hands all around me. Die if you like, but don't make others die. Suicides like the ones about to be committed here are sublime, but suicide is limited and won't tolerate being extended; the moment suicide hurts your nearest and dearest, it's known as murder. Think of those little blond heads, think of that old white hair. Listen, just a moment ago, Enjolras told me he saw a dismal fifth-floor window, lit up by a candle, down at the corner of the rue du Cygne, and silhouetted against the windowpane was the wobbling shadow of the head of an old woman who looked as though she'd spent the night sitting up waiting. Maybe she's the mother of one of you. Well, then, let that man leave now, and let him hurry up and say to his mother: Mother, here I am! Let him rest assured, we'll get the job done here just the same. When you support your nearest and dearest through your labor, you no longer have the right to sacrifice yourself. That is deserting the family, that is. And what about those who have daughters, and those who have sisters! Have you thought about that? You get yourselves killed, you're dead, fine, and tomorrow? Young girls who have no bread—that's a terrible thing. A man begs, a woman sells. Ah, those lovely creatures, so graceful and so sweet with their flowery bonnets, who sing and chatter and fill the house with chaste life, who are like a living perfume, who prove the existence of angels in heaven through the purity of virgins on earth, your Jeanne, your Lise, your Mimi, those adorable and decent creatures who are your blessing and your pride—my God, they'll be going hungry! What do you want me to say? There's a market in human flesh, and it's not with your ghostly hands fluttering around them that you will stop them heading for it! Think of the street, think of the pavement crawling with men strutting past, think of the shops in front of which women come and go in the mud in revealing frocks. Those women, too, were once pure. Think of your sisters, those of you who have sisters. Misery, prostitution, police officers, Saint-Lazare[1]—that's what those beautiful delicate girls will come to, those fragile marvels of modesty, of kindness and beauty, fresher than lilacs in the month of May. So, you've gone and got yourselves killed! Right! You're not around anymore! Fine. You wanted to deliver the people from the monarchy, but you hand your girls over to the police instead. Friends, beware, have some compassion. Women, poor sorry women—we don't usually think about them much. We rely on the fact that women haven't received the same education as men, we prevent them from reading, we prevent them from thinking, we prevent them from getting mixed up in politics—won't you prevent them from going to the morgue tonight to identify your bodies? Look, those who have families need to be good boys and just shake our hands and go, and let us do what has to be done here on our own. I'm well aware it takes courage to leave, it's hard; but the harder it is, the more commendable it is. You say: I've got a gun, I'm at the barricade, too bad, I'm staying. Too bad is soon said. My friends, there is a day after, you won't be there on that day after, but your families will be. All that suffering! Listen, a pretty apple-cheeked baby brimming with health, who babbles, and jabbers away, and laughs, and smells so sweet when you give them a kiss—do you know what happens to that baby when it's abandoned? I saw one once, a little thing, knee-high to a grasshopper. His father had died. Some poor people had taken him in out of charity but they didn't have enough bread for themselves. The child was always hungry. It was winter. He didn't cry. They saw him go up to the stove where there was never a fire and where the pipe, you know, was puttied with yellow clay. The child picked off a bit of this clay with his little fingers and ate it. His breathing was labored, his face livid, his legs like jelly, his stomach swollen. He said nothing. They spoke to him, he didn't answer. He died. They took him to the Necker hospice[2] to die, that's where I saw him. I was an intern at that hospice. Now, if there are any fathers among you, fathers who have the pleasure of taking their child's little hand in their good strong hand for a walk on Sundays, let each of these fathers imagine that this child is his own. That poor little toddler, I remember him well, it seems to me I can still see him when he was on the dissecting table naked, with his ribs poking out under his skin like graves under grass in a cemetery. They found what looked like mud in his stomach. There was ash in his teeth. Come on, let's examine our consciences, let's listen to our hearts. The statistics show that the mortality rate among abandoned infants is fifty-five percent. I repeat, we're talking about women here, we're talking about mothers, we're talking about girls, we're talking about little nippers. Are we talking about you here? We know very well who you are; we know very well that you are all brave men, for Christ's sake! We know very well that your souls are full of the joy and the glory of giving your lives for the great cause; we know very well that you feel you've been handpicked to die usefully and magnificently and that each of you is clinging to his part in the triumph. Well and good. But you are not alone in this world. There are other beings you have to think of. You must not be selfish."

Everyone hung their heads glumly.

Ah, the strange contradictions of the human heart in its most sublime moments! Combeferre, who spoke thus, was not an orphan. He remembered the mothers of others but forgot his own. He was going to get himself killed. He was "selfish."

Marius, feverish, his stomach empty, his every hope shed, one after the other, stranded in grief, the darkest of shipwrecks, awash with violent emotions, and feeling the end near, had sunk deeper and deeper into that visionary stupor that always preludes the fatal hour when it is willed and welcomed.

A physiologist could have studied in him the growing symptoms of that febrile self-absorption, known and classified by science, which is to suffering what sensual fulfillment is to pleasure. Despair, too, has its ecstasy. Marius had reached that point. He took part in everything as though he were outside it; as we said before, things happening right in front of him seemed remote; he could make out the whole, but not the details. He saw everyone's coming and going as through a burning glare. He heard voices talking as though at the bottom of an abyss.

But one thing unsettled him. There was one part of the picture that got through to him, causing him to snap out of his stupor. All he wanted to do now was to die and he was not about to be thrown off track; but the thought occurred to him, in his heartsick sleepwalking state, that, in disappearing yourself, you were not actually prohibited from saving someone else.

He spoke up: "Enjolras and Combeferre are right!" he said. "No pointless sacrifices. I'm with them and we need to be quick about it. Combeferre has made the most important point. There are among you those who have families—mothers, sisters, wives, children. Let those men break ranks."

No one budged.

"Married men and those supporting families, out now!" repeated Marius.

His authority was great. Enjolras was well and truly the chief of the barricade, but Marius was its savior.

"I order you!" barked Enjolras.

"I implore you," said Marius.

So, stirred by Combeferre's speech, shaken by Enjolras' command, moved by Marius's prayer, those heroic men began to denounce each other.

"That's right," said a young man to an older man. "You're the father of a family. Off you go."

"You're the one who should go," replied the man. "You've got your two sisters to feed."

And an incredible row broke out. Those men were fighting *not* to be turned away from death's door.

"Let's get a move on," said Courfeyrac. "In a quarter of an hour it will all be too late."

"Citizens," Enjolras went on, "the Republic starts here and universal suffrage[3] rules. You yourselves elect who should go."

They did as they were told. After a few minutes, five men had been unanimously elected and broke ranks.

"There are five of you!" wailed Marius.

There were only four uniforms.

"Well, then," the five chorused, "one of us has to stay."

And the five of them fought to stay and to find reasons why the others should not stay. The unbelievably generous squabbling began again.

"You've got a wife who loves you."

"You've got your poor old mother."

"You don't have a father or a mother anymore, so what's going to happen to your three little brothers?"

"You're the father of five children."

"You have the right to live, you're only seventeen, that's too young."

Those great revolutionary barricades were places where heroes came together. The implausible was natural there. Those men did not amaze one another.

"Hurry up!" Courfeyrac said again.

Someone down among the men cried out to Marius: "You choose who should stay."

"Yes," said the five. "We'll do whatever you say."

Marius did not think he could feel anything anymore, any fresh emotion, and yet at the very idea of marking a man for death his blood rushed to his heart and he would have gone a white shade of pale if that were possible.

He walked over to the five men who were all beaming at him, and each man, with his eyes full of that great flame that we see at the beginnings of history in the men of Thermopylae, cried out to him: "Me! Me! Me!"

And Marius, stupidly, counted them; there were still five! Then his eyes dropped to the four uniforms. In that second, a fifth uniform fell, as though from the sky, on top of the four others. The fifth man was saved.

Marius raised his eyes and recognized Monsieur Fauchelevent. Jean Valjean had just entered the barricade.

Whether through information obtained, whether through instinct or chance, he had arrived via Mondétour lane. Thanks to his National Guard uniform, he had got through easily.

The scout placed by the insurgents in the rue Mondétour had not given the alarm over a lone National Guard. He had let him enter the street, telling him-self: "It's probably a reinforcement or, at the worst, a prisoner." The moment was too grave for the sentinel to let himself be distracted from his duty or from his observation post.

When Jean Valjean entered the redoubt, no one noticed him, all eyes being riveted on the five chosen men and the four uniforms. Jean Valjean had himself seen and understood and had silently stripped off his coat and thrown it on the pile with the others.

The emotion was indescribable.

"Who is that man?" asked Bossuet.

"A man," replied Combeferre, "who saves others."

Marius added in a grave voice: "I know him."

This assurance was enough for everyone. Enjolras turned toward Jean Val-jean.

"Citizen, welcome."

And he added: "You know we are going to die."

Jean Valjean, without answering, helped the insurgent he had saved get into his uniform.

## V. THE VIEW FROM THE TOP OF THE BARRICADE

Everyone's situation, at that fatal hour and in that inexorable place, found its ul-timate expression and pinnacle in the supreme melancholy of Enjolras.

Enjolras had the fullness of the revolution inside him; yet he was incom-plete, inasmuch as the absolute can be; there was too much of Saint-Just about him and not enough Anacharsis Clootz.[1] Still, his mind, in the Society of the Friends of the ABC, had ended up being galvanized to some extent by the ideas of Combeferre. Little by little, for some time, he had been moving away from strict dogma and venturing into the wider fields of progress, and he had even come to accept, as a definitive and magnificent evolution, the transformation of the great Republic of France into the vast republic of humanity. As for the im-mediate means, given that it was a violent situation, he wanted them to be vio-lent; in that, he had not wavered; and he was still of that epic and formidable school that can be summed up one word: ninety-three.

Enjolras was standing on the cobblestone stairs, with his elbow on the bar-rel of his carbine, thinking; he was shivering, as though buffeted by gusts of wind passing over him; places where death lurks produce these effects of vibra-tions. From his eyes, full of an inward gaze, a kind of smoldering fire streamed. All of a sudden, he raised his head, and his blond hair fell back like the hair of the angel of peace on the somber quadriga of stars; it was like a lion's mane star-tled and flaming out into a halo, and Enjolras cried out: "Citizens, do you picture the future to yourselves? The city streets flooded with lights, green branches hanging over the doorsteps, the nations like sisters, men just, old men blessing children, the past loving the present, thinkers enjoying complete liberty, believers enjoying complete equality, for religion the sky, God a priest needing no intermediary, human conscience once more an altar, no more hatred, the fraternity of workshop and school, notoriety as penalty enough and as reward, work for all; for all, the law, over all, peace, no more bloodshed, no more wars, mothers happy! To tame matter is the first step; to realize the ideal is the second. Think what progress has already done. Once upon a time the early human races looked with terror as the hydra passed before their eyes blowing over the waters, the dragon spewed fire, and the griffin, that monster of the air, flew with the wings of an eagle and the claws of a tiger; frightening beasts that were above man. But man set his snares, the sacred snares of intelligence, and he wound up catching these monsters in them.

"We have tamed the hydra, it is now called the steamer; we have tamed the dragon, it is now called the locomotive; we are on the point of taming the griffin, we already have him in our grip, it is now called the air balloon. The day this Promethean travail is finished, when man will finally have harnessed to his will the triple chimera of antiquity—hydra, dragon, griffin—he will be master of water, fire, and air and he will be for the rest of animate creation what the ancient gods once were for him. Courage, forward march! Citizens, what are we headed for? For science made government, for the force of things become the sole public force, for the law of nature having its own sanctions and penalties within itself and being promulgated by evidence, for a dawning of truth that corresponds to the dawning of day. We are headed for the union of peoples; we are headed for the unity of mankind. No more fictions; no more parasites. The real ruled by the true—that is the goal. Civilization will hold its courts on the peaks of Europe and, later, at the center of the continents in a great parliament of intelligence. Something of the sort has already been seen. The Amphictyons[2] held two sessions a year, one in Delphi, home of the gods, the other in Thermopylae, home of the heroes. Europe will have its Amphictyons; the globe will have its Amphictyons. France bears this sublime future in its loins. This is where the gestation of the nineteenth century is happening. What Greece began is worthy of being finished by France. Listen to me, you, Feuilly, valiant worker, man of the people, man of the peoples. I venerate you. Yes, you clearly see future times; yes, you are right. You had no father and no mother of your own, Feuilly; you adopted humanity as mother, and as father you adopted justice. You are going to die here—that is, to triumph. Citizens, whatever happens today, through our defeat every bit as much as through our victory, we will bring about a revolution. Just as conflagrations light up the whole city, revolutions light up the whole human race. And what revolution are we going to bring about? I just told you: the revolution of the True. From the political standpoint, there is only one principle: the sovereignty of man over himself. This sovereignty I have over myself is known as Liberty. Wherever two or more such sovereignties gather together, the State begins. But in this gathering together, there is no abdication. Each sovereignty concedes a certain portion of itself to form the common right. This portion is the same for all. The identical nature of the concession that each makes to all is known as Equality. Common right is nothing more nor less than the protection of all shining on the right of each. This protection of all over each is known as Fraternity. The point of intersection of all these aggregate sovereignties is known as Society. This intersection being a junction, the point is a node. Hence what is known as the social bond. Some say social contract; which is the same thing, the word *contract* being etymologically formed by the notion of a bond. Let's understand each other in regard to equality; for if liberty is the high point, equality is the base. Equality, citizens, is not the leveling of all the vegetation, a society of tall blades of grass and short oak trees, a community of envies leaping at each other's throats; it is, in civic terms, all aptitudes having the same opportunity; in political terms, all votes having the same weight; in religious terms, all consciences having the same right. Equality has an organ: free and compulsory education. The right to the alphabet—that's where we have to start. Primary school imposed on everyone, secondary school offered to everyone—that's the rule. From the school that is identical springs the equal society. Yes, education! Light! Light! Everything comes from light and everything comes down to it. Citizens, the nineteenth century is great, but the twentieth century will be happy. Then there will be nothing left of the old history; there will be no more fear, like there is today, of conquest, invasion, usurpation, rivalry between nations by force of arms, civilization interrupted by some marriage of kings, a birth in the hereditary tyrannies, the division of nations by congress, dismemberment through the downfall of some dynasty, some battle between two religions going head to head, like two billy goats in the shadows, on the bridge of the infinite; they will not have to fear any more famine, exploitation, prostitution caused by distress, misery caused by unemployment, and the scaffold, and the blade, and battles and all the armed robberies caused by chance in the forest of events. You could almost say: There will be no more events. People will be happy. The human race will live up to its law, just as the terrestrial globe lives up to its law; harmony will be reestablished between the soul and the star. The soul will gravitate around the truth, just as the star does around the light. Friends, the moment we have reached, this moment in which I am speaking to you, is a somber moment; but this is the terrible price the future exacts. A revolution is a tollgate. Oh, the human race will be delivered, lifted up and consoled! We swear to it on this barricade. Where will the cry of love go up from if not from the height of sacrifice? O, my brothers, this is the very spot where those who think and those who suffer come together as one; this barricade is not made of cobblestones, or wooden beams, or scrap iron; it is made of two heaps, a heap of ideas and a heap of pain. Misery meets the ideal here. The day embraces the night here and says to it: I am going to die with you and you will be born again with me. From this embracing of all sorrows springs faith. Suffering brings its agony here, and ideas their immortality. This agony and this immortality are going to mingle and compose our death. Brothers, whoever dies here dies in the radiance of the future, and we will enter a grave entirely lit up by dawn."

Enjolras broke off at this point rather than stopped; his lips moved silently as though he were continuing to talk to himself, which made the men watch him closely, straining to hear him still. There was no applause, but the whispering went on for a long time afterward. Words being breath, the rustling of minds is like the rustling of leaves.

## VI. Marius Haggard, Javert Laconic

Let us tell you what was passing through Marius's mind.

Remember how he was feeling. Everyone was now a dream to him. His judgment was clouded. Marius, we must insist, was standing in the shadow of those great dark wings that flap open over any soul at death's door. He felt he had both feet in the grave; it seemed to him that he was already on the other side of the great divide and he only looked on the faces of the living, now, with the eyes of a dead man.

How did Monsieur Fauchelevent get there? Why was he there? What was he there for? Marius did not ask himself any of these questions. In any case, our despair has the peculiarity of wrapping itself around others as it does us, so it seemed only logical to him that everybody had come to die.

Only, he thought of Cosette with a wrench.

On top of that, Monsieur Fauchelevent did not speak to him, did not look at him, did not even look as though he had heard when Marius piped up and said: "I know him."

As for Marius, Monsieur Fauchelevent's attitude relieved him and, if we could use such a word for such sensations, we would have to say it gratified him. Marius had always felt that it was absolutely unthinkable for him to say anything to this enigmatic man who was, to him, both ambiguous and imposing at once. It was also a very long while since he had clapped eyes on the man, and for someone as timid and reserved as Marius, that made it even more unthinkable.

The five chosen men left the barricade via Mondétour lane; they looked exactly like National Guards. One of them walked away in tears. Before they left, they hugged those who remained.

When the five men sent back to life had gone, Enjolras went on to the man condemned to death. He walked into the downstairs room. Javert was musing as he stood, tied to the post.

"Is there anything you need?" Enjolras asked him.

Javert merely answered: "When are you going to kill me?"

"You'll just have to wait. We need all the cartridges we've got right now."

"Then, give me a drink," said Javert.

Enjolras himself presented him with a glass of water and, as Javert was still bound, helped him drink.

"Is that all?" Enjolras went on.

"I'm not too comfortable at this post," replied Javert. "It wasn't very nice of you to make me spend the night here. Tie me up however you like, but you could lay me down on a table, like that other man."

And with a toss of the head he indicated the corpse of Monsieur Mabeuf.

There was, you will recall, a great long table at the back of the room on which they had cast bullets and made cartridges. All the cartridges having been made and all the powder having been used, this table was now free.

On Enjolras' orders, four insurgents untied Javert from the post. While he was being untied, a fifth man held a bayonet to his chest. His hands were left tied behind his back, a thin but strong whipcord was wound around his feet that allowed him to take small steps of about fifteen inches, like those of a man mounting the scaffold, and he was walked to the end of the room, where he was laid out and tightly bound around his waist.

For greater security, they added the sort of trussing known in jail as a *martingale,* or goat-tying, to the systems of ligatures that already made any escape impossible. In goat-tying, a rope is tied around the neck before being pulled tight down to the waist, where it is split in two, passing between the legs before coming up and joining the hands again behind the back.

While Javert was being tied up in this fashion, a man on the doorstep was eyeing him with intense attention. The shadow that the man cast made Javert turn his head. He looked up and recognized Jean Valjean. He did not even flinch. He proudly lowered his eyelids and merely said: "Only to be expected."

## VII. THE SITUATION GETS WORSE

It was getting light fast. But not a window was opened, not a door stood ajar; it was sunrise, but no one was rising. As you know, the end of the rue de la Chanvrerie opposite the barricade had been evacuated by the troops; it seemed free and lay open to passersby with an air of sinister tranquillity. The rue Saint-Denis was as mute as the avenue of the Sphinxes in Thebes.[1] There wasn't a living soul at the junction, which was turning white in reflected sunlight. Nothing is as gloomy as bright sunshine in deserted streets.

They couldn't see anything, but they could hear all right. Some mysterious movement was taking place a certain distance away. It was clear that the critical moment was coming. As they had done the night before, the scouts fell back; only, this time, all of them did so.

The barricade was stronger than for the first attack. Since the five had left, it had been raised even higher.

On the advice of the scout who had been keeping an eye on Les Halles, Enjolras, fearing a surprise attack from the rear, took a serious step. He had them barricade the narrow little Mondétour laneway, which had remained open till then. They pulled up the cobblestones the length of a few more houses for the purpose. The barricade, now walled in on three streets, in front on the rue de la Chanvrerie, to the left on the rue du Cygne and the rue de la Petite-Truanderie, to the right on the rue Mondétour, really was now almost impregnable; it is true that they were fatally hemmed in. It had three fronts, but no longer an exit.

"A fortress—and a mousetrap," Courfeyrac quipped, laughing.

Enjolras got them to pile up about thirty paving stones, "ripped up for spares," said Bossuet, next to the cabaret door.

The silence was now so profound on the side where the attack would surely come that Enjolras got everyone to take up their positions once more.

A ration of eau-de-vie was distributed all round.

Nothing is weirder than a barricade gearing up for an assault. Each man chooses his place as though at the theater to see a show. There is a lot of leaning, leaning across, leaning on, leaning shoulder to shoulder. There are those who make stalls out of paving stones. Over there, a bit of wall is in the way, they move away from it; here is a niche that can offer protection, they take cover inside it. The left-handed are precious; they take positions unsuitable for everyone else. Many arrange themselves to fight sitting down. They want to be at ease for killing and comfortable for dying. In the dismal war of June 1848, one insurgent, an awe-inspiring shot who was fighting from the top of a roof garden, had himself brought a Voltaire armchair[2] up there; a blast of grapeshot found him seated in it.

As soon as the chief orders everyone to man their stations, all chaotic movement ceases; no more skirmishing with one another; no more nattering huddles; no more private conversations; no more standing aloof; whatever is in everyone's minds converges and turns into waiting for the assailant. A barricade before danger erupts is chaos; in danger, discipline. Peril produces order.

As soon as Enjolras had taken up his double-barreled carbine and positioned himself at a sort of battlement he had reserved for himself, everyone shut up. Little dry crackling noises sounded all along the cobblestone wall. It was the sound of muskets being cocked.

But otherwise the insurgents' bearing was prouder and more confident than ever; the extravagance of self-sacrifice is galvanizing; they no longer had any hope, but they had despair. Despair is a last weapon that sometimes brings victory; Virgil said so. Supreme resources emerge from extreme resolves. Hurtling headlong into death is sometimes the only way to escape going down with the ship; the coffin lid can become a lifeline.

Just like the night before, everyone's attention was directed at, we might almost say drawn to, the end of the street, now visible in the light.

The wait was not long. Things started stirring again distinctly over by Saint-Leu but it was not like the movement involved in the first attack. A rattling of chains, the disquieting juddering of some great mass, a clanking of brass bouncing over cobblestones, a sort of solemn din, announced that some sinister scrap heap was approaching. There was a shudder in the bowels of those peaceful streets, cut out and built as they are for the fruitful circulation of interests and ideas, not made for the monstrous rumble of war.

The fixed stare all the combatants had pinned on the end of the street turned savage. A piece of cannon appeared.

Gunners were pushing the piece; the gun tube had been moved forward on the gun carriage and was now in position, ready to fire; two gunners supported the gun carriage, four were at the wheels; others followed with the caisson. You could see the lit fuse smoking.

"Fire!" cried Enjolras.

The whole barricade fired, the detonation was frightening; an avalanche of smoke covered and obliterated the gun and the men; after a few seconds, the cloud dispersed and the cannon and the men reappeared; the gun operators managed—slowly, correctly, and without haste—to roll the gun into place facing the barricade head on. Not one had been hit. Then the gun captain, pressing down on the breech ring to elevate the range of the barrel, started to point the cannon with the gravity of an astronomer training a telescope.

"Bravo, cannoneers!" shouted Bossuet.

And the whole barricade clapped. A moment later, squarely emplaced smack bang in the middle of the street, straddling the gutter, the gun was *en batterie* ready for action. A formidable maw was now open on the barricade.

"All right, look alive!" said Courfeyrac. "There's the brute. The light tap is about to become a punch in the face. The army is reaching its great paw out to us. The barricade is about to be seriously rocked. The fusillade puts out feelers, the cannonade clobbers."

"It's an eight-pounder, new model, bronze," added Combeferre. "With guns like this one, all you have to do is exceed the ratio of ten parts tin to a hundred copper, even by a fraction, and they are liable to burst. Too much tin in cast guns makes them oversensitive. So they sometimes have hollows and chambers in the bore. To obviate the danger and be able to force out the load, we might well have to go back to the fourteenth-century process of hooping, and strengthen the cylinder from the outside with a series of unsoldered steel rings, from the breech down to the trunnions. Meanwhile, you do what you can to alleviate the defect; you can even identify where the holes and hollows in the bore of a gun tube are by using calipers. But there's a better way and that's Gribeauval's 'movable star.'"

"In the sixteenth century," observed Bossuet, "they rifled grooves in their gun tubes."

"Yes," replied Combeferre, "rifling increases the ballistic momentum, but decreases the accuracy of the aim. On top of that, at close range, the trajectory isn't level enough, the parabolic curve is accentuated, the path of the projectile is not straight enough to be able to hit any intermediary objects, though that is essential in combat, and its importance only increases with the proximity of the enemy and the firing speed. The lack of tension in the curve of the projectile used in the sixteenth-century rifled cannon was due to the weakness of the charge; weak charges, for this kind of engine of siege warfare, are imposed by the necessities of ballistics, such as, for instance, preserving the gun carriages. To sum up, that despot, the cannon, can't do all it would like to; strength is a great weakness. A cannonball does only six hundred leagues an hour; light does seventy thousand leagues a second. That is the superiority of Jesus Christ over Napoléon."

"Reload arms!" said Enjolras. How would the shell of the barricade behave under cannon fire? Would the charge breach it? That was the question. While the insurgents were reloading their fusils, the gunners were loading the cannon.

There was intense anxiety in the redoubt. The charge was fired, the detonation exploded.

"Present!" cried a jubilant voice.

And at the same time as the cannonball struck the barricade, Gavroche tumbled inside. He had come via the rue du Cygne and had nimbly hurdled the auxiliary barricade that fronted the maze of the Petite-Truanderie.

Gavroche had a greater impact on the barricade than the cannonball.

The ball lost itself in the jumble of debris. The very most it did was smash one of the wheels of the bus and polish off the old Anceau cart. Seeing which, the barricade started to laugh.

"Get on with it!" Bossuet shouted to the gunners.

## VIII. THE GUNNERS GET THEMSELVES TAKEN SERIOUSLY

Everyone milled around Gavroche. But he didn't have time to relate anything. Marius, shuddering, took him aside.

"What are you doing here?"

"Hang on!" said the boy. "What about you?"

And he looked Marius in the eye with epic effrontery. His eyes grew bigger and shone with the light of the pride he felt inside. It was in a harsh tone that Marius continued: "Who told you to come back? Did you at least take my letter to the right address?"

Gavroche was not entirely without remorse on the letter score. In his haste to get back to the barricade, he had palmed it off instead of delivering it. He was forced to admit to himself that he had entrusted it a tad rashly to that stranger whose face he couldn't even see properly. It is true that the man was bareheaded, but that was not enough. In a word, he gave himself a bit of a talking to and he was afraid of what Marius would say. To avoid trouble, he took the easy way out: He lied abominably.

"Citizen, I gave the letter to the porter. The lady was sleeping. She'll get the letter when she wakes up."

Marius had two aims in sending the letter: to say farewell to Cosette and to save Gavroche. He would have to be content with half of what he wanted.

The sending of his letter and the presence of Monsieur Fauchelevent in the barricade suddenly struck him as quite a coincidence. He pointed Monsieur Fauchelevent out to Gavroche.

"Do you know that man?"

"No," said Gavroche.

Gavroche had, in fact, only seen Jean Valjean at night, as we know.

The morbid and unhealthy suspicions that had begun to take shape in Marius's mind evaporated. Did he have any idea what Monsieur Fauchelevent's political views were? Perhaps Monsieur Fauchelevent was a republican. Hence his perfectly natural presence in the fight.

Meanwhile Gavroche was already at the other end of the barricade shouting: "My gun!" Courfeyrac made them hand it over to him.

Gavroche warned "the comrades," as he called them, that the barricade was surrounded. He had had great difficulty getting through. A battalion of the line whose stacks of arms were in the Petite-Truanderie was watching the rue du Cygne side; on the opposite side, the Municipal Guard occupied the rue des Prêcheurs. Directly facing them they had the bulk of the army.

This information delivered, Gavroche added: "I authorize you to tan their hides."

Meanwhile Enjolras stuck to his battlement, ears pricked, eyes peeled.

The assailants, no doubt a trifle unhappy with their cannonball shot, had not repeated it.

A company of infantry of the line had come to take up the end of the street behind the gun. The soldiers were ripping up the roadway and building a little low wall with the paving stones, a kind of retaining wall, a sort of breastwork hardly more than eighteen inches high, facing the barricade. At the corner to the left of this breastwork, you could see the head of the column of a suburban battalion massed in the rue Saint-Denis.

Enjolras at his lookout thought he could make out the particular noise made when canisters of case shot are being taken out of caissons, and he saw the gun captain change the aim and swing the mouth of the cannon slightly to the left. Then the cannoneers began to load the gun. The gun captain himself grabbed the slow match and brought it to the touchhole.

"Heads down, get back to the wall!" cried Enjolras. "All of you on your knees, all the way along the barricade!"

The insurgents had quit their posts when Gavroche turned up and they were scattered outside the tavern; they now ran helter-skelter toward the barricade, but before Enjolras' order could be executed, the gun was fired with the frightening rattle of a volley of shot. Which is exactly what it was.

The charge had been directed at the opening in the redoubt, had ricocheted off the wall there and killed two men and wounded three others. If this continued the barricade was no longer tenable. It was not grapeshot-proof. There was a rumble of dismay.

"Let's at least see that doesn't happen twice," said Enjolras.

And, lowering his carbine, he aimed at the gunner captain who, at that moment, was bent over the breech of the cannon, adjusting and finally setting the aim.

The gunner captain was a handsome gunnery sergeant, incredibly young, sandy-haired, with a really sweet face and an intelligent look appropriate to that fearsome predestined weapon that, in its very perfection of horror, must surely wind up killing off war.

Combeferre, standing next to Enjolras, studied the young man.

"What a shame!" said Combeferre. "What a hideous thing all this butchery is! Anyway, when there are no more kings, there will be no more war. Enjolras, you're aiming at that sergeant, but you aren't looking at him. You can see for yourself, he's a dashing young man, he is fearless, you can see he's a thinker, these young artillerymen are extremely well educated; he has a father, a mother, a family, he's probably in love, he can't be any more than twenty-five years old; he could be your brother."

"He is," said Enjolras.

"Yes," Combeferre went on, "and mine, too. So, then, let's not kill him."

"Leave me alone. We do what we have to."

And a tear rolled slowly down Enjolras' marble cheek.

At the same time, he squeezed the trigger of his carbine. The flash shot out. The artilleryman spun round a couple of times, his arms stretched out in front of him and his head raised as though to gulp in air, then he tipped over sideways on the gun and remained motionless. They could see his back, and the stream of blood gushing from a hole in the middle of it. The bullet had passed clean through his chest. He was dead.

He had to be carted away and replaced. This did actually buy them a few extra minutes.

### IX. Putting That Old Poacher's Skill to Use Along with the Infallible Shot That Influenced the 1796 Conviction

Opinions flew past each other through the barricade. The gun was about to be fired again. They could not hold out for a quarter of an hour in that grapeshot. It was absolutely necessary to absorb the shock of the fire. Enjolras launched this command: "We have to get a mattress over there."

"We don't have a spare," said Combeferre. "The wounded have taken them."

Jean Valjean, sitting apart on a curbstone at the corner of the tavern, his musket between his knees, had not taken part in anything that had happened up to that moment. He seemed not to hear the combatants saying around him: "There's one gun doing nothing."

At the order given by Enjolras, he got to his feet.

You will recall that when they had rallied in the rue de la Chanvrerie, an old woman, foreseeing bullets, had stuck her mattress in front of her window. This window, a garret window, was in the roof of a six-story house located a bit farther along from the barricade. The mattress, placed sideways and resting at the bottom on two clothes poles, was held at the top by two ropes which, from a distance, looked to be two lines tied to nails driven into the window frame of the dormer. These two ropes could clearly be seen against the sky like hairs.

"Can anyone lend me a double-barreled carbine?" said Jean Valjean.

Enjolras, who had just reloaded his, handed it to him. Jean Valjean aimed at the dormer and fired. One of the two mattress ropes was cut. The mattress now hung only by a thread. Jean Valjean fired the second shot. The second rope whipped the dormer window. The mattress slid down between the two clothes poles and fell to the street. The barricade applauded. Every voice shouted: "There's your mattress."

"Yes," said Combeferre, "but who's going to go and get it?"

The mattress had in fact fallen outside the barricade between the besieged and the besiegers. Now, the death of the gunner sergeant had stirred up the troops and the soldiers had, for some moments, been lying flat on their stomachs behind the line of paving stones they had put up, and to make up for the enforced silence of the gun that sat quietly waiting while its servicing was reorganized, they had opened fire on the barricade. The insurgents did not return fire, in order to save their ammunition. The fusillade broke against the barricade; but the street, which it filled with bullets, was horrifyingly dangerous.

Jean Valjean ducked out through the opening, stepped into the street, dashed through the hail of bullets, raced to the mattress, grabbed it, loaded it onto his back, and returned to the barricade. He himself placed the mattress in the opening, wedging it against the wall in such a way that the artillerymen could not see it.

That done, they awaited the volley of grapeshot. It was not long coming.

The cannon spewed out its bundle of buckshot with a roar. But this time there was no ricochet. The shot aborted on the mattress. The desired effect was obtained. The barricade was maintained.

"Citizen," said Enjolras to Jean Valjean, "the Republic thanks you."

Bossuet marveled, laughing. He yelled: "How immoral for a mattress to have so much power. It's the triumph of what yields over what mows down. But, never mind: Glory be to the mattress that cancels out a cannon!"

## X. Daybreak

At that very moment, Cosette woke up.

Her room was small, clean, understated, with a long window facing east over the rear courtyard of the house.

Cosette had no idea what was happening in Paris. She had not been there the day before and had already gone back up to her room when Toussaint had said: "It looks like there's a bit of a row on."

Cosette had not slept long but she had slept well. She had had sweet dreams which might have had something to do with the fact that her little bed was extremely white. Someone who was Marius had appeared to her in the light. She woke with the sun in her eyes and at first this felt like a continuation of the dream.

Her first thoughts as she came out of the dream were happy. She felt completely reassured. Just like Jean Valjean a few hours before, she was going through that spirited reaction that involves absolute rejection of unhappiness. She began to hope with all her might, without knowing why. Then she felt a pang. It was now three days since she had seen Marius. But she told herself he must have received her letter by now, he knew where she was, and that he was so clever, he would find a way of getting to her. And this would happen today at the latest, and perhaps that very morning. It was already broad daylight, but as the sun's rays were perfectly horizontal she thought it was still early, but that she should get up anyway—to welcome Marius.

She felt that she could not live without Marius and that, consequently, this was all that was needed and that Marius would come. No objection was admissible. All this was certain. It was already monstrous enough to have suffered for three days. No Marius for three days—that was horrible of the good Lord. But now that she had survived the ordeal, which was obviously His idea of a joke, Marius would turn up and would bring good news. That's what it is to be young; the young quickly dry their eyes; they find pain pointless and simply don't put up with it. Youth is the smile of the future, faced with a stranger which is itself. It is natural for it to be happy. It is as though it hopes as it breathes.

Besides, Cosette could not quite remember what Marius had told her about being away, which was supposed to be only for a day, and what explanation he had given her. Everyone has noticed how swiftly a coin you drop on the ground rolls away and hides and how cleverly it makes itself unfindable. There are thoughts that play the same trick on us; they curl up in a corner of our brains and that's that; they are lost; impossible to set memory on them again. Cosette was a bit cross with the feeble useless effort her memory was making. She told herself it was very naughty of her and perfectly reprehensible to have forgotten words uttered by Marius.

She got out of bed and performed those two ablutions of the soul and of the body: her prayers and her toilette.

It is all right, at a pinch, to take the reader into a bridal chamber, but not into a virgin's bedroom. Poetry would hardly dare, prose should not.

It is the inside of a flower not yet opened, it is a whiteness glowing in the shade, it is the intimate cell of a closed lily, which should remain unseen by any man as long as it has not yet been seen by the sun. A budding woman is sacred. This innocent bed that throws off its bedclothes, this adorable semi-nudity that is frightened of itself, this white foot that takes refuge in a slipper, this bosom that veils itself in front of a mirror as though the mirror had eyes, this chemise that rushes back up to hide a shoulder whenever a piece of furniture creaks or a carriage goes by, these ribbons tied, these hooks and eyes fastened, these laces pulled tight, these starts and jumps, these little frissons of cold and modesty, this exquisite alarm at every movement, this very nearly flapping anxiety where there is nothing to fear, layers of clothing as lovely as clouds at dawn—it is not right or proper that all this be recounted; it is already too much to refer to it.

Man's eye should be even more worshipful before the rising of a young girl than before the rising of a star. The possibility of reaching out and touching should only increase respect. The down on a peach, the frost on a plum, the radiate crystal of a snowflake, a butterfly's wing powdered with feathers, are coarse things beside this chastity that does not even know it is chaste. A young girl is merely a glimmer of a dream that has not yet turned into a statue. Her alcove is hidden in the dark part of the ideal. The indiscreet touch of a gaze roughs up this dim half-light. Here, to contemplate is to profane.

And so we will show nothing of the exquisite intimate fuss involved in Cosette's awakening.

An eastern tale has it that the rose was made white by God, but that when Adam looked at it as it was beginning to open, it was ashamed and went pink. We are among those who feel tongue-tied before young girls and flowers, finding both sacred.

Cosette got dressed pretty fast, combed and did her hair, which was a very simple business in those days when women did not puff up their curls and their coils with little cushions and tiny rolls or stick crinolines in their hair. Then she opened the window and ran her eyes all around, hoping to be able to turn up something of the street, a corner of a house, a patch of pavement, and be able to watch for Marius there. But you could not see anything of the outside. The rear courtyard was wrapped around by fairly high walls with only a few gardens beyond them for a vista. Cosette declared those gardens hideous; for the first time in her life, she found flowers ugly. The tiniest strip of gutter at the crossroads would have been more to her liking. She decided to look at the sky instead, as though she thought Marius could just as easily come that way.

Suddenly, she dissolved in tears. Not out of moodiness, but because her hopes were dashed by dejection over her current situation. She vaguely felt some nameless horror looming. These things are, indeed, in the air. She told herself she was not sure of anything, that losing sight of each other was the same as losing each other; and the idea that Marius could very well come back to her from out of the sky no longer seemed lovely, but sinister, to her.

Then, as is the way with such black clouds, calm returned, and hope, and a sort of unconscious smile expressing trust in God.

The rest of the household was still in bed. A provincial silence reigned. Not a shutter was pushed open. The porter's lodge was shut. Toussaint was not up yet, and Cosette quite naturally thought that her father was still sleeping. She must indeed have suffered a lot and she must be suffering a lot still, for she told herself her father had been rotten; but she counted on Marius. For such a light to go out was, of course, impossible. At times she heard what sounded like dull tremors some distance away and she said to herself: "It's funny they're opening and shutting the portes cochères so early in the morning." This was the cannon fire battering the barricade.

A few feet below Cosette's window, in the old blackened cornice of the wall, there was a nest of swifts; the overhang of the nest jutted out a bit from the cornice, so that from above you could see inside this little paradise. The mother bird was there, fanning her wings over her brood; the father flapped around, then went off and came back, bringing food in his beak and kisses. The rising sun turned to gold this happy thing; the great law, Go and multiply, was there, smiling and serene, and the whole sweet mystery blossomed in the glory of the morning. Cosette, her hair in the sun, her soul in fantasyland, lit up inside by love and outside by the dawn, leaned over sort of automatically and, almost without daring to admit she was thinking of Marius at the same time, settled in to watching the birds, this family, this male and this female, this mother and these babies, in the deep turmoil a nest throws a virgin into.

## XI. THE GUNSHOT THAT MISSES NOTHING BUT KILLS NO ONE

The assailants' fire continued. Musketry alternated with grapeshot, without actually doing too much damage, if the truth be known. Only the top of the façade of Corinthe suffered; the crossbar on the upper-story casement and the attics in the roof, riddled with buckshot and biscayens, slowly warped. The combatants who had posted themselves up there had to leap out of the way. In any case, this is a tactic of barricade attack: keep firing away for a long time in order to exhaust the insurgents' ammunition if they make the mistake of returning fire. When you see, by the slowing down in their firing rate, that they are running out of balls and powder, that is when you storm in. Enjolras had not fallen into the trap; the barricade did not retaliate.

At each volley, Gavroche stuck his tongue in his cheek, a sign of utmost contempt.

"That's it," he said, "rip up the canvas, we need lint."

Courfeyrac scoffed at the grapeshot for its ineffectiveness and said to the cannon: "You're losing your touch, old boy."

There is as much intrigue in battle as at a ball. The silence of the redoubt was probably beginning to worry the besiegers, causing them to fear some unexpected development, and they were probably feeling the need to see clearly through that heap of cobblestones and to know what was going on behind that impassable wall that took fire without returning it. The insurgents suddenly saw a helmet shining in the sun on top of a neighboring roof. A sapper was backed up against a tall chimney stack and he looked to be there as a sentinel. He could see straight down into the barricade.

"Now there's an overseer we could do without," said Enjolras.

Jean Valjean had given Enjolras his carbine back, but he still had his musket.

Without saying a word, he aimed at the sapper, and a second later, the helmet, struck by a bullet, fell clattering to the street. The startled soldier scuttled out of sight fast.

A second observer took his place. This one was an officer. Jean Valjean, who had reloaded his gun, aimed at the newcomer and sent the officer's helmet flying off to join the soldier's. This time the warning was understood. Nobody appeared on the roof again and they gave up spying on the barricade.

"Why didn't you kill the man?" Bossuet asked Jean Valjean.

Jean Valjean did not answer.

## XII. DISORDER, A SUPPORTER OF ORDER

Bossuet murmured in Combeferre's ear:

"He didn't answer my question."

"He's a man who does good with bullets," said Combeferre.

Those who have retained any memory of that already remote time know that the National Guards from the suburbs always came down hard on insurrections. They were particularly fierce and fearless in those days of June 1832. Many a good cabaret owner from Pantin or Les Vertus or La Cunette, whose "establishment" had been put out of action by the riot, took sides and fought like lions when they saw their dance floor deserted and got themselves killed to save the order represented by the open-air dive. In those days, at once bourgeois and heroic, faced with ideas that had their knights, commercial interests had their knights-errant. The prosaic nature of the motive did not detract in any way from the bravery of the move. The fall in value of a pile of écus had bankers singing the "Marseillaise." Blood was lyrically shed for the good of the cash register; and the shop, that vast diminutive of the homeland, was defended with Spartan gusto.

At bottom, we hasten to say, there was nothing funny about any of this. It was deadly serious. The different social elements had entered into battle, in anticipation of the day when they would enter into balance.

Another sign of the times was the way anarchy got mixed up in governmentalism (the barbarous name then given to the party of correctness). People were for order with insubordination. The drums would suddenly beat out capricious rappels at the command of some colonel or other of the National Guard; many a captain would suddenly open fire, just like that, acting on a hunch; many a National Guard fought "for the heck of it"—and for reasons best known to themselves. In critical moments, on the "big days," people did not so much listen to leaders as to their own instincts. In the army of order there were veritable guerrillas, some brandishing the sword like Fannicot; others the pen, like Henri Fonfrède.[1]

Civilization, sadly represented at the time more by a conglomeration of vested interests than by any set of principles, was, or believed itself to be, in peril; it raised the cry of alarm; each and every man decided he was central to it and defended it, rushed to its aid and protected it, however he saw fit; and every man and his dog took it upon himself to save society.

The zeal sometimes went as far as extermination. Many a platoon of National Guards set themselves up, on their own private authority, as a court-martial and would then try and execute in five minutes any insurgent taken prisoner. It was a kangaroo court of the kind that had killed Jean Prouvaire.

This ferocious lynch law[2] is not something any party has the right to reproach others with, for it is applied by the republic in America just as much as by the monarchy in Europe. Lynch law led to terrible blunders. On one day of rioting, a young poet named Paul-Aimé Garnier[3] was actually pursued through the place Royale with a bayonet at his backside and escaped only by taking refuge under the porte cochère of no. 6. They shouted: "There goes another one of those Saint-Simonians!" And they would have killed him. He happened to be carrying a volume of the duc de Saint-Simon's memoirs under his arm. A National Guard had read the word *Saint-Simon* on the cover and had cried: Kill him!

On June 6, 1832, a suburban company of National Guards, commanded by the same Captain Fannicot referred to above, got themselves decimated in the rue de la Chanvrerie—on a whim and for the thrill of it. This incident, singular as it was, was recorded by the judicial investigation opened in the aftermath of the insurrection of 1832. Captain Fannicot, a bold and impatient bourgeois, a sort of condottiere[4] of order, a fanatical and rebellious governmentalist of the kind described above, could not resist the impulse to open fire before it was time in his overweening ambition to take the barricade all on his own, that is, with his company. Exasperated by the appearance of the red flag, followed by the old black coat, which he took for the black flag, he blamed out loud the generals and corps leaders, who were holding council and did not consider that the decisive moment of the assault had arrived and thereby let "the insurrection stew in its own juice," as the famous expression of one of them went. As for himself, he thought the barricade was ripe for the taking, and since what is ripe must fall, he decided to have a go.

He commanded men as resolute as he was—*enragés,* fanatics, in the word of one witness. His company, the very one that had shot down the poet Jean Prouvaire, was the first of the battalion posted at the corner of the street. The moment they were least expecting it, the captain launched his men against the barricade. This movement, executed with more goodwill than strategy, cost the Fannicot company dearly. Before they had got two thirds of the way down the street, they were greeted by a general discharge from the barricade. Four men, the most daring, who had run ahead, were struck down point-blank at the very foot of the redoubt, and this courageous throng of National Guards, all very brave men but with no military stamina, had to fall back after some hesitation, leaving fifteen corpses behind them on the pavement. That moment of hesitation gave the insurgents the time to reload their weapons and a second discharge, most murderous, hit the company before they could regain the corner of the street, their cover. At one point they were caught between two volleys of shot and copped the volley from the field gun *en batterie* which, the gunners not having any orders, had kept firing without interruption. The intrepid and imprudent Fannicot was one of those who died in this hail of grapeshot. He was killed by the cannon, that is, by order.

This attack, which was more furious than serious, angered Enjolras.

"The idiots!" he said. "They're getting their men killed and using up our ammunition for nothing!"

Enjolras spoke like the true riot general he was. Insurrection and its repression do not fight on equal terms. Insurrection, promptly exhaustible, has only a limited number of shots to fire and only a limited number of combatants to lose. An emptied cartridge pouch, a man down, can't be replaced. Repression, having the army, does not count men and, having Vincennes,[5] does not count shots. Repression has as many regiments as the barricade has men and as many arsenals as the barricade has cartridge boxes. And so they are struggles of one against one hundred, which always end in the crushing of the barricades; unless revolution, suddenly rearing up, comes and throws its flaming archangel's blade into the balance. This does happen. Then there is a general uprising, the streets start to boil over, popular redoubts proliferate, all Paris ripples with an intense thrill, the *quid divinum*[6] is unleashed, an August 10 is in the air, a July 29[7] is in the air, a wondrous light appears, the yawning maw of force backs away and the army, that lion, sees in front of it, steady on its feet and tranquil, that prophet, France.

## XIII. PASSING GLIMMERS

In the chaos of feelings and passions that go into defending a barricade, there is a bit of everything; there is bravery, youth, honor, enthusiasm, idealism, conviction, the relentlessness of the gambler, and, especially, flashes of hope.

One of these flashes, one of these faint stirrings of hope, suddenly ran through the barricade of the rue de la Chanvrerie, at the most unexpected moment.

"Listen," Enjolras, still on the watch, suddenly cried, "it seems to me that Paris is waking up."

It is undeniable that for an hour or two on the morning of June 6, the insurrection experienced a certain upswing. The obstinacy of the Saint-Merry tocsin rekindled a few vague urges. In the rue du Poirier and the rue des Gravilliers, barricades got under way. In front of the porte Saint-Martin a young man armed with a carbine attacked a cavalry squadron single-handedly. Out in the open, in the middle of the boulevard, he went down on one knee, raised his weapon to his shoulder, fired, killed the captain of the squadron, and turned on his heel, quipping: "There's another one who won't do us any more harm." He was promptly run through with a saber. In the rue Saint-Denis, a woman fired on the Municipal Guard from behind a lowered venetian blind. At each shot you could see the slats of the blind quivering. A fourteen-year-old boy was stopped in the rue de la Cossonnerie with his pockets full of cartridges. Several posts were attacked. At the entrance to the rue Bertin-Poirée, an extremely lively and completely unpredictable fusillade greeted a regiment of cuirassiers at the head of which marched General Cavaignac de Baragne.[1] In the rue Planche-Mibray, they hurled shards of old crockery and household utensils at the troops from the rooftops. This was a bad sign and when the incident was reported to Maréchal Soult, Napoléon's old lieutenant became dreamy, remembering Suchet's Saragossa dictum:[2] "We're finished when the old women empty their chamber pots on our heads."

These general symptoms, presenting just when the riot was thought to be contained, this outbreak of angry fever, gaining the upper hand again, these sparks, flying around here and there above the dense masses of combustible material known as the faubourgs of Paris—all this taken together worried the top brass. They rushed to put out the fire before it spread. They delayed the attack on the Maubuée, la Chanvrerie, and Saint-Merry barricades until the crackling flames could be put out, so as to have nothing else to tackle but those three, and to be able to finish them in one go. Columns were sent out into the fermenting streets, sweeping the main ones, sounding out the small ones, right and left, sometimes slowly and cautiously, other times charging along. The troops broke down the doors of houses from which there had been firing. At the same time cavalry maneuvers dispersed the throngs on the boulevards. This repression was not accomplished without noise, without that tumultuous racket peculiar to clashes between the army and the people. This was exactly what Enjolras had picked up, in the intervals between the cannonade and the musketry. On top of that, he had seen wounded men going past the end of the street on stretchers and he said to Courfeyrac: "Those wounded men aren't ours."

Hope did not last long; the glimmer quickly dimmed. In less than half an hour, what was in the air had evaporated, it was like lightning without the thunder, and the insurgents again felt crushed by that sort of lead weight that the indifference of the people drops on deserted die-hards.

The general movement that seemed to have been vaguely taking off had aborted; and the attention of the minister of war and the strategy of the generals could now focus on the three or four barricades still standing.

The sun rose on the horizon.

An insurgent called out to Enjolras: "We're hungry here. Are we really going to die like this without eating?"

Enjolras, still leaning on his battlement and without taking his eyes off the end of the street, nodded his head in the affirmative.

## XIV. In Which You Will Read
### the Name of Enjolras' Mistress

Courfeyrac, sitting on a paving stone next to Enjolras, continued to abuse the cannon, and every time that gloomy cloud of projectiles known as grapeshot passed with its monstrous noise, he greeted it with an outburst of irony.

"You're wearing your lungs out, you poor old brute, you worry me, you're wasting your breath. That's not thunder. That's a cough."

And those around him chuckled.

Courfeyrac and Bossuet, whose valiant good humor grew with the danger, swapped jokes instead of food, like Madame Scarron,[1] and, since wine was lacking, poured good cheer all round.

"I have to hand it to Enjolras," said Bossuet. "His imperturbable temerity stuns me. He lives alone, which makes him, perhaps, a little sad. Enjolras moans about the greatness that keeps him single. The rest of us all more or less have mistresses that drive us mad, in other words, make us brave. When you're as lovesick as a tiger, the least you can do is fight like a lion. It's a way of getting our own back for the tricks our little grisettes play on us. Roland gets himself killed to rile Angélique.[2] All our acts of heroism derive from our women. A man without a woman is like a pistol without a hammer; it's women that get men fired up. But, well, Enjolras doesn't have a woman. He's not lovesick, yet he still finds a way to be intrepid. It's unheard of—that you can be as cold as ice and as bold as fire."

Enjolras did not look as though he was listening but if anyone had been close to him, they would have heard him mutter in an undertone: *Patria*.

Bossuet was still laughing when Courfeyrac cried out: "Here's something new!"

And, putting on the voice of a court crier, he added: "I'm known as Eight-Pounder."

Indeed, a new character had just entered the stage. It was a second piece of ordnance. The gunners rapidly maneuvered this second piece into position *en batterie* next to the first. This was the beginning of the end.

A few moments later the two guns, swiftly served, fired straight at the redoubt; the fire of the platoon of the line and of the suburbs supported the artillery.

Another cannonade could be heard some distance away. At the same time as the two guns were relentlessly battering the redoubt in the rue de la Chanvrerie, two other pieces of ordnance, one positioned on the rue Saint-Denis, the other on the rue Aubry-le-Boucher, were peppering the barricade Saint-Merry. The four cannons echoed each other dolefully.

The barking of those dour dogs of war was like calling and answering.

One of the two guns now battering the barricade in the rue de la Chanvrerie was firing grapeshot and the other cannonballs.

The gun firing cannonballs was pointed a little high and the angle of fire was calculated so that the cannonball struck the rim of the upper ridge of the barricade, flattened it, and scattered the shattered cobblestones over the insurgents in bursts of shot.

This process was meant to drive the combatants off the top of the redoubt and force them to huddle together inside it; in other words, it heralded the main assault.

Once the combatants were driven from the top of the barricade by the cannonballs and from the windows of the tavern by the grapeshot, the attacking columns could risk entering the street without being targeted, perhaps even without being seen, swiftly scale the redoubt, as they had done the night before, and, who knows? perhaps take it by surprise.

"We absolutely must do something about those guns," said Enjolras, and he shouted, "Open fire on the gunners!"

Everyone was ready. The barricade, which had remained silent for so long, opened fire wildly, seven or eight discharges followed each other in a fit of rage and jubilation, the street filled with blinding smoke and, after a few minutes, through this fog all streaked with flames, two thirds of the gunners could vaguely be made out lying under the wheels of the guns. Those who had remained standing continued to serve the guns with rigid composure; but the firing had slackened its pace.

"This is working well," said Bossuet to Enjolras. "Success."

Enjolras shook his head and replied: "Another fifteen minutes of such success and there won't be ten cartridges left in the barricade."

It would seem that Gavroche heard this remark.

## XV. GAVROCHE OUTSIDE

Courfeyrac suddenly saw someone at the foot of the barricade, outside, in the street, under the rain of cannonballs.

Gavroche had taken a bottle carrier from the tavern, had gone out through the exit, and was busy quietly emptying into his carrier the full cartridge pouches of the National Guards who had been killed on the talus of the redoubt.

"What are you doing out there?" said Courfeyrac.

Gavroche stuck his nose up.

"Citizen, I'm filling my carrier."

"Can't you see the grapeshot?"

Gavroche replied: "So, it's raining. What of it?"

Courfeyrac yelled: "Get back!"

"Presently," said Gavroche.

And he bounded into the street.

You will recall that, in falling back, the Fannicot company had left behind them a trail of corpses. Some twenty dead lay strewn about here and there over the pavement all the way down the street. Some twenty cartridge pouches for Gavroche. A supply of cartridges for the barricade.

The smoke was as thick as fog in the street. Anyone who has seen a cloud fall into a mountain gorge between two sheer cliff faces can imagine what the smoke was like, how compressed it was and how seemingly thickened by the two gloomy rows of tall houses. It rose slowly and was endlessly topped up; hence a gradual darkening that turned even broad daylight a dense white. The combatants could hardly see each other from one end of the street to the other, even though the street was very short.

This obscurity, probably intentional and calculated by the army chiefs who were supposed to be directing the assault on the barricade, was useful to Gavroche.

Under the folds of this veil of smoke, and thanks to his smallness, he was able to advance a fair way into the street without being seen. He robbed seven or eight cartridge pouches without much danger.

He crawled along on his stomach, galloped on all fours, holding his carrier in his teeth, twisted, slid, wriggled, snaked from one dead body to the next, and emptied each cartridge pouch or cartridge box the way a monkey opens a nut.

From the barricade, which he was still fairly close to, no one dared yell out to him to come back for fear of calling attention to him.

On one body, which was that of a corporal, he found a powder horn.

"In case of thirst," he said, ramming it in his pocket.

Forging ever onward, he came to the point where the fog from the fusillade became transparent. So much so that the skirmishers from the suburbs, massed at the corner of the street, suddenly pointed out to each other this thing stirring in the smoke.

Just as Gavroche was divesting a sergeant lying over a curbstone of his cartridges, a bullet struck the corpse.

"Well, I never!" said Gavroche. "Now they're killing my dead on me."

A second bullet made the pavement next to him glitter with sparks. A third knocked over his carrier. Gavroche peered around and saw that it was coming from the suburbans at the end of the street.

He scrambled to his feet and stood erect. With his hair to the wind, his hands on his hips, and his eyes fixed on the National Guards that were shooting, he sang:

They're ugly in Nanterre,
That's the fault of Voltaire,[1]
And dumb in Palaiseau,
That's the fault of Rousseau.[2]

Then he picked up his carrier, put back in the cartridges that had fallen out, without losing a single one, and, advancing toward the fusillade, went and stripped another cartridge pouch. There a fourth bullet also missed him. Gavroche sang:

I am not the lord mayor,
That's the fault of Voltaire,
I'm only a sparrow,
That's the fault of Rousseau.[3]

A fifth bullet only succeeded in dragging a third verse out of him:

Joy is my nature,
That's the fault of Voltaire,
Misery is my trousseau,
That's the fault of Rousseau.[4]

This went on for some little time.

The spectacle was horrifying and mesmerizing. Gavroche, shot at, was taunting the shooting. He looked like he was really enjoying himself. It was the sparrow pecking at the hunters. He responded to each discharge with a verse. They went on firing at him and they went on missing him. The National Guards and the soldiers laughed as they aimed at him. He lay down, then got up, he hid in a doorway, then leaped out, disappeared, reappeared, ran away, came back, responded to the volley of grapeshot by thumbing his nose, and meanwhile looted cartridges, emptied cartridge pouches, and filled his pannier. The insurgents, breathless with anxiety, followed him with their eyes. The barricade trembled; he sang. This was not a child, it was not a man; it was a strange fairy larrikin. You would have said the invulnerable dwarf of the mêlée. The bullets chased him, but he was nimbler than they were. Like Roger the Dodger, he was playing some frightening private game of hide-and-seek with death; every time the pug-nosed face of the specter came close, the gamin gave him the flick.

One bullet, though, better aimed or more treacherous than the others, ended up hitting the will-o'-the-wisp child. They saw Gavroche totter, then he crumpled. The whole barricade let out a cry; but there was something of An-taeus in this pygmy. For a gamin to hit the pavement is like a giant hitting the ground; Gavroche had only fallen the better to rise again; he stayed sitting there on his haunches and, with a long trickle of blood streaking his face, he lifted up both arms in the air, turned his head to where the bullet had come from, and began singing:

> I fell from the air,
> That's the fault of Voltaire,
> Nose in gutter, though,
> That's the fault of—[5]

He did not finish. A second bullet from the same sniper cut him off. This time he fell face first onto the pavement and did not stir again. That great little soul had taken wing.

### XVI. HOW YOU GO FROM BEING A BROTHER TO A FATHER

At that very moment in the Luxembourg gardens—for the eye of the drama must be everywhere at once—there were two little boys holding each other by the hand. One of them could have been seven years old, the other five. Having been soaked by the rain, they were walking along the paths on the sunny side, the older one leading the little one; they were pale and in rags and they looked like wild birds. The little one said: "I'm really hungry."

The older boy, already a bit protective, pulled his brother along by the left hand and held a stick in his right.

They were alone in the garden. The garden was empty, the gates were closed as a police measure in response to the insurrection. The troops that had bivouacked there had been called away by the requirements of combat.

How did the boys get there? Perhaps they had escaped from some unlocked guardhouse; perhaps, somewhere in the neighborhood—at the barrière d'Enfer or on the esplanade of the Observatoire or in the neighboring square over-looked by the pediment on which you can read: *invenerunt parvulum pannis invo-lutum*[1]—there was some run-down booth set up by street players that they had run away from; perhaps, the night before, they had managed to evade the garden keepers at closing time and had spent the night in one of those huts where people sit around reading the newspapers. The fact is that they were wandering around like strays, apparently on their own. Wandering around like a stray apparently on your own means you are lost. These poor little boys were, in fact, lost.

The two boys were the same two boys Gavroche had gone to some trouble over and that the reader will recall. Children of the Thénardiers, rented out to mother Magnon, attributed to Monsieur Gillenormand, and now leaves dropped by all those rootless trees and tumbled along the ground by the wind.

Their clothes, clean in the days of mother Magnon—that had served her as a prospectus in regard to Monsieur Gillenormand—had turned to tatters.

These little creatures now belonged to the statistics of "abandoned children"—children that the police report, pick up, mislay, and find once more on the streets of Paris.

It took the mayhem of such a day for the two miserable little waifs to end up in the gardens. If the wardens had spotted them, they'd have chased the ragamuffins away. Poor kids are not allowed in public gardens; yet people ought to reflect that they too, like all children, have a right to flowers.

These two were there thanks to the gates being shut. They were breaking the law. They had sneaked into the gardens and stayed there. Closed gates do not mean the keepers are suddenly off-duty, surveillance is meant to continue; but it slackens off and takes a nap; and the keepers themselves, stirred up by the general public anxiety and more concerned about what was happening outside than inside, had stopped watching the garden and had not spotted the two tiny delinquents.

It had rained the night before and even a little that morning. But in June downpours are of no account. You hardly notice, an hour after a storm, that the beautiful bright day earlier shed tears. In summer the ground dries as fast as a child's cheek.

At around the time of the summer solstice, the light at the height of noon is piercing, so to speak. It gobbles up everything. It applies itself to the ground and smothers it in a sort of suction action. It is as though the sun is thirsty. A shower is a glass of water; rain is immediately drunk. In the morning, everything was streaming, in the afternoon, everything is shining in a powdery haze.

Nothing is as wonderful as green foliage washed by the rain and dried by the sun; it is like freshness served hot. Gardens and meadows, with water in their roots and sunshine in their flowers, turn into incense burners and smolder away, releasing all their perfumes at once. Everything laughs and sings and offers itself. You feel sweetly drunk. Spring is a taste of paradise; the sun helps human beings to bide their time.

There are those who ask for nothing more, living beings who, having bright blue skies above, say: This is enough; dreamers absorbed in wonder, drawing from nature-worship an indifference to good and bad, contemplators of the cosmos radiantly distracted from mankind who just don't understand how anybody can worry about the hunger of some, the thirst of others, the nakedness of the poor in winter, about the lymphatic curvature of a tiny spine, about the straw pallet, about the garret, the dungeon, and the rags of shivering young girls, when a person can just dream away idly under the trees; peaceful and terrible souls, mercilessly content. The funny thing is, the infinite is enough for them. That great need of mankind's, the finite, which allows itself to be embraced, is something they know nothing about. The finite, which allows that sublime travail, progress, is not something they ever think about. The indefinite, which is born of the half-human, half-divine combination of the infinite and the finite, escapes them. Provided they are face-to-face with immensity, they smile. Never joy, always ecstasy. To lose themselves is what they live for. For them the history of humanity is a mere cadastral survey; the All is not in it; the true All remains beyond it; what's the point of worrying about that minor detail, man? Man suffers, that's possible; but just look at Aldebaran[2] on the rise! The mother has no more milk, the newborn baby dies, I know nothing about that, but just look at this marvelous rosette made by a slice of fir tree examined under the microscope! What's the most beautiful Malines lace compared to that! These thinkers forget to love. The zodiac is such a big thing for them that it prevents them from seeing the child crying. God eclipses their souls. This is a family of minds, at once both small and great. Horace was one of them, Goethe was another, La Fontaine, perhaps; magnificent egoists of the infinite, unruffled onlookers of pain, who don't see Nero if the weather's nice, people for whom the sun hides the stake, who would gladly watch the guillotine at work in order to study some effect of light in it, who hear neither the cry, nor the sob, nor the death rattle, nor the tocsin, for whom everything is fine since the month of May exists, people who, as long as there are clouds of purple and gold above their heads, declare themselves satisfied and are determined to be happy until the stars stop shining and the birds stop singing.

These are the darkly radiant. They have no idea they are to be pitied. Of course, they are. Whoever does not weep, does not see. We have to admire them and pity them, as you would pity and admire anyone who is at once both night and day, with no eyes beneath their eyebrows but a star, instead, in the middle of their forehead.

The indifference of such thinkers is, according to some, a superior philosophy. So be it; but this brand of superiority is a little wobbly. You can be immortal and lame; witness Vulcan.[3] You can be more than man and less than man. The immense incomplete exists in nature. Who knows whether the sun isn't a blind man?

But then, heavens! Who can you trust? *Solem quis dicere falsum audeat?*[4] So certain geniuses themselves, certain almighty human beings, star men, might actually get things wrong? That which sits up there, at the top, at the summit, at the zenith, that which pours so much light over the earth, might actually see little, see badly, see not at all? Isn't this cause for despair? No. But what is above the sun, then? God.

On June 6, 1832, at around eleven o'clock in the morning, solitary and empty of people, the Luxembourg was lovely. The quincunxes and parterres sent each other balms and dazzling displays through the light. The branches of trees, wild in the midday brightness, seemed to be trying to embrace each other. Warblers were making a racket in the sycamores, sparrows were triumphant, woodpeckers were climbing right up the chestnut trees giving little taps of their beaks in holes in the bark. The flowerbeds accepted the legitimate royalty of the lilies; the most noble of perfumes is the perfume given off by whiteness. You breathed in the peppery smell of pinks. The old crows of Marie de Médicis' were amorous in the great trees. The sun lit up the tulips and turned them gold and crimson, tulips being nothing more than every variety of flame made flower. All around the tulip beds the bees whirled, sparks from the flame-flowers. Everything was grace and gaiety, even the impending rain; that recidivist, which the lilies of the valley and the honeysuckles would lap up, was not at all off-putting; the swallows were flying low, sweetly menacing. Whoever was around inhaled happiness; life smelled good; all of this nature gave off candor, succor, support, fatherliness, tenderness, a golden yellow freshness of dawn. The thoughts falling from the sky were as soft as a little child's hand when you kiss it.

The statues under the trees, naked and white, had frocks of shade riddled with light; these goddesses were all in tatters of sunshine; sunbeams hung from them on all sides. Around the great pond, the ground was already so dry again, it was almost burnt. There was enough wind to raise little riots of dust here and there. A few yellow leaves, left over from the previous autumn, merrily chased each other, like gamins playing.

The abundance of light had something indescribably reassuring about it. Life, sap, heat, fragrance, spilled over; you could feel the hugeness of the spring underlying creation; in all these puffs of air saturated with love, in this to-ing and fro-ing of reverberations and reflections, in this wildly extravagant spree of sunbeams, in this endless outpouring of liquid gold, you could feel the prodigality of the inexhaustible; and, behind this splendor, as behind a curtain of flame, you caught a glimpse of God, that millionaire in stars.

Thanks to the sand, there was not a trace of mud; thanks to the rain, there was not a speck of ash. The bouquets of flowers had just had a wash; all the velvets, all the satins, all the enamels, all the golds that come from out of the ground in the form of flowers were impeccable. This magnificence was clean. The great silence of happy nature filled the gardens. A celestial silence compatible with a thousand different melodies, the cooing of nests, the buzzing of swarms, the palpitations of the wind. All the harmony of the season came together in a gracious whole; spring's entrances and exits were taking place in the desired order; the lilacs were nearly finished, the jasmine was starting to come out; some flowers were late, some insects early; the vanguard of the red butterflies of June were fraternizing with the rear guard of the white butterflies of

May. The plane trees were getting new skins. The breeze was carving waves in the magnificent hugeness of the chestnut trees. It was splendid. A veteran of the neighboring barracks, peering through the fence, said: "Here's spring in full dress, shouldering arms."

All of nature was breakfasting; creation was at table; it was time; the great blue tablecloth had been laid over the sky and the great green tablecloth over the ground; the sun shone *a giorno*. God was serving the universal meal. Every being had its food or its fodder. The wood pigeon found hemp seed, the chaffinch found millet, the goldfinch found chickweed, the robin redbreast found worms, the bee found flowers, the fly found infusoria, the greenfinch found flies. Of course they all took a bite of each other, which is the mystery of the mixing of bad with good; but not one creature had an empty stomach.

The two little abandoned boys had almost got as far as the big pond, but they were a bit overwhelmed by all this light, and they tried to hide—an instinct of the poor and weak in the face of magnificence, even when impersonal; they ducked behind the swans' shelter and stayed there.

Now and then, at intervals, when the wind came on, you could vaguely hear cries, a noise, a sort of tumultuous jangling, which was gunfire, and dull knocking sounds, which were cannon blasts. There was smoke over the rooftops around Les Halles. A bell, which seemed to be calling, was ringing far away in the distance.

The boys did not seem to hear these sounds. The little one repeated in a small voice from time to time: "I'm hungry."

Almost at the same moment as the boys, another pair approached the great pond. This was a burgher of about fifty, leading by the hand a burgher of about six. No doubt a father with his son. The burgher of six was holding a big brioche.

In those days, certain houses near the park in the rue Madame and the rue d'Enfer had keys to the Luxembourg, which the residents used when the gates were closed, a special dispensation since done away with. This father-and-son duo no doubt came from one of those houses. The two little boys saw "the gentleman" coming and hid a bit more.

The man was a bourgeois. The same one, perhaps, that Marius in his lovesick state had heard one day advising his son "to avoid excess" at this same great pond. He had an affable and high-minded air and a mouth that, never shut, was always smiling. This mechanical smile, produced by too much jaw and too little skin, bares the teeth more than the soul. The child, with his brioche that he had mauled but not finished, looked stuffed. He was decked out as a National Guard because of the riot and the father had stayed decked out as a bourgeois because of prudence.

Father and son had stopped at the pond where the two swans were frolicking. The bourgeois seemed to have a special admiration for the swans. He resembled them in the sense that he walked just like them. For the moment, the swans were swimming, which is their principal talent, and they were superb.

If the two poor little boys had listened and been old enough to understand, they would have been able to reap the words of a grave man. The father was saying to his son: "The wise man lives content with little. Look at me, son. I don't go in for pomp. You never see me with coats spangled with gold brocade or bedizened with precious stones. I leave such fake glamour to unruly souls."

Here the loud shouting that came from over near Les Halles burst out with a redoubling of bell and clamor.

"What's that?" asked the child.

The father replied: "Those are saturnalia."[6]

All of a sudden, he spotted the two little ragamuffins, motionless behind the little green swan house.

"That is where it starts," he said.

After a pause he added: "Anarchy has entered the garden."

Meanwhile the son took a bite of the brioche, spat it out again, and started to cry.

"What are you crying for?" asked the father.

"I'm not hungry anymore," said the child.

The father's smile grew wider.

"One doesn't need to be hungry to eat a cake."

"I'm sick of my cake. It's stale."

"Don't you want any more?"

"No."

The father showed him the swans.

"Throw it to these web-footed creatures."

The child hesitated. Not wanting any more of your cake is no reason to give it away.

The father went on: "Be humane. We must have pity on animals."

And, taking his son's cake away from him, he threw it in the pond. The cake fell fairly close to the edge. The swans were a long way off, in the middle of the pond, and busy with some prey. They had not seen the bourgeois or the brioche.

The bourgeois, feeling that the cake was in danger of sinking, and stirred to action by such a pointless shipwreck, started jerking his arms as though sending signals and wound up attracting the swans' attention.

They saw something floating, veered like the ships they are, and headed slowly for the brioche with the smug majesty appropriate to white creatures.

"Swans swan about," said the bourgeois, delighted at his wit.

At that moment the distant tumult of the city was suddenly amplified again. This time, the sound was sinister. There are gusts of wind that speak more distinctly than others. The one blowing at that moment clearly brought drumrolls, uproar, platoon fire, and the lugubrious call and answer of the tocsin and the cannon. This coincided with a black cloud that promptly hid the sun.

The swans had not yet reached the brioche.

"Let's go home," said the father, "they're attacking the Tuileries."

He grabbed his son's hand again. Then he went on: "From the Tuileries to the Luxembourg, there is only the distance that separates royalty from the peerage;[7] it's not far. It's going to rain musket balls."

He looked at the cloud.

"And perhaps it's even going to rain rain, too. The heavens are joining in. The younger branch is doomed.[8] Let's go home, quick."

"I wanted to see the swans eat the brioche," wailed the child.

The father replied: "That would be imprudent."

And he hauled away his little bourgeois. The son, regretting the swans, kept his head turned toward the pond until a flowerbed hid it from him.

Meanwhile, at the same time as the swans, the two little strays headed for the brioche. It was floating on the water. The little one watched the cake, the big one watched the bourgeois walking away.

Father and son entered the maze of pathways that leads to the great steps by the stand of trees on the rue Madame side.

As soon as they were no longer in sight, the elder boy swiftly lay flat on his stomach on the rounded lip of the pond and, clinging to this with his left hand, leaning over the water, close to falling in, he held his stick out toward the cake with his right hand. The swans, seeing the enemy, stepped up the pace and in stepping up the pace, produced a kind of breastplate effect beneficial to the little fisherman; the water in front of the swans flowed back, and one of these soft concentric ripples gently pushed the brioche toward the little boy's stick. As the swans came up, the stick touched the cake. The boy gave it a quick shove, hooked in the brioche, scared off the swans, seized the cake, and straightened up. The cake was sopping wet; but they were hungry and thirsty. The elder boy broke the brioche into two pieces, a big one and a small one, took the small one for himself and gave the big one to his brother, telling him: "There, stick that in your cake-hole."

## XVII. Mortuus Pater Filium Moriturum Expectat[1]

Marius had flown out of the barricade. Combeferre had followed hot on his heels. But it was too late. Gavroche was dead. Combeferre brought the pannier of cartridges back. Marius brought the child.

"Alas!" he thought. "What his father did for my father, I'm doing for the son. Only Thénardier brought my father back alive. I'm bringing the boy back dead."

When Marius went back into the redoubt with Gavroche in his arms, his face, like the child's, was covered in blood. Just as he had swooped down to pick Gavroche up, a bullet had grazed his skull; he had not even noticed.

Courfeyrac took off his cravat and bandaged Marius's forehead with it.

They laid Gavroche out on the same table as Mabeuf and spread the black shroud over the two dead bodies. It was big enough for both the old man and the child.

Combeferre distributed the cartridges from the pannier that he had brought back. That gave each man fifteen shots to fire.

Jean Valjean was still in the same place, motionless on his curbstone. When Combeferre handed him his fifteen cartridges, he shook his head.

"That's a queer bird for you," Combeferre whispered to Enjolras. "He's managed to get himself into the barricade but he doesn't want to fight."

"That doesn't stop him from defending it," retorted Enjolras.

"Heroism has its oddballs," Combeferre shot back.

And Courfeyrac, who had overheard, added: "He's a different kettle of fish from old father Mabeuf."

It should be noted that the fire battering the barricade hardly disturbed the men inside it. Those who have never been through the whirlwind of this kind of war can't begin to imagine the strange moments of tranquillity that are part and parcel of the convulsions. People come and go, they chat, crack jokes, sit around. Someone we know once heard a combatant say to him in the middle of a volley of grapeshot: "It's like a bachelors' picnic in here." The redoubt in the rue de la Chanvrerie, we repeat, seemed incredibly calm inside. Every possible development, every possible phase of action, had come to an end—or was about to. The position had gone from critical to threatening and was doubtless about to go from threatening to desperate. The grimmer the situation became, the darker the barricade glowed with the bloodred light of heroism. Enjolras gravely ruled over it in the attitude of a young Spartan dedicating his naked blade to the dark genius Epidotas.

Combeferre, with an apron tied round his waist, was tending the wounded; Bossuet and Feuilly were making cartridges using the powder horn collected by Gavroche from the dead corporal, and Bossuet was saying to Feuilly: "We'll soon be catching the coach for another planet"; Courfeyrac was laying out and arranging, as carefully as a young girl tidying her little workbasket, a whole arsenal of weaponry over the few cobblestones he had reserved for himself next to Enjolras: his sword stick, his musket, two horse pistols, and a handheld knuckle-duster pistol. Jean Valjean was silently staring at the wall opposite. A worker was tying a broad-brimmed straw hat of mother Hucheloup's on his head with some string, "for fear of sunstroke," he said. The young men of the Cougourde d'Aix were nattering away gaily among themselves as though keen to speak patois one last time. Joly, who had taken down the widow Hucheloup's mirror, was examining his tongue. A few combatants, having stumbled on some crusts of more or less moldy bread in a drawer, were wolfing them down. Marius was worrying about what his father was going to say to him.

## XVIII. THE VULTURE TURNS INTO THE PREY

There is one psychological fact peculiar to barricades that we must underline. No characteristic of this surprising street warfare should be omitted.

Whatever the strange interior tranquillity just mentioned, the barricade, for those who remain inside it, remains no less unreal, a hallucination.

There is something of the apocalypse in civil war, with all the mists of the unknown swirling in to mingle with those savage blazes; revolutions are sphinxes and anyone who has lived through a barricade feels like they have lived through a dream.

What you feel in those places, as we have shown with Marius—and we will see the consequences—is both larger and smaller than life. Once out of a barricade, you no longer have any idea what you saw there. You did terrible things, but you don't remember. You were surrounded by conflicting ideas that had human faces; but your head was in the light of the future. There were corpses lying prone and phantoms on their feet. The passing hours were colossal and felt like the hours of eternity. You lived in death. Shadows passed. What were they? You saw hands with blood on them; there was an unbearable deafening; there was also a terrible silence; there were open mouths shouting and other open mouths that kept quiet; you were in smoke, in the darkness perhaps. You think you felt the sinister ooze of unknown depths; you look at something red you have under your fingernails. You don't remember anymore.

Let's get back to the rue de la Chanvrerie. All of a sudden, between two shots, they heard the distant sound of the hour striking.

"Midday," said Combeferre.

The twelve strokes had not finished sounding when Enjolras sprang straight to his feet and yelled from the top of the barricade in a voice of thunder: "Take cobblestones up into the house. Line the downstairs and attic windowsills with them. Half the men on the muskets, the other half on the cobblestones. Not a minute to lose."

A platoon of sappers, axes over their shoulders, had just appeared in battle order at the end of the street.

This could only be the head of a column; and what column was it? The attacking column, obviously, the sappers charged with demolishing the barricade having always to precede the soldiers charged with scaling it.

They were obviously coming to the moment that Monsieur de Clermont-Tonnerre,[1] in 1822, called "the choker trick."

Enjolras' order was executed with the due haste peculiar to ships and barricades, the only two places of combat where escape is impossible. In less than a minute, two thirds of the cobblestones that Enjolras had had piled at the door of Corinthe had been taken up to the first floor and the attic, and before another minute had passed, these cobblestones, artistically packed one on top of the other, walled up half the height of the window on the first floor as well as the dormer windows in the roof. A few gaps, carefully arranged at intervals by Feuilly, the chief builder, would allow the muzzles of the muskets to pass through. This arming of the windows was all the easier to do as the grapeshot had ceased. The two field guns were now firing cannonballs at the middle of the roadblock to make a hole in it and, if possible, a breach, for the assault.

When the cobbles destined for the final defense were in place, Enjolras had them carry up to the first floor the bottles he had placed under the table where Mabeuf lay.

"So, who's going to drink that?" Bossuet asked him.

"They are," said Enjolras.

Then they barricaded the window downstairs and they held at the ready the iron crossbars that served to bar the tavern door from the inside at night. The fortress was complete. The barricade was the rampart, the tavern was the keep.

With the remaining cobblestones they blocked up the opening.

As defenders of a barricade are always obliged to stint on their ammunition, and the besiegers know this, the besiegers go about putting the finishing touches on their arrangements with a sort of irritating leisureliness, exposing themselves prematurely to fire, though more in appearance than in reality, and making themselves comfortable. Preparations for attack are always made with a certain methodical slowness; after which, all hell breaks loose.

This slow pace allowed Enjolras to review everything and perfect everything. He felt that since men like these were to die, their death should be a masterpiece.

He said to Marius: "We are the two leaders. I'm going to give the last orders inside. You, stay outside and keep watch."

Marius posted himself to keep watch on the crest of the barricade. Enjolras had the door to the kitchen, which, as you will recall, was now the field hospital, nailed up.

"So the wounded won't get spattered," he said.

He gave his final instructions in the downstairs room in a voice that was clipped, but profoundly calm; Feuilly listened and answered on everyone's behalf.

"On the first floor, hold your axes ready to cut off the staircase. Have you got them?"

"Yes," said Feuilly.

"How many?"

"Two axes and a poleax."

"Good. There are twenty-six of us combatants left standing. How many muskets are there?"

"Thirty-four."

"Eight too many. Keep the eight guns loaded like the rest and at hand. Swords and pistols at your belts. Twenty men at the barricade. Six in ambush at the attic windows and the window on the first floor to open fire on the assailants through the loopholes in the cobblestones. Let not a single useless worker remain here. Shortly, when the drum beats the charge, let the twenty from below rush the barricade. The first men in will get the best places."

These provisions made, he turned to Javert and said to him: "I haven't forgotten you."

And, placing a pistol on the table, he added: "The last one out of here will put a bullet in this spy's skull."

"Here?" asked a voice.

"No, let's not mix his corpse up with ours. You can climb over the small barricade in Mondétour lane. It's only four feet high. The man's well trussed-up. You will take him there and you will execute him there."

Only one man, at that moment, was even more imperturbable than Enjolras. It was Javert. Here Jean Valjean appeared. He had been mixed up with the group of insurgents. He stepped away from them and said to Enjolras: "You are the commander?"

"Yes."

"You thanked me a moment ago."

"In the name of the Republic. The barricade has two saviors: Marius Pontmercy and you."

"Do you think I deserve a reward?"

"Of course."

"All right, then, I'm asking for one."

"What?"

"To blow that man's brains out myself."

Javert raised his head, saw Jean Valjean, gave an imperceptible nod and said: "That is only right."

As for Enjolras, he had started to reload his carbine; he cast his eyes around him: "Any complaints?"

And he turned to Jean Valjean: "Take the snitch."

Jean Valjean did, in fact, take possession of Javert by plunking himself down on the end of the table. He grabbed the pistol and a faint clicking sound announced that he had cocked it. Almost at the same moment, a bugle call was heard.

"On guard!" cried Marius from the top of the barricade.

Javert started to laugh with that noiseless laugh peculiar to him, and staring hard at the insurgents, he said to them: "You're hardly any better off than I am."

"Everyone outside!" cried Enjolras.

The insurgents leaped outside in an uproar and, as they left, were stabbed in the back, if you'll forgive the expression, by these words of Javert's: "See you soon!"

## XIX. JEAN VALJEAN GETS HIS REVENGE

When Jean Valjean was alone with Javert, he undid the rope that held the prisoner secure around the waist, the knot of which was under the table. Then he signaled to him to get up. Javert did as he was told, but with that indefinable smile in which the supremacy of shackled authority is condensed.

Jean Valjean seized Javert by the martingale as you would grab a beast of burden by the breast strap, and, dragging him after him, walked out of the tavern slowly, for Javert, hobbled at the legs, could only take very small steps.

Jean Valjean had his pistol in his fist. They went through the trapeze formed by the inside of the barricade like this. The insurgents, all geared up for the imminent attack, had their backs turned.

Marius, alone, positioned at the left end of the roadblock, saw them go by. This pair formed by the victim and the executioner was lit up for him by the sepulchral light in his soul.

Jean Valjean made Javert climb over the small entrenchment of Mondétour lane, which he did with some difficulty, trussed up as he was, though he did not let go of him for a single instant. When they had climbed over this little roadblock, they found themselves alone together in the lane. No one could see them now. The elbow made by the houses hid them from the insurgents. The corpses removed from the barricade made a terrible mound a few feet away.

You could make out in the heap of the dead a livid face, hair flowing down, a hand shot through, and a half-bared woman's breast. That was Éponine.

Javert looked sideways at the dead woman and, profoundly calm, said in an undertone: "It seems to me I know that girl."

Then he turned to Jean Valjean.

Jean Valjean stuck his pistol under his arm and leveled a look at Javert that needed no words to say: Javert, it's me.

Javert answered: "Take your revenge."

Jean Valjean pulled a knife out of his fob pocket and flicked it open.

"A pigsticker!" cried Javert. "You're right. That's more your style."

Jean Valjean cut the martingale yoked around Javert's neck, then he cut the ropes around his wrists, then, bending down, he cut the string around his feet; and, straightening up again, he said to him: "You are free."

Javert was not easily amazed. Yet, completely in control of himself as he was, he could not escape a surge of inner turmoil. He stood stock-still, mouth agape.

Jean Valjean elaborated: "I don't think I'll be getting out of here alive. But if, by chance, I do get out, I go by the name of Fauchelevent, rue de l'Homme-Armé, number seven."

Javert gave a tiger's scowl that pulled up the corners of his mouth, and he snarled between clenched teeth: "Watch out."

"Off you go," said Jean Valjean.

Javert went on: "You said Fauchelevent, rue de l'Homme-Armé?"

"Number seven."

Javert repeated to himself: "Number seven."

He buttoned up his overcoat again, put some military stiffness back between his shoulder blades, did a half turn, folded his arms, supporting his chin with one hand, and began to walk in the direction of Les Halles. Jean Valjean watched him go. After a few steps, Javert turned round and shouted at Jean Valjean: "I don't like this. Kill me, instead, why don't you."

Javert himself did not notice that he no longer addressed Jean Valjean with the familiarity of contempt.

"Keep going," said Jean Valjean.

Javert walked very slowly away. A moment later, he turned the corner of the rue des Prêcheurs.

When Javert had disappeared, Jean Valjean fired the pistol in the air. Then he returned to the barricade and said: "Done."

Meanwhile, what had happened is this:

Marius, busier with the outside than the inside, had not till then looked too closely at the spy tied up in the dark at the back of the downstairs room.

When he saw him in broad daylight, clambering over the barricade to go to his death, he recognized him. A memory suddenly sprang to mind. He remembered the inspector of the rue de Pontoise and the two pistols he had given him, which he, Marius, had used in this very barricade; and he not only remembered the face, but he remembered the name.

This recollection, though, was hazy and confused like everything going on in his mind. It was not a statement he put to himself, but a question. "Isn't that the inspector of police who told me his name was Javert?"

Perhaps there was still time to intervene on the man's behalf? But he had to know first of all if it really was Javert.

Marius called out to Enjolras, who had just positioned himself at the other end of the barricade.

"Enjolras!"

"What?"

"What's the name of that man?"

"Who?"

"The police officer. Do you know his name?"

"Naturally. He told us himself."

"So what's his name?"

"Javert."

Marius straightened up.

At that moment, the pistol shot was heard. Jean Valjean reappeared and cried out: "Done."

A dark chill ran through Marius's heart.

## XX. THE DEAD ARE RIGHT BUT THE LIVING ARE NOT WRONG

The barricade's death throes were about to begin.

Everything concurred in the tragic majesty of this supreme moment; a thousand mysterious roaring sounds in the air, the breath of the armed masses set in motion in streets that could not be seen, the intermittent galloping of cavalry, the heavy rattling of artillery on the move, platoon fire and cannon fire crossing each other in the labyrinth of Paris, the smoke from the battle rising all golden above the rooftops, unidentifiable, vaguely terrible cries in the distance, lightning flashes of menace everywhere, the tocsin of Saint-Merry that now sounded like sobbing, the sweetness of the season, the splendor of the sky full of sun and clouds, the beauty of the day, and the appalling silence of the houses.

For since the night before, the two rows of houses of the rue de la Chanvrerie had become two great walls; staunchly savage walls. Doors shut, windows shut, shutters shut.

In those days, so different from our own, when the people finally felt the time had come to have done either with a situation that had gone on too long, or with a charter granted or some piece of law, when universal anger had spread throughout the atmosphere, when the city consented to the pulling up of its pavements, when insurrection made the bourgeoisie smile by whispering its watchword in its ear, then the ordinary householder, immersed in rioting, so to speak, was the auxiliary of the combatant, and the house fraternized with the improvised fortress that leaned on it. When the situation was not ripe, when insurrection was decidedly not agreed to, when the masses disowned the movement, then that was it for the combatants, the city turned into a desert around the revolt, hearts and minds frosted over, refuges were walled off, and the street turned itself into a defile to assist the army in taking the barricade.

You can't shock a people into going any faster than they want to go. Woe betide the man who tries to force their hand! A people won't let themselves be pushed around. They will just abandon an insurrection to its own devices. The insurgents become lepers. A house is a cliff face, a door is rejection, a façade is a wall. The wall sees, hears, and will have none of it. It could crack open a bit and save you. But no. The wall is a judge. It looks at you and condemns you. What a grim sight these closed houses are! They look dead but they are alive. Life, which seems to be suspended there, goes on inside just the same. No one has come out for twenty-four hours, but they are all in there. On the inside of that solid rock, they come and go, go to bed, get up; they are one happy family in there; they eat in there and they drink; they are frightened in there, too, which is a terrible thing! Fear excuses such terrible inhospitality; it merges with alarm, an extenuating circumstance. Sometimes, and this has been seen, fear even becomes a passion; fright can turn to fury, just as prudence can turn to rage; hence the very profound expression, *moderate extremists.* There are flare-ups of utter terror from which rage issues like gloomy smoke. "What do these people want? They're never satisfied. They compromise men of peace. As if we haven't had enough revolutions as it is! What have they come here for? Let them get themselves out of it. Too bad for them. It's their own fault. They've only got what they had coming to them. It's nothing to do with us. Look at our poor street riddled with bullets. They're a bunch of vermin. Whatever you do, don't open the door." And the house takes on the look of a tomb. The insurgent at the door is about to die; he sees the grapeshot and the drawn sabers coming; if he cries out, he knows that they can hear him, but that no one will come; there are walls there that could protect him, there are men there who could save him, and the walls have ears of flesh and the men have hearts of stone.

Who is to blame?

No one and everyone.

The imperfect times in which we live.

It is always at its own risk that a utopia transforms itself into an insurrection and goes from a philosophical protest to an armed protest, turning from Minerva to Pallas.[1] The utopia that gets impatient and turns into a riot knows what awaits it; it almost always arrives too soon. So it resigns itself and stoically accepts disaster in place of triumph. It serves those who denounce it without complaining, even exonerating them, and its magnanimity lies in agreeing to desertion. It is indomitable in the face of any obstacle, yet easy on ingratitude.

Is it ingratitude, though?

Yes, from the standpoint of the human race.

No, from the standpoint of the individual.

Progress is mankind's modus vivendi. Progress is the name we give to the regular life of the human race; Progress is the name we give to the collective step the human race takes. Progress marches onward; it makes the great human and earthly journey toward the heavenly and the divine; it has its halts where it rallies the flock lagging behind; it has its stops where it meditates beside some splendid Canaan that suddenly unveils its promised land; it has its nights where it sleeps; and one of the poignant preoccupations of the thinker is to see shadow over the human soul and to grope around in the dark without being able to wake dozing progress up.

"Maybe God is dead," Gérard de Nerval[2] said one day to the writer of these lines, confusing God with progress and taking the interruption in movement for the death of the Supreme Being.

Whoever despairs is wrong. Progress invariably wakes up and has always marched on, so to speak, even as it dozes, for it has grown. When we see it on its feet again, we find it taller. To be always peaceful is no more the province of progress than of a river; don't throw up a dam there, don't throw in a rock; any obstruction makes the water roil and makes humanity boil over. This produces turmoil; but after such turmoil, we recognize that a certain amount of ground has been covered. Until order, which is simply universal peace, is established, until harmony and unity reign, Progress will have revolutions as stopovers along the way.

So what is Progress? We just said. The continuous life of peoples.

Now, it sometimes happens that the momentary life of individuals puts up some resistance to the eternal life of the human race.

Let's admit without bitterness that the individual has his own distinct self-interest, and can without committing a crime make that interest clear and defend it; the present has its excusable dose of egotism; the life of the moment has its rights and is not bound to sacrifice itself endlessly to the future. The generation currently taking its turn on this earth is not obliged to shorten its passage for the generations to come, who are its equals, after all, and will later have their turn. "I exist," murmurs that someone known as Everyman. "I am young and I am in love, I am old and I want to rest, I am a family man, I work, I am doing well, I am doing a roaring trade, I have houses to rent, I have money invested in the government, I am happy, I have a wife and kids, I love all that, I want to live, leave me alone . . ." And so, at certain times, a frigid cold shoulder is shown the magnanimous vanguards of the human race.

Utopia, in any case—let's agree on this—quits its radiant sphere in making war. Tomorrow's truth borrows its method—battle—from yesterday's lie. The future acts like the past. The pure idea turns into assault and battery. It muddies its heroism with a violence that it is only right it should answer for—a casual and expedient violence that goes against principles and for which it is fatally punished. Utopia does battle as insurrection, the old military code in its fist; it shoots down spies, it executes traitors, it does away with living beings and hurls them into unknown darkness. It deals in death, which is a serious matter. It looks as though utopia no longer has faith in radiance, its irresistible and incorruptible strength. It smites with the blade. Now, no blade is simple. Every sword is double-edged; whoever wounds with one edge, wounds himself with the other.

This reservation made, and made in all severity, we can't help but admire, whether they succeed or not, the glorious fighters for the future, utopia's confidants. Even when they miscarry, they are venerable, and it is, perhaps, in their failure that they are most majestic. Victory, when it falls in with progress, deserves the applause of the peoples of the world; but a heroic defeat deserves their compassion. The one is magnificent, the other, sublime. For us, who prefer martyrdom to success, John Brown is greater than Washington, Pisacane is greater than Garibaldi.[3]

Someone has to stand up for the vanquished after all.

People are unjust toward these great assayers of the future when they miscarry.

People accuse revolutionaries of sowing fear. Every barricade seems the work of terrorists. Their theories are found incriminating, their aims are treated with suspicion, their ulterior motives are regarded with mistrust, their scruples are condemned. They are accused of raising, piling up, and packing a whole heap of miseries, sorrows, iniquities, grievances, and despairs against the reigning social order and of dredging up great blocks of darkness from out of the dregs as battlements that they can entrench themselves behind to fight. People shout at them: That pavement you're ripping up is the road to hell. They could well answer: That is why our barricade is made of good intentions.

The best thing, of course, is the peaceful solution. To sum up, we might agree that when you see those paving stones, you think of the bear in its pit, the monster in its lair, and that is the sort of goodwill that raises society's hackles. But it is up to society to save itself; it is to its own goodwill that we appeal. No violent remedy is necessary. Study evil amicably, note it, then cure it. That is what we urge society to do.

Whatever the case may be, even when they have fallen, especially when they have fallen, those men are honorable who, at the four corners of the globe, their eyes fixed on France, fight for the great cause with the inflexible logic of the ideal; they give their lives as a pure sacrifice for progress; they carry out the will of Providence; they commit a religious act. At the appointed hour, with as much disinterestedness as an actor who comes in on cue, following the divine script, they step into the grave. And they accept this hopeless fight and their own stoical disappearance as a means of bringing the magnificent movement of humanity irresistibly begun on July 14, 1789, to its splendid and supreme universal conclusion. The French Revolution is a move made by God.

On top of this, though, there are—and we really should add this distinction to the distinctions already mentioned in an earlier chapter—accepted insurrections that go by the name of revolutions; and rejected revolutions that go by the name of riots. An insurrection that breaks out is an idea that sits for its exam before the people. If the people don't give it a pass, the idea withers on the vine, the insurrection is a mere brawl.

To go to war at every summons and every time utopia desires it is not the way of the peoples of the world. Nations do not always, at any given moment, have the temperament of heroes and martyrs.

They are positive. Insurrection is repugnant to them, a priori; first, because it often ends in disaster; second, because it always starts off with an abstraction.

For the beautiful thing is that it is always for the ideal, and for the ideal alone, that those who do devote themselves devote themselves. Insurrection is enthusiasm. Enthusiasm can lose its temper; hence the taking up of arms. But every insurrection that targets a government or a regime aims higher. So, for example, and we must insist on this, what the chiefs of the insurrection of 1832 were fighting against, and in particular the young enthusiasts of the rue de la Chanvrerie, was not Louis-Philippe exactly. Most of them, chatting unguardedly, did justice to the king's good points, standing as he did with one foot in the monarchy and the other in the revolution; none of them hated him. But what they were attacking was the younger branch of divine right in Louis-Philippe, just as they had attacked the elder branch in Charles X; and what they wanted to overthrow in overthrowing royalty in France, as we explained, was the usurpation of man over man and of privilege over justice throughout the world. Paris without a king results in a world without despots. That is how they reasoned. Their goal was no doubt remote, perhaps vague, and it receded the more they strained after it; but it was grand.

That is the way it is. And people sacrifice themselves for these visions, which, for those sacrificed, are almost always illusions, but illusions in which, on the whole, all human certainty is mixed up. Insurgents wax lyrical about and gild the insurrection. They throw themselves into that tragic mess and get drunk on what they are about to do. Who knows? Maybe they will succeed. They are but few; they have a whole army arrayed against them; but they are defending right, the law of nature, justice, truth, the sovereignty of each man over himself, from which no abdication is possible; and, if need be, they will die like the three hundred Spartans. It is not Don Quixote they have in mind, but Leonidas.[4] And they forge ahead and, once they are committed, there is no going back, so they rush headlong, hoping for an unheard-of victory— complete revolution, unbridled progress, the betterment of the human race, universal deliverance; and, if the worst comes to the worst, Thermopylae.

These sparring matches on behalf of progress often fail and we have just explained why. The hordes rebel against the training of the knights-errant. These ponderous masses, the multitudes, vulnerable because of their very weight, are scared of adventure; and there is something of the adventure in the ideal.

Besides, we should not forget, there are interests involved, ones not too friendly to the ideal and the romantic. Sometimes the stomach paralyzes the heart.

The greatness and beauty of France is that it develops less of a paunch than other peoples; it can tighten its belt more easily. It is the first awake, last asleep. It steams ahead out front. It is a seeker.

This is because France is an artist.

The ideal is nothing but the culmination of logic, just as the beautiful is nothing but the acme of the true. Artistic peoples are also consistent peoples. To love beauty is to seek the light. This is why the torch of Europe, that is, of civilization, was carried first by Greece, who passed it on to Italy, who passed it on to France. Divine trailblazers of peoples! *Vitae lampada tradunt!*[5]

The wonderful thing is that the poetry of a people is part and parcel of its progress. The degree of civilization is measured by the degree of imagination. Only, a civilizing people must remain a virile people. Corinth, yes; Sybaris, no.[6] Those who become effeminate become degenerate. You have to be neither a dilettante nor a virtuoso; but you have to be an artist. When it comes to civilization, the thing is not to refine but to sublimate. On this condition, you can provide the human race with a model of the ideal.

The modern ideal has its classic example in art and its means in science. It is through science that we will realize that august vision of the poets: social beauty. We will remake Eden by learning what $a + b$ equals. At this point in civilization, the exact is an essential element of the marvelous, and artistic emotion is not merely served but completed by the organ of science; dream must be able to add up. Art, which conquers, must have as its fulcrum science, which does the walking. The sturdiness of the mount is important. The modern spirit is the genius of Greece with the genius of India under it, driving; Alexander on an elephant.

Races petrified in dogma or demoralized by lucre are unfit to lead civilization. Genuflecting to idols or to the dollar atrophies the walking muscle and the galvanizing will. Hieratic or mercantile absorption diminishes a people's radiance, lowers its horizon by lowering its level, and deprives it of that understanding, at once human and divine, of the universal goal, which makes nations missionaries. Babylon has no ideal. Carthage has no ideal. Athens and Rome have and keep, even through all the nocturnal depths of the centuries, the glories of civilization.

France has the same quality of people as Greece and Italy. It is Athenian in its beauty and Roman in its grandeur. On top of this, it is good. It gives itself. It is more likely than any other people to be inclined to devotion and self-sacrifice. Only, this inclination comes and goes. And that is the great danger for those who run when France wants only to walk, or who walk when France wants to stop for a breather. France has its relapses into materialism, and, at certain moments, the ideas that clog that sublime brain have nothing left in them that recalls French greatness and are the size, instead, of a Missouri or a South Carolina.[7] What can you do? The giant plays the dwarf; vast France has its fantasies of being small. That's all there is to it.

There is nothing to be said on that score. People, like stars, have the right to an eclipse. And all is well as long as the light comes back and the eclipse does not degenerate into darkness. Dawn and resurrection are synonyms. The reappearance of the light is identical to the persistence of the self.

Let's note these facts calmly. Death at the barricade, or a grave in exile, is an acceptable possible outcome for devotion. The true name for devotion is disinterestedness. Let the deserted let themselves be deserted, let the exiled let themselves be exiled; and let us restrict ourselves to imploring the great peoples of the world not to step back too far when they step back. They must not, under pretext of some return to reason, go too far downhill.

Matter exists, the moment exists, interests exist, the stomach exists; but the stomach must not be the sole guiding light. The life of the moment has its rights, we accept that, but life everlasting has its rights, too. Alas! Having risen does not stop you from falling. We see this in history more often than we would like. A nation is illustrious; it tastes the ideal, then it gorges on muck and finds it good; and if we ask it how come it is abandoning Socrates for Falstaff, it answers: It's just that I love statesmen.

One last word before we return to the fray.

A battle like the one we are currently describing is nothing but a convulsive lurch toward the ideal. Fettered progress is unhealthy and has epileptic fits that end in tragedy. This disease of progress, civil war, is something we have been forced to encounter on our travels. It is one of the fatal stages, at once act and interlude, in this tragedy that pivots around one of society's damned and whose true title is: *Progress.*

Progress!

This cry that we often let out is the only thing we have in mind, and at the point in the tragedy that we have reached, the idea it embodies having more than one more ordeal to go through yet, we may perhaps be allowed, if not to lift the veil on it, then at least to let its light shine through clearly.

The book that the reader has before his eyes at this moment, is, from one end to the other, as a whole and in its every detail, whatever its irregularities, its exceptions or shortcomings, a step from bad to good, from the unjust to the just, from the false to the true, from night to day, from appetite to awareness, from rottenness to life; from bestiality to duty, from hell to heaven, from nothingness to God. Starting point: matter; end point: the soul. A hydra in the beginning, an angel at the end.

## XXI. Heroes

All of a sudden the drum beat the charge.

The attack was a tornado. The night before, in the dark, the barricade had been approached as silently as if by a boa. Now, in broad daylight, in that wide-mouthed street, surprise was decidedly impossible, the gloves were off, the cannon had begun roaring, the army was hurling itself at the barricade. Fury had now turned to skill. A powerful column of infantry of the line, interspersed at equal intervals by National Guards and Municipal Guards on foot, and supported by dense masses that could be heard but not seen, poured into the street at a run, drums beating, bugles blaring, bayonets fixed, sappers at the head, and, imperturbable under the projectiles, made it to the top of the barricade with the force of a bronze beam against a wall.

The wall held.

The insurgents fired frantically. The scaled barricade shook a mane of lightning flashes. The assault was so frenzied that for a moment the barricade was overrun with assailants; but it shook off the soldiers the way a lion shakes off dogs and was covered in besiegers the way a cliff gets covered in foam— only to reappear a second later, sheer, black, and forbidding.

Forced to fall back, the column remained massed in the street, out in the open, but it was truly frightening and it retorted to the redoubt with a terrifying volley of musketry. Anyone who has seen fireworks will recall the spray made by the crossfire of flashing explosions known as a bouquet. Picture this bouquet as horizontal rather than vertical, bearing a bullet, a ball, a piece of buckshot or a biscayan at the tip of each of its jets of fire, and scattering death in its clusters of thunderclaps. The barricade was underneath.

On both sides, equal resolution. The bravery was almost barbaric, mixed up as it was with a sort of heroic ferocity that began with self-sacrifice. Those were the days when a National Guardsman fought with the dash of a Zouave.[1] The troops wanted to put an end to it all; the insurrection wanted to put up a fight. The acceptance of dying in the fullness of youth and in the fullness of health turns fearlessness into frenzy. Each and every man in the mêlée had that larger-than-life quality that comes with the final hour. The street was strewn with dead bodies.

The barricade had Enjolras at one end and Marius at the other. Enjolras, carrying as he did the whole barricade in his head, held himself in reserve, saving his strength and keeping under cover; three soldiers in a row fell beneath his battlement without even seeing him. Marius was fighting out in the open. He made himself a target. He stood with more than half his body showing above the top of the redoubt. There is no more violent profligate than a miser who takes the bit between the teeth, there is no more frightening man in action than a dreamer. Marius was both awesome and oblivious. He did battle as though he were in a dream. You would have taken him for a phantom firing a gun.

The cartridges of the men besieged were running out; not so, their acid wit. In this sepulchral whirlwind they found themselves in, they laughed.

Courfeyrac was bareheaded.

"What happened to your hat?" Bossuet asked him.

Courfeyrac replied: "They finally got rid of it for me with cannon fire."

When not making wisecracks, they spoke of higher things.

"Does anyone," cried Feuilly bitterly, "understand these men"—and he rattled off names, well-known names, even famous names, some from the old army[2]—"who promised to come and join us, who swore they would help us, and who were bound to do so in all honor, these men who were to have been our generals and who have deserted us!"

And Combeferre merely replied, with a grave smile: "There are people who observe rules of honor the way you and I observe the stars—from afar."

There were so many ripped cartridges strewn about the interior of the barricade, it looked as if it had snowed.

The assailants had the numbers; the insurgents had the position. They were at the top of a high wall, and they shot down point-blank any soldiers stumbling around among the dead and the wounded or tangled up in the steep slope of the barricade itself. Built as it was and wonderfully well shored up, the barricade truly was one of those places where a handful of men hold a whole legion in check. Yet, constantly reinforced and swelling under the rain of balls, the attacking column was getting inexorably nearer and, now, little by little, step by step, but beyond the shadow of a doubt, the army was tightening round the barricade like the screw on a winepress.

There was assault after assault. The horror got worse and worse.

At that point, on those heaps of cobblestones in the rue de la Chanvrerie, a fight worthy of a Trojan wall broke out. These men, wild-eyed, in tatters, exhausted, who had not eaten for twenty-four hours, who had not slept, who had only a few shots left to fire, who fumbled in their empty pockets for cartridges, almost all of them wounded, head or arm bandaged with a dirty bit of rust-colored cloth, who had holes in their coats through which the blood ran, who were barely armed with lousy flintlock muskets and old chipped sabers, these men turned into Titans. The barricade was approached, assailed, and scaled ten times and yet not taken.

To get any idea of this struggle, you need to imagine a pile of terrible courages set alight, and that you are watching blaze. It was not a fight, it was the inside of a furnace; mouths breathed flames there; faces were extraordinary, the human form seemed transmuted, the combatants flashing flames, and it was amazing to see these salamanders of the fray moving around in all that red smoke. We decline to describe the successive and simultaneous scenes in this grandiose slaughter. Only an epic has the right to fill twelve hundred lines with one battle.

You could be forgiven for thinking it was the hell the Brahmins talk about, the most fearsome of the seventeen abysses, which the Veda[3] calls the Forest of Swords.

They fought hand to hand, foot to foot, with pistols, with sabers, with fists, from a distance, from close up, from above, below, everywhere at once, from the roofs of the houses, from the windows of the tavern, from the basement windows of the cellars that some of them had slipped down into. It was one against sixty. The façade of Corinthe, half-demolished, was hideous to behold. The window, speckled with shot, had lost both glass and frame, and was just a shapeless hole, crazily stopped up with cobbles. Bossuet was killed; Feuilly was killed; Courfeyrac was killed; Joly was killed; Combeferre, run through with three thrusts of a bayonet to the chest just as he was lifting up a wounded soldier, only had time to look up at the sky before he breathed his last.

Marius, still fighting, was so peppered with wounds, particularly to the head, that his face was lost in blood and looked for all the world as though it was covered in a red handkerchief.

Enjolras alone was unscathed. Whenever he had no more weapon, he swung his hand to left and right and an insurgent stuck some kind of blade in his fist. All he had left out of four swords—one more than François I had at Marignano[4]—was a stump.

Homer says: "Then Diomed cut the throat of Axylus, son of Teuthranis, who lived in happy Arisbe; Euryalus, son of Mecisteus, wiped out Dresos and Opheltios, then turned and went for Aesepus and Pedasus, twins the naiad Abarbarea bore the lofty Bucolion; Ulysses overthrows Pidytes of Percote; Antilochus, Ablerus; Polypaetes, Astyalus; Polydamas, Otus of Cyllend; and Teucer, Aretaon. Meganthis dies under the thrust of Euripylus's spear. Agamemnon, king of heroes, brings down Elatos, born in the high hill town bathed in the sound of the River Satnois."[5] In our old poems of high deeds, Esplandian attacks the giant Marquis Swantibore with a flaming mortise ax, and the latter defends himself by stoning the knight with towers he uproots.[6] Our ancient frescoes show us the two ducs[7] de Bretagne and de Bourbon, armed, emblazoned, and accoutred for war, on horseback and approaching each other, battle-ax in hand, masked in iron, booted in iron, gloved in iron, the one caparisoned in ermine, the other draped in azure; Bretagne, with his lion between the two horns of his crown, Bourbon, helmeted in a monstrous fleur-de-lis with a visor. But to be superb, you don't have to wear the ducal morion, black quartz, like Yvon,[8] or hold a living flame in your fist, like Esplandian, or, like Phyles, father of Polydamas, to have brought back from Ephyrae good solid armor, a gift from Euphetes,[9] king of men; it is enough to give your life out of some conviction or sense of loyalty. This naïve little soldier, yesterday a peasant from the

Beauce or the Limousin, who prowls around the nannies in the Luxembourg with his cabbage-cutter at his side, that pale young student bending over a bit of anatomy or a book, a blond adolescent who trims his beard with scissors—take them both, breathe a bit of a sense of duty into them, set them opposite each other in Boucherat square or in the cul-de-sac Planche-Mibray, and let the one fight for his flag and let the other fight for his ideal; and let them both imagine that they are fighting for their homeland. The fight will be colossal; and the shadow cast, in that great epic field where humanity thrashes about, by this footslogger and this jumped-up bonesetter as they battle it out, will equal the shadow cast by Megaryon, king of Lycia, land of tigers, wrestling gigantic Ajax, equal of the gods.

## XXII. Inch by Inch

When there were no more chiefs left alive except Enjolras and Marius at the two ends of the barricade, the center, which Courfeyrac, Joly, Bossuet, Feuilly, and Combeferre had held for so long, folded. The cannon, without making a passable breach, had put a real dent in the middle of the redoubt; there, the top of the wall had been hit by cannonballs and had crumbled; and the rubble that had fallen, inside and outside, had piled up to create two sorts of taluses on either side of the roadblock, one inside, the other outside. The outside talus offered an inclined plane for the assailants to walk up.

A final assault was now attempted there and this assault was successful. The mass bristling with bayonets hurled themselves forward like gymnasts, irresistibly, and the dense battlefront of the attacking column appeared through the smoke at the top of the steep slope. This time the jig was up. The group of insurgents defending the center withdrew willy-nilly.

At that point a grim love of life flared up in some. Targeted by that forest of fusils, several did not want to die. This is a moment when the instinct of self-preservation lets out its howl and the beast rears its head again in the man. They were driven back to the tall six-story house that formed the back of the redoubt. This house might mean salvation. The house was barricaded and as though walled off from top to bottom. Before the troops of the line got inside the redoubt, there was time for a door to open and shut, it could happen in a flash, and the door of the house, suddenly cracked open and shut again at once, meant life for these desperate men. At the back of the house, there were streets, possible flight, open space. They started hammering on the door with the butts of their guns and with their feet, calling out, yelling, begging, pleading with their hands clasped together in entreaty. Nobody opened. From the dormer window on the third floor, the death's head watched them steadily.

But Enjolras and Marius and seven or eight others who had rallied around them lunged forward and covered them. Enjolras had shouted at the soldiers: "Stay back!" When one officer had failed to obey, Enjolras had killed the officer. Enjolras was now in the tiny inner courtyard, with his back to the house of Corinthe, sword in one hand, carbine in the other, holding open the tavern door, which he barred to the assailants. He cried to the desperate men: "There's only one door open—this is it." And, covering them with his body, alone facing an entire battalion, he got them through behind him. They all rushed inside. Enjolras, executing with his carbine, which he was now wielding like a cane, the maneuver that practioners of the martial art of cane fencing know as *la rose couverte,* hoed into the bayonets around him and in front of him and stepped inside last. There was one awful moment when the soldiers were trying to get in and the insurgents were trying to shut the door on them. The door was finally shut with such violence that when it slammed back into its frame, the five severed fingers of a soldier who had clung on were revealed, jammed in the doorway.

Marius had remained outside. A bullet had just shattered his collarbone; he felt himself fainting and falling. At that moment, with his eyes already closed, he was jolted by the shock of a vigorous hand grabbing him, and in the moment before he lost consciousness, he barely had time to think this thought, which merged with one last memory of Cosette: "I've been taken prisoner. I'll be shot."

Enjolras, not seeing Marius among those who had taken refuge in the cabaret, had the same idea. But they were at that point where each man has only enough time to think of his own death. Enjolras secured the bar on the door and locked and bolted it with a double turn of the key and the padlock, while the soldiers outside banged furiously on the other side of the door with the butts of their muskets, the sappers with their axes. The assailants had converged on the door. The cabaret siege had begun.

The soldiers, we have to say, were full of rage.

The death of the gunner sergeant had whipped them into a fury and then, something even more disastrous during the few hours that preceded the attack, the rumor spread among them that the insurgents mutilated prisoners and that in the cabaret lay the corpse of a soldier with his head cut off. This kind of deadly rumor is the normal accompaniment to civil wars and it was a bogus report of the sort that later brought about the catastrophe of the rue Transnonain.

When the door was barricaded, Enjolras said to the others: "Let's make them pay through the nose for us."

Then he went over to the table where Mabeuf and Gavroche were laid out. You could see two straight stiff shapes under the black cloth, one big, the other little, and the two faces were vaguely outlined beneath the cold folds of the shroud. A hand emerged from below the pall, dangling toward the floor. It was the old man's.

Enjolras bent down and kissed that venerable hand, just as he had kissed the man's forehead the night before. These were the only two kisses he had ever given in his life.

To cut a long story short, the barricade had fought like a gate to Thebes, and the cabaret now fought like a house in Saragossa. Such resistance is tough going. There is no mercy. No possible negotiation. People are willing to die as long as they get to kill. When Suchet says, "Capitulate," Palafox replies, "After the war of cannon, the war of knives." Nothing was lacking in the storming of the cabaret Hucheloup: neither the cobblestones raining down from the window and the roof on the besiegers and aggravating the soldiers by horribly mangling them, nor the shots from the cellars and the garrets, nor the fury of the attack, nor the rage of the defense, nor, in the end, when the door gave way, the frenetic madness of the extermination. The assailants, hurtling into the cabaret, their feet tangled up and tripping over the panels of the door which had been battered in and thrown on the floor, found not one combatant inside. The spiral staircase had been hacked away with an ax and was lying, prone, in the middle of the downstairs room, where a few wounded men were breathing their last; anyone who had not been killed was up on the first floor, and there, through the hole in the ceiling, which had been the entry for the staircase, a terrifying volley of shots burst out. This was the last of the cartridges. When they had all burned out, when the fearsome men at death's door had no more powder and no more bullets, each one grabbed two of the bottles Enjolras had put aside, and they stood and faced the escalade with those appallingly fragile clubs. The bottles contained aqua fortis—concentrated nitric acid. We do no more than tell it like it was when we describe the awful carnage. The besieged, alas, uses anything he can as a weapon. Greek fire did not dishonor Archimedes; boiling pitch did not dishonor Bayard.[1] All war is horrifying, and there is absolutely nothing to choose from in any of it. The besiegers' musketry, although hampered and directed upward from below, was murderous. The rim of the hole in the ceiling was soon surrounded by the heads of the dead from which long lines of blood streamed, red and fuming. The racket was indescribable; trapped and burning smoke almost blanketed the fight in total darkness. No words can express horror at that pitch. There were no men left in that now infernal struggle. It was no longer a matter of giants versus colossi. It was more like something out of Milton and Dante than Homer.[2] Fiends attacked, specters resisted.

It was the heroism of monsters.

## XXIII. Orestes on a Fast and Pylades[1] Drunk

At last, giving each other a leg up, enlisting the support of the skeleton of the staircase, climbing up the walls, clinging to the ceiling, tearing to pieces the last to resist, at the very edge of the hatch, twenty or so besiegers, soldiers, National Guards, Municipal Guards, most of them disfigured by wounds to the face in the awful ascent, blinded by blood, furious, wild as savages, burst into the room on the upper floor, in a whirl. There was only one man left standing there—Enjolras. Cartridgeless, swordless, all he had left in his hands was the barrel of his carbine, whose butt he had smashed on the heads of those scrambling in. He had put the billiard table between the assailants and himself; had backed into a corner of the room and there, eyes proud, head held high, that stump of a weapon in his fist, he was still frightening enough for no one to come near him. A cry went up: "That's the chief. He's the one who killed the gun captain. Since he's placed himself here, this is the place for him. Let him stay here. We'll shoot him on the spot."

"Go ahead!" said Enjolras.

And, throwing down the stump of his carbine and folding his arms, he offered his chest.

Daring to die well always moves other men. As soon as Enjolras folded his arms, accepting the end, the deafening clamor of the struggle died down in the room, and the chaos suddenly abated in a sort of sepulchral solemnity. It was as if the threatening majesty of Enjolras, disarmed and motionless, weighed on the tumult, and that, if only by the authority of his tranquil gaze, this young man, who alone had no wound, superb, cruel, dashing, indifferent as though invulnerable, was forcing that sinister mob to kill him with respect. His beauty, at that moment enhanced by his dignity, was resplendent, and, as though he could no more feel than be wounded after the terrible twenty-four hours that had just elapsed, he was fresh and rosy. It was, perhaps, about him that a witness was speaking when he said later before the ensuing court-martial: "There was one insurgent I heard them call Apollo." A National Guard who was aiming at Enjolras lowered his weapon, saying: "I feel like I'm about to shoot a flower."

Twelve men formed a platoon in the corner opposite Enjolras and readied their muskets in silence.

Then a sergeant shouted: "Take aim!"

An officer intervened.

"Wait."

And addressing Enjolras: "Would you like us to put a blindfold over your eyes?"

"No."

"Was it really you who killed the gunner sergeant?"

"Yes."

Grantaire had just woken up a few seconds ago.

Grantaire had been sleeping, as you will recall, since the day before in the room at the top of the cabaret, sitting on a chair, slumped over a table.

He had staged, as convincingly as possible, that old metaphor: dead drunk.

The ghastly poison consisting of absinthe, stout, and spirits had thrown him into a lethargic state. His table being small and of no use in the barricade, they had left him to it. He was still in the same position, his chest doubled over the table, his head lying flat on his arms, surrounded by glasses, tankards, and bottles. He slept the shattering sleep of the sluggish bear and the satiated leech. Nothing had gotten through, neither the shooting, nor the cannonballs, nor the volleys of shot that found their way through the casement window into the room where he was, nor the almighty racket of the assault. Only, he responded occasionally to the cannon with a snore. He seemed to be waiting for a bullet to come and save him the trouble of waking up. Several dead bodies were lying around him; and, at first glance, nothing distinguished him from death's heavy sleepers.

Noise does not wake up a drunk, it is silence that rouses him. This peculiarity has been observed more than once. The fall of everything, all around him, only accentuated Grantaire's annihilation; collapse rocked him like a cradle. The sort of break in the tumult provoked by Enjolras jolted him out of his heavy sleep. It is the effect of a galloping carriage that suddenly comes to a halt. Anyone sleeping inside wakes up. Grantaire shot to his feet with a start, stretched his arms, rubbed his eyes, looked around, yawned, and understood.

Drunkenness coming to an end is like a curtain ripped down. You see, all at once and altogether, all that it was hiding. Everything suddenly crams back into your memory, and the drunk, who doesn't have a clue what has happened in the last twenty-four hours, no sooner opens his eyes than he is up to speed. Things come rushing back with abrupt lucidity, the annihilation caused by drunkenness, a sort of condensation steaming up over the brain and blinding it, evaporates and gives way to a clear and clean grasp of reality.

Relegated as he was to a corner and more or less protected behind the billiard table, Enjolras had the eyes of the soldiers riveted on him. They had not even spotted Grantaire and the sergeant was getting ready to repeat the order: "Take aim!" when, all of a sudden, they heard a powerful voice shouting right next to them: "Long live the Republic! I'm with them."

Grantaire had risen to his feet.

The immense blazing light of the fight which he had completely missed, had not taken part in, appeared in the startling gaze of the drunk, transfigured.

He repeated: "Long live the Republic!" Then he crossed the room with steady tread and went and planted himself beside Enjolras in front of the raised guns.

"You might as well kill two birds with the one stone," he said.

And, turning to Enjolras gently, he said to him: "All right with you?"

Enjolras shook his hand with a smile. He was still smiling when the explosion ripped through the silence. Enjolras was riddled with eight shots, but remained with his back against the wall as though the bullets had nailed him to it. Only, he dropped his head. Grantaire, mowed down, crashed to his feet.

A few moments later, the soldiers dislodged the last insurgents who had taken refuge at the top of the house. They fired through a wooden trellis in the attic. They fought inside the roof. They threw bodies out the windows, some of them still alive. Two light infantrymen, who were trying to right the smashed bus, were killed by two carbine shots fired from the attic. A man in a smock was hurled headlong out of there with a bayonet stuck in his guts, and was moaning in agony on the ground. A soldier and an insurgent slid down the tiled roof slope together and would not let go of each other, and fell, locked together in a ferocious embrace. Similar struggle in the cellar. Cries, shots, savage shuffling. Then silence. The barricade was taken.

The soldiers began searching the surrounding houses and going after the fugitives.

## XXIV. PRISONER

Marius was indeed a prisoner. A prisoner of Jean Valjean.

The hand that had gripped him from behind just as he was about to fall and which he had felt as he lost consciousness was Jean Valjean's.

Jean Valjean had taken no part in the fight except to expose himself to danger. Without him, at that ultimate stage of the battle to the death, no one would have spared a thought for the wounded. Thanks to him, everywhere at once as he was in the carnage like some angel of salvation, those who fell were lifted up, carried into the downstairs room, and patched up. In the intervals in between, he repaired the barricade. But nothing bearing any resemblance to a blow or an attack, not even some kind of self-defense, came from his hands. He stayed silent and gave succor. And the amazing thing is, he had only a few scratches. Bullets would have nothing to do with him. If suicide had any part in what he had dreamed of when he came into this sepulchre, on that score he had not succeeded. But we doubt he had been thinking of suicide, which is an irreligious act.

In the thick fog of combat, Jean Valjean did not appear to see Marius; the fact is he did not take his eyes off him. When a shot brought Marius down, Jean Valjean sprang with the agility of a tiger, fell upon him as upon some prey, and carried him off.

The whirlwind of the attack was so violently centered on Enjolras and on the cabaret door at that particular moment that nobody saw Jean Valjean holding Marius senseless in his arms as he crossed the now unpaved field of the barricade and disappeared behind the corner of the house of Corinthe.

You will recall that this corner formed a sort of headland on the street; it protected a few square feet of terrain from balls and shot and from eyes, too. In fires, similarly, there is sometimes a room that does not burn, and in the wildest seas, a calm spot in the lee of a promontory or at the end of a cul-de-sac of reefs. It was in this recess in the inner trapezium of the barricade that Éponine had lain dying.

There Jean Valjean stopped; he let Marius slide to the ground, leaned back against the wall and cast his eyes about him. The situation was appalling.

For the moment, for maybe two or three minutes, this bit of wall was a refuge; but how could they get out of this massacre? He remembered the anguish he had felt in the rue Polonceau eight years before, and how he had managed to escape; that was hard then, today it was impossible. He had in front of him that implacable and mute six-story house that seemed to be inhabited only by the dead man leaning out of his window; on his right, he had the fairly low barricade that closed off the rue de la Petite-Truanderie; getting over that obstacle looked easy, but beyond the crest of the roadblock you could see the tips of a row of bayonets. These were the troops of the line, posted on the far side of that barricade and on the lookout. It was obvious that getting over the barricade meant going looking for platoon fire and that any head that risked poking out over the top of the wall of cobblestones would serve as a target for sixty musket shots. On his left, he had the field of combat. Death lurked around the corner of the wall.

What was to be done? Only a bird could have gotten away from the place.

And he had to decide swiftly, find an expedient, make a decision. They were fighting a few feet away from him; happily everyone was fiercely intent on hammering away at a single point, the door of the tavern; but if one soldier, just one, got the idea of going around the house, or attacking its flank, it would all be over.

Jean Valjean looked at the house in front of him, he looked at the barricade beside him, then he looked at the ground, with the violence of ultimate extremity, in desperation, as though he could drill a hole with his eyes.

He looked so hard, something vaguely plausible occurred to him in the midst of his agony and took shape at his feet, as though causing the thing required to sprout was one of the powers of looking. He saw, a few feet away, at the base of the small roadblock so mercilessly guarded and watched from outside, under a collapsed heap of cobblestones that partly hid it, an iron grate lying down flat, level with the ground. This grate, made of sturdy crossbars, was about two feet square. The cobblestone frame that held it in place had been ripped out and it was, so to speak, unsealed. Through the bars you could see an obscure opening, something like the flue of a chimney or the cylinder of a cistern. Jean Valjean dashed forward. The art of escape he'd once mastered rushed back to his brain like a flash of light. He cleared away the stones, lifted out the grate, loaded Marius, inert as a corpse, onto his shoulders, and with this burden on his back, he dropped down into this sort of luckily fairly shallow well, using his elbows and his knees, let the heavy iron trapdoor fall shut over his head and the stones roll back over it again, and found his footing on the flagstone surface ten feet below ground. And all this was done the way you do things when you are delirious, with the strength of a giant and the speed of an eagle; it hardly took a few minutes.

Jean Valjean found himself, with Marius still senseless, in a sort of long underground corridor.

There, profound peace, absolute silence, night.

The impression that he had earlier had falling from the street into the convent came back to him. Only, what he was carrying with him today was not Cosette anymore, but Marius.

He could only dimly now hear above him, like a faint murmur, the awful tumult of the tavern being stormed.

# BOOK TWO

# LEVIATHAN'S BOWELS

## I. LAND IMPOVERISHED BY THE SEA

Paris throws twenty-five million a year into the sea. And that is not a metaphor. How, and in what way? Day and night. With what aim? With no aim. With what thought? With no thought. What for? For nothing. By means of what organ? By means of its bowels. What do you mean, its bowels? Its sewers.

Twenty-five million is the most conservative estimate of the approximate figures provided by specialized science.

Science, having groped about for a long time, now knows that the most fertilizing and the most effective of manures is human manure. The Chinese, we have to say to our shame, got on to this before we did. No Chinese peasant, so Eckeberg[1] tells us, goes to town without bringing back, at the two ends of his bamboo pole, two buckets full of what we call crap. Thanks to human manure, the soil in China is as fresh as it was in the days of Abraham. Chinese wheat harvests yield up to one hundred and twenty times the amount of seed. There is no guano as fertile as the excreta of a capital. A big city is the most potent of dung beetles. Put the city to work manuring the plain and you just can't fail. If our gold is dung, our dung, on the other hand, is gold.

What do we do with this gold dung? We sweep it into the void.

We send out convoys of ships, at great cost, to harvest the droppings of petrels and penguins at the South Pole, and the supply of incalculable opulence that we have to hand we send into the sea. If all the human and animal manure that the world loses was put back in the soil instead of being tossed out to sea, it would be enough to feed the world.

These heaps of filth piled up by the curbstones on street corners, these cartloads of muck bouncing along the streets at night, these awful cans the night carters trundle along the roadways, these fetid streams of subterranean feculence that the pavement hides from you—do you know what all this is? It is meadows in flower, it is green grass, it is parsley, sage, marjoram, and thyme, it is wild game, it is cattle, it is the satisfied lowing of great bullocks at evening, it is fragrant hay, golden wheat, it is bread on your table, it is hot blood in your veins, health, joy, life. Which is how that mysterious creation that spells transformation on earth and transfiguration in heaven wants it.

Stick the stuff back in the great crucible and you will have your abundance. Feed the plains and you feed mankind.

You have the power to lose this wealth and find me ridiculous into the bargain. That would be the crowning glory of your ignorance.

Statistics show that France alone pays out half a billion every year to the Atlantic through the mouths of its rivers. Take note: With this five hundred million you could cover a quarter of our budget outlays. Man is so smart that he prefers to chuck this five hundred million in the gutter. It is the people's very substance that is being carried away, here drop by drop, there in gushing torrents, by the miserable vomiting of our sewers into the rivers and the copious vomiting of our rivers into the ocean. Every time our cesspools hiccup, it costs us a thousand francs. This has two results: The soil is impoverished and the water is contaminated. Hunger is delivered by the furrow and disease by the river.

It is well-known, for instance, that at this point in time, the Thames is poisoning London. When it comes to Paris, they have recently had to move most of the sewer outlets downstream past the last bridge.

A twin tubular apparatus, provided with valves and sweeping sluices, sucking in and driving back, an elementary drainage system as simple as a human lung, and which is already fully operational in several counties in England, would suffice to bring into our towns the pure water of our fields and to send back to our fields the rich water of the towns, and this simple two-way movement, the simplest in the world, would let us hold on to the five hundred million we throw away. And that would be that.

The current process does harm in trying to do good. The intention is good, the result is woeful. We think we are sanitizing the city, but we are depleting the population. A sewer is a misunderstanding. When drainage, with its twin function of restoring what it takes, has everywhere replaced the sewer, which is a simple impoverishing wash, then, this being combined with the givens of a new social economy, the produce of the earth will be increased tenfold and the problem of destitution will be radically reduced. Add to this the elimination of parasites, and it will be resolved.

Meanwhile public wealth is going down the drain into the river and the waste goes on. Waste is the word. Europe is ruining itself this way through exhaustion.

As for France, we have just revealed the figures. Now, as Paris contains a twenty-fifth of the total French population and as Parisian guano is the richest of the lot, we are underestimating Paris's share in the loss of the half billion France expels annually when we put it at twenty-five million. That twenty-five million, spent on aid and on pleasure, would double the splendor of Paris. But the city squanders it in cesspools. So that we could well say that the great prodigality of Paris, its wondrous festiveness, its Folie Beaujon,[2] its orgy of profusion, its gold slipping through its fingers by the bucketload, its sumptuousness, its luxury, its magnificence—is its sewers.

This is how, in the blindness of a bad political economy, we drown and let the well-being of all stream away and disappear in swallow holes. There ought to be Saint-Cloud nets[3] for the public wealth.

Economically, the situation can be summed up like this: Paris is a leaky bucket.

Paris, this model city, this blueprint of the well-made capital that every nation tries to copy, this metropolis of the ideal, this august homeland of initiative, of drive and enterprise, this center and home of the mind, this nation city, this hive of the future, this marvelous amalgam of Babylon and Corinth, would make a peasant from Fuhkien[4] shrug his shoulders, from the viewpoint we have just pointed out.

Imitate Paris and you will ruin yourself. In any case, particularly in this immemorial and insane wastefulness, Paris itself imitates.

For this surprising ineptitude is not new; it is no youthful idiocy. The ancients acted like the moderns. "The cesspools of Rome," says Liebig,[5] "soaked up the entire well-being of the Roman peasant." When the countryside around Rome was ruined by the Roman sewers, Rome wore out Italy, and when it had dragged Italy down into its cesspool, it poured Sicily in, then Sardinia, then Africa. The sewers of Rome engulfed the world. That cesspool offered its engulfment to the city and the world. *Urbi et orbi.*[6] Eternal City, bottomless sewer.

In this, as in other things, Rome sets the example. It is an example Paris follows, with all the stupidity peculiar to cities of genius.

For the requirements of the operation we have just described, Paris has another Paris below it; a Paris of sewers, which has its streets, its crossroads, its squares, its dead ends, its arteries, and its traffic consisting of muck, minus the human form.

For we must flatter no one and nothing, not even a great people; wherever nothing is lacking, ignominy sits next to sublimeness; and if Paris contains Athens, the city of light, Tyre, the city of power, Sparta, the city of virtue, Nineveh, the city of wonder, it also contains Lutetia,[7] the city of slime.

Besides, the mark of its greatness also lies here, with the titanic sink of Paris achieving, among the monuments, that strange ideal achieved within humanity by men like Machiavelli, Bacon, and Mirabeau:[8] awe-inspiring vileness.

The basement of Paris, if the eye could penetrate its surface, would reveal a colossal coral reef. A sponge hardly has any more pores and passages than the clump of earth six leagues around on which the great antique city rests. Not counting the catacombs, which are like a separate cellar, not counting the tangled latticework of gas mains, and forgetting the vast tubular system for distributing running water that ends in public drinking fountains, the sewers alone make up a prodigious dark network under both banks of the river; a labyrinth whose thread is its downhill slope.

It is there, in the dank mist, that the rat pops up, apparently the product of Paris in labor.

## II. THE ANCIENT HISTORY OF THE SEWER

If you imagine Paris lifted up like a lid, the underground network of sewers would, from a bird's-eye view, describe a sort of great tree, grafted onto the river and spanning both banks. On the right bank, the ring sewer would be the trunk of the tree, the secondary pipelines would be the smaller branches, and the dead ends would be the twigs.

This figure is only very sketchy and half exact, the right angle, which is the most common angle in this type of underground ramification, being very rare in the plant world.

We could get a more plausible image of this strange geometric plan by assuming that we can see, spread flat over a dark background, some kind of bizarre oriental alphabet in a great scrambled mess, whose deformed letters are welded together in an apparent jumble, apparently at random, some by their corners, others by their ends.

Sinks and sewers played a great role in the Middle Ages, in the late Roman Empire, and in the ancient Orient. The plague was born in them, despots died in them. The multitudes regarded these beds of putrefaction with an almost religious fear as monstrous cradles of death. The vermin pit of Benares is no less dizzying than the lion's den of Babylon.[1] Tiglath-Pileser, king of Assyria, swore by the sink of Nineveh, according to the rabbinical books. It was from the Münster sewer that Jan van Leiden brought out his fake moon, and it is from the cesspit of Kekhscheb that his oriental double, Mokanna, the veiled prophet from the Persian province of Khorassan, brought out his fake sun.[2]

The history of mankind is reflected in the history of its cesspools. The Gemoniae[3] told the story of Rome. The Paris sewer has been an awesome old thing. It has been a sepulchre, it has been a refuge. Crime, intelligence, social protest, freedom of conscience, thought, theft, all that human laws pursue or have pursued, has hidden in this hole; the Maillotins[4] in the fourteenth century, highwaymen in the fifteenth, the Huguenots in the sixteenth, Morin's visionary Illuminati[5] in the seventeenth, the Chauffeurs,[6] those brigands who burned their victims' feet to make them talk, in the eighteenth. A hundred years ago, the nocturnal thrust of the dagger surfaced there, the crook in danger slipped down into it; the wood had its cave, Paris had its sewer. Gangsters, that Gallic *picareria*,[7] accepted the sewer as a branch of the Cour des Miracles,[8] and in the evening, scathing and fierce, ducked back down under the Maubuée vomitorium as into an alcove.

It was only natural that those whose place of daily work was the cul-de-sac Vide-Gousset—Empty Pocket—or the rue Coupe-Gorge—Cutthroat—had as their nocturnal abode the culvert of the Chemin-Vert or sheltered corner of Hurepoix. Whence a welter of memories. All kinds of phantoms haunt these long lonely passages; everywhere putrefaction and miasma; here and there a vent through which Villon on the inside chats with Rabelais[9] on the outside.

The sewer, in the old Paris, was the meeting place of all exhaustion and all enterprise. Political economics sees refuse there, social philosophy sees residue.

The sewer is the conscience of the city. Everything converges and clashes there. In this leaden place, there is darkness but there are no more secrets. Every thing has its true form, or at least its final form. A heap of crap has this going for it: It does not lie. Naïveté has taken refuge there, Basil's mask is found down there, but you can see the pasteboard and strings and the inside as well as the outside, and it is enhanced by honest muck. Scapin's false nose[10] is nearby. Every bit of the filth of civilization, once it is of no more use, falls into this pit of truth where the immense social slide ends; it is swallowed up in it, but on display. This jumble is a confession. Here, no more false appearances, no possible covering up; crap takes off its shirt in an absolute laying bare, a routing of illusions and mirages; nothing is more than what is, cutting the sinister figure of what comes to an end. Reality and disappearance. Down there, the bottom of a bottle avows drunkenness, the handle of a basket tells of domesticity; there, the apple core that once gave itself literary opinions goes back to being an apple core; the head on the five-franc piece frankly turns to verdigris, Caïaphas's spit meets Falstaff's vomit,[11] the gold louis from the gambling den bumps into the nail with the suicide's bit of rope still hanging off it, a livid fetus rolls by wrapped in the sequins that danced at the last Mardi Gras at the Opéra, a judge's wig that has judged men grovels next to a bit of rot that was once Maggie's skirt. This is more than fraternity, it is being on intimate terms. All that was once carefully made up is now smeared and laid on with a trowel. The last veil is ripped off. A sewer is a cynic. It tells all.

This sincerity of muck pleases us, and is restful for the soul. When you have passed your time on earth enduring the spectacle of high and mighty airs put on by reasons of state, oaths, political wisdom, human justice, professional probity, the strict requirements of position, incorruptible robes, it is a relief to step into a sewer and see the sludge that rightly belongs there.

It teaches us something at the same time. As we said a moment ago, history passes through the sewer. The Saint Bartholomews[12] filter into it, drop by drop, seeping through the cobblestones. The great public assassinations, the political and religious butcheries, travel through this subterranean passage of civilization, pushing their cadavers along. To the eye of the dreamer, all the historic murderers are there, in the hideous gloom, on their knees, with a fold of their shrouds as apron, dourly mopping up their work. Louis XI is there with Tristan, François I is there with Duprat, Charles IX is there with his mother, Richelieu is there with Louis XIII, Louvois[13] is there, Letellier is there, Hébert and Maillard[14] are there, scraping stones and trying to make all traces of their actions disappear. You can hear the broom of these specters beneath these vaults. You breathe in the enormous fetidness of social catastrophes. You can see reddish gleams in the corners. A terrible water flows there in which bloody hands have been washed.

The social observer should step into these shadows. They are part of his laboratory. Philosophy is the microscope of thought. Everything tries to run away from it but nothing escapes it. To prevaricate is useless. What side of yourself do you show by prevaricating? The shame side. Philosophy pursues evil with its probing eye and will not let it escape into nothingness. In the erasure of things that disappear, in the diminishing of things that vanish, philosophy recognizes everything. It reconstructs the purple from the bit of rag and the woman from the tatters. With the cesspool it reconstructs the city, with the muck it reconstructs the morals and customs. From the shard it completes the amphora, the pitcher. It recognizes by the imprint of a fingernail on a piece of parchment the difference that distinguishes the Jewry of the Judengasse from the Jewry of the Ghetto.[15] It retrieves from what remains what has been, the good, the bad, the false, the true, the bloodstain of the law court, the inkblot in the cave, the blob of tallow in the house of ill repute, the ordeals endured, the welcome temptations, the orgies spewed out, the kink that people have acquired in abasing themselves, the trace of prostitution in souls their own coarseness made them capable of, and on the jacket of the porters of Rome, the mark of Messalina's dig[16] in the ribs.

### III. BRUNESEAU

The Paris sewer was legendary in the Middle Ages. In the sixteenth century Henri II[1] tried some exploratory soundings but they were aborted. Not even a hundred years ago, as Mercier[2] can attest, the cesspit was left to its own devices and went its own way.

That was the old Paris for you, given up to carping, dithering, and groping around in the dark. It was not terribly bright for quite some time. Later, 1789 showed how towns can get some sense into them. But in the good old days, the capital did not have much of a head; it did not know how to do business, either morally or materially, and had no more idea how to get rid of its rubbish than its abuses. Everything was too hard, everything was called into question. The sewer, for instance, rebelled against any itinerary. People could not get their bearings in the waste dump network any more than they could make themselves understood in the city; up above, the unintelligible babble, down below, an inextricable tangle; beneath the confusion of tongues lay the confusion of cellars; Daedalus replicated Babel.[3]

Sometimes the sewer of Paris took it upon itself to overflow, as though this undervalued Nile was suddenly rocked by anger. It is pretty revolting, but sometimes the sewer flooded. This stomach of civilization occasionally had trouble digesting, the cesspit gurgled back up into the city's gullet, and Paris had an aftertaste of its gutter. These instances of resemblance between the sewer and remorse had a good side; they were warnings; very badly received warnings, though, with the city fuming over its sludge having such gall and not accepting that what you dump can come back to haunt you. Get rid of it better.

The flood of 1802 is still a living memory for Parisians of eighty. The muck spread out in a cross at the place des Victoires where the statue of Louis XIV stands; it entered the rue Saint-Honoré through the two sewer mouths in the Champs-Élysées, the rue Saint-Florentin through the Saint-Florentin sewer, the rue Pierre-à-Poisson through the sewer of the Sonnerie, the rue Popincourt through the sewer of the Chemin-Vert, and the rue de la Roquette through the sewer of the rue de Lappe; it filled the gutters of the rue des Champs-Élysées to a depth of thirty-five centimeters; and, at midday, through the vomitorium of the Seine performing its function in reverse, it penetrated the rue Mazarine, the rue de l'Échaudé, and the rue des Marais, where it stopped after going 109 meters, just a few feet short of the house Racine once lived in, respecting, of the seventeenth century, the poet more than the king. It attained its maximum depth in the rue Saint-Pierre, where it rose to a level of three feet above the flagstones of the waterspout, and its maximum reach in the rue Saint-Sabin, where it spread out for 238 meters.

At the beginning of this century, the Paris sewer was still a mysterious place. Sludge can never smell sweet; but here its reputation was so bad as to strike fear. Paris was vaguely aware that it had a terrible cellar under it. People talked about it as though it were the monstrous bog of Thebes, which teemed with scolopendra, gargantuan sea monsters fifteen feet long, and which could easily have served as a bathtub for Behemoth.[4] The great boots of the sewer workers never ventured beyond certain known points. This was still not long after the days when the garbage collectors' carts, on which Sainte-Foix fraternized with the marquis de Créqui,[5] were simply emptied straight into the sewer. As for any cleaning operation, this was left to storm water, which gummed up the works more than flushed them out. Rome let a little poetry stick, still, to its cloaca, and called it the Gemoniae; Paris insulted its and called it the Stink Hole. Science and superstition were in agreement as to its horror. The Stink Hole was no less averse to hygiene than to legend. The Goblin Monk[6] had hatched under the fetid arch of the Mouffetard sewer; the cadavers of the Marmousets[7] had been thrown into the sewer of the Barillerie; Fagon[8] had attributed the fearful malignant fever of 1685 to the big open hole in the Marais sewer, which remained gaping until 1833 in the rue Saint-Louis practically in front of the inn sign for the Messager Galant. The manhole in the rue de la Mortellerie was famous for the plagues that came out of it; with its grate of pointy iron bars simulating a row of teeth, it was as deadly in that street as a dragon's maw blowing hell over mankind. The popular imagination seasoned the somber Parisian sink with an unspeakably hideous dose of the boundless. The sewer was a bottomless pit. The sewer was the Barathrum,[9] the gorge outside Athens into which criminals were cast. The idea of exploring these pestilential regions did not occur even to the police. To tempt that unknown, to throw a plumb line into that shadowland, to go on a voyage of discovery into that abyss, who would have dared? It was terrifying. Someone did turn up, though. The cesspit had its Christopher Columbus.

On a day in 1805, on one of the rare appearances the emperor put in in Paris, the minister of the interior, a Decrès or a Crétet[10] or someone, came to the master's morning levee. You could hear the clatter of the swords in the Carrousel of all those amazing soldiers of the mighty republic and the mighty empire; there was a glut of heroes tripping over themselves at Napoléon's door—men from the Rhine, from the Scheldt, the Adige, and the Nile; companions of Joubert, Desaix, Marceau, Hoche, Kléber; balloonists from Fleurus, grenadiers from Mayence, pontoniers from Genoa, hussars that the pyramids had gazed upon, artillerymen Junot's cannonballs had spattered, cuirassiers who had stormed the battle fleet at anchor in the Zuyder Zee; some had followed Bonaparte over the bridge at Lodi, others had been with Murat in the trenches of Mantua, still others had gone before Lannes in the sunken road of Montebello. The whole army of those days was there, in the courtyard of the Tuileries, represented by a squad or a platoon, and was guarding Napoléon while he rested. It was the splendid time when the Grande Armée had Marengo behind it and Austerlitz ahead of it. "Sire," said the minister of the interior to Napoléon, "yesterday I saw the boldest man in your empire." "Who is this man?" the emperor promptly asked, "and what has he done?" "It's what he wants to do, sire." "Which is what?" "To visit the sewers of Paris."

This man existed and his name was Bruneseau.[11]

## IV. DETAILS NOBODY KNOWS

The visit took place. It was a formidable campaign; a nocturnal battle against plague and asphyxiation. It was, at the same time, a voyage of discovery. One of the survivors of the expedition, a smart sewer worker, very young at the time, was still a few years ago telling anyone who'd listen the curious details that Bruneseau thought it best to leave out of his report to the prefect of police as unworthy of the administrative style. Disinfecting procedures were very rudimentary in those days. Bruneseau had only just got past the first sections of the underground network when eight out of the twenty workers with him refused to go any farther. The operation was complicated; the visit involved cleaning, so clean they must, but at the same time, they had to survey: to note the water inlets, to count the grates and the grids, to detail the connecting pipes, to jot down the currents at drainage divides, to identify the respective capacities of the various basins, to probe the small sewers grafted onto the main sewer, to measure the height under the keystone of each tunnel along with the width both at the spring of the vault and level with the floor, and last, to determine the different levels at the right of each water inlet, both from the sewer floor and from the street surface. They made painful headway. It was not uncommon for the stepladders to sink into three feet of mud. The lanterns kept flickering and going out in the noxious vapors. From time to time they would have to carry out a sewer worker who had fainted. At certain places there would be a sheer drop. The ground would have given way, the flagstones would have crumbled, the sewer would have turned into a sinkhole; there was nothing solid left; one man promptly disappeared and they had great difficulty pulling him out. On Fourcroy's[1] advice, they lit at intervals, in spots sufficiently cleaned, great cages full of tow soaked in resin. In some places the wall was covered with gnarled funguses that looked for all the world like tumors; the stone itself seemed sick in that unbreathable environment.

Bruneseau proceeded downstream on his exploratory expedition. At the parting of the two water mains from the Grand-Hurleur, he deciphered the date 1550 on a jutting stone, indicating the point reached by Philibert Delorme,[2] who was given the job by Henri II of visiting the underground waste dumps of Paris. This stone was the sixteenth century's mark on the sewer. Bruneseau also found the seventeenth century's handiwork in the Ponceau conduit and in the conduit from the rue Vieille-du-Temple, both vaulted between 1600 and 1650, as well as the eighteenth century's handiwork in the west section of the collector canal, laid down and vaulted in 1740. These two vaults, especially the more recent one, the one from 1740, were more cracked and decrepit than the masonry of the ring sewer, which dated from 1412, a time when the bubbling brook of Ménilmontant was elevated to the rank of main sewer of Paris, a promotion analogous to a peasant's becoming premier valet de chambre to the king; something like Gros-Jean transformed into Lebel.

Here and there, notably under the Palais de Justice, they thought they recognized the cavities of old dungeons cut into the sewer itself. Ghastly *in pace*.[3] An iron collar hung in one of these cells. They walled them all up. Some finds were bizarre; among others, the skeleton of an orangutan that had disappeared from the Jardin des Plantes in 1800, a vanishing act probably connected to the famous and incontestable appearance of the devil in the rue des Bernardins in the last year of the eighteenth century. The poor devil had ended up drowning in the sewer.

Under the long vaulted corridor that ends in the Arche-Marion, a rag-and-bone man's sack, perfectly preserved, was the admiration of connoisseurs. Everywhere the mud, which the sewer workers had come to handle fearlessly, abounded in precious objects, gold and silver jewelry, precious stones, coins. If a giant had sifted through this cloaca, he would have collected the riches of centuries in his sieve. At the parting of the two branches of the rue du Temple and the rue Sainte-Avoye, they picked up a singular Huguenot medallion in copper, bearing on one side a pig capped with a cardinal's hat and on the other, a wolf wearing a tiara on its head.

The most surprising encounter was at the entrance to what was called the Grand Sewer. This inlet had previously been closed by a grate of which only the hinges remained. From one of these hinges hung a sort of grimy shapeless rag, a remnant of something no doubt caught there as it was going by, floating in the dark, that had wound up being torn to shreds. Bruneseau held up his lantern and examined this shred. It was of very fine cambric and they made out at one of the least worn corners a heraldic crown embroidered above these seven letters: LAVBESP. The crown was a marquis's coronet and the seven letters stood for "Laubespine."[4] They realized that what they were looking at was a piece of Marat's shroud. Marat, in his youth, had had his share of love affairs. This was when he was part of the household of the comte d'Artois in his capacity as a physician to the stables. From his love affair with a great lady, which is a matter of historical record, he had kept this bedsheet. At his death, as it was the only remotely fine linen he had at his place, they had buried him in it. Old women had bundled up the tragic friend of the people for the grave in these swaddling clothes that had known the pleasures of the flesh.

Bruneseau moved on. They left the flap of cloth where it was, without finishing it off. Out of scorn or respect? Marat deserved both. And then again, destiny was imprinted clearly enough on it for anyone to hesitate to touch it. Besides, what is entombed should be left where it chooses to be. In a word, the relic was strange. A marquise had slept in it; Marat had rotted in it; it had passed through the Panthéon only to wind up down with the sewer rats. This intimate boudoir rag, whose every crease Watteau[5] would once have drawn with delight, had wound up worthy of Dante's penetrating glare.

The complete visit of the foul underground waste dump of Paris took seven years, from 1805 to 1812. As he wended his way, Bruneseau designed, directed, and brought to completion substantial public works; in 1808, he lowered the canal floor of the Ponceau drain and, creating new lines everywhere, drove the sewer under the rue Saint-Denis as far as the fontaine des Innocents in 1809; under the rue Froidmanteau and La Salpêtrière in 1810; under the rue Neuve-des-Petits-Pères, the rue du Mail, the rue de l'Écharpe, and the place Royale in 1811; and under the rue de la Paix and the chaussée d'Antin in 1812. At the same time, he had the entire network disinfected and cleaned. From the second year on, Bruneseau took on his son-in-law, Nargaud, as his assistant.

That is how, at the beginning of this century, the old society cleaned up its double backside and performed its sewer's toilette. That was one act cleaned up, at least.

Tortuous, fissured, unpaved, cracked, sliced up by quagmires, jolted by sharp bends, rising and falling without rhyme or reason, fetid, feral, savage, submerged in darkness, with scars on its flagstones and gashes on its walls, appalling—such was, in retrospect, the antique sewer of Paris.

Ramifications in all directions, crisscrossing trenches, connecting drainpipes, junctions like crow's-feet, stars as in saps, ceca, culs-de-sac, vaults covered with saltpeter, putrid sinkholes, scurfy scabs oozing over the walls, drips dripping from the ceiling, darkness; nothing equaled the horror of this old crypt, the digestive apparatus of Babylon, lair, pit, chasm bored through by streets, titanic molehill where the mind seems to see prowling through the shadows, in filth that once was splendor, that enormous blind mole, the past. This, we repeat, was the sewer of days gone by.

## V. Current Progress

Today the sewer is clean, cold, upright, correct. It practically achieves the ideal of what is understood in England by the word *respectable*. It is decent and dull; straight as a die; we might almost say immaculate. It is like a supplier who has become a councillor of state. You can almost see clearly in it. The muck behaves itself there. At first glance, you could mistake it for one of those underground tunnels once so common and so handy for the flight of monarchs and princes, in the good old days, "when the people loved their kings." The current sewer is a beautiful sewer; the pure style reigns there; the classic rectilinear alexandrine, driven out of poetry, seems to have taken refuge in architecture, apparently fusing with each and every stone in this long, gloomy, whitish vault; every overflow pipeline is an arcade; the rue de Rivoli has its imitators even in the cloaca. In any case, if the geometric line has a place anywhere, it is surely in the stercorary trenches of a great city. There, everything must be subordinate to the shortest path. The sewer has today taken on a certain official aspect. Even the police reports of which it is sometimes the object now show respect for it. The terms used to describe it in administrative language are elevated and dignified. What was once known as a gut is now a gallery; what was once known as a hole is now a light shaft. Villon would no longer recognize his antiquated bolthole. This network of cellars, of course, still has its time-honored population of rodents, more teeming than ever; from time to time, a rat, old whiskers, risks popping his head out of the sewer window to examine the Parisians; but these very vermin are becoming tame, satisfied as they are with their subterranean palace. The cloaca has nothing left now of its primitive ferocity. The rain, which befouled the sewer of bygone days, washes today's sewer clean. But don't rely on it too much. Miasmas still inhabit it. It is more hypocritical than irreproachable. The prefecture of police and the health department have toiled in vain. Despite all the cleansing processes, it gives off a faintly suspect odor, like Tartuffe after confession.[1]

Let's agree, though, since cleaning is, all things considered, a tribute that the sewer pays to civilization, and since, from this point of view, Tartuffe's conscience is an advance on Augeas's stable,[2] the sewer of Paris has most certainly improved.

It is more than an advance; it is a transmutation. Between the old sewer and the current sewer, there has been a revolution. Who brought about this revolution? The man everyone forgets, but whom we have named, Bruneseau.

## VI. FUTURE PROGRESS

The excavation of the Paris sewer was no mean feat. They worked on it for the last ten centuries without being able to finish the job any more than they were able to finish Paris. The sewer, in fact, reaps all the aftereffects of the growth of Paris. It is a sort of dark polyp with a thousand antennae sitting in the earth and growing down below at the same time as the city above. Every time the city carves out a street, the sewer stretches out an arm. The old monarchy only built 23,300 meters of sewers; that's as far as Paris had got by January 1, 1806. From that period, which we will talk about again shortly, the work was usefully and energetically resumed and continued. Napoléon built—the figures are curious—4,804 meters; Louis XVIII, 5,709; Charles X, 10,836; Louis-Philippe, 89,020; the Republic of 1848, 23,381; the current regime, 70,500; in all, at the present time, 226,610 meters, or sixty leagues of sewers, form Paris's enormous entrails. Obscure ramification, always in labor; an immense construction project that goes unnoticed.

As you can see, the underground maze of Paris is today ten times what it was at the beginning of the century. It is hard to imagine all the perseverance and effort required to bring this cloaca to the point of relative perfection it has now attained. It was with great difficulty that the old monarchical provostship and, in the last ten years of the eighteenth century, the revolutionary mayoralty, managed to tunnel out the five leagues of sewers that existed before 1806. All kinds of obstacles got in the way of this operation, some to do with the nature of the soil, others inherent in the very prejudices of the working population of Paris. Paris is built on a deposit strangely resistant to the pick, to mud, to the plumb bob, to manhandling. There is nothing harder to drill through and penetrate than the geological formation that the marvelous historical formation known as Paris sits on top of; as soon as work, in any shape or form, begins and ventures into that nappe of alluvial sediment, subterranean resistance abounds in the form of liquid clays, springs, hard rock, the soft deep silt that the special science calls "mustard." The pick makes slow headway in those calcareous plates alternating with very thin veins of potter's clay and layers of schist containing sheets encrusted with oyster shells contemporary with the preadamite oceans. Sometimes a stream abruptly causes a vault under construction to cave in and floods the workers; or a marl slide occurs, moving with the fury of a waterfall and shattering the great wooden support beams like glass. Only very recently, at Villette, when they needed to take the main sewer under the canal Saint-Martin without interrupting navigation and without emptying the canal, a fissure opened in the canal basin, water suddenly rose in the subterranean work site at a rate faster than the pumps could pump it out; they had to get a diver to look for the fissure, which turned out to be in the neck of the main basin, and they had a hell of a job blocking it up. Elsewhere, close to the Seine, and even some distance from the river, at Belleville, Grande-Rue, and the Lunière Arcade, for instance, you come across quicksand where a man can drop out of sight in a trice. Add suffocation from miasmas, entombment from landslides, the earth suddenly caving in. Add typhus slowly permeating the workers. In our day, after having dug out the Clichy gallery and provided it with a track for holding a water main to take water from the Ourcq, works executed in a cutting ten meters deep; after having survived all the landslides and often putrid excavations to vault over the Bièvre River[1] from the boulevard de l'Hôpital as far as the Seine; after having endeavored to rescue Paris from the torrential waters of Montmartre and to provide a runoff for the fluvial pond, nine hectares across, which used to stagnate near the barrière des Martyrs; after having built the sewer line from the barrière Blanche to the Aubervilliers road in four months flat, working day and night, at a depth of eleven meters; after having built an underground sewer in the rue Barre-du-Bec, without a cutting, six meters below ground—something never before seen—the foreman Monnot dropped dead. After having vaulted three thousand meters of sewers over every bit of the city, from the rue Traversière-Saint-Antoine to the rue de Lourcine; after having drained off, through the Arbalète drain, the storm water that used to flood the Censier-Mouffetard junction; after having built the Saint-Georges sewer on dry stone revetment and concrete in shifting sands; after having directed the awe-inspiring lowering of the floor of the Notre-Dame-de-Nazareth drain, the engineer, Duleau, dropped dead. There are no bulletins for these particular acts of bravery, even though they are rather more useful than the mindless bloodbaths of the battlefield.

The sewers of Paris in 1832 were far from being what they are today. Bruneseau had set things in motion, but it needed cholera[2] to spur the vast reconstruction that has taken place since. It may come as a shock to know, for example, that in 1821, part of the ring sewer known as the Grand Canal, as in Venice, was still stagnating out in the open, in the rue des Gourdes. It was not until 1823 that the city of Paris found in its purse the 266,080 francs and 6 centimes needed to cover over this vile abcess. The three absorbing dead wells of the Combat, the Cunette, and Saint-Mandé, with their overflow pipes, their machinery, their sumps, and their purifying connecting drains, date only from 1836. The intestinal waste dump of Paris has been completely revamped, becoming, as we said, ten times what it was a quarter of a century ago.

Thirty years ago, at the time of the insurrection of June 5 and 6, it was still, in many places, practically the old sewer. A very large number of streets, today cambered, were then very uneven tracks. You very often saw, at the dip where the sides of a street or an intersection ended, wide square grates with big bars whose iron shone, burnished by the feet of the crowd. These were dangerous and slippery for carriages and caused horses to take a tumble. The official language of the department of civil engineering gave these dips and grates the expressive term *cassis*—black currants. In 1832, in a whole host of streets— rue de l'Étoile, Saint-Louis, du Temple, Vieille-du-Temple, Notre-Dame-de-Nazareth, Folie-Méricourt, quai aux Fleurs, rue du Petit-Musc, de Normandie, Pont-aux-Biches, des Marais, faubourg Saint-Martin, rue Notre-Dame-des-Victoires, faubourg Montmartre, rue Grange-Batelière, in the Champs-Élysées, rue Jacob, rue de Tournon—the old gothic cloaca still cynically flashed its gaping chops. These were enormous gaps in stone building blocks, occasionally surrounded by curbstones, in a show of monumental effrontery.

Paris, in 1806, was practically still at the same sewer figures as that recorded in May 1663: 10,384 meters. After Bruneseau, on January 1, 1832, it had 40,300 meters. From 1806 to 1831, they had built 750 meters on average a year; since then they have built eight and even ten thousand meters of galleries of masonry every year using small materials with a bath of hydraulic cement poured over a concrete base. At two hundred francs a meter, the sixty leagues of sewers of today's Paris represent forty-eight million francs.

Apart from the economic progress that we indicated at the beginning, serious public hygiene issues are linked to this immense problem, the Paris sewer.

Paris lies between two sheets, a sheet of water and a sheet of air. The sheet of water, which lies fairly deep underground but is already being explored by two bores, is provided by a layer of green sandstone lying between chalk and Jurassic limestone; this layer may be represented by a disk with a radius of twenty-five leagues; a whole host of rivers and streams trickle into it; when you drink a glass of the water from the Grenelle well, you are drinking the Seine, the Marne, the Yonne, the Oise, the Aisne, the Cher, the Vienne, and the Loire. The sheet of water is healthy; it comes from the sky first of all, then from the ground; the sheet of air is unhealthy, it comes from the sewer. All the miasmas of the cloaca blend into the air the city breathes—hence its bad breath. Air taken from above a pile of manure—this has been scientifically observed—is purer than air taken from above Paris. Eventually, with the help of progress, mechanisms currently being developed, together with our growing enlightenment, will allow us to use the sheet of water to purify the sheet of air—meaning, we will wash the sewer. By washing the sewer, of course, we mean restoring the muck to the earth; sending the dung back to the soil to fertilize the fields. This simple act will mean a decrease in misery and an increase in health for the whole social community. At the present time, diseases from Paris spread out over a radius of fifty leagues around the Louvre, taken as the hub of this pestilential wheel.

You could say that, for ten centuries, the cloaca has been the disease of Paris. The sewer is the vice the city has in its blood. The people's instinct has never been wrong. The job of sewer worker was once almost as perilous, and almost as repulsive for the people, as the job of slaughterer in an abattoir, a job tainted with horror and long abandoned to the executioner. It needed high pay to persuade a mason to disappear into that fetid sap; the well-sinker's ladder thought twice before it plunged in; a proverb had it that "to go down into the sewer is to step into the grave"; and all sorts of hair-raising legends, as we said, once covered with horror that colossal sink; dreaded putrescent swamp that bears the trace of the revolutions of the terrestrial globe just as it does the revolutions of men, and in which vestiges of all the cataclysms are to be found, from shells dating back to the Flood right down to Marat's flap of rag.

# BOOK THREE

# IT MAY BE MUCK,
# BUT IT IS STILL THE SOUL

## I. THE CLOACA AND ITS SURPRISES

It was in the Paris sewer that Jean Valjean found himself.

A further resemblance between Paris and the sea. As in the ocean, the diver can disappear there.

The transition was startling. Smack bang in the middle of the city, Jean Valjean had left the city behind; and, in the twinkling of an eye, the time it took to lift up a lid and put it back down again, he had gone from broad daylight to utter darkness, from midday to midnight, from hubbub to silence, from the whirlwind of thunder and lightning to the stagnation of the tomb, and, through even more amazing twists and turns than those of the rue Polonceau, from the most extreme peril to the most absolute safety.

It meant tumbling abruptly into a vault; disappearing into the oubliette of Paris; quitting the streets where death lurked everywhere for a sort of sepulchre where there was life—a strange moment. He remained apparently dazed for a few seconds, listening, stunned. The trapdoor of salvation had suddenly opened under him. A heavenly goodness had in a way taken him by stealth in one of those fabulous ambushes of Providence.

Only, the wounded man did not stir, and Jean Valjean had no idea whether the man he was carrying into this pit was alive or dead.

His first sensation was of blindness. Suddenly, he could not see a thing. It also felt as though he'd gone deaf in one minute flat. He could not hear a thing. The frenetic storm of murder that was raging a few feet above him did not reach him, as we said, thanks to the thick chunk of earth that separated him from it, except in a muted indistinct way, like rumbling at a great depth. He felt that the ground was solid beneath his feet; that was all, but it was enough. He stretched out one arm, then the other, touching the wall on either side, and realized the corridor was narrow; he slipped, and realized the flagstones were wet. He advanced a foot cautiously, fearing a hole, a well, some kind of gulf; he found that the flagging continued. A terrible stink alerted him to where he was.

After a few moments, he was no longer blind. A trickle of light fell from the air vent through which he had slipped and his eyes adjusted to the vault. He began to make something out. The tunnel where he was holed up—no other words could express the situation better—was walled in behind him. It was one of those dead ends that the technical language terms a branch pipe. In front of him stood another wall, a wall of darkness. The light from the air vent died out ten or twelve feet in front of Jean Valjean and barely cast a wan whiteness over a few meters of the damp sewer wall. Beyond that, the opacity was massive; to penetrate further into it seemed horrible, to step into it felt like being swallowed up. But you could sink into this wall of mist and it had to be done. It had to be done very quickly, even. Jean Valjean thought that the grate he had spotted under the paving stones could also be spotted by the soldiers and that there was every chance it would be. They could hop down into the well, too, and search it. There was not a minute to lose. He had deposited Marius on the ground and now he gathered him up again—this being the right phrase—and threw him over his shoulders once more and set out, stepping resolutely into the darkness.

The reality was that they were not as safe as Jean Valjean had thought. Perils of another kind, no less great, were perhaps awaiting them. After the blazing whirlwind of combat came the cavern of miasmas and traps; after chaos, the cesspit. Jean Valjean had fallen from one circle of hell into another.

When he had gone fifty paces, he had to stop. A question presented itself. The corridor ended in another narrow tunnel which it met side-on. Which way should he go? Left or right? How could a man get his bearings in this black labyrinth? The labyrinth, as we noted earlier, has a thread, which is its downward slope. Following the downward slope means reaching the river. Jean Valjean caught on instantly.

He told himself that he was probably in the sewer at Les Halles; that if he chose the left fork and followed the slope he would, in about fifteen minutes, reach some outlet opening on to the Seine between the Pont-au-Change and the Pont-Neuf—meaning, he would pop up in broad daylight at the most crowded spot in Paris. Maybe he would come out in some sunny stretch of a public square. Imagine the stupor of the bystanders seeing two men covered in blood emerging from out of the ground beneath their feet. The cops would arrive, there'd be a call to arms at the nearest guardhouse. They'd be nabbed before they fully surfaced. Better to sink into the maze, trust to that blackness, and rely on Providence for an exit. He went back up the slope and took the right.

When he had turned the corner of the gallery, the distant gleam from the air vent disappeared, the curtain of darkness fell back over him and he went blind again. But he forged ahead regardless and as fast as his legs would carry him. Marius's arms were hanging around his neck and his feet dangling behind him. He had hold of both arms with one hand and groped along the wall with the other. Marius's cheek touched his own and stuck to it like glue, being covered in blood. He felt a warm stream that came from Marius flow over him and seep into his clothes. Yet a damp warmth in the ear pressed against the wounded man's mouth indicated there was still breath and consequently, life. The corridor through which Jean Valjean was now wending his way was not as narrow as the first. Jean Valjean walked along it, though pretty painfully. The rains of the night before had not yet run off and they formed a small torrent in the middle of the channel floor, and he was forced to hug the wall to keep his feet out of the water. And so, on he staggered in the dark. He was like one of those nocturnal creatures groping through the invisible, lost underground in the veins of shadow.

And yet, little by little, either because distant air vents were sending a bit of flickering light into this opaque mist, or because his eyes were getting used to the dark, some feeble sight returned and he began to be vaguely aware again, here of the wall he was touching, there of the vault he was passing under. The pupil dilates in the night and ends up finding a kind of daylight there, just as the soul dilates in misery and ends up finding God.

Finding his way was hard. The layout of the sewers reflects, so to speak, the layout of the streets lying on top. In the Paris of the day there were two thousand two hundred streets. Try to imagine this forest of dark branches known as the sewer underneath that. Placed end to end, the sewer system existing at the time would have measured eleven leagues in length. As we said earlier, the current network is no less than sixty leagues long.

Jean Valjean had gone wrong from the start. He thought he was under the rue Saint-Denis and it is a shame he wasn't. Under the rue Saint-Denis, there is an old stone sewer dating from Louis XIII's day that runs straight into the main sewer, known as the Grand Égout, the Grand Sewer, with only a single sharp turn, on the right-hand side, under the old Cour des Miracles, and a single connecting drain, the Saint-Martin sewer, whose four intersecting arms form a cross. But the Petite-Truanderie gallery, whose inlet was near the Corinthe tavern, has never been connected to the underground passage under the rue Saint-Denis; it ends in the Montmartre sewer and that was where Jean Valjean was tangled up. There, opportunities to get lost abounded. The Montmartre sewer is one of the most labyrinthine in the old network. Luckily Jean Valjean had left behind him the sewer of Les Halles, whose geometric layout shows like a whole bevy of interlocking topgallant masts; but he had ahead of him more than one tricky encounter and more than one street corner—for these are streets—

popping up in the dark like a question mark: first, on his left, the vast Plâtrière sewer, a sort of Chinese puzzle, shoving and scrambling its chaotic jumble of T-intersections and Z-bends under the Hôtel des Postes and under the rotunda at the wheat market and as far as the Seine, where it ends in a Y; second, on his right, the curved tunnel of the rue du Cadran with its three teeth, which are so many dead ends; third, on his left, the Mail branch line, complicated very near the entrance by a sort of fork and zigzagging along to end in the great outfall basin of the Louvre, where it breaks up into sections and branches out in all directions; last, on his right, the dead-end tunnel of the rue de Jeûneurs. This was without counting the tiny offshoots here and there before you get to the ring sewer, which alone could lead him to some exit far enough away to be safe.

If Jean Valjean had had any idea of the above, he would quickly have realized just by feeling the wall that he was not in the underground gallery of the rue Saint-Denis. Instead of the old hewn stone, instead of the ancient architecture, which was noble and regal even in the sewer, with channel floor and water courses of granite and rich lime mortar, the latter costing over four hundred livres per meter, he would have felt beneath his hand the then-contemporary crumminess, the economic expedient, the millstone rock of a hydraulic mortar bed over a layer of concrete that costs a mere two hundred francs a meter, bourgeois masonry known as small materials. But he knew nothing about any of that.

He forged ahead, anxious but calm, seeing nothing, knowing nothing, absorbed in random chance, that is, engulfed by Providence.

By degrees, we have to say, horror crept over him. The shadows that enveloped him entered his mind. He was walking through a puzzle. The cloaca aqueduct is glumly forbidding; it weaves around, dizzyingly intertwining. It is pretty grim being caught up in this Paris of darkness. Jean Valjean was obliged to find, almost to invent, his route without seeing it. Within this unknown, every step he risked could be his last. How would he ever get out of there? Would he find a way out? Would he find it in time? Would this colossal subterranean sponge with alveoli of stone let itself be penetrated and pierced through? Would he stumble across some unexpected knot of obscurity in there? Would they come to a part where they would get stuck and stay there, stranded? Would Marius die there of a hemorrhage and himself of starvation? Would they wind up getting lost in there, the two of them, and end up as two skeletons in some pocket of that black night? He did not know. He asked himself all this but could not give himself any answers. The bowels of Paris are bottomless. He was, like the prophet, in the belly of the monster whale.

Suddenly he had a jolt. At the most unpredictable moment and without his having stopped walking in a straight line, he noticed he was no longer going uphill; the water of the stream churned at his heels instead of coming at his toes. The sewer was now running downward. How come? Was he about to suddenly hit the Seine? The danger of that was great, but the peril of going back was even greater. He forged ahead.

It was not toward the Seine that he was heading. The hump formed by the soil of Paris on the right bank empties one of its sides into the Seine and the other into the Grand Sewer. The ridge of the hump that determines which way the water flows follows an extremely capricious line. The culmination point, which is the point at which the runoff divide occurs, is above the rue Michel-le-Comte in the Sainte-Avoye sewer, close to the boulevards in the Louvre sewer, and close to Les Halles in the Montmartre sewer. It was this culmination point that Jean Valjean had reached. He was heading for the ring sewer. He was on the right track. But he didn't know it.

Whenever he came to a side drain, he groped around the opening and if he found it was not as wide as the tunnel he was in, he did not go into it but continued on his way, judging, rightly, that a narrower passage would end in a dead end and could only take him away from the goal, that is, the way out. And so he avoided the fourfold trap laid out for him in the darkness by the four mazes mentioned above.

At a certain moment he realized that he had moved away from under the Paris petrified by the riot, where the barricades had brought traffic to a standstill, and back under the normal Paris, alive and bustling. He suddenly heard a noise like thunder overhead—distant, but continuous. It was the rumbling of carriages.

He had been walking for about half an hour, at least according to his inner reckoning, and had not yet thought about resting. The only thing he'd done was change the hand supporting Marius. The darkness was deeper than ever, but this deep darkness reassured him.

All of a sudden he saw his shadow in front of him. It stood out against a feeble, almost indistinct red patch that vaguely turned the channel floor at his feet and the vault over his head crimson, as it slid to left and right over the two slimy walls of the tunnel. Stunned, he wheeled round.

Behind him, in the section of tunnel he had just traversed, at a distance that seemed to him immense, a sort of horrible star was flaring, lighting up the dense darkness, and it looked to be watching him.

It was the dark star of the police rising in the sewer. Behind this star, moving around confusedly, were eight or ten black shapes, erect, indistinct, terrifying.

## II. Explanation

During the day of June 6, a battue of the sewers had been ordered. It was feared that they might be used as a refuge by the vanquished, and the prefect, Gisquet, was supposed to scour the hidden Paris while General Bugeaud swept the public Paris; a twin operation that demanded a twin strategy from the public force represented by the army up above and the police down below. Three platoons of officers and sewer workers explored the subterranean streets of Paris, the first, the right bank, the second, the left bank, the third, the Île de la Cité. The officers were armed with carbines, clubs, swords, and daggers.

What was at that moment directed at Jean Valjean was the lantern of the right bank patrol.

This patrol had just been through the curved gallery and the three dead ends lying under the rue du Cadran. While they were waving their lantern around at the back of those dead ends, Jean Valjean had stumbled on the entrance to the gallery in his path, had found it narrower than the main tunnel, and had not gone in. He had disregarded it. The police officers, reemerging from the Cadran gallery, had thought they heard the noise of footfalls coming from the direction of the ring sewer. They were right, these were Jean Valjean's footsteps. The sergeant in command of the patrol had held up his lantern and the squad had started peering into the mist over where the noise had come from.

This was a moment beyond words for Jean Valjean.

Luckily, if he could see the lantern clearly, the lantern could not clearly see him. It was light and he was shadow. He was a very long way off and merged into the black darkness of the place. He flattened himself against the wall and stopped, dead-still.

In any case, he had no idea what it was that was moving around behind him. Lack of sleep, lack of food, emotional turmoil had thrown him, too, into a hallucinatory state. He saw a flaring light and around that flaring light, specters. What were they? He didn't have a clue.

Jean Valjean having stopped, the noise also stopped. The men on patrol listened and heard nothing, they looked and saw nothing. They conferred.

In those days, at that point in the Montmartre sewer, there was a sort of square known as the service junction, since done away with because of the small inland lake formed by the torrential runoff that collected there in violent storms. The platoon was able to huddle together in this space. Jean Valjean saw the specters form a sort of circle. They brought their mastiff heads together and whispered.

The outcome of this confabulation of guard dogs was that they had been mistaken, that there had been no noise, that no one was there, that there was no point trying to tackle the ring sewer, that it would be a waste of time, but that they needed to get cracking toward Saint-Merry, that if there was anything to be done and any loudmouth troublemakers, or *bousingots,* to track down, it was in that quarter.

From time to time the different parties slap new soles on their old insults. In 1832, the word *bousingot* filled the interim between the word *Jacobin,* which was old hat, and the word *démagogue,* or rabble-rouser, which was then almost unused but which has since done such an excellent job.

The sergeant gave the order to veer off to the left toward the downhill slope to the Seine. If it had occurred to them to split into two squads and cover both directions at once, Jean Valjean would have been caught. His fate was hanging by a thread. It is likely that instructions from the prefecture, anticipating that there could be a fight, one involving a fair number of insurgents, had ruled out the patrol's splintering. The patrol set off again, leaving Jean Valjean behind them. Of all this movement, Jean Valjean saw nothing except the eclipse of the lantern which suddenly swung round the other way.

Before going off, the sergeant, to ease the conscience of the police officers, fired his carbine in the direction they were abandoning—at Jean Valjean. The explosion rolled through the basin, echoing along the way, as though the titanic tunnel's gut were rumbling. A chunk of plaster fell into the stream and made the water splash a few feet from where he stood, alerting Jean Valjean to the fact that the musket ball had struck the vault above his head.

Slow and measured footsteps reverberated along the channel for a while, but they were more and more dampened the farther away they got; the pack of black shapes slunk into the gloom, a glimmer of light wavered and fluttered, turning the curved arch of the vault a kind of red, before dwindling and disappearing; silence once more fell, profound, blindness and deafness again took hold of the darkness, and Jean Valjean, not yet daring to move again, stayed for a long time with his back to the wall, ears pricked, eyes wide open, watching the vanishing phantom patrol.

## III. The Man Tailed

We must do the police of the day justice and acknowledge that, even in the gravest political situations, they carried out their duty imperturbably as far as maintenance of roads and waterways and surveillance went. A riot was not in their eyes a reason for giving malefactors free rein and neglecting society just because the government was in peril. Ordinary duty was performed correctly through extraordinary duty and was in no way disturbed by it. In the middle of a totally unpredictable political event that had taken off, under pressure of a possible revolution, without letting himself be distracted by mere insurrections and barricades, a policeman would "tail" a thief.

It was precisely something of the kind that happened on the afternoon of June 6 down by the Seine, on the embankment of the right bank, a bit beyond the pont des Invalides.

There is no embankment there today. The whole look of the place has changed.

On this embankment, two men a certain distance apart looked to be eyeing each other, with one avoiding the other. The one up ahead was trying to get away, the one bringing up the rear was trying to close the gap.

It was like a game of chess being played at a distance, silently. Neither man seemed in a hurry; they both walked slowly as though each of them feared to cause his partner to step up the pace if he showed too much haste. It made you think of a hungry predator following its prey, but trying to look as though it wasn't. The prey was cunning and kept on his guard.

The requisite distance between a hounded weasel and the mastiff hounding it was observed. The man trying to escape was a scrawny skinny-necked weed, the man going after him was a tall strapping man who looked hard as nails, and would no doubt be hard as nails if you went up against him.

The first, feeling himself to be the weaker, avoided the second, but he avoided him in a profoundly furious fashion; anyone observing him closely would have seen his eyes shining with the glum hostility of a man in flight and with all the menace there is in fear.

The embankment was deserted and cut-off, there was no one going by; not even a boatman or a longshoreman on the barges moored here and there.

You could not easily spot the two men except from the quai opposite, and for anyone studying them at that distance, the man in front would have looked as though his hackles were up, ragged and skulking as he was, fretful and shivering under a tattered smock, and the other man, like some classic official, wearing the overcoat of authority buttoned up to the chin. The reader would perhaps recognize the two men if they could see them a little closer.

What was the second man's objective? Probably to dress the first man in something warmer.

When a man dressed by the state pursues a man in rags, it is to turn him, too, into a man dressed by the state. Only, the color is the crux of the matter. To be dressed in blue is glorious; to be dressed in red[1] is rather unpleasant. There is such a thing as low-life crimson. It was probably some unpleasantness and a shade of crimson of the kind that the first man hoped to elude.

If the second man let him walk ahead and had not yet seized him, it was, to all appearances, in the hopes of seeing him wind up at some important rendezvous with some gang worth nabbing with him that would amount to a good haul all around. This delicate operation is known as tailing.

What makes such a conjecture perfectly plausible is that the buttoned-up man, spotting from the embankment an empty fiacre going past, signaled to the driver, and the driver understood, evidently realized with whom he was dealing, turned around and began to follow the two men from the quai at a slow trot. This was not picked up by the shady character in rags walking ahead.

The fiacre rolled along under the trees of the Champs-Élysées. You could see the driver's upper body above the parapet, whip in hand.

One of the secret instructions issued by the police to their officers contains this article: "Always have a hire car to hand, just in case."

While maneuvering, each on his side, with irreproachable strategy, the two men approached a ramp on the quai that went down to the embankment and which, in those days, allowed coach drivers coming from Passy to go down to the river to water their horses. This ramp has been removed since, in the interests of symmetry; the horses die of thirst, but the eye is flattered.

It seemed most likely that the man in the smock would run up this ramp in order to escape down the Champs-Élysées, a place adorned with trees, but also, on the other hand, heavily dotted with police officers, where the other man would have a helping hand.

This point of the quai is not very far from the house brought from Moret to Paris in 1824 by Colonel Brack, and known as the house of François I.[2] A guardhouse sits right alongside it.

To the great surprise of his observer, the hounded man did not take the ramp to the watering place. He kept going along the embankment beside the quai. His position was becoming visibly critical. Apart from throwing himself in the Seine, what was he going to do?

No way back up to the quai now; no more ramp, no stairs; and they were very close to the bend in the Seine near the pont d'Iéna, where the embankment got narrower and narrower, tapering off in a skinny tongue before vanishing underwater. There he would inevitably find himself trapped between the sheer wall on his right, the river on his left and in front of him, and the powers that be at his heels.

It is true that the end of the embankment was hidden from sight by a heap of rubble six or seven feet high produced by some demolition or other. But was the man actually hoping to hide effectively behind a heap of rubble anyone could just walk around? The expedient would have been puerile. Surely he wouldn't dream of it. The innocence of crooks has its limits.

The heap of debris made a sort of elevation at the water's edge that extended as a promontory right up to the wall of the quai.

The man being followed reached this knoll and rounded it so that he couldn't be seen anymore by the other man.

The latter could not see but neither could he be seen; he took advantage of that fact to abandon all dissimulation and step up the pace. In a few seconds he had reached the mound of rubble and turned it. There, he stopped in his tracks, stunned. The man he was hunting was no longer to be seen. The man in the smock had disappeared into thin air.

The embankment barely went on for another thirty paces from the heap of rubble before it dived below the water that lapped against the quai wall. The fugitive could not have thrown himself into the Seine or scaled the quai without being seen by the man following him. What had become of him?

The man with the buttoned-up coat walked to the very end of the embankment and stayed there a moment lost in thought, wildly clenching and unclenching his fists, his eyes darting about like a ferret's. All of a sudden he slapped himself on the forehead. At the point where the ground ended and the water began, he had just clapped eyes on an iron gate, wide and low-lying, arched, fitted with a heavy lock and three massive hinges. This gate, a sort of door cut into the bottom of the quai, opened onto the river as much as onto the embankment. A blackish stream flowed at the bottom. This stream disgorged into the Seine.

On the other side of its heavy rusted iron bars you could make out a sort of tunnel, vaulted and black.

The man folded his arms and gave the gate a look of resentment.

Looking was not enough. He then tried to push it open; he rattled it, it resisted without budging. Yet it most likely had just been opened, even if he hadn't heard a sound, which was pretty strange for such a rusty grate; but it had certainly been closed again. This showed that the man this door had just opened for had, not a hook, but a key.

This obvious fact came to the man in a flash, prompting him to shake the gate as hard as he could, and forcing out of him this roar of indignation: "The nerve of it! A government key!"

Then, instantly calming down, he gave vent to a whole inner world of ideas in a flurry of monosyllables spat out with almost ironic emphasis: "Well! Well! Well! Well!"

That said, hoping for who knows what—either to see the man emerge again or to see other men go in—he posted himself on the lookout behind the heap of rubble with the patient rage of a pointer.

For its part, the fiacre, which mirrored all his movements, had come to a halt above him alongside the parapet. The driver, foreseeing a long wait, fitted the muzzles of his horses into the nosebag of oats, wet at the bottom, which is so familiar to Parisians, being—this said in brackets—something the various governments sometimes apply to them. The rare passersby on the pont d'Iéna, before moving on, turned their heads to gaze for a moment at those two motionless features of the landscape, the man on the embankment, the fiacre on the quai.

## IV. He, Too, Bears His Cross

Jean Valjean had continued on his course once more and did not stop again.

The going was more and more laborious. The level of the tunnels varies, the average height being about five feet six inches, based on a man's height. Jean

Valjean was forced to bend over so as not to bang Marius against the vaulted ceiling; he had to duck at every step, then straighten up again, groping the wall constantly. The dampness of the stones and the sliminess of the floor meant they were useless as supports, for either hands or feet. He stumbled in the city's hideous shit heap. The intermittent reflections from the air vents appeared only at very widely spaced intervals and the light was so wan that daylight was like moonlight; all the rest was mist, miasma, opacity, blackness. Jean Valjean was hungry and thirsty; thirsty, especially; and that place, like the sea, is full of water that can't be drunk. His strength, which, as we know, was prodigious and barely diminished a fraction with age thanks to his chaste and sober life, was beginning to give way. He was getting tired and as his strength diminished, the weight of his burden grew. Marius, who was perhaps dead, weighed heavily as inert bodies do. Jean Valjean was carrying him in such a way that his chest was not squashed and he could breathe as freely as possible. He could feel the rats darting between his legs. One of them was frightened enough to bite him. From time to time a breath of fresh air came to him through the covers of the manholes and revived him.

It might have been three in the afternoon when he reached the ring sewer. At first he was amazed at the sudden widening. He suddenly found himself in a gallery where his outstretched hands did not reach the walls on either side and beneath a vault that his head did not touch. The Grand Sewer is, indeed, eight feet wide and seven feet high.

At the point where the Montmartre sewer joins the Grand Sewer, two other underground galleries, that of the rue de Provence and that of the Abattoir, intersect and form a square. Having to choose between these four lanes anyone less wise would have been undecided. Jean Valjean took the widest, meaning the ring sewer. But this is where the question returned: uphill or downhill? He sensed the situation was urgent and that it was now vital to get to the Seine whatever the risk. In other words, to go downhill. He took the left.

And just as well for him that he did. For it would be a mistake to think that the ring sewer has two exits, one somewhere at Bercy, the other somewhere at Passy, and that it is, as its name would suggest, the underground ring around the Paris of the right bank. The Grand Sewer, you must remember, is nothing more than the old Ménilmontant stream and it ends, if you go up it, in a dead end— that is, in its old starting point, which was its spring, at the foot of the Ménilmontant knoll. It is not directly connected to the drain that collects the Paris runoff starting from the Popincourt quartier and emptying into the Seine through the Amelot sewer above the old Île Louviers. This drain, which completes the outfall sewer, is separated from it, under the rue Ménilmontant itself, by a solid wall that marks the drainage divide between the upstream and downstream runoff. If Jean Valjean had gone up the gallery, then after huge effort, shattering fatigue, gasping his last, in darkness, he would have hit a wall. He would have been sunk.

At a pinch, by retracing his steps a short distance and taking the Filles-du-Calvaire tunnel, on the condition of not hesitating at the underground bifurcation under the Boucherat junction but taking the Saint-Louis tunnel instead, then, on the left, the Saint-Gilles tunnel, then, by turning right and avoiding the Saint-Sébastien gallery, he would have been able to get to the Amelot sewer and from there, as long as he didn't go astray in the sort of F-formation under the Bastille, he would have reached the outlet on the Seine near the Arsenal. But, to do that, he would have had to know the enormous coral reef that is the sewer inside out, along with all its ramifications and all its interconnections. Well, we said before and we'll say it again, he knew nothing about this grisly network of tunnels in which he was wending his way; and if anyone had asked him what he was in, he would have answered: In the dark.

His instinct served him well. Going downhill did indeed mean possible salvation.

He left behind on his right the two tunnels that branch out in a claw shape under the rue Laffitte and the rue Saint-Georges and the long forked tunnel of the chaussée d'Antin.

A bit beyond a tributary that was most likely the Madeleine drain, he paused. He was very weary. A pretty big air vent, probably the manhole in the rue d'Anjou, provided an almost sharp light. With movements as gentle as those of a man handling his own wounded brother, Jean Valjean laid Marius down on the bank of the sewer. Marius's bloody face looked to be lying at the bottom of a grave in the white light from the air vent. His eyes were closed, his matted hair stuck to his temples like dried brushes that had been dipped in the color red, his hands hung down, lifeless, his limbs were cold, there was coagulated blood at the corners of his mouth. A clot of blood had built up in the knot of his cravat; his shirt was sinking into in his wounds, the cloth of his coat was rubbing against the gaping gashes in his living flesh. Jean Valjean pulled his clothes aside with the tips of his fingers and placed his hand on his chest; his heart was still beating. Jean Valjean ripped up his own shirt, bandaged the wounds as best he could and stanched the flowing blood; then, bending over the still-unconscious and almost unbreathing Marius in the twilit gloom, he glared at him with inexpressible hatred.

In disturbing Marius's clothes, he had found in his pockets two things: the bread forgotten there since the day before and Marius's wallet. He ate the bread and opened the wallet. In the first compartment he found the four lines written by Marius. You will recall them:

My name is Marius Pontmercy. Take my body to my grandfather, Monsieur Gillenormand, rue des Filles-du-Calvaire, no. 6, in the Marais.

Jean Valjean read these four lines in the light of the air vent and remained for a moment as though absorbed in himself, repeating to himself in a murmur: "rue des Filles-du-Calvaire, number six, Monsieur Gillenormand." He put the wallet back in Marius's pocket. He had eaten, his strength had returned; he put Marius on his back again, carefully rested his head on his right shoulder, and began descending the sewer again.

The Grand Sewer, aligned following the riverbed of the Ménilmontant valley, is almost two leagues long. It is paved for a considerable part of its course.

But this torch of Paris street names which we are shining for the reader's benefit on Jean Valjean's subterranean course, was not available to Jean Valjean. Nothing told him which part of the city he was crossing or what way he had come. Only the growing faintness of the pools and points of light he came across periodically showed him that the sun was withdrawing from the footpath above and day was gradually coming to a close; and the rumbling of the carriages overhead, having gone from endless to intermittent, then almost ceasing altogether, made him conclude that he was no longer under the center of Paris, but was approaching some out-of-the-way area somewhere near the outer boulevards or the quais furthest away. Wherever there are fewer houses and fewer streets, the sewer has fewer air vents. The darkness was getting thicker around Jean Valjean. He continued to forge ahead, though, regardless, groping in the gloom.

This gloom promptly became terrible.

## V. With Sand as with Women, There Is a Kind of Fineness That Is Perfidious

He felt that he was stepping into water and that he had beneath his feet not pavement now, but mud.

It sometimes happens, on certains stretches of Breton or Scottish coast, that a man, a traveler or a fisherman, trudging along the beach at low tide far from shore, suddenly realizes he has been struggling for some minutes. The sand is like pitch underfoot; his soles stick to it; it's no longer sand, it's glue. The beach is perfectly dry, but with every step a person takes, as soon as he lifts his foot, the footprint it leaves fills with water. The eye, though, has not registered any change; the vast wide beach is all of a piece and peaceful, everywhere the sand looks the same, nothing distinguishes solid ground from ground that no longer is; the little gleeful cloud of sandflies continues to hop tumultuously over the wayfarer's feet. The man follows his route, forges straight ahead, leaning in toward the ground, tries to get closer to the hinterland. He is not worried. What's there to worry about? Only, he feels somehow as though his feet are getting heavier with each step he takes. Suddenly, he sinks. He sinks by two or three inches. Clearly he is not on the right track; he stops to get his bearings. All of a sudden he looks at his feet. His feet have disappeared. The sand has buried them. He pulls his feet out of the sand, he tries to retrace his steps, he swivels round; he sinks deeper. The sand comes up to his ankles, he yanks himself out and throws himself to the left, the sand comes halfway up his calves, he throws himself to the right, the sand comes up to the backs of his knees. Then he recognizes with unspeakable terror that he is caught in quicksand and that that awful medium in which a man can no more walk than a fish can swim is lying under him. He chucks away his load if he has one, he lightens himself like a ship in distress. It is already too late, the sand is above his knees.

He calls out, he waves his hat or his handkerchief, the sand is gaining on him more and more; if the beach is deserted, if the land is too far away, if the sandbank is too notorious, if there is no hero about, then that's it, he is condemned to being sucked down and buried alive. He is condemned to that appalling interment—long, inexorable, implacable, impossible to slow down or speed up, going on for hours, never-ending—that grabs you as you stand, free and in the pink of health, and pulls you by the feet and, at every effort you make, at every cry you let out, drags you under a bit farther; that seems to punish you for your resistance by redoubling its grip, that pulls a man slowly into the ground, leaving him all the time in the world to gaze at the horizon, the trees, the lush green countryside, the smoke from villages in the plain, the sails of ships out on the sea, the birds flying about and singing, the sun, the sky. Being sucked down is the sepulchre turned into the watery grave of a tide rising up from the ends of the earth to attack the living. Every minute means further entombment. The poor bastard tries to sit down, to lie down, to crawl; every move he makes buries him; he straightens up, he sinks down; he feels himself being engulfed; he screams, implores, cries out to the clouds, wrings his hands, despairs. There he is waist-deep in the sand; the sand reaches his chest; he is no more than a bust now. He raises his arms, groans furiously, clutches at the beach with his nails, tries to hold on to that ash, leans on his elbows to tear himself out of that soft sheath, sobs frantically; the sand rises. The sand reaches his shoulders, the sand reaches his neck; only his face is visible now. His mouth shouts, the sand fills it; silence. His eyes still gaze, the sand shuts them; darkness. Then his forehead diminishes, a bit of hair flutters above the sand; a hand pops up, pokes a hole in the surface of the beach, flaps and shakes, then disappears. A man has been sinisterly erased.

Sometimes the rider gets sucked down with the horse; sometimes the carter gets sucked down with the cart; all sink beneath the beach. It is a shipwreck out of water. It is land drowning the man. Land, permeated by the ocean, becomes a trap. It offers itself as a plain and opens itself up like a wave. The abyss goes in for such treachery.

This fatal experience, always possible on this or that ocean beach, was also possible, thirty years ago, in the sewer of Paris. Before the major works begun in 1833 got off the ground, the underground network of Paris was subject to sudden cave-ins.

The water trickled down into certain underlying pockets of particularly friable soil; the channel floor, whether made of paving as in the old sewers, or of hydraulic cement over concrete as in the new galleries, having lost its support, buckled. A buckle in a floor of this nature means a crack; a crack means collapse. The channel floor would give way over a certain distance. This crevasse, a gap that was a gully of sludge, was known in the specialized language as *subsidence*. What is subsidence? It is the quicksand of the seaside suddenly encountered under the ground; it is the beach of Mont Saint-Michel[1] in a sewer. The saturated soil behaves as though molten; all of its molecules are in suspension in a soft medium; it is not soil and it is not water. And this, sometimes to very great depth. There is nothing more awful than such an encounter. If water is predominant, death is swift, you are simply swallowed up; if soil is predominant, death is slow, you are sucked down inch by inch.

Can you imagine such a death? If being sucked down is appalling on a beach by the sea, what can it be like in the cloaca? Instead of the open air, bright sunlight, broad daylight, that clear horizon, those vast sounds, those free clouds raining down life, those boats just visible in the distance, hope in all its forms, people probably going by, help possible up until the last minute—instead of all that, deafness, blindness, a black vault, the inside of a grave all ready and waiting, death in a bog under a lid, slow suffocation by feculence, a stone box where asphyxiation opens its claws in the mire and grabs you by the throat; fetid air mingling with your death rattle; slime instead of sand, sulphured hydrogen instead of a hurricane, ordure instead of the ocean! And you call out, and you grind your teeth, and you writhe, and struggle, and agonize, with this enormous city that is completely ignorant of all this, sitting there just above your head!

No words can express the horror of dying like this! Death sometimes redeems its atrociousness by a certain terrible dignity. At the stake, in a shipwreck, a person can be grand; in flames as in foam, a superb attitude is possible; you are transfigured in going down into the abyss. But not here. Death is dirty. Expiring here is humiliating. The last things you see floating by are base. Muck is synonymous with shame. It is small, ugly, vile. Die in a tun of marsala,[2] like Clarence, if you have to; in the night-carter's ditch, like d'Escoubleau, no, that is horrible. To struggle in it is ghastly; while you are fighting for your life, you squelch around paddling. It is dark enough to be hell, viscous enough to be no more than a slime pit, and the dying man can't tell whether he will turn into a specter or a toad. Everywhere else the sepulchre is sinister; here it is grotesque.

The depth of subsidences varied, as well as their length and density, depending on how bad the quality of the subsoil was. Sometimes a subsidence was two or three feet deep, sometimes eight or ten; occasionally, the bottom could not be found. The muck would be almost solid in one place, almost liquid in another. In the Lunière subsidence,[3] it would have taken a man a day to disappear, whereas he would have been devoured in five minutes flat in the Phélippeaux bog. Sludge's load-bearing capacity varies with its density. A child can get away where a man is sunk. The first law of salvation is to shed any kind of weight. Chuck your tool bag or your sack or your hod. That was the first thing a sewer worker did when he felt the ground giving way under him.

Subsidences had different causes: the friability of the soil; a landslide at a depth below human reach; the violent showers of summer; the endless downpours of winter; long drizzle patches. Sometimes the weight of neighboring houses on a marly or sandy ground bore down on the vaults of the underground galleries and caused them to warp, or else the sewer floor would burst and crack under the crushing pressure. The compression caused by the Panthéon obliterated in this way, a century ago, a section of the vaults of montagne Sainte-Geneviève. When a sewer slumped under pressure from houses, the chaos occasionally translated at street level as a sort of sawtoothed split between paving stones; this rent would snake all the way along the cracked vault and then, since the problem was visible, it could be promptly fixed. Just as often, the internal ravages did not reveal themselves by any external scar. In which case, woe betide the sewer workers. Stepping carelessly into the caved-in sewer, they could lose their lives there. The old records make mention of well sinkers buried alive in this way in subsidences. They list several names, among others the name of a sewerman who got bogged down when the sewer caved in under the square in the rue Carême-Prenant, a man named Blaise Poutrain. This Blaise Poutrain was the brother of Nicolas Poutrain, who was the last ditch-digger of the cemetery nicknamed the Slaughterhouse of the Innocents in 1785, the period when that particular cemetery died.

There was also the young and dashing vicomte d'Escoubleau[4] we just referred to, one of the heroes of the siege of Lérida, where they mounted the attack in silk stockings, violins leading the way. D'Escoubleau, surprised one night at his cousin's, the duchesse de Sourdis, drowned in a quagmire in the Beautrellis sewer, where he had sought refuge from the duc. Madame de Sourdis, when told of his death, asked for her smelling salts and forgot to weep, she was so busy sniffing the salts. In such cases, no love can hold up; the cloaca snuffs it out. Hero refuses to wash Leander's dead body. Thisbe holds her nose in front of Pyramus[5] and lets out a: "Pooh!"

## VI. THE SUBSIDENCE

Jean Valjean found himself faced with a subsidence. This type of cave-in was then frequent in the subsoil of the Champs-Élysées, which did not really lend itself to hydraulic works and was not very good at preserving underground structures because of its excessive fluidity. For inconsistency this fluidity is even worse than the sands of the quartier Saint-Georges, which could only be defeated by a layer of dry stone revetment over concrete; even worse than the clay beds contaminated with gas of the quartier des Martyrs, which are so waterlogged that the passage could only be dug out under the gallery des Martyrs by means of a cast-iron pipe. When, in 1836, they demolished, in order to rebuild it, the old stone sewer under the faubourg Saint-Honoré where we see Jean Valjean tangled up at this moment, the quicksand that forms the subsoil of the Champs-Élysées right down to the Seine was such an obstacle that the operation lasted close on six months, to the great hue and cry of local residents, especially those residents who owned mansions[1] or coaches. The work was more than grueling; it was downright dangerous. It is true that it rained for four and a half months and that the Seine flooded three times.

The subsidence that Jean Valjean encountered was caused by the downpour the day before. The paved floor, poorly supported by the underlying sand, had buckled and blocked the flow of storm water, producing a flood. Seepage had occurred and collapse had followed. The broken-up floor had subsided into the sludge. For how long a stretch? Impossible to say. It was darker here than anywhere else. It was a mud hole in a cavern of pitch-black night.

Jean Valjean felt the pavement give way under him. He stepped into the mire. It was water on the surface, sludge at the bottom. He had to get through it. To go back the way he had come was out of the question. Marius was dying and Jean Valjean worn out. What other way was there? Jean Valjean plowed on. Besides, the bog did not seem too deep for the first few steps. But the farther he advanced, the deeper his feet sank in. He was soon knee-deep in sludge and more than knee-deep in water. He trudged on, holding Marius as high as he could with both arms above the water. The sludge now came up over his knees and the water to his waist. It was already too late to turn back. He was sinking deeper and deeper. The sludge was dense enough to hold one man's weight but evidently could not bear two. Separately, Marius and Jean Valjean would have had a chance to get out. Jean Valjean continued to advance, holding up the dying man who was, perhaps, already a corpse.

The water came up to his armpits; he felt himself foundering; he could hardly move, the muck was so deep. Its density, which was its load-bearing support, was also the obstacle. He kept Marius aloft and, with an unbelievable show of strength, made headway; but he was sinking fast. Now only his head was out of water and the arms that held Marius aloft. In old paintings of the Flood, you'll see a mother holding her child in the same manner.

He sank even deeper, throwing his head back to avoid swallowing water and to be able to breathe; to anyone there in the darkness he would have looked like a mask floating in the dark; he dimly caught sight of Marius's head hanging down above him and his livid face; he made a desperate effort and thrust his foot out; his foot hit something solid. A foothold. High time.

He straightened up and twisted round and rooted himself firmly on that support in a kind of fit of fury. It was, for him, like the first step of a flight of stairs leading back up to life.

The support, encountered in the muck just in the nick of time, just as he was about to go under, was the start of the other side of the sewer floor that had folded without breaking up and buckled under the water like a board, in one piece. A well-built pavement forms an arch and is good and solid like this. This fragment of the floor, partly submerged but solid, was a veritable ramp and, once he was on the ramp, Jean Valjean climbed up the inclined plane to the other side of the bog.

Emerging from the water, he hit a rock and fell to his knees. This seemed fitting to him and he stayed there a while, his soul plunged in we know not what words to God.

He got to his feet, shivering, frozen, rank, bent under the dying man he was lugging, all streaming with muck, his soul full of a strange light.

## VII. SOMETIMES WE HAVE RUN AGROUND WHEN WE THINK WE HAVE LANDED

He set out again once more.

But if he had not left his life behind in the subsidence, he seemed to have left his strength there. That last supreme effort had polished him off. He was now so weary that every three or four steps he was forced to stop to get his breath and he would lean against the wall. Once, he had to sit down on the bank of the channel to change Marius's position and he thought he would never get up. But if his vigor was gone, his spirit was not. He got up.

He walked on in desperation, almost fast, went about a hundred paces in this fashion without lifting his head, almost without breathing, when all of a sudden he banged into a wall. He had reached a sharp bend in the sewer and, arriving at the turn with his head down, had struck the wall. He looked up and at the end of the tunnel up ahead, in front of him, a long way down, a very long way down, he saw a light. It was not the terrible light of before; it was good, white light. It was daylight. Jean Valjean could see the way out.

A damned soul suddenly spotting the way out of Gehenna,[1] from the middle of the blazing furnace of hell, would feel what Jean Valjean then felt. They would fly frantically with the stumps of their burned wings toward that radiant door. Jean Valjean no longer felt tired, he no longer felt Marius's weight, his calves once more became calves of steel, he didn't walk, he ran. As he approached, the exit stood out more and more distinctly. It was a circular arch, not as high as the vault, which got smaller by degrees, and not as wide as the gallery, which got narrower at the same time that the vault got lower. The tunnel ended like the inside of a funnel, tightening severely in imitation of the gates of houses of detention—logical in a jail, illogical in a sewer and since corrected.

Jean Valjean reached the exit. There, he stopped. It was indeed an outlet, but there was no way out.

The arch was sealed off by a heavy gate and this gate, which, to all appearances, rarely turned on its oxidized hinges, was held fast in its stone frame by a heavy lock, red with rust, that looked like an enormous brick. You could see the keyhole and the robust sliding bolt driven deep into the iron staple. The lock was visibly locked with a double turn. It was one of those fortress locks that were rampant in the old lock-crazy Paris.

Beyond the gate, there was the open air, the river, sunlight, the embankment, very narrow but wide enough to get away, the distant quais, Paris, that bottomless pit where a person can so easily hide, the wide horizon, freedom. To the right, downriver, you could make out the pont d'Iéna, and, on the left, upriver, the pont des Invalides; the spot would have been just right for waiting till nightfall and escaping. It was one of the most deserted places in Paris: the embankment fronting the Gros-Caillou. Flies came and went through the bars of the gate.

It might have been eight-thirty in the evening. The day was coming to a close.

Jean Valjean laid Marius down along the wall on the dry part of the floor channel, then went up to the gate and gripped the bars with both hands; the shaking was frenetic, the shock nonexistent. The gate did not budge. Jean Valjean seized each bar, one by one, hoping to be able to tear out the least sturdy and use it as a lever to lift up the gate or break the lock. Not one bar shifted. A tiger's teeth are no firmer in their sockets. No lever; no possible purchase. The obstacle was invincible. There was no way of opening the gate.

Must he end it all there, then? What to do? What would happen to them? Should he go back, do the frightening course he had already covered all over again? He did not have the strength. Besides, how could he cross that bog once more when it was a miracle they had got through it in the first place? And after the bog, what about the police patrol? He would not escape that lot twice, that much was certain. And, anyway, where would he go? What direction would he take? Following the downhill slope did not mean reaching the goal. Should a person make it to some other exit, he would find it blocked off by some other plug or grate. All the exits were indubitably sealed off in this fashion. Chance had unsealed the grate by which they had entered, but obviously all the other sewer outlets and manholes were shut tight. They had only succeeded in escaping into a prison.

The jig was up. All that Jean Valjean had done was useless. God would not have it.

They were caught, the two of them, in the gloomy immense web of death, and Jean Valjean could feel that horrible spider running along the trembling black threads in the darkness.

He turned his back to the gate and flopped down on the stone floor, flattened rather than sitting, next to the ever-motionless Marius, and his head sank between his knees. No way out. As far as anguish went, this was the last straw.

Who did he think of in his profound devastation? Not of himself, nor of Marius. He thought of Cosette.

## VIII. The Torn Bit of Coat

In the middle of his annihilation a hand clapped on his shoulder and a voice that was low said to him: "Go you halves."

Was there someone in that gloom? Nothing is more dreamlike than despair. Jean Valjean thought he was dreaming. He had not heard any footsteps. Was it possible? Could it be? He looked up. A man was planted in front of him.

This man was dressed in a smock; he was barefoot; he was holding his shoes in his left hand; he had obviously taken them off to approach Jean Valjean without being heard.

Jean Valjean was not in doubt for a moment. As unforeseen as the encounter was, the man was known to him. The man was Thénardier.

Although woken up, so to speak, with a start, Jean Valjean was used to being on the alert and on the lookout for unexpected blows that you have to swiftly parry, and he once more and without further ado regained his presence of mind. Besides, the situation could hardly get any worse; at a certain level of distress a crescendo is no longer possible and even Thénardier could not make the night any blacker.

There was a moment's silence.

Thénardier raised his right hand to his forehead and shaded his eyes with it; then he knitted his eyebrows together as he blinked, which, along with a slight pursing of the mouth, typifies the sagacious attention of a man straining to place another man. He did not succeed. Jean Valjean, as we say, had his back to the light and was in any case so disfigured, so covered with mud and blood, that at high noon he would have been unrecognizable. On the other hand, lit up from the front by the light coming through the gate which shone full in his face, the light of a cellar, it is true, livid but sharp in its lividity, Thénardier, as the lively if trite metaphor has it, stood out plain as day to Jean Valjean. This imbalance in the situation was enough to ensure Jean Valjean had an advantage in the

mysterious duel that was about to begin between the two men in their two opposing camps. In the encounter that took place, Jean Valjean was veiled and
Thénardier unmasked.

Jean Valjean saw right away that Thénardier did not recognize him.

They studied each other for a moment in the half-light as though each was
taking the other's measure. Thénardier was the first to break the silence.

"How are you going to get out?"

Jean Valjean did not answer. Thénardier went on: "No way you can pick the
lock. You've got to get out of here, though."

"That's true," said Jean Valjean.

"Well, then, go you halves."

"What do you mean?"

"You've killed the man; fine. Me, I've got the key."

Thénardier pointed to Marius. He continued: "I don't know you, but I'd
like to help you. Only, you've got to be a friend."

Jean Valjean began to understand. Thénardier took him for a murderer.
Thénardier resumed: "Listen, comrade. You didn't kill this geezer without seeing what he had in his pockets. Give me my half. And I'll open the gate for you."

And pulling a huge key halfway out from under his badly torn smock, he
added: "Would you like to see how the key to freedom's made? Here it is."

Jean Valjean "stayed dumb"—the expression is Corneille the elder's[1]—to
the point of doubting that what he saw was real. It had to be Providence taking
on a horrible guise, with the good angel crawling out of the ground in the form
of Thénardier.

Thénardier thrust his fist into a big pocket hidden under his smock, fished
around, pulled out a rope, and held it out to Jean Valjean.

"Here," he said. "I'll throw in the rope while I'm at it."

"A rope, what for?"

"You'll need a stone, too, but you'll find plenty outside. There's a heap of
rubble out there."

"A stone, what for?"

"Idiot. If you're going to throw this mug in the river, you'll need a rope and
a stone; without 'em, it'll bob up and float on the water."

Jean Valjean took the rope. There is no one who hasn't taken what they are
offered without thinking.

Thénardier snapped his fingers as though he'd just had a brain wave:

"Ah, right, comrade, while I think of it: How the hell did you manage to get
out of the bog back there? I wasn't taking any chances myself. Pooh! You stink."

After a pause, he added: "I'm asking you questions but you're right not to
answer. It's your bit of an apprenticeship for the cursed quarter of an hour in
front of the examining magistrate. And then again, if you don't talk at all, you

don't run the risk of talking too loud. It's all the same to me. Just because I can't see your face and don't know your name, you'd be wrong to think I don't know who you are and what you want. I know all right. You've knocked this gentleman around a bit and now you'd like to tuck him away somewhere safe. What you need is the river, the great cover-upper-of-stuff-ups. I'm about to get you out of your predicament. Help out a mate in trouble, that's right up my alley."

While applauding Jean Valjean for holding his tongue, he was clearly trying to get him to speak. He gave his shoulder a shove to try and get a look at him side-on, and cried, though without raising his voice above the middle register he favored: "Speaking of that boghole, you're a bit finicky, aren't you? Why didn't you just dump the geezer in there?"

Jean Valjean remained silent. Thénardier went on, hoisting the old rag that served him as a cravat up as far as his Adam's apple, a gesture that completes the capable air of a man to be reckoned with: "Actually, you probably acted wisely. When the workers come tomorrow to patch up the hole they'd have found the poor sucker left there, for sure, and bit by bit, one way or another, they'd have been able to sniff you out and track you down. Someone's come through the sewer? Who? How'd he get out? Where? Did anyone see him come out? The police have got eyes in the back of their heads. The sewer's treacherous and gives you away. Such a find is a rarity, it attracts attention, not many people use the sewer to go about their business, whereas the river's anybody's. The river, that's the real cemetery in this town. After a month, they fish up your man for you in the Saint-Cloud nets. So, who gives two hoots? It's a decaying carcass, for Christ's sake! Who killed the man? Paris. And the law doesn't even put up a notice. You did the right thing."

The more loquacious Thénardier was, the more mute Jean Valjean. Thénardier shoved his shoulder again.

"Now, to conclude our business. We'll divvy it up. You've seen my key, now show me your dough."

Thénardier was haggard, smelly, sleazy, a bit threatening, yet friendly. One thing was strange; Thénardier's manner was not natural; he didn't look entirely at ease; while he didn't exactly affect an air of mystery, he kept his voice low; from time to time he placed a finger over his mouth and murmured: sshhh! It was hard to guess why. There was no one there but the two of them. Jean Valjean thought that other bandits were perhaps hidden in some recess, not far away, and that Thénardier was not too keen to share any spoils with them.

Thénardier resumed: "Let's get it over with, then. How much did this dunce here have in his pouch?"

Jean Valjean felt around in his pockets.

It was, as you will recall, his custom to always have money on him. The grim life of expediency that he was condemned to lead made this a rule for him. This time, however, he was caught off guard. In donning his National Guard uniform the night before, gloomily absorbed as he was, he had forgotten to take his wallet with him. All he had was a few loose coins in his waistcoat pocket. It only amounted to thirty or so francs! He turned his pocket inside out, all soaked with muck, and then set out a gold louis, two five-franc pieces, and five or six *gros sous* on the curb of the channel floor.

Thénardier thrust out his bottom lip with a significant twist of the neck.

"You didn't kill him for much," he said.

He started to pat, in all familiarity, Jean Valjean's pockets, followed by Marius's pockets. Jean Valjean, concerned above all with keeping his back to the light, let him go ahead. While he handled Marius's coat, Thénardier, with the dexterity of a conjurer and unbeknownst to Jean Valjean, managed to tear off a strip that he hid under his smock, probably thinking that this piece of cloth could later serve him to identify the man killed and the killer. Otherwise he did not come up with a sou more than the thirty francs.

"It's true," he said, "the two of you together, that's all you're good for."

And, forgetting his phrase "go you halves," he took the lot.

He did hesitate a bit before the *gros sous* but, upon reflection, took those, too, grumbling: "Bugger it! It's knifing people too cheap."

This done, he pulled the key out of his smock once more.

"Now, friend, you can go. It's just like at the fair here, you pay as you go. You've paid, now go."

And he started to laugh.

In offering a stranger the aid of this key and getting some man other than himself out through the gate, did he have the pure and disinterested intention of saving a murderer? That is something you may be forgiven for doubting.

Thénardier helped Jean Valjean get Marius back on his shoulders, then he headed for the gate on his bare feet, tiptoeing, beckoning to Jean Valjean to follow him; he peered outside, placed a finger to his lips and remained sort of suspended for a few seconds; the inspection done, he put the key in the lock. The bolt slid and the gate turned. There was no squeaking, no grating. It happened very smoothly. Clearly, the gate and the hinges were carefully oiled and opened more often than you would have thought. The smoothness was sinister; you could feel in it the furtive comings and goings, the silent entrances and exits of nocturnal men and the wolflike tread of crime. The sewer was evidently in cahoots with some mysterious gang. That taciturn gate was a receiver of stolen goods—a "fence."

Thénardier cracked the gate open, left just enough room for Jean Valjean to squeeze through, then shut it again, turned the key twice in the lock, and plunged back into the darkness, quiet as a breath. He seemed to walk with the velvet pads of a tiger. A moment later, that repulsive savior had melted back into the invisible.

Jean Valjean found himself outside.

## IX. MARIUS LOOKS TO BE DEAD TO ONE WHO KNOWS

He let Marius slide down onto the embankment. They were outside!

The miasmas, the darkness, the horror, were behind him. The healthful, pure, vital, joyful, freely breathable air flooded him. All around him was silence, but the lovely silence of the sun going down in the bright blue sky. Twilight had fallen; night, that great liberator, the friend of all those who need the cover of darkness to surface from some torment, was on the way. The sky offered itself everywhere you looked as an enormous calm. The river lapped at his feet with the soft smack of a kiss. You could hear the overhead dialogue of birds in their nests bidding each other good evening in the elms of the Champs-Élysées. A few stars, feebly punctuating the pale blue of the zenith and visible only to day-dreamers, made barely perceptible points of splendor in the infinite vastness.

It was that undecided and exquisite hour that says neither yes nor no. It was already dark enough for a person to be able to be lost from sight in it at some remove and still light enough for a person to be recognizable up close.

For a few seconds, Jean Valjean was irresistibly overcome by all that awesome yet soft serenity; such moments of forgetting occur; suffering stops harassing the miserable; all worry slips away; peace wraps the dreamer like night; and in the glow of twilight the soul twinkles with stars, mimicking the sky as it lights up. Jean Valjean could not help but contemplate this vast bright darkness above him; pensive, he bathed in ecstasy and prayer within the magnificent silence of the eternal heavens. Then, swiftly, as though a sense of duty was coming back to him, he bent down to Marius and, scooping up some water in the palm of his hand, gently threw a few drops over his face. Marius's eyelids did not lift; but he breathed through his half-open mouth.

Jean Valjean was about to plunge his hand in the river again when all of a sudden he felt strangely uneasy, as you do when you know someone is behind you, even though you can't see them. We have talked about this feeling, which everyone is familiar with, before. He wheeled round.

Someone was indeed behind him, just as there had been a moment ago.

A tall man, wrapped in a long redingote, with his arms folded, the lead knob of a club showing in his right hand, was standing a few feet behind Jean Valjean as he crouched over Marius.

There in the gloaming, it seemed to be a sort of apparition. A simple man would have been frightened of it because of the gathering dark, and a reflective man because of the club. Jean Valjean knew that it was Javert.

The reader has no doubt guessed that Thénardier's tracker was none other than Javert. Javert, after his unhoped-for exit from the barricade, had gone to the prefecture of police, had given a verbal report to the prefect in person during a brief audience, then had immediately resumed his duties, which involved— you will remember the note seized on him earlier—a certain surveillance of the right bank embankment at the Champs-Élysées, which had excited the attention of the police for some time. There, he had spotted Thénardier and followed him. You know the rest.

You will also understand that the gate that so obligingly opened for Jean Valjean was a bit of cunning on Thénardier's part. Thénardier could smell that Javert was still around; a watched man has a scent that does not let him down; he had to throw the bloodhound a bone. A murderer, what a godsend! It meant cutting his losses, which is an option a person must never turn down. Thénardier, in shoving Jean Valjean outside in his stead, gave the police a bit of bait, threw them off his own scent, got himself overlooked in a much bigger haul, rewarded Javert for waiting, which always placates a police spy, earned himself thirty francs, and found a means, one he was certainly counting on, of bolting with the aid of this diversion.

Jean Valjean had gone from one pitfall to another.

These two encounters, one right after the other, first Thénardier, then Javert, shook him up.

Javert did not recognize Jean Valjean, who, as we say, did not look himself at the moment. He kept his arms folded, quietly ensured his club was firmly in hand, and said in a calm, brisk voice: "Who are you?"

"Me."

"Who is me?"

"Jean Valjean."

Javert stuck the club between his teeth, bent his knees, leaned forward, placed his two powerful hands on Jean Valjean's shoulders, clamping them like two vices, examined him and saw that it was him. Their faces were almost touching. Javert's gaze was terrible.

Jean Valjean remained inert under Javert's grip like a lion submitting to the claws of a lynx.

"Inspector Javert," he said, "you've got me. Besides, since this morning, I've considered myself your prisoner. I didn't give you my address in order to try and get away from you. Take me. Only, grant me one thing."

Javert seemed not to hear. He bored into Jean Valjean with his hard stare. His puckered chin pushed his lips up toward his nose, a sign of fierce musing. Finally, he let go of Jean Valjean, straightened up all in one go, took his club fully in hand, and, as in a dream, murmured more than spoke these questions: "What are you doing here? And who is this man?"

He continued using *vous* rather than *tu* in addressing Jean Valjean.

Jean Valjean answered, and the sound of his voice seemed to wake Javert: "He is precisely what I wanted to speak to you about. Do what you like with me, but first help me get him home. That's all I ask you."

Javert's face tensed the way it did whenever anyone believed him capable of some concession. Yet he did not say no.

He bent down again, pulled a handkerchief from his pocket, and wiped Marius's bloody forehead.

"This man was at the barricade," he said in a small voice, as though speaking to himself. "He's the one they called Marius."

A first-class spy, the man had observed all, heard all, absorbed all, and retained all, believing himself about to die; he went on spying even at death's door; even with one foot in the grave, he went on taking notes.

He seized Marius's hand, looked for a pulse.

"He's one of the wounded," said Jean Valjean.

"He's one of the dead," said Javert.

Jean Valjean answered: "No. Not yet."

"So, you carried him here from the barricade?" observed Javert.

He must have been very preoccupied indeed for him not to dwell on this troubling rescue via the sewer, not even to notice Jean Valjean's silence at his question.

Jean Valjean, for his part, seemed to have only one thought. He resumed: "He lives in the Marais, rue des Filles-du-Calvaire, with his grandfather— I forget the name."

Jean Valjean fumbled in Marius's coat, pulled out the wallet, opened it at the page penciled in by Marius, and handed it to Javert.

There was still enough light floating in the air to be able to read by. Javert, moreover, had the catlike phosphorescence of night owls in his eyes. He deciphered the few lines written by Marius and muttered: "Gillenormand, rue des Filles-du-Calvaire, number six."

Then he yelled: "Driver!"

You will remember the fiacre was waiting, just in case.

Javert held onto Marius's wallet.

A moment later, the carriage, which had come down the watering-hole ramp, was on the embankment, Marius was lifted onto the back seat, and Javert was sitting next to Jean Valjean on the front seat.

When the door was shut again, the fiacre pulled away rapidly, going back along the quais in the direction of the Bastille.

They turned off the quais and into the streets. The driver, a black silhouette on his box, whipped his bony horses. Icy silence inside the fiacre. Marius, motionless, his body propped up against the back corner, his head lolling on his chest, arms dangling, legs stiff, appeared to be waiting now only for a coffin;

Jean Valjean seemed to be made of shadow, and Javert, of stone; and in this carriage full of night, whose interior turned a livid white, as though struck by intermittent lightning, every time it passed a lamp, chance seemed to have brought together in grim confrontation three tragic immobilities, the corpse, the specter, and the statue.

## X. RETURN OF THE SON PRODIGAL WITH HIS LIFE

At every jolt from the pavement, a drop of blood fell from Marius's hair. Night had closed in by the time the fiacre pulled up at no. 6, rue des Filles-du-Calvaire.

Javert was first to set foot on the ground, took in at a glance the number above the porte cochère, and lifting up the heavy wrought-iron knocker, embellished in the old-fashioned way with a billy goat and a satyr clashing, gave it a violent bang. One side of the double door cracked open a little and Javert gave it a shove. The porter stuck his head out, yawning, vaguely awake, candle in hand.

Everyone in the house was asleep. They go to bed early in the Marais, especially on days when there's a riot on. This good old quartier, scared stiff by the revolution, takes refuge in sleep, just as children, when they hear the bogeyman coming, quickly duck their heads under the covers.

Meanwhile, Jean Valjean and the driver lifted Marius out of the fiacre, Jean Valjean holding him under the armpits and the driver under the knees.

While he was carrying Marius in this fashion, Jean Valjean slipped a hand under his clothes, which were pretty much torn to shreds, and felt his chest to reassure himself that his heart was still beating. It was even beating a little less feebly as if the motion of the carriage had produced a certain return to life.

Javert called out to the porter in the tone appropriate for the government to take with the porter of a troublemaker: "Anyone here by the name of Gillenormand?"

"That's here. What do you want with him?"

"We've brought his son home for him."

"His son?" said the porter in a daze.

"He's dead."

Jean Valjean, who came up behind Javert, ragged and dirty, and whom the porter regarded with some horror, motioned to him with his head that he was not. The porter did not seem to understand either Javert's words or Jean Valjean's signs.

Javert continued: "He's been at the barricade, and now, here he is."

"At the barricade!" cried the porter.

"He's gone and got himself killed. Go and wake up the father."

The porter did not budge.

"Go on, then!" Javert barked.

And he added: "There will be a funeral here tomorrow."

For Javert, the usual incidents of the public highway were classified according to category, which is the basis of foresight and oversight, and every eventuality had its pigeonhole; the possible facts were filed away in drawers, so to speak, from where they emerged, as the occasion arose, in variable quantities; there was, in the street, a bit of a racket, a bit of a riot, a bit of a carnival, a bit of a funeral.

The porter went no further than waking up Basque. Basque woke up Nicolette, Nicolette woke up Aunt Gillenormand. As for the grandfather, they let him sleep on, telling themselves he'd find out soon enough.

They carried Marius up to the first floor, without anyone, moreover, knowing anything about it in the other parts of the house, and they laid him out on an old sofa in Monsieur Gillenormand's antechamber; and while Basque went off to look for a doctor and Nicolette opened the linen cupboards, Jean Valjean felt Javert tap him on the shoulder. He understood and went back downstairs with Javert following hot on his heels.

The porter watched them leave just as he had watched them arrive, in drowsy horror. They climbed back up into the fiacre, and the driver onto his box.

"Inspector Javert," said Jean Valjean, "grant me one more thing."

"What?" asked Javert rudely.

"Let me go back to my place for a moment. After that, you can do what you like with me."

Javert remained silent for a few moments, with his chin tucked into the collar of his coat; then he pulled down the window in front.

"Driver," he said, "rue de l'Homme-Armé, number seven."

## XI. The Absolute, Rocked

They did not open their mouths again the entire trip.

What did Jean Valjean want? To finish what he had started; to warn Cosette, to tell her where Marius was, perhaps give her some other useful information, and make, if he could, certain final arrangements. As for himself, as for what concerned him personally, it was all over; he had been nabbed by Javert and did not resist; anyone else, in such a situation, might perhaps have thought vaguely of the rope that Thénardier had given him and of the bars of the first dungeon that he would enter; but since the bishop, Jean Valjean, when confronted by any violence, including against himself, felt a profoundly religious hesitation. We cannot stress this point enough.

Suicide, that mysterious assault and battery against the unknown, which may to a certain extent involve the death of the soul, was impossible for Jean Valjean.

At the entrance to the rue de l'Homme-Armé, the fiacre stopped. The street was too narrow for carriages to be able to go in. Javert and Jean Valjean got down.

The driver humbly pointed out to "Monsieur l'inspecteur" that the Utrecht velvet of his carriage was all stained by the blood of the murdered man and by the mud of the murderer. That was what he had understood, anyway. He added that some kind of compensation was due to him. At the same time, pulling his notebook out of his pocket, he begged Monsieur l'inspecteur to have the goodness to write down for him "a bit of a statement to that effect." Javert pushed away the notebook the driver held out to him and said: "How much do you need, being on standby and the trip itself included?"

"There's seven and a quarter hours," answered the driver, "and my velvet was brand-new. Eighty francs, Monsieur l'inspecteur."

Javert took four napoléons out of his pocket and sent the fiacre packing.

Jean Valjean thought Javert intended to conduct him on foot to the Blancs-Manteaux guardhouse or the Archives guardhouse, which are both close by. They stepped into the street. It was, as usual, deserted. Javert followed Jean Valjean. They reached no. 7. Jean Valjean knocked. The door opened.

"Good," said Javert. "Go up."

He added with a strange expression, as though it cost him quite an effort to speak in such a way: "I'll wait for you here."

Jean Valjean looked at Javert. This way of doing things was not at all in Javert's repertoire. Yet the fact that Javert now displayed a sort of arrogant confidence, the confidence of a cat allowing a mouse the freedom of the length of its claw, resolved as Jean Valjean was to give himself up and have done with it— this could hardly surprise him much. He pushed the door, stepped into the house, shouted to the porter, who was in bed and had pulled the cord from his bed without getting up, "It's me!" and mounted the stairs.

When he reached the first floor, he paused. All painful paths have their stations. The window on the landing, which was a sash window, was open. As in many old houses, the stairway let in the light and looked onto the street. The streetlamp, standing exactly opposite, threw light on the stairs and that meant economizing on lighting.

Jean Valjean, either to take a breath of air, or simply without thinking, stuck his head out the window, and leaned out over the street. It is a short street and the lamp lit it from one end to the other. Jean Valjean felt suddenly dizzy with amazement; there was no one there anymore.

Javert had gone.

## XII. THE GRANDFATHER

Basque and the porter had carried Marius into the salon and he was still stretched out motionless on the sofa where they had first laid him. The doctor, who had been sent for, had come running. Aunt Gillenormand had got out of bed.

Aunt Gillenormand came and went, aghast, clutching her hands, unable to do anything but mutter: "God, is it possible?" She added an occasional: "Everything will be covered in blood!" When the initial horror had subsided, a certain philosophical attitude toward the situation came over her and was translated into this exclamation: "It was bound to end this way!" She did not go so far as the "I told you so!" that is customary on such occasions.

On the doctor's orders, a camp bed had been set up next to the sofa. The doctor examined Marius and, after establishing that there was a persistent pulse, that the wounded man had no deep stab wounds in his chest, and that the blood at the corner of his mouth came from his nasal cavity, he had him laid out flat on the bed, without a pillow, his head level with his body, and even a bit lower, and his chest bare to facilitate breathing. At the sight of them undressing Marius, Mademoiselle Gillenormand withdrew. She began saying her rosary in her room.

Marius had no internal injuries; a bullet, absorbed by his wallet, had swerved and raked across his ribs in a hideous gash but without going deep, and so without danger. The long trip underground had completed the dislocation of his broken collarbone and there were serious complications there. His arms had saber cuts. No scar disfigured his face; his head, on the other hand, was badly hacked about; what would become of these head wounds? Did they stop at the scalp? Did they eat into the skull? It was not yet possible to say. One grave symptom was that they had caused unconsciousness and you don't always recover from unconsciousness of the kind. The hemorrhaging, moreover, had worn the wounded man out. But below the waist, the lower part of his body had been protected by the barricade.

Basque and Nicolette ripped up linen and prepared bandages; Nicolette sewed them, Basque rolled them up. There being no lint, the doctor had stanched the blood flowing from the wounds with wads of cotton wool for the time being. Beside the bed, three candles burned on a table where the surgical instruments were spread out. The doctor washed Marius's face and hair with cold water. A full bucket turned red in an instant. The porter stood by, his candle in hand, providing the light.

The doctor seemed lost in sad thoughts. From time to time, he shook his head as though answering some question he had silently put to himself. They were a bad sign for the sick man, these mysterious conversations the doctor had with himself.

Just as the doctor was wiping Marius's face and gently touching his still-closed lids, a door opened at the back of the salon and a long pale figure appeared. It was the grandfather.

For two days the riot had strongly agitated, outraged, and preoccupied Monsieur Gillenormand. He had not been able to sleep a wink the night before and had had a fever all day. That evening, he had gone to bed far earlier than usual, advising that everything in the house be locked up, and he had finally dozed off from sheer fatigue

Old men's sleep is fragile; Monsieur Gillenormand's room was next door to the salon, and no matter what precautions they may have taken, the noise had woken him up. Surprised at the crack of light he saw under his door, he had gotten out of bed and groped his way along.

He was standing at the half-open door, with one hand on the doorknob, his head tipped forward a little and wobbling, his body wrapped tightly in a white dressing gown as rigid and wrinkle-free as a shroud, astonished; and he looked like a phantom peering into a tomb.

He saw the bed, and on the mattress this young man covered in blood, white with a waxy whiteness, eyes closed, mouth agape, lips pale, naked to the waist, slashed to ribbons with dark red wounds, lying there motionless under harsh light.

The grandfather shivered from head to toe, as much as ossified limbs can shiver, and his eyes, their corneas yellow due to his great age, filmed over with a sort of glassy gleam. His whole face instantly took on the ashen boniness of a skeleton's head, his arms fell dangling as though a spring in them had broken, and his stupor expressed itself in the way he spread the fingers of his two badly shaking old hands, his knees buckled forward, showing his poor bare legs bristling with white hairs through the gap in his dressing gown, and he murmured: "Marius!"

"Monsieur," said Basque, "they have just brought Monsieur home. He was at the barricade and—"

"He's dead!" cried the old man in a terrible voice. "Ah! The rascal!"

Then a sort of sepulchral transfiguration made this centenarian stand as tall and erect as a young man.

"Monsieur," he said, "you are the doctor. Begin by telling me one thing. He is dead, isn't he?"

The doctor, in a paroxysm of anxiety, remained silent.

Monsieur Gillenormand wrung his hands with a frightening burst of laughter.

"He's dead! He's dead! He got himself killed at the barricades! Out of hatred for me! It's to spite me that he did that! Ah, bloodsucker! This is the way he comes back to me! Misery of my life, he's dead!"

He went to the window, flung it open wide as though he was suffocating, and, standing facing the darkness, he started talking to the night out there in the street: "Riddled with holes, sabered, butchered, exterminated, hacked to pieces, carved up! You see that, the little rogue! He knew very well that I was waiting for him, and that I had them fix up his room and that I had them hang his portrait from when he was a little boy by my bed! He knew very well that he only had to come back and that I'd been calling him back for years and that I spent every night in my corner by the fire with my hands on my knees not knowing what to do, losing my mind worrying about him! You knew all that very well, and that you only had to come home and say, 'It's me' and you'd be master of the house and that I'd do whatever you said and that you could do whatever you liked with your old codger of a grandfather! You knew that very well, and you said: 'No, he's a royalist, I won't go!' And off you went to the barricades, and you got yourself killed out of spite! To get revenge for what I said to you about Monsieur le duc de Berry! That's what's so despicable! Go to bed, then, and sleep soundly. He is dead. That's what I've got to wake up to."

The doctor, who was beginning to worry on both scores, left Marius for a moment and went over to Monsieur Gillenormand and took his arm. The grandfather spun round, looked at him with widened bloodshot eyes, and said to him calmly: "Monsieur, I thank you. I am calm, I am a man, I saw the death of Louis XVI, I know how to bear up under events. There is one thing that is terrible, though, and that is to think that it is your newspapers that do all the damage. You can have all the scribblers, gasbags, lawyers, orators, tribunes, debates, progress, enlightenment, rights of man, freedom of the press you want, and this is how they bring your children back home for you! Ah, Marius! It's abominable! Killed! Dead before me! A barricade! Ah, the little cur! Doctor, you live in the neighborhood, I believe? Oh, I know you well. I see your cabriolet going by from my window. Let me tell you something. You'd be mistaken to think I'm angry. One does not get angry at a dead man. That would be stupid. I raised this child, you see. I was already old when he was still only a toddler. He used to play in the Tuileries with his little spade and his little chair, and so the keepers would not scold him, I'd get my cane and fill in the holes he made in the ground with his spade as he made them. One day he yelled, 'Down with Louis XVIII!' and off he went. It's not my fault. He was all rosy and blond. His mother is dead. Have you noticed how all little children are blond? Where does that come from? He is the son of one of those brigands of the Loire. But children are innocent of the crimes of their fathers. I remember when he was just this high. He could never manage to pronounce the *d*s. He chattered away so sweetly and so unintelligibly you'd have thought he was a bird. I remember once, in front of the Farnese Hercules, they all stood around in a circle to marvel at him and admire him, he was so beautiful, that child! He had a head like the ones in paintings. I put on my gruff voice for him, I frightened him with my cane, but he knew very well that it was all just in fun. In the morning, when he used to come into my room, I would growl at him, but for me it was like sunshine streaming in. You can't defend yourself against these little mites. They take hold of you, they hold on to you, they never let go of you. The truth is that there never was a little love like that child there. Now, what do you have to say for your Lafayettes, your Benjamin Constants, and your Tirecuir de Corcelles,[1] that have gone and killed him for me! It can't go on like this."

He went over to Marius, still livid and motionless, the doctor once more by his side, and he began to wring his hands again. The white lips of the old man moved as though they had a will of their own, and let slip, like the exhalations of a death rattle, almost indistinct words that could barely be heard: "Ah, heartless! Ah, clubbist![2] Ah, scoundrel! Ah, Septembrist!" Reproaches made tonelessly by a dying man to a corpse.

Little by little, as inner eruptions will always out, he strung his words together again in a sequence, but the grandfather appeared to have no strength left to utter them; his voice was so subdued and faint that it seemed to come from the other side of an abyss: "I don't care, I'll die, too, I will. And don't tell me that in all Paris there wasn't some little vixen who'd have been glad to make this miserable wretch happy! A young rascal who, instead of having fun and enjoying life, took himself off to fight and got himself shot to bits like a noodle! And who for? What for? For the republic! Instead of going dancing at the Chaumière, as young people are supposed to! What's the good of being twenty years old, I ask you. The republic, what a load of poppycock! Poor mothers, go and make pretty boys, why don't you! So that's that, he's dead. That'll be two graves under the porte cochère. So this is how you spruce yourself up for the fine eyes of this General Lamarque! A sword-slinger! A blatherskite! Fancy getting yourself killed for a dead man! If that isn't enough to drive a man mad! Go and figure that out! At twenty years old! And without turning a hair to see if he was leaving someone behind! So now we poor old blighters are forced to die all alone. Croak in your corner, old owl! Well, then, actually, so much the better, it's what I was hoping for, it will kill me stone dead. I'm too old, I'm a hundred years old, I'm a hundred thousand years old, I earned the right to be dead long ago. This blow will do the trick. So, it's over, what luck! What's the good of making him sniff ammonia and all these other drugs? You're wasting your time, you numskull of a quack! Get out of there, he's dead, dead as a doornail. Take it from me—I'm one who knows, I'm dead, too. He hasn't done it by halves. Yes, these are ghastly times, ghastly, ghastly, and here is what I think of you, of your ideas, of your systems, of your masters, of your oracles, of your doctors, of your little pipsqueaks of writers, of your weasels of philosophers, and of all the revolutions that have terrified the flocks of crows in the Tuileries for the last sixty years! And since you showed no mercy in getting yourself killed like this, I won't even feel any grief at your death, do you hear, you assassin!"

At that moment, Marius's eyelids slowly lifted, and his eyes, still filmy with drowsy amazement, rested on Monsieur Gillenormand.

"Marius!" cried the old man. "Marius! My darling Marius! My dear boy! My beloved son! You've opened your eyes, you are looking at me, you are alive, thank you!"

And he promptly passed out.

# BOOK FOUR

# JAVERT DERAILED

## I. JAVERT DERAILED

Javert had walked away from the rue de l'Homme-Armé with slow tread.

He walked with his head down for the first time in his life, and also for the first time in his life with his hands behind his back. Until that day, Javert had only ever adopted, of Napoléon's two poses, the one that expresses resolution, arms folded over the chest; the one that expresses uncertainty, hands behind the back, was unknown to him. Now a change had occurred; his whole person, slow and somber, was stamped with anxiety.

He plunged into the silent streets. Yet he was headed in only one direction. He took a shortcut to the Seine, reached the quai des Ormes, followed the quai, passed La Grève and stopped, at some distance from the place du Châtelet guardhouse, at the corner of the pont Notre-Dame. There, between the pont Notre-Dame and the Pont-au-Change, on the one hand, and between the quai de la Mégisserie and the quai aux Fleurs, on the other, the Seine forms a sort of squared-off lake crossed by a rapid.

This point of the Seine is dreaded by bargemen. Nothing is more dangerous than this rapid, confined in those days and churned up by the piles of the bridge mill, since demolished. The two bridges, being so close to each other, increase the peril; the water rushes mightily under the arches. It rolls there in wide and terrible corrugations; it gathers and builds; the torrent charges at the piles of the bridges as though to rip them out with fat liquid ropes. Men who fall in there never reappear; the best swimmers drown.

Javert leaned on the parapet with both elbows, his chin in both hands, and while his nails mechanically raked through his thick sideburns, he reflected.

A new thing, a revolution, a catastrophe, had just taken place deep inside him and he had good grounds for examining himself. Javert was in appalling pain. For some hours now, Javert had stopped being a simple man. He was deeply troubled; that brain, so limpid in its blindness, had lost its transparency; there was a cloud in the crystal. Javert felt duty splitting in two in his conscience and he could not dodge the fact. When he had run into Jean Valjean so unexpectedly on the bank of the Seine, he had felt something like a wolf catching its prey again—but also like a dog that once more finds his master.

He saw two roads before him, both equally straight, but he saw two of them; and this terrified him, for he had never in his life known more than one straight line. And what made the anguish more poignant was that the two roads were radically opposed. One of the two straight lines ruled out the other. Which of the two was the true one? His situation was more than he could bear.

To owe your life to a malefactor, to accept this debt and pay it back, to be, in spite of yourself, on a par with a fugitive from justice and to pay him back for a good deed done by another good deed; to let him say to you, "Off you go" and to say to him in turn, "You're free," to sacrifice duty, that all-encompassing obligation, to personal motives, and to feel in those personal motives something that was also all-encompassing and, perhaps, superior; to betray society in order to remain true to your conscience—that all these absurd things should happen and should come and heap themselves upon him, absolutely floored him.

One thing had amazed him and that was that Jean Valjean had spared him; and one thing had petrified him, and that was that he, Javert, had spared Jean Valjean.

What had he come to? He looked for himself but could not find himself anymore.

What was he to do now? To hand over Jean Valjean was bad; to let Jean Valjean go free was bad. In the first case, the man of the law would fall lower than the man of the galleys; in the second, a convict would rise above the law and trample it underfoot. Both cases meant dishonor for him, Javert. Whichever course he took, there was a fall. Destiny has certain extreme overhangs that loom, sheer, over the abyss of the impossible and beyond which life is no more than a free fall. Javert was standing on one of those overhangs.

One of the things worrying him was being made to think. The very violence of all these contradictory emotions forced him to do so. Thinking was not something he was used to and it was oddly painful.

Thinking always involves a certain amount of inner revolt and he was annoyed at having anything like that in him.

Thinking, on any subject at all outside the narrow circle of his functions, would have been pointless and tiring for him no matter what; but thinking about the day that had just run its course was torture. Yet he had to look inside his conscience after such a series of shake-ups and give an account of himself.

What he had just done sent a shiver down his spine. He—he, Javert—had seen fit to decide, contrary to all police regulations, contrary to the whole social and judicial system, contrary to the code as a whole, in favor of a release; that had suited him; he had substituted his personal concerns for public concerns. Wasn't that beyond the pale? Every time he faced this unspeakable action that he had committed head-on, he shuddered from head to toe. What could he reconcile himself to doing? There was only one resort left to him: to return swiftly to the rue de l'Homme-Armé and have Jean Valjean locked up. It was clear that this was what had to be done. He could not do it.

Something barred the way to him on that side. Something? What? Could there be anything else in the world besides law courts, binding verdicts, the police, and authority? Javert was shattered.

A galley slave, sacred! A convict justice could not seize! And this, due to Javert!

That Javert and Jean Valjean, the man made to ruthlessly mete out punishment and the man made to submit to it, that these two men, who were the two sides of the same coin known as the legal system, had come to this, to both place themselves above the law—wasn't this terrifying?

What then! Would such outrages be allowed to happen and no one be punished! Would Jean Valjean be allowed to be stronger than the entire social order, to be free and he, Javert, continue to eat the government's bread!

His thoughts gradually became unbearably black.

He could also have reproached himself somewhat over the insurgent who was taken back to the rue des Filles-du-Calvaire while he was at it; but he didn't think of that. The lesser fault got lost in the bigger one. Besides, the insurgent was obviously dead and, legally, death puts an end to pursuit.

Jean Valjean, that was what was weighing on his mind.

Jean Valjean threw him. All the axioms that had propped up his whole life collapsed before that man. Jean Valjean's generosity toward him, Javert, devastated him. Other deeds that he remembered and that he had once dismissed as lies and acts of madness, came back to him now as real facts. Monsieur Madeleine reappeared behind Jean Valjean and the two figures merged into one—one that was to be revered. Javert felt that something awful was seeping into his soul, admiration for a convict. Respect for a galley slave, was that possible? He shuddered at it, yet could not shake it off. There was no point trying to fight it; he was reduced to admitting, in his deepest heart, the sublimeness of that poor miserable bastard. This was monstrous.

A benevolent malefactor, a compassionate convict, gentle, helpful, clement, doing good in return for bad, offering forgiveness in return for hate, favoring pity over revenge, preferring to be destroyed himself to destroying his enemy, saving the one who had brought him down, kneeling at the pinnacle of virtue, closer to an angel than a man! Javert was forced to admit that this monster existed. It could not go on like this.

Of course, and we must insist on this, he had not surrendered without resisting this monster, this loathsome angel, this vile hero, who outraged him almost as much as he amazed him. Twenty times, when he was in that carriage face-to-face with Jean Valjean, the legal tiger in him had roared. Twenty times he had been tempted to throw himself at Jean Valjean, to seize him and devour him, that is, arrest him. What could be simpler, in effect? To shout out at the first guardhouse they came to: "Here is a fugitive from justice who has returned illegally!" To call the gendarmes and tell them, "This man is yours!" and then be on his way, to leave the damned outcast there, forget about the rest, not get involved, not interfere in anything again. This man is forever a prisoner of the law; the law will do with him what it likes. What could be more just? Javert had told himself all that; he had tried to carry on regardless, to act, to apprehend the man, and, then as now, he had not been able to; and every time his hand had shot up convulsively toward Jean Valjean's collar, his hand had dropped again, as though under an enormous weight, and in the back of his mind, a voice, a strange voice, cried out to him: "Go on, then. Hand over your savior. Then have them bring you Pontius Pilate's washbasin[1] and wash your claws."

His thoughts then turned back to himself, and beside Jean Valjean ennobled, he saw himself, Javert, demeaned. A convict was his benefactor!

And another thing, why had he allowed that man to let him live? He had every right to be killed, at that barricade. He ought to have exercised that right. Rallied the other insurgents to his aid against Jean Valjean, got himself shot by force, that would have been better.

His supreme anguish was the evaporation of all certainty. He felt torn up by the roots, annihilated. The code was now a mere stub in his hand. He was facing scruples of an unknown kind. An emotional revelation was taking shape within him and it was entirely distinct from assertion of the law, till then his sole measuring stick. To keep to his former honesty was no longer enough. A whole order of unexpected acts surged up and subjugated him. A whole new world appeared to his soul: kindness accepted and returned, devotion, miséricorde, leniency, the havoc wreaked on austerity by pity, acceptance of other people, no more definitive condemnation, no more damnation, the possibility of a tear pearling in the eye of the law, some indefinable sense of justice according to God's rules that was the reverse of justice according to man. He saw in the darkness the terrifying sun of an unknown morality dawning; and he was appalled and dazzled by it. Like an owl forced to gaze out of an eagle's eyes.

He told himself that it was true, then, that there were exceptions, that authority could be unseated, that the rules could be brought up short by a deed, that not everything was framed within the text of the code, that the unforeseen commanded obedience, that the virtue of a convict could present a snare for the virtue of a public servant, that the monstrous could be divine, that destiny set up these kinds of ambushes, and he thought with despair that even he had not been safe from a surprise.

He was forced to acknowledge that goodness existed. This convict had been good. And he had just been good himself, which was unheard of. Clearly, he was becoming depraved. He found himself spineless. He horrified himself.

The ideal for Javert was not to be humane, to be great, to be sublime; it was to be irreproachable. Well, he had just faltered.

How had he come to this? How had all this happened? He could not have said how, not even to himself. He took his head in his two hands but it was no good, he could not manage to explain it to himself.

He had certainly always had the intention of handing Jean Valjean back over to the law, whose captive Jean Valjean was, while he, Javert, was its slave. He had not admitted to himself for a single instant, while he held him, that he was thinking of letting him go. It was in a way without his being aware of it that his hand had opened and released him.

All kinds of puzzling new doors began to crack open before his eyes. He put himself questions and gave himself answers, and his answers scared him. He asked himself this: "This convict, this desperado, whom I pursued to the point of persecution, and who had me under his foot, and could have taken his revenge, and who should have done, every bit as much out of resentment as for his security, in granting me life, in sparing me, what did he do? His duty? No. Something more. And me, in sparing him in turn, what did I do? My duty? No. Something more. So there is something more than duty?" This is where he became alarmed; his balance was out of whack, the scales tipped; one of the scale pans toppled into the abyss, the other flew off up into the heavens; and Javert was no less horrified by the one on high than by the one down below. Without in the least being what is known in the world as a Voltairean, or a philosopher, or a skeptic, being, on the contrary, instinctively respectful of the established Church, he knew it only as an august fragment of the social whole; law and order was his dogma and was enough for him; since he had come of age and become a public servant, he had poured just about all his religion into the police, being, and here we use the terms without the least irony and in their most serious sense, being, as we say, a spy the way another man is a priest. He had a superior, one Monsieur Gisquet; till that day he had barely given a thought to that other superior, God.

This new chief, God, he sensed unexpectedly and this disturbed him.

He was disoriented by this unforeseen presence; he did not know what to do with this particular superior, aware as he was that the subordinate is bound always to bow and scrape, that he must not disobey or blame or discuss, and that, in relation to a superior who throws him too much, the inferior has no other recourse than to hand in his resignation. But how do you go about handing in your resignation to God?

Be that as it may, and it was always to this that he came back, one fact overruled all else for him and that was that he had just committed a terrible offense. He had just turned a blind eye to a recidivist in breach of his ban. He had just set a galley slave free. He had just robbed the laws of a man who was theirs by rights. He had done that. He could not understand himself anymore. He was not sure he was himself. The very reasons for his action escaped him, all that was left of them was vertigo. He had lived till that moment on the sort of blind faith that engenders a dour probity. That faith was leaving him, that probity was letting him down. All that he had believed was coming apart at the seams. Truths he wanted nothing to do with obsessed him inescapably. From now on, he had to be another man. He was suffering the strange pangs of a conscience suddenly operated on for cataracts. He could see what he hated seeing. He felt emptied, useless, cut off from his past life, demoted, dissolved. Authority was dead in him. He had no reason to go on living. What a terrible situation! To be moved!

To be granite, and to have doubts! To be the very statue of punishment, cast all of a piece in the mold of the law, and to suddenly realize that under your breast of bronze you have something absurd and unruly that almost resembles a heart! To come to this—returning good for good—even though you have told yourself till then that this particular good was bad! To be a watchdog and lick! To be ice and melt! To be a vise and turn into a hand! To suddenly feel your fingers opening! To let go—appalling! A human projectile, no longer knowing what path to take and recoiling!

To be obliged to admit to yourself: that infallibility is not infallible, that there may be error in dogma, that the code does not have the last word, society is not perfect, authority is ambiguous and can vacillate, the immutable can crack, judges are only men, the law can be mistaken, the courts can be wrong! To see a fissure in the immense blue of the firmament!

What was happening inside Javert was the diverting of a rectilinear conscience, the throwing off course of a soul, the smashing of a probity irresistibly launched straight ahead and shattering against God. Of course, this was strange. That the engine driver of order, that the mechanic of authority, mounted on the blind iron horse of the straight and narrow, could be thrown by a shaft of light! That the incommutable, the direct, the correct, the geometric, the passive, the perfect, could bend! That there was for the locomotive a road to Damascus!

God, who is always within man, and resistant, He the true conscience, to the false, stopping the spark from going out, ordering the sunbeam to remember the sun, enjoining the soul to recognize the true absolute when faced with the fictitious absolute; indestructible humanity, the inadmissible human heart, that splendid phenomenon, the most beautiful perhaps of our inner wonders, did Javert understand it? Did Javert fathom it? Did Javert even register it? Obviously not. But the pressure of the incomprehensible, the incontestable, was so great he felt his skull cracking open.

He was more a victim of this miracle than transfigured by it. He endured it, exasperated. He only saw in all that an immense difficulty in being. It seemed to him that from that point on, his breathing would be forever labored. To have the unknown hanging over his head was not something he was used to.

Until now all that had been hanging over him had been, in his eyes, a clean, simple, limpid surface; nothing unknown or obscure there; nothing that wasn't defined, coordinated, linked, precise, exact, circumscribed, limited, closed; completely foreseen. Authority was something flat; no falling there, no vertigo before it. Javert had never seen the unknown except down below. The irregular, the unexpected, the disorderly unlocking of chaos, the possibility of sliding into an abyss—this is what happened in lower realms, to rebels, to rotters, to those poor bastards, the dregs. Now Javert was tipping over backward and he was suddenly scared by this unheard-of apparition: an abyss up above. Hell! A person was completely demolished! A person was absolutely thrown! What could a man hold on to? What a man was convinced of was crumbling!

What! The chink in society's armor could be found by some magnanimous outcast! What! An honest servant of the law could suddenly find himself caught between two crimes, the crime of letting a man get away and the crime of arresting him! All was not clear in the instructions given to the public servant by the government! Duty could have dead ends! Jesus Christ! All this was real! Was it true that a former crook, buckled under the weight of his convictions, could straighten out and end up being in the right? Was it conceivable? Were there really cases, then, where the law should back off in the face of crime transfigured, and stammer its excuses?

Yes, it had happened! And Javert saw him! And Javert touched him! And not only could he not deny it, but he had a hand in it. These things were real. It was abominable that real facts could wind up getting so twisted.

If the facts did their duty, they would stick to being evidence in law; the facts are God-given. Was anarchy now about to descend from on high?

And so—with the distortion caused by anguish and the optical illusion caused by extreme dismay, anything that might have checked and corrected his impression evaporated, and society, and the human race, and the whole world, now looked to him to be simply hideous—and so punishment, the thing judged, the force due to legislation, the decrees of the sovereign courts, the magistracy, the government, prevention and repression, official wisdom, legal infallibility, the principle of authority, all the dogmas on which rest political and civilian security, sovereignty, justice, the logic devolving from the code, the social absolute, public truth, all that was now wreckage, rubble, chaos; himself,

Javert, the keeper of order, incorruptibility at the service of the police, the heaven-sent mastiff guarding society, was defeated and floored; and on this whole ruin, there was one man left standing, with a green cap on his head and a halo over his brow; this was the shattering upheaval, spinning him head over heels, to which he had come; this was the terrifying vision now lodged in his soul.

That this could be bearable. No.

It was a violent state, if ever there was one. There were only two ways out. One was to go resolutely to Jean Valjean and to slam the jailbird back in the dungeon. The other . . .

Javert pushed off from the parapet and, holding his head high this time, set out with firm tread for the guardhouse indicated by a lantern at a corner of the place du Châtelet.

When he got there, he saw a police officer through the window and went in. Merely by the way they push open the guardhouse door, policemen recognize each other. Javert gave his name, showed his card to the sergeant, and sat down at the guardhouse table, where a candle was burning. On the table there was also a pen, a lead inkwell, and spare paper for eventual police reports and the statements of the night patrols.

This table, always completed by its straw chair, is an institution; it exists in all police stations; it is invariably adorned with a boxwood saucer full of sawdust and a little pasteboard cup full of red sealing wafers, an example of the lower official style. It is with that table that state literature begins.

Javert took the pen and a sheet of paper and began to write. This is what he wrote:

### SOME OBSERVATIONS FOR THE GOOD OF THE SERVICE

First: I beg Monsieur le préfet to cast his eyes on this.

Second: The detainees coming from the initial hearing take their shoes off and remain barefoot on the flagstones while they are being searched. Several cough on returning to prison. This entails hospital expenses.

Third: Tailing is good, with relays of officers at intervals, but for important occasions, there ought to be at least two officers who do not lose sight of one another, so that if, for any reason, an officer takes sick on the job, the other can keep watch over him and stand in for him.

Fourth: It is hard to explain why the special regulations of Les Madelonnettes prison ban prisoners from having a chair, even when they pay for it.

Fifth: At Les Madelonnettes, there are only two bars on the canteen window, which allows the woman running the canteen to let the prisoners touch her hand.

Sixth: The detainees, known as barkers, that call the other detainees to the visitors' room, make the prisoner pay them two sous to call out their name clearly. This is theft.

Seventh: For a dropped thread, ten sous are held back from a prisoner in the weaving workshop; this is an abuse on the part of the contractor, since the cloth is just as good.

Eighth: It is annoying that visitors to La Force prison have to cross the cour des Mômes to get to the visitors' room of Sainte-Marie-l'Egyptienne.

Ninth: It is a fact that every day, in the prefecture courtyard, one hears gendarmes recounting the interrogations of those held by the magistrates. For a gendarme, who should be beyond reproach, to repeat what he has heard in the examining magistrate's chamber, amounts to serious disorderly conduct.

Tenth: Madame Henry is an honest woman; her canteen is extremely clean; but it is bad for a woman to be posted at the trapdoor leading down to solitary. This is not worthy of the Conciergerie of a great civilization.

Javert wrote these lines in his calmest, most correct handwriting, not leaving out a comma, and making the paper screech firmly under his pen. Below the last line he signed:

Javert.
Inspector—1st class.

At the police station of the place du Châtelet.
June 7, 1832, approximately one o'clock in the morning.

Javert dried the fresh ink, folded the sheet of paper like a letter, sealed it, wrote on the back *Note for the administration,* left it on the table, and walked out of the station. The door with its glass panels and iron bars swung shut behind him.

Once more he crossed the place du Châtelet diagonally, regained the quai, and went back with automatic precision to the very spot he had left a quarter of an hour earlier; he leaned there and found himself again in the same position on the same flagstone of the parapet. It was as though he had not stirred.

The darkness was now pitch black. It was that deathly moment that follows midnight. A ceiling of clouds hid the stars. The sky was just a sinister density. The houses of the Cité no longer had a single light in them; no one was out walking; the streets and the quais were deserted as far as the eye could see; Notre-Dame and the towers of the Palais de Justice were outlined like features of the night. A streetlamp turned the rim of the quai red. The silhouettes of the bridges were distorted in the mist, one behind the other. Rain had swollen the river.

The spot where Javert was leaning was, as you will recall, located right above the rapid of the Seine, right over that fearful swirling whirlwind that spirals this way, then that, like an endless screw.

Javert poked his head over and looked. Everything was black. You could not make anything out. You could hear the noise of the foam; but you could not see the river. Now and then, a glimmer of light flashed in those dizzying depths and dimly snaked along, the water having the power, on the blackest of nights, to take the light who knows where and turn it into a death adder. The glimmer of light vanished and everything became indistinct again; immensity seemed to open out there. What you had below you was not water, it was a yawning chasm. The quai wall, abrupt, confused, merging into the vapor, suddenly hidden, struck you as being a cliff of infinity.

You could not see a thing, but you could feel the hostile coldness of the water and smell the staleness of the wet stones. A savage breath rose from that abyss. The swelling of the river more guessed at than seen, the tragic whispering of the waves, the gloomy enormity of the arches of the bridge, the easily imaginable fall into that somber void, all that darkness was full of horror.

Javert stood dead still for some minutes, gazing at this window on darkness; he studied the invisible with a fixedness that was like attention. The water gurgled. All of a sudden, he took off his hat and placed it on the edge of the quai. A moment later, a figure appeared, tall and black, which from a distance anyone still out and about could well have taken for a phantom, standing on the parapet, leaning toward the Seine, then it straightened up and fell straight into the darkness; there was a muted splash; and the shadow alone was in on the secret of the convulsions this obscure form made as it disappeared beneath the water.

# BOOK FIVE

# GRANDSON AND GRANDFATHER

## I. IN WHICH WE ONCE MORE SEE THE TREE WITH THE ZINC PLASTER

Some little time after the events we have just related, old Boulatruelle experienced a strong emotion.

Old Boulatruelle is the Montfermeil road-mender we have already caught sight of in the dark sections of this book.

Boulatruelle, you may remember, was a man with many and varied troubles on his mind. He broke stones and fleeced travelers on the highway. A road worker and a robber, he had a dream; he believed in treasures buried deep in the Montfermeil forest. He hoped one day to find money in the ground at the foot of a tree; meanwhile, he enjoyed looking for it in the pockets of those passing through.

And yet, for the moment, he was prudently lying low. He had just had a narrow escape. He had been, as we know, picked up in the Jondrette dive along with the other bandits. Vice can be useful: It was his drunkenness that saved him. They never could clear up whether he was there as robber or robbed. The case was dismissed due to lack of evidence, based on his clearly observable state of intoxication on the night of the ambush, and he was set free. He got away to the woods again. He went back to his old road between Gagny and Lagny to carry out graveling, on behalf of the state and under the surveillance of the administration, keeping his head down, a little downcast, extremely pensive, and with slightly cold feet as far as robbery went, since that activity had nearly sunk him, but turning all the more tenderly to drink, which had just saved his neck.

As for the strong emotion he experienced shortly after being back under the turf roof of his road-mender's hut again, this was it:

One morning, shortly before daybreak, as he was making his way as usual to his work, and perhaps to his hideout, Boulatruelle spotted a man among the branches and though he could only see his back, the man's bulk, it seemed to him, from a distance, through the dim light, was not entirely unfamiliar to him. Boulatruelle may have been a drunk but his memory was intact and lucid, an indispensable defensive weapon when a man is somewhat at odds with the legal order.

"Where the devil have I seen that man before?" he asked himself.

But he could not provide himself with an answer, except that he looked like someone who had left a dim trace in his mind.

Nonetheless, apart from the man's identity, which he could not quite put his finger on, Boulatruelle made some connections and calculations. The man was not from around there. He had come there from somewhere else. On foot, obviously. No public conveyance passes at that hour at Montfermeil. He had walked all night. Where had he come from? From somewhere not far away. For he had neither a haversack nor a bundle. From Paris no doubt. Why was he in this wood? Why was he there at such an hour? What had he come there to do?

Boulatruelle thought about the treasure. By dint of digging into his memory he vaguely remembered having had a similar jolt already, several years before, in relation to a man who struck him as very possibly the same man.

While he chewed this over, he had, under the very weight of his meditation, bowed his head, which is only natural, but not too clever. When he looked up again, there was no one in sight. The man had melted into the forest and into the gloom.

"Bugger!" said Boulatruelle. "I'll find him again, but. I'll find out which parish this particular parishioner hails from. This stroller, up at the crack of dawn, has a why and a wherefore, and I'll find out what it is. There are no secrets in my woods without me sticking my nose in."

He grabbed his pickax, which was very sharp.

"Now this," he muttered, "is just the thing for plowing through dirt—or a man."

And, following the path the man must have taken as exactly as he could, the way you tie one thread to another thread, he set off through the undergrowth.

When he had gone a hundred yards, day was starting to break and came to his aid. Footprints left in the sand here and there, grass flattened underfoot, ferns crushed, young branches bent back in the scrub and straightening out again at a graciously slow pace, like the arms of a pretty woman stretching out on waking, more or less pointed the way. He followed it, then he lost it. Time passed. He delved further into the woods and came to a kind of knoll. An early-morning hunter going by along a path in the distance, whistling jauntily, gave him the idea of climbing up a tree. Though old, he was agile. There was a very tall beech tree nearby, worthy of Virgil's Tityrus,[1] and of Boulatruelle. Boulatruelle climbed the beech as high as he could.

It was a good idea. Exploring the lonely expanse over where the wood is completely tangled and wild, Boulatruelle suddenly spotted his man.

Hardly had he spotted him when he lost sight of him again.

The man went, or rather slipped, into a fairly remote glade, camouflaged by tall trees, a place Boulatruelle knew well, though, having noticed, near a big pile of millstones, a sick chestnut tree bandaged with a zinc plaster nailed straight onto the bark. This glade is the clearing known as the Blaru grounds in days gone by. The pile of stones that could be seen there thirty years ago, intended for who knows what use, is doubtless still there today. Nothing can beat a pile of stones for longevity—unless it is a paling fence. It is always only temporary. What a good reason for it to stay where it is!

Boulatruelle, going hell for leather in his excitement, practically fell out of the tree climbing down. The lair had been found, now it was just a matter of bagging the game. The famous treasure of his dreams was probably there.

It was no mean feat getting to the glade. The well-trodden paths that zigzag crazily all over the place took a good quarter of an hour; the straight path through the thicket, which is incredibly thick, extremely thorny, and extremely aggressive, took a good half an hour. Boulatruelle made the mistake of not reckoning on this. He believed in the straight line—a respectable optical illusion, but one that causes a lot of people to come unstuck. The thicket, spiky as it was, seemed to him to be the right way.

"We'll take the wolves' rue de Rivoli," he said.

Boulatruelle was used to straying; this time he made the mistake of going straight.

He threw himself with gusto into the mêlée of the undergrowth.

He had to tackle holly, nettles, hawthorn, dog roses, thistles, the crankiest of brambles, and got himself scratched to bits.

At the bottom of a ravine, he found water that he had to wade through.

He finally reached the Blaru glade after a good forty minutes, sweating, soaked, out of breath, clawed to bits, ferocious.

No one in the glade.

Boulatruelle ran to the pile of stones. It was in place. It had not been carted away.

As for the man, he had vanished into the forest. He had escaped. Where to? Which way? In what thicket? Impossible to guess.

And, most poignantly, behind the pile of stones, in front of the tree with the zinc plaster, there was freshly dug dirt, a forgotten or abandoned pick, and a hole.

The hole was empty.

"Thief!" cried Boulatruelle, showing the horizon his two fists.

## II. MARIUS, EMERGING FROM CIVIL WAR, GEARS UP FOR DOMESTIC WAR

For a long while Marius was neither dead nor alive. For several weeks he had a fever accompanied by delirium and serious symptoms of brain damage caused more by the concussion resulting from the wounds to the head than by the wounds themselves.

He repeated Cosette's name for whole nights on end in the morbid loquacity induced by fever and with the grim obstinacy of approaching death. The size of certain injuries was a serious danger, pus suppurating from open wounds always being susceptible to being resorbed, and consequently killing the patient, under certain atmospheric conditions; at every change in the weather, at the least storm, the doctor became anxious. "Above all else, don't excite him," he would repeat. The bandages were complex and difficult, for fixing pads and cloth in place with surgical tape or sticking plaster had not yet been dreamed up at the time. Nicolette used up a sheet "as big as a ceiling," she said, for lint. It was not without a struggle that the chlorinated lotions and the silver nitrate finally got the better of the gangrene. As long as there was danger, Monsieur Gillenormand stayed by his grandson's bedside, distraught and, like Marius, neither dead nor alive.

Every day and sometimes twice a day, a white-haired gentleman, very well dressed, according to the description provided by the porter, came to hear the latest on the wounded man and left a fat packet of lint for bandages.

At last, on September 7, three months to the day from the painful night he was brought back dying to his grandfather's home, the doctor declared that he was out of danger. Convalescence began. Marius, though, had to stay lying down on a chaise longue for over two months still, on account of the complications produced by the fractured collarbone. There is always one last wound that does not want to heal and so prolongs the bandaging to the great annoyance of the patient.

On the other hand, this long illness and convalescence saved him from prosecution. In France, there is no rage, not even official rage, that six months won't snuff out. Riots, in the current state of society, are so much everybody's fault that they are followed by a certain need to turn a blind eye.

We might add that the unspeakable directive issued by Gisquet enjoining doctors to denounce the wounded, having outraged public opinion, and not only public opinion but the king first and foremost, the wounded were shielded and protected by this outrage; and, with the exception of those who had been taken prisoner in actual combat, the courts-martial did not dare disturb any of them. And so they left Marius in peace.

Monsieur Gillenormand went through every possible anguish at first, and after that every possible ecstasy. They had a lot of trouble preventing him from spending every night by the wounded man's side; he had his great big armchair wheeled in next to Marius's bed; he demanded that his daughter use the best linen in the house to make poultices and bandages with. Mademoiselle Gillenormand, wise elder daughter that she was, managed to find a way of sparing the very best linen, while letting the old man think his wishes were respected. Monsieur Gillenormand would not allow anyone to explain to him that for making lint, cambric is not as good as coarse cloth and new cloth is not as good as used cloth. He watched all the dressing operations, while Mademoiselle Gillenormand absented herself for modesty's sake. When they hacked away the dead flesh with scissors, he would wince: "Ouch! Ouch!" Nothing could be more touching than to see him handing the patient a cup of herbal tea with his slight senile tremor. He overwhelmed the doctor with questions without realizing that his questions were always the same ones.

The day the doctor told him that Marius was out of danger, the poor man went delirious. He gave his porter three louis as a bonus. That evening, when he went up to his room, he danced a gavotte, clicking his thumb and index finger like castanets, and he sang the following song:

Jeanne[1] was born in Fougère,
A real nest for a shepherdess;
I love her petticoat
     Little rogue.

Love, you live in her;
For it is in her eyes
That you put your quiver,
     Scoffer!

Me, I sing of her, and love
More than Diana, even,
Jeanne and her hard Breton
     Nipples.[2]

Then he knelt on a chair and Basque, who watched him through the door, which was ajar, felt sure he prayed.

Until then, he hadn't believed in God for a moment.

At each new stage of improvement, as recovery became more and more marked, the old man ranted and raved. He did all sorts of wildly gay things, quite unconsciously; he ran up and down the stairs without knowing why. A neighbor, and a pretty one at that, was quite stunned one morning to receive a huge bouquet; it was Monsieur Gillenormand who had sent it. The husband threw a jealous fit. Monsieur Gillenormand tried to pull Nicolette onto his knees. He called Marius Monsieur le baron. He cried out: "Long live the Republic!"

At every turn, he asked the doctor: "There's no danger anymore, is there?" He would look at Marius with a grandmother's gaze. He would sit and brood over him as he ate. He did not know himself anymore, he no longer counted. Marius was the master of the house, there was abdication in the old man's joy, he was his grandson's grandson.

In the state of delight he was in, he was the most venerable of children. From fear of tiring or annoying the convalescent, he would stand behind him and beam down at him. He was happy, joyful, thrilled, charming, young. His white hair added sweet majesty to the shiny bright light that lay over his face. When grace tackles wrinkles, it is adorable. There is an indefinable dawning in radiant old age.

As for Marius, while letting himself be bandaged and cared for, he had only one idea in his head: Cosette. Since the fever and delirium had left him, he no longer uttered that name, and a person could be forgiven for thinking that he no longer thought about her. He kept his mouth shut, precisely because his heart would have leaped out of it.

He did not know what had become of Cosette; the whole business of the rue de la Chanvrerie was like a cloud in his memory; almost indistinct shadows flitted through his mind, Éponine, Gavroche, Mabeuf, the Thénardiers, all his friends grimly mixed up with the smoke of the barricade; the strange cameo rôle of Monsieur Fauchelevent in that gory episode struck him as a riddle in a tempest; he did not understand a thing about his own life, he did not know how or through whom he had been saved and no one around him knew, either; all they had been able to tell him was that he had been brought back to the rue des Filles-du-Calvaire at night in a fiacre; past, present, future, everything inside him was now no more than the fog of a vague idea, but in this mist there was one fixed point, a clear and precise outline, something carved in stone, a resolution, a desire: to find Cosette again. For him, the idea of life itself could not be separated from the idea of Cosette; he had decreed in his heart that he would not accept one without the other and he was unshakably determined to demand of anyone or anything that wanted to force him to live, whoever and whatever they might be—his grandfather, fate, hell—the restitution of his lost Eden.

He did not hide the obstacles from himself.

We might underline one detail here: He was not won over or much softened by all the tender loving care his grandfather showed him. In the first place, he was not entirely aware of its extent; then, in his sick man's daydreams, which were perhaps still feverish, he mistrusted sweetness of the sort as something new and strange aimed at bringing him to heel. He remained coldly unmoved by it. The grandfather smiled his poor old smile for nothing. Marius said to himself that, yes, everything was all right as long as he, Marius, did not say anything and went along with things; but that as soon as Cosette came up, he would see a different face and that his grandfather's true feelings would then betray themselves. The gloves would be off then; just watch the old family issues rear their ugly head again, and the clash between their positions, and every sarcastic remark and every objection all at once, Fauchelevent, Coupelevent, wealth, poverty, destitution, the old millstone around the neck, the future. Violent resistance; conclusion, refusal. Marius was steeling himself in advance.

And then, the more he recovered, the more his old grievances crept up on him, the more the old ulcers of his memory reopened, he thought once more about the past, Colonel Pontmercy once more came between Monsieur Gillenormand and himself, Marius; he told himself there was no real kindness to hope for from someone who had been so unjust and so hard on his father. And with health, a kind of bitter harshness toward his grandfather returned. The old man quietly took it on the chin and suffered in silence.

Monsieur Gillenormand noticed that since he had been brought home to him and since he had regained consciousness, Marius had not once called him father—though he did not show that he noticed this. Marius did not call him monsieur, true; but he found a way of saying neither one nor the other by using a certain manner of circumlocution. A crisis was obviously brewing.

As almost always happens in such cases, Marius, to try his hand, skirmished before giving battle. This is known as seeing how the land lies. One morning it so happened that Monsieur Gillenormand, over a newspaper that had fallen into his hands, spoke lightly of the Convention and let fall a casual royalist remark about Danton, Saint-Just, and Robespierre.

"The men of '93 were giants," said Marius sternly. The old man shut up and did not breathe a whisper for the rest of the day.

Marius had always had in his mind's eye the inflexible grandfather of his early years, and so he saw this silence as a profound concentration of anger and foresaw from it a fierce struggle, and he stepped up his preparations for battle in the innermost recesses of his mind.

He decided that if his grandfather refused, he would rip off his bandages, dislocate his collarbone, expose and open whatever wounds he still had, and push away all food. His wounds were his ammunition. He would have Cosette or die.

He waited for the right moment with the sly patience of the sick. That moment arrived.

### III. MARIUS ATTACKS

One day, while his daughter was tidying up the cups and vials on the marble top of the chest of drawers, Monsieur Gillenormand leaned over Marius and said to him in the most loving tone: "You see, my darling Marius, if I were you, I'd be eating meat now rather than fish. Fried sole is excellent at the start of convalescence, but to get a sick man on his feet, there's nothing like a good chop."

Marius, who had regained almost all his strength, gathered it together, sat up, drove his balled fists into the bedclothes, looked his grandfather straight in the eye as fiercely as he could and said: "That brings me to something I want to say to you."

"Which is?"

"That I wish to marry."

"It's all taken care of," said the grandfather. And he burst out laughing.

"What do you mean it's all taken care of?"

"Yes, it's all taken care of. You shall have her, your little lass."

Marius, stunned and overcome with dizziness, trembled in every limb.

Monsieur Gillenormand went on: "Yes, you shall have her, your beautiful pretty little girl. She comes every day in the form of an old gentleman to hear your latest news. Since you were wounded, she has passed her time weeping and making lint. I made inquiries. She lives in the rue de l'Homme-Armé, number seven. Ah, so at last the truth's out! Ah, you want her! Well, then, you shall have her. That's got you! You'd devised your little plot, you said to yourself: 'I'm going to come right out with it to this grandfather of mine, this embalmed mummy of the Regency[1] and the Directoire, this has-been of an old rake, this Dorante who's turned into Géronte;[2] he's had his lighter moments, too, he has, and his love affairs, and his grisettes, and his Cosettes; he's strutted around in his finery like a peacock, he's spread his wings, he's sown his wild oats—surely he must remember what it was like. We'll soon see. Let the battle begin.' So! You take the bull by the horns. That's good. I offer you a chop and you answer: 'By the way, I wish to marry.' Now, that's what I call a leap! Ah! You were all set on a bit of a tiff! You didn't know I was an old coward. What have you got to say about that? You're nettled. You didn't expect to find your grandfather even more of a fool than you are, did you? You're losing the thread of the speech you were going to make me, Monsieur the attorney, that's irritating. Well, then, too bad, rant away. I'm doing what you want, that's shut you up, hasn't it, you imbecile! Listen. I've made my inquiries, I'm sly, too, you know; she's lovely, she's good, it's not true about the lancer, she's made heaps of lint, she's a gem, she adores you. If you had died, there would have been three of us; her bier would have accompanied mine. I had a strong notion, as soon as you were better, to plant her right here at your bedside, but it's only in novels that one sticks young girls without further ado by the beds of the pretty wounded lads they've got their eye on. It's just not done. What would your aunt have said? You were quite naked three quarters of the time, my good man. Ask Nicolette, who wouldn't leave you for a second if she had anything to do with it. And, then, what would the doctor have said? A pretty girl doesn't cure a fever. In the end, everything's fine, let's not talk about it any further, it's said, it's done, it's taken care of, she's yours. Such is my ferocity. You see, I saw that you didn't love me, and I said: 'What can I do to make that particular animal love me?' I said: 'Hold on, I've got my little Cosette at hand, I'll give her to him, then he'll have to love me a little, or tell me why not.' Ah, you thought the old boy was going to kick up a stink, raise the roof, shout no, and raise my cane and shake it at love's young dream. Not a bit of it. Cosette, well and good; love, well and good. I ask nothing more. Monsieur, do take the trouble to marry yourself off. Be happy, my dear beloved boy."

That said, the old man burst into tears.

And he took Marius's head and cradled it with both arms against his breast, and they both wept. This is one of the ultimate forms of happiness.

"Father!" cried Marius.

"Ah! So you do love me, after all!" cried the old man.

There was an ineffable moment. They choked and could not speak.

Finally the old man stammered: "There you are then! He finally said it. He called me father."

Marius pulled his head away from his grandfather and said, softly: "But, Father, now that I'm doing so well, it seems to me I could be allowed to see her."

"That's taken care of, too, you'll see her tomorrow."

"Father!"

"What?"

"Why not today?"

"Well, today, then. Today it is. You called me Father three times, that's got to be worth that much. I'll see to it. She shall be brought to you. It's taken care of, I tell you. This has already been set to verse. It's the denoument of the elegy in André Chénier's *Le Jeune malade*—the André Chénier[3] who had his throat cut by the bast—by the giants of '93."

Monsieur Gillenormand thought he saw a slight frown on Marius's brow, though Marius, we have to say, was actually no longer listening to him, floating off as he was in ecstasy, with his mind a lot more on Cosette than on 1793. The grandfather, trembling at having introduced André Chénier so clumsily, rushed on: "'His throat cut' is not the right way to put it. The fact is that the great revolutionary geniuses, who were not bad men, that is incontestable, who were heroes, heavens! found that André Chénier embarrassed them a bit, and so they had him guilloti—that is to say, those great men, on the seventh of Thermidor,[4] in the interests of public safety, begged André Chénier to be good enough to—"

Monsieur Gillenormand could not go on; his own sentence stuck in his throat, and not being able to either finish it or retract it, while his daughter fluffed up Marius's pillow behind him, overcome by such surges of emotion, the old man hurled himself out of the bedroom, as fast as his age would allow him, slammed the door shut behind him and, purple in the face, choking, foaming at the mouth, his eyes popping out of his head, found himself nose to nose with the honest Basque, who was polishing boots in the antechamber. He grabbed Basque by the collar and shouted furiously right in his face: "By the hundred thousand Javottes of the devil, those brigands assassinated him!"

"Who, Monsieur?"

"André Chénier!"

"Yes, Monsieur," said Basque, appalled.


### IV. Mademoiselle Gillenormand Winds Up Deciding It Is Not Such a Bad Thing That Monsieur Fauchelevent Came with Something Under His Arm

Cosette and Marius saw each other again. How this meeting went we will refrain from saying. There are things we should not try to depict, among others, the sun.

The whole family, including Basque and Nicolette, were gathered together in Marius's room when Cosette came in. She appeared at the door; she looked as though she were standing in a luminous cloud of mist. At precisely that moment, the grandfather was about to blow his nose; he stopped short, kept his nose in his handkerchief, and eyed Cosette over the top of it: "Adorable!" he cried.

Then he loudly blew his nose.

Cosette was intoxicated, rapt, frightened, in seventh heaven. She was also as terrified as a person can be by happiness. She stuttered, pale as anything, red as anything, wanting to throw herself into Marius's arms yet not daring to, ashamed to love openly in front of all these people. People are merciless with happy lovers, hanging around when lovers most want to be alone. Lovers have no need of people at all.

With Cosette, behind her, a white-haired man had come, looking grave yet smiling, but with a small, heartbreaking smile. It was "Monsieur Fauchelevent," otherwise known as Jean Valjean.

He was "very well decked out," as the porter had said, entirely dressed in black and in new clothes, with a white cravat.

The porter would never in a blue moon have guessed that this upstanding bourgeois, most likely a notary, was the terrifying man hauling cadavers who had loomed at his door on the night of June 7, in rags, covered in mud, hideous, haggard, his face caked in blood and muck, supporting the unconscious Marius by the armpits; yet his porter's nose was aroused. When Monsieur Fauchelevent turned up with Cosette, the porter could not help saying to his wife in private:

"I don't know why, but I can't help feeling I've seen that face somewhere before."

Monsieur Fauchelevent, in Marius's room, stood back from the others, as though aloof, close to the door. He had under his arm a parcel not unlike an octavo volume wrapped in paper. The wrapping paper was greenish and looked moldy.

"Does that gentleman always go about with books under his arm like that?" Mademoiselle Gillenormand asked Nicolette in a low voice; she did not like books.

"Well," answered Monsieur Gillenormand, who had heard her, in the same low tone, "he's a savant. What of it? He can't help it! Monsieur Boulard,[1] whom I knew, never walked around without a book either, and that way he always had a book close to his heart."

And, bowing, he said out loud: "Monsieur Tranchelevent—"

Father Gillenormand did not do it deliberately, but inattention to proper names was an aristocratic way of his.[2]

"Monsieur Tranchelevent, I have the honor of asking you on behalf of my grandson, the baron Marius Pontmercy, for Mademoiselle's hand."

"Monsieur Tranchelevent" inclined his head.

"Enough said," said the grandfather.

And, turning to Marius and Cosette, with both arms opened wide in blessing, he cried: "Permission granted to adore each other."

Those two did not need to be told twice. Too bad about the crowd! The cooing began. They whispered to each other, Marius leaning forward on his chaise longue, Cosette standing close by him.

"Oh, my God!" murmured Cosette, "I can't believe I'm seeing you again. It is you! It is you, Monsieur! Fancy going off and fighting like that! What on earth for? It's horrible. For four months, I was dead. Oh, it was so spiteful of you to have been in that battle! What did I ever do to you? I forgive you, but you needn't think you'll be doing anything like that again. A moment ago, when they told us to come over, I thought I was going to die again, but this time of joy. I was so sad! I didn't take the time to dress properly, I must look a fright. Whatever will your family say, seeing me with a collar all crumpled? Well, say something! You're letting me do all the talking. We're still in the rue de l'Homme-Armé. It seems that your shoulder was in a terrible state. They told me you could have put your fist inside. And then it seems they cut the flesh with scissors. That was so awful. I cried so much, my eyes have disappeared. It's funny how you can suffer like that. Your grandfather looks so nice! Don't move, don't lean on your elbow; careful, you'll hurt yourself. Oh, I'm so happy! So, our troubles are over! I'm quite giddy. There are all sorts of things I wanted to tell you but I can't remember any of them. Do you still love me? We live at the rue de l'Homme-

Armé. It doesn't have a garden. I made lint all the time, here, Monsieur, see, it's all your fault, I've got calluses on my fingers."

"Angel!" crooned Marius.

*Angel* is the only word in the language that can't be worn out. No other word could resist the merciless use that those in love put it to.

Then, as there were other people present, they broke off and did not say another word to each other, merely touching each other's hand gently. Monsieur Gillenormand turned to all those in the room and shouted: "Talk among yourselves, the rest of you! Make some noise, over there in the wings. Come on, a bit of hubbub, for heaven's sake! So these children can yap at their ease."

And, going over to Marius and Cosette, he said to them in a very low voice: "Call each other *tu*. Don't be embarrassed."

Aunt Gillenormand watched this irruption of light in her quaint old home in amazement. Her amazement had nothing aggressive about it; it was not in the least the scandalized, envious attitude of an owl gazing upon two turtledoves; hers was the dazed eye of a poor innocent of fifty-seven; it was life that had missed out gazing on that triumph, love.

"Mademoiselle Gillenormand the elder," her father said to her, "I told you this would happen."

He remained silent for a moment before adding: "Look at the happiness of others."

Then he turned to Cosette: "She's so pretty! She's so pretty! She's a Greuze.[3] So, you're going to have this all to yourself, then, you cheeky rascal! Ah, young scallywag, you've got off lightly with me, you're happy, but if I were fifteen years younger, we'd cross swords to see who'd get her. Come now! I am in love with you, Mademoiselle. That's only natural. It's your right. Ah, what a beautifully pretty charming little wedding this is going to be! Saint-Denis du Saint-Sacrement is our parish, but I'll get a dispensation so that you can marry at Saint-Paul. It's a better church. It was built by the Jesuits. It's smarter. It's just opposite the Cardinal de Birague fountain. The masterpiece of Jesuit architecture is in Namur. A place called Saint-Loup. You must go there when you're married. It's worth the trip. Mademoiselle, I am entirely on your side, I want girls to marry, they're made for it. There is a certain Saint Catherine[4] that I'd still like to see with her hair down. To stay a maid is all very well, but it's chilly. The Bible says: Go and multiply. To save the people, you need Joan of Arc; but to make the people, you need a Mère Gigogne.[5] So marry, you beauties. I really don't see the point of remaining a maid. I'm well aware there's a chapel set apart in church and there's a lot of hot air about the sorority of the Virgin;[6] but, heavens above, a pretty husband, a brave boy, and, after a year, a big blond nipper that sucks heartily on your nipples, one with nice rolls of fat on his thighs, that gropes and grabs fistfuls of your breast with his little pink paws, laughing like the dawn—surely that's better than holding a candle at vespers and singing *Turris eburnea!*[7]

The grandfather did a pirouette on his ninety-year-old heels and began to speak again, like a spring springing back:

So, to stop the flow of your daydreams,
Alcippe, it's true, then, in a little you'll be married.[8]

"Speaking of which!"

"What, Father?"

"Didn't you have a close friend?"

"Yes, Courfeyrac."

"What's happened to him?"

"He died."

"That's just as well."

He sat beside them, made Cosette sit, and took their four hands in his old hands, gnarled as they were.

"She is exquisite, this little cutie. She is a masterpiece, this Cosette here! She is very much the ingénue and very much the grande dame at once. She will only be a baroness, which is demeaning, for she was born a marquise. Now those are what I call eyelashes for you! My children, get it into your thick noggins that this is for real. Love one another. Be silly with love. Love is mankind's silliness and God's wit. Adore one another. Only," he added, all at once darkening, "what a sorry state of affairs! Now that I think about it! More than half of what I have is in a life annuity; while I'm alive, that'll hold out all right, but after my death, you won't get a sou! Your beautiful white hands, Madame la baronne, will have the honor of scraping and saving to make ends meet."

Here a grave and tranquil voice was heard to say: "Mademoiselle Euphrasie Fauchelevent has six hundred thousand francs."

It was the voice of Jean Valjean.

He had not yet uttered a word, no one seemed to realize he was still there, standing as he was, straight and motionless, behind all these happy people.

"Who is the Mademoiselle Euphrasie in question?" asked the grandfather, alarmed.

"I am," answered Cosette.

"Six hundred thousand francs!" replied Monsieur Gillenormand.

"Less fourteen or fifteen thousand francs perhaps," said Jean Valjean.

And he placed on the table the packet that Aunt Gillenormand had mistaken for a book. Jean Valjean himself opened the packet; it was a bundle of banknotes. They flicked through them and counted them. There were five hundred notes of a thousand francs and one hundred and sixty-eight of five hundred. In all, five hundred and eighty-four thousand francs.

"Now there's a good book for you," said Monsieur Gillenormand.

"Five hundred and eighty-four thousand francs!" murmured the aunt.

"This arranges things pretty nicely—isn't that so, Mademoiselle Gillenormand the elder?" the grandfather crowed. "That little devil Marius, he's plucked a millionaire grisette for you from off the tree of dreams! So now you can trust in young people's love affairs! Male students find female students worth six hundred thousand francs. Cherubino does better than Rothschild."[70]

"Five hundred and eighty-four thousand francs!" Mademoiselle Gillenormand repeated in a hushed voice. "Five hundred and eighty-four thousand francs! You might as well say six hundred thousand while you're at it!"

As for Marius and Cosette, they gazed at each other the whole time and paid scant attention to this tiny detail.

## V. You Are Better off Putting Your Money in a Certain Forest Than Leaving It with a Certain Notary

You will no doubt have realized, without having to be told at length, that, after the Champmathieu affair, Jean Valjean had made it to Paris, thanks to the initial escape that lasted a few days, and to withdraw in time from Laffitte's the sum earned by him under the name of Monsieur Madeleine at Montreuil-sur-mer; and that, fearing recapture, which in fact was only a little while off, he had hidden and buried this sum in the forest of Montfermeil in the place known as the Blaru grounds. The sum, six hundred and thirty thousand francs, all in banknotes, did not take up much space and was contained in only one box. To preserve the box from damp, he had put it inside an oak casket full of chestnut shavings. In the same casket he had put his other treasure, the bishop's candlesticks. You will recall that he had carried off the candlesticks when he escaped from Montreuil-sur-mer. The man spotted one night by Boulatruelle was Jean Valjean. Later, whenever Jean Valjean needed money, he came and got some in the Blaru glade. Hence the absences we have mentioned. He had a pick somewhere among the briars in a hiding place he alone knew about. When he saw that Marius was getting better, feeling that the time was coming when the money might be useful, he had gone and got it and it was him again whom Boulatruelle had seen in the woods, but this time in the morning, not at night. Boulatruelle inherited the pickax.

The real sum was five hundred and eighty-four thousand five hundred francs. Jean Valjean kept the five hundred francs for himself. "We'll see what happens later," he said.

The difference between this sum and the six hundred and thirty thousand francs withdrawn from Laffitte's represented ten years' expenses, from 1823 to 1833. The five years' stay in the convent had only cost five thousand francs.

Jean Valjean put the two silver candlesticks on the mantelpiece, where they shone to Toussaint's great admiration.

On top of this, Jean Valjean knew that he had been delivered from Javert. It had been mentioned in his hearing, and he had confirmed the fact in the *Moniteur,* which had published it, that a police inspector named Javert had been found drowned under a washerwomen's boat between the Pont-au-Change and the Pont-Neuf and that a note left by this man, otherwise irreproachable and highly esteemed by his chiefs, indicated that he had committed suicide in a bout of insanity.

"In actual fact," thought Jean Valjean, "since he had me there and yet let me go, he must have been mad already."

## VI. THE TWO OLD MEN DO ALL THEY CAN, EACH IN HIS OWN WAY, TO SEE THAT COSETTE IS HAPPY

The wedding preparations were all under way. The doctor was consulted and declared that it could take place in February. This was in December. A few blissful weeks of perfect happiness rolled by.

The grandfather was far from being the least happy. He would sit gazing at Cosette for a quarter of an hour at a stretch.

"What an outrageously pretty girl!" he would cry. "And she looks so sweet and so good! No need to say cross my heart and hope to die, this is the loveliest girl I've ever seen in my life. Later on, she'll be as virtuous as can be, with a whiff of violets about her. She is grace itself, don't you know! You couldn't help but live nobly with such a creature. Marius, my boy, you are a baron, you are rich, stop this pettifogging, I beseech you."

Cosette and Marius had suddenly stepped out of the sepulchre and into paradise. The transition had been pretty abrupt and they would have been dazed had they not been dazzled.

"Can you make head or tail of it?" Marius said to Cosette.

"No," Cosette answered, "but it seems to me the good Lord is looking down on us."

Jean Valjean did everything, smoothed everything, reconciled everything, made everything easy. He rushed toward Cosette's happiness with as much eagerness and apparent joy as Cosette herself.

As he had been a mayor, he knew how to resolve a delicate problem that he alone was in on the secret of: Cosette's civil status. To baldly state her origins, who knows? It might well have prevented the marriage. He got Cosette out of all difficulties, though. He arranged a whole family of dead people for her, a sure way of not incurring any untoward claim. Cosette was all that remained of an otherwise extinct family; she was not his own daughter but the daughter of a different Fauchelevent. Two Fauchelevent brothers had been gardeners at the Petit-Picpus convent. They went to the convent: The best information and the most respectable testimonials abounded; the good sisters had little aptitude or inclination for delving into questions of paternity, and without meaning any harm, had never really known exactly which of the two Fauchelevents little Cosette was the daughter of. They said what they were required to say and said it with gusto. A notary's affidavit was drawn up. Cosette became Mademoiselle Euphrasie Fauchelevent before the law. She was declared an orphan on both her father's and her mother's sides. Jean Valjean engineered things so that he was designated Cosette's guardian, under the name of Fauchelevent, with Monsieur Gillenormand as surrogate guardian.

As for the five hundred and eighty-four thousand francs, this was a legacy left to Cosette by a dead person who wished to remain anonymous. The original legacy had been five hundred and ninety-four thousand francs, but ten thousand francs had been spent on the education of Mademoiselle Euphrasie, of which five thousand had been paid to the convent itself. This legacy, deposited in the hands of a third party, was to be handed to Cosette when she came of age or when she married. Altogether this arrangement was most acceptable, as we see, especially with an extra income of over half a million. There were, in fact, a few disparities here and there, but nobody saw them; one of the interested parties had his eyes blindfolded by love, the others by the six hundred thousand francs.

Cosette learned that she was not the daughter of the man she had so long called father. He was merely a relation; a different Fauchelevent was her real father. At any other time, this would have devastated her. But at this ineffably wonderful moment in her life, the news was just a patch of shadow, a small dark cloud, and she felt so much joy that the cloud soon dissolved. She had Marius. The young man surged to the fore, the old man faded into the background. Such is life.

And then, Cosette had been accustomed to finding herself surrounded by unanswered questions for many a long year; anyone who has had a mysterious childhood is always ready to give certain things up. But she continued to call Jean Valjean father.

In her rapture, Cosette was wild about old Gillenormand. It is true that he showered her with compliments and gifts. While Jean Valjean was busy building a normal place for Cosette in society and possession of an unassailable status, Monsieur Gillenormand saw to the wedding presents. Nothing amused him like being extravagantly generous. He had given Cosette a dress of Binche guipure lace which had come down to him from his very own grandmother.

"This is back in fashion again," he said. "Vintage clothes are all the rage, and the young women of my dotage dress like the old women of my childhood."

He rummaged through his respectable potbellied Coromandel lacquer chests of drawers, which had not been opened in years. "Let's get these old dowagers to cough up," he said. "Let's see what they've got in their paunches." He noisily violated bulging drawers full of the outfits of all his wives, all his mistresses, all his grandmothers. Pekins, damasks, lampases, painted moires, gowns of gros de Tours flambé damask, handkerchiefs from India embroidered with a washable gold, bits of reversible silk velvets known as dauphines, bobbin-made point de Gênes lace and needle-made point d'Alençon lace, sets of jewels in old goldplate and silverplate, ivory sweet boxes decorated with microscopic battles, frippery, ribbons—he lavished the lot on Cosette. Cosette, marveling, frantic with love for Marius and wild with gratitude for Monsieur Gillenormand, dreamed of boundless happiness decked out in satin and velvet. Her stock of wedding presents appeared to her held aloft by seraphim. Her soul reeled off into the blue on wings of Mechlin lace.

The intoxication of the lovers, we say again, was equaled only by the ecstasy of the grandfather. It was as though there was a brass band playing in the rue des Filles-du-Calvaire.

Every morning, a new offering of bric-a-brac from the grandfather to Cosette. All possible frills and flounces bloomed splendidly around her.

One day Marius, who was given to talking seriously in the midst of his happiness, said apropos who knows what incident: "The men of the Revolution are so great, they already have the luster of the centuries, like Cato and Phocion, and every one of them already seems like a figure of antiquity."

"Antique moiré!" cried the old man. "Thank you, Marius. That's exactly what I was after."

And the next day a magnificent gown of antique moiré the color of tea was added to Cosette's stock of wedding presents. The grandfather derived wisdom from these fine confections: "Love is all very well, but you need this with it. You need the useless for happiness. Happiness is only the bare necessity. Season it for me with a good pinch of the superfluous. A palace and her heart. Her heart and the Louvre. Her heart and the great fountains of Versailles. Give me my shepherdess but try and see to it that she's a duchesse with it. Bring me Phyllis crowned with cornflowers and throw in a hundred thousand francs a year, while you're at it. Show me a pastoral scene as far as the eye can see from under a colonnade of marble. I go along with the pastoral and with the fairyland enchantment of marble and gold, too. Plain unadulterated happiness is like plain unadulterated bread: You eat, but you don't dine. I want the superfluous, the useless, the extravagant, the too-much, something that serves no purpose at all. I remember seeing in Strasbourg cathedral a clock[1] as tall as a three-story house that marked the hour, that was good enough to mark the hour, but that didn't look as though it was made for the task; for, after striking midday or midnight—midday, the hour of sun, midnight, the hour of love—or any other hour you please, it gave you the moon and the stars, the earth and the sea, the birds and the fish, Phoebus and Phoebe,[2] and a swarm of things that popped out of a niche, and the twelve apostles, and the emperor Charles V,[3] and Éponine and Sabinus,[4] and a host of little gilded chaps that played the trumpet, to boot. Not counting the ravishing chimes that it scattered into the air all the time without anyone knowing why. Can a paltry bare dial that merely tells the time compete with that? Myself, I side with the great clock of Strasbourg, and I prefer it to the cuckoo clock of the Black Forest any day."

Monsieur Gillenormand raved most especially about the wedding, and all the Louis XV vaudeville routines of the eighteenth century passed willy-nilly into his panegyrics.

"You don't know anything about the art of fêtes. You don't know how to put on a really wonderful celebration these days," he cried. "This nineteenth century of yours has no gumption. It lacks excess. It knows nothing about what is rich, it knows nothing about what is noble. In all things it is so tightfisted. Your Third Estate is insipid, colorless, odorless, and shapeless. What your bourgeoise who are starting out, as they say, dream of: a pretty boudoir freshly decorated, rosewood and calico. Make way! Make way! Old Grigou is marrying old maid Grippesou,[5] that skinflint. Talk about sumptuousness and splendor! They have stuck a gold louis to a candle. There you have the age in a nutshell. I ask only to run away beyond the Sarmatians. Ah, as early as 1787, I foresaw that all was lost the day I saw the duc de Rohan,[6] prince de Léon, duc de Chabot, duc de Mont-bazon, marquis de Soubise, vicomte de Thouars, peer of France, trot off to Longchamp[7] in a boneshaker! See what fruit it has born. In this century, they wheel and deal, they play the stock exchange, they earn money, and they are stingy. They polish and varnish the surface; they are all turned out immaculately, washed, soaped, raked, shaved, combed, waxed, smoothed down, rubbed, brushed, cleaned outwardly, irreproachable, polished like a pebble, discreet, neat and tidy, and at the same time, by my true love's virtue! if they don't have dung heaps and cesspits at the bottom of their consciences that'd make a cow-girl that blows her nose with her fingers step back in horror. I grant these times this motto: Dirty cleanliness. Marius, don't get annoyed, let me have my say, I'm not bad-mouthing the people, you see, I can't stop talking about this people of yours, but don't mind me if I give the bourgeoisie a bit of a pummeling. I'm part of it. Who loves well lashes well. On that note, I say quite frankly, nowadays people marry but they no longer know how to marry. Ah, it's true, I miss the nicety of the old ways. I miss everything about them. The elegance, the chivalry, the charming courtly manners, the delightful luxury everyone went in for, the way music was part of the wedding, symphony at the top, drumming at

the bottom, the dances, the joyful faces around the table, the convoluted madri-
gals, the songs, the crackers, the belly laughs, every man and his dog there, the
ribbons tied in big bows. I miss the bride's garter. The bride's garter is the cousin
of the chastity belt. What does the Trojan War turn on? Helen's garter,[8] by Jove!
What are they fighting for, why does the divine Diomedes smash that great
bronze helmet with its ten points over Meriones' head, why do Achilles and
Hector paint each other all over with fine strokes of the pick? Because Helen let
Paris take her garter. With Cosette's garter, Homer would have made the *Iliad*.
He'd stick an old chatterbox like me in his poem and he'd call him Nestor.[9] My
friends, in the old days, in the good old days, they knew how to marry; they'd
have a good solid contract[10] and after that a good solid spread. As soon as Cujas
went out, Gamache[11] came in. But, heavens! That's because the stomach is an
agreeable animal that demands its due and wants its wedding, too. You dined
well, and you had at your table a beautiful neighbor without a chemisette who
didn't mind showing a bit of cleavage! Oh, the wide laughing mouths, how gay
we were in those days! Youth was a bouquet; every young man ended in a
branch of lilac or a bunch of roses; even if you were a warrior, you were a shepherd; and if, by chance, you were a captain of dragoons, you'd find a way of
being called Florian.[12] We were keen to be pretty, we embellished ourselves, we
decked ourselves out in crimson. A bourgeois looked like a flower, a marquis
looked like a gem. We didn't have stirrups, we didn't have boots. We were
spruce, glossy, iridescent, brushed with gold, all aflutter, dapper, dashing. But
that did not stop you from having your sword by your side. A hummingbird—
beak and claws. Those were the days of Rameau's *Les Indes galantes*.[13] One side of
the century was its delicacy, the other, its magnificence; and, saints above! we
had fun. Today, they're so serious. The bourgeois is a miser, his wife is a prude;
your century is dire. They'd chase away the Graces for flashing too much
bosom. Alas! They hide beauty as though it were ugly. Since the Revolution,
everyone's been wearing pants, even the dancing girls; a strolling player must
be grave; your rigadoons are doctrinaire. A person has to be stately. You would
be most annoyed not to have your chin in your cravat. The ideal of some twirp
of twenty about to marry is to be like Monsieur Royer-Collard.[14] And do you
know what the world's coming to with that kind of stateliness? To being small.
Listen and learn: Joy is not only joyful, it is big. So be in love with gusto, for
God's sake! So get married, when you marry, with all the fever and giddiness
and uproar and mayhem of happiness! Gravity at church, fair enough. But, as
soon as mass is over, damn it! the new bride must be surrounded by a swirling
dream. A wedding should be royal and fabulous; it should take its ceremony for
a stroll from the cathedral of Rheims to the pagoda of Chanteloup.[15] I can't
stand a halfhearted wedding. For pity's sake! Be on Olympus, at least that day.
Be gods. Ah, you could be sylphs, those divinities, the Pleasures, Argyraspides;[16]
and yet you are gutless wonders! My friends, every new bridegroom should be

a prince Aldobrandini.[17] Take advantage of this one minute of your life to soar off into the empyrean with the swans and the eagles, even if it means dropping back down into the bourgeois world of frogs the next day. Don't stint on the bonds of marriage, don't cut back on its splendors; don't skimp on the one day you are to shine. A wedding is not housework. Oh! If I had my way, it would be gallantly chic. You would hear violins in the trees. This is how I see it: sky blue and silver. I would bring the rustic divinities into the fête, I would summon the dryads and the nereids. The sea goddess Amphitrite's wedding day, a pink cloud, nymphs with tremendous hairdos but otherwise completely naked, a member of the Académie offering the goddess quatrains, a chariot drawn by sea monsters.

> Triton trotted ahead and from his conch he drew
> Sounds so ravishing, he ravished young and old, too.[18]

"Now that's a proper program for a fête for you, or I'm a Dutchman, by jingo!"

While the grandfather was in full lyrical flight, enjoying the sound of his own voice, Cosette and Marius were practically swooning in intoxication, now that they could gulp each other in freely by gazing.

Aunt Gillenormand studied all this with her unflappable placidity. She had had a certain dose of emotion in the space of five or six months; Marius back home; Marius carried back home covered in blood, Marius carried back home from some barricade, Marius dead, then alive, Marius reconciled, Marius engaged, Marius about to marry a pauper, Marius about to marry a millionaire. The six hundred thousand francs had been her latest surprise. Then she reverted to her usual indifference, the lack of interest of a first communicant. She regularly went to church services, said her rosary, read her prayer book, which she called a Euchologion, whispered *Ave*s[19] in one corner of the house while they were whispering *I love you*s in the other, looked on Marius and Cosette as two shadows. She was the shadow.

There is a certain state of inert asceticism in which the soul, neutralized by torpor, foreign to what might be called the business of living, does not pick up any human impressions, whether pleasant or painful—with the exception of earthquakes and other disasters. "This kind of devoutness," said old Gillenormand to his daughter, "corresponds to a head cold. You can't smell anything of life. No bad odor, but also, no good."

Still, the six hundred thousand francs had taken care of the old maid's indecision. Her father had acquired the habit of taking so little account of her that he had not consulted her when consenting to Marius's marriage. He had acted impetuously, as was his wont, having only one thought, now that he had gone from being a despot to being a slave, and that was to make Marius happy. As for the lad's aunt, that that aunt should exist and that she might have an opinion was not something he had considered for a moment, and though she was as docile as a lamb, this had hurt her feelings. A tad rebellious deep within, though unrufflable without, she had said to herself: "My father has settled the question of the marriage without me; I will settle the question of the inheritance without him." She, in fact, was rich and the father was not. And so she reserved her decision on that score. It is likely that if it had been a poor match, she would have left it poor. "Too bad for Monsieur, my nephew! If he wants to marry a beggar, let him be a beggar himself." But Cosette's half million tickled the aunt and changed her position in regard to this particular pair of lovers. A person owes six hundred thousand francs some consideration and it was obvious that she could not do otherwise than to leave her fortune to these young people, since they no longer needed it.

It was arranged that the couple would live at the grandfather's. Monsieur Gillenormand absolutely insisted on giving them his room, the nicest in the house. "It will rejuvenate me," he declared. "It is an old scheme of mine. I always planned to liven up my room." He filled the room with a swag of old gentlemanly knickknacks. He had a new ceiling put up and hung with an extraordinary fabric he happened to have a bolt of and which he thought was from Utrecht, velvet bear's ear flowers on a satiny buttercup yellow background.

"It was with some of this fabric," he said, "that the bed of the duchesse d'Anville was draped at La Roche-Guyon."[20]

On the mantelpiece he planted a Saxony figurine holding a muff over her bare stomach.

Monsieur Gillenormand's library became the attorney's chambers Marius needed, chambers, you will remember, being required by the rules of the order.

## VII. Dream Effects Fusing into Happiness

The lovers saw each other every day. Cosette came along with Monsieur Fauchelevent. "It's doing things the wrong way round," said Mademoiselle Gillenormand, "for the intended to come to the groom's home and be courted like this." But Marius's convalescence had become a habit and the rue des Filles-du-Calvaire armchairs, better for tête-à-têtes than the straw-bottomed chairs of the rue de l'Homme-Armé, had firmly established it. Marius and Monsieur Fauchelevent saw each other but did not speak to each other. It seemed that this was some sort of agreement. Every girl needs a chaperone. Cosette would not have been able to come without Monsieur Fauchelevent. For Marius, Monsieur Fauchelevent was the condition on which he saw Cosette. He accepted him. By bringing up certain political questions, vaguely and without going into particulars, to do with the general improvement in everyone's lot, they managed to say a bit more than yes or no to each other.

Once, on the subject of education, which Marius thought should be free and compulsory, spread far and wide in all its forms, lavished on all like the air and the sun, in a word, breathable by the whole population, they were in complete agreement and almost chatted. Marius noticed on that occasion that Monsieur Fauchelevent spoke well and even with a certain linguistic flair. Yet he was lacking some indefinable quality. Monsieur Fauchelevent was something less than a man of the world—and something more.

Inwardly and at the back of his mind, Marius surrounded this Monsieur Fauchelevent, who was to him simply benevolent and cold, with all sorts of silent questions. At times, he had doubts about his own memories. There was a hole in his memory, a black spot, an abyss hollowed out by four months at death's door. Many things had gotten lost down it. He had even got to the point of wondering if it was really true that he had seen Monsieur Fauchelevent, such a serious and calm man, at the barricade.

And this was not the only blank spot that the comings and goings of the past had left in his mind. It would be wrong to think that he was freed from all those obsessions of memory that force us, even when we are happy, even when we are satisfied, to look back in melancholy. The head that does not turn round toward horizons that have vanished can neither think nor love. At times, Marius covered his face with his hands and the vague but tumultuous past would travel across the dim twilight in his brain. He saw Mabeuf fall again, he heard Gavroche sing under the grapeshot, he felt the coldness of Éponine's forehead against his lips; Enjolras, Courfeyrac, Jean Prouvaire, Combeferre, Bossuet, Grantaire, all his friends rose before him, then evaporated. All these beloved beings, sorrowful, valiant, charming, or tragic—were they dreams? Had they actually existed? The riot had wreathed everything in its smoke. Those great fevers produce great dreams. He questioned himself; he patted himself down; he was dizzy from all those vanished realities. Where had they all gone? Was it really true that they were all dead? A tumble in the dark had carried all away, except for him. All that seemed to him to have disappeared as though behind a theater curtain. Curtains do come down like that on life. God skips to the next act.

And what about him? Was he actually the same man? He, the pauper, was rich; he, the abandoned, had a family; he, the hopeless, was marrying Cosette. He felt like he had been through a tomb, going in black and coming out white. But the others had stayed there. At certain moments, all these creatures from the past came back from the dead and formed a ring around him and cast a shadow over him like a dark cloud; then he would think of Cosette and he became serene once more; but nothing less than this felicity was needed to erase that catastrophe.

Monsieur Fauchelevent very nearly had a place among those vanished beings. Marius found it hard to believe that the Fauchelevent of the barricade was the same as this Fauchelevent of flesh and blood, so gravely seated by Cosette's side. The first was probably one of those nightmares that came and went during his hours of delirium. In any case, both of them being unapproachable, there was no way Marius could put a question of any kind to Monsieur Fauchelevent. The idea did not even occur to him. We have already pointed out this typical detail.

For two men to have a common secret, yet, through a sort of tacit agreement not exchange a single word on the subject, is not as rare as you might think. Only once did Marius make an attempt of the kind. Bringing up the rue de la Chanvrerie in conversation, he turned to Monsieur Fauchelevent and asked him: "You know the street well, don't you?"

"What street?"

"The rue de la Chanvrerie."

"I have no idea what the name of the street is," answered Monsieur Fauchelevent in the most natural tone in the world.

The answer, which had to do with the name of the street and not the street itself, appeared to Marius more conclusive than it was.

"Obviously," he thought, "I must have been dreaming. I must have had a hallucination. It's someone who looks like him. Monsieur Fauchelevent was not there."

## VIII. TWO MEN WHO CAN'T BE FOUND

The enchantment, great as it was, did not wipe other preoccupations from Marius's mind. While the wedding was gearing up and while waiting for the agreed-upon day to arrive, he had some tricky and thorough retrospective investigations carried out.

He owed gratitude on several sides; he owed some to his father, he owed some to himself. There was Thénardier; there was the unknown man who had brought him, Marius, back to Monsieur Gillenormand's. Marius was keen to find these two men, not intending to marry, be happy, and forget them, and fearing that these debts of duty if unpaid would cast a shadow over his life, so luminous now. He was not the sort of person who could leave all these arrears overdue behind him, and he wanted, before joyfully embarking on the future, to have paid the past's bill.

That Thénardier was a scoundrel in no way detracted from the fact that he had saved Colonel Pontmercy's life. Thénardier was a crook to everyone else but Marius. And Marius, knowing nothing about what really happened on the battlefield of Waterloo, did not know this specific fact, which was that his father was, in relation to Thénardier, in the strange situation of owing the man his life without owing him gratitude.

None of the sundry agents Marius employed managed to pick up Thénardier's scent. All traces seemed to have been obliterated on that side. Mother
Thénardier had died in prison during the preliminary inquiry pending trial.
Thénardier and his daughter Azelma, the two sole survivors of the woeful clan,
had melted back into the shadows. The fathomless pit of the social Unknown had
silently closed over those beings. You could no longer even see on the surface
that quivering and trembling, those faint concentric circles that announce that
something has fallen in and that a probe might be thrown in after them.

With mother Thénardier dead, Boulatruelle out of harm's way, Claquesous
vanished into thin air, the principal accused broken out of jail, the legal proceedings relating to the ambush in the Gorbeau slum had more or less aborted.
The affair had been left up in the air. The bench of the circuit court had had
to make do with two underlings, Panchaud, alias Printanier, alias Bigrenaille,
and Demi-liard, alias Deux-milliards, who had been sentenced in the presence
of the parties involved to ten years in the galleys. A verdict of hard labor in
perpetuity had been delivered against their accomplices who had escaped and
did not appear. Thénardier, chief and ringleader, had been sentenced to death,
also in absentia. This sentence was the only thing left of Thénardier, casting
its sinister glow on his buried name, like a candle next to a bier. Besides, by
causing Thénardier to dive back down into the lowest depths for fear of being
seized again, the sentence only added to the thick layer of murk that covered
the man.

As for the other one, the unidentified stranger who had saved Marius's life,
the investigation initially yielded some results, then stalled. They managed to
find the fiacre that had brought Marius back to the rue des Filles-du-Calvaire
on the night of June 6. The driver declared that on June 6, according to a police
officer's orders, he had "parked," from three o'clock in the afternoon till nightfall, on the quai des Champs-Élysées, above the outlet of the Grand Sewer;
that, at around nine o'clock in the evening, the sewer gate that opens onto the
riverbank had opened; that a man had emerged from it, carrying on his shoulders another man, who looked to be dead; that, on the officer's orders, he, the
driver, had accommodated "all those people" in his fiacre; that they had first
gone to the rue des Filles-du-Calvaire; that they had put the dead man down
there—that was Monsieur Marius—that he, the driver, recognized him perfectly, even though he was alive "this time round"; that, after that, they had got
back in his cab, that he had whipped his horses, that, a few feet from the porte
des Archives, they'd shouted at him to stop, that there, in the street, they had
paid him and left him and that the officer had taken the other man with him,
that he did not know anything more; that it had been a very dark night.

Marius, as we said, remembered nothing. He only remembered being
grabbed from behind by a very strong hand just as he was falling backward into

the barricade; then everything was a blank. He had only recovered consciousness at Monsieur Gillenormand's.

He got bogged down in conjectures. He could not doubt his own identity.
Yet how come, having fallen in the rue de la Chanvrerie, he had been picked up
by the police officer on the bank of the Seine near the pont des Invalides?
Somebody had carried him from Les Halles quartier to the Champs-Élysées.
How? Through the sewer. Unheard-of devotion! Somebody? Who?

It was this man that Marius was looking for. Of this man, who was his savior, nothing; not a trace; not the slightest sign.

Although forced to tread very carefully here, Marius pushed his investigations as far as the prefecture of police. There, the information obtained did not
lead to any enlightenment, any more than elsewhere. The prefecture knew less
than the cabdriver. They were not aware of any arrest carried out on June 6 at
the gate of the Grand Sewer; they had received no officer's report about such an
action, which, at the prefecture, was regarded as a fable—a fable they attributed
to the driver. A driver looking for a tip is capable of anything, even of imagination. The action had definitely happened, though, and Marius could not doubt
it, unless he doubted his own identity, as we were saying a moment ago. Everything, in this strange puzzle, was inexplicable.

The man, the mystery man, who the driver had seen coming out of the
gate of the Grand Sewer carrying the unconscious Marius on his back, and
whom the police officer on the lookout had arrested in the act of rescuing an
insurgent—what had become of him? What had become of the officer himself?
Why had this officer maintained his silence? Had the man succeeded in escaping? Had he bribed the officer? Why didn't the man give Marius some sign of
life, when Marius was in his eternal debt? The man's disinterestedness was no
less staggering than his devotion. Why didn't the man reappear? Maybe he was
above a reward, but no one is above gratitude. Was he dead? What sort of man
was he? What did he look like? No one could say. The driver answered: "It was
a very dark night." Basque and Nicolette, flabbergasted, had been riveted by
their young master all covered in blood. The porter, whose candle had shed
light on the tragic arrival of Marius, was alone in noticing the man in question,
but the only description he gave of him was this: "The man was awful."

In the hope of making use of them in his investigations, Marius had had
preserved the bloodstained clothes he had on when he had been brought home
to his grandfather's. On examining the coat, it was noticed that there was an odd
tear. A bit was missing.

One evening, Marius was talking, in front of Cosette and Jean Valjean,
about the whole peculiar episode, of the endless information he had gathered,
and the pointlessness of his efforts. The stony face of "Monsieur Fauchelevent"
irritated him. He cried out with a vehemence that almost had the ringing tone

of anger: "Yes, that man, whoever he is, was sublime. Do you know what he did, Monsieur? He intervened, like the archangel. He would have had to hurl himself into the middle of the fray, steal me away, open up the sewer, drag me down into it, carry me through it! He would have had to go more than a league and a half, through hideous underground tunnels, bent over, buckled under, in the dark, in the cesspool, more than a league and a half, Monsieur, with a corpse on his back! And with what aim? With the single aim of saving the corpse. And the corpse was me. He said to himself: 'There is perhaps a glimmer of life in there yet; I'm going to risk my own existence for that miserable spark!' And his existence—he didn't just risk it once, but twenty times! And every step of the way was dangerous. The proof is that, when he came out of the sewer, he was arrested. Did you know, Monsieur, that this man did all that? And with no reward waiting for him. What was I? An insurgent. What was I? One of the defeated. Oh, if Cosette's six hundred thousand francs were mine—"

"They are yours," Jean Valjean cut in.

"Well, then," Marius resumed, "I would give them all to find that man!"

Jean Valjean said nothing.

# BOOK SIX

# A SLEEPLESS NIGHT

## I. FEBRUARY 16, 1833[1]

The night of the sixteenth of February, 1833, was a blessed night. Above its shadow sat the open sky. It was Marius and Cosette's wedding night.

The day had been wonderful.

It had not been the sky blue fête of the grandfather's dreams, a spectacular fairyland with a welter of cherubs and cupids over the married couple's heads, a wedding worthy of featuring in a frieze above a door; but it had been sweet and happy.

The fashion for weddings in 1833 was not what it is today. France had not yet borrowed from England the supreme refinement of abducting your wife, running off as soon as you are out the church door, hiding your happiness in shame and generally behaving like a bankrupt emulating the ravishment portrayed in the Song of Songs.[2] They had not yet realized how terribly chaste, exquisite, and decent it is to go bumping your taste of paradise about in a post chaise, to chop your secret pleasure up with clickety-clacks, to take a bed in an inn as the nuptial bed and leave behind, in the banal alcove at so much a night, the most sacred of life's memories all jumbled up indiscriminately with the tête-à-tête you had with the stagecoach driver and the servant at the inn.

In this second half of the nineteenth century in which we live, the mayor and his sash, the priest and his chasuble,[3] the law and God, are no longer enough; we have to top them up with the Longjumeau postilion: blue jacket with red lapels and bell-shaped buttons; badge worn as an armband, green leather breeches, curses directed at Norman horses with knotted tails, imitation galloons, oilskin hat, big powdered hair, enormous whip, and sturdy boots. France has not yet carried elegance as far as the English nobility, who shower down-at-the-heel slippers and old worn-out shoes on the married couple's post barouche, in memory of Churchill, later Marlborough,[4] or Malbrouck, who was assailed on his wedding day by the wrath of an aunt that brought him luck. The old shoes and the slippers are not yet part of our nuptial celebrations. But, patience; with good taste continuing to spread, we will get there. In 1833, a hundred years ago, the act of marriage was not performed at a brisk trot.

They still imagined in those days, oddly enough, that a wedding was an intimate social fête, that a patriarchal banquet did not spoil the domestic solemnity, that gaiety, even when excessive, provided it remained decent, did not hurt happiness, and that, in the end, it was noble and good that the fusion of two destinies from which a family would emerge should begin at home, and that the nuptial chamber should be a witness from that moment on to the union. And they had the cheek to marry at home.

The wedding reception took place, then, after this now-outdated fashion, at Monsieur Gillenormand's.

As natural and normal as the business of marrying may be, there is always some complication with the banns to be published, the acts to be drawn up, the *mairie,* the church. They could not be ready before February 16.

Now, we note this detail for the sheer satisfaction of being precise, it so happened that February 16 was a Mardi Gras, Shrove Tuesday. Hesitations, scruples, particularly on the part of Aunt Gillenormand.

"A Mardi Gras!" cried the grandfather. "So much the better. There is a proverb:

A Mardi Gras wedding match
And you'll avoid ungrateful brats.[5]

"Let's carry on regardless. The sixteenth it is! You don't want to put it back, do you, Marius?"

"No, of course not!" replied the lover.

"Let's get married, then," said the grandfather.

And so the wedding took place on the sixteenth, notwithstanding the public festivities. It rained that day, but there is always a little pocket of blue in the sky at the service of happiness, which lovers see even when the rest of creation is huddled under an umbrella.

The night before, Jean Valjean had handed Marius the five hundred and eighty-four thousand francs in the presence of Monsieur Gillenormand. The marriage being based on joint ownership of property, the acts were straightforward.

Toussaint was now of no use to Jean Valjean; Cosette had inherited her and had promoted her to the rank of lady's maid. As for Jean Valjean, there was in the Gillenormand house a lovely room done up just for him, and Cosette had said to him so irresistibly, "Father, please, I implore you," that she had more or less got him to promise he would come and live in it.

A few days before the day fixed for the wedding, Jean Valjean had had an accident; he had injured his right thumb. It was not serious and he would not allow anyone to look at it, or bandage it, or even to see that he was in pain, not even Cosette. But it had forced him nonetheless to wrap up his hand in some linen and to wear his arm in a sling, and so had prevented him from signing anything. Monsieur Gillenormand, as Cosette's surrogate guardian, had stood in for him.

We will not take the reader either to the *mairie* or to the church. It is not done to follow two lovers as far as that, the usual practice being to turn one's back to the drama as soon as a bridegroom's sprig is safely in its buttonhole. We will restrict ourselves to noting an incident that, although unnoticed by the wedding party, marked the trip from the rue des Filles-du-Calvaire to the church of Saint-Paul.[6]

At the time, the north end of the rue Saint-Louis was being repaved. It was cordoned off from the rue du Parc-Royal on. This meant it was impossible for the two wedding cars to go directly to Saint-Paul's. There was no choice but to change the itinerary, and the simplest thing to do was to turn off at the boulevard. One of the guests observed that it was Mardi Gras and that the place would be packed with carriages there. "Why?" asked Monsieur Gillenormand. "Because of the masks."[7] "Splendid!" said the grandfather. "Let's go that way. These young people are getting married. They're about to enter the serious business of life. Getting a look at a bit of a masquerade will set them up nicely."

They took the boulevard. The first of the wedding berlins contained Cosette and Aunt Gillenormand, Monsieur Gillenormand, and Jean Valjean. Marius, still kept apart from his fiancée, according to custom, came only in the second. The nuptial cortège, on leaving the rue des Filles-du-Calvaire, joined the long procession of carriages that formed an endless chain from the Madeleine to the Bastille and from the Bastille to the Madeleine.

Masks were to be seen all over the boulevard. It could rain all it liked, as often as it liked, Paillasse, Pantaloon, and Gilles[8] were not about to call it a day. In the good-humored atmosphere of the winter of 1833, Paris had disguised itself as Venice.[9] You don't see Mardi Gras like that anymore. All that exists now being one great carnival, there is no carnival anymore.

The side alleys were choked with people out and about and windows were crammed with the curious. The loggias that crown the peristyles of the theaters were overflowing with onlookers. Apart from the masks, they were lapping up the parade, peculiar to Mardi Gras and Longchamp, of vehicles of all kinds—fiacres, *citadines*, covered breaks known as *tapissières*, charabancs, carioles, gigs, all rolling along in orderly fashion, rigorously hooked up to each other by police regulations as though running on rails. Anyone sitting in these vehicles is at once spectator and spectacle. Police constables on the sides of the boulevard were keeping these two interminable parallel lines moving in opposite directions and watching closely to ensure that nothing hampered the twin flow of the two streams of cars running upstream and downstream, either toward the chaussée d'Antin or toward the faubourg Saint-Antoine. The emblazoned carriages of the peers of France and the ambassadors stuck to the middle of the road where they could come and go untrammeled. Certain magnificent and rowdy cortèges, notably the Fat Ox,[10] the special model of a prize ox, enjoyed the same privilege. In this gay Paris, England cracked its whip; the post chaise of Lord Seymour,[11] harassed by a vulgar nickname, rolled along with much racket.

In the double line, which Municipal Guards galloped up and down like sheepdogs, honest-to-goodness family berlingots,[12] loaded up with great-aunts and grandmothers, displayed at their doors clusters of fresh-faced children in disguise, seven-year-old Pierrots, six-year-old Pierrettes,[13] ravishing little creatures who, sensing that they were officially part of the public rejoicing, were pervaded by the dignity of the harlequinade and were as grave as public servants.

From time to time a traffic jam occurred somewhere in the procession of vehicles, and one or the other of the two lines would stop just long enough for the knot to be disentangled; one carriage held up was enough to bring the whole line to a standstill. Then they would resume their course.

The wedding coaches were in the line heading toward the Bastille and hugging the right side of the boulevard. Where the rue du Pont-aux-Choux comes in, there was a halt. Almost at the same moment, on the other shoulder, the line going the other way toward the Madeleine also stopped.

These cars, or, to be more precise, these cartloads of masks, are only too familiar to Parisians. If they were missing from a Mardi Gras or a mid-Lent carnival,[14] people would see something sinister in it and they would say: "There's something behind this. The ministry's probably about to go." A heap of Cassandras, Harlequins, and Columbines, jigging past over the heads of the onlookers, every possible grotesque from the Turk to the Savage, Hercules ferrying marquises, fishwives who would make Rabelais block his ears just as the maenads[15] caused Aristophanes to lower his gaze, hemp wigs, pink costumes, loud swaggerers' hats, buffoonish glasses, pirates' cocked hats teased by butterflies, shouts hurled at pedestrians, hands on hips, brazen posturing, bare shoulders, masked faces, unfettered shamelessness; a chaotic profusion of effrontery driven about by a coach driver with flowers in his hair—that is the institution in a nutshell.

Greece needed Thespis's chariot, France needs Vadé's fiacre.[16]

Everything can be parodied, even parody. The saturnalia, that grimace of antique beauty, gets bigger and bigger all the time until it turns into Mardi Gras; and the bacchanal, once crowned with vines, flooded with sunshine, and showing marble breasts in divine semi-nakedness, has today gone flabby under the wet rags of the north and has ended up calling itself a *chie-en-lit*, a shit-a-bed, or shambles of the more demoniac kind.

The tradition of cars of masks—masked revelers—goes back as far as the earliest years of the monarchy. Louis XI's accounts allocate to the bailiff "twenty sous minted at Tours for three coaches for boulevard masquerades." In our time, these boisterous piles of creatures usually get themselves lugged about in some ancient contraption where they clutter the top deck, or they tumultuously overwhelm a government landau with its hood folded back. Twenty of them pile in a car built for six. There they are, on the box, on the folding seat, on the sides of the hood, on the trailing arm. They even straddle the carriage lanterns. They stand, lie, sit, legs curled up, legs dangling; the women camp on the men's knees. You can see the frantic pyramid they form in the distance over the teeming heads. These cartloads are mountains of merriment in the middle of the throng. Collé, Panard, and Piron,[17] those masters of vaudeville, come from here, spiced up with a bit of slang. The vulgar catechism is spat at the people from up there. That fiacre, which has ballooned with its load, has an air of conquest. Hubbub is out in front, hurly-burly brings up the rear. They scream and shout up there, they practice their scales, they howl, they explode, they wriggle with glee; hilarity roars up there, sarcasm blazes, joviality flaunts itself as though born to the purple; two nags drag farce along up there flourishing as apotheosis; it is the triumphal cart of Laughter.

A laughter too cynical to be frank. And indeed that laughter is suspect. That laughter has a mission. Its job is to prove to Parisians that there is such a thing as a carnival.

These gaudy cars, which exude a brooding darkness you can feel, give the philosopher pause for thought. There is a whiff of the government about them. In them we can put our finger on the mysterious affinity between public figures and public women—prostitutes.

That depraved acts should stack up to yield a total of gaiety; that ignominy piled on top of opprobrium should entice a people; that espionage, propping prostitution up like a caryatid, should amuse the hordes by confronting them; that the crowd should enjoy seeing go by, on the four wheels of a fiacre, this monstrous living heap, tattered tinsel, half trash, half light, barking and singing; that people should applaud this glory that is made up of every kind of disgrace; that there should be no fête for the multitudes unless the police parade among them these sorts of hydras of jubilation with twenty heads—yes, that is sad. But what can you do about it? These tumbrels of beribboned and flower-bedecked slime are both insulted and amnestied by public laughter. The laughter of all is complicit in the universal degradation. Certain unwholesome fêtes cause the people to disintegrate and degenerate into plebs; and plebs, like tyrants, require buffoons. The king has Roquelaure, the people have Paillasse[18] the clown. Paris is the great city of the madcap, whenever it is not the great city of the sublime. The carnival is part of politics there. Paris, let's admit it, is only too happy to let infamy provide it with comedy. It asks of its masters—when it has masters— only one thing: dress up the muck for us. Rome was of the same temperament. Rome loved Nero. Nero was a colossal float hauler.

Chance would have it, as we said, that one of this amorphous gaggles of masked men and women, trundling along in a vast barouche, stopped on the left of the boulevard just as the wedding cortège stopped on the right. From the opposite side of the boulevard, the car with the masks was facing the car with the bride.

"Look!" said a mask. "A wedding."

"A sham wedding," said another mask. "We're the real thing."

And, too far away to be able to call out to the wedding party, and also fearing to be stopped by the police, the two masks looked elsewhere.

The whole masked cartload had enough on their plates a moment later when the multitude began to boo it, which is the crowd's seal of approval in masquerades; and the two masks that had just spoken had to stand up to everyone else along with their cohorts and needed all the projectiles in the Les Halles repertoire to respond to the enormous barbs hurled at them by the people. An alarming exchange of metaphors occurred between masks and throng.

Meanwile, two other masks in the same car, an old-fashioned-looking Spaniard with an outsize nose and an enormous black mustache, and a skinny fishwife of a young girl wearing an eye mask, or *loup*, had also noticed the wedding party, and while their companions and the passersby were busy insulting each other, they carried on a dialogue in a muted tone.

Their private conversation was covered by the tumult and swallowed up by it. Gusts of rain had drenched the wide-open car; the February wind is not warm; all the while answering the Spaniard, the fishwife, in her low-cut dress, shivered, chortled, and coughed.

This is how the dialogue went:

"Well, I never!"

"What, pop?"

"You see that old geezer?"

"What old geezer?"

"There, in the first caravan of that wedding party, on our side."

"The one with his arm hooked up in a black cravat?"

"Yes."

"Well?"

"I'm sure I know him."

"Ah!"

"I'll be hanged and I'll eat my hat if I'm not acquainted with that *pantinois* of a Parisian there."

"It's today that Paris is Pantin."[19]

"Can you see the bride, if you lean forward?"

"No."

"What about the groom?"

"There's no groom in that caravan."

"Bah!"

"Unless it's the other old geezer."

"Lean right over and try and get a gander at the bride."

"I can't."

"Never mind, the old geezer with the thing on his mitt, I'm sure I know him."

"And what's it to you if you do know him?"

"You never know. It might come in handy!"

"I don't give two hoots about any old geezer, myself."

"Don't I know it!"

"You can know him all you like."

"How in hell did he get to be at a wedding?"

"We're at it too, good as."

"Where's it come from, this wedding party?"

"How would I know?"

"Listen."

"What?"

"There's something you have to do."

"What?"

"Hop down from our caravan and tail the wedding party."

"What for?"

"To find out where they're going and what they're up to. Hurry up and get down, go on, hop it, my little elf, you're the young one."

"I can't leave the carriage."

"Why not?"

"I've been hired."

"Bugger!"

"I owe the prefecture my day as a fishwife."

"That's true."

"If I leave the carriage the first inspector that claps eyes on me'll arrest me. You know very well."

"Yes, I know."

"Today, I've been bought by that show-off, the governor."

"Never mind. That old geezer's getting my goat."

"Old geezers always get your goat. And you're not even a young girl."

"He's in the front car."

"So?"

"In the bride's caravan."

"What of it?"

"So he's the father."

"What's that to me?"

"I'm telling you he's the father."

"He isn't the only father in the world."

"Listen."

"What?"

"I can hardly get out unless I'm masked. Here I'm hidden, no one knows I'm here. But tomorrow, that's it for the masks. It's Ash Wednesday. I'll be lucky if I don't get nabbed. I'll have to crawl back into my hole. You, you're free."

"Not so free."

"Freer than me."

"So what?"

"I want you to try and find out where that wedding party's going."

"Where it's going?"

"Yes."

"I know."

"So where's it going?"

"To the Cadran Bleu."

"In the first place, that's not the way."

"Well, then! To La Rapée."[20]

"Or somewhere else."

"It's free. Weddings are free."

"That's not all there is to it. I tell you, I want you to try and find out for me what's going on with that wedding party that the old geezer's part of, and where that wedding party lives."

"Not on your life! Talk about rich. You'd think there was nothing to it—one week later, finding a wedding party that went by in Paris at Mardi Gras! Like looking for a needle in a lousy haystack! Can it even be done?"

"Doesn't matter, I want you to give it a go. You hear me, Azelma?"

The two lines began moving again in opposite directions on either side of the boulevard, and the car with the masks lost sight of the bride's "caravan."

## II. JEAN VALJEAN STILL HAS HIS ARM IN A SLING

To have your dreams come true. To whom is that given? There must be elections for this in heaven; we are all candidates without knowing it; the angels vote. Cosette and Marius had been elected.

Cosette, at the *mairie* and in church, was at once stunning and moving. It was Toussaint, with a little help from Nicolette, who had dressed her.

Cosette wore her gown of Binche guipure lace over a taffeta petticoat, a veil in point d'Angleterre lace, a necklace of fine pearls, a crown of orange blossoms;[1] all this was in white and, in all this whiteness, she shone. It was exquisite candor opening and being transfigured into luminosity. She looked like a virgin on her way to becoming a goddess.

Marius's beautiful hair was lustrous and perfumed; you could see faint lines here and there under the thick curls that were the scars from the barricade.

The grandfather, superb, his head held high, uniting more than ever in his toilette and in his manners all the elegance of the days of Barras,[2] gave Cosette away. He replaced Jean Valjean who, because he still had his arm in that sling, could not give the bride his hand.

Jean Valjean, in black, followed behind, smiling.

"Monsieur Fauchelevent," the grandfather said to him, "what a great day it is. I vote for an end to affliction and chagrin. There should be no sadness anywhere from now on. Good Lord! I decree joy! Bad has no right to exist. The fact that there are unhappy men truly does shame the blue of the skies above. Bad does not come from man, who is, at bottom, good. All forms of human misery have, as their administrative seat and central government, hell—in other words, the devil's Tuileries. Good, now I'm talking like a demagogue! As for me, I don't have any political opinions anymore; let all men be rich, that is, full of joy, that's all I ask for."

When all phases of the ceremony were fully completed, after every possible "yes" had been uttered before the mayor and before the priest, after the registers at the municipality and at the sacristy had been signed, after their rings had been exchanged, after they had knelt together elbow to elbow under the canopy of white moiré in the smoke from the censer, hand in hand, admired and envied by all, Marius in black, she in white, preceded by the Swiss Guard with his colonel's epaulets striking the flagstones with his halberd, between two rows of marveling onlookers, they reached the portal of the church, whose double doors were open, ready to climb back into the carriage again now that it was all over, Cosette still could not believe it. She looked at Marius, she looked at the crowd, she looked at the sky; it seemed she was afraid to wake up. Her stunned and anxious air made her even more mysteriously enchanting. For the return journey, they got into the same carriage together, with Marius next to Cosette and Monsieur Gillenormand and Jean Valjean sitting opposite. Aunt

Gillenormand had taken a step back and was in the second carriage. "My children," the grandfather was saying, "here you are Monsieur le baron and Madame la baronne with a living of thirty thousand pounds a year." And Cosette, leaning up close into Marius, caressed his ear with this angelic whisper: "So it's true. My name is Marius. I am Madame You."

Those two shone. They had reached that irreversible and unrepeatable moment, the dazzling point where youth and joy meet and achieve perfection. They were the very embodiment of Jean Prouvaire's poem; together they did not have forty years between them. It was marriage made sublime; those two children were as innocent as two white lilies. They did not see each other, they contemplated each other. Cosette perceived Marius in a glory; Marius perceived Cosette on an altar. And on that altar and in that glory, the two apotheoses merging, somewhere in the background, who knows how—perhaps behind a cloud for Cosette, in a blaze for Marius—there lay the ideal thing, the real thing, the rendezvous of the kiss and the dream, the nuptial pillow.

All the torment they had felt came back to them as intoxication. It seemed to them that the heartache, the sleepless nights, the tears, the anguish, the horror, the despair, having turned to caresses and rays of light, made the moment that was approaching even lovelier; and that their sorrows were so many servants dressing their joy for the occasion. How good to have suffered! Their unhappiness formed a halo over their happiness. The long agony of their love ended in an ascension.

Both their souls were under the same spell, nuanced with voluptuous anticipation in Marius and with modest awe in Cosette. They whispered quietly to each other: We'll go back and see our little garden in the rue Plumet again. The folds of Cosette's frock flowed over Marius's legs.

A day like this is an ineffable mixture of dream and certainty. You possess and you assume. You still have enough time ahead of you to guess. Being at midday dreaming of midnight on such a day is an overwhelming emotion. The delight these two hearts felt spilled over onto the crowd and gave the onlookers a joyful lift.

People stopped in the rue Saint-Antoine in front of Saint-Paul's to peer through the carriage windows and watch the orange blossom quiver on Cosette's head.

Then the party went back to the rue des Filles-du-Calvaire—their home. Marius, with Cosette at his side, climbed the stairs, triumphant and beaming, the same stairs he had been dragged up half dead. The poor, gathered together in front of the door and receiving a share of their purses, blessed them. There were flowers everywhere. The house was no less filled with fragrance than the church; after the incense, roses. They thought they could hear voices singing in infinity; they had God in their hearts; destiny appeared to them as a ceiling of stars; they saw above their heads a glimmer of the rising sun. All of a sudden, the clock rang out. Marius gazed at Cosette's lovely bare arms and the pink bits you could vaguely make out through the lace of her bodice, and Cosette, seeing Marius look, began to blush to the roots of her hair.

A good number of old friends of the Gillenormand family had been invited and they buzzed around Cosette, vying with each other to call her Madame la baronne.

The officer Théodule Gillenormand, now captain, had come up from Chartres, where he was in charge of the garrison, to attend the wedding of his cousin Pontmercy. Cosette did not recognize him.

He, for his part, accustomed to being found good-looking by the ladies, did not remember Cosette any more than any other woman.

"How right I was not to believe that story about the lancer!" old Gillenormand said to himself.

Cosette had never been more loving to Jean Valjean. She was as one with old Gillenormand; while he elevated joy into aphorisms and maxims, she gave off love and goodness like a perfume. Happiness wants everyone to be happy.

Talking to Jean Valjean, she once more hit the note she'd struck in the days when she was a little girl. She enveloped him with her smile.

A banquet had been set up in the dining room. Lighting as bright as natural light is the required seasoning for great joy. Haze and dimness are not accepted by the happy. They do not consent to being black. Night, yes; dark, no. If you don't have sunlight, you have to make it.

The dining room was ablaze with cheery brilliance. In the center, above the dazzling white table, there was a Venetian chandelier with flat crystal drops and every kind of colored bird, blue, violet, red, green, perched among the candles; around the chandelier, candelabra, on the wall, reflecting lamps with three or four branches; mirrors, crystal, glassware, tableware, porcelain, faience, ceramics, goldplate, silverware, everything sparkled and rejoiced. The spaces between the candelabra were filled with bouquets, so that wherever there wasn't a light there was a flower. In the antechamber, three violins and a flute softly played Haydn's quartets.

Jean Valjean sat down on a chair in the salon, behind the door where one of the door panels folded back on him in such a way as virtually to hide him. A few moments before everyone took their seats at the table, Cosette came, as though on a sudden impulse, to give him a low curtsy, spreading out her bridal frock with both hands and, with a lovingly impish look, she asked him: "Father, are you happy?"

"Yes," said Jean Valjean, "I'm happy."

"Well then, laugh."

Jean Valjean started to laugh.

A few seconds later, Basque announced that dinner was served.

The guests, preceded by Monsieur Gillenormand, who gave his arm to Cosette, filed into the dining room and spread out, taking their appointed places around the table.

Two big armchairs had been placed to right and left of the bride, the first for Monsieur Gillenormand, the second for Jean Valjean. Monsieur Gillenormand took his seat. The other armchair remained empty.

All eyes sought "Monsieur Fauchelevent." He was not there anymore. Monsieur Gillenormand called out to Basque.

"Do you know where Monsieur Fauchelevent is?"

"Monsieur," answered Basque, "exactly. Monsieur Fauchelevent said to tell Monsieur that he is suffering a little from his sore hand and that he could not dine with Monsieur le baron and Madame la baronne. He said he begged to be excused. He said he'd come tomorrow morning. He's just left."

That empty armchair put a damper on the exuberance of the wedding feast momentarily. But if Monsieur Fauchelevent was not there, Monsieur Gillenormand was, and the grandfather shone enough for two. He declared that Monsieur Fauchelevent was right to go to bed early if he was in pain, but that it was only a scratch. This declaration was all that was needed. Besides, what is one dark patch in such a deluge of joy? Cosette and Marius were in one of those blessed selfish moments when you can't see anything but happiness. And then, Monsieur Gillenormand had an idea.

"By Jove, this armchair is empty. Come here, Marius. Your aunt has a right to you, but she'll let you. This armchair is for you. It's legal and it's nice. Fortunatus next to Fortunata."

General applause. And so Marius took Jean Valjean's place next to Cosette; and things worked out in such a way that Cosette, at first sad about Jean Valjean's absence, ended up being happy about it. If Marius were to sit in for Him, Cosette would not have missed the Lord Himself. She placed her sweet little foot, shod in white satin, on Marius's.

With the armchair occupied, Monsieur Fauchelevent was erased; and nothing was lacking. And, five minutes later, the whole table was laughing from one end to the other with all the gusto of forgetting.

At dessert, Monsieur Gillenormand got to his feet, a glass of champagne in hand, only half full so that the tremor of his ninety-two years would not cause it to spill, and toasted the health of the bride and groom.

"You will not escape two sermons," he cried. "This morning you had the curé's, tonight you shall have the grandfather's. Bear with me. I'm going to give you a word of advice: Adore one another. I won't beat about the bush, I'll go straight to the point: Be happy. The only wise creatures in all of creation are the turtledoves. The philosophers say: Joy in moderation. I say: Let your joy run wild. Be madly, passionately in love. Be rabid. The philosophers drivel on. I'd like to ram their philosophy down their throats. Can there be too many perfumes, too many rosebuds opening, too many nightingales singing, too many green leaves, too many dawns in life? Can you love one another too much? Can you please one another too much? Look out, Estelle, you're too pretty! Look out, Némorin,[3] you're too handsome! What piffle! Can you enchant each other too much, kiss and cuddle each other too much, bewitch each other too much? Can you be too alive? Can you be too happy? Joy in moderation. What poppycock! Down with the philosophers! Wisdom is jubilation. Let you jubilate, let us jubilate. Are we happy because we are good, or are we good because we are happy? Is the Sancy diamond called the Sancy[4] because it once belonged to Harley de Sancy or because it weighs a hundred and six carats? I don't have a clue. Life is full of such problems. The important thing is to have the Sancy, and happiness. Let's be happy without quibbling. Let's blindly obey the sun. What is the sun? It is love. Whoever says love, says woman. Ah! Ah! Now, there's one thing that's omnipotent and it is woman. Ask this rabble-rouser of a Marius if he is not a slave to this little tyrant of a Cosette. And of his own accord, the coward! Woman! There is no Robespierre who can hold out, woman rules. I am no longer a royalist except when it comes to that particular royalty. What is Adam? He is the kingdom of Eve. No '89 for Eve. There was the royal scepter surmounted by a fleur-de-lis, there was the imperial scepter surmounted by a globe, there was Charlemagne's scepter which was iron, there was the Great Louis's scepter which was gold, the Revolution twisted them between its thumb and forefinger like worthless wisps of straw. It's finished, it's broken, it's on the ground, there is no more scepter. But you try and give me any revolution against this little embroidered hankie that smells of patchouli! I'd like to see you at it. Just you try. Why is it so solid? Because it's a bit of cloth. Ah, you are the nineteenth century? Well, then, what of it? We were the eighteenth, we were! And we were every bit as stupid as you. Don't imagine you've changed much in the universe, just because your *trousse-galant,* as they used to call it, now goes by the name of cholera morbus,[5] and just because your *bourrée* goes by the name of the *cachucha.* In the end, we can't help but love women always. I defy you to get out of that one. These she-devils are our angels. Yes, love, women, kissing—it is a circle I defy you to get out of. As for me, I'd like to get back in. Which of you has seen the star Venus, that great coquette of the void, the Célimène of the ocean, rising in the infinite sky, calming all below her, gazing down on the flowing waters like a woman? The ocean, now there's a rude Alceste.[6] Well, then, he can grumble all he likes; Venus appears, and he can't help but smile. The silly brute submits. We are all the same. Rage, fury, thunderbolts, spume up to the rafters. A woman enters the scene, a star rises; you fall flat on your face! Marius was fighting six months ago, now he's marrying. And so he should. Yes, Marius, yes, Cosette, you are right. Live life to the full for one another, cuddle each other to death, make us die of rage that we can't do the same, idolize one another to bits. Take all the little bits of bliss that there are on this earth in your two beaks and make yourselves a nest out of them for life. By Jove, to love and be loved, that's the great miracle of being young! Don't think for a second that you invented it. I, too, have dreamed, I have mooned about, I have sighed; I, too, have had my pocket full of moonbeams. Love has a right to a long white beard. Methuselah[7] is a mere toddler next to Cupid. For sixty centuries men and women have gotten out of trouble by loving each other. The devil, who is cunning, took to hating man; man, who is even more cunning, took to loving woman. In this way, he did himself more good than the devil did him harm. This particular bit of shrewdness was stumbled on in the earliest days of our earthly paradise. My friends, the invention goes back a long way, but it is always brand-new. Take advantage of it. Be Daphnis and Chloë while you're waiting to play Philemon and Baucis.[8] Behave in such a way that when you are with each other, nothing is lacking, and Cosette is the sun for Marius and Marius is the world for Cosette. Cosette, let the good weather for you be your husband's smile; Marius, let the rain for you be your wife's tears. And let it never rain in your home. You picked the lucky number in the lottery—love in the sacrament; you win first prize, hang on tight to it, put it under lock and key, don't waste it, adore one another, and to hell with the rest. Believe what I tell you. It's common sense. Common sense can't lie. Be a religion to each other.

"Everyone has their own way of worshipping God. Struth! The best way to worship God is to love your wife. I love you! That's my catechism for you. Whoever loves is orthodox. Henri IV's favorite swearword puts sanctity between a blowout and drunkenness. *Ventre-saint-gris!* Holy-Grey-Guts, indeed! I don't follow the religion of that swearword. Woman has been left out. That amazes me for a curse coming from Henri IV. My friends, long live woman! I am old, so they tell me; it's amazing how much younger I feel I'm growing again! I'd like to go and listen to musettes in the woods. These children here, who manage to be beautiful and happy, make my head swim. I'd get well and truly married myself if someone would have me. It's impossible to imagine that God made us for anything else but this: to idolize, to bill and coo, to strut and plume, to be pigeons, to be cocks, to peck at our loves from morning to night, to gaze at our reflections in our little woman, to be proud, to be triumphant, to puff ourselves up; that's what life is all about. That, whether you like it or not, is what we used to think, we old-timers, in our day, when we were the young blades. Ah, blow me down if there weren't charming women about in those days, and the pretty little faces, and the slips of girls! I wreaked havoc. So, love one another. If we didn't love one another, I really can't see the good in having a spring; and, as for myself, I'd ask the good Lord to pack up all the beautiful things he lays out before us and take them back and stick the flowers and the birds and the pretty girls back in his box. My children, receive this old boy's blessing."

The evening was lively, gay, genial. The grandfather's sovereign good humor set the tone for the whole fête and everyone tuned themselves according to this very nearly centenarian cordiality. They danced a little, they laughed a lot; it was a good-natured wedding. You could have invited good old Once Upon a Time to it. In any case, he was there in the person of old Gillenormand.

There was tumult, then silence. The bride and groom disappeared. A bit after midnight, the Gillenormand household turned into a temple.

We will stop there. On the threshold of wedding nights, an angel stands, smiling, a finger to its lips. The soul enters into contemplation before this sanctuary where the celebration of love takes place.

There must be glimmers above houses like this one. The joy they contain must escape through the stones of the walls as light and dimly streak the darkness. This sacred and fateful celebration is simply bound to send a celestial shimmer into infinity. Love is the sublime crucible in which a man and a woman melt together; the one being, the triple being, the final being, the human trinity, result. This birth of two souls in one must move deep night. The lover is priest, the rapt virgin filled with fear. Something of this joy travels up to God. Wherever there is a real marriage, meaning where there is love, the ideal is involved. A nuptial bed creates a pocket of dawn light in the darkness. If it were given to our eye of flesh and blood to see the fearsome and lovely sights of the higher life, we would probably see the forms of the night, winged strangers, the blue bystanders of the invisible, bend down, a throng of dark heads, over the luminous house, satisfied, blessing, pointing out to each other, sweetly alarmed, the virgin bride, and wearing the reflection of human bliss on their divine faces. If, at that supreme moment, the newlyweds, dazed with sensual rapture and believing themselves alone, were to listen, they would hear in their room the muted sound of fluttering wings. Perfect happiness implies the solidarity of angels. This little dark nook is overhung by the whole heavens. When two mouths, sanctified by love, come together to create, that ineffable kiss is simply bound to set the mysterious stars shuddering throughout immensity.

This is the real bliss. There is no joy beyond these joys. Love is the sole ecstasy here. Everything else weeps.

To love or to have loved is enough. Don't ask for anything more. There is no other pearl to be found in the shadowy folds of life. To love is an achievement.

## III. THE INSEPARABLE

What had happened to Jean Valjean?

Immediately after giving Cosette a laugh, at her sweet behest, with no one paying him any attention, Jean Valjean had gotten to his feet and gained the antechamber, unseen. This was the same room that he had entered, eight months before, black with mud, blood, and gunpowder, bringing the grandson home to his grandfather. The old woodwork was garlanded with leaves and flowers; the musicians were sitting on the sofa where they had laid Marius. Basque, in black habit, short breeches, white stockings, and white gloves, was laying crowns of roses around each of the dishes they were about to serve. Jean Valjean had shown him his arm in a sling, had asked him to explain his absence for him, and left.

The windows of the dining room looked out onto the street. Jean Valjean stood motionless in the dark for a few minutes under those blazing windows, listening. The muffled noise reached him. He heard the exalted and brilliant speech of the grandfather, the violins, the clatter of the plates and clink of the glasses, the peals of laughter, and in all this gay uproar he clearly made out Cosette's sweet joyful voice.

He left the rue des Filles-du-Calvaire and turned to go back to the rue de l'Homme-Armé.

The way he took was the rue Saint-Louis, the rue Culture-Sainte-Catherine, and the rue des Blancs-Manteaux; it was a little longer, but it was the way he had gotten used to coming, every day for the past three months, from the rue de l'Homme-Armé to the rue des Filles-du-Calvaire, with Cosette, thereby avoiding the congestion and mud of the rue Vieille-du-Temple. The fact that Cosette had come this way ruled out every other route for him.

Jean Valjean arrived home. He lit his candle and went upstairs. The apartment was empty. Even Toussaint was not there now. Jean Valjean's footsteps made more of a noise than usual through the rooms. All the cupboards were open. He went into Cosette's room. There were no sheets on the bed. The pillow of drill, without pillowcase and without lacework, was placed on the folded blankets at the foot of the mattress, of which you could see the ticking and on which no one would be sleeping ever again. All the little feminine objects Cosette held so dear had been taken away; only the heavy furniture and the four walls remained. Toussaint's bed was also stripped. A single bed was made up and seemed to be waiting for someone, and that someone was himself, Jean Valjean.

Jean Valjean looked at the walls, shut a few of the cupboard doors, wandered about from room to room. Then he found himself back in his room, and he put his candle down on a table.

He had taken his arm out of the sling and was using his right hand as though it did not hurt a bit.

He went over to his bed, and his eyes fell—was it by chance? was it intentional?—on the "inseparable," which Cosette had been jealous of—the little trunk that never left his side. On June 4, when he'd arrived at the rue de l'Homme-Armé, he had put it on an occasional table beside the bed. He bounded over to this table, took a key from his pocket, and opened the suitcase.

He slowly pulled out the clothes in which, ten years before, Cosette had left Montfermeil; first, the little black dress, then the black fichu, then the good old chunky children's shoes that Cosette could still almost get into, her feet were so small, then the child's vest of good thick fustian, then the knitted petticoat, then the smock with pockets, then the woolen stockings. These stockings, still gracefully molded to the shape of little legs, were scarcely any longer than Jean Valjean's hand. All the things were black. It was he who had brought these clothes to Montfermeil for her. As he took them out of the suitcase, he laid them on the bed. He was thinking. He was remembering. It was winter, a very cold December, she was shivering half-naked in her rags, her poor little feet red raw in clogs. He, Jean Valjean, had got her to take off those tatters and to put on this mourning outfit. The mother must have been happy in her grave to see her daughter wearing mourning for her, and especially to see that she was all dressed up and that she was warm. He thought about the forest of Montfermeil; they had crossed it together, Cosette and he; he thought about the weather at the time, about the leafless trees, about the birdless woods, about the sunless sky; that hadn't mattered, it was lovely. He arranged the tiny old clothes on the bed, the fichu next to the petticoat, the stockings beside the shoes, the little vest beside the dress, and he looked at them, one by one. She was only just so high, she had her big doll in her arms, she had put her gold louis in the pocket of this smock, she was laughing, they were walking together hand in hand, she had nobody in all the world but him.

Then his venerable white head dropped onto the bed, his stoical old heart broke, he buried his face, so to speak, in Cosette's clothes, and if anyone had passed on the stairs at that moment, they would have heard the sound of heartrending sobs.

## IV. IMMORTALE JECUR[1]

The old tremendous struggle, of which we have seen several phases, started all over again.

Jacob wrestled with the angel[2] for only one night. Alas! How many times have we seen Jean Valjean seized in the dark in hand-to-hand combat by his conscience and fighting desperately against it!

An unbelievable struggle! At certain moments, you lose your footing; at other times, the ground gives way. How many times had his conscience, in a frenzy to be good, tackled him and brought him down! How many times had the truth, inexorable, planted its knee on his chest! How many times, bowled over by the light, had he begged it for mercy! How many times had that implacable light, lit within him and over him by the bishop, dazzled him by force when all he wanted was to be blind! How many times had he got back on his feet to resume the fight, pinned to the rock, leaning back on sophism, dragged through the dust, sometimes toppling his conscience underneath him, sometimes toppled by it! How many times, after some equivocation, after a bout of the treacherous and specious reasoning of self-interest, had he heard his angry conscience shout in his ear: "It's a setup! Miserable bastard!" How many times had his recalcitrant thoughts convulsively railed under the obviousness of duty! Resisting God. Sweating like a man dying. All the secret wounds that he alone felt bleeding! All the flaying alive of his lamentable existence! How many times had he gotten back up covered in blood, bruised, broken, enlightened, despair in his heart, serenity in his soul! and, conquered, felt himself the conqueror. And, after having torn him apart, tortured him and broken him, his conscience, standing over him, fearsome, luminous, tranquil, would quietly say to him: "Now go in peace!"

But, coming out of such a grim struggle, what gloomy peace, alas!

That particular night, though, Jean Valjean felt he was fighting his last fight. A question presented itself, one that stabbed him through the heart.

Predestined paths are not all straight; they don't evolve into a rectilinear avenue in front of the predestined; they have their blind alleys, dead ends, obscure twists and turns, disturbing crossroads offering alternative paths. Jean Valjean was poised this moment at the most perilous of such crossroads.

He had come to the final crossing of good and evil. That was the dark intersection he now had before his eyes. And, once again, as in past painful crises, two roads opened up before him; one tempting, the other terrifying. Which one should he take?

The terrifying one was recommended by the mysterious pointing finger that we all see whenever we stare straight into the shadows.

Jean Valjean, yet again, had the choice between the frightening haven and the beckoning ambush. Can it be true, then? That the soul can be cured; but fate, no. What an appalling thing! An incurable destiny!

The question that presented itself was this:

How was Jean Valjean going to conduct himself in the face of Cosette and Marius's happiness? A happiness he himself had wanted, that he himself had made; he was the one who had stabbed himself in the guts with it, and, at this moment, looking back on it, he could feel the sort of satisfaction an armorer would have felt, recognizing his trademark on a blade as he yanked it, all fuming, out of his chest.

Cosette had Marius, Marius possessed Cosette. They had it all, even wealth. And it was his doing.

But this happiness, now that it existed, now that it was there—what was he going to do with it, he, Jean Valjean? Was he to impose himself on this happiness? Was he to treat it as belonging to him? There was no doubt that Cosette belonged to another; but was he, Jean Valjean, to hold back all that he could hold back from Cosette? Was he to remain the sort of father, rarely seen but respected, that he had been till then? Was he to quietly worm his way into Cosette's house? Was he to bring his past into that future, without saying a word? Was he to just turn up there as though he had the right and go and take a seat, disguised, at that luminous hearth? Was he to take the hands of those innocents in his two tragic hands, smiling at them all the while? Was he to put his feet up on the peaceful firedogs of the Gillenormand salon, dragging along behind them as they did the shaming shadow of the law? Was he to cast in his lot with Cosette and Marius? Was he to deepen the darkness over his head and the cloud over theirs? Was he to put his third of catastrophe in with their two shares of bliss? Was he to continue to keep quiet? In a word, was he to be the sinister mute of destiny beside those two happy souls?

You have to be used to the twists of fate and being caught up in them to dare lift your eyes when certain questions appear in all their horrible starkness. Good or evil are behind the stern question mark. What are you going to do? asks the sphinx.[3]

The habit of undergoing trials by fire is one Jean Valjean had acquired. He looked the sphinx full in the face. He examined the merciless problem from every angle.

Cosette, that lovely presence, was the life raft in this shipwreck. What was he to do? Cling on, or let go? If he clung on, he would escape disaster, he would clamber back into the sunlight, he would let the bitter water run off his clothes and his hair, he would be saved, he would live. If he let go? Then, the abyss.

And so he held dolorous counsel with his thoughts. Or, more exactly, he struggled; he thrashed around furiously inside himself, now against his will, now against his conviction.

It was just as well for Jean Valjean that he had been able to cry. That perhaps brightened him. But the beginning was fierce. A storm more violent than the one that had once driven him to Arras broke inside him. The past came back to him in a showdown with the present; he compared and he sobbed. Once the floodgates of tears were opened, the desperate man doubled up in pain.

He felt blighted.

Alas, in this unrelenting brawl between our egoism and our duty, when we thus recoil step by step before our immutable ideal, bewildered, dogged, exasperated at yielding, fighting tooth and nail, hoping for some escape route, looking for a way out, what brusque and sinister resistance the wall at our backs puts up! To feel the holy shadow barring the way! The inexorable invisible, what an obsession!

We are never done, then, with conscience. Make up your mind what to do with it, Brutus; make up your mind what to do with it, Cato.[4] It is without end, being God. We throw into this bottomless pit a lifetime of labor, we throw into it our fortune, we throw into it our wealth, we throw into it our success, we throw into it our liberty or our country, we throw into it our well-being, we throw into it our repose, we throw into it our joy. More! More! More! Empty the vessel! Tip out the urn! We are forced in the end to throw in our hearts. Somewhere in the mists of the old underworld there is a barrel like that.

Can't a person be forgiven for refusing in the end? Can the inexhaustible have a right? Aren't endless chains beyond human endurance? Who, then, would blame Sisyphus or Jean Valjean for saying: "That's enough!" The compliance of matter is limited by friction; isn't there a limit to the compliance of the soul? If perpetual motion is impossible, is perpetual devotion really due?

The first step is nothing; it is the last step that is hard. What was the Champmathieu affair beside the marriage of Cosette and all that it implied? What was this: to go back to jail, beside this: to sink into oblivion?

O, first step on the way down, how gloomy you are! O, second step, how black you are! How could he not turn his head the other way this time?

Martyrdom is a kind of moral purification, a corrosive kind of purification. It is a form of torture that crowns. You can consent to it for the first hour or so; you sit down on the throne of red-hot iron, you set the crown of red-hot iron on your head, you accept the globe of red-hot iron, you take the scepter of red-hot iron, but you still have to put on the mantle of flames; and isn't there a moment when the miserable flesh revolts and when you abdicate the torment?

At last Jean Valjean began to feel the calmness of utter devastation. He weighed, he reflected, he considered the alternatives presented by the mysterious balance of light and shadow. To impose his jail term on these two dazzling children, or to himself bring about his own irremediable demise. On one side, the sacrifice of Cosette, on the other, of himself.

What solution did he choose? What decision did he make? What was, in his heart of hearts, his final answer to the incorruptible interrogation of fate? What door did he decide to open? What side of his life did he make up his mind to close off and condemn? Between all these unfathomable sheer drops that surrounded him, what was his choice? What extremity did he accept? To which of these gulfs did he give the nod?

His dizzying reverie lasted all night.

He stayed there till daybreak, in the same position, bent double over his bed, prostrate under the enormity of fate, perhaps crushed, alas! his fists clenched, his arms stretched out at right angles like a crucified man taken down from the cross and cast facedown on the ground. He stayed twelve hours, the twelve hours of a long winter's night, frozen, without lifting his head and without uttering a word. He was as still as a corpse, while his thoughts rolled on the ground or soared, now like a hydra, now like an eagle. To have seen him motionless like this you would have thought he was dead; but all of a sudden he shuddered convulsively and his mouth, stuck to Cosette's clothes, kissed them; then you could see that he was alive.

Who is this "you?" Since Jean Valjean was alone, and there was no one there?

The You who is in the darkness.

# BOOK SEVEN

# THE LAST DROP IN THE CHALICE[1]

## I. THE SEVENTH CIRCLE[1] AND THE EIGHTH HEAVEN

The day after a wedding is lonely. One respects the reverential silence of the happy couple. And also, a little, the fact that they don't go to sleep till late and then sleep in. The clamor of visits and congratulations does not begin till later. On the morning of February 17, it was a bit after midday when Basque, busy "doing his antechamber," with cloth and feather duster under his arm, heard a light rap at the door. The person had not rung the bell, which was discreet on such a day. Basque opened up and saw Monsieur Fauchelevent. He ushered him into the salon, which was still in a cluttered mess and looked like the battlefield of the previous night's jubilation.

"Heavens, Monsieur," observed Basque, "we've woken up rather late."

"Is your master up?" asked Jean Valjean.

"How is Monsieur's arm?" asked Basque.

"Better. Is your master up?"

"Which one? The old one or the new one?"

"Monsieur Pontmercy."

"Monsieur le baron?" said Basque, drawing himself up.

One is especially a baron for one's servants. Something of the glory is reflected on them; they have what a philosopher would call a spattering of title, and this flatters them. Marius, we might mention in passing, a militant republican—and he had proved it—was now a baron in spite of himself. A minor revolution had taken place in the family over this title; it was now Monsieur Gillenormand who insisted on it, and Marius who made light of it. But Colonel Pontmercy had written: "My son will bear my title." Marius asserted. And then again, Cosette, in whom the woman was beginning to dawn, was thrilled to be a baroness.

"Monsieur le baron?" Basque repeated. "I'll go and see. I'll go and tell him Monsieur Fauchelevent is here."

"No. Don't tell him it is me. Tell him that someone wants to talk to him in private but don't give the name."

"Ah!" said Basque.

"I want to give him a surprise."

"Ah!" Basque said again, giving himself his second "Ah!" as an explanation of the first.

And he went out. Jean Valjean stood alone.

The salon, as we say, was in chaos. It looked as though, if you cocked your ear, you would still have been able to hear the faint noise of the wedding. On the parquet floor there were all sorts of flowers that had fallen from the garlands and out of people's coiffures. The candles had burned down to stubs and added stalactites of wax to the crystals of the chandeliers. Not a single piece of furniture was in its proper place. In the corners, three or four armchairs, pushed together to form a circle, looked as though they were carrying on chatting. The whole thing was cheerful as can be. A certain grace lingers on after a party has died. It had been happy. Over these chairs in disarray, among these wilting flowers, under these extinguished lights, all thoughts had been of joy. The sun had taken over from the chandelier, and gaily entered the room.

A few minutes ticked away. Jean Valjean stood rooted to the spot right where Basque had left him. He was very pale. His eyes were hollow and so sunken in their sockets from lack of sleep that they had almost disappeared. His black coat had the tired wrinkles of a garment that had stayed up all night. The elbows had gone white with that fluffy down that friction leaves on fabric. Jean Valjean looked down at the window outlined on the parquet floor at his feet by the sun.

There was a noise at the door, he looked up. Marius stepped in, his head high, laughter on his lips, some indefinable light over his face, his forehead radiant, his eyes triumphant. He, too, had not slept a wink.

"It's you, Father!" he cried when he saw Jean Valjean. "That idiot of a Basque with his mysterious air! But you've come too early. It's only half past twelve. Cosette is still sleeping."

That word *father*, said to Monsieur Fauchelevent by Marius, meant: supreme bliss. There had always been, as we know, a wall, a certain coldness and constraint between them, ice to be broken or melted. Marius had reached that point of intoxication where the wall drops and the ice melts, and Monsieur Fauchelevent was now for him, as for Cosette, a father.

He went on; the words spilled out of him, which is a feature of such heavenly paroxysms of joy: "I'm so happy to see you! If you only knew how much we missed you yesterday! Hello, father. How's your hand? Better, I think?"

And, satisfied with the positive response he had given himself, he rushed on: "We talked about you a lot, the two of us. Cosette loves you so much! You haven't forgotten that your room is here. We don't want any more of this rue de l'Homme-Armé. We don't want any more of it at all. How could you go and live in a street like that, when it is sick, and crotchety, and ugly, and fenced off at one end, and where a person is cold, where a person can't even get in? You will come and move in here. And this very day, too. Or you'll have to deal with Cosette. She means to lead us all by the nose, I warn you. You saw your room, it's right next to ours, it looks out on the garden; the lock has been fixed, the bed's made up, it's all ready, all you have to do is come over. Cosette has placed a big old bergère covered in Utrecht velvet by your bed and she said to it: "Open your arms to him." Every spring, in the stand of acacias outside your windows, a nightingale comes. You'll have him in a couple of months. You'll have his nest to your left and ours to your right. By night he will sing and by day Cosette will talk. Your room faces full south. Cosette will arrange your books there for you, your *Voyages* of Captain Cook, and the other one, Vancouver's,[2] all your things. There is, I believe, a small suitcase to which you are attached; I've selected a place of honor for it. You've won over my grandfather, you go together well. We'll all live together. Do you play whist? You'll make my grandfather jump for joy if you play whist. You're the one who'll take Cosette out walking on my days in court, you'll give her your arm, you know, like you used to do, before, in the Luxembourg. We are absolutely determined to be deliriously happy. And you'll be deliriously happy, too, at our happiness, do you hear, father? Speaking of which, are you having breakfast with us today?"

"Monsieur," said Jean Valjean, "I have something to tell you. I am an ex-convict."

The mind has limits beyond which it can't perceive sharp sounds any more than the ear can. Those words: "I am an ex-convict," coming from the mouth of Monsieur Fauchelevent and entering Marius's ears, exceeded the limits of the possible. Marius did not hear. It seemed to him that something had just been said to him, but he did not know what. He stood openmouthed.

He realized then that the man talking to him was frightening. In his happy daze, he had not till that moment noticed that terrible pallor.

Jean Valjean untied the black cravat that was supporting his right arm, untied the cloth wrapped round his hand, laid bare his thumb and showed it to Marius.

"There's nothing wrong with my hand," he said.

Marius looked at the thumb.

"There's never been anything wrong with it," Jean Valjean went on.

There was indeed no trace of a wound. Jean Valjean pursued: "It was best for me not to be at your wedding. I've stayed out of it as much as I could. I feigned this wound so as not to commit forgery, so as not to introduce a void into the marriage certificates, so as to get out of signing."

Marius stammered: "What does this mean?"

"It means," said Jean Valjean, "that I was in the galleys."

"You're driving me mad!" Marius cried, horrified.

"Monsieur Pontmercy," said Jean Valjean, "I spent nineteen years in the galleys. For theft. Then I was sentenced to life. For theft. For a second offense. At the present time, I am in breach of ban."

Marius could recoil from reality all he liked, reject the facts, resist the evidence; he was compelled to yield. He started to understand, and as always happens in such cases, his understanding went further. He shuddered with a ghastly inner flash; an idea, which made him shake, crossed his mind. He glimpsed a deformed destiny in the future—his own.

"Tell all, tell all!" he yelled. "You are Cosette's father!"

And he stepped back in a movement of unsayable horror.

Jean Valjean raised his head in an attitude of such nobility that he seemed to grow as tall as the ceiling.

"It is essential that you believe me here, Monsieur, and although the oath of the likes of us is not admitted in court . . ."

Here he paused, and then, with a sort of sovereign and sepulchral authority he added, slowly articulating and emphasizing every syllable: "You will believe me. Cosette's father—me! Before God, no. Monsieur le baron Pontmercy, I am a peasant from Faverolles. I used to earn my living pruning trees. My name is not Fauchelevent, my name is Jean Valjean. I am nothing to Cosette. Rest assured."

Marius stuttered: "Who can prove to me—"

"I can. Since I'm telling you."

Marius looked at this man. He was grim and tranquil. No lie could possibly emerge from such calm. What is ice-cold is sincere. You could feel the truth in this coldness of the grave.

"I believe you," said Marius.

Jean Valjean dipped his head as though taking note of this and continued: "What am I to Cosette? A passerby. Ten years ago, I didn't know she existed. I love her, it's true. When you've known a child when she was small, being yourself old already, you can't help but love them. When you are old, you feel like a grandfather to all little children. You may, it seems to me, assume that I have something akin to a heart. She was an orphan. Without father or mother. She needed me. So that is why I began to love her. Children are so weak that the first person to come along, even a man like me, can be their protector. That's the duty I carried out in relation to Cosette. I don't think you can really call such a small thing a good deed; but if it is a good deed, well then, let's say that I did it. Make a note of this extenuating circumstance. Today Cosette is passing out of my life; we are going our separate ways. From now on I can do nothing more for her. She is Madame Pontmercy. Her savior has changed. And Cosette has gained by the change. All is well. As for the six hundred thousand francs, you haven't mentioned them to me but I know what you're thinking—it's a trust. How did this trust come into my hands? Does it matter? I'm handing over the trust. Nothing more can be asked of me. I complete the restitution in saying my real name. That, too, is my business. But, for my sake, I want you to know who I am."

And Jean Valjean looked Marius full in the face.

What Marius felt was turbulent and incoherent. Certain of destiny's blasts create such tidal waves in our souls.

We have all had such troubled moments in which everything inside us breaks up; we say whatever comes into our heads, which is not always exactly what we should say. There are sudden revelations that we just cannot bear and that make our heads spin like lousy wine. Marius was so stupefied by the new situation that had been revealed to him that he spoke to the man almost as if he resented him for making the confession.

"But in the end," he shouted, "why are you telling me all this? What's forcing you to? You could have kept the secret to yourself. No one's denouncing you, or pursuing you, or tracking you down, are they? You have some reason for making such a revelation of your own volition. Get on with it. There's something else. What's the reason you're making this confession? What's your motive?"

"What's my motive?" answered Jean Valjean in such a low and muffled voice that he seemed to be talking to himself more than to Marius. "What motive, indeed, could this convict have for coming and saying: 'I am a convict'? Well, yes! My motive is strange. It's out of honesty. Listen, what is really unlucky is that I have these strings here in my heart that keep me bound. It is especially when you are old that these strings are sturdy. Life falls apart completely all around you; they hold fast. If I could have ripped out these strings, broken them, untied the knot or cut it, gone far away, I'd have been saved; all I'd have had to do is leave; there are plenty of stagecoaches in the rue du Bouloi; you're happy, I take myself off. I've tried to break them, these strings, I've tugged at them, but they've held firm, they haven't snapped, I was merely tearing my heart out with them. So then I said: 'I can't live anywhere but here. I must stay.' Well, yes, but you're right, I'm an idiot, why not just stay? You offer me a room in the house, Madame Pontmercy is fond of me, she says to that armchair: 'Open your arms to him'; your grandfather asks nothing better than to have me, he thinks we go well together, we'll all live together, eat together, I'll give my arm to Cosette—to Madame Pontmercy, sorry, force of habit—we'll have but one roof, one table, one fire, the same corner of the fireplace in winter, the same walks in summer. That is joy, that is, that is happiness, that is everything, that is. We'll live as a family. As a family!"

At this word, Jean Valjean became fierce. He folded his arms, studied the floor at his feet as though he would have liked to disappear through the floorboards into a hole, and his voice suddenly boomed: "As a family! No! I'm not part of any family. I'm not part of yours. I'm not part of the family of man. In houses where people are at home, I'm the odd one out. There are families, but that's not for me. I'm the unlucky one; I'm on the outside, looking in. Did I have a father and a mother? I almost doubt it. The day I married off that child, it was all over, I saw her happy, and that she was with the man she loves, and that there was a good old man there, a marriage of two angels, every joy about the house, and that this was good, and I said to myself: 'You, stay out.' I could lie, it's true, fool the lot of you, remain Monsieur Fauchelevent. As long as it was for her, I was able to lie; but now that it would be for myself, I must not do it. All I had to do was keep quiet, it's true, and everything would carry on. You ask me what's forcing me to speak? A funny thing—my conscience. It would have been so easy to keep quiet, though. I've spent the night trying to persuade myself to do just that; you are hearing my confession, and what I have come to tell you is so extraordinary that you have a right to hear it; so, yes, I spent the night coming up with reasons, I came up with some very good reasons, I did all I could, naturally. But there are two things I didn't manage to pull off: I didn't manage to snap the strings that keep me bound, riveted, stuck here, by my heart; and I didn't manage to silence the one who whispers to me when I am alone. That's why I came to confess everything to you this morning. Everything, or as good as. There are things I could say, but they're pointless and concern only me; I'll keep those things to myself. The essential, you know. So, I've taken my secret and I've brought it to you. And I've ripped it open before your very eyes. It wasn't an easy decision to make. I struggled with myself all night. Ah, you think I didn't tell myself that this wasn't the Champmathieu affair, that in concealing my name I wasn't doing anyone any harm, that the name Fauchelevent was given to me by Fauchelevent himself in gratitude for a service rendered, and that I could very well hang on to it, and that I'd be happy in this room you're offering me, that I wouldn't be in the way, that I'd be in my little corner, and that, while you had Cosette, I, I'd have the knowledge that I was in the same house as her. Everyone would have had their due of happiness. For me to go on being Monsieur Fauchelevent would have been better for everyone. Yes, except for my soul. There was joy all around me, but the bottom of my soul stayed black. It's not enough to be happy, you have to be content. If I'd gone on being Monsieur Fauchelevent, if I'd kept my true face hidden, in the middle of your flourishing, I'd have been an enigma; in the middle of your bright sunlight, I'd have been in darkness; without warning you, quite simply, I'd have brought the penal colony into your home, I'd have sat at your table with the thought that, if you knew who I was, you'd drive me away; I'd have let myself be waited on by servants who, if they'd known, would have said: 'How horrible!' I'd have brushed you with my elbow when you have a right to want no part of it, I'd have cheated you of your handshakes! Respect in your house would have been split between a venerable white head and a branded white head; in your most intimate moments, when all hearts would have believed themselves to be completely open, each for the others, when all four of us would have been together, your grandfather, you two, and myself, there would have been a stranger in your midst! I'd have been alongside you in your existence, worrying only about how to keep the lid on my terrible well. I, a dead man, would have forced myself on you, the living. As for her, I'd have sentenced her to me for life. You, Cosette, and I, we'd have been three heads in the one green lifer's cap! Doesn't it make you shudder? Where I'm only the most stricken of men, I'd have been the most monstrous. And this crime, I'd have committed it every day! And this lie, I'd have told it every day! And this face of darkness, I'd have worn it over my face every day! And my stain, I'd have given you your share of it every day! Every day! To you my dearly beloved, to you my children, to you my innocents! You think keeping quiet is nothing? You think staying silent is simple? No, it's not simple. There is a silence that lies. And my lie, and my fraud, and my unworthiness, and my cowardice, and my treachery, and my crime—I would have drained it all to the dregs, I'd have spat it back up, then drunk it again, I'd have finished at midnight and started again at midday, and my good morning would have been a lie, and my good evening would have been a lie, and I'd have slept on it, and I'd have eaten it with my bread, and I'd have looked Cosette in the face, and I'd have answered the angel's smile with the smile of the damned, and I'd have been a vile imposter! What for? To be happy. To be happy—me! Do I have the right to be happy? I am one of life's outsiders, Monsieur."

Jean Valjean stopped. Marius was listening. Such trains of thought and heartache cannot be interrupted. Jean Valjean dropped his voice once more, but it was no longer muted, it was ominous.

"You ask me why I'm speaking out? I haven't been denounced, or pursued, or tracked down, you say. Oh yes I have! I've been denounced! Yes, I've been pursued! Yes, I've been tracked down! Who by? By myself. I'm the one barring my way myself, and I drag myself along, and I push and shove myself, and I arrest myself, and I restrain myself, and when a man holds himself in custody, he won't get away."

And, seizing his own coat in his clenched fist and holding it out to Marius: "You see this fist, here?" he went on. "Wouldn't you say it's holding this collar in such a way as to not let go of it? Well then! Conscience is like a fist of another kind! If you want to be happy, Monsieur, you must never have a sense of duty; for the moment you do, it becomes implacable. You'd think it was punishing you for seeing it; but no: It rewards you, for it puts you in a hell where you can feel God beside you. No sooner have you torn your heart out than you are at peace with yourself."

And, with poignant emphasis, he added: "Monsieur Pontmercy, this is not common sense, but I am an honest man. In debasing myself in your eyes I rise in mine. This has already happened to me once before, but it was less painful then; it was nothing. Yes, an honest man. I would not be if, through my fault, you had continued to esteem me; now that you despise me, I am. I have a curse on me that means never being able to have any but stolen consideration, such consideration humiliates me and overwhelms me inside, and so, for me to respect myself, I have to be despised by others. Then I can hold my head up. I am a convict who obeys his conscience. I'm well aware that this seems unlikely. But what do you want me to do about it? That's how it is. I've made commitments to myself; I keep them. There are encounters that bind us, there are random events that drive us to do our duty. You see, Monsieur Pontmercy, I've been through a bit in life."

Jean Valjean paused again and swallowed his saliva with effort as though his words had a bitter aftertaste, before he resumed: "When you have such horror hanging over you, you don't have the right to make others share in it unwittingly, you don't have the right to contaminate them with your pestilence, you don't have the right to push them over the edge of your precipice without their realizing, you don't have the right to trundle your red convict smock around on them, you don't have the right to burden another's happiness on the sly with your own misery. To go up to those who are well and press your invisible ulcer against them in the shadows—that is abhorrent. Fauchelevent gave me his name in vain. I don't have the right to use it. He was able to give it to me; I wasn't able to take it. A name is an identity. You see, Monsieur, I have thought a bit, I have read a bit, even though I'm a peasant; and I know a thing or two. You see I can express myself properly. I've given myself an education of my own. So then, yes, taking away a name and sticking yourself under it is dishonest. The letters of the alphabet can be swiped like a purse or a watch. To be a forged signature in flesh and blood, to be a living picklock, to enter the homes of decent people by picking their locks, never to look openly, always to squint, to be rotten to the core inside, no! no! no! no! Better to suffer, to bleed, to weep, to tear your skin off your flesh with your nails, to spend your nights tossing and turning in anguish, to gnaw away at yourself, guts and soul. That's why I'm here telling you all this. Of my own volition, as you say."

He gulped in air painfully and then tossed out these final words: "Once upon a time I stole a loaf of bread to live; today, to live, I will not steal a name."

"To live!" Marius broke in. "You don't need that name to live?"

"Ah, I know what I'm saying," answered Jean Valjean, nodding slowly several times.

There was a silence. Both kept quiet, each deeply absorbed in thought. Marius had gone and sat himself down at a table and was leaning with the corner of his mouth hooked on a curled finger. Jean Valjean was pacing up and down. He stopped in front of a mirror and stood dead still. Then, as though obeying some inner argument, he spoke, staring in the mirror without seeing himself: "Whereas now, I'm relieved!"

He began to move again and strode to the other end of the drawing room. As he turned round, he realized that Marius was watching him pace. So then he said to him in a tone no words can describe: "I drag one leg a bit. Now you know why."

Then he turned all the way round to face Marius squarely.

"And now, Monsieur, picture this: I said nothing, I remained Monsieur Fauchelevent, I took my place among you, I am part of the family, I'm in my room, I come down and have breakfast in the morning in my slippers, in the evening we go off to a show together, the three of us, I accompany Madame Pontmercy to the Tuileries and to the place Royale, we are together, you think of me as the same as you; one fine day, I'm here, you're here, we're chatting away, we're laughing, suddenly you hear a voice shout: 'Jean Valjean!' And you see the awful hand of the police shoot out of the shadows and promptly rip off my mask!"

He clammed up again. Marius had leaped to his feet. Jean Valjean went on: "What do you say to that?"

Marius's silence was his answer.

"You see I'm right not to keep my silence. Listen, be happy, be in seventh heaven, be an angel's angel, live in the sun, and be satisfied with that, and don't worry how a poor doomed man goes about getting things off his chest and doing his duty; you have a most miserable man before you, Monsieur."

Marius slowly crossed the room and when he was close to Jean Valjean, held out his hand. But Marius had to reach out and take that other hand that did not reach for his. Jean Valjean just stood there and it felt to Marius like he was squeezing a hand of marble.

"My grandfather has friends," said Marius. "I'll get you your pardon."

"There's no point," said Jean Valjean. "They think I'm dead, that's enough. The dead aren't subject to surveillance. They are supposed to rot quietly away. Death, that's the same thing as a pardon."

And, disengaging his hand from Marius, who was hanging on to it, he added with a sort of ruthless dignity: "Besides, doing my duty, now that's the friend I can turn to; and I need only one pardon and that is from my conscience."

At that moment, at the far end of the room, the door cracked open gently and Cosette poked her head in. Only her sweet face was visible; her hair was beautifully tousled, her eyelids were still swollen from sleep. She moved like a bird darting its head out of its nest, looked first at her husband, then at Jean Valjean, and cried to them with a laugh, so that you felt as if you saw a smile deep inside a rose: "I bet you're talking politics! Talk about silly, when you could be with me!"

Jean Valjean gave a start.

"Cosette—" Marius stammered.

And he broke off. Both men looked guilty.

Cosette, radiant, continued to look from one to the other. There were glints of paradise in her eyes.

"I've caught you in the very act," said Cosette. "I just heard, through the door, my father Fauchelevent saying: 'Conscience... Doing my duty...' That's politics, that is. I won't have it. You really shouldn't be talking politics the very next day. It's not right."

"You're wrong, Cosette," answered Marius. "We're talking business. We're discussing the best way to invest your six hundred thousand francs..."

"That's not everything," Cosette interrupted. "I'm coming in. Do you want me here?"

And, slipping resolutely through the door, she stepped into the salon. She was wearing a loose white peignoir with lots of pleats and bell sleeves, which fell to her feet. In the golden skies of old Gothic paintings there are similarly charming sacks for bagging angels in.

She studied herself from head to toe in the big mirror, then cried out in a burst of ineffable ecstasy: "Once upon a time there was a king and a queen. Oh, I'm so happy!"

That said, she curtseyed to Marius and to Jean Valjean.

"So, there," she said. "I'm going to sit myself down alongside you in an armchair, we'll be having breakfast in half an hour, you can talk all you like, I'm well aware men have to talk, I'll be very good."

Marius took her arm and said lovingly to her: "We're talking business."

"Speaking of which," answered Cosette, "I opened my window and a bunch of *pierrots* just popped up in the garden. Birds, not masks. Today is Ash Wednesday, but not for the birds."

"I mean it, we're talking business. Off you go, my darling Cosette, leave us a moment. We're talking numbers. You'll be bored."

"You've put on a gorgeous cravat this morning, Marius. You look most dashing, my lord. No, I won't be bored."

"I assure you, you will."

"Not if it's you two. I won't understand you, but I'll listen to you. When a girl hears the voices she loves, she doesn't need to understand the words they are saying. To be here, together, that's all I want. I'm staying here with you and that's that!"

"You are my darling Cosette! But you can't!"

"I can't?"

"No."

"Very well," Cosette replied. "I would have given you some news. I would have told you that my grandfather is still sleeping, that your aunt is at mass, that the chimney in my father Fauchelevent's room smokes, that Nicolette has had the chimney sweep round, that Toussaint and Nicolette have already had a fight, that Nicolette pokes fun at Toussaint's stutter. Now you'll know nothing. Ah, I can't, you say? I, too, will have my turn, you'll see, Monsieur, at saying: 'You can't.' Who will get a telling off then? Please, my sweet Marius, let me stay here with the two of you."

"I swear we need to be on our own."

"Well then, do I count as anyone?"

Jean Valjean did not utter a word. Cosette turned to him.

"First of all, Father, I'd like you to come and give me a kiss. What are you doing standing over there saying nothing, instead of taking my side? Where did I get such a father? You can see very well that I'm extremely unhappy at home. My husband beats me. So come here, give me a kiss immediately."

Jean Valjean went over. Cosette turned back to Marius.

"As for you, I poke my tongue at you."

Then she held out her forehead to Jean Valjean. Jean Valjean took a step toward her. Cosette shrank back.

"Father, you're white. Is your arm hurting you?"

"It's better," said Jean Valjean.

"Did you sleep badly?"

"No."

"Are you sad?"

"No."

"Give me a kiss. If you're well, if you're sleeping well, if you're happy, I won't scold you."

And once again, she held out her forehead to him. Jean Valjean planted a kiss on this forehead with its heavenly reflection.

"Smile."

Jean Valjean did what he was told. It was the smile of a specter.

"Now defend me against my husband."

"Cosette!—" said Marius.

"Get angry, Father. Tell him I have to stay. Surely people can talk in front of me. You must think I'm a real ninny. What you have to say must be pretty astounding! Business, investing money in a bank, that is really something! Men play at being mysterious over nothing. I want to stay. I'm very pretty this morning. Look at me, Marius."

And with an adorable shrug of the shoulders, she shot Marius an absolutely exquisite sulky look. Something like lightning flashed between those two. That someone else was there just did not matter.

"I love you!" said Marius.

"I adore you!" said Cosette.

And they fell irresistibly into each other's arms.

"And now," Cosette resumed, readjusting a pleat in her peignoir with a triumphant little pout, "I'm staying."

"No you're not," Marius replied in an imploring tone. "There's something we have to finish."

"So it's still no?"

Marius assumed a grave tone of voice: "I assure you, Cosette, you can't stay."

"Ah, you're putting on your manly voice, Monsieur. Very well, I'll be off. You, Father, did not support me. Monsieur mon mari, Monsieur mon papa, you are tyrants. I'm going to tell Grandfather. If you think I'll be coming back, you are very much mistaken. I am proud. I will wait for you to come to me, now. You'll see that it's you who'll be bored without me. I'm off, thank you all the same."

And off she went.

Two seconds later, the door opened again, her fresh rosy face poked once more round the door, and she yelled at them: "I am very angry."

The door shut again and darkness returned. It was as though a ray of sunshine had gone astray and, without realizing it, had flashed through the night. Marius made sure the door was properly shut.

"Poor Cosette!" he murmured. "When she finds out—"

At these words, a shiver ran down Jean Valjean's entire body. He fixed Marius with a wild-eyed stare.

"Cosette! Oh, yes, that's true, you'll tell all this to Cosette. That's right. Fancy, I didn't think of that. A person can only face one thing at a time, you have no strength left for anything else. Monsieur, I beseech you, I entreat you, Monsieur, give me your most sacred word, don't tell her. Isn't it enough that you know yourself? I've been able to tell it myself without being forced into it, I would have told the world, told everyone, I wouldn't have cared less. But her! She doesn't know anything about anything, it would appall her. A convict, for God's sake! A person would be forced to explain to her, to tell her: 'That means a man who's been in the galleys.' She saw a chain gang going past one day. Oh, my God!"

He collapsed into an armchair and hid his face in his hands. You couldn't hear him, but from the way his shoulders shook, you could see he was crying. Silent tears, terrible tears.

You suffocate when you sob. A sort of convulsion seized him, he flopped back against the back of the chair trying to breathe, letting his arms hang down and letting Marius see his face flooded with tears, and Marius heard him murmur, so low that his voice seemed to come from fathomless depths: "Oh, I wish I was dead!"

"Rest assured," said Marius, "I'll keep your secret for myself alone."

And, less moved to pity, perhaps, than he should have been, but obliged for the past hour to accustom himself to the dreadful shock of seeing a convict gradually superimpose himself on Monsieur Fauchelevent before his very eyes, little by little overtaken by this grim reality and led by the downhill trend of the situation to note the gulf that had just opened between this man and himself, Marius added: "I can't possibly not say something about the trust you have so faithfully and so honorably handed over. That was an act of probity. It's only right that you be given a reward. You decide on the amount yourself, and you will have it. Don't be afraid of asking too much."

"Thank you, Monsieur," answered Jean Valjean softly.

He remained pensive for a moment, mechanically running the tip of his forefinger over the nail of his thumb, then he spoke up: "That just about does it. There is one last thing I—"

"What?"

Jean Valjean seemed to have one last hesitation and, tonelessly, almost breathlessly, he stammered out rather than spoke these words: "Now that you know, do you think, Monsieur, you who are the master, that I should not see Cosette anymore?"

"I think that would be best," replied Marius coldly.

"I won't see her again," murmured Jean Valjean.

And he headed for the door. He placed his hand on the doorknob, the spring bolt yielded, the door cracked open, Jean Valjean opened it just wide enough to squeeze through, remained motionless for a second, then shut the door again and turned back to face Marius.

He was no longer pale, he was white. There were no more tears in his eyes, but a sort of tragic fire. His voice had become strangely calm again.

"Listen, Monsieur," he said, "if you like, I'll come and see her. I assure you that I want to very much. If I hadn't been so keen to see Cosette, I would not have made the confession I've just made to you, I'd have gone away; but since I want to stay wherever Cosette is and go on seeing her, I had to make a clean breast of it to you in all honesty. You follow my reasoning, don't you? It's not hard to understand. You see, it's over nine years that I've had her by my side. We lived at first in that slum on the boulevard, after that in the convent, after that near the Luxembourg. That's where you saw her for the first time. You remember her fluffy blue hat. After that we were in the quartier des Invalides where there was a fence and a garden. Rue Plumet. I lived in a little rear courtyard from where I could hear her on the piano. That is my life for you. We never left each other's side. That lasted nine years and one month. I was like her father and she was my little girl. I don't know if you follow me, Monsieur Pontmercy, but to go off now, not see her anymore, not talk to her anymore, not have anything anymore—that would be hard. If you don't see any harm in it, I'll come and see Cosette from time to time. I won't come often. I won't stay long. You can tell them to stick me in the little room downstairs. On the ground floor. I'm happy to come in the back door, the one for the servants, but that might startle them. It would be better, I think, if I came in the front door the same as everyone else. Monsieur, truly. I'd like very much to go on seeing Cosette for a while. As rarely as you like. Put yourself in my place, that's all I have left. And then, you have to be careful. If I no longer ever came, that would have a bad effect, people would find that funny. For instance, what I could do is come in the evening, when night is about to fall."

"You will come every evening," said Marius, "and Cosette will be waiting for you."

"You are good, Monsieur," said Jean Valjean.

Marius bowed to Jean Valjean, happiness saw despair to the door, and the two men parted.

## II. THE OBSCURITIES A REVELATION MAY CONTAIN

Marius was shattered.

The sort of distance he had always felt for the man he used to see Cosette with was now explained for him. There was something indefinably enigmatic about that character that his instinct had warned him about. The enigma turned out to be the most shameful disgrace, jail. This Monsieur Fauchelevent was the convict Jean Valjean.

To abruptly find such a secret in the midst of his happiness was like discovering a scorpion in a nest of turtledoves. Was Marius and Cosette's happiness from now on condemned to such kinship? Was it a fait accompli? Was acceptance of this man part of the marriage that had been consummated? Wasn't there anything that could now be done? Had Marius also married the convict?

It is all very well to be crowned with light and joy, it is all very well to savor life's great golden hour, happy love; such shocks would force even an archangel in his ecstasy, even a demigod in his glory, to quake.

As always happens in changes of perspective of this kind, where the earth shifts under our feet, Marius wondered if he wasn't himself at fault somewhere here? Had he lacked astuteness? Had he lacked prudence? Had he unintentionally let things go to his head? A little, perhaps. Had he embarked on this amorous adventure that had ended in his marriage to Cosette a bit too carelessly to take in his surroundings? He took stock—which is the way it goes: By a series of successive stocktakings of ourselves by ourselves, life gets us to mend our ways little by little—he took stock of the fanciful and visionary side of his nature, a sort of inner cloud cover peculiar to many organisms and that, in the paroxysms of passion and of pain, expands, changing the temperature of the soul and invading the whole man, to the point where there is nothing left of him but a conscience blanketed by haze. We have more than once pointed out this characteristic feature of Marius's makeup as an individual. He recalled that, in the intoxication of his love, in the rue Plumet, for six or seven ecstatic weeks, he had not even spoken to Cosette of the baffling drama that had taken place in the Gorbeau slum, in which the victim had taken the odd course of keeping quiet during the struggle and of running away after it. Why hadn't he spoken about it to Cosette? Yet it was all so close and so frightening. Why hadn't he even mentioned the Thénardiers to her and, especially, the day he had run into Éponine? He now almost had trouble explaining to himself his silence at the time. He did register it, though. He remembered his giddy exhilaration, his intoxication with Cosette, how love absorbed everything, how they'd kidnapped each other and carried each other off into the ideal, and perhaps, also, as the imperceptible dose of reason mixed in with that violent and wonderful state of the soul, a vague and nameless instinct to hide and to wipe from his memory that fearful episode he did not want to go near, in which he did not want to play any kind of rôle, which he himself shunned and in which he could be neither narrator nor witness without also being accuser. Besides, those few weeks had gone by in a flash; they hadn't had time for anything but love. In the end, when he weighed everything up, turned it over, examined it, if he had told Cosette about the Gorbeau ambush, if he had named the Thénardiers to her, what would the consequences have been? Even if he had discovered that Jean Valjean was a convict, would that have changed him, Marius? Would it have changed her, Cosette? Would he have withdrawn? Would he have adored her any the less? Would he have married her any the less? No. Would it have changed anything that had happened? No. Nothing to regret, then, nothing to reproach himself for. All was well. There is a god for those drunks known as lovers. Blind, Marius had followed the course he would have followed with his eyes wide open. Love had blindfolded him, to take him where? To paradise.

But this paradise was complicated from now on by an infernal contact.

Marius's erstwhile sense of distance from this man, from this Fauchelevent–*cum*–Jean Valjean, was now mixed with horror. In this horror, we have to say, there was some pity and even a certain amazement.

This thief, this recidivist thief, had restored a trust of six hundred thousand francs. He was the only one to know about the secret trust. He could have kept it all, yet he had handed it all over.

On top of that, he had himself revealed his situation of his own accord. Nothing obliged him to. If anyone knew who he was, it was his own doing. There was in that confession more than the acceptance of humiliation, there was the acceptance of danger. For a condemned man, a mask is not a mask, it is a refuge. He had given up that refuge. A false name means security; he had cast off that false name. He, a galley slave, could have hidden himself away forever in a respectable family; he had resisted the temptation. And for what motive? The scruples of conscience. He had explained this himself in the irresistible voice of truth. To sum up, whatever this Jean Valjean was, his was unarguably a conscience that was stirring. There was some mysterious rehabilitation already at work there, and to all appearances, for a long time already, scruples had had this man under strict control. Such attacks of justness and goodness are not given to vulgar natures. The stirring of conscience is the grandeur of the soul.

Jean Valjean was sincere. This sincerity, which was visible, palpable, indisputable, evident even in the pain that it caused him, made further information pointless and lent weight to all the man said. Here, for Marius, a strange turning of tables occurred. What came from Monsieur Fauchelevent? Distrust. What emanated from Jean Valjean? Trust.

In this mysterious balance sheet that the reflective Marius was drawing up for Jean Valjean, he noted the credit, he noted the debit, and he tried to reach a balance. But all this was happening in a storm. In endeavoring to get a clear picture of the man and pursuing Jean Valjean, so to speak, in his innermost thoughts, he kept losing him and finding him again in an inescapable haze.

The honesty in handing over the trust, the probity of the confession, that was good. It was like a break in the clouds, but then the clouds would turn black again. As muddled as Marius's memories were, a shadow of them came back to him.

What exactly was that business in the Jondrette garret all about? Why, at the arrival of the police, instead of lodging a complaint, did the man make his escape? Here Marius found the answer. Because the man was a fugitive from justice in breach of ban.

Another question: Why had the man come to the barricade? For now Marius distinctly saw that episode again, resurfacing like indelible ink over a flame. This man was at the barricade. He didn't fight, though. So what had he come there to do? Before this question a specter rose up, and gave the answer. Javert. Marius recalled perfectly clearly at that moment the funereal vision of Jean Valjean dragging the trussed-up Javert beyond the barricade, and he could still hear the awful pistol shot ringing out from around the corner of the petite rue Mondétour. There was probably hate between that spy and this galley slave. One was in the other's way. Jean Valjean had gone to the barricade to take his revenge. He had got there late. He doubtless knew that Javert was held prisoner there. The Corsican vendetta[1] had spread among the dregs in certain sectors of the underworld and was the rule there; it is so simple that it doesn't even shock semi-reformed souls; and people like that are so made that a criminal, in the process of repenting, may be scrupulous about theft but not about revenge. Jean Valjean had killed Javert. At least that much seemed clear.

Finally, one last question; but this one had no answer. Marius felt this question like a jab to the heart. How was it that Jean Valjean's existence had rubbed shoulders so long with Cosette's? What was this somber game of Providence that had placed this child in such close contact with this man? Could there also be coupling chains, forged up above, and does God amuse himself by pairing an angel with a demon? Can crime and innocence be roommates in the mysterious prison of misery and destitution? In that parade of the condemned known as human destiny, can two heads come together, one naïve, the other fearsome, one all bathed in the divine white washes of dawn, the other forever blanched by the glimmer of endless lightning? Who could have decided on this inexplicable pairing? In what way, as the result of what miracle, could a shared life have been set up between the heavenly little girl and the doomed old man? Who could have tied the lamb to the wolf, and, even more incomprehensible, tethered the wolf to the lamb? For the wolf loved the lamb, for the savage one adored the frail one, for over the course of nine years, the angel had had the monster to lean on. Cosette's childhood and adolescence, her coming into the world, her virginal growth toward life and the light, had been protected by that warped devotion. Here, the questions peeled off, so to speak, into countless puzzles, abysses opened at the bottom of abysses, and Marius could no longer lean over Jean Valjean without vertigo. So what was this sheer cliff of a man, then?

The old symbols from Genesis[2] are eternal; in human society, as it exists, until the day that a greater clarity shall change it, there are and always will be two men, the one on top, the other subterranean; the one who follows good is Abel; the one who follows bad is Cain. Who was this loving Cain? Who was this felon so religiously absorbed in the adoration of a virgin, watching over her, raising her, keeping her, dignifying her, and enveloping her, himself impure, in purity? What was this cesspit that had revered such innocence to the point of not leaving a stain on her? Who was this Jean Valjean who had seen to Cosette's education? What was this figure of darkness whose sole concern had been to protect a rising star from all shadow and from all cloud?

There lay Jean Valjean's secret; and there lay God's secret.

Faced with this twin secret, Marius shrank back. The one in a way reassured him about the other. God was as visible in this enterprise as Jean Valjean. God has His instruments. He uses whatever tool He pleases. He is not answerable to man. Do we know the ways of God? Jean Valjean had worked on Cosette. He had more or less made that soul. This was incontestable. So, what then? The worker was awful, but his work was wonderful. God performs His miracles however He sees fit. He had built the lovely Cosette, and He had put Jean Valjean to work to do it. It had pleased Him to choose this strange collaborator. What account have we to ask of Him? Is it the first time that manure has helped spring make a rose?

Marius gave himself these answers and told himself that they were right. On all the points we have just listed, he had not dared press Jean Valjean—without admitting to himself that he simply did not dare. He adored Cosette. He possessed Cosette, Cosette was splendidly unsullied. That was enough for him. What further clarification did he need? Cosette was a ray of light. Does light need to be clarified? He had everything; what more could he want? Isn't everything enough? Jean Valjean's personal affairs were none of his business. In crouching over the fatal shadow of that man, he clung to the solemn declaration the poor miserable man had made: "I am nothing to Cosette. Ten years ago, I didn't know she existed."

Jean Valjean had just been passing through. He had said so himself. Well then, let him keep going. Whatever he was, his rôle was over. Marius was there from now on to carry out the job of Providence by Cosette's side. Cosette had soared off into the blue to find her mate, her lover, her spouse, her celestial male. In taking flight, winged and transfigured, Cosette was leaving behind her on the ground, empty and hideous, her chrysalis, Jean Valjean. Into whatever circle of ideas Marius spiraled off, he always came back to a certain feeling of horror for Jean Valjean. A sacred horror perhaps, for, as we just pointed out, he sensed a *quid divinum*[3] in this man. But, no matter what he did, and no matter what extenuating circumstances he looked for, he could not avoid falling back on this: The man was a convict; that is, the one who does not even have a place on the social ladder, being below the lowest rung. Below the lowest of men comes the convict. The convict is no longer the like of the living, so to speak. The law has stripped him of all the amount of humanity it can deprive a man of. On penal questions, Marius, though he remained a democrat, was still stuck on the side of the ruthless legal system and he had, about those whom the law strikes, all the ideas of the law. He had not yet, we have to say, gone all the way as far as progress goes. He had not yet come to distinguish between what is written by man and what is written by God, between the law and justice. He had not examined and weighed up the right man claims to dispose of the irrevocable and the irreparable. He was not revolted by the notion of *vindicte*[4]— prosecution and punishment. He found it perfectly natural that certain infringements of the written law be followed by eternal punishments, and he accepted social damnation as civilized procedure. That was as far as he had got, though he reserved the right to advance infallibly later, his nature being good and basically entirely made up of latent progress.

In this conceptual environment, Jean Valjean looked disfigured and repulsive to him. He was the reprobate. He was the convict. This word was for him like a trumpet blast at the Last Judgment;[5] and, after thinking about Jean Valjean for a long time, his final movement was to turn his head away. *Vade retro*[6]— get thee behind me.

Marius, it must be acknowledged and even underlined, even while interrogating Jean Valjean to the point where Jean Valjean had said to him, "You are hearing my confession," had not, however, put two or three decisive questions to him. It was not that they had not occurred to him, but he had been frightened of them. The Jondrette garret? The barricade? Javert? Who knows how far such revelations might have gone? Jean Valjean did not seem like a man who would shrink from the truth, and who knows whether Marius, after goading him on, would not have wanted to gag him? In certain extreme situations, surely all of us have wanted to block our ears after posing a question so we don't hear the answer. It is especially when we love someone that we experience this sort of cowardice. It is not wise to question sinister situations to the nth degree, especially when the indissoluble side of our own life is fatally involved. From Jean Valjean's desperate explanations, some unbearable light might be shone, and who knows whether this hideous clarity might not even reflect on Cosette? Who knows whether a sort of infernal glimmer might not remain on that angelic brow? The flare of light in a thunderstorm is still lightning. Fate has such interlocking connections whereby innocence itself is stamped with crime by the grim law of bleeding reflections. The purest natures may forever preserve the lurid reflections of some horrible association. Rightly or wrongly, Marius had been afraid. He already knew too much. He sought to turn a deaf ear rather than to find out more. Distraught, he carried Cosette off in his arms and shut his eyes to Jean Valjean.

That man was of the night, of the living and terrible night. How could Marius dare to try and plumb the depths? It is terrifying, questioning the shadows. Who knows what they might answer? The dawn could be blackened by it forever.

In this frame of mind, it was a gut-wrenching torment for Marius to think that the man would have any further contact whatever with Cosette. These fearful questions, in the face of which he had recoiled, yet which might have given rise to a final and implacable decision—he could almost have kicked himself now for not having asked them. He thought he'd been too kind, too soft, we might as well say it, too weak. This weakness had led him to make a foolish concession. He'd let himself be moved. He'd been wrong. He should have thrown Jean Valjean out, purely and simply. Jean Valjean meant playing with fire, he should have done it, and rid his house of the man. He was angry with himself, he was angry with this sudden whirlwind of emotions that had deafened him, blinded him, and swept him away. He was unhappy with himself.

What was he to do now? Jean Valjean's visits were profoundly repugnant to him now. What was the good of having the man there at his place? What could he do? Here, his head spun, he did not want to dig any deeper; he did not want to go into it any further, he did not want to probe his own feelings. He had made a promise, he had let himself be carried away into making a promise; Jean Valjean had his promise; even with a convict, especially with a convict, a man must keep his word. Still, his first duty was to Cosette. In short, he was racked with repulsion, which dominated everything.

Marius rolled this whole set of ideas around confusedly in his mind, going from one idea to the next and stirred by all of them. Hence his deep commotion. It was not easy for him to hide this commotion from Cosette, but love is a talent and Marius managed.

On top of this, he put questions to Cosette, apparently aimlessly, and she, candid as a dove is white, did not suspect a thing; he talked to her about her childhood and her youth and he convinced himself more and more that all that a man can be that is good, fatherly, and respectable, this convict had been for Cosette. All that Marius had glimpsed and assumed was real. That sinister stinging nettle had loved and protected this lily.

# BOOK EIGHT

# DUSK FALLS

## I. THE ROOM DOWN BELOW

The next day, at nightfall, Jean Valjean knocked on the porte cochère of the Gillenormand house. It was Basque who received him. Basque just happened to be in the courtyard at the appointed time—as though under orders. It sometimes happens that a servant is told: "Keep an eye out for Monsieur So-and-so when he comes."

Basque, without waiting for Jean Valjean to approach, addressed him: "Monsieur le baron asked me to ask Monsieur if he would like to go up or stay downstairs?"

"I'll stay downstairs," answered Jean Valjean.

Basque, who was in any case absolutely respectful, opened the door of the downstairs room, saying: "I'll go and let Madame know."

The room Jean Valjean stepped into was a damp vaulted chamber on the ground floor, serving as a storeroom, as the occasion arose; it looked onto the street and was tiled with red tiles and only dimly lit by one barred window.

The room was not one of those that are bothered by the broom, the ceiling brush, or the duster. Dust was safe there. The persecution of spiders had not been established there, either. A lovely big spiderweb, nice and black and adorned with dead flies, fanned out over one of the windowpanes. Small and low-ceilinged, the room was furnished with a heap of empty bottles piled in a corner. The walls, which had been washed with a yellow ocher limewash, were peeling off in big chunks of plaster. At the back, there was a wooden fireplace painted black with a narrow mantelpiece. A fire had been lit in it; which indicated that someone had counted on Jean Valjean's answer being: "I'll stay downstairs."

Two armchairs had been placed on either side of the fireplace. Between the armchairs, in guise of a carpet, an old bedside rug had been spread showing more warp than wool. For light, the room had the fire in the fireplace and the dying light coming through the window.

Jean Valjean was tired. For several days he had not eaten or slept. He dropped into one of the armchairs. Basque came back, placed a burning candle on the mantelpiece, and withdrew. Jean Valjean, his head drooping and his chin on his chest, did not notice Basque or the candle.

All of a sudden, he rose with a start. Cosette was behind him. He had not seen her come in, but he had felt her come in. He turned round. He looked at her. She was adorably beautiful. But it was not her beauty that he was contemplating with that deeply penetrating gaze, it was her soul.

"Well," said Cosette, "the very idea! Father, I knew you were unusual, but I would never have expected this. Marius tells me it's you who came up with the idea that I receive you down here."

"Yes, it was my idea."

"I expected that answer. Well, I warn you I'm going to make a scene. But first things first. Father, give me a kiss."

And she turned her cheek. Jean Valjean did not move a muscle.

"You just stand there. I take note. Action of the guilty. But it doesn't matter, I forgive you. Jesus Christ said: Turn the other cheek. So here it is."

And she turned the other cheek. Jean Valjean did not stir. It seemed as though his feet were nailed to the floor.

"This is getting serious," said Cosette. "What have I done to you? I declare I'm baffled. You owe it to me to make amends. You'll eat with us."

"I've eaten."

"That's not true. I'll get Monsieur Gillenormand to scold you. Grandfathers are made to scold fathers. Come along. Come up with me to the drawing room. This minute."

"I can't."

Here Cosette lost a bit of ground. She stopped her bossing and moved on to asking questions.

"But why ever not? And you choose the ugliest room in the house to see me in. It's horrible here."

"You know, Cos—"

Jean Valjean corrected himself.

"You know, Madame, I am peculiar, I have my whims."

Cosette clapped her little hands together.

"Madame! . . . You called me madame! . . . This is new! What does this mean?"

Jean Valjean flashed her the heartbreaking smile he sometimes resorted to.

"You wanted to be madame. And now you are."

"Not to you, Father."

"Don't call me father anymore."

"What?"

"Call me Monsieur Jean. Jean, if you like."

"You aren't father anymore? I'm not Cosette anymore? Monsieur Jean? What is this about? Well, this is a development! What on earth's happened? Look me in the face a little, why don't you. And you don't want to live with us! And you don't want my room! What have I done to you? What have I done to you? Has something happened?"

"Nothing."

"Well, then?"

"Everything is as usual."

"So why are you changing your name?"

"You've certainly changed yours."

He smiled again with the same smile and added: "Since you are Madame Pontmercy, surely I can be Monsieur Jean."

"I just don't understand. This whole thing is idiotic. I'll ask my husband if you have permission to be Monsieur Jean. I hope he won't allow you. You are seriously hurting my feelings. A person can have whims, but he is not to give his little Cosette grief. That's not nice. You have no right to be mean, when you are so good."

He did not answer. She briskly grabbed both his hands and, with an irresistible movement, brought them to her face and pressed them against her neck under her chin—a gesture of profound tenderness.

"Oh!" she said to him. "Be good!"

And she went on: "This is what I call being good: being nice, coming here to live, resuming our nice little promenades, there are birds here just like in the rue Plumet; living with us, leaving that hole of a place in the rue de l'Homme-Armé, not putting on charades for us to work out, being like everyone else, having dinner with us, having breakfast with us, being my father."

He pulled his hands away.

"You don't need a father anymore, you have a husband."

Cosette flew off the handle.

"I don't need a father anymore! What can a person say to nonsense like that!"

"If Toussaint was here," Jean Valjean began, as though casting about for an authoritative reference and grasping at straws, "she would be the first to agree that it's true that I've always had my own funny ways. That's nothing new. I've always liked my own dark corner."

"But it's cold here. You can hardly see. It is abominable, this wanting to be Monsieur Jean. I don't want you to be formal with me."

"A moment ago, on my way here," replied Jean Valjean, "I saw a piece of furniture in the rue Saint-Louis. In a cabinetmaker's. If I were a pretty woman I'd make myself a present of that piece, there. A really nice dressing table—modern style. What you call rosewood, I think. Inlaid. Fairly big mirror. And drawers. Very pretty."

"Boo! Nasty old bear!" Cosette replied.

And with staggering sweetness, gritting her teeth and baring them in a snarl, she hissed at Jean Valjean. It was one of the Graces mimicking a cat.

"I am furious!" she said. "Since yesterday you've all been driving me mad. I am well and truly riled. I just don't understand. You don't defend me against Marius. Marius doesn't take my side against you. I am all on my own. I do a room up nicely. If I could have put the good Lord in it for good measure, I would have. I'm left stuck with my room. My tenant skips out on me. I order a nice little dinner from Nicolette. No one wants your dinner, Madame. And my father Fauchelevent wants me to call him Monsieur Jean, and for me to receive him in an awful, ugly, moldy old cellar where the walls have beards and where, for crystal, there are empty bottles and for curtains, there are spiderwebs! You are unusual, I agree, it's just like you, but people who have just married are granted a reprieve. You should not have gone back to being unusual quite so soon. I suppose you think you'll be very happy in your abominable rue de l'Homme-Armé. I was pretty desperate there, myself! What have you got against me? You are really hurting my feelings a great deal. Shame on you!"

And, suddenly serious, she stared hard at Jean Valjean and added: "Are you annoyed with me for being happy?"

Naïveté, unwittingly, sometimes goes deep. This question, straightforward for Cosette, was profoundly complex for Jean Valjean. Cosette wanted to lash out; her claws tore.

Jean Valjean went pale. He didn't answer for a moment, then, in a toneless voice, talking to himself, he murmured: "Her happiness, that was my life's sole purpose. Now, God can sign me out. Cosette, you're happy; my time is up."

"Ah, you called me Cosette!" cried Cosette.

And she threw herself around his neck. Jean Valjean, distraught, hugged her frantically to his chest. It almost felt to him like he was taking her back.

"Thank you, Father!" said Cosette.

Jean Valjean was getting so carried away his heart was about to break. He gently disentangled himself from Cosette's arms and grabbed his hat.

"What now?" asked Cosette.

Jean Valjean replied: "I'll leave you, Madame, they're waiting for you."

And, from the doorway, he added: "I called you Cosette. Tell your husband it won't happen again. Forgive me."

Jean Valjean went out, leaving Cosette dumbfounded by this enigmatic farewell.

## II. OTHER STEPS BACK

The following day, at the same time, Jean Valjean came again.

Cosette did not ask him any questions, did not act amazed anymore, no longer cried that she was cold, no longer spoke of the drawing room; she avoided saying either father or Monsieur Jean. She let him address her formally. She let him call her madame. Only, she was a little less joyful. She would have been sad, had she been capable of sadness.

More than likely she had had one of those conversations with Marius in which the beloved man says what he wants to, explains nothing, yet satisfies the beloved woman. The curiosity of people in love does not extend too far beyond their love.

The downstairs room had spruced itself up a bit. Basque had done away with the bottles and Nicolette with the spiders.

Every day that followed brought Jean Valjean at the same time. He came every single day, not having the strength to take Marius's words other than literally. Marius arranged things so that he was always out when Jean Valjean called. The household accommodated itself to Monsieur Fauchelevent's new mode of being. Toussaint smoothed things over. She never got tired of saying: "Monsieur has always been like that." The grandfather issued this decree: "The man is an original." And that was that. Anyway, at ninety, no new bond is possible; everything is packed tight, a newcomer is an encumbrance. There is no room left; every habit has been acquired. Monsieur Fauchelevent, Monsieur Tranchelevent—old man Gillenormand asked for nothing more than to be released from "that monsieur." He added: "Nothing is more common than these originals; the place is crawling with them. They get up to all kinds of mad antics. For no reason. The marquis de Canaples was worse. He bought a palace just so he could live in the attic. People do the strangest things."

No one glimpsed the sinister dark side. Who, in any case, could have guessed such a thing? There are swamps in India where the water looks weird, inexplicably quivering when there is no breeze, whipped up when it should be calm. You look at this surface bubbling away apparently without a cause; you don't see the hydra scuttling along the bottom.

A lot of men have a secret monster like this, an ache that they feed, a dragon that gnaws away at them, a despair that haunts their nights. Such a man looks like any other, comes and goes. You do not know that he has a frightening parasitic pain inside him with a thousand teeth, living inside the miserable wretch and killing him, for he is dying of it. You do not know that this man is a bottomless pit. One where the water is still, but deep. From time to time, a disturbance no one can fathom shows on the surface. A mysterious wrinkle puckers up, then vanishes, then reappears; a bubble of air rises and bursts. It is not much, but it is terrifying. It is the unknown beast breathing.

Certain strange habits, like arriving just as others are leaving, staying in the background while others are showing off, blending into the wall on all occasions, seeking out the lonely lane, preferring the deserted street, not joining in conversations, avoiding crowds and special occasions, seeming fairly well-off yet living in poverty, having your key in your pocket and your candle at the porter's no matter how rich you are, entering by the back door, going up the back stairs—all these insignificant little oddities, wrinkles, air bubbles, fleeting ripples on the surface, often rise up from forbidding depths.

Several weeks went by this way. A new life gradually took hold of Cosette, with the ties marriage creates, the visits, the care of the house, life's new pleasures, those weighty matters. Cosette's pleasures were not costly; they consisted of a single pleasure: being with Marius. Stepping out with him, staying in with him, this was the great occupation of her life. For them it was an endlessly novel joy to saunter out arm in arm into the sun, out into the street, without hiding, in front of everyone, the two of them together all on their own. Cosette had a minor setback. Toussaint could not get along with Nicolette, the pairing of two old maids being impossible, and she took herself off. The grandfather was in fine fettle; Marius had a few cases to plead here and there; alongside the newly married couple Aunt Gillenormand peacefully led the marginal life that was all she required. Jean Valjean came every day.

With familiarity gone, with this *vous* instead of *tu*, with this *madame* and this *Monsieur Jean*, he was a different person for Cosette. The care he had himself taken to get her to let go of him was doing its work on her. She was more and more lively and less and less loving. She was still very fond of him, though, and he felt that. One day she suddenly said to him: "You used to be my father, and now you aren't my father anymore; you used to be my uncle, and now you aren't my uncle anymore; you used to be Monsieur Fauchelevent, and now you are just plain Jean. So who are you really? I don't like all this. If I didn't know how good you were, I'd be frightened of you."

He still lived in the rue de l'Homme-Armé, not being able to bring himself to move from the quartier where Cosette lived.

At first, he would spend only a couple of minutes with Cosette at a time, then he would go away. Little by little he developed the habit of staying longer. It was as though he was taking advantage of the authorization provided by the days as they got longer. He arrived earlier and left later.

One day Cosette accidentally called him: "Father." A flash of joy lit up Jean Valjean's somber old face. He pulled her up: "Call me Jean."

"Ah, that's right," she said and burst out laughing. "Monsieur Jean."

"That's more like it," he said.

And he turned his head away so that she could not see him drying his eyes.

### III. They Remember the Garden in the Rue Plumet

That was the last time. After that momentary flash of light, complete extinction was achieved. No more familiarity, no more greeting with a kiss, never again that word, so profoundly sweet: "Father!" At his own behest and with his own complicity, he was gradually driven away from every happiness; and he endured this misery that, after having lost Cosette completely in one day, he then had to lose her all over again a bit at a time.

The eye ends up adapting to dingy cellar light. In a word, his daily glimpse of Cosette was enough for him. His whole life was concentrated in those moments. He would sit next to her and look at her in silence or else he would talk to her about days long gone, about her childhood, about the convent, about her little friends at the time.

One afternoon—it was one of the first days of April, already hot, still fresh, that time of the year when the sun is so jaunty, the gardens around Marius and Cosette's windows seemed visibly to be waking up, the hawthorn was about to break out, a jeweled array of wallflowers was spreading out over the old walls, pink snapdragons yawned in the cracks between the stones, lovely little daisies and buttercups were just starting to push up through the grass, white butterflies made their first appearance of the year, and the wind, that fiddler at life's eternal wedding, tried out in the trees the first notes of that great dawn symphony the old poets used to call renewal—Marius said to Cosette: "We said we'd go back and see our garden in the rue Plumet. Let's go. We shouldn't be ungrateful."

And off they flew into the spring like two swallows. The garden in the rue Plumet had the same effect on them as the dawn. Already in their lives they had behind them something like the springtime of their love. The house in the rue Plumet still belonged to Cosette, having been taken out on a lease. They went through the garden and through the house. There, they found themselves again, and lost themselves again. That evening, at the usual time, Jean Valjean went to the rue des Filles-du-Calvaire.

"Madame has gone out with Monsieur and is not back yet," Basque told him.

He sat down in silence and waited for an hour. Cosette did not come home. He bowed his head and went on his way.

Cosette was so intoxicated by her walk with Marius in "their garden," and so overjoyed at having "lived in her past for a whole day," that she could talk of nothing else the next day. It never occurred to her that she had not seen Jean Valjean.

"How did you get there?" Jean Valjean asked her.

"On foot."

"And how did you get back?"

"In a fiacre."

For some little time Jean Valjean had noticed the cramped life the young couple led. It made him cranky. Marius's economizing was severe, and Jean Valjean meant the word in its absolute sense. He hazarded a question:

"Why don't you have your own carriage? A pretty coupé would only set you back five hundred francs a month. You're rich."

"I don't know," replied Cosette.

"It's like Toussaint," Jean Valjean went on. "She's gone. But you haven't replaced her. Why not?"

"Nicolette's enough."

"But you need a lady's maid."

"I have Marius, don't I?"

"You ought to have a house of your own, servants of your own, a carriage, a box at the theater. Nothing is too good for you. Why not take advantage of the fact that you're rich? Wealth only adds to happiness." Cosette did not answer.

Jean Valjean's visits did not get any shorter. Far from it. When it is the heart that is slipping, you don't stop on the way down.

Whenever Jean Valjean wanted to prolong his visit and make her forget the time, he would praise Marius; he would find him handsome, noble, courageous, witty, eloquent, good. Cosette would outdo him. Jean Valjean would start again. They never dried up. Marius—that word was inexhaustible; those six letters spoke volumes. This way, Jean Valjean managed to stay for a lòng while. To see Cosette, to forget by her side, was so sweet to him! It was the dressing of his wound. It happened several times that Basque had to come twice to say: "Monsieur Gillenormand has sent me to remind Madame la baronne that dinner is served."

On those days, Jean Valjean would return home in a very thoughtful mood.

Was there, then, some truth in that comparison with the chrysalis that had popped into Marius's mind? Was Jean Valjean, in fact, a chrysalis who would dig his heels in and would go on coming over to visit his butterfly?

One day he stayed even longer than usual. The next day, he noticed that there was no fire in the grate. "Right!" he thought. "No fire." And he furnished himself with this explanation: "It's quite simple. It's now April. The cold is over."

"God! It's cold in here!" cried Cosette, as she came in.

"No, it's not," said Jean Valjean.

"So it was you who told Basque not to light a fire?"

"Yes. Soon it will be May."

"But we light fires up until the month of June. In this cellar, you have to light them all year round."

"I thought we wouldn't need a fire."

"Another one of your funny ideas!" Cosette scolded.

The day after that, there was a fire. But the two armchairs had been moved away across the room next to the door.

"What is that supposed to mean?" thought Jean Valjean.

He went to get the armchairs and put them back in their usual place by the fireside. Still, the fact that the fire had been lit again encouraged him. He made their chat last even longer than usual. As he got up to go, Cosette said to him: "My husband said a funny thing to me yesterday."

"What was that?"

"He said to me: 'Cosette, we have thirty thousand livres in income. Twenty-seven from you, and the three that my grandfather gives me.' I said: 'That makes thirty.' He went on: 'Would you have the courage to live on three thousand?' I said: 'Yes, on nothing. As long as it was with you.' And then I asked: 'Why are you asking?' He answered: 'I just wanted to see.'"

Jean Valjean could think of nothing to say. Cosette probably expected him to give her some explanation; he listened to her in mournful silence. He returned to the rue de l'Homme-Armé so profoundly absorbed that he got the door wrong and instead of going into his place, he went into the place next door. It was only after climbing nearly two flights of stairs that he realized his mistake and went downstairs again.

His mind was racked with surmise. It was clear that Marius had his doubts about the origins of those six hundred thousand francs, that he feared some illicit source. Who knows? Perhaps he had even found out that the money came from him, Jean Valjean, and was hesitating in the face of a suspect fortune, loath to accept it as his own, preferring for them to remain poor, he and Cosette, than to enjoy a tainted wealth.

On top of this, Jean Valjean was vaguely beginning to feel he was being turned away.

The following day, when he stepped into the downstairs room he had a kind of jolt. The armchairs had disappeared. There was not even a chair.

"What!" cried Cosette on entering. "No armchairs! What on earth has happened to the armchairs?"

"They're not here anymore," replied Jean Valjean.

"That's a bit much!"

Jean Valjean stammered: "I told Basque to take them away."

"The reason being?"

"I'll only be staying a few minutes today."

"Staying only a little while is no reason for staying standing up."

"I think Basque needed armchairs for the drawing room."

"What for?"

"No doubt you're having people over this evening."

"We're not having anyone."

Jean Valjean could not say another word. Cosette gave a shrug.

"Fancy getting them to take the armchairs away! The other day you had the fire put out. You really are quite peculiar!"

"Adieu," murmured Jean Valjean.

He did not say: "Adieu, Cosette." But he did not have the strength to say: "Adieu, Madame."

He went away, crushed. This time the meaning was all too clear. The next day, he did not come. Cosette did not even notice till that evening.

"Fancy," she said. "Monsieur Jean didn't come today."

Her heart gave a slight lurch, but she scarcely registered it, immediately distracted as she was by a kiss from Marius.

The day after that, he did not come. Cosette did not give it a thought; she whiled away her evening and slept away her night as if nothing had happened, and only thought about it when she woke up. She was so happy! She sent Nicolette off swiftly to Monsieur Jean's to see if he was sick and to see why he hadn't turned up the night before. He was not sick. He was busy. He would come soon. Just as soon as he could. In any case, he was going on a short trip. Madame might remember that it was his habit to go on trips from time to time. No one should worry on his account. No one should give him a thought.

Nicolette, on entering Monsieur Jean's, had repeated to him the exact words her mistress had used. That Madame was sending her to see "why Monsieur Jean had not come the night before."

"It's been two days since I was last there," said Jean Valjean softly.

But the observation was lost on Nicolette, who didn't breathe a word of it to Cosette.


## IV. ATTRACTION AND EXTINGUISHMENT

During the late spring and early summer of 1833, occasional passersby in the Marais, shopkeepers, loungers idling on doorsteps, noticed an old man neatly dressed in black, who, every day at around the same time, at dusk, would come out of the rue de l'Homme-Armé near the rue Sainte-Croix-de-la-Bretonnerie, go past the rue des Blancs-Manteaux as far as the rue Culture-Sainte-Catherine and, having reached the rue de l'Écharpe, turn left into the rue Saint-Louis.

There he would walk slowly, his head thrust forward, seeing nothing, hearing nothing, his eyes immutably fixed on a point that was always the same, that seemed to him to be glittering with stars, and yet was nothing more than the corner of the rue des Filles-du-Calvaire. The closer he got to that street corner, the brighter his eyes would grow; a sort of joy would light up his pupils like an inner dawn; he looked fascinated and overcome with emotion, his lips would move slightly, as though he were talking to someone he could not see, he would smile vaguely and slow his pace to a crawl. You would have said that, while he wanted to get there, he was afraid of the moment when he would be quite close. When there were no more than a few houses between himself and this street that seemed to draw him like a magnet, his steps would slow down to such an extent that at times you could be forgiven for thinking he had stopped walking. His wobbling head and his staring eyes reminded you of a compass needle seeking the magnetic pole. However long he managed to defer his arrival, he had to arrive some time; he would reach the rue des Filles-du-Calvaire; then he would stop, he would shake, he would poke his head round the corner of the end house with a sort of grim timidity and there he would gaze into the street, and in that tragic gaze there was something that resembled the bedazzlement of the impossible and the reflection of a paradise that was shut. Then a tear that had gathered slowly in the corner of his eye would grow big enough to fall and would slide down his cheek and sometimes stop at his mouth. The old man would taste its bitterness. He would stay like this for a few minutes as though turned to stone; then he would go back the way he had come just as slowly, and the farther away he got the more the light in his eyes would go out.

Little by little, the old man stopped going as far as the corner of the rue des Filles-du-Calvaire; he would stop halfway down the rue Saint-Louis; sometimes a bit farther away, sometimes a bit closer. One day, he stayed at the corner of the rue Culture-Sainte-Catherine and gazed at the rue des Filles-du-Calvaire from afar. Then he silently shook his head from side to side as though he were denying himself something, and he retraced his steps.

Soon, he did not even go as far as the rue Saint-Louis. He would get to the rue Pavée, shake his head, and turn back; then he would go no farther than the rue des Trois-Pavillons; then he would not go beyond the rue des Blancs-Manteaux. He was like the pendulum of a clock that has stopped being wound up, whose swings get shorter and shorter before stopping altogether.

Every day, he left his place at the same time, he set out on the same route, but he no longer finished it and, without perhaps realizing it, he made it shorter and shorter all the time. His whole face expressed this one idea: What's the use? His eyes were dead; the light had gone out. The tear, too, had dried up; it no longer gathered in the corner of his eye; that thoughtful eye was dry. The old man's head was always thrust forward; his chin quivered at times; the folds on his thin neck would break your heart. Sometimes, when the weather was bad, he would have his umbrella tucked under his arm, but he would not open it. The good women of the quartier would say: "That man's an innocent." Children would follow him, laughing.

# BOOK NINE

# SUPREME DARKNESS, SUPREME DAWN

## I. PITY FOR THE UNHAPPY, BUT INDULGENCE FOR THE HAPPY

It is a terrible thing to be happy! How we content ourselves with it! How easily we find it to be the be-all and end-all! How easily, having attained that false aim of life, happiness, we forget the real aim, duty!

We must say, though, that it would be wrong to blame Marius.

Marius, as we explained, had not put any questions to Monsieur Fauchelevent before his marriage, and since then had been afraid to put any to Jean Valjean. He had regretted the promise he had let the man drag out of him. He had told himself over and over that he was wrong to make that concession to despair. He had restricted himself to gradually banishing Jean Valjean from the house and erasing him as much as possible from Cosette's mind. He had always in a way stood between Cosette and Jean Valjean, sure that this way she would not notice the man and would not think about him. It was more than erasure, it was an eclipse.

Marius did what he judged necessary and right. He believed he had serious reasons for pushing Jean Valjean out of the way, without harshness, but without weakness—the same serious reasons we have already seen and others we will see later. Having met by chance, during a trial in which he was acting for the defense, a former clerk from the banking house of Laffitte, without looking for it he had obtained mysterious information that he had not, if the truth be known, been able to delve into any further, out of that very respect for the secret he had promised to keep, and out of consideration for Jean Valjean's precarious situation. He believed, at that particular moment, that he had a grave duty to perform, which was the restitution of the six hundred thousand francs to someone he was looking for as discreetly as possible. Meanwhile, he refrained from touching the money.

As for Cosette, she was not in on any of these secrets; but it would be hard to condemn her, either. There was an all-powerful magnetism between herself and Marius that made her, instinctively and almost automatically, do whatever Marius wanted. She sensed that Marius wanted something in regard to "Monsieur Jean" and she fell into line. Her husband did not have to say a word to her; she felt the vague, but clear, pressure of his tacit intentions, and blindly complied. Her compliance here consisted in not remembering whatever Marius forgot. She did not need to make any effort to do this. Without herself knowing why, and without being in any way to blame, her soul had so thoroughly become her husband's that whatever was covered in darkness in Marius's thoughts, grew dim in hers.

Let's not go too far, though; in relation to Jean Valjean, this disregard and this erasure were only superficial. She was more unthinking than oblivious. In her heart of hearts, she was very fond of the man she had so long called her father. But she loved her husband even more. That is what had somewhat tipped her heart's balance in favor of one side only.

It sometimes happened that Cosette spoke of Jean Valjean and expressed amazement. Then Marius would calm her down: "He's away, I think. Didn't he say he was going on a trip?"

"That's true," Cosette thought. "He was in the habit of disappearing like this. But not for so long."

Two or three times she sent Nicolette around to the rue de l'Homme-Armé to find out whether Monsieur Jean was back from his trip. Jean Valjean had her say he was still away.

Cosette did not inquire any further, having only one need on this earth, Marius. We should say further that, on their side, Marius and Cosette had been away. They had gone to Vernon. Marius had taken Cosette to his father's grave.

Marius had little by little taken Cosette away from Jean Valjean. Cosette had let it happen.

Besides, what people call much too harshly, in certain cases, the ingratitude of children is not always as reprehensible as you might think. It is the ingratitude of nature. Nature, as we have already said elsewhere, "looks straight ahead." Nature divides the living into those on the way in and those on the way out. Those on the way out are turned toward the darkness, those on the way in toward the light. Whence a gap that, for the old, is fatal, and, for the young, involuntary. This gap is at first imperceptible, but it slowly increases like all dividing branches. The smaller branches, without breaking off the trunk, grow away from it. It is not their fault. Youth goes where there is joy, festivity, bright lights, love. Old age goes to the end. They do not lose sight of each other, but they lose their hold on each other. Young people feel the cooling effect of life; old people that of the grave. Let's not blame the poor children.

## II. LAST FLICKERINGS OF A LAMP WITH NO OIL

One day Jean Valjean went downstairs, took three steps into the street, sat down on a curbstone, on that same curbstone where Gavroche, on the night of June 5, had found him musing; he stayed there for a few minutes, then went back up. This was the last swing of the pendulum. The next day, he did not leave his room. The day after that, he did not leave his bed.

His concierge, who prepared his frugal meal, a bit of cabbage and a few potatoes with a bit of streaky bacon, looked at the brown earthenware plate and cried: "But you didn't eat yesterday, you poor dear man!"

"Yes, I did," replied Jean Valjean.

"The plate's still full."

"Look at the water pitcher. It's empty."

"That proves you drank; it doesn't prove you ate."

"Well, then," said Jean Valjean, "what if I was only hungry for water?"

"That's called thirst and, when you don't eat at the same time, it's called fever."

"I'll eat tomorrow."

"Or on Trinity Sunday. Why not today? Do you hear anyone else say: 'I'll eat tomorrow!' Fancy leaving me my plate full without touching it! And my red potatoes were so good!"

Jean Valjean took the old woman's hand: "I promise you I'll eat them," he said to her in his benign voice.

"I'm not happy with you," answered the concierge.

Jean Valjean hardly saw any human being apart from this good woman. There are streets in Paris that no one walks down and houses where no one comes. He was in one of those streets and in one of those houses.

In the days when he still went out, he had bought a little copper crucifix for a few sous from a coppersmith and he had hung it on a nail facing his bed. That particular gallows, the holy rood, is always good to see.

A week went by without Jean Valjean's taking a step even inside his room. He kept to his bed. The concierge said to her husband: "That old fellow from upstairs doesn't get up anymore, doesn't eat anymore, he won't last long. He's got his sorrows, that one has. You can't tell me his daughter hasn't made a bad match."

The porter returned in the tone of husbandly supremacy: "If he's rich, he can get a doctor. If he's not rich, he can do without. If he doesn't get a doctor, he'll die."

"And if he gets one?"

"He'll die."

The concierge began to scratch away at the grass that was growing in what she called her pavement with a knife, and while tearing out the grass, she mumbled: "That's a shame. An old man who's so clean! He's as white as a plucked chicken."

She saw a local doctor going by at the end of the street and took it upon herself to ask him in.

"It's on the second floor," she told him. "You can go straight in. Since the old fellow doesn't stir from his bed anymore, the key's always in the door."

The doctor saw Jean Valjean and spoke to him. When he came back downstairs, the concierge intercepted him: "Well, then, doctor?"

"Your sick man is very sick indeed."

"What's he got?"

"Everything—and nothing. That's a man who, to all appearances, has lost someone dear to him. A person can die of that."

"What did he tell you?"

"He told me he was in good health."

"Will you come back again, doctor?"

"Yes," answered the doctor. "But someone other than me has to come back."

### III. A FEATHER CRUSHES THE MAN WHO LIFTED FAUCHELEVENT'S CART

One evening, Jean Valjean had trouble lifting himself up on his elbow; he took his wrist and couldn't find the pulse; his breathing was shallow and stopped now and then; he realized that he was weaker than he had ever yet been. So, under pressure no doubt from some ultimate overriding concern, he made an effort, sat up, and got dressed. He put on his old workingman's gear. Not going out anymore, he had reverted to it and preferred it. He had to stop several times as he was dressing and the sheer effort of getting his arms into the sleeves of his jacket made the sweat roll down his forehead.

Since he had been on his own, he had put his bed in the antechamber so as to occupy the deserted apartment as little as possible. He opened the suitcase and pulled out Cosette's little bundle of clothes. He spread them out on the bed.

The bishop's candlesticks were in their place on the mantelpiece. He took two beeswax candles out of a drawer and put them in the candlesticks. Then, though it was still broad daylight, in summer, he lit them. You sometimes see candles blazing away like this in the middle of the day in rooms where dead people lie.

Every step he took going from one piece of furniture to the other wore him out and he was forced to sit down. It was not the normal fatigue that expends strength in order to renew it; it was the last vestige of what motion was possible; it was life exhausted and running out drop by drop in overwhelming efforts never to be made again.

One of the chairs on which he now dropped had been placed in front of the mirror, so fatal for him, so providential for Marius, in which he had read Cosette's writing on the blotter backward. He saw himself in the mirror but did not recognize himself. He looked eighty years old; before Marius's marriage, you would scarcely have given him fifty; this year had cost him thirty. What he had on his forehead was not the wrinkles of age, but the mysterious mark of death. You could sense there the gouging of that pitiless claw. His cheeks sagged; the skin on his face was the color that makes it look like there is dirt over it already; both corners of his mouth were turned down like the mask the ancients used to carve on tombs; he stared into space with an air of reproach; you would have taken him for one of those great tragic figures whose rôle is to lament someone.

He was in that place, the last phase of desolation, where sorrow no longer flows down like a fountain; it has, so to speak, coagulated; the soul is blocked by a sort of clot of despair.

Night had come. With great difficulty he dragged a table and the old armchair over to the fireplace and placed on the table a quill pen, ink, and paper.

That done, he fainted. When he regained consciousness, he was thirsty. Not being able to lift up the water pitcher, he tilted it painfully toward his mouth and gulped a mouthful down.

Then he turned toward the bed and, still sitting down, for he could not remain on his feet, he looked at the tiny black dress and all those little objects so dear to his heart. Such contemplation can go on for hours that fly by like minutes. All of a sudden he shivered; he felt the cold coming over him; he leaned on the table, which the bishop's candlesticks lit, and he took up the pen.

As neither the pen nor the ink had been used for a long time, the pen nib was bent and the ink was dry. He had to get up and put a few drops of water in the ink, which he could only do by stopping and sitting down two or three times; and then he was forced to write with the back of the pen. He wiped his forehead from time to time.

His hand was shaking. He slowly wrote the lines that follow:

Cosette, I bless you. I am going to explain to you. Your husband was right in giving me to understand that I ought to clear off; yet he was a little mistaken in what he believed, but he was right. He is a very good man. Always love him with all your heart when I am dead. Monsieur Pontmercy, always love my beloved child. Cosette, they will find this note, here is what I want to tell you, you will see the figures, if I have the strength to remember them, listen carefully, the money really does belong to you. Here is the whole story: White jet comes from Norway, black jet comes from England, black glass beads come from Germany. Jet is lighter, more precious, more dear. We can make imitations in France just as in Germany. You need a small anvil two inches square and a spirit lamp to soften the wax. The wax used to be made with resin and lamp black and cost four francs a pound. I came up with the idea of making it with shellac and turpentine. It costs no more than thirty sous and is a lot better. Loops are made with a violet glass that you stick onto a small black iron plate frame using the wax. The glass should be violet for iron jewelry and black for gold jewelry. Spain buys a lot of it. That is the place for jet . . .

Here he broke off, the pen fell from his fingers, one of those desperate sobs came over him that sometimes rose up from the very depths of his being, the poor man took his head in his hands and brooded.

"Oh!" he cried inside (lamentable cries, heard by God alone), "it's over. I won't see her again. She is a smile that brushed over me. I am about to go into that dark night without even seeing her again. Oh, to hear her voice, touch her dress, look at her, my girl, that angel, if only for a minute, an instant! And then die! Dying is nothing, what is unbearable is dying without seeing her. She would give me a smile, she would have a word with me. Would that hurt anyone? No, it's over, forever. Here I am, all alone. My God! My God! I will never see her again."

At that moment someone knocked on his door.

## IV. Bottle of Ink That Only Manages to Whiten

That same day, or, more precisely, that same evening, as Marius had just left the table and retired to his office to study a case file, Basque had handed him a letter, saying: "The person who wrote the letter is in the antechamber."

Cosette had taken the grandfather's arm and was taking a turn in the garden.

A letter, like a man, can look bad. Coarse paper, clumsy folding, the mere sight of certain missives puts you off. The letter Basque had brought was of this sort.

Marius took it. It smelled of tobacco. Nothing evokes a memory like a smell. Marius recognized the tobacco. He looked at the address: *To Monsieur, Monsieur le baron Pontmerci. At his private hotel.* Recognizing the tobacco made him recognize the handwriting. You could say that amazement has its flashes of insight. Marius was, as it were, illuminated by one of those flashes.

The sense of smell, that mysterious aide-mémoire, instantly brought a whole world back to him. This was indeed the paper, the way of folding, the watery tone of the ink, it was indeed the familiar handwriting; and more than anything else it was the tobacco. The Jondrette garret appeared before him.

What a strange stroke of luck! One of the two trails he had been hoping to find for so long, the one he'd gone to so much trouble over even recently and that he'd thought forever cold, had come to offer itself to him of its own accord.

He eagerly unsealed the letter and read:

> Monsieur le baron,
>
> If the Supreme Being had gven me the talent for it, I could have been the baron Thénard, member of the institute (académie des ciences), but I am not. I merely bare the same name as him, happy if this reminder recomends me to the excellense of your bounties. The kindness you honor me with will be resiprocated. I am in posseshion of a secret conserning an individual. This individual conserns you. I hold the secret at your disposal desiring to have the honor of being yuseful to you. I will give you the simple meens of chasing from your honorable famly this individual who has no right to it, Madame la barone being of high birth. The sanktuary of virtu could never coabit any longer with crime without abdickating.
>
> I await in the entechamber the orders of Monsieur le baron.
>
> With respeck.

The letter was signed "THÉNARD."

This signature was not false. It was merely somewhat abbreviated.

Besides, the gobbledygook and the spelling rounded off the revelation. The certificate of origin was complete. There could be no doubt whatsoever.

Marius's emotion was profound. After the initial surge of surprise, he felt a surge of happiness. If he could only find the other man now, the one who had saved his life, he would have nothing more to wish for.

He opened a drawer in his secretaire, pulled out a few banknotes, shoved them in his pocket, closed the secretaire again and rang. Basque opened the door a little.

"Show him in," said Marius.

Basque announced: "Monsieur Thénard."

A man entered. Fresh surprise for Marius. The man who entered was someone he had never seen before in his life.

This man, who was old on top of everything else, had a bulbous nose, a chin that disappeared into his cravat, green goggles with a double shade of green taffeta over his eyes, hair slicked down flat over his forehead to his eyebrows like the wigs of high-life English coach drivers. His hair was gray. He was dressed in black from head to foot, in a very threadbare but clean black; a bunch of charms, hanging out of his fob pocket, suggested a watch. He held an old hat in his hand. He walked with a stoop, and the curve of his back was accentuated by the very low bow he gave.

What was striking at first sight was that the man's coat, although carefully buttoned up, was too big for him and seemed to have been made for someone else.

Here a short digression is necessary. There was in Paris at the time, in a shady old dive in the rue Beautreillis, near the Arsenal, an ingenious Jew whose business it was to turn a scoundrel into a respectable man. Not for too long, which might have been uncomfortable for the scoundrel. The change was a set change in full view of the audience, for a day or two, at the rate of thirty sous a day, by means of a costume as closely as possible resembling ordinary average respectability. The costume hirer was called the Changer; the crooks of Paris had given him the name and did not know him by any other. He had a fairly complete wardrobe in stock. The rags with which he decked people out were roughly convincing. He had specialties and general categories; from every nail in his shop, a social condition hung, worn and crumpled; here, a magistrate's garb, there a priest's, there a banker's, in one corner a retired soldier's, elsewhere that of a man of letters, further away a statesman's. The man was the wardrobe master for the immense drama that skulduggery staged in Paris. His dive was the dressing room from which theft emerged and to which daylight robbery returned. A rogue in tatters showed up at this changing room, put down thirty sous, and chose the outfit that suited him, depending on the rôle he wanted to play that day, and when he went back downstairs, that rogue was suddenly somebody. The next day, the costume was faithfully returned and the Changer, who trusted robbers with all his stock, was never robbed. These clothes had one drawback, though: They didn't fit, not being made for those who wore them; they were too tight on this one, baggy on that one, didn't fit anyone. Any crook who was bigger or smaller than the human average was ill at ease in the Changer's costumes. You had to be not too fat and not too skinny. The Changer only catered to normal men. He had taken the measure of the species in the person of the first thug to happen along, who was neither thick nor thin, neither tall nor small. Whence the sometimes difficult adaptations that the Changer's customers had to try and get away with as best they could. Too bad for the exceptions! The statesman's outfit, for instance, which was black from top to bottom and consequently most seemly, would have been too big for Pitt and too small for Castelcicala.[1] The garb of the statesman was described as follows in the Changer's catalogue, which we quote: "A coat of black cloth, trousers of black woolskin, a waistcoat of silk, boots, and linen." In the margin was written "Ex-ambassador" and a note that we also transcribe: "In a separate box, a wig properly frizzed, green spectacles, charms, and two small quill tubes one inch long wrapped in cotton." All this went with the statesman, ex-ambassador. The whole costume was, if we may use the word, tired; the seams were going white, a sort of buttonhole was opening up on one of the elbows, and, on top of this, a button was missing on the breast of the coat; but this was a mere detail, for the statesman's hand had always to be inside his coat over his heart, the purpose being to hide the missing button.

If Marius had been familiar with the occult institutions of Paris, he would immediately have recognized, on the back of the visitor that Basque had just shown in, the statesman's outfit borrowed from the Take-that-one-down-for-me of the Changer.

Marius's disappointment at seeing a man enter who was not the man he was expecting, turned to displeasure with the newcomer. He looked him up and down while the character was busy bowing exaggeratedly, and he asked him in a crisp tone: "What do you want?"

The man answered with an amiable grimace not unlike a crocodile's grin: "It does not seem possible to me that I have not already had the honor of seeing Monsieur le baron about town. I really do think I met him in particular, a few years ago, at Madame la princesse Bagration's and in the salons of his lordship the vicomte Dambray,[2] peer of France."

It is always a good tactic in crooked dealings to seem to recognize someone you don't know. Marius paid close attention to the man's speech. He focused on the accent and the gestures, but his disappointment only grew; this man's was a nasal tone, absolutely unlike the sharp dry voice he was expecting. He was completely thrown.

"I do not know," he said, "either Madame Bagration or Monsieur Dambray. I have never in my life set foot in either's house."

The reply was gruff. The character, gracious even so, insisted.

"Then it must have been at Chateaubriand's that I saw Monsieur! I know Chateaubriand very well. A most affable man. He sometimes says to me: Thénard, my friend, won't you have a drink with me?"

Marius's forehead became more and more stern: "I have never had the honor of being received at Monsieur de Chateaubriand's. Let's get to the point. What do you want?"

Confronted by the harder tone of voice, the man bowed even lower.

"Monsieur le baron, deign to hear me out. In America, in a region close to Panama, there is a village called La Joya. This village consists of a lone house. A big, square, three-story house made of bricks baked in the sun, each side of the square five hundred feet long, each floor set back twelve feet from the floor below so that every floor has a terrace in front of it that runs round the entire building; at the center an inner courtyard where the provisions and munitions are kept; no windows, only loopholes, no door, only ladders, ladders to go up from the ground to the first terrace, and from the first to the second, and from the second to the third, ladders to go down into the inner courtyard; no doors on the rooms, only trapdoors, no stairs to the rooms, only ladders; at night, they shut the trapdoors, they take away the ladders, they level blunderbusses and carbines out the loopholes; no means of gaining entry; a house by day, a citadel by night, eight hundred inhabitants, and that's the village for you. Why so many precautions? Because the region's dangerous; it's full of cannibals. So why do people go there? Because it's a marvelous region; it's where you find gold."

"What are you getting at?" Marius broke in, having shifted from disappointment to impatience.

"This, Monsieur le baron. I am a tired old ex-diplomat. The old world has given me an appetite. I'd like to try savages."

"And?"

"Monsieur le baron, selfishness makes the world go round. The landless peasant woman who works by the day turns round when a stagecoach goes by, the landowning peasant woman laboring in her own field doesn't turn round. The poor man's dog barks at the rich man, the rich man's dog barks at the poor man. Every man for himself. Self-interest, that's man's purpose in life. And gold is the lodestone."

"So? Get to the point."

"I'd like to go and set myself up in La Joya. There are three of us. I have a missus and a young lady—a very beautiful girl. The voyage is long and dear. I need a bit of money."

"What's this got to do with me?" asked Marius.

The stranger poked his neck up out of his cravat in a movement peculiar to the vulture, and replied with a smile twice as big: "Could it be that Monsieur le baron has not read my letter?"

This was very nearly the case. The fact is that the contents of the epistle had glanced off Marius. He had taken in the writing more than what it said. He could hardly remember a word of it. For a moment now a new suspicion had been aroused by a new clue falling into place. He had noticed that detail: "a missus and a young lady." He fixed a piercing eye on the stranger. An examining magistrate could not have done better. He was almost lying in wait for him. He kept his answer brief: "Be more specific."

The stranger thrust both hands in both fob pockets, threw back his head without straightening up his spine, but scrutinizing Marius in turn through the green glare of his glasses.

"Right you are, Monsieur le baron. I will be more specific. I have a secret to sell you."

"A secret!"

"A secret."

"That concerns me?"

"Somewhat."

"What is this secret?"

Marius examined the man more and more intensely as he listened to him.

"I'll begin gratis," said the stranger. "You'll see that I'm worth your while."

"Go on."

"Monsieur le baron, you have under your roof a thief and a murderer."

Marius jumped.

"Under my roof? No!" he said.

The stranger brushed his hat with his elbow, imperturbable, and went on: "Murderer and thief. Note, Monsieur le baron, that I am not talking here about deeds that are old, bygone, null and void, that can be canceled out by statutory limitation in the eye of the law, and by repentance in the eye of God. I'm talking about recent deeds, current deeds, deeds justice is still ignorant of, even as we speak. I shall proceed. This man has insinuated himself into your confidence, and almost into your family, under a false name. I am going to tell you his real name. And tell it to you for nothing."

"I'm listening."

"His name is Jean Valjean."

"I know."

"I am going to tell you, also for nothing, who he is."

"Go on."

"He is an ex-convict."

"I know."

"You know since I had the honor of telling you."

"No. I knew beforehand."

Marius's cold tone, that double retort "I know," his terseness, so unamenable to dialogue, stirred mute fury in the stranger. He shot Marius a furtive look of rage, immediately extinguished. As fast as it was, that look was the kind you recognize when you have seen it before; it did not escape Marius. Certain flashes of fire can only come from certain souls; the eye, that cellar window of thought, is set ablaze; glasses hide nothing; you might as well stick a pane of glass on hell.

The stranger went on, smiling: "I would not allow myself to contradict Monsieur le baron. In any case, you must see that I am well informed. Now, what I am about to tell is known to myself alone. It concerns the fortune of Madame la baronne. It is an extraordinary secret. It is for sale. I offer it to you first. Dirt cheap. Twenty thousand francs."

"I know that secret just as I know the others," said Marius.

The character felt the need to lower his price a little: "Monsieur le baron, say ten thousand francs and I'll talk."

"I repeat that you have nothing to tell me. I know what you want to say."

There was a fresh flash in the man's eyes. He shouted: "I still have to eat today. It's an extraordinary secret, I tell you. Monsieur le baron, I am going to talk. I am talking. Give me twenty francs."

Marius stared at him: "I know your extraordinary secret, just as I knew the name Jean Valjean, just as I know your name."

"My name?"

"Yes."

"That's not hard, Monsieur le baron. I had the honor of writing it for you and of telling it to you. Thénard."

"—dier."

"Huh?"

"Thénardier."

"Who's that?"

When in danger, the porcupine bristles, the scarab plays dead, the old guard forms a square; this man started to laugh. Then he brushed a speck of dust from his coat sleeve with a flick. Marius continued: "You are also the workingman Jondrette, the comedian Fabantou, the poet Genflot, the Spaniard don Alvarez, and mother Balizard."

"Mother what?"

"And you used to keep a greasy spoon of a place in Montfermeil."

"A greasy spoon! Never!"

"And I tell you, you are Thénardier."

"I deny it."

"And you are a beggar of a man. Here."

And Marius, pulling a banknote out of his pocket, threw it in his face.

"Thanks! Pardon! Five hundred francs! Monsieur le baron!"

And the man, overcome, bowing and scraping, grabbed the note and examined it.

"Five hundred francs!" he repeated, flabbergasted. And he stammered under his breath: "A serious scrap of paper!"

Then abruptly: "All right! You're on!" he cried. "Let's make ourselves comfortable."

And, with the swiftness of a monkey, tossing his hair back, ripping off his glasses, taking out of his nose and pocketing the two quill tubes we mentioned a moment ago, and which we have already seen as it happens on another page of this book, he took his face off as you take off a hat.

His eyes lit up; his forehead, uneven, deeply lined, lumpy, hideously wrinkled at the top, cleared, his nose regained its beaklike sharpness; the ferocious and acute profile of the man of prey reappeared.

"Monsieur le baron is infallible," he said in a clear voice free of any nasal twang. "I am Thénardier."

And he straightened up his hunched back.

Thénardier, for it was indeed he, was strangely taken aback; he'd have been rocked, if that were possible for him. He had come to deliver a shock, and it was he who had received one. This humiliation had been compensated for by five hundred francs, and, all in all, he accepted it; but he was no less stunned.

He was seeing this baron Pontmercy for the very first time, and, despite his disguise, this baron Pontmercy recognized him, and recognized him good and proper. And not only did this baron know exactly who Thénardier was, but he seemed to know all about Jean Valjean, too. Who was this practically beardless young man, so glacial and so generous, who knew people's names, who knew all their names, and who opened his purse to them, who bullied crooks about like a judge and who paid them like a mug?

Thénardier, you will recall, although once living next door to Marius, had never set eyes on him, which happens often enough in Paris; he had once vaguely heard his daughters talking about a very poor young man named Marius who lived in the house. He had written him the letter we know about, without knowing him. There was no possible connection in his mind between that Marius and this Monsieur le baron Pontmercy.

As for the name Pontmercy, you will recall that, on the battlefield of Waterloo, he had only caught the last two syllables, for which he had always held the legitimate contempt we owe to mere thanks.

Otherwise, through his daughter Azelma, whom he had set on the trail of the newly married couple of February 16, and through his own digging, he had managed to find out a lot of things and, from the depths of his darkness, he had succeeded in seizing more than one mysterious thread. He had, by dint of industry, discovered, or, at the very least, by dint of induction, divined, who the man was that he had encountered on a certain day in the Grand Sewer. From the man, he had easily arrived at the name. He knew that Madame la baronne Pontmercy was Cosette. But on that score he intended to be discreet. Who was Cosette? He himself did not really know. He caught a whiff of bastardy, Fantine's story having always struck him as fishy; but what was the good of bringing it up? To get his silence paid for? He had, or thought he had, something better than that for sale. And, to all appearances, to come along, without proof, and make this revelation to the baron Pontmercy: "Your wife is a bastard"— well, it would only succeed in attracting the husband's boot to the revealer's backside.

To Thénardier's way of thinking, the conversation with Marius had not yet got off the ground. He had had to retreat, modify his strategy, abandon one position, change tack; but nothing essential had yet been jeopardized, and he had five hundred francs in his pocket. Moreover, he had something decisive to say, and even vis-à-vis this baron Pontmercy, well informed and well armed as he was, he felt himself to be in a strong position. For men of Thénardier's ilk, all dialogue is a battle. In the one that was about to begin, how did he stand? He did not know who he was talking to, but he knew what he was talking about. He swiftly made this internal review of his forces, and after agreeing, "I am Thénardier," he hung fire.

Marius had remained pensive. So, he had Thénardier at last. The man whom he had wanted so badly to find once more was there. So, he would be able to honor Colonel Pontmercy's injunction. He felt humiliated that that hero had owed anything to this crook, and that the bill of exchange drawn on Marius by his father from the bottom of the grave should have been outstanding till that day. It also seemed to him, in the complex state his mind was in over Thénardier, that there was good reason to avenge the colonel for the misfortune of having been saved by such a scoundrel. But whatever else happened, he was satisfied. Finally, he was going to free the colonel's shade from the clutches of this unworthy creditor, and it seemed to him that he was about to release his father's memory from debtors' jail.

Alongside this duty, he had another, which was to throw light if possible on the source of Cosette's fortune. The opportunity seemed to present itself. Thénardier did perhaps know something. It might be useful to sound the man out. He would start with that.

Thénardier had slipped the "serious scrap of paper" into his fob pocket and was looking at Marius with an almost tender sweetness. Marius broke the silence.

"Thénardier, I've told you what your name is. Now, your secret, what you've come to tell me, would you like me to tell you what it is? I know more about it than you do. Jean Valjean, as you say, is a murderer and a thief. A thief, since he robbed a rich manufacturer, Monsieur Madeleine, whose ruin he caused. A murderer, since he murdered the police officer, Javert."

"I don't understand, Monsieur le baron," said Thénardier.

"I'll make myself clearer. Listen. Some time around 1822, in an arrondissement of the Pas-de-Calais, there was a man who had had some kind of scrape with the law some time before and who, under the name of Monsieur Madeleine, got back on his feet and rehabilitated himself. This man became a just man, in the full force of the term. With an industry, the manufacture of black glass beads, he made the fortune of a whole town. As for his personal fortune, he made that, too, but only secondarily, and in a way, incidentally. He was a foster father to the poor. He founded hospitals, opened schools, visited the sick, provided for daughters, supported widows, adopted orphans; he was the guardian, so to speak, of the district. He turned down the cross, he was appointed mayor. A freed convict knew the secret about a sentence that was incurred by this man; he denounced him and had him arrested, and took advantage of the arrest to come to Paris, to Laffitte, the banker's, and withdraw, using a false signature—I heard this from the cashier himself—a sum of more than half a million, belonging to Monsieur Madeleine. This convict, who robbed Monsieur Madeleine, is Jean Valjean. As for the other deed, you have nothing to tell me there, either. Jean Valjean killed the police officer Javert; he shot him with a pistol. I, who am speaking to you now, was there."

Thénardier threw Marius the withering look of a beaten man who once more suddenly has his hand on victory and has just clawed back in one go all the ground he had lost. But the smile was back in place immediately; the inferior can only enjoy an obsequious triumph in front of the superior and Thénardier contented himself with saying to Marius: "Monsieur le baron, we are on the wrong track."

And he emphasized this phrase by giving his bunch of charms an expressive twirl.

"What?" Marius returned. "Do you contest it? Those are the facts."

"Those are fantasies; you're dreaming. The confidence with which Monsieur le baron honors me makes it my duty to say so. Truth and justice, first and foremost. I don't like seeing people accused unjustly. Monsieur le baron, Jean Valjean did not rob Monsieur Madeleine, and Jean Valjean did not kill Javert."

"That's a good one! How do you work that out?"

"Two reasons."

"Which are? Go on."

"The first is this: He didn't rob Monsieur Madeleine, given that he, Jean Valjean, is himself Monsieur Madeleine."

"What are you talking about?"

"And the second is this: He didn't murder Javert, given that the man who killed Javert is Javert."

"What do you mean?"

"That Javert committed suicide."

"Prove it! Prove it!" Marius shrieked, losing control.

Thénardier went on, scanning his sentence in the manner of a classical alexandrine: "The-po-lice-off-i-cer-Ja-vert-was-found-drown-ed-un-der-a-boat-at-the-Pont-au-Change."

"So prove it, then!"

Thénardier pulled from his side pocket a large gray paper envelope that looked as if it contained folded pages of different sizes.

"I have my file," he said, calmly.

And he added: "Monsieur le baron, for your sake, I wanted to know my Jean Valjean backward. I say that Jean Valjean and Madeleine are the same man, and I say that Javert had no killer other than Javert, and when I say something, it's because I have proof. Not handwritten proof, handwriting is suspicious, writing is lax, but proof in print."

As he spoke, Thénardier extracted from the envelope two editions of newspapers, yellowed, faded, and highly saturated with tobacco. One of these two newspapers, torn at the creases and falling apart in squared-off strips, looked a lot older than the other.

"Two facts, two pieces of proof," said Thénardier. And he handed Marius the two newspapers unfolded and spread out.

These two newspapers are familiar to the reader. One, the older one, an edition of the *Drapeau blanc* of July 25, 1823, the text of which can be found on page 301 of this book, established that Monsieur Madeleine and Jean

Valjean were identical. The other, a *Moniteur* of June 15, 1832, recorded Javert's suicide, adding that it resulted from a report by Javert to the prefect that, having been made a prisoner in the barricade in the rue de la Chanvrerie, he had owed his life to the magnanimity of an insurgent who, while holding him with his pistol, instead of blowing his brains out, had fired into the air.

Marius read. Here was evidence, certain date, irrefutable proof; these two newspapers had not been printed expressly to support Thénardier's story: The note published in the *Moniteur* was an official communiqué of the prefecture of police. Marius could not doubt it. The bank clerk's information was false and he himself had been mistaken. Jean Valjean, suddenly looming large, emerged from the cloud cover. Marius could not hold back a cry of joy: "So then, that poor unfortunate man is a wonderful man! That whole fortune really did belong to him! He is Madeleine, the salvation of a whole region! He is Jean Valjean, the savior of Javert! He is a hero! He is a saint!"

"He is not a saint, and he is not a hero," said Thénardier. "He is a murderer and a thief."

And he added in the voice of a man who feels he is gaining the upper hand: "Let's calm down, shall we?"

Thief, murderer, these words that Marius had thought banished, returned and crashed over him like a shower of ice.

"Still?" he said.

"Still!" said Thénardier. "Jean Valjean did not rob Monsieur Madeleine, but he is still a thief. He did not kill Javert, but he is still a murderer."

"You're not talking," Marius shot back, "about that miserable petty theft of forty years ago, expiated, as appears from your very own newspapers, by a whole lifetime of repentance, self-denial, and good?"

"I say murder and theft, Monsieur le baron. And I repeat that I'm talking about current deeds. What I have to reveal to you is absolutely unknown. It's a scoop. And maybe it's where you'll find the source of the fortune cunningly offered by Jean Valjean to Madame la baronne. I say cunningly, for, through a donation of the kind, to slip into an honorable household, the comforts of which he will share, and, by the same token, cover up his crime, to enjoy the fruits of his theft, bury his name, and create himself a family—that would not be particularly inept."

"I could interrupt you here," observed Marius, "but go on."

"Monsieur le baron, I will tell you all, leaving the reward to your generosity. This secret is worth its weight in gold. You'll say to me: 'Why didn't you go to Jean Valjean?' For a very simple reason: I know that he has dispossessed himself, and dispossessed himself in your favor, and I find the scheme ingenious; but he no longer has a sou, he would just show me his empty pockets, and since

I need some money for my trip to La Joya, I prefer you, you have the lot, to him—he has nothing. I'm a little weary, allow me to take a seat."

Marius sat down and gestured for him to sit.

Thénardier settled into a padded chair, took back the two newspapers, thrust them back in the envelope, and muttered, tapping the *Drapeau blanc* with his nail: "I went to a lot of trouble to get this one." That done, he crossed his legs and lay back in his chair, in the manner of a man who is sure of what he is saying; then he took the plunge and tackled the subject gravely, stressing every word with great emphasis: "Monsieur le baron, the sixth of June, 1832, roughly a year ago, the day of the riot, there was a man in the Grand Sewer of Paris, over where the sewer comes out at the Seine, between the pont des Invalides and the pont d'Iéna."

Marius abruptly brought his chair closer to Thénardier's. Thénardier registered the movement and went on at the slow pace of an orator who holds his audience in the palm of his hand and feels his enemy squirming under his words: "This man was forced to go into hiding, though for reasons that have nothing to do with politics, and he'd taken the sewer as his place of residence and had a key to it. It was, I repeat, the sixth of June; it could have been eight o'clock in the evening. The man heard a noise in the sewer. He was pretty startled and he hugged the wall and watched. It was the noise of footsteps, someone was walking in the shadows, someone was coming his way. The funny thing was that there was another man in the sewer—someone other than himself. The sewer exit was not far away. A bit of light coming through the gate allowed him to recognize the newcomer and to see that the man was carrying something on his back. He was walking hunched over. The man walking hunched over was an ex-convict and what he was lugging on his shoulders was a corpse. Case of being caught red-handed in the act of murder, if ever there was one. As for the theft, it goes without saying; you don't kill a man for free. The convict was going to throw the corpse in the river. A fact to note is that before reaching the exit gate, the convict, who came from way down the sewer, had to have encountered a dreadful bog where it would seem he could well have left the corpse, but the very next day, the sewer workers working on the quagmire would have found the murdered man and that was not how the murderer wanted it. He preferred to get through the bog, with his burden, and he must have worked horribly hard at it, you could not put your life more completely at risk. I don't understand how he got out of there alive."

Marius's chair came even closer. Thénardier took advantage of this to take a deep breath. He pursued: "Monsieur le baron, a sewer is not the Champ de Mars. There's nothing there, not even room. When there are two men in there, they have to run into each other. And that's what happened. The resident and the man passing through were forced to say hello to each other, regretfully on both sides. The blow-in said to the resident: 'You can see what's on my back, I've got to get out, you have the key, give it to me.' This convict was a man of terrible strength. There was no refusing him. Yet the one with the key parlayed, solely to gain time. He examined the dead man, but he couldn't see anything, except that he was young, well turned out, apparently rich, and all disfigured by blood. While he chatted, he was able to tear off a piece of the murdered man's coat at the back, without the murderer being any the wiser. Supporting evidence, you understand; a way of getting back on the trail of things and pinning the crime on the criminal. He put the supporting evidence in his pocket. After which he opened the gate, let the man out with his load on his back, shut the gate again, and bolted, not caring too much to get mixed up in the episode as it happens and especially not wanting to be there when the murderer chucked his victim into the river. Now you get it. The one lugging the corpse is Jean Valjean; the one with the key is speaking to you at this very moment; and the bit of coat—"

Thénardier finished his sentence by pulling out of his pocket and flourishing, at eye level, between both thumbs and forefingers, a strip of black cloth that was in shreds and covered with dark stains.

Marius had got to his feet, pale, barely breathing, his eye fixed on the piece of black cloth, and, without uttering a word, without taking his eyes off this tatter, he backed toward the wall and, with his right hand stretched out behind him, groped for the key in the lock of a cupboard next to the fireplace. He found the key, opened the cupboard, and thrust his arm in without looking and without taking his startled eyes off the fragment of cloth Thénardier held up.

Meanwhile Thénardier went on: "Monsieur le baron, I have very good reason to think that the young man assassinated was a wealthy foreigner, lured by Jean Valjean into a trap while he was carrying an enormous sum on him."

"The young man was me, and here is the coat!" cried Marius as he threw an old black coat all covered in blood on the parquet floor.

Then ripping the fragment out of Thénardier's hands, he crouched over the coat and brought the torn fragment to the mutilated panel. The tear fitted perfectly, the strip completed the coat. Thénardier was petrified. What he thought was: "I'll be buggered!"

Marius straightened up, shivering, desperate, radiant. He fumbled in his pocket and strode, furious, over to Thénardier, handing him, practically ramming into his face a fist filled with notes of five hundred francs and one thousand francs.

"You are a thorough bastard! You are a liar, a defamer, a cur. You came to accuse a man, but you've only vindicated him; you wanted to sink him, but you've only succeeded in glorifying him. You are the thief! You are the murderer! I saw you, Thénardier Jondrette, in that hole on the boulevard de l'Hôpital, I've got enough on you to send you to jail and beyond, if I wanted to. Here, here's a thousand francs, racketeer scum that you are!"

And he threw a thousand-franc note at Thénardier.

"Ah, Jondrette Thénardier, vile reprobate! Let this be a lesson to you, you peddler of secrets, mystery merchant, rummager in the dark, miserable bastard! Take these five hundred francs while you're at it and get out! Waterloo is the only thing saving your hide!"

"Waterloo!" snorted Thénardier, pocketing the five hundred francs along with the thousand francs.

"Yes, you murderous swine! You saved the life of a colonel—"

"A general," said Thénardier, lifting his head.

"A colonel!" Marius shot back in a fit of rage. "I wouldn't give two hoots for a general. And to think you came *here* to commit your evil deeds! I tell you, you have committed every crime in the book. Get out! Get out of my sight! Go and crawl under a rock! Just be happy, that's all I ask. You monster! Here's another three thousand francs. Take it. You'll leave tomorrow at the latest for America, with your daughter; for your wife is dead, you lying worm! I'll see to it that you set sail, you crook, and I'll count you out twenty thousand francs at the dock! Go and get yourself hanged somewhere else!"

"Monsieur le baron," replied Thénardier bowing to the ground, "eternal gratitude."

And Thénardier scuttled away, comprehending nothing, stunned and thrilled at this soft pummeling with bags of gold, this thunderclap bursting over his head in banknotes.

Thunderstruck he was, but content, too; and he would have been very sorry to have had a lightning rod to protect him against this particular bolt from the blue.

Let's wash our hands of the man without further ado. Two days after the events we are relating at the moment, he left, thanks to Marius, for America, under a false name, with his daughter Azelma, armed with a draft for twenty thousand francs to be drawn in New York. The moral destitution of Thénardier, that bourgeois manqué, was irremediable; he was in America what he had been in Europe. Contact with a mean man is sometimes all it takes to corrupt a good deed and cause something bad to spring from it. With the money from Marius, Thénardier made himself a slave trader.[3]

As soon as Thénardier was out the door, Marius ran to the garden where Cosette was still ambling.

"Cosette! Cosette!" he yelled. "Come! Come quickly. We must get cracking. Basque, a fiacre! Cosette, hurry. Oh, my God! He was the one who saved my life! We mustn't lose a minute! Put your shawl on."

Cosette thought he'd gone mad, and did as she was told.

He couldn't breathe, he placed his hand on his heart to slow the beating. He paced to and fro with great strides, he kissed Cosette: "Ah, Cosette! What a sorry man I am!" he said.

Marius was overcome. He began to have an inkling of how incredibly lofty and solemn a figure this Jean Valjean was. An unheard-of virtue appeared to him, supreme and meek, humble in its immensity. The convict was transfigured into Christ. Marius was completely dazzled by this wonder. He did not know exactly what he saw, only that it was great.

In an instant, a fiacre was at the door.

Marius handed Cosette up and leaped in.

"Driver," he said, "rue de l'Homme-Armé, number seven."

The fiacre set off.

"Ah, what happiness!" said Cosette. "Rue de l'Homme-Armé. I didn't dare bring it up anymore. We're going to see Monsieur Jean."

"Your father, Cosette! Your father, more than ever. Cosette, I think I can guess what happened. You told me you never got the letter I sent you via Gavroche. It must have fallen into his hands. Cosette, he went to the barricade to save me. As his great need is to be an angel, just like that, in passing, he saved others there. He saved Javert. He pulled me out of that inferno in order to hand me to you. He carried me on his back through that appalling sewer. Ah, I'm a monstrous ingrate. Cosette, after being your salvation, he was mine. Just imagine. There was an awful quagmire, one you could drown in a hundred times over, one that could drown you in the sludge, Cosette! He got me through it. I'd passed out; I saw nothing, I heard nothing, I didn't have a clue what was happening to me. We're going to bring him back, have him here with us, whether he likes it or not, he won't be leaving us ever again. Let's hope he's at home! Let's hope we find him! I'll spend the rest of my life at his feet. Yes, that must be it, you see, Cosette? Gavroche must have handed my letter to him, instead of you. That explains everything. You understand."

Cosette did not understand a word.

"You're right," she said.

Meanwhile the fiacre rolled along.

## V. Night with Day Behind It

At the knock he heard at his door, Jean Valjean turned round.

"Come in," he croaked.

The door opened. Cosette and Marius appeared. Cosette rushed into the room. Marius stayed on the landing, leaning against the doorway.

"Cosette!" said Jean Valjean, and he rose in his chair, his arms open wide and shaking, haggard, pale, looking like death, but with an immense joy in his eyes.

Cosette, choked with emotion, fell on Jean Valjean's breast.

"Father!" she said.

Jean Valjean was overwhelmed; he stuttered: "Cosette! It's her! You, Madame! It's you! Oh, God!"

And, hugged tight in Cosette's arms, he cried: "It's you! You're here! So you forgive me!"

Marius closed his eyes to stop the tears flowing, took a step forward and murmured between lips convulsively pressed together to stop the sobs: "My father!"

"And you, too, you forgive me!" said Jean Valjean.

Marius could find no words and Jean Valjean spoke again: "Thank you."

Cosette tore off her shawl and threw her hat on the bed.

"They're in the way."

And, sitting on the old man's knees, she brushed aside his white hair in the sweetest gesture and kissed his forehead. Jean Valjean just sat there, bewildered.

Cosette, who had only a very dim idea of what was going on, kissed him and caressed him more intently, as though she wanted to pay off Marius's debt. Jean Valjean stammered: "How stupid can you be! I thought I'd never see her again. Just imagine, Monsieur Pontmercy, the moment you came in, I was saying to myself: It's finished. There's her little dress, I am a miserable man, I'll never see Cosette again. I was saying that the very moment you were coming up the stairs. What an idiot I was! See what an idiot I am! But we don't take the good Lord into account. The good Lord says: You think they're going to abandon you, nincompoop! No, no, that's not how it's going to happen. Let's see, there's a poor old man that needs an angel. And the angel comes; and a man sees his Cosette again, a man sees his little Cosette again! Ah, I was so unhappy!"

For a moment he could not speak, then he went on: "I really did need to see Cosette for just a moment from time to time. A heart needs a bone to gnaw on. But I was all too well aware I wasn't wanted. I resigned myself to it: They don't need you, stay in your corner, a man doesn't have the right to go on forever. Ah, God be blessed, I'm seeing her again! You know, Cosette, your husband is very handsome? Ah, that's a pretty embroidered collar you have there, lovely. I like that pattern. Your husband chose it, didn't he? And then, you must have cashmeres. Monsieur Pontmercy, let me call her Cosette. It won't be for long."

And Cosette came back: "How mean to have left us like that! Where on earth did you go? Why did you stay away so long? Once, your trips only lasted three or four days. I sent Nicolette over, but they always told her: 'He's away.' How long have you been back? Why didn't you let us know? Do you know you've changed a lot? Ah, wicked father! He was sick and we didn't know! Here, Marius, feel how cold his hand is!"

"So here you are! Monsieur Pontmercy, you forgive me!" Jean Valjean repeated.

At those words, coming once more from Jean Valjean, all that was welling up in Marius's heart found an outlet and he burst out: "Cosette, do you hear that? Typical! He asks me to forgive him. And do you know what he did for me, Cosette? He saved my life! He did more than that. He gave me you. And after saving me, and after giving me you, Cosette, what did he do with himself? He sacrificed himself. That's the kind of man he is. And to me the oblivious, the pitiless, the guilty, the ungrateful wretch, he says: Thank you! Cosette, if I spent my whole life at this man's feet, it would be too little. The barricade, the sewer, the furnace, the cesspit—he went through it all for me, for you, Cosette! He carried me through every form of death, driving death away from me and accepting it for himself. Every form of courage, every form of virtue, every form of heroisim, every form of saintliness, he has the lot! Cosette, this man is an angel!"

"Shhhh! Shhh!" Jean Valjean whispered. "Why say all that?"

"But what about you!" shouted Marius with a fury verging on veneration. "Why didn't you say anything? It's your fault, too. You save people's lives, and you hide it from them! You do more than that, you slander yourself while you're pretending to unmask yourself. It's appalling."

"I told the truth," answered Jean Valjean.

"No," Marius retorted, "the truth is the whole truth and that you did not tell. You were Monsieur Madeleine. Why didn't you say so? You saved Javert, why didn't you say so? I owe my life to you, why didn't you say so?"

"Because I thought as you did. I felt you were right. I had to go away. If you'd known about that sewer business, you would have made me stay with you. So I had to keep quiet. If I had spoken out, it would've upset everything."

"Upset what! Upset who?" returned Marius. "You don't think you're going to stay here, do you? You're coming with us. My God! When I think it was only by accident that I learned all this! You're coming with us. You are part of us. You are her father and mine. You're not spending another day in this hellhole of a place. Don't imagine that you'll still be here tomorrow."

"Tomorrow," said Jean Valjean, "I won't be here, but I won't be at your place, either."

"What do you mean by that?" replied Marius. "Oh, no, we won't allow any more trips. You're not leaving us again. You belong to us. We won't let you go."

"This time, it's for keeps," chipped in Cosette. "We have a carriage down below. I'm kidnapping you. If necessary, I'll use force."

And, laughing, she made as though to lift the old man up in her arms.

"Your room's still there at our place," she went on. "If you only knew how lovely the garden is at the moment! The azaleas are coming along nicely. The paths are all sanded with river sand; there are little violet-colored shells in it. You'll eat my strawberries. I water them myself. And no more Madame, and no more Monsieur Jean, we are in a republic, everybody says *tu*, don't they, Marius? There's been a change of program. If you only knew, Father, I had a terrible thing happen, there was a robin redbreast that had built its nest in a hole in the wall, and a horrible cat went and ate it on me. My poor pretty little robin redbreast, who used to stick its head in the window and look at me! I cried over it. I could have killed the cat! But no one is going to cry anymore now. Everyone is going to laugh, everyone is going to be happy. You're going to come with us. Grandfather will be so pleased! You'll have your patch in the garden, you'll grow things in it, and we'll see if your strawberries are as good as mine. And then, I'll do whatever you like, and you'll do whatever I say."

Jean Valjean listened to her without understanding what she was saying. He was listening to the music of her voice more than the meaning of her words; one of those big tears, which are the somber pearls of the soul, slowly gathered in his eye. He murmured: "The proof that God is good, is that she is here."

"My darling father!" said Cosette.

Jean Valjean went on: "It's all too true that it would be lovely to live together. They have trees full of birds. I'd stroll around with Cosette. To be one of the living, say good morning to each other, call out to each other in the garden, how sweet that is. We'd see each other from first thing in the morning. We'd each have our own little corner. She would get me to eat her strawberries, I would get her to pick my roses. It would be lovely. Only—"

He broke off, and said softly: "What a shame."

The tear did not fall, it went back in, and Jean Valjean replaced it with a smile. Cosette took both the old man's hands in hers.

"My God!" she said. "Your hands are even colder. Are you sick? Are you in pain?"

"Me? No," answered Jean Valjean. "I feel very well. Only—"

He stopped himself.

"Only what?"

"I'm going to die in a little while."

Cosette and Marius shuddered.

"To die!" cried Marius.

"Yes, but that's nothing," said Jean Valjean.

He took a breath, smiled, and went on: "Cosette, you were talking to me, go on, talk some more, so your little robin redbreast is dead, talk, so I can hear your voice!"

Marius looked at the old man, petrified. Cosette let out a heartrending cry.

"Father! My darling father! You shall live. You are going to live. I want you to live, do you hear me!"

Jean Valjean lifted his head to her in adoration.

"Ah, yes, forbid me to die. Who knows? Perhaps I'll obey. I was dying when you arrived. That stopped me, I felt like I was born again."

"You're full of strength and life," cried Marius. "You don't really imagine that people die just like that? You've had your sorrows, you won't have any more. It is I who beg your forgiveness, and on my knees, to boot! You are going to live, and to live with us, and to live a long time. We will take you home. There are two of us here who will have only one thought from now on—your happiness!"

"You see," Cosette said, in tears. "Marius says you won't die."

Jean Valjean went on smiling.

"If you were to take me back, Monsieur Pontmercy, would that mean I was not what I am? No, God thought the same as you and I did, and He doesn't change His mind. It's best that I take myself off. Death is a good arrangement. God knows better than we do what we need. That you be happy, that Monsieur Pontmercy have Cosette, that youth marry morning, that there be lilacs and nightingales around you, my children, that your life be a beautiful lawn in sunlight, that all the enchantments of heaven fill your soul, and that now I, I who am good for nothing, I die—all this is surely only right and good. You see, be reasonable, there's nothing left now, I feel absolutely sure that it's over. An hour ago, I fainted. And then, last night, I drank that pitcher full of water over there. How good your husband is, Cosette! You're much better off with him than with me."

There was a noise at the door. It was the doctor coming in.

"Hello and goodbye," said Jean Valjean. "Here are my poor children."

Marius went over to the doctor. He addressed this single word to him: "Monsieur?" But the way he said it involved the whole question.

The doctor answered that question with a glance that said it all.

"Just because you don't like the way things are," said Jean Valjean, "that's no reason to be unfair to God."

There was a silence. All hearts were heavy. Jean Valjean turned to Cosette. He began to contemplate her as though he wanted to take her in for all eternity. Even at the dark depth to which he had already descended, he could still feel ecstasy in gazing at Cosette. The glow from that sweet face lit up his own pale face. Even at death's door, a person can still be dazzled.

The doctor felt his pulse.

"Ah, it's you that he needed!" he murmured, looking at Cosette and Marius.

And, bending over to Marius's ear, he whispered: "Too late."

Jean Valjean, almost without ceasing to gaze at Cosette, considered Marius and the doctor with serenity. They heard these words, barely audible, come from his lips: "Dying is nothing; what's terrible is not to live."

All of a sudden, he stood up. These surges of strength are sometimes a sign of dying. He walked with firm tread to the wall, pushed Marius and the doctor aside when they tried to help him, took down the small copper crucifix from the wall where it was hanging, came back and sat down with all the ease of movement of a man in his prime, and said in a loud voice, laying the crucifix on the table: "There is the great martyr."

Then his chest sank, his head swayed, as though the intoxication of the grave had taken hold of him, and his hands, lying on his knees, began to claw at the fabric of his trousers.

Cosette held him by the shoulders and sobbed, and tried to talk to him but could not do it. Among the words that mingled with that mournful saliva that accompanies tears, they could make out words such as these: "Father! Don't leave us. Can we really have found you again only to lose you?"

It could be said that death meanders in its throes. It comes and goes, moves toward the grave, then turns back toward life. There is groping in the act of dying.

Jean Valjean gathered strength again after this semi-blackout, shook his head as though to shake off the dark, and became almost completely lucid again. He grabbed a piece of Cosette's sleeve and kissed it.

"He's coming back! Doctor, he's coming back!" cried Marius.

"You are good, the two of you," said Jean Valjean. "I'll tell you what hurt me. What hurt me, Monsieur Pontmercy, is that you didn't want to touch the money. That money really is your wife's. I'm going to explain to you, my children, that's even the real reason I'm so pleased to see you. Black jet comes from England, white jet comes from Norway. All of this is in that note over there, that you'll read. For bracelets, I invented a way of replacing soldered metal loops with slightly open metal loops. It's prettier, better, and cheaper. You see all the money that can be made. Cosette's fortune is well and truly hers. I give you these details to put your minds at rest."

The concierge had come up and was watching by the door, which was ajar. The doctor sent her away, but he could not prevent the good woman from calling out to the dying man before she disappeared: "Would you like a priest?"

"I have one," said Jean Valjean.

And, with his finger, he seemed to be pointing to a spot above his head where you would have sworn he saw someone. It is likely, in fact, that the bishop was there with him in his agony.

Cosette gently slid a pillow behind his back. Jean Valjean went on: "Monsieur Pontmercy, have no fear, I implore you. The six hundred thousand francs really are Cosette's. I'll have lived my life in vain if you don't enjoy them! We got to the stage where we were turning out very good glass beads. We could compete with what is known as Berlin jewelry. You can't, for instance, equal the black glass of Germany. A gross, which contains twelve hundred well-cut stones, only costs three francs."

When a being that is dear to us is about to die, you look at them with a look that clings to them in an effort to hold them back. Both Cosette and Marius, speechless with anguish, not knowing what to say to death, desperate and trembling, stood before him, Cosette giving Marius her hand.

Jean Valjean was fading fast, from one moment to the next. He was going down; he was getting closer to that dark horizon. His breath had become intermittent, broken up by a faint death rattle. He had trouble moving his arm, his feet had lost all movement and at the same time as the misery of his limbs and the crushing of his body was growing, all the majesty of his soul was rising and unfurling across his forehead. The light of the unknown world was already visible in his eyes.

His face grew white and at the same time he smiled. Life was no longer there, there was something else. His breath died away, his gaze widened. He was a corpse with wings you could feel.

He signaled to Cosette to approach, then to Marius; it was clearly the final minute of the final hour, and he began to talk to them in a voice so weak it seemed to come from far away, and from that moment, it was as though there was a wall between them and him.

"Come here, come here both of you. I love you dearly. Oh, it's good to die this way! You, too, you love me, my Cosette. I knew all along that you still felt affection for your good old boy. How sweet of you to have put that pillow behind my back! You will cry for me a bit, won't you? Not too much. I don't want you to be overcome with sorrow. You must live life to the hilt, my children. I forgot to tell you, you make even more on the buckles without tongues than on all the rest. The gross, the twelve dozen, used to cost ten francs and sell for sixty. It really was a good business. So you really shouldn't be surprised at that six hundred thousand francs, Monsieur Pontmercy. It's honest money. You can be rich in all tranquillity. You must have a carriage, from time to time a box at the theater, beautiful ball gowns, my Cosette, and then give your good friends good dinners, be very happy. I was writing to Cosette a moment ago. She'll find my letter. It is to her that I bequeath those two candlesticks on the mantelpiece. They're silver; but for me, they are gold, they are diamond; they change the candles you put in them into altar candles. I don't know if the man who gave them to me is pleased with me up there. I did what I could. My children, you won't forget that I'm a pauper, you'll bury me in the first plot of ground you come across beneath a stone to mark the spot. That is my wish. No name on the stone. If Cosette wants to come and see me for a while sometimes, it will make me happy. You, too, Monsieur Pontmercy. I have to confess I have not always loved you; forgive me, please. Now the two of you are but one for me. I am very grateful to you. I feel that you make Cosette happy. If you only knew, Monsieur Pontmercy, her beautiful rosy cheeks, they were my joy in life: Whenever I saw her a bit pale, I was sad. There's a five-hundred-franc note in the chest of drawers. I haven't touched it. It's for the poor. Cosette, you see your little dress, over there on the bed? Do you recognize it? Yet it's only ten years ago. How time flies! We have been pretty happy. It's over. My children, don't cry, I'm not going far. I'll see you from there. You'll only have to look up at night and you'll see me smile. Cosette, do you remember Montfermeil? You were in the woods, you were scared stiff; do you remember how I took the handle of the bucket? That was the first time I touched your poor little hand. It was so cold! Ah, you had red hands in those days, Mademoiselle; they are nice and white now. And the big doll! Do you remember? You called her Catherine. You were sorry you didn't bring her to the convent! How you made me laugh at times, my sweet angel! When it rained, you used to launch bits of straw in the gutters and watch them sail away. One day, I gave you a wickerwork bat and a shuttlecock with yellow, blue, and green feathers. You've forgotten it, I know. You were so mischievous when you were little! You were always playing. You'd stick cherries over your ears. That's all in the past. The forests where you went with your little girl, the trees where we would stroll, the convents where we hid, the games, the good hard laughs of childhood, that is shadow now. I thought all that belonged to me. That's where I was so stupid. Those Thénardiers were a nasty lot. You must forgive them. Cosette, the time has come to tell you your mother's name. Her name was Fantine. Hang on to that name: Fantine. Go down on your knees every time you say it. She suffered so much. She loved you dearly. She had as much unhappiness as you have happiness. Those are God's lots. He is up there, he sees every one of us, and he knows what he's doing up there in the middle of his great stars. So, I'm going away, my children. Love one another dearly, always. Nothing else in the world really matters but that: to love one another. You will think sometimes of the poor old man who died here. O, my Cosette! It's not my fault, is it, if I didn't see you all this time lately. It broke my heart. I would go just to the corner of your street, I must have had quite an effect on the people who saw me go by, I was like a madman, once I went out without a hat. My children, I can't see too clearly anymore now, I still had things to say, but never mind. Think of me sometimes. You are among the blessed. I don't know what's the matter with me, I see light. Come closer. I die happy. Give me your dearly beloved heads, so I can lay my hands on them."

Cosette and Marius fell to their knees, distraught, choking with tears, each with one of Jean Valjean's hands on their head. Those august hands no longer stirred. He had fallen backward, the light from the two candlesticks shone on him; his white face looked up at the sky, he let Cosette and Marius cover his hands with kisses; he was dead.

The night was starless and black as pitch. Doubtless, in the dark, some vast angel was standing by with wings outspread, waiting for his soul.

## VI. The Grass Hides and the Rain Erases

In the cemetery of Père-Lachaise, close to the common grave, far from the elegant quartier of this city of sepulchres, far from all those fantastic tombs that show off death's ghastly fashions in the face of eternity, in a deserted corner, along an old wall, under a great yew tree on which birdwood climbs, among the couch grass and the moss and the bindweed, there is a stone. This stone is no more exempt than the others from the leprosy of time, of mold, of lichen, and of bird droppings. Water turns it green, the air turns it black. It is not near any path and no one likes going over that way, because the grass is high and your feet get instantly wet. When there is a bit of sun, the lizards come out. There is, all around, a rustling of wild oats. In spring, the warblers sing in the tree.

This stone is completely bare. The only idea in cutting it was to meet the bare requirements of a grave, and no further care was taken than to make the stone long enough and narrow enough to cover a man.

There is no name on it for you to read.

Only, many years ago already, someone's hand wrote four lines of verse on it in chalk, lines that gradually became illegible under the rain and the dust, and that have probably now been erased:

He sleeps. Though fate for him was truly odd,
He lived. He died when his angel was gone;
The thing just happened of its own accord,
As night comes on when day is done.[1]

# NOTES

1. **Hauteville House:** Hugo's residence-in-exile on the Channel island of Guernsey under the reign of Napoléon III. Hugo had left France soon after the coup d'état that made "prince-president" Napoléon Bonaparte Emperor Napoléon II in December 1851. Hugo's exile was voluntary—the imperial government claimed it bore no ill will toward the most famous author in France, but documents discovered after the fall of the Second Empire indicate that Hugo's exile was as prudent as it was dramatic. After living briefly in Brussels and then on the island of Jersey, Hugo established himself on Guernsey, purchasing Hauteville House in 1856 as a means of rendering his position as a foreign resident of British territory more secure. Hugo did not return to France until 1870, when the French defeat in the Franco-Prussian War brought an end to the Second Empire.

PART ONE: FANTINE

BOOK ONE: A JUST MAN
*I: Monsieur Myriel*

1. **Myriel was bishop of Digne:** Hugo based his bishop on Charles-François-Melchior-Bienvenu de Miollis (1753–1838), bishop of Digne from 1805 to 1831. Like his fictional counterpart, Miollis was known for the simplicity of his lifestyle and his attention to the poorest members of his diocese. Miollis also welcomed a convict named Pierre Maurin, who had spent five years in prison for stealing a loaf of bread (with aggravating circumstances). Several details of Bishop Myriel's life are inventions of the novelist and were even criticized by conservative Catholics, who saw Myriel's lifestyle as a rebuke of the Church, and by the surviving members of Miollis's family.

   The town of Digne was also a fortuitous location for Bishop Myriel's good works, given that *digne* means "worthy" in French. The bishop's name may suggest other meanings. The *-iel* ending recalls the traditional names of the archangels (Gabriel, Raphael, Michael, Uriel). The name also has a certain assonance with *miel*, "honey."

2. *noblesse de robe:* the hereditary class of magistrates who made up the *parlements,* the law courts of ancien régime France. The *robins* were considered one rung below the *noblesse d'épée,* the nobility of the sword, the dukes, counts, and so on, of the old feudal-military order.

3. **tragic scenes of '93:** The year 1793, the fourth year of the French Revolution, saw some of the bloodiest episodes of the era, from the trial and execution of Louis XVI in January to Marie Antoinette's in October, as well as the beginning of the Terror. Hugo's last novel, *Quatre-vingt-treize* (Ninety-three), a story of political conflict in revolutionary Brittany, was published in 1874.

4. **émigrés:** Usually taken to refer to aristocrats, the term can refer to anyone who fled France for political reasons during the Revolution.

5. **1804:** In 1804, Consul for Life Napoléon Bonaparte, de facto dictator of France since 1799, became emperor of the French. The coronation of December 2 was officiated by Pope Pius VII in the cathedral of Notre-Dame de Paris.

6. **curé of Brignolles:** The title *curé,* curate, was used to describe almost any priest, as was the courtesy title *abbé,* abbot. Brignolles is a small town in the Provence region. The place names Hugo cites throughout the novel are mostly real, from the Midi to the Paris region later on in the story.

7. **Cardinal Fesch:** Joseph Fesch (1763–1839), Napoléon's uncle—his mother's younger half brother—was named archbishop of Lyon and ambassador to the Vatican by his nephew.

8. **the Midi:** the south of France.

9. **Monseigneur:** literally, "my lord," the formal title used to address bishops; the humble Myriel, unlike his housekeeper, prefers the less pompous *Monsieur.*

10. **imperial decree, which ranked bishops . . . field marshals:** Napoléon was highly conscious of issues of rank and protocol and in arranging the etiquette of his new imperial court.

*II: Monsieur Myriel Becomes Monseigneur Bienvenu*

1. **Monseigneur Henri Puget . . . abbé of Simore:** bishop of Digne (1708–28) and abbot of Simore. Under the ancien régime, bishops often held one or (usually) more abbeys, which supplemented their incomes.

2. **Charles Brûlart de Genlis, archbishop prince of Embrun . . . lord bishop of Senez:** In the early Middle Ages, Embrun was a free city ruled by the archbishop, who was recognized as a prince. The title was used as a courtesy after Embrun officially became subject to the French Crown in the sixteenth century. Under the ancien régime, several bishoprics carried with them secular titles and offices—such as lord bishops and bishop barons, described below—and even political authority. As was increasingly the case in the eighteenth century, the archbishop of Genlis was from an aristocratic family; Crillon and Sabran in particular were great names of the French nobility; Antoine de Mes-

grigny, Capuchin bishop of Grasse, was both a Capuchin monk and a priest, a status more common in the Middle Ages than in later eras. Philippe de Vendôme, grand prior of France, descended from César de Vendôme, an acknowledged bastard of King Henri IV and Gabrielle d'Estrées. Philippe (1655–1727), in spite of his clerical status, had a prominent military career, being named grand prior of the Knights of Malta before succeeding his elder brother as the fourth and last Duc de Vendôme. The abbey of Saint-Honoré de Lérins was one of many that provided an income to the princely warrior-monk.

3. **Manosque, and Sisteron:** two cities in the Provence region of France, within Bishop Myriel's diocese.

4. **imperial senator:** Napoléon created the Senate in imitation of Rome, in order to give the gloss of a constitutional order to his government and as a means to honor high-ranking or prestigious citizens. Senators were provided with substantial endowments, often including country houses or châteaux, such as the "magnificent senatorial seat" mentioned here. The senator in question received his *sénatorerie* in return for supporting Bonaparte's seizure of power in the coup d'état of the Eighteenth Brumaire of November 9, 1799—18 brumaire, year VII, according to the Revolutionary calendar still in effect—that brought Bonaparte to power. The Consulate (with Bonaparte as first consul and then consul for life) replaced the Directoire.

5. **Council of Five Hundred:** Under the Directoire government that followed the fall of Robespierre and the Convention, the Council of the Five Hundred was the lower and larger of the two legislative bodies, paired with the Conseil des Anciens, or Council of Elders.

6. **Monsieur Bigot de Préameneu:** Félix Bigot de Préameneu (1747–1825), Napoléon's *ministre des cultes,* or minister of public worship, also one of the authors of the Napoleonic Code.

7. **"the Durance at Château-Arnoux":** The Durance River flows down through the Alps to the Rhone, crossing much of Bishop Myriel's diocese, including the city of Château-Arnoux.

8. **Things were not good with Rome at that point:** After Napoléon had restored the Catholic Church to its official place in French society by the Concordat of 1801 and Pius VII had officiated at Napoléon's coronation of December 1, 1804, the relationship between Paris and Rome steadily deteriorated (see note 2, p. 1204). Caesar is the senator's flattering reference to the still-new emperor of the French.

*III: A Good Bishop for a Hard Bishopric*

1. **Senez . . . once an episcopal city:** The town of Senez lost its episcopal status in the reorganization of the French church in 1790.

2. **"the right to mow . . . else":** I.e., those widows and orphans would have been allowed to sell their hay at the highest prices possible, without competititon from their neighbors.

3. **engraved stationery:** or *papier timbré*, stamped paper, which bore the official government stamp and was required for all legal documents. A metaphor for the expense of lawsuits.

*IV: He Puts His Money Where His Mouth Is*

1. **a peerage . . . grandfather:** Under the Restoration, the Charter, or constitution, provided for a bicameral legislature of elected deputies in the lower house, and a Chamber of Peers, appointed by the king, with a limited number of hereditary seats.
2. **"Saint Augustine":** Saint Augustine (354–430) was one of the Fathers of the Church.
3. **ultra-royalist and an ultra-Voltairean at once:** not so rare a combination, as many aristocrats before and after the Revolution superficially affected the cynical subversiveness of Voltaire while clinging to the ultra-royalist politics that ensured their position and authority.
4. **"tax on doors and windows":** effectively a luxury tax on home owners, it was, as the bishop implies, a grossly regressive and unfair tax.
5. **public prosecutor:** Under the royal governments before and after the Revolution, public prosecutors were extremely powerful, especially in local governments.
6. **You may think you are indifferent to the death penalty:** Opposition to the death penalty was a lifelong cause of Hugo, surviving all of his political permutations. His novel *The Last Day of a Condemned Man* (1829), a first-person narrative of a man facing execution, was a powerful and eloquent condemnation of the death penalty.
7. **Maistre . . . Beccaria:** The conservative count Joseph de Maistre (1753–1821) was one of the leading politcal theorists of legitimacy and conservatism in post-Napoleonic France; Marquis Cesare di Beccaria (1738–94) was an Italian philosopher and politician whose treatise *On Crime and Punishment* (1764) advocated penal reform and the abolition of torture and the death penalty.

*V: How Monseigneur Bienvenu Made His Cassocks Last Too Long*

1. **canon . . . grand-vicars:** subalterns of bishops. Canons were priests associated with various chapters of a cathedral; grand-vicars assisted bishops in conducting the business of their dioceses.
2. **purple overcoat, purple stockings:** Purple was the traditional color associated with bishops; like the three golden "spinach-seed" tassels, these are Myriel's rare displays of his office.
3. **As he made his cassocks last a very long time:** During his years at Hauteville House, Hugo adopted the practice of turning his old coats inside out, as an object lesson in frugality to his middle-class peers.
4. **"a Trappist":** The Trappist monks were known for the extreme austerity of their living conditions.

5. **this passage in Genesis:** Genesis 1:2.
6. **Flavius Josephus:** Jewish historian (ca. 37–ca. 95) whose magnum opus, *Jewish Antiquities,* chronicled the Jewish people from Creation to the reign of Nero. The Chaldean Bible that Hugo refers to is an Aramaic translation of the Pentateuch, rediscovered and published in Bologna in 1482.
7. **Hugo, bishop of Ptolemaïs:** Hugo's relationship to the bishop-theologian Charles-Louis Hugo (1667–1739) was a family tradition that does not stand up to close genealogical examination.
8. **Oh, Thou who art! . . . the most beautiful:** Hugo's list of many names of God in the Bible ends with "Mercy," *Miséricorde* in French, *Misericordia* in Latin, the most beautiful of all the names of God.

*VI: How He Protected His House*

1. **a huge bergère:** an upholstered armchair.
2. **forty-two francs and ten sous:** The franc was established as the basic unit of currency in 1795, but the names of old currencies persisted well into the nineteenth century. The term *livre,* or pound, was used interchangeably with *franc* through most of the nineteenth century. A *sou* was worth five centimes, so twenty sous equaled one franc, or one livre; a five-franc coin was often called a *pièce de cent sous,* a hundred-sous coin. The reader will also encounter the *écu,* a coin worth three francs, and the gold *louis,* worth twenty francs.
3. **abbé of Grand-Champ, Order of Cîteaux:** Following the monastic rule established by Saint Robert of Molesme, the first abbot of Cîteaux, the Cistercian monasteries, such as the abbey of Grand-Champ, were known for their austerity.
4. **appointed by the king:** According to the long-established tradition of Gallicanism, the French monarchs controlled the vast majority of clerical appointments in their kingdom. This tradition survived the Revolution and well into the nineteenth century.
5. **two wax candles:** wax candles, as opposed to the cheaper tallow variety found in most poor homes.
6. **Tournefort . . . Linnaeus:** Joseph Pitton de Tournefort (1656–1708), Bernard de Jussieu (1699–1777), and Charles de Linné (1707–78), who used the Latinized name of Linnaeus when publishing his learned treatises, were all famous botanists.
7. **"Nisi Dominus custodierit domum, in vanum vigilant qui custodiunt eam":** "If a house is not watched over by the Lord, those who watch over it do so in vain."

*VII: Cravatte*

1. **Gaspard Bès's gang of crooks:** Gaspard Bès was a bandit, captured and executed in 1781. Cravatte is an invention of Hugo.
2. **Piedmont:** not just the region but at the time a separate country, part of the Kingdom of Savoy.
3. **Joug-de-l'Aigle:** literally, the Eagle's Yoke, a high mountain pass in the French Alps.

4. **to sing a Te Deum:** A Te Deum is a mass of thanksgiving to God.
5. **Our Lady of Embrun:** I.e., the Cathedral of Notre Dame d'Embrun.

*VIII: Philosophy After a Drink or Two*

1. **Epicurus:** a Greek philosopher of the third century B.C.E. who advocated the pursuit of contentment in life.
2. **Pigault-Lebrun:** Guillaume-Charles-Antoine Pigault de l'Épiney (1753–1835), who published under the name Pigault-Lebrun, was known for his scandalously libertine and antireligious writings, largely forgotten today.
3. **"the marquis d'Argen, Pyrrhon, Hobbes, and Monsieur Naigeon":** A comically ignorant hodgepodge of names. The Marquis d'Argen (1704–71) was best known for his wit, largely forgotten today; Pyrrhon (third century B.C.E.) was one of the first of the Greek skeptic philosphers; the English philosopher Thomas Hobbes (1588–1679), one of the most influential of European philosophers, is best known for his *Leviathan* and his assertion that life, in the state of nature, is nasty, brutish, and short; Monsieur Naigeon was a publisher and friend of Diderot.
4. **"Diderot":** Denis Diderot (1713–84), along with Voltaire and Rousseau one of the greatest figures of the French Enlightenment. An archrationalist and atheist, Diderot was best known in his time as the co-editor (with d'Alembert) of the *Encyclopédie,* the great compendium of Enlightenment rationalism; he was also an essayist, playwright, and novelist. The senator's opinions on Diderot reveal him to be a man of dangerously little knowledge.
5. **"even more of a bigot than Voltaire":** bigot in the sense of the French word *bigot,* meaning someone of narrow-minded and intolerant religious orthodoxy. If anyone could be less of a bigot than the deist Voltaire, it was the atheist Diderot.
6. **"Needham":** Jean Turberville Needham (1713–81) is best remembered today as a target for Voltaire's satire, directed at Needham's belief in spontaneous generation.
7. *"fiat lux":* Genesis 1:3, "Let there be light."
8. **"The** *fas* **and the** *nefas"*: good and evil, or right and wrong.
9. **"Tertullian":** a classical writer and early convert to Christianity (ca. 160–240).
10. *"Moniteur":* the quasi-official journal of government proceedings from 1799 to 1901.
11. *"Inter pocula":* "among drinkers," i.e., among friends.
12. **"Panthéon":** During the Revolution, the Church of Saint Geneviève was renamed the Panthéon and dedicated as the mausoleum of heroes of the nation. The great Revolutionary orator Mirabeau was the first man interred there, followed by the disinterred remains of Voltaire. After being restored to its original purpose as a church by the Restoration government in 1815, the building was converted back into a national mausoleum in 1884, just in time to receive the mortal remains of Victor Hugo.
13. **"Sardanapalus or Vincent de Paul":** two antithetical figures: Sardanapalus

was, according to legend and Lord Byron, the debauched last king of Babylon; Saint Vincent de Paul (1576–1660) founded two religious orders, one of priests, one of nuns, dedicated to active service to the poor. Vincent was known for his personal humility and gentle piety.

14. *"niente"*: Italian for "nothing."

15. **"Cato . . . Stephen . . . Joan of Arc"**: three martyrs to principle. The Roman senator Cato the Younger (95–46 B.C.E.) fled Rome and later killed himself rather than submit to Julius Caesar; Saint Stephen was martyred by stoning in first-century Jerusalem; Saint Joan of Arc, "the Maid of Orléans," was a peasant girl from Lorraine who presented herself to the court of King Charles VIII and announced that God had sent her to drive the English out of France. After leading the French armies to near-total victory, Joan was abandoned to the English, who tried her as a heretic and burned her at the stake in 1431.

## IX: The Brother as the Sister Tells It

1. **Telemachus . . . Minerva**: i.e., scenes from *Télémaque,* or *Telemachus, Son of Odysseus,* a widely read novel by François de La Mothe-Fénelon (1656–1715), archbishop of Cambrai and tutor to the grandchildren of Louis XIV, who borrowed from Homer to craft a moral lesson for the duke of Burgundy, heir presumptive to the throne.

## X: The Bishop Before an Unknown Light

1. **the National Convention**: the legislative body that governed the First Republic after the abolition of the monarchy in September 1792. It was the Convention that tried and executed Louis XVI and Marie Antoinette, made war on Austria and Prussia, and eventually gave rise to the infamous Comité de Salut Public. Danton and Robespierre were the great leaders of the Convention. It was under the Convention that such egalitarian measures as using only the familiar, informal *tu* form and the titles of *citoyen* and *citoyenne* replaced *monsieur* and *madame.*

2. **a semi-regicide**: Those members of the National Convention—the majority—who voted for the execution of Louis XVI were known as regicides. Some voted for exile, some for death with a suspended sentence, which was a symbolic vote that amounted to exile. Those who did not vote for the death penalty for the "tyrant" were viewed with suspiscion as being lukewarm in Revolutionary sentiment, a distinctly unhealthy position. With the return of the legitimate princes in 1814, and even more so after the Hundred Days, many regicides faced prosecution and were usually sentenced to exile.

3. **Azrael, the Mohammedan angel of the sepulchre**: Azrael, the archangel of death, is never mentioned in the Qu'ran but is part of several extracanonical traditions.

4. **"fatal return of the past known as 1814"**: i.e., the return of the Bourbon monarchy, albeit in a much-changed form.

5. **" '93"**: See note 3, p. 1196.
6. **"Louis XVII"**: the son of Louis XVI and Marie Antoinette; recognized as King Louis XVII (1785–95) by royalists, he was in fact the great-grandson of Louis XV. Declared a ward of the Republic after his father's execution, he was raised in the Temple prison by brutal guardians, forbidden to see his mother and sister even while they were in the same compound. The boy, who died in 1795, was known to royalists as "the Martyr of the Temple."
7. **"Cartouche's brother"**: Cartouche, born Louis-Dominique Bourguignon (1693–1721) was a Parisian bandit chief whose trial and subsequent public torture and execution in Paris in 1721—he was broken on a spiked wheel on the place de Grève—was a public spectacle, giving rise to a legend that made Cartouche seem larger than life. For Hugo, for whom the fight against the death penalty was lifelong and futile, such judicial spectacles, whether it was the wheel or the guillotine, were barbaric and dehumanizing.
8. **"the place de Grève"**: Today known as the place de l'Hôtel de Ville, on the right bank, the place de Grève was the site of public torture and executions from the Middle Ages until 1830, when it was given its present name.
9. *"Sinite parvulos"*: from the Gospel of Mark 10:14, "Suffer the little children to come unto me."
10. **"dauphin of Barabbas and the dauphin of Herod"**: i.e., the children of the guilty. Barrabas was the criminal whose life was spared by Pontius Pilate at the demands of the Passover crowds, who thus abandoned Jesus Christ to crucifixion.
11. **"draped in the fleur-de-lis"**: The lily was the symbol of the French royal family from Louis IX (Saint Louis, born 1214, reigned 1226–70) to the Bourbons.
12. **"gala-standard berlin"**: A *berlin* was a large, elegant carriage, of the sort used in public processions.
13. *"Vermis sum"*: from Psalm 21, "I am a worm and no man."
14. **"Marat applauding the guillotine"**: As a journalist and politician, Jean-Paul Marat (1743–93) was known for the exceptional violence of his rhetoric, including his role in inciting the September Massacres and the campaign against the moderate Girondins. His assassination in the bath by the royalist Charlotte Corday on July 13, 1793, memorialized in David's hagiographic painting, made him a martyr to the Revolution. His remains were placed in the Panthéon, only to be removed scarcely a year later after the fall of Robespierre.
15. **"Bossuet . . . Protestants"**: Jacques-Bénigne Bossuet (1627–1704), bishop of Meaux, one of the leading clerics of Louis XIV's reign. A gifted writer and orator, Bossuet was a staunch supporter of both Catholic orthodoxy and royal power. The Te Deum is a mass of thanksgiving in the Catholic Church. While Bossuet sought to bring Protestants back to the Catholic Church, the government often took more violent measures such as G—— alludes to. Dragonnades refers to a policy by which Protestants were forced to provide lodging to soldiers (specifically dragoons, the cavalry), who were tacitly encouraged to harass their hosts into converting, often resulting in violence. More than two

hundred thousand French Protestants, or Huguenots, fled France as a result of such policies.

16. **"Carrier . . . marquis de Louvois":** Face-to-face with the royalist Bishop Myriel, G—— compares the excesses of the Revolution to those of Louis XIV's persecution of the Huguenots in the late seventeenth century. Jean-Baptist Carrier (1757–94) was one of the most infamous prosecutors of the Terror, operating chiefly in the city of Nantes. Among his innovations were mass executions by drowning, in which boats carrying as many as one hundred bound prisoners were sunk in the Loire; he also invented the *mariage républicain*, in which a man and a woman judged guilty of counterrevolutionary activities were tied together and thrown into the river. Carrier was eventually executed for his excesses after the fall of Robespierre. Nicolas-Auguste de la Baume, Marquis de Montrevel (1636–1716), was a notorious persecutor of Protestants, as was Nicolas Lamoignon-Bâville (1648–1724). Antoine Fouquier-Tinville served as chief prosecutor for the trials supervised by the Committee for Public Safety, including Marie Antoinette's; he was executed with Robespierre and Saint-Just after 9 Thermidor. Stanislas-Marie Maillard (1763–94) took part in many of the violent popular revolts of the Revolution, including the fall of the Bastille and the September Massacres, where he led the mob that murdered prisoners of the Abbaye prison. The duc Gaspard de Saulx-Tavannes (1509–73), Marshal of France, was one of the instigators of the Saint Bartholomew's Day Massacre, one of the bloodiest incidents of the religious wars of the sixteenth century. *Le père Duchêne* was a newspaper edited by Jacques-René Hébert (1757–94), one of the most radical and violent of revolutionaries and a rival of Robespierre. Le père Le Tellier (1648–1719) was confessor to Louis XIV and encouraged the king's harsh repression of Protestants and Jansenists (see note 2, p. 1254) alike. He was not related to François-Michel Le Tellier, Marquis de Louvois (1641–91); as minister of war and Louis's closest adviser, Louvois encouraged and executed many of those policies, specifically the *dragonnades*. Jourdan-Coupe-Tête, Jourdan the Head Chopper, refers to Mathieu Jouve Jourdan (1749–94); a former butcher and soldier, Jourdan made his mark during the fall of the Bastille, when he is believed to have murdered the governor, the marquis de Launay; he was one of the most violent members of the mob that invaded Versailles on October 5, 1789, but it was in Avignon in 1791 that he earned his sobriquet: At the head of still another extralegal mob, he supervised the beheading of as many as sixty people. Jourdan was eventually arrested and executed by the Committee for Public Safety.

17. **"Marie Antoinette, archduchess and queen":** Archduke and archduchess were the titles given to the children of the reigning Austrian Hapsburgs, Marie Antoinette's family.

18. **"poor Huguenot . . . Louis le Grand":** The Huguenots lived under the protection of Henri IV's 1598 Edict of Nantes. Louis XIV—Louis le Grand, as G—— calls him with some irony—repealed the edict in 1685, giving rise to legal and social persecutions, such as the *dragonnades* referred to above, that led

to the mass emigration of Protestants to England, Holland, Germany, and even the American colonies.

19. **"Tantalus":** In Greek mythology, Tantalus was condemned to stand in a pool of water while suffering from a painful thirst. Whenever he stooped to drink, the water would recede from his reach. The verb "tantalize" comes from this myth.

20. **"Your blessing," said the bishop:** one of the most controversial scenes in *Les Misérables* when the novel was published. The surviving family of Bishop de Miollis was particularly offended that the character so clearly modeled on their saintly ancestor should ask the blessing of a character like G——.

21. **"red bonnet" . . . "hat":** The "red bonnet" is the Phrygian cap, favored by the *sans-culottes* in imitation of the one worn by freed slaves in ancient Rome; the red hat refers to the cardinal's hat.

## XI: A Qualification

1. **"philosopher bishop" or "patriot priest":** two classic archetypes of the late-eighteenth-century French church. The "philosopher bishop," the aristocratic prelate who flouted his vows of poverty, chastity, and humility, is epitomized by Talleyrand (see note 13, p. 1211), appointed to the bishopric of Autun just before the Revolution, who was known chiefly for his wit, his elegance, his gambling, and his womanizing; some thirty years his senior, Archbishop Dillon of Narbonne lived a princely lifestyle in a château near Paris, with his mistress, his stable and kennel for hunting, and massive debts. The "patriot priest" was the curé who adopted the principles of Revolution: the abbé Emmanuel Joseph Sieyès (1748–1836), author of the famous pamphlet *Qu'est-ce que le tiers état?* (What Is the Third Estate?) was more committed to the principles of Rousseau and Locke than to the Gospel, while the abbé Henri Grégoire (1750–1831) was committed to both the Church and the Republic; Grégoire was a defender of the rights of minorities, including Protestants and Jews, and devoted considerable energy to the abolition of slavery and the slave trade. Some have speculated that the abbé Grégoire was one of the models for the Conventionist G——; Grégoire was in fact a member of the Convention, absent on the day of the vote regarding Louis XVI's sentence, and was a sincere believer.

2. **The arrest of the pope . . . July 5–6, 1809:** The tempestuous relationship between Pius VII, who had presided over Napoléon's imperial coronation, culminated in the pope's being forcibly taken from the Vatican to Fontainebleau, where he remained a prisoner until January 1814.

3. **the synod of the bishops:** The Concile National was held in June 1811 in an attempt to circumvent the pope's refusal to recognize bishops appointed by the emperor. Monseigneur de Miollis attended the council and, along with the majority, supported the pope against Napoléon.

4. **Ultramontane . . . Gallican:** The Gallican tradition maintained the independence of the Catholic Church in France vis-à-vis Rome, surviving the Revolution well into the nineteenth century to the reign of Napoléon III; the Ultramontane (from the Latin for "beyond the mountains," i.e., south of the

Alps, Rome) favored the authority of the pope over national interests. Monseigneur de Miollis was an Ultramontane.

5. **refused to go and gawk:** After Napoléon landed on the coast at Fréjus, near Cannes, in March 1815, huge crowds—many of them cheering—turned out along his route north to Paris, which passed near Digne.

6. **having a command in Provence ... determined to let him get away:** Many in the French military had only grudgingly accepted the return of the Bourbons in 1814 and were sympathetic to Napoléon's return, many of them far more enthusiastically than the bishop's rather noncommittal brother. Bishop de Miollis's brothers were a Napoleonic general and a magistrate.

7. **The year 1812 comes along ... In 1815, as the ultimate disasters were in the air:** This passage describes the long decline of Napoléon, from the disastrous Russian campaign of 1812 to his defeat at the hands of the Allies during the 1813 German campaign, culminating in the French defeat at Leipzig in October; the "cowardly" and "taciturn legislative body" refers to the imperial Senate, which remained passive as the Allies approached Paris in March 1814, only to proclaim Napoléon's fall under the leadership of Talleyrand. Napoléon finally agreed to abdicate when a number of his top generals, notably Maréchal Marmont, Duc de Raguse, publicly defected; many Bonapartists considered Marmont and his fellows to be "treacherous marshals." The "ultimate disasters" are, of course, events leading up to the emperor's last stand at Waterloo, where Allied armies led by Wellington put an end to the Napoleonic saga.

8. **a legionnaire of Austerlitz:** The French defeat of the combined forces of Austria, Prussia, and Russia at Austerlitz on December 2, 1805, was one of Napoléon's greatest victories. Coming on the anniversary of his coronation, it consolidated his power at home and, for a time, shattered his European opposition.

9. **eagle:** symbol of the new French Empire.

10. **the imperial profile had vanished:** The returning Bourbons maintained the Legion of Honor, created by Bonaparte in 1803 to honor valor in warfare, but Napoléon's profile was effaced from the medal, as it was from coinage.

11. **"three toads":** apparently a dismissive reference to the three fleurs-de-lis that were a traditional symbol of the French monarchy.

12. **"That gouty old bastard":** Louis XVIII suffered from gout and obesity; the pigtail is a reference to the king's old-fashioned, powdered hairstyle.

13. **Prussia and England:** not only traditional enemies of France, but two countries that Napoléon particularly despised and distrusted.

## XII: Monseigneur Bienvenu's Solitude

1. **Saint Francis de Sales:** As Roman Catholic bishop of Geneva, Sales (1567–1622) sought to convert Protestants back to the Catholic faith.

2. **cadets:** i.e., its subalterns.

3. **metropolis:** in the Roman Catholic Church, an archbishop's diocese.

4. **subdeacon:** Such clerical "livings" were much sought after by young clerics, al-

though many of the abuses of clerical livings were weeded out by Revolutionary and Napoleonic reforms.

5. **more abbés than priests:** i.e., leaning more toward politics and the secular life than spiritual and pastoral duties; again, such cases were far more common under the ancien régime than in the nineteenth century. Ambition was certainly present in the French Church in Hugo's time, but it tended to aim toward bishoprics and cardinal's hats rather than the diplomatic posts and ministerial portfolios of earlier ages.

6. **conclavist:** i.e., a member of the College of Cardinals, which meets in a papal conclave to elect a new pope.

7. **the Rota:** one of the highest of the canonical courts in the Church.

8. **a pallium:** a scarflike ecclesiastical garment worn by certain prelates, usually archbishops.

9. **Perrette:** an allusion to a fable of La Fontaine: Perrette, a careless famer's wife, dreaming of everything she will buy with the proceeds from the sale of her milk, trips and spills the milk pail balanced on her head.

10. **Juvenal and Tacitus:** Juvenal's *Satires,* along with the *Annals* of Tacitus, were part of Hugo's rigorous classical education. The two authors are frequent points of reference in *Les Misérables.*

11. **Moses . . . Napoléon:** It was typical of the French Romantics to include Napoléon among the historic geniuses who changed the world.

12. **a sham Corneille write *Tiridate:*** Jean-Gilbert de Campistron (1656–1723), whose *Tiridate* debuted at the Théâtre Français in 1691. Hugo was a great admirer of Corneille, whose work he vastly preferred to that of his contemporary Racine.

13. **some military Prudhomme:** an allusion to Wellington. Prudhomme and *prudhommerie* came to refer to banal mediocrity in nineteenth-century France, following the writer and illustrator Henri Monnier's hugely successful caricature of the 1830s. Monnier's Monsieur Prudhomme was well intentioned but also pretentious, vain, and ignorant. Hugo refers to *prudhommerie* frequently in *Les Misérables.*

14. **Sambre-et-Meuse army:** During the Revolution, armies were given the names of the new *départements* to replace the old system of aristocratic and provincial names.

15. **Mousqueton's . . . Claude's:** Mousqueton was the valet of Porthos in *The Three Musketeers;* Hugo held the successors of Caesar Augustus, including Claudius (10 B.C.E.–54), in low esteem, as the reader will see throughout *Les Misérables.*

### XIII: What He Believed

1. ***Credo in Patrem:*** the opening phrase of the Apostle's Creed in Latin: "I believe in the Father . . ."

2. ***quia multum amavit:*** an allusion to Christ's public forgiveness of Mary Magdelene, from Luke 7:47: "Because she has loved much . . ."

3. **the Brahmans:** in Hinduism, the Brahman spirit is the eternal and transcendent spirit underlying all life.
4. **"Who . . . the earth?":** Ecclesiastes 3:19–21.
5. **Saint Francis of Assisi and Marcus Aurelius:** Saint Francis (1181–1226) is traditionally associated with benevolence toward animals; the Roman emperor Marcus Aurelius (121–180), author of the *Meditations,* is recognized as a philosopher of the Stoic tradition.
6. **Pope Gregory XVI:** Pope from 1831 to 1846, the traditionalist Gregory was so opposed to modernism that he forbade the construction of railways in the Papal States. He took a similarly conservative view of politics, though it should be noted that, like Hugo, he was a vocal opponent of slavery.

*XIV: What He Thought*

1. **Swedenborg or Pascal:** The Swedish scientist Emanuel Swedenborg (1688–1722) underwent a religious conversion at the age of fifty, when he claimed to have spoken to God and visited heaven and hell in mystic visions; his writings inspired a great number of followers in Europe. The mathematician and philosopher Blaise Pascal (1623–62) died at the age of thirty-nine while composing notes for a defense of the Christian faith; those notes, published under the title *Pensées,* remain one of the greatest expressions of religious thought in the French language. Pascal suffered from poor health all his life, certain symptoms of which may have been interpreted as madness.
2. **Elijah's mantle:** In 2 Kings 2:8, the prophet Elijah, in company with Elisha, approaches the river Jordan. He rolls up his mantle and strikes the water. The water immediately divides, and Elijah and Elisha cross on dry land. Suddenly, a chariot of fire and horses of fire appear and Elijah is lifted up to heaven in a whirlwind. As Elijah is lifted up, his mantle falls to the ground and Elisha picks it up.
3. **Saint Teresa and Saint Jerome:** Saint Teresa of Ávila (1515–82) was a Spanish nun who experienced mystic visions; Saint Jerome (ca. 340–419), who translated the Hebrew Old Testament and the Greek New Testament into the Latin Vulgate Bible, is counted as one of the Fathers of the Church.
4. *Love one another:* from the Gospel of John (13:34–35): "A new command I give you: Love one another. As I have loved you, so you must love one another."
5. **Lucretius . . . Dante:** Hugo had named the Roman philosopher-poets Lucretius, Saint-Paul, and Dante "giants of the human spirit" in his essay "William Shakespeare." He learned of the Indian philosopher Manu through a translation of *The Laws of Manu,* which had been published in Paris in 1840.

BOOK TWO: THE FALL
*I: The Night After a Day's Walk*

1. **the *mairie:*** the town hall and probably the residence of the mayor.
2. **General Drouot:** Antoine Drouot (1774–1847), one of Napoléon's most loyal

generals, accompanied Napoléon to Elba and then on his return during the Hundred Days.

3. **Napoléon's proclamation:** i.e., announcing his return from Elba and his intention to retake his imperial throne.

4. **Juan Gulf:** the site of Napoléon's landing after his escape from Elba, roughly midway between Cannes and Nice.

5. **General Bertrand . . . the good burghers:** Général Comte Henri-Gatien Bertrand (1773–1844) may have proved himself Napoléon's most loyal follower. Named grand marshal of the palace by the emperor in November 1813, Bertrand followed Napoléon not just to Elba but to post-Waterloo exile on Saint Helena, where he remained until Bonaparte's death. He became one of the chief propagandists of the Napoleonic legend, and when King Louis-Philippe decided to bring Napoléon's remains back to France in 1840, it was Bertrand who headed the mission. Hugo refers here to a legend by which Bertrand is said to have paved the way for Napoléon's return to Paris by handing out honors (*croix d'honneur,* i.e., of the Legion of Honor) and money ("fistfuls of napoléons," the name by which the twenty-franc "louis" was known under the Empire).

6. **"twelve leagues":** thirty-six miles.

7. **"Jean Valjean":** In the long genesis of his novel, Hugo changed the name of his hero several times, all versions based on the idea that the common name of *Jean* stood for an everyman: Jean Tréjean, John Veryjohn, a very ordinary man. The *val-* of Jean Valjean suggests "John is worth John," or "John is as good as any other John."

8. **the wars of religion:** At the end of the sixteenth century, clashes between Protestants and Catholics erupted into civil war, coming to a head when the Protestant King Henri IV inherited the throne from his cousin, Charles IX, last of the Valois dynasty. The wars ended when Henri converted to Catholicism, reasoning, according to legend, that Paris was well worth a mass.

9. **"four sous":** twenty centimes (see note 2, ch. VI, p. 1199).

## II: Prudence Is Recommended to Wisdom

1. **Duty:** i.e., *le Devoir,* the duty of Christians.

2. **the Fathers and Doctors:** the theologians, scholars, and philosophers recognized as authorities by the Catholic Church: Saint Augustine, Saint Jerome, Saint Thomas Aquinas, etc.

## III: The Heroism of Passive Obedience

1. **"Toulon":** a large Mediterranean port that was the site of shipyards where prisoners given sentences to forced labor (*forçats*) were imprisoned.

2. **"my yellow passport":** Passports were required for internal travel in France at the time; Jean Valjean's passport marks him as a convict even though he has served his sentence.

3. **"bishop of the Majore, in Marseilles"**: Sainte-Marie-la-Majeure, known as La Majore, is the cathedral of Marseilles, rebuilt in the 1850s.

4. **"a pointed thing, gold, on his head"**: the ceremonial bishop's miter.

5. **a man shipwrecked on the *Medusa***: a famous shipwreck in 1814, memorialized in one of the most famous paintings of the era (see note 18, p. 1212).

6. **"The red *paletot*"**: the garment worn by prisoners at Toulon. Hugo noted all the details of prison life Jean Valjean describes in a visit to Toulon in 1839.

*VI: Jean Valjean*

1. **Brie:** the agricultural region east and southeast of Paris.

2. **Vlajean . . . "voilà Jean":** Jean Vlajean was one of the names Hugo considered for his hero. There is, in *voilà Jean,* "Behold Jean," an echo of Pilate's presentation of Christ to the crowd in Jerusalem: *Ecce homo,* "Behold the man" (John 19:5).

3. **twenty-four sous a day:** one franc, twenty centimes per day; the pay for this skilled labor is the most Jean Valjean earns in a year before taking his unskilled jobs out of season.

4. **Montenotte:** April 12, 1796, an early victory over the Austrians for the twenty-seven-year-old general still known, and still referring to himself, as Buona-parte, as seen below.

5. **from the Directoire to the Five Hundred:** The Directoire was the executive body that gave the government its name, the Council of the Five Hundred was the larger and more powerful chamber of the bicameral legislature.

6. **Floréal 2, Year IV:** the date according to the Revolutionary calendar, which counted from the fall of the monarchy in 1792.

7. **Bicêtre prison:** a notorious prison in Paris, where prisoners bound for Toulon were shackled together for the journey. Hugo described the process in detail in *The Last Day of a Condemned Man.*

8. **Saint-Sulpice:** a seventeenth-century church in today's sixth arrondissement, near the Luxembourg gardens. Hugo lived nearby with his mother and brothers after his parents' separation.

9. **Claude Gueux:** a real-life prisoner who was put to death for attacking a prison guard; he was the subject of Hugo's short 1834 book *Claude Gueux.*

*VII: Despair from the Inside*

1. **Ignorantine friars:** an order founded with the mission of providing free education to poor children.

2. **galley slave:** The first prisoners sent to Toulon in the sixteenth century were in fact galley slaves, sentenced to work the oars of galley ships; the terms *galérien* and *galères* were still used long after sails had replaced oars and prisoners worked in the shipyards rather than on ships. Official use of the term *forçat,* for one sentenced to forced labor, began in the late eighteenth century.

3. **rue Montorgueil near Les Halles:** The former marketplace of Paris, the

working-class neighborhood around Les Halles will play an important role later in the novel.

4. **one of Puget's wonderful caryatids**: The caryatids of sculptor Pierre-Henri Puget (1624–90) can still be seen on the façade of Toulon's town hall.

### IX: Fresh Grievances

1. **in Grasse . . . a distillery**: Then as now, the Provençal city of Grasse was a center of the perfume industry.

### XIII: Petit-Gervais

1. **Savoyard:** i.e., a boy from the Kingdom of Savoy, made up of territory now found in northern Italy and southeastern France, including the cities of Torino and Chambéry. Petits Savoyards traditionally worked as chimney sweeps.

BOOK THREE: IN THE YEAR 1817
*I: The Year 1817*

1. **the twenty-second year of his reign**: Louis XVIII insisted that his reign dated from the death of Louis XVII in the Temple prison in 1795 (see note 6, p. 1202). This was a point of contention between the royalists and those who warily accepted his and his family's return to a royal throne.

    This chapter was added to the novel during the revisions of 1860. There are a few inaccuracies in this long list of Hugo's memories of Restoration Paris, and Hugo sometimes seems to be amusing himself with ironic depictions of people or events as he seeks to conjure up the political and cultural atmosphere of Restoration Paris for his Second Empire readers.

    Several critics have pointed out that 1817 is also the year in which Victor Hugo entered several public poetry competitions, thus marking his debut as a professional writer.

2. **Monsieur Bruguière de Sorsum:** (1773–1823) a minor poet and translator of Shakespeare.

3. **azure and fleurs-de-lis:** the traditional banner of the French kings.

4. **the comte Lynch:** As Hugo describes, Jean-Baptiste Lynch was the first government official to welcome the Bourbons, in the person of the duc d'Angoulême (see following note), back to France, several days before Napoléon's abdication. Lynch had been in contact with royalist agents for some months as the imperial government steadily weakened. He was later rewarded with a title and a seat in the Chamber of Peers (see note 1, ch. IV, p. 1198).

5. **Monsieur le duc d'Angoulême:** Louis de France, the elder son (1755–1844) of the comte d'Artois, the future Charles X, second in line to the throne after the childless Louis XVIII and his father.

6. **Napoléon was on Saint Helena . . . having his old riding habits turned:** Bona-

parte's British jailers on the island of Saint Helena refused even the smallest gesture that would acknowledge their prisoner's former status, including providing cloth in the color that had been his imperial livery. Their stubbornness was matched by Bonaparte's, who went to great lengths before giving in.

7. **Pellegrini sang . . . Odry did not yet exist:** The Italian singer Pellegrini actually made his Parisian debut in 1819; Potier and Odry were well-known comic actors during the Restoration.

8. **Madame Saqui . . . Forioso:** two famous tightrope walkers.

9. **There were still Prussians in France:** as well as Austrian, Russian, and British soldiers, who made up the occupying armies who remained in France until 1819.

10. **Monsieur Delalot:** the royalist editor of the *Journal des débats,* one of the most important newspapers of the nineteenth century. The royalist influence of Delalot was an exception to the publication's long liberal tradition.

11. **legitimacy:** The doctrine adopted by the great European powers at the Congress of Vienna, legitimacy sought to restore a pre-Napoleonic, pre-Revolutionary status quo by replacing royal families on thrones usurped by Napoléon, his family, and his allies. Wellington and Metternich were the great symbols of legitimacy in the first half of the nineteenth century.

12. **Pleignier, Carbonneau, and Tolleron:** three men convicted of plotting to blow up the Tuileries Palace in 1816; subsequently executed. The ritual of cutting off their hands was part of the punishment prescribed for lèse-majesté.

13. **The prince de Talleyrand . . . Louis serving him as deacon:** Charles-Maurice de Talleyrand-Périgord (1754–1838) was one of the legendary figures of the Revolutionary and Napoleonic eras; a great aristocrat, a onetime bishop, a revolutionary politician, and above all a political survivor, Talleyrand served virtually every government from the Constituent Assembly through the July Monarchy, reaching the peak of his influence as foreign minister of France, first to Napoléon and then, having helped orchestrate the emperor's downfall, to Louis XVIII. The Congress of Vienna was a triumph for Talleyrand before Napoléon's return from Elba cost him his standing with the allies. On July 14, 1790, as bishop of Autun and one of the leading members of the Constituent Assembly, Talleyrand had officiated at a mass of celebration dedicated to the Federation of French citizens and their volunteer militias performed on the Champ de Mars. He was assisted in that mass by a priest named Abbé Joseph Louis (1755–1837). Thanks largely to Talleyrand's protection, the abbé Louis, more interested in economics than theology, had a long career in government, serving as minister of finance under the Restoration and later for Louis-Philippe.

14. **the Champ de Mai:** On June 1, 1815, as allied armies massed in Belgium, Napoléon sought to rally Parisians to his cause with a grandiose pageant celebrating French military history from the Merovingian era—when military assemblies were known as *champs de mai*—to his own pre-Russian victories. The "eagles and bees" that decorated the gold-leafed wooden columns were the

imperial symbols. During the post-Waterloo occupation, allied armies camped in bivouacs on the Champ de Mars and the Champs-Élysées and in the Boulogne and Vincennes woods.

15. **Gros Caillou:** a neighborhood just to the east of the Champ de Mars.

16. **the Touquet edition of Voltaire:** That particular edition of Voltaire in fact appeared in 1821; the entrepreneurial publisher also marketed a "snuffbox *à la Charte*" with the text of the 1814 Constitution engraved on its lid.

17. **the murder committed by Dautun:** Charles Dautun murdered his brother in 1814 and was beheaded for it in 1816.

18. **the *Medusa*:** The frigate *Medusa* sank in 1816, a wreck made famous by the scandal of the ship's captain, Chaumareix, fleeing first, and more so by the painting by Géricault, *Le Radeau de la Méduse* (The Raft of the Medusa), which dramatically depicts survivors clinging to a raft as a rescue ship, the *Argus*, approaches in the distance. It was one of the most famous paintings of the era.

19. **Colonel Selves:** A French officer whose name in fact was Sèves; in 1816, he traveled to Egypt, where he converted to Islam and entered the military under the name Suleiman Pasha.

20. **Messier:** Charles Messier (1730–1817) was the naval astronomer who worked on the roof of the Hôtel de Cluny, on the left bank, since restored and established as a museum of medieval history.

21. **The duchesse de Duras:** Claire de Kersaint (1778–1829), Duchesse de Duras, known as a bit of a bluestocking, received visitors, most notably Chateaubriand, in her small salon in the Abbaye-aux-Bois, boulevard Raspail. Her novel *Ourika* is the story of an African girl raised as the companion to the daughter of French aristocrats and of her unhappy romance with a young French nobleman. *Ourika* was in fact written in 1820 and published in 1824.

22. **The *N*s . . . the Louvre:** Napoléon had had large *N*s carved into the walls of the Louvre; they were replaced by double *L*s.

23. **The pont d'Austerlitz . . . Jardin du Roi:** a neighborhood on what was then the western edge of Paris took its name from Napoléon's great victory of 1805; the Jardin du Roi, today known as the Jardin des Plantes, is in the same neighborhood. Not all such Napoleonic memories were erased from Paris.

24. **Louis XVIII . . . Mathurin Bruneau:** Louis XVIII was the most learned of the three brothers who were the last Bourbon kings of France and knew Horace and other classical authors well. Even with Napoléon on Saint Helena, his partisans and his popularity were real concerns. Mathurin Bruneau (1784–?) was the con man son of a clogmaker (*sabotier*), who, after having impersonated a nobleman and royal cousin named Charles de Navarre, declared himself to be the long-lost dauphin of Louis XVI and Marie Antoinette and thus the rightful king of France. He was soon arrested and imprisoned for vagrancy and fraud.

25. **The Académie Française . . . essay prize:** The fifteen-year-old Hugo submitted an ode to this competition.

26. **Monsieur Bellart ... Courier's sarcasm:** Nicolas Bellart (1761–1825) served as *procureur général* of Paris under the Restoration. One of his deputies, Jacques-Nicolas de Broë, would in 1821 attempt a legal prosecution of the liberal, anticlerical pamphleteer Paul-Louis Courier (1782–1825).

27. **A Chateaubriand impersonator named Marchangy ... d'Arlincourt:** François-René, Vicomte de Chateaubriand (1768–1848), one of the most influential writers and politicians of the early nineteenth century. His short novel *René* was one of the first and most important texts of French Romanticism. He was also a leading politician, ambassador, and advocate of moderately conservative, constitutional monarchism. Chateaubriand was much admired by the young royalist Victor Hugo, who declared when he began writing poetry at age fourteen, "I want to be Chateaubriand or nothing." When the two finally met in 1820, Chateaubriand called Hugo *"l'enfant sublime"* but, according to legend, did not like him. Louis-Antoine Marchangy and the vicomte d'Arlincourt aspired, and failed, to replicate Chateaubriand's succes in literature and politics.

28. *Claire d'Albe* and *Malek-Adel* ... **Madame Cottin:** Madame Cottin was a successful but largely forgotten popular novelist. Malek-Adel was also the name of a character in her novel *Mathilde*.

29. **The Institut de France ... Napoléon Bonaparte:** The Revolutionary government had created the Institut de France in 1795 to replace the academies of the ancien régime; Napoléon Bonaparte had been invited to join the institute, ostensibly in recognition of his contribution to scholarship through the Egyptian expedition of 1798–99.

30. **a naval school at Angoulême:** The landlocked town of Angoulême is some distance from the ocean.

31. **Franconi's posters:** In the 1780s, the Italian-born Antonio Franconi (1737–1836) started a successful circus in Paris, which was carried on by his sons.

32. **Monsieur Paër ... Edmond Géraud:** Ferdinand Paër (1771–1839) and Edmond Géraud (1775–1821) were moderately successful composers during the early years of the Restoration.

33. **The *Nain jaune* turned into the *Miroir*:** The *Nain jaune* (Yellow Dwarf) was a satiric newspaper published from 1814 to 1815; also satiric, the *Miroir*, which appeared from 1821 to 1823, was not directly related to the *Nain jaune*.

34. **The Café Lemblin ... Café Valois:** two cafés in the Palais-Royal where politically like-minded habitués would gather—former officers of the Grande Armée at Lemblin's, aging returned émigrés at the Café Valois.

35. **Monsieur le duc de Berry ... Louvel:** The duc de Berry was the younger son of the comte d'Artois. As the duchesse d'Angoulême, the wife of his elder brother and daughter of Louis XVI, was past childbearing age, the younger prince's marriage was a matter of state concern. He was married to his distant cousin Marie-Caroline de Bourbon-Sicile, daughter of the king of Naples and Sicily. The duc de Berry was assassinated at the Opéra by Louvel in 1820; the fact that his young wife was pregnant was taken by royalists as a sign of divine favor for the Bourbon monarchy.

36. **Madame de Staël:** Germaine Necker, Baronesse de Stäel-Holstein, was one of

the most famous and influential women of the Revolutionary era; she died on July 14, 1817. Rich, ambitious, and well connected, she made her salon a center of anti-Bonapartist opinion; the First Consul ordered her exile from France in 1803. Her books *De l'Allemagne* and *Dix Années d'exil* were critiques of his autocratic, unconstitutional government. She is best remembered today for her romantic fiction, especially the novels *Corinne* and *Delphine*.

37. **Mademoiselle Mars:** Jeanne-Marguerite Salvetat (1779–1847), known as Mademoiselle Mars, was the leading actress of the Comédie-Française from 1803 on. Mademoiselle Mars was Napoléon's favorite actress and briefly his mistress. Later in her career, she would play Doña Sol in Hugo's *Hernani* (1830). (See note 5, p. 1280).

38. **The *Constitutionnel* was constitutional:** i.e., liberal.

39. **The *Minerve:*** was in fact first published in 1818.

40. **the turncoat press . . . the outlaws of 1815:** One of the "outlaws of 1815" was General Léopold Hugo, who held the fortified city of Thionville for months after Napoléon's abdication.

41. **David had lost his talent . . . lost his genius:** The painter Jacques-Louis David (1748–1825) had joined the Revolutionary cause with fervor, become an ally of Robespierre, and voted for the execution of Louis XVI and Marie Antoinette as a member of the Convention, before finally ingratiating himself to Napoléon. He was exiled in 1816. The playwright Antoine-Vincent Arnault (1766–1834) was a fervent and very public supporter of Napoléon during the Hundred Days; the premiere of his play *Germanicus* in 1817 was highly politicized. Lazare Carnot (1753–1823) was famous for his integrity and his republican convictions; having rallied to Napoléon during the Hundred Days, he was banished by the Bourbons. Nicolas-Jean de Dieu Soult (1769–1851) was named marshal of France and duc de Dalmatie by Napoléon; minister of war during the Hundred Days, he was exiled from 1815 to 1819, and eventually enjoyed a successful political career under Louis-Philippe.

42. **Everyone knows that letters . . . rarely reach him:** It is worth recalling here that Hugo wrote this chapter while in exile himself.

43. **Descartes . . . banished:** The philosopher René Descartes (1596–1650) settled in Holland in 1629, seeking to avoid the interference of the Church, but of his own volition, not due to a legal banishment. He remained in Holland until 1649, when Queen Christina of Sweden invited him to her court at Stockholm, where he fell ill and died.

44. **Whether you said "regicides" or "voters" . . . "Napoléon" or "Buonaparte":** The divide between the various political factions of post-Napoleonic France: republicans, revolutionaries, and Bonapartists on one side and royalists on the other: "regicides or voters" refers to those members of the Convention who voted for the death penalty for Louis XVI; "enemies or allies" to the occupying allied forces, who were viewed as allies by supporters of the Bourbons and as enemies of the nation to those, republicans and imperialists, who resented the return of the monarchy; to use Napoléon's first name only was to implicitly recognize the Empire as legal and valid, while dismissing him as

"Buonaparte" relegated him to the status of usurper and military adventurer, however successful.

45. **All reasonable people agreed:** Writing in 1860, Hugo looks back with some irony on the revolutions that followed 1817: 1830, 1848, and the coup d'état of 1851 that established the Second Empire of Napoléon III.

46. *Redivivus . . . the statue of Henri IV: redivivus,* Latin for "resurrected." In 1818, the statue of Henri IV that had been removed by the Revolutionary government was replaced on its pedestal on the Île de la Cité. The adolescent Victor Hugo won a prize for an ode dedicated to the rechristened statue of the first Bourbon king of France. The statue was cast in bronze obtained by melting down the statue of Napoléon from the top of the Vendôme column.

47. **Monsieur Pieté:** The royalist deputy's house in the rue Thérèse served as a meeting place for a large group of ultra-royalists, called Ultras.

48. **Bacot:** The politician René Bacot was a Bonapartist turned Ultra. Hugo exaggerates his political influence.

49. **The ultra-royalists . . . "Waterside Conspiracy":** An ephemeral conspiracy of Ultra extremists who met in the Tuileries Garden, along the bank of the Seine, to plan their fanciful kidnapping of Louis XVIII, whom they hoped to force to abdicate in favor of his more conservative brother, Monsieur the comte d'Artois. The degree of Artois' complicity is doubtful, and the plotters were eventually released, but the minister of police, Decazes (see below), successfully used the plot to create a rift between the two brothers, thus strengthening his own position in the king's circle.

50. **The ex-army officers . . . Trogoff:** L'Épingle Noire (The Black Needle) was a secret group of Bonapartist officers who began meeting in 1817. In 1820, several members, including Delaverderie and Trogoff, were charged with plotting against the government.

51. **Monsieur Decazes . . . prevailed:** Élie Decazes (1780–1860), an ambitious bureaucrat who became the favorite of Louis XVIII; he was viewed with great hostility by the Ultras, who managed to bring about his downfall following the assassination of the duc de Berry.

52. **Chateaubriand . . . *La Monarchie selon la Charte:*** As a conservative constitutional monarchist, Chateaubriand was viewed with hostility by the Ultras to his right and the liberals to his left. *La Monarchie selon la Charte* had in fact been published in 1816.

53. **preferred Lafon to Talma:** an allusion to the failings of critics, as Talma (François-Joseph Talma, but always referred to by only one name; 1763–1826) was generally recognized as the greatest actor of his time, while Lafon was largely forgotten by 1860.

54. **Monsieur de Féletz . . . Monsieur Hoffmann:** Féletz and Hoffmann were literary critics. Hoffmann wrote a negative review of Hugo's first published collection of verse in 1822.

55. **Charles Nodier:** One of the leading figures of early French Romanticism, Nodier acted as a patron to the youthful poet Hugo in the 1820s.

56. **Divorce was abolished:** Divorce had been legalized under the First Republic

and continued to be legal, if rare, under the empire; it was outlawed again under the Bourbon Restoration. Hugo's parents had begun divorce proceedings in 1814, but the return of the Bourbons meant that they remained married until Madame Hugo's death in 1821.

57. **the king of Rome:** the son of Napoléon and Marie-Louise von Hapsburg; recognized as Napoléon II by loyal Bonapartists, he was known as the duke of Neipperg in Austria. He lived at Schönbrunn, his grandfather's palace outside Vienna, and died there of tuberculosis in 1832, at the age of twenty-one.

58. **Madame:** Marie-Thérèse de Bourbon (1778–1851), daughter of Louis XVI and Marie Antoinette; wife of her cousin the duc d'Angoulême. Known as the Orphan of the Temple (*l'Orphéline du Temple*), she had seen first her father, then her mother taken away to the guillotine and her brother taken away to be raised as a ward of the Republic, before she was sent to her Austrian relatives in return for French prisoners of war in 1795, at the age of seventeen. Known as Madame Royale, she was held in quasi-religious veneration by royalists and quietly pressured her uncle Louis XVIII to rid the government of the Revolutionary survivors she regarded as her parents' murderers.

59. **Monsieur le duc d'Orléans:** Louis-Philippe de Bourbon-Orléans (1773–1850), cousin of the royal family and first prince of the blood royal (*premier prince du sang*). The duke's popularity was doubly troubling to the royal family, as his family had been considered an alternative to the elder branch of the Bourbons since the 1790s, especially in 1814 and again in 1815. For Madame Royale, the duke's popularity was especially disturbing since his father had embraced the Revolution, renouncing his title and calling himself Philippe-Égalité. The renegade duke had been elected to the Convention and voted for his cousin's execution before being arrested and beheaded himself. Louis-Philippe would in fact take the throne from Charles X after the July Revolution of 1830.

60. **the dome of the Invalides:** The Hôtel des Invalides was built as a hospital and convalescent home for wounded soldiers by Louis XIV, including a church with a dome covered in gold leaf.

61. **Monsieur de Trinquelague ... Monsieur de Salaberry was not happy:** conservative politicians of middling importance. Clausel de Montals was a politically conservative priest who used his sermons and writings to promote the same legitimist politics as did his brother, the Ultra deputy Clausel de Coussergues.

62. **Picard:** Molière was an actor as well as a playwright. In spite of the Académie's opinions, Picard was already largely forgotten in 1862.

63. **the Odéon:** The changing names of this theater, founded in 1782, reflect the dramatic changes in French politics.

64. **Cugnet de Montarlot:** a Napoleonic officer prosecuted for his membership in the secret society Le Lion Dormant (The Sleeping Lion); he was acquitted, along with his codefendants.

65. **Fabvier . . . Bavoux:** Charles-Nicolas Fabvier (1782–1855) was a member of the Épingle Noire (see note 50, p. 1215). Banished in 1820, he made his way to Athens, where he served as a general in the Greek insurgency against the Turks. He returned to France after the July Revolution and was named a lieutenant general and a peer. Like Hugo, he served in the Legislative Assembly of the Second Republic and retired from politics on the declaration of the Second Empire. Nicolas Bavoux was a professor of law who used his classroom as a forum to passionately critique the Restoration government. Fired in 1819, he was subsequently prosecuted for sedition and acquitted.

66. **Pélicier:** Hugo seems to have invented this minor act of commercial fraud by Pélicier, the publisher of Hugo's first poetry collection, *Odes et poésies diverses* (1822), with whom he later had a falling-out.

67. **Monsieur Charles Loyson:** After having taken first prize in an 1817 poetry competition in which Hugo received only an honorable mention, Charles de Loyson died in 1820, at age twenty-nine.

68. **Cardinal Fesch . . . the diocese of Lyon:** Napoléon had named his uncle Joseph Fesch (see note 7, p. 1196) archbishop of Lyon, which seat the cardinal refused to officially resign even though he had been living in exile in Rome ever since his nephew's final defeat. Monsieur de Pins would serve as de facto archbishop of Lyon until his death in 1837.

69. **the valley of Dappes:** The Swiss had ceded this valley in the Juras to Bonaparte in 1804, and the Congress of Vienna had returned it to Switzerland. The French government, however, resisted and did not officially give up control until 1863.

70. **Saint-Simon:** An indirect descendant of the seventeenth-century memorialist of the court of Louis XIV, the comte Henri de Saint-Simon (1760–1825) advocated social reform through industrialization and progressivism, guided by a sense of Christian fraternity. His work would inspire a utopian community after his death.

71. **a celebrated Fourier . . . a Fourier the future will remember:** The scientist Joseph Fourier (1768–1830) would in fact be eclipsed by the utopian socialist Charles Fourier (1772–1837), whose work would inspire the Phalanstery movement in the United States, most notably Brook Farm.

72. **David d'Angers:** Not to be confused with the painter Jacques-Louis David, the sculptor David d'Angers established his reputation with a statue commissioned by the government in 1816.

73. **The abbé Caron . . . Lamennais:** The abbé Caron had befriended and protected Félicité de Lamennais (1782–1854), who published the first part of his *Essay on Indifference in Matters of Religion* in 1817. The two priests were briefly neighbors of Madame Hugo and her sons, and Lamennais sought—unsuccessfully—to convert the teenage Victor to the orthodox Catholicism he was then preaching. Lamennais stressed (among other things) the social value of the Christian religion. Lamennais later became a champion of the poor and an advocate of republicanism.

74. **Monsieur de Vaublanc:** The comte de Vaublanc (1756–1845), as minister of the interior to Louis XVIII, had effective control of the Institut de France, including nominations to the Académie Française.

75. **The faubourg Saint-Germain and the pavillon Marsan:** The elegant faubourg Saint-Germain neighborhood, corresponding roughly to today's seventh arrondissement, was a metaphor for the ultra-royalist, ancien régime aristocrats who lived there. Those social and political conservatives placed their hopes in Louis XVIII's brother, the comte d'Artois, who would become Charles X in 1824 and who resided in a wing of the Tuileries palace known as the pavillon Marsan.

76. **Monsieur Delavau:** It is typical of the Ultras that religious devotion should be the chief qualification for political office; minister of police was the office held by Decazes, whom the Ultras held responsible for Louis XVIII's supposed liberalism. Delavau was named to head the police when the conservative Villèle (see note 2, ch. VII, p. 1228) replaced Decazes in 1821.

77. **Dupuytren and Récamier:** Both Guillaume Dupuytren (1777–1835) and Joseph-Claude Récamier (1774–1852) were famous surgeons, but Récamier was a devout Christian, while Dupuytren was reputed to be an atheist.

78. **Cuvier:** Georges Cuvier (1769–1832), a naturalist whose studies of fossils made him one of the founders of modern biology and paleontology.

79. **bigots:** in the French sense of the term, persons of inflexible religious orthodoxy.

80. **François de Neufchâteau . . . Parmentier's memory:** Nicolas-Louis François de Neufchâteau (1750–1828) had briefly served as minister of the interior and was an amateur agronomist and sometime poet. He had championed the cause of Antoine-Augustin Parmentier (1737–1813), the agronomist who had popularized the cultivation of the potato in France long after it had spread through Europe. As a member of the Académie Française, Neufchâteau had taken an interest—albeit a self-centered one—in the young poet Victor Hugo (see note 2, ch. IV, p. 1281).

81. **The abbé Grégoire:** The abbé Grégoire (see note 1, p. 1204) was denounced by royalists as a regicide, even though he had been absent from the Convention on the day of the vote.

82. **Monsieur Royer-Collard:** Pierre-Paul Royer-Collard (1763–1845), a scholar and politician; as a moderate constitutional monarchist, Royer-Collard was prepared to accept innovation in politics but not in the French language.

83. **the pont d'Iéna:** named for Napoléon's victory over the Prussians at Jena. The occupying Prussians had planned to blow up the bridge in a bid to reclaim their national pride; after Blücher's initial attempt failed, Louis XVIII sent word to the duke of Wellington, the chief of the Allied forces, that he intended to have his carriage driven to the middle of the bridge, ready to go up with the bridge, if Blücher followed through with his plans. Wellington reined the Prussians in. Louis understood the importance of such symbolism in maintaining the support of the army for his new government.

84. **Blücher:** Gebhard Leberecht Blücher, Prince von Wahlstatt (1742–1819), the commander of the Prussian forces in the 1815 coalition. His arrival at Waterloo decisively turned the battle against the French. An aggressive soldier, he was known by his troops as "Vorwärts!" (Forward!).

85. **the comte d'Artois:** the ultra-royalist Charles-Philippe de Bourbon, the youngest brother of Louis XVI and Louis XVIII, known as Monsieur under the Restoration; his attempts to turn back the political clock after his accession to the throne as Charles X, in 1824, would eventually provoke the July Revolution of 1830. Charles died in exile in Prague in 1836.

86. **"Bonaparte and Talma . . . arm in arm":** Bonaparte was a great admirer of the actor Talma, who was rumored to have coached the general turned politician in his public appearances. Their trips to the Bal-Sauvage, a public ball, must have been early in Bonaparte's career, as he became increasingly conscious of his public image as his power increased through the Consulate and Empire.

87. **the deserters of Ligny and Quatre-Bras:** On June 16, 1815, two days before Waterloo, Napoléon planned an offensive against the divided Allied armies. He would attack the Prussians under Blücher at Ligny, while Ney would attack the Anglo-Dutch forces at Quatre-Bras. Napoléon successfully pushed back the Germans, but Ney's relative inaction did no damage to Wellington's forces. Blücher managed to preserve his cavalry, which arrived at Waterloo just in time to decisively turn the battle in the Allies' favor. The word *deserters* conveys Hugo's still-strong emotions about the Napoleonic era, some fifty years after the fact.

## II: A Double Foursome

1. **to study in Paris . . . born in Paris:** Hugo himself was born in Besançon but studied in Paris.

2. **"Oscar":** Here, and in the following paragraphs, Hugo mocks the early Romantic literature, chiefly influenced by Sir Walter Scott in "Scandinavian or Caledonian" (i.e., Scottish) settings with heroes named Oscar, Adolph, Gustave, etc. *Adolphe* was a popular autobiographically inspired novel (1816) by Benjamin Constant, inspired by his own affair with Madame de Staël (*Corinne,* 1807, gives her side of the story). Hugo's own novel *Han d'Islande* betrays some of the same influences.

3. *Ossian:* a collection of poems published in London in the early 1760s by James Macpherson, a Scotsman who claimed to have discovered and translated the epic story of "Ossian" from the original Scots Gaelic. Before Macpherson's poems were discovered to be his own invention, they enjoyed a huge success all over Europe. Napoléon and Chateaubriand were great admirers of the Ossianic saga.

4. **Favorite, so named because she had been to England:** *favorite* being a term used to describe a royal mistress.

5. **nom de guerre:** A classic trope of the nineteenth-century demimonde is the single name adopted by the courtesan.

6. **Jungfrau:** The German word *Jungfrau* means "maiden" or "virgin." The exact reference here is unclear.

7. **Gascon:** The Pyrenean province of Gascony, in southwestern France, was said to produce proud, boastful people. Edmond Rostand's Cyrano de Bergerac is based on the traditional stereotype.

8. **the Directoire:** In the chaotic 1790s, it is not difficult to imagine a child born in the circumstances Hugo creates for Fantine.

9. **working girls:** not quite courtesans, "working girls," or *grisettes*, refers to young working-class women—seamstresses, shopgirls, laundresses—who were the mistresses of students, struggling artists, and young men of their own class. They provided young men company in cheap restaurants, the *parterres* of theaters, and the public balls of Montmartre and the suburbs. In nineteenth-century Paris, especially in its literary representations, the *grisette* occupies a place above the common prostitute but below the dancers, actresses, and grand courtesans of the demimonde.

10. **four thousand francs annual income:** not a princely sum, but a substantial income for a student, even a thirty-year-old student. Compare to the twenty-four sous a day Jean Valjean earns for his manual labor, less than five hundred francs a year.

11. **the montagne Sainte-Geneviève:** the hill rising up on the left bank of the Seine, topped by the Panthéon. It is used here as a synonym for the Latin Quarter, home of the Sorbonne and its students.

12. **"the noggin at thirty, the knees at forty":** i.e., "When the hair goes by thirty, the knees go by forty." Already wrinkled and losing his teeth, Tholomyès is philosophical about his precocious old age.

### III: Four by Four

1. **today we say Fécamp ... Saint-Cloud:** Fécamp is a small Norman town on the coast of the English Channel; Saint-Cloud, on the western outskirts of Paris, was the site of a royal château with magnificent gardens and park including an elaborate man-made cascade or waterfall. Saint-Cloud was the preferred residence of Marie Antoinette and the Bonapartes. The park was open to the public provided they were decently dressed. The château was demolished after sustaining heavy damage during the siege of Paris in 1870, but the park remains.

2. *folies champêtres:* i.e., pastoral amusements, a romantic image of innocent youth at play in the fields.

3. **Castaing:** Dr. Castaing was executed in 1823 for poisoning two of his best friends in order to inherit their estates.

4. **Puteaux ... Neuilly:** The four couples' day in the country takes them on a tour of the western suburbs of Paris, some of which, such as Passy, are now part of Paris itself.

5. **the knight of Labouïsse:** Known as the *poète de l'hymène,* Jean-Pierre de

Labouïsse-Rochefort was especially well-known for the poetry he dedicated to his wife, Eléanore.

6. **Delvincourt and Monsieur Blondeau:** two professors of law at the University of Paris. Étienne-Claude Delvincourt (1762–1831) was the dean of the law school and a royalist; Jean-Hyacinthe Blondeau (1784–1854) was a specialist in Roman law.

7. **Galatea's flight beneath the willows:** not Pygmalion's Galatea but a reference to Virgil's *Eclogues,* in which the flirtatious nymph Galatea tempts a young shepherd to abandon his flock and follow her into the woods.

8. **Erigone:** The lover of the wine god Bacchus, Erigone took the form of a bunch of grapes to seduce him.

9. **Canebière:** a wide street that runs through the "Old Marseilles" section of the city, down to the port.

10. **the vicomtesse de Cette:** perhaps a reference to Ermengarde de Narbonne, a twelfth-century noblewoman who is said to have maintained a "court of love."

11. **Coustou:** Nicolas Coustou (1658–1733), a sculptor.

12. **Psyche and Venus:** Psyche, though so beautiful she caused the goddess Venus to be jealous, was a mere mortal.

*IV: Tholomyès Is So Cheery He Sings a Spanish Ditty*

1. **"The embarkation for Cythera!" cries Watteau . . . for good measure:** Antoine Watteau (1684–1721) was the great painter of the *fête galante; The Embarkation for Cythera* is one of his most famous paintings. Nicolas Lancret (1690–1743) was a less successful imitator of Watteau. For Diderot, see note 4, p. 1200. Honoré d'Urfé's novel *Astrée* is set in fifth-century Gaul, complete with Druids.

2. **the Bien National:** or national property; the term *bien national* originated with the Revolution, when the estates and properties of émigrés and others judged guilty of political crimes were confiscated and, when possible, sold to provide revenue to the government.

3. **Bourguin:** Those who had supply contracts with Napoléon's armies often made fortunes in dubious dealings and inflated prices. Such characters are staples of literature of the era, especially Balzac's *Comédie humaine.*

4. **the anchorite:** i.e., a hermit.

5. **a Turcaret metamorphosed into Priapus:** Turcaret was the title character of a 1709 play by Alain-René Lesage, a sharply satirical portrait of a greedy financier. Priapus was the Roman god of male fertility and a symbol of lust.

6. **the abbé de Bernis:** A fixture of the court of Louis XV, the poet-priest Bernis was the protégé of both the duc de Choiseul, Louis's powerful minister, and the marquise de Pompadour, his even more powerful mistress. His poems often described romantic pastoral scenes such as two peasant lovers and a "swing that hung from two chestnuts."

7. **Greuze:** Jean-Baptiste Greuze (1725–1804), one of the most popular painters of the late eighteenth century.

8. **the old *gallega* song:** "Soy de Badajoz. / Amor me llama. / Toda mi alma / Es en mis ojos / Porque enseñas / A tus piernas."
9. **from Passy to the barrière de l'Étoile:** Then a leafy suburb, Passy is now part of the sixteenth arrondissement of Paris; the barrière de l'Étoile is now the place de l'Étoile.
10. **Beaujon heights:** On a rise north of the Champs-Élysées, on the site of the estate of the banker Nicolas Beaujon, a sort of amusement park had been built in the late eighteenth century, including a *montagne russe,* an early form of the roller coaster.

*V: At Bombarda's*

1. **Bombarda:** a real restaurant of the Restoration era.
2. **Molière:** Born Jean-Baptiste Poquelin (1622), Molière created comedies and characters—the religious hypocrite Tartuffe, the misanthrope Alceste, Monsieur Jourdain of *The Would-be Gentleman*—who are frequent points of reference for Hugo and his readers. The verse quoted here is from *L'Étourdi* (*The Blunderer*). Molière, Racine, and Corneille are considered to be the three greatest playwrights of the Golden Age under Louis XIV.
3. **Their feet ... were able:** "Ils faisaient sous la table / Un bruit, un trique-trac de pieds epouvantable."
4. **The Marly horses:** The Marly horses, originally sculpted by Guillaume Coustou for the gardens of the royal château Marly, were moved to the Champs-Élysées during the Revolution.
5. **the white flag ... Tuileries:** the royal flag indicating that the king was in residence.
6. **The place de la Concorde ... place Louis XV:** The place Louis XV was rebaptized place de la Révolution by the Convention in 1792, then place de la Concorde after the fall of Robespierre; it reverted to its Bourbon name in 1815, and back to the place de la Concorde in 1830.
7. **the silver fleur-de-lis ... not yet disappeared:** i.e., the Bourbons were still fairly popular.
8. **the Hundred Days:** *les Cent Jours,* the name given to Napoléon's 1815 return to power.
9. **our Père de Gand:** Louis XVIII fled to Ghent (Gand in French), Belgium, as Napoléon approached Paris after his escape from Elba.
10. **Give us back ... our Father:** "Rendez-nous notre père de Gand, / Rendez-nous notre père."
11. **faubourg folk ... good bourgeois:** *Faubourgs* (suburbs) were home to the working and artisan classes, as opposed to the more affluent—and respectably royalist—bourgeois who could afford to live in Paris.
12. **the great carré Marigny:** a square roughly in the middle of the Champs-Élysées.
13. **the prefect of police, Anglès:** Jules Anglès (1778–1828) held that office from

1815 until 1821. His name will appear frequently through the first part of the novel. He was succeeded by Guy Delavau (see note 76, p. 1218).

14. **Minerva:** the Roman name for Athena, goddess of wisdom.

15. **the tenth of August:** the final fall of Louis XVI in 1792, when Parisian crowds invaded the Tuileries palace and forced the royal family to ask for the protection of the National Assembly, effectively an abdication by the king.

16. **Austerlitz:** Napoléon's first great military victory as emperor; see note 8, p. 1205.

17. **Danton's mainstay:** The great Revolutionary orator Georges-Jacques Danton (1759–94), known as the *Mirabeau du peuple,* was immensely popular with the Parisian working classes. Danton became Robespierre's great rival for power in the Convention. He was guillotined in April 1794, only a few months before Robespierre's fall.

18. **turn the first rue Greneta . . . into the Caudine Forks:** The rue Greneta, in the district of Les Halles, was the site of a popular insurrection in 1839; the Caudine Forks are a narrow mountain gorge in southern Italy where the Roman army was trapped and defeated by the Samnites in the fourth century B.C.E. "To pass through the Caudine Forks" is a proverbial expression in France, meaning to go through an almost impossible situation.

19. **the "Carmagnole":** a popular song of the French Revolution, its lyrics directly threatened Louis XVI and Marie Antoinette. The "Marseillaise," which became the French national anthem, began as a marching song for Revolutionary armies, its lyrics more broadly denouncing tyranny.

*VI: A Chapter Where Everyone Adores One Another*

1. **Saint-Jacques-du-Haut-Pas:** a parish church on the southern edge of the Latin Quarter, in the rue Saint-Jacques.

*VII: The Wisdom of Tholomyès*

1. **"Grimod de la Reynière . . . Talleyrand":** Alexandre Grimod de la Reynière advocated "the pleasures of the table" under the Restoration. Talleyrand, the post-Revolutionary *grand seigneur,* cultivated an image of aristocratic *desinvoltura;* he was said to have frequently admonished his underlings to show no zeal (*"Pas de zèle!"*) in their diplomatic communications.

2. **"Jesus Christ made a pun . . . city of Toryna":** a reference to Matthew 16:18, "You are Peter and on this rock I shall build my Church." Moses' pun about Isaac—according to a tradition by which Moses was the author of the book of Genesis—is that Isaac means "he who laughs," because Abraham laughed when God told him that he would have a son when he was a hundred years old and his wife was ninety-three. The playwright Aeschylus pointed out that Polynices, whose name means "many victories" or "many quarrels," fought many battles. Cleopatra's pun about Octavius does not translate well, but the sense of it, that Octavius was no warrior but an ineffectual political schemer,

was rendered moot when Octavius's forces defeated those of Cleopatra and Mark Antony at Actium, near the city of Toryna.

3. **"the prudence of Amphiaraüs"**: a Greek warrior given the gift of prophecy by the gods; he went into battle against Thebes in spite of having foreseen his own death.

4. *"Est modus in rebus"*: from Horace, roughly, "In all things, moderation."

5. **"Gula punishes Gulax"**: I.e., gluttony is its own punishment.

6. **"Munatius Demens ... quaestor of parricide"**: "Parricide" may be a reference to Nero, i.e., Munatius Demens, whose name suggests dementia, madness, is the judge (*quatator*) who metes out justice in the name of a murderer.

7. **"Sulla or Origen of Alexandria"**: Sulla was a second-century-B.C.E. Roman general and dictator who abdicated his poltical power; Origen of Alexandria, one of the Fathers of the Church, believed so strongly in the renunciation of earthly pleasures that he castrated himself.

8. **"Prospero"**: Félix is usually associated with the Latin, "happy."

9. **"Woman is perfidious and devious"**: an echo of Hugo's *Le Roi s'amuse* (The King Takes His Pleasure). According to legend, King Francis I scratched a verse along those lines [into a wooden window frame at Chambord: "Souvent femme varie / Bien fol qui s'y fie" (A woman is fickle / 'tis folly to trust her). Hugo used the phrase at a key point in his play. In Verdi's *Rigoletto*, the verse becomes the Italian *La donna è mobile.*

10. *"Nunc te, Bacche, canam!"*: The citation from Virgil's *Eclogues*, "And now, Bacchus, I shall sing of you!," is not Spanish but Latin.

11. **"handed the apple, like Venus"**: According to the Greek myth, the Trojan War began when Paris was called upon to hand a golden apple to the most beautiful of the goddesses. When he chose Aphrodite (Venus), she gave him the love of Helen, the most beautiful woman in the world and the wife of the king of Sparta.

12. **"to Liège for corks or to Pau for gloves"**: The Belgian industrial town of Liège was known for its manufacture of gloves, among other things; corks came from the southwest of France, around the city of Pau.

13. **"Marguerite"**: Hugo had briefly thought of naming this character Marguerite, which is derived from the Greek word for "pearl."

14. **"Clermont-Tonnerre"**: The Clermont-Tonnerre family was one of the greatest of the French aristocracy. The historically minded students seem to be alluding to some medieval scheme to win the papacy for one of them, which is not at all improbable.

15. **The Father ... money back**: "Les pères dindons donnèrent / De l'argent à un agent / Pour que mons Clermont-Tonnerre / Fût fait pape à la Saint-Jean; / Mais Clermont ne put pas être / Fait pape, n'étant pas prêtre; / Alors leur agent rageant / Leur rapporta leur argent."

16. **"Elleviou"**: François Elleviou (1769–1842) was a famous singer at the Parisian theaters Comédie Italienne and Opéra-Comique.

17. **"O Luxembourg ... allée de l'Observatoire"**: The Parisian Tholomyès sings

the glories of what nature is to be found in Paris, from the Luxembourg gardens to the allée de l'Observatoire and the rue Madame, which run alongside them. Like his *Eclogues,* Virgil's *Georgics* celebrate the rural life.

## VIII: Death of a Horse

1. **"Edon's"**: another real restaurant of Restoration Paris, one that Hugo had frequented with his brothers as a boy.
2. *"glaces"*: The French word *glace* refers to both ice cream and decorative mirrors.
3. **"Descartes or Spinoza"**: For Descartes, see note 43, p. 1214; Baruch Spinoza (1632–77) was born in Holland of Portuguese-Jewish parents. His rationalist philosophy is often seen as a precursor to the Enlightenment.
4. **"Désaugiers"**: a composer of popular songs.
5. **"Ber— . . . Choux"**: Arnaud Berquin (1747–91) wrote sentimental and moralistic books for children. Joseph de Berchoux (1760–1839) is best known for his long poem *La Gastronomie* (1801), which celebrated the pleasures of the table and good company.
6. **"Munophis of Elephanta . . . Thygelion of Cheroneus"**: these names seem to be inventions of Hugo.
7. **"Apuleius"**: a second-century Roman author.
8. *"Nil sub sole novum"*: Ecclesiastes 1:10.
9. *"amor omnibus idem"*: from the *Georgics,* the sense is that love is a tyrant for everyone.
10. **"Aspasia . . . Samos"**: Aspasia is a legendary figure said to have exerted enormous political influence over Pericles in fifth-century-B.C.E. Athens. She is variously described as being Pericles' lover and his wife; others describe her as a prostitute and brothel keeper. One legend claims that Pericles declared war against Samos to gratify his mistress.
11. **"Manon Lescaut"**: the prostitute heroine of the abbé Prévost's immensely popular 1733 novel.
12. **"Prometheus"**: the Titan who stole fire from the gods and gave it to mortals; as punishment, he was chained to a mountain, where vultures pecked at his liver for all eternity.
13. **a mare from Beauce**: The Beauce is a vast agricultural region south of Paris.
14. **She was . . . the mongrel!**: "Elle était de ce monde où coucous et carrosses / Ont le même destin; / Et, rosse, elle a vécu ce que vivent les rosses, / L'espace d'un matin!"

## IX: Happy Ending to Happiness

1. **"The Toulouse diligence"**: i.e., the public coach bound for Toulouse, in southwest France. The firm Laffitte et Caillard ran the diligence service from Paris to Toulouse and other routes.

BOOK FOUR: TO ENTRUST IS SOMETIMES TO ABANDON
*I: One Mother Meets Another*

1. **Homer ... Caliban:** In Homer's *Odyssey,* Polyphemus is the Cyclops who traps Odysseus and his sailors in his cave. Caliban, in Shakespeare's *Tempest,* is the half-human slave of Prospero, who once tried to rape Prospero's daughter, Miranda, and who rebels against his master.
2. **King Louis-Philippe:** Louis-Philippe d'Orléans (born 1773, reigned 1830 to 1848, died in exile in 1850) took the throne after the July 1830 Revolution. His eighteen-year reign was scorned by both the left and the right as *la monarchie bourgeoise;* many artists saw it as a triumph of crass middle-class materialism, nicely incarnated by Tholomyès as described here. In spite of his scorn, Hugo served in the Chamber of Peers under Louis-Philippe and was friendly with the king and his family.
3. **Cosette ... Euphrasie:** One sees in these different but similar names the difference between the child's father and mother. Euphrasie suggests the Greco-Latin roots of *eu-* ("good" or "well") plus *phras-* (from the Greek verb for "to tell"), while Cosette suggests the French verb *causer,* to speak easily and informally.

*II: Initial Sketch of Two Shady Characters*

1. *Clélie* ... **Madame Barthélémy-Hadot:** Hugo traces the decline of the novel from the seventeenth century to his own. Mademoiselle de Scudéri (usually Scudéry, 1607–1701) wrote enormously successful, metaphorical romances, such as *Clélie,* in the mode of the *précieuses* of the age; more widely read today is her contemporary Madame de La Fayette (1634–93), whose *La Princesse de Clèves* is considered the first psychological novel. In spite of the gentle scorn Hugo directs at Mesdames Bournon-Malarme and Barthélémy-Hadot, Yves Gohin notes that Hugo read their novels as a child and teenager. It is also worth noting that Hugo does not include such novelists as Stendhal, Balzac, or for that matter Madame de Staël or George Sand. A very distinct type of popular, romantic novel is targeted here.
2. **Pigault-Lebrun:** See note 2, p. 1200.
3. **Megaera ... from Pamela:** Megaera was one of the three Furies; the French word *mégère* translates roughly as "shrew." Pamela was the heroine of Samuel Richardson's 1740 novel of the same name, which was hugely successful in France and a frequent point of reference of French Romantic literature.
4. **Éponine ... Gulnare:** "Éponine" was in fact the name of a Gaulish heroine who aided her husband, Sabinus, in his fight against the invading Romans (see note 4, p. 1326). "Gulnare" suggests the Scandinavian–New Caledonian influences as for Oscar and Alfred (see note 2, p. 1219).
5. **Ducray-Duminil:** François-Guillaume Ducray-Duminil (1761–1819), another popular novelist.

*III: The Lark*

1. **a caution:** i.e., a legal judgment marking him as a debtor.

BOOK FIVE: THE DESCENT
*II: Madeleine*

1. **Madeleine:** The religious overtones of the name, derived from Mary Magdalene's, are unmistakable.
2. **an Oratorian father named Fouché:** Another of the legendary figures of the era, Joseph Fouché (1763–1820) made his name as a ruthless enforcer of Revolutionary politics and policies (including overseeing the execution of more than a thousand "counterrevolutionaries" in barely three months). He ruthlessly enforced official atheism under the Convention. This reputation and a talent for espionage made Fouché the powerful minister of police for the Directoire and most of the Napoleonic empire. During the Hundred Days, Fouché played the royalists against the imperialists until deciding to side with the Bourbons. The Bourbons' gratitude to the regicide did not last, however, and Fouché died in Trieste in 1821 after five years of exile from France. Contrary to legend, Fouché was a lay teacher in an Oratorian school and never took holy orders.
3. **the *Moniteur:*** the official journal of government proceedings from 1795 to 1901.
4. **chevalier of the Légion d'Honneur:** Knight of the Legion of Honor; the Bourbons had retained the Napoleonic institution, cheapening it, in the eyes of true Bonapartists, by awarding it indiscriminately.

*III: Sums Deposited with Laffitte*

1. **Laffitte:** Jacques Laffitte (1767–1844) served as governor of the Banque de France under the Empire and personal banker to Napoléon; he sided with the liberal opposition under the Restoration and supported the advent of Louis-Philippe to the throne in 1830.

*IV: Monsieur Madeleine in Mourning*

1. **microscopic faubourg Saint-Germain:** i.e., the local aristocracy (see note 2, ch. VII, p. 1266).

*V: Dim Flashes of Lightning on the Horizon*

1. **a kind of Styx:** In Greek mythology, the river Styx is one of the three rivers of the underworld.
2. **Brutus meets Vidocq:** Junius Brutus led a conspiracy of Roman senators to assassinate Julius Caesar out of a sense of duty to the Republic (Hugo's father

briefly took the name to demonstrate his Republican devotion). The legendary Eugène-François Vidocq (1775–1857), the "Napoléon de la police," was a former convict who became a secret agent of the French police. The true details of Vidocq's career are ambiguous, though he is generally regarded as having been ruthless and effective. He was the inspiration for the character of Vautrin in Balzac's *Comédie humaine*.

3. **Joseph de Maistre:** See note 7, p. 1198.

4. **"ultra"—ultra-royalist—newspapers:** The Ultras took their name from the adjective *ultraroyaliste*; they were said to be *"plus royalistes que le roi,"* more monarchist than the monarch.

### VI: Father Fauchelevent

1. **"Ten louis":** two hundred francs.

### VII: Fauchelevent Becomes a Gardener in Paris

1. **the Saint-Antoine quartier of Paris:** the *faubourg Saint-Antoine*, a mostly working-class neighborhood on the (then) eastern edge of Paris on the right bank of the Seine.

2. **Monsieur de Villèle:** Jean-Baptiste Joseph de Villèle (1773–1854), a leader of the more conservative royalists under the Restoration, Villèle served as prime minister from 1822 to 1828.

### VIII: Madame Victurnien Spends Thirty-five Francs on Morality

1. **a red cap . . . to the Jacobins:** i.e., left a Bernardine monastery for the Jacobin club, the radical Paris political association that was the seat of power of Robespierre. The club had affiliates in many provincial towns.

2. **a bigot:** See note 5, ch. VIII, p. 1200.

### IX: Madame Victurnien's Success

1. **twelve sous a day:** i.e., sixty centimes a day.

### X: Continued Success

1. **the postage costs of which were ruining her:** At the time, postage was paid by the recipient of a letter, so the Thénardiers' epistolary "bombardment" was a further expense for Fantine.

2. **"two napoléons":** two louis, or forty francs.

*XI: Christus Nos Liberavit*

1. **Christus nos liberavit:** "Christ has made us free." Hugo used this phrase from Paul's letter to the Galatians (5:1) as the epigraph to his royalist ode *À la liberté*.

*XII: The Idleness of Monsieur Bamatabois*

1. **the struggle of the South American republics . . . Morillo:** The Spanish colonial empire was crumbling in the 1820s under an independence movement led by Simon Bolívar (1783–1830). General Pablo Morillo (1775–1837) led the forces that unsuccessfully fought to reestablish Spanish control.

*XIII: The Answer to Some of the Municipal Police's Questions*

1. **stamped paper:** I.e., *papier timbré;* see note 3, ch. III, p. 1198.
2. **a property owner and voter:** Under the Restoration, the voting franchise was restricted to those who paid a certain amount of taxes.

BOOK SIX: JAVERT
*I: The Beginning of Rest*

1. **the bas-reliefs at Rheims:** The Wise and Foolish Virgins (*vierges sages et folles*) are typical examples of religious art of the Middle Ages.
2. **Laënnec:** The physician René Laënnec (1781–1826) invented the stethoscope.

*II: How Jean Can Turn Into Champ*

1. **"Cochepaille and Chenildieu":** *Cochepaille* suggests a contraction of *cochon,* "pig," or *coucher,* "to sleep," and *paille,* straw; *Chenildieu,* as Hugo later specifies, comes from "Je renie Dieu," "I renounce God." Their slangy names are typical of criminals and prisoners as represented in literature. Balzac and Eugène Sue used similar milieus in their fiction.

BOOK SEVEN: THE CHAMPMATHIEU AFFAIR
*I: Sister Simplice*

1. **Lazarist sisters:** The Lazarists, like the Sisters of Charity, follow the Vincentian model of public service (see below).
2. **a Capuchin nun or an Ursuline:** The Capuchins are followers of the Franciscan rule; Ursuline nuns are typically devoted to teaching young girls or the care of the sick.
3. **White Friar:** a member of the Carmelite order.
4. **Vincent de Paul:** a seventeenth-century priest who founded what would become the Vincentian orders (see note 13, p. 1200).

5. **Abbé Sicard . . . Massieu:** Father Sicard (1742–1822) spent his life teaching the deaf. Massieu, we can assume, is a colleague or student.

### III: A Storm on the Brain

1. **Dante Alighieri . . . a sinister door:** In Dante's *Inferno*, the author-narrator stands before the gates of hell, above which is inscribed "Abandon All Hope, Ye Who Enter Here." Dante's work is a frequent point of reference for Hugo.
2. **letters of credit that he held:** i.e., IOUs for loans that Jean Valjean had made to local businessmen in difficulty; the debts are thus erased.

### VI: Sister Simplice Is Put to the Test

1. **We'll buy some . . . my love is true:**
> Nous achèterons de bien belles choses
> En nous promenant le long des faubourgs.
>
> Les bleuets sont bleus, les roses sont roses,
> Les bleuets sont bleus, j'aime mes amours.
>
> La vierge Marie auprès de mon poêle
> Est venue hier en manteau brodé;
> Et m'a dit:—Voici, caché sous mon voile,
> Le petit qu'un jour tu m'as demandé.
> Courez à la ville, ayez de la toile,
> Achetez du fil, achetez un dé.
>> Nous achèterons de bien belles choses
>> En nous promenant le long des faubourgs.
>
> Bonne sainte Vierge, auprès de mon poêle
> J'ai mis un berceau de rubans orné;
> Dieu me donnerait sa plus belle étoile,
> J'aime mieux l'enfant que tu m'as donné.
> Madame, que faire avec cette toile?
> Faites en trousseau pour mon nouveau-né.
>> Les bleuets sont bleus, les roses sont roses,
>> Les bleuets sont bleus, j'aime mes amours.
>
> Lavez cette toile.—Où?—Dans la rivière.
> Faites-en, sans rien gâter ni salir,
> Une belle jupe avec sa brassière
> Que je veux broder et de fleurs emplir.
>> L'enfant n'est plus là, madame, qu'en faire?
>> Faites-en un drap pour m'ensevelir.
>
> Nous achèterous de bien belles choses
> En nous promenant le long des faubourgs.
> Les bleuets sont bleus, les roses sont roses,
> Les bleuets sont bleus, j'aime mes amours.

*VII: The Traveler Arrives Only to Get Ready to Leave Again*

1. **"Monsieur de Conzié":** one of the "philosopher bishops" (see note 1, p. 1204) of the ancien régime.

*VIII: Preferential Admission*

1. **no doubt by mistake, *June 11, Year II*:** The date given is a blend of the Gregorian and Revolutionary calendars. Such mistakes were not uncommon in the various changes introduced by the Revolution.

*IX: A Place Where Convictions Are About to Shape Up*

1. **there was a crucifix . . . at the time he was convicted:** The Revolutionary governments were secular; Catholicism was the official religion of the ancien régime, the Empire, and the Restoration governments.
2. *a temple of Melpomene:* Melpomene was the muse of tragedy in Greek mythology.
3. *those gentle Levites:* In the Hebrew tradition, the Levites were the guardians of the Temple.
4. **Bénigne Bossuet:** a prelate whose writings and orations were considered masterpieces of the French language as well as of religious thought; see note 15, p. 1202.
5. **cunning bit of antonomasia:** a rhetorical device that uses a paraphrase or euphemism to refer to an individual or group or a proper name to refer to some individual or group.
6. **the immorality of the Romantic school:** In the early 1820s, when this scene takes place, the young and still conservative Victor Hugo was not yet the leader of the most "satanic" elements of liberal romanticism, and he was never as far right as the *Oriflamme*. One wonders how what was still a relatively obscure literary movement could have driven the illiterate Champmathieu/"Jean Valjean" to commit a crime.
7. **the *Oriflamme* and the *Quotidienne*:** two ultra-royalist newspapers; an *oriflamme* was a banner carried into battle by armies in the medieval and early modern eras.
8. **the tale of Théramènes:** from Racine's *Phèdre*, one of the most famous passages in French literature; Théramènes's monologue recounts for Theseus the death of his son Hippolytus, whom Theseus had called on Neptune to punish because of his erroneous belief that Hippolytus had attempted to seduce his stepmother, Phaedra, when in fact it was Theseus's wife who had attempted to seduce his son.

*X: The Strategy of Denial*

1. **"the Enfants-Rouges":** an orphanage once located in the Third Arrondissement where the children were dressed in red.

2. **"a good sort who never went to dances":** I.e., the public balls were frequented by *grisettes* and young men like Tholomyès.
3. **"Shrove Tuesday":** the day before Ash Wednesday, better known as Mardi Gras. The religious connotations were still more important than those of the Carnival in nineteenth-century France.

*XI: Champmathieu More and More Amazed*

1. **"the three letters T.F.P.":** Convicts sent to Toulon were branded with the letters *TF*, for *travaux forcés*, or "forced labor"; those sentenced to hard labor for life, like Chenildieu, were branded with *TFP*, *travaux forcés perpetuels*, "perpetual forced labor."

BOOK EIGHT: AFTERSHOCK
*III: Javert Satisfied*

1. **this monstrous Saint Michael:** According to Christian tradition, the Archangel Saint Michael, or Michel, is God's warrior, first of the angels, and chief of the heavenly hosts. Michael famously expelled Satan from heaven, an image frequently reproduced in art. Saint Michael was one of the angels who spoke to Joan of Arc, making him one of the patron saints of France from the fifteenth century onward.

*V: A Suitable Grave*

1. **a galley slave:** The term *galérien* outlasted the use of the galleys in the French navy; the term was used frequently in place of the proper term of *forçat* for one sentenced to forced labor.
2. **the *Drapeau Blanc*:** the *White Flag*, still another legitimist newspaper; note the lady's pronunciation "Buonapartists"; the Italian pronunciation emphasized Napoléon's foreignness.

PART TWO: COSETTE

BOOK ONE: WATERLOO
*I: What You Meet with When You Come from Nivelles*

1. **Last year, 1861, on a lovely morning in May:** Hugo did in fact travel to Waterloo in May 1861, in order to confirm his understanding of the battle. Even though, as he wrote in a letter, he would say only "a word" (*un mot*) about Waterloo in *Les Misérables,* he wanted to be sure of his accuracy.
2. **On the horizon . . . looked like a lion:** The king of Holland ordered a lion built on top of a hill at Waterloo in recognition of the service of his son, the prince of Orange, who had been wounded in the battle.

*II: Hougoumont*

1. **Hougoumont:** the old fortified manor house was the site of a key skirmish within the larger battle.
2. **Henri IV:** The first Bourbon reigned from 1590 to 1610.
3. **Napoléon sent his brother Jérôme:** Jérôme Bonaparte (1784–1860), Napoléon's youngest brother, was named king of Westphalia by his elder brother.
4. **the divisions of Guilleminot, Foy, and Bachelu:** Général Comte Armand-Charles Guilleminot (1774–1840); Général Baron Gilbert Bachelu (1777–1849), and Général Comte Maximilien Foy (1775–1825). Foy would have the most significant post-Napoleonic career, as an opposition leader in the Chamber of Deputies, from 1819 until his death. His funeral became the scene of a protest against the Bourbon government.
5. *Conde de Rio Maïor. Marques y Marquesa de Almagro* (**Habana**): a vestige of the era when Belgium was known as the Spanish Netherlands, ruled by the Spanish branch of the Hapsburgs.
6. **the first French style that preceded Le Nôtre:** André Le Nôtre (1613–1700), the landscape architect who popularized the formal French garden, most notably at Versailles.

*III: June 18, 1815*

1. **June 18, 1815:** the day of the battle of Waterloo.
2. **So that Waterloo could be the end of Austerlitz ... a bit of rain:** A key part of the Napoleonic legend was the "sun of Austerlitz." The battle of Austerlitz began in a heavy fog. The French soldiers advanced in spite of it, and when the sun suddenly burned off the mist, the Russian and Austrian troops were stunned to find a massive French force virtually on top of them. At Waterloo, by contrast, the heavy rains and muddy ground prevented Napoléon from executing his plans as he would have wished.
3. **Blücher:** commander of the Prussian forces in 1815; see note 84, p. 1219.
4. **Aboukir:** During General Bonaparte's ill-fated Egyptian 1798–99 campaign under the Directoire, there were two battles at Aboukir, near Alexandria. At the first, Nelson decimated the French fleet, which had just left Bonaparte's army; at the second, Napoléon's cannons repulsed a landing of Turkish troops backed by the British navy.
5. **Wellington:** The commander of the allied armies, Arthur Wellesley, Duke of Wellington (1769–1852), had made his name and earned his dukedom by driving the French out of Spain in 1812–13. Waterloo made him one of the most powerful men in Europe.
6. **Napoléon's ... point of view:** Napoléon's point of view was given by *Mémoires pour servir à l'histoire de France sous Napoléon*, written according to Napoléon's dictation and published by the loyal generals who had accompanied him in his

final exile, including Bertrand, Montholon, and Gourgaud, and published in six volumes from 1823 to 1825; the *Mémorial de Sainte-Hélène* by Emmanuel de Las Cases was enormously popular when published in 1826. The glittering array of historians who gave the "opposite point of view" were those Hugo read or reviewed in exile, such as Charras (see note 1, p. 1235), Quinet, Adolphe Thiers, and Vaulabelle.

## IV: A

1. **the College of Brienne:** Napoléon Bonaparte had attended the military academy at Brienne thanks to a royal scholarship from 1778 to 1785 (from the age of nine to sixteen).
2. **the Marengo sword:** Marengo (Italy), site of a great victory over the Austrians for First Consul Bonaparte on July 14, 1800.
3. **Babylon sacked . . . diminishes Titus:** "Babylon sacked" alludes to Alexander's conquest of the city in his war against the Persian king Darius III; "Rome in chains" refers to Caesar's establishment of the dictatorship in the ancient republic; "Jerusalem massacred" to Titus Flavius Vespasianus's harsh repression of the Jewish rebellion in the year 70, during which the Great Temple of Jerusalem was razed. Titus did not actually succeed his father, Vespasian, as emperor until 79.

## V: The Quid Obscurum of Battles

1. **Ney:** Michel Ney (1769–1815) was one of Napoléon's favorite generals, nicknamed *"le brave des braves."* Named marshal of the Empire in 1804, he played decisive roles in the battles of Elchingen, Eylau, and the Moskova. He was made duc d'Elchingen in 1808 and prince de la Moskova in 1813. Ney rallied to the Bourbons in 1814, and when Napoléon landed at Juan Gulf after escaping from Elba, Ney promised Louis XVIII that he would bring Napoléon back to Paris in an iron cage. He rode south from Paris, but—in no small part due to the obvious sentiments of his troops—reconciled with his emperor when they met. After the return of the Bourbons, Ney was arrested, tried, and shot by a firing squad.
2. **something for Salvator Rosa, not for Gribeauval:** The Italian painter and poet Salvator Rosa (1615–73) specialized in battle scenes; Jean-Baptiste Vauquette de Gribeauval (1715–89) was a famous officer in the artillery.
3. *Quid obscurum, quid divinum:* something obscure, something divine.
4. **Van der Meulen:** The Dutch painter Antoine-François van der Meulen (1634–90) came to France at the invitation of Louis XIV, who admired his depictions of battle.
5. **This is what gives Folard . . . Polybius:** The military theorist Jean-Charles de Folard (1669–1752) was best known for a treatise refuting an ancient Greek predecessor, the historian Polybius (ca. 200–120 B.C.E.).

*VI: Four O'clock in the Afternoon*

1. **as Charras says:** Jean-Baptiste Charras (1810–65), a military officer elected to the Chamber of Deputies of the Second Republic in 1848. Exiled by Louis-Napoléon in 1852, he wrote his *Histoire de la Campagne de 1815: Waterloo* in Brussels, where it was published in 1857. This was Hugo's primary source for his retelling of the battle.

2. **Wellington shouted . . . Talavera, Vitoria, and Salamanca:** victories of Wellington's armies in the Portuguese and Spanish campaigns. General Hugo fought at Talavera and Vitoria.

*VII: Napoléon in a Good Mood*

1. *Ridet Caesar, Pompeius flebit:* "Caesar laughed, Pompey wept"—a reference to the battle of Pharsalus, where Caesar and his armies, including the Fulminatrix Legion (the Thundering Legion), defeated the forces of Pompey the Great in 48 B.C.E. It is not clear if Hugo took this phrase from some classical source or paraphrased it, but he was quite capable of composing a Latin phrase on his own. It is interesting to note that although Napoléon lost the battle, he is still compared to Caesar, while the victorious Wellington is a Pompey who "this time did not have to weep."

2. **Bertrand:** See note 5, p. 1208.

3. **Soult:** Imperial general named duc de Dalmatia by Napoléon; see note 6, p. 1304, also note 1, ch. XI, p. 1237.

4. **Fleury de Chaboulon:** Napoléon's secretary.

5. **Gourgaud:** one of the contributors to the *Mémoires pour servir à l'histoire de France sous Napoléon* (see note 6, p. 1233).

6. **Benjamin Constant:** Benjamin Constant de Robeque (1767–1830) was born in Lausanne, Switzerland, and emigrated to France under the Directoire. Initially a supporter of Bonaparte, he became a critic of the Empire under the influence of his lover, Madame de Staël, and both were exiled in 1803. In 1815, Napoléon asked him to draft a new constitution for the Empire as a gesture to liberals. After the Bourbons returned, his political activity was limited to the opposition press. He is best remembered today for his novel *Adolphe*, an autobiographical account of his affair with Madame de Staël.

7. **the mysterious trip from the isle of Elba to France:** The question of how Napoléon managed to escape from Elba largely undetected is still somewhat controversial.

8. **the white cockade:** A cockade was a small cloth badge worn with a military hat. The question of whether the military would wear white (Bourbon) or tricolor (associated with the Revolution) cockades was a major point of dispute as the return of the Bourbons was negotiated in 1814 and 1815. Civilian supporters of royalist and constitutionalist causes showed their politics through cockades as well. The politics of the cockade were also important in the early Revolutionary years.

9. **the amaranth strewn with bees:** Napoléon's personal heraldry, distinct from the imperial eagle. The bee was chosen as it was believed to have been a symbol of the Merovingian kings.

10. *Scabra rubigine:* i.e., a coarse rust, from Virgil's *Georgics,* a reference to what remains after a battle.

### VIII: The Emperor Puts a Question to Lacoste, the Guide

1. **Grouchy's delay:** General Emmanuel de Grouchy (1766–1847) had concentrated his forces on a wing of the Prussian army, rather than joining the main battle; this was seen as one of the reasons the close battle turned against the French.

2. **Beresina, Leipzig, and Fontainebleau:** three of the greatest disasters of Napoléon's career. At the crossing of the half-frozen Beresina River in November 1812, during the Grande Armée's retreat from Moscow, already devastated by difficult battles, lack of food, and the Russian winter, the army lost more than ten thousand men, either killed by the pursuing Cossacks or drowning in an attempt to cross the bridges hastily constructed by the French engineers. Leipzig was a catastrophic, arguably fatal, defeat for Napoléon at the hands of the allies in October 1813. Napoléon had withdrawn to Fontainebleau when the allies reached Paris in March 1814; while his emissaries were negotiating the possibility of Napoléon retaining the throne in return for abandoning conquered territories, some of his most trusted generals defected, making his abdication inevitable.

3. **the final overthrow of England . . . canceling out Agincourt:** Hugo sums up five hundred years of enmity between France and England. Edward III of England defeated Philippe VI of France at Crécy in 1346, the first major battle of the Hundred Years' War. In 1356, the Black Prince not only defeated the French but captured King Jean II at Poitiers. Malplaquet was a costly, even Pyrrhic, victory for the English and their Austrian allies over the forces of Louis XIV during the War of the Spanish Succession in 1709. The duke of Marlborough drove the French out of Belgium after the battle of Ramillies, in 1607. Napoléon, the man from Marengo, would delete the legendary English victory at Agincourt in 1415, the battle for which, according to Shakespeare, Henry V rallied his troops with his Saint Crispin's Day speech: "We few, we happy few, we band of brothers" (*Henry V,* act 4, scene 3).

### IX: The Unexpected

1. **the great redoubt of the Moskowa:** On September 7, 1812, at Borodino on the Moskowa River outside the Russian capital, 130,000 French troops attacked 135,000 Russians based in a large fortification or redoubt. The bloodiest single battle of the Napoleonic wars, one of the bloodiest in European history, it resulted in almost thirty thousand casualties for the French, fifty thousand for the Russians. After the Russian retreat, Napoléon entered Moscow.

2. **Murat was missing:** Joachim Murat (1767–1815) owed his reputation more to his reckless courage than his skill as a general. Married to Napoléon's imperious and ambitious sister Caroline, Murat was named grand duke of Berg and Cleves before taking the place of his brother-in-law Joseph on the throne of Naples. After an unsuccessful attempt to retain his throne in 1814, he rallied to Napoléon during the Hundred Days, but was prevented from reaching France by an Austrian army at Tolentino in northern Italy, on May 2. He was eventually captured and shot by forces loyal to the Bourbon king of Naples.

3. **the old Orphic sagas:** i.e., Greek mythology. Orpheus, the son of the muse Calliope, was given a lyre by Apollo and taught song and poetry to mortals.

## X: The Plateau of Mont-Saint-Jean

1. **the prince de Condé . . . Louis XVIII at Ghent:** The prince de Condé was the Bourbons' cousin; he took refuge at Malines, Belgium, while the king waited for the outcome of Waterloo at Ghent.

## XI: Bad Guide for Napoléon, Good Guide for Bülow

1. **the duc de Dalmatia:** General Nicolas-Jean de Dieu Soult (1769–1851), named marshal of the Empire in 1804 and duc de Dalmatia in 1808 (Napoléon liked to give his generals and ministers foreign titles to emphasize the breadth of his conquests and his empire). Soult was named minister of war by Louis XVIII in 1814 but rallied to Napoléon in 1815. Exiled until 1819, Soult served the government of Louis-Philippe in several capacities, including minister of war, foreign minister, and prime minister.

## XIII: The Catastrophe

1. **the Uhlans:** traditionally the Polish cavalry; both the Prussian and Austrian armies had corps of Uhlans in the nineteenth century.

2. **The Grande Armée:** a term Napoléon used inconsistently to describe his own forces from 1805, during the march toward Austerlitz, up until Waterloo.

3. *Hoc erat in fatis:* "Thus was their fate."

## XIV: The Last Square

1. **Ulm, Wagram, Jena, Friedland:** some of Napoléon's greatest military victories.

2. **Cambronne:** Pierre-Jacques-Étienne Cambronne (1770–1842) volunteered for the Revolutionary armies and rose up through the ranks through courage, talent, and his devotion to Napoléon, whom he followed to Elba in 1814 and back to France in 1815. After he had married an Englishwoman and been named a viscount by Louis XVIII, he both denied and affirmed the *mot* that had made him famous. According to his own accounts and those of eyewitnesses, he may have said, in response to calls to surrender, "The Guard dies, it does not sur-

render!" or "Bastards [*bougres*] like us don't give up!" In fact, Cambronne was forced to surrender after being seriously wounded and was taken prisoner by the English.

3. **"Shit!":** *"Merde!"*; Hugo was criticized for including this word in his novel; he defended it by pointing out that it was *"le misérable des mots."* Hugo prized the "soldierly energy" of "Shit!" to the other responses reported.

### XV: Cambronne

1. **among all these giants, there was a Titan:** i.e., one even greater than the giants. The Titans were the race of Greek gods who preceded the Olympians.

2. **round off Leonidas with Rabelais:** i.e., to end the battle with the earthy and unshakable good humor typical of the French. Leonidas was the Spartan king who led his three hundred men to certain death at Thermopylae; François Rabelais (1494–1553) was one of the greatest writers of the French Renaissance. His comic novels *Pantagruel* and *Gargantua* combine broad humor, frequently scatological and sexual, with the humanistic ideals of the Renaissance.

3. **Aeschylus:** a playwright of ancient Greece (ca. 535–456 B.C.E.), considered the father of tragedy.

4. **the way Rouget de l'Isle . . . the "Marseillaise":** Claude-Joseph Rouget de l'Isle (1760–1836) wrote the "Marseillaise" in one night, in April 1792.

5. **like Danton talking or Kléber roaring:** Danton was the great popular orator of the French Revolution. The force of his rhetoric and his popularity with the Parisian masses were such that Robespierre refused to allow him to speak in his own defense while on trial. Jean-Baptiste Kléber (1753–1800) was known for his fierceness in battle. He served under Bonaparte during the Egyptian campaign and remained behind to command the French forces when Bonaparte returned to France to arrange the coup d'état of 18 Brumaire. Kléber had negotiated the French evacuation when he was assassinated in Cairo in January 1800.

### XVI: Quot Libras in Duce?

1. ***Quot Libras in Duce?:*** "What does the chief weigh?," i.e., "What is the value of a leader?"

2. **Jomini . . . Müffling . . . Charras:** three historians of the Napoleonic era. Antoine-Henri Jomini (1779–1869) served under Ney until he was passed over for promotion by Berthier in 1813; he defected to the Russians and served as the czar's aide-de-camp. He wrote several works of military history while serving in the Russian military. Karl von Müffling was a Prussian general who served as Blücher's liaison to Wellington at Waterloo; he subsequently published an account of the battle. Charras (see note 1, ch. VI, p. 1235) was Hugo's primary source for details about Waterloo.

3. **above Blücher . . . Goethe and above Wellington . . . Byron:** Hugo, known first and foremost as a poet, firmly believed in the social value of the poet, the

prophet and priest of humanity. Left unsaid is which French poet is greater than Napoléon, the greatest general.

4. **God, who likes an antithesis:** Hugo was also fond of antitheses.

5. **the Barrême of the war . . . Michelangelo:** Barrême was a scientist, making Napoléon Bonaparte the inspired genius as opposed to the technician of war that was Wellington, the *prudhomme militaire* (see note 13, p. 1206).

6. **Beaulieu . . . Mélas:** a succession of Austrian generals defeated by Bonaparte in Italy. All of them commanded Austrian forces in the battles listed in the following note in the years before the Empire.

7. **Lodi . . . Arcola:** a string of Napoleonic victories over the Austrians in Italy: the defeat of the Austrians at Lodi in 1796; Montebello in 1800; Montenotte in 1796; Arcola outside Mantua in 1796; Marengo in 1800.

8. **another young Wurmser:** another unflattering reference to Wellington, as a member of the "military academe."

9. **Lord Bathurst:** British minister of war at the time of Waterloo.

10. **Essling and Rivoli:** two more victories. The French defeated the Austrians at Essling, just outside of Vienna in 1809; Rivoli was another defeat of the Austrians in January 1797. General Masséna, Duc de Rivoli and Prince d'Essling, played a key role in both battles.

11. **1688 and our 1789:** the two great revolutions and their consequences were often compared to each other after 1789.

12. **Bautzen:** The 1813 victory over Prussian and Russian forces was a hard-fought one for the French.

13. **Virgil before the fatal plain of Philippi:** another reference to the *Georgics.* The plain of Philippi in Greece was site of the final defeat of Brutus and Cassius by Mark Antony and Octavius in 42 B.C.E.

*XVII: Do We Have to Think Waterloo Was a Good Thing?*

1. **it is July 14, 1789, attacked via March 20, 1815:** It was on March 20 that Napoléon returned to Paris from Elba.

2. **the Brunswicks . . . the Bourbons:** the royal houses of "legitimist" Europe aligned against Bonaparte: the Brunswicks (Hanovers) of Great Britain, the Nassaus of Holland, the Romanoffs of Russia, the Hohenzollerns of Prussia, the Hapsburgs of Austria, and the Bourbons of France.

3. **Louis XVIII's granting the Charter:** Upon returning to France, Louis XVIII agreed to recognize a written constitution, known as the Charter, or Charte.

4. **Bonaparte places a coachman . . . the throne of Sweden:** The detractors of Napoléon's brother-in-law Joachim Murat, named king of Naples in 1809, claimed that he had begun as a mere groom; he was in fact a cavalry soldier. The sergeant Napoléon placed on the throne of Sweden was Jean-Jules-Baptiste Bernadotte (1763–1844), who began as a sergeant before rising to the rank of general in the Revolutionary armies; in 1810, the Swedish parliament, seeking to curry favor with Napoléon, elected him the prince-heir of the

childless Charles XIII. When the political and military tide turned against Napoléon, Bernadotte went with it. Bernadotte's descendants still hold the throne of Sweden.

5. **Louis XVIII at Saint-Ouen:** It was at Saint-Ouen, on the road from Rouen to Paris, that Louis XVIII negotiated the final details of his return to power, including official recognition of the 1790 Declaration of the Rights of Man.

6. **turn Foy . . . into an orator:** General-Comte Maximillien-Sébastien Foy (1775–1825) became one of the leaders of liberal opposition in the Chamber of Deputies after serving in the Revolutionary and imperial armies. His public funeral became a demonstration against the government of Charles X.

7. **the man who bounded over the Alps . . . doddering old invalid of father Élysée:** Napoléon's crossing of the Alps with an entire army in 1800 was part of the Napoleonic legend, immortalized in a famous painting by Jacques-Louis David. The doddering invalid refers to Louis XVIII; father Élysée was his personal physician. Besides being a gout sufferer, the king suffered from crippling obesity and generally poor health.

8. **including, they say, the baton of the maréchal de France:** The presentation of the marshal's baton, an honor reserved to the greatest defenders of the realm, to the conqueror of French armies was obviously done with as little fanfare as possible.

## XVIII: A Fresh Bout of Divine Right

1. **The Corsican became . . . the man from the Béarn:** Henri IV (born 1553, reigned 1589–1610), founder of the Bourbon dynasty, born in the Kingdom of Navarre in modern southwestern France (*le Béarnais*) was a popular figure even among the revolutionaries. In the French national imagination, the earthy warrior, noble and generous, was the embodiment of what a king should be.

2. **The flag . . . was white:** The white flag, like the white cockade, was a symbol of the Bourbon dynasty.

3. **Hartwell's:** Hartwell was the country estate in Kent, England, where Louis XVIII, known as the comte de Lille, spent the last years of his exile.

4. **People talked about Bouvines and Fontenoy:** two great military victories for ancien régime France—Bouvines in 1214, Fontenoy in 1745.

5. **Europe wore the white cockade:** I.e., Europe supported the return of the Bourbons.

6. **Trestaillon:** Jacques Dupont took the name of Trestaillon as one of the leaders of the "White Terror," a series of often bloody reprisals against revolutionaries and imperialists (and sometimes Protestants and Jews), in Nîmes; though a national phenomenon, the *Terreur blanche* was especially violent in the south (Nîmes, Avignon, and Toulouse).

7. **non pluribus impar:** "Inferior to None," the personal heraldic motto of Louis XIV, as the "sunburst" and its rays represent the Sun King.

8. **Maison Rouge:** Under the ancien régime, the company known as the Maison Rouge had been, essentially, the royal bodyguard.

9. **The arc du Carrousel . . . the duc d'Angoulême:** Napoléon had built the triumphal arch in the place du Carrousel in 1806; a statue of the duc d'Angoulême, elder son of the future Charles X and thus heir presumptive to the throne, gave the Napoleonic monument a legitimist gloss.

10. **The cemetery of the Madeleine . . . '93:** The bodies of Louis XVI and Marie Antoinette were thrown into a mass grave near the place de la Madeleine. The Restoration government went to great lengths to recover the remains of the royal martyrs.

11. **the moat of Vincennes . . . the duc d'Enghien:** Louis-Antoine-Henri de Bourbon-Condé, Duc d'Énghien, cousin of the Bourbons and prince of the blood royal, was shot in the dry moat of Vincennes castle on March 21, 1804, after having been kidnapped on German territory by Bonaparte's order. Considered an act of political terrorism by most of Europe, it was this execution that prompted the famous political aphorism, variously attributed to Talleyrand and Fouché, "It's worse than a crime, it is a mistake." Napoléon was actually crowned in December 1804, but it was in March that the Senate, under the instigation of Fouché, proposed that the consul for life be named emperor of the French.

12. **Pope Pius VII:** Elected to the papacy in 1800, Pius VII had come to France to officiate at the coronation of Napoléon, who had restored Catholicism to its official place in French society; their entente was short-lived, however; Napoléon steadily absorbed the Papal States into his Empire, and in 1809 the pope was forcibly taken from Rome to Fontainebleau as Napoléon's prisoner.

13. **in Schönbrunn Castle . . . the king of Rome:** Napoléon had named his son king of Rome almost upon his birth in 1811. In 1814, Marie-Louise took him back to her father's palace in Vienna and quickly lost interest in her and her son's claims to the imperial throne. Known in Austria as the duke of Reichstadt, Napoléon II died of tuberculosis at the age of twenty-one.

14. **Article 14:** the broadly written article of the Charter of 1814 that established the powers of the king as head of state.

15. **People's imaginations:** The Napoleonic legend never faded among many old soldiers and peasants, who saw Napoléon as the conqueror who had reestablished peace at home and glory abroad. The legend grew stronger after Bonaparte died in 1821.

16. **a Holy Alliance:** An alliance of European powers (mainly Russia, Prussia, Austria, and France) formed during the Congress of Vienna, the Holy Alliance became an expression of counterrevolutionary monarchism, its chief accomplishment being the restoration of the absolute monarchy in Spain in 1823. After the death in 1825 of Czar Alexander I of Russia, whose mystic idealism had provided the background of its founding, the Alliance ceased to function.

17. **Hudson Lowe . . . Montchenu:** At Longwood, the house on Saint Helena where he was kept prisoner, the former emperor constantly complained of the treatment he received at the hands of Sir Hudson Lowe, the British governor of the island. The Marquis de Montchenu was the French commissioner to Saint Helena.

18. **Alexander:** Czar Alexander I of Russia had been fascinated by Napoléon, and the two emperors had reached a fragile entente before the issue of Poland reignited their enmity.

19. **Bonapartist liberalism:** Many Bonapartists, whether from conviction or resentment against the Bourbons, became members of the liberal opposition. Much of this liberalism proved ephemeral when Louis-Philippe replaced the Bourbons in 1830.

20. **The Congress of Vienna:** In 1814, the powers of Europe, dominated by Great Britain, Russia, Austria, and Prussia, convened in Vienna to redraw the political map of Europe. Talleyrand had managed to negotiate relatively favorable terms for France before news of Napoléon's return reached the Congress. The post-Waterloo treaties of 1815 were much harsher for the French, including loss of territory, foreign occupation, and huge indemnities.

*XIX: The Battlefield by Night*

1. *sic vos non vobis:* an allusion to Virgil's satire of a plagiarist: "Thus you [do] not for yourself," i.e., one who takes undeserved credit.

2. **marquis de Fervacques:** The 1544 battle of Cérisoles (Ceresole Alba, in northern Italy) was a victory for the French under Francis I over the forces of Charles V Hapsburg (see note 1, ch. IV, p. 1255). The source of Hugo's anecdote about the marquis de Fervacques is unclear.

3. **Turenne . . . the Palatinate:** Henri de La Tour d'Auvergne, Vicomte de Turenne (1611–75), was one of the great French generals of the seventeenth century. His armies laid waste to the German principality of the Palatinate in 1672.

4. **Hoche and Marceau:** Louis-Lazare Hoche (1768–97) and François-Sévérin Marceau (1769–96), contemporaries of Bonaparte and, like him, wunderkind generals of the Revolutionary armies. Napoléon believed that had they lived, they might have been his rivals. Hoche died of tuberculosis, Marceau of wounds received in battle.

BOOK TWO: THE SHIP *ORION*
*I: Number 24601 Becomes Number 9430*

1. **Number 24601:** According to the Hugo legend, 24601 is a tribute to the day the great poet was conceived (June 24, 1801), on a mountaintop in the Vosges. He was born on February 26, 1802.

2. **the *Drapeau blanc:*** Hugo imitated the style of the two royalist newspapers the *Drapeau blanc* and the *Journal de Paris* in his pastiches. The *Drapeau blanc* (White Flag) was more staid than the sensationalist *Journal de Paris.*

3. **the patriarch of Ferney:** Voltaire spent much of the last half of his life on an estate at Ferney, near the Swiss border, in case prudence dictated an absence from French territory.

4. **the *Constitutionnel:*** an opposition newspaper that favored a more liberal, constitutional monarchy; sometimes considered anticlerical.

*II: In Which You Will Read Two Lines of Verse That Are Perhaps the Devil's*

1. **a bad Norman monk named Tryphon:** Tryphon, his verses, and the Montfermeil legend about the devil's treasure all seem to have been invented out of whole cloth by Hugo.
2. **Dig . . . things:** "Fodit, et in fossa thesauros condit opaca / As, nummos, lapides, cadaver, simulacra, nihilque."
3. **Roger Bacon:** The English monk, philosopher, and scientist (ca. 1215–90) was the first European to record a recipe for gunpowder.
4. **Charles VI:** or Charles the Mad, reigned from 1368 to 1422.

*III: How the Chain on the Shackles Must Have Undergone Preparatory Treatment to Be Shattered Like That with One Whack of the Hammer*

1. **"the war with Spain":** With the backing of the Holy Alliance, France sent a military force to reestablish the authority of Ferdinand VII, who had been forced by the Spanish parliament, the Cortes, to accept a liberal constitution. The French forces under the duc d'Angoulême met little resistance, as the king was more popular than the Cortes. The war was considered a "big family affair," as the Spanish Bourbons were descended from a grandson of Louis XIV.
2. **"the hero of Andujar":** The city of Andujar was the site of the treaty that put an end to the Spanish War. The treaty was not as severe as many conservatives had hoped.
3. **very real terrorism of the Holy Office:** i.e., the Spanish Inquisition.
4. ***descamisados:*** literally, "shirtless ones," i.e., the peasantry and the working class.
5. **the generalissimo son of France:** I.e., the duc d'Angoulême; the title *Fils de France* was a relic of the ancien régime.
6. **the prince de Carignan:** The Carignan family was the French branch of the royal house of Savoy, Charles-Albert took the throne in 1823; his grandson, Victor Emmanuel, was the first king of unified Italy in 1870.
7. **Koblenz:** Under the leadership of the prince de Condé and later the comte d'Artois, armies of émigrés gathered at Koblenz in 1789–92. The battle to restore divine-right monarchs was seen by many as a religious duty.
8. **the war of 1808 . . . Saragossa:** Napoléon's attempted conquest of Spain was far more difficult than Angoulême's intervention on behalf of the king. The city of Saragossa fell only after a long and bloody siege.
9. **Palafox:** José de Rebolledo Palafox y Melzi was the Spanish officer who became chief of the Spanish resistance to Napoléon; he was captured at Saragossa.
10. **Rostopchine . . . Ballesteros:** As governor of Moscow, it was Count Rostopchine who decided to burn the city rather than allow the French army to oc-

cupy and pillage it in 1812; Francisco Ballesteros had earned his military reputation in the resistance to Napoléon's occupation but quickly surrendered to the duc d'Angoulême and the Banque de France.

11. **1823 sowed the seeds of 1830:** I.e., the apparent triumph of legitimacy led to the reactionary decrees of July 1830, which would provoke the July Revolution and the final collapse of the Bourbon monarchy.

12. **de Ruyter:** Michael de Ruyter (1613–77), a Dutch admiral and naval hero.

BOOK THREE: KEEPING THE PROMISE MADE TO THE DEAD WOMAN
*I: The Issue of Water at Montfermeil*

1. **a *liard*:** an old copper coin worth less than a sou.

*II: Two Portraits Completed*

1. **the abbé Delille:** Jacques Delille (1738–1813), a poet and translator of Virgil's *Georgics*.
2. **Voltaire . . . oddly, Saint Augustine:** The abbés Raynal (1713–96) and Parny (1753–1813) were well-known figures of the Enlightenment, friends of Voltaire; Saint Augustine (354–430), of course, is the odd man out.
3. **the Champ d'Asile fund:** a fund started to support an ultimately unsuccessful colony of Napoleonic veterans in Texas.

*VI: Which Perhaps Proves Boulatruelle's Intelligence*

1. **His massive berlin:** The *berline* was a large, often open carriage, often used in public ceremonies or parades.
2. **a scholar's smile:** Witty and well-read, Louis XVIII fancied himself an intellectual.
3. **the Golden Fleece . . . wide blue sash:** The French king is adorned with the highest chivalric orders of Europe. The Golden Fleece of Spain was established by Charles V in the sixteenth century; the French order of Saint Louis by Louis XIV in 1693; the Order of the Holy Spirit (Saint-Ésprit), also French, dated from the reign of Henri III; the "blue sash" is the *cordon bleu* of the Order of the Holy Spirit.
4. **quartier Saint-Marceau:** a then working-class neighborhood in the southeastern part of the city.
5. **le duc d'Havré:** one of Louis XVIII's most trusted courtiers.
6. **Monsieur le comte d'Anglès:** See note 13, p. 1222.
7. ***The Two Convicts:*** a melodrama that in fact debuted at the Porte Saint-Martin theater in 1822.

*VIII: Unpleasantness of Putting Up a Pauper Who Might Just Be Rich*

1. **Monsieur Laffitte:** Jacques Laffitte (1767–1844), a Parisian banker who played an important role in the liberal opposition from 1815 until his death.
2. **a moujik:** a Russian peasant.
3. **the duchesse de Berry:** Marie-Caroline de Bourbon-Sicile (1798–1870), the widow of Charles X's younger son, the duc de Berry, and mother of his posthumous son, known as the duc de Bordeaux, designated even before his birth as the heir to the Bourbons. See note 35, p. 1213, and note 9, ch. IV, p. 1291.
4. **the *Courrier français*:** a liberal weekly newspaper appeared under that name from 1819 to 1821, one of several over the course of the nineteenth century.
5. **orange blossom:** French brides traditionally wear orange blossoms in their hair.

*IX: Thénardier in Operation*

1. **doors and windows:** Houses were taxed according to the number of doors and windows they had, a sort of luxury tax (see note 4, ch. IV, p. 1198).
2. **the little Prussian pigtail . . . the crown of laurel:** On louis and napoléons, see note 2, p. 1228. The Prussian pigtail designates the old-fashioned hairstyle favored by the Bourbons; the crown of laurel, the classical sign of the victor, was plainly visible in Napoléon's profile on imperial coinage.

BOOK FOUR: THE OLD GORBEAU SLUM
*I: Maître Gorbeau*

1. **La Salpêtrière . . . the barrière de l'Italie:** La Salpetrière was (and is) a large hospital located on the eastern edge of the city, on the south side of the Seine; the barrière d'Italie, roughly at the site of today's place d'Italie, marked the southeastern edge of the city.
2. **Châtelet:** Once the site of a small defensive fortress on the Right Bank, the Châtelet served as both a prison and a court of criminal law throughout the Revolutionary period. It was demolished by Napoléon's order in 1808.
3. **Two names anticipated by La Fontaine:** Jean de La Fontaine (1621–95), one of the most celebrated of French writers; his *Fables* contained brilliant social and political satire. *Le Corbeau et le renard* is one of his most famous works.
4. **Maître Corbeau . . . Hello! etc.:** "Maître Corbeau, sur un dossier perché, / Tenait dans son bec une saisie executoire; / Maître Renard, par l'odeur alléché, / Lui fit à peu près cette histoire: / Hé! bonjour! etc."
5. **Louis XV . . . Madame Du Barry:** The legendary debauchery of Louis XV (born 1710, reigned 1715–1775) was such that it is difficult to tell which stories about it are apocryphal. This anecdote, which includes royal, aristocratic, and clerical decadence, does seem too good to be true. The papal nuncio was essentially the Vatican's ambassador to the French court; the cardinal de La Roche-Aymon (1697–1777) was the archbishop of Reims and grand almoner of

France; Louis' affair with the former prostitute Jeanne Bécu, Comtesse du Barry, whose political influence was wildly exaggerated by propagandists, was the nadir of his satyric adventures.

6. **Bicêtre:** a notorious prison on what was then the southeastern boundary of Paris.

7. **"the murder of the barrière de Fontainebleau":** the barrière de Fontaine-bleau, near today's place d'Italie. In 1827, Hugo saw a young man named Ulbach executed for the murder of a young farm girl on the suburban outskirts of Paris.

8. **the mean and shameful place de Grève:** the site of public executions until 1830, today known as the place de l'Hotel de Ville, on the Right Bank.

9. **the Orléans railway station:** now the Gare d'Austerlitz.

BOOK FIVE: A MUTE PACK OF HOUNDS FOR A DIRTY HUNT
*I: The Zigzags of Strategy*

1. **the author of this book . . . has been absent from Paris:** It was in December 1851—only a few days after Louis-Napoléon Bonaparte had successfully managed a coup d'état that made him Emperor Napoléon III—that Hugo boarded a train for Brussels. He would not return to Paris until 1870, spending most of the intervening decades on the British island of Jersey. During his absence, the Second Empire, in the person of Baron Haussmann, would effect the transformations Hugo describes in this passage.

2. **Saint-Étienne-du-Mont:** a church on top of montagne Sainte-Geneviève, just behind the Panthéon.

*II: It Is a Good Thing the Austerlitz Bridge Takes Vehicles*

1. **This is . . . sells tiles:** "De Goblet fils c'est ici la fabrique; / Venez choisir des cruches et des brocs, / Des pots à fleurs, des tugaux, de la brique. / A tout venant le Cœur vend des Carreaux."

*III: See the 1727 Map of Paris*

1. **See the 1727 Map of Paris:** There is something of a wink in this chapter title as Hugo departs from his geographical realism to describe a fictional neighborhood and convent. Up until Jean Valjean and Cosette cross the Austerlitz bridge, their path follows real streets of pre-Haussmann Paris, following the western edge of the city from the barrière de Fontainebleau to the Seine. Hugo modeled the Petit-Picpus neighborhood after the faubourg Saint-Antoine and the convent after one in the faubourg Saint-Marceau. The streets surrounding the convent are likewise inventions of the author.

*X: In Which It Is Explained How Javert Came Up Empty*

1. **the triumphant entry into Bayonne:** the return of the victorious duc d'An-goulême from Spain; see note 1, ch. III, p. 1243.
2. **Seine-et-Oise:** the *département* just northwest of Paris, where Montfermeil is lo-cated.
3. **Danton . . . Arcis-sur-Aube:** Danton (see note 17, p. 1223), in the spring of 1794, did not take seriously enough the threat posed by Robespierre's consolidation of power in the Convention. By the time Danton returned from his country home to Paris, Robespierre had triumphed and Danton's fate was sealed. He was guillotined on April 5, 1794.

BOOK SIX: PETIT-PICPUS
*II: The Rule of Martin Verga*

1. **Martin Verga:** Hugo created an imaginary religious order based on the name of a fifteenth-century Spanish Cistercian, Martin de Vargas, who instigated re-forms within the order but did not found a new rule.
2. **Bernardines:** i.e., Cistercians, among the strictest of monastic orders. As Hugo explains, the monastery of Cîteaux, and thus the Cistercian order, was founded in 1098 by Saint Robert de Molesme, who wanted to reestablish strict obedi-ence to the monastic rules laid down by Saint Benedict (ca. 480–ca. 547), the founder of the Western tradition of monasticism. Robert was eclipsed by the prestige of his successor as abbot of Cîteaux, Saint Bernard (1090–1138), who founded a number of filial abbeys, most notably Clairvaux. As Hugo indicates, a number of medieval religious orders were founded as an attempt to return to the original rule of Saint Benedict.
3. **he was old and . . . hermit:** Hugo seems to be playing on the old French proverb "When the devil gets old, he'll become a monk." One of the abbeys Saint Bene-dict founded is the famous abbey of Monte Cassino, previously the site of a pagan temple dedicated to Apollo.
4. **Ladies of the Blessed Sacrament:** This was a real convent in the rue Neuve-Sainte-Geneviève, on the left bank, that Hugo had originally thought to use as Jean Valjean's retreat before deciding to invent a convent, and even a fictional order, in order to avoid offending any real religious communities.
5. **Philip di Neri . . . Pierre de Bérulle:** Philip di Neri (1515–95) was founder of the order of the Oratory in Italy. Pierre de Bérulle (1575–1629) founded the French Oratory.

*III: The Austerities*

1. **mademoiselles de Sainte-Aulaire and de Bélissen:** Sainte-Aulaire and de Bélissen were the names of well-known families of the French aristocracy, as were the Choiseuls and the Sérents, mentioned later.

2. **Talbot:** the family name of the earls of Shrewsbury, several of whom remained in the Catholic Church after the Reformation.

*IV: Fun*

1. **There . . . in prison:** "Il est arrivé un coup de bâton. / C'est Polichinelle qui l'a donné au chat. / Ça ne lui a pas fait de bien, ça lui a fait du mal. / Alors une dame a mis Polichinelle en prison."

*V: Entertainment*

1. **the *Lives of the Saints:*** Several books were devoted to the stories of Catholic saints. Hugo may refer here to Dom Mabillon's *Lives of the Benedictine Saints* (see note 1, ch. III, p. 1253) or to the *Lives of the Saints of the Order of Saint Benedict* by Marguerite de Blemeur (see note 1, p. 1249), supposed ancestress of Mother Innocent.

2. ***Nemo regulas . . . communicabit:*** "No one shall discuss our rules or our institution with outsiders."

3. **Montmorencys:** The Montmorencys claimed direct descent from one of Charlemagne's barons.

4. **Monseigneur de Quélen:** Louis-Hyancinthe de Quélen (1778–1839), archbishop of Paris from 1821 until his death.

5. **Monsieur le duc de Rohan:** Louis-François-Auguste de Rohan-Chabot (1788–1833), known as the prince de Léon before succeeding his father as duc de Rohan; one of the most elegant young men of the *grand monde,* he shocked his family and friends by entering the priesthood after the death of his young wife in 1815. He was named archbishop of Auch in 1828 and later cardinal archbishop of Besançon. He was the model for the elegant bishop of Agde in Stendhal's *The Red and the Black.* Hugo knew the ducal archbishop in the 1820s.

*VI: The Little Convent*

1. **the Ladies of Sainte-Aure:** The small community of Sainte-Aure occupied a house next to the Benedictine convent Hugo based Petit-Picpus on; it was destroyed and disbanded during the Revolution.

2. **Madame de Beaufort d'Hautpoul and Madame la marquise Dufresne:** Again Hugo has used real names in his invented convent.

3. **Madame de Genlis:** As a shocking and ostentatious gesture of modernity, the duc d'Orléans, later known as Philippe-Égalité, hired the comtesse de Genlis (1746–1830), who was also his mistress, as tutor for his children, including the future King Louis-Philippe, in the 1780s. During the Revolution, she emigrated to England, where she supported herself by writing novels. She entered her "ferociously devout phase" on returning to France in 1800. Napoléon gave her a pension and, it was widely believed, employed her as a spy among her circle of friends.

4. *Imparibus meritis . . . tua perdas:* "Three bodies of unequal merit hang from the branches; / Dismas and Gesmas and the power of the divine; / Dismas wishes to go on high; unhappy Gesmas will go below; / Let our bodies and our goods be protected by the Supreme Power. / Recite these verses so that theft shall not deprive you of what is yours."

5. **Dismas and Gestas:** According to extracanonical tradition, Dismas and Gestas were the two thieves crucified along with Jesus on the hill at Golgotha. Gestas, on Jesus's left, mocked the Son of God for not saving his own life. Dismas asked Christ for mercy and went to heaven.

6. **the vicomte de Gestas:** It would seem an odd thing to brag about, but such claims were not unheard of. An eighteenth-century duc de Lévis claimed that his family descended from the biblical Levi.

7. **the Hospitaller order:** Several orders of nuns were described as *hospitalières,* that is, dedicated to the care of the sick.

*VII: A Few Silhouettes in the Shadows*

1. **Marguerite de Blemeur:** a seventeenth-century (1618–96) nun and scholar who wrote the *Lives of the Saints of the Order of Saint Benedict.*

2. **the Dacier of the Order:** its scholar, Anne Dacier (1647–1720), was an accomplished woman of letters who translated classical authors from Sappho and Aristophanes to Plautus and Terence.

3. **Mademoiselle Gauvain . . . Mademoiselle de Siguenza:** Several of the names Hugo gives here have resonance in his own life. Gauvain, for example, was the real family name of his longtime mistress, Juliette Drouet. Cogolludo, Cifuentes, and Siguenza were fiefs granted to Hugo's father by Joseph Bonaparte in Spain; Miltière and Laudinière were properties purchased by General Hugo under the Restoration; Auverné near Nantes was the birthplace of Hugo's mother, Sophie Trébuchet.

4. **the Isle of Bourbon . . . Roze:** Réunion, in the Indian Ocean, now an overseas department (Département d'Outre-Mer, DOM) of France. The chevalier Roze was Nicolas Roger Roze (1675–1733), who worked heroically to alleviate the conditions in Marseilles during the plague of 1720.

*VIII: Post Corda Lapides*

1. *Post corda lapides:* "After the hearts, the stones."

2. **a *jeu de paume* . . . "eleven thousand devils":** The *jeu de paume* (predecessor of the tennis court) was another landmark on the left bank near the convent of the rue Neuve-Sainte-Geneviève.

*IX: A Century Under a Wimple*

1. **the abbey of Fontevrault:** sometimes Fontevraud, an unusual abbey that was both a monastery and a nunnery. The Plantagenets supported the abbey, and several members of the family—Henry II, Eleanor of Aquitaine, and Richard the Lion-Hearted—are buried there. It was turned into a prison in 1804.

2. **Monsieur de Miromesnil:** Armand-Thomas Hue de Miromesnil (1723–96), keeper of the seals for most of the reign of Louis XVI (1774–87).

3. **the Bernardines were right up there:** a reference to the great age of libertinage in the eighteenth century; the implication is that Bernardine monks of aristocratic origin were as elegant and worldly as young officers of the musketeers. While the *abbé mondain* is a common literary and historical figure of the Enlightenment, it is unusual to see monks described in this way.

4. **giving Molière an idea:** It is not clear what play Hugo might be referring to, but farces about lovers' misunderstandings are not unusual in Molière's work.

## X: Origins of Perpetual Adoration

1. **In 1649, the Blessed Sacrament . . . with this pious aim:** Hugo seems to have invented the incident involving the desecration of the Eucharist, but he has once again used real people in his fictional creation. Catherine de Bar (1614–98), known as Mother Mechthilde du Saint-Sacrement, was a well known, influential abbess in the seventeenth century. She did in fact found a convent dedicated to the adoration of the Blessed Sacrament, in the rue du Bac, in 1653. The comtesse de Châteauvieux was a friend and supporter of Mother Mechthilde.

## XI: End of the Petit-Picpus

1. *Volaverunt:* "They have flown away."

2. **Julia Alpinula:** the inscription of a tombstone found in a Roman excavation in Switzerland: "Here I lie, I lived for twenty-three years."

3. **Joseph de Maistre . . . Voltaire:** Joseph de Maistre (see note 7, p. 1198) was as devoted to orthodox Catholicism as he was to absolute monarchy; Voltaire's hostility to the Catholic Church was legendary.

4. **Calas:** The *affaire Calas* was a criminal trial in which a Protestant, Jean Calas, was convicted of the murder of his son in spite of inconclusive evidence. In Toulouse, where relations between Catholics and Protestants remained hostile well into the nineteenth century, Calas was suspected of having wanted to stop his son from converting to Catholicism. Calas was executed in 1762, but Voltaire was able to have his conviction posthumously overturned three years later.

BOOK SEVEN: A PARENTHESIS

1. **A Parenthesis:** Yves Gohin notes that Hugo's Belgian publisher, Lacroix, asked him to delete this section from the novel, which was growing to an alarming length. Hugo at first agreed, then protested, "I cannot introduce a convent into *Les Misérables* only to praise it. There must be some reservations."

## I: The Convent as an Abstract Idea

1. **the infinite:** The idea of the infinite, *l'infini*—the limitless nature of the sky, the ocean, God, love, hate, the natural world—fascinated the Romantics.

2. **a hideous side ... and a sublime side:** an apparent allusion to Hugo's theory of the *grotesque*, his fascination with the duality of *laideur* (ugliness) and *beauté* in a single person, feeling, or entity. Hugo elaborated on his idea of the *grotesque* in the preface to his play *Cromwell;* the play is in fact remembered because of the preface. The best-known example is probably Quasimodo of *Notre-Dame de Paris,* whose hideous physical appearance hides the sublime and infinite love he bears for Esmeralda. See also page 423, where the image of the bleeding Christ is described as "hideous and magnificent."

## II: The Convent as Historical Fact

1. **what mistletoe is to oak:** Mistletoe is a parasite on oak.
2. **seraphim:** the highest order of angels, who live in the presence of God.
3. **a whiff of the East:** French and European writers of the Romantic era, indeed the entire nineteenth century, were fascinated by the "Orient." The references in this paragraph to the aga khan of heaven, the seraglio (the harem), the odalisque, and the eunuch are all manifestations of this exotic imagining of the East.
4. **aga khan of heaven:** The aga khan was the ruler of the Ismalian sect of Muslims; here the reference is more vaguely meant to indicate a Muslim equivalent of an archbishop.
5. **seraglio:** In the harem, or seraglio, the odalisques (concubines) of the sultan were guarded by eunuchs.
6. **The *in pace* replaced the leather bag:** The *in pace* is a cell used as a means of discipline in convents. The "leather bag" refers to the legendary means of execution favored by Ottoman sultans, in this case for adulterous wives or insolent concubines: The victim was sewn into a leather bag and thrown, alive, into the waters of the Bosporus.
7. **Jean-Jacques:** Rousseau's last name was not necessary, especially for those who saw him as a virtual prophet, as did many Romantics.
8. **Diderot:** Denis Diderot (see note 4, ch. VIII, p. 1200), with Voltaire and Rousseau, is considered the greatest of the *philosophes.* He is best known for directing and editing the *Encyclopédie* and writing novels such as *Jacques the Fatalist and His Master, Rameau's Nephew,* and the scandalous, posthumously published *The Nun.*
9. **Voltaire on Calas, Labarre, and Sirven:** As in the *affaire Calas* (see page 421), Jacques de Labarre and the Protestant Sirvens were convicted of crimes before Voltaire took up their cause. At the age of sixteen, the chevalier de Labarre (1746–66) was accused of blasphemy for the desecration of a statue of the Virgin Mary. He was condemned to have his hand cut off and his tongue cut out before being burned at the stake; on appeal the sentence was reduced to simple decapitation. Voltaire (among others) fought in vain to stop his execution, which was the last for a charge of blasphemy under the ancien régime. The Sirvens, husband and wife, were accused of murdering their daughter in order to prevent her from converting to Catholicism. In this case, the couple fled to Switzerland before being arrested and were condemned to death in absentia. Voltaire succeeded in his efforts to have their sentence overturned.

10. **Tacitus, too ... "that poor Holofernes":** The works of the Roman senator and historian Tacitus (ca. 56–117) chronicled the lives of five Caesars, including Nero. In the book of Judith, in the Catholic Old Testament (excluded by the Protestant and Jewish canons), Holofernes was the Assyrian general sent by Nebuchadnezzar to subdue the rebellious Jerusalem. As his armies starved the city by siege, the beautiful and pious widow Judith made her way to his tent, seduced him, and gave him wine until he fell asleep, at which point she cut off his head, which she carried back to Jerusalem in triumph. The story of Judith and Holofernes inspired painters from Rembrandt to Klimt and several operas.

11. *oubliettes:* these cells evocatively derive their name from the French verb *oublier,* "to forget."

### III: On What Conditions We Can Respect the Past

1. **put the handles back on the aspersoria and the sabers:** Aspersoria are vessels made to carry holy water. Paired with sabers, the image suggests forced conversions to Christianity in early medieval Europe.

2. **Haruspices:** Haruspices were Etruscan, and later, Roman, priests who specialized in reading the entrails of sacrificed animals.

3. *Bos cretatus:* a reference to the satires of Juvenal, in which the author mocks the superficial religious practices of his contemporaries. If a white bull was required for sacrifice but unavailable, a bull of some other color was simply whitened with chalk.

4. **the city of 1789, of 1830, of 1848:** the French revolutions that toppled, respectively, Louis XVI and the ancien régime, Charles X and the Charter of 1815, and finally Louis-Philippe and the July Monarchy.

5. **fakirs, bonzes ... talapoins, and dervishes:** Muslim, Hindu, and Eastern Orthodox clerics are lumped together in a scornful comparison to those living in Catholic cloisters.

### VI: Absolute Goodness of Prayer

1. **Marcus Aurelius:** (121–180) Roman emperor (from 161 until his death) and stoic philosopher, author of the *Meditations.*

2. **lyceum:** Aristotle's school in Athens. The French word *lycée,* secondary school, is derived from "lyceum."

### VII: Precautions to Take in Laying Blame

1. **Caiaphas as bishop ... Tiberius as emperor:** Caiaphus was the high priest of Jerusalem at the time of Christ's trial; he continued to persecute early Christians after the Crucifixion. Draco, the Athenian ruler (seventh century B.C.E.), is remembered as the creator of unreasonably harsh laws. The adjective draconian derives from his name. Trimalcion was from the *Satyricon* of the first-

century Roman author Petronius; Trimalcion, or Trimalchio, is a pompous nouveau riche Roman who flaunts his wealth and his shallow understanding of literature and philosophy. Trimalcion as "lawmaker" or legislator recalls the senator of Part One, and would have had great resonance for readers of France under the July Monarchy and the Second Empire. Tiberius (42 B.C.E.–A.D. 37) succeeded Caesar Augustus as Roman emperor (14–37). His reign was marked by the execution of political enemies and legendary debauchery on the island of Capri.

2. **Cenobitism:** i.e., those living in cloistered religious communities.

*VIII: Faith, Law*

1. **Thales:** Thales of Miletus (ca. 624–546 B.C.E.); a pre-Socratic philospher regarded as the founder of the Greek schools of philosophy and science.

2. **The abbé of La Trappe . . . Horace's lines with him:** the abbey of La Trappe became famous for its strict of observance of the Cistercian rule. A philosophical fatalism unites the austere monk of La Trappe with the poet of first-century Rome.

3. **Leibniz at prayer . . . Voltaire at worship:** The German mathematician and philosopher Gottfried Leibniz (1646–1716) was a rationalist and firm believer in God. In *Candide* (1756), Voltaire made Dr. Pangloss the satirically reductive voice of Leibniz's philosophical optimism in "this the best of all possible worlds." The deist Voltaire believed in the "watchmaker god" who had created a brilliant machine but was indifferent to its operations, including prayer.

4. *Deo erexit Voltaire:* "A monument to God, erected by Voltaire," the inscription on the church Voltaire had built in the village of Ferney (see note 3, ch. I, p. 1242). Whatever his hostility to politicized religious institutions such as the Catholic Church (the object of his legendary motto *"Écrasez l'Infame,"* "Crush the Infamous One"), he believed that religion was necessary to provide moral guidance to the masses. He also promoted such cottage industries as pottery and watch-making in Ferney, as work was also necessary to social order. It is worth noting that Voltaire's church is dedicated to God, not to any religion or saint.

BOOK EIGHT: CEMETERIES TAKE WHAT THEY ARE GIVEN
*I: In Which the Way to Enter a Convent Is Dealt With*

1. **a *tabellion:*** A *tabellion* was a sort of copy clerk who made and preserved copies of important legal documents for attorneys. Fauchelevent's oft-referenced illiteracy should be understood as ignorance rather than an inability to read; he was unlettered rather than illiterate.

*III: Mother Innocent*

1. **"Dom Mabillon" . . . "Me neither":** Dom Mabillon (1623–1707), a Benedictine monk and scholar, author of *The Lives of the Benedictine Saints.* We will not fol-

low Mother Innocent through all twists and turns of her erudition, which, though Hugo gently mocks it, was his own as well. Yves Gohin attributes this scene to Hugo's love of reading dictionaries, in this case Louis Moreri's *Catholic Encyclopedia,* first published in 1649. Several of the authorities and examples Mother Innocent cites are erroneous or simply inventions of Hugo's. Old man Fauchelevent's uncomprehending goodwill ("Me neither") toward Merlonus Horstius confirms Hugo's lighthearted touch in this scene, in which one can see the hand of Hugo the playwright.

2. **"a Jansenist, Madame de Béthune"**: The ducal Béthune family descended from the family of Sully, the great minister of Henri IV. The Jansenists were Catholic reformers who believed in austerity and predestination. The movement was ferociously opposed by the Vatican, the powerful Jesuits, and Louis XIV. Largely stamped out in the early eighteenth century, Jansenism continued to trouble the religious and political establishment for many years.

3. *"Hanc igitur oblationem"*: "With this sacrifice." In the Catholic Church, these words begin the prayer with which the officiant presents the host, the body of Christ.

4. **"the emp—Buonaparte"**: Father Fauchelevent is careful to use the appropriate language to describe the usurper.

5. *"Stat crux dum volvitur orbis"*: "The cross remains standing as the world turns."

6. **"he brought down Abelard at the Council of Sens"**: In a celebrated theological quarrel, the scholar and theologian Pierre Abelard (1079–1142), best remembered as the lover of Héloïse, debated the more orthodox Bernard of Clairvaux before a Church tribunal at Sens. The council ruled in favor of Bernard and condemned Abelard as a heretic.

7. **"King Louis the Young"**: i.e., Louis VII, born 1120, reigned 1137–1180.

8. **"Eugenius III"**: pope from 1145 to 1153, he gave the Knights Templar—i.e., the Temple—an official status in the Church and sponsored the Second Crusade.

9. **"Monte Cassino"**: the site of Saint Benedict's first abbey; see note 3, p. 1247.

10. **"the Basil of the West"**: Basil of Caesarea, or Saint Basil the Great (ca. 330–79), one of the fathers of the Eastern and Roman churches.

11. **"the Huguenot king Henri IV"**: Mother Innocent, after more than two hundred years, seems suspicious of the sincerity of Henri IV's conversion (see note 8, p. 1208). Henri's confessor, Father Coton, persuaded the earthy Béarnais to refrain from using blasphemous expletives, at least in the priest's presence.

12. **"Martin of Tours"**: Saint Martin of Tours (ca. 316–97), the first Christian bishop of Tours and an influential figure in the early Church. While serving as an officer in the Roman cavalry, Martin came upon a beggar shivering in the cold. He cut his cloak in half and gave half to the beggar. That night he had a dream of Jesus wearing his cloak, and when he awoke his cloak was whole again. Martin declared himself a soldier of Christ, quit the army, and took holy orders.

*IV: In Which Jean Valjean Looks as Though He Has Read Austin Castillejo*

1. **If the monk Austin Castillejo . . . get her out again:** At the height of his power, Charles V (1500–58), Holy Roman Emperor (1530–58) and King of Spain (1516–56), controlled Austria and much of Germany, the Low Countries, the Franche-Comté, much of Italy, and the Spanish possessions in the Americas. After his abdication in 1556 due to ill health—his Spanish possessions went to his son, Philip II of Spain, his German titles to his brother—Charles lived at the Spanish monastery of San Yuste, near Extremadura, Spain. The anecdote about a mistress named La Plombes, as well as its source, Austin Castillejo, are inventions of Hugo.

*V: It's Not Enough to Be a Drunk to Be Immortal*

1. **the dome of the Invalides:** i.e., the golden dome of the Hôtel des Invalides.
2. **Montparnasse Cemetery:** a small cemetery near today's Montparnasse train station, much smaller than the sprawling Père-Lachaise on the eastern edge of the city.
3. **"For the philosophers . . . the Supreme Being":** The deist *philosophes* described God in non-Christian terms, as did Robespierre, who invented the cult of the Supreme Being, l'Être suprême, to combat the atheism of certain revolutionaries while remaining distinct from the Catholic Church.
4. **"You're a peasant, I'm a Parisian":** In French, especially in the nineteenth century, *peasant* (*paysan*) had less of a class connotation than simply meaning someone from the country, though the Parisian gravedigger is certainly supercilious.
5. **"a porter at the Prytanée":** A Jesuit college in the town of La Flèche from 1604, the Prytanée school became a military school in 1762, was closed during the Revolution and reopened by Napoléon. The gravedigger's father must have been an ambitious doorman to have had money to lose in the stock market.
6. **"cooks in the Croix-Rouge":** i.e., the servants of the neighborhood known as the Croix-Rouge, just west of the church of Saint-Sulpice.

*VI: Between Four Planks*

1. **"*Qui dormiunt . . . semper*":** the call of the priest and the response of the altar boy constituting the Latin burial rite of the Catholic Church: "Those who sleep in the dirt shall awaken, some in eternal life, some in shame that they shall see forever."
2. **"*De profundis*":** "From the depths," Psalm 130: "From the depths I cried out to you, O Lord."
3. **"*Requiem . . . Domine*":** "Give him eternal rest, O Lord."
4. **"*Et lux . . . ei*":** "And let an eternal light illuminate him."
5. **"*Requiescat in pace*":** "Rest in peace."

*VIII: A Successful Interrogation*

1. **Monsieur de Latil . . . brother to the king:** Before his brother Louis XVIII died, making him Charles X, the Comte d'Artois was known as "Monsieur," according to the Bourbon tradition. As his confessor, Jean-Baptiste de Latil (1761–1839) was promoted by the new king to the archbishopric of Rheims just in time to officiate at the coronation.
2. **Leo XII:** Annibale della Genga succeeded Pius VII as pope in 1823.

*IX: Enclosure*

1. **royalist paper money of '93:** Antirevolutionary activity was particularly strong in the west of France, in Bretagne and the Vendée region, which gave the its name to the movement and its military forces, the Vendéens, or, as they called themselves, l'Armée Catholique et Royale de la France. Jean Nicolas Stofflet (1753–96), one of the leaders of the Vendéen movement, was captured and shot by government troops in 1796.

2.

| × | × | × | × | *Armée Catholique* | × | × | × | × |
|---|---|---|---|---|---|---|---|---|
| × | | | | | | | | × |
| × | | | *De par la Roi* | | | | | × |
| × | | | *Bon commercable de* dix LIVRES | | | | | × |
| × | | | *pour objets fournis à l'armée* | | | | | × |
| | | | rembousable à la paix. | | | | | |
| × | | | Série 3.      *     No. 103090 | | | | | × |
| | | | *   * | | | | | |
| × | | | *Stofflet.* | | | | | × |
| × | × | × | × | *et Royale* | × | × | × | × |

3. **assignat from La Vendée:** The Vendéens issued assignats, paper money, in imitation of the Revolutionary government. Revolutionary assignats devalued quickly and those of the Vendée even faster.
4. **the Chouan party:** Allies of the Vendéens, the Chouan rebels took their name from the word for *owl* in the Breton dialect. Beginning in 1791, Chouan insurgents began a guerrilla war against the government. They outlasted the Vendéens, making a last effort at insurrection as late as 1799. Hugo's last novel, *Ninety-three*, tells the story of a Chouan faction at war with the armies of the Convention.
5. **lacerated by discipline:** i.e., by the scourge with which certain religious practiced self-mortification.

PART THREE: MARIUS

BOOK ONE: PARIS STUDIED DOWN TO ITS MINUTEST ATOM
*I: Parvulus*

1. *Parvulus:* Latin for child.
2. *Homuncio:* little man. Plautus was a Roman playwright of the third century B.C.E. whose comedies are a frequent point of reference in *Les Misérables* (see especially page 487 and note 3, ch. X, pp. 1260–61).

*II: A Few of His Distinguishing Marks*

1. **dwarf:** In royal and princely courts of the Middle Ages and Renaissance, dwarves were frequently employed as fools or jesters and, according to classical tradition, used their status to point out the foibles of the mighty, as with Shakespeare's fool in *King Lear.* The dwarf-jester Triboulet is the protagonist of Hugo's play *Le Roi s'amuse* (The King Takes His Pleasure), which inspired Verdi's *Rigoletto.*
2. **cherub of the gutter:** For French readers, especially in Hugo's time, cherub, *chérubin,* had a double meaning: not only the Cupid-like angel but also the insolent, Puck-like character in Beaumarchais' *Mariage de Figaro.*
3. **fiacres:** one-horse hansom cabs that took their name from the place Saint-Fiacre, thought to be the place where the first carriages for hire were found.
4. **his fabulous monster:** According to Yves Gohin, this monster is a memory of Hugo's childhood, when he and his brother Eugène would frighten each other with tales of a monster who lived in the well of their house.
5. **Talleyrand:** The celebrated diplomat (see note 13, p. 1211) was as well known for his sharp wit in society as for his unscrupulous survival skills in politics.

*III: He Is Nice*

1. **Mademoiselle Mars:** See note 37, p. 1214.
2. *De Profundis* **to carnival numbers:** i.e., from religious hymns to bawdy ditties. Carnival, culminating in Mardi Gras, was celebrated with much more fervor in the nineteenth century, just as Lent was observed more scrupulously.
3. **Rabelais:** See note 2, ch. XV, p. 1238.
4. **Adamastor:** a monster imagined by the sixteenth-century Portuguese poet Luíz Vaz de Camões as a metaphor for the dangers of seafaring.

*IV: He Can Be Useful*

1. **Prudhomme and Fouillou:** not specific people but personifications of two types: Prudhomme, from "prudent man" (see note 13, p. 1206), the cautious, complacent, and self-satisfied man so typical of the French bourgeoisie of the July Monarchy and the Second Empire, and Fouillou, from the verb *fouiller,* "to

search" or "to dig," the resourceful and self-reliant—sometimes slippery—type, like Figaro.

2. **an Ionian or a Boeotian:** The Ionians, in modern-day Turkey, and the Boeotians (i.e., the Thebans) revolted against the Persian Empire in the fifth and fourth centuries B.C.E.

## V: His Boundaries

1. ***Urbis amator . . .* like Flaccus:** *urbis amator,* one who loves the city; *ruris amator,* one who loves the country. An allusion to the Epistles of Horace, specifically a letter the poet (Quintus Horatius Flaccus) wrote to a friend, Fuscus, in Rome.

2. **Glacière, Cunette . . . the Pierre-Plate de Châtillon:** As with the list of suburban villages at the end of the chapter, many of these sites can still be seen on a map of Paris and its outskirts. Of special note is the "hideous Grenelle wall riddled with bullet holes." The *mur de Grenelle*—a since-demolished vestige of the medieval defensive wall—was the site of military executions by firing squad. Besides Hugo's lifelong abhorrence of the death penalty, this was the site and method of execution of General Lahorie, Hugo's godfather and his mother's lover, convicted of plotting against Napoléon in 1812.

3. **Ivry, Gentilly . . . Gonesse:** Many of these suburbs have since been absorbed into the municipality of Paris itself.

## VI: A Bit of History

1. **"the swallows of the pont d'Arcole":** a real group of homeless children who lived under the bridge and foraged through Paris like Fagin's gang in the 1850s.

2. **Louis XIV . . . naval fleet:** The Sun King wanted a fleet to compete with the trading and exploration of the Spanish, Dutch, and English; his great minister Jean-Baptiste Colbert (1619–83) built it for him.

3. **intendants and the parliaments:** the royal administrators and law courts of the various provinces and cities of France.

4. **Barbier:** Edmond-Jean-François Barbier (1689–1771), a Parisian lawyer and diarist whose *Journal* bears witness to Parisian life for almost fifty years, from 1718 to 1763.

## VII: The Gamin Would Have His Place in the Caste System of India

1. **a little work entitled *Claude Gueux:*** *Claude Gueux* was in fact an 1834 novel by Hugo himself. He had already used the word *gamin* in *Notre-Dame de Paris;* it is quite possible he forgot in the thirty-year interval between that novel and *Les Misérables.*

2. **No festival comes near La Grève:** Executions were performed in the place de Grève until 1830.

3. **Sanson and the abbé Montès:** The Sanson family were the chief executioners in Paris from 1688 to 1847, the office passing from father to son. The abbé

Montès was the chief almoner for the prisons of Paris under the Restoration and the July Monarchy.

4. **Lacenaire . . . Debacker:** Like the rest of the criminals named in this chapter, Lacenaire was a real person. Pierre François Lacenaire (1803–36) was the well-educated son of a prosperous merchant in Lyon; arrested for two murders—and a third that he had attempted—Lacenaire managed to make himself a celebrity in prison, writing poetry and his memoirs before his execution was carried out. Hugo would have been thirteen when he saw Dautun executed for the murder of his brother in 1816 (see note 17, p. 1212). Papavoine was executed for murdering two children in the Bois de Vincennes. Tolleron was one of those executed in an 1816 plot to blow up the Tuileries Palace. Avril was Lacenaire's friend and accomplice. Louvel assassinated the duc de Berry in 1820 (see note 35, p. 1213). Delaporte was a highwayman executed in 1824; Castaing (1793–1824) murdered two of his friends in order to inherit their fortunes. Bories was one of four soldiers condemned to death for plotting a republican coup in the plot of the "Sergents de Rochelle." Jean-Martin is a mistaken reference to Paul-Louis Martin, who was beheaded for murdering his father in 1820. Madame Lecouffé pushed her son to murder an old lady so that they could rob her. Castaing, Bories, Martin, Dautun, and Papavoine were mentioned in Hugo's *Last Day of a Condemned Man.* The details of the criminal named Debacker are elusive.

5. **To be left-handed:** According to an old European superstition, the left hand was associated with the devil, the right with God.

*VIII: In Which You Will Read a Delightful Saying of the King's*

1. **the boats of washerwomen:** Laundresses worked on rafts anchored on the Seine, to take advantage of the flowing water.

2. **Eleusinian lamentations of the Panathenaea:** The Panathenaea was a festival in ancient Athens that included song and poetry contests and, every fourth year, competitive games. The Eleusinians were associated with the cult of Demeter and Persephone. *Evoe* was an invocation to the wine god Bacchus, used in orgies and celebrations.

3. **From 1815 to 1830 . . . pears on walls:** The turkeys are caricatures of the Bourbons Louis XVIII and Charles X, while Louis-Philippe was mocked for his pear-shaped head.

4. **a gold louis . . . "The pear's on that, too":** i.e., the royal profile on the twenty-franc coin.

5. **curés:** literally curates, but used as a catchall term for priests.

6. **rue de l'Université:** one of the main streets of the elegant faubourg Saint-Germain.

7. **Tantalus:** See note 19, p. 1204.

8. **the Pont-Neuf:** the oldest existing bridge in Paris, on the western tip of the Île de la Cité.

## IX: The Old Soul of Gaul

1. **Poquelin, son of Les Halles:** Jean-Baptiste Poquelin, known as Molière (see note 2, p. 1222), was the son of a prosperous upholsterer in the commercial district around Les Halles; he was baptized in the Saint-Eustache church, with the young king Louis XIV as his godfather.

2. **Beaumarchais:** Pierre-Caron de Beaumarchais (1732–99) was both the creator and alter ego of Figaro, the hero of *The Barber of Seville* and *The Marriage of Figaro*.

3. **Camille Desmoulins:** Beginning his career with public harangues in the garden of the Palais-Royal, Desmoulins (1760–94) became one of the most ardent revolutionaries, serving as Danton's secretary in the first republican government in 1792. Desmoulins was appalled by the excesses of the Terror and became a critic of Robespierre, which proved fatal. He was guillotined along with Danton in April 1794.

4. **Championnet:** Jean-Étienne Championnet (1762–1800) rose from simple soldier to general in less than ten years. "Flooded the porticoes" of churches is Hugo's insolent—*gaminesque*—allusion to a verse of Racine's *Athalie,* in which the phrase is used, obviously in a quite different sense. As commander of the army that took Naples in 1798, Championnet persuaded the archbishop to celebrate the miracle of Saint Januarius (San Gennaro), in which the prelate holds up a vial of the saint's dried blood and declares that it has turned back to liquid.

5. **the Theban boy:** an apparent reference to Hercules, whose mother was the wife of the king of Thebes and who killed the Nemean lion as a youth and wore the skin as a trophy for the rest of his life.

6. **the drummer Barra:** Joseph Barra or Bara (1780–93), a legendary martyr of the Republic, was killed by Chouan troops in 1793 after he refused to say "Vive le roi" and instead cried out "Vive la République!" Robespierre quickly adopted the boy's death as a symbol of republican devotion and royalist brutality.

7. **the warhorse in the Scriptures:** Job 39:19–22: "Do you give the horse his strength and endow his neck with splendor? . . . He laughs at fear."

## X: Ecce Paris, Ecce Homo

1. *Ecce Paris, Ecce Homo:* "Behold Paris, Behold the Man"; an echo of John 19:5: "And Pilate said unto them, Behold the man!"

2. *graeculus* **of Rome:** *graeculus* means "little Greek."

3. **Paris has its Capitol . . . the Panthéon:** Hugo believed that Paris was the heir to Rome, as Rome had been heir to Athens, the center of the civilized world. His comparison begins at the top of the political and social order, by directly comparing the symbols of the government (the Capitol and the Hôtel de Ville), of religion (the Parthenon and Notre-Dame), etc. The Sorbonne is apparently set apart for satire, as an Asinarium, or donkey shed, the "house of asses." Hugo descends from the highest to the lowest aspects of Parisian society and com-

pares the city to the Rome he knew from his readings of classical texts, especially Plautus, whose comedies provide many of the characters in Hugo's long comparison. Only those citations that have some broader echo in *Les Misérables* or Hugo's life and work are explained here.

4. **Rameau's nephew and Curculion the parasite:** In Diderot's novel *Le Neveu de Rameau*, the nephew of the great eighteenth-century composer is presented as a philosophical observer of French society as he survives on the invitations and sometimes reluctant generosity of friends and acquaintants. Curculion the Parasite is a Roman social type from Plautus.

5. **Café Anglais:** in the boulevard des Italiens, a center of fashionable nightlife for most of the nineteenth century.

6. *Quis ... pallio:* From Plautus' play *Epidicus:* "Who stops me in my path, taking me by the cloak."

7. **Mademoiselle Lenormand:** Marie Anne Adelaide Lenormand (1772–1843) was a famous fortune-teller in Paris.

8. **séances:** Fascinated by the supernatural (and haunted by the death of his favorite daughter, Léopoldine, in 1843), Hugo participated in séances at Hauteville House in Jersey.

9. **puts a grisette on the throne:** a reference to Madame du Barry, who was a prostitute before being elevated to the rank of royal mistress.

10. **Messalina:** The legendary sexual appetites and adventures of Claudius' empress fascinated Hugo, among others.

11. *Contra ... oblivisci:* "Against the Gracchi, we have the Tiber. To drink from the Tiber is to forget sedition."

12. **Tartuffe's posturing ... Priapus' "hiccups":** Tartuffe, the sanctimonious hypocrite who lusts for his benefactor's wife, was one of Molière's most enduring characters; Priapus, the Greco-Roman god of male fertility, often incarnated male lustiness in popular Roman literature and theater.

13. **David d'Angers, Balzac, and Charlet:** The sculptor David d'Angers, the novelist Honoré de Balzac, and the painter and engraver Nicolas-Toussaint Charlet all used contemporary Paris and Parisians as the subjects of their work. Hugo delivered Balzac's eulogy at the Père-Lachaise cemetery in 1850.

## XI: Railing, Reigning

1. **"To please you, O Athenians!" cried Alexander:** The source of this quote, apparently referring to the Macedonian Alexander's conquest of Athens, is unclear.

2. **the Tennis Court Oath:** the celebrated moment of June 20, 1789, when the deputies of the Third Estate declared themselves the representatives of the French nation and vowed that they would not disband until they had established a constitution for France. Within a few days, Louis XVI recognized the former Estates General, with its divisions of the nobility, the clergy, and the common people, as the National Assembly. The ancien régime was legally a thing of the past.

3. **night of August 4:** a dramatic session of the National Assembly on August 4, 1789, when the deputies abolished all fiscal and social privileges of the nobility.

4. **Washington . . . Garibaldi:** From George Washington to Giuseppe Garibaldi, who as Hugo wrote was working to unify Italy, these men were heros of nineteenth-century liberalism: Tadeusz Kościuszko (1746–1817) fought in the American Revolution before returning to his native Poland to lead an unsuccessful revolt against Russian rule; Kościuszko died in exile. Simon Bolívar was the great hero of South American independence from Spain. Markos Botzaris (1788–1823) was a leader of the Greek revolt against Ottoman rule. Rafael del Riego (1784–1823) was a leader of the liberal revolt against the king of Spain in 1822. Manin (1804–57) was a leader of the Risorgimento and early advocate of Italian nationalism. Carlos Antonio López (1796–1867) was the first president of Paraguay. Hugo considered the Abolitionist John Brown a hero and martyr. The persons and places named in these passages relate to the movements for independence and liberalism, often republicanism, in Europe (Greece, Italy, Spain, and Hungary) and across South America in the nineteenth century.

5. **Boston in 1779 . . . Palermo in 1860:** Just as Boston is the cradle of American liberty, the other cities and sites named represent republican and independence movements across Europe in the nineteenth century. "Pest in 1848" refers to the Hungarian uprising against the Hapsburgs. The island of St. Léon was a stronghold for the liberal Spanish insurgents in 1820. In Palermo in 1860, Giuseppe Garibaldi led an uprising against the reactionary Bourbon rulers of the Kingdom of the Two Sicilies.

6. **Byron dies at Missolonghi:** Lord Byron traveled to Greece in 1824 to join the fight for independence, but died of a fever and subsequent bleedings before he could join in combat.

7. **Mazet dies in Barcelona:** Dr. Mazet was one of a group of French physicians who traveled to Barcelona in 1821 in order to study and help fight an epidemic of yellow fever; Mazet died after contracting the disease himself. Hugo's 1822 poem "Le Dévouement" was inspired by Mazet and the other members of the humanitarian expedition.

8. **Mirabeau's feet . . . Robespierre:** After a decidedly ambiguous early life, Honoré-Gabriel Riqueti, comte de Mirabeau, became one of the heroes of the Revolution due to his powerful speeches to the National Assembly. Robespierre was doomed when he became tyrant in the name of republicanism.

9. **Pascal . . . Molière:** In Hugo's view, the poets, writers, and thinkers who sought to enlighten (see p. 486) their readers were the true priests of humanity.

10. **Bouginier's nose . . . *Crédéville is a thief:*** two popular instances of Parisian graffiti that took on lives of their own as the French traveled through Europe. Legend has it that *"Crédéville voleur"* is in fact written at the top of an Egyptian pyramid.

11. **Montesquieu . . . Danton:** A chronological list of the writers who over the course of the eighteenth century made it possible for Danton to act on his daring. Montesquieu's (1689–1755) *L'Esprit des lois* (On the Spirit of Laws) is one

of the founding documents of the Enlightenment and of modern political science. The mathematician marquis de Condorcet (1749–94), called the last of the *philosophes*, joined the (relatively) moderate Girondin faction in the Convention. Arouet is Voltaire's real name.

12. **"Daring!" is a *fiat lux*:** Danton rallied the Convention and the Parisian populace to a war footing in 1792, as German and French royalist troops prepared to cross the Rhine, with a passionate speech calling for courageous daring: *"De l'audace, encore de l'audace et toujours de l'audace!" Fiat lux* refers to the first chapter of Genesis: "Let there be light!"

13. **the torch of Prometheus to Cambronne's stunted pipe:** Prometheus brought fire, and thus light (enlightenment), to mortals; in Hugo's view, Cambronne's refusal to surrender (*"Merde!"*) was a stand against the governments represented by the armies in the field.

## XII: *The Future Latent in the People*

1. ***Fex urbis*, cries Cicero:** i.e., the dregs of the city.
2. ***mob*, adds Burke:** The conservative, traditionalist Edmund Burke supported American independence but was resolutely hostile to the French Revolution.

## XIII: *Petit-Gavroche*

1. **About eight or nine years:** thus, in 1831 or 1832. The July Revolution has in the interim deposed the Bourbons in favor of a new government and new constitution under Louis-Philippe d'Orléans.
2. **the boulevard, the Cirque, the Porte Saint-Martin:** Gavroche, the theatergoer, cab fetcher, and errand runner, haunts the elegant district of theaters like the Porte Saint-Martin and the Cirque around the *grands boulevards* on the right bank.

BOOK TWO: THE GRAND BOURGEOIS
*I: Ninety Years Old and All Thirty-two Teeth*

1. **the Temple:** The onetime fortress of the Knights Templar, the Temple was part of the Marais neighborhood, as was the place des Vosges, home of the Hugo family from 1832 to 1848 and today the site of the Victor Hugo Museum. The last remnants of the Temple were destroyed over the course of the nineteenth century.
2. **the new Tivoli quartier:** Also called the *quartier de l'Europe*, for the place de l'Europe, the name Tivoli comes from the Tivoli Gardens, which once occupied the area around today's Gare Saint-Lazare.
3. **a true and complete bourgeois:** the *grande bourgeoisie*, the wealthy Parisians who lived off private fortunes and were quite content, in the idealized case of Monsieur Gillenormand, with their status in the Second Order.

4. *a sensible fellow* and *Nature:* With *sensibilité* and *Nature,* some of the vocabulary, if not the spirit, of Rousseau seems to have entered into Monsieur Gillenormand's vocabulary.

5. **"The Opéra *danseuses* are rose-pink cannibals":** the image of dancers, who were, like actresses, considered part of the demimonde. The verb *manger,* "to eat," was used to describe the way they devoured their lovers' fortunes, a literary tradition that ran from *Manon Lescaut* to Zola's *Nana.* Monsieur Gillenormand longs to be their victim once again.

6. **"The Caribbeans":** from the indigenous tribe that inhabited the islands of the Caribbean Sea; i.e., the "natives" or "savages" of European imagination.

*II: Like Master, Like Abode*

1. **a boudoir:** not, as is often thought, a bedroom, but a small sitting room, traditionally the site of adulterous assignations. Boudoirs are usually associated with women.

2. **Monsieur de Vivonne:** The duc de Vivonne, later duc de Rochechouart, was a great favorite of Louis XIV, who made him Général des Galères, essentially head of the French navy, because of both his military service and the fact that he was the brother of the royal mistress, Madame de Montespan.

3. **the man of the court . . . and the man of the robe:** a distinction between the *noblesse de cour,* or *d'épée,* and the *noblesse de robe,* the class of magistrates whose offices could be purchased until 1789. Before dedicating his fortune to the acquisition of mistresses, Monsieur Gillenormand could easily have purchased the second sort of nobility, but he is proud of his own place in the bygone social order.

4. **Jordaens:** Jacob Jordaens, a seventeenth-century Flemish painter.

5. **the Incroyables:** Also called *muscadins,* the *Incroyables* were the male counterpart of the *merveilleuses,* whose number included Joséphine de Beauharnais, part of an extravagant and debauched high society that flourished after the fall of the puritanical Robespierre.

*III: Luc-Esprit*

1. **La Camargo and La Sallé:** Marie-Anne Camargo (1710–70) and Marie Sallé (1707–56) were dancers at the Opéra. Voltaire wrote an ode to them that began: *"Ah! Camargo, que vous êtes brillante! / Mais que Sallé, grands Dieux, est ravissante!"*

2. **Guimard:** Marie-Madeleine Guimard (1743–1816), known simply as La Guimard, was one of the most celebrated *danseuses-courtisanes* of the eighteenth century, whose lovers included the prince de Soubise and the bishop of Orléans.

3. **Longchamp:** The racetrack at Longchamp was a gathering place for high society from the mid-1750s on.

4. **Madame de Boufflers:** Both the marquise de Boufflers and her cousin by mar-

riage, the comtesse de Boufflers, were leading figures in Parisian high society in the late eighteenth century.

5. **Corbière! Humann! Casimir Périer!:** Jacques-Joseph de Corbière was the son of a carpenter who became minister of the interior from 1821 to 1824; Georges Humann was, like Casimir Périer (see note 26, p. 1290), a banker and politician; Humann served as minister of finance several times under the July Monarchy, the first time in 1832. For the old-fashioned Monsieur Gillenormand, a bourgeois minister is a ludicrous notion.

6. **Luc-Esprit:** i.e., Saint Luke the Evangelist, and *esprit,* "spirit," as in Saint-Esprit, the Holy Spirit. *Esprit* also means "wit," especially in the libertine eighteenth century so dear to Monsieur Gillenormand.

*IV: An Aspiring Centenarian*

1. **duc de Nivernais . . . duc de Nevers:** Louis-Jules Mancini-Mazarini (1716–98), the last duc de Nivernais, was the grandson of the duc de Nevers. Monsieur Gillenormand apparently finds the older title more impressive.

2. **"blue sash":** the *cordon bleu* of the Order of the Saint-Esprit, the highest heraldic decoration of the French monarchy.

3. **Catherine II:** In spite of her reputation as an "enlightened despot," Catherine the Great participated in the partitioning of Poland in 1772 and 1792 and the final absorption of Poland into Russia, Prussia, and Austria in 1795.

4. **"Bestuchef's yellow dye . . . Lamotte's drops":** the "gold elixir from Bestuchef" and "Lamotte's drops" were believed to be cures for the "catastrophes of love," i.e., venereal disease.

*V: Basque and Nicolette*

1. **"by turning . . . into an annuity":** I.e., he purchased a life annuity, a *rente viagère,* that would last his lifetime but leave very little for his heirs.

2. **"national property":** Beginning in 1790, the properties of *émigrés,* the Catholic Church, and eventually anyone accused of betraying the nation were confiscated and sold to provide revenue for the state.

3. *tiers consolidé:* In 1797, the Directory government, faced with a huge public debt, declared that all outsanding government securities would be paid out only at one third of their value. Like the rue Quincampoix, the traditional location of bankers in ancien régime France, such vulgar matters of finance are beneath Monsieur Gillenormand's attention.

4. **Nimois . . . Picard:** i.e., from the region around Nîmes, Picardie, the Franche-Comté, or Poitou.

5. **Bayonne . . . Basque:** The city of Bayonne is in the eastern part of the Pyrenees range, on the edge of the Basque country.

6. *cordon bleu:* here meaning a master chef.

*VI: In Which We Catch a Glimpse of La Magnon and Her Two Little Boys*

1. **"Monsieur le duc d'Angoulême"**: illegitimate son (1573–1650) of Charles IX (born 1550, reigned 1560–74). Such antiquated gossip was relatively well known among the readers of historical memoirs like Monsieur Gillenormand and Victor Hugo.
2. **"knight of Malta"**: The crusading order of the Knights Hospitaller of Saint John of Jerusalem were given the island of Malta in 1560. In the eighteenth century, the military-religious order was a convenient honorific to bestow on younger (and bastard) sons, thus limiting the number of eligible heirs to diminishing estates.
3. *"Sylvae sint consule dignae"*: a pun based on a verse from Virgil's *Bucolics*: "Even the woods are worthy of consul."
4. **a soldier of fortune**: For a traditionalist like Monsieur Gillenormand, the soldiers of the Grande Armée were little better than pirates or highwaymen.

*VII: Golden Rule: Only Receive Visitors in the Evening*

1. **dog-ear style**: The *oreilles de chien* hairstyle, worn long and framing the face on each side, was favored by the young dandies known as *Incroyables* in the 1790s.
2. **the faubourg Saint-Germain . . . the Marais**: The faubourg Saint-Germain, the left bank neighborhood around the boulevard Saint-Germain, was the aristocratic neighborhood of choice from the mid-eighteenth through the nineteenth centuries. The Marais, built around the place des Vosges, had been the most fashionable address in the seventeenth century; by the July Monarchy, it suggested a sort of faded gentility.

*VIII: Two Do Not Make a Pair*

1. **bigotry**: See note 5, p. 1200; bigotry is meant in the French sense, referring to a rigid, generally conservative set of religious beliefs.
2. **the Confraternity of the Virgin**: Groups such as this, quasi-religious orders for laypeople, thrived in the renewal of devout Catholicism that occurred among the French under the Restoration and especially the July Monarchy.
3. **Agnus Deis and the Ave Marias**: "Lamb of God" and "Hail Mary," prayers of the Catholic Church.

BOOK THREE: GRANDFATHER AND GRANDSON
*I: An Old-World Salon*

1. **Monsieur de Bonald and even Monsieur Bengy-Puy-Vallée**: two paragons of ultra-royalism under the Restoration. The vicomte de Bonald (1754–1840) was an influential writer and legislator; Monsieur Bengy-Puy-Vallée was rather more obscure, and there may be some irony in the pairing of these two names.
2. **la baronne de T——**: There is no obvious model for the baroness, but ambas-

sadorships, particularly to a capital as important as Berlin, were typically given only to the highest nobility under the ancien régime.

3. **"a very mixed bag":** i.e., the Restoration court, which included members of the imperial aristocracy.

4. **the Jacobinism of Louis XVIII:** Compared to his family and the ultra-royalists, Louis XVIII, who deemed 1814 the nineteenth year of his reign, was considered a moderate for his conciliatory pragmatism. Hugo barely exaggerates the attitude of the Ultras.

5. **Monsieur, later Charles X:** Monsieur, the comte d'Artois, was far more conservative than his elder brother, and his succession to the throne in 1824 was seen by the Ultras as a chance to turn back the historical clock.

6. **"the federates":** the name given volunteers for the regional National Guards in the early years of the Revolution. It was the federates of Marseilles who first sang the "Marseillaise," which these lyrics parody.

7. **Pull . . . flag!:** "Renforcez dans vos culottes / Le bout d'chems' qui vous pend. / Qu'on n' dis pas qu' les patriotes / Ont arboré l'dropeau blanc!"

8. **the Dessolles ministry . . . Deserre:** The marquis de Dessolles was president of the Council of Ministers (prime minister) from 1817 to 1819; Élie Decazes, who had become the favorite of Louis XVIII—who called him *"mon cher fils"*—was minister of the interior; and George Deserre was minister of justice. All three were moderately liberal politicians.

9. **To shore up . . . pot:** "Pour raffermir letrone ébranlé sur sa base, / Il faut changer de sol, et de serre et de case."

10. ***Damas, Sabran, Gouvion-Saint-Cyr:*** The marquis de Gouvion-Saint-Cyr (1764–1830) and the baron de Damas (1785–1862) were both aristocrats who served in the imperial armies and then the Restoration government, Damas succeeding Saint-Cyr as minister of war under Louis XVIII. The inclusion of Sabran in this list is not clear.

11. **"Ça ira":** a popular and violent revolutionary song that celebrated the hanging of aristocrats from the lampposts of Paris. The denizens of Madame de T——'s salon have replaced the aristocrats with "Buonapartists" in their lyrics.

12. **Ah! . . . lampposts!:** "Ah! ça ira! ça ira! ça ira! / Les buonapartist' à la lanterne!"

13. **Fualdès affair:** In 1817, Antoine-Bernadin Fualdès, a former public prosecutor (*procureur impérial*) under the Napoleonic government, was brutally murdered in Rodez. Two men named Bastide and Jausion were arrested, convicted, and executed in Toulouse in 1818. The sensational case was closely followed throughout France.

14. **"the brothers and friends":** a mocking allusion to the Revolutionary ideal of *fraternité.*

15. **the comte de Lamothe-Valois . . . strange amnesties:** Antoine-Nicolas Lamothe, or Lamotte, a fraudulent count who married Jeanne de Valois-Saint-Rémy (1756–91), the descendant of a bastard of the Valois dynasty. The comte de Lamothe-Valois and his wife had been the principal orchestrators of the "Necklace Affair," an ancien régime scandal that had badly damaged the public image of the royal family, hence the "strange amnesties."

16. **Marigny, brother of La Pompadour:** Louis XV had made his mistress's brother, Abel Poisson, the marquis de Marigny.

17. **Monsieur le prince de Soubise:** The prince de Soubise was a member of the Rohan family, who claimed descent from the ancient kings of Brittany. He was the father-in-law (and cousin) of the prince de Guéménée, whose bankruptcy in 1782 was still another scandal for the court aristocracy.

18. **Du Barry, godfather of La Vaubernier:** "Godfather" could not be used more ironically. Jean du Barry was the patron and brother-in-law of Madame du Barry, née Jeanne Bécu, Vaubernier being the name of her father, a monk at the Picpus monastery in Paris. Du Barry married the beautiful young prostitute to his elder brother, the comte du Barry, in order to give her entry into high society and thus a better clientele. She eventually became the mistress of Louis XV.

19. **Monsieur le maréchal de Richelieu's:** Monsieur le maréchal de Richelieu was one of the celebrated *grands seigneurs* and libertines of the eighteenth century. The ducs de Richelieu were the (indirect) descendants and heirs of the cardinal de Richelieu.

20. **Mercury:** Hermes in Greek mythology, the messenger god was also a thief and a prankster.

21. **the king of Prussia . . . marquis de Brandenburg:** By tradition, monarchs traveling in foreign lands used assumed names in order to facilitate protocol— Louis XVIII in exile was known as the comte de Lille. Louis XVIII, the alleged Jacobin, considered himself the scion of the oldest dynasty in Europe and first among equals with other monarchs, and thus alienated the rulers of the countries that had restored him to his throne with his "refined impertinence"—when Czar Alexander I arrived for a meeting, Louis never asked him to sit down. Marquis (margrave) de Brandenburg was the ancient title of the Hohenzollerns before they became electors and then kings of Prussia.

22. *Courrier français:* a liberal-leaning newspaper (several newspapers of various political stripes have been published with that title).

23. **Monsieur de Talleyrand:** Monsieur Gillenormand, and Hugo, take their inspiration from Chateaubriand, who, having seen the clubfooted Talleyrand and Fouché arriving for an audience with Louis XVIII after Waterloo, later wrote, "And then Vice entered, supported by Crime, M. de Talleyrand leaning on the arm of M. Fouché."

24. **brigand of the Loire:** After Waterloo and Napoléon's abdication, the soldiers loyal to him retreated beyond the Loire River before officially surrendering.

*II: One of the Red Ghosts of the Time*

1. **Vernon:** a small town on the Seine in Normandy, about forty miles from Paris. Colonel Baron Pontmercy's exile has certain parallels with that of General Count Hugo, although the author's father lived in Blois, on the banks of the Loire, and the woman he lived with was his mistress, not an old servant.

2. **Soulange-Bodin:** Étienne Soulange-Bodin (1774–1846) made great advances in botany.

3. **Georges Pontmercy:** There are many indirect parallels between the careers of Marius's father and Victor Hugo's. Both were simple soldiers who rose through the ranks through battlefield promotions. Both fought in Germany and then in Italy, but General Hugo remained in Italy, where he eventually became Joseph Bonaparte's aide-de-camp before following *le roi Joseph* to Spain in 1808, remaining there until 1813. In 1814, General Hugo was sent to command the fortified town of Thionville, where he held out against the allies even after Napoléon had surrendered and embarked for Elba. During the Hundred Days, Napoléon sent him back to Thionville, which he again held after the final abdication. It was only in November 1815, some five months after Napoléon had been shipped off to Saint Helena, that General Hugo surrendered.

4. **fought at Spires . . . Mayence:** battles of the Revolutionary armies in the early 1790s. Pontmercy's military career follows Napoléon to Waterloo, making it somewhat more glamorous than General Hugo's, which was spent mostly in the Napoleonic quagmire in Spain.

5. **Houchard's rear guard . . . Audernach:** General Jean-Nicolas Houchard (1740–1793) was guillotined in November 1793, after attempting a strategic retreat to Audernach that turned into a rout of French armies by the forces of the prince of Hesse.

6. **Joubert:** Barthélemy Catherine Joubert (1769–99), Napoléon's successor commanding the Army of Italy, was defeated by the Austrians and their Russian allies before being killed at the battle of Novi in August 1799.

7. **Berthier's . . . Lodi:** Prince Louis-Alexandre Berthier (1753–1815) was Napoléon's chief of staff and closest confidant. Lodi was a significant victory (May 1796) in establishing General Bonaparte's reputation as the heroic commander of the Army of Italy.

8. **the red, white, and blue:** i.e., the tricolor flag that was still the symbol of the Consulate.

9. **Wettingen:** an early French victory in the 1805 campaign that culminated in the defeat of Austria and Russia at Austerlitz.

10. **Wurmser taken prisoner in Mantua . . . Mack in Ulm:** three Austrian generals forced to surrender to French armies: Wurmser at Mantua in 1797; Mélas in Alexandria in June 1800; and Mack at Ulm, in Germany, in 1805, a prelude to Napoléon's victory at Austerlitz.

11. **Eylau:** a hard-won victory over the Russians and Prussians (February 1807); it was Eylau and even more so the victory at Friedland the following June that led Czar Alexander to accept negotiations, leading to the meeting of the two emperors at Tilsit in July.

12. **captain Louis Hugo:** Hugo's poem "Le Cimetière d'Eylau" tells the story of the captain's heroic stance.

13. **Moscow, then the Beresina:** The scorched-earth tactic of the Russians made the taking of Moscow (September 1812) a Pyrrhic victory. Forced to retreat,

the already weakened Grande Armée was trapped, on November 26, between a pursuing Russian force and the Beresina River, where the ice proved too weak to support the planned passage of the army. As the engineering corps raced to fashion a bridge, more than 10,000 French troops were killed, either by drowning or by Cossacks.

14. **Lützen, Bautzen ... Gelenhausen:** battles of the 1813 campaign in Germany, all victories except for the battle of Leipzig (October 16–19), also known as the Battle of Nations, which forced Napoléon to retreat to French territory for the last time.

15. **Montmirail, Château-Thierry . . . Laon:** battles of the defensive "French Campaign" as Napoléon's armies fell back in the face of the allied advance toward Paris. As with his résumé of the German campaign, Hugo ends his list of Pyrrhic victories with a defeat, that of the battle of Laon on March 10.

16. **Eight days before the capitulation:** General Marmont signed an armistice with the Allies at 2 A.M. on March 31, 1814; allied armies entered Paris later that day, while Napoléon retreated to Fontainebleau. On April 3, the imperial legislature pronounced Napoléon's removal as emperor; on April 4, he abdicated, under the condition that his four-year-old son be recognized as Emperor Napoléon II, under the regency of Empress Marie-Louise; the Allies refused his conditions; on April 6, Napoléon abdicated unconditionally while his senate, under the leadership of Talleyrand, voted a proclamation recognizing Louis XVIII as king of the French. Pontmercy's refusal to surrender recalls General Hugo's holdout at Thionville.

17. **half pay:** One of the great blunders of the first Restoration was, in 1814, to place large numbers of officers on half pay (*demi-solde*), a quasi-official retirement with inadequate pension. This policy made the army far more receptive to Napoléon's return from Elba.

18. **King Louis XVIII . . . recognized neither . . . title as baron:** Like Pontmercy's, the title granted to General Hugo (count of Siguenza and Sifuentes) was never officially registered in Paris and was thus unrecognized by the Restoration.

19. **Sir Hudson Lowe:** governor of Saint Helena, the final villain of the Napoleonic saga.

20. **"The greatest families are forced to do it":** Napoléon aggressively encouraged marriages between the old nobility of the faubourg Saint-Germain and the new nobility of his marshals, generals, and colonels.

21. **the legacy from Mademoiselle Gillenormand:** French law closely governed questions of inheritance.

22. **hiding behind a pillar:** When their parents had a falling-out, the very young Victor Hugo would hide behind a pillar at Saint-Sulpice in order to see his future wife, Adèle Foucher, attending mass in the company of her mother.

*III: Requiescant—R.I.P.*

1. **the salon of Madame de T——**: this crowded salon is something of a reflection of the atmosphere the adolescent Victor Hugo grew up in. Madame Hugo liked to blame her failed marriage on her royalist principles, and if the company she kept was far less grand than Madame de T——'s guests (Beauffremont, Clermont-Tonnerre, and la Luzerne are some of the great names of the old aristocracy), the Revolution and Empire were vilified by Hugo's mother and her friends. While most of the baroness's guests are real people, only those who played some larger role in history or Hugo's life are discussed here. As the title of the chapter makes clear, Madame de T—— and her guests are living relics of another time.

2. **Trestaillon**: leader of a violent royalist reaction—*the Terreur blanche*—in the south of France (see note 6, ch. XVIII, p. 1240).

3. **The bailiff of Ferrette . . . on his way to Monsieur de Talleyrand's**: Talleyrand, a rich European celebrity, had a house that was a gathering place for those elements of Parisian high society who were less ideological than Madame de T—— and her guests. For an old libertine like the bailiff of Ferrette, Talleyrand's house would have been far more agreeable.

4. **the comte d'Artois**: In his pre-Revolutionary youth, the future Charles X had been the only Bourbon of his generation to uphold the family tradition of libertinage. Time and the death of his favorite mistress led him back to the Church.

5. **Aristotle . . . La Guimard**: According to a medieval legend, the Athenian courtesan Campaspe, or Phyllis, the mistress of Alexander the Great, seduced Aristotle and, as proof of his love, demanded that he allow her to ride his back while he crawled on all fours. For medieval moralists, this was a warning of the perfidy of woman, the dangers of desires of the flesh, and the arrogance of human intellect. "La Guimard" refers to one of the famous courtesans of the eighteenth century (see note 2, ch. III, p. 1264).

6. **the abbé Frayssinous**: Denis-Antoine-Luc Frayssinous (1765–1841), an intimate of Charles X.

7. **advocate of the saints**: In the "trials" that determine if a candidate is fit for sainthood, the advocate of the saints pleads the case of the nominee, while the devil's advocate offers the counterevidence.

8. **Chateaubriand**: *Le Conservateur* was the Ultra newspaper Chateaubriand contributed to when he was dismssed from Louis XVIII's government in 1816, which in turn inspired the young and still royalist Hugo brothers to found *Le Conservateur littéraire* in 1818.

9. **hating the Encyclopedia**: Diderot's *Encyclopédie* of 1751–72.

10. **White—legitimist—Paris society**: i.e., commited to the Bourbons.

11. **Chateaubriand . . . Père Duchesne**: As with Louis XVIII's "Jacobinism," the conservative but constitutional monarchist Chateaubriand can be compared to the violently revolutionary *Père Duchesne* (see note 16, p. 1203) only by almost fanatical ultra-royalists.

12. **Comte Beugnot:** Jacques-Claude Beugnot (1761–1835) came from an old family of the robe nobility but served both the Napoleonic and Restoration governments.

13. **The "noble" salons of today . . . to their credit:** Hugo is apparently referring to the Paris of 1860–62, when the futility of royalism made those who adhered to it admirable, while " 'noble' salons" did nothing to opppose the tyranny of Louis-Napoléon.

14. **the duchesses de Longueville and de Chevreuse:** heroines of the Fronde, the period of aristocratic rebellion against Cardinal Mazarin, who animate the memoirs of the ducs de La Rochefoucauld and Saint-Simon.

15. **"besmirched by the usurper":** The "usurper" is, of course, Napoléon, who required his courtiers to address him as "Your Majesty" and "Sire."

16. **Methuselah informed Epimenides:** Methuselah lived for 967 years, according to the book of Genesis, while in Greek legend, Epimenides fell asleep in a cave for fifty-seven years.

17. **The time . . . since Koblenz:** the German city where royalist émigrés organized an ultimately unsuccessful counterrevolutionary invasion of France.

18. **the advent of Monsieur de Villèle:** The appointment of Villèle to the post of prime minister was seen as a triumph for the Ultras, even if he eventually proved too pragmatic for the Right.

19. **revenants:** literally, "those who have returned"; this is also the French word for ghosts.

20. *ci-devants:* The term used to describe "former" noblemen during the Revolution, *ci-devant* came to refer to those aristocrats who clung to the traditions of the ancien régime.

21. **the nobility of the Crusades:** The ideal of the French aristocracy under the ancien régime, when custom dictated that only those who could prove four hundred years of noble ancestry could be presented at court. In the eighteenth century, some notoriously creative geneaologies were used to gain access to court.

22. **Fontenoy . . . Marengo:** battles of the ancien régime and the Empire, respectively.

23. **Monsieur de Martainville:** a royalist playwright and actor (1776–1830) who is best remembered as the founder of the Ultra newspaper *Le Drapeau blanc.*

24. **Fiévée . . . Agier:** Joseph Fiévée was a journalist who tacked his sails to the prevailing wind, switching from Bonapartism to royalism in 1815. Agier was the leader of a large faction of conservatives in the Chamber of Deputies.

25. **After the fifth of September . . . the eighth of July:** an apparent reference to a decree of the Convention on September 5, 1793, which authorized the arrest of "suspects" practically on the whim of Revolutionary authorities, making noble status a virtual crime in itself. July 8, 1815, was the day Louis XVIII returned to Paris after Waterloo. In terms of both numbers and official persecutions, it is a gross exaggeration to compare the *Terreur blanche* to the *Terreur rouge* of 1793–94.

26. **Monsieur de Vaublanc:** minister of the interior to Louis XVIII.

27. **The Congregation:** The Chevaliers de la Foi, or Knights of Faith, a mostly aristocratic group committed first to the Church and second to politics, became an almost mythical force in the popular political imagination under the Restoration. The Congregation plays a large role in Stendhal's *Le Rouge et le noir*—far larger, probably, than it ever played in fact.

*VI: What It Is to Have Met a Churchwarden*

1. **the *Moniteur*:** the quasi-official newspaper of virtually every French government from 1789 to 1901. Bonaparte was especially conscious of the usefulness of such an outlet.

2. **the *Mémorial de Sainte-Hélène*:** Emmanuel de Las Cases served as an officer in the Napoleonic armies before following Napoléon to Saint Helena. Although ordered by the British to leave after a year, Las Cases had sufficient time to interview Napoléon and gather the notes he would use in composing the *Mémorial*, a hagiographic account of the Napoleonic epic. A huge success from the moment of its publication, the *Mémorial* was one of the most important factors in shaping Napoléon's legend in the 1820s.

3. **the bulletins of the Grande Armée:** The bulletins were official accounts of the actions of Napoléon's army. A key tool of imperial propaganda, the bulletins were sometimes praised for their writing; Hugo's "Homeric stanzas" more likely refers to the content than the style. The bulletins were recognized as propaganda at the time; the saying "to lie like the bulletins" became common among soldiers.

4. **Mirabeau . . . Danton:** some of the greatest figures of the Revolution. Mirabeau (1749–91) was the famous orator who dominated the Constituent Assembly. Pierre Vergniaud (1753–93) was one of the leading figures of the Girondist faction, moderate republicans who were eclipsed by the more radical Jacobins. Vergniaud was among those executed after the Jacobins triumphed in the spring of 1793. On Saint-Just, see note 1, ch. V, p. 1316. Robespierre, the leader of the Jacobins, was overthrown in the coup of 9 Thermidor, July 28, 1794. On Desmoulins, see note 3, ch. IX, p. 1260. On Danton, see note 17, p. 1223.

5. **the monster who was his sisters' lover . . . poisoner of Jaffa:** such was the royalist propaganda against Napoléon, that he and his brothers committed incest with their sisters; "ham actor" refers to the rumors that Napoléon had been taught how to perform in public by the actor Talma (see note 53, p. 1215). The legend of the "poisoner of Jaffa" refers to the Egyptian campaign of 1798–99. Napoléon supposedly poisoned the well at a camp in Jaffa (Haifa) in order to eliminate sick soldiers who were slowing his retreat after encountering an overwhelming Turkish force.

6. **Charlemagne . . . the Committee of Public Safety:** some of the most powerful rulers of France. Charlemagne (ca. 750–814), the first Holy Roman emperor, is claimed by the French as a king. Louis XI (born 1423, reigned 1461–83), the Spider King, patiently and ruthlessly consolidated royal power in the wake of

the Hundred Years' War. Hugo helped promote the legend of Louis XI in *Notre-Dame de Paris*. Henri IV was the first Bourbon king and the grandfather of Louis XIV (born 1638, reigned 1643–1715). Cardinal de Richelieu (1585–1642), the loyal and ruthless prime minister of Louis XIII, worked to strengthen the monarchy. The Committee of Public Safety was the executive component of the Convention, the means through which Robespierre ruled the country.

7. **Baron Marius Pontmercy:** Like Marius, it was only after his father's death in 1829 that Hugo began to use the title of "Baron Hugo," to which he was entitled according to the strict rules of the imperial nobility, his elder brothers being the comte (Abel) and vicomte (Edmond) Hugo.

8. **Géronte's gaiety . . . the melancholy Werther:** The name Géronte was traditionally used for the character of the patriarch in French theater, including by Molière; Werther was the classic Romantic hero of Goethe's *The Sorrows of Young Werther,* a brooding youth in love with an unattainable woman.

## VII: A Bit of Skirt

1. **a good-looking officer:** With his mustache, his "girl's waist," and his decorative saber, Lieutenant Théodule is a classic dandy of the era.

2. **on top:** The cheapest seats on a public coach were those on the top deck, the roof of the carriage itself, which had no protection from the elements.

3. **Théodule:** Théodule, which can suggest "one who praises God," is a name well suited to please Mademoiselle Gillenormand, even if the young officer would prefer the more fashionable "Alfred."

4. **Argus snored all night:** Argus was the hundred-eyed, all-seeing demigod of Greek mythology.

## VIII: Marble Versus Granite

1. **rogues, cutthroats, red caps, thieves:** the royalists' image of the revolutionaries; on red caps, see note 21, 1204.

2. **Louis XVIII had been dead four years:** Louis XVIII died in 1824.

3. **the duc de Berry:** the royalist martyr assassinated in 1820; see note 35, p. 1213.

4. **sixty pistoles:** a coin worth ten livres, or francs. The word was rarely used in the nineteenth century.

BOOK FOUR: FRIENDS OF THE ABC
*I: A Group That Nearly Became History*

1. **the German Tugendbund . . . The Cougourde:** The Tugendbund (League of Virtue) was formed in 1808 as a response to the French domination of Germany. Its members sought to promote German nationalism and to fight Napoléon. The Italian Carbonari also formed as a resistance movement in response to the rule of Joachim Murat around 1810. Carbonari groups formed in

different parts of Italy, demanding greater liberalism and—in the north—combating Austrian influence. In Savoy and Naples, Carbonari succeeded in forcing the monarchs to grant constitutions. Ironically, Louis-Napoléon Bonaparte was a member of the Carbonari before becoming heir to his uncle's throne and Hugo's nemesis. The Cougourde, a secret organization of republicans, had only begun to form under the July Monarchy; like their fictional contemporaries in the Friends of the ABC, they were "at the embryo stage."

2. **Castratus ad castrata . . . hanc Petram:** "From castrato to the camp." The eunuch Narses was made a general by the Byzantine emperor Justinian. *Barbari et Barbarini:* "What the barbarians didn't take, the Barbarini will"; in the seventeenth century, the aristocratic Roman Barbarini family appropriated a number of antiquities for their palace. *Feuros y fuegos:* "Rights and hearths!" was the motto of Spanish liberals in the revolt of 1823. *Tu es Petrus . . . hanc Petrum:* Jesus' words to Peter: "You are Peter and on this rock I shall build my Church" (see note 2, p. 1223).

3. **Les Halles . . . Café Musain:** The great Halles of Paris were still the site of the central market. Corinthe was one of the independent city-states of ancient Greece. The place Saint-Michel was not the modern square on the left bank of the Seine but on the site of today's place Edmond Rostand, just outside the Luxembourg gardens.

4. **the main ones:** The nine Friends of the ABC are generally seen as reflections of different aspects of Victor Hugo.

5. **Antinous:** The lover of the Roman emperor Hadrian, Antinous is one of the classic images of male beauty from antiquity.

6. **Gracchus . . . Saint-Just:** The Gracchi were two brothers who served as tribunes in Rome; both sought to reform land ownership in favor of the poor, and both were persecuted by the patrician class. The youthful Saint-Just (see note 1, ch. V, p. 1316) was a leader of the Revolution who was executed before his thirtieth birthday.

7. **Evadné's bare breast . . . Harmodius:** Hugo seems to have confused his allusions here. Evadné was a beautiful young woman loved by Apollo who rejected the god in favor of the warrior Capane; when Capane was killed in battle, Evadné threw herself on his funeral pyre. Harmodius and Aristogeiton hid their daggers in flowers during a procession in order to take revenge on Hipparch, who had seduced the sister of Harmodius.

8. **the gallant cherubs of Beaumarchais . . . Ezekiel:** Cherubino is a charming, Puck-like character, a boy traditionally played by a young woman, in Beaumarchais' *Marriage of Figaro.* The "awesome cherubim" in the Old Testament Book of Ezekiel are fierce and unearthly creatures who guard the heavens.

9. **Homo et Vir:** two Latin words for "man." *Vir* connotes the traditional masculine, or virile, qualities of the Roman citizen.

10. **Arago . . . Geoffroy Saint-Hilaire:** Dominique-François Arago (1786–1853) was a pioneering physicist and astronomer, director of the Paris Observatory; Étienne Geoffroy Saint-Hilaire (1772–1844) taught zoology at the University of Paris.

11. **Saint-Simon with Fourier:** See notes 70 and 71, p. 1217.

12. **Puységur and Deleuze:** two proponents of magnetism; followers of Mesmer.
13. **issues of education:** Hugo was a constant advocate of education reform throughout his life.
14. **Jehan:** a typical affectation of Romantic youth in the 1820s and '30s. Hugo's *Notre-Dame de Paris* was a part of both "that most necessary study of the Middle Ages" and the "touch of whimsy" that went along with it.
15. **André Chénier:** a royalist journalist who was arrested and executed in 1794; his Romantic poetry was not published until 1819, after which he became a hero to Hugo's generation.
16. **Corneille to Racine . . . Agrippa d'Aubigné:** Hugo also preferred Corneille to Racine. Agrippa d'Aubigné (1552–1630) was a Huguenot poet who drew on his knowledge of the Bible to compose poetic laments on France torn apart by the Wars of Religion.
17. **Greece . . . Italy:** five European nations viewed as oppressed by foreigners: the Greeks and Romanians by the Ottoman Empire; the Poles by Russia; Hungary and Italy by the Austrian Hapsburgs.
18. **1772:** the first of three partitions of Poland in the eighteenth century by Russia, Prussia, and Austria ("that crime of three"). Upon the third partition, in 1795, Poland ceased to exist. At the Congress of Vienna, Czar Alexander I declared that a free Poland was a mortal threat to Russia and essentially annexed the country. Hugo called for a free Poland in one of his first speeches before the Chamber of Peers, in 1846.
19. *ne varietur:* "without exception."
20. **One of the false ideas . . . that particle:** The "nobiliary particle" was not as insignificant as Hugo claims, but it was far more important after the Revolution than before and probably more important to the bourgeoisie than to the aristocracy.
21. **the *Minerve*:** a conservative newspaper.
22. *quasi cursores:* "like runners."
23. **paladin:** i.e., a champion, a defender.
24. **the bloody tumult of June 1822:** During a demonstration against a new law concerning the voting franchise (in June 1820, not 1822), a young student named Lallemand was shot on the place du Carrousel; his funeral subsequently turned into a thousands-strong rally, with an even larger crowd joining a demonstration afterward.
25. **a square cap:** i.e., the mortarboard traditionally worn by university students.
26. **Monsieur Delvincourt:** dean of the law school in Paris; see note 6, ch. III, p. 1221.
27. **Bossuet:** seventeenth-century theologian and orator; see note 15, p. 1202.
28. **the *malade imaginaire*:** i.e., the hypochondriac, from the title of one of Molière's masterpieces.
29. *feuillants,* **royalists, doctrinaires:** some of the different factions of the French Revolution. The *feuillants* were moderate royalists who split from the Jacobins; they were close in ideology to the *doctrinaires,* who believed in a constitutional monarchy.

30. **Loizerolles:** According to a royalist legend, the aristocratic Loizerolles took the place of his son in a Revolutionary prison and was guillotined.
31. **Pollux . . . Pechméja:** a reference to some legendary male friendships. Pollux with Castor, Patroclus with Achilles, Nisus with Euryale (in The *Iliad*), Eudamidas was the friend of Charixane in the work of the Roman poet Lucian. The modern example is Jean de Pechméja (1741–85), who was so devoted to his friend Dr. Dubrueil that he cared for the doctor through a fatal and contagious illness and died two weeks after the doctor did.
32. **Orestes and Pylades:** Orestes, son of Agamemnon, king of Mycenae, was raised with Pylades, the son of a foreign king. When Orestes returned to his homeland to avenge his father's murder at the hands of his wife and her lover, Pylades encouraged his friend not to falter in avenging his father by killing his mother.

*II: Blondeau's Funeral Oration, by Bossuet*

1. **Blondeau:** the name of a law professor in Paris in the 1830s.
2. *Erudimini qui judicatis terram:* "Educate yourselves, you who would judge the earth."

*III: The Amazement of Marius*

1. **Bewigged tragedy:** the classical seventeenth-century tragedies of Racine, Corneille, and their lesser brethren.
2. **Aeschylus:** See note 3, ch. XV, p. 1238.
3. **Jean-Jacques and Thérèse:** Jean-Jacques Rousseau and his mistress, Thérèse Levasseur. The "little creatures" refers to the five children they had, all of whom, according to a legend started by Rousseau himself, were abandoned by their father at a foundling hospital.
4. *Initium sapientiae:* "the beginning of wisdom."

*IV: The Back Room of the Café Musain*

1. **"the Heidelberg tun":** a giant wine cask (or tun) at Heidelberg Castle, which held 58,100 gallons of wine.
2. **"Ecclesiastes says: 'All is vanity' ":** Ecclesiastes 1:1–2.
3. **"Caligula . . . Roastbeef ":** Part of the legend of the mad Roman emperor Caligula, originally recorded by Suetonius, is that he hoped to make his favorite horse, Incitatus, a consul of Rome. The epicurean king Charles II (born 1630, reigned 1660–85) of England may have made a pun about barons of beef and sirloins, but he never knighted or ennobled any cuts of meat.
4. **"Diogenes' mantle":** Diogenes chose to live in abject poverty.
5. **"Strongylion":** a famous Greek sculptor of fifth-century B.C.E. Athens.
6. **"battle of Pydna:** the battle in 168 B.C.E. at Pydna in Macedonia (now in Greece) that established Rome as a power on the Hellenic peninsula.
7. **"Clovis's Tolbiac":** The battle at Tolbiac (ca. 500), now Zülpich in Germany,

established Clovis and his Franks as the most powerful of the Germanic tribes. According to Saint Gregory of Tours, Clovis promised to convert to Christianity if he won the battle.

8. *"Si volet usus"*: "If custom wills it."

9. **"Phocion, or Coligny"**: Phocion was the elected leader (strategos) of Athens at the time of the Macedonian expansion by Philip and Alexander; he was executed for treason after he advocated cooperation with the Macedonians. Gaspard de Coligny (1519–72) was a naval hero and confidant of Henri II, and a leader of the Huguenot party under the regency of Catherine de Médicis. He was killed during the Saint Bartholomew's Day massacre.

10. **"Pisistratus"**: an Athenian ruler popular for his economic reforms.

11. **"Philetas"**: a poet and grammarian who lived ca. 500 B.C.E.

12. **"An Alexis decapitated . . . Paul stomped on"**: palace coups in Russia were the stuff of legend; many czars died mysterious deaths.

13. **"the Abattoir"**: "the slaughterhouse," a real Parisian tavern.

14. **"Cleopatra"**: a reference to the ruse Cleopatra used to reach Julius Caesar: She had herself rolled up in a carpet, which was brought to the Roman conqueror as a gift.

15. **"gesture of Hippocrates . . . Artaxerxes's hodgepodge"**: The Greek physician Hippocrates refused to treat Artaxerxes, king of Persia, in spite of the latter's offers of magnificent gifts, because the Persians were the enemies of Athens.

16. **"Vaud . . . Gex"**: The border between the French region of Gex and the Swiss canton of Vaud was established by treaty in 1815.

17. **"Staub's"**: Staub was the most fashionable tailor in Paris.

18. **"Vignemale . . . Cybele's headdress"**: Vignemale is the highest peak in the Pyrenees; Cybele is another name for Rhea, mother of the Olympian gods.

19. **"Pan"**: Pan is the goat god of the mountains who taught humans to play the flute.

20. **"Io . . . Pissevache"**: The nymph Io was a daughter of the river god Inachus; Pissevache is a waterfall in the French Alps.

21. **"Touquet Charter"**: See note 16, p. 1212.

22. **"François I . . . Louis XIV"**: Francis I died in 1547, Louis XIV in 1715. It is not clear who Hugo means by "Desmarets."

*V: The Horizon Expands*

1. **"Bonaparte's fatal number"**: 18 Brumaire, the coup that brought Bonaparte to power.

2. *"Quia nominor leo"*: "because my name is lion"; from a Greek fable that portrayed the lion as king of the beasts.

3. **"Justinian"**: The emperor Justinian (ca. 482–565) rewrote the laws of the Byzantine Empire.

4. **"Pascal's lightning wit"**: This wit is best represented in Pascal's *Lettres provinciales,* which satirized the Jesuits.

5. **"Newton's mathematics"**: Bonaparte began his military career as an artillery officer, a position that required a great deal of mathematical precision.

6. **"Tilsit"**: the first imperial summit between Napoléon and Alexander I of Russia in July 1807.

7. **"Laplace"**: Pierre-Simon Laplace (1749–1827) was a mathematician, physicist, and astronomer.

8. **"Merlin"**: Philippe-Antoine Merlin (1754–1838), known as Merlin de Douai for his hometown, was a Revolutionary politician known for his legal scholarship and as an orator.

9. **"Cromwell . . . curtain tassel"**: These two anecdotes, apparently referring to the frugality of the English and French dictators, are of unknown origin.

10. **"If Caesar . . . I love my mother more"**: Combeferre has apparently rewritten and politicized "J'aime mieux ma mie," a famous love song from Molière's *Misanthrope:* "Si César m'avait donné / La gloire et la guerre, / Et qu'il me fallût quitter / L'amour de ma mère, / Je dirais au grand César: / Reprends ton sceptre et ton char, / J'aime mieux ma mère, ô gué! / J'aime mieux ma mère."

11. **"Citizen"**: this form of address had significant political connotations in post-Revolutionary France.

*VI: Res Angusta*

1. ***Res Angusta:*** "straitened (financial) circumstances."

BOOK FIVE: THE VIRTUES OF ADVERSITY
*II: Marius Poor*

1. **Rousseau's:** one of the cheap greasy spoons of the Latin Quarter.

*III: Marius Grown Up*

1. **this Septembrist:** one of Monsieur Gillenormand's catchall terms for a Revolutionary; it refers to the September massacres of 1792.

2. **Monsieur Magimel:** a contemporary bookseller and publisher.

*IV: Monsieur Mabeuf*

1. **the Furies . . . the Eumenides:** The Greeks called the Furies (the Erinyes), the goddesses of vengeance and retribution, the Eumenides because the act of speaking their names could draw their wrath.

2. **The July Revolution:** In July 1830, Charles X and his ministers attempted to push through a number of restrictive laws, most notably against freedom of the press, that provoked an uprising in Paris. Within three days (*Les Trois glorieuses*) it became clear that the government could not survive. Charles abdicated, and his son the duc d'Angoulême renounced his right to succession. An interim government offered the throne of a constitutional monarchy to Louis-Philippe d'Orléans.

3. **the village of Austerlitz:** Now part of Paris, the village named for Napoléon's

greatest victory was then on the eastern edge of Paris, where the Gare d'Austerlitz now stands.

### V: Poverty, Misery's Good Neighbor

1. **Comte Pajol . . . Fririon:** Pierre-Claude Pajol (né Pajot) (1772–1844), a Napoleonic general and count who fought at Waterloo. General Bellavesne (1770–1826) lost a leg to a cannonball—Marius could not have visited him in the early years of the July Monarchy. General Baron Fririon (1766–1840) retired from combat in 1811 and was later named governor of the Hôtel des Invalides.
2. **a book like Job:** God tested Job's faith with a series of disasters.

### VI: The Substitute

1. **the *Quotidienne:*** a royalist newspaper.
2. **a conflict between the minister of war:** The details of what was probably a specific incident are not clear, but there were any number of political conflicts—ranging from rallies to riots to insurrections—in Paris in the 1830s and '40s.
3. ***"descamisados":*** See note 4, ch. III, p. 1243.
4. **"Carnot said . . . Fouché answered":** a famous exchange between Carnot (see note 41, p. 1214) and Fouché (see note 2, ch. II, p. 1227) during Fouché's brief period of influence following the Second Restoration in 1815. Fouché had persuaded the comte d'Artois and a few other Ultras that only a former Jacobin could purify France of its remaining Jacobins. Carnot was among the former colleagues of the Convention, Directory, and Empire that Fouché ordered into exile, before the Ultras procured his exile in turn.
5. ***"Hernani":*** With tongue in cheek, Hugo mocks the reaction to his own play of 1830, which was enormously controversial for its complete break with the traditions of French theater (hence, "not even written in French!"). The antithesis was one of Hugo's favorite literary devices.
6. **"Benjamin Constant":** See note 6, p. 1235.
7. **"the *Drapeau blanc* . . . Martainville":** See note 23, p. 1272.
8. **"Sieyès":** On the "patriot priest" Joseph Sieyès (1748–1836), see note 1, p. 1204. Sieyès was one of the most influential voices of the Revolution, from 1788 until 1799. He expected to exercise great influence over General Bonaparte after the Brumaire coup d'état but found himself ignored by the first consul. Napoléon named him senator.
9. **"hats like Henri IV":** As the Empire progressed, Napoléon became more preoccupied with ceremony and stagecraft. At one point, the official Senate uniforms resembled costumes of the late Renaissance.

BOOK SIX: THE CONJUNCTION OF TWO STARS
*I: The Nickname as a Way of Forming Family Names*

1. **the Sicambri:** a Germanic tribe related to the Franks.
2. **fled like some Parthian:** According to ancient tradition, Parthian soldiers continued fighting even in retreat.

*II: Lux Facta Est*

1. *Lux facta est:* Genesis 1:3: "and there was light."
2. **Raphael . . . Jean Goujon:** two masters of Renaissance art, the Italian painter Raphael (1483–1520) and the French sculptor Goujon (1510–65), whose work can still be seen on the façades of the Louvre and in the Musée Carnavalet.

*IV: Beginning of a Great Sickness*

1. **"Beware of extremes, son":** a phrase that could have served as the unofficial motto of the July Monarchy, which always sought the *juste milieu,* or wise middle ground, between the Ultraism of the monarchists and republicanism like that of the Friends of the ABC.
2. **"Marcos Obregon de la Ronda . . . *Gil Blas*":** an allusion to a rather strange incident in Hugo's early career. The academician François de Neufchâteau (1750–1828; see note 80, p. 1218) had hired the young prodigy Victor Hugo to write an article on *Gil Blas.* Hugo was unaware that he was being hired as a ghostwriter and was shocked and indignant to see his work published under the name of Neufchâteau, who had been dead more than thirty years when Hugo took this mild literary revenge.

*VI: Taken Prisoner*

1. **Petrarch . . . Dante:** Both Petrarch and his friend Dante were haunted by the images of beautiful women, Petrarch by Laura and Dante by Beatrice.
2. **"Audry de Puyraveau":** Pierre-François Audry de Puyraveau (1773–1852). A leading legislator of the Left, he was a member of the opposition under the Restoration and—when the July Monarchy he had helped bring to power proved too conservative—to the Orléanist governments.
3. **Frédérick:** The actor Frédérick Lemaître (1800–76) was so well-known that only a first name was needed. His role as the bandit Robert Macaire in the play *L'Auberge des Adrets* was his signature.
4. **Quicherat:** Louis Quicherat (1799–1884), a linguist who published Latin-French and French-Latin dictionaries.

*VII: Adventures of the Letter* U *Open to Conjecture*

1. **Leonidas or Spartacus:** heroes of antiquity, typical subjects of statues in the Luxembourg gardens.

*VIII: Even War Invalids Can Be Happy*

1. **A fresh Prairial breeze:** i.e., spring; Prairial was one of the months of the Revolutionary calendar.
2. **the nymphs . . . Theocritus:** Virgil's *Georgics* and *Eclogues* celebrated the pleasures of the rural life. The ancient Greek poet Theocritus also specialized in bucolic poetry.
3. **Isis:** queen of the Egyptian gods.
4. **Bartholo . . . Cherubino:** I.e., the neophyte lover is already jealous. In Beaumarchais' *Barber of Seville,* Figaro helps the count elope with Suzanne in spite of her jealous supervision by her aged guardian, Bartholo; in *The Marriage of Figaro,* Cherubino is a young boy with a precocious interest in women (see note 8, p. 1275).
5. **a Louis XV uniform:** i.e., an old-fashioned uniform. Louis XV died in 1774, so it would have been quite possible to see a veteran of his reign in the 1830s.
6. **reject of Mars:** i.e., one wounded in battle, Mars being the god of war.

*IX: Eclipse*

1. **"gentleman from the first floor":** First-floor apartments—one level above the street—were the most expensive in most buildings.

BOOK SEVEN: PATRON-MINETTE
*I: Mines and Miners*

1. **Jean-Jacques . . . lantern:** Diogenes walked with a lantern and, when asked why, announced that he was searching for an honest man. Rousseau's pick is part of Hugo's own mining metaphor.
2. **Calvin grabs Socin by the hair:** Jean Calvin (1509–64) was born in France before fleeing to Geneva, where he found a political atmosphere more congenial to his Protestantism; the Italian Leo Socin (1525–62) rejected the divinity of Jesus Christ, the existence of the Holy Spirit, and the utility of the sacraments.
3. **John Huss . . . Babeuf:** The Czech Jon Huss (1369–1415) was convicted of heresy and burned at the stake. On Martin Luther (1483–1546) and René Descartes, see note 43, p. 1214. On Condorcet, see note 11, pp. 1262–63. On Marat, see note 14, p. 1202. François-Noël Babeuf (1760–97), who called himself Gracchus, agitated for greater protosocialist reforms during the Revolution; he was eventually executed as an "agitator" by the Directoire.
4. **Saint-Simon, Owen, and Fourier:** On Saint-Simon and Fourier, see notes 70

and 71, p. 1217. Robert Owen (1771–1858) founded a cooperative agricultural community in England.

5. *Inferi:* a Latin word for hell.

## *II: The Dregs*

1. **the Ugolinos:** According to a legend that grew out of Dante's *Inferno,* the Pisan count Hugolino (ca. 1220–89; Ugolino in Italian) was convicted of treason and imprisoned, with his young sons but without food, in the tower of Pisa; he eventually resorted to cannibalism. The sculptor Auguste Rodin portrayed the Hugolinos in his *Gates of Hell.*
2. **Lacenaire:** a famous thief and murderer; see note 4, ch. VII, p. 1259.
3. **Babeuf . . . Cartouche:** for Babeuf, see note 3, ch. I, p. 1282; for the criminal Cartouche, see note 7, p. 1202.
4. **Marat . . . Schinderhannes:** On Marat, see note 14, p. 1202; Schinderhannes was the leader of a gang of thieves; he was eventually captured and executed in 1803.

## *III: Babet, Gueulemer, Claquesous, and Montparnasse*

1. **the Farnese Hercules:** a famous Roman statue of Hercules belonging to the Farneses. Copies of the statue were popular in the elegant gardens of seventeenth- and eighteenth-century France.
2. **a Creole:** here, a European born in the tropics, usually the Caribbean.
3. **Maréchal Brune:** Guillaume-Marie-Anne Brune (1763–1815), a Revolutionary general who served under Napoléon just long enough to be named a marshal of France. He was murdered by royalists in 1815.
4. **Bobèche's . . . Bobino's:** popular circuses in late-eighteenth- and nineteenth-century Paris.
5. **turned this Abel into a Cain:** i.e., turned him into a criminal (Genesis 4).

## *IV: Composition of the Troupe*

1. **Proteus:** a Greek sea god known for his shape-shifting; the source of the adjective "protean."
2. **the great Vidocq:** See note 2, ch. V, p. 1227.
3. **Coco-Lacour:** Like Vidocq, Coco-Lacour was a legendary figure, a criminal employed by the police. Even fewer details are known about Coco-Lacour's career.
4. *département* **of the Seine:** at the time, Paris and its environs.
5. *Ambubaïarum collegia . . . mimde:* "Troops of flute players, drug sellers, beggars, and actresses." From Horace's *Satires.*

BOOK EIGHT: THE BAD PAUPER
*I: Marius Looks for a Girl in a Hat and Meets a Man in a Cap*

1. **"Chaumière"**: like Mabille and the Sceaux Ball, public dances popular with students and grisettes.

*II: A Find*

1. **Whether . . . its lair**: "Qu'il luise ou qu'il luiserne, / L'ours rentre en sa caverne."

*III: Quadrifrons*

1. **Quadrifrons**: "four-faced."
2. *square opposite the Chamber of Deputies:* The Chamber of Deputies was located in the Palais-Bourbon, on the Left Bank, across the Seine from the place de la Concorde.
3. *elector:* Until 1848, only those who paid a certain level of taxes were eligible to vote.
4. *Saint-Jacques-du-Haut-Pas:* a parish church in rue Saint-Jacques, roughly on the border between the Latin Quarter and faubourg Saint-Marceau.

*IV: A Rose in Misery*

1. **I'm hungry . . . Jacquot!**: "J'ai faim, mon père. / Pas de fricot. / J'ai froid, ma mère. / Pas de tricot. / Grelotte, / Lolotte! / Sanglote, / Jacquot."

*VI: Feral Man in His Lair*

1. **Wagramme/Elot**: the battles of Wagram (1809) and Eylau (1807), misspelled.
2. **Lavater**: a Swiss theologian (1741–1801) who promoted the study of physiognomy, the belief that a person's character could be read in the face.
3. **Ducray-Duminil**: a mediocre novelist, popular during Hugo's childhood.

*VII: Strategies and Tactics*

1. **"Rothschild"**: Jacob Rothschild (1792–1868) was the banking family's representative in France.
2. **"I suppress the freedom of the press"**: an ironic echo of the deposed Charles X in the absolute monarch of the Gorbeau slum.

*IX: Jondrette Very Nearly Weeps*

1. **"Student of Talma"**: the great French actor of the early nineteenth century; see note 53, p. 1215.

2. **"Mademoiselle Mars"**: the great actress of the early nineteenth century (see note 37, p. 1214).

3. **Célimène . . . Belisarius:** Célimène is the self-centered coquette of Molière's *Misanthrope,* Elmira is the heroine of *Tartuffe,* and Belisarius is the hero of a play of the same name by Marmontel.

### X: Rates for Cabs: Two Francs an Hour

1. **La Force:** The former Parisian palace of the ducs de La Force had been turned into a prison in the seventeenth century.

### XII: Use of Monsieur Leblanc's Five-Franc Piece

1. **"Croesus":** Greek king whose wealth became proverbial.
2. **"not even a quarter yet":** Rents were paid quarterly in Paris at the time.

### XIII: Solus cum Solo, in Loco Remoto, Non Cogitabantur Orare Pater Noster

1. **Solus cum Solo . . . Pater Noster:** "All alone, it does not occur to him to say the Our Father."
2. **the benevolence of a Brahmin:** the aristocratic, priestly caste of India.

### XIV: Where a Police Officer Gives a Lawyer a Couple of Punches

1. **"little muscadin":** i.e., a little dandy.

### XVI: Where You Will Find the Words of an English Tune Fashionable in 1832

1. **Our love . . . last forever!:** "Nos amours ont duré tout une semaine, / Mais que du bonheur les instants sont courts! / S'adorer huit jours, c'était bien la peine! / Le temps des amours devrait durer toujours! / Devrait durer toujours! devrait durer toujours!"
2. **You leave me . . . all the way:** "Vous me quittez pour aller à la gloire, / Mon triste cœur suivra partout vos pas."

### XVII: Marius's Five-Franc Piece Put to Use

1. **Diogenes . . . Cartouche:** Diogenes used his lantern to search for an honest man, the antithesis of Cartouche or Jondrette.
2. **one of the hats . . . Charles X's consecration:** Charles X's coronation in 1825 was a deliberately antiquated ceremony.

### XX: The Ambush

1. **"your fancy Sakoski loafers":** Sakoski was a fashionable shoemaker, with a shop in the gallery of the Palais-Royal.

2. **"David at Bruqueselles"**: The Revolutionary and Bonapartist painter Jacques-Louis David (see note 41, p. 1214) was exiled to Brussels (which Jondrette mispronounces in French) after the return of the Bourbons.

3. **"Desnoyers"**: a fashionable restaurant in the chaussée d'Antin neighborhood.

4. **"Benvenuto Cellinis . . . Villons"**: The sculptor and goldsmith Cellini (1500–71) led a scandalous life, including a charge of manslaughter and numerous sex scandals; François Villon (ca. 1431–after 1463), the legendary brig-and-poet of the fifteenth century, was a habitual criminal who wrote some of the most beautiful poetry of the French Middle Ages.

*XXI: You Should Always Arrest the Victims First*

1. **Frederick II on parade at Potsdam**: i.e., Frederick the Great (born 1712, reigned 1740–86), king of Prussia and military commander. Potsdam, outside Berlin, was his preferred residence.

*XXII: The Little Boy Who Cried Out in Part Three*

1. **The Little Boy**: the child crying in the cradle when Jean Valjean arrived to take Cosette.

2. **King Get-the-boot-in . . . A' huntin' crows**: "Le roi Coupdesabot / S'en allait à la chasse, / À la chasse aux corbeaux—"

3. **"Saint-Lazare"**: in the nineteenth century, a women's prison, especially for prostitutes and petty thieves.

4. **"Les Madelonnettes"**: a women's prison in a former convent attached to La Force.

5. **King Get-the-boot-in . . . two sous**: "Le roi Coupdesabot / S'en allait à la chasse, / À la chasse aux corbeaux, / Monté sure des échasses. / Quand on passait dessous, / On lui payait deux sous."

PART FOUR: THE IDYLL OF THE RUE PLUMET
AND THE EPIC OF THE RUE SAINT-DENIS

BOOK ONE: A FEW PAGES OF HISTORY
*I: Well Cut*

1. **the July Revolution**: From his ascension to the throne in 1824, Charles X and his Ultra allies had consistently attempted to increase the power of the throne, effectively attempting to reinstate the ancien régime. In July 1830, royal decrees dissolving the Chamber of Deputies and suppressing the liberty of the press and other civil liberties provoked a coup d'état that in the space of three days—*les Trois Glorieuses*—brought down the government and established Louis-Philippe d'Orléans on the throne.

2. **Caesar for Prusias . . . king of Yvetot**: Prusias was a king in Italy in the second

century B.C.E. who offered to violate the rules of hospitality by killing his guest Hannibal in order to ingratiate himself to the Romans. The king of Yvetot was a legendary figure from French history, an image revived by a popular song by Pierre-Jean Béranger in the early nineteenth century, referring to someone with an inflated idea of his merit and importance.

3. **the Stuarts after the Protector:** The Stuarts, in the person of Charles II, son of the executed Charles I, returned to the English throne after the fall of the Protectorate of Oliver Cromwell.

4. **Louis XVII reigned on the ninth of Thermidor:** The son of Louis XVI and Marie Antoinette was still a prisoner of the republican government at the time of the coup d'état of 9 Thermidor (July 28, 1794). The boy died in June 1795, under the Convention.

5. **the July Ordinances:** the retrogressive laws through which Charles X attempted to neuter the Chamber of Deputies and restrict freedom of the press. Those laws sparked the July uprising that became a revolution.

6. **the spectral calm of Charles I:** the king of England beheaded in 1629.

7. **Charles X . . . square table:** According to legend, Charles X, making his way to Cherbourg in order to board a ship to exile in England, met with his councillors, but the meeting was delayed as a round table was cut into a square, the better to accommodate the seating arrangements dictated by court protocol.

8. **Guillaume du Vair after the Day of the Barricades:** A reference to the Wars of Religion: In May 1588, a riot, incited by the Catholic duc de Guise, broke out at the news that King Henri III intended to designate the Protestant Henri, king of Navarre, as his heir. The king and his court were forced to flee the city, which was left in control of Guise and the Holy League. This was the first time that barricades were constructed in the capital. Guillaume du Vair, as his speech indicates, remained a firm supporter of the monarchy.

9. **Machiavelli:** Niccolò Machiavelli (1469–1527), whose *The Prince* is viewed as a handbook of political cynicism.

*II: Badly Stitched Together*

1. **Iturbide:** Agustin de Iturbide (1783–1824), a Mexican-born officer who joined the independence movement, eventually declaring himself emperor of Mexico in 1822. He attempted to govern as an autocrat and was soon deposed by the army. Driven into exile, he returned to Mexico in the hope of returning to power but was arrested and executed almost immediately.

2. **House of Brunswick:** Usually called the House of Hanover, the British kings called to the throne after the death of Queen Anne in fact were descended from a branch of the ducal House of Brunswick.

3. **England in 1688:** i.e., the Glorious Revolution that replaced the would-be authoritarian James II with his daughter Mary and her husband, William of Orange.

4. **The 221:** i.e., the 221 liberal deputies, the majority that Charles X had attempted to dissolve with the July Ordinances. Lafayette, a national hero whose

reputation had been polished by the passage of time, lent his support to the new Orléans monarchy, making a speech at the Hôtel de Ville of Paris in 1830, just as he had in 1789.

5. **The Hôtel de Ville . . . replaced the cathedral of Rheims:** The ceremonies that installed Louis-Philippe on the throne took place at the town hall of Paris rather than at Rheims Cathedral, where French kings had been crowned for almost a thousand years, an antiquated tradition that Charles X had attempted to revive in 1825.

*III: Louis-Philippe*

1. **Son of a father:** Louis-Philippe's father, the duc d'Orléans (1747–93), first prince of the blood royal, ostentatiously joined the Revolution, probably hoping to replace his cousin, Louis XVI, on the throne. He renamed himself Philippe-Égalité, renounced his royal privileges, and was elected to the Convention, where he voted for the execution of Louis. He himself was guillotined only a few months later.

2. **first prince of the blood:** In the elaborate system of etiquette developed by the Bourbons, the first prince of the blood held the third rank at court, after the *"fils de France"* and *"petits fils de France,"* the sons and grandsons of the king.

3. **daring against Austria at Ancona . . . paying off Pritchard:** events of Louis-Philippe's reign that loomed large in Hugo's lifetime but are largely forgotten now. Austrian influence in Italy and English meddling in Spanish politics were seen as a threat to French interests, just as the European powers resisted putting an Orléans prince on the throne of the new nation of Belgium.

4. **a general at Valmy . . . Jemappes:** As the sons of the Revolutionary duke, Louis-Philippe and his younger brothers had enlisted in the Revolutionary armies. The battles of Jemappes (November 1792) and Valmy (September 1792) were victories for the republican army over the Austro-German forces. Louis-Philippe served as a competent junior officer, neither a private nor a general, in both battles.

5. **Poland and Hungary:** The causes of Polish resistance to Russia and Hungarian resistance to Austria were popular among European liberals.

6. **"les polonois" and said "les hongraïs":** Standard French spelling (and pronunciation) changed during the years of Revolution and Empire; in 1830, the correct spelling was *les Polonais* and *les Hongrois*.

7. **Henri III . . . his dagger:** At the time of the Wars of Religion, Henri III was under constant threat of assassination.

8. **the rue Transnonain:** In April 1834, a troop of soldiers under General Bugeaud (see note 5, p. 1305) was fired on in the rue Transnonain, near Les Halles. The soldiers stormed the house and killed several occupants. Accounts differ as to whether those killed were connected to the shooting, and the actual shooters are believed to have escaped via the roof. A government inquiry cleared the soldiers, but in the popular mind, the "massacre of the rue Transnonain" was another black mark against the government.

9. **Belgium rejected:** When the Belgians gained independence from the Dutch in 1830, a faction in Brussels offered the Belgian throne to Louis-Philippe's younger son. The Orléans were reluctantly persuaded to refuse in deference to English and German concerns. A marriage was arranged between one of Louis-Philippe's daughters and the German prince who became King Léopold I.

10. **Algeria conquered too brutally:** The conquest of Algeria was France's opening move in the European colonization of Africa. It had begun under Charles X and was continued by the July Monarchy.

11. **Abd-el-Kader:** Abd-el-Kader (1808–85) was an Algerian emir and Muslim theologian who became the leader of the anti-French resistance. Throughout the 1830s he negotiated a series of truces with the French, none of which was kept.

12. **profound tenderness . . . for his family:** Hugo had the chance to witness the Orléans as a family; as the most famous writer in France in the late 1830s and early 1840s, he was a frequent guest of the royal family. He was especially friendly with the duc d'Orléans (1810–42), heir to the throne, and his wife.

13. **Marie d'Orléans:** Louis-Philippe's daughter (1813–39), a sculptress. Charles, Duc d'Orléans (1394–1465), was an accomplished poet.

14. **Metternich:** Klemens von Metternich (1773–1859), the powerful Austrian politician who was, with Wellington, one of the living symbols of conservatism in the early nineteenth century.

15. **He had been banned, errant, poor:** As heir to his father's fortune, Louis-Philippe was the owner of the richest princely domains in France, which of course had been confiscated by the Revolution. After fleeing the Revolution (see below), he took refuge at Reichenau in Switzerland and worked as a tutor and schoolteacher.

16. **Adélaïde:** Louis-Philippe's formidable and fiercely loyal younger sister, known as Mademoiselle Adélaïde (1777–1847), was her brother's closest adviser; she frequently encouraged his ambition and stiffened his resolve.

17. **the last iron cage:** Hugo had used the iron cages of Louis XI in *Notre-Dame de Paris.*

18. **Dumouriez's:** Charles-François Dumouriez (1739–1823), the Revolutionary general, had been Louis-Philippe's commander in the Revolutionary armies. When Dumouriez defected to the Austrians in April 1793, Louis-Philippe followed his example and took refuge in Switzerland.

19. **"Young man!":** i.e., the terrible republican had addressed the erstwhile prince and future king in familiar and friendly terms.

20. **Monsieur de Chartres:** The eldest son of the duc d'Orléans had been called the duc de Chartres under the ancien régime.

21. **Capet:** The royal family was called Capet during the Revolution, after Hugh Capet, the tenth-century ancestor of the Bourbons.

22. **a witness beyond all possible doubt:** Hugo himself.

23. **The laws of September:** Following Fieschi's attempted assassination (see below), the government passed laws intending to strengthen the prosecution of

suspected antigovernment plots; Hugo argues that the laws were sufficiently open to public scrutiny.

24. **Louis Blanc:** A leading early socialist, Blanc (1811–82) served, like Hugo, in the governments of the Second and Third Republics and spent the intervening years of the Second Empire in exile. Although the two shared similar concerns about the welfare of the poor, Blanc was well to Hugo's left.

25. **La Grève . . . barrière Saint-Jacques:** In 1830, the site of public executions was moved from the place de Grève, in the center of Paris, to the barrière Saint-Jacques, on the southern edge of the city.

26. **Casimir Périer:** a banker and politician (1777–1832), Louis-Philippe's prime minister (1831–32); a liberal under the Restoration and supporter of the July Revolution. Périer's conservatism in office was an early indicator that the July Monarchy would not be as liberal as many had hoped. One of his most significant acts was the severe repression of a revolt of unemployed silk workers in Lyon in 1831.

27. **Beccaria:** See note 7, p. 1198. The Italian philosopher was an advocate of penal reform and an opponent of the death penalty.

28. **the Fieschi plot:** The Corsican Giuseppe Fieschi (1790–1836) built a *machine infernale*—twenty-four rifles rigged to fire simultaneously—along a planned parade route, hoping to assassinate the king and the royal family in July 1835. The king and his family were unhurt, but twenty bystanders were killed. At his trial Fieschi and his coconspirators were proven to have been acting out of "exalted" republican beliefs, but no link to any larger movement or group could be proved. All three were guillotined.

29. **Louis IX:** Louis IX was revered in his time as a protector of the common people; he was canonized for leading a crusade.

30. **two tombs in exile:** This chapter, which looks back on the July Monarchy, is clearly an addition of Hugo's 1860 revisions; this passage refers to Hugo's own self-exile under the Second Empire of Napoléon III. Louis-Philippe died in England in 1850.

*IV: Cracks Beneath the Foundation*

1. **a Vendéen:** a royalist insurgent during the Revolution.

2. **To the rights of man:** a reference to the Declaration of the Rights of Man, proclaimed by the National Assembly in 1789.

3. **as Venice died:** General Bonaparte and the republican armies put an end to the polite political fiction of the Venetian Republic in 1797.

4. **Lafayette had to be used to defend Polignac:** I.e., without Lafayette's intervention, Polignac would have been assassinated, if not executed.

5. **the year 1832 had begun:** A repetition in miniature of the chapter "In the Year 1817." Of greatest importance for *Les Misérables* is the economic distress of the working classes of Paris and Lyon and the increasing conservatism of the French government, disappointing many liberals and humiliating Lafayette, who had lent his prestige to the July Revolution.

6. **Brussels chasing Nassau out:** I.e., the Belgians had revolted against the Dutch rule established by the Congress of Vienna in 1815.

7. **Poland:** An attempted revolt against Russian rule in Poland had been brutally repressed by Czar Nicholas I, who annexed the country outright in 1831.

8. **the cross torn down from Notre-Dame:** A republican manifestation turned violently anticlerical in 1831; the cathedral was damaged, and the palace of the archbishop was destroyed (see note 1, ch. V, p. 1305).

9. **the duchesse de Berry in the Vendée:** The widow of Charles X's murdered son and mother of the child known to royalists as Henri V, the duchess attempted to provoke a royalist insurrection in the Vendée. She was quickly captured and imprisoned and lost her status as a royalist icon when she was discovered to be pregnant.

*V: Deeds from Which History Emerges and Which History Ignores*

1. **Bonaparte's proclamation to the Army of Italy:** I.e., in the spring of 1796, the newly appointed commander of the Army of Italy assured his troops that they would share in the spoils of victory.

2. **Quénisset:** In 1841, Quénisset attempted to assassinate the duc d'Aumale, son of Louis-Philippe.

3. **"Babouvist! . . . smell Gisquet:** On the revolutionary Babeuf, whose followers were called "Babouvists," see note 3, ch. I, p. 1282. Joseph-Henri Gisquet (1792–1866) was the prefect of the Paris police from 1831 to 1836.

4. **jacquerie:** a reference to the fourteenth-century peasant revolts of central France.

5. **Saint-Eustache:** the parish church of the district around Les Halles.

6. **the Court of Peers:** a special inquest tribunal made up of members of the Chamber of Peers.

7. **Unité . . . *Populaire*:** Several of the names of the sections have historical resonance. For Barra, see note 6, p. 1260. Tadeusz Kościuszko (1746–1817) was a leader of the anti-Russian resistance in Poland. On Caius Gracchus, see note 6, p. 1275. The fall of the Girondins was the ultimate triumph of the Jacobins over the moderates. On Hoche and Marceau, see note 4, p. 1242.

8. **the insurrection of April 1834:** A revolt of unemployed silk workers in Lyon began on April 9; over the course of a week, more than six hundred insurgents and soldiers were killed. On the thirteenth, Parisian workers and those sympathetic to them rioted in Paris. The massacre of the rue Transnonain took place in the wake of this unrest.

9. *Pluviôse, Year XL:* The Revolutionary calendar dated from the fall of the Bourbon monarchy in 1792, so 1832 is the Year XL.

10. **The Pikes . . . Ça ira:** Pikes were the weapon of choice during the insurrections of 1789–92. On the phrygian cap, see note 21, p. 1204. January 21 was the day of Louis XVI's execution in 1793. "Ça ira" was a revolutionary song (see note 11, p. 1267).

11. **Belfort, Lunéville, and Épinal movements:** Republican soldiers in these three

important forts in western France rebelled in sympathy with the Lyonnais silk workers in April 1834.

12. **"Tree of Liberty"**: a custom of the Revolution.

13. **Ennius:** Latin poet of the second century B.C.E.

14. **"sybilline wine"**: The source of sybilline wine is unclear, but it suggests an allusion to the Greek oracles known as "sybils," thus wine that gives the gift of prophecy.

15. *Ingens:* power.

### VI: Enjolras and His Lieutenants

1. **"polytechnic students"**: Students of the École Polytechnique were traditionally in the front rank of the protests and insurrections of nineteenth-century Paris.

2. **"Dupuytren's"**: See note 77, p. 1218.

3. **"the Contrat Social . . . my constitution for the Year II"**: Grantaire offers his republican bona fides by loosely citing some of the founding documents of the Revolution, such as Rousseau's *Du Contrat social* (1768) and the revolutionary constitution (there was no constitution voted in 1794/Year II, but there was in 1793/Year I and 1795/Year III; Grantaire quotes the former). Louis-Marie Prud'homme was a relatively obscure journalist during the Revolution who became a supporter of the Bourbons during the Restoration. A curious name to cite alongside that of Rousseau.

4. **"assignat"**: See note 3, p. 1256.

5. **"Hébertist"**: the most radical faction of the Revolution of 1789.

### BOOK TWO: ÉPONINE
### I: The Lark's Field

1. *salle des pas perdus:* i.e., a waiting room.

2. **men like Escousse and Lebras:** Barely twenty, Escousse and Lebras made and carried out a suicide pact in 1832 when a play they had cowritten failed.

3. **Ruisdael:** Jacob van Ruisdael (1629–82), a Dutch landscape painter.

### II: Embryonic Development of Crimes in Prison Incubators

1. **Némorin . . . Schinderhannes:** Némorin was the hero-lover of a Romantic novel, *Estelle and Némorin;* on the criminal Schinderhannes; see note 4, ch. II, p. 1283; that is, Montparnasse would rather seduce Éponine than work with Thénardier and their accomplices.

2. **the Salon:** a juried exposition of art sponsored by the government.

### IV: Marius's Apparition

1. **Gans and Savigny:** two German law professors who disputed the theories of Hegel as applied to law. Karl Marx studied with both men.

2. **Ophelia:** In Shakespeare's *Hamlet,* Ophelia is driven mad by Hamlet's own growing madness.

BOOK THREE: THE HOUSE IN THE RUE PLUMET
*I: The House with a Secret Entrance*

1. **the parliament of Paris:** the largest and most powerful of the law courts of the
   ancien régime.
2. **"a little house":** In the grand tradition of libertinage, great aristocrats and their
   wealthy imitators built or bought small houses expressly for the purpose of
   assignations.
3. **Mansart . . . Watteau:** François Mansart (1598–1666), an influential architect;
   Watteau (see note 1, p. 1221) was the great late-baroque painter of the *fête
   galante;* the rocaille, or rococo, interior and the stolid exterior, which suggests
   the wig of the staid magistrate, make the house a metaphor for the secret love
   affairs it was built for.
4. **the hospital:** i.e., from extreme poverty, from dying in a charity hospital.
5. **rue de l'Ouest . . . rue de l'Homme-Armé:** The rue de l'Ouest, today absorbed
   into the rue d'Assas, was near the Luxembourg gardens; the rue de l'Homme-
   Armé was on the western edge of the Marais.

*II: Jean Valjean as a National Guard*

1. **man of means, was in the National Guard:** Those with sufficient assets to
   qualify as voters were required to serve periodically in the National Guard.
2. **local *mairie:*** Each arrondissement had a mayor and *mairie.*
3. **the comte de Lobau:** the Napoleonic general and count Georges Mouton
   (1770–1838), loyal to Napoléon, briefly exiled by the Bourbons, named marshal and peer of France by Louis-Philippe.

*III: Foliis ac Frondibus*

1. ***Foliis ac Frondibus:*** leaves and branches.
2. **Floréal:** month of the revolutionary calendar, roughly April 20–May 19, named
   for the bloom of spring flowers.

*IV: Gate Change*

1. **Paphos:** In Greek mythology, Paphos, on the island of Crete, was the place
   where Aphrodite stepped out of the sea.
2. **Lamoignon . . . Le Nôtre:** I.e., the *parlementaire* takes himself for a second
   Chrétien-François Lamoignon (1613–1700), president of the Paris *parlement*
   under Louis XIV, and his gardener for André Le Nôtre, the landscape architect
   of the Versailles gardens.
3. **camera obscura:** Latin for "dark chamber," an optic device, invented in the

eighteenth century, that used the play of light through a lens to project an image inside a box.

*V: The Rose Realizes She Is an Engine of War*

1. **a hat by Gérard . . . Herbaut:** two fashionable milliners in Restoration Paris.

*VIII: The Chain Gang*

1. **"La Vestale" . . . Désaugiers's:** The songwriter Marc-Antoine Désaugiers (1772–1827) was also a theater owner, enormously successful with vaudeville and other popular theater. "La Vestale" dates from 1807.
2. **the Gemoniae:** the Gemonian Stairs, or Stairs of Mourning, which led from the Forum down to the Tiber in ancient Rome. A site of public execution, used with the intent of publicly shaming the criminals after their death. The corpses of the executed were left there to rot.

BOOK FIVE: WHOSE END IS NOTHING LIKE ITS BEGINNING
*II: Cosette's Fears*

1. *Euryanthe:* Karl Maria von Weber's 1823 opera.

*III: Embellished by Toussaint's Comments*

1. **"like it was the Bastille":** The Bastille was a massive military fortress and arsenal.

*VI: The Old Are Made for Going Out at the Right Moment*

1. **One kiss, and that was everything:** The overgrown garden of the rue Plumet is generally taken as a remembrance of a similar garden attached to the house where Victor Hugo lived as a child, where he would play with his future wife, Adèle Foucher.

BOOK SIX: PETIT-GAVROCHE
*I: Nasty Trick of the Wind*

1. **the maréchale de la Mothe-Houdancourt:** an apparent reference to Saint-Simon's *Mémoires;* an influential aristocrat who married each of her three daughters to dukes.

*II: In Which Petit-Gavroche Puts Napoléon the Great to Good Use*

1. **the first great epidemic of the century:** An epidemic of cholera swept through Paris in 1832.

2. **worthy of meeting Faust on the Brocken:** In Goethe's *Faust*, the hero meets the devil on top of the Brocken, the highest peak in northern Germany, which had a long history of being associated with witches and Walpurgis Night.

3. **Saint Martin . . . cloak:** See note 12, p. 1254.

4. **the Iowas and the Botocudos:** references to indigenous peoples of Brazil.

5. **the Conciergerie:** the massive medieval fortress on the Île de la Cîté, a former royal palace turned prison. It was where prisoners of the Revolution, most famously Marie Antoinette, awaited the tumbrils that would take them to the guillotine.

6. **red-tails of the *grand siècle:*** The painter and engraver Jacques Callot (1592–1635) was actually a generation older than Molière (1622–73); he often chose scenes from lower-class life as the subject of his drawings. Molière sometimes worked into his comedies the argot of the working class from the Les Halles neighborhood he had grown up in, most notably in *Le bourgeois gentilhomme*.

7. **a member of the Institut, commander in chief of the Army of Egypt:** i.e., Napoléon Bonaparte. The elephant, which stood in the place de la Bastille from 1814 until 1846, was a plaster model of an intended monument to the Egyptian campaign.

8. **this stovepipe:** The July Column was inaugurated in 1840.

9. **a child caught sleeping:** Hugo gives no record of this incident, but several such occasions noted in *Les Misérables* were based on fact.

10. **the great tun of Heidelberg:** See note 1, ch. IV, p. 1277.

11. **Jonas . . . the biblical whale:** the Old Testament book of Jonah, in which God sends a whale to punish Jonah's disobedience.

12. **The claque . . . the boulevards:** An old tradition in the French theater, claques were groups who went to applaud or to jeer a play, depending on their taste, their relationship to the author, or—most commonly—who was paying them. Paid claques were used especially by and against Hugo at the tempestuous premiere of *Hernani* in 1830. Gavroche is bragging a bit by claiming to have nothing to do with the popular theaters of the boulevards (see note 14 below).

13. **Paul de Kock:** An immensely prolific popular novelist, Paul de Kock (1793–1871) wrote many novels and almost two hundred plays for vaudeville and the popular theater. His work treated the lower classes of Paris with a combination of humor and sentimentality.

14. **the Théâtre Ambigu:** One of the boulevard theaters Gavroche claimed to disdain, the Théâtre Ambigu, in the boulevard du Temple, specialized in vaudeville, comedy, and melodrama.

15. **what the good storyteller Perrault calls "fresh meat":** from *Petit Poucet* (*Tom Thumb* in English) by Charles Perrault (1628–1703), the cry with which the ogre hunts Tom and his brothers.

*III: The Ups and Downs of Escape*

1. **Milton glimpsed behind Berquin:** John Milton (1697–74) painted a vision of hell in *Paradise Lost*; Arnaud Berquin (1747–91) wrote sentimental and moralistic books for children.
2. **Desrues . . . the Endormeurs gang:** Antoine-François Desrues (1744–77), a famous con man and murderer, broken on the wheel in 1777.
3. *"Qu'il mourut":* from Corneille's play *Horace*. Corneille was one of Hugo's favorite playwrights.
4. **the nearby clock of Saint Paul:** the church of Saint-Paul on the rue Saint-Antoine, near the place des Vosges.
5. **the argot of the Temple:** i.e., of the neighborhood around the Temple; see note 1, ch. I, p. 1263.
6. **Poulailler and Cartouche:** two famous criminals. On Cartouche, see note 7, p. 1202. Poulailler was an eighteenth-century bandit who preyed on prosperous farms and became something of a legend in popular imagination.
7. **the language of Racine . . . André Chénier:** Hugo vastly preferred the poetry of Chénier (see note 15, p. 1276) to the classical verse of Racine.
8. **survivors from the *Medusa*:** See note 18, p. 1212.

BOOK SEVEN: SLANG
*I: Origins*

1. **thirty-four years ago:** a reference to Hugo's 1830 novel *Le Dernier Jour d'un condamné* (The Last Day of a Condemned Man), an eloquent statement against the death penalty as well as an intriguingly written first-person monologue of a man facing imminent execution.
2. **Balzac and Eugène Sue:** Balzac's 1847 *Splendeurs et misères des courtisanes* (The Splendor and Misery of Courtesans) and *Les Misérables* both drew inspiration from Eugène Sue's *Les Mystères de Paris* (The Mysteries of Paris), an immensely popular and successful novel when published as a serial in 1842–43 that is rarely read today.
3. *Montpellier available, Marseilles:* i.e., goods or produce from those cities.
4. **the phrenologist:** Phrenologists claimed to be able to discern a person's character according to the shape and contours of the skull. Belief in phrenology was fairly widespread in the nineteenth century.
5. **the Hôtel de Rambouillet meets the Cour des Miracles:** The salons of the Hôtel de Rambouillet, the Parisian town house of the marquise de Rambouillet, formed the center of an elite literary culture in the seventeenth century that is often seen as part of the movement of *préciosité*, especially the sentimental and affected language invented by the *précieuses* to speak of love. The Cour des Miracles played an important role in Hugo's *Notre-Dame de Paris*. In that novel, set in late medieval Paris, the Cours des Miracles were gathering places for thieves, beggars and the homeless. They took their name from the fact that

many beggars who claimed some disability were "miraculously" cured when returning there.

6. **Monsieur de Montmorency a** *bourgeois:* The Montmorencys were one of the oldest families of the French nobility. The meaning of *bourgeois* was changing.

7. **Jean Bart, Duquesne, Suffren, and Duperré:** historic French admirals. The privateer Jean Bart (1650–1702) was named a naval officer by Louis XIV; Admiral Abraham Duquesne (1610–88); Bailli de Suffren (1729–88) was admiral of the French Navy during the American Revolution; Guy Victor Duperré (1775–1845) served under the Restoration and July Monarchy.

8. **Plautus:** a Roman comic playwright whose work Hugo knew well; see note 3, ch. X, pp. 1260–61.

9. **Molière . . . Levantine:** In *Le bourgeois gentilhomme,* Molière used the Levantine patois—a dialect used by Mediterranean sailors from different countries to communicate with one another—in a famous scene.

## *II: Roots*

1. **the red-hot brand of the executioner:** Those condemned to hard labor, as at Toulon, were branded, with either the letters *TF,* for *Travaux forcés,* for limited terms, or *TFP, Travaux forcés perpetuels,* for life sentences.

2. **Mandrin:** The bandit Louis Mandrin (1725–55) gained a Robin Hood–esque reputation because he limited his thefts to the rich, especially the hated tax collectors known as *fermiers généraux.* He was also a smuggler, selling heavily taxed goods, especially tobacco, far cheaper than legitimate merchants could. He was captured and, because the *fermiers généraux* hated him so much, broken on the wheel.

3. **Villon:** See note 4, ch. XX, p. 1286.

4. **La Fontaine's:** Jean de La Fontaine (1621–95), author of the *Fables.*

5. **the poor poacher Survincent:** Hugo visited several prisons in Paris, including the Châtelet (see note 2, ch. I, p. 1245), and is almost certainly quoting a prisoner he met there.

6. **"Langleviel La Beaumelle":** Voltaire often used his wit and his pen to take revenge on those who had insulted him. Many of these targets are remembered only because they attracted the great man's contempt.

## *III: Slang That Cries and Slang That Laughs*

1. **Turgot:** Anne-Robert Turgot (1727–81), the most prominent of the physiocrats, who unsuccessfully attempted to institute significant reforms as Louis XVI's minister of finance.

2. **weirdly subversive writings . . . the dregs:** It is unclear to whose writings Hugo is referring, but the prince de Conti (Louis-François de Bourbon-Conti, 1727–1776), prince of the blood royal, had a reputation for sponsoring writers who tested the limits of royal censors, including Rousseau and Beaumarchais.

3. **Restif de la Bretonne:** Nicolas-Edme Restif de la Bretonne (1734–1806) came to Paris from the provinces and studied the lower classes and darker corners of Parisian society.

4. *The Robbers:* play by Johann von Schiller (1759–1805), a romantic playwright and poet whom Hugo admired.

5. **a fourteenth of July, a tenth of August:** days of popular insurrection during the Revolution: July 14, 1789, was the day the Bastille was stormed by what is usually called a mob; on August 10, 1792, civilians, National Guard, and soldiers invaded the Tuileries Palace, and the king and the royal family were forced to ask for the protection of the National Assembly, making it the last day of the monarchy.

6. **The wagons that carried . . . in 1848:** i.e., during the revolution of 1848.

*IV: The Two Duties: To Watch and to Hope*

1. **imams to converse with Bonaparte inside the great pyramid:** a singularly romantic image of Bonaparte's 1798–99 Egyptian campaign.

BOOK EIGHT: ENCHANTMENT AND DESOLATION
*I: Broad Daylight*

1. **the Jungfrau:** one of the highest peaks in the Alps. Hugo plays on multiple images of purity: two white birds meeting on a snow-covered peak, the name of which translates as "virgin."

*IV: A Cab Rolls in English and Yelps Like a Mutt in Slang*

1. **It's not . . . Daddy's neck:** "Nous n'sommes pas le jour de l'an, / À bécoter papa, maman."

2. **the Île des Cygnes:** a small artificial island in the Seine.

3. **My arms . . . won't come again:** "Mon bras si dodu, / Ma jambe bien faite, / Et le temps perdu."

*VI: Marius Falls to Earth and Gives Cosette His Address*

1. **the Faublases and the Prudhommes:** a reference to two fictional characters representing a certain fatuous pseudointellectualism. Faublas refers to the chevalier de Faublas (1760–97), the libertine hero of the comic novels by Jean-Baptiste Louvetin in the 1780s and '90s. Prudhomme refers to Monnier's caricatural bourgeois (see note 13, p. 1206).

2. **Busiris:** a tyrannical king in Greek mythology, slain by Hercules.

*VII: Old Heart and Young Heart Face-to-Face*

1. **Monsieur Humblot-Conté, peer of France:** an obscure deputy and supporter of the July Revolution (1776–1845) who was named to the Chamber of Peers

by Louis-Philippe and immortalized by Monsieur Gillenormand's royalist indignation.

2. **"prefer sabreurs to saber-draggers"**: i.e., he prefers a real soldier to a uniformed dandy like Théodule.

3. **Garat:** probably Dominique-Joseph Garat (1749–1833), a journalist and politician.

4. **"Molière overlooked this one"**: i.e., the absurdity of a young man asking pity from an old man, as in a scene in a farce.

5. **"run up debts without even telling me to pay them"**: For Monsieur Gillenormand, debts should be a fact of life for any healthy young man.

6. **"permission to marry"**: The question is not a mere formality. The age of majority for men was twenty-five; Marius would have needed the permission of his grandfather (and legal guardian) to enter into any legal contract.

7. **"help storm the Louvre"**: i.e., did Marius help bring down the Bourbons in July 1830.

8. **"to replace the monument of Monsieur le duc de Berry"**: It was in fact in 1844 that a memorial on the site of the duke's assassination was replaced by a fountain.

9. **"twelve hundred livres"**: i.e., the six hundred pistoles that Marius has always returned to his aunt.

10. **"A real Pamela"**: the heroine of Samuel Richardson's immensely popular novel; see note 3, ch. II, p. 1226.

BOOK NINE: WHERE ARE THEY GOING?
*I: Jean Valjean*

1. **Pépin or Morey:** another anachronism. Pépin and Morey were the accomplices of Fieschi in the plot against Louis-Philippe in 1835.

*II: Marius*

1. **What devastates Othello . . . Candide:** Shakespeare's Othello is driven to a murderous rage by the slightest evidence of infidelity on the part of Desdemona; Voltaire's simple Candide is incapable of anger against Cunégonde.

2. **General Lamarque's funeral:** Jean-Maximilien Lamarque (1770–1832) was a volunteer soldier in the Revolutionary Army and rose to the rank of general under Napoléon. Exiled after Waterloo for having rallied to Napoléon, he returned to France in 1818 and was elected to the Chamber of Deputies in 1828. A liberal democrat and ally of Lafayette, he was one of the 221 who resisted the July Ordinances (see note 5, p. 1287). Under the July Monarchy, he remained a member of the opposition, and was particularly noted for his rhetorical support of the Poles, the Greeks, and other oppressed peoples. He died a victim of the cholera epidemic of 1832. His funeral was in fact the trigger for the *journée* described here as the "epic of the rue Saint-Denis." Hugo's biographer Graham Robb points out that in 1832, Victor Hugo barely noticed the insurrection.

Although vaguely sympathetic to republicanism and the sufferings of the poor, Hugo—the man Robb describes as being, in 1832, "a tax-paying, property-owning father of four with timorous leanings to the left"—dismissed the *journée* as "follies drowned in blood."

### III: Monsieur Mabeuf

1. **"Round by the Arsenal"**: The Arsenal stands on the right bank, just east of the Marais.

### BOOK TEN: JUNE 5, 1832
### I: The Issue on the Surface

1. **Philinte versus Alceste**: In Molière's *Misanthrope,* Alceste is the protagonist of unyielding principle who refuses to compromise with the hypocrisies of the society he lives in; his best friend, Philinte, urges him to compromise in order to fit in more comfortably with those around him.
2. **the happy medium**: *le juste milieu,* which supporters of the July Monarchy saw as a wise stance based on Aristotle's "golden mean." Its detractors on the right and left saw it as Hugo did, as lukewarm political water.
3. **Jean Chouan . . . Jeanne**: Jean Chouan was the nom de guerre of Jean Cottereau, a leader of the Chouan movement (the "war of the bushes" Hugo refers to; see note 4, p. 1256). A worker (*ouvrier*) known only as Jeanne was one of the leaders of the insurrection of June 5 (see note 3, p. 1304).
4. **The setting up of Philippe V in Spain**: a reference to the War of Spanish Succession (1701–14), when Louis XIV won a hugely expensive and bloody war against the English and their allies in order to affirm his grandson's claim to the Spanish throne.

### II: The Heart of the Matter

1. **according to whether it is the king or the Convention . . . Bonaparte defends the true**: On August 10, 1792, the Tuileries were invaded by a Parisian mob aided by the National Guard; the Swiss Guard was the royal family's last line of defense. On Vendémiaire 14, Year IV (October 5, 1795), a royalist insurgency surrounded the Tuileries, then occupied by the Convention. General Bonaparte led the counterstrike, driving back 25,000 royalists with well-placed cannon fire.
2. **Terray . . . Turgot**: Joseph (l'abbé) Terray (1715–78), minister of finance for Louis XV from 1769 to 1774; like his successor, Turgot (see note 1, p. 1297), he attempted dramatic budgetary reforms, but without the innovations toward representative government that earned Turgot Hugo's approbation.
3. **Ramus assassinated by schoolboys**: Petrus Ramus, or Pierre de La Ramée (1515–72), a humanist philosopher and theologian, was an enormously popu-

lar and controversial professor at the Sorbonne; having converted to Calvinism, he was murdered during the Saint Bartholomew's Day Massacre, possibly by university students.

4. **Rousseau driven out of Switzerland:** Several of Rousseau's books contained sharp critiques of organized religion that angered Catholics and Protestants; he emigrated to England from Switzerland in 1765 when that hostility led to, among other things, his house being pelted with stones.

5. **Israel versus Moses . . . sailors versus Christopher Columbus:** In the Old Testament (Numbers 16) a number of elders challenge the authority of Moses. On "Athens versus Phocion," see note 9, p. 1278: "Rome versus Scipio": probably a reference to Scipio Africanus, consul at the time of the Gracchi (see note 6, p. 1275), who was found murdered in his bed. "The soldiers versus Alexander": Alexander the Great faced dissent among his officers and soldiers several times. "Sailors versus Christopher Columbus": During Columbus's first voyage, he faced a near munity from sailors who believed their ships were lost.

6. **"Death to the Salt Taxes":** The *gabelle,* a tax on salt, was one of the most regressive and hated taxes of the ancien régime.

7. **Saint Bartholomew killers . . . La Vendée is one big Catholic riot:** On the Saint-Bartholomew's Day massacres, see note 16, p. 1203. Those responsible for the massacres of the religious wars, like all those mentioned in these lines, were practicing violence for dubious political causes. "September cutthroats": the September massacres of the Revolution; one of the most famous victims was Marie Antoinette's friend the princesse de Lamballe. "Avignon slaughterers": See note 16, p. 1203. "Assassins of Coligny": See note 3, ch. III, p. 1311. "Assassins of Brune": See note 3, ch. III, p. 1283. The Miquelet militias were Spanish guerrillas who fought against Napoleonic forces. The Verdets and the Chevaliers du Brassard were royalists who took an active part in the *Terreur blanche* in the south of France; they took their name from the green (*vert*) cockades and armbands (*brassards*) they wore, the color and symbol of the comte d'Artois, who was known to be more conservative than his brother the king. "Cadenette-wearing soldiers": young royalists, fops, and Incroyables who practiced clandestine violence on revolutionaries after the fall of Robespierre. "Companions of Jesus" (*les compagnons de Jéhu;* they apparently preferred an archaic spelling) were another group that made up the *Terreur blanche.* Hugo saw the Vendée in starkly different terms when younger.

8. **Hébert versus Danton:** Jacques-René Hébert (1757–94) was the leader of the *enragé* faction of the Revolution that attacked Danton under the Convention. Robespierre found Hébert a useful weapon against Danton, but when Hébert started attacking Robespierre, he was arrested and guillotined.

9. **Polignac . . . Camille Desmoulins:** Jules de Polignac (1780–1847) became prime minister to Charles X in August 1829. An Ultra of long standing (and the son of Marie Antoinette's controversial favorite, the duchesse de Polignac), Polignac encouraged the king's intransigence in the face of the Chamber of Deputies. He was seen as responsible for the July Ordinances that provoked

the revolution of 1830. Camille Desmoulins (1760–94) became one of the leading orators of the Revolution; closely allied to Danton, he was arrested and executed with him in April 1794.

10. **there was Juvenal:** Juvenal (ca. 50–ca. 125) was the author of the *Satires,* which sharply critiqued all aspects of Roman society. He couched his political critiques by referring to past emperors, but they were sharp enough to bring about his exile to Syene, in Egypt (near modern Aswan).

11. **the Gracchi:** Roman brothers who attempted reforms to aid the poor; see note 6, page 1275.

12. **the man of the *Annals:*** Tacitus, whose *Annals* offered a scathing indictment of the emperors from Tiberius to Nero.

13. **the mighty exile of Patmos:** traditionally believed to be Saint John the Evangelist, the author of the Book of Revelation (or Apocalypse), written while the author was living in exile on the Greek island of Patmos.

14. **the Neros:** i.e., the Caesars, of whom Nero was the last and worst of a corrupt line beginning with Tiberius.

15. **The Ciceronian period:** The Roman senator and orator Cicero solidified his public reputation as the prosecutor of Gaius Lucius Verres, accused of corruption while serving as governor of Sicily.

16. **Tiberii:** i.e., Tiberius and his successors Caligula, Claudius, and Nero, the subjects of Tacitus's *Annals.*

17. **the Sicilian pirates . . . the Rubicon:** I.e., Caesar's great achievements cover the sin of crossing the Rubicon with his armies to seize dictatorial powers and effectively end the Roman Republic.

18. **Vitellius . . . Sulla:** Vitellius (15–69) held the title of emperor for barely six months before being deposed and killed by the forces of Vespasian; Lucius Cornelius Sulla (138–78 B.C.E.), often called Sylla, used his military successes to seize power in Rome as dictator. He was in many ways a precursor of Julius Caesar.

19. **Claudius and under Domitian:** Many Roman historians portrayed Claudius (born 10 B.C.E., reigned 41–54) as weak and manipulated by his wives—including Messalina and Agrippina—and flatterers. Besides being an incompetent ruler, Domitian (born 51, reigned 81–96) was said to have persecuted Christians and Jews. Some believe the Book of Revelation was written under his reign, as a response to his persecutions.

20. **Caracalla . . . Heliogabalus:** Caracalla (born 186, reigned 211–217) was one of the most brutal of Roman rulers; Commodus (born 161, reigned 180–92) was known as a weak, capricious, and incompetent ruler; Heliogabalus (born 203, reigned 218–222) was known for his eccentric debauchery, and his cruelty became the stuff of legend.

21. **Masaniello . . . Spartacus:** Masaniello, or Tommaso Aniello (1622–47), was a fisherman who became the leader of a Neopolitan revolt against Spanish rule in 1647; he was eventually betrayed and assassinated by those who had been his followers, and the revolt failed. The legend of the gladiator-slave Spartacus (ca. 120–ca. 70 B.C.E.), who led a briefly successful slave revolt against the

Roman government and army, was enormously popular with nineteenth-century liberals and revolutionaries.

22. **Gaster:** an allusion to Rabelais, who refers to the stomach as "Monsieur Gaster."

23. **Buzançais:** In 1847, during a year of extremely poor harvests in France, a group of peasants attacked a landowner who refused to lower the price of his wheat. Three men were hanged as a result.

24. **no Alps ... the Asturias:** The Jura Mountains in eastern France rise up against the Alps, much as the Asturias do in northern Spain against the larger and more imposing Pyrenees.

*III: A Burial: An Occasion for Rebirth*

1. **Foy, his predecessor:** Maximilien-Sébastien Foy (1775–1825), like Lamarque, rose up through the ranks to become a general and fought at Waterloo. In the Chamber of Deputies, Foy became an influential orator and leader of the liberal opposition. His funeral procession, like Lamarque's seven years later, became the occasion for antigovernment protests.

2. **the comte Gérard and the comte Drouet:** Maurice-Étienne Gérard (1773–1852) and Jean-Baptiste Drouet (1765–1844) both rallied to Napoléon during the Hundred Days and fought at Waterloo. Both had significant political careers under the July Monarchy.

3. **maréchaux *in petto:*** meaning Napoléon had planned to promote them but had not yet done so.

4. **The treaties of 1815:** Following Napoléon's return from Elba and Waterloo, the European allies demanded greater concessions from France in terms of territory, indemnity, and postwar occupation of France than they had in 1814.

5. **the faubourg Saint-Antoine:** Then on the eastern edge of Paris on the right bank (in today's eleventh and twelfth arrondissements), the faubourg Saint-Antoine was one of the poorest quarters of Paris. Its populace was associated with many of the *journées* of the French Revolution (including the taking of the Bastille, June 20 and August 10, 1792).

6. **the sectionnaires:** The *sections* were administrative districts of Paris drawn up by the Revolutionary governments, with names like Amis du peuple, les Piques, and les Brutus. The section meetings were used to rally crowds for demonstrations and insurrections. They were suppressed in 1795, in favor of the twelve arrondissements.

7. **refugees of all nations:** Lamarque was noted for his interest in the liberal movement across Europe (see note 2, ch. II, p. 1299).

8. **place Louis XV:** In 1830, the great square between the Tuileries and the Champs-Élysées had been renamed the place de la Concorde.

9. **legitimist intrigues ... the duc de Reichstadt:** I.e., Partisans of both the elder branch of the Bourbon family and Napoléon's son (who died on July 22, 1832) saw a chance to retake the throne from Louis-Philippe.

10. **the Vendôme column:** A symbol of Napoleonic, and French, military glory,

the great column in the place Vendôme was made from the bronze of Austrian and Russian cannons captured at Austerlitz and melted down. The Bourbons removed the statue of Napoléon from the top of the column in 1814. Hugo's 1827 poem "Ode à la Colonne de Vendôme" is seen as an indicator of his shifting politics, from royalism to liberalism.

11. **the duc de Fitz-James:** Descended from the duke of Berwick, the illegitimate son of James II of England who took refuge in France in 1688, the Fitz-Jameses were one of the great families of the aristocracy. The duke's refusal to remove his hat as the funeral procession passes is seen as a sign of disrespect.

12. **the Gallic cock:** adopted as a national symbol by the July Monarchy.

13. **a red flag . . . a red cap:** a symbol of republicanism, as the "pike topped a red cap," the Phrygian cap, specifically recalled the bloodiest episodes of the Revolution of 1789–92.

14. **Exelmans:** Rémy-Joseph Exelmans (1775–1852) was known as one of the fiercest partisans of Napoléon. Louis-Napoléon would name him a marshal of France and senator of the Second Empire just before his death.

15. **"Lamarque to the Panthéon!" "Lafayette to the Hôtel de Ville!":** The Panthéon had been redesignated a national mausoleum by the July Monarchy after having been restored to its religious function—as the church of Sainte-Geneviève—by the Bourbons. Lafayette's public appearances at the Hôtel de Ville had been key moments in the revolutions of 1789 and 1830.

16. **the narrow arm of the Seine:** The small branch of the Seine between the right bank and the Île Louviers was filled in to create the quai Morland in 1847.

*IV: The Seething of Days Gone By*

1. **an imperceptible white stripe:** I.e., the color of the Bourbons, of royalism, is reduced to a bare minimum.

2. **yataghans:** long daggers with curved blades.

3. **no. 50 . . . Jeanne and his one hundred and six companions:** At 50, rue Saint-Merry (or Saint-Merri), at the intersection of the rue Saint-Martin, a worker whose name is recorded only as Jeanne led one of the strongest points of resistance to the National Guard. Jeanne and twenty other survivors were later deported.

4. **the Hôtel Dieu . . . prefecture of police:** a charity hospital founded in the seventh century; it was then housed in a building next to Notre-Dame, since destroyed by Haussmann's renovations. The prefecture of police faces the cathedral.

5. **the tocsin of Saint-Merry:** I.e., an alarm signal was being rung with the bells of the church of Saint-Merry.

6. **maréchal Soult:** Nicolas-Jean de Dieu Soult (1769–1851), duc de Dalmatie, had been one of Napoléon's closest generals. After a brief exile during the Restoration, he was restored to his military rank and named peer of France by Charles

X in 1827; he served as minister of war (1830–34, 1840–45), minister of foreign affairs (1839–40), and twice as prime minister (1832–34, 1845–47) under Louis-Philippe.

## V: Originality of Paris

1. **In 1831:** In February 1831, a memorial service for the assassinated duc de Berry provoked a Republican riot that culminated in the sacking of the archbishop's palace on the Île de la Cité.
2. **the insurrection of May 12, 1839:** Under the leadership of Auguste Blanqui, several hundred socialists and republicans invaded the Hôtel de Ville; the insurrection lasted only a few hours.
3. **Armand Carrel . . . maréchal Clauzel:** Armand Carrel (1800–36), the editor and publisher of the liberal *National,* in fact did not support the insurrection of June 1832. Marshal Bertrand Clauzel (1772–1842) had served in the army with Lamarque and served as a pallbearer at his funeral. As implied by the reference to Anne Radcliffe below, Hugo is reporting rumors rather than facts.
4. **that Anne Radcliffe:** Anne Radcliffe (1764–1832) was one of the first and most successful of Gothic novelists. Her work was extremely popular in France.
5. **Lobau and Bugeaud:** Georges Mouton, marshal count Lobau (see note 3, ch. II, p. 1293) was responsible for putting down the insurrections of the 1830s as commander of the National Guard. Thomas-Robert Bugeaud de la Piconnerie (1784–1849) was a general and deputy; placed in charge of a brigade of the National Guard during the insurrection of 1834, he earned the nickname "butcher of the rue Transnonain" (see note 8, p. 1288).
6. **Lagrange, the man from Lyon:** Charles Lagrange, one of the leaders of the silk workers' insurrection of 1834 (see note 8, ch. V, p. 1291).

BOOK ELEVEN: THE ATOM FRATERNIZES WITH THE HURRICANE
*I: Some Insights . . . on This Poetry*

1. **You can't . . . Pointy-hatted hood!:** "La nuit on ne voit rien, / Le jour on voit très bien, / D'un écrit apocryphe / Le bourgeois s'ébouriffe, / Pratiquez la vertu, / Tutu chapeau pointu!"
2. **Monsieur Baour-Lormian:** "one of the Forty," i.e., a member of the Académie Française.

## II: Gavroche on the March

1. **"Let impure blood flood our furrows!":** *"Qu'un sang impur abreuve nos sillons,"* the last line of the chorus of the "Marseillaise."
2. **Scotland has its trios of witches:** a reference to the "weird sisters" of *Macbeth,* Act I, scene iii: "All hail, Macbeth! thou shalt be king hereafter!"
3. **the king of Rome . . . the duc de Bordeaux . . . Louis XVII:** three heirs de-

prived of their birthright by revolution. On the king of Rome, see note 57, p. 1216. Charles X's grandson, the posthumous son of the assassinated duc de Berry, had been named duc de Bordeaux by Louis XVIII; he was known to royalists as Henri V after his grandfather Charles X and his uncle, the duc d'Angoulême, abdicated. Louis XVII was a son of Louis XVI and Marie Antoinette.

4. **the Hôtel Lamoignon:** one of the great Renaissance town houses—*hôtels particuliers*—of the Marais; the Lamoignons were one of the most notable families of the *noblesse de robe*. It now houses the Bibliothèque Historique de la Ville de Paris.

### III: A Wigmaker's Just Indignation

1. **Prudhomme:** Henri Monnier's satirical portrait of the typical Parisian bourgeois; see note 13, p. 1206.
2. **"The emperor was only ever wounded once" . . . "At Ratisbon":** At the battle of Regensburg, Germany (Ratisbonne in French), in April 1809, Napoléon was struck in the heel by a Austrian bullet. Comparisons to Achilles were inevitable.
3. **a Pindaric tone:** Pindar was a lyric poet in Greece (fifth century B.C.E.).

### IV: The Boy Marvels at the Old Man

1. **"Long live Poland!":** The cause of Polish independence was enormously popular among French liberals and romantics.
2. **"para bellum":** from a Latin axiom, *"Si vis pacem, para bellum"*: "If you want peace, prepare for war."

### V: The Old Man

1. **Here's the moon . . . one boot:**
Voici la lune qui paraît,
Quand irons-nous dans la forêt?
> Demandait Charlot à Charlotte.
>> Tou tou tou
>> Pour Chatou.
Je n'ai qu'un Dieu, qu'un roi, qu'un liard et qu'une botte.
> Pour avoir bu de grand matin
> La rosée à même le thym,
> Deux moineaux étaient en ribote.
>> Zi zi zi
>> Pour Passy.
Je n'ai qu'un Dieu, qu'un roi, qu'un liard et qu'une botte.
> Et ces deux pauvres petits loups
> Comme deux grives étaient soûls;
> Un tigre en riait dans sa grotte.
>> Don don don
>> Pour Meudon.

Je n'ai qu'un Dieu, qu'un roi, qu'un liard et qu'une botte.
  L'un jurait et l'autre sacrait.
  Quand irons-nous dans la forêt?
  Demandait Charlot à Charlotte.
    Tin tin tin
    Pour Pantin.
Je n'ai qu'un Dieu, qu'un roi, qu'un liard et qu'une botte.

BOOK TWELVE: CORINTHE

1. **Corinthe:** after the ancient Greek city-state, one of the leaders of the cities allied against Spartan domination.

*I: History of Corinthe from Its Foundation*

1. **Saint-Eustache . . . rue de la Petite-Truanderie:** The rue Rambuteau was built in 1838–39. Many of the streets Hugo names still exist; the rue Saint-Denis, the rue de la Grande-Truanderie, and the rue du Cygne can easily be found on a map of Paris.
2. **old Théophile:** a probable allusion to the poet Théophile de Viau (1590–1626), but Yves Gohin has identifed the source of the couplet as Viau's contemporary the poet Marc-Antoine de Saint-Amant (1594–1661).
3. **Here bobs . . . hanged himself:** "Là branle le squelette horrible / D'un pauvre amant qui se pendit."
4. **Mathurin Régnier:** Another contemporary of Viau and Saint-Amant, Régnier (1573–1613) is best remembered for his *Satires*.
5. **Natoire:** Charles-Joseph Natoire (1700–77), a popular rococo painter.
6. **She passes . . . into her mouth:** "Elle étonne à dix pas, elle épouvante à deux, / Une verrue habite en son nez hasardeux; / On tremble à chaque instant qu'elle ne vous la mouche, / Et qu'un beau jour son nez ne tombe dans la bouche."
7. **"Revel if you can and eat if you dare":** A parody of a famous line from Corneille's *Héraclius: "Dévine, si tu peux, et choisis, si tu l'oses"*—"Guess if you can, and choose if you dare."

*II: Preliminary Gaieties*

1. **hooded friars call *bini:*** In certain monastic orders, lay brothers wore a hat instead of a cowl. *Bini* refers to two who share virtually everything.
2. **"of the funeral orations":** Bossuet, the Eagle of Meaux, who gave Laigle his nickname, was known for his funeral orations (see note 15, p. 1202).
3. **"That great mound of oyster shells":** I.e., the jaded cynic Grantaire, who has just eaten a bad oyster and who finds himself repulsed by erudition, sees the library as a pile of discarded, useless things. It is worth recalling here that even Grantaire is a reflection of some part of Victor Hugo. The Bibliothèque de

France (now the Bibliothèque Nationale de France) was then located in the rue Richelieu, in a building that today still houses several collections of the BNF.

4. **"The Gauls covet Clusium . . . the Sabines did to you":** The city-state of Clusium, in Tuscany, was an ally of Rome when the Gauls under the leadership of Brennus invaded Italy ca. 400 B.C.E. Brennus and his Gauls eventually conquered and sacked Rome. The Romans agreed to pay Brennus a ransom of one thousand pounds of gold in return for his evacuation. As the Gaulish general and the Roman leaders argued over the accuracy of the scales, Brennus threw his sword onto the balance and cried: *"Vae victis!,"* "Woe unto the vanquished!" The city of Alba, the tribes of the Fidenae, the Sabines, etc., were all victims of Rome's military aggression.

5. **"the lean cock . . . of Uri, or for the fat cock . . . of Glaris":** two Swiss cantons that, according to legend, decided a disputed border according to the crowing of cocks. The people of Uri did not feed their rooster, so it awoke and crowed earlier.

6. **"Caesar dies . . . strikes him with a comet":** In the days following Caesar's death, a comet was visible, seen as a sign of Caesar's apotheosis.

7. **"the comet of 1811":** The Great Comet of 1811 was visible to the naked eye for more than 250 days. It was seen in retrospect as an omen of Napoléon's coming invasion of Russia.

8. **"the hanging of the prince de Condé":** The scandalous life of the last prince de Condé, Louis VI Henri-Joseph de Bourbon-Condé (1756–1830), came to a mysterious end when he was found hanged in his château of Chantilly. The father of the duc d'Enghien (see note 11, p. 1241), he was a cousin of the Bourbons and an uncle of Louis-Philippe d'Orléans, a dissolute alcoholic with a fondness for inelegant prostitutes. Nonetheless, suspicion for his death fell on everyone from the royal family—whose son, the duc d'Aumale, became the richest individual in France upon his great-uncle's death—to his last mistress, the former prostitute Madame la baronne de Feuchères, who inherited two million francs and several estates.

9. **"a German princeling":** The minor princes of the three hundred–plus German principalities that made up the former Holy Roman Empire inspired a standard comic figure in the eighteenth and nineteenth centuries.

10. **"seraglios . . . odalisques":** Grantaire (or Hugo) seems to have confused his orientalist fantasies; the houri is usually the companion found in Paradise, while odalisques were found in seraglios (harems).

11. **"the month of Prairial":** the early-summer month of the old revolutionary calendar, roughly May 20–June 18.

12. ***"Tymbraes Apollo":*** i.e., "a mad Apollo." Grantaire has made a Latinate pun based on the French word *timbré,* teched.

13. **"Night, and Death . . . Psyche":** Psyche was so beautiful that Venus was jealous. It is unclear if Hugo is referring to a specific version of the story from Greek mythology or elaborating upon it.

*III: Night Begins to Fall on Grantaire*

1. *"Non licet omnibus adire Corinthum":* a play on a verse from Horace: "It is not permitted to everyone [omnibus] to reach Corinth."
2. **"a Gothic Pygmalion":** The sculptor Pygmalion fell in love with his own statue Galatea. Venus took pity on him, answered his prayers, and brought the statue to life.
3. **"Titian's mistress":** Such famous paintings as *Flora* and *A Young Woman at Her Toilet* are believed to represent Titian's mistress.
4. **"I am Capitoul . . . of flower games":** The capitouls of Toulouse were the municipal magistrates of the city, elected from the most notable members of the bourgeoisie; although their fuctions were limited by the creation of a royal *parlement,* the Capitolum remained a very prestigious institution. "Flower games" refers to a prestigious poetry competition, dating back to the fourteenth century, held by the Académie des Jeux Floraux de Toulouse; in 1820, the eighteen-year-old Victor Hugo was named "maitre ès jeux" by the Académie, an honor he shared with Ronsard, Voltaire, and Chateaubriand.
5. **died at Thermopylae . . . with Cromwell:** On Leonidas and the battle of Thermopylae, see note 2, ch. XV, p. 1238. In 1649, Oliver Cromwell (1599–1658) led a Roundhead army into Ireland, where royalist partisans of Charles II had allied themselves with Catholic nationalists. He laid siege to the port town of Drogheda; when the town fell, Cromwell ordered his troops to kill every officer and every Catholic priest in the town.

*VI: While Waiting*

1. **This one:**

Vous rappelez-vous notre douce vie,
Lorsque nous étions si jeunes tous deux,
Et que nous n'avions au cœur d'autre envie
Que d'être bien mis et d'être amoureux.

Lorsqu'en ajoutant votre âge a mon âge,
Nous ne comptions pas à deux quarante ans,
Et que, dans notre humble et petit ménage,
Tout, même l'hiver, nous était printemps?

Beaux jours! Manuel était fier et sage,
Paris s'asseyait à de saints banquets,
Foy lançait la foudre, et votre corsage
Avait une épingle où je me piquais.

Tout vous contemplait. Avocat sans causes,
Quand je vous menais au Prado dîner,
Vous étiez jolie au point que les roses
Me faisaient l'effet de se retourner.

Je les entendais dire: Est-elle belle!
Comme elle sent bon! quels cheveux à flots!
Sous son mantelet elle cache une aile;
Son bonnet charmant est à peine éclos.

J'errais avec toi, pressant ton bras souple.
Les passants croyaient que l'amour charmé
Avait marié, dans notre heureux couple,
Le doux mois d'avril au beau mois de mai.

Nous vivions cachés, contents, porte close,
Dévorant l'amour, bon fruit défendu;
Ma bouche n'avait pas dit une chose
Que déja ton cœur avait répondu.

La Sorbonne était l'endroit bucolique
Où je t'adorais du soir au matin.
C'est ainsi qu'une âme amoureuse applique
La carte du Tendre au pays latin.

O place Maubert! O place Dauphine!
Quand, dans le taudis frais et printanier,
Tu tirais ton bas sur ta jambe fine,
Je voyais un astre au fond du grenier.

J'ai fort lu Platon, mais rien ne m'en reste
Mieux que Malebranche et que Lamennais;
Tu me démontrais la bonté céleste
Avec une fleur que tu me donnais.

Je t'obéissais, tu m'étais soumise.
O grenier doré! te lacer! te voir!
Aller et venir des l'aube en chemise,
Mirant ton front jeune à ton vieux miroir!

Et qui donc pourrait perdre la mémoire
De ces temps d'aurore et de firmament,
De rubans, de fleurs, de gaze et de moire,
Où l'amour bégaye un argot charmant?

Nos jardins étaient un pot de tulipe;
Tu masquais la vitre avec un jupon;
Je prenais le bol de terre de pipe,
Et je te donnais la tasse en japon.

Et ces grands malheurs qui nous faisaient rire!
Ton manchon brûlé, ton boa perdu!
Et ce cher portrait du divin Shakspeare
Qu'un soir pour souper nous avons vendu!

J'étais mendiant, et toi charitable;
Je baisais au vol tes bras frais et ronds.
Dante in-folio nous servait de table
Pour manger gaîment un cent de marrons.

Le première fois qu'en mon joyeux bouge
Je pris un baiser à ta lèvre en feu,
Quand tu t'en allas décoiffée et rouge,
Je restai tout pâle et je crus en Dieu!

Te rappeles-tu nos bonheurs sans nombre,
Et tous ces fichus changés en chiffons?
Oh! que de soupirs, de nos cœrs pleins d'ombre,
Se sont envolés dans les cieux profonds!

2. **The Tender card:** The Carte du Tendre, the Map of the Tender, i.e., an allegorical map of tender sentiments, was an invention of the seventeenth-century *précieuses;* see note 5, ch. I, p. 1296.
3. **Malebranche and Lamennais:** two important Catholic philosophers, Nicolas Malebranche (1638–1715) and Félicité de Lamennais (1782–1854).

*VIII: Several Question Marks Regarding a Man Named Le Cabuc Who Was Perhaps Not Le Cabuc*

1. **the Themis of antiquity:** the goddess of justice.
2. **"no more Satan . . . no more Michael":** I.e., when the progess of humanity and the human spirit has brought an end to evil, there will no longer be a need for God's warrior, Michael, the avenging archangel.

BOOK THIRTEEN: MARIUS STEPS INTO THE SHADOWS
*I: From the Rue Plumet to the Quartier Saint-Denis*

1. **Black coats and round hats . . . caked with dirt:** I.e., the bourgeoisie had given way to the working class.

*III: The Extreme Edge*

1. **no longer Montmirail or Champaubert:** two battles during the defensive French campaign of 1814; Colonel Pontmercy fought at Montmirail, but no mention is made of Champaubert.
2. **Timoleon versus the tyrant:** The fourth-century-B.C.E. Corinthian politician and general traveled to Syracuse, in Sicily, in order to help liberate the city from the tyrant Hicetas, who was backed by Carthage.
3. **Brutus . . . Coligny:** Brutus was the executioner of Julius Caesar. Étienne Marcel (ca. 1315–1358) was the Parisian official (provost of merchants) who led the Estates General as a member of the Third Estate in 1355 and '56. Arnold of Blankenheim may be a reference to a leader of the Swiss revolt against the Hapsburgs. Gaspard de Coligny was a leader of the Protestant faction during the Wars of Religion, killed during the Saint Bartholomew's Day Massacre.

4. **Ambiorix, by Artevelde, by Marnix, by Pelagius:** Ambiorix led the Gauls against Caesar and the Roman legions. Jacques d'Artevelde (or Jakob van Artevelde) (ca. 1285–1345) led the Flemish against French domination. Philippe de Marnix (1540–98) led the Dutch in a revolt against Spanish rule. Pelagius, king of Asturias in northern Spain, fought against the Moorish invasion of the eighth century.

5. **drive out the Englishman:** perhaps a reference to Joan of Arc, or to Colonel Pontmercy fighting against Wellington.

6. *Prometheus Bound* **begins, Aristogeiten ends:** In Aeschylus's play *Prometheus Bound,* the Titan who gave fire to mortals in defiance of the gods and was in punishment chained to a mountainside, where vultures pecked at his liver, is presented as a rebel against the unreasonable authority of Zeus. The theme of the rebel Titan captured the Romantic imaginations of Goethe, Byron, and Shelley. Hugo attributes the overthrow of the tyrant Hipparchus by the Aristogeiten and Harmodius (see note 7, p. 1275) to the influence of Aeschylus, but it appears that the play was written after Hipparchus's assassination.

7. **Thrasybulus:** general who overthrew the Athenian oligarchy and restored democracy in 411 B.C.E. Hugo compares the effect of Diderot and the Enlightenment on the Revolution, when writers (poets) lit the way for politicians, to the ancient Greeks.

8. **"because he is a Bourbon":** "parce qu'il est Bourbon," given as the ultimate rationale for the execution of Louis XVI. He was guilty of tyranny simply because he was a Bourbon.

BOOK FOURTEEN: THE GRANDEURS OF DESPAIR
*I: The Flag—Act One*

1. **Here come the suburbs:** Gavroche, the proud Parisian, mocks the National Guard troops from the suburbs who have come under General Bugeaud to fight against Parisians.

2. **My nose . . . Cock-a-doodle-do:** "Mon nez est en larmes, / Mon ami Bugeaud, / Prêt-moi tes gendarmes / Pour leur dire un mot. / Encapote bleue, / La poule au shako, / Voici la banlieue! / Co-cocorico!"

3. **the statue of the Commendatore:** a reference to Mozart's *Don Giovanni,* in which the statue-ghost of the commendatore avenges Don Giovanni's seduction of his daughter by dragging the libertine down to hell.

*VI: The Agony of Death After the Agony of Life*

1. **At the sight . . . Run! he said:** "En voyant Lafayette / Le gendarme répète / Sauvons-nous! sauvons-nous! sauvons-nous!"

*VII: Gavroche a Profound Calculator of Distances*

1. **"I'll be back in plenty of time":** At this point in the manuscript, a note of Hugo's reads, "Here the Peer of France interrupted [his writing], and the exile continued: 30 December, 1860, Guernsey."

BOOK FIFTEEN: THE RUE DE L'HOMME-ARMÉ
*IV: Gavroche's Excessive Zeal*

1. **The bird . . . Lon la:**
> L'oiseau médit dans les charmilles,
> Et prétend qu'hier Atala
> Avec un russe s'en alla.
> > Où vont les belles filles,
> > > Lon la.
> Mon ami pierrot, tu babilles,
> Parce que l'autre jour Mila
> Cogna sa vitre, et m'appela.     Où vont, etc.
> Les drôlesses sont fort gentilles;
> Leur poison qu'm'ensorcela
> Griserait monsieur Orfila.     Où vont, etc.
> J'aime l'amour et ses bisbilles,
> J'aime Agnès, j'aime Paméla,
> Lise en m'allumant se brûla.     Où vont, etc.
> Jadis, quand je vis les mantilles
> De Suzette et de Zéila,
> Mon âme à leurs plis se mêla.     Où vont, etc.
> Amour; quand, dans l'ombre où tu brilles,
> Tu coiffes de roses Lola,
> Je me damnerais pour cela.     Où vont, etc.
> Jeanne, à ton miroir tu t'habilles!
> Mon cœur un beau jour s'envola;
> Je crois que c'est Jeanne qui l'a.     Où vont, etc.
> Le soir, en sortant des quadrilles,
> Je morte aux étoiles Stella
> Et je leur dis; regardez-la.     Où vont, etc.

2. **But there are . . . Lon la:**
> Mais il reste encor des bastilles,
> Et je vais mettre le holà
> Dans l'ordre public que voilà
> > Où vont les belles filles,
> > > Lon la.
> Quelqu'un vent-il jouer aux quilles?
> Tout l'ancien monde s'écroula
> Quand la grosse boule roula     Où vont, etc.

> Vieux bon peuple, à coups de béquilles,
> Cassons ce Louvre où s'étala
> La monarchie en falbala.          Où vont, etc.
> Nous en avons forcé les grilles,
> Le roi Charles-Dix ce jour-là
> Tenait mal et se décolla.          Où vont, etc.

PART FIVE: JEAN VALJEAN

BOOK ONE: WAR BETWEEN FOUR WALLS
*I: The Charybdis of the Faubourg Saint-Antoine and the Scylla of the Faubourg du Temple*

1. **Charybdis . . . Scylla:** in Greek mythology, two monsters who lived on either side of a narrow, dangerous passage, traditionally located in the Strait of Messina between Italy and Sicily. Scylla lived on the rocks, Charybdis in a whirlpool.

2. **the fatal insurrection of June 1848:** The July Monarchy had fallen in February, and Victor Hugo had been elected to the Constituent Assembly of the new republic. On June 23, after a turbulent spring, widespread unemployment led to a revolt of Parisian workers in the northern and eastern parts of the city. Barricades were erected in the faubourgs Saint-Denis, Saint-Antoine, and Saint-Jacques. Insurgents broke into the Hugos' apartment in the place des Vosges, intending to loot and burn it, but stopped when they learned whose home it was. The repression of the riots was chiefly the responsibility of General Cavaignac, but Hugo, as a member of the legislative committee appointed to oversee the reestablishment of order, took an active part in the government's counterinsurgency efforts, even accompanying troops to the barricaded streets. By midnight of June 26, the insurgency was effectively crushed. An estimated 1,500 insurgents had been killed; 15,000 more would be deported.

3. **mob rule rises up against the Demos:** Hugo draws a distinction between the mob, or *ochlocracy*—a Renaissance neologism based on ancient Greek—and the orderly rule of the *demos*/democracy. As with the distinction between plebs and the people, the difference is fine and based on circumstance.

4. **Saint Jerome . . . *Fex urbis, lex orbis:*** "From the dregs of the city comes the law of the world." Saint Jerome (ca. 342–419) is one of the Fathers of the Roman and Eastern Churches. His translation of the Bible from Greek into Latin formed the basis of the Vulgate Bible of the Roman Catholic Church.

5. **the fearful square that witnessed July 14:** The place de la Bastille was traditionally the western boundary of the faubourg Saint-Antoine.

6. **Sisyphus . . . pottery:** symbols of great suffering. Sisyphus was condemned to roll a rock up a hill every day; when he reached the top of the hill, the rock would roll down and he would start again. In the Book of Job (2:7–9), Satan afflicts Job with terrible sores; Job's faith is unshaken as he takes up a "shard of pottery" to scrape his skin.

7. **Ossa heaped upon the Pelion:** two mountains in Greece; in mythology, the rebellious young giants Otus and Elphiates put Mount Pelion on top of Mount Ossa in an attempt to reach Olympus but were killed by Apollo before reaching the home of the gods; to put Pelion on top of Ossa proverbially refers to a massive but futile effort.

8. **Thermidor 9 . . . Prairial:** Thermidor 9 was the date of the coup d'état against Robespierre (July 28, 1794). For "August 10," see note 5, p. 1296. "Brumaire 18" refers to Bonaparte's 1799 coup d'état, and "January 21" to the execution of Louis XVI. "Vendémiaire" refers to the attempted royalist insurrection of October 5, 1795, and "Prairial" to the Jacobins' triumph over the Girondins in the spring of 1793.

9. **it was Sinai:** It was at the top of Mount Sinai that God spoke to Moses and gave him the Ten Commandments (Exodus 19–24).

10. **the "Carmagnole" . . . the "Marseillaise":** Two revolutionary songs: "La Marseillaise" had been banned by the Empire and Restoration governments after having been the national anthem from 1795 to 1804; the July Monarchy put an end to legal interdictions, but the song would not become the national anthem again until the Third Republic of 1870. The "Carmagnole," more specifically antiroyalist than the "Marseillaise," which calls for the defense of the *patrie,* never had any official status; new verses were written during the successive revolutions and insurrections of the nineteenth century.

11. **the generals of Africa:** In 1848, the generals who put down the June insurrection had made their military reputations in Algeria, most notably Louis Eugène Cavaignac (1802–57).

12. **Zaatcha and Constantine:** two battles the French fought against Algerian resistance, Constantine in 1836 and Zaatcha in 1849.

13. **Cournet, the other Barthélemy:** Frédéric Cournet (1801–52) was a naval officer who became involved in politics after he retired; Emmanuel Barthélemy had, as Hugo relates, a less savory history. The two men were both living in exile in London, where Barthélemy insulted Cournet, provoking the duel that killed the latter. Barthélemy was later convicted of killing two people in that mysterious, passionate adventure Hugo alludes to and was hanged in London.

*II: What Is There to Do in a Bottomless Pit but Talk?*

1. **"Harmodius . . . Sand":** On Harmodius and Aristogeiton, see note 7, p. 1275; Brutus led the Roman senators who assassinated Caesar. Chereas was one of the Praetorian guards who assassinated Caligula. Stephanus assassinated the emperor Domitian (see note 19, p. 1302). Cromwell, as the leader of the Puritan or Roundhead rebels of the English rebellion, bore the greatest responsibility for the death of King Charles I in 1649. Charlotte Corday assassinated the Revolutionary leader Jean-Paul Marat in 1793. The German nationalist Ludwig Sand (1795–1820) murdered the German playwright (and Russian agent) August von Kotzebue in 1819.

2. **the *Georgics*:** Virgil's poetic celebration of rural life and a frequent point of reference for Hugo, who was no doubt familiar with each of the early-nineteenth-century translations Combeferre names.

3. **"Zoïlus insults Homer . . . Fréron insults Voltaire":** Zoïlus (fourth century B.C.E.) was one of the earliest critics of Homer; Maevius was a hostile contemporary critic of Virgil, known only because Virgil and Horace mockingly answered his criticisms. Jean Donneau de Visé (1638–1710), a minor playwright and critic, was hostile to Molière and Racine but, like Hugo, a great admirer of Corneille. Alexander Pope (1688–1744) published an edition of Shakespeare's plays that included corrections of the poetic meter and rewrites of certain verses, which could certainly be taken as an insult. The journalist and critic Élie Fréron (1718–76) conducted a long and public battle with Voltaire.

4. **"that rapist of the Rubicon":** Caesar's crossing of the Rubicon with his armies violated Roman law and tradition; it was the irrevocable step in bringing the Roman Republic to an end with Caesar's dictatorship.

5. **"Eutropius":** a fourth-century Roman historian, the author of *Breviarium historiae Romanae,* widely read by Latin scholars from the Middle Ages onward.

6. **"O Cydathenaeum . . . from Edapteon":** cities of ancient Greece. Bossuet seems to be mocking the bourgeois, who do not know what he is talking about, and himself and his friends, who do.

*IV: Five Fewer, One More*

1. **"Saint-Lazare":** a women's prison, frequently used to incarcerate prostitutes.

2. **"the Necker hospice":** a hospital built by Jacques Necker (1732–1804), the father of Madame de Staël and Louis XVI's minister of finance (1776–81 and 1788–90), and his wife, Suzanne (1739–94), who was known for her generosity to charity hospitals.

3. **"universal suffrage":** Hugo was an advocate of universal suffrage under the ephemeral Second Republic.

*V: The View from the Top of the Barricade*

1. **Saint-Just . . . Anacharsis Clootz:** Saint-Just, an acolyte of Robespierre, was too devoted to the ideology of revolution and not enough to the benefits revolution offered to mankind. The Prussian nobleman Jean-Baptiste Clootz (1755–94), who took the name Anacharis when he emigrated to Paris to join the French Revolution and proclaimed himself "orator of mankind," advocated international revolution for the benefit of all mankind. Clootz's militant atheism offended Robespierre, who sent him to the guillotine with the Hébertists (see note 5, p. 1292).

2. **"The Amphictyons":** The Amphictyons were representatives of the leading Greek city-states who met to decide common religious festivals and military concerns. The numerous wars between the cities involved belie the notion that this was a model for European cooperation.

*VII: The Situation Gets Worse*

1. **the avenue of the Sphinxes in Thebes:** The road from Luxor Temple to Karnak Temple in Thebes is lined with statues of sphinxes.
2. **a Voltaire armchair:** a low armchair with a high, reclining backrest, so named in the early nineteenth century by an anonymous pioneer in the art of marketing.

*XII: Disorder, a Supporter of Order*

1. **Fannicot . . . Henri Fonfrède:** Henri Fonfrède was the son of Conventionist, a journalist who opposed the Bourbon Restoration, and loyal supporter of the July Monarchy as a constitutional monarchy. He spent most of his life and career in Bordeaux, only briefly attempting to launch a Parisian newspaper in 1836. The story of National Guard Captain Fannicot is given according to Hugo's reading of the government account of the June insurrection.
2. **lynch law:** perhaps from Colonel William Lynch, a Virginia politician of the Revolutionary era who practiced summary justice with the approval of the Virginia General Assembly; the term came to be used to describe the practice of vigilantism more generally.
3. **Paul-Aimé Garnier:** Hugo ascribes to a young poet (1820–46) of his acquaintance a nearly tragic but comic episode of his own life, as he walked home during the 1834 insurrection holding a volume of the seventeenth-century memorialist and was mistaken for a follower of the nineteenth-century utopian social reformer (see note 70, p. 1217). Number 6 place Royale (called the place des Vosges since 1848) was the residence of the Hugos from 1832 to 1848; the house now contains the Victor Hugo Museum.
4. **condottiere:** after the legendary companies of mercenaries of fifteenth- and sixteenth-century Italy.
5. **Vincennes:** a medieval château on the western edge of Paris, officially a royal residence, used largely as a prison and arsenal from the seventeenth century on.
6. **the *quid divinum:*** the "divine thing."
7. **an August 10 . . . a July 29:** the coups d'états that brought down Louis XVI (August 10, 1792) and his brother Charles X (July 29, 1830), respectively.

*XIII: Passing Glimmers*

1. **General Cavaignac de Baragne:** Jacques-Marie, Vicomte de Cavaignac and Baron de Baragne, the uncle of Louis-Eugène de Cavaignac, who was the head of the National Guard in 1848 (see note 2, p. 1314).
2. **Suchet's Saragossa dictum:** On the difficulties of the French army in Spain, see note 8, p. 1243.

*XIV: In Which You Will Read the Name of Enjolras' Mistress*

1. **Madame Scarron:** Before she became the pious and morganatic wife of Louis XIV, Françoise d'Aubigné (1635–1719) was married to the impoverished but witty poet Paul Scarron (1610–1660) and served as hostess in his salon. After Scarron died, she was named governess of the bastard children of Louis XIV and Madame de Montespan. The king granted her the title of marquise de Maintenon, the name by which she is best known.

2. **Roland . . . Angélique:** names typical of young lovers in romantic novels.

*XV: Gavroche Outside*

1. **the fault of Voltaire:** Gavroche's song mocks the conservatives who blame the Enlightenment and the Revolution for all the ills of society, firing mockery back at the armed bourgeois. Hugo wrote the lyrics following an 1817 song by Bérenger.

2. **They're ugly . . . of Rousseau:** "On est laid à Nanterre / C'est la faute à Voltaire, / Et bête à Palaiseau, / C'est la faute à Rousseau."

3. **I am not . . . of Rousseau:** "Je ne suis pas notaire, / C'est la faute à Voltaire; / Je suis petit oiseau, / C'est la faute à Rousseau."

4. **Joy is . . . of Rousseau:** "Joie est mon caractère, / C'est la faute à Voltaire; / Misère est mon trousseau, / C'est la faute à Rousseau."

5. **I fell . . . fault of—:** "Je suis tombé par terre, / C'est la faute à Voltaire, / La nez dans le ruisseau, / C'est la faute à—"

*XVI: How You Go from Being a Brother to a Father*

1. *invenerunt parvulum pannis involutum:* Luke 2:12: "And they found a little child wrapped in swaddling clothes" (Hugo inadvertently changed the Latin future tense to the past), the inscription on the Hôpital Saint-Vincent-de-Paul (see note 13, p. 1200), an orphanage that then stood in the avenue Denfert-Rochereau.

2. **Aldebaran:** the brightest star in the constellation Taurus, sometimes called the Bull's-Eye. Aldebaran was also, in a noncanonical tradition, a fallen angel.

3. **Vulcan:** i.e., Hephestes, the ugly, misshapen god of volcanoes and fire. The blacksmith of Olympus was also the god of iron, arms, and armor.

4. *Solem quis dicere falsum audeat?:* "Who would dare to say that the sun is deceitful?" from Virgil's *Georgics.*

5. **Marie de Médicis:** The Florentine Marie de Médicis, queen of Henri IV and mother of Louis XIII, built the Luxembourg palace and gardens for her Parisian residence; they were completed in 1625.

6. **"saturnalia":** i.e., an immoral celebration, comparable for this prudhommesque bourgeois to a Roman orgy.

7. **"separates royalty from the peerage":** The Luxembourg was the meeting place of the Chamber of Peers.

8. **"The younger branch is doomed"**: Louis-Philippe and the Orléans family were descended from the duc d'Orléans, younger brother of Louis XIV, thus the "younger branch" of the royal family.

*XVII: Mortuus Pater Filium Moriturum Expectat*

1. **Mortuus . . . expectat:** "The dead father awaits the son who is also to die."

*XVIII: The Vulture Turns into the Prey*

1. **Monsieur de Clermont-Tonnerre:** The comte de Clermont-Tonnerre was minister of war from 1823 to 1827.

*XX: The Dead Are Right but the Living Are Not Wrong*

1. **turning from Minerva to Pallas:** The goddess of wisdom gained the name Pallas when she killed a giant (in some versions a Titan identified with war) and took his name as one of her own.
2. **Gérard de Nerval:** a poet and writer (1802–55).
3. **John Brown . . . Garibaldi:** John Brown (1800–59) was hanged after leading an unsuccessful attack on Harper's Ferry. Carlo Pisacane (1818–57) was killed in an attempted republican revolt in the Kingdom of Naples; Giuseppe Garibaldi (1807–82), the primary military leader of the Risorgimento, lived largely in retirement once unification was achieved.
4. **not Don Quixote . . . but Leonidas:** i.e., not the delusional would-be knight of Cervantes tilting at windmills but Leonidas, who leads his men to inevitable but honorable defeat.
5. *Vitae lampada tradunt!:* "They pass the torch of life from one to another!"; an allusion to a poem by Lucretius.
6. **Corinth, yes; Sybaris, no:** The Greek city-states of Corinth and Sybaris grew rich from trade, but while the Sybarites fell into luxurious decadence, the Corinthians remained honorable and virile. The adjective *sybaritic* comes from the legend of Sybaris.
7. **Missouri or a South Carolina:** The choice of two slave states is almost certainly a reflection of Hugo's growing interest in the question of emancipation throughout the 1850s.

*XXI: Heroes*

1. **the dash of a Zouave:** Taking their name from a Berber tribe that had allied with the French in Algeria, the Zouaves were an elite unit of infantry in the French army.
2. **"Does anyone" . . . from the old army:** Hugo's unwonted reluctance to name names is intriguing.

3. **the Veda:** the sacred texts of Hinduism.
4. **François I had at Marignano:** The French victory under Francis I at Marignan (Marignano, Italy) led the way to the French capture of Milan.
5. **"Then Diomed . . . River Satnois":** from the *Iliad*. This passage is not a quote but a summary of characters and events in Homer's epic.
6. **Esplandian attacks . . . towers he uproots:** a story taken from a Spanish novel of the sixteenth century.
7. **the two ducs:** Hugo's romantic image of a chivalric battle (or tournament) seems to refer to the early Middle Ages, when Bretagne (Brittany) was independent of the French crown.
8. **Yvon:** a Breton spelling of Yves.
9. **Phyles . . . Euphetes:** more allusions to heroes of the *Iliad*, as are Megaryon and Ajax below.

*XXII: Inch by Inch*

1. **Greek fire . . . Bayard:** Among the weapons the ancient Greek scientist Archimedes is credited with inventing is Greek fire, a flaming liquid that could be projected onto enemy ships. Boiling pitch, or tar, was frequently used as a defensive weapon in the time of Pierre Terrail, the chevalier Bayard (1476–1524), the French military hero who epitomized the martial virtues of the early Renaissance.
2. **Milton and Dante than Homer:** i.e., more like a vision of hell than a tale of heroic military action.

*XXIII: Orestes on a Fast and Pylades Drunk*

1. **Orestes . . . Pylades:** the archetypal male friendship of Orestes (the abstemious Enjolras) and Pylades (the drunken Grantaire).

BOOK TWO: LEVIATHAN'S BOWELS

1. **Leviathan's:** Leviathan was a biblical sea monster, variously described as a great serpent and a great fish.

*I: Land Impoverished by the Sea*

1. **Eckeberg:** Captain Charles Gustav Eckeberg (1716–84), a Swedish officer who wrote a book entitled *The Art of Chinese Husbandry*.
2. **Folie Beaujon:** The house and gardens of the financier Nicolas Beaujon were famous for their extravagance. See also note 10, ch. IV, p. 1222.
3. **Saint-Cloud nets:** Downriver from Paris, nets were set up to prevent large objects, including bodies, from floating downriver and obstructing navigation.
4. **Fuhkien:** or Fujian, a province in southern China.

5. **Liebig:** Justus Liebig (1803–73), a German chemist who specialized in agricultural methods.

6. **Urbi et orbi:** "To the city and to the world."

7. **if Paris contains . . . Lutetia:** Tyre was the capital of the commercial empire of the ancient Phoenicians; Nineveh was the capital of the Assyrian empire; Lutetia, the Latin name for the city that became Paris (*Lutèce* in French) was believed to come from the Latin *lutum,* mud.

8. **Machiavelli, Bacon, and Mirabeau:** historical figures of combined genius and moral corruption: Machiavelli's *The Prince* made his name a byword for political cynicism (see note 9, p. 1287); the English essayist, scientist, and political philosopher Francis Bacon (1561–1626) had an equivocal reputation ranging from an arrest for debts to a history of opportunism to his sex life; Honoré-Gabriel de Mirabeau's scandalous personal life preceded his reputation as a statesman.

*II: The Ancient History of the Sewer*

1. **Benares . . . Babylon:** Benares is the modern city of Varanasi in India; "the lion's den of Babylon" refers to the Book of Daniel, when the prophet is cast into a pit of lions for refusing to renounce God and is miraculously protected from harm.

2. **Tiglath-Pileser . . . his fake sun:** Tiglath-Pileser was the name of three Assyrian kings; the source of Hugo's assertion about "the sink of Nineveh" cannot be found. Jan van Leyden (ca. 1510–36) was a leader of the Anabaptist movement, an eccentric who claimed the city of Münster was the kingdom of Zion and he was king. The eighth-century Persian prophet Mokanna (or al-Muqanna) claimed to be the reincarnation of God and wore a veil because (he claimed) his face emitted rays of light as powerful as the sun.

3. **Gemoniae:** On the Gemonian Staircase in Rome, see note 2, p. 1294.

4. **Maillotins:** The Maillotins were a group who rebelled against taxation in the late fourteenth century.

5. **Morin's visionary Illuminati:** Simon Morin, a mystic and minor writer, became convinced he was the son of God. He was arrested and burned at the stake in 1663. His followers—*les illuminés*—are not related to the Bavarian Illuminati of the following century.

6. **Chauffeurs:** From the French verb *chauffer,* "to heat," chauffeurs practiced political terror in Brittany and the Vendée during the Revolution, and various groups, including the bandit chief Schinderhannes, extorted money from their victims by literally holding their feet to the fire.

7. **that Gallic *picareria:*** from the Spanish *picaro,* adventurer, Hugo's apparent neologism refers to a collection of vagrants (*truands*) and petty thieves.

8. **the Cour des Miracles:** see note 5, ch. I, p. 1296.

9. **Villon . . . Rabelais:** I.e., the criminal-poet Villon lived outside the law, whereas the humanist Rabelais lived and wrote near but within its edges.

10. **Basil's mask . . . Scapin's false nose:** Basil and Scapin were traditional names

for farcical characters in popular theater, cunning or cowardly valets and peasants. Their masks refer to the tradition of the Italian commedia dell'arte.

11. **Caïaphas's . . . vomit:** I.e., the sacred meets the profane. When Christ was brought before the Jewish high priest Caiaphas for trial, he was spit upon by Caiaphas's soldiers, not the priest himself; Falstaff is the cheerful drunk of Shakespeare's *Henry IV* and *Henry V.*

12. **The Saint Bartholomews:** the Saint Bartholomew's Day massacre and similar acts of political violence.

13. **Louis XI . . . Louvois:** The darker legends of French kings are presented along with their advisers, their *âmes damnés* in French. The Spider King, Louis XI, loomed large in the romantic imagination as a cruel, even sadistic figure (in *Notre-Dame de Paris,* he is depicted taunting Cardinal Balue, who languishes in an iron cage). The king's adviser, Tristan l'Hermite, is portrayed as his henchman. Antoine Duprat (1463–1535) was the detested adviser of François I, known for his aggressive taxation and harsh persecution of Protestants; Hugo's portrayal of François I in *Le Roi s'amuse* (The King Takes His Pleasure) as a corrupt and dissolute monarch abusing his authority was a far cry from the usual portrayal of François as a gallant Renaissance prince. Charles IX (born 1550, reigned 1560–74) is popularly portrayed as the weak and vacillating puppet of his domineering mother, Catherine de Médicis (1519–89), who has been held responsible for the Saint Bartholomew's Day Massacre of 1572. Cardinal de Richelieu dominated the reign of Louis XIII and ruthlessly crushed opposition to royal authority. Louvois and Letellier were advisers of Louis XIV who promoted harsh policies against the Protestant Huguenots (see note 15, p. 1202).

14. **Hébert and Maillard:** The revolutionaries are linked with the royal malefactors above chiefly for their part in the September massacres.

15. **the Jewry of the Ghetto:** Hugo refers to the original Ghetto, the Jewish quarter in Venice, and the Judengasse of German cities.

16. **the mark of Messalina's dig:** the legendary sexual appetite of Claudius's empress Messalina fascinated Hugo, among others.

### III: Bruneseau

1. **Henri II:** son of François I, husband of Catherine de Médicis, and father of the last three Valois kings of France (born 1519, reigned 1547–59).

2. **Mercier:** Louis-Sébastien Mercier (1740–1814), a prolific author best remembered for his *Tableau de Paris,* in which he examined virtually every observable facet of Paris society, from the highest to the lowest.

3. **Daedalus replicated Babel:** Daedalus, the father of Icarus, designed the Labyrinth of Crete, where the Minotaur was kept. Babel was the site of the tower men built in an attempt to reach heaven; the arrogance of the effort angered God, who destroyed the tower and invented different languages so that mankind could never cooperate on such a venture again.

4. **Behemoth:** from the Book of Job. Behemoth is the largest, fiercest animal of the

land, as Leviathan (see note 1, Book Two, p. 1320) is the largest and most fearsome creature in the sea.

5. **Sainte-Foix . . . Créqui:** two notoriously libertine aristocrats of the late eighteenth century.

6. **The Goblin Monk:** a Parisian ghost story dating back at least to the seventeenth century; a ghost or demon who walked the streets at night.

7. **Marmousets:** derisive but undeserved nickname given to the counselors of King Charles VI, known as Charles the Mad (born 1368, reigned 1380–1422). When the young king's madness left his rapacious uncles in charge, the Marmousets were driven from power and from Paris but not actually killed, as Hugo implies.

8. **Fagon:** Guy-Crescent Fagon (1638–1718), first physician to Louis XIV, was known for his interest in public health.

9. **Barathrum:** a deep pit or ravine into which criminals were thrown in ancient Athens, either as a means of execution or after their execution, according to various sources.

10. **a Decrès or a Crétet:** Denis Decrès (1761–1820) was Napoléon's minister of the marine for all of the consular and imperial eras; Emmanuel Crétet (1747–1809) was minister of the interior from 1806 until his death.

11. **Bruneseau:** Pierre-Emmanuel Bruneseau (1751–1819) was a municipal inspector for the city of Paris who reformed the sewer system.

*IV: Details Nobody Knows*

1. **Fourcroy's:** Antoine-François de Fourcroy (1755–1809), a chemist and member of the Convention. Fourcroy held a number of positions in successive revolutionary governments, including director of public works.

2. **Philibert Delorme:** An architect employed by François I and Henri II, Delorme is best known for designing the Tuileries palace for Catherine de Médicis.

3. *in pace:* small cells; see note 6, p. 1251.

4. **"Laubespine":** It is known that Marat had treated the marquise de l'Aubespine as a patient; whether their relationship progressed further is not clear.

5. **Watteau:** See note 1, p. 1221.

*V: Current Progress*

1. **Tartuffe after confession:** I.e., Molière's religious hypocrite could not be trusted even in the confessional.

2. **Augeas's stable:** One of Hercules' twelve labors was to clean the stables of King Augeas, the largest in the world.

*VI: Future Progress*

1. **the Ourcq . . . Bièvre River:** The Ourcq is a small river that flows into the Marne northeast of Paris; the Bièvre is a tributary of the Seine that runs from the southeastern part of the city. In 1912, it was canalized into an underground aquaduct.
2. **cholera:** the same cholera epidemic that killed General Lamarque.

BOOK THREE: IT MAY BE MUCK, BUT IT IS STILL THE SOUL
*III: The Man Tailed*

1. **to be dressed in red:** i.e., the red smock (see note 6, ch. III, p. 1209) worn by prisoners at Toulon and other prisons.
2. **the house brought from Moret . . . François I:** a house that was rebuilt stone by stone on the right bank, roughly across the Seine from the Hôtel des Invalides.

*V: With Sand as with Women, There Is a Kind of Fineness That Is Perfidious*

1. **the beach of Mont Saint-Michel:** The beaches around the tidal island of Mont Saint-Michel contain many patches of quicksand.
2. **Die in a tun of marsala:** According to legend, featured in Shakespeare's *Richard III,* the duke of Clarence was drowned in a butt (a container measuring about one hundred gallons) of malmsey wine after having been found guilty of plotting against his brother King Edward IV.
3. **the Lunière subsidence:** As with the Phélippeaux bog below, Hugo is referring to sewers in different parts of Paris.
4. **d'Escoubleau:** The vicomte d'Escoubleau de Sourdis lived from 1593 to 1645.
5. **Hero . . . Pyramus:** Hero and Leander, along with Thisbe and Pyramus, were pairs of lovers from classical mythology and literature.

*VI: The Subsidence*

1. **residents who owned mansions:** i.e., the wealthier residents who owned the private town houses in the elegant quartier.

*VII: Sometimes We Have Run Aground When We Think We Have Landed*

1. **Gehenna:** the word for hell in Jewish tradition.

*VIII: The Torn Bit of Coat*

1. **Corneille the elder's:** Pierre Corneille (1606–84); the quote comes from his *Cinna.* His younger brother Thomas (1625–1709) was also a playwright.

*XII: The Grandfather*

1. **"Benjamin Constants, and your Tirecuir de Corcelles":** like Lafayette, liberal politicians who are anathema to old Gillenormand.
2. **"clubbist":** i.e., a member of one of the revolutionary clubs, Robespierre's Jacobins or Danton's Cordeliers.

BOOK FOUR: JAVERT DERAILED
*I: Javert Derailed*

1. **"Pontius Pilate's washbasin":** In Matthew 27:24, Pilate ceremoniously washes his hands, signifying his abandonment of Jesus to the people of Jerusalem.

BOOK FIVE: GRANDSON AND GRANDFATHER
*I: In Which We Once More See the Tree with the Zinc Plaster*

1. **Virgil's Tityrus:** from the *Eclogues.*

*II: Marius, Emerging from Civil War, Gears Up for Domestic War*

1. **Jeanne:** Like the Jeanne Monsieur Gillenormand sings of, Juliette Drouet was a Bretonne born in Fougères.
2. **Jeanne . . . Nipples:**  Jeanne est née à Fougère,
   Vrai nid d'une bergère;
   J'adore son jupon,
      Fripon.
   Amour, tu vis en elle;
   Car c'est dans sa prunelle
   Que tu mets ton carquois,
      Narquois!
   Moi, je la chante, et j'aime,
   Plus que Diane même,
   Jeanne et ses durs tetons
      Bretons.

*III: Marius Attacks*

1. **"the Regency":** The Regency (1715–23), the period when Philippe d'Orléans (1674–1723), a nephew of Louis XIV, ruled France in the name of the five-year-old Louis XV (born 1710, reigned 1715–1774), great-grandson of the Sun King, was remembered as a time of great libertinage. Monsieur Gillenormand is not old enough to have seen the Regency, though he strives to keep its spirit alive.
2. **"Dorante . . . Géronte":** traditional names of youth (Dorante) and old age (Géronte) in traditional French comedy.
3. **"André Chénier":** The royalist Gillenormand and his Romantic grandson can find common ground in the poetry of Chénier (see note 15, p. 1276).

4. **"Thermidor"**: Chénier was in fact guillotined on 7 Thermidor, Year II (July 25, 1794), only two days before Robespierre himself was arrested in the coup of 9 Thermidor.

### IV: Mademoiselle Gillenormand . . . Under His Arm

1. **"Monsieur Boulard"**: probably Antoine-Marie-Henri Boulard (1754–1825); a Parisian lawyer and friend of many *philosophes*, he left a library of five hundred thousand volumes.
2. **Father Gillenormand . . . aristocratic way of his**: The inability, real or affected, to correctly recall a social inferior's name is a trope of eighteenth- and nineteenth-century French literature.
3. **"a Greuze"**: See note 7, ch. IV, p. 1221.
4. **"a certain Saint Catherine"**: Traditionally, an unmarried woman was said to "take Saint Catherine's veil" at age twenty-five, a reference to her quasi-official status as an old maid.
5. **"Mère Gigogne"**: Another traditional figure of folklore, Mère Gigogne, literally Mother Cricket, is a woman with a large family.
6. **"sorority of the Virgin"**: one of the lay religious organizations that were very popular during the July Monarchy.
7. *"Turris eburnea"*: "Ivory tower," from a sacred song dedicated to the Virgin Mary.
8. **So, to stop . . . married**: "Ainsi, bornant le cours de tes rêvasseries. / Alcippe, il est donc vrai, dans peu tu te maries."
9. **"Cherubino . . . Rothschild"**: I.e., the innocent, cherublike Marius unwittingly does better business than the famous banker.

### VI: The Two Old Men . . . Cosette Is Happy

1. **"Strasbourg cathedral a clock"**: The famous astronomical clock of Strasbourg Cathedral dates from the sixteenth century.
2. **"Phoebus and Phoebe"**: alternate names for Apollo, god of the sun, and Artemis, goddess of the moon. The names derive from the Greek word for "light" or "pure."
3. **"Charles V"**: See note 1, ch. IV, p. 1255.
4. **"Éponine and Sabinus"**: The Gaulish chieftain Sabinus led a revolt against Roman occupation in the year 68, after which he hid in the forest for nine years. His wife, Éponine, protected and supplied him in his hiding places. Both were captured, then publicly tortured and executed by the emperor Vespasian, as an example to Roman subjects.
5. **"Old Grigou . . . old maid Grippesou"**: traditional names for misers. *Grippesou* means "penny-pincher."
6. **"the duc de Rohan"**: The string of titles associated with only one member of the Rohan family gives an idea of their status.
7. **"Longchamp"**: The racetrack at Longchamp was a gathering place for Parisian high society from the mid-eighteeth century.

8. **"The Trojan War . . . Helen's garter"**: Monsieur Gillenormand recalls Homer's *Iliad* and *Odyssey* to pay a compliment to Cosette.

9. **"Nestor"**: In the *Iliad,* Nestor is a counselor to younger warriors and a generous host to Odysseus's son Telemachus.

10. **"a good solid contract"**: By tradition and by law, marriage contracts were standard in France. Under the ancien régime, among families with means, the signing of the marriage contract was a ceremony in itself, hence the "good solid spread."

11. **"Cujas . . . Gamache"**: Jacques Cujas (1520–90) was a great legal scholar of the Renaissance; Gamache is a character in *Don Quixote* associated with a wedding party. Monsieur Gillenormand advocates a festive celebration once the legal formalities of marriage are disposed of.

12. **"Florian"**: from the Latin word for flowers; even soldiers were poetic. Edmond Rostand's Cyrano de Bergerac, a swordsman and poet, is probably the best-known incarnation of this very French archetype.

13. **"Rameau's *Les Indes galantes*"**: Rameau's 1735 opera takes the broadest definition of the Indies, presenting five love stories in five exotic—i.e., non-European, settings, in Turkey, Peru, Persia, and North America.

14. **"Monsieur Royer-Collard"**: The constitutional monarchist Pierre-Paul Royer-Collard (1763–1845) was a highly respected scholar, philosopher, and politician. Naturally, Monsieur Gillenormand has no use for him.

15. **"cathedral of Rheims . . . Chanteloup"**: The majestic Gothic cathedral of Rheims was the traditional site of the coronation of French kings; Chanteloup was the legendary château of the duc de Choiseul, prime minister of Louis XV and the epitome of the *grand seigneur* of the eighteenth century. The château has been razed, but the forty-four-meter-tall pagoda, an example of the decorative *folies* that decorated great French gardens at the time, still stands.

16. **"Argyraspides"**: an elite corps of the army of Alexander the Great. Monsieur Gillenormand seems to reach for half-remembered allusions to the classical era to regret the banality of his grandson's generation.

17. **"prince Aldobrandini"**: The Aldobrandini were one of the great noble families of Italy.

18. **Triton . . . old, too:** "Tritton troittait devant, et tirait de sa conque / Des sons si ravissants qu'il ravissants quiconque."

19. **Euchologion . . . *Aves*:** The Euchologion is a prayer book usually associated with the Eastern Orthodox Church. *"Aves"* are recitations of the "Ave Maria," the "Hail Mary."

20. **"the duchesse d'Anville . . . La Roche-Guyon"**: The duchesse de La Rochefoucauld d'Anville and her son the duc de La Rochefoucauld were two of the leading members of the liberal, enlightened nobility of the late eighteenth century. La Roche-Guyon was their château outside Paris.

BOOK SIX: A SLEEPLESS NIGHT
*I: February 16, 1833*

1. **February 16, 1833:** the first night Victor Hugo and Juliette Drouet spent together.
2. **the Song of Songs:** sometimes called the Song of Solomon, the great poetic celebration of love of the Old Testament.
3. **the mayor and his sash, the priest and his chasuble:** After the Revolution, French law required that all marriages be civil ceremonies, performed by the mayor of an arrondissement or one of his representatives. Almost all couples, in the early nineteenth century, complemented the civil ceremony with a religious one.
4. **Churchill, later Marlborough:** John Churchill was the great English general of the War of Spanish Succession (and a direct ancestor of Winston Churchill). He was named duke of Marlborough by Queen Anne.
5. **A Mardi Gras . . . brats:** "Mariage un Mardi Gras, / N'aura point d'enfants ingrats."
6. **the church of Saint-Paul:** In the rue Saint-Antoine, very near the Hugos' house in the place des Vosges, the church of Saint-Paul is where Léopoldine Hugo was married in 1843, only months before her death.
7. **"the masks":** i.e., those taking part in the celebrations of carnival, when masks and full costumes were traditional.
8. **Paillasse, Pantaloon, and Gilles:** clowns and fools of vaudeville and other popular theatrical traditions, and typical costumes of carnival.
9. **Paris had disguised itself as Venice:** The carnival celebrations of Venice were the most celebrated of Europe.
10. **Fat Ox:** one of the traditional images of carnival and Mardi Gras parades.
11. **Lord Seymour:** The very wealthy Edward Seymour (1805–85), the future duke of Somerset, spent a considerable amount of time in Paris, where he had a reputation for extravagant spending and low company.
12. **berlingots:** The Berlingot is a mocking reference to the family's berlin-style carriage.
13. **Pierrots . . . Pierrettes:** Pierrot the clown or fool and Pierrette are stock characters in popular theater.
14. **mid-Lent carnival:** mid-Lent, or Laetare Sunday, the fourth Sunday of Lent, to give people a respite from the restrictions of the season.
15. **maenads:** a sect of women who worshipped Dionysus, working themselves into an ecstatic frenzy as part of their ritual.
16. **Greece needed . . . Vadé's fiacre:** Thespis is traditionally the father of acting in classical theater; the popular songwriter Joseph Vadé (1719–57) wrote songs in the coarse language of the working-class *poissardes,* the market women of Les Halles.
17. **Collé, Panard, and Piron:** three eighteenth-century playwrights of vaudeville and the popular theater.

18. **Roquelaure . . . Paillasse:** The duc de Roquelaure (1617–83) became a favorite of Louis XIV because of his wit. Paillasse was a clown who took his name from the Italian word for clown, *pagliaccio.*

19. **"Paris is Pantin":** I.e., carnival is the season of reversal, so Paris is disguised as the working-class suburb of Pantin.

20. **"the Cadran Bleu . . . La Rapée":** famous restaurants of Restoration Paris.

### II: *Jean Valjean Still Has His Arm in a Sling*

1. **a crown of orange blossoms:** the traditional headdress of French brides.

2. **the days of Barras:** i.e., the Directory, for Paul de Barras (1755–1829) was one of the leading political figures of the era.

3. **"Estelle . . . Némorin":** *Estelle et Némorin,* an eighteenth-century novel, later the subject of an opera by Berlioz.

4. **"the Sancy":** one of the crown jewels of France, originally purchased by Harlay de Sancy from the king of Portugal in 1580.

5. **"cholera morbus":** Monsieur Gillenormand would likely be horrified to know that this disease is now known by the even more inelegant name of gastroenteritis.

6. **"Célimène . . . Alceste":** from Molière's *Misanthrope,* Célimène is the self-centered coquette who breaks the heart of the inflexible Alceste.

7. **"Methuselah":** In the Old Testament, Methuselah lives to the age of 967.

8. **"Daphnis and Chloë . . . Philemon and Baucis":** from classical literature, the two couples represent young love and a love that has lasted into old age.

### IV: *Immortale Jecur*

1. **Immortale jecur:** "the indestructable liver," a reference to the myth of Prometheus, who was condemned to have a vulture tear at his liver for eternity. To the ancient Greeks, the liver was the physical site of feelings and emotions, so the modern parallel is one of a constantly broken heart.

2. **Jacob wrestled with the angel:** Jacob wrestled all night with an angel while returning to Canaan with his family (Genesis 32).

3. **asks the sphinx:** The Sphinx, in Greek myth, would kill and eat anyone who could not answer her riddle. Oedipus finally answered, and the monster killed herself.

4. **Brutus . . . Cato:** two of the Roman senators who resisted Julius Caesar. Cato decided to kill himself rather than surrender, Brutus to assassinate Caesar.

### BOOK SEVEN: THE LAST DROP IN THE CHALICE

1. **the Chalice:** probably from Socrates' cup of hemlock, the image of the chalice as a symbol of inevitable suffering is proverbial in French.

*I: The Seventh Circle and the Eighth Heaven*

1. **the Seventh Circle:** reference to Dante's *Divine Comedy*, in which hell (Inferno) is divided into circles and heaven (Paradiso) into concentric spheres.
2. *Voyages* **of Captain Cook . . . Vancouver's:** Accounts by explorers and travelers were enormously popular in the eighteenth and nineteenth centuries.

*II: The Obscurities a Revelation May Contain*

1. **The Corsican vendetta:** The generations-long blood feuds of Corsica held an exotic fascination for French Romantics. Balzac, Mérimée, and Maupassant all used the vendetta in their fiction.
2. **The old symbols from Genesis:** Hugo seems to be alluding to the "mark and curse of Cain," Genesis 4, when God condemns Cain, the murderer of his brother, Abel, and the first criminal in human history, to wander the earth bearing the visible mark of God's judgment.
3. **a** *quid divinum:* a "divine thing."
4. *vindicte:* from the Latin word *vindicta,* "vengeance," the idea that justice should be society's retribution.
5. **a trumpet blast at the Last Judgment:** Revelations 8: Seven angels blow seven trumpets to announce the Apocalypse.
6. *Vade retro:* from the Gospel of Mark (8:33): "Get thee behind me, Satan."

BOOK NINE: SUPREME DARKNESS, SUPREME DAWN
*IV: Bottle of Ink That Only Manages to Whiten*

1. **too big for Pitt . . . Castelcicala:** William Pitt the Younger (1759–1806), the English statesman and prime minister (1783–1801, 1804–06); and the ambassador of the Neapolitan Bourbons, Fabrizio Ruffio, prince of Castelcicala (1767–1832).
2. **la princesse Bagration's . . . the vicomte Dambray:** two notables of the Parisian *grand monde.* The princess Bagration was the widow of a rich Russian general who established herself in Paris in the 1820s. The vicomte Dambray, a son of the minister of justice of Louis XVIII, refused to recognize the July government. Thénardier assumes that Baron Pontmercy would be flattered by his assumptions.
3. **a slave trader:** As evidenced by the repeated references to John Brown, Hugo had become a committed opponent of slavery in the 1850s.

*VI: The Grass Hides and the Rain Erases*

1. **He sleeps . . . is done:** "Il dort. Quoique le sort fût pour lui bien étrange, / Il vivait. Il mourut quand il n'eut plus son ange. / La chose simplement d'elle-même arriva, / Comme la nuit se fait lorsque le jour s'en va."

ABOUT THE TRANSLATOR

JULIE ROSE's acclaimed translations include Alexandre Dumas's *The Knight of Maison-Rouge* and Racine's *Phèdre*, as well as works by Paul Virilio, Jacques Rancière, Chantal Thomas, and many others. She is a recipient of the PEN medallion for translation and the New South Wales Premier's Translation Prize.

# MODERN LIBRARY IS ONLINE AT WWW.MODERNLIBRARY.COM

## MODERN LIBRARY ONLINE IS YOUR GUIDE TO CLASSIC LITERATURE ON THE WEB

## THE MODERN LIBRARY E-NEWSLETTER

Our free e-mail newsletter is sent to subscribers, and features sample chapters, interviews with and essays by our authors, upcoming books, special promotions, announcements, and news. To subscribe to the Modern Library e-newsletter, visit **www.modernlibrary.com**

## THE MODERN LIBRARY WEBSITE

Check out the Modern Library website at **www.modernlibrary.com** for:

- The Modern Library e-newsletter
- A list of our current and upcoming titles and series
- Reading Group Guides and exclusive author spotlights
- Special features with information on the classics and other paperback series
- Excerpts from new releases and other titles
- A list of our e-books and information on where to buy them
- The Modern Library Editorial Board's 100 Best Novels and 100 Best Nonfiction Books of the Twentieth Century written in the English language
- News and announcements

Questions? E-mail us at **modernlibrary@randomhouse.com**. For questions about examination or desk copies, please visit the Random House Academic Resources site at **www.randomhouse.com/academic.**